You are always in my heart.

The American Short Story

THE American SHORT STORY

A Treasury of the Memorable and Familiar
By the Great American Writers from
Washington Irving to Saul Bellow

EDITED BY
THOMAS K. PARKES

STATE STREET PRESS
ANN ARBOR, MICHIGAN

Published by Galahad Books
A division of BBS Publishing Corporation
450 Raritan Center Parkway
Edison, NJ 08837

This edition distributed by State Street Press

Library of Congress Catalog Number: 94-77197

ISBN: 0-681-64687X

Printed in the United States of America.

To my ghost editor, N. C. S.,
who always imagines the best

Acknowledgements

The Publisher has made every effort to trace the ownership of all copyrighted stories. While expressing regret for any error unintentionally made, the Publisher will be pleased to make the necessary correction in future editions of the book.

"Silent Snow, Secret Snow" by Conrad Aiken. Copyright 1932 by Conrad Aiken. Copyright renewed 1960 by Conrad Aiken. Reprinted by permission of Brandt & Brandt Literary Agents, Inc.

"I'm a Fool" by Sherwood Anderson. Reprinted by permission of Harold Ober Associates Incorporated. Copyright © 1922 by Dial Publishing Co., Inc. Copyright renewed 1949 by Eleanor Copenhaver Anderson.

"Tell Me How Long The Train's Been Gone" from TELL ME HOW LONG THE TRAIN'S BEEN GONE by James Baldwin. Used by permission of Doubleday, a division of Bantam Doubleday Dell Publishing Group, Inc.

"A Silver Dish" copyright © 1978 by Saul Bellow. Reprinted by permission of Harriet Wasserman Literary Agency, as agent for the author.

"The Devil and Daniel Webster" by Stephen Vincent Benet copyright 1936 by the Curtis Publishing Company. Copyright renewed © 1964 by Thomas C. Benet, Stephanie B. Mahin, and Rachel Benet Lewis. Reprinted by permission of Brandt & Brandt Literary Agents, Inc.

"There Will Come Soft Rains" reprinted by permission of Don Congdon Associates, Inc. Copyright © 1950, renewed 1977 by Ray Bradbury.

"A Christmas Memory" from A CHRISTMAS MEMORY by Truman Capote. Copyright © 1956 by Truman Capote. Reprinted by permission of Random House, Inc.

"The Country Husband" by John Cheever. Copyright © 1977, 1978 by John Cheever, reprinted with the permission of Wylie, Aitken & Stone Inc. First published in *The New Yorker.*

"Christ in Concrete" by Pietro Di Donato courtesy of the Estate of Pietro Di Donato.

"A Rose for Emily" from COLLECTED STORIES OF WILLIAM FAULKNER by William Faulkner. Copyright © 1930 and renewed 1958 by William Faulkner.

"Afternoon of a Faun" By Edna Ferber. Copyright © 1921, 1924. Copyright renewed © 1948, 1952. Reprinted by permission of Robert G. Sugarman, trustee for the Edna Ferber Literary Trust.

"Babylon Revisited" reprinted with permission of Charles Scribner's Sons, an imprint of Macmillan Publishing Company, from TAPS AT REVEILLE by F. Scott Fitzgerald. Copyright 1931 by The Curtis Publishing Company. Copyright renewed 1959 by Francis Scott Fitzgerald Lanahan.

"The Snows of Kilimanjaro" reprinted with permission of Charles Scribner's Sons, an imprint of Macmillan Publishing Company, from THE SHORT STORIES OF ERNEST HEMINGWAY. Copyright 1936 by Ernest Hemingway. Copyright renewed © 1964 by Mary Hemingway.

"The Lottery" from THE LOTTERY by Shirley Jackson Copyright © 1948, 1949 by Shirley Jackson and copyright renewed © 1976, 1977 by Laurence Hyman, Barry Hyman, Mrs. Sarah Webster and Mrs. Joanne Schnurer. Reprinted by permission of Farrar, Straus & Giroux, Inc.

"The Golden Honeymoon" reprinted with the permission of Charles Scribner's Sons, an imprint of Macmillan Publishing Company from THE BEST SHORT STORIES OF RING LARDNER. Copyright 1922 and renewed 1950 by Ellis A Lardner.

"The Magic Barrel" from THE MAGIC BARREL by Bernard Malamud. Copyright © 1954, 1958 and copyright renewed © 1982, 1986 by Bernard Malamud. Reprinted by permission of Farrar, Straus & Giroux, Inc.

"A Deal in Wheat" by Frank Norris courtesy of Bantam, Doubleday, Dell & Company.

"A Good Man is Hard to Find" from A GOOD MAN IS HARD TO FIND AND OTHER STORIES, copyright 1953 by Flannery O'Connor and renewed 1981 by Regina O'Connor, reprinted by permission of Harcourt Brace & Company.

"Imagine Kissing Pete" copyright © 1960 by United States Trust Company of New York, as trustee under the will of John O'Hara. Copyright renewed 1988 by Wylie O'Hara Doughty.

"Where Are You Going, Where have You Been?" copyright © 1970 by Joyce Carol Oates. Reprinted by permission of John Hawkins & Associates, Inc.

"Big Blonde" copyright 1929, renewed © 1957 by Dorothy Parker, "Faute de Mieux", copyright 1928, renewed © 1956 by Dorothy Parker, from THE PORTABLE DOROTHY PARKER by Dorothy Parker, Introduction by Brendan Gill. Used by permission of Viking Penguin, a division of Penguin Books USA, Inc.

"Flowering Judas" from FLOWERING JUDAS AND OTHER STORIES, copyright 1930 and renewed 1958 by Katherine Anne Porter, reprinted by permission of Harcourt Brace & Company.

"Daring Young Man on the Flying Trapeze" by William Saroyan courtesy of The William Saroyan Foundation.

"Gimpel the Fool" by Isaac Bashevis Singer, translated by Saul Bellow, copyright 1953 by The Partisan Review, renewed © 1981 by Isaac Bashevis Singer, from A TREASURY OF YIDDISH STORIES by Irving Howe and Eliezer Greenberg. Used by permission of Viking Penguin, a division of Penguin Books USA Inc.

"The Red Pony" from THE RED PONY by John Steinbeck. Copyright 1933, 1937, 1938 © renewed 1961, 1965, 1966 by John Steinbeck. Used by permission of Viking Penguin, a division of Penguin Books USA Inc.

"The Secret Life of Walter Mitty" copyright © 1942 James Thurber. Copyright © 1970 Helen Thurber & Rosemary A. Thurber. From MY WORLD–AND WELCOME TO IT, published by Harcourt Brace & Co.

"Pigeon Feathers" from PIGEON FEATHERS AND OTHER STORIES by John Updike. Copyright © 1959, 1960, 1961, 1962, by John Updike. Reprinted by permission of Alfred A. Knopf, Inc.

"Welcome to the Monkey House" from WELCOME TO THE MONKEY HOUSE by Kurt Vonnegut, Jr. Copyright © 1961 by Kurt Vonnegut Jr. Used by permission of Delacorte Press/ Seymour Lawrence, a division of Bantam Doubleday Dell Publishing Group, Inc.

"The Death of a Traveling Salesman" from A CURTAIN OF GREEN AND OTHER STORIES, copyright 1941 and renewed 1969 by Eudora Welty, reprinted by permission of Harcourt Brace & Company.

"The Mission of Jane" reprinted with the permission of Charles Scribner's Sons, an imprint of Macmillan Publishing Company from THE COLLECTED SHORT STORIES OF EDITH WHARTON Volume I edited by Richard W. B. Lewis. Copyright © 1968 William R. Tyler.

"The Lost Boy" from THE HILLS BEYOND by Thomas Wolfe, copyright 1935, 1936, 1937, 1939, 1941 by Maxwell Perkins as Executor, renewed 1969 by Paul Gitlin, Administrator of the Estate of Thomas Wolfe. Reprinted by permission.

Contents

Introduction

As a literary genre, the short story is far less ancient than poetry or drama, having its origins in the early 1800s. Despite its roots in European folk tales and particularly in the Germanic tales of Gothic horror, the short story was refined and reconceived by American writers such as Nathaniel Hawthorne, Edgar Allan Poe, and Henry James, each of whom added his distinctive signature to this evolving form of fiction. In general, these writers defined a successful tale, or short story, as one that achieves a single, dramatic effect. Even today, many short story writers strive for this single effect.

The Beginning of the Short Story: Romanticism

The Romantic movement began in Europe during the late eighteenth century and flowered in the works of such poets as Wordsworth and Coleridge in England, Hugo in France, and Heine in Germany. When Romanticism crossed the Atlantic to Puritan New England, however, American writers placed their own distinctive mark on it. America's first great quartet of fiction writers—Washington Irving, Hawthorne, Poe, and Herman Melville—were radically different from one another, yet they all remained true to various Romantic precepts: a fascination with the medieval past, inclusion of Gothic touches, a reliance on private symbols and complex allegorical formulations, and an emphasis on imagination and emotion rather than reason as a means to determining truth. Within this inherited framework, however, they explored distinctively American themes: man's relationship to nature—in particular, the wild expanses of the American continent; the coexistence of sin and innocence in the American character; the moral ambiguity and psychosocial instability of their characters' world. Irving's stories, which he called "sketches," were a combination of Gothic tale and short essay, but set in purely American locales. He achieved enormous popularity both in the United States and abroad, introducing readers to a peculiarly American Romantic vision of headless horsemen and twenty-year slumbers. Hawthorne abandoned Gothic trappings and blended allegory with traces of historical realism to explore the psychology of guilt and desire in Puritan New England, while Poe recast the Gothic in dream-like narratives to explore the psychopathology of terror. Melville's shorter works often share Hawthorne's brooding tone and Poe's haunting atmosphere, but he was preoccupied by metaphysical questions of evil and innocence in his characters.

Post Civil War Stories: Regionalism, Humor, Realism, and Naturalism

The popularity of these Romantic short story writers gave rise to the publication of several influential literary magazines in the United States. *Harper's Magazine* was first published in 1850; the *Atlantic Monthly* began in 1857; and *Scribner's Monthly* was founded in 1870. With these and other magazines as a conduit for their work, nineteenth century American writers began producing stories in greater quantity and diversity. Confronted with a national cataclysm, many of these post-Civil War writers rebelled against the precepts of Romanticism, which they regarded as escapist. They wanted instead to treat real events in familiar social settings featuring ordinary characters—characteristics of a new style that became known as Realism in both America and Europe. Writers of Realistic fiction during this period include Ambrose Bierce and Edward Everett Hale, both of whom focused on war experiences, Mark Twain (the pen name of Samuel Clemens), Bret Harte, and Sarah Orne Jewett. Realists also also rejected the flamboyantly metaphoric prose style of European Romanticism in favor of a plainer, more oral and colloquial style. Writers such as Joel Chandler Harris, Twain, and Jewett, in particular, featured regional settings—the deep South, the Midwest, and the coast of Maine, respectively—and speech patterns that reflected the growing interest in and accessibility to the farther corners of the country.

As the short story's popularity increased in late nineteenth century America, the surprise ending became the most extreme expression of the genre's "single effect." Frank Stockton, Henry Van Dyke, Thomas Aldrich, and especially O. Henry established their reputations as masters of this literary device, and it became so celebrated that for a time a story without a surprise ending was a surprise.

As cities became industrialized and urban poverty spread, some writers, often following the theoretical lead of France's Emile Zola, began to feel that even social Realism was too soft a style. These writers, known as Naturalists, treated more sordid settings and plots than the Realists, and operated under the assumption that humans are controlled not by their free choices but by the outside forces of heredity and social environment. Frank Norris, Hamlin Garland, Stephen Crane, Theodore Dreiser, and Sherwood Anderson (in his early work) were preeminent Naturalists. Jack London, too, is often considered a Naturalist, though his stories, set mostly in the far North, characteristically focus on the conflict between humans and the anonymous forces of nature.

Also writing toward the turn of the century, Henry James brought a different focus to bear on Realism. James' studies of the interior workings of individual consciousness established a tradition of psychological Realism in American fiction. His story "The Turn of the Screw," which on first reading seems to be a Gothic ghost story in the tradition of Irving and Poe, is at a richer level a study of the psychology of terror and sexual repression, raising a question that critics still argue: are the story's ghosts real or a product of hysterical psychological projections?

James's friend and protégé, Edith Wharton, followed his lead in the exploration of consciousness, writing close interior studies of characters firmly entrenched in the upper levels of American society. As writers who define reality primarily in terms of the subjective mind's responses, James and Wharton were forerunners of the literary movement known as Modernism.

Post World War I Stories: The Lost Generation, Modernism, and the Rise of the South

World War I, no less than the Civil War, changed America's social order and literature. Though late to enter the conflict, Americans came to experience much of the same disillusionment that was produced on the European continent where it was fought. The terror and death, the mud and poison gas, the shifts in borders and alliances, combined to produce a sense of social breakdown, a feeling of individual helplessness that reflected a widespread lack of faith in the political and religious ideals that once governed society. Writers, faced with the spectacle of democratic, Christian nations destroying one another and engulfed in the despair engendered by this carnage, left the United States after the war for Europe, as if to be closer both to the altar of art and the remnants of devastation. These temporary expatriates, often known as the "Lost Generation," included F. Scott Fitzgerald, Ernest Hemingway, and Dorothy Parker. Though they lived for a time abroad, they set many of their stories in the United States and continued to focus on American themes: the conflict with nature was ever-present in Hemingway's work, and Fitzgerald and Parker explored characters mired in social and psychological alienation, damaged or destroyed from within.

The Modernist tradition that these writers represent repudiated nineteenth century depictions of reality as a social phenomenon. More and more, they looked to the self, no matter how imperfectly defined, as the sole measuring stick for truth and knowledge. Their stories no longer strove for a single effect but courted multiple, even contradictory possiblities for meaning in a world filled with irresolution and skepticism. Their protagonists were often socially and psychologically alienated, cast adrift in a fragmented cultural order that had yet to be understood.

Regionalism was still evident in stories of this period of ironic indeterminism. William Saroyan, for example, wrote evocatively of his California and its inhabitants. More notably, the South produced writers who, having lived within a ruined social order since the end of the Civil War, could now explore this legacy of racial guilt and communal loss for a broader, national audience. Haunted by the ghosts of doomed ancestors, William Faulkner, Katherine Anne Porter, Eudora Welty, Thomas Wolfe, and, later, Flannery O'Connor each wrote in this rich Southern tradition, often incorporating Gothic touches, grotesque characters, mythic analogues, and local color into symbol-laden stories of a failed plantation culture.

From the Present to the Future: The City, the Suburbs, and Beyond

World War II and its aftermath, the Cold War, exerted a new and powerful influence on the American short story. The threat of nuclear destruction, the disintegration of the family unit, a growing awareness of anti-Semitism and racial bigotry, the assassination of public figures, the horrors of the Vietnam War—these changes and raw realities were reflected in the work of writers of the post World War II period.

Several prominent writers based in New York and Chicago—Saul Bellow, Bernard Malamud, Truman Capote, James Baldwin, and Isaac Bashevis Singer—began publishing at this time. Singer's stories were often explorations of a vanishing Yiddish culture, clever blendings of legend and reality that explored the Jewish identity. Malamud and Bellow also wrote of the Jewish experience, usually concentrating on the more familiar and intimate aspects of daily life. Baldwin's stories dealt with the alienation of being black in a white world, but the modern condition of estrangement found a more general narrative register in the suburban stories of John Cheever and John Updike. These last two writers offer a satiric look at the unexceptional, often finding epiphanies in the trivial moments of everyday life. Their characters do not face the blunt social oppression of Baldwin's, but rather pass their days in a state of fear and loneliness that contrasts sharply with the outward comfort of their lives.

This vague loneliness and suburban angst is magnified to a terrifying condition of psychological instability and mental illness in many of the stories of Joyce Carol Oates. Still more disturbing is Shirley Jackson's story "The Lottery," which presents barbaric madness as an underlying condition in the human social order. Jackson's frightening world of the village scapegoat is only a few steps away from the short story subgenre of science fiction, which can be seen as either an attempt to escape from the grim realities of the present or as a method of assimilating the overwhelming surge of scientific knowledge that has come to characterize the late twentieth century. Ray Bradbury and Kurt Vonnegut both leave the anxious present for the imaginary future in their writing, but for both the problems of the present—alienation, loneliness, and fear—prove to be timeless.

From its beginnings in the early nineteenth century to the present, the American short story has evolved in theme and form, taking shape and reinventing itself with the nation that has produced so many distinguished practitioners. A varied and flexible genre, the short story over time has explored and questioned the major concerns of American life. One aspect of the genre remains constant, however: whether writers attempt to produce a single effect or illuminate a small corner of human existence, the short story works as a mirror to reflect the constantly changing nature of American society, and both the visionary aspirations and moral uncertainties of the American character.

WASHINGTON IRVING

[1783–1859]

Rip Van Winkle

A POSTHUMOUS WRITING OF DIEDRICH KNICKERBOCKER

(First published in *The Sketchbook of Geoffrey Crayon, Gent.*, May, 1819.)

By Woden, God of Saxons,
From whence comes Wensday, that is Wodensday,
Truth is a thing that ever I will keep
Unto thylke day in which I creep into
My sepulchre–"

CARTWRIGHT

WHOEVER HAS MADE a voyage up the Hudson must remember the Kaatskill mountains. They are a dismembered branch of the great Appalachian family, and are seen away to the west of the river, swelling up to a noble height, and lording it over the surrounding country. Every change of season, every change of weather, indeed, every hour of the day, produces some change in the magical hues and shapes of these mountains, and they are regarded by all the good wives, far and near, as perfect barometers. When the weather is fair and settled, they are clothed in blue and purple, and print their bold outlines on the clear evening sky; but, sometimes, when the rest of the landscape is cloudless, they will gather a hood of gray vapors about their summits, which, in the last rays of the setting sun, will glow and light up like a crown of glory.

At the foot of these fairy mountains, the voyager may have descried the light smoke curling up from a village, whose shingle-roofs gleam among the trees, just where the blue tints of the upland melt away into the fresh green of the nearer landscape. It is a little village of great antiquity, having been founded by some of the Dutch colonists, in the early times of the province, just about the beginning of the government of the good Peter Stuyvesant, (may he rest in peace!) and there were some of the houses of the original settlers standing within a few years, built of small yellow bricks brought from Holland, having latticed windows and gable fronts, surmounted with weather-cocks.

In that same village, and in one of these very houses (which, to tell the precise truth, was sadly time-worn and weather-beaten), there lived many years since, while the country was yet a province of Great Britain, a simple good-natured fellow of the name of Rip Van Winkle. He was a descendant of the Van Winkles who figured so gallantly in the chivalrous days of Peter Stuyvesant, and accompanied him to the siege of Fort Christina. He inherited, however, but little of the martial character of his ancestors. I have observed that he was a simple, good-natured man; he was, moreover, a kind neighbor, and an obedient, hen-pecked husband. Indeed, to the latter circumstance might be owing that meekness of spirit which gained him such universal popularity; for those men are most apt to be obsequious and conciliating abroad, who are under the discipline of shrews at home. Their tempers, doubtless, are rendered pliant and malleable in the fiery furnace of domestic tribulation; and a curtain lecture is worth all the sermons in the world for teaching the virtues of patience and long-suffering. *A* termagant wife may, therefore, in some respects, be considered a tolerable blessing; and if so, Rip Van Winkle was thrice blessed.

Certain it is, that he was a great favorite among all the good wives of the village, who, as usual, with the amiable sex, took his part in all family squabbles; and never failed, whenever they talked those matters over in their evening gossipings, to lay all the blame on Dame Van Winkle. The children of the village, too, would shout with joy whenever he approached. He assisted at their sports, made their playthings, taught them to fly kites and shoot marbles, and told them long stories of ghosts, witches, and Indians. Whenever he went dodging about the village, he was surrounded by a troop of them, hanging on his skirts, clambering on his back, and playing a thousand tricks on him with impunity; and not a dog would bark at him throughout the neighborhood.

The great error in Rip's composition was an insuperable aversion to all kinds of profitable labor. It could not be from the want of assiduity or perseverance; for he would sit on a wet rock, with a rod as long and heavy as a Tartar's lance, and fish all day without a murmur, even though he should not be encouraged by a single nibble. He would carry a fowling-piece on his shoulder for hours together, trudging through woods and swamps, and up hill and down dale, to shoot a few squirrels or wild pigeons. He would never refuse to assist a neighbor even in the roughest toil, and was a foremost man at all country frolics for husking Indian corn, or building stone fences; the women of the village, too, used to employ him to run their errands, and to do such little odd jobs as their less obliging husbands would not do for them. In a word Rip was ready to attend to anybody's business but his own; but as to doing family duty, and keeping his farm in order, he found it impossible.

In fact, he declared it was of no use to work on his farm; it was the most pestilent little piece of ground in the whole country; everything about it went wrong, and would go wrong, in spite of him. His fences were continually falling to pieces; his cow would either go astray, or get among the cabbages; weeds were sure to grow quicker in his fields than anywhere else; the rain always made a point of setting in just as he had some out-door work to do; so that though his patrimonial estate had dwindled away under his management, acre by acre, until there was little more left than a mere patch of Indian corn and potatoes, yet it was the worst conditioned farm in the neighborhood.

His children, too, were as ragged and wild as if they belonged to nobody. His son Rip, an urchin begotten in his own likeness, promised to inherit the habits, with the old clothes of his father. He was generally seen trooping like a colt at his mother's heels, equipped in a pair of his father's cast-off galligaskins, which he had much ado to hold up with one hand, as a fine lady does her train in bad weather.

Rip Van Winkle, however, was one of those happy mortals, of foolish, well-oiled dispositions, who take the world easy, eat white bread or brown, whichever can be got with least thought or trouble, and would rather starve on a penny than work for a pound. If left to himself, he would have whistled life away in perfect contentment; but his wife kept continually dinning in his ears about his idleness, his carelessness, and the ruin he was bringing on his family. Morning, noon, and night, her tongue was incessantly going, and everything he said or did was sure to produce a torrent of household eloquence. Rip had but one way of replying to all lectures of the kind, and that, by frequent use, had grown into a habit. He shrugged his shoulders, shook his head, cast up his eyes, but said nothing. This, however, always provoked a fresh volley from his wife; so that he was fain to draw off his forces, and take to the outside of the house--the only side which, in truth, belongs to a hen-pecked husband.

Rip's sole domestic adherent was his dog Wolf, who was as much henpecked as his master; for Dame Van Winkle regarded them as companions in idleness, and even looked upon Wolf with an evil eye, as the cause of his master's going so often astray. True it is, in all points of spirit befitting an honorable dog, he was as courageous an animal as ever scoured the woods—but what courage can withstand the ever-during and all-be-setting terrors of a woman's tongue? The moment Wolf entered the house his crest fell, his tail drooped to the ground, or curled between his legs, he sneaked about with a gallows air, casting many a sidelong glance at Dame Van Winkle, and at the least flourish of a broomstick or ladle, he would fly to the door with yelping precipitation.

Times grew worse and worse with Rip Van Winkle as years of matrimony rolled on; a tart temper never mellows with age, and a sharp tongue is the only edged tool that grows keener with constant use. For a long while he used to console himself, when driven from home, by frequenting a kind of perpetual club of the sages, philosophers, and other idle personages of the village; which held its sessions on a bench before a small inn, designated by a rubicund portrait of His Majesty George the Third. Here they used to sit in the shade through a long lazy summer's day, talking listlessly over village gossip, or telling endless sleepy stories about nothing. But it would have been worth any statesman's money to have heard the profound discussions that sometimes took place, when by chance an old newspaper fell into their hands from some passing traveller. How solemnly they would listen to the contents, as drawled out by Derrick Van Bummel, the schoolmaster, a dapper learned little man, who was not to be daunted by the most gigantic word in the dictionary; and how sagely they would deliberate upon the public events some months after they had taken place.

The opinions of this junto were completely controlled by Nicholas Vedder, a patriarch of the village, and landlord of the inn, at the door of which he took his seat from morning till night, just moving sufficiently to avoid the sun and keep in the shade of a large tree; so that the neighbors could tell the hour by his movements as accurately as by a sun-dial. It is true he was rarely heard to speak, but smoked his pipe incessantly. His adherents, however (for every great man has his adherents), perfectly understood him, and knew how to gather his opinions. When any thing that was read or related displeased him, he was observed to smoke his pipe vehemently, and to send forth short, frequent and angry puffs; but when pleased, he would inhale the smoke slowly and tranquilly, and emit it in light and placid clouds; and sometimes, taking the pipe from his mouth, and letting the fragrant vapor curl about his nose, would gravely nod his head in token of perfect approbation.

From even this stronghold the unlucky Rip was at length routed by his termagant wife, who would suddenly break in upon the tranquillity of the assemblage and call the members all to naught; nor was that august personage, Nicholas Vedder himself, sacred from the daring tongue of this terrible virago, who charged him outright with encouraging her husband in habits of idleness.

Poor Rip was at last reduced almost to despair; and his only alternative, to escape from the labor of the farm and clamor of his wife, was to take gun in hand and stroll away into the woods. Here he would sometimes seat himself at the foot of a tree, and share the contents of his wallet with Wolf, with whom he sympathized as a fellow-sufferer in persecution. "Poor Wolf," he would say, "thy mistress leads thee a dogs life of it; but never mind, my lad, whilst I live thou shalt never want a friend to stand by thee!" Wolf would wag his tail, look wistfully in his master's face, and if dogs can feel pity I verily believe he reciprocated the sentiment with all his heart.

In a long ramble of the kind on a fine autumnal day, Rip had unconsciously scrambled to one of the highest parts of the Kaatskill mountains. He was after his favorite sport of squirrel shooting, and the still solitudes had echoed and re-echoed with the reports of his gun. Panting and fatigued, he threw himself, late in the afternoon, on a green knoll, covered with mountain herbage, that crowned the brow of a precipice. From an opening between the trees he could overlook all the lower country for many a mile of rich woodland. He saw at a distance the lordly Hudson, far, far below him, moving on its silent but majestic course, with the reflection of a purple cloud, or the sail of a lagging bark, here and there sleeping on its glassy bosom, and at last losing itself in the blue highlands.

On the other side he looked down into a deep mountain glen, wild, lonely, and shagged, the bottom filled with fragments from the impending cliffs, and scarcely lighted by the reflected rays of the setting sun. For some time Rip lay musing on this scene; evening was gradually advancing; the mountains began to throw their long blue shadows over the valleys; he saw that it would be dark long before he could reach the village, and he heaved a heavy sigh when he thought of encountering the terrors of Dame Van Winkle.

As he was about to descend, he heard a voice from a distance, hallooing, "Rip Van Winkle! Rip Van Winkle!" He looked round, but could see nothing but a crow winging its solitary flight across the mountain. He thought his fancy must have deceived him, and turned again to descend, when he heard the same cry ring through the still evening air: "Rip Van Winkle! Rip Van Winkle!"—at the same time Wolf bristled up his back, and giving a low growl, skulked to his master's side, looking fearfully down into the glen. Rip now felt a vague apprehension stealing over him; he looked anxiously in the same direction, and perceived a strange figure slowly toiling up the rocks, and bending under the weight of something he carried on his back. He was surprised to see any human being in this lonely and unfrequented place, but supposing it to be some one of the neighborhood in need of his assistance, he hastened down to yield it.

On nearer approach he was still more surprised at the singularity of the stranger's appearance. He was a short square-built old fellow, with thick bushy hair, and a grizzled beard. His dress was of the antique Dutch fashion—a cloth jerkin strapped round the waist—several pair of breeches, the outer one of ample volume, decorated with rows of buttons down the sides, and bunches at the knees. He bore on his shoulder a stout keg, that seemed full of liquor, and made signs for Rip to approach and assist him with the load. Though rather shy and distrustful of this new acquaintance, Rip complied with his usual alacrity; and mutually relieving one another, they clambered up a narrow gully, apparently the dry bed of a mountain torrent. As they ascended, Rip every now and then heard long rolling peals, like distant thunder, that seemed to issue out of a deep ravine, or rather cleft, between lofty rocks, toward which their rugged path conducted. He paused for an instant, but supposing it to be the muttering of one of those transient thundershowers which often take place in mountain heights, he proceeded. Passing through the ravine, they came to a hollow, like a small amphitheatre, surrounded by perpendicular precipices, over the brinks of which impending trees shot their branches, so that you only caught glimpses of the azure sky and the bright evening cloud. During the whole time Rip and his companion had labored on in silence; for though the former marvelled greatly what could be the object of carrying a keg of liquor up this wild mountain, yet there was something strange and incomprehensible about the unknown, that inspired awe and checked familiarity.

On entering the amphitheatre, new objects of wonder presented themselves. On a level spot in the centre was a company of odd-looking personages playing at ninepins. They were dressed in a quaint outlandish fashion; some wore short doublets, others jerkins, with long knives in their belts, and most of them had enormous breeches, of similar style with that of the guide's. Their visages, too, were peculiar: one had a large beard, broad face, and small piggish eyes; the face of another seemed to consist entirely of nose, and was surmounted by a white sugar-loaf hat set off with a little red cock's tail. They all had beards, of various shapes and colors. There was one who seemed to be the commander. He was a stout old gentleman, with a weather-beaten countenance; he wore a laced doublet, broad belt and hanger, high-crowned hat and feather, red stockings, and high-heeled shoes, with roses in them. The whole group reminded Rip of the figures in an old Flemish painting, in the parlor of Dominie Van Shaick, the village parson, and which had been brought over from Holland at the time of the settlement.

What seemed particularly odd to Rip was, that though these folks were evidently amusing themselves, yet they maintained the gravest faces, the most mysterious silence, and were, withal, the most melancholy party of pleasure he had ever witnessed. Nothing interrupted the stillness of the scene but the noise of the balls, which, whenever they were rolled, echoed along the mountains like rumbling peals of thunder.

As Rip and his companion approached them, they suddenly desisted from their play, and stared at him with such fixed statue-like gaze, and such strange, uncouth, lack-lustre countenances, that his heart turned within him, and his knees smote together. His companion now emptied the contents of the keg into large flagons, and made signs to him to wait upon the company. He obeyed with fear and trembling; they quaffed the liquor in profound silence, and then returned to their game.

By degrees Rip's awe and apprehension subsided. He even ventured, when no eye was fixed upon him, to taste the beverage, which he found had much of the flavor of excellent Hollands. He was naturally a thirsty soul, and was soon tempted to repeat the draught. One taste provoked another;

and he reiterated his visits to the flagon so often that at length his senses were overpowered, his eyes swam in his head, his head gradually declined, and he fell into a deep sleep.

On waking, he found himself on the green knoll whence he had first seen the old man of the glen. He rubbed his eyes—it was a bright sunny morning. The birds were hopping and twittering among the bushes, and the eagle was wheeling aloft, and breasting the pure mountain breeze. "Surely," thought Rip, "I have not slept here all night." He recalled the occurrences before he fell asleep. The strange man with a keg of liquor—the mountain ravine—the wild retreat among the rocks—the woe-begone party at ninepins—the flagon—"Oh! that flagon! that wicked flagon!" thought Rip—"what excuse shall I make to Dame Van Winkle!"

He looked round for his gun, but in place of the clean well-oiled fowling-piece, he found an old firelock lying by him, the barrel incrusted with rust, the lock falling off, and the stock worm-eaten. He now suspected that the grave roysters of the mountain had put a trick upon him, and, having dosed him with liquor, had robbed him of his gun. Wolf, too, had disappeared, but he might have strayed away after a squirrel or partridge. He whistled after him and shouted his name, but all in vain; the echoes repeated his whistle and shout, but no dog was to be seen.

He determined to revisit the scene of the last evening's gambol, and if he met with any of the party, to demand his dog and gun. As he rose to walk, he found himself stiff in the joints, and wanting in his usual activity. "These mountain beds do not agree with me," thought Rip, "and if this frolic should lay me up with a fit of the rheumatism, I shall have a blessed time with Dame Van Winkle." With some difficulty he got down into the glen: he found the gully up which he and his companion had ascended the preceding evening; but to his astonishment a mountain stream was now foaming down it, leaping from rock to rock, and filling the glen with babbling murmurs. He, however, made shift to scramble up its sides, working his toilsome way through thickets of birch, sassafras, and witch-hazel, and sometimes tripped up or entangled by the wild grapevines that twisted their coils or tendrils from tree to tree, and spread a kind of network in his path.

At length he reached to where the ravine had opened through the cliffs to the amphitheatre; but no traces of such opening remained. The rocks presented a high impenetrable wall, over which the torrent came tumbling in a sheet of feathery foam, and fell into a broad deep basin, black from the shadows of the surrounding forest. Here, then, poor Rip was brought to a stand. He again called and whistled after his dog; he was only answered by the cawing of a flock of idle crows, sporting high in air about a dry tree that overhung a sunny precipice; and who, secure in their elevation, seemed to look down and scoff at the poor man's perplexities. What was to be done? The morning was passing away, and Rip felt famished for want of his breakfast. He grieved to give up his dog and gun; he dreaded to meet his wife; but it would not do to starve among the mountains. He shook his head, shouldered the rusty firelock, and, with a heart full of trouble and anxiety, turned his steps homeward.

As he approached the village he met a number of people, but none whom he knew, which somewhat surprised him, for he had thought himself acquainted with everyone in the country round. Their dress, too, was of a different fashion from that to which he was accustomed. They all stared at him with equal marks of surprise, and whenever they cast their eyes upon him, invariably stroked their chins. The constant recurrence of this gesture induced Rip, involuntarily, to do the same, when, to his astonishment, he found his beard had grown a foot long!

He had now entered the skirts of the village. A troop of strange children ran at his heels, hooting after him, and pointing at his gray beard. The dogs, too, not one of which he recognized for an old acquaintance, barked at him as he passed. The very village was altered; it was larger and more populous. There were rows of houses which he had never seen before, and those which had been his familiar haunts had disappeared. Strange names were over the doors—strange faces at the windows—everything was strange. His mind now misgave him; he began to doubt whether both he and the world around him were not bewitched. Surely this was his native village, which he had left but the day before. There stood the Kaatskill mountains—there ran the silver Hudson at a distance—there was every hill and dale precisely as it had always been. Rip was sorely perplexed—"That flagon last night," thought he, "has addled my poor head sadly!"

It was with some difficulty that he found the way to his own house, which he approached with silent awe, expecting every moment to hear the shrill voice of Dame Van Winkle. He found the house gone to decay—the roof fallen in, the windows shattered, and the doors off the hinges. A half-starved dog that looked like Wolf was skulking about it. Rip called him by name, but the cur snarled, showed his teeth, and passed on. This was an unkind cut indeed—"My very dog," sighed poor Rip, "has forgotten me!"

He entered the house, which, to tell the truth, Dame Van Winkle had always kept in neat order. It was empty, forlorn, and apparently abandoned. This desolateness overcame all his connubial fears—he called loudly for his wife and children—the lonely chambers rang for a moment with his voice, and then all again was silence.

He now hurried forth, and hastened to his old resort, the village inn—but it too was gone. A large rickety wooden building stood in its place, with great gaping windows, some of them broken and mended with old hats and petticoats, and over the door was painted, "the Union Hotel, by Jonathan Doolittle." Instead of the great tree that used to shelter the quiet little Dutch inn of yore, there now was reared a tall naked pole, with something on the top that looked like a red night-cap, and from it was fluttering a flag, on which was a singular assemblage of stars and stripes—all this was strange and incomprehensible. He recognized on the sign, however, the ruby face of King George, under which he had smoked so many a peaceful pipe; but even this was singularly metamorphosed. The red coat was changed for one of blue and buff, a sword was held in the hand instead of a sceptre, the head was decorated with a cocked hat, and underneath, was painted in large characters, GENERAL WASHINGTON.

There was, as usual, a crowd of folk about the door, but none that Rip recollected. The very character of the people seemed changed. There was a busy, bustling, disputatious tone about it, instead of the accustomed phlegm and drowsy tranquillity. He looked in vain for the sage Nicholas Vedder, with his broad face, double chin, and fair long pipe, uttering clouds of tobacco-smoke instead of idle speeches; or Van Bummel, the schoolmaster, doling forth the contents of an ancient newspaper. In place of these, a lean, bilious-looking fellow, with his pockets full of handbills, was haranguing vehemently about rights of citizens—elections—members of Congress—liberty—Bunker's Hill—heroes of seventy-six—and other words, which were a perfect Babylonish jargon to the bewildered Van Winkle.

The appearance of Rip, with his long grizzled beard, his rusty fowling-piece, his uncouth dress, and an army of women and children at his heels, soon attracted the attention of the tavern politicians. They crowded round him, eying him from head to foot with great curiosity. The orator bustled up to him, and, drawing him partly aside, inquired "On which side he voted?" Rip stared in vacant stupidity. Another short but busy little fellow pulled him by the arm, and, rising on tiptoe, inquired in his ear, "Whether he was Federal or Democrat?" Rip was equally at a loss to comprehend the question; when a knowing, self-important old gentleman, in a sharp cocked hat, made his way through the crowd, putting them to the right and left with his elbows as he passed, and planting himself before Van Winkle, with one arm akimbo, the other resting on his cane, his keen eyes and sharp hat penetrating, as it were, into his very soul, demanded in an austere tone, "What brought him to the election with a gun on his shoulder, and a mob at his heels, and whether he meant to breed a riot in the village?"—"Alas! gentlemen," cried Rip, somewhat dismayed, "I am a poor quiet man, a native of the place, and a loyal subject of the king, God bless him!"

Here a general shout burst from the bystanders—"A tory! a tory! a spy! a refugee! hustle him! away with him!" It was with great difficulty that the self-important man in the cocked hat restored order; and, having assumed a tenfold austerity of brow, demanded again of the unknown culprit, what he came there for, and whom he was seeking? The poor man humbly assured him that he meant no harm, but merely came there in search of some of his neighbors, who used to keep about the tavern.

"Well—who are they?—name them."

Rip bethought himself a moment, and inquired. "Where's Nicholas Vedder?"

There was a silence for a little while, when an old man replied in a thin piping voice, "Nicholas Vedder! why, he is dead and gone these eighteen years! There was a wooden tombstone in the churchyard that used to tell all about him, but that's rotten and gone too."

"Where's Brom Dutcher?"

"Oh, he went off to the army in the beginning of the war; some say he was killed at the storming of Stony Point—others say he was drowned in a squall at the foot of Antony's Nose. I don't know—he never came back again."

"Where's Van Bummel, the schoolmaster?"

"He went off to the wars too, was a great militia general, and is now in Congress."

Rip's heart died away at hearing of these sad changes in his home and friends, and finding himself thus alone in the world. Every answer puzzled him too, by treating of such enormous lapses of time, and of matters which he could not understand: war—congress—Stony Point;—he had no courage to ask after any more friends, but cried out in despair, "Does nobody here know Rip Van Winkle?"

"Oh, Rip Van Winkie!" exclaimed two or three, "Oh, to be sure! that's Rip Van Winkle yonder, leaning against the tree."

Rip looked, and beheld a precise counterpart of himself, as he went up the mountain: apparently as lazy, and certainly as ragged. The poor fellow was now completely confounded. He doubted his own identity, and whether he was himself or another man. In the midst of his bewilderment, the man in the cocked hat demanded who he was, and what was his name?

"God knows," exclaimed he, at his wit's end; "I'm not myself—I'm somebody else—that's me yonder—no—that's somebody else got into my shoes—I was myself last night, but I fell asleep on the mountain, and they've changed my gun, and every thing's changed, and I'm changed, and I can't tell my name, or who I am!"

The bystanders began now to look at each other, nod, wink significantly, and tap their fingers against their foreheads. There was a whisper, also, about securing the gun, and keeping the old fellow from doing mischief, at the very suggestion of which the self-important man in the cocked hat retired with some precipitation. At this critical moment a fresh, comely woman pressed through the throng to get a peep at the gray-bearded man. She had a chubby child in her arms, which, frightened at his looks, began to cry. "Hush, Rip," cried she, "hush, you little fool; the old man won't hurt you." The name of the child, the air of the mother, the tone of her voice, all awakened a train of recollections in his mind. "What is your name, my good woman?" asked he.

"Judith Gardenier."

"And your father's name?"

"Ah, poor man, Rip Van Winkle was his name, but it's twenty years since he went away from home with his gun, and never has been heard of since—his dog came home without him; but whether he shot himself, or was carried away by the Indians, nobody can tell. I was then but a little girl."

Rip had but one question more to ask; but he put it with a faltering voice:

"Where's your mother?"

"Oh, she too had died but a short time since; she broke a bloodvessel in a fit of passion at a New England peddler."

There was a drop of comfort, at least, in this intelligence. The honest man could contain himself no longer. He caught his daughter and her child in his arms. "I am your father!" cried he—"Young Rip Van Winkle once—old Rip Van Winkle now!—Does nobody know poor Rip Van Winkle?"

All stood amazed, until an old woman, tottering out from among the crowd, put her hand to her brow, and peering under it in his face for a moment, exclaimed, "Sure enough! it is Rip Van Winkle—it is himself! Welcome home again, old neighbor—Why, where have you been these twenty long years?"

Rip's story was soon told, for the whole twenty years had been to him but as one night. The neighbors stared when they heard it; some were seen to wink at each other, and put their tongues in their cheeks; and the self-important man in the cocked hat, who, when the alarm was over, had returned to the field, screwed down the corners of his mouth, and shook his head—upon which there was a general shaking of the head throughout the assemblage.

It was determined, however, to take the opinion of old Peter Vanderdonk, who was seen slowly advancing up the road. He was a descendant of the historian of that name, who wrote one of the earliest accounts of the province. Peter was the most ancient inhabitant of the village, and well versed in all the wonderful events and traditions of the neighborhood. He recollected Rip at once, and corroborated his story in the most satisfactory manner. He assured the company that it was a fact, handed down from his ancestor the historian, that the Kaatskill mountains had always been haunted by strange beings. That it was affirmed that the great Hendrick Hudson, the first discoverer of the river and country, kept a kind of vigil there every twenty years, with his crew of the *Half-Moon;* being permitted in this way to revisit the scenes of his enterprise, and keep a guardian eye upon the river, and the great city called by his name. That his father had once seen them in their old Dutch dresses playing at ninepins in a hollow of the mountain; and that he himself had heard one summer afternoon, the sound of their balls, like distant peals of thunders.

To make a long story short, the company broke up, and returned to the more important concerns of the election. Rip's daughter took him home to live with her; she had a snug, well-furnished house, and a stout cheery farmer for a husband, whom Rip recollected for one of the urchins that used to climb upon his back. As to Rip's son and heir, who was the ditto of himself, seen leaning against the tree, he was employed to work on the farm; but evinced an hereditary disposition to attend to anything else but his business.

Rip now resumed his old walks and habits; he soon found many of his former cronies, though all rather the worse for the wear and tear of time, and preferred making friends among the rising generation, with whom he soon grew into great favor.

Having nothing to do at home, and being arrived at that happy age when a man can be idle with impunity, he took his place once more on the bench at the inn door, and was reverenced as one of the patriarchs of the village, and a chronicle of the old times "before the war." It was some time before he could get into the regular track of gossip, or could be made to comprehend the strange events that had taken place during his torpor. How that there had been a revolutionary war—that the country had thrown off the yoke of old England—and that, instead of being a subject of his Majesty George the Third, he was now a free citizen of the United States. Rip, in fact, was no politician; the changes of states and empires made but little impression on him; but there was one species of despotism under which he had long groaned, and that was—petticoat government. Happily that was at an end; he had got his neck out of the yoke of matrimony, and could go in and out whenever he pleased, without dreading the tyranny of Dame Van Winkle. Whenever her name was mentioned, however, he shook his head, shrugged his shoulders, and cast up his eyes; which might pass either for an expression of resignation to his fate, or joy at his deliverance.

He used to tell his story to every stranger that arrived at Mr. Doolittle's hotel. He was observed, at first, to vary on some points every time he told it, which was, doubtless, owing to his having so recently awaked. It at last settled down precisely to the tale I have related, and not a man, woman, or child in the neighborhood, but knew it by heart. Some always pretended to doubt the reality of it, and insisted that Rip had been out of his head, and that this was one point on which he always remained flighty. The old Dutch inhabitants, however, almost universally gave it full credit. Even to this day they never hear a thunderstorm of a summer afternoon about the Kaatskill, but they say Hendrick Hudson and his crew are at their game of ninepins; and it is a common wish of all hen-pecked husbands in the neighborhood, when life hangs heavy on their hands, that they might have a quieting draught out of Rip Van Winkle's flagon.

The Legend of Sleepy Hollow

(First published in *The Sketchbook of Geoffrey Crayon, Gent.*, February, 1820.)

A pleasing land of drowsy head it was,
Of dreams that wave before the half-shut eye;
And of gay castles in the clouds that pass,
For ever flushing round a summer sky.

CASTLE OF INDOLENCE

IN THE BOSOM of one of the spacious coves which indent the eastern shore of the Hudson, at that broad expansion of the river denominated by the ancient Dutch navigators the Tappan Zee, and where they always prudently shortened sail, and implored the protection of St. Nicholas when they crossed, there lies a small market-town or rural port, which by some is called Greensburgh, but which is more generally and properly known by the name of Tarry Town. This name was given, we are told, in former days, by the good housewives of the adjacent country, from the inveterate propensity of their husbands to linger about the village tavern on market days. Be that as it may, I do not vouch for the fact, but merely advert to it, for the sake of being precise and authentic. Not far from this village, perhaps about two miles, there is a little valley, or rather lap of land, among high hills, which is one of the quietest places in the whole world. A small brook glides through it, with just murmur enough to lull one to repose; and the occasional whistle of a quail or tapping of a woodpecker, is almost the only sound that ever breaks in upon the uniform tranquillity.

I recollect that, when a stripling, my first exploit in squirrel-shooting was in a grove of tall walnut-trees that shades one side of the valley. I had wandered into it at noon time, when all nature is peculiarly quiet, and was startled by the roar of my own gun, as it broke the Sabbath stillness around, and was prolonged and reverberated by the angry echoes. If ever I should wish for a retreat, whither I might steal from the world and its distractions, and dream quietly away the remnant of a troubled life, I know of none more promising than this little valley.

From the listless repose of the place, and the peculiar character of its inhabitants, who are descendants from the original Dutch settlers, this sequestered glen has long been known by the name of SLEEPY HOLLOW, and its rustic lads are called the Sleepy Hollow Boys throughout all the neighboring country. A drowsy dreamy influence seems to hang over the land, and to pervade the very atmosphere. Some say that the place was bewitched by a high German doctor, during the early days of the settlement; others, that an old Indian chief, the prophet or wizard of his tribe, held his powwows there before the country was discovered by Master Hendrick Hudson. Certain it is, the place still continues under the sway of some witching power, that holds a spell over the minds of the good people, causing them to walk in a continual reverie. They are given to all kinds of marvelous beliefs; are subject to trances and visions; and frequently see strange sights, and hear music and voices in the air. The whole neighborhood abounds with local tales, haunted spots, and twilight superstitions; stars shoot and meteors glare oftener across the valley than in any other part of the country, and the nightmare, with her whole nine fold, seems to make it the favorite scene of her gambols.

The dominant spirit, however, that haunts this enchanted region, and seems to be commander-in-chief of all the powers of the air, is the apparition of a figure on horseback without a head. It is said by some to be the ghost of a Hessian trooper, whose head had been carried away by a cannon-ball, in some nameless battle during the Revolutionary War; and who is ever and anon seen by the country folk, hurrying along in the gloom of night, as if on the wings of the wind. His haunts are not confined to the valley, but extend at times to the adjacent roads, and especially to the vicinity of a church at no great distance. Indeed, certain of the most authentic historians of those parts, who have been careful in collecting and collating the floating facts concerning this specter, allege that the body of the trooper, having been buried in the churchyard, the ghost rides forth to the scene of battle in nightly quest of his head; and that the rushing speed with which he sometimes passes along the Hollow, like a midnight blast, is owing to his being belated, and in a hurry to get back to the churchyard before daybreak.

Such is the general purport of this legendary superstition, which has furnished materials for many a wild story in that region of shadows; and the specter is known at all the country firesides by the name of the Headless Horseman of Sleepy Hollow.

It is remarkable that the visionary propensity I have mentioned is not confined to the native inhabitants of the valley, but is unconsciously imbibed by everyone who resides there for a time. However wide awake they may have been before they entered that sleepy region, they are sure, in a little time, to inhale the witching influence of the air, and begin to grow imaginative—to dream dreams, and see apparitions.

I mention this peaceful spot with all possible laud; for it is in such little retired Dutch valleys, found here and there embosomed in the great state of New York, that population, manners, and customs remain fixed; while the great torrent of migration and improvement, which is making such incessant changes in other parts of this restless country, sweeps by them unobserved. They are like those little nooks of still water which border a rapid stream; where we may see the straw and bubble riding quietly at anchor, or slowly revolving in their mimic harbor, undisturbed by the rush of the passing current. Though many years have elapsed since I trod the drowsy shades of Sleepy Hollow, yet I question whether I should not still find the same trees and the same families vegetating in its sheltered bosom.

In this by-place of nature there abode, in a remote period of American history, that is to say, some thirty years since, a worthy wight of the name of Ichabod Crane; who sojourned, or, as he expressed it, "tarried," in Sleepy Hollow, for the purpose of instructing the children of the vicinity. He was a native of Connecticut; a state which supplies the Union with pioneers for the mind as well as for the forest, and sends forth yearly its legions of frontier woodmen and country schoolmasters. The cognomen of Crane was not inapplicable to his person. He was tall, but exceedingly lank, with narrow shoulders, long arms and legs, hands that dangled a mile out of his sleeves, feet that might have served for shovels, and his whole frame most loosely hung together. His head was small, and flat at top, with huge ears, large green glassy eyes, and a long snipe nose, so that it looked like a weather-cock, perched upon his spindle neck, to tell which way the wind blew. To see him striding along the profile of a hill on a windy day, with his clothes bagging and fluttering about him, one might have mistaken him for the genius of famine descending upon the earth, or some scarecrow eloped from a corn-field.

His school-house was a low building of one large room, rudely constructed of logs; the windows partly glazed, and partly patched with leaves of old copy-books. It was most ingeniously secured at vacant hours, by a withe twisted in the handle of the door, and stakes set against the window-shutters; so that, though a thief might get in with perfect ease, he would find some embarrassment in getting out; an idea most probably borrowed by the architect, Yost Van Houten, from the mystery of an eel-pot. The school-house stood in a rather lonely but pleasant situation, just at the foot of a woody hill, with a brook running close by, and a formidable birch-tree growing at one end of it. From hence the low murmur or his pupils'voices, conning over their lessons, might be heard. in a drowsy summer's day, like the hum of a bee-hive; interrupted now and then by the authoritative voice of the master, in the tone of menace or command; or, peradventure, by the appalling sound of the birch, as he urged some tardy loiterer along the flowery path of knowledge. Truth to say, he was a conscientious man, and ever bore in mind the golden maxim, "Spare the rod and spoil the child." Ichabod Crane's scholars certainly were not spoiled.

I would not have it imagined, however, that he was one of those cruel potentates of the school, who joy in the smart of their subjects; on the contrary, he administered justice with discrimination rather than severity; taking the burthen off the backs of the weak, and laying it on those of the strong. Your mere puny stripling, that winced at the least flourish of the rod, was passed by with indulgence; but the claims of justice were satisfied by inflicting a double portion on some little tough, wrong-headed, broad-skirted Dutch urchin, who sulked and swelled and grew dogged and sullen beneath the birch. All this he called "doing his duty by their parents"; and he never inflicted a chastisement without following it by the assurance, so consolatory to the smarting urchin, that "he would remember it and thank him for it the longest day he had to live."

When school-hours were over, he was even the companion and playmate of the larger boys; and on holiday afternoons would convoy some of the smaller ones home, who happened to have pretty sisters, or good housewives for mothers, noted for the comforts of the cupboard. Indeed, it behoved him to keep on good terms with his pupils. The revenue arising from his school was small, and would have been scarcely sufficient to furnish him with daily bread, for he was a huge feeder, and though lank, had the dilating powers of an anaconda; but to help out his maintenance, he was, according to country custom in those parts, boarded and lodged at the houses of the farmers, whose children he instructed. With these he lived successively a week at a time; thus going the rounds of the neighborhood, with all his worldly effects tied up in a cotton handkerchief.

That all this might not be too onerous on the purses of his rustic patrons, who are apt to consider the costs of schooling a grievous burden, and schoolmasters as mere drones, he had various ways of rendering himself both useful and agreeable. He assisted the farmers occasionally in the lighter labors of their farms; helped to make hay; mended the fences; took the horses to water; drove the cows from pasture; and cut wood for the winter fire. He laid aside, too, all the dominant dignity and absolute sway with which he lorded it in his little empire, the school, and became wonderfully gentle and ingratiating. He found favor in the eyes of the mothers by petting the children, particularly the youngest; and like the lion bold, which whilom so magnanimously the lamb did hold, he would sit with a child on one knee, and rock a cradle with his foot for whole hours together.

In addition to his other vocations, he was the singing-master of the neighborhood, and picked up many bright shillings by instructing the young folks in psalmody. It was a matter of no little vanity to him, on Sundays, to take his station in front of the church gallery, with a band of chosen singers; where, in his own mind, he completely carried away the psalm from the parson. Certain it is, his voice resounded far above all the rest of the congregation; and there are peculiar quavers still to be heard in that church, and which may even be heard half a mile off, quite to the opposite side of the mill-pond, on a still Sunday morning, which are said to be legitimately descended from the nose of Ichabod Crane. Thus, by divers little make-shifts, in that ingenious way which is commonly denominated "by hook and by crook," the worthy pedagogue got on tolerably enough, and was thought, by all who understand nothing of the labor of head-work, to have a wonderfully easy life of it.

The schoolmaster is generally a man of some importance in the female circle of a rural neighborhood; being considered a kind of idle gentleman-like personage, of vastly superior taste and accomplishments to the rough country swains, and, indeed, inferior in learning only to the parson. His appearance, therefore, is apt to occasion some little stir at the tea-table of a farm-house and the addition of a supernumerary dish of cakes or sweetmeats, or peradventure the parade of a silver teapot. Our man of letters, therefore, was peculiarly happy in the smiles of all the country damsels. How he would figure among them in the churchyard between services on Sundays! gathering grapes for them from the wild vines that overran the surrounding trees; reciting for their amusement all the epitaphs on the tombstones; or sauntering with a whole bevy of them along the banks of the adjacent mill-pond; while the more bashful country bumpkins hung sheepishly back, envying his superior elegance and address.

From his half-itinerant life, also, he was a kind of traveling gazette, carrying the whole budget of local gossip from house to house; so that his appearance was always greeted with satisfaction. He was, moreover, esteemed by the women as a man of great erudition, for he had read several books quite through, and was a perfect master of Cotton Mather's *History of New England Witchcraft,* in which, by the way, he most firmly and potently believed.

He was, in fact, an odd mixture of small shrewdness and simple credulity. His appetite for the marvelous, and his powers of digesting it, were equally extraordinary; and both had been increased by his residence in this spell-bound region. No tale was too gross or monstrous for his capacious swallow. It was often his delight, after his school was dismissed in the afternoon, to stretch himself on the rich bed of clover, bordering the little brook that whimpered by his school-house, and there con over old Mather's direful tales, until the gathering dusk of the evening made the printed page a mere mist before his eyes. Then, as he wended his way by swamp and stream and awful woodland, to the farm-house where he happened to be quartered, every sound of nature, at that witching hour, fluttered his excited imagination: the moan of the whip-poor-will* from the hill-side; the boding cry of the tree-toad, that harbinger of storm; the dreary hooting of the screech-owl, or the sudden rustling in the thicket of birds frightened from their roost. The fire-flies, too, which sparkled most vividly in the darkest places, now and then startled him, as one of uncommon brightness would stream across

*The whip-poor-will is a bird which is only heard at night. It receives its name from its note, which is thought to resemble those words.

his path; and if by chance a huge blackhead of a beetle came winging his blundering flight against him, the poor varlet was ready to give up the ghost, with the idea that he was struck with a witch's token. His only resource on such occasions, either to drown thought or drive away evil spirits, was to sing psalm tunes;—and the good people of Sleepy Hollow, as they sat by their doors of an evening, were often filled with awe at hearing his nasal melody, "in linked sweetness long drawn out," floating from the distant hill, or along the dusky road.

Another of his sources of fearful pleasure was to pass long winter evenings with the old Dutch wives, as they sat spinning by the fire, with a row of apples roasting and spluttering along the hearth, and listen to their marvelous tales of ghosts and goblins, and haunted fields, and haunted brooks, and haunted bridges, and haunted houses, and particularly of the headless horseman, or Galloping Hessian of the Hollow, as they sometimes called him. He would delight them equally by his anecdotes of witchcraft, and of the direful omens and portentous sights and sounds in the air, which prevailed in the earlier times of Connecticut; and would frighten them woefully with speculations upon comets and shooting stars; and with the alarming fact that the world did absolutely turn round, and that they were half the time topsy-turvy!

But if there was a pleasure in all this, while snugly cuddling in the chimney-corner of a chamber that was all of a ruddy glow from the crackling wood fire, and where, of course, no specter dared to show its face, it was dearly purchased by the terrors of his subsequent walk homewards. What fearful shapes and shadows beset his path amidst the dim and ghastly glare of a snowy night!—With what wistful look did he eye every trembling ray of light streaming across the waste fields from some distant window!—How often was he appalled by some shrub covered with snow, which, like a sheeted specter, beset his very path!—How often did he shrink with curdling awe at the sound of his own steps on the frosty crust beneath his feet! and dread to look over his shoulder, lest he should behold some uncouth being tramping close behind him!—and how often was he thrown into complete dismay by some rushing blast, howling among the trees, in the idea that it was the Galloping Hessian on one of his nightly scourings!

All these, however, were mere terrors of the night, phantoms of the mind that walk in darkness; and though he had seen many specters in his time, and been more than once beset by Satan in divers shapes, in his lonely perambulations, yet daylight put an end to all these evils; and he would have passed a pleasant life of it, in despite of the devil and all his works, if his path had not been crossed by a being that causes more perplexity to mortal man than ghosts, goblins, and the whole race of witches put together, and that was—a woman.

Among the musical disciples who assembled one evening in each week to receive his instructions in psalmody, was Katrina Van Tassel, the daughter and only child of a substantial Dutch farmer. She was a blooming lass of fresh eighteen; plump as a partridge; ripe and melting and rosy-cheeked as one of her father's peaches, and universally famed, not merely for her beauty, but her vast expectations. She was, withal, a little of a coquette, as might be perceived even in her dress, which was a mixture of ancient and modern fashions, as most suited to set off her charms. She wore ornaments of pure yellow gold, which her great-great-grandmother had brought over from Saardam; the tempting stomacher of the olden time; and withal a provokingly short petticoat, to display the prettiest foot and ankle in the country round.

Ichabod Crane had a soft and foolish heart towards the sex, and it is not to be wondered at that so tempting a morsel soon found favor in his eyes, more especially after he had visited her in her paternal mansion. Old Baltus Van Tassel was a perfect picture of a thriving, contented, liberal-hearted farmer. He seldom, it is true, sent either his eyes or his thoughts beyond the boundaries of his own farm; but within those, everything was snug, happy, and well-conditioned. He was satisfied with his wealth, but not proud of it; and piqued himself upon the hearty abundance, rather than the style in which he lived. His stronghold was situated on the banks of the Hudson, in one of those green, sheltered, fertile nooks, in which the Dutch farmers are so fond of nestling. A great elm-tree spread its broad branches over it, at the foot of which bubbled up a spring of the softest and sweetest water, in a little well formed of a barrel, and then stole sparkling away through the grass to a neighboring brook that bubbled along among alders and drawf willows. Hard by the farm-house was a vast barn that might have served for a church, every window and crevice of which seemed bursting forth with the treasures of the farm; the flail was busily resounding within it from morning to night; swallows and martins skimmed twittering about the eaves; and rows of pigeons, some with one eye turned up, as if watching the weather, some with their heads under their wings, or buried in their bosoms, and others swelling, and cooing, and bowing about their dames, were enjoying the sunshine on the roof. Sleek unwieldy porkers were grunting in the repose and abundance of their pens, whence sallied forth now and then troops of sucking pigs, as if to snuff the air. A stately squadron of snowy geese were riding in an adjoining pond, convoying whole fleets of ducks; regiments of turkeys were gobbling through the farm-yard, and guinea-fowls fretting about it, like ill-tempered house-wives, with their peevish, discontented cry. Before the barn door strutted the gallant cock, that pattern of a husband, a warrior, and a fine gentleman, clapping his burnished wings, and crowing in the pride and gladness of his heart—sometimes tearing up the earth with his feet, and then generously calling his ever-hungry family of wives and children to enjoy the rich morsel which he had discovered.

The pedagogue's mouth watered as he looked upon his sumptuous promise of luxurious winter fare. In his devouring mind's eye he pictured to himself every roasting-pig running about with a pudding in his belly, and an apple in his mouth; the pigeons were snugly put to bed in a comfortable pie, and tucked in with a coverlet of crust; the geese were swimming in their own gravy; and the ducks pairing cozily in dishes, like snug married couples, with a decent competency of onion sauce. In the porkers he saw carved out the future sleek side of bacon and juicy relishing ham; not a turkey but he beheld daintily trussed up, with its gizzard under its wing, and, peradventure, a necklace of savory sausages; and even bright chanticleer himself lay sprawling on his back in a side dish, with uplifted claws, as if craving that quarter which his chivalrous spirit disdained to ask while living.

As the enraptured Ichabod fancied all this, and as he rolled his great green eyes over the fat meadow-lands, the rich fields of wheat, of rye, of buckwheat, and Indian corn, and the orchards burthened with ruddy fruit, which surrounded the warm tenement of Van Tassel, his heart yearned after the damsel who was to inherit these domains, and his imagination expanded with the idea, how they might be readily turned into cash, and the money invested in immense tracts of wild land, and shingle palaces in the wilderness. Nay, his busy fancy already realized his hopes, and presented to him the blooming Katrina, with a whole family of children, mounted on the top of a wagon loaded with household trumpery, with pots and kettles dangling beneath; and he beheld himself bestriding a pacing mare, with a colt at her heels, setting out for Kentucky, Tennessee, or the Lord knows where.

When he entered the house, the conquest of his heart was complete. It was one of those spacious farm-houses, with high-ridged, but lowly sloping roofs, built in the style handed down from the first Dutch settlers; the low projecting eaves forming a piazza along the front, capable of being closed up in bad weather. Under this were hung flails, harness, various utensils of husbandry, and nets for fishing in the neighboring river. Benches were built along the sides for summer use; and a great spinning-wheel at one end, and a churn at the other, showed the various uses to which this important porch might be devoted. From this piazza the wondering Ichabod entered the hall, which formed the center of the mansion and the place of usual residence. Here rows of resplendent pewter, ranged on a long dresser, dazzled his eyes. In one corner stood a huge bag of wool ready to be spun; in another, a quantity of linsey-woolsey just from the loom; ears of Indian corn, and strings of dried apples and peaches, hung in gay festoons along the wall, mingled with the gaud of red peppers; and a door left ajar gave him a peep into the best parlor, where the claw-footed chairs and dark mahogany tables shone like mirrors; and irons, with their accompanying shovel and tongs, glistened from their covert of asparagus tops; mock oranges and conch-shells decorated the mantel-piece; strings of various colored birds' eggs were suspended above it; a great ostrich egg was hung from the center of the room, and a corner-cupboard, knowingly left open, displayed immense treasures of old silver and well-mended china.

From the moment Ichabod laid his eyes upon these regions of delight, the peace of his mind was at an end, and his only study was how to gain the affections of the peerless daughter of Van Tassel. In this enterprise, however, he had more real difficulties than generally fell to the lot of a knight-errant of yore, who seldom had anything but giants, enchanters, fiery dragons, and such like easily conquered adversaries, to contend with; and had to make his way merely through gates of iron and brass, and walls of adamant, to the castle keep, where the lady of his heart was confined; all which he achieved as easily as a man would carve his way to the center of a Christmas pie, and then the lady gave him her hand as a matter of course. Ichabod, on the contrary, had to win his way to the heart of a country coquette, beset with a labyrinth of whims and caprices, which were forever presenting new difficulties and impediments; and he had to encounter a host of fearful adversaries of real flesh and blood, the numerous rustic admirers who beset every portal to her heart, keeping a watchful and angry eye upon each other, but ready to fly out in the common cause against any new competitor.

Among these the most formidable was a burly, roaring, roistering blade, of the name of Abraham, or, according to the Dutch abbreviation, Brom Van Brunt, the hero of the country round, which rang with his feats of strength and hardihood. He was broad-shouldered and double-jointed, with short curly black hair, and a bluff but not unpleasant countenance, having a mingled air of fun and arrogance. From his Herculean frame and great powers of limb, he had received the nickname of BROM BONES, by which he was universally known. He was famed for great knowledge and skill in horsemanship, being as dexterous on horseback as a Tartar. He was foremost at all races and cockfights, and, with the ascendency which bodily strength acquires in rustic life, was the umpire in all disputes, setting his hat on one side, and giving his decisions with an air and tone admitting of no gainsay or appeal. He was always ready for either a fight or frolic, but had more mischief than ill-will in his composition; and, with all his overbearing roughness, there was a strong dash of waggish good humor at bottom. He had three or four boon companions, who regarded him as their model, and at the head of whom he scoured the country, attending every scene of feud or merriment for miles round. In cold weather he was distinguished by a fur cap, surmounted with a flaunting fox's tail; and when the folks at a country gathering descried this well-known crest at a distance, whisking about among a squad of hard riders, they always stood by for a squall. Sometimes his crew would be heard dashing along past the farm-houses at midnight, with hoop and halloo, like a troop of Don Cossacks, and the old dames, startled out of their sleep, would listen for a moment, till the hurry-scurry had clattered by, and then exclaim, "Ay, there goes BROM BONES and his gang!" The neighbors looked upon him with a mixture of awe, admiration, and good-will; and when any madcap prank or rustic brawl occurred in the vicinity, always shook their heads and warranted Brom Bones was at the bottom of it.

This rantipole hero had for some time singled out the blooming Katrina for the object of his uncouth gallantries, and though his amorous toyings were something like the gentle caresses and endearments of a bear, yet it was whispered that she did not altogether discourage his hopes. Certain it is, his advances were signals for rival candidates to retire, who felt no inclination to cross a lion in his amours; insomuch that when his horse was seen tied to Van Tassel's paling on a Sunday night, a sure sign that his master was courting, or, as it is termed, "sparking," within, all other suitors passed by in despair, and carried the war into other quarters.

Such was the formidable rival with whom Ichabod Crane had to contend, and, considering all things, a stouter man than he would have shrunk from the competition, and a wiser man would have despaired. He had, however, a happy mixture of pliability and perseverance in his nature; he was in form and spirit like a supple-jack,–yielding, but tough; though he bent, he never broke; and though he bowed beneath the slighest pressure, yet, the moment it was away–jerk! he was as erect, and carried his head as high as ever.

To have taken the field openly against his rival would have been madness; for he was not a man to be thwarted in his amours, any more than that stormy lover, Achilles. Ichabod, therefore, made his advances in a quiet and gently insinuating manner. Under cover of his character of singing-master, he made frequent visits at the farm-house; not that he had anything to apprehend from the meddlesome interference of parents, which is so often a stumbling-block in the path of lovers. Balt Van Tassel was an easy, indulgent soul; he loved his daughter better even than his pipe, and, like a reasonable man and an excellent father, let her have her way in everything. His notable little wife, too, had enough to do to attend to her housekeeping, and manage her poultry; for, as she sagely observed, ducks and geese are foolish things, and must be looked after, but girls can take care of themselves. Thus, while the busy dame bustled about the house, or plied her spinning-wheel at one end of the piazza, honest Balt would sit smoking his evening pipe at the other, watching the achievements of a little wooden warrior, who, armed with a sword in each hand, was most valiantly fighting the wind on the pinnacle of the barn. In the meantime, Ichabod would carry on his suit with the daughter by the side of the spring under the great elm, or sauntering along in the twilight, that hour so favorable to the lover's eloquence.

I profess not to know how women's hearts are wooed and won. To me they have always been matters of riddle and admiration. Some seem to have but one vulnerable point, or door of access; while others have a thousand avenues, and may be captured in a thousand different ways. It is a great triumph of skill to gain the former, but a still greater proof of generalship to maintain possession of the latter, for a man must battle for his fortress at every door and window. He who wins a thousand common hearts is therefore entitled to some renown; but he who keeps undisputed sway over the heart of a coquette, is indeed a hero. Certain it is, this was not the case with the redoubtable Brom Bones; and from the moment Ichabod Crane made his advances, the interests of the former evidently declined: his horse was no longer seen tied at the palings on Sunday nights, and a deadly feud gradually arose between him and the preceptor of Sleepy Hollow.

Brom, who had a degree of rough chivalry in his nature, would fain have carried matters to open warfare, and have settled their pretensions to the lady, according to the mode of those most concise and simple reasoners, the knights-errant of yore—by single combat: but Ichabod was too conscious of the superior might of his adversary to enter the lists against him; he had overheard a boast of Bones, that he "would double the school-master up, and lay him on a shelf of his own school-house"; and he was too wary to give him an opportunity. There was something extremely provoking in this obstinately pacific system; it left Brom no alternative but to draw upon the funds of rustic waggery in his disposition, and to play off boorish practical jokes upon his rival. Ichabod became the object of whimsical persecution to Bones and his gang of rough riders. They harried his hitherto peaceful domains; smoked out his singing-school, by stopping up the chimney; broke into the school-house at night, in spite of his formidable fastenings of withe and window stakes, and turned everything topsy-turvy; so that the poor schoolmaster began to think all the witches in the country held their meetings there. But what was still more annoying, Brom took all opportunities of turning him into ridicule in the presence of his mistress, and had a scoundrel dog whom he taught to whine in the most ludicrous manner, and introduced as a rival of Ichabod's to instruct her in psalmody.

In this way matters went on for some time, without producing any material effect on the relative situation of the contending powers. On a fine autumnal afternoon, Ichabod, in pensive mood, sat enthroned on the lofty stool whence he usually watched all the concerns of his little literary realm. In his hand he swayed a ferule, that scepter of despotic power; the birch of justice reposed on three nails behind the throne, a constant terror to evildoers; while on the desk before him might be seen sundry contraband articles and prohibited weapons, detected upon the persons of idle urchins; such as half-munched apples, pop-guns, whirligigs, fly-cages, and whole legions of rampant little paper game-cocks. Apparently there had been some appalling act of justice recently inflicted, for his scholars were all busily intent upon their books, or slyly whispering behind them with one eye kept upon the master; and a kind of buzzing stillness reigned throughout the school-room. It was suddenly interrupted by the appearance of a Negro, in tow-cloth jacket and trousers, a round-crowned fragment of a hat, like the cap of Mercury, and mounted on the back of a ragged, wild, half-broken colt, which he managed with a rope by way or halter. He came clattering up to the school door with an invitation to Ichabod to attend a merry-making, or "quilting frolic," to be held that evening at Mynheer Van Tassel's; and having delivered his message with that air of importance and effort at fine language which a Negro is apt to display on petty embassies of the kind, he dashed over the brook, and was seen scampering away up the hollow, full of the importance and hurry of his mission.

All was now bustle and hubbub in the late quiet school-room. The scholars were hurried through their lessons without stopping at trifles; those who were nimble skipped over half with impunity, and those who were tardy had a smart application now and then in the rear, to quicken their speed, or help them over a tall word. Books were flung aside without being put away on the shelves; inkstands were overturned, benches thrown down, and the whole school was turned loose an hour before the usual time, bursting forth like a legion of young imps, yelping and racketing about the green in joy at their early emancipation.

The gallant Ichabod now spent at least an extra half-hour at his toilet, brushing and furbishing up his best, and indeed only suit of rusty black, and arranging his locks by a bit of broken looking-glass that hung up in the school-house. That he might make his appearance before his mistress in the true style of a cavalier, he borrowed a horse from the farmer with whom he was domiciliated, a choleric old Dutchman, of the name of Hans Van Ripper, and, thus gallantly mounted, issued forth like a knight-errant in quest of adventures. But it is meet I should, in the true spirit of romantic story, give some account of the looks and equipments of my hero and his steed. The animal he bestrode was a broken-down plough-horse that had outlived almost everything but his viciousness. He was gaunt and shagged, with a ewe neck and a head like a hammer; his rusty mane and tail were tangled and knotted with burrs; one eye had lost its pupil, and was glaring and spectral; but the other had the gleam of a genuine devil in it. Still he must have had fire and mettle in his day, if we may judge from the name he bore of Gunpowder. He had, in fact, been a favorite steed of his master's, the choleric Van Ripper, who was a furious rider, and had infused, very probably, some of his own spirit into the animal; for, old and broken-down as he looked, there was more of the lurking devil in him than in any young filly in the country.

Ichabod was a suitable figure for such a steed. He rode with short stirrups, which brought his knees nearly up to the pommel of the saddle; his sharp elbows stuck out like grasshoppers; he carried his whip perpendicularly in his hand, like a scepter, and, as his horse jogged on, the motion of his arms was not unlike the flapping of a pair of wings. A small wool hat rested on the top of his nose, for so his scanty strip of forehead might be called; and the skirts of his black coat fluttered out almost to the horse's tail. Such was the appearance of Ichabod and his steed, as they shambled out of the gate of Hans Van Ripper, and it was altogether such an apparition as is seldom to be met with in broad daylight.

It was, as I have said, a fine autumnal day, the sky was clear and serene, and nature wore that rich and golden livery which we always associate with the idea of abundance. The forests had put on their sober brown and yellow, while some trees of the tenderer kind had been nipped by the frosts into brilliant dyes of orange, purple, and scarlet. Streaming files of wild ducks began to make their appearance high in the air; the bark of the squirrel might be heard from the groves of beech and hickory nuts, and the pensive whistle of the quail at intervals from the neighboring stubble field.

The small birds were taking their farewell banquets. In the fulness of their revelry, they fluttered, chirping and frolicking, from bush to bush and tree to tree, capricious from the very profusion and variety around them. There was the honest cock-robin, the favorite game of stripling sportsmen, with its loud, querulous note; and the twittering blackbirds flying in sable clouds; and the golden-winged woodpecker, with his crimson crest, his broad black gorget, and splendid plumage; and the cedar-bird, with its red-tipt wings and yellow-tip tail, and its little monteiro cap of feathers; and the blue jay, that noisy coxcomb, in his gay light-blue coat and white underclothes; screaming and chattering, nodding and bobbing and bowing, and pretending to be on good terms with every songster of the grove.

As Ichabod jogged slowly on his way, his eye, ever open to every symptom of culinary abundance, ranged with delight over the treasures of jolly autumn. On all sides he beheld vast stores of apples; some hanging in oppressive opulence on the trees; some gathered into baskets and barrels for the market; others heaped up in rich piles for the cider-press. Further on he beheld great fields of a Indian corn, with its golden ears peeping from their leafy coverts, and holding out the promise of cakes and hasty-pudding; and the yellow pumpkins lying beneath them, turning up their fair round bellies to the sun, and giving ample prospects of the most luxurious of pies; and anon he passed the fragrant buckwheat fields breathing the odor of the bee-hive, and as he beheld them, soft anticipations stole over his mind of dainty slapjacks, well buttered, and garnished with honey or treacle, by the delicate little dimpled hand of Katrina Van Tassel.

Thus feeding his mind with many sweet thoughts and "sugared suppositions

tions," he journeyed along the sides of a range of hills which look out upon some of the goodliest scenes of the mighty Hudson. The sun gradually wheeled his broad disc down into the west. The wide bosom of the Tappan Zee lay motionless and glassy, except that here and there a gentle undulation waved and prolonged the blue shadow of the distant mountain. A few amber clouds floated in the sky, without a breath of air to move them. The horizon was of a fine golden tint, changing gradually into a pure apple-green, and from that into the deep blue of the mid-heaven. A slanting ray lingered on the woody crests of the precipices that overhung some parts of the river, giving greater depth to the dark-gray and purple of their rocky sides. A sloop was loitering in the distance, dropping slowly down with the tide, her sail hanging uselessly against the mast; and as the reflection of the sky gleamed along the still water, it seemed as if the vessel was suspended in the air.

It was towards evening that Ichabod arrived at the castle of the Heer Van Tassel, which he found thronged with the pride and flower of the adjacent country. Old farmers, a spare leathern-faced race, in homespun coats and breeches, blue stockings, huge shoes, and magnificent pewter buckles. Their brisk withered little dames, in close crimped caps, long-waisted short gowns, homespun petticoats, with scissors and pincushions, and gay calico pockets hanging on the outside. Buxom lasses, almost as antiquated as their mothers, excepting where a straw hat, a fine riband, or perhaps a white frock, gave symptoms of city innovation. The sons, in short square-skirted coats with rows of stupendous brass buttons, and their hair generally queued in the fashion of the times, especially if they could procure an eel-skin for the purpose, it being esteemed throughout the country as a potent nourisher and strengthener of the hair.

Brom Bones, however, was the hero of the scene, having come to the gathering on his favorite steed Daredevil, a creature like himself, full of mettle and mischief, and which no one but himself could manage. He was, in fact, noted for preferring vicious animals, given to all kinds of tricks, which kept the rider in constant risk of his neck, for he held a tractable, well-broken horse as unworthy of a lad of spirit.

Fain would I pause to dwell upon the world of charms that burst upon the enraptured gaze of my hero, as he entered the state parlor of Van Tassel's mansion. Not those of the bevy of buxom lasses, with their luxurious display of red and white; but the ample charms of a genuine Dutch country tea-table in the sumptuous time of autumn. Such heaped-up platters of cakes of various and almost indescribable kinds, known only to experienced Dutch housewives! There was the doughty dough-nut, the tenderer oly koek, and the crisp and crumbling cruller; sweet-cakes and short-cakes, ginger-cakes and honey-cakes, and the whole family of cakes. And then there were apple-pies and peach-pies and pumpkin-pies; besides slices of ham and smoked beef; and, moreover, delectable dishes of preserved plums, and peaches, and pears, and quinces; not to mention broiled shad and roasted chickens; together with bowls of milk and cream, all mingled higgledy-piggledy, pretty much as I have enumerated them, with the motherly tea-pot sending up its clouds of vapor from the midst—Heaven bless the mark! I want breath and time to discuss this banquet as it deserves, and am too eager to get on with my story. Happily, Ichabod Crane was not in so great a hurry as his historian, but did ample justice to every dainty.

He was a kind and thankful creature, whose heart dilated in proportion as his skin was filled with good cheer; and whose spirits rose with eating as some men's do with drink. He could not help, too, rolling his large eyes round him as he ate, and chuckling with the possibility that he might one day be lord of all this scene of almost unimaginable luxury and splendor. Then he thought, how soon he'd turn his back upon the old school-house, snap his fingers in the face of Hans Van Ripper and every other niggardly patron, and kick any itinerant pedagogue out of doors that should dare to call him comrade!

Old Baltus Van Tassel moved about among his guests with a face dilated with content and good humor, round and jolly as the harvest moon. His hospitable attentions were brief, but expressive, being confined to a shake of the hand, a slap on the shoulder, a loud laugh, and a pressing invitation to "fall to, and help themselves."

And now the sound of the music from the common room or hall summoned to the dance. The musician was an old gray-headed Negro, who had been the itinerant orchestra of the neighborhood for more than half a century. His instrument was as old and battered as himself. The greater part of the time he scraped on two or three strings, accompanying every movement of the bow with a motion of the head; bowing almost to the ground, and stamping with his foot whenever a fresh couple were to start.

Ichabod prided himself upon his dancing as much as upon his vocal powers. Not a limb, not a fiber about him was idle; and to have seen his loosely hung frame in full motion, and clattering about the room, you would have thought Saint Vitus himself, that blessed patron of the dance, was figuring before you in person. He was the admiration of all the Negroes; who, having gathered, of all ages and sizes, from the farm and the neighborhood, stood forming a pyramid of shining black faces at every door and window, gazing with delight at the scene, rolling their white eye-balls, and showing grinning rows of ivory from ear to ear. How could the flogger of urchins be otherwise than animated and joyous? the lady of his heart was his partner in the dance, and smiling graciously in reply to all his amorous oglings; while Brom Bones, sorely smitten with love and jealousy, sat brooding by himself in one corner.

When the dance was at an end, Ichabod was attracted to a knot of the sager folks, who, with old Van Tassel, sat smoking at one end of the piazza, gossiping over former times, and drawing out long stories about the war.

This neighborhood, at the time of which I am speaking, was one of those highly favored places which abound with chronicle and great men. The British and American line had run near it during the war; it had, therefore, been the scene of marauding, and infested with refugees, cow-boys, and all kinds of border chivalry. Just sufficient time had elapsed to enable each story-teller to dress up his tale with a little becoming fiction, and, in the indistinctness of his recollection, to make himself the hero of every exploit.

There was the story of Doffue Martling, a large bluebearded Dutchman, who had nearly taken a British frigate with an old iron nine-pounder from a mud breastwork, only that his gun burst at the sixth discharge. And there was an old gentleman who shall be nameless, being too rich a mynheer to be lightly mentioned, who, in the battle of White Plains, being an excellent master of defense, parried a musketball with a small sword, insomuch that he absolutely felt it whiz round the blade, and glance off at the hilt; in proof of which he was ready at any time to show the sword, with the hilt a little bent. There were several more that had been equally great in the field, not one of whom but was persuaded that he had a considerable hand in bringing the war to a happy termination.

But all these were nothing to the tales of ghosts and apparitions that succeeded. The neighborhood is rich in legendary treasures of the kind. Local tales and superstitions thrive best in these sheltered long-settled retreats; but are trampled under-foot by the shifting throng that forms the population of most of our country places. Besides, there is no encouragement for ghosts in most of our villages, for they have scarcely had time to finish their first nap, and turn themselves in their graves, before their surviving friends have traveled away from the neighborhood; so that when they turn out at night to walk their rounds, they have no acquaintance left to call upon. This is perhaps the reason why we so seldom hear of ghosts except in our long-established Dutch communities.

The immediate cause, however, of the prevalence of supernatural stories in these parts, was doubtless owing to the vicinity of Sleepy Hollow. There was a contagion in the very air that blew from that haunted region; it breathed forth an atmosphere of dreams and fancies infecting all the land. Several of the Sleepy Hollow people were present at Van Tassel's, and, as usual, were doling out their wild and wonderful legends. Many dismal tales were told about funeral trains, and mourning cries and wailings heard and seen about the great tree where the unfortunate Major Andre was taken, and which stood in the neighborhood. Some mention was made also of the woman in white, that haunted the dark glen at Raven Rock, and was often heard to shriek on winter nights before a storm, having perished there in the snow. The chief part of the stories, however, turned upon the favorite specter of Sleepy Hollow, the headless horseman, who had been heard several times of late, patrolling the country; and, it was said, tethered his horse nightly among the graves in the churchyard.

The sequestered situation of this church seems always to have made it a favorite haunt of troubled spirits. It stands on a knoll surrounded by locust-trees and lofty elms, from among which its decent white-washed walls shine modestly forth, like Christian purity, beaming through the shades of retirement. A gentle slope descends from it to a silver sheet of water, bordered by high trees, between which peeps may be caught at the blue hills of the Hudson. To look upon its grass-grown yard, where the sunbeams seem to sleep so quietly, one would think that there at least the dead might rest in peace. On one side of the church extends a wide woody dell, along which raves a large brook among broken rocks and trunks of fallen trees. Over a deep black part of the stream, not far from the church, was formerly thrown a wooden bridge; the road that led to it, and the bridge itself, were thickly shaded by overhanging trees, which cast a gloom about it, even in the daytime; but occasioned a fearful darkness at night. Such was one of the favorite haunts of the headless horseman, and the place where he was most frequently encountered. The tale was told of old Brouwer, a most heretical disbeliever in ghosts, how he met the horseman returning from his foray into Sleepy Hollow, and was obliged to get up behind him; how they galloped over bush and brake, over hill and swamp, until they reached the bridge; when the horseman suddenly turned into a skeleton, threw old Brouwer into the brook, and sprang away over the tree-tops with a clap of thunder.

This story was immediately matched by a thrice marvelous adventure of Brom Bones, who made light of the Galloping Hessian as an arrant jockey. He affirmed that, on returning one night from the neighboring village of Sing-Sing, he had been overtaken by this midnight trooper; that he had offered to race with him for a bowl of punch, and should have won it too, for Daredevil beat the goblin horse all hollow, but, just as they came to the church bridge, the Hessian bolted, and vanished in a flash of fire.

All these tales, told in that drowsy undertone with which men talk in the dark, the countenances of the listeners only now and then receiving a casual gleam from the glare of a pipe, sank deep in the mind of Ichabod. He repaid them in kind, with large extracts from his invaluable author, Cotton Mather, and added many marvelous events that had taken place in his native state of Connecticut, and fearful sights which he had seen in his nightly walks about Sleepy Hollow.

The revel now gradually broke up. The old farmers gathered together their families in their wagons, and were heard for some time rattling along the hollow roads, and over the distant hills. Some of the damsels mounted on pillions behind their favorite swains, and their light-hearted laughter, mingling with the clatter of hoofs, echoed along the silent woodlands, sounding fainter and fainter until they gradually died away—and the late scene of noise and frolic was all silent and deserted. Ichabod only lingered behind, according to the custom of country lovers, to have a *tête-à-tête* with the heiress, fully convinced that he was now on the high road to success. What passed at this interview I will not pretend to say, for in fact I do not know. Something, I fear me, must have gone wrong, for he certainly sallied forth, after no very great interval, with an air quite desolate and chop-fallen. Oh, these women! these women! Could that girl have been playing off any of her coquettish tricks?—Was her encouragement of the poor pedagogue all a mere sham to secure her conquest of his rival?—Heaven only knows, not I!—Let it suffice to say, Ichabod stole forth with the air of one who had been sacking a hen-roost, rather than a fair lady's heart. Without looking to the right or left to notice the scene of rural wealth on which he had so often gloated, he went straight to the stable, and with several hearty cuffs and kicks, roused his steed most uncourteously from the comfortable quarters in which he was soundly sleeping, dreaming or mountains of corn and oats, and whole valleys of timothy and clover.

It was the very witching time of night that Ichabod, heavy-hearted and crest-fallen, pursued his travels homewards, along the sides of the lofty hills which rise above Tarry Town, and which he had traversed so cheerily in the afternoon. The hour was as dismal as himself. Far below him the Tappan Zee spread its dusky and indistinct waste of waters, with here and there the tall mast of a sloop riding quietly at anchor under the land. In the dead hush of midnight he could even hear the barking of the watch-dog from the opposite shore of the Hudson; but it was so vague and faint as only to give an idea of his distance from this faithful companion of man. Now and then, too, the long-drawn crowing of a cock, accidentally awakened, would sound far, far off, from some farm-house away among the hills—but it was like a dreaming sound in his ear. No signs of life occurred near him, but occasionally the melancholy chirp of a cricket, or perhaps the guttural twang of a bull-frog, from a neighboring marsh, as if sleeping uncomfortably, and turning suddenly in his bed.

All the stories of ghosts and goblins that he had heard in the afternoon now came crowding upon his recollection. The night grew darker and darker; the stars seemed to sink deeper in the sky, and driving clouds occasionally hid them from his sight. He had never felt so lonely and dismal. He was, moreover, approaching the very place where many of the scenes of the ghost-stories had been laid. In the center of the road stood an enormous tulip-tree, which towered like a giant above all the other trees of the neighborhood, and formed a kind of landmark. Its limbs were gnarled and fantastic, large enough to form trunks for ordinary trees, twisting down almost to the earth, and rising again into the air. It was connected with the tragical story of the unfortunate André, who had been taken prisoner hard by; and was universally known by the name of Major André's tree. The common people regarded it with a mixture of respect and superstition, partly out of sympathy for the fate of its ill-starred namesake and partly from the tales of strange sights and doleful lamentations told concerning it.

As Ichabod approached this fearful tree, he began to whistle; he thought his whistle was answered; it was but a blast sweeping sharply through the dry branches. As he approached a little nearer, he thought he saw something white hanging in the midst of the tree–he paused and ceased whistling; but on looking more narrowly, perceived that it was a place where the tree had been scathed by lightning, and the white wood laid bare. Suddenly he heard a groan–his teeth chattered, and his knees smote against the saddle; it was but the rubbing of one huge bough upon another, as they were swayed about by the breeze. He passed the tree in safety, but new perils lay before him.

About two hundred yards from the tree a small brook crossed the road, and ran into a marshy and thickly wooded glen, known by the name of Wiley's Swamp. A few rough logs, laid side by side, served for a bridge over this stream. On that side of the road where the brook entered the wood, a group of oaks and chestnuts, matted thick with wild grapevines, threw a cavernous gloom over it. To pass this bridge was the severest trial. It was at this identical spot that the unfortunate André was captured, and under the covert of those chestnuts and vines were the sturdy yeomen concealed who surprised him. This has ever since been considered a haunted stream, and fearful are the feelings of the schoolboy who has to pass it alone after dark.

As he approached the stream, his heart began to thump; he summoned up, however, all his resolution, gave his horse half a score of kicks in the ribs, and attempted to dash briskly across the bridge; but instead of starting forward, the perverse old animal made a lateral movement, and ran broadside against the fence. Ichabod, whose fears increased with the delay, jerked the reins on the other side, and kicked lustily with the contrary foot: it was all in vain; his steed started, it is true, but it was only to plunge to the opposite side of the road into a thicket of brambles and alder-bushes. The schoolmaster now bestowed both whip and heel upon the starveling ribs of old Gunpowder, who dashed forward, snuffling and snorting, but came to a stand just by the bridge, with a suddenness that had nearly sent his rider sprawling over his head. Just at this moment a plashy tramp by the side of the bridge caught the sensitive ear of Ichabod. In the dark shadow of the grove, on the margin of the brook, he beheld something huge, mis-shapen, black and towering. It stirred not, but seemed gathered up in the gloom, like some gigantic monster ready to spring upon the traveler.

The hair of the affrighted pedagogue rose upon his head with terror. What was to be done? To turn and fly was now too late; and besides, what chance was there of escaping ghost or goblin, if such it was, which could ride upon the wings of the wind? Summoning up, therefore, a show of courage, he demanded in stammering accents–"Who are you?" He received no reply. He repeated his demand in a still more agitated voice. Still there was no answer. Once more he cudgelled the sides of the inflexible Gunpowder, and, shutting his eyes, broke forth with involuntary fervor into a psalm tune. Just then the shadowy object of alarm put itself in motion, and with a scramble and a bound, stood at once in the middle of the road. Though the night was dark and dismal, yet the form of the unknown might now in some degree be ascertained. He appeared to be a horseman of large dimensions, and mounted on a black horse of powerful frame. He made no offer of molestation or sociability, but kept aloof on one side of the road, jogging along on the blind side of old Gunpowder, who had now got over his fright and waywardness.

Ichabod, who had no relish for this strange midnight companion, and bethought himself of the adventure of Brom Bones with the Galloping Hessian, now quickened his steed, in hopes of leaving him behind. The stranger, however, quickened his horse to an equal pace. Ichabod pulled up, and fell into a walk, thinking to lag behind–the other did the same. His heart began to sink within him; he endeavored to resume his psalm tune, but his parched tongue clove to the roof of his mouth, and he could not utter a stave. There was something in the moody and dogged silence of this pertinacious companion that was mysterious and appalling. It was soon fearfully accounted for. On mounting a rising ground, which brought the figure of his fellow-traveler in relief against the sky, gigantic in height, and muffled in a cloak, Ichabod was horror-struck on perceiving that he was headless!—but his horror was still more increased on observing that the head, which should have rested on his shoulders, was carried before him on the pommel of the saddle: his terror rose to desperation; he rained a shower of kicks and blows upon Gunpowder, hoping, by a sudden movement, to give his companion the slip–but the specter started full jump with him. Away then they dashed, through thick and thin; stones flying and sparks flashing at every bound. Ichabod's flimsy garments fluttered in the air, as he stretched his long lank body away over his horse's head, in the eagerness of his flight.

They had now reached the road which turns off to Sleepy Hollow, but Gunpowder, who seemed possessed with a demon, instead of keeping up it, made an opposite turn, and plunged headlong down the hill to the left. This road leads through a sandy hollow, shaded by trees for about a quarter of a mile, where it crosses the bridge famous in goblin story, and just beyond swells the green knoll on which stands the white-washed church.

As yet the panic of the steed had given his unskilful rider an apparent advantage in the chase; but just as he had got half way through the hollow, the girths of the saddle gave way, and he felt it slipping from under him. He seized it by the pommel, and endeavored to hold it firm, but in vain; and had just time to save himself by clasping old Gunpowder round the neck, when the saddle fell to the earth, and he heard it trampled underfoot by his pursuer. For a moment the terror of Hans Van Ripper's wrath passed across his mind—for it was his Sunday saddle; but this was no time for petty fears; the goblin was hard on his haunches; and (unskilful rider that he was!) he had much ado to maintain his seat; sometimes slipping on one side, sometimes on the other, and sometimes jolted on the high ridge of his horse's back-bone, with a violence that he verily feared would cleave him asunder.

An opening in the trees now cheered him with the hopes that the church bridge was at hand. The wavering reflection of a silver star in the bosom of the brook told him that he was not mistaken. He saw the walls of the church dimly glaring under the trees beyond. He recollected the place where Brom Bones' ghostly competitor had disappeared. "If I can but reach that bridge," thought Ichabod, "I am safe." Just then he heard the black steed panting and blowing close behind him; he even fancied that he felt his hot breath. Another convulsive kick in the ribs, and old Gunpowder sprang upon the bridge; he thundered over the resounding planks; he gained the opposite side; and now Ichabod cast a look behind to see if his pursuer should vanish, according to rule, in a flash of fire and brimstone. Just then he saw the goblin rising in his stirrups, and in the very act of hurling his head at him. Ichabod endeavored to dodge the horrible missile, but too late. It encountered his cranium with a tremendous crash—he was tumbled head-long into the dust, and Gunpowder, the black steed, and the goblin rider passed by like a whirlwind.

The next morning the old horse was found without his saddle and with the bridle under his feet, soberly cropping the grass at his master's gate. Ichabod did not make his appearance at breakfast—dinner-hour came, but no Ichabod. The boys assembled at the school-house, and strolled idly about the banks of the brook; but no schoolmaster. Hans Van Ripper now began to feel some uneasiness about the fate of poor Ichabod and his saddle. An inquiry was set on foot, and after diligent investigation they came upon his traces. In one part of the road leading to the church was found the saddle trampled in the dirt; the tracks of horses' hoofs deeply dented in the road, and evidently at furious speed, were traced to the bridge, beyond which, on the bank of a broad part of the brook, where the water ran deep and black, was found the hat of the unfortunate Ichabod, and close beside it a shattered pumpkin.

The brook was searched, but the body of the schoolmaster was not to be discovered. Hans Van Ripper, as executor of his estate, examined the bundle, which contained all his worldly effects. They consisted of two shirts and a half; two stocks for the neck; a pair or two of worsted stockings; an old pair of corduroy small clothes; a rusty razor; a book of psalm tunes, full of dog's ears; and a broken pitch-pipe. As to the books and furniture of the school-house, they belonged to the community, excepting Cotton Mather's *History of Witchcraft,* a New England Almanac, and a book of dreams and fortune-telling; in which last was a sheet of foolscap much scribbled and blotted in several fruitless attempts to make a copy of verses in honor of the heiress of Van Tassel. These magic books and the poetic scrawl were forthwith consigned to the flames by Hans Van Ripper; who from that time forward determined to send his children no more to school, observing that he never knew any good come of this same reading and writing. Whatever money the schoolmaster possessed, and he had received his quarter's pay but a day or two before, he must have had about his person at the time of his disappearance.

The mysterious event caused much speculation at the church on the following Sunday. Knots of gazers and gossips were collected in the churchyard, at the bridge, and at the spot where the hat and pumpkin had been found. The stories of Brouwer, of Bones, and a whole budget of others, were called to mind; and when they had diligently considered them all, and compared them with the symptoms of the present case, they shook their heads, and came to the conclusion that Ichabod had been carried off by the Galloping Hessian. As he was a bachelor, and in nobody's debt, nobody troubled his head any more about him: the school was removed to a different quarter of the Hollow, and another pedagogue reigned in his stead.

It is true, an old farmer, who had been down to New York on a visit several years after, and from whom this account of the ghostly adventure was received, brought home the intelligence that Ichabod Crane was still alive; that he had left the neighborhood, partly through fear of the goblin and Hans Van Ripper, and partly in mortification at having been suddenly dismissed by the heiress; that he had changed his quarters to a distant part of the country; had kept school and studied law at the same time; he had been admitted to the bar, turned politician, electioneered, written for the newspapers, and finally had been made a justice of the Ten-pound Court. Brom Bones, too, who shortly after his rival's disappearance conducted the blooming Katrina in triumph to the altar, was observed to look exceedingly knowing whenever the story of Ichabod was related, and always burst into a hearty laugh at the mention of the pumpkin; which led some to suspect that he knew more about the matter than he chose to tell.

The old country wives, however, who are the best judges of these matters, maintain to this day that Ichabod was spirited away by supernatural means; and it is a favorite story often told about the neighborhood round the winter evening fire. The bridge became more than ever an object of superstitious awe, and that may be the reason why the road has been altered of late years, so as to approach the church by the border of the mill-pond. The school-house, being deserted, soon fell to decay, and was reported to be haunted by the ghost of the unfortunate pedagogue; and the plough-boy, loitering homeward of a still summer evening, has often fancied his voice at a distance, chanting a melancholy psalm tune among the tranquil solitudes of Sleepy Hollow.

Postscript

FOUND IN THE HANDWRITING OF MR. KNICKERBOCKER

The preceding tale is given, almost in the precise words in which I heard it related at a Corporation meeting of the ancient city of Manhattoes, at which were present many of its sagest and most illustrious burghers. The narrator was a pleasant, shabby, gentlemanly old fellow, in pepper-and-salt clothes, with a sadly humorous face; and one whom I strongly suspected of being poor—he made such efforts to be entertaining. When his story was concluded, there was much laughter and approbation, particularly from two or three deputy aldermen, who had been asleep the greater part of the time. There was, however, one tall, dry-looking old gentleman, with beetling eye-brows, who maintained a grave and rather a severe face throughout: now and then folding his arms, inclining his head, and looking down upon the floor, as if turning a doubt over in his mind. He was one of your wary men, who never laugh, but upon good grounds—when they have reason and the law on their side. When the mirth of the rest of the company had subsided, and silence was restored, he leaned one arm on the elbow of his chair, and sticking the other akimbo demanded with a slight but exceedingly sage motion of the head, and contraction of the brow, what was the moral of the story, and what it went to prove?

The story-teller, who was just putting a glass of wine to his lips, as a re-freshment after his toils, paused for a moment, looked at his inquirer with an air of infinite deference, and, lowering the glass slowly to the table, ob-served that the story was intended most logically to prove:—

"That there is no situation in life but has its advantages and pleasures—provided we will but take a joke as we find it:

"That, therefore, he that runs races with goblin troopers is likely to have rough riding of it.

"Ergo, for a country schoolmaster to be refused the hand of a Dutch heiress is a certain step to high preferment in the state."

The cautious old gentleman knit his brows tenfold closer after this ex-planation, being sorely puzzled by the ratiocination of the syllogism: while, methought, the one in pepper-and-salt eyed him with something of a triumphant leer. At length he observed that all this was very well; but still he thought the story a little on the extravagant—there were one or two points on which he had his doubts.

"Faith sir," replied the story-teller, "as to that matter, I don't believe one half of it myself."

D. K.

NATHANIEL HAWTHORNE

[1804–1864]

Rappaccini's Daughter

(FROM THE WRITINGS OF AUBÉPINE)

(First published in *The Democratic Review*, December, 1844; first book publication in 1846.)

WE DO NOT remember to have seen any translated specimens of the productions of M. de l'Aubépine—a fact the less wondered at, as his very name is unknown to many of his own countrymen as well as to the student of foreign literature. As a writer, he seems to occupy an unfortunate position between the Transcendentalists (who, under one name or another, have their share in all the current literature of the world) and the great body of pen-and-ink men who address the intellect and sympathies of the multitude. If not too refined, at all events too remote, too shadowy, and unsubstantial in his modes of development to suit the taste of the latter class, and yet too popular to satisfy the spiritual or metaphysical requisitions of the former, he must necessarily find himself without an audience, except here and there an individual or possibly an isolated clique. His writings, to do them justice, are not altogether destitute of fancy and originality; they might have won him greater reputation but for an inveterate love of allegory, which is apt to invest his plots and characters with the aspect of scenery and people in the clouds, and to steal away the human warmth out of his conceptions. His fictions are sometimes historical, sometimes of the present day, and sometimes, so far as can be discovered, have little or no reference either to time or space. In any case, he generally contents himself with a very slight embroidery of outward manners,—the faintest possible counterfeit of real life,—and endeavors to create an interest by some less obvious peculiarity of the subject. Occasionally a breath of Nature, a raindrop of pathos and tenderness, or a gleam of humor, will find its way into the midst of his fantastic imagery, and make us feel as if, after all, we were yet within thc limits of our native earth. We will only add to this very cursory notice that M. de l'Aubépine's productions, if the reader chance to take them in precisely the proper point of view, may amuse a leisure hour as well as those of a brighter man; if otherwise, they can hardly fail to look excessively like nonsense.

Our author is voluminous; he continues to write and publish with as much praiseworthy and indefatigable prolixity as if his efforts were crowned with the brilliant success that so justly attends those of Eugene Sue. His first appearance was by a collection of stories in a long series of volumes entitled "Contes deux fois racontées." The titles of some of his more recent works (we quote from memory) are as follows: "Le Voyage Céleste à Chemin de Fer," 3 tom., 1838; "Le nouveau Père Adam et la nouvelle Mère Eve," 2 tom., 1839; "Roderic; ou le Serpent à l'estomac," 2 tom., 1840; "Le Culte du Feu," a folio volume of ponderous research into the religion and ritual of the old Persian Ghebers, published in 1841; "La Soirée du Château en Espagne," 1 tom., 8 vo, 1842; and "L'Artiste du Beau; ou le Papillon Mécanique," 5 tom., 4to, 1843. Our somewhat wearisome perusal of this startling catalog of volumes has left behind it a certain personal affection and sympathy, though by no means admiration, for M. de l'Aubépine; and we would fain do the little in our power towards introducing him favorably to the American public. The ensuing tale is a translation of his "Beatrice; ou la Belle Empoisonneuse," recently published in "La Revue Anti-Aristrocratique." This journal, edited by the Comte de Bearhaven, has for some years past led the defense of liberal principles and popular rights with a faithfulness and ability worthy of all praise.

A young man, named Giovanni Guasconti, came, very long ago, from the more southern region of Italy, to pursue his studies at the University of Padua. Giovanni, who had but a scanty supply of gold ducats in his pocket, took lodgings in a high and gloomy chamber of an old edifice which looked not unworthy to have been the palace of a Paduan noble, and which, in fact, exhibited over its entrance the armorial bearings of a family long since extinct. The young stranger, who was not unstudied in the great poem of his country, recollected that one of the ancestors of this family, and perhaps an occupant of this very mansion, had been pictured by Dante as a partaker of the immortal agonies of his Inferno. These reminiscences and associations, together with the tendency to heartbreak natural to a young man for thc first time out of his native sphere, caused Giovanni to sigh heavily as he looked around the desolate and ill-furnished apartment.

"Holy Virgin, signor!" cried old Dame Lisabetta, who, won by the youth's remarkable beauty of person, was kindly endeavoring to give the chamber a habitable air, "what a sigh was that to come out of a young man's heart! Do you find this old mansion gloomy? For the love of Heaven, then, put your head out of the window, and you will see as bright sunshine as you have left in Naples."

Guaseonti mechanically did as the old woman advised, but could not quite agree with her that the Paduan sunshine was as cheerful as that of Southern Italy. Such as it was, however, it fell upon a garden beneath the window and expended its fostering influences on a variety of plants, which seemed to have been cultivated with exceeding care.

"Does this garden belong to the house?" asked Giovanni.

"Heaven forbid, signor, unless it were fruitful of better pot herbs than any that grow there now," answered old Lisabetta. "No; that garden is cultivated by the own hands of Signor Giacomo Rappaccini, the famous doctor, who, I warrant him, has been heard of as far as Naples. It is said that he distils these plants into medicines that are as potent as a charm. Oftentimes you may see the signor doctor at work, and perchance the signora, his daughter, too, gathering the strange flowers that grow in the garden."

The old woman had now done what she could for the aspect of the chamber; and, commending the young man to the protection of the saints, took her departure.

Giovanni still found no better occupation than to look down into the garden beneath his window. From its appearance, he judged it to be one of those botanic gardens which were of earlier date in Padua than elsewhere in Italy or in the world. Or, not improbably, it might once have been the pleasure-place of an opulent family; for there was the ruin of a marble fountain in the center, sculptured with rare art, but so woefully shattered that it was impossible to trace the original design from the chaos of remaining fragments. The water, however, continued to gush and sparkle into the sunbeams as cheerfully as ever. A little gurgling sound ascended to the young man's window, and made him feel as if the fountain were an immortal spirit that sung its song unceasingly and without heeding the vicissitudes around it, while one century embodied it in marble and another scattered the perishable garniture on the soil. All about the pool into which the water subsided grew various plants, that seemed to require a plentiful supply of moisture for the nourishment of gigantic leaves, and, in some instances, flowers gorgeously magnificent. There was one shrub in particular, set in a marble vase in the midst of the pool, that bore a profusion of purple blossoms, each of which had the luster and richness of a gem; and the whole together made a show so resplendent that it seemed enough to illuminate the garden, even had there been no sunshine. Every portion of the soil was peopled with plants and herbs, which, if less beautiful, still bore tokens of assiduous care, as if all had their individual virtues, known to the scientific mind that fostered them. Some were placed in urns, rich with old carving, and others in common garden pots; some crept serpent-like along the ground or climbed on high, using whatever means of ascent was offered them. One plant had wreathed itself round a statue of Vertumnus, which was thus quite veiled and shrouded in a drapery of hanging foilage, so happily arranged that it might have served a sculptor for a study.

While Giovanni stood at the window he heard a rustling behind a screen of leaves, and became aware that a person was at work in the garden. His figure soon emerged into view, and showed itself to be that of no common laborer, but a tall, emaciated, sallow, and sickly looking man, dressed in a scholar's garb of black. He was beyond the middle term of life, with gray hair, a thin, gray beard, and a face singularly marked with intellect and cultivation, but which could never, even in his more youthful days, have expressed much warmth of heart.

Nothing could exceed the intentness with which this scientific gardener examined every shrub which grew in his path: it seemed as if he was looking into their inmost nature, making observations in regard to their creative essence, and discovering why one leaf grew in this shape and another in that, and wherefore such and such flowers differed among themselves in hue and perfume. Nevertheless, in spite of this deep intelligence on his part, there was no approach to intimacy between himself and these vegetable existences. On the contrary, he avoided their actual touch or the direct inhaling of their odors with a caution that impressed Giovannia most disagreeably; for the man's demeanor was that of one walking among malignant influences, such as savage beasts, or deadly snakes, or evil spirits, which, should he allow them one moment of license, would wreak upon him some terrible fatality. It was strangely frightful to the young man's imagination to see this air of insecurity in a person cultivating a garden, that most simple and innocent of human toils, and which had been alike the joy and labor of the unfallen parents of the race. Was this garden, then, the Eden of the present world? And this man, with such a perception of harm in what his own hands caused to grow,—was he the Adam?

The distrustful gardener, while plucking away the dead leaves or pruning the too luxuriant growth of the shrubs, defended his hands with a pair of thick gloves. Nor were these his only armor. When, in his walk through the garden, he came to the magnificent plant that hung its purple gems beside the marble fountain, he placed a kind of mask over his mouth and nostrils, as if all this beauty did not conceal a deadlier malice; but, finding his task still too dangerous, he drew back, removed the mask, and called loudly, but in the infirm voice of a person affected with inward disease:

"Beatrice! Beatrice!"

"Here am I, my father. What would you?" cried a rich and youthful voice from the window of the opposite house—a voice as rich as a tropical sunset, and which made Giovanni, though he knew not why, think of deep hues of purple or crimson and of perfumes heavily delectable. "Are you in the garden?"

"Yes, Beatrice," answered the gardener, "and I need your help."

Soon there emerged from under a sculptured portal the figure of a young girl, arrayed with as much richness of taste as the most splendid of the flowers, beautiful as the day, and with a bloom so deep and vivid that one shade more would have been too much. She looked redundant with life, health, and energy; all of which attributes were bound down and compressed, as it were, and girdled tensely, in their luxuriance, by her virgin zone. Yet Giovanni's fancy must have grown morbid while he looked down into the garden; for the impression which the fair stranger made upon him was as if here were another flower, the human sister of those vegetable ones, as beautiful as they, more beautiful than the richest of them, but still to be touched only with a glove, nor to be approached without a mask. As Beatrice came down the garden path, it was observable that she handled and inhaled the odor of several of the plants which her father had most seduously avoided.

"Here, Beatrice," said the latter, "see how many needful offices require to be done to our chief treasure. Yet, shattered as I am, my life might pay the penalty of approaching it so closely as circumstances demand. Henceforth, I fear, this plant must be consigned to your sole charge."

"And gladly will I undertake it," cried again the rich tones of the young lady, as she bent towards the magnificent plant and opened her arms as if to embrace it. "Yes, my sister, my splendor, it shall be Beatrice's task to nurse and serve thee; and thou shalt reward her with thy kisses and perfumed breath, which to her is as the breath of life."

Then, with all the tenderness in her manner that was so strikingly expressed in her words, she busied herself with such attentions as the plant seemed to require; and Giovanni, at his lofty window, rubbed his eyes and almost doubted whether it were a girl tending her favorite flower, or one sister performing the duties of affection to another. The scene soon terminated. Whether Dr. Rappaccini had finished his labors in the garden, or that his watchful eye had caught the stranger's face, he now took his daughter's arm and retired. Night was already closing in; oppressive exhalations seemed to proceed from the plants and steal upward past the open window; and Giovanni, closing the lattice, went to his couch and dreamed of a rich flower and beautiful girl. Flower and maiden were different, and yet the same, and fraught with some strange peril in either shape.

But there is an influence in the light of morning that tends to rectify whatever errors of fancy, or even of judgment, we may have incurred during the sun's decline, or among the shadows of the night, or in the less wholesome glow of moonshine. Giovanni's first movement, on starting from sleep, was to throw open the window and gaze down into the garden which his dreams had made so fertile of mysteries. He was surprised and a little ashamed to find how real and matter-of-fact an affair it proved to be, in the first rays of the sun which gilded the dewdrops that hung upon leaf and blossom, and, while giving a brighter beauty to each rare flower, brought everything within the limits of ordinary experience. The young man rejoiced that, in the heart of the barren city, he had the privilege of overlooking this spot of lovely and luxuriant vegetation. It would serve, he said to himself, as a symbolic language to keep him in communion with Nature. Neither the sickly and thoughtworn Dr. Giacomo Rappaccini, it is true, nor his brilliant daughter, were now visible; so that Giovanni could not determine how much of the singularity which he attributed to both was due to their own qualities and how much to his wonder-working fancy; but he was inclined to take a most rational view of the whole matter.

In the course of the day he paid his respects to Signor Pietro Baglioni, professor of medicine in the university, a physician of eminent repute, to whom Giovanni had brought a letter of introduction. The professor was an elderly personage, apparently of genial nature, and habits that might almost be called jovial. He kept the young man to dinner, and made himself very agreeable by the freedom and liveliness of his conversation, especially when warmed by a flask or two of Tuscan wine. Giovanni, conceiving that men of science, inhabitants of the same city, must needs be on familiar terms with one another, took an opportunity to mention thc name of Dr. Rappaccini. But the professor did not respond with so much cordiality as he had anticipated.

"Ill would it become a teacher of the divine art of medicine," said Professor Pietro Baglioni, in answer to a question of Giovanni, "to with hold due and well-considered praise of a physician so eminently skilled as Rappaccini; but, on the other hand, I should answer it but scantily to my conscience were I to permit a worthy youth like yourself, Signor Giovanni, the son of an ancient friend, to imbibe erroneous ideas respecting a man who might hereafter chance to hold your life and death in his hands. The truth is, our worshipful Dr. Rappaccini has as much science as any member of the faculty—with perhaps one single exception—in Padua, or all Italy; but there are certain grave objections to his professional character."

"And what are they?" asked the young man.

"Has my friend Giovanni any disease of body or heart, that he is so inquisitive about physicians?" said the professor, with a smile. "But as for Rappaccini, it is said of him—and I, who know the man well, can answer for its truth—that he cares infinitely more for science than for mankind. His patients are interesting to him only as subjects for some new experiment. He would sacrifice human life, his own among the rest, or whatever else was dearest to him, for the sake of adding so much as a grain of mustard seed to the great heap of his accumulated knowledge."

"Methinks he is an awful man indeed," remarked Guasconti, mentally recalling the cold and purely intellectual aspect of Rappaccini. "And yet, worshipful professor, is it not a noble spirit? Are there many men capable of so spiritual a love of science?"

"God forbid," answered the professor, somewhat testily; "at least, unless they take sounder views of the healing art than those adopted by Rappaccini. It is his theory that all medicinal virtues are comprised within those substances which we term vegetable poisons. These he cultivates with his own hands, and is said even to have produced new varieties of poison, more horribly deleterious than Nature, without the assistance of this learned person, would ever have plagued the world withal. That the signor doctor does less mischief than might be expected with such dangerous substances is undeniable. Now and then, it must he owned, he has effected, or seemed to effect, a marvelous cure; but, to tell you my private mind, Signor Giovanni, he should receive little credit for such instances of success,–they being probably the work of chance,–but should be held strictly accountable for his failures, which may justly be considered his own work."

The youth might have taken Baglioni's opinions with many grains of allowance had he known that there was a professional warfare of long continuance between him and Dr. Rappaccini, in which the latter was generally thought to have gained the advantage. If the reader be inclined to judge for himself, we refer him to certain black-letter tracts on both sides, preserved in the medical department of the University of Padua.

"I know not, most learned professor," returned Giovanni, after musing on what had been said of Rappaccini's exclusive zeal for science,–"I know not how dearly this physician may love his art; but surely there is one object more dear to him. He has a daughter."

"Aha!" cried the professor, with a laugh. "So now our friend Giovanni's secret is out. You have heard of this daughter, whom all the young men in Padua are wild about, though not half a dozen have ever had the good hap to see her face. I know little of the Signora Beatrice save that Rappaccini is said to have instructed her deeply in his science, and that, young and beautiful as fame reports her, she is already qualified to fill a professor's chair. Perchance her father destines her for mine! Other absurd rumors there be, not worth talking about or listening to. So now, Signor Giovanni, drink off your glass of lachryma."

Guasconti returned to his lodgings somewhat heated with the wine he had quaffed, and which caused his brain to swim with strange fantasies in reference to Dr. Rappaccini and the beautiful Beatrice. On his way, happening to pass by a florist's he bought a fresh bouquet of flowers.

Ascending to his chamber, he seated himself near the window, but within the shadow thrown by the depth of the wall, so that he could look down into the garden with little risk of being discovered. All beneath his eye was a solitude. The strange plants were basking in the sunshine, and now and then nodding gently to one another, as if in acknowledgment of sympathy and kindred. In the midst, by the shattered fountain, grew the magnificent shrub, with its purple gems clustering all over it; they glowed in the air, and gleamed back again out of the depths of the pool, which thus seemed to overflow with colored radiance from the rich reflection that was steeped in it. At first, as we have said, the garden was a solitude. Soon, however,–as

Giovanni had half hoped, half feared, would be the case,—a figure appeared beneath the antique sculptured portal, and came down between the rows of plants, inhaling their various perfumes as if she were one of those beings of old classic fable that lived upon sweet odors. On again beholding Beatrice, the young man was even startled to perceive how much her beauty exceeded his recollection of it; so brilliant, so vivid, was its character, that she glowed amid the sunlight, and, as Giovanni whispered to himself, positively illuminated the more shadowy intervals of the garden path. Her face being now more revealed than on the former occasion, he was struck by its expression of simplicity and sweetness,—qualities that had not entered into his idea of her character, and which made him ask anew what manner of mortal she might be. Nor did he fail again to observe, or imagine, an analogy between the beautiful girl and the gorgeous shrub that hung its gemlike flowers over the fountain,—a resemblance which Beatrice seemed to have indulged a fantastic humor in heightening, both by the arrangement of her dress and the selection of its hues.

Approaching the shrub, she threw open her arms, as with a passionate ardor, and drew its branches into an intimate embrace—so intimate that her features were hidden in its leafy bosom and her glistening ringlets all intermingled with the flowers.

"Give me thy breath, my sister," exclaimed Beatrice; "for I am faint with common air. And give me this flower of thine, which I separate with gentlest fingers from the stem and place it close beside my heart."

With these words the beautiful daughter of Rappaccini plucked one of the richest blossoms of the shrub, and was about to fasten it in her bosom. But now, unless Giovanni's draughts of wine had bewildered his senses, a singular incident occurred. A small orange-colored reptile, of the lizard or chameleon species, chanced to be creeping along the path, just at the feet of Beatrice. It appeared to Giovanni,—but, at the distance from which he gazed, he could scarcely have seen anything so minute,—it appeared to him, however, that a drop or two of moisture from the broken stem of the flower descended upon the lizard's head. For an instant the reptile contorted itself violently, and then lay motionless in the sunshine. Beatrice observed this remarkable phenomenon, and crossed herself, sadly, but without surprise; nor did she therefore hesitate to arrange the fatal flower in her bosom. There it blushed, and almost glimmered with the dazzling effect of a precious stone, adding to her dress and aspect the one appropriate charm which nothing else in the world could have supplied. But Giovanni, out of the shadow of his window, bent forward and shrank back, and murmured and trembled.

"Am I awake? Have I my senses?" said he to himself. "What is this being? Beautiful shall I call her, or inexpressibly terrible?"

Beatrice now strayed carelessly through the garden, approaching closer beneath Giovanni's window, so that he was compelled to thrust his head quite out of its concealment in order to gratify the intense and painful curiosity which she excited. At this moment there came a beautiful insect over the garden wall; it had, perhaps, wandered through the city, and found no flowers or verdure among those antique haunts of men until the heavy perfumes of Dr. Rappaccini's shrubs had lured it from afar. Without alighting on the flowers, this winged brightness seemed to be attracted by Beatrice, and lingered in the air and fluttered about her head. Now, here it could not be but that Giovanni Guasconti's eyes deceived him. Be that as it might, he fancied that, while Beatrice was gazing at the insect with childish delight, it grew faint and fell at her feet; its bright wings shivered; it was dead–from no cause that he could discern, unless it were the atmosphere of her breath. Again Beatrice crossed herself and sighed heavily as she bent over the dead insect.

An impulsive movement of Giovanni drew her eyes to the window. There she beheld the beautiful head of the young man–rather a Grecian than an Italian head, with fair, regular features, and a glistening of gold among his ringlets–gazing down upon her like a being that hovered in mid air. Scarcely knowing what he did, Giovanni threw down the bouquet which he had hitherto held in his hand.

"Signora," said he, "there are pure and healthful flowers. Wear them for the sake of Giovanni Guasconti."

"Thanks, signor," replied Beatrice, with her rich voice, that came forth as it were like a gush of music, and with a mirthful expression half childish and half woman-like. "I accept your gift, and would fain recompense it with this precious purple flower; but if I toss it into the air it will not reach you. So Signor Guasconti must even content himself with my thanks."

She lifted the bouquet from the ground, and then, as if inwardly ashamed at having stepped aside from her maidenly reserve to respond to a stranger's greeting, passed swiftly homeward through the garden. But few as the moments were, it seemed to Giovanni, when she was on the point of vanishing beneath the sculptured portal, that his beautiful bouquet was already beginning to wither in her grasp. It was an idle thought; there could be no possibility of distinguishing a faded flower from a fresh one at so great a distance.

For many days after this incident the young man avoided the window that looked into Dr. Rappaccini's garden, as if something ugly and monstrous would have blasted his eyesight had he been betrayed into a glance. He felt conscious of having put himself, to a certain extent, within the influence of an unintelligible power by the communication which he had opened with Beatrice. The wisest course would have been, if his heart were in any real danger, to quit his lodgings and Padua itself at once; the next wiser, to have accustomed himself, as far as possible, to the familiar and daylight view of Beatrice—thus bringing her rigidly and systematically within the limits of ordinary experience. Least of all, while avoiding her sight, ought Giovanni to have remained so near this extraordinary being that the proximity and possibility even of intercourse should give a kind of substance and reality to the wild vagaries which his imagination ran riot continually in producing. Guasconti had not a deep heart—or, at all events, its depths were not sounded now; but he had a quick fancy, and an ardent Southern temperament, which rose every instant to a higher fever pitch. Whether or no Beatrice possessed those terrible attributes, that fatal breath, the affinity with those so beautiful and deadly flowers which were indicated by what Giovanni had witnessed, she had at least instilled a fierce and subtle poison into his system. It was not love, although her rich beauty was a madness to him; nor horror, even while he fancied her spirit to be imbued with the same baneful essence that seemed to pervade her physical frame; but a wild offspring of both love and horror that had each parent in it, and burned like one and shivered like the other. Giovanni knew not what to dread; still less did he know what to hope; yet hope and dread kept a continual warfare in his breast, alternately vanquishing one another and starting up afresh to renew the contest. Blessed are all simple emotions, be they dark or bright! It is the lurid intermixture of the two that produces the illuminating blaze of the infernal regions.

Sometimes he endeavored to assuage the fever of his spirit by a rapid walk through the streets of Padua or beyond its gates: his footsteps kept time with the throbbings of his brain, so that the walk was apt to accelerate itself to a race. One day he found himself arrested; his arm was seized by a portly personage, who had turned back on recognizing the young man and expended much breath in overtaking him.

"Signor Giovanni! Stay, my young friend!" cried he. "Have you forgotten me? That might well be the case if I were as much altered as yourself."

It was Baglioni, whom Giovanni had avoided ever since their first meeting, from a doubt that the professor's sagacity would look too deeply into his secrets. Endeavoring to recover himself, he stared forth wildly from his inner world into the outer one and spoke like a man in a dream.

"Yes; I am Giovanni Guasconti. You are Professor Pietro Baglioni. Now let me pass!"

"Not yet, not yet, Signor Giovanni Guasconti," said the professor, smiling, but at the same time scrutinizing the youth with an earnest glance. "What! did I grow up side by side with your father? and shall his son pass me like a stranger in these old streets of Padua? Stand still, Signor Giovanni; for we must have a word or two before we part."

"Speedily, then, most worshipful professor, speedily," said Giovanni, with feverish impatience. "Does not your worship see that I am in haste?"

Now, while he was speaking there came a man in black along the street, stooping and moving feebly like a person in inferior health. His face was all overspread with a most sickly and sallow hue, but yet so pervaded with an expression of piercing and active intellect that an observer might easily have overlooked the merely physical attributes and have seen only his wonderful energy. As he passed, this person exchanged a cold and distant salutation with Baglioni, but fixed his eyes upon Giovanni with an intentness that seemed to bring out whatever was within him worthy of notice. Nevertheless, there was a peculiar quietness in the look, as if taking merely a speculative, not a human, interest in the young man.

"It is Dr. Rappaccini!" whispered the professor when the stranger had passed. "Has he ever seen your face before?"

"Not that I know," answered Giovanni, starting at the name.

"He *has* seen you! he must have seen you!" said Baglioni, hastily. "For some purpose or other, this man of science is making a study of you. I know that look of his! It is the same that coldly illuminates his face as he bends over a bird, a mouse, or a butterfly, which, in pursuance of some experiment, he has killed by the perfume of a flower; a look as deep as Nature itself, but without Nature's warmth of love. Signor Giovanni, I will stake my life upon it, you are the subject of one of Rappaccini's experiments!"

"Will you make a fool of me?" cried Giovanni, passionately. "*That*, signor professor, were an untoward experiment."

"Patience! patience!" replied the imperturbable professor. "I tell thee, my poor Giovanni, that Rappaccini has a scientific interest in thee. Thou hast fallen into fearful hands! And the Signora Beatrice,—what part does she act in this mystery?"

But Guasconti, finding Baglioni's pertinacity intolerable, here broke away, and was gone before the professor could again seize his arm. He looked after the young man intently and shook his head.

"This must not be," said Baglioni to himself. "The youth is the son of my old friend, and shall not come to any harm from which the arcana of medical science can preserve him. Besides, it is too insufferable an impertinence in Rappaccini, thus to snatch the lad out of my own hands, as I may say, and make use of him for his infernal experiments. This daughter of his! It shall be looked to. Perchance, most learned Rappaccini, I may foil you where you little dream of it!"

Meanwhile Giovanni had pursued a circuitous route, and at length found himself at the door of his lodgings. As he crossed the threshold he was met by old Lisabetta, who smirked and smiled, and was evidently desirous to attract his attention; vainly, however, as the ebullition of his feelings had momentarily subsided into a cold and dull vacuity. He turned his eyes full upon the withered face that was puckering itself into a smile, but seemed to behold it not. The old dame, therefore, laid her grasp upon his cloak.

"Signor! signor!" whispered she, still with a smile over the whole breadth of her visage, so that it looked not unlike a grotesque carving in wood, darkened by centuries. "Listen, signor! There is a private entrance into the garden!"

"What do you say?" exclaimed Giovanni, turning quickly about, as if an inanimate thing should start into feverish life. "A private entrance into Dr. Rappaccini's garden?"

"Hush! hush! not so loud!" whispered Lisabetta, putting her hand over his mouth. "Yes; into the worshipful doctor's garden, where you may see all his fine shrubbery. Many a young man in Padua would give gold to be admitted among those flowers."

Giovanni put a piece of gold into her hand.

"Show me the way," said he.

A surmise, probably excited by his conversation with Baghoni, crossed his mind, that this interposition of old Lisabetta might perchance be connected with the intrigue, whatever were its nature, in which the professor seemed to suppose that Dr. Rappaccini was involving him. But such a suspicion, though it disturbed Giovanni, was inadequate to restrain him. The instant that he was aware of the possibility of approaching Beatrice, it seemed an absolute necessity of his existence to do so. It mattered not whether she were angel or demon; he was irrevocably within her sphere, and must obey the law that whirled him onward, in ever-lessening circles, towards a result which he did not attempt to foreshadow; and yet, strange to say, there came across him a sudden doubt whether this intense interest on his part were not delusory; whether it were really of so deep and positive a nature as to justify him in now thrusting himself into an incalculable position; whether it were not merely the fantasy of a young man's brain, only slightly or not at all connected with his heart.

He paused, hesitated, turned half about, but again went on. His withered guide led him along several obscure passages, and finally undid a door, through which, as it was opened, there came the sight and sound of rustling leaves, with the broken sunshine glimmering among them. Giovanni stepped forth, and, forcing himself through the entanglement of a shrub that wreathed its tendrils over the hidden entrance, stood beneath his own window in the open area of Dr. Rappaccini's garden.

How often is it the case that, when impossibilities have come to pass and dreams have condensed their misty substance into tangible realities, we find ourselves calm, and even coldly self-possessed, amid circumstances which it would have been a delirium of joy or agony to anticipate! Fate delights to thwart us thus. Passion will choose his own time to rush upon the scene, and lingers sluggishly behind when an appropriate adjustment of events would seem to summon his appearance. So was it now with Giovanni. Day after day his pulses had throbbed with feverish blood at the improbable idea of an interview with Beatrice, and of standing with her, face to face, in this very garden, basking in the Oriental sunshine of her beauty, and snatching from her full gaze the mystery which he deemed the riddle of his own existence. But now there was a singular and untimely equanimity within his breast. He threw a glance around the garden to discover if Beatrice or her father were present, and, perceiving that he was alone, began a critical observation of the plants.

The aspect of one and all of them dissatisfied him; their gorgeousness seemed fierce, passionate, and even unnatural. There was hardly an individual shrub which a wanderer, straying by himself through a forest, would not have been startled to find growing wild, as if an unearthly face had stared at him out of the thicket. Several also would have shocked a delicate instinct by an appearance of artificialness indicating that there had been such commixture, and, as it were, adultery, of various vegetable species, that the production was no longer of God's making, but the monstrous offspring of man's depraved fancy, glowing with only an evil mockery of beauty. They were probably the result of experiment, which in one or two cases had succeeded in mingling plants individually lovely into a compound possessing the questionable and ominous character that distinguished the whole growth of the garden. In fine, Giovanni recognized but two or three plants in the collection, and those of a kind that he well knew to be poisonous. While busy with these contemplations he heard the rustling of a silken garment, and, turning, beheld Beatrice emerging from beneath the sculptured portal.

Giovanni had not considered with himself what should be his deportment; whether he should apologize for his intrusion into the garden, or assume that he was there with the privity at least, if not by the desire, of Dr. Rappaccini or his daughter; but Beatrice's manner placed him at his ease, though leaving him still in doubt by what agency he had gained admittance. She came lightly along the path and met him near the broken fountain. There was surprise in her face, but brightened by a simple and kind expression of pleasure.

"You are a connoisseur in flowers, signor," said Beatrice, with a smile, alluding to the bouquet which he had flung her from the window. "It is no marvel, therefore, if the sight of my father's rare collection has tempted you to take a nearer view. If he were here, he could tell you many strange and interesting facts as to the nature and habits of these shrubs; for he has spent a lifetime in such studies, and this garden is his world."

"And yourself, lady," observed Giovanni, "if fame says true,—you likewise are deeply skilled in the virtues indicated by these rich blossoms and these spicy perfumes. Would you deign to be my instructress, I should prove an apter scholar than if taught by Signor Rappaccini

"Are there such idle rumors?" asked Beatrice, with the music of a pleasant laugh. "Do people say that I am skilled in my father's science of plants?

What a jest is there! No; though I have grown up among these flowers, I know no more of them than their hues and perfume; and sometimes methinks I would fain rid myself of even that small knowledge. There are many flowers here, and those not the least brilliant, that shock and offend me when they meet my eye. But pray, signor, do not believe these stories about my science. Believe nothing of me save what you see with your own eyes."

"And must I believe all that I have seen with my own eyes?" asked Giovanni, pointedly, while the recollection of former scenes made him shrink. "No, signora; you demand too little of me. Bid me believe nothing save what comes from your own lips."

It would appear that Beatrice understood him. There came a deep flush to her cheek; but she looked full into Giovanni's eyes, and responded to his gaze of uneasy suspicion with a queenlike haughtiness.

"I do so bid you, Signor," she replied. "Forget whatever you may have fancied in regard to me. If true to the outward senses, still it may be false in its essence; but the words of Beatrice Rappaccini's lips are true from the depths of the heart outward. Those you may believe."

A fervor glowed in her whole aspect and beamed upon Giovanni's consciousness like the light of truth itself; but while she spoke there was a fragrance in the atmosphere around her, rich and delightful, though evanescent, yet which the young man, from an indefinable reluctance, scarcely dared to draw into his lungs. It might be the odor of the flowers. Could it be Beatrice's breath which thus embalmed her words with a strange richness, as if by steeping them in her heart? A faintness passed like a shadow over Giovanni and flitted away; he seemed to gaze through the beautiful girl's eyes into her transparent soul, and felt no more doubt or fear.

The tinge of passion that had colored Beatrice's manner vanished; she became gay, and appeared to derive a pure delight from her communion with the youth not unlike what the maiden of a lonely island might have felt conversing with a voyager from the civilized world. Evidently her experience of life had been confined within the limits of that garden. She talked now about matters as simple as the daylight or summer clouds, and now asked questions in reference to the city, or Giovanni's distant home, his friends, his mother, and his sisters—questions indicating such seclusion, and such lack of familiarity with modes and forms, that Giovanni responded as if to an infant. Her spirit gushed out before him like a fresh rill that was just catching its first glimpse of the sunlight and wondering at the reflections of earth and sky which were flung into its bosom. There came thoughts, too, from a deep source, and fantasies of a gemlike brilliancy, as if diamonds and rubies sparkled upward among the bubbles of the fountain. Ever and anon there gleamed across the young man's mind a sense of wonder that he should be walking side by side with the being who had so wrought upon his imagination, whom he had idealized in such hues of terror, in whom he had positively witnessed such manifestations of dreadful attributes,—that he should be conversing with Beatrice like a brother, and should find her so human and so maidenlike. But such reflections were only momentary; the effect of her character was too real not to make itself familiar at once.

In this free intercourse they had strayed through the garden, and now, after many turns among its avenues, were come to the shattered fountain, beside which grew the magnificent shrub, with its treasury of glowing blossoms. A fragrance was diffused from it which Giovanni recognized as identical with that which he had attributed to Beatrice's breath, but incomparably more powerful. As her eyes fell upon it, Giovanni beheld her press her hand to her bosom as if her heart were throbbing suddenly and painfully.

"For the first time in my life," murmured she, addressing the shrub, "I had forgotten thee."

"I remember, signora," said Giovanni, "that you once promised to reward me with one of these living gems for the bouquet which I had the happy boldness to fling to your feet. Permit me now to pluck it as a memorial of this interview."

He made a step towards the shrub with extended hand; but Beatrice darted forward, uttering a shriek that went through his heart like a dagger. She caught his hand and drew it back with the whole force of her slender figure. Giovanni felt her touch thrilling through his fibers.

"Touch it not!" exclaimed she, in a voice of agony. "Not for thy life! It is fatal!"

Then, hiding her face, she fled from him and vanished beneath the sculptured portal. As Giovanni followed her with his eyes, he beheld the emaciated figure and pale intelligence of Dr. Rappaccini, who had been watching the scene, he knew not how long, within the shadow of the entrance.

No sooner was Guasconti alone in his clamber than the image of Beatrice came back to his passionate musings, invested with all the witchery that had been gathering around it ever since his first glimpse of her, and now likewise imbued with a tender warmth of girlish womanhood. She was human; her nature was endowed with all gentle and feminine qualities; she was worthiest to be worshipped; she was capable, surely, on her part, of the height and heroism of love. Those tokens which he had hitherto considered as proofs of a frightful peculiarity in her physical and moral system were now either forgotten, or, by the subtle sophistry of passion transmitted into a golden crown of enchantment, rendering Beatrice the more admirable by so much as she was the more unique. Whatever had looked ugly was now beautiful; or, if incapable of such a change, it stole away and hid itself among those shapeless half ideas which throng the dim region beyond the daylight of our perfect consciousness. Thus did he spend the night, nor fell asleep until the dawn had begun to awake the slumbering flowers in

Dr. Rappaccini's garden, whither Giovanni's dreams doubtless led him. Up rose the sun in his due season, and, flinging his beams upon the young man's eyelids, awoke him to a sense of pain. When thoroughly aroused, he became sensible of a burning and tingling agony in his hand—in his right hand—the very hand which Beatrice had grasped in her own when he was on the point of plucking one of the gemlike flowers. On the back of that hand there was now a purple print like that of four small fingers, and the likeness of a slender thumb upon his wrist.

Oh, how stubbornly does love,—or even that cunning semblance of love which flourishes in the imagination, but strikes no depth of root into the heart,—how stubbornly does it hold its faith until the moment comes when it is doomed to vanish into thin mist! Giovanni wrapped a handkerchief about his hand and wondered what evil thing had stung him, and soon forgot his pain in a reverie of Beatrice.

After the first interview, a second was in the inevitable course of what we call fate. A third; a fourth; and a meeting with Beatrice in the garden was no longer an incident in Giovanni's daily life, but the whole space in which he might be said to live; for the anticipation and memory of that ecstatic hour made up the remainder. Nor was it otherwise with the daughter of Rappaccini. She watched for the youth's appearance, and flew to his side with confidence as unreserved as if they had been playmates from early infancy—as if they were such playmates still. If, by any unwonted chance, he failed to come at the appointed moment, she stood beneath the window and sent up the rich sweetness of her tones to float around him in his chamber and echo and reverberate throughout his heart: "Giovanni! Giovanni! Why tarriest thou? Come down!" And down he hastened into that Eden of poisonous flowers.

But, with all this intimate familiarity, there was still a reserve in Beatrice's demeanor, so rigidly and invariably sustained that the idea of infringing it scarcely occurred to his imagination. By all appreciable signs, they loved; they had looked love with eyes that conveyed the holy secret from the depths of one soul into the depths of the other, as if it were too sacred to be whispered by the way; they had even spoken love in those gushes of passion when their spirits darted forth in articulated breath like tongues of long-hidden flame; and yet there had been no seal of lips, no clasp of hands, nor any slightest caress such as love claims and hallows. He had never touched one of the gleaming ringlets of her hair; her garment—so marked was the physical barrier between them—had never been waved against him by a breeze. On the few occasions when Giovanni had seemed tempted to overstep the limit, Beatrice grew so sad, so stern, and withal wore such a look of desolate separation, shuddering at itself, that not a spoken word was requisite to repel him. At such times he was startled at the horrible suspicions that rose, monster-like, out of the caverns of his heart and stared him in the face;

his love grew thin and faint as the morning mist, his doubts alone had substance. But, when Beatrice's face brightened again after the momentary shadow, she was transformed at once from the mysterious, questionable being whom he had watched with so much awe and horror; she was now the beautiful and unsophisticated girl whom he felt that his spirit knew with a certainty beyond all other knowledge.

A considerable time had now passed since Giovanni's last meeting with Baglioni. One morning, however, he was disagreeably surprised by a visit from the professor, whom he had scarcely thought of for whole weeks, and would willingly have forgotten still longer. Given up as he had long been to a pervading excitement, he could tolerate no companions except upon condition of their perfect sympathy with his present state of feeling. Such sympathy was not to be expected from Professor Baglioni.

The visitor chatted carelessly for a few moments about the gossip of the city and the university, and then took up another topic.

"I have been reading an old classic author lately," said he, "and met with a story that strangely interested me. Possibly you may remember it. It is of an Indian prince, who sent a beautiful woman as a present to Alexander the Great. She was as lovely as the dawn and gorgeous as the sunset; but what especially distinguished her was a certain rich perfume in hcr breath—richer than a garden of Persian roses. Alexander, as was natural to a youthful conqueror, fell in love at first sight with this magnificent stranger; but a certain sage physician, happening to be present, discovered a terrible secret in regard to her."

"And what was that?" asked Giovanni, turning his eyes downward to avoid those of the professor.

"That this lovely woman," continued Baglioni, with emphasis, "had been nourished with poisons from her birth upward, until her whole nature was so imbued with them that she herself had become the deadliest poison in existence. Poison was her element of life. With that rich perfume of her breath she blasted the very air. Her love would have been poison—her embrace death. Is not this a marvelous tale?"

"A childish fable," answered Giovanni, nervously starting from his chair. "I marvel how your worship finds time to read such nonsense among your graver studies."

"By the by," said the professor, looking uneasily about him, "what singular fragrance is this in your apartment? Is it the perfume of your gloves ? It is faint, but delicious; and yet, after all, by no means agreeable. Were I to breathe it long, methinks it would make me ill. It is like the breath of a flower; but I see no flowers in the chamber."

"Nor are there any," replied Giovanni, who had turned pale as the professor spoke; "nor, I think, is there any fragrance except in your worship's imagination. Odors, being a sort of element combined of the sensual and the spiritual, are apt to deceive us in this manner. The recollection of a perfume, the bare idea of it, may easily be mistaken for a present reality."

"Ay; but my sober imagination does not often play such tricks," said Baglioni; "and, were I to fancy any kind of odor, it would be that of some vile apothecary drug, wherewith my fingers are likely enough to be imbued. Our worshipful friend Rappaccini, as I have heard, tinctures his medicaments with odors richer than those of Araby. Doubtless, likewise, thc fair and learned Signora Beatrice would minister to her patients with draughts as sweet as a maiden's breath; but woe to him that sips them!"

Giovanni's face evinced many contending emotions. The tone in which the professor alluded to the pure and lovely daughter of Rappaccini was a torture to his soul; and yet the intimation of a view of her character, opposite to his own, gave instantaneous distinctness to a thousand dim suspicions, which now grinned at him like so many demons. But he strove hard to quell them and to respond to Baglioni with a true lover's perfect faith.

"Signor professor," said he, "you were my father's friend; perchance, too, it is your purpose to act a friendly part towards his son. I would fain feel nothing towards you save respect and deference; but I pray you to observe, signor, that there is one subject on which we must not speak. You know not the Signora Beatrice. You cannot, therefore, estimate the wrong—the blasphemy, I may even say—that is offered to her character by a light or injurious word."

"Giovanni! my poor Giovanni!" answered the professor, with a calm expression of pity, "I know this wretched girl far better than yourself. You shall hear the truth in respect to the poisoner Rappaccini and his poisonous daughter; yes, poisonous as she is beautiful. Listen; for, even should you do violence to my gray hairs, it shall not silence me. That old fable of the Indian woman has become a truth by the deep and deadly science of Rappaccini and in the person of the lovely Beatrice."

Giovanni groaned and hid his face.

"Her father," continued Baglioni, "was not restrained by natural affection from offering up his child in this horrible manner as the victim of his insane zeal for science; for, let us do him justice, he is as true a man of science as ever distilled his own heart in an alembic. What, then, will be your fate? Beyond a doubt you are selected as the material of some new experiment. Perhaps the result is to be death; perhaps a fate more awful still. Rappaccini, with what he calls the interest of science before his eyes, will hesitate at nothing."

"It is a dream," muttered Giovanni to himself: "surely it is a dream."

"But," resumed the professor, "be of good cheer, son of my friend. It is not yet too late for the rescue. Possibly we may even succeed in bringing back this miserable child within the limits of ordinary nature, from which her father's madness has estranged her. Behold this little silver vase! It was wrought by the hands of the renowed Benvenuto Cellini, and is well worthy to be a love gift to the fairest dame in Italy. But its contents are invaluable. One little sip of this antidote would have rendered the most virulent poisons of the Borgias innocuous. Doubt not that it will be as efficacious against those of Rappaccini. Bestow the vase, and the precious liquid within it, on your Beatrice, and hopefully await the result."

Baglioni laid a small, exquisitely wrought silver vial on the table and withdrew, leaving what he had said to produce its effect upon the young man's mind.

"We will thwart Rappaccini yet," thought he, chuckling to himself, as he descended the stairs; "but, let us confess the truth of him, he is a wonderful man—a wonderful man indeed; a vile empiric, however, in his practice, and therefore not to be tolerated by those who respect the good old rules of the medical profession."

Throughout Giovanni's whole acquaintance with Beatrice, he had occasionally, as we have said, been haunted by dark surmises as to her character; yet so thoroughly had she made herself felt by him as a simple, natural, most affectionate, and guileless creature, that the image now held up by Professor Baglioni looked as strange and incredible as if it were not in accordance with his own original conception. True, there were ugly recollections connected with his first glimpses of the beautiful girl; he could not quite forget the bouquet that withered in her grasp, and the insect that perished amid the sunny air, by no ostensible agency save the fragrance of her breath. These incidents, however, dissolving in the pure light of her character, had no longer the efficacy of facts, but were acknowledged as mistaken fantasies, by whatever testimony of the senses they might appear to be substantiated. There is something truer and more real than what we can see with the eyes and touch with the finger. On such better evidence had Giovanni founded his confidence in Beatrice, though rather by the necessary force of her high attributes than by any deep and generous faith on his part. But now his spirit was incapable of sustaining itself at the height to which the early enthusiasm of passion had exalted it; he fell down, grovelling among earthly doubts, and defiled therewith the pure whiteness of Beatrice's image. Not that he gave her up; he did but distrust. He resolved to institute some decisive test that should satisfy him, once for all, whether there were those dreadful peculiarities in her physical nature which could not be supposed to exist without some corresponding monstrosity of soul. His eyes, gazing down afar, might have deceived him as to the lizard, the insect, and the flowers; but if he could witness, at the distance of a few paces the sudden blight of one fresh and healthful flower in Beatrice's hand there would be room for no further question. With this idea he hastened to the florist's and purchased a bouquet that was still gemmed with the morning dew-drops.

It was now the customary hour of his daily interview with Beatrice. Before descending into the garden, Giovanni failed not to look at his figure in the mirror,–a vanity to be expected in a beautiful young man, yet, as displaying itself at that troubled and feverish moment, the token of a certain shallowness of feeling and insincerity of character. He did gaze, however, and said to himself that his features had never before possessed so rich a grace, nor his eyes such vivacity, nor his cheeks so warm a hue of superabundant life.

"At least," thought he, "her poison has not yet insinuated itself into my system. I am no flower to perish in her grasp."

With that thought he turned his eyes on the bouquet, which he had never once laid aside from his hand. A thrill of indefinable horror shot through his frame on perceiving that those dewy flowers were already beginning to droop; they wore the aspect of things that had been fresh and lovely yesterday. Giovanni grew white as marble, and stood motionless before the mirror, staring at his own reflection there as at the likeness of something frightful. He remembered Baglioni's remark about the fragrance that seemed to pervade the chamber. It must have been the poison in his breath! Then he shuddered–shuddered at himself. Recovering from his stupor, he began to watch with curious eye a spider that was busily at work hanging its web from the antique cornice of the apartment, crossing and recrossing the artful system of interwoven lines–as vigorous and active a spider as ever dangled from an old ceiling. Giovanni bent towards the insect, and emitted a deep, long breath. The spider suddenly ceased its toil; the web vibrated with a tremor originating in the body of the small artisan. Again Giovanni sent forth a breath, deeper, longer, and imbued with a venomous feeling out of his heart: he knew not whether he were wicked, or only desperate. The spider made a convulsive gripe with his limps and hung dead across the window.

"Accursed! accursed!" muttered Giovanni, addressing himself. "Hast thou grown so poisonous that this deadly insect perishes by thy breath?"

At that moment a rich, sweet voice came floating up from the garden.

"Giovanni! Giovanni! It is past the hour! Why tarriest thou? Come down!"

"Yes," muttered Giovanni again. "She is the only being whom my breath may not slay! Would that it might!"

He rushed down, and in an instant was standing before the bright and loving eyes of Beatrice. A moment ago his wrath and despair had been so fierce that he could have desired nothing so much as to wither her by a glance; but with her actual presence there came influences which had too real an existence to be at once shaken off: recollections of the delicate and benign power of her feminine nature, which had so often enveloped him in a religious calm; recollections of many a holy and passionate outgush of her heart, when the pure fountain had been unsealed from its depths and made visible in its transparency to his mental eye; recollections which, had

Giovanni known how to estimate them, would have assured him that all this ugly mystery was but an earthly illusion, and that, whatever mist of evil might seem to have gathered over her, the real Beatrice was a heavenly angel. Incapable as he was of such high faith, still her presence had not utterly lost its magic. Giovanni's rage was quelled into an aspect of sullen insensibility. Beatrice, with a quick spiritual sense, immediately felt that there was a gulf of blackness between them which neither he nor she could pass. They walked on together, sad and silent, and came thus to the marble fountain and to its pool of water on the ground, in the midst of which grew the shrub that bore gemlike blossoms. Giovanni was affrighted at the eager enjoyment—the appetite, as it were—with which he found himself inhaling the fragrance of the flowers.

"Beatrice," asked he, abruptly, "whence came this shrub?"

"My father created it," answered she, with simplicity.

"Created it! created it!" repeated Giovanni. "What mean you, Beatrice?"

"He is a man fearfully acquainted with the secrets of Nature," replied Beatrice; "and, at the hour when I first drew breath, this plant sprang from the soil, the offspring of his science, of his intellect, while I was but his earthly child. Approach it not!" continued she, observing with terror that Giovanni was drawing nearer to the shrub. "It has qualities that you little dream of. But I, dearest Giovanni,—I grew up and blossomed with the plant and was nourished with its breath. It was my sister, and I loved it with a human affection; for, alas!—hast thou not suspected it?—there was an awful doom."

Here Giovanni frowned so darkly upon her that Beatrice paused and trembled. But her faith in his tenderness reassured her, and made her blush that she had doubted for an instant.

"There was an awful doom," she continued, "the effect of my father's fatal love of science, which estranged me from all society of my kind. Until Heaven sent thee, dearest Giovanni, oh, how lonely was thy poor Beatrice!"

"Was it a hard doom?" asked Giovanni, fixing his eyes upon her.

"Only of late have I known how hard it was," answered she, tenderly. "Oh, yes; but my heart was torpid, and therefore quiet."

Giovanni's rage broke forth from his sullen gloom like a lightning flash out of a dark cloud.

"Accursed one!" cried he, with venomous scorn and anger. "And, finding thy solitude wearisome, thou hast severed me likewise from all the warmth of life and enticed me into thy region of unspeakable horror!"

"Giovanni!" exclaimed Beatrice, turning her large bright eyes upon his face. The force of his words had nor found its way into her mind; she was merely thunderstruck.

"Yes, poisonous thing!" repeated Giovanni, beside himself with passion. "Thou hast done it! Thou hast blasted me! Thou hast filled my veins with poison! Thou hast made me as hateful, as ugly, as loathsome and deadly a creature as thyself—a world's wonder of hideous monstrosity! Now, if our breath be happily as fatal to ourselves as to all others, let us join our lips in one kiss of unutterable hatred, and so die!"

"What has befallen me?" murmured Beatrice, with a low moan out of her heart. "Holy Virgin, pity me, a poor heart-broken child!"

"Thou,—dost thou pray?" cried Giovanni, still with the same fiendish scorn. "Thy very prayers, as they come from thy lips, taint the atmosphere with death. Yes, yes; let us pray! Let us to church and dip our fingers in the holy water at the portal! They that come after us will perish as by a pestilence! Let us sign crosses in the air! It will be scattering curses abroad in the likeness of holy symbols!"

"Giovanni," said Beatrice, calmly, for her grief was beyond passion, "why dost thou join thyself with me thus in those terrible words? I, it is true, am the horrible thing thou namest me. But thou,—what hast thou to do, save with one other shudder at my hideous misery to go forth out of the garden and mingle with thy race, and forget that there ever crawled on earth such a monster as poor Beatrice?"

"Dost thou pretend ignorance?" asked Giovanni scowling upon her. "Behold! this power have I gained from the pure daughter of Rappaccini."

There was a swarm of summer insects flitting through the air in search of the food promised by the flower odors of the fatal garden. They circled round Giovanni's head, and were evidently attracted towards him by the same influence which had drawn them for an instant within the sphere of several of the shrubs. He sent forth a breath among them, and smiled bitterly at Beatrice as at least a score of the insects fell dead upon the ground.

"I see it! I see it!" shrieked Beatrice. "It is my father's fatal science! No, no, Giovanni; it was not I! Never! never! I dreamed only to love thee and be with thee a little time, and so to let thee pass away, leaving but thine image in mine heart; for Giovanni, believe it, though my body be nourished with poison, my spirit is God's creature, and craves love as its daily food. But my father,—he has united us in this fearful sympathy. Yes; spurn me, tread upon me, kill me! Oh, what is death after such words as thine? But it was not I. Not for a world of bliss would I have done it."

Giovanni's passion had exhausted itself in its outburst from his lips. There now came across him a sense, mournful, and not without tenderness, of the intimate and peculiar relationship between Beatrice and himself. They stood, as it were, in an utter solitude, which would be made none the less solitary by the densest throng of human life. Ought not, then, the desert of humanity around them to press this insulated pair closer together? If they should be cruel to one another, who was there to be kind to them? Besides, thought Giovanni, might there not still be a hope of his returning within the limits of ordinary nature, and leading Beatrice, the redeemed Beatrice, by the hand O, weak, and selfish, and unworthy spirit, that could dream of an earthly union and earthly happiness as possible, after such deep love had been so bitterly wronged as was Beatrice's love by Giovanni's blighting words! No, no; there could be no such hope. She must pass heavily, with that broken heart, across the borders of Time–she must bathe her hurts in some fount of paradise, and forget her grief in the light of immortality, and *there* be well.

But Giovanni did not know it.

"Dear Beatrice," said he, approaching her, while she shrank away as always at his approach, but now with a different impulse, "dearest Beatrice, our fate is not yet so desperate. Behold! there is a medicine, potent, as a wise physician has assured me, and almost divine in its efficacy. It is composed of ingredients the most opposite to those by which thy awful father has brought this calamity upon thee and me. It is distilled of blessed herbs. Shall we not quaff it together, and thus be purified from evil?"

"Give it me!" said Beatrice, extending her hand to receive the little silver vial which Giovanni took from his bosom. She added, with a peculiar emphasis, "I will drink; but do thou await the result."

She put Baglioni's antidote to her lips; and, at the same moment, the figure of Rappaccini emerged from the portal and came slowly towards the marble fountain. As he drew near, the pale man of science seemed to gaze with a triumphant expression at the beautiful youth and maiden, as might an artist who should spend his life in achieving a picture or a group of statuary and finally be satisfied with his success. He paused; his bent form grew erect with conscious power; he spread out his hands over them in the attitude of a father imploring a blessing upon his children; but those were the same hands that had thrown poison into the stream of their lives. Giovanni trembled. Beatrice shuddered nervously, and pressed her hand upon her heart.

"My daughter," said Rappaccini, "thou art no longer lonely in the world. Pluck one of those precious gems from thy sister shrub and bid thy bridegroom wear it in his bosom. It will not harm him now. My science and the sympathy between thee and him have so wrought within his system that he now stands apart from common men, as thou dost, daughter of my pride and triumph, from ordinary women. Pass on, then, through the world, most dear to one another and dreadful to all besides!"

"My father," said Beatrice, feebly,–and still as she spoke she kept her hand upon her heart,–"wherefore didst thou inflict this miserable doom upon thy child?"

"Miserable!" exclaimed Rappaccini. "What mean you, foolish girl? Dost thou deem it misery to be endowed with marvelous gifts against which no power nor strength could avail an enemy–misery, to be able to quell the mightiest with a breath—misery, to be as terrible as thou art beautiful? Wouldst thou, then, have preferred the condition of a weak woman, exposed to all evil and capable of none?"

"I would fain have been loved, not feared," murmured Beatrice, sinking down upon the ground. "But now it matters not. I am going, father, where the evil which thou hast striven to mingle with my being will pass away like a dream—like the fragrance of these poisonous flowers, which will no longer taint my breath among the flowers of Eden. Farewell, Giovanni! Thy words of hatred are like lead within my heart; but they, too, will fall away as I ascend. Oh, was there not, from the first, more poison in thy nature than in mine?"

To Beatrice,—so radically had her earthly part been wrought upon by Rappaccini's skill—as poison had been life, so thc powerful antidote was death; and thus the poor victim of man's ingenuity and of thwarted nature, and of the fatality that attends all such efforts of perverted wisdom, perished there, at the feet of her father and Giovanni. Just at that moment Professor Pietro Baglioni looked forth from the window, and called loudly, in a tone of triumph mixed with horror, to the thunderstricken man of science,—

"Rappaccini! Rappaccini! and is *this* the upshot of your experiment!"

EDGAR ALLEN POE

[1809–1849]

The Fall of the House of Usher

(First published in *Burton's Gentleman's Magazine*, September, 1839; first book publication in 1845.)

Son coeur est un luth suspendu;
Sitôt qu'on le touche il résonne.
—DE BÉRANGER

DURING THE WHOLE of a dull, dark, and soundless day in the autumn of the year, when the clouds hung oppressively low in the heavens, I had been passing alone, on horseback, through a singularly dreary tract of country, and at length found myself, as the shades of the evening drew on, within view of the melancholy House of Usher. I know not how it was—but, with the first glimpse of the building, a sense of insufferable gloom pervaded my spirit. I say insufferable; for the feeling was unrelieved by any of that half-pleasurable, because poetic, sentiment with which the mind usually receives even the sternest natural images of the desolate or terrible. I looked upon the scene before me—upon the mere house, and the simple landscape features of the domain—upon the bleak walls—upon the vacant eye-like windows—upon a few rank sedges—and upon a few white trunks of decayed trees—with an utter depression of soul which I can compare to no earthly sensation more properly than to the after-dream of the reveller upon opium—the bitter lapse into every-day life—the hideous dropping off of the veil. There was an iciness, a sinking, a sickening of the heart—an unredeemed dreariness of thought which no goading of the imagination could torture into aught of the sublime. What was it—I paused to think—what was it that so unnerved me in the contemplation of the House of Usher? It was a mystery all insoluble; nor could I grapple with the shadowy fancies that crowded upon me as I pondered. I was forced to fall back upon the unsatisfactory conclusion, that while, beyond doubt, there *are* combinations of very simple natural objects which have the power of thus affecting us, still the analysis of this power lies among considerations beyond our depth. It was possible, I reflected, that a mere different arrangement of the particulars of the scene, of the details of the picture, would be sufficient to modify, or perhaps to annihilate its capacity for sorrowful impression; and, acting upon this idea, I reined my horse to the precipitous brink of a black and lurid tarn that lay in unruffled lustre by the dwelling, and gazed down—but with a shudder even more thrilling than before—upon the remodelled and inverted images of the gray sedge, and the ghastly tree-stems, and the vacant and eye-like windows.

Nevertheless, in this mansion of gloom I now proposed to myself a sojourn of some weeks. Its proprietor, Roderick Usher, had been one of my boon companions in boyhood; but many years had elapsed since our last meeting. A letter, however, had lately reached me in a distant part of the country—a letter from him—which, in its wildly importunate nature, had admitted of no other than a personal reply. The MS. gave evidence of nervous agitation. The writer spoke of acute bodily illness—of a mental disorder which oppressed him—and of an earnest desire to see me, as his best and indeed his only personal friend, with a view of attempting, by the cheerfulness of my society, some alleviation of his malady. It was the manner in which all this, and much more, was said—it was the apparent *heart* that went with his request—which allowed me no room for hesitation; and I accordingly obeyed forthwith what I still considered a very singular summons.

Although, as boys, we had been even intimate associates, yet I really knew little of my friend. His reserve had been always excessive and habitual. I was aware, however, that his very ancient family had been noted, time out of mind, for a peculiar sensibility of temperament, displaying itself, through long ages, in many works of exalted art, and manifested, of late, in repeated deeds of munificent yet unobtrusive charity, as well as in a passionate devotion to the intricacies, perhaps even more than to the orthodox and easily recognizable beauties, of musical science. I had learned, too, the very remarkable fact, that the stem of the Usher race, all time-honored as it was, had put forth, at no period, any enduring branch; in other words, that the entire family lay in the direct line of descent, and had always, with very trifling and very temporary variation, so lain. It was this deficiency, I considered, while running over in thought the perfect keeping of the character of the premises with the accredited character of the people, and while speculating upon the possible influence which the one, in the long lapse of centuries, might have exercised upon the other—it was this deficiency, perhaps, of collateral issue, and the consequent undeviating transmission, from sire to son, of the patrimony with the name, which had, at length, so identified the two as to merge the original title of the estate in the quaint and equivocal appellation of the 'House of Usher'—an appellation which seemed to include, in the minds of the peasantry who used it, both the family and the family mansion.

I have said that the sole effect of my somewhat childish experiment—that of looking down within the tarn—had been to deepen the first singular impression. I here can be no doubt that the consciousness of the rapid increase of my superstition—for why should I not so term it?—served mainly to accelerate the increase itself. Such, I have long known, is the paradoxical law of all sentiments having terror as a basis. And it might have been for this reason only, that, when I again uplifted my eyes to the house itself, from its image in the pool, there grew in my mind a strange fancy—a fancy so ridiculous, indeed, that I but mention it to show the vivid force of the sensations which oppressed me. I had so worked upon my imagination as really to believe that about the whole mansion and domain there hung an atmosphere peculiar to themselves and their immediate vicinity—an atmosphere which had no affinity with the air of heaven, but which had reeked up from the decayed trees, and the gray wall, and the silent tarn—a pestilent and mystic vapor, dull, sluggish, faintly discernible, and leaden-hued.

Shaking off from my spirit what *must* have been a dream, I scanned more narrowly the real aspect of the building. Its principal feature seemed to be that of an excessive antiquity. The discoloration of ages had been great. Minute fungi overspread the whole exterior, hanging in a fine tangled webwork from the eaves. Yet all this was apart from any extraordinary dilapidation. No position of the masonry had fallen; and there appeared to be a wild inconsistency between its still perfect adaptation of parts, and the crumbling condition of the individual stones. In this there was much that reminded me of the specious totality of old wood-work which has rotted for long years in some neglected vault, with no disturbance from the breath of the external air. Beyond this indication of extensive decay, however, the fabric gave little token of instability. Perhaps the eye of a scrutinizing observer might have discovered a barely perceptible fissure, which, extending from the roof of the building in front, made its way down the wall in a zigzag direction, until it became lost in the sullen waters of the tarn.

Noticing these things, I rode over a short causeway to the house. A servant in waiting took my horse, and I entered the Gothic archway of the hall. A valet, of stealthy step, thence conducted me, in silence, through many dark and intricate passages in my progress to the *studio* of his master. Much that I encountered on the way contributed, I know not how, to heighten the vague sentiments of which I have already spoken. While the objects around me—while the carvings of the ceilings, the sombre tapestries of the walls, the ebon blackness of the floors, and the phantasmagoric armorial trophies which rattled as I strode, were but matters to which, or to such as which, I had been accustomed from my infancy—while I hesitated not to acknowledge how familiar was all this—I still wondered to find how unfamiliar were the fancies which ordinary images were stirring up. On one of the staircases, I met the physician of the family. His countenance, I thought, wore a mingled expression of low cunning and perplexity. He accosted me with trepidation and passed on. The valet now threw open a door and ushered me into the presence of his master.

The room in which I found myself was very large and lofty. The windows were long, narrow, and pointed, and at so vast a distance from the black oaken floor as to be altogether inaccessible from within. Feeble gleams of encrimsoned light made their way through the trellissed panes, and served to render sufficiently distinct the more prominent objects around; the eye, however, struggled in vain to reach the remoter angles of the chamber, or the recesses of the vaulted and fretted ceiling. Dark draperies hung upon the walls. The general furniture was profuse, comfortless, antique, and tattered. Many books and musical instruments lay scattered about, but failed to give any vitality to the scene. I felt that I breathed an atmosphere of sorrow. An air of stern, deep, and irredeemable gloom hung over and pervaded all.

Upon my entrance, Usher arose from a sofa on which he had been lying at full length, and greeted me with a vivacious warmth which had much in it, I at first thought, of an overdone cordiality—of the constrained effort of the *ennuyé* man of the world. A glance, however, at his countenance convinced me of his perfect sincerity. We sat down; and for some moments, while he spoke not, I gazed upon him with a feeling half of pity, half of awe. Surely, man had never before so terribly altered, in so brief a period, as had Roderick Usher! It was with difficulty that I could bring myself to admit the identity of the wan being before me with the companion of my early boyhood. Yet the character of his face had been at all times remarkable. A cadaverousness of complexion; an eye large, liquid, and luminous beyond comparison; lips somewhat thin and very pallid but of a surpassingly beautiful curve; a nose of a delicate Hebrew model, but with a breadth of nostril unusual in similar formations; a finely moulded chin, speaking, in its want of prominence, of a want of moral energy; hair of a more than web-like softness and tenuity;—these features, with an inordinate expansion above the regions of the temple, made up altogether a countenance not easily to be forgotten. And now in the mere exaggeration of the prevailing character of these features, and of the expression they were wont to convey, lay so much of change that I doubted to whom I spoke. The now ghastly pallor of the skin, and the now miraculous lustre of the eye, above all things startled and even awed me. The silken hair, too, had been suffered to grow all unheeded, and as, in its wild gossamer texture, it floated rather than fell about the face, I could not, even with effort, connect its Arabesque expression with any idea of simple humanity.

In the manner of my friend I was at once struck with an incoherence—an inconsistency; and I soon found this to arise from a series of feeble and futile struggles to overcome an habitual trepidancy—an excessive nervous agitation. For something of this nature I had indeed been prepared, no less by his letter, than by reminiscences of certain boyish traits, and by conclusions deduced from his peculiar physical confirmation and temperament.

His action was alternately vivacious and sullen. His voice varied rapidly from a tremulous indecision (when the animal spirits seemed utterly in abeyance) to that species of energetic concision—that abrupt, weighty, unhurried, and hollow-sounding enunciation—that leaden, self-balanced, and perfectly modulated guttural utterance, which may be observed in the lost drunkard, or the irreclaimable eater of opium, during the periods of his most intense excitement.

It was thus that he spoke of the object of my visit, of his earnest desire to see me, and of the solace he expected me to afford him. He entered, at some length, into what he conceived to be the nature of his malady. It was, he said, a constitutional and a family evil, and one for which he despaired to find a remedy—a mere nervous affection, he immediately added, which would undoubtedly soon pass off. It displayed itself in a host of unnatural sensations. Some of these, as he detailed them, interested and bewildered me; although, perhaps, the terms and the general manner of their narration had their weight. He suffered much from a morbid acuteness of the senses; the most insipid food was alone endurable; he could wear only garments of certain texture; the odors of all flowers were oppressive; his eyes were tortured by even a faint light; and there were but peculiar sounds, and these from stringed instruments, which did not inspire him with horror.

To an anomalous species of terror I found him a bounden slave. 'I shall perish,' said he, 'I *must* perish in this deplorable folly. Thus, thus, and not otherwise, shall I be lost. I dread the events of the future, not in themselves, but in their results. I shudder at the thought of any, even the most trivial, incident, which may operate upon this intolerable agitation of soul. I have, indeed, no abhorrence of danger, except in its absolute effect—in terror. In this unnerved, in this pitiable, condition I feel that the period will sooner or later arrive which I must abandon life and reason together, in some struggle with the grim phantasm, FEAR.'

I learned, moreover, at intervals, and through broken and equivocal hints, another singular feature of his mental condition. He was enchained by certain superstitious impressions in regard to the dwelling which he tenanted, and whence, for many years, he had never ventured forth—in regard to an influence whose supposititious force was conveyed in terms too shadowy here to be re-stated—an influence which some peculiarities in the mere form and substance of his family mansion had, by dint of long sufferance, he said, obtained over his spirit—an effect which the *physique* of the gray walls and turrets, and of the dim tarn into which they all looked down, had, at length, brought about upon the *morale* of his existence.

He admitted, however, although with hesitation, that much of the peculiar gloom which thus afflicted him could be traced to a more natural and far more palpable origin—to the severe and long-continued illness—indeed to the evidently approaching dissolution—of a tenderly beloved sister, his sole companion for long years, his last and only relative on earth. 'Her decease,' he said, with a bitterness which I can never forget, 'would leave him (him, the hopeless and the frail) the last of the ancient race of the Ushers.' While he spoke, the lady Madeline (for so was she called) passed through a remote portion of the apartment, and, without having noticed my presence, disappeared. I regarded her with an utter astonishment not unmingled with dread; and yet I found it impossible to account for such feelings. A sensation of stupor oppressed me as my eyes followed her retreating steps. When a door, at length, closed upon her, my glance sought instinctively and eagerly the countenance of the brother; but he had buried his face in his hands, and I could only perceive that a far more than ordinary wanness had overspread the emaciated fingers through which trickled many passionate tears.

The disease of the lady Madeline had long baffled the skill of her physicians. A settled apathy, a gradual wasting away of the person, and frequent although transient affections of a partially cataleptical character were the unusual diagnosis. Hitherto she had steadily borne up against the pressure of her malady, and had not betaken herself finally to bed; but on the closing in of the evening of my arrival at the house, she succumbed (as her brother told me at night with inexpressible agitation) to the prostrating power of the destroyer; and I learned that the glimpse I had obtained of her person would thus probably be the last I should obtain–that the lady, at least while living, would be seen by me no more.

For several days ensuing, her name was unmentioned by either Usher or myself; and during this period I was busied in earnest endeavors to alleviate the melancholy of my friend. We painted and read together, or I listened, as if in a dream, to the wild improvisations of his speaking guitar. And thus, as a closer and still closer intimacy admitted me more unreservedly into the recesses of his spirit, the more bitterly did I perceive the futility of all attempt at cheering a mind from which darkness, as if an inherent positive quality, poured forth all objects of the moral and physical universe in one unceasing radiation of gloom.

I shall ever bear about me a memory of the many solemn hours I thus spent alone with the master of the House of Usher. Yet I should fail in any attempt to convey an idea of the exact character of the studies, or of the occupations, in which he involved me, or led me the way. An excited and highly distempered ideality threw a sulphureous lustre over all. His long improvised dirges will ring forever in my ears. Among other things, I hold painfully in mind a certain singular perversion and amplification of the wild air of the last waltz of Von Weber. From the paintings over which his elaborate fancy brooded, and which grew, touch by touch, into vaguenesses at which I shuddered the more thrillingly, because I shuddered knowing not why–from these paintings (vivid as their images now are before me) I would in vain endeavor to educe more than a small portion which should lie within the compass of merely written words. By the utter simplicity, by the nakedness of his designs, he arrested and overawed attention. If ever mortal painted an idea, that mortal was Roderick Usher. For me at least, in the circumstances then surrounding me, there arose out of the pure abstractions which the hypochondriac contrived to throw upon his canvas, an intensity of intolerable awe, no shadow of which felt I ever yet in the contemplation of the certainly glowing yet too concrete reveries of Fuseli.

One of the phantasmagoric conceptions of my friend, partaking not so rigidly of the spirit of abstraction, may be shadowed forth, although feebly, in words. A small picture presented the interior of an immensely long and rectangular vault or tunnel, with low walls, smooth, white, and without interruption or device. Certain accessory points of the design served well to convey the idea that this excavation lay at an exceeding depth below the surface of the earth. No outlet was observed in any portion of its vast extent, and no torch or other artificial source of light was discernible; yet a flood of intense rays rolled throughout, and bathed the whole in a ghastly and inappropriate splendor.

I have just spoken of that morbid condition of the auditory nerve which rendered all music intolerable to the sufferer, with the exception of certain effects of stringed instruments. It was, perhaps, the narrow limits to which he thus confined himself upon the guitar which gave birth, in great measure, to the fantastic character of his performances. But the fervid *facility* of his *impromptus* could not be so accounted for. They must have been, and were, in the notes, as well as in the words of his wild fantasias (for he not unfrequently accompanied himself with rhymed verbal improvisations), the result of that intense mental collectedness and concentration to which I have previously alluded as observable only in particular moments of the highest artificial excitement. The words of one of these rhapsodies I have easily remembered. I was, perhaps, the more forcibly impressed with it as he gave it, because, in the under or mystic current of its meaning, I fancied that I perceived, and for the first time, a full consciousness on the part of Usher of the tottering of his lofty reason upon her throne. The verses, which were entitled 'The Haunted Palace,' ran very nearly, if not accurately, thus:—

I

In the greenest of our valleys,
By good angels tenanted,
Once a fair and stately palace—
Radiant palace—reared its head.
In the monarch Thought's dominion!
It stood there!
Never seraph spread a pinion
Over fabric half so fair.

II

Banners yellow, glorious, golden,
On its roof did float and flow
(This—all this—was in the olden
Time long ago);
And every gentle air that dallied,
In that sweet day,
Along the ramparts plumed and pallid,
A winged odor went away.

III

Wanderers in that happy valley
Through two luminous windows saw
Spirits moving musically
to a lute's well-tuned law;
Round about a throne, where sitting
(Porphyrogene!)
In state his glory well befitting,
The ruler of the realm was seen.

IV

And all with pearl and ruby glowing
Was the fair palace door,
Through which came flowing, flowing, flowing
And sparkling evermore,
A troop of Echoes whose sweet duty
Was but to sing,
In voices of surpassing beauty,
The wit and wisdom of their king.

V

But evil things, in robes of sorrow,
Assailed the monarch's high estate;
(Ah, let us mourn, for never morrow
Shall dawn upon him, desolate!)
And, round about his home, the glory
That blushed and bloomed
Is but a dim-remembered story
Of the old time entombed.

VI

And travellers now within that valley,
Through the red-litten windows see
Vast forms that move fantastically
To a discordant melody;
While, like a rapid ghastly river,
Through the pale door;
A hideous throng rush out forever,
And laugh—but smile no more.

I well remember that suggestions arising from this ballad led us into a train of thought wherein there became manifest an opinion of Usher's which

I mention not so much on account of its novelty (for other men* have thought thus), as on account of the pertinacity with which he maintained it. This opinion in its general form, was that of the sentience of all vegetable things. But, in his disordered fancy, the idea had assumed a more daring character, and trespassed, under certain conditions, upon the kingdom of inorganization I lack words to express the full extent, or the earnest *abandon* of his persuasion. The belief, however, was connected (as I have previously hinted) with the gray stones of the home of his forefathers. The conditions of the sentence had been here, he imagined, fulfilled in the method of collocation of these stones–in the order of their arrangement, as well as in that of the many *fungi* which overspread them, and of the decayed trees which stood around—above all, in the long undisturbed endurance of this arrangement, and in its reduplication in the still waters of the tarn. Its evidence–the evidence of the sentience–was to be seen, he said (and I here started as he spoke), in the gradual yet certain condensation of an atmosphere of their own about the waters and the walls. The result was discoverable, he added, in that silent yet importunate and terrible influence which for centuries had moulded the destinies of his family, and which made *him* what I now saw him–what he was. Such opinions need no comment, and I will make none.

Our books–the books which, for years, had formed no small portion of the mental existence of the invalid–were, as might be supposed, in strict keeping with this character of phantasm. We pored together over such works as the 'Ververt et Chartreuse' of Gresset; the 'Belphegor' of Machiavelli; the 'Heaven and Hell' of Swedenborg; the 'Subterranean Voyage of Nicholas Klimm' of Holberg; the 'Chiromancy' of Robert Flud, of Jean D'Indaginé, and of Dela Chambre; the 'Journey into the Blue Distance of Tieck'; and the 'City of the Sun of Campanella.' One favorite volume was a small octavo edition of the 'Directorium Inquisitorium,' by the Dominican Eymeric de Gironne; and there were passages in Pomponius Mela, about the old African Satyrs and Egipans, over which Usher would sit dreaming for hours. His chief delight, however, was found in the perusal of an exceedingly rare and curious book in quarto Gothic–the manual of a forgotten church–the *Vigilioe Mortuorum secundum Chorum Ecclesioe Maguntinoe.*

I could not help thinking of the wild ritual of this work, and of its probable influence upon the hypochondriac, when, one evening, having informed me abruptly that the lady Madeline was no more, he stated his intention of preserving her corpse for a fortnight (previously to its final interment), in one of the numerous vaults within the main walls of the building. The worldly reason, however, assigned for this singular proceeding, was one

*Watson, Dr. Percival, Spallanzani, and especially the Bishop of Landaff.–See 'Chemical Essays,' vol. v.

which I did not feel at liberty to dispute. The brother had been led to his resolution (so he told me) by consideration of the unusual character of the malady of the deceased, of certain obtrusive and eager inquiries on the part of her medical men, and of the remote and exposed situation of the burial-ground of the family. I will not deny that when I called to mind the sinister countenance of the person whom I met upon the staircase, on the day of my arrival at the house, I had no desire to oppose what I regarded as at best but a harmless, and by no means an unnatural, precaution.

At the request of Usher, I personally aided him in the arrangements for the temporary entombment. The body having been encoffined, we two alone bore it to its rest. The vault in which we placed it (and which had been so long unopened that our torches, half smothered in its oppressive atmosphere, gave us little opportunity for investigation) was small, damp, and entirely without means of admission for light: lying, at great depth, immediately beneath that portion of the building in which was my own sleeping apartment. It had been used, apparently, in remote feudal times, for the worst purposes of a donjon-keep, and, in later days, as a place of deposit for powder, or some other highly combustible substance, as a portion of its floor, and the whole interior of a long archway through which we reached it, were carefully sheathed with copper. The door, of massive iron, had been, also, similarly protected. Its immense weight caused an unusually sharp, grating sound, as it moved upon its hinges.

Having deposited our mournful burden upon tressels within this region of horror, we partially turned aside the yet unscrewed lid of the coffin, and looked upon the face of the tenant. A striking similitude between the brother and sister now first arrested my attention; and Usher, divining, perhaps, my thoughts, murmured out some few words from which I learned that the deceased and himself had been twins, and that sympathies of a scarcely intelligible nature had always existed between them. Our glances, however, rested not long upon the dead—for we could not regard her unawed. The disease which had thus entombed the lady in the maturity of youth, had left, as usual in all maladies of a strictly cataleptical character, the mockery of a faint blush upon the bosom and the face, and that suspiciously lingering smile upon the lip which is so terrible in death. We replaced and screwed down the lid, and, having secured the door of iron, made our way, with toil, into the scarcely less gloomy apartments of the upper portion of the house.

And now, some days of bitter grief having elapsed, an observable change came over the features of the mental disorder of my friend. His ordinary manner had vanished. His ordinary occupations were neglected or forgotten. He roamed from chamber to chamber with hurried, unequal, and objectless step. The pallor of his countenance had assumed, if possible, a more ghastly hue—but the luminousness of his eye had utterly gone out. The once occasional huskiness of his tone was heard no more; and a tremulous quaver, as if of extreme terror, habitually characterized his utterance. There were times, indeed, when I thought his unceasingly agitated mind was laboring with some oppressive secret, to divulge which he struggled for the necessary courage. At times, again, I was obliged to resolve all into the mere inexplicable vagaries of madness, for I beheld him gazing upon vacancy for long hours, in an attitude of the profoundest attention, as if listening to some imaginary sound. It was no wonder that his condition terrified—that it infected me. I felt creeping upon me, by slow yet certain degrees, the wild influences of his own fantastic yet impressive superstitions.

It was, especially, upon retiring to bed late in the night of the seventh or eighth day after the placing of the lady Madeline within the donjon, that I experienced the full power of such feelings. Sleep came not near my couch—while the hours waned and waned away. I struggled to reason off the nervousness which had dominion over me. I endeavored to believe that much, if not all of what I felt, was due to the bewildering influence of the gloomy furniture of the room—of the dark and tattered draperies, which, tortured into motion by the breath of a rising tempest, swayed fitfully to and fro upon the walls, and rustled uneasily about the decorations of the bed. But my efforts were fruitless. An irrepressible tremor gradually pervaded my frame; and, at length, there sat upon my very heart an incubus of utterly causeless alarm. Shaking this off with a gasp and a struggle, I uplifted myself upon the pillows, and, peering earnestly within the intense darkness of the chamber, hearkened—I know not why, except that an instinctive spirit prompted me—to certain low and indefinite sounds which came, through the pauses of the storm, at long intervals, I knew not whence. Overpowered by an intense sentiment of horror, unaccountable yet unendurable, I threw on my clothes with haste (for I felt that I should sleep no more during the night), and endeavored to arouse myself from the pitiable condition into which I had fallen, by pacing rapidly to and fro through the apartment.

I had taken but few turns in this manner, when a light step on an adjoining staircase arrested my attention. I presently recognized it as that of Usher. In an instant afterward he rapped, with a gentle touch, at my door, and entered, bearing a lamp. His countenance was, as usual, cadaverously wan—but, moreover, there was a species of mad hilarity in his eyes—an evidently restrained *hysteria* in his whole demeanor. His air appalled me—but any thing was preferable to the solitude which I had so long endured, and I even welcomed his presence as a relief.

'And you have not seen it?' he said abruptly, after having stared about him for some moments in silence—'you have not then seen it?—but, stay! you shall.' Thus speaking, and having carefully shaded his lamp, he hurried to one of the casements, and threw it freely open to the storm.

The impetuous fury of the entering gust nearly lifted us from our feet. It was, indeed, a tempestuous yet sternly beautiful night, and one wildly singular in its terror and its beauty. A whirlwind had apparently collected its force in our vicinity; for there were frequent and violent alterations in the direction of the wind; and the exceeding density of the clouds (which hung so low as to press upon the turrets of the house) did not prevent our perceiving the life-like velocity with which they flew careering from all points against each other, without passing away into the distance. I say that even their exceeding density did not prevent our perceiving this–yet we had no glimpse of the moon or stars, nor was there any flashing forth of the lightning. But the under surfaces of the huge masses of agitated vapor, as well as all terrestrial objects immediately around us, were glowing in the unnatural light of a faintly luminous and distinctly visible gaseous exhalation which hung about and enshrouded the mansion.

'You must not–you shall not behold this!' said I, shuddering, to Usher, as I led him, with a gentle violence, from the window to a seat. These appearances, which bewilder you, are merely electrical phenomena not uncommon–or it may be that they have their ghastly origin in the rank miasma of the tarn. Let us close this casement;–the air is chilling and dangerous to your frame. Here is one of your favorite romances. I will read, and you shall listen:–and so we will pass away this terrible night together.

The antique volume which I had taken up was the 'Mad Trist' of Sir Launcelot Canning; but I had called it a favorite of Usher's more in sad jest than in earnest; for, in truth, there is little in its uncouth and unimaginative prolixity which could have had interest for the lofty and spiritual ideality of my friend. It was, however, the only book immediately at hand; and I indulged a vague hope that the excitement which now agitated the hypochondriac, might find relief (for the history of mental disorder is full of similar anomalies) even in the extremeness of the folly which I should read. Could I have judged, indeed, by the wild overstrained air of vivacity with which he hearkened, or apparently hearkened, to the words of the tale, I might well have congratulated myself upon the success of my design.

I had arrived at that well-known portion of the story where Ethelred, the hero of the Trist, having sought in vain for peaceable admission into the dwelling of the hermit, proceeds to make good an entrance by force. Here, it will be remembered, the words of the narrative run thus:

'And Ethelred, who was by nature of a doughty heart, and who was now mighty withal, on account of the powerfulness of the wine which he had drunken, waited no longer to hold parley with the hermit, who, in sooth, was of an obstinate and maliceful turn, but, feeling the rain upon his shoulders, and fearing the rising of the tempest, uplifted his mace outright, and, with blows, made quickly room in the plankings of the door for his gauntleted hand; and now pulling therewith sturdily, he so cracked, and ripped, and tore all asunder, that the noise of the dry and hollow-sounding wood alarumed and reverberated throughout the forest.'

At the termination of this sentence I started and, for a moment, paused; for it appeared to me (although I at once concluded that my excited fancy had deceived me)—it appeared to me that, from some very remote portion of the mansion, there came, indistinctly to my ears, what might have been, in its exact similarity of character, the echo (but a stifled and dull one certainly) of the very cracking and ripping sound which Sir Launcelot had so particularly described. It was, beyond doubt, the coincidence alone which had arrested my attention; for, amid the rattling of the sashes of the casements, and the ordinary commingled noises of the still increasing storm, the sound, in itself, had nothing, surely, which should have interested or disturbed me. I continued the story:

'But the good champion Ethelred, now entering within the door, was sore enraged and amazed to perceive no signal of the maliceful hermit; but, in the stead thereof, a dragon of a scaly and prodigious demeanor, and of a fiery tongue, which sate in guard before a palace of gold, with a floor of silver; and upon the wall there hung a shield of shining brass with this legend enwritten—

Who entereth herein, a conqueror hath bin;
Who slayeth the dragon, the shield he shall win.

And Ethelred uplifted his mace, and struck upon the head of the dragon, which fell before him, and gave up his pesty breath, with a shriek so horrid and harsh, and withal so piercing, that Ethelred had fain to close his ears with his hands against the dreadful noise of it, the like whereof was never before heard.'

Here again I paused abruptly, and now with a feeling of wild amazement—for there could be no doubt whatever that, in this instance, I did actually hear (although from what direction it proceeded I found it impossible to say) a low and apparently distant, but harsh, protracted, and most unusual screaming or grating sound—the exact counterpart of what my fancy had already conjured up for the dragon's unnatural shriek as described by the romancer.

Oppressed, as I certainly was, upon the occurrence of this second and most extraordinary coincidence, by a thousand conflicting sensations, in which wonder and extreme terror were predominant, I still retained sufficient presence of mind to avoid exciting, by any observation, the sensitive nervousness of my companion. I was by no means certain that he had noticed the sounds in question; although, assuredly, a strange alteration had, during the last few minutes, taken place in his demeanor. From a position fronting my own, he had gradually brought round his chair, so as to sit with his face to the door of the chamber; and thus I could but partially perceive his features, although I saw that his lips trembled as if he were murmuring inaudibly. His head had dropped upon his breast–yet I knew that he was not asleep, from the wide and rigid opening of the eye as I caught a glance of it in profile. The motion of his body, too, was at variance with this idea–for he rocked from side to side with a gentle yet constant and uniform sway. Having rapidly taken notice of all this, I resumed the narrative of Sir Launcelot, which thus proceeded:

'And now, the champion, having escaped from the terrible fury of the dragon, bethinking himself of the brazen shield, and of the breaking up of the enchantment which was upon it, removed the carcass from out of the way before him, and approached valorously over the silver pavement of the castle to where the shield was upon the wall; which in sooth tarried not for his full coming, but fell down at his feet upon the silver floor, with a mighty great and terrible ringing sound.'

No sooner had these syllables passed my lips, than–as if a shield of brass had indeed, at the moment, fallen heavily upon a floor of silver–I became aware of a distinct, hollow, metallic, and clangorous, yet apparently muffled, reverberation. Completely unnerved, I leaped to my feet; but the measured rocking movement of Usher was undisturbed. I rushed to the chair in which he sat. His eyes were bent fixedly before him, and throughout his whole countenance there reigned a stony rigidity. But, as I placed my hand upon his shoulder, there came a strong shudder over his whole person; a sickly smile quivered about his lips; and I saw that he spoke in a low, hurried, and gibbering murmur, as if unconscious of my presence. Bending closely over him, I at length drank in the hideous import of his words.

'Now hear it?–yes, I hear it, and *have* heard it. Long–long–long–many minutes, many hours, many days, have I heard it–yet I dared not–oh, pity me, miserable wretch that I am!–I dared not–I *dared* not speak! *We have put her living in the tomb!* Said I not that my senses were acute? I *now* tell you that I heard her first feeble movements in the hollow coffin. I heard them–many, many days ago–yet I dared not–*I dared not speak!* And now–to-night–Ethelred–ha! ha!–the breaking of the hermit's door, and the death-cry of the dragon, and the clangor of the shield–say, rather, the rending of her coffin, and the grating of the iron hinges of her prison, and her struggles within the coppered archway of the vault! Oh! whither shall I fly? Will she not be here anon? Is she not hurrying to upbraid me for my haste? Have I not heard her footstep on the stair? Do I not distinguish that heavy and horrible beating of her heart? Madman!'–here he sprang furiously to his feet, and shrieked out his syllables, as if in the effort he were giving up his soul–*'Madman! I tell you that she now stands without the door!'*

As if in the superhuman energy of his utterance there had been found the potency of a spell, the huge antique panels to which the speaker pointed threw slowly back, upon the instant, their ponderous and ebony jaws. It was the work of the rushing gust–but then without those doors there *did* stand the lofty and enshrouded figure of the lady Madeline of Usher. There was blood upon her white robes, and the evidence of some bitter struggle upon every portion of her emaciated frame. For a moment she remained trembling and reeling to and fro upon the threshold—then, with a low moaning cry, fell heavily inward upon the person of her brother, and in her violent and now final death-agonies, bore him to the floor a corpse, and a victim to the terrors he had anticipated.

From that chamber, and from that mansion, I fled aghast. The storm was still abroad in all its wrath as I found myself crossing the old causeway. Suddenly there shot along the path a wild light, and I turned to see whence a gleam so unusual could have issued; for the vast house and its shadows were alone behind me. The radiance was that of the full, setting, and blood-red moon, which now shone vividly through that once barely discernible fissure, of which I have before spoken as extending from the roof of the building, in a zigzag direction, to the base. While I gazed, this entire orb of the satellite burst at once upon my sight—my brain reeled as I saw the mighty walls rushing asunder—there was a long tumultuous shouting sound like the voice of a thousand waters—and the deep and dank tarn at my feet closed sullenly and silently over the fragments of the '*House of Usher.*'

The Murders in the Rue Morgue

(First published in *Graham's Magazine*,
April, 1841; first book publication in 1845.)

What song the Syrens sang, or what name Achilles assumed when he hid himself among women, although puzzling questions, are not beyond all conjecture.

SIR THOMAS BROWNE, *Urn-Burial*

THE MENTAL FEATURES discoursed of as the analytical, are, in themselves, but little susceptible of analysis. We appreciate them only in their effects. We know of them, among other things, that they are always to their possessor, when inordinately possessed, a source of the liveliest enjoyment. As the strong man exults in his physical ability, delighting in such exercises as call his muscles into action, so glories the analyst in that moral activity which *disentangles*. He derives pleasure from even the most trivial occupations bringing his talents into play. He is fond of enigmas, of conundrums, of hieroglyphics; exhibiting in his solutions of each a degree of acumen which appears to the ordinary apprehension preternatural. His results, brought about by the very soul and essence of method, have, in truth, the whole air of intuition. The faculty of re-solution is possibly much invigorated by mathematical study, and especially by that highest branch of it which, unjustly, and merely on account of its retrograde operations, has been called, as if *par excellence*, analysis. Yet to calculate is not in itself to analyze. A chess-player, for example, does the one without effort at the other. It follows that the game of chess, in its effects upon mental character, is greatly misunderstood. I am not now writing a treatise, but simply prefacing a somewhat peculiar narrative by observations very much at random; I will, therefore, take occasion to assert that the higher powers of the reflective intellect are more decidedly and more usefully tasked by the unostentatious game of draughts than by all the elaborate frivolity of chess. In this latter, where the pieces have different and *bizarre* motions, with various and variable values, what is only complex is mistaken (a not unusual error) for what is profound. The *attention* is here called powerfully into play. If it flag for an instant, an oversight is committed, resulting in injury or defeat. The possible moves being not only manifold but involute, the chances of such oversights are multiplied; and in nine cases out of ten it is the more concentrative rather than the more acute player who conquers. In draughts, on the contrary, where the moves are unique and have but little variation, the probabilities of inadvertence are diminished, and the mere attention being left comparatively unemployed, what advantages are obtained by either party are obtained by superior *acumen*. To be less abstract—Let us suppose a game of draughts where the pieces are reduced to four kings, and where, of course, no oversight is to be expected. It is obvious that here the victory can be decided (the players being at all equal) only by some *recherché* movement, the result of some strong exertion of the intellect. Deprived of ordinary resources, the analyst throws himself into the spirit of his opponent, identifies himself therewith, and not unfrequently sees thus, at a glance, the sole methods (sometimes indeed absurdly simple ones) by which he may seduce into error or hurry into miscalculation.

Whist has long been noted for its influence upon what is termed the calculating power; and men of the highest order of intellect have been known to take an apparently unaccountable delight in it, while eschewing chess as frivolous. Beyond doubt there is nothing of a similar nature so greatly tasking the faculty of analysis. The best chess-player in Christendom *may* be little more than the best player of chess; but proficiency in whist implies capacity for success in all these more important undertakings where mind struggles with mind. When I say proficiency, I mean that perfection in the game which includes a comprehension of *all* the sources whence legitimate advantage may be derived. These are not only manifold but multiform, and lie frequently among recesses of thought altogether inaccessible to the ordinary understanding. To observe attentively is to remember distinctly; and, so far, the concentrative chess-player will do very well at whist; while the rules of Hoyle (themselves based upon the mere mechanism of the game) are sufficiently and generally comprehensible. Thus to have a retentive memory, and to proceed by "the book," are points commonly regarded as the sum total of good playing. But it is in matters beyond the limits of mere rule that the skill of the analyst is evinced. He makes, in silence, a host of observations and inferences. So, perhaps, do his companions; and the difference in the extent of the information obtained, lies not so much in the validity of the inference as in the quality of the observation. The necessary knowledge is that of *what* to observe. Our player confines himself not at all; nor, because the game is the object, does he reject deductions from things external to the game. He examines the countenance of his partner, comparing it carefully with that of each of his opponents. He considers the mode of assorting the cards in each hand; often counting trump by trump, and honor by honor, through the glances bestowed by their holders upon each. He notes every variation of face as the play progresses, gathering a fund of thought from the differences in the expression of certainty, of surprise, of triumph, or chagrin. From the manner of gathering up a trick he judges whether the person taking it can make another in the suit. He recognizes what is played through feint, by the air with which it is thrown upon the table. A casual or inadvertent word; the accidental dropping or turning of a card, with the accompanying anxiety or carelessness in regard to its concealment; the counting of the tricks, with the order of their arrangement; embarrassment, hesitation, eagerness or trepidation—all afford, to his apparently intuitive perception, indications of the true state of affairs. The first two or three rounds having been played, he is in full possession of the contents of each hand, and thenceforward puts down his cards with as absolute a precision of purpose as if the rest of the party had turned outward the faces of their own.

The analytical power should not be confounded with simple ingenuity; for while the analyst is necessarily ingenious, the ingenious man is often remarkably incapable of analysis. The consecutive or combining power, by which ingenuity is usually manifested, and to which the phrenologists (I believe erroneously) have assigned a separate organ, supposing it a primitive faculty, has been so frequently seen in those whose intellect bordered otherwise upon idiocy, as to have attracted general observation among writers on morals. Between ingenuity and the analytic ability there exists a difference far greater, indeed, than that between the fancy and the imagination, but of a character very strictly analogous. It will be found, in fact, that the ingenious are always fanciful, and the *truly* imaginative never otherwise than analytic.

The narrative which follows will appear to the reader somewhat in the light of a commentary upon the propositions just advanced.

Residing in Paris during the spring and part of the summer of 18–, I there became acquainted with a Monsieur C. Auguste Dupin. This young gentleman was of an excellent—indeed of an illustrious family, but, by a variety of untoward events, had been reduced to such poverty that the energy of his character succumbed beneath it, and he ceased to bestir himself in the world, or to care for the retrieval of his fortunes. By courtesy of his creditors, there still remained in his possession a small remnant of his patrimony; and, upon the income arising from this, he managed, by means of a rigorous economy, to procure the necessaries of life, without troubling himself about its superfluities. Books, indeed, were his sole luxuries, and in Paris these are easily obtained.

Our first meeting was at an obscure library in the Rue Montmartre, where the accident of our both being in search of the same very rare and very remarkable volume, brought us into closer communion. We saw each other again and again. I was deeply interested in the little family history which he detailed to me with all that candor which a Frenchman indulges whenever mere self is the theme. I was astonished, too, at the vast extent of his reading; and, above all, I felt my soul enkindled within me by the wild fervor, and the vivid freshness of his imagination. Seeking in Paris the objects I then sought, I felt that the society of such a man would be to me a treasure beyond price; and this feeling I frankly confided to him. It was at length arranged that we should live together during my stay in the city; and as my worldly circumstances were somewhat less embarrassed than his own, I was permitted to be at the expense of renting, and furnishing in a style which suited the rather fantastic gloom of our common temper, a time-eaten and grotesque mansion, long deserted through superstitions into which we did not inquire, and tottering to its fall in a retired and desolate portion of the Faubourg St. Germain.

Had the routine of our life at this place been known to the world, we should have been regarded as madmen—although, perhaps, as madmen of a harmless nature. Our seclusion was perfect. We admitted no visitors. Indeed the locality of our retirement had been carefully kept a secret from my own former associates; and it had been many years since Dupin had ceased to know or be known in Paris. We existed within ourselves alone.

It was a freak of fancy in my friend (for what else shall I call it?) to be enamored of the Night for her own sake; and into this *bizarrerie*, as into all his others, I quietly fell; giving myself up to his wild whims with a perfect *abandon*. The sable divinity would not herself dwell with us always; but we could counterfeit her presence. At the first dawn of the morning we closed all the massy shutters of our old building; lighted a couple of tapers which, strongly perfumed, threw out only the ghastliest and feeblest of rays. By the aid of these we then busied our souls in dreams—reading, writing, or conversing, until warned by the clock of the advent of the true Darkness. Then we sallied forth into the streets, arm and arm, continuing the topics of the day, or roaming far and wide until a late hour, seeking, amid the wild lights and shadows of the populous city, that infinity of mental excitement which quiet observation can afford.

At such times I could not help remarking and admiring (although from his rich ideality I had been prepared to expect it) a peculiar analytic ability in Dupin. He seemed, too, to take an eager delight in this exercise—if not exactly in its display—and did not hesitate to confess the pleasure thus derived. He boasted to me, with a low chuckling laugh, that most men, in respect to himself, wore windows in their bosoms, and was wont to follow up such assertions by direct and very startling proofs of his intimate knowledge of my own. His manner at these moments was frigid and abstract; his eyes were vacant in expression; while his voice, usually a rich tenor, rose into a treble which would have sounded petulantly but for the deliberateness and entire distinctness of the enunciation. Observing him in these moods, I often dwelt meditatively upon the old philosophy of the Bi-Part Soul, and amused myself with the fancy of a double Dupin—the creative and the resolvent.

Let it not be supposed, from what I have just said, that I am detailing any mystery, or penning any romance. What I have described in the Frenchman was merely the result of an excited, or perhaps of a diseased, intelligence. But of the character of his remarks at the periods in question an example will best convey the idea.

We were strolling one night down a long dirty street, in the vicinity of the Palais Royal. Being both, apparently, occupied with thought, neither of us had spoken a syllable for fifteen minutes at least. All at once Dupin broke forth with these words:

"He is a very little fellow, that's true, and would do better for the *Théâtre des Variétiés.*"

"There can be no doubt of that," I replied unwittingly, and not at first observing (so much had I been absorbed in reflection) the extraordinary manner in which the speaker had chimed in with my meditations. In an instant afterwards I recollected myself, and my astonishment was profound.

"Dupin," said I, gravely, "this is beyond my comprehension. I do not hesitate to say that I am amazed, and can scarcely credit my senses. How was it possible you should know I was thinking of——?" Here I paused, to ascertain beyond a doubt whether he really knew of whom I thought.

——"of Chantilly," said he, "why do you pause? You were remarking to yourself that his diminutive figure unfitted him for tragedy."

This was precisely what had formed the subject of my reflections. Chantilly was a *quondam* cobbler of the Rue St. Denis, who, becoming stage-mad, had attempted the *rôle* of Xerxes, in Crébillon's tragedy so called, and been notoriously Pasquinaded for his pains.

"Tell me, for Heaven's sake," I exclaimed, "the method–if method there is–by which you have been enabled to fathom my soul in this matter." In fact I was even more startled than I would have been willing to express.

"It was the fruiterer," replied my friend, "who brought you to the conclusion that the mender of soles was not of sufficient height for Xerxes *et id genus omne.*"

"The fruiterer!–you astonish me–I know no fruiterer whomsoever."

"The man who ran up against you as we entered the street–it may have been fifteen minutes ago."

I now remembered that, in fact, a fruiterer, carrying upon his head a large basket of apples, had nearly thrown me down, by accident, as we passed from the Rue C––into the thoroughfare where we stood; but what this had to do with Chantilly I could not possibly understand.

There was not a particle of *charlatanerie* about Dupin. "I will explain," he said, "and that you may comprehend all clearly, we will first retrace the course of your meditations, from the moment in which I spoke to you until that of the *rencontre* with the fruiterer in question. The larger links of the chain run thus–Chantilly, Orion, Dr. Nichols, Epicurus, Stereotomy, the street stones, the fruiterer."

There are few persons who have not, at some period of their lives, amused themselves in retracing the steps by which particular conclusions of their own minds have been attained. The occupation is often full of interest; and he who attempts it for the first time is astonished by the apparently illimitable distance and incoherence between the starting point and the goal. What, then, must have been my amazement when I heard the Frenchman speak what he had just spoken, and when I could not help acknowledging that he had spoken the truth. He continued:

"We had been talking of horses, if I remember right, just before leaving the Rue C——. This was the last subject we discussed. As we crossed into this street, a fruiterer, with a large basket upon his head, brushing quickly past us, thrust you upon a pile of paving-stones collected at a spot where the causeway is undergoing repair. You stepped upon one of the loose fragments, slipped, slightly strained your ankle, appeared vexed or sulky, muttered a few words, turned to look at the pile, and then proceeded in silence. I was not particularly attentive to what you did; but observation has become with me, of late, a species of necessity.

"You kept your eyes upon the ground—glancing, with a petulant expression, at the holes and ruts in the pavement (so that I saw you were still thinking of the stones), until we reached the little alley called Lamartine, which has been paved, by way of experiment, with the overlapping and riveted blocks. Here your countenance brightened up, and, perceiving your lips move, I could not doubt that you murmured the word 'stereotomy,' a term very affectedly applied to this species of pavement. I knew that you could not say to yourself 'stereotomy' without being brought to think of atomies, and thus of the theories of Epicurus; and since, when we discussed this subject not very long ago, I mentioned to you how singularly, yet with how little notice, the vague guesses of that noble Greek had met with confirmation in the late nebular cosmogony, I felt that you could not avoid casting your eyes upwards to the great *nebula* in Orion, and I certainly expected that you would do so. You did look up; and I was now assured that I had correctly followed your steps. But in that bitter *tirade* upon Chantilly, which appeared in yesterday's '*Musée*,' the satirist, making some disgraceful allusions to the cobbler's change of name upon assuming the buskin, quoted a Latin line about which we have often conversed. I mean the line

Perdidit antiquum litera prima sonum

I had told you that this was in reference to Orion, formerly written Urion; and, from certain pungencies connected with this explanation, I was aware that you could not have forgotten it. It was clear, therefore, that you would not fail to combine the two ideas of Orion and Chantilly. That you did combine them I saw by the character of the smile which passed over your lips. You thought of the poor cobbler's immolation. So far, you had been stooping in your gait; but now I saw you draw yourself up to your full height. I was then sure that you reflected upon the diminutive figure of Chantilly. At this point I interrupted your meditations to remark that as, in fact, he *was* a very little fellow—that Chantilly—he would do better at the *Théâtre des Variétés*."

Not long after this, we were looking over an evening edition of the "Gazette des Tribunaux," when the following paragraphs arrested our attention.

EXTRAORDINARY MURDERS.—This morning, about three o'clock, the inhabitants of the Quartier St. Roch were aroused from sleep by a succession of terrific shrieks, issuing, apparently, from the fourth story of a house in the Rue Morgue, known to be in the sole occupancy of one Madame L'Espanaye, and her daughter, Mademoiselle Camille L'Espanaye. After some delay, occasioned by a fruitless attempt to procure admission in the usual manner, the gateway was broken in with a crowbar, and eight or ten of the neighbors entered, accompanied by two *gendarmes*. By this time the cries had ceased; but, as the party rushed up the first flight of stairs, two or more rough voices, in angry contention, were distinguished, and seemed to proceed from the upper part of the house. As the second landing was reached, these sounds, also, had ceased, and everything remained perfectly quiet. The party spread themselves, and hurried from room to room. Upon arriving at a large back chamber in the fourth story (the door of which, being found locked, with the key inside, was forced open), a spectacle presented itself which struck every one present not less with horror than with astonishment.

"The apartment was in the wildest disorder—the furniture broken and thrown about in all directions. There was only one bedstead; and from this the bed had been removed, and thrown into the middle of the floor. On a chair lay a razor, besmeared with blood. On the hearth were two or three long and thick tresses of gray human hair, also dabbled in blood, and seeming to have been pulled out by the roots. Upon the floor were found four Napoleons, an earring of topaz, three large silver spoons, three smaller of *métal d' Alger*, and two bags, containing nearly four thousand francs in gold. The drawers of a *bureau*, which stood in one corner, were open, and had been, apparently, rifled, although many articles still remained in them. A small iron safe was discovered under the *bed* (not under the bedstead). It was open, with the key still in the door. It had no contents beyond a few old letters, and other papers of little consequence.

"Of Madame L'Espanaye no traces were here seen; but an unusual quantity of soot being observed in the fireplace, a search was made in the chimney, and (horrible to relate!) the corpse of the daughter, head downwards, was dragged therefrom; it having been thus forced up the narrow aperture for a considerable distance. The body was quite warm. Upon examining it, many excoriations were perceived, no doubt occasioned by the violence with which it had been thrust up and disengaged. Upon the face were many severe scratches, and, upon the throat, dark bruises, and deep indentations of finger-nails, as if the deceased had been throttled to death.

"After a thorough investigation of every portion of the house, without farther discovery, the party made its way into a small paved yard in the rear of the building, where lay the corpse of the old lady, with her throat so entirely cut that, upon an attempt to raise her, the head fell off. The body, as well as the head, was fearfully mutilated—the former so much so as scarcely to retain any semblance of humanity.

"To this horrible mystery there is not as yet, we believe, the slightest clue."

The next day's paper had these additional particulars.

"*The Tragedy in the Rue Morgue.* Many individuals have been examined in relation to this most extraordinary and frightful affair" (the word '*affaire*' has not yet, in France, that levity of import which it conveys with us), "but nothing whatever has transpired to throw light upon it. We give below all the material testimony elicited.

"*Pauline Dubourg,* laundress, deposes that she has known both the deceased for three years, having washed for them during that period. The old lady and her daughter seemed on good terms—very affectionate towards each other. They were excellent pay. Could not speak in regard to their mode or means of living. Believed that Madame L. told fortunes for a living. Was reputed to have money put by. Never met any persons in the house when she called for the clothes or took them home. Was sure that they had no servant in employ. There appeared to be no furniture in any part of the building except in the fourth story.

"*Pierre Moreau,* tobacconist, deposes that he has been in the habit of selling small quantities of tobacco and snuff to Madame L'Espanaye for nearly four years. Was born in the neighborhood, and has always resided there. The deceased and her daughter had occupied the house in which the corpses were found, for more than six years. It was formerly occupied by a jeweler, who under-let the upper rooms to various persons. The house was the property of Madame L. She became dissatisfied with the abuse of the premises by her tenant, and moved into them herself, refusing to let any portion. The old lady was childish. Witness had seen the daughter some five or six times during the six years. The two lived an exceedingly retired life—were reputed to have money. Had heard it said among the neighbors that Madame L. told fortunes—did not believe it. Had never seen any person enter the door except the old lady and her daughter, a porter once or twice, and a physician some eight or ten times.

"Many other persons, neighbors, gave evidence to the same effect. No one was spoken of as frequenting the house. It was not known whether there were any living connections of Madame L. and her daughter. The shutters of the front windows were seldom opened. Those in the rear were always closed, with the exception of the large back room, fourth story. The house was a good house—not very old.

"*Isidore Musèt, gendarme*, deposes that he was called to the house about three o'clock in the morning, and found some twenty or thirty persons at the gateway, endeavoring to gain admittance. Forced it open, at length, with a bayonet—not with a crowbar. Had but little difficulty in getting it open, on account of its being a double or folding gate, and bolted neither at bottom nor top. The shrieks were continued until the gate was forced—and then suddenly ceased. They seemed to be screams of some person (or persons) in great agony—were loud and drawn out, not short and quick. Witness led the way upstairs. Upon reaching the first landing, heard two voices in loud and angry contention—the one a gruff voice, the other much shriller—a very strange voice. Could distinguish some words of the former, which was that of a Frenchman. Was positive that it was not a woman's voice. Could distinguish the words '*sacré*' and '*diable*.' The shrill voice was that of a foreigner. Could not be sure whether it was the voice of a man or of a woman. Could not make out what was said, but believed the language to be Spanish. The state of the room and of the bodies was described by this witness as we described them yesterday.

"*Henri Duval*, a neighbor, and by trade a silversmith, deposes that he was one of the party who first entered the house. Corroborates the testimony of Musèt in general. As soon as they forced an entrance, they reclosed the door, to keep out the crowd, which collected very fast, notwithstanding the lateness of the hour. The shrill voice, the witness thinks, was that of an Italian. Was certain it was not French. Could not be sure that it was a man's voice. It might have been a woman's. Was not acquainted with the Italian language. Could not distinguish the words, but was convinced by the intonation that the speaker was an Italian. Knew Madame L. and her daughter. Had conversed with both frequently. Was sure that the shrill voice was not that of either of the deceased.

"—*Odenheimer restaurateur*. This witness volunteered his testimony. Not speaking French, was examined through an interpreter. Is a native of Amsterdam. Was passing the house at the time of the shrieks. They lasted for several minutes—probably ten. They were long and loud—very awful and distressing. Was one of those who entered the building. Corroborated the previous evidence in every respect but one. Was sure that the shrill voice was that of a man—of a Frenchman. Could not distinguish the words uttered. They were loud and quick—unequal—spoken apparently in fear as well as in anger. The voice was harsh—not so much shrill as harsh. Could not call it a shrill voice. The gruff voice said repeatedly '*sacré*,' '*diable*' and once '*mon Dieu*.'

"*Jules Mignaud*, banker, of the firm of Mignaud et Fils, Rue Deloraine. Is the elder Mignaud. Madame L'Espanaye had some property. Had opened an account with his banking house in the spring of the year—— (eight years previously). Made frequent deposits in small sums. Had checked for nothing until the third day before her death, when she took out in person the sum of 4000 francs. This sum was paid in gold, and a clerk sent home with the money.

"*Adolphe Le Bon*, clerk to Mignaud et Fils, deposes that on the day in question, about noon, he accompanied Madame L'Espanaye to her residence with the 4000 francs, put up in two bags. Upon the door being opened, Mademoiselle L. appeared and took from his hands one of the bags, while the old lady relieved him of the other. He then bowed and departed. Did not see any person in the street at the time. It is a byestreet—very lonely.

"*William Bird*, tailor, deposes that he was one of the party who entered the house. Is an Englishman. Has lived in Paris two years. Was one of the first to ascend the stairs. Heard the voices in contention. The gruff voice was that of a Frenchman. Could make out several words but cannot now remember all. Heard distinctly '*sacré*' and '*mon Dieu*.' There was a sound at the moment as if of several persons struggling—a scraping and scuffling sound. The shrill voice was very loud—louder than the gruff one. Is sure that it was not the voice of an Englishman. Appeared to be that of a German. Might have been a woman's voice. Does not understand German.

"Four of the above-named witnesses, being recalled, deposed that the door of the chamber in which was found the body of Mademoiselle L. was locked on the inside when the party reached it. Everything was perfectly silent—no groans or noises of any kind. Upon forcing the door no person was seen. The windows, both of the back and front room, were down and firmly fastened from within. A door between the two rooms was closed, but not locked. The door leading from the front room into the passage was locked, with the key on the inside. A small room in the front of the house, on the fourth story, at the head of the passage, was open, the door being ajar. This room was crowded with old beds, boxes, and so forth. These were carefully removed and searched. There was not an inch of any portion of the house which was not carefully searched. Sweeps were sent up and down the chimneys. The house was a four-story one, with garrets (*mansardes*). A trap-door on the roof was nailed down very securely—did not appear to have been opened for years. The time elapsing between the hearing of the voices in contention and the breaking open of the room door, was variously stated by the witnesses. Some made it as short as three minutes—some as long as five. The door was opened with difficulty.

"*Alfonzo Garcio*, undertaker, deposes that he resides in the Rue Morgue. Is a native of Spain. Was one of the party who entered the house. Did not proceed upstairs. Is nervous, and was apprehensive of the consequences of agitation. Heard the voices in contention. The gruff voice was that of a

Frenchman. Could not distinguish what was said. The shrill voice was that of an Englishman—is sure of this. Does not understand the English language, but judges by the intonation.

"*Alberto Montani*, confectioner, deposes that he was among the first to ascend the stairs. Heard the voices in question. The gruff voice was that of a Frenchman. Distinguished several words. The speaker appeared to be expostulating. Could not make out the words of the shrill voice. Spoke quick and unevenly. Thinks it the voice of a Russian. Corroborates the general testimony. Is an Italian. Never conversed with a native of Russia.

"Several witnesses, recalled, here testified that the chimneys of all the rooms on the fourth story were too narrow to admit the passage of a human being. By 'sweeps' were meant cylindrical sweeping-brushes, such as are employed by those who clean chimneys. These brushes were passed up and down every flue in the house. There is no back passage by which any one could have descended while the party proceeded up stairs. The body of Mademoiselle L'Espanaye was so firmly wedged in the chimney that it could not be got down until four or five of the party united their strength.

"*Paul Dumas*, physician, deposes that he was called to view the bodies about daybreak. They were both then lying on the sacking of the bedstead in the chamber where Mademoiselle L. was found. The corpse of the young lady was much bruised and excoriated. The fact that it had been thrust up the chimney would sufficiently account for these appearances. The throat was greatly chafed. There were several deep scratches just below the chin, together with a series of livid spots which were evidently the impression of fingers. The face was fearfully discolored, and the eyeballs protruded. The tongue had been partially bitten through. A large bruise was discovered upon the pit of the stomach, produced, apparently, by the pressure of a knee. In the opinion of M. Dumas, Mademoiselle L'Espanaye had been throttled to death by some person or persons unknown. The corpse of the mother was horribly mutilated. All the bones of the right leg and arm were more or less shattered. The left *tibia* much splintered, as well as all the ribs of the left side. Whole body dreadfully bruised and discolored. It was not possible to say how the injuries had been inflicted. A heavy club of wood, or a broad bar of iron—a chair—any large, heavy, and obtuse weapon would have produced such results, if wielded by the hands of a very powerful man. No woman could have inflicted the blows with any weapon. The head of the deceased, when seen by witness, was entirely separated from the body, and was also greatly shattered. The throat had evidently been cut with some very sharp instrument—probably with a razor.

"*Alexandre Etienne*, surgeon, was called with M. Dumas to view the bodies. Corroborated the testimony, and the opinions of M. Dumas.

"Nothing farther of importance was elicited, although several other persons were examined. A murder so mysterious, and so perplexing in all its particulars, was never before committed in Paris—if indeed a murder has been committed at all. The police are entirely at fault—an unusual occurrence in affairs of this nature. There is not, however, the shadow of a clue apparent."

The evening edition of the paper stated that the greatest excitement still continued in the Quartier St. Roch—that the premises in question had been carefully re-searched, and fresh examinations of witnesses instituted, but all to no purpose. A postscript, however, mentioned that Adolphe Le Bon had been arrested and imprisoned—although nothing appeared to criminate him, beyond the facts already detailed.

Dupin seemed singularly interested in the progress of this affair—at least so I judged from his manner, for he made no comments. It was only after the announcement that Le Bon had been imprisoned, that he asked me my opinion respecting the murders.

I could merely agree with all Paris in considering them an insoluble mystery. I saw no means by which it would be possible to trace the murderer.

"We must not judge of the means," said Dupin, "by this shell of an examination. The Parisian police, so much extolled for *acumen*, are cunning, but no more. There is no method in their proceedings, beyond the method of the moment. They make a vast parade of measures; but, not unfrequently, these are so ill adapted to the objects proposed, as to put us in mind of Monsieur Jourdain's calling for his *robe-de-chambre—pour mieux entendre la musique*. The results attained by them are not unfrequently surprising, but, for the most part, are brought about by simple diligence and activity. When these qualities are unavailing, their schemes fail. Vidocq, for example, was a good guesser, and a persevering man. But, without educated thought, he erred continually by the very intensity of his investigations. He impaired his vision by holding the object too close. He might see, perhaps, one or two points with unusual clearness, but in so doing he, necessarily, lost sight of the matter as a whole. Thus there is such a thing as being too profound. Truth is not always in a well. In fact, as regards the more important knowledge, I do believe that she is invariably superficial. The depth lies in the valleys where we seek her, and not upon the mountain-tops where she is found. The modes and sources of this kind of error are well typified in the contemplation of the heavenly bodies. To look at a star by glances—to view it in a side-long way, by turning towards it the exterior portions of the *retina* (more susceptible of feeble impressions of light than the interior), is to behold the star distinctly—is to have the best appreciation of its luster—a luster which grows dim just in proportion as we turn our vision *fully* upon it. A greater number of rays actually fall upon the eye in the latter case, but, in the former, there is the more refined capacity for comprehension. By undue profundity we perplex and enfeeble thought; and it is possible to make even Venus herself vanish from the firmament by a scrutiny too sustained, too concentrated, or too direct.

"As for these murders, let us enter into some examinations for ourselves, before we make up an opinion respecting them. An inquiry will afford us amusement" (I thought this an odd term, so applied, but said nothing), "and, besides, Le Bon once rendered me a service for which I am not ungrateful. We will go and see the premises with our own eyes. I know G——, the Prefect of Police, and shall have no difficulty in obtaining the necessary permission."

The permission was obtained, and we proceeded at once to the Rue Morgue. This is one of those miserable thoroughfares, which intervene between the Rue Richelieu and the Rue St. Roch. It was late in the afternoon when we reached it; as this quarter is at a great distance from that in which we resided. The house was readily found; for there were still many persons gazing up at the closed shutters, with an objectless curiosity, from the opposite side of the way. It was an ordinary Parisian house, with a gateway, on one side of which was a glazed watch-box, with a sliding panel in the window, indicating a *loge de concierge*. Before going in we walked up the street, turned down an alley, and then, again turning, passed in the rear of the building–Dupin, meanwhile, examining the whole neighborhood, as well as the house, with a minuteness of attention for which I could see no possible object.

Retracing our steps, we came again to the front of the dwelling, rang, and, having shown our credentials, were admitted by the agents in charge. We went upstairs–into the chamber where the body of Mademoiselle L'Espanaye had been found, and where both the deceased still lay. The disorders of the room had, as usual, been suffered to exist. I saw nothing beyond what had been stated in the "Gazette des Tribunaux." Dupin scrutinized everything–not excepting the bodies of the victims. We then went into the other rooms, and into the yard: a *gendarme* accompanying us throughout. The examination occupied us until dark, when we took our departure. On our way home my companion stopped in for a moment at the office of the daily papers.

I have said that the whims of my friend were manifold, and that *Je les ménageais:*–for this phrase there is no English equivalent. It was his humor, now, to decline all conversation on the subject of the murder, until about noon the next day. He then asked me, suddenly, if I had observed anything *peculiar* at the scene of the atrocity.

There was something in his manner of emphasizing the word "peculiar," which caused me to shudder, without knowing why.

"No, nothing *peculiar*," I said; "nothing more, at least, than we both saw stated in the paper."

"The 'Gazette,'" he replied, "has not entered, I fear, into the unusual horror of the thing. But dismiss the idle opinions of this print. It appears to me that this mystery is considered insoluble, for the very reason which should cause it to be regarded as easy of solution—I mean for the *outré* character of its features. The police are confounded by the seeming absence of motive—not for the murder itself—but for the atrocity of the murder. They are puzzled, too, by the seeming impossibility of reconciling the voices heard in contention, with the facts that no one was discovered upstairs but the assassinated Mademoiselle L'Espanaye, and that there were no means of egress without the notice of the party ascending. The wild disorder of the room; the corpse thrust, with the head downwards, up the chimney; the frightful mutilation of the body of the old lady; these considerations, with those just mentioned, and others which I need not mention, have sufficed to paralyze the powers, by putting completely at fault the boasted *acumen*, of the government agents. They have fallen into the gross but common error of confounding the unusual with the abstruse. But it is by these deviations from the plane of the ordinary, that reason feels its way, if at all, in its search for the true. In investigations such as we are now pursuing, it should not be so much asked 'what has occurred,' as 'what has occurred that has never occurred before.' In fact, the facility with which I shall arrive, or have arrived, at the solution of this mystery, is in the direct ratio of its apparent insolubility in the eyes of the police."

I stared at the speaker in mute astonishment.

"I am now awaiting," continued he, looking towards the door of our apartment—"I am now awaiting a person who, although perhaps not the perpetrator of these butcheries, must have been in some measure implicated in their perpetration. Of the worst portion of the crimes committed, it is probable that he is innocent. I hope that I am right in this supposition; for upon it I build my expectation of reading the entire riddle. I look for the man here—in this room—every moment. It is true that he may not arrive; but the probability is that he will. Should he come, it will be necessary to detain him. Here are pistols; and we both know how to use them when occasion demands their use."

I took the pistols, scarcely knowing what I did, or believing what I heard, while Dupin went on, very much as if in a soliloquy. I have already spoken of his abstract manner at such times. His discourse was addressed to myself; but his voice, although by no means loud, had that intonation which is commonly employed in speaking to some one at a great distance. His eyes, vacant in expression, regarded only the wall.

"That the voices heard in contention," he said, "by the party upon the stairs, were not the voices of the women themselves, was fully proved by the evidence. This relieves us of all doubt upon the question whether the old lady could have first destroyed the daughter, and afterward have committed suicide. I speak of this point chiefly for the sake of method; for the strength of Madame L'Espanaye would have been utterly unequal to the task of thrusting her daughter's corpse up the chimney as it was found; and the nature of the wounds upon her own person entirely preclude the idea of self-destruction. Murder, then, has been committed by some third party; and the voices of this third party were those heard in contention. Let me now advert–not to the whole testimony respecting these voices–but to what was *peculiar* in that testimony. Did you observe anything peculiar about it?"

I remarked that, while all the witnesses agreed in supposing the gruff voice to be that of a Frenchman, there was much disagreement in regard to the shrill, or, as one individual termed it, the harsh voice.

"That was the evidence itself," said Dupin, "but it was not the peculiarity of the evidence. You have observed nothing distinctive. Yet there *was* something to be observed. The witnesses, as you remark, agreed about the gruff voice; they were here unanimous. But in regard to the shrill voice, the peculiarity is–not that they disagreed–but that, while an Italian, an Englishman, a Spaniard, a Hollander, and a Frenchman attempted to describe it, each one spoke of it as that *of a foreigner*. Each is sure that it was not the voice of one of his own countrymen. Each likens it–not to the voice of an individual of any nation with whose language he is conversant–but the converse. The Frenchman supposes it the voice of a Spaniard, and 'might have distinguished some words *had he been acquainted with the Spanish*.' The Dutchman maintains it to have been that of a Frenchman; but we find it stated that '*not understanding French this witness was examined through an interpreter*.' The Englishman thinks it the voice of a German, and '*does not understand German*.' The Spaniard 'is sure' that it was that of an Englishman, but 'judges by the intonation' altogether, '*as he has no knowledge of the English*.' The Italian believes it the voice of a Russian, but '*has never conversed with a native of Russia*.' A second Frenchman differs, moreover, with the first, and is positive that the voice was that of an Italian; but, *not being cognizant of that tongue*, is, like the Spaniard, 'convinced by the intonation.' Now, how strangely unusual must that voice have really been, about which such testimony as this *could* have been elicited!–in whose *tones*, even, denizens of the five great divisions of Europe could recognize nothing familiar! You will say that it might have been the voice of an Asiatic–of an African. Neither Asiatics nor Africans abound in Paris; but, without denying the inference, I will now merely call your attention to three points. The voice is termed by one witness 'harsh rather than shrill.' It is represented by two others to have been 'quick and *unequal*.' No words–no sounds resembling words–were by any witness mentioned as distinguishable.

"I know not," continued Dupin, "what impression I may have made, so far, upon your own understanding; but I do not hesitate to say that legitimate deductions even from this portion of the testimony–the portion respecting the gruff and shrill voices–are in themselves sufficient to engender a suspicion which should give direction to all farther progress in the investigation of the mystery. I said 'legitimate deductions'; but my meaning is not thus fully expressed. I designed to imply that the deductions are the *sole* proper ones, and that the suspicion arises *inevitably* from them as the single result. What the suspicion is, however, I will not say just yet. I merely wish you to bear in mind that, with myself, it was sufficiently forcible to give a definite form—certain tendency—to my inquiries in the chamber.

"Let us now transport ourselves, in fancy, to this chamber. What shall we first seek here? The means of egress employed by the murderers. It is not too much to say that neither of us believe in præternatural events. Madame and Mademoiselle L'Espanaye were not destroyed by spirits. The doers of the deed were material, and escaped materially. Then how? Fortunately, there is but one mode of reasoning upon the point, and that mode *must* lead us to a definite decision.—Let us examine, each by each, the possible means of egress. It is clear that the assassins were in the room where Mademoiselle L'Espanaye was found, or at least in the room adjoining, when the party ascended the stairs. It is then only from these two apartments that we have to seek issues. The police have laid bare the floors, the ceilings, and the masonry of the walls, in every direction. No *secret* issues could have escaped their vigilance. But not trusting to *their* eyes, I examined with my own. There were, then, no secret issues. Both doors leading from the rooms into the passage were securely locked, with the keys inside. Let us turn to the chimneys. These, although of ordinary width for some eight or ten feet above the hearths, will not admit, throughout their extent, the body of a large cat. The impossibility of egress, by means already stated, being thus absolute, we are reduced to the windows. Through those of the front room no one could have escaped without notice from the crowd in the street. The murderers *must* have passed, then, through those of the back room. Now, brought to this conclusion in so unequivocal a manner as we are, it is not our part, as reasoners, to reject it on account of apparent impossibilities. It is only left for us to prove that these apparent 'impossibilities' are, in reality, not such.

"There are two windows in the chamber. One of them is unobstructed by furniture, and is wholly visible. The lower portion of the other is hidden from view by the head of the unwieldy bedstead which is thrust close up against it. The former was found securely fastened from within. It resisted the utmost force of those who endeavored to raise it. A large gimlet-hole had been pierced in its frame to the left, and a very stout nail was found fitted therein, nearly to the head. Upon examining the other window, a similar nail was seen similarly fitted in it; and a vigorous attempt to raise this sash, failed also. The police were now entirely satisfied that egress had not been in these directions. And, *therefore*, it was thought a matter of supererogation to withdraw the nails and open the windows.

"My own examination was somewhat more particular, and was so for the reason I have just given—because here it was, I knew, that all apparent impossibilities *must* be proved to be not such in reality.

"I proceeded to think thus—*à posteriori*. The murderers *did* escape from one of these windows. This being so, they could not have refastened the sashes from the inside, as they were found fastened;—the consideration which put a stop, through its obviousness, to the scrutiny of the police in this quarter. Yet the sashes *were* fastened. They *must*, then, have the power of fastening themselves. There was no escape from this conclusion. I stepped to the unobstructed casement, withdrew the nail with some difficulty, and attempted to raise the sash. It resisted all my efforts, as I had anticipated. A concealed spring must, I now knew, exist; and this corroboration of my idea convinced me that my premises, at least, were correct, however mysterious still appeared the circumstances attending the nails. A careful search soon brought to light the hidden spring. I pressed it, and, satisfied with the discovery, forbore to upraise the sash.

"I now replaced the nail and regarded it attentively. A person passing out through this window might have reclosed it, and the spring would have caught—but the nail could not have been replaced. The conclusion was plain, and again narrowed in the field of my investigations. The assassins *must* have escaped through the other window. Supposing, then, the springs upon each sash to be the same, as was probable, there *must* be found a difference between the nails, or at least between the modes of their fixture. Getting upon the sacking of the bedstead, I looked over the head-board minutely at the second casement. Passing my hand down behind the board, I readily discovered and pressed the spring, which was, as I had supposed, identical in character with its neighbor. I now looked at the nail. It was as stout as the other, and apparently fitted in the same manner—driven in nearly up to the head.

"You will say that I was puzzled; but, if you think so, you must have misunderstood the nature of the inductions. To use a sporting phrase, I had not been once 'at fault.' The scent had never for an instant been lost. There was no flaw in any link of the chain. I had traced the secret to its ultimate result,—and that result was *the nail.* It had, I say, in every respect, the appearance of its fellow in the other window; but this fact was an absolute nullity (conclusive as it might seem to be) when compared with the consideration that here, at this point, terminated the clue. 'There *must* be something wrong,' I said, 'about the nail.' I touched it; and the head, with about a quarter of an inch of the shank, came off in my fingers. The rest of the shank was in the gimlet-hole, where it had been broken off. The fracture was an old one (for its edges were incrusted with rust), and had apparently been accomplished by the blow of a hammer, which had partially imbedded, in the top of the bottom sash, the head portion of the nail. I now carefully replaced this head portion in the indentation whence I had taken it, and the resemblance to a perfect nail was complete—the fissure was invisible. Pressing the spring, I gently raised the sash for a few inches; the head went up with it, remaining firm in its bed. I closed the window, and the semblance of the whole nail was again perfect.

"The riddle, so far, was now unriddled. The assassin had escaped through the window which looked upon the bed. Dropping of its own accord upon his exit (or perhaps purposely closed), it had become fastened by the spring; and it was the retention of this spring which had been mistaken by the police for that of the nail,—farther inquiry being thus considered unnecessary.

"The next question is that of the mode of descent. Upon this point I had been satisfied in my walk with you around the building. About five feet and a half from the casement in question there runs a lightning-rod. From this rod it would have been impossible for any one to reach the window itself, to say nothing of entering it. I observed, however, that the shutters of the fourth story were of the peculiar kind called by Parisian carpenters *ferrades*—a kind rarely employed at the present day, but frequently seen upon very old mansions at Lyons and Bordeaux. They are in the form of an ordinary door (a single, not a folding door), except that the upper half is latticed or worked in open trellis—thus affording an excellent hold for the hands. In the present instance these shutters are fully three feet and a half broad. When we saw them from the rear of the house, they were both about half open—that is to say, they stood off at right angles from the wall. It is probable that the police, as well as myself, examined the back of the tenement; but, if so, in looking at these *ferrades* in the line of their breadth (as they must have done), they did not perceive this great breadth itself, or, at all events, failed to take it into due consideration. In fact, having once satisfied themselves that no egress could have been made in this quarter they would naturally bestow here a very cursory examination. It was clear to me, however, that the shutter belonging to the window at the head of the bed, would, if swung fully back to the wall, reach to within two feet of the lightning-rod. It was also evident that, by exertion of a very unusual degree of activity and courage, an entrance into the window, from the rod, might have been thus effected.—By reaching to the distance of two feet and a half (we now suppose the shutter open to its whole extent) a robber might have taken a firm grasp upon the trellis-work. Letting go, then, his hold upon the rod, placing his feet securely against the wall, and springing boldly from it, he might have swung the shutter so as to close it, and, if we imagine the window open at the time, might even have swung himself into the room.

"I wish you to bear especially in mind that I have spoken of a *very* unusual degree of activity as requisite to success in so hazardous and so difficult a feat. It is my design to show you, first, that the thing might possibly have been accomplished:—but, secondly and *chiefly*, I wish to impress upon your understanding the *very extraordinary*—the almost præternatural character of that agility which could have accomplished it.

"You will say, no doubt, using the language of the law, that 'to make out my case' I should rather undervalue, than insist upon a full estimation of the activity required in this matter. This may be the practice in law, but it is not the usage of reason. My ultimate object is only the truth. My immediate purpose is to lead you to place in juxtaposition that *very unusual* activity of which I have just spoken, with that *very peculiar* shrill (or harsh) and *unequal* voice, about whose nationality no two persons could be found to agree, and in whose utterance no syllabification could be detected."

At these words a vague and half-formed conception of the meaning of Dupin flitted over my mind. I seemed to be upon the verge of comprehension, without power to comprehend—as men, at times, find themselves upon the brink of remembrance, without being able, in the end, to remember. My friend went on with his discourse.

"You will see," he said, "that I have shifted the question from the mode of egress to that of ingress. It was my design to suggest that both were effected in the same manner, at the same point. Let us now revert to the interior of the room. Let us survey the appearances here. The drawers of the bureau, it is said, had been rifled, although many articles of apparel still remained within them. The conclusion here is absurd. It is a mere guess—a very silly one—and no more. How are we to know that the articles found in the drawers were not all these drawers had originally contained? Madame L'Espanaye and her daughter lived an exceedingly retired life—saw no company—seldom went out—had little use for numerous changes of habiliment. Those found were at least of as good quality as any likely to be possessed by these ladies. If a thief had taken any, why did he not take the best—why did he not take all? In a word, why did he abandon four thousand francs in gold to encumber himself with a bundle of linen ? The gold *was* abandoned. Nearly the whole sum mentioned by Monsieur Mignaud, the banker, was discovered, in bags, upon the floor. I wish you, therefore, to discard from your thoughts the blundering idea of *motive*, engendered in the brains of the police by that portion of the evidence which speaks of money delivered at the door of the house. Coincidences ten times as remarkable as this (the delivery of the money, and murder committed within three days upon the party receiving it), happen to all of us every hour of our lives, without attracting even momentary notice. Coincidences, in general, are great stumbling-blocks in the way of that class of thinkers who have been educated to know nothing of the theory of probabilities—that theory to which the most glorious objects of human research are indebted for the most glorious of illustration. In the present instance, had the gold been gone, the fact of its delivery three days before would have formed something more than a coincidence. It would have been corroborative of this idea of motive. But, under the real circumstances of the case, if we are to suppose gold the motive of this outrage, we must also imagine the perpetrator so vacillating an idiot as to have abandoned his gold and his motive together.

"Keeping now steadily in mind the points to which I have drawn your attention—that peculiar voice, that unusual agility, and that startling absence of motive in a murder so singularly atrocious as this—let us glance at the butchery itself. Here is a woman strangled to death by manual strength, and thrust up a chimney, head downwards. Ordinary assassins employ no such modes of murder as this. Least of all, do they thus dispose of the murdered. In the manner of thrusting the corpse up the chimney, you will admit that there was something *excessively outré*—something altogether irreconcilable with our common notions of human action, even when we suppose the actors the most depraved of men. Think, too, how great must have been that strength which could have thrust the body *up* such an aperture so forcibly that the united vigor of several persons was found barely sufficient to drag it *down*!

"Turn, now, to other indications of the employment of a vigor most marvelous. On the hearth were thick tresses—very thick tresses—of gray human hair. These had been torn out by the roots. You are aware of the great force necessary in tearing thus from the head even twenty or thirty hairs together. You saw the locks in question as well as myself. Their roots (a hideous sight!) were clotted with fragments of the flesh of the scalp—sure token of the prodigious power which had been exerted in uprooting perhaps half a million of hairs at a time. The throat of the old lady was not merely cut, but the head absolutely severed from the body: the instrument was a mere razor. I wish you also to look at the *brutal* ferocity of these deeds. Of the bruises upon the body of Madame L'Espanaye I do not speak. Monsieur Dumas, and his worthy coadjutor Monsieur Etienne, have pronounced that they were inflicted by some obtuse instrument; and so far these gentlemen are very correct. The obtuse instrument was clearly the stone pavement in the yard, upon which the victim had fallen from the window which looked in upon the bed. This idea, however simple it may now seem, escaped the police for the same reason that the breadth of the shutters escaped them—because, by the affair of the nails, their perceptions had been hermetically sealed against the possibility of the windows having ever been opened at all.

"If now, in addition to all these things, you have properly reflected upon the odd disorder of the chamber, we have gone so far as to combine the ideas of an agility astounding, a strength superhuman, a ferocity brutal, a butchery without motive, a *grotesquerie* in horror absolutely alien from humanity, and a voice foreign in tone to the ears of men of many nations, and devoid of all distinct or intelligible syllabification. What result, then, has ensued? What impression have I made upon your fancy?"

I felt a creeping of the flesh as Dupin asked me the question. "A madman," I said, "has done this deed–some raving maniac, escaped from a neighboring *Maison de Santé.*"

"In some respects," he replied, "your idea is not irrelevant. But the voices of madmen, even in their wildest paroxysms, are never found to tally with that peculiar voice heard upon the stairs. Madmen are of some nation, and their language, however incoherent in its words, has always the coherence of syllabification. Besides, the hair of a madman is not such as I now hold in my hand. I disentangled this little tuft from the rigidly clutched fingers of Madame L'Espanaye. Tell me what you can make of it."

"Dupin!" I said, completely unnerved; "this hair is most unusual—this is no *human* hair."

"I have not asserted that it is," said he; "but, before we decide this point, I wish you to glance at the little sketch I have here traced upon this paper. It is a *facsimile* drawing of what has been described in one portion of the testimony as 'dark bruises, and deep indentations of fingernails,' upon the throat of Mademoiselle L'Espanaye, and in another (by Messrs. Dumas and Etienne), as a 'series of livid spots, evidently the impression of fingers.'

"You will perceive," continued my friend, spreading out the paper upon the table before us, "that this drawing gives the idea of a firm and fixed hold. There is no *slipping* apparent. Each finger has retained–possibly until the death of the victim–the fearful grasp by which it originally imbedded itself. Attempt, now, to place all your fingers, at the same time, in the respective impressions as you see them."

I made the attempt in vain.

"We are possibly not giving this matter a fair trial," he said. "The paper is spread out upon a plane surface; but the human throat is cylindrical. Here is a billet of wood, the circumference of which is about that of the throat. Wrap the drawing around it and try the experiment again."

I did so; but the difficulty was even more obvious than before.

"This," I said, "is the mark of no human hand."

"Read now," replied Dupin, "this passage from Cuvier."

It was a minute anatomical and generally descriptive account of the large fulvous Orang-Outang of the East Indian Islands. The gigantic stature, the prodigious strength and activity, the wild ferocity, and the imitative propensities of these mammalia are sufficiently well known to all. I understood the full horrors of the murder at once.

"The description of the digits," said I, as I made an end of reading, "is in exact accordance with this drawing. I see that no animal but an Orang-Outang, of the species here mentioned, could have impressed the indentations as you have traced them. This tuft of tawny hair, too, is identical in character with that of the beast of Cuvier. But I cannot possibly comprehend the particulars of this frightful mystery. Besides, there were *two* voices heard in contention, and one of them was unquestionably the voice of a Frenchman."

"True; and you will remember an expression attributed almost unanimously, by the evidence, to this voice,—the expression, '*mon Dieu!*' This, under the circumstances, has been justly characterized by one of the witnesses (Montani, the confectioner), as an expression of remonstrance or expostulation. Upon these two words, therefore, I have mainly built my hopes of a full solution of the riddle. A Frenchman was cognizant of the murder. It is possible—indeed it is far more than probable—that he was innocent of all participation in the bloody transactions which took place. The Orang-Outang may have escaped from him. He may have traced it to the chamber; but, under the agitating circumstances which ensued, he could never have recaptured it. It is still at large. I will not pursue these guesses—for I have no right to call them more—since the shades of reflection upon which they are based are scarcely of sufficient depth to be appreciable by my own intellect, and since I could not pretend to make them intelligible to the understanding of another. We will call them guesses then, and speak of them as such. If the Frenchman in question is indeed, as I suppose, innocent of this atrocity, this advertisement, which I left last night, upon our return home, at the office of 'Le Monde' (a paper devoted to the shipping interest, and much sought by sailors), will bring him to our residence."

He handed me a paper, and I read thus:

CAUGHT—*In the Bois de Boulogne, early in the morning of the—inst.* (the morning of the murder), *a very large, tawny Orang-Outang of the Bornese species. The owner (who is ascertained to be a sailor, belonging to a Maltese vessel), may have the animal again, upon identifying it satisfactorily, and paying a few charges arising from its capture and keeping. Call at No.—, Rue—, Faubourg St. Germain—au troisième.*

"How was it possible," I asked, "that you should know the man to be a sailor, and belonging to a Maltese vessel?"

"I do *not* know it," said Dupin. "I am not *sure* of it. Here, however, is a small piece of ribbon, which from its form, and from its greasy appearance, has evidently been used in tying the hair in one of those long *queues* of which sailors are so fond. Moreover, this knot is one which few besides sailors can tie, and is peculiar to the Maltese. I picked the ribbon up at the foot of the lightning-rod. It could not have belonged to either of the deceased. Now if, after all, I am wrong in my induction from this ribbon, that the Frenchman was a sailor belonging to a Maltese vessel, still I can have done no harm in saying what I did in the advertisement. If I am in error, he will merely suppose that I have been misled by some circumstance into which he will not take the trouble to inquire. But if I am right, a great point is gained. Cognizant although innocent of the murder, the Frenchman will naturally hesitate about replying to the advertisement—about demanding the Orang-Outang. He will reason thus:—'I am innocent; I am poor; my Orang-Outang is of great value—to one in my circumstances a fortune of itself—why should I lose it through idle apprehensions of danger? Here it is, within my grasp. It was found in the Bois de Boulogne—at a vast distance from the scene of that butchery. How can it ever be suspected that a brute beast should have done the deed? The police are at fault—they have failed to procure the slightest clue. Should they even trace the animal, it would be impossible to prove me cognizant of the murder, or to implicate me in guilt on account of that cognizance. Above all, *I am known*. The advertiser designates me as the possessor of the beast. I am not sure to what limit his knowledge may extend. Should I avoid claiming a property of so great value, which it is known that I possess, I will render the animal, at least, liable to suspicion. It is not my policy to attract attention either to myself or to the beast. I will answer the advertisement, get the Orang-Outang, and keep it close until this matter has blown over.'"

At this moment we heard a step upon the stairs.

"Be ready," said Dupin, "with your pistols, but neither use them nor show them until at a signal from myself."

The front door of the house had been left open, and the visitor had entered, without ringing, and advanced several steps upon the staircase. Now, however, he seemed to hesitate. Presently we heard him descending. Dupin was moving quickly to the door, when we again heard him coming up. He did not turn back a second time, but stepped up with decision and rapped at the door of our chamber.

"Come in," said Dupin, in a cheerful and hearty tone.

A man entered. He was a sailor, evidently,—a tall, stout, and muscular-looking person, with a certain dare-devil expression of countenance, not altogether unprepossessing. His face, greatly sunburnt, was more than half hidden by whisker and *mustachio*. He had with him a huge oaken cudgel, but appeared to be otherwise unarmed. He bowed awkwardly, and bade us "good evening," in French accents, which, although somewhat Neufchatelish, were still sufficiently indicative of a Parisian origin.

"Sit down, my friend," said Dupin. "I suppose you have called about the Orang-Outang. Upon my word, I almost envy you the possession of him; a remarkably fine, and no doubt a very valuable animal. How old do you suppose him to be?"

The sailor drew a long breath, with the air of a man relieved of some intolerable burthen, and then replied, in an assured tone:

"I have no way of telling—but he can't be more than four or five years old. Have you got him here?"

"Oh no; we had no conveniences for keeping him here. He is at a livery stable in the Rue Dubourg, just by. You can get him in the morning. Of course you are prepared to identify the property?"

"To be sure I am, sir."

"I shall be sorry to part with him," said Dupin.

"I don't mean that you should be at all this trouble for nothing, sir," said the man. "Couldn't expect it. Am very willing to pay a reward for the finding of the animal—that is to say, anything in reason."

"Well," replied my friend, "that is all very fair, to be sure. Let me think!—what should I have? Oh! I will tell you. My reward shall be this. You shall give me all the information in your power about these murders in the Rue Morgue."

Dupin said the last words in a very low tone, and very quietly. Just as quietly, too, he walked towards the door, locked it, and put the key in his pocket. He then drew a pistol from his bosom and placed it, without the least flurry, upon the table.

The sailor's face flushed up as if he were struggling with suffocation. He started to his feet and grasped his cudgel; but the next moment he fell back into his seat, trembling violently, and with the countenance of death itself. He spoke not a word. I pitied him from the bottom of my heart.

"My friend," said Dupin, in a kind tone, "you are alarming yourself unnecessarily—you are indeed. We mean you no harm whatever. I pledge you the honor of a gentleman, and of a Frenchman, that we intend you no injury. I perfectly well know that you are innocent of the atrocities in the Rue Morgue. It will not do, however, to deny that you are in some measure implicated in them. From what I have already said, you must know that I have had means of information about this matter—means of which you could never have dreamed. Now the thing stands thus. You have done nothing which you could have avoided—nothing, certainly, which renders you culpable. You were not even guilty of robbery, when you might have robbed with impunity. You have nothing to conceal. You have no reason for concealment. On the other hand you are bound by every principle of honor to confess all you know. An innocent man is now imprisoned, charged with that crime of which you can point out the perpetrator."

The sailor had recovered his presence of mind, in a great measure, while Dupin uttered these words; but his original boldness of bearing was all gone.

"So help me God," said he, after a brief pause, "I *will* tell you all I know about this affair;—but I do not expect you to believe one half I say—I would be a fool indeed if I did. Still, I *am* innocent, and I will make a clean breast if I die for it."

What he stated was, in substance, this. He had lately made a voyage to the Indian Archipelago. A party, of which he formed one, landed at Borneo, and passed into the interior on an excursion of pleasure. Himself and a companion had captured the Orang-Outang. This companion dying, the animal fell into his own exclusive possession. After great trouble, occasioned by the intractable ferocity of his captive during the home voyage, he at length succeeded in lodging it safely at his own residence in Paris, where, not to attract towards himself the unpleasant curiosity of his neighbors, he kept it carefully secluded, until such time as it should recover from a wound in the foot, received from a splinter on board ship. His ultimate design was to sell it.

Returning home from some sailors' frolic on the night, or rather in the morning of the murder, he found the beast occupying his own bedroom, into which it had broken from a closet adjoining, where it had been, as was thought, securely confined. Razor in hand, and fully lathered, it was sitting before a looking-glass, attempting the operation of shaving, in which it had no doubt previously watched its master through the keyhole of the closet. Terrified at the sight of so dangerous a weapon in the possession of an animal so ferocious, and so well able to use it, the man, for some moments, was at a loss what to do. He had been accustomed, however, to quiet the creature, even in its fiercest moods, by the use of a whip, and to this he now resorted. Upon sight of it, the Orang-Outang sprang at once through the door of the chamber, down the stairs, and thence, through a window, unfortunately open, into the street.

The Frenchman followed in despair; the ape, razor still in hand, occasionally stopping to look back and gesticulate at its pursuer, until the latter had nearly come up with it. It then again made off. In this manner the chase continued for a long time. The streets were profoundly quiet, as it was nearly three o'clock in the morning. In passing down an alley in the rear of the Rue Morgue, the fugitive's attention was arrested by a light gleaming from the open window of Madame L'Espanaye's chamber, in the fourth story of her house. Rushing to the building, it perceived the lightning-rod, clambered up with inconceivable agility, grasped the shutter, which was thrown fully back against the wall, and, by its means, swung itself directly upon the headboard of the bed. The whole feat did not occupy a minute. The shutter was kicked open again by the Orang-Outang as it entered the room.

The sailor, in the meantime, was both rejoiced and perplexed. He had strong hopes of now recapturing the brute, as it could scarcely escape from the trap into which it had ventured, except by the rod, where it might be intercepted as it came down. On the other hand, there was much cause for anxiety as to what it might do in the house. This latter reflection urged the man still to follow the fugitive. A lightning-rod is ascended without difficulty, especially by a sailor; but, when he had arrived as high as the window, which lay far to his left, his career was stopped; the most that he could accomplish was to reach over so as to obtain a glimpse of the interior of the room. At this glimpse he nearly fell from his hold through excess of horror. Now it was that those hideous shrieks arose upon the night, which had startled from slumber the inmates of the Rue Morgue. Madame L'Espanaye and her daughter, habited in their night clothes, had apparently been arranging some papers in the iron chest already mentioned, which had been wheeled into the middle of the room. It was open, and its contents lay beside it on the floor. The victims must have been sitting with their backs toward the window; and, from the time elapsing between the ingress of the beast and the screams, it seems probable that it was not immediately perceived. The flapping-to of the shutter would naturally have been attributed to the wind.

As the sailor looked in, the gigantic animal had seized Madame L'Espanaye by the hair (which was loose, as she had been combing it), and was flourishing the razor about her face, in imitation of the motions of a barber. The daughter lay prostrate and motionless; she had swooned. The screams and struggles of the old lady (during which the hair was torn from her head) had the effect of changing the probably pacific purposes of the Orang-Outang into those of wrath. With one determined sweep of its muscular arm it nearly severed her head from her body. The sight of blood inflamed its anger into frenzy. Gnashing its teeth, and flashing fire from its eyes, it flew upon the body of the girl, and imbedded its fearful talons in her throat, retaining its grasp until she expired. Its wandering and wild glances fell at this moment upon the head of the bed, over which the face of its master, rigid with horror, was just discernible. The fury of the beast, who no doubt bore still in mind the dreaded whip, was instantly converted into fear. Conscious of having deserved punishment, it seemed desirous of concealing its bloody deeds, and skipped about the chamber in an agony of nervous agitation; throwing down and breaking the furniture as it moved, and dragging the bed from the bedstead. In conclusion, it seized first the corpse of the daughter, and thrust it up the chimney, as it was found; then that of the old lady, which it immediately hurled through the window headlong.

As the ape approached the casement with its mutilated burthen, the sailor shrank aghast to the rod, and, rather gliding than clambering down it, hurried at once home—dreading the consequences of the butchery, and gladly abandoning, in his terror, all solicitude about the fate of the Orang-Outang. The words heard by the party upon the staircase were the Frenchman's exclamations of horror and affright, comingled with the fiendish jabberings of the brute.

I have scarcely anything to add. The Orang-Outang must have escaped from the chamber, by the rod, just before the breaking of the door. It must have closed the window as it passed through it. It was subsequently caught by the owner himself, who obtained for it a very large sum at the *Jardin des Plantes*. Le Bon was instantly released, upon our narration of the circumstances (with some comments from Dupin) at the *bureau* of the Prefect of Police. This functionary, however well disposed to my friend, could not altogether conceal his chagrin at the turn which affairs had taken, and was fain to indulge in a sarcasm or two, about the propriety of every person minding his own business.

"Let them talk," said Dupin, who had not thought it necessary to reply. "Let him discourse; it will ease his conscience. I am satisfied with having defeated him in his own castle. Nevertheless, that he failed in the solution of this mystery, is by no means that matter for wonder which he supposes it; for, in truth, our friend the Prefect is somewhat too cunning to be profound. In his wisdom is no *stamen*. It is all head and no body, like the pictures of the Goddess Laverna,—or, at best, all head and shoulders, like a codfish. But he is a good creature after all. I like him especially for one master stroke of cant, by which he has attained his reputation for ingenuity. I mean the way he has '*de nier ce qui est, et d'expliquer ce qui n'est pas.*'"*

*Rousseau, *Nouvelle Héloïse.*

The Purloined Letter

(First published in *The Gift,* January, 1845;
first book publication in 1845.)

Nil sapientiæ odiosius acumine nimio.
SENECA

AT PARIS, JUST after dark one gusty evening in the autumn of 18–, I was enjoying the twofold luxury of meditation and a meerschaum, in company with my friend C. Auguste Dupin, in his little back library, or book-closet, *au troisième, No. 33, Rue Dunôt, Faubourg St. Germain.* For one hour at least we had maintained a profound silence; while each, to any casual observer, might have seemed intently and exclusively occupied with the curling eddies of smoke that oppressed the atmosphere of the chamber. For myself, however, I was mentally discussing certain topics which had formed matter for conversation between us at an earlier period of the evening. I mean the affair of the Rue Morgue, and the mystery attending the murder of Marie Rogêt. I looked upon it, therefore, as something of a coincidence, when the door of our apartment was thrown open and admitted our old acquaintance, Monsieur G——, the Prefect of the Parisian police.

We gave him a hearty welcome; for there was nearly half as much of the entertaining as of the contemptible about the man, and we had not seen him for several years. We had been sitting in the dark, and Dupin now arose for the purpose of lighting a lamp, but sat down again, without doing so, upon G——'s saying that he had called to consult us, or rather to ask the opinion of my friend, about some official business which had occasioned a great deal of trouble.

"If it is any point requiring reflection," observed Dupin, as he forebore to enkindle the wick, "we shall examine it to better purpose in the dark."

"That is another of your odd notions," said the Prefect, who had a fashion of calling everything "odd" that was beyond his comprehension, and thus lived amid an absolute legion of "oddities."

"Very true," said Dupin, as he supplied his visitor with a pipe, and rolled towards him a comfortable chair.

"And what is the difficulty now?" I asked. "Nothing more in the assassination way, I hope?"

"Oh no; nothing of that nature. The fact is, the business is very simple indeed, and I make no doubt that we can manage it sufficiently well ourselves; but then I thought Dupin would like to hear the details of it, because it is so excessively *odd.*"

"Simple and odd," said Dupin.

"Why, yes; and not exactly that, either. The fact is, we have all been a good deal puzzled because the affair *is* so simple, and yet baffles us altogether."

"Perhaps it is the very simplicity of the thing which puts you at fault," said my friend.

"What nonsense you *do* talk!" replied the Prefect, laughing heartily.

"Perhaps the mystery is a little *too* plain," said Dupin.

"Oh, good heavens! who ever heard of such an idea?"

"A little *too* self-evident."

"Ha! ha! ha!–ha! ha! ha!–ho! ho! ho!"–roared our visitor, profoundly amused, "oh, Dupin, you will be the death of me yet!"

"And what, after all, *is* the matter on hand ?" I asked.

"Why, I will tell you," replied the Prefect, as he gave a long, steady, and contemplative puff, and settled himself in his chair. "I will tell you in a few words; but, before I begin, let me caution you that this is an affair demanding the greatest secrecy, and that I should most probably lose the position I now hold, were it known that I confided it to any one."

"Proceed," said I.

"Or not," said Dupin.

"Well, then; I have received personal information, from a very high quarter, that a certain document of the last importance, has been purloined from the royal apartments. The individual who purloined it is known; this beyond a doubt; he was seen to take it. It is known, also, that it still remains in his possession."

"How is this known?" asked Dupin.

"It is clearly inferred," replied the Prefect, "from the nature of the document, and from the non-appearance of certain results which would at once arise from its passing *out* of the robber's possession;–that is to say, from his employing it as he must design in the end to employ it."

"Be a little more explicit," I said.

"Well, I may venture so far as to say that the paper gives its holder a certain power in a certain quarter where such power is immensely valuable." The Prefect was fond of the cant of diplomacy.

"Still I do not quite understand," said Dupin.

"No? Well; the disclosure of the document to a third person, who shall be nameless, would bring in question the honor of a personage of most exalted station; and this fact gives the holder of the document an ascendancy over the illustrious personage whose honor and peace are so jeopardized."

"But this ascendancy," I interposed, "would depend upon the robber's knowledge of the loser's knowledge of the robber. Who would dare–"

"The thief," said G––, "is the Minister D––, who dares all things, those unbecoming as well as those becoming a man. The method of the theft was not less ingenious than bold. The document in question–a letter, to be frank–had been received by the personage robbed while alone in the royal *boudoir*. During its perusal she was suddenly interrupted by the entrance of the other exalted personage from whom especially it was her wish to conceal it. After a hurried and vain endeavor to thrust it in a drawer, she was forced to place it, open as it was, upon a table. The address, however, was uppermost, and, the contents thus unexposed, the letter escaped notice. At this juncture enters the Minister D——. His lynx eye immediately perceives the paper, recognizes the handwriting of the address, observes the confusion of the personage addressed, and fathoms her secret. After some business transactions, hurried through in his ordinary manner, he produces a letter somewhat similar to the one in question, opens it, pretends to read it, and then places it in close juxtaposition to the other. Again he converses, for some fifteen minutes, upon the public affairs. At length, in taking leave, he takes also from the table the letter to which he had no claim. Its rightful owner saw, but, of course, dared not call attention to the act, in the presence of the third personage who stood at her elbow. The minister decamped; leaving his own letter–one of no importance–upon the table."

"Here, then," said Dupin to me, "you have precisely what you demand to make the ascendancy complete–the robber's knowledge of the loser's knowledge of the robber."

"Yes," replied the Prefect; "and the power thus attained has, for some months past, been wielded, for political purposes, to a very dangerous extent. The personage robbed is more thoroughly convinced, every day, of the necessity of reclaiming her letter. But this, of course, cannot be done openly. In fine, driven to despair, she has committed the matter to me."

"Than whom," said Dupin, amid a perfect whirlwind of smoke, "no more sagacious agent could, I suppose, be desired, or even imagined."

"You flatter me," replied the Prefect; "but it is possible that some such opinion may have been entertained."

"It is clear," said I, "as you observe, that the letter is still in possession of the minister; since it is this possession, and not any employment of the letter, which bestows the power. With the employment the power departs.

"True," said G——; "and upon this conviction I proceeded. My first care was to make thorough search of the minister's hotel; and here my chief embarrassment lay in the necessity of searching without his knowledge. Beyond all things, I have been warned of the danger which would result from giving him reason to suspect our design."

"But," said I, "you are quite *au fait* in these investigations. The Parisian police have done this thing often before."

"Oh yes; and for this reason I did not despair. The habits of the minister gave me, too, a great advantage. He is frequently absent from home all night.

His servants are by no means numerous. They sleep at a distance from their master's apartment, and, being chiefly Neapolitans, are readily made drunk. I have keys, as you know, with which I can open any chamber or cabinet in Paris. For three months a night has not passed, during the greater part of which I have not been engaged, personally, in ransacking the D—— hotel. My honor is interested, and, to mention a great secret, the reward is enormous. So I did not abandon the search until I had become fully satisfied that the thief is a more astute man than myself. I fancy that I have investigated every nook and corner of the premises in which it is possible that the paper can be concealed."

"But is it not possible," I suggested, "that although the letter may be in possession of the minister, as it unquestionably is, he may have concealed it elsewhere than upon his own premises?"

"This is barely possible," said Dupin. "The present peculiar condition of affairs at court, and especially of those intrigues in which D—is known to be involved, would render the instant availability of the document–its susceptibility of being produced at a moment's notice–a point of nearly equal importance with its possession."

"Its susceptibility of being produced?" said I.

"That is to say, of being *destroyed*," said Dupin.

"True," I observed; "the paper is clearly then upon the premises. As for its being upon the person of the minister, we may consider that as out of the question."

"Entirely," said the Prefect. "He has been twice waylaid, as if by footpads, and his person rigorously searched under my own inspection."

"You might have spared yourself this trouble," said Dupin. "D——, I presume, is not altogether a fool, and, if not, must have anticipated these waylayings, as a matter of course."

"Not *altogether* a fool," said G——, "but then he's a poet, which I take to be only one remove from a fool."

"True," said Dupin, after a long and thoughtful whiff from his meerschaum, "although I have been guilty of certain doggerel myself."

"Suppose you detail," said I, "the particulars of your search."

"Why, the fact is, we took our time, and we searched *everywhere*. I have had long experience in these affairs. I took the entire building, room by room; devoting the nights of a whole week to each. We examined, first, the furniture of each apartment. We opened every possible drawer; and I presume you know that, to a properly trained police agent, such a thing as a *secret* drawer is impossible. Any man is a dolt who permits a 'secret' drawer to escape him in a search of this kind. The thing is *so* plain. There is a certain amount of bulk–of space–to be accounted for in every cabinet. Then we have accurate rules. The fiftieth part of a line could not escape us. After the cabinets we took the chairs. The cushions we probed with the fine long needles you have seen me employ. From the tables we removed the tops."

"Why so?"

"Sometimes the top of a table, or other similarly arranged piece or furniture, is removed by the person wishing to conceal an article; then the leg is excavated, the article deposited within the cavity, and the top replaced. The bottoms and tops of bedposts are employed in the same way."

"But could not the cavity be detected by sounding?" I asked.

"By no means, if, when the article is deposited, a sufficient wadding of cotton be placed around it. Besides, in our case, we were obliged to proceed without noise."

"But you could not have removed–you could not have taken to pieces *all* articles of furniture in which it would have been possible to make a deposit in the manner you mention. A letter may be compressed into a thin spiral roll, not differing much in shape or bulk from a large knitting needle, and in this form it might be inserted into the rung of a chair, for example. You did not take to pieces all the chairs?"

"Certainly not; but we did better–we examined the rungs of every chair in the hotel, and, indeed, the jointings of every description of furniture, by the aid of a most powerful microscope. Had there been any traces of recent disturbance we should not have failed to detect it instantly. A single grain of gimlet-dust, for example, would have been as obvious as an apple. Any disorder in the gluing–any unusual gaping in the joints–would have sufficed to insure detection."

"I presume you looked to the mirrors, between the boards and the plates, and you probed the beds and the bedclothes, as well as the curtains and carpets."

"That of course; and when we had absolutely completed every particle of the furniture in this way, then we examined the house itself. We divided its entire surface into compartments, which we numbered, so that none might be missed; then we scrutinized each individual square inch throughout the premises, including the two houses immediately adjoining, with the microscope, as before."

"The two houses adjoining!" I exclaimed; "you must have had a great deal of trouble."

"We had; but the reward offered is prodigious."

"You include the *grounds* about the houses?"

"All the grounds are paved with brick. They gave us comparatively little trouble. We examined the moss between the bricks, and found it undisturbed."

"You looked among D——'s papers, of course, and into the books of the library?"

"Certainly; we opened every package and parcel; we not only opened every book, but we turned over every leaf in each volume, not contenting ourselves with a mere shake, according to the fashion of some of our police officers. We also measured the thickness of every book-*cover*, with the most accurate admeasurement, and applied to each the most jealous scrutiny of the microscope. Had any of the bindings been recently meddled with, it would have been utterly impossible that the fact should have escaped observation. Some five or six volumes, just from the hands of the binder, we carefully probed, longitudinally, with the needles."

"You explored the floors beneath the carpets?"

"Beyond doubt. We removed every carpet, and examined the boards with the microscope."

"And the paper on the walls?"

"Yes."

"You looked into the cellars?"

"We did."

"Then," I said, "you have been making a miscalculation, and the letter is *not* upon the premises, as you suppose."

"I fear you are right there," said the Prefect. "And now, Dupin, what would you advise me to do?"

"To make a thorough research of the premises."

"That is absolutely needless," replied G——. "I am not more sure that I breathe than I am that the letter is not at the hotel."

"I have no better advice to give you," said Dupin. "You have, of course, an accurate description of the letter?"

"Oh yes!"—And here the Prefect, producing a memorandum book proceeded to read aloud a minute account of the internal, and especially of the external appearance of the missing document. Soon after finishing the perusal of this description, he took his departure, more entirely depressed in spirits than I had ever known the good gentleman before.

In about a month afterwards he paid us another visit, and found us occupied very nearly as before. He took a pipe and a chair and entered into some ordinary conversation. At length I said:

"Well, but G——, what of the purloined letter? I presume you have at last made up your mind that there is no such thing as overreaching the minister?"

"Confound him, say I—yes; I made the re-examination, however, as Dupin suggested—but it was all labor lost, as I knew it would be."

"How much was the reward offered, did you say?" asked Dupin.

"Why, a very great deal—a *very* liberal reward—I don't like to say how much, precisely; but one thing I *will* say, that I wouldn't mind giving my individual check for fifty thousand francs to any one who could obtain me that letter. The fact is, it is becoming of more and more importance every day; and the reward has been lately doubled. If it were trebled, however, I could do no more than I have done."

"Why, yes," said Dupin, drawlingly, between the whiffs of his meerschaum, "I really–think, G—, you have not exerted yourself–to the utmost in this matter. You might–do a little more, I think, eh?"

"How?–in what way?"

"Why–puff, puff–you might–puff, puff–employ counsel in the matter, eh?–puff, puff, puff. Do you remember the story they tell of Abernethy ?"

"No; hang Abernethy!"

"To be sure! hang him and welcome. But, once upon a time, a certain rich miser conceived the design of sponging upon this Abernethy for a medical opinion. Getting up, for this purpose, an ordinary conversation in a private company, he insinuated his case to the physician, as that of an imaginary individual.

"'We will suppose,' said the miser, 'that his symptoms are such and such; now, doctor, what would *you* have directed him to take?'

"'Take!' said Abernethy, 'why, take *advice*, to be sure.'"

"But," said the Prefect, a little discomposed, "I am *perfectly* willing to take advice, and to pay for it. I would *really* give fifty thousand francs to any one who would aid me in the matter."

"In that case," replied Dupin, opening a drawer, and producing a checkbook, "you may as well fill me up a check for the amount mentioned. When you have signed it, I will hand you the letter."

I was astounded. The Prefect appeared absolutely thunder-stricken. For some minutes he remained speechless and motionless, looking incredulously at my friend with open mouth, and eyes that seemed starting from their sockets; then, apparently recovering himself in some measure, he seized a pen, and after several pauses and vacant stares, finally filled up and signed a check for fifty thousand francs, and handed it across the table to Dupin. The latter examined it carefully and deposited it in his pocketbook; then, unlocking an *escritoire*, took thence a letter and gave it to the Prefect. This functionary grasped it in a perfect agony of joy, opened it with a trembling hand, cast a rapid glance at its contents, and then, scrambling and struggling to the door, rushed at length unceremoniously from the room and from the house, without having uttered a syllable since Dupin had requested him to fill up the check.

When he had gone, my friend entered into some explanations.

"The Parisian police," he said, "are exceedingly able in their way. They are persevering, ingenious, cunning, and thoroughly versed in the knowledge which their duties seem chiefly to demand. Thus, when G— detailed to us his mode of searching the premises at the Hôtel D—, I felt entire confidence in his having made a satisfactory investigation–so far as his labors extended."

"So far as his labors extended?" said I.

"Yes," said Dupin. "The measures adopted were not only the best of their kind, but carried out to absolute perfection. Had the letter been deposited within the range of their search, these fellows would, beyond a question, have found it."

I merely laughed—but he seemed quite serious in all that he said.

"The measures, then," he continued, "were good in their kind, and well executed; their defect lay in their being inapplicable to the case, and to the man. A certain set of highly ingenious resources are, with the Prefect, a sort of Procrustean bed, to which he forcibly adapts his designs. But he perpetually errs by being too deep or too shallow for the matter in hand; and many a schoolboy is a better reasoner than he. I knew one about eight years of age whose success at guessing in the game of 'even and odd' attracted universal admiration. This game is simple, and is played with marbles. One player holds in his hand a number of these toys, and demands of another whether that number is even or odd. If the guess is right, the guesser wins one; if wrong, he loses one. The boy to whom I allude won all the marbles of the school. Of course he had some principle of guessing; and this lay in mere observation and admeasurement of the astuteness of his opponents. For example, an arrant simpleton is his opponent, and, holding up his closed hand, asks, 'Are they even or odd?' Our schoolboy replies, 'odd' and loses; but upon the second trial he wins, for he then says to himself, 'the simpleton had them even upon the first trial, and his amount of cunning is just sufficient to make him have them odd upon the second; I will therefore guess odd';—he guesses odd, and wins. Now, with a simpleton a degree above the first, he would have reasoned thus: 'This fellow finds that in the first instance I guessed odd, and, in the second, he will propose to himself upon the first impulse, a simple variation from even to odd, as did the first simpleton; but then a second thought will suggest that this is too simple a variation, and finally he will decide upon putting it even as before. I will therefore guess even';—he guesses even, and wins. Now this mode of reasoning in the schoolboy, whom his fellows termed 'lucky,'—what, in its last analysis, is it?"

"It is merely," I said, "an identification of the reasoner's intellect with that of his opponent."

"It is," said Dupin; "and, upon inquiring of the boy by what means he effected the *thorough* identification in which his success consisted, I received answer as follows: 'When I wish to find out how wise, or how stupid, or how good, or how wicked is any one, or what are his thoughts at the moment I fashion the expression of my face, as accurately as possible, in accordance with the expression of his, and then wait to see what thoughts or sentiments arise in my mind or heart, as if to match or correspond with the expression.' This response of the schoolboy lies at the bottom of all the spurious profundity which has been attributed to Rochefoucauld, to La Bougive, to Machiavelli, and to Campanella."

"And the identification," I said, "of the reasoner's intellect with that of his opponent, depends, if I understand you aright, upon the accuracy with which the opponent's intellect is admeasured."

"For its practical value it depends upon this," replied Dupin; "and the Prefect and his cohort fail so frequently, first, by default of this identification, and, secondly, by ill-admeasurement, or rather through non-admeasurement, of the intellect with which they are engaged. They consider only their *own* ideas of ingenuity; and, in searching for anything hidden, advert only to the modes in which *they* would have hidden it. They are right in this much—that their own ingenuity is a faithful representative of that of *the mass;* but when the cunning of the individual felon is diverse in character from their own, the felon foils them, of course. This always happens when it is above their own, and very usually when it is below. They have no variation of principle in their investigations; at best, when urged by some unusual emergency—by some extraordinary reward—they extend or exaggerate their old modes of *practice*, without touching their principles. What, for example, in this case of D——, has been done to vary the principle of action ? What is all this boring, and probing, and sounding, and scrutinizing with the microscope, and dividing the surface of the building into registered square inches—what is it all but an exaggeration *of the application* of the one principle or set of principles of search, which are based upon the one set of notions regarding human ingenuity, to which the Prefect, in the long routine of his duty, has been accustomed? Do you not see he has taken it for granted that *all* men proceed to conceal a letter,—not exactly in a gimlet-hole bored in a chair-leg—but, at least, in *some* out-of-the-way hole or corner suggested by the same tenor of thought which would urge a man to secrete a letter in a gimlet-hole bored in a chair-leg? And do you not see also, that such *recherchés* nooks for concealment are adapted only for ordinary occasions, and would be adopted only by ordinary intellects; for, in all cases of concealment, a disposal of the article concealed—a disposal of it in this *recherché* manner,—is, in the very first instance, presumable and presumed; and thus its discovery depends, not at all upon the acumen, but altogether upon the mere care, patience, and determination of the seekers; and where the case is of importance—or, what amounts to the same thing in the political eyes, when the reward is of magnitude,—the qualities in question have *never* been known to fail. You will now understand what I mean in suggesting that, had the purloined letter been hidden anywhere within the limits of the Prefect's examination—in other words, had the principle of its concealment been comprehended within the principles of the Prefect—its discovery would have been a matter altogether beyond question. This functionary, however, has been thoroughly mystified; and the remote source of his defeat lies in the supposition that the minister is a fool, because he has acquired renown as a poet. All fools are poets; this the Prefect *feels;* and he is merely guilty of a *non distributio medii* in thence inferring that all poets are fools."

"But is this really the poet?" I asked. "There are two brothers, I know; and both have attained reputation in letters. The minister I believe has written learnedly on the Differential Calculus. He is a mathematician, and no poet."

"You are mistaken; I know him well; he is both. As poet *and* mathematician, he would reason well; as mere mathematician, he could not have reasoned at all, and thus would have been at the mercy of the Prefect."

"You surprise me," I said, "by these opinions, which have been contradicted by the voice of the world. You do not mean to set at naught the well-digested idea of centuries. The mathematical reason has long been regarded as *the* reason *par excellence.*"

"'*Il y a à parier*,'" replied Dupin, quoting from Chamfort, "'*que toute idée publique, toute convention reçue, est une sottise, car elle a convenu au plus grand nombre.*' The mathematicians, I grant you, have done their best to promulgate the popular error to which you allude, and which is none the less an error for its promulgation as truth. With an art worthy a better cause, for example, they have insinuated the term 'analysis' into application to algebra. The French are the originators of this particular deception; but if a term is of any importance–if words derive any value from applicability–then 'analysis' conveys 'algebra' about as much as, in Latin, '*ambitus*' implies 'ambition,' '*religio*' 'religion,' or '*homines honesti*,' a set of *honorable* men."

"You have a quarrel on hand, I see," said I, "with some of the algebraists of Paris; but proceed."

"I dispute the availability, and thus the value, of that reason which is cultivated in any special form other than the abstractly logical. I dispute, in particular, the reason educed by mathematical study. The mathematics are the science of form and quantity; mathematical reasoning is merely logic applied to observation upon form and quantity. The great error lies in supposing that even the truths of what is called *pure* algebra, are abstract or general truths. And this error is so egregious that I am confounded at the universality with which it has been received. Mathematical axioms are *not* axioms of general truth. What is true of *relation*–of form and quantity–is often grossly false in regard to morals, for example. In this latter science it is very usually *un*true that the aggregated parts are equal to the whole. In chemistry also the axiom fails. In the consideration of motive it fails; for two motives, each of a given value, have not, necessarily, a value when united, equal to the sum of their values apart. There are numerous other mathematical truths which are only truths within the limits of *relation*. But the mathematician argues, from his *finite truths*, through habit, as if they were of an absolutely general applicability–as the world indeed imagines them to be. Bryant, in his very learned 'Mythology,' mentions an analogous source of error, when he says that 'although the Pagan fables are not believed, yet we forget ourselves continually, and make inferences from them as existing realities.' With the algebraists, however, who are Pagans themselves, the 'Pagan fables' *are* believed, and the inferences are made, not so much through lapse of memory, as through an unaccountable addling of the brains. In short, I never yet encountered the mere mathematician who could be trusted out of equal roots, or one who did not clandestinely hold it as a point of his faith that $x^2 + px$ was absolutely and unconditionally equal to q. Say to one of these gentlemen, by way of experiment, if you please, that you believe occasions may occur where $x^2 + px$ is *not* altogether equal to q, and, having made him understand what you mean, get out of his reach as speedily as convenient, for, beyond doubt, he will endeavor to knock you down.

"I mean to say," continued Dupin, while I merely laughed at his last observations, "that if the minister had been no more than: a mathematician, the Prefect would have been under no necessity of giving me this check. I knew him, however, as both mathematician and poet, and my measures were adapted to his capacity, with reference to the circumstances by which he was surrounded. I knew him as a courtier, too, and as a bold *intrigant*. Such a man, I considered, could not fail to be aware of the ordinary policial modes of action. He could not have failed to anticipate–and events have proved that he did not fail to anticipate—the waylayings to which he was subjected. He must have foreseen, I reflected, the secret investigations of his premises. His frequent absences from home at night, which were hailed by the Prefect as certain aids to his success, I regarded only as *ruses*, to afford opportunity for thorough search to the police, and thus the sooner to impress them with the conviction to which G—, in fact, did finally arrive–the conviction that the letter was not upon the premises. I felt, also that the whole train of thought, which I was at some pains in detailing to you just now, concerning the invariable principle of policial action in searches for articles concealed–I felt that this whole train of thought would necessarily pass through the mind of the minister. It would imperatively lead him to despise all the ordinary *nooks* of concealment. *He* could not, I reflected, be so weak as not to see that the most intricate and remote recess of his hotel would be as open as his commonest closets to the eyes, to the probes, to the gimlets, and to the microscopes of the Prefect. I saw, in fine, that he would be driven, as a matter of course, to *simplicity*, if not deliberately induced to it as a matter of choice. You will remember, perhaps, how desperately the Prefect laughed when I suggested, upon our first interview, that it was just possible this mystery troubled him so much on account of its being so *very* self-evident."

"Yes," said I, "I remember his merriment well. I really thought he would have fallen into convulsions."

"The material world," continued Dupin, "abounds with very strict analogies to the immaterial; and thus some color of truth has been given to the rhetorical dogma, that metaphor, or simile, may be made to strengthen an argument, as well as to embellish a description. The principle of the *vis inertiæ*, for example, seems to be identical in physics and metaphysics. It is not more true in the former, that a large body is with more difficulty set in motion than a smaller one, and that its subsequent *momentum* is commensurate with this difficulty, than it is, in the latter, that intellects of the vaster capacity, while more forcible, more constant, and more eventful in their movements than those of inferior grade, are yet the less readily moved, and more embarrassed and full of hesitation in the first few steps of their progress. Again: have you ever noticed which of the street signs, over the shop doors, are the most attractive of attention?"

"I have never given the matter a thought," I said.

"There is a game of puzzles," he resumed, "which is played upon a map. One party playing requires another to find a given word—the name of town, river, state or empire—any word, in short, upon the motley and perplexed surface of the chart. A novice in the game generally seeks to embarrass his opponents by giving them the most minutely-lettered names; but the adept selects such words as stretch, in large characters, from one end of the chart to the other. These, like the over-largely lettered signs and placards of the street, escape observation by dint of being excessively obvious; and here the physical oversight is precisely analogous with the moral inapprehension by which the intellect suffers to pass unnoticed those considerations which are too obtrusively and too palpably self-evident. But this is a point, it appears, somewhat above or beneath the understanding of the Prefect. He never once thought it probable, or possible, that the minister had deposited the letter immediately beneath the nose of the whole world, by way of best preventing any portion of that world from perceiving it.

"But the more I reflected upon the daring, dashing, and discriminating ingenuity of D——; upon the fact that the document must always have been *at hand*, if he intended to use it to good purpose; and upon the decisive evidence, obtained by the Prefect, that it was not hidden within the limits of that dignitary's ordinary search—the more satisfied I became that, to conceal this letter, the minister had resorted to the comprehensive and sagacious expedient of not attempting to conceal it at all.

"Full of these ideas, I prepared myself with a pair of green spectacles, and called one fine morning, quite by accident, at the ministerial hotel. I found D—— at home, yawning, lounging, and dawdling, as usual, and pretending to be in the last extremity of *ennui*. He is, perhaps, the most really energetic human being now alive—but that is only when nobody sees him.

"To be even with him, I complained of my weak eyes, and lamented the necessity of the spectacles, under cover of which I cautiously and thoroughly surveyed the apartment, while seemingly intent only upon the conversation of my host.

"I paid special attention to a large writing-table near which he sat, and upon which lay confusedly, some miscellaneous letters and other papers, with one or two musical instruments and a few books. Here, however, after a long and very deliberate scrutiny, I saw nothing to excite particular suspicion.

"At length my eyes, in going the circuit of the room, fell upon a trumpery filigree card-rack of pasteboard, that hung dangling by a dirty blue ribbon, from a little brass knob just beneath the middle of the mantelpiece. In this rack, which had three or four compartments, were five or six visiting cards and a solitary letter. This last was much soiled and crumpled. It was torn nearly in two, across the middle—as if a design, in the first instance, to tear it entirely up as worthless, had been altered, or stayed, in the second. It had a large black seal, bearing the D—— cipher *very* conspicuously, and was addressed, in a diminutive female hand, to D——, the minister, himself. It was thrust carelessly, and even, as it seemed, contemptuously, into one of the upper divisions of the rack.

"No sooner had I glanced at this letter, than I concluded it to be that of which I was in search. To be sure, it was, to all appearance, radically different from the one of which the Prefect had read us so minute a description. Here the seal was large and black, with the D—— cipher; there it was small and red, with the ducal arms of the S—— family. Here, the address, to the minister, was diminutive and feminine; there the superscription, to a certain royal personage, was markedly bold and decided; the size alone formed a point of correspondence. But, then, the *radicalness* of these differences, which was excessive; the dirt; the soiled and torn condition of the paper, so inconsistent with the *true* methodical habits of D——, and so suggestive of a design to delude the beholder into an idea of the worthlessness of the document; these things, together with the hyperobtrusive situation of this document, full in the view of every visitor, and thus exactly in accordance with the conclusions to which I had previously arrived; these things, I say, were strongly corroborative of suspicion, in one who came with the intention to suspect.

"I protracted my visit as long as possible, and, while I maintained a most animated discussion with the minister, on a topic which I knew well had never failed to interest and excite him, I kept my attention really riveted upon the letter. In this examination, I committed to memory its external appearance and arrangement in the rack; and also fell, at length, upon a discovery which set at rest whatever trivial doubt I might have entertained. In scrutinizing the edges of the paper, I observed them to be more *chafed* than seemed necessary. They presented the *broken* appearance which is manifested when a stiff paper, having been once folded and pressed with a folder, is refolded in a reversed direction, in the same creases or edges which had formed the original fold. This discovery was sufficient. It was clear to me that the letter had been turned, as a glove, inside out, redirected, and resealed. I bade the minister good morning, and took my departure at once, leaving a gold snuff-box upon the table.

"The next morning I called for the snuff-box, when we resumed, quite eagerly, the conversation of the preceding day. While thus engaged, however, a loud report, as if of a pistol, was heard immediately beneath the windows of the hotel and was succeeded by a series of fearful screams, and the shoutings of a mob. D–– rushed to a casement, threw it open, and looked out. In the meantime, I stepped to the card-rack, took the letter, put it in my pocket, and replaced it by a *facsimile* (so far as regards externals), which I had carefully prepared at my lodgings; imitating the D–– cipher, very readily, by means of a seal formed of bread.

"The disturbance in the street had been occasioned by the frantic behavior of a man with a musket. He had fired it among a crowd of women and children. It proved, however, to have been without ball, and the fellow was suffered to go his way as a lunatic or a drunkard. When he had gone, D–– came from the window, whither I had followed him immediately upon securing the object in view. Soon afterwards I bade him farewell. The pretended lunatic was a man in my own pay."

"But what purpose had you," I asked, "in replacing the letter by a *facsimile?* Would it not have been better, at the first visit, to have seized it openly, and departed?"

"D––," replied Dupin, "is a desperate man, and a man of nerve. His hotel, too, is not without attendants devoted to his interests. Had I made the wild attempt you suggest, I might never have left the ministerial presence alive. The good people of Paris might have heard of me no more. But I had an object apart from these considerations. You know my political prepossessions. In this matter, I act as a partisan of the lady concerned. For eighteen months the minister has had her in his power. She has now him in hers; since, being unaware that the letter is not in his possession, he will proceed with his exactions as if it was. Thus will he inevitably commit himself, at once, to his political destruction. His downfall, too, will not be more precipitate than awkward. It is all very well to talk about the *facilis descensus Averni;* but in all kinds of climbing, as Catalani said of singing, it is far more easy to get up than to come down. In the present instance I have no sympathy–at least no pity–for him who descends. He is that *monstrum horrendum*, an unprincipled man of genius. I confess, however, that I should like very well to know the precise character of his thoughts, when, being defied by her whom the Prefect terms 'a certain personage,' he is reduced to opening the letter which I left for him in the card-rack."

"How? Did you put anything particular in it?"

"Why–it did not seem altogether right to leave the interior blank–that would have been insulting. D——, at Vienna once, did me an evil turn, which I told him, quite good-humoredly, that I should remember. So, as I knew he would feel some curiosity in regard to the identity of the person who had outwitted him, I thought it a pity not to give him a clue. He is well acquainted with my MS., and I just copied into the middle of the blank sheet the words–

'——Un dessein si funeste,
S'il n'est digne d'Atrée, est digne de Thyeste.'
They are to be found in Crébillon's 'Atrée.'"

HERMAN MELVILLE

[1819–1891]

Benito Cereno

(First published in *Putnam's Monthly*,
October, 1855; first book publication in 1868.)

IN THE YEAR 1799, Captain Amasa Delano, of Duxbury in Massachusetts, commanding a large sealer and general trader, lay at anchor with a valuable cargo in the harbor of St Maria—a small, desert, uninhabited island toward the southern extremity of the long coast of Chile. There he had touched for water.

On the second day, not long after dawn, while lying in his berth, his mate came below, informing him that a strange sail was coming into the bay. Ships were then not so plenty in those waters as now. He rose, dressed, and went on deck.

The morning was one peculiar to that coast. Everything was mute and calm; everything gray. The sea, though undulated into long roods of swells, seemed fixed, and was sleeked at the surface like waved lead that has cooled and set in the smelter's mold. The sky seemed a gray surtout. Flights of troubled gray fowl, kith and kin with flights of troubled gray vapors among which they were mixed, skimmed low and fitfully over the waters, as swallows over meadows before storms. Shadows present, foreshadowing deeper shadows to come.

To Captain Delano's surprise, the stranger, viewed through the glass, showed no colors, though to do so upon entering a haven, however uninhabited in its shores, where but a single other ship might be lying, was the custom among peaceful seamen of all nations. Considering the lawlessness and loneliness of the spot, and the sort of stories at that day associated with those seas, Captain Delano's surprise might have deepened into some uneasiness had he not been a person of a singularly undistrustful good nature, not liable except on extraordinary and repeated incentives, and hardly then, to indulge in personal alarms any way involving the imputation of malign evil in man. Whether, in view of what humanity is capable, such trait implies, along with a benevolent heart, more than ordinary quickness and accuracy of intellectual perception, may be left to the wise to determine.

But whatever misgivings might have obtruded on first seeing the stranger would almost, in any seaman's mind, have been dissipated by observing that the ship, in navigating into the harbor, was drawing too near the land, a sunken reef making out off her bow. This seemed to prove her a stranger, indeed, not only to the sealer, but the island; consequently she could be no wonted freebooter on that ocean. With no small interest Captain Delano continued to watch her—a proceeding not much facilitated by the vapors partly mantling the hull, through which the far matin light from her cabin streamed equivocally enough; much like the sun—by this time hemisphered on the rim of the horizon, and, apparently, in company with the strange ship entering the harbor—which, wimpled by the same low, creeping clouds, showed not unlike a Lima intrigante's one sinister eye peering across the Plaza from the Indian loophole of her dusk *saya-y-manta*.

It might have been but a deception of the vapors, but the longer the stranger was watched the more singular appeared her maneuvers. Erelong it seemed hard to decide whether she meant to come in or no—what she wanted, or what she was about. The wind, which had breezed up a little during the night, was now extremely light and baffling, which the more increased the apparent uncertainty of her movements.

Surmising at last that it might be a ship in distress, Captain Delano ordered his whaleboat to be dropped, and, much to the wary opposition of his mate, prepared to board her, and, at the least, pilot her in. On the night previous, a fishing party of the seamen had gone a long distance to some detached rocks out of sight from the sealer, and, an hour or two before daybreak, had returned, having set with no small success. Presuming that the stranger might have been long off soundings, the good captain put several baskets of the fish, for presents, into his boat, and so pulled away. From her continuing too near the sunken reef deeming her in danger, calling to his men he made all haste to apprise those on board of their situation. But, some time ere the boat came up, the wind, light though it was, having shifted, had headed the vessel off, as well as partly broken the vapors from about her.

Upon gaining a less remote view, the ship, when made signally visible on the verge of the leaden-hued swells, with the shreds of fog here and there raggedly furring her, appeared like a whitewashed monastery after a thunderstorm, seen perched upon some dun cliff among the Pyrenees. But it was no purely fanciful resemblance which now, for a moment, almost led Captain Delano to think that nothing less than a shipload of monks was before him. Peering over the bulwarks were what really seemed, in the hazy distance, throngs of dark cowls; while, fitfully revealed through the open portholes, other dark moving figures were dimly descried, as of Black Friars pacing the cloisters.

Upon a still nigher approach, this appearance was modified, and the true character of the vessel was plain—a Spanish merchantman of the first class, carrying Negro slaves, amongst other valuable freight, from one colonial port to another. A very large, and in its time, a very fine vessel, such as in those days were at intervals encountered along that main; sometimes superseded Acapulco treasure ships, or retired frigates of the Spanish king's navy, which, like superannuated Italian palaces, still, under a decline of masters, preserved signs of former state.

As the whaleboat drew more and more nigh, the cause of the peculiar pipe-clayed aspect of the stranger was seen in the slovenly neglect pervading her. The spars, ropes, and great part of the bulwarks looked woolly from long unacquaintance with the scraper, tar, and the brush. Her keel seemed laid, her ribs put together, and she launched, from Ezekiel's Valley of Dry Bones.

In the present business in which she was engaged, the ship's general model and rig appeared to have undergone no material change from their original warlike and Froissart pattern. However, no guns were seen.

The tops were large, and were railed about with what had once been octagonal network, all now in sad disrepair. These tops hung overhead like three ruinous aviaries, in one of which was seen perched, on a ratline, a white noddy, a strange fowl so called from its lethargic, somnambulistic character, being frequently caught by hand at sea. Battered and moldy, the castellated forecastle seemed some ancient turret long ago taken by assault, and then left to decay. Toward the stern, two high-raised quarter galleries—the balustrades here and there covered with dry tindery sea moss—opening out from the unoccupied state cabin, whose deadlights, for all the mild weather, were hermetically closed and calked—these tenantless balconies hung over the sea as if it were the grand Venetian canal. But the principal relic of faded grandeur was the ample oval of the shieldlike sternpiece, intricately carved with the arms of Castile and Leon, medallioned about by groups of mythological or symbolical devices, uppermost and central of which was a dark satyr in a mask holding his foot on the prostrate neck of a writhing figure, likewise masked.

Whether the ship had a figurehead, or only a plain beak, was not quite certain, owing to canvas wrapped about that part, either to protect it while undergoing a refurbishing, or else decently to hide its decay. Rudely painted or chalked, as in a sailor freak, along the forward side of a sort of pedestal below the canvas, was the sentence, SEGUID VUESTRO JEFE ('follow your leader'); while upon the tarnished headboards near by appeared, in stately capitals, once gilt, the ship's name *SAN DOMINICK*, each letter streakingly corroded with tricklings of copper-spike rust; while, like mourning weeds, dark festoons of sea grass slimily swept to and fro over the name with every hearselike role of the hull.

As, at last, the boat was hooked from the bow along toward the gangway amidship, its keel, while yet some inches separated from the hull, harshly grated as on a sunken coral reef. It proved a huge bunch of conglobated barnacles adhering below the water to the side like a wen—a token of baffling airs and long calms passed somewhere in those seas.

Climbing the side, the visitor was at once surrounded by a clamorous throng of whites and blacks, but the latter outnumbering the former more than could have been expected, Negro transportation ship as the stranger in port was. But, in one language, and as with one voice, all poured out a common tale of suffering; in which the Negresses, of whom there were not a few, exceeded the others in their dolorous vehemence. The scurvy, together with the fever, had swept off a great part of their number, more especially the Spaniards. Off Cape Horn they had narrowly escaped shipwreck; then, for days together, they had lain tranced without wind; their provisions were low; their water next to none; their lips that moment were baked.

While Captain Delano was thus made the mark of all eager tongues, his one eager glance took in all faces, with every other object about him.

Always upon first boarding a large and populous ship at sea, especially a foreign one, with a nondescript crew such as Lascars or Manila men, the impression varies in a peculiar way from that produced by first entering a strange house with strange inmates in a strange land. Both house and ship—the one by its walls and blinds, the other by its high bulwarks like ramparts—hoard from view their interiors till the last moment, but in the case of the ship there is this addition: that the living spectacle it contains, upon its sudden and complete disclosure, has, in contrast with the blank ocean which zones it, something of the effect of enchantment. The ship seems unreal; these strange costumes, gestures, and faces but a shadowy tableau just emerged from the deep, which directly must receive back what it gave.

Perhaps it was some such influence, as above is attempted to be described, which, in Captain Delano's mind, heightened whatever, upon a staid scrutiny, might have seemed unusual, especially the conspicuous figures of four elderly grizzled Negroes, their heads like black, doddered willow tops, who, in venerable contrast to the tumult below them, were crouched, sphinxlike, one on the starboard cathead, another on the larboard, and the remaining pair face to face on the opposite bulwarks above the mainchains. They each had bits of unstranded old junk in their hands, and, with a sort of stoical self-content, were picking the junk into oakum, a small heap of which lay by their sides. They accompanied the task with a continuous, low monotonous chant, droning and druling away like so many gray-headed bagpipers playing a funeral march.

The quarter-deck rose into an ample elevated poop, upon the forward verge of which, lifted, like the oakum-pickers, some eight feet above the general throng, sat along in a row, separated by regular spaces, the crosslegged figures of six other blacks, each with a rusty hatchet in his hand, which, with a bit of brick and a rag, he was engaged like a scullion in scouring, while between each two was a small stack of hatchets, their rusted edges turned forward awaiting a like operation. Though occasionally the four oakum-pickers would briefly address some person or persons in the crowd below, yet the six hatchet-polishers neither spoke to others nor breathed a whisper among themselves, but sat intent upon their task, except at intervals, when, with the peculiar love in Negroes of uniting industry with pastime, two and two they sideways clashed their hatchets together, like cymbals, with a barbarous din. All six, unlike the generality, had the raw aspect of unsophisticated Africans.

But that first comprehensive glance which took in those ten figures, with scores less conspicuous, rested but an instant upon them, as, impatient of the hubbub of voices, the visitor turned in quest of whomsoever it might be that commanded the ship.

But as if not unwilling to let nature make known her own case among his suffering charge, or else in despair of restraining it for the time, the Spanish captain, a gentlemanly, reserved-looking, and rather young man to a stranger's eye, dressed with singular richness but bearing plain traces of recent sleepless cares and disquietudes, stood passively by, leaning against the mainmast, at one moment casting a dreary, spiritless look upon his excited people, at the next an unhappy glance toward his visitor. By his side stood a black of small stature, in whose rude face, as occasionally, like a shepherd's dog, he mutely turned it up into the Spaniard's, sorrow and affection were equally blended.

Struggling through the throng, the American advanced to the Spaniard, assuring him of his sympathies, and offering to render whatever assistance might be in his power. To which the Spaniard returned for the present but grave and ceremonious acknowledgments, his national formality dusked by the saturnine mood of ill-health.

But losing no time in mere compliments, Captain Delano, returning to the gangway, had his basket of fish brought up, and as the wind still continued light, so that some hours at least must elapse ere the ship could be brought to the anchorage, he bade his men return to the sealer and fetch back as much water as the whaleboat could carry, with whatever soft bread the steward might have, all the remaining pumpkins on board, with a box of sugar and a dozen of his private bottles of cider.

Not many minutes after the boat's pushing off, to the vexation of all, the wind entirely died away, and, the tide turning, began drifting back the ship helplessly seaward. But trusting this would not long last, Captain Delano sought, with good hopes, to cheer up the strangers, feeling no small satisfaction that, with persons in their condition, he could—thanks to his frequent voyages along the Spanish Main—converse with some freedom in their native tongue.

While left alone with them, he was not long in observing some things tending to heighten his first impressions; but surprise was lost in pity, both for the Spaniards and blacks, alike evidently reduced from scarcity of water and provisions, while long-continued suffering seemed to have brought out the less good-natured qualities of the Negroes, besides at the same time impairing the Spaniard's authority over them. But, under the circumstances, precisely this condition of things was to have been anticipated. In armies, navies, cities, or families, in nature herself, nothing more relaxes good order than misery. Still, Captain Delano was not without the idea that had Benito Cereno been a man of greater energy, misrule would hardly have come to the present pass. But the debility, constitutional or induced by hardships bodily and mental, of the Spanish captain was too obvious to be overlooked. A prey to settled dejection, as if long mocked with hope he would not now indulge it even when it had ceased to be a mock, the prospect of that day, or evening at furthest, lying at anchor, with plenty of water for his people, and a brother captain to counsel and befriend, seemed in no perceptible degree to encourage him. His mind appeared unstrung, if not still more seriously affected. Shut up in these oaken walls, chained to one dull round of command whose unconditionality cloyed him, like some hypochondriac abbott he moved slowly about, at times suddenly pausing, starting, or staring, biting his lip, biting his fingernail, flushing, paling, twitching his beard, with other symptoms of an absent or moody mind. This distempered spirit was lodged, as before hinted, in as distempered a frame. He was rather tall, but seemed never to have been robust, and now with nervous suffering was almost worn to a skeleton. A tendency to some pulmonary complaint appeared to have been lately confirmed. His voice was like that of one with lungs half gone—hoarsely suppressed, a husky whisper. No wonder that, as in this state he tottered about, his private servant apprehensively followed him. Sometimes the Negro gave his master his arm, or took his handkerchief out of his pocket for him; performing these and similar offices with that affectionate zeal which transmutes into something filial or fraternal acts in themselves but menial, and which has gained for the Negro the repute of making the most pleasing body servant in the world; one, too, whom a master need be on no stiffly superior terms with, but may treat with familiar trust—less a servant than a devoted companion.

Marking the noisy indocility of the blacks in general, as well as what seemed the sullen inefficiency of the whites, it was not without humane satisfaction that Captain Delano witnessed the steady good conduct of Babo.

But the good conduct of Babo, hardly more than the ill-behavior of others, seemed to withdraw the half-lunatic Don Benito from his cloudy languor. Not that such precisely was the impression made by the Spaniard on the mind of his visitor. The Spaniard's individual unrest was, for the present, but noted as a conspicuous feature in the ship's general affliction. Still, Captain Delano was not a little concerned at what he could not help taking for the time to be Don Benito's unfriendly indifference towards himself. The Spaniard's manner, too, conveyed a sort of sour and gloomy disdain, which he seemed at no pains to disguise. But this the American in charity ascribed to the harassing effects of sickness, since, in former instances, he had noted that there are peculiar natures on whom prolonged physical suffering seems to cancel every social instinct of kindness, as if, forced to black bread themselves, they deemed it but equity that each person coming nigh them should, indirectly, by some slight or affront, be made to partake of their fare.

But erelong Captain Delano bethought him that, indulgent as he was at the first in judging the Spaniard, he might not after all have exercised charity enough. At bottom it was Don Benito's reserve which displeased him, but the same reserve was shown towards all but his faithful personal attendant. Even the formal reports which, according to sea usage, were, at stated times, made to him by some petty underling, either a white, mulatto, or black, he hardly had patience enough to listen to without betraying contemptuous aversion. His manner upon such occasions was, in its degree, not unlike that which might be supposed to have been his imperial countryman's, Charles V, just previous to the anchoritish retirement of that monarch from the throne.

This splenetic disrelish of his place was evinced in almost every function pertaining to it. Proud as he was moody, he condescended to no personal mandate. Whatever special orders were necessary, their delivery was delegated to his body servant, who in turn transferred them to their ultimate destination, through runners, alert Spanish boys or slave boys, like pages or pilot fish within easy call continually hovering round Don Benito. So that to have beheld this undemonstrative invalid gliding about, apathetic and mute, no landsman could have dreamed that in him was lodged a dictatorship beyond which, while at sea, there was no earthly appeal.

Thus the Spaniard, regarded in his reserve, seemed the involuntary victim of mental disorder. But, in fact, his reserve might, in some degree, have proceeded from design. If so, then here was evinced the unhealthy climax of that icy though conscientious policy more or less adopted by all commanders of large ships, which, except in signal emergencies, obliterates alike the manifestation of sway with every trace of sociality, transforming the man into a block or rather into a loaded cannon, which, until there is call for thunder, has nothing to say.

Viewing him in this light, it seemed but a natural token of the perverse habit induced by a long course of such hard self-restraint that, notwithstanding the present condition of his ship, the Spaniard should still persist in a demeanor which, however harmless or, it may be, appropriate, in a well-appointed vessel such as the *San Dominick* might have been at the outset of the voyage, was anything but judicious now. But the Spaniard, perhaps, thought that it was with captains as with gods: reserve, under all events, must still be their cue. But probably this appearance of slumbering dominion might have been but an attempted disguise to conscious imbecility—not deep policy, but shallow device. But be all this as it might, whether Don Benito's manner was designed or not, the more Captain Delano noted its pervading reserve, the less he felt uneasiness at any particular manifestation of that reserve towards himself.

Neither were his thoughts taken up by the captain alone. Wonted to the quiet orderliness of the sealer's comfortable family of a crew, the noisy confusion of the *San Dominick*'s suffering host repeatedly challenged his eye. Some prominent breaches, not only of discipline but of decency, were observed. These Captain Delano could not but ascribe, in the main, to the absence of those subordinate deck officers to whom, along with higher duties, is intrusted what may be styled the police department of a populous ship. True, the old oakum-pickers appeared at times to act the part of monitorial constables to their countrymen, the blacks, but though occasionally succeeding in allaying trifling outbreaks now and then between man and man, they could do little or nothing toward establishing general quiet. The *San Dominick* was in the condition of a transatlantic emigrant ship, among whose multitude of living freight are some individuals, doubtless, as little troublesome as crates and bales, but the friendly remonstrances of such with their ruder companions are of not so much avail as the unfriendly arm of the mate. What the *San Dominick* wanted was, what the emigrant ship has, stern superior officers. But on these decks not so much as a fourth mate was to be seen.

The visitor's curiosity was roused to learn the particulars of those mishaps which had brought about such absenteeism, with its consequences, because, though deriving some inkling of the voyage from the wails which at the first moment had greeted him, yet of the details no clear understanding had been had. The best account would, doubtless, be given by the captain. Yet at first the visitor was loath to ask it, unwilling to provoke some distant rebuff. But, plucking up courage, he at last accosted Don Benito, renewing the expression of his benevolent interest, adding that, did he (Captain Delano) but know the particulars of the ship's misfortunes, he would, perhaps be better able in the end to relieve them. Would Don Benito favor him with the whole story.

Don Benito faltered, then, like some somnambulist suddenly interfered with, vacantly stared at his visitor, and ended by looking down on the deck. He maintained this posture so long that Captain Delano, almost equally disconcerted, and involuntarily almost as rude, turned suddenly from him, walking forward to accost one of the Spanish seamen for the desired information. But he had hardly gone five paces, when, with a sort of eagerness, Don Benito invited him back, regretting his momentary absence of mind, and professing readiness to gratify him.

While most part of the story was being given, the two captains stood on the after part of the main deck, a privileged spot, no one being near but the servant.

'It is now a hundred and ninety days,' began the Spaniard, in his husky whisper, 'that this ship, well officered and well manned, with several cabin passengers–some fifty Spaniards in all–sailed from Buenos Ayres bound to Lima, with a general cargo, hardware, Paraguay tea and the like–and,' pointing forward, 'that parcel of Negroes, now not more than a hundred and fifty, as you see, but then numbering over three hundred souls. Off Cape Horn we had heavy gales. In one moment, by night, three of my best officers, with fifteen sailors, were lost, with the mainyard, the spar snapping under them in the slings as they sought, with heavers, to beat down the icy sail. To lighten the hull, the heavier sacks of maté were thrown into the sea, with most of the water pipes lashed on deck at the time. And this last necessity it was, combined with the prolonged detentions afterwards experienced, which eventually brought about our chief causes of suffering. When–'

Here there was a sudden fainting attack of his cough, brought on, no doubt, by his mental distress. His servant sustained him, and, drawing a cordial from his pocket, placed it to his lips. He a little revived. But, unwilling to leave him unsupported while yet imperfectly restored, the black with one arm still encircled his master, as the same time keeping his eye fixed on his face, as if to watch for the first sign of complete restoration, or relapse, as the event might prove.

The Spaniard proceeded, but brokenly and obscurely, as one in a dream.

–'Oh, my God! rather than pass through what I have, with joy I would have hailed the most terrible gales; but–'

His cough returned and with increased violence; this subsiding, with reddened lips and closed eyes he fell heavily against his supporter.

'His mind wanders. He was thinking of the plague that followed the gales,' plaintively sighed the servant; 'my poor, poor master!' wringing one hand, and with the other wiping the mouth. 'But be patient, *señor*,' again turning to Captain Delano, 'these fits do not last long; master will soon be himself.'

Don Benito reviving, went on; but, as this portion of the story was very brokenly delivered, the substance only will be set down.

It appeared that after the ship had been many days tossed in storms off the Cape, the scurvy broke out, carrying off numbers of the whites and blacks. When at last they had worked round into the Pacific, their spars and sails were so damaged, and so inadequately handled by the surviving mariners, most of whom were become invalids, that, unable to lay her northerly course by the wind, which was powerful, the unmanageable ship for successive days and nights was blown northwestward, where the breeze suddenly deserted her, in unknown waters to sultry calms. The absence of the water pipes now proved as fatal to life as before their presence had menaced it. Induced, or at least aggravated, by the more than scanty allowance of water, a malignant fever followed the scurvy, with the excessive heat of the lengthened calm making such short work of it as to sweep away, as by billows, whole families of the Africans, and a yet larger number, proportionally, of the Spaniards, including, by a luckless fatality, every remaining officer on board. Consequently, in the smart west winds eventually following the calm, the already rent sails, having to be simply dropped, not furled, at need, had been gradually reduced to the beggars' rags they were now. To procure substitutes for his lost sailors, as well as supplies of water and sails, the captain, at the earliest opportunity, had made for Baldivia, the southernmost civilized port of Chile and South America, but upon nearing the coast the thick weather had prevented him from so much as sighting that harbor. Since which period, almost without a crew, and almost without canvas and almost without water, and at intervals giving its added dead to the sea, the *San Dominick* had been battledored about by contrary winds, inveigled by currents, or grown weedy in calms. Like a man lost in woods, more than once she had doubled upon her own track.

'But throughout these calamities,' huskily continued Don Benito, painfully turning in the half-embrace of his servant, 'I have to thank those Negroes you see, who, though to your inexperienced eyes appearing unruly, have, indeed, conducted themselves with less of restlessness than even their owner could have thought possible under such circumstances.'

Here he again fell faintly back. Again his mind wandered, but he rallied, and less obscurely proceeded.

'Yes, their owner was quite right in assuring me that no fetters would be needed with his blacks; so that while, as is wont in his transportation, those Negroes have always remained upon deck–not thrust below, as in the Guineamen–they have, also, from the beginning, been freely permitted to range within given bounds at their pleasure.'

Once more the faintness returned–his mind roved–but, recovering, he resumed:

'But it is Babo here to whom, under God, I owe not only my own preservation, but likewise to him, chiefly, the merit is due of pacifying his more ignorant brethren, when at intervals tempted to murmurings.'

'Ah, master,' sighed the black, bowing his face, 'don't speak of me; Babo is nothing; what Babo has done was but duty.'

'Faithful fellow!' cried Captain Delano. 'Don Benito, I envy you such a friend; slave I cannot call him.'

As master and man stood before him, the black upholding the white,

Captain Delano could not but bethink him of the beauty of that relationship which could present such a spectacle of fidelity on the one hand and confidence on the other. The scene was heightened by the contrast in dress, denoting their relative positions. The Spaniard wore a loose Chile jacket of dark velvet; white smallclothes and stockings, with silver buckles at the knee and instep; a high-crowned sombrero of fine grass; a slender sword, silver mounted, hung from a knot in his sash—the last being an almost invariable adjunct, more for utility than ornament, of a South American gentleman's dress to this hour. Excepting when his occasional nervous contortions brought about disarray, there was a certain precision in his attire curiously at variance with the unsightly disorder around, especially in the belittered ghetto, forward of the mainmast, wholly occupied by the blacks.

The servant wore nothing but wide trousers, apparently, from their coarseness and patches, made out of some old topsail; they were clean, and confined at the waist by a bit of unstranded rope, which, with his composed, deprecatory air at times, made him look something like a begging friar of St Francis.

However unsuitable for the time and place, at least in the blunt-thinking American's eyes, and however strangely surviving in the midst of all his afflictions, the toilette of Don Benito might not, in fashion at least, have gone beyond the style of the day among South Americans of his class. Though on the present voyage sailing from Buenos Ayres, he had avowed himself a native and resident of Chile, whose inhabitants had not so generally adopted the plain coat and once plebeian pantaloons, but, with a becoming modification, adhered to their provincial costume, picturesque as any in the world. Still, relatively to the pale history of the voyage, and his own pale face, there seemed something so incongruous in the Spaniard's apparel as almost to suggest the image of an invalid courtier tottering about London streets in the time of the plague.

The portion of the narrative which perhaps most excited interest, as well as some surprise, considering the latitudes in question, was the long calms spoken of, and more particularly the ship's so long drifting about. Without communicating the opinion, of course, the American could not but impute at least part of the detentions both to clumsy seamanship and faulty navigation. Eying Don Benito's small, yellow hands, he easily inferred that the young captain had not got into command at the hawsehole, but the cabin window; and if so, why wonder at incompetence, in youth, sickness, and gentility united?

But, drowning criticism in compassion, after a fresh repetition of his sympathies, Captain Delano, having heard out his story, not only engaged, as in the first place, to see Don Benito and his people supplied in their immediate bodily needs, but, also now further promised to assist him in procuring a large permanent supply of water, as well as some sails and rigging; and, though it would involve no small embarrassment to himself, yet he would spare three of his best seamen for temporary deck officers, so that without delay the ship might proceed to Conception, there fully to refit for Lima, her destined port.

Such generosity was not without its effect, even upon the invalid. His face lighted up; eager and hectic, he met the honest glance of his visitor. With gratitude he seemed overcome.

'This excitement is bad for master,' whispered the servant, taking his arm, and with soothing words gently drawing him aside.

When Don Benito returned, the American was pained to observe that his hopefulness, like the sudden kindling in his cheek, was but febrile and transient.

Erelong, with a joyless mien, looking up towards the poop, the host invited his guest to accompany him there, for the benefit of what little breath of wind might be stirring.

As, during the telling of the story, Captain Delano had once or twice started at the occasional cymbaling of the hatchet-polishers, wondering why such an interruption should be allowed, especially in that part of the ship, and in the ears of an invalid; and moreover, as the hatchets had anything but an attractive look, and the handlers of them still less so, it was, therefore, to tell the truth, not without some lurking reluctance, or even shrinking, it may be, that Captain Delano, with apparent complaisance, acquiesced in his host's invitation. The more so since, with an untimely caprice of punctilio, rendered distressing by his cadaverous aspect, Don Benito, with Castilian bows, solemnly insisted upon his guest's preceding him up the ladder leading to the elevation, where, one on each side of the last step, sat for armorial supporters and sentries two of the ominous file. Gingerly enough stepped good Captain Delano between them, and in the instant of leaving them behind, like one running the gantlet, he felt an apprehensive twitch in the calves of his legs.

But when, facing about, he saw the whole file, like so many organ-grinders, still stupidly intent on their work, unmindful of everything beside, he could not but smile at his late fidgety panic.

Presently, while standing with his host looking forward upon the decks below, he was struck by one of those instances of insubordination previously alluded to. Three black boys, with two Spanish boys, were sitting together on the hatches, scraping a rude wooden platter in which some scanty mess had recently been cooked. Suddenly one of the black boys, enraged at a word dropped by one of his white companions, seized a knife, and, though called to forbear by one of the oakum-pickers, struck the lad over the head, inflicting a gash from which blood flowed.

In amazement, Captain Delano inquired what this meant. To which the pale Don Benito dully muttered that it was merely the sport of the lad.

'Pretty serious sport, truly,' rejoined Captain Delano. 'Had such a thing happened on board the *Bachelor's Delight*, instant punishment would have followed.'

At these words the Spaniard turned upon the American one of his sudden, staring, half-lunatic looks, then, relapsing into his torpor, answered, 'Doubtless, doubtless, *señor.*'

Is it, thought Captain Delano, that this hapless man is one of those paper captains I've known, who by policy wink at what by power they cannot put down? I know no sadder sight than a commander who has little of command but the name.

'I should think, Don Benito,' he now said, glancing toward the oakum-picker who had sought to interfere with the boys, 'that you would find it advantageous to keep all your blacks employed, especially the younger ones, no matter at what useless task, and no matter what happens to the ship. Why, even with my little band, I find such a course indispensable. I once kept a crew on my quarter-deck thrumming mats for my cabin, when, for three days, I had given up my ship–mats, men, and all–for a speedy loss, owing to the violence of a gale, in which we could do nothing, but helplessly drive before it.'

'Doubtless, doubtless,' muttered Don Benito.

'But,' continued Captain Delano, again glancing upon the oakum-pickers and then at the hatchet-polishers, near by, 'I see you keep some, at least, of your host employed.'

'Yes,' was again the vacant response.

'Those old men there, shaking their pows from their pulpits,' continued Captain Delano, pointing to the oakum-pickers, 'seem to act the part of old dominies to the rest, little heeded as their admonitions are at times. Is this voluntary on their part, Don Benito, or have you appointed them shepherds to your flock of black sheep?'

'What posts they fill, I appointed them,' rejoined the Spaniard, in an acrid tone, as if resenting some supposed satiric reflection.

'And these others, these Ashantee conjurers here,' continued Captain Delano, rather uneasily eying the brandished steel of the hatchet-polishers, where in spots, it had been brought to a shine, 'this seems a curious business they are at, Don Benito?'

'In the gales we met,' answered the Spaniard, 'what of our general cargo was not thrown overboard was much damaged by the brine. Since coming into calm weather, I have had several cases of knives and hatchets daily brought up for overhauling and cleaning.'

'A prudent idea, Don Benito. You are part owner of ship and cargo, I presume; but none of the slaves, perhaps?'

'I am owner of all you see,' impatiently returned Don Benito, 'except the main company of blacks, who belonged to my late friend, Alexandro Aranda.'

As he mentioned this name, his air was heartbroken; his knees shook; his servant supported him.

Thinking he divined the cause of such unusual emotion, to confirm his surmise Captain Delano after a pause said: 'And may I ask, Don Benito, whether–since awhile ago you spoke of some cabin passengers–the friend, whose loss so afflicts you, at the outset of the voyage accompanied his blacks?'

'Yes.'

'But died of the fever?'

'Died of the fever. Oh, could I but–'

Again quivering, the Spaniard paused.

'Pardon me,' said Captain Delano, lowly, 'but I think that, by a sympathetic experience, I conjecture, Don Benito, what it is that gives the keener edge to your grief. It was once my hard fortune to lose, at sea, a dear friend, my own brother, then supercargo. Assured of the welfare of his spirit, its departure I could have borne like a man, but that honest eye, that honest hand–both of which had so often met mine–and that warm heart–all, all–like scraps to the dogs–to throw it all to the sharks! It was then I vowed never to have for fellow voyager a man I loved, unless, unbeknown to him, I had provided requisite in case of a fatality, for embalming his mortal part for interment on shore. Were your friend's remains now on board this ship, Don Benito, not thus strangely would the mention of his name affect you.'

'On board this ship?' echoed the Spaniard. Then with horrified gestures, as directed against some specter, he unconsciously fell into the ready arms of his attendant, who, with a silent appeal toward Captain Delano, seemed beseeching him not again to broach a theme so unspeakably distressing to his master.

This poor fellow now, thought the pained American, is the victim of that sad superstition which associates goblins with the deserted body of man, as ghosts with an abandoned house. How unlike are we made! What to me, in like case, would have been a solemn satisfaction, the bare suggestion, even, terrifies the Spaniard into his trance. Poor Alexandro Aranda! what would you say could you here see your friend–who on former voyages, when you for months were left behind, has, I dare say, often longed and longed for one peep at you–not transported with terror at the least thought of having you anyway nigh him.

At this moment, with a dreary graveyard toll betokening a flaw, the ship's forecastle bell, smote by one of the grizzled oakum-pickers, proclaimed ten o'clock through the leaden calm, when Captain Delano's attention was caught by the moving figure of a gigantic black emerging from the general crowd below and slowly advancing towards the elevated poop. An iron collar was about his neck, from which depended a chain thrice wound round his body, the terminating links padlocked together at a broad band of iron, his girdle.

'How like a mute Atufal moves,' murmured the servant.

The black mounted the steps of the poop, and, like a brave prisoner brought up to receive sentence, stood in unquailing muteness before Don Benito, now recovered from his attack.

At the first glimpse of his approach, Don Benito had started; a resentful shadow swept over his face, and, as with the sudden memory of bootless rage, his white lips glued together.

This is some mulish mutineer, thought Captain Delano, surveying, not without a mixture of admiration, the colossal form of the Negro.

'See, he waits your question, master,' said the servant.

Thus reminded, Don Benito, nervously averting his glance as if shunning, by anticipation, some rebellious response, in a disconcerted voice, thus spoke:

'Atufal, will you ask my pardon now?'

The black was silent.

'Again, master,' murmured the servant, with bitter upbraiding eying his countryman; 'Again, master; he will bend to master yet.'

'Answer,' said Don Benito, still averting his glance, 'say but the one word, *pardon*, and your chains shall be off.'

Upon this, the black, slowly raising both arms, let them lifelessly fall, his links clanking, his head bowed; as much as to say, 'No, I am content.'

'Go,' said Don Benito, with inkept and unknown emotion.

Deliberately as he had come, the black obeyed.

'Excuse me, Don Benito,' said Captain Delano, 'but this scene surprises me; what means it, pray?'

'It means that that Negro alone, of all the band, has given me peculiar cause of offense. I have put him in chains; I–'

Here he paused; his hand to his head, as if there were a swimming there, or a sudden bewilderment of memory had come over him; but meeting his servant's kindly glance seemed reassured, and proceeded:

'I could not scourge such a form. But I told him he must ask my pardon. As yet he has not. At my command, every two hours he stands before me.'

'And how long has this been?'

'Some sixty days.'

'And obedient in all else? And respectful?'

'Yes.'

'Upon my conscience, then,' exclaimed Captain Delano, impulsively, 'he has a royal spirit in him, this fellow.'

'He may have some right to it,' bitterly returned Don Benito, 'he says he was king in his own land.'

'Yes,' said the servant, entering a word, 'those slits in Atufal's ears once held wedges of gold; but poor Babo here, in his own land, was only a poor slave; a black man's slave was Babo, who now is the white's.'

Somewhat annoyed by these conversational familiarities, Captain Delano turned curiously upon the attendant, then glanced inquiringly at his master; but, as if long wonted to these little informalities, neither master nor man seemed to understand him.

'What, pray, was Atufal's offense, Don Benito?' asked Captain Delano; 'if it was not something very serious, take a fool's advice, and, in view of his general docility, as well as in some natural respect for his spirit, remit him his penalty.'

'No, no, master never will do that,' here murmured the servant to himself, 'proud Atufal must first ask master's pardon. The slave there carries the padlock, but master here carries the key.'

His attention thus directed, Captain Delano now noticed for the first time that, suspended by a slender silken cord from Don Benito's neck, hung a key. At once, from the servant's muttered syllables, divining the key's purpose, he smiled and said: 'So, Don Benito—padlock and key—significant symbols, truly.'

Biting his lip, Don Benito faltered.

Though the remark of Captain Delano, a man of such native simplicity as to be incapable of satire or irony, had been dropped in playful allusion to the Spaniard's singularly evidenced lordship over the black, yet the hypochondriac seemed some way to have taken it as a malicious reflection upon his confessed inability thus far to break down, at least on a verbal summons, the entrenched will of the slave. Deploring this supposed misconception, yet despairing of correcting it, Captain Delano shifted the subject; but finding his companion more than ever withdrawn, as if still sourly digesting the lees of the presumed affront above mentioned, by and by Captain Delano likewise became less talkative, oppressed, against his own will, by what seemed the secretive vindictiveness of the morbidly sensitive Spaniard. But the good sailor, himself of a quite contrary disposition, refrained on his part alike from the appearance as from the feeling of resentment, and if silent, was only so from contagion.

Presently the Spaniard, assisted by his servant, somewhat discourteously crossed over from his guest, a procedure which, sensibly enough, might have been allowed to pass for idle caprice of ill-humor had not master and man, lingering round the corner of the elevated skylight, begun whispering together in low voices. This was unpleasing. And more: the moody air of the Spaniard, which at times had not been without a sort of valetudinarian stateliness, now seemed anything but dignified, while the menial familiarity of the servant lost its original charm of simple-hearted attachment.

In his embarrassment, the visitor turned his face to the other side of the ship. By so doing, his glance accidentally fell on a young Spanish sailor, a coil of rope in his hand, just stepped from the deck to the first round of the mizzen rigging. Perhaps the man would not have been particularly noticed were it not that, during his ascent to one of the yards, he, with a sort of covert intentness, kept his eye fixed on Captain Delano, from whom, presently, it passed, as if by a natural sequence, to the two whisperers.

His own attention thus redirected to that quarter, Captain Delano gave a slight start. From something in Don Benito's manner just then, it seemed as if the visitor had, at least partly, been the subject of the withdrawn consultation going on—a conjecture as little agreeable to the guest as it was flattering to the host.

The singular alternations of courtesy and ill-breeding in the Spanish captain were unaccountable, except on one of two suppositions—innocent lunacy, or wicked imposture.

But the first idea, though it might naturally have occurred to an indifferent observer, and, in some respect, had not hitherto been wholly a stranger to Captain Delano's mind, yet, now that, in an incipient way, he began to regard the stranger's conduct something in the light of an intentional affront, of course the idea of lunacy was virtually vacated. But if not a lunatic, what then? Under the circumstances, would a gentleman, nay, any honest boor, act the part now acted by his host? The man was an imposter. Some lowborn adventurer, masquerading as an oceanic grandee, yet so ignorant of the first requisites of mere gentlemanhood as to be betrayed into the present remarkable indecorum. That strange ceremoniousness, too, at other times evinced, seemed not uncharacteristic of one playing a part above his real level. Benito Cereno—Don Benito Cereno—a sounding name. One, too, at that period not unknown, in the surname, to supercargoes and sea captains trading along the Spanish Main, as belonging to one of the most enterprising and extensive mercantile families in all those provinces, several members of it having titles; a sort of Castilian Rothschild, with a noble brother, or cousin, in every great trading town of South America. The alleged Don Benito was in early manhood, about twenty-nine or thirty. To assume a sort of roving cadetship in the maritime affairs of such a house, what more likely scheme for a young knave of talent and spirit? But the Spaniard was a pale invalid. Never mind. For even to the degree of simulating mortal disease, the craft of some tricksters has been known to attain. To think that, under the aspect of infantile weakness, the most savage energies might be couched—those velvets of the Spaniard but the silky paw to his fangs.

From no train of thought did these fancies come; not from within, but from without; suddenly, too, and in one throng, like hoarfrost, yet as soon to vanish, as the mild sun of Captain Delano's good nature regained its meridian.

Glancing over once more towards his host—whose side face, revealed above the skylight, was now turned towards him—he was struck by the profile, whose clearness of cut was refined by the thinness incident to ill-health, as well as ennobled about the chin by the beard. Away with suspicion. He was a true offshoot of a true hidalgo Cereno.

Relieved by these and other better thoughts, the visitor, lightly humming a tune, now began indifferently pacing the poop, so as not to betray to Don Benito that he had at all mistrusted incivility, much less duplicity; for such mistrust would yet be proved illusory, and by the event, though, for the present, the circumstance which had provoked that distrust remained unexplained. But when that little mystery should have been cleared up, Captain Delano thought he might extremely regret it did he allow Don Benito to become aware that he had indulged in ungenerous surmises. In short, to the Spaniard's black-letter text, it was best, for a while, to leave open margin.

Presently, his pale face twitching and overcast, the Spaniard still supported by his attendant, moved over towards his guest, when, with even more than his usual embarrassment, and a strange sort of intriguing intonation in his whisper, the following conversation began:

'*Señor*, may I ask how long you have lain at this isle?'

'Oh, but a day or two, Don Benito.'

'And from what port are you last?'

'Canton.'

'And there, *señor*, you exchanged your sealskins for teas and silks, I think you said?'

'Yes. Silks, mostly.'

'And the balance you took in specie, perhaps?'

Captain Delano, fidgeting a little, answered, 'Yes; some silver; not a very great deal, though.'

'Ah—well. May I ask how many men have you, *senor*?'

Captain Delano slightly started, but answered, 'About five-and-twenty, all told.'

'And at present, *señor*, all on board, I suppose?'

'All on board, Don Benito,' replied the Captain, now with satisfaction.

'And will be tonight, *señor*?'

At this last question, following so many pertinacious ones, for the soul of him Captain Delano could not but look very earnestly at the questioner, who, instead of meeting the glance, with every token of craven discomposure dropped his eyes to the deck; presenting an unworthy contrast to his servant, who, just then, was kneeling at his feet, adjusting a loose shoe buckle, his disengaged face meantime, with humble curiosity, turned openly up into his master's downcast one.

The Spaniard, still with a guilty shuffle, repeated his question:

'And—will be tonight, *señor*?'

'Yes, for aught I know,' returned Captain Delano—'But nay,' rallying himself into fearless truth, 'some of them talked of going off on another fishing party about midnight.'

'Your ships generally go—go more or less armed, I believe, *señor*?'

'Oh, a six-pounder or two, in case of emergency,' was the intrepidly indifferent reply, 'with a small stock of muskets, sealing spears, and cutlasses, you know.'

As he thus responded, Captain Delano again glanced at Don Benito, but the latter's eyes were averted, while, abruptly and awkwardly shifting the subject, he made some peevish allusion to the calm, and then, without apology, once more, with his attendant, withdrew to the opposite bulwarks, where the whispering was resumed.

At this moment, and ere Captain Delano could cast a cool thought upon what had just passed, the young Spanish sailor before mentioned was seen descending from the rigging. In act of stooping over to spring inboard to the deck, his voluminous, unconfined frock, or shirt, of coarse woolen, much spotted with tar, opened out far down the chest, revealing a soiled under-garment of what seemed the finest linen, edged, about the neck, with a narrow blue ribbon, sadly faded and worn. At this moment the young sailor's eye was again fixed on the whisperers, and Captain Delano thought he observed a lurking significance in it, as if silent signs, of some Freemason sort, had that instant been interchanged.

This once more impelled his own glance in the direction of Don Benito, and, as before, he could not but infer that himself formed the subject of the conference. He paused. The sound of the hatchet polishing fell on his ears. He cast another swift side look at the two. They had the air of conspirators. In connection with the late questionings, and the incident of the young sailor, these things now begat such return of involuntary suspicion that the singular guilelessness of the American could not endure it. Plucking up a gay and humorous expression, he crossed over to the two rapidly, saying: 'Ha, Don Benito, your black here seems high in your trust, a sort of privy councilor, in fact.'

Upon this, the servant looked up with a good-natured grin, but the master started as from a venomous bite. It was a moment or two before the Spaniard sufficiently recovered himself to reply; which he did, at last, with cold constraint: 'Yes, *señor*, I have trust in Babo.'

Here Babo, changing his previous grin of mere animal humor into an intelligent smile, not ungratefully eyed his master.

Finding that the Spaniard now stood silent and reserved, as if involuntarily, or purposely giving hint that his guest's proximity was inconvenient just then, Captain Delano, unwilling to appear uncivil even to incivility itself, made some trivial remark and moved off, again and again turning over in his mind the mysterious demeanor of Don Benito Cereno.

He had descended from the poop, and, wrapped in thought, was passing near a dark hatchway leading down into the steerage, when, perceiving motion there, he looked to see what moved. The same instant there was a sparkle in the shadowy hatchway and he saw one of the Spanish sailors, prowling there, hurriedly placing his hand in the bosom of his frock, as if hiding something. Before the man could have been certain who it was that was passing, he slunk below out of sight. But enough was seen of him to make it sure that he was the same young sailor before noticed in the rigging.

What was that which so sparkled? thought Captain Delano. It was no lamp—no match—no live coal. Could it have been a jewel? But how come sailors with jewels?—or with silk-trimmed undershirts either? Has he been robbing the trunks of the dead cabin passengers? But if so he would hardly wear one of the stolen articles on board ship here. Ah, ah—if, now, that was indeed, a secret sign I saw passing between this suspicious fellow and his captain awhile since; if I could only be certain that, in my uneasiness, my senses did not deceive me, then—

Here, passing from one suspicious thing to another, his mind revolved the strange questions put to him concerning his ship.

By a curious coincidence, as each point was recalled, the black wizards of Ashantee would strike up with their hatchets, as in ominous comment on the white stranger's thoughts. Pressed by such enigmas and portents, it would have been almost against nature had not, even into the least distrustful heart, some ugly misgivings obtruded.

Observing the ship, now helplessly fallen into a current, with enchanted sails drifting with increased rapidity seaward, and noting that, from a lately intercepted projection of the land, the sealer was hidden, the stout mariner began to quake at thoughts which he barely durst confess to himself. Above all, he began to feel a ghostly dread of Don Benito. And yet, when he roused himself, dilated his chest, felt himself strong on his legs, and coolly considered it—what did all these phantoms amount to?

Had the Spaniard any sinister scheme, it must have reference not so much to him (Captain Delano) as to his ship (the *Bachelor's Delight*). Hence the present drifting away of the one ship from the other, instead of favoring any such possible scheme, was, for the time at least, opposed to it. Clearly any suspicion combining such contradictions must need be delusive. Beside, was it not absurd to think of a vessel in distress—a vessel by sickness almost dismanned of her crew—a vessel whose inmates were parched for water—was it not a thousand times absurd that such a craft should, at present, be of a piratical character; or her commander, either for himself or those under him, cherish any desire but for speedy relief and refreshment? But, then, might not general distress, and thirst in particular, be affected? And might not that same undiminished Spanish crew, alleged to have perished off to a remnant, be at that very moment lurking in the hold? On heart-broken pretense of entreating a cup of cold water, fiends in human form had got into lonely dwellings, nor retired until a dark deed had been done.

And among the Malay pirates it was no unusual thing to lure ships after them into their treacherous harbors, or entice boarders from a declared enemy at sea, by the spectacle of thinly manned or vacant decks, beneath which prowled a hundred spears with yellow arms ready to upthrust them through the mats. Not that Captain Delano had entirely credited such things. He had heard of them—and now, as stories, they recurred. The present destination of the ship was the anchorage. There she would be near his own vessel. Upon gaining that vicinity, might not the *San Dominick*, like a slumbering volcano, suddenly let loose energies now hid?

He recalled the Spaniard's manner while telling his story. There was a gloomy hesitancy and subterfuge about it. It was just the manner of one making up his tale for evil purposes, as he goes. But if that story was not true, what was the truth? That the ship had unlawfully come into the Spaniard's possession? But in many of its details, especially in reference to the more calamitous parts, such as the fatalities among the seamen, the consequent prolonged beating about, the past sufferings from obstinate calms and still continued suffering from thirst; in all these points, as well as others, Don Benito's story had corroborated not only the wailing ejaculations of the indiscriminate multitude, white and black, but likewise—what seemed impossible to be counterfeit—by the very expression and play of every human feature which Captain Delano saw. If Don Benito's story was throughout an invention, then every soul on board, down to the youngest Negress, was his carefully drilled recruit in the plot: an incredible inference. And yet, if there was ground for mistrusting his veracity, that inference was a legitimate one.

But those questions of the Spaniard. There, indeed, one might pause. Did they not seem put with much the same object with which the burglar or assassin, by daytime, reconnoiters the walls of a house? But, with ill purposes to solicit such information openly of the chief person endangered, and so, in effect, setting him on his guard—how unlikely a procedure was that? Absurd, then, to suppose that those questions had been prompted by evil designs. Thus, the same conduct which in this instance had raised the alarm, served to dispel it. In short, scarce any suspicion or uneasiness, however apparently reasonable at the time, which was not now with equal apparent reason dismissed.

At last he began to laugh at his former forebodings, and laugh at the strange ship for, in its aspect, someway siding with them, as it were; and laugh, too, at the odd-looking blacks, particularly those old scissors-grinders, the Ashantees; and those bed-ridden old knitting women, the oakum-pickers; and almost at the dark Spaniard himself, the central hobgoblin of all.

For the rest, whatever in a serious way seemed enigmatical was now good-naturedly explained away by the thought that, for the most part, the poor invalid scarcely knew what he was about; either sulking in black vapors, or putting idle questions without sense or object. Evidently, for the present the man was not fit to be intrusted with the ship. On some benevolent plea withdrawing the command from him, Captain Delano would yet have to send her to Conception, in charge of his second mate, a worthy person and good navigator—a plan not more convenient for the *San Dominick* than for Don Benito; for, relieved from all anxiety, keeping wholly to his cabin, the sick man, under the good nursing of his servant, would, probably, by the end of the passage, be in a measure restored to health, and with that he should also be restored to authority.

Such were the American's thoughts. They were tranquilizing. There was a difference between the idea of Don Benito's darkly preordaining Captain Delano's fate and Captain Delano's lightly arranging Don Benito's. Nevertheless, it was not without something of relief that the good seaman presently perceived his whaleboat in the distance. Its absence had been prolonged by unexpected detention at the sealer's side, as well as its returning trip lengthened by the continual recession of the goal.

The advancing speck was observed by the blacks. Their shouts attracted the attention of Don Benito, who, with a return of courtesy approaching Captain Delano, expressed satisfaction at the coming of some supplies, slight and temporary as they must necessarily prove.

Captain Delano responded, but while doing so, his attention was drawn to something passing on the deck below: among the crowd climbing the landward bulwarks, anxiously watching the coming boat, two blacks, to all appearances accidentally incommoded by one of the sailors, violently pushed him aside, which the sailor someway resenting, they dashed him to the deck, despite the earnest cries of the oakum-pickers.

'Don Benito,' said Captain Delano quickly, 'do you see what is going on here? Look!'

But, seized by his cough, the Spaniard staggered, with both hands to his face, on the point of falling. Captain Delano would have supported him, but the servant was more alert, who, with one hand sustaining his master, with the other applied the cordial. Don Benito restored, the black withdrew his support, slipping aside a little, but dutifully remaining within call of a whisper. Such discretion was here evinced as quite wiped away, in the visitor's eyes, any blemish of impropriety which might have attached to the attendant from the indecorous conferences before mentioned, showing, too, that if the servant were to blame it might be more the master's fault than his own, since, when left to himself, he could conduct thus well.

His glance called away from the spectacle of disorder to the more pleasing one before him, Captain Delano could not avoid again congratulating his host upon possessing such a servant, who, though perhaps a little too forward now and then, must upon the whole be invaluable to one in the invalid's situation.

'Tell me, Don Benito,' he added, with a smile—'I should like to have your man here myself—what will you take for him? Would fifty doubloons be any object?'

'Master wouldn't part with Babo for a thousand doubloons,' murmured the black, overhearing the offer and taking it in earnest, and, with the strange vanity of a faithful slave appreciated by his master, scorning to hear so paltry a valuation put upon him by a stranger. But Don Benito, apparently hardly yet completely restored, and again interrupted by his cough, made but some broken reply.

Soon his physical distress became so great, affecting his mind, too, apparently, that, as if to screen the sad spectacle, the servant gently conducted his master below.

Left to himself, the American, to while away the time till his boat should arrive, would have pleasantly accosted some one of the few Spanish seamen he saw, but recalling something that Don Benito had said touching their ill conduct, he refrained, as a shipmaster indisposed to countenance cowardice or unfaithfulness in seamen.

While, with these thoughts, standing with eye directed forward towards that handful of sailors, suddenly he thought that one or two of them returned the glance and with a sort of meaning. He rubbed his eyes and looked again, but again seemed to see the same thing. Under a new form, but more obscure than any previous one, the old suspicions recurred, but, in the absence of Don Benito, with less of panic than before. Despite the bad account given of the sailors, Captain Delano resolved forthwith to accost one of them. Descending the poop, he made his way through the blacks, his movement drawing a queer cry from the oakum-pickers, prompted by whom, the Negroes, twitching each other aside, divided before him, but, as if curious to see what was the object of his deliberate visit to their ghetto, closing in behind in tolerable order, followed the white stranger up. His progress thus proclaimed as by mounted kings-at-arms, and escorted as by a Kaffir guard of honor, Captain Delano, assuming a good-humored, offhanded air, continued to advance; now and then saying a blithe word to the Negroes, and his eye curiously surveying the white faces, here and there sparsely mixed in with the blacks, like stray white pawns venturously involved in the ranks of the chessmen opposed.

While thinking which of them to select for his purpose, he chanced to observe a sailor seated on the deck engaged in tarring the strap of a large block, a circle of blacks squatted round him inquisitively eying the process.

The mean employment of the man was in contrast with something superior in his figure. His hand, black with continually thrusting it into the tarpot held for him by a Negro, seemed not naturally allied to his race, a face which would have been a very fine one but for its haggardness. Whether this haggardness had aught to do with criminality could not be determined, since, as intense heat and cold, though unlike, produce like sensations, so innocence and guilt, when, through casual association with mental pain stamping any visible impress, use one seal—a hacked one.

Not again that this reflection occurred to Captain Delano at the time, charitable man as he was. Rather another idea. Because observing so singular a haggardness combined with a dark eye, averted as in trouble and shame, and then again recalling Don Benito's confessed ill opinion of his crew, insensible, he was operated upon by certain general notions which, while disconnecting pain and abashment from virtue, invariably link them with vice.

If, indeed, there be any wickedness on board this ship, thought Captain Delano, be sure that man there has fouled his hand in it, even as now he fouls it in the pitch. I don't like to accost him. I will speak to this other, this old Jack here on the windlass.

He advanced to an old Barcelona tar, in ragged red breeches and dirty nightcap, cheeks trenched and bronzed, whiskers dense as thorn hedges. Seated between two sleepy-looking Africans, this mariner, like his younger shipmate, was employed upon some rigging—splicing a cable—the sleepy-looking blacks performing the inferior function of holding the outer parts of the ropes for him.

Upon Captain Delano's approach, the man at once hung his head below its previous level; the one necessary for business. It appeared as if he desired to be thought absorbed with more than common fidelity in his task. Being addressed, he glanced up, but with what seemed a furtive, diffident air, which sat strangely enough on his weather-beaten visage, much as if a grizzly bear, instead of growling and biting, should simper and cast sheep's eyes. He was asked several questions concerning the voyage—questions purposely referring to several particulars in Don Benito's narrative, not previously corroborated by those impulsive cries greeting the visitor on first coming on board. The questions were briefly answered, confirming all that remained to be confirmed of the story. The Negroes about the windlass joined in with the old sailor, but, as they became talkative, he by degrees became mute, and at length quite glum, seemed morosely unwilling to answer more questions, and yet, all the while, this ursine air was somehow mixed with his sheepish one.

Despairing of getting into unembarrassed talk with such a centaur, Captain Delano, after glancing round for a more promising countenance but seeing none, spoke pleasantly to the blacks to make way for him, and so, amid various grins and grimaces, returned to the poop, feeling a little strange at first, he could hardly tell why, but upon the whole with regained confidence in Benito Cereno.

How plainly, thought he, did that old whiskerando yonder betray a consciousness of ill desert. No doubt when he saw me coming he dreaded lest

I, apprised by his captain of the crew's general misbehavior, came with sharp words for him, and so down with his head. And yet—and yet, now that I think of it, that very old fellow, if I err not, was one of those who seemed so earnestly eying me here awhile since. Ah, these currents spin one's head round almost as much as they do the ship. Ha, there now's a pleasant sort of sunny sight; quite sociable, too.

His attention had been drawn to a slumbering Negress, partly disclosed through the lacework of some rigging, lying, with youthful limbs carelessly disposed, under the lee of the bulwarks, like a doe in the shade of a woodland rock. Sprawling at her lapped breasts was her wide-awake fawn, stark naked, its black little body half lifted from the deck, crosswise with its dam's; its hands, like two paws, clambering upon her; its mouth and nose ineffectually rooting to get at the mark; and meantime giving a vexatious half-grunt, blending with the composed snore of the Negress.

The uncommon vigor of the child at length roused the mother. She started up, at a distance racing Captain Delano. But as if not at all concerned at the attitude in which she had been caught, delightedly she caught the child up, with maternal transports, covering it with kisses.

There's naked nature, now, pure tenderness and love, thought Captain Delano, well pleased.

This incident prompted him to remark the other Negresses more particularly than before. He was gratified with their manners: like most uncivilized women, they seemed at once tender of heart and tough of constitution, equally ready to die for their infants or fight for them. Unsophisticated as leopardesses, loving as doves. Ah! thought Captain Delano, these, perhaps, are some of the very women whom Ledyard saw in Africa, and gave such a noble account of.

These natural sights somehow insensibly deepened his confidence and ease. At last he looked to see how his boat was getting on, but it was still pretty remote. He turned to see if Don Benito had returned, but he had not.

To change the scene, as well as to please himself with a leisurely observation of the coming boat, stepping over into the mizzen-chains, he clambered his way into the starboard quarter-gallery—one of those abandoned Venetian-looking water balconies previously mentioned—retreats cut off from the deck. As his foot pressed the half-damp, half-dry sea mosses matting the place, and a chance phantom cat's-paw—an islet of breeze, unheralded, unfollowed—as this ghostly cat's-paw came fanning his cheek; as his glance fell upon the row of small, round deadlights—all closed liked coppered eyes of the coffined—and the state-cabin door, one connecting with the gallery, even as the deadlights had once looked out upon it, but now calked fast like a sarcophagus lid; and to a purple-black, tarred-over, panel, threshold, and post; and he bethought him of the time when that state cabin and this state balcony had heard the voices of the Spanish king's officers, and the forms of the Lima viceroy's daughters had perhaps leaned where he stood—as these and other images flitted through his mind as the cat's-paw through the calm, gradually he felt rising a dreamy inquietude, like that of one who alone on the prairie feels unrest from the repose of the noon.

He leaned against the carved balustrade, again looking off toward his boat, but found his eye falling upon the ribbon grass, trailing along the ship's water line, straight as a border of green box, and parterres of seaweed, broad ovals and crescents, floating nigh and far, with what seemed long formal alleys between, crossing the terraces of swells, and sweeping round as if leading to the grottoes below. And overhanging all was the balustrade by his arm, which, partly stained with pitch and partly embossed with moss, seemed the charred ruin of some summerhouse in a grand garden long running to waste.

Trying to break one charm, he was but becharmed anew. Though upon the wide sea, he seemed in some far inland country, prisoner in some deserted château, left to stare at empty grounds and peer out at vague roads where never wagon or wayfarer passed.

But these enchantments were a little disenchanted as his eye fell on the corroded mainchains. Of an ancient style, massy and rusty in link, shackle and bolt, they seemed even more fit for the ship's present business than the one for which she had been built.

Presently he thought something moved nigh the chains. He rubbed his eyes, and looked hard. Groves of rigging were about the chains; and there, peering from behind a great stay, like an Indian from behind a hemlock, a Spanish sailor, a marlinespike in his hand, was seen, who made what seemed an imperfect gesture towards the balcony, but immediately, as if alarmed by some advancing step along the deck within, vanished into the recesses of the hempen forest like a poacher.

What meant this? Something the man had sought to communicate, unbeknown to anyone, even to his captain. Did the secret involve aught unfavorable to his captain? Were those previous misgivings of Captain Delano's about to be verified? Or, in his haunted mood at the moment, had some random, unintentional motion of the man, while busy with the stay as if repairing it, been mistaken for a significant beckoning?

Not unbewildered, again he gazed off for his boat. But it was temporarily hidden by a rocky spur of the isle. As with some eagerness he bent forward, watching for the first shooting view of its beak, the balustrade gave way before him like charcoal. Had he not clutched an outreaching rope he would have fallen into the sea. The crash, though feeble, and the fall, though hollow, of rotten fragments, must have been overheard. He glanced up. With sober curiosity peering down upon him was one of the old oakum-pickers, slipped from his perch to an outside boom, while below the old Negro, and, invisible to him, reconnoitering from a porthole like a fox from the mouth of its den, crouched the Spanish sailor again. From something suddenly suggested by the man's air, the mad idea now darted into Captain Delano's mind that Don Benito's plea of indisposition, in withdrawing below, was but a pretense: that he was engaged there maturing his plot, of which the sailor, by some means gaining an inkling had a mind to warn the stranger against, incited, it may be, by gratitude for a kind word on first boarding the ship. Was it from foreseeing some possible interference like this that Don Benito had, beforehand, given such a bad character of his sailors, while praising the Negroes, though, indeed, the former seemed as docile as the latter the contrary? The whites, too, by nature, were the shrewder race. A man with some evil design, would he not be likely to speak well of that stupidity which was blind to his depravity, and malign that intelligence from which it might not be hidden? Not unlikely, perhaps. But if the whites had dark secrets concerning Don Benito, could then Don Benito be any way in complicity with the blacks? But they were too stupid. Besides, who ever heard of a white so far a renegade as to apostatize from his very species almost, by leaguing in against it with Negroes? These difficulties recalled former ones. Lost in their mazes, Captain Delano, who had now regained the deck, was uneasily advancing along it when he observed a new face; an aged sailor seated crosslegged near the main hatchway. His skin was shrunk up with wrinkles like a pelican's empty pouch, his hair frosted, his countenance grave and composed. His hands were full of ropes, which he was working into a large knot. Some blacks were about him obligingly dipping the strands for him, here and there, as the exigencies of the operation demanded.

Captain Delano crossed over to him and stood in silence surveying the knot, his mind, by a not uncongenial transition, passing from its own entanglements to those of the hemp. For intricacy, such a knot he had never seen in an American ship, nor indeed any other. The old man looked like an Egyptian priest making Gordian knots for the temple of Ammon. The knot seemed a combination of double-bowline-knot, treble-crown-knot, back-handed-well-knot, knot-in-and-out-knot and jamming knot.

At last, puzzled to comprehend the meaning of such a knot, Captain Delano addressed the knotter: 'What are you knotting there, my man?'

'The knot,' was the brief reply, without looking up.

'So it seems; but what is it for?'

'For someone else to undo,' muttered back the old man, plying his fingers harder than ever, the knot being now nearly completed.

While Captain Delano stood watching him, suddenly the old man threw the knot towards him, saying in broken English—the first heard in the ship—something to this effect: 'Undo it, cut it, quick.' It was said lowly, but with such condensation of rapidity, that the long, slow words in Spanish, which had preceded and followed, almost operated as covers to the brief English between.

For a moment, knot in hand, and knot in head, Captain Delano stood mute, while, without further heeding him, the old man was now intent upon other ropes. Presently there was a slight stir behind Captain Delano. Turning, he saw the chained Negro, Atufal, standing quietly there. The next moment the old sailor rose, muttering, and, followed by his subordinate Negroes, removed to the forward part of the ship, where in the crowd he disappeared.

An elderly Negro, in a clout like an infant's, and with a pepper-and-salt head and a kind of attorney air, now approached Captain Delano. In tolerable Spanish, and with a good-natured, knowing wink, he informed him that the old knotter was simple-witted, but harmless, often playing his odd tricks. The Negro concluded by begging the knot, for of course the stranger would not care to be troubled with it. Unconsciously, it was handed to him. With a sort of *congé*, the Negro received it, and, turning his back, ferreted into it like a detective custom-house officer after smuggled laces. Soon, with some African words equivalent to pshaw, he tossed the knot overboard.

All this is very queer, thought Captain Delano, with a qualmish sort of emotion; but, as one feeling incipient seasickness, he strove, by ignoring the symptoms, to get rid of the malady. Once more he looked off for his boat. To his delight, it was now again in view, leaving the rocky spur astern.

The sensation here experienced, after at first relieving his uneasiness, with unforeseen efficacy soon began to remove it. The less distant sight of that well-known boat—showing it, not as before, half blended with the haze but with outline defined, so that its individuality, like a man's, was manifest; that boat, *Rover* by name, which, though now in strange seas, had often pressed the beach of Captain Delano's home, and, brought to its threshold for repairs, had familiarly lain there, as a Newfoundland dog; the sight of that household boat evoked a thousand trustful associations, which, contrasted with previous suspicions, filled him not only with lightsome confidence, but somehow with half humorous self-reproaches at his former lack of it.

'What, I, Amasa Delano—Jack of the Beach, as they called me when a lad—I, Amasa, the same that, duck-satchel in hand, used to paddle along the waterside to the schoolhouse made from the old hulk—I, little Jack of the Beach, that used to go berrying with cousin Nat and the rest—I to be murdered here at the ends of the earth on board a haunted pirate ship by a horrible Spaniard? Too nonsensical to think of! Who would murder Amasa Delano? His conscience is clean. There is someone above. Fie, fie, Jack of the Beach! you are a child indeed; a child of the second childhood, old boy; you are beginning to dote and drool, I'm afraid.'

Light of heart and foot, he stepped aft, and there was met by Don Benito's servant, who, with a pleasing expression responsive to his own present feelings, informed him that his master had recovered from the effects of his coughing fit, and had just ordered him to go present his compliments to his good guest, Don Amasa, and say that he (Don Benito) would soon have the happiness to rejoin him.

There now, do you mark that? again thought Captain Delano, walking the poop. What a donkey I was. This kind gentleman who here sends me his kind compliments, he, but ten minutes ago, dark-lantern in hand, was dodging round some old grindstone in the hold, sharpening a hatchet for me, I thought. Well, well; these long calms have a morbid effect on the mind, I've often heard, though I never believed it before. Ha! glancing towards the boat, there's *Rover*, a good dog, a white bone in her mouth. A pretty big bone though, seems to me.–What? Yes, she has fallen afoul of the bubbling tide rip there. It sets her the other way, too, for the time. Patience.

It was now about noon, though, from the grayness of everything, it seemed to be getting towards dusk.

The calm was confirmed. In the far distance, away from the influence of land, the leaden ocean seemed laid out and leaded up, its course finished, soul gone, defunct. But the current from landward, where the ship was, increased, silently sweeping her further and further towards the tranced waters beyond.

Still, from his knowledge of those latitudes, cherishing hopes of a breeze, and a fair and fresh one, at any moment, Captain Delano, despite present prospects, buoyantly counted upon bringing the *San Dominick* safely to anchor ere night. The distance swept over was nothing, since, with a good wind, ten minutes' sailing would retrace more than sixty minutes' drifting. Meantime, one moment turning to mark *Rover* fighting the tide rip and the next to see Don Benito approaching, he continued walking the poop.

Gradually he felt a vexation arising from the delay of his boat; this soon merged into uneasiness, and at last–his eye falling continually, as from a stage box into the pit, upon the strange crowd before and below him, and by and by recognizing there the face, now composed to indifference, of the Spanish sailor who had seemed to beckon from the mainchains–something of his old trepidations returned.

Ah, thought he, gravely enough, this is like the ague: because it went off, it follows not that it won't come back.

Though ashamed of the relapse, he could not altogether subdue it; and so, exerting his good nature to the utmost, insensibly he came to a compromise.

Yes, this is a strange craft, a strange history, too, and strange folks on board. But–nothing more.

By way of keeping his mind out of mischief till the boat should arrive, he tried to occupy it with turning over and over, in a purely speculative sort of way, some lesser peculiarities of the captain and crew. Among others, four curious points recurred:

First, the affair of the Spanish lad assailed with a knife by the slave boy; an act winked at by Don Benito. Second the tyranny in Don Benito's treatment of Atufal, the black, as if a child should lead a bull of the Nile by the ring in his nose. Third, the trampling of the sailor by the two Negroes, a piece of insolence passed over without so much as a reprimand. Fourth, the cringing submission to their master of all the ship's underlings, mostly blacks, as if by the least inadvertence they feared to draw down his despotic displeasure.

Coupling these points, they seemed somewhat contradictory. But what then, thought Captain Delano, glancing towards his now nearing boat—what then? Why, Don Benito is a very capricious commander. But he is not the first of the sort I have seen, though it's true he rather exceeds any other. But as a nation—continued he in his reveries—these Spaniards are all an odd set; the very word Spaniard has a curious, conspirator, Guy-Fawkish twang to it. And yet I dare say Spaniards in the main are as good folks as any in Duxbury, Massachusetts. Ah good! At last *Rover* has come.

As, with its welcome freight, the boat touched the side, the oakum-pickers, with venerable gestures, sought to restrain the blacks, who, at the sight of three gurried water casks in its bottom and a pile of wilted pumpkins in its bow, hung over the bulwarks in disorderly raptures.

Don Benito, with his servant, now appeared, his coming, perhaps, hastened by hearing the noise. Of him Captain Delano sought permission to serve out the water, so that all might share alike, and none injure themselves by unfair excess. But sensible, and, on Don Benito's account, kind as this offer was, it was received with what seemed impatience; as if aware that he lacked energy as a commander, Don Benito, with the true jealousy of weakness, resented as an affront any interference. So, at least, Captain Delano inferred.

In another moment the casks were being hoisted in, when some of the eager Negroes accidentally jostled Captain Delano where he stood by the gangway, so that, unmindful of Don Benito, yielding to the impulse of the moment, with good-natured authority he bade the black stand back, to enforce his words making use of a half-mirthful, half-menacing gesture. Instantly the blacks paused, just where they were, each Negro and Negress suspended in his or her posture, exactly as the word had found them—for a few seconds continuing so—while, as between the responsive posts of a telegraph, an unknown syllable ran from man to man among the perched oakum-pickers. While the visitor's attention was fixed by this scene, suddenly the hatchet-polishers half rose, and a rapid cry came from Don Benito.

Thinking that at the signal of the Spaniard he was about to be massacred, Captain Delano would have sprung for his boat, but paused, as the oakum-pickers, dropping down into the crowd with earnest exclamations, forced every white and every Negro back, at the same moment, with gestures friendly and familiar, almost jocose, bidding him, in substance, not be a fool. Simultaneously the hatchet-polishers resumed their seats, quietly as so many tailors, and at once, as if nothing had happened, the work of hoisting the casks was resumed, white and blacks singing at the tackle.

Captain Delano glanced towards Don Benito. As he saw his meager form in the act of recovering itself from reclining in the servant's arms, into which the agitated invalid had fallen, he could not but marvel at the panic by which himself had been surprised, on the darting supposition that such a commander, who, upon a legitimate occasion, so trivial too, as it now appeared, could lose all self-command, was, with energetic iniquity, going to bring about his murder.

The casks being on deck, Captain Delano was handed a number of jars and cups by one of the steward's aids, who, in the name of his captain, entreated him to do as he had proposed—dole out the water. He complied, with republican impartiality as to this republican element, which always seeks one level, serving the oldest white no better than the youngest black, excepting, indeed, poor Don Benito, whose condition, if not rank, demanded an extra allowance. To him, in the first place, Captain Delano presented a fair pitcher of the fluid, but, thirsting as he was for it, the Spaniard quaffed not a drop until after several grave bows and salutes, a reciprocation of courtesies which the sight-loving Africans hailed with clapping of hands.

Two of the less wilted pumpkins being reserved for the cabin table, the residue were minced up on the spot for the general regalement. But the soft bread, sugar, and bottled cider Captain Delano would have given the whites alone, and in chief Don Benito, but the latter objected; which disinterestedness not a little pleased the American; and so mouthfuls all around were given alike to whites and blacks, excepting one bottle of cider, which Babo insisted upon setting aside for his master.

Here it may be observed that as, on the first visit of the boat, the American had not permitted his men to board the ship, neither did he now, being unwilling to add to the confusion of the decks.

Not uninfluenced by the peculiar good humor at present prevailing, and for the time oblivious of any but benevolent thought, Captain Delano, who from recent indications counted upon a breeze within an hour or two at furthest, dispatched the boat back to the sealer, with orders for all the hands that could be spared immediately to set about rafting casks to the watering place and filling them. Likewise he bade word be carried to his chief officer that if against present expectation, the ship was not brought to anchor by sunset, he need be under no concern; for as there was to be a full moon that night, he (Captain Delano) would remain on board ready to play the pilot, come the wind soon or late.

As the two Captains stood together observing the departing boat—the servant, as it happened, having just spied a spot on his master's velvet sleeve, and silently engaged rubbing it out—the American expressed his regrets that the *San Dominick* had no boats, none, at least, but the unseaworthy old hulk of the longboat, which, warped as a camel's skeleton in the desert and almost as bleached, lay pot-wise inverted amidships, one side a little tipped, furnishing a subterraneous sort of den for family groups of the blacks, mostly women and small children, who, squatting on old mats below, or perched above in the dark dome on the elevated seats, were descried, some distance within, like a social circle of bats sheltering in some friendly cave, at intervals, ebon flights of naked boys and girls three or four years old darting in and out of the den's mouth.

'Had you three or four boats now, Don Benito,' said Captain Delano, 'I think that, by tugging at the oars, your Negroes here might help along matters some. Did you sail from port without boats, Don Benito?'

'They were stove in the gales, *señor*.'

'That was bad. Many men, too, you lost then. Boats and men. Those must have been hard gales, Don Benito.'

'Past all speech,' cringed the Spaniard.

'Tell me, Don Benito,' continued his companion with increased interest, 'tell me, were these gales immediately off the pitch of Cape Horn?'

'Cape Horn?—who spoke of Cape Horn?'

'Yourself did, when giving me an account of your voyage,' answered Captain Delano, with almost equal astonishment at this eating of his own words, even as he ever seemed eating his own heart, on the part of the Spaniard. 'You yourself, Don Benito, spoke of Cape Horn,' he emphatically repeated.

The Spaniard turned, in a sort of stooping posture, pausing an instant as one about to make a plunging exchange of elements, as from air to water.

At this moment a messenger boy, a white, hurried by, in the regular performance of his function carrying the last expired half-hour forward to the forecastle from the cabin timepiece, to have it struck at the ship's large bell.

'Master,' said the servant, discontinuing his work on the coat sleeve and addressing the rapt Spaniard with a sort of timid apprehensiveness, as one charged with a duty the discharge of which, it was foreseen, would prove irksome to the very person who had imposed it and for whose benefit it was intended, 'master told me never mind where he was, or how engaged, always to remind him, to a minute, when shaving-time comes. Miguel has gone to strike the half-hour afternoon. It is *now*, master. Will master go into the cuddy?'

'Ah—yes,' answered the Spaniard, starting, as from dreams into realities, then, turning upon Captain Delano, he said that erelong he would resume the conversation.

'Then if master means to talk more to Don Amasa,' said the servant, 'why not let Don Amasa sit by master in the cuddy, and master can talk, and Don Amasa can listen, while Babo here lathers and strops.'

'Yes,' said Captain Delano, not unpleased with this sociable plan, 'yes, Don Benito, unless you had rather not, I will go with you.'

'Be it so, *señor*.'

As the three passed aft, the American could not but think it another strange instance of his host's capriciousness, this being shaved with such uncommon punctuality in the middle of the day. But he deemed it more than likely that the servant's anxious fidelity had something to do with the matter, inasmuch as the timely interruption served to rally his master from the mood which had evidently been coming upon him.

The place called the cuddy was a light deck cabin formed by the poop, a sort of attic to the large cabin below. Part of it had formerly been the quarters of the officers, but since their death all the partitionings had been thrown down and the whole interior converted into one spacious and airy marine hall; for absence of fine furniture and picturesque disarray of odd appurtenances, somewhat answering to the wide, cluttered hall of some eccentric bachelor squire in the country, who hangs his shooting jacket and tobacco pouch on deer antlers, and keeps his fishing rod, tongs, and walking stick in the same corner.

The similitude was heightened, if not originally suggested, by glimpses of the surrounding sea, since, in one aspect, the country and the ocean seem cousins-german.

The floor of the cuddy was matted. Overhead, four or five old muskets were stuck into horizontal holes along the beams. On one side was a claw-footed old table lashed to the deck, a thumbed missal on it, and over it, a small, meager crucifix attached to the bulkhead. Under the table lay a dented cutlass or two with a hacked harpoon, among some melancholy old rigging, like a heap of poor friars' girdles. There were also two long, sharp-ribbed settees of Malacca cane, black with age, and uncomfortable to look at as inquisitors' racks, with a large, misshapen armchair, which, furnished with a rude barber's crotch at the back, working with a screw, seemed some grotesque engine of torment. A flag locker was in one corner, open, exposing various colored buntings, some rolled up, others half unrolled, still others tumbled. Opposite was a cumbrous washstand of black mahogany, all of one block, with a pedestal like a font, and over it a railed shelf, containing combs, brushes, and other implements of the toilet. A torn hammock of stained grass swung near, the sheets tossed, and the pillow wrinkled up like a brow, as if whoever slept here slept but illy, with alternate visitations of sad thoughts and bad dreams.

The further extremity of the cuddy, overhanging the ship's stern, was pierced with three openings, windows or portholes, according as men or cannon might peer, socially or unsocially, out of them. At present neither men nor cannon were seen, though huge ringbolts and other rusty iron fixtures of the woodwork hinted of twenty-four-pounders.

Glancing towards the hammock as he entered, Captain Delano said, 'You sleep here, Don Benito?'

'Yes, *señor*, since we got into mild weather.'

'This seems a sort of dormitory, sitting room, sail loft, chapel, armory, and private closet all together, Don Benito,' added Captain Delano, looking round.

'Yes, *señor*; events have not been favorable to much order in my arrangements.'

Here the servant, napkin on arm, made a motion as if waiting his master's good pleasure. Don Benito signified his readiness, when, seating him at the Malacca armchair, and for the guest's convenience drawing opposite one of the settees, the servant commenced operations by throwing back his master's collar and loosening his cravat.

There is something in the Negro which, in a peculiar way, fits him for avocations about one's person. Most Negroes are natural valets and hairdressers, taking to the comb and brush congenially as to the castinets, and flourishing them apparently with almost equal satisfaction. There is, too, a smooth tact about them in this employment with a marvelous, noiseless, gliding briskness, not ungraceful in its way, singularly pleasing to behold, and still more so to be the manipulated subject of. And above all is the great gift of good humor. Not the mere grin or laugh is here meant. Those were unsuitable. But a certain easy cheerfulness, harmonious in every glance and gesture, as though God had set the whole Negro to some pleasant tune.

When to this is added the docility arising from the unaspiring contentment of a limited mind, and that susceptibility of blind attachment sometimes inhering in indisputable inferiors, one readily perceives why those hypochondriacs, Johnson and Byron—it may be, something like the hypochondriac Benito Cereno—took to their hearts, almost to the exclusion of the entire white race, their servingmen, the Negroes, Barber and Fletcher. But if there be that in the Negro which exempts him from the inflicted sourness of the morbid or cynical mind, how, in his most prepossessing aspects, must he appear to a benevolent one? When at ease with respect to exterior things, Captain Delano's nature was not only benign, but familiarly and humorously so. At home, he had often taken rare satisfaction in sitting in his door, watching some free man of color at his work or play. If on a voyage he chanced to have a black sailor, invariably he was on chatty and half-gamesome terms with him. In fact, like most men of a good, blithe heart, Captain Delano took to Negroes, not philanthropically, but genially, just as other men to Newfoundland dogs.

Hitherto, the circumstances in which he found the *San Dominick* had repressed the tendency. But in the cuddy, relieved from his former uneasiness, and, for various reasons, more sociably inclined than at any previous period of the day, and seeing the colored servant, napkin on arm, so debonair about his master, in a business so familiar as that of shaving too, all his old weakness for Negroes returned.

Among other things, he was amused with an odd instance of the African love of bright colors and fine shows, in the black's informally taking from the flag locker a great piece of bunting of all hues and lavishly tucking it under his master's chin for an apron.

The mode of shaving among the Spaniards is a little different from what it is with other nations. They have a basin, specifically called a barber's basin, which on one side is scooped out, so as accurately to receive the chin, against which it is closely held in lathering, which is done, not with a brush, but with soap dipped in the water of the basin and rubbed on the face.

In the present instance salt water was used for lack of better, and the parts lathered were only the upper lip and low down under the throat, all the rest being cultivated beard.

The preliminaries being somewhat novel to Captain Delano, he sat curiously eying them, so that no conversation took place, nor, for the present, did Don Benito appear disposed to renew any.

Setting down his basin, the Negro searched among the razors, as for the sharpest, and having found it, gave it an additional edge by expertly stropping it on the firm smooth, oily skin of his open palm; he then made a gesture as if to begin, but midway stood suspended for an instant, one hand elevating the razor, the other professionally dabbling among the bubbling suds on the Spaniard's lank neck. Not unaffected by the close sight of the gleaming steel, Don Benito nervously shuddered; his usual ghastliness was heightened by the lather, which lather, again, was intensified in its hue by the contrasting sootiness of the Negro's body. Altogether the scene was somewhat peculiar, at least to Captain Delano, nor, as he saw the two thus postured, could he resist the vagary that in the black he saw a headsman, and in the white a man at the block. But this was one of those antic conceits, appearing and vanishing in a breath, from which, perhaps, the best-regulated mind is not always free.

Meantime the agitation of the Spaniard had a little loosened the bunting from around him, so that one broad fold swept curtainlike over the chair arm to the floor, revealing, amid a profusion of armorial bars and ground color—black, blue, and yellow—a closed castle in a blood-red field diagonal with a lion rampant in a white.

'The castle and the lion,' exclaimed Captain Delano—'why, Don Benito, this is the flag of Spain you use here. It's well it's only I, and not the King, that sees this,' he added, with a smile, 'but'—turning towards the black—'it's all one, I suppose, so the colors be gay'; which playful remark did not fail somewhat to tickle the Negro.

'Now, master,' he said, readjusting the flag, and pressing the head gently further back into the crotch of the chair, 'now, master,' and the steel glanced nigh the throat.

Again Don Benito faintly shuddered.

'You must not shake so, master. See, Don Amasa, master always shakes when I shave him. And yet master knows I never yet have drawn blood, though it's true if master will shake so I may some of these times. Now master,' he continued. 'And now, Don Amasa, please go on with your talk about the gale, and all that; master can hear, and, between times, master can answer.'

'Ah yes, these gales,' said Captain Delano; 'but the more I think of your voyage, Don Benito, the more I wonder, not at the gales, terrible as they must have been, but at the disastrous interval following them. For here, by your account, have you been these two months and more getting from Cape Horn to St Maria, a distance which I myself with a good wind, have sailed in a few days. True, you had calms, and long ones, but to be becalmed for two months, that is, at least, unusual. Why, Don Benito, had almost any other gentleman told me such a story, I should have been disposed to a little incredulity.'

Here an involuntary expression came over the Spaniard, similar to that just before on the deck, and whether it was the start he gave, or a sudden gawky roll of the hull in the calm, or a momentary unsteadiness of the servant's hand, however it was, just then the razor drew blood, spots of which stained the creamy lather under the throat; immediately the black barber drew back his steel, and, remaining in his professional attitude, back to Captain Delano, and face to Don Benito, held up the trickling razor, saying, with a sort of half humorous sorrow, 'See, master–you shook so–here's Babo's first blood.'

No sword drawn before James the First of England, no assassination in that timid king's presence, could have produced a more terrified aspect than was now presented by Don Benito.

Poor fellow, thought Captain Delano, so nervous he can't even bear the sight of barber's blood; and this unstrung, sick man, is it credible that I should have imagined he meant to spill all my blood, who can't endure the sight of one little drop of his own? Surely, Amasa Delano, you have been beside yourself this day. Tell it not when you get home, sappy Amasa. Well, well, he looks like a murderer, doesn't he? More like as if himself were to be done for. Well, well, this day's experience shall be a good lesson.

Meantime, while these things were running through the honest seaman's mind, the servant had taken the napkin from his arm, and to Don Benito had said–'But answer Don Amasa, please, master, while I wipe this ugly stuff off the razor, and strop it again.'

As he said the words, his face was turned half round, so as to be alike visible to the Spaniard and the American, and seemed, by its expression, to hint that he was desirous, by getting his master to go on with the conversation, considerately to withdraw his attention from the recent annoying accident. As if glad to snatch the offered relief, Don Benito resumed, rehearsing to Captain Delano that, not only were the calms of unusual duration, but the ship had fallen in with obstinate currents, and other things he added, some of which were but repetitions of former statements, to explain how it came to pass that the passage from Cape Horn to St Maria had been so exceedingly long, now and then mingling with his words incidental praises, less qualified than before, to the blacks, for their general good conduct. These particulars were not given consecutively, the servant, at convenient times, using his razor, and so, between the intervals of shaving, the story and panegyric went on with more than usual huskiness.

To Captain Delano's imagination, now again not wholly at rest, there was something so hollow in the Spaniard's manner, with apparently some reciprocal hollowness in the servant's dusky comment of silence, that the idea flashed across him that possibly master and man, for some unknown purpose were acting out, both in word and deed, nay, to the very tremor of Don Benito's limbs, some juggling play before him. Neither did the suspicion of collusion lack apparent support, from the fact of those whispered conferences before mentioned. But then, what could be the object of enacting this play of the barber before him? At last, regarding the notion as a whimsey, insensibly suggested, perhaps, by the theatrical aspect of Don Benito in his harlequin ensign, Captain Delano speedily banished it.

The shaving over, the servant bestirred himself with a small bottle of scented waters, pouring a few drops on the head, and then diligently rubbing, the vehemence of the exercise causing the muscles of his face to twitch rather strangely.

His next operation was with comb, scissors, and brush, going round and round, smoothing a curl here, clipping an unruly whisker hair there, giving a graceful sweep to the temple lock, with other impromptu touches evincing the hand of a master, while, like any resigned gentleman in barber's hands, Don Benito bore all much less uneasily, at least, than he had done the razoring; indeed, he sat so pale and rigid now that the Negro seemed a Nubian sculptor finishing off a white statue head.

All being over at last, the standard of Spain removed, tumbled up, and tossed back into the flag locker, the Negro's warm breath blowing away any stray hair which might have lodged down his master's neck, collar and cravat readjusted, a speck of lint whisked off the velvet lapel—all this being done, backing off a little space, and pausing with an expression of subdued self-complacency, the servant for a moment surveyed his master, as, in toilette at least, the creature of his own tasteful hands.

Captain Delano playfully complimented him upon his achievement, at the same time congratulating Don Benito.

But neither sweet waters, nor shampooing, nor fidelity, nor sociality, delighted the Spaniard. Seeing him relapsing into forbidding gloom, and still remaining seated, Captain Delano, thinking that his presence was undesired just then, withdrew, on pretense of seeing whether, as he had prophesied, any signs of a breeze were visible.

Walking forward to the mainmast, he stood awhile thinking over the scene, and not without some undefined misgivings, when he heard a noise near the cuddy, and turning, saw the Negro, his hand to his cheek. Advancing, Captain Delano perceived that the cheek was bleeding. He was about to ask the cause, when the Negro's wailing soliloquy enlightened him.

'Ah, when will master get better from his sickness; only the sour heart that sour sickness breeds made him serve Babo so, cutting Babo with the razor because, only by accident, Babo had given master one little scratch, and for the first time in so many a day, too. Ah, ah, ah,' holding his hand to his face.

Is it possible, thought Captain Delano; was it to wreak in private his Spanish spite against this poor friend of his that Don Benito, by his sullen manner, impelled me to withdraw? Ah this slavery breeds ugly passions in man.–Poor fellow!

He was about to speak in sympathy to the Negro, but with a timid reluctance he now re-entered the cuddy.

Presently master and man came forth, Don Benito leaning on his servant as if nothing had happened.

But a sort of love quarrel, after all, thought Captain Delano.

He accosted Don Benito, and they slowly walked together. They had gone but a few paces, when the steward–a tall, rajah-looking mulatto, Orientally set off with a pagoda turban formed by three or four Madras handkerchiefs wound about his head, tier on tier–approaching with a salaam, announced lunch in the cabin.

On their way thither, the two captains were preceded by the mulatto, who, turning round as he advanced, with continual smiles and bows, ushered them on, a display of elegance which quite completed the insignificance of the small bareheaded Babo, who, as if not unconscious of inferiority, eyed askance the graceful steward. But, in part, Captain Delano imputed his jealous watchfulness to that peculiar feeling which the full-blooded African entertains for the adulterated one. As for the steward, his manner, if not bespeaking much dignity of self-respect, yet evidenced his extreme desire to please, which is doubly meritorious, as at once Christian and Chesterfieldian.

Captain Delano observed with interest that while the complexion of the mulatto was hybrid, his physiognomy was European–classically so.

'Don Benito,' whispered he, 'I am glad to see this usher-of-the-golden-rod of yours; the sight refutes an ugly remark once made to me by a Barbados planter, that when a mulatto has a regular European face, look out for him; he is a devil. But see, your steward here has features more regular than King George's of England, and yet there he nods, and bows, and smiles, a king, indeed—the king of kind hearts and polite fellows. What a pleasant voice he has, too.'

'He has, *señor.*'

'But tell me, has he not, so far as you have known him, always proved a good, worthy fellow?' said Captain Delano, pausing, while with a final genuflexion the steward disappeared into the cabin; 'come, for the reason just mentioned, I am curious to know.'

'Francesco is a good man,' a sort of sluggishly responded Don Benito, like a phlegmatic appreciator, who would neither find fault nor flatter.

'Ah, I thought so. For it were strange indeed, and not very creditable to us whiteskins, if a little of our blood mixed with the African's should, far from improving the latter's quality, have the sad effect of pouring vitriolic acid into black broth—improving the hue, perhaps, but not the wholesomeness.'

'Doubtless, doubtless, *señor,* but'—glancing at Babo—'not to speak of Negroes, your planter's remark I have heard applied to the Spanish and Indian intermixtures in our provinces. But I know nothing about the matter,' he listlessly added.

And here they entered the cabin.

The lunch was a frugal one. Some of Captain Delano's fresh fish and pumpkins, biscuit and salt beef, the reserved bottle of cider, and the *San Dominick's* last bottle of Canary.

As they entered, Francesco, with two or three colored aids, was hovering over the table giving the last adjustments. Upon perceiving their master they withdrew, Francesco making a smiling *congé,* and the Spaniard, without condescending to notice it, fastidiously remarking to his companion that he relished not superfluous attendance.

Without companions, host and guest sat down, like a childless married couple, at opposite ends of the table, Don Benito waving Captain Delano to his place, and, weak as he was, insisting upon that gentleman being seated before himself.

The Negro placed a rug under Don Benito's feet, and a cushion behind his back, and then stood behind, not his master's chair, but Captain Delano's. At first, this a little surprised the latter. But it was soon evident that, in taking his position, the black was still true to his master, since by facing him he could the more readily anticipate his slightest want.

'This is an uncommonly intelligent fellow of yours, Don Benito,' whispered Captain Delano across the table.

'You say true, *señor.*'

During the repast, the guest again reverted to parts of Don Benito's story, begging further particulars here and there. He inquired how it was that the scurvy and fever should have committed such wholesale havoc upon the whites, while destroying less than half of the blacks. As if this question reproduced the whole scene of plague before the Spaniard's eyes, miserably reminding him of his solitude in a cabin where before he had had so many friends and officers round him, his hand shook, his face became hueless, broken words escaped; but directly the same memory of the past seemed replaced by insane terrors of the present. With starting eyes he stared before him at vacancy. For nothing was to be seen but the hand of his servant pushing the Canary over towards him. At length a few sips served partially to restore him. He made random reference to the different constitution of races, enabling one to offer more resistance to certain maladies than another. The thought was new to his companion.

Presently Captain Delano, intending to say something to his host concerning the pecuniary part of the business he had undertaken for him, especially—since he was strictly accountable to his owners—with reference to the new suit of sails, and other things of that sort, and naturally preferring to conduct such affairs in private, was desirous that the servant should withdraw, imagining that Don Benito for a few minutes could dispense with his attendance. He, however, waited awhile, thinking that, as the conversation proceeded, Don Benito, without being prompted, would perceive the propriety of the step.

But it was otherwise. At last catching his host's eye, Captain Delano, with a slight backward gesture of his thumb, whispered, 'Don Benito, pardon me, but there is an interference with the full expression of what I have to say to you.'

Upon this the Spaniard changed countenance, which was imputed to his resenting the hint, as in some way a reflection upon his servant. After a moment's pause, he assured his guest that the black's remaining with them could be of no disservice; because since losing his officers he had made Babo (whose original office, it now appeared, had been captain of the slaves) not only his constant attendant and companion, but in all things his confidant.

After this, nothing more could be said; though indeed Captain Delano could hardly avoid some little tinge of irritation upon being left ungratified in so inconsiderable a wish, by one, too, for whom he intended such solid services. But it is only his querulousness, thought he, and so, filling his glass, he proceeded to business.

The price of the sails and other matters was fixed upon. But while this was being done, the American observed that, though his original offer of assistance had been hailed with hectic animation, yet now when it was reduced to a business transaction, indifference and apathy were betrayed. Don Benito, in fact, appeared to submit to hearing the details more out of regard to common propriety than from any impression that weighty benefit to himself and his voyage was involved.

Soon his manner became still more reserved. The effort was vain to seek to draw him into social talk. Gnawed by his splenetic mood, he sat twitching his beard, while to little purpose the hand of his servant, mute as that on the wall, slowly pushed over the Canary.

Lunch being over, they sat down on the cushioned transom, the servant placing a pillow behind his master. The long continuance of the calm had now affected the atmosphere. Don Benito sighed heavily, as if for breath.

'Why not adjourn to the cuddy,' said Captain Delano; 'there is more air there.' But the host sat silent and motionless.

Meantime his servant knelt before him with a large fan of feathers. And Francesco, coming in on tiptoes, handed the Negro a little cup of aromatic waters, with which at intervals he chafed his master's brow, smoothing the hair along the temples as a nurse does a child's. He spoke no word. He only rested his eye on his master's as if, amid all Don Benito's distress, a little to refresh his spirit by the silent sight of fidelity.

Presently the ship's bell sounded two o'clock, and through the cabin windows a slight rippling of the sea was discerned, and from the desired direction.

'There,' exclaimed Captain Delano, 'I told you so, Don Benito, look!'

He had risen to his feet, speaking in a very animated tone, with a view the more to rouse his companion. But though the crimson curtain of the stern window near him that moment fluttered against his pale cheek, Don Benito seemed to have even less welcome for the breeze than the calm.

Poor fellow, thought Captain Delano, bitter experience has taught him that one ripple does not make a wind, any more than one swallow a summer. But he is mistaken for once. I will get his ship in for him, and prove it.

Briefly alluding to his weak condition, he urged his host to remain quietly where he was, since he (Captain Delano) would with pleasure take upon himself the responsibility of making the best use of the wind.

Upon gaining the deck, Captain Delano started at the unexpected figure of Atufal, monumentally fixed at the threshold, like one of those sculptured porters of black marble guarding the porches of Egyptian tombs.

But this time the start was, perhaps, purely physical. Atufal's presence, singularly attesting docility even in sullenness, was contrasted with that of the hatchet-polishers, who in patience evinced their industry; while both spectacles showed that, lax as Don Benito's general authority might be, still, whenever he chose to exert it, no man so savage or colossal but must, more or less, bow.

Snatching a trumpet which hung from the bulwarks, with a free step Captain Delano advanced to the forward edge of the poop, issuing his orders in his best Spanish. The few sailors and many Negroes, all equally pleased, obediently set about heading the ship towards the harbor.

While giving some directions about setting a lower stunsail, suddenly

Captain Delano heard a voice faithfully repeating his orders. Turning, he saw Babo, now for the time acting, under the pilot, his original part of captain of the slaves. This assistance proved valuable. Tattered sails and warped yards were soon brought into some trim. And no brace or halyard was pulled but to the blithe songs of the inspirited Negroes.

Good fellows, thought Captain Delano, a little training would make fine sailors of them. Why see, the very women pull and sing too. These must be some of those Ashantee Negresses that make such capital soldiers, I've heard. But who's at the helm? I must have a good hand there.

He went to see.

The *San Dominick* steered with a cumbrous tiller, with large horizontal pulleys attached. At each pulley end stood a subordinate black, and between them, at the tillerhead, the responsible post, a Spanish seaman, whose countenance evinced his due share in the general hopefulness and confidence at the coming of the breeze.

He proved the same man who had behaved with so shamefaced an air on the windlass.

'Ah–it is you, my man,' exclaimed Captain Delano–'well, no more sheep's-eyes now; look straight forward and keep the ship so. Good hand, I trust? And want to get into the harbor, don't you?'

The man assented with an inward chuckle, grasping the tillerhead firmly. Upon this, unperceived by the American, the two blacks eyed the sailor intently.

Finding all right at the helm, the pilot went forward to the forecastle to see how matters stood there.

The ship now had way enough to breast the current. With the approach of evening, the breeze would be sure to freshen.

Having done all that was needed for the present, Captain Delano, giving his last orders to the sailors, turned aft to report affairs to Don Benito in the cabin, perhaps additionally incited to rejoin him by the hope of snatching a moment's private chat while the servant was engaged upon deck.

From opposite sides, there were, beneath the poop, two approaches to the cabin, one further forward than the other, and consequently communicating with a longer passage. Marking the servant still above, Captain Delano, taking the nighest entrance–the one last named, and at whose porch Atufal still stood–hurried on his way, till, arrived at the cabin threshold, he paused an instant, a little to recover from his eagerness. Then, with the words of his intended business upon his lips, he entered. As he advanced toward the seated Spaniard, he heard another footstep, keeping time with his. From the opposite door, a salver in hand, the servant was likewise advancing.

'Confound the faithful fellow,' thought Captain Delano; 'what a vexatious coincidence.'

Possibly the vexation might have been something different, were it not for the brisk confidence inspired by the breeze. But even as it was he felt a slight twinge, from a sudden indefinite association in his mind of Babo with Atufal.

'Don Benito,' said he, 'I give you joy; the breeze will hold, and will increase. By the way, your tall man and timepiece, Atufal, stands without. By your order, of course?'

Don Benito recoiled, as if at some bland satirical touch delivered with such adroit garnish of apparent good breeding as to present no handle for retort.

He is like one flayed alive, thought Captain Delano; where may one touch him without causing a shrink.

The servant moved before his master, adjusting a cushion; recalled to civility, the Spaniard stiffly replied: 'You are right. The slave appears where you saw him, according to my command, which is that if at the given hour I am below he must take his stand and abide my coming.'

'Ah now, pardon me, but that is treating the poor fellow like an ex-king indeed. Ah, Don Benito,' smiling, 'for all the license you permit in some things, I fear lest, at bottom, you are a bitter hard master.'

Again Don Benito shrank, and this time, as the good sailor thought, from a genuine twinge of his conscience.

Again conversation became constrained. In vain Captain Delano called attention to the now perceptible motion of the keel gently cleaving the sea; with lackluster eye, Don Benito returned words few and reserved.

By and by, the wind having steadily risen, and still blowing right into the harbor, bore the *San Dominick* swiftly on. Rounding a point of land, the sealer at distance came into open view.

Meantime Captain Delano had again repaired to the deck, remaining there some time. Having at last altered the ship's course so as to give the reef a wide berth, he returned for a few moments below.

I will cheer up my poor friend this time, thought he.

'Better and better, Don Benito,' he cried as he blithely re-entered: 'there will soon be an end to your cares, at least for a while. For when, after a long, sad voyage, you know, the anchor drops into the haven, all its vast weight seems lifted from the captain's heart. We are getting on famously, Don Benito. My ship is in sight. Look through this side light here; there she is, all a-taunt-o! *The Bachelor's Delight*, my good friend. Ah, how this wind braces one up. Come, you must take a cup of coffee with me this evening. My old steward will give you as fine a cup as ever any sultan tasted. What say you, Don Benito, will you?'

At first, the Spaniard glanced feverishly up, casting a longing look towards the sealer, while, with mute concern his servant gazed into his face. Suddenly the old ague of coldness returned, and dropping back to his cushions he was silent.

'You do not answer. Come, all day you have been my host; would you have hospitality all on one side?'

'I cannot go,' was the response.

'What? it will not fatigue you. The ships will lie together as near as they can without swinging foul. It will be little more than stepping from deck to deck, which is but as from room to room. Come, come, you must not refuse me.'

'I cannot go,' decisively and repulsively repeated Don Benito.

Renouncing all but the last appearance of courtesy, with a sort of cadaverous sullenness, and biting his thin nails to the quick, he glanced, almost glared, at his guest, as if impatient that a stranger's presence should interfere with the full indulgence of his morbid hour. Meantime the sound of the parted waters came more and more gurglingly and merrily in at the windows; as reproaching him for his dark spleen, as telling him that, sulk as he might, and go mad with it, nature eared not a jot, since whose fault was it, pray?

But the foul mood was now at its depth, as the fair wind at its height.

There was something in the man so far beyond any mere unsociality or sourness previously evinced that even the forbearing good nature of his guest could no longer endure it. Wholly at a loss to account for such demeanor, and deeming sickness with eccentricity, however extreme, no adequate excuse, well satisfied, too, that nothing in his own conduct could justify it, Captain Delano's pride began to be roused. Himself became reserved. But all seemed one to the Spaniard. Quitting him, therefore, Captain Delano once more went to the deck.

The ship was now within less than two miles of the sealer. The whaleboat was seen darting over the interval.

To be brief, the two vessels, thanks to the pilot's skill, erelong in neighborly style lay anchored together.

Before returning to his own vessel, Captain Delano had intended communicating to Don Benito the smaller details of the proposed services to be rendered. But as it was, unwilling anew to subject himself to rebuffs, he resolved, now that he had seen the *San Dominick* safely moored, immediately to quit her, without further allusion to hospitality or business. Indefinitely postponing his ulterior plans, he would regulate his future actions according to future circumstances. His boat was ready to receive him; but his host still tarried below. Well, thought Captain Delano, if he has little breeding, the more need to show mine. He descended to the cabin to bid a ceremonious, and, it may be, tacitly rebukeful adieu. But to his great satisfaction, Don Benito, as if he began to feel the weight of that treatment with which his slighted guest had, not indecorously, retaliated upon him, now, supported by his servant, rose to his feet, and grasping Captain Delano's hand, stood tremulous, too much agitated to speak. But the good augury hence drawn was suddenly dashed by his resuming all his previous reserve with augmented gloom, as, with half-averted eyes, he silently reseated himself on his cushions. With a corresponding return of his own chilled feelings, Captain Delano bowed and withdrew.

He was hardly midway in the narrow corridor, dim as a tunnel, leading from the cabin to the stairs, when a sound, as of the tolling for execution in some jailyard, fell on his ears. It was the echo of the ship's flawed bell striking the hour, drearily reverberated in this subterranean vault. Instantly, by a fatality not to be withstood, his mind, responsive to the portent, swarmed with superstitious suspicions. He paused. In images far swifter than these sentences, the minutest details of all his former distrusts swept through him.

Hitherto, credulous good nature had been too ready to furnish excuses for reasonable fears. Why was the Spaniard, so superfluously punctilious at times, now heedless of common propriety in not accompanying to the side his departing guest? Did indisposition forbid? Indisposition had not forbidden more irksome exertion that day. His last equivocal demeanor recurred. He had risen to his feet, grasped his guest's hand, motioned toward his hat; then, in an instant, all was eclipsed in sinister muteness and gloom. Did this imply one brief repentant relenting at the final moment from some iniquitous plot, followed by remorseless return to it? His last glance seemed to express a calamitous yet acquiescent farewell to Captain Delano forever. Why decline the invitation to visit the sealer that evening? Or was the Spaniard less hardened than the Jew, who refrained not from supping at the board of him whom the same night he meant to betray? What imported all those daylong enigmas and contradictions, except they were intended to mystify, preliminary to some stealthy blow? Atufal, the pretended rebel but punctual shadow, that moment lurked by the threshold without. He seemed a sentry, and more. Who, by his own confession had stationed him there? Was the Negro now lying in wait?

The Spaniard behind—his creature before: to rush from darkness to light was the involuntary choice.

The next moment, with clenched jaw and hand, he passed Atufal, and stood unharmed in the light. As he saw his trim ship lying peacefully at anchor and almost within ordinary call; as he saw his household boat, with familiar faces in it, patiently rising and falling on the short waves by the *San Dominick's* side; and then, glancing about the decks where he stood, saw the oakum-pickers still gravely plying their fingers, and heard the low, buzzing whistle and industrious hum of the hatchet-polishers still bestirring themselves over their endless occupation; and more than all, as he saw the benign aspect of nature taking her innocent repose in the evening, the screened sun in the quiet camp of the west shining out like the mild light from Abraham's tent—as charmed eye and ear took in all these, with the chained figure of the black, clenched jaw and hand relaxed. Once again he smiled at the phantoms which had mocked him, and felt something like a tinge of remorse that, by harboring them even for a moment, he should by implication have betrayed an atheist doubt of the ever-watchful Providence above.

There was a few minutes' delay, while, in obedience to his orders, the boat was being hooked along to the gangway. During this interval, a sort of saddened satisfaction stole over Captain Delano at thinking of the kindly offices he had that day discharged for a stranger. Ah, thought he, after good actions one's conscience is never ungrateful, however much so the benefited party may be.

Presently his foot, in the first act of descent into the boat, pressed the first round of the side ladder, his face presented inward upon the deck. In the same moment he heard his name courteously sounded, and, to his pleased surprise, saw Don Benito advancing—an unwonted energy in his air, as if, at the last moment, intent upon making amends for his recent discourtesy. With instinctive good feeling, Captain Delano, withdrawing his foot, turned and reciprocally advanced. As he did so, the Spaniard's nervous eagerness increased, but his vital energy failed, so that, the better to support him, the servant, placing his master's hand on his naked shoulder, and gently holding it there, formed himself into a sort of crutch.

When the two captains met, the Spaniard again fervently took the hand of the American, at the same time casting an earnest glance into his eyes, but, as before, too much overcome to speak.

I have done him wrong, self-reproachfully thought Captain Delano; his apparent coldness has deceived me; in no instance has he meant to offend.

Meantime, as if fearful that the continuance of the scene might too much unstring his master, the servant seemed anxious to terminate it. And so, still presenting himself as a crutch, and walking between the two captains, he advanced with them towards the gangway; while still, as if full of kindly contrition, Don Benito would not let go the hand of Captain Delano but retained it in his, across the black's body.

Soon they were standing by the side, looking over into the boat, whose crew turned up their curious eyes. Waiting a moment for the Spaniard to relinquish his hold, the now embarrassed Captain Delano lifted his foot to overstep the threshold of the open gangway, but still Don Benito would not let go his hand. And yet, with an agitated tone, he said, 'I can go no further; here I must bid you adieu. Adieu, my dear, dear Don Amasa. Go—go!' suddenly tearing his hand loose, 'go, and God guard you better than me, my best friend.'

Not unaffected, Captain Delano would now have lingered, but, catching the meekly admonitory eye of the servant, with a hasty farewell he descended into his boat, followed by the continual adieus of Don Benito, standing rooted in the gangway.

Seating himself in the stern, Captain Delano, making a last salute, ordered the boat shoved off. The crew had their oars on end. The bowsmen pushed the boat a sufficient distance for the oars to be lengthwise dropped. The instant that was done, Don Benito sprang over the bulwarks, falling at the feet of Captain Delano; at the same time calling towards his ship, but in tones so frenzied that none in the boat could understand him. But, as if not equally obtuse, three sailors, from different and distant parts of the ship, splashed into the sea, swimming after their captain, as if intent upon his rescue.

The dismayed officer of the boat eagerly asked what this meant. To which Captain Delano, turning a disdainful smile upon the unaccountable Spaniard, answered that, for his part, he neither knew nor cared; but it seemed as if Don Benito had taken it into his head to produce the impression among his people that the boat wanted to kidnap him. 'Or else—give way for your lives,' he wildly added, starting at a clattering hubbub in the ship, above which rang the tocsin of the hatchet-polishers, and seizing Don Benito by the throat he added, 'this plotting pirate means murder!' Here, in apparent verification of the words, the servant, a dagger in his hand, was seen on the rail overhead, poised, in the act of leaping, as if the desperate fidelity to befriend his master to the last; while, seemingly to aid the black, the three white sailors were trying to clamber into the hampered bow. Meantime, the whole host of Negroes, as if inflamed at the sight of their jeopardized captain, impended in one sooty avalanche over the bulwarks.

All this, with what preceded and what followed, occurred with such involutions of rapidity that past, present, and future seemed one.

Seeing the Negro coming, Captain Delano had flung the Spaniard aside, almost in the very act of clutching him, and, by the unconscious recoil shifting his place, with arms thrown up so promptly grappled the servant in his descent, that with the dagger presented at Captain Delano's heart, the black seemed of purpose to have leaped there as to his mark. But the weapon was wrenched away, and the assailant dashed down into the bottom of the boat, which now, with disentangled oars, began to speed through the sea.

At this juncture, the left hand of Captain Delano, on one side, again clutched the half-reclined Don Benito, heedless that he was in a speechless faint, while his right foot, on the other side, ground the prostrate Negro, and his right arm pressed for added speed on the after oar, his eye bent forward, encouraging his men to their utmost.

But here the officer of the boat, who had at last succeeded in beating off the towing sailors, and was now, with face turned aft, assisting the bowsman at his oar, suddenly called to Captain Delano to see what the black was about, while a Portuguese oarsman shouted to him to give heed to what the Spaniard was saying.

Glancing down at his feet, Captain Delano saw the free hand of the servant aiming with a second dagger—a small one, before concealed in his wool—with this he was snakishly writhing up from the boat's bottom at the heart of his master, his countenance lividly vindictive, expressing the centered purpose of his soul; while the Spaniard, half-choked, was vainly shrinking away, with husky words, incoherent to all but the Portuguese.

That moment, across the long-benighted mind of Captain Delano, a flash of revelation swept, illuminating, in unanticipated clearness, his host's whole mysterious demeanor, with every enigmatic event of the day, as well as the entire past voyage of the *San Dominick.* He smote Babo's hand down, but his own heart smote him harder. With infinite pity he withdrew his hold from Don Benito. Not Captain Delano, but Don Benito, the black in leaping into the boat, had intended to stab.

Both the black's hands were held, as, glancing up towards the *San Dominick,* Captain Delano, now with scales dropped from his eyes, saw the Negroes, not in misrule, not in tumult, not as if frantically concerned for Don Benito, but, with mask torn away, flourishing hatchets and knives in ferocious piratical revolt. Like delirious black dervishes, the six Ashantees danced on the poop. Prevented by their foes from springing into the water, the Spanish boys were hurrying up to the upmost spars, while such of the few Spanish sailors not already in the sea, less alert, were descried, helplessly mixed in, on deck with the blacks.

Meantime Captain Delano hailed his own vessel, ordering the ports up, and the guns run out. But by this time the cable of the *San Dominick* had been cut, and the fag end, in lashing out, whipped away the canvas shroud about the beak, suddenly revealing, as the bleached hull swung round towards the open ocean, death for the figurehead, in a human skeleton, chalky comment on the chalked words below, FOLLOW YOUR LEADER.

At the sight, Don Benito, covering his face, wailed out: ' 'Tis he, Aranda! my murdered, unburied friend!'

Upon reaching the sealer, calling for ropes, Captain Delano bound the Negro who made no resistance, and had him hoisted to the deck. He would then have assisted the now almost helpless Don Benito up the side; but Don Benito, wan as he was, refused to move, or be moved, until the Negro should have been first put below out of view. When, presently assured that it was done, he no more shrank from the ascent.

The boat was immediately dispatched back to pick up the three swimming sailors. Meantime, the guns were in readiness, though, owing to the *San Dominick* having glided somewhat astern of the sealer, only the aftermost one could be brought to bear. With this, they fired six times, thinking to cripple the fugitive ship by bringing down her spars, but only a few inconsiderable ropes were shot away. Soon the ship was beyond the gun's range, steering broad out of the bay, the blacks thickly clustering round the bowsprit, one moment with taunting cries towards the whites, the next with upthrown gestures hailing the now dusky moors of the ocean–cawing crows escaped from the hand of the fowler.

The first impulse was to slip the cables and give chase. But, upon second thoughts, to pursue with whaleboat and yawl seemed more promising.

Upon inquiring of Don Benito what firearms they had on board the *San Dominick*, Captain Delano was answered that they had none that could be used, because, in the earlier stages of the mutiny, a cabin passenger, since dead, had secretly put out of order the locks of what few muskets there were. But with all his remaining strength Don Benito entreated the Americans not to give chase, either with ship or boat, for the Negroes had already proved themselves such desperadoes that, in case of a present assault, nothing but a total massacre of the whites could be looked for. But, regarding this warning as coming from one whose spirit had been crushed by misery, the American did not give up his design.

The boats were got ready and armed. Captain Delano ordered his men into them. He was going himself when Don Benito grasped his arm.

'What! have you saved my life, *señor*, and are you now going to throw away your own?'

The officers also, for reasons connected with their interests and those of the voyage, and a duty owing to the owners, strongly objected against their commander's going. Weighing their remonstrances a moment, Captain Delano felt bound to remain; appointing his chief mate—an athletic and resolute man, who had been a privateer's-man—to head the party. The more to encourage the sailors, they were told that the Spanish captain considered his ship good as lost; that she and her cargo, including some gold and silver, were worth more than a thousand doubloons. Take her, and no small part should be theirs. The sailors replied with a shout.

The fugitives had now almost gained an offing. It was nearly night, but the moon was rising. After hard, prolonged pulling, the boats came up on the ship's quarters, at a suitable distance laying upon their oars to discharge their muskets. Having no bullets to return, the Negroes sent their yells. But upon the second volley, Indianlike, they hurtled their hatchets. One took off a sailor's fingers. Another struck the whaleboat's bow, cutting off the rope there, and remaining stuck in the gunwale like a woodman's ax. Snatching it, quivering, from its lodgement, the mate hurled it back. The returned gauntlet now stuck in the ship's broken quarter-gallery, and so remained.

The Negroes giving too hot a reception, the whites kept a more respectful distance. Hovering now just out of reach of the hurtling hatchets, they, with a view to the close encounter which must soon come, sought to decoy the blacks into entirely disarming themselves of their most murderous weapons in a hand-to-hand fight, by foolishly flinging them, as missiles, short of the mark, into the sea. But, erelong perceiving the stratagem, the Negroes desisted, though not before many of them had to replace their lost hatchets with handspikes, an exchange which, as counted upon, proved, in the end, favorable to the assailants.

Meantime, with a strong wind the ship still clove the water, the boats alternately falling behind and pulling up to discharge fresh volleys.

The fire was mostly directed towards the stern, since there, chiefly, the Negroes at present were clustering. But to kill or maim the Negroes was not the object. To take them, with the ship, was the object. To do it, the ship must be boarded, which could not be done by boats while she was sailing so fast.

A thought now struck the mate. Observing the Spanish boys still aloft, high as they could get, he called to them to descend to the yards, and cut adrift the sails. It was done. About this time, owing to causes hereafter to be shown, two Spaniards, in the dress of sailors and conspicuously showing themselves, were killed, not by volleys, but by deliberate marksman's shots; while, as it afterwards appeared, by one of the general discharges Atufal, the black, and the Spaniard at the helm likewise were killed. What, now, with the loss of the sails and loss of leaders, the ship became unmanageable to the Negroes.

With creaking masts, she came heavily round to the wind, the prow slowly swinging into view of the boats, its skeleton gleaming in the horizontal moonlight and casting a gigantic ribbed shadow upon the water, One extended arm of the ghost seemed beckoning the whites to avenge it.

'Follow your leader!' cried the mate; and, one on each bow, the boats boarded. Sealing-spears and cutlasses crossed hatchets and handpikes. Huddled upon the longboat amidships, the Negresses raised a wailing chant, whose chorus was the clash of the steel.

For a time, the attack wavered, the Negroes wedging themselves to beat it back, the half-repelled sailors, as yet unable to gain a footing, fighting as troopers in the saddle, one leg sideways flung over the bulwark and one without, plying their cutlasses like carters' whips. But in vain. They were almost overborne, when, rallying themselves into a squad as one man, with a huzzah they sprang inboard, where, entangled, they involuntarily separated again. For a few breaths' space there was a vague, muffled, inner sound, as of submerged swordfish rushing hither and thither through shoals of blackfish. Soon, in a reunited band, and joined by the Spanish seamen, the whites came to the surface, irresistibly driving the Negroes towards the stern. But a barricade of casks and sacks, from side to side, had been thrown up by the mainmast. Here the Negroes faced about, and though scorning peace or truce, yet fain would have had respite. But, without pause overleaping the barrier, the unflagging sailors again closed. Exhausted, the blacks now fought in despair. Their red tongues lolled, wolflike, from their black mouths. But the pale sailors' teeth were set; not a word was spoken, and, in five minutes more, the ship was won.

Nearly a score of the Negroes were killed. Exclusive of those by the balls, many were mangled; their wounds—mostly inflicted by the long-edged sealing-spears, resembling those shaven ones of the English at Preston Pans, made by the poled scythes of the Highlanders. On the other side, none were killed, though several were wounded, some severely, including the mate. The surviving Negroes were temporarily secured, and the ship, towed back into the harbor at midnight, once more lay anchored.

Omitting the incidents and arrangements ensuing, suffice it that, after two days spent in refitting, the ships sailed in company for Conception, in Chile, and thence for Lima, in Peru; where, before the viceregal courts, the whole affair, from the beginning, underwent investigation.

Though, midway on the passage, the ill-fated Spaniard, relaxed from constraint, showed some signs of regaining health with free-will, yet, agreeably to his own foreboding, shortly before arriving at Lima, he relapsed, finally becoming so reduced as to be carried ashore in arms. Hearing of his story and plight, one of the many religious institutions of the City of Kings opened an hospitable refuge to him, where both physician and priest were his nurses, and a member of the order volunteered to be his one special guardian and consoler, by night and by day.

The following extracts, translated from one of the official Spanish documents, will, it is hoped, shed light on the preceding narrative, as well as, in the first place, reveal the true port of departure and true history of the *San Dominick's* voyage down to the time of her touching at the island of St Maria.

But ere the extracts come it may be well to preface them with a remark.

The document selected, from among many others, for partial translation, contains the deposition of Benito Cereno, the first taken in the case. Some disclosures therein were at the time held dubious, for both learned and natural reasons. The tribunal inclined to the opinion that the deponent, not undisturbed in his mind by recent events, raved of some things which could never have happened. But subsequent depositions of the surviving sailors, bearing out the revelations of their captain in several of the strangest particulars, gave credence to the rest. So that the tribunal, in its final decision, rested its capital sentences upon statements which, had they lacked confirmation, it would have deemed it but duty to reject.

I, DON JOSÉ DE ABOS AND PADILLA, His Majesty's Notary for the Royal Revenue, and Register of this Province, and Notary Public of the Holy Crusade of this Bishopric, etc.

Do certify and declare, as much as is requisite in law, that, in the criminal cause commenced the twenty-fourth of the month of September, in the year seventeen hundred and ninety-nine, against the Negroes of the ship *San Dominick*, the following declaration before me was made:

Declaration of the first witness, DON BENITO CERENO.

The same day, and month, and year, His Honor, Doctor Juan Martínez de Rozas, Councilor of the Royal Audience of this Kingdom, and learned in the law of this Intendency, ordered the captain of the ship *San Dominick,* Don Benito Cereno, to appear, which he did in his litter, attended by the monk Infelez, of whom he received the oath, which he took by God, our Lord, and a sign of the Cross, under which he promised to tell the truth of whatever he should know and should be asked; and being interrogated agreeably to the tenor of the act commencing the process, he said that, on the twentieth of May last, he set sail with his ship from the port of Valparaiso, bound to that of Callao, loaded with the produce of the country beside thirty cases of hardware and one hundred and sixty blacks of both sexes, mostly belonging to Don Alexandro Aranda, gentleman, of the city of Mendoza; that the crew of the ship consisted of thirty-six men beside the persons who went as passengers; that the Negroes were in part as follows:

[*Here, in the original, follows a list of some fifty names, descriptions, and ages, compiled from certain recovered documents of Aranda's, and also from recollections of the deponent, from which portions only are extracted.*]

– One, from about eighteen to nineteen years, named José, and this was the man that waited upon his master, Don Alexandro, and who speaks well the Spanish, having served him four or five years; . . . a mulatto, named Francesco, the cabin steward, of a good person and voice, having sung in the Valparaiso churches, native of the province of Buenos Ayres, aged about thirty-five years. . . . A smart Negro, named Dago, who had been for many years a gravedigger among the Spaniards, aged forty-six years. . . . Four old Negroes, born in Africa, from sixty to seventy, but sound, calkers by trade, whose names are as follows: the first was named Muri, and he was killed (as was also his son named Diamelo); the second, Nacta; the third, Yola, likewise killed; the fourth, Ghofan; and six full-grown Negroes, aged from thirty to forty-five, all raw, and born among the Ashantees–Matiluqui, Yan, Lecbe, Mapenda, Yambaio, Akim; four of whom were killed; . . . a powerful Negro named Atufal, who being supposed to have been a chief in Africa, his owner set great store by him. . . . And a small Negro of Senegal, but some years among the Spaniards, aged about thirty, which Negro's name was Babo; . . . that he does not remember the names of the others, but that still expecting the residue of Don Alexandro's papers will be found, will then take due account of them all, and remit to the court; . . . and thirty-nine women and children of all ages.

[*The catalogue over, the deposition goes on:*]

. . . That all the Negroes slept upon deck, as is customary in this navigation, and none wore fetters, because the owner, his friend Aranda, told him that they were all tractable; . . . that on the seventh day after leaving port, at three o'clock in the morning, all the Spaniards being asleep except the two officers on the watch, who were the boatswain, Juan Robles, and the carpenter, Juan Bautista Gayete, and the helmsman and his boy, the Negroes revolted suddenly, wounded dangerously the boatswain and the carpenter, and successively killed eighteen men of those who were sleeping upon deck, some with handspikes and hatchets, and others by throwing them alive overboard, after tying them; that of the Spaniards upon deck they left about seven, as he thinks, alive and tied, to maneuver the ship, and three or four more, who hid themselves, remained also alive. Although in the act of revolt the Negroes made themselves masters of the hatchway, six or seven wounded went through it to the cockpit, without any hindrance on their part; that during the act of revolt the mate and another person, whose name he does not recollect, attempted to come up through the hatchway, but, being quickly wounded, were obliged to return to the cabin; that the deponent resolved at break of day to come up the companionway, where the Negro Babo was, being the ringleader, and Atufal, who assisted him, and having spoken to them, exhorted them to cease committing such atrocities, asking them, at the same time what they wanted and intended to do, offering, himself, to obey their commands; that notwithstanding this, they threw, in his presence, three men, alive and tied, overboard; that they told the deponent to come up and that they would not kill him; which having done, the Negro Babo asked him whether there were in those seas any Negro countries where they might be carried, and he answered them, No; that the Negro Babo afterwards told him to carry them to Senegal, or to the neighboring islands of St Nicholas, and he answered that this was impossible on account of the great distance, the necessity involved of rounding Cape Horn, the bad condition of the vessel, the want of provisions, sails, and water; but that the Negro Babo replied to him he must carry them in anyway, that they would do and conform themselves to everything the deponent should require as to eating and drinking; that after a long conference, being absolutely compelled to please them, for they threatened to kill all the whites if they were not, at all events, carried to Senegal, he told them that what was most wanting for the voyage was water, that they would go near the coast to take it, and thence they would proceed on their course; that the Negro Babo agreed to it, and the deponent steered towards the intermediate ports, hoping to meet some Spanish or foreign vessel that would save them; that within ten or eleven days they saw the land, and continued their course by it in the vicinity of Nasca; that the deponent observed that the Negroes were now restless and mutinous because he did not effect the taking in of water, the Negro Babo having required, with threats, that it should be done, without fail, the following day; he told him he saw plainly that the coast was steep, and the rivers designated in the maps were not to be found, with other reasons suitable to the circumstances, that the best way would be to go to the island of Santa Maria, where they might water easily, it being a solitary island, as the foreigners did; that the deponent did not go to Pisco, that was near, nor make any other port of the coast, because the Negro Babo had intimated to him several times that he would kill all the whites the very moment he should perceive any city, town, or settlement of any kind on the shores to which they should be carried; that having determined to go to the island of Santa Maria, as the deponent had planned, for the purpose of trying whether, on the passage or near the island itself, they could find any vessel that should favor them, or whether he could escape from it in a boat to the neighboring coast of Arruco, to adopt the necessary means he immediately changed his course, steering for the island; that the Negroes Babo and Atufal held daily conferences, in which they discussed what was necessary for their design of returning to Senegal, whether they were to kill all the Spaniards, and particularly the deponent; that eight days after parting from the coast of Nasca, the deponent being on the watch a little after daybreak, and soon after the Negroes had their meeting, the Negro Babo came to the place where the deponent was and told him that he had determined to kill his master, Don Alexandro Aranda, both because he and his companions could not otherwise be sure of their liberty, and that, to keep the seamen in subjection, he wanted to prepare a warning of what road they should be made to take did they or any of them oppose him, and that, by means of the death of Don Alexandro, that warning would best be given, but that what this last meant the deponent did not at the time comprehend, nor could not, further than that the death of Don Alexandro was intended; and moreover the Negro Babo proposed to the deponent to call the mate Raneds, who was sleeping in the cabin, before the thing was done, for fear, as the deponent understood it, that the mate, who was a good navigator, should be killed with Don Alexandro and the rest; that the deponent, who was a friend from youth of Don Alexandro, prayed and conjured, but all was useless, for the Negro Babo answered him that the thing could not be prevented, and that all the Spaniards risked their death if they should attempt to frustrate his will in this matter or any other; that, in this conflict, the deponent called the mate, Raneds, who was forced to go apart, and immediately the Negro Babo commanded the Ashantee Martinqui and the Ashantee Lecbe to go and commit the murder; that those two went down with hatchets to the berth of Don Alexandro, that, yet half alive and mangled, they dragged him on deck; that they were going to throw him overboard in that state, but the Negro Babo stopped them, bidding the murder be completed on the deck before him, which was done, when, by his orders, the body was carried below, forward; that nothing more was seen of it by the deponent for three days; . . . that Don Alonzo Sidonia, an old man, long resident at Valparaiso, and lately appointed to a civil office in Peru, whither he had taken passage, was at the time sleeping in the berth opposite Don Alexandro's; that awakening at his cries, surprised them, and at the sight of the Negroes with their bloody hatchets in their hands, he threw himself into the sea through a window which was near him, and was drowned, without it being in the power of the deponent to assist or take him up; . . . that a short time after killing Aranda, they brought upon deck his german-cousin, of middle-age, Don Francisco Masa, of Mendoza and the young Don Joaquín, Marqués de Aramboalaza, then lately from Spain, with his Spanish servant Ponce, and the three young clerks of Aranda, José Mozairi, Lorenzo Bargas, and Hermenegildo Gandix, all of Cádiz; that Don Joaquín and Hermenegildo Gandix, the Negro Babo, for purposes hereafter to appear, preserved alive, but Don Francisco Masa, José Mozairi, and Lorenzo Bargas, with Ponce the servant, beside the boatswain, Juan Robles, the boatswain's mates, Manuel Viscaya and Roderigo Hurta, and four of the sailors the Negro Babo ordered to be thrown alive into the sea, although they made no resistance nor begged for anything else but mercy; that the boatswain, Juan Robles, who knew how to swim, kept the longest above water, making acts of contrition, and, in the last words he uttered, charged this deponent to cause mass to be said for his soul to our Lady of Succor; . . . that, during the three days which followed, the deponent, uncertain what fate had befallen the remains of Don Alexandro, frequently asked the Negro Babo where they were, and, if still on board, whether they were to be preserved for interment ashore, entreating him so to order it; that the Negro Babo answered nothing till the fourth day, when, at sunrise, the deponent coming on deck, the Negro Babo showed him a skeleton, which had been substituted for the ship's proper figurehead—the image of Christopher Colón, the discoverer of the New World; that the Negro Babo asked him whose skeleton that was, and whether, from its whiteness, he should not think it a white's, that, upon discovering his face, the Negro Babo, coming close, said words to this effect: 'Keep faith with the blacks from here to Senegal, or you shall in spirit, as now in body, follow your leader,' pointing to the prow; . . . that the same morning the Negro Babo took by succession each Spaniard forward, and asked him whose skeleton that was, and whether, from its whiteness, he should not think it a white's; that each Spaniard covered his face; that then to each the Negro Babo repeated the words in the first place said to the deponent; . . . that they (the Spaniards), being then assembled aft, the Negro Babo harangued them, saying that he had now done all; that the deponent (as navigator for the Negroes) might pursue his course, warning him and all of them that they should, soul and body, go the way of Don Alexandro if he saw them (the Spaniards) speak or plot anything against them (the Negroes)–a threat which was repeated every day; that, before the events last mentioned, they had tied the cook to throw him overboard, for it is not known what thing they heard him speak, but finally the Negro Babo spared his life, at the request of the deponent; that a few days after, the deponent, endeavoring not to omit any means to preserve the lives of the remaining whites, spoke to the Negroes of peace and tranquillity, and agreed to draw up a paper, signed by the deponent and the sailors who could write, as also by the Negro Babo, for himself and all the blacks, in which the deponent obliged himself to carry them to Senegal, and they not to kill any more, and he formally to make over to them the ship, with the cargo, with which they were for that time satisfied and quieted. . . . But the next day, the more surely to guard against the sailors' escape, the Negro Babo commanded all the boats to be destroyed but the longboat, which was unseaworthy, and another, a cutter in good condition, which, knowing it would yet be wanted for towing the water casks, he had it lowered down into the hold.

[*Various particulars of the prolonged and perplexed navigation ensuing here follow, with incidents of a calamitous calm, from which portion one passage is extracted, to wit:*]

– That on the fifth day of the calm, all on board suffering much from the heat and want of water, and five having died in fits, and mad, the Negroes became irritable, and for a chance gesture, which they deemed suspicious– though it was harmless–made by the mate, Raneds, to the deponent in the act of handing a quadrant, they killed him; but that for this they afterwards were sorry, the mate being the only remaining navigator on board, except the deponent.

– That omitting other events which daily happened, and which can only serve uselessly to recall past misfortunes and conflicts, after seventy-three day's navigation, reckoned from the time they sailed from Nasca, during which they navigated under a scanty allowance of water, and were afflicted with the calms before mentioned, they at last arrived at the island of Santa Maria, on the seventeenth of the month of August, at about six o'clock in the afternoon, at which hour they cast anchor very near the American ship *Bachelor's Delight*, which lay in the same bay, commanded by the generous Captain Amasa Delano; but at six o'clock in the morning they had already descried the port, and the Negroes became uneasy, as soon as at distance they saw the ship, not having expected to see one there; that the Negro Babo pacified them, assuring them that no fear need be had; that straightway he ordered the figure on the bow to be covered with canvas, as for repairs, and had the decks a little set in order; that for a time the Negro Babo and the Negro Atufal conferred; that the Negro Atufal was for sailing away but the Negro Babo would not, and, by himself, cast about what to do; that at last he came to the deponent proposing to him to say and do all that the deponent declares to have said and done to the American captain; . . . that the Negro Babo warned him that if he varied in the least, or uttered any word, or gave any look that should give the least intimation of the past events or present state, he would instantly kill him, with all his companions, showing a dagger which he carried hid, saying something which, as he understood it, meant that the dagger would be alert as his eye; that the Negro Babo then announced the plan to all his companions, which pleased them; that he then, the better to disguise the truth, devised many expedients, in some of them uniting deceit and defense; that of this sort was the device of the six Ashantees before named, who were his bravoes; that them he stationed on the break of the poop, as if to clean certain hatchets (in cases, which were part of the cargo), but in reality to use them, and distribute them at need, and at a given word he told them; that, among other devices, was the device of presenting Atufal, his right-hand man, as chained, though in a moment the chains could be dropped; that in every particular he informed the deponent what part he was expected to enact in every device, and what story he was to tell on every occasion, always threatening him with instant death if he varied in the least; that, conscious that many of the Negroes would be turbulent, the Negro Babo appointed the four aged Negroes, who were calkers, to keep what domestic order they could on the decks; that again and again he harangued the Spaniards and his companions, informing them of his intent and of his devices, and of the invented story that this deponent was to tell, charging them lest any of them varied from the story; that these arrangements were made and matured during the interval of two or three hours between their first sighting the ship and the arrival on board of Captain Amasa Delano; that this happened about half-past seven o'clock in the morning, Captain Amasa Delano coming in his boat, and all gladly receiving him, that the deponent, as well as he could force himself, acting then the part of principal owner and a free captain of the ship, told Captain Amasa Delano, when called upon, that he came from Buenos Ayres, bound to Lima, with three hundred Negroes; that off Cape Horn, and in a subsequent fever, many Negroes had died; that also, by similar casualties, all the sea officers and the greatest part of the crew had died.

[*And so the deposition goes on, circumstantially recounting the fictitious story dictated to the deponent by Babo, and through the deponent imposed upon Captain Delano, and also recounting the friendly offers of Captain Delano, with other things, but all of which is here omitted. After the fictitious story, etc., the deposition proceeds:*]

– that the generous Captain Amasa Delano remained on board all the day, till he left the ship anchored at six o'clock in the evening, deponent speaking to him always of his pretended misfortunes, under the forementioned principles, without having had it in his power to tell a single word or give him the least hint, that he might know the truth and state of things, because the Negro Babo, performing the office of an officious servant with all the appearance of submission of the humble slave, did not leave the deponent one moment; that this was in order to observe the deponent's actions and words, for the Negro Babo understands well the Spanish, and besides, there were thereabout some others who were constantly on the watch, and likewise understood the Spanish; . . . that upon one occasion, while deponent was standing on the deck conversing with Amasa Delano, by a secret sign the Negro Babo drew him (the deponent) aside, the act appearing as if originating with the deponent; that then, he being drawn aside, the Negro Babo proposed to him to gain from Amasa Delano full particulars about his ship, and crew, and arms; that the deponent asked 'For what?' that, the Negro Babo answered he might conceive; that, grieved at the prospect of what might overtake the generous Captain Amasa Delano, the deponent at first refused to ask the desired questions, and used every argument to induce the Negro Babo to give up this new design; that the Negro Babo showed the point of his dagger, that after the information had been obtained the Negro Babo again drew him aside, telling him that that very night he (the deponent) would be captain of two ships, instead of one, for that, great part of the American's ship's crew being to be absent fishing, the six Ashantees, without anyone else, would easily take it; that at this time he said other things to the same purpose; that no entreaties availed; that, before Amasa Delano's coming on board, no hint had been given touching the capture of the American ship; that to prevent this project the deponent was powerless; . . .–that in some things his memory is confused, he cannot distinctly recall every event; . . .–that as soon as they had cast anchor at six of the clock in the evening, as has before been stated, the American captain took leave, to return to his vessel; that upon a sudden impulse, which the deponent believes to have come from God and his angels, he after the farewell had been said, followed the generous Captain Amasa Delano as far as the gunwale, where he stayed, under pretense of taking leave, until Amasa Delano should have been seated in his boat; that, on shoving off, the deponent sprang from the gunwale into the boat, and fell into it, he knows not how, God guarding him; that—

[*Here, in the original, follows the account of what further happened at the escape, and how the* San Dominick *was retaken, and of the passage to the coast; including in the recital many expressions of 'eternal gratitude' to the 'generous Captain Amasa Delano.' The deposition then proceeds with recapitulatory remarks, and a partial renumeration of the Negroes, making record of their individual part in the past events, with a view to furnishing, according to command of the court, the data whereon to found the criminal sentences to be pronounced. From this portion is the following;*]

– That he believes that all the Negroes, though not in the first place knowing to the design of revolt, when it was accomplished, approved it. . . . That the Negro José, eighteen years old, and in the personal service of Don Alexandro, was the one who communicated the information to the Negro Babo about the state of things in the cabin, before the revolt; that this is known, because, in the preceding midnight, he used to come from his berth, which was under his master's, in the cabin, to the deck where the ringleader and his associates were, and had secret conversations with the Negro Babo, in which he was several times seen by the mate; that, one night, the mate drove him away twice; . . . that this same Negro José was the one who, without being commanded to do so by the Negro Babo, as Lecbe and Martinqui were, stabbed his master, Don Alexandro, after he had been dragged half-lifeless to the deck; . . . that the mulatto steward, Francesco, was of the first band of revolters, that he was, in all things, the creature and tool of the Negro Babo; that, to make his court, he, just before a repast in the cabin, proposed to the Negro Babo poisoning a dish for the generous Captain Amasa Delano; this is known and believed, because the Negroes have said it; but that the Negro Babo, having another design, forbade Francesco; . . . that the Ashantee Lecbe was one of the worst of them, for that, on the day the ship was retaken, he assisted in the defense of her with a hatchet in each hand, with one of which he wounded in the breast the chief mate of Amasa Delano, in the first act of boarding; this all knew; that, in sight of the deponent, Lecbe struck with a hatchet, Don Francisco Masa, when, by the Negro Babo's orders, he was carrying him to throw him overboard alive, beside participating in the murder, before mentioned, of Don Alexandro Aranda and others of the cabin passengers; that, owing to the fury with which the Ashantees fought in the engagement with the boats, but this Lecbe and Yan survived; that Yan was bad as Lecbe; that Yan was the man who, by Babo's command, willingly prepared the skeleton of Don Alexandro, in a way the Negroes afterwards told the deponent, but which he, so long as reason is left him, can never divulge; that Yan and Lecbe were the two who, in a calm by night, riveted the skeleton to the bow; this also the Negroes told him; that the Negro Babo was he who traced the inscription below it; that the Negro Babo was the plotter from first to last; he ordered every murder, and was the helm and keel of the revolt; that Atufal was his lieutenant in all, but Atufal with his own hand committed no murder, nor did the Negro Babo; . . . that Atufal was shot, being killed in the fight with the boats, ere boarding; . . . that the Negresses, of age, were knowing to the revolt, and testified themselves satisfied at the death of their master, Don Alexandro; that, had the Negroes not restrained them, they would have tortured to death, instead of simply killing, the Spaniards slain by command of the Negro Babo; that the Negresses used their utmost influence to have the deponent made away with; that, in the various acts of murder, they sang songs and danced—not gaily, but solemnly, and before the engagement with the boats, as well as during the action, they sang melancholy songs to the Negroes, and that this melancholy tone was more inflaming than a different one would have been, and was so intended; that all this is believed, because the Negroes have said it. . . .—that of the thirty-six men of the crew, exclusive of the passengers (all of whom are now dead), which the deponent had knowledge of, six only remained alive, with four cabin boys and ship boys, not included with the crew; . . .—that the Negroes broke an arm of one of the cabin boys and gave him strokes with hatchets.

[*Then follow various random disclosures referring to various periods of time. The following are extracted;*]

— That during the presence of Captain Amasa Delano on board, some attempts were made by the sailors, and one by Hermenegildo Gandix, to convey hints to him of the true state of affairs, but that these attempts were ineffectual, owing to fear of incurring death, and, furthermore, owing to the devices which offered contradictions to the true state of affairs, as well as owing to the generosity and piety of Amasa Delano incapable of sounding such wickedness; . . . that Luys Galgo, a sailor about sixty years of age, and formerly of the king's navy, was one of those who sought to convey tokens to Captain Amasa Delano; but his intent, though undiscovered, being suspected, he was, on a pretense, made to retire out of sight, and at last into the hold, and there was made away with. This the Negroes have since said; . . . that one of the ship boys feeling, from Captain Amasa Delano's presence, some hopes of release, and not having enough prudence, dropped some chance word respecting his expectations, which being overheard and understood by a slave boy with whom he was eating at the time, the latter struck him on the head with a knife, inflicting a bad wound, but of which the boy is now healing; that likewise, not long before the ship was brought to anchor, one of the seamen steering at the time endangered himself by letting the blacks remark some expression in his countenance, arising from a cause similar to the above, but this sailor, by his heedful after conduct, escaped; . . . that these statements are made to show the court that from the beginning to the end of the revolt it was impossible for the deponent and his men to act otherwise than they did; . . .–that the third clerk, Hermenegildo Gandix, who before had been forced to live among the seamen, wearing a seaman's habit, and in all respects appearing to be one for the time, he, Gandix, was killed by a musket ball fired through mistake from the boats before boarding; having in his fright run up the mizzen rigging, calling to the boats–'don't board,' lest upon their boarding the Negroes should kill him; that this inducing the Americans to believe he some way favored the cause of the Negroes, they fired two balls at him, so that he fell wounded from the rigging, and was drowned in the sea; . . .–that the young Don Joaquín, Marqués de Aramboalaza, like Hermenegildo Gandix, the third clerk, was degraded to the office and appearance of a common seaman; that upon one occasion when Don Joaquín shrank, the Negro Babo commanded the Ashantee Lecbe to take tar and heat it, and pour it upon Don Joaquín's hands; . . .–that Don Joaquín was killed owing to another mistake of the Americans, but one impossible to be avoided, as, upon the approach of the boats, Don Joaquín, with a hatchet tied edge out and upright to his hand, was made by the Negroes to appear on the bulwarks; whereupon, seen with arms in his hands and in a questionable attitude, he was shot for a renegade seaman; . . .–that on the person of Don Joaquín was found secreted a jewel, which, by papers that were discovered, proved to have been meant for the shrine of our Lady of Mercy in Lima, a votive offering, beforehand prepared and guarded, to attest his gratitude when he should have landed in Peru, his last destination, for the safe conclusion of his entire voyage from Spain; . . .–that the jewel, with the other effects of the late Don Joaquín, is in the custody of the brethren of the Hospital de Sacerdotes, awaiting the disposition of the honorable court; . . .–that, owing to the condition of the deponent, as well as the haste in which the boats departed for the attack, the Americans were not forewarned that there were, among the apparent crew, a passenger and one of the clerks disguised by the Negro Babo; . . .–that, beside the Negroes killed in action, some were killed after the capture and reanchoring at night, when shackled to the ringbolts on deck; that these deaths were committed by the sailors, ere they could be prevented. That as soon as informed of it, Captain Amasa Delano used all his authority, and in particular with his own hand struck down Martínez Gola, who having found a razor in the pocket of an old jacket of his which one of the shackled Negroes had on, was aiming it at the Negro's throat; that the noble Captain Amasa Delano also wrenched from the hand of Bartholomew Barlo a dagger, secreted at the time of the massacre of the whites, with which he was in the act of stabbing a shackled Negro, who, the same day, with another Negro, had thrown him down and jumped upon him; . . .—that, for all events, befalling through so long a time, during which the ship was in the hands of the Negro Babo, he cannot here give account, but that what he has said is the most substantial of what occurs to him at present, and is the truth under the oath which he has taken; which declaration he affirmed and ratified, after hearing it read to him.

He said that he is twenty-nine years of age, and broken in body and mind; that when finally dismissed by the court, he shall not return home to Chile but betake himself to the monastery on Mount Agonia without; and signed with his honor, and crossed himself, and, for the time, departed as he came, in his litter, with the monk Infelez, to the Hospital de Sacerdotes.

BENITO CERENO.

DOCTOR ROZAS.

If the deposition have served as the key to fit into the lock of the complications which precede it, then, as a vault whose door has been flung back, the *San Dominick's* hull lies open today.

Hitherto the nature of this narrative, besides rendering the intricacies in the beginning unavoidable, has more or less required that many things, instead of being set down in the order of occurrence, should be retrospectively or irregularly given; this last is the case with the following passages, which will conclude the account:

During the long, mild voyage to Lima, there was, as before hinted, a period during which the sufferer a little recovered his health, or, at least in some degree, his tranquillity. Ere the decided relapse which came, the two captains had many cordial conversations—their fraternal unreserve in singular contrast with former withdrawments.

Again and again it was repeated how hard it had been to enact the part forced on the Spaniard by Babo.

'Ah, my dear friend,' Don Benito once said, 'at those very times when you thought me so morose and ungrateful, nay, when, as you now admit, you half thought me plotting your murder, at those very times my heart was frozen; I could not look at you, thinking of what, both on board this ship and your own, hung, from other hands, over my kind benefactor. And as God lives, Don Amasa, I know not whether desire for my own safety alone could have nerved me to that leap into your boat, had it not been for the thought that, did you, unenlightened, return to your ship, you, my best friend, with all who might be with you, stolen upon that night in your hammocks, would never in this world have wakened again. Do but think how you walked this deck, how you sat in this cabin, every inch of ground mined into honeycombs under you. Had I dropped the least hint, made the least advance towards an understanding between us, death, explosive death—yours as mine—would have ended the scene.'

'True, true,' cried Captain Delano, starting, 'you have saved my life, Don Benito, more than I yours; saved it, too, against my knowledge and will.'

'Nay, my friend,' rejoined the Spaniard, courteous even to the point of religion, 'God charmed your life, but you saved mine. To think of some things you did—those smilings and chattings, rash pointings and gesturings. For less than these, they slew my mate, Raneds; but you had the Prince of Heaven's safe conduct through all ambuscades.'

'Yes, all is owing to Providence, I know: but the temper of my mind that morning was more than commonly pleasant, while the sight of so much suffering, more apparent than real, added to my good-nature, compassion, and charity, happily interweaving the three. Had it been otherwise, doubtless, as you hint, some of my interferences might have ended, unhappily enough. Besides, those feelings I spoke of enabled me to get the better of momentary distrust, at times when acuteness might have cost me my life, without saving another's. Only at the end did my suspicions get the better of me, and you know how wide of the mark they then proved.'

'Wide, indeed,' said Don Benito, sadly; 'you were with me all day; stood with me, sat with me, talked with me, looked at me, ate with me, drank with me; and yet, your last act was to clutch for a monster, not only an innocent man, but the most pitiable of all men. To such degree may malign machinations and deceptions impose. So far may even the best man err in judging the conduct of one with the recesses of whose condition he is not acquainted. But you were forced to it, and you were in time undeceived. Would that, in both respects, it was so ever, and with all men.'

'You generalize, Don Benito; and mournfully enough. But the past is passed; why moralize upon it? Forget it. See, yon bright sun has forgotten it all, and the blue sea, and the blue sky; these have turned over new leaves.'

'Because they have no memory,' he dejectedly replied; 'because they are not human.'

'But these mild trades that now fan your cheek, do they not come with a human-like healing to you? Warm friends, steadfast friends are the trades.'

'With their steadfastness they but waft me to my tomb, *señor*,' was the foreboding response.

'You are saved,' cried Captain Delano, more and more astonished and pained; 'you are saved: what has cast such a shadow upon you?'

'The Negro.'

There was silence, while the moody man sat, slowly and unconsciously gathering his mantle about him, as ir it were a pall.

There was no more conversation that day.

But if the Spaniard's melancholy sometimes ended in muteness upon topics like the above, there were others upon which he never spoke at all; on which, indeed, all his old reserves were piled. Pass over the worst, and, only to elucidate, let an item or two of these be cited. The dress, so precise and costly, worn by him on the day whose events have been narrated, had not willingly been put on. And that silver-mounted sword, apparent symbol of despotic command, was not, indeed, a sword, but the ghost of one. The scabbard, artificially stiffened, was empty.

As for the black–whose brain, not body, had schemed and led the revolt, with the plot–his slight frame, inadequate to that which it held, had at once yielded to the superior muscular strength of his captor, in the boat. Seeing all was over, he uttered no sound, and could not be forced to. His aspect seemed to say: since I cannot do deeds, I will not speak words. Put in irons in the hold with the rest, he was carried to Lima. During the passage, Don Benito did not visit him. Nor then, nor at any time after, would he look at him. Before the tribunal he refused. When pressed by the judges he fainted. On the testimony of the sailors alone rested the legal identity of Babo.

Some months after, dragged to the gibbet at the tail of a mule, the black met his voiceless end. The body was burned to ashes; but for many days, the head, that hive of subtlety, fixed on a pole in the plaza, met, unabashed, the gazes of the whites, and across the Plaza looked towards St Bartholomew's church, in whose vaults slept then, as now, the recovered bones of Aranda, and across the Rimac bridge looked towards the monastery, on Mount Agonia without; where, three months after being dismissed by the court, Benito Cereno, borne on the bier, did, indeed, follow his leader.

EDWARD EVERETT HALE

[1822–1909]

The Man Without a Country

(First published in *Atlantic Monthly*,
December, 1863; first book publication in 1868.)

I SUPPOSE THAT very few casual readers of the *New York Herald* of August 13th observed, in an obscure corner, among the "Deaths," the announcement:

"NOLAN. Died, on board U. S. Corvette *Levant*, Lat. 2° 11" S., Long. 131° W., on the 11th of May, Philip Nolan."

I happened to observe it, because I was stranded at the old Mission-House in Mackinac, waiting for a Lake Superior steamer which did not choose to come, and I was devouring, to the very stubble, all the current literature I could get hold of, even down to the deaths and marriages in the *Herald*. My memory for names and people is good, and the reader will see, as he goes on, that I had reason enough to remember Philip Nolan. There are hundreds of readers who would have paused at that announcement, if the officer of the *Levant* who reported it had chosen to make it thus: "Died, May 11th, The Man Without a Country."' For it was as "The Man Without a Country" that poor Philip Nolan had generally been known by the officers who had him in charge during some fifty years, as indeed, by all the men who sailed under them. I dare say there is many a man who has taken wine with him once a fortnight, in a three years' cruise, who never knew that his name was "Nolan," or whether the poor wretch had any name at all.

There can now be no possible harm in telling this poor creature's story. Reason enough there has been till now, ever since Madison's Administration went out in 1817, for very strict secrecy, the secrecy of honor itself, among the gentlemen of the navy who have had Nolan in successive charge. And certainly it speaks well for the *esprit de corps* of the profession and the personal honor of its members, that to the press this man's story has been wholly unknown,—and, I think, to the country at large also. I have reason to think, from some investigations I made in the Naval Archives when I was attached to the Bureau of Construction, that every official report relating to him was burned when Ross burned the public buildings at Washington. One of the Tuckers, or possibly one of the Watsons, had Nolan in charge at the end of the war; and when, on returning from his cruise, he reported at Washington to one of the Crowninshields,—who was in the Navy Department when he came home,—he found that the Departrnent ignored the whole business. Whether they really knew nothing about it, or whether it was a *Non mi ricordo*, determined on as a piece of policy, I do not know. But this I do know, that since 1817, and possibly before, no naval officer has mentioned Nolan in his report of a cruise.

But, as I say, there is no need for secrecy any longer. And now the poor creature is dead, it seems to me worth while to tell a little of his story, by way of showing young Americans of today what it is to be

A MAN WITHOUT A COUNTRY

Philip Nolan was as fine a young officer as there was in the "Legion of the West," as the Western division of our army was then called. When Aaron Burr made his first dashing expedition down to New Orleans in 1805, at Fort Massac, or somewhere above on the river, he met, as the Devil would have it, this gay, dashing, bright young fellow, at some dinner party, I think. Burr marked him, talked to him, walked with him, took him a day or two's voyage in his flat-boat, and, in short, fascinated him. For the next year barrack-life was very tame to poor Nolan. He occasionally availed of the permission the great man had given him to write to him. Long, high-worded, stilted letters the poor boy wrote and re-wrote and copied. But never a line did he have in reply from the gay deceiver. The other boys in the garrison sneered at him, because he sacrificed in this unrequited affection for a politician the time which they devoted to Monongahela, sledge, and high-low-jack. Bourbon, euchre, and poker were still unknown. But one day Nolan had his revenge. This time Burr came down the river, not as an attorney seeking a place for his office, but as a disguised conqueror. He had defeated I know not how many district attorneys; he had dined at I know not how many public dinners; he had been heralded in I know not how many Weekly Arguses; and it was rumored that he had an army behind him and an empire before him. It was a great day—his arrival—to poor Nolan. Burr had not been at the fort an hour before he sent for him. That evening he asked Nolan to take him out in his skiff, to show him a cane-brake or a cotton-wood tree, as he said,—really to seduce him; and by the time the sail was over, Nolan was enlisted body and soul. From that time, though he did not yet know it, he lived as "A Man Without a Country."

What Burr meant to do I know no more than you, dear reader. It is none of our business just now. Only, when the grand catastrophe came, and Jefferson and the House of Virginia of that day undertook to break on the wheel all the possible Clarences of the then House of York, by the great treason-trial at Richmond, some of the Iesser fry in that distant Mississippi Valley, which was farther from us than Puget's Sound is today, introduced the like novelty on their provincial stage, and, to while away the monotony of the summer at Fort Adams, got up, for *spectacles*, a string of court-martials on the officers there. One and another of the colonels and majors were tried, and, to fill out the list, little Nolan, against whom, Heaven knows, there was evidence enough—that he was sick of the service, had been willing to be false to it, and would have obeyed any order to march anywhither with anyone who would follow him, had the order only been signed, "By command of His Exc. A. Burr." The courts dragged on. The big flies escaped,—rightly for all I know. Nolan was proved guilty enough, as I say; yet you and I would never have heard of him, reader, but that, when the president of the court asked him at the close, whether he wished to say anything to show that he had always been faithful to the United States, he cried out, in a fit of frenzy:

"Damn the United States! I wish I may never hear of the United States again!"

I suppose he did not know how the words shocked old Colonel Morgan, who was holding the court. Half the officers who sat in it had served through the Revolution, and their lives, not to say their necks, had been risked for the very idea which he so cavalierly cursed in his madness. He, on his part, had grown up in the West of those days, in the midst of "Spanish plot," "Orleans plot," and all the rest. He had been educated on a plantation, where the finest company was a Spanish officer or a French merchant from Orleans. His education, such as it was, had been perfected in commercial expeditions to Vera Cruz, and I think he told me his father once hired an Englishman to be a private tutor for a winter on the plantation. He had spent half his youth with an older brother, hunting horses in Texas; and, in a word, to him, "United States" was scarcely a reality. Yet he had been fed by "United States" for all the years since he had been in the army. He had sworn on his faith as a Christian to be true to "United States" which gave him the uniform he wore, and the sword by his side. Nay, my poor Nolan, it was only because "United States" had picked you out first as one of her own confidential men of honor, that "A. Burr" cared for you a straw more than for the flat-boat men who sailed his ark for him. I do not excuse Nolan; I only explain to the reader why he damned his country, and wished he might never hear her name again.

He never did hear her name but once again. From that moment, September 23, 1807, till the day he died, May 11, 1863, he never heard her name again. For that half century and more he was a man without a country.

Old Morgan, as I said, was terribly shocked. If Nolan had compared George Washington to Benedict Arnold, or had cried, "God save King George," Morgan would not have felt worse. He called the court into his private room, and returned in fifteen minutes, with a face like a sheet, to say,—

"Prisoner, hear the sentence of the Court. The Court decides, subject to the approval of the President that you never hear the name of the United States again."

Nolan laughed. But nobody else laughed. Old Morgan was too solemn and the whole room was hushed dead as night for a minute. Even Nolan lost his swagger in a moment. Then Morgan added: "Mr. Marshal, take the prisoner to Orleans in an armed boat, and deliver him to the naval commander there."

The marshal gave his orders, and the prisoner was taken out of court.

"Mr. Marshal," continued old Morgan, "see that no one mentions the United States to the prisoner. Mr. Marshal, make my respects to Lieutenant Mitchell at Orleans, and request him to order that no one shall mention the United States to the prisoner while he is on board ship. You will receive your written orders from the officer on duty here this evening. The court is adjourned without day."

I have always supposed that Colonel Morgan himself took the proceedings of the court to Washington City, and explained them to Mr. Jefferson. Certain it is that the President approved them,–certain, that is, if I may believe the men who say they have seen his signature. Before the *Nautilus* got round from New Orleans to the Northern Atlantic coast with the prisoner on board, the sentence had been approved and he was a man without a country.

The plan then adopted was substantially the same which was necessarily followed ever after. Perhaps it was suggested by the necessity of sending him by water from Fort Adams and Orleans. The Secretary of the Navy–it must have been the first Crowninshield, though he is a man I do not remember–was requested to put Nolan on board a Government vessel bound on a long cruise, and to direct that he should be only so far confined there as to make it certain that he never saw or heard of the country. We had few long cruises then, and the navy was very much out of favor; and as almost all of this story is traditional, as I have explained, I do not know certainly what his first cruise was. But the commander to whom he was intrusted–perhaps it was Tingey or Shaw, though I think it was one of the younger men,–we are all old enough now–regulated the etiquette and the precautions of the affair, and according to his scheme they were carried out, I suppose, till Nolan died.

When I was second officer of the *Intrepid* some thirty years after, I saw the original paper of instructions. I have been sorry ever since that I did not copy the whole of it. It ran, however, much in this way:

"Washington," (with the date, which
must have been late in 1807.)

"Sir,–You will receive from Lt. Neale the person of Philip Nolan, late a Lieutenant in the United States Army.

"This person on his trial by court-martial expressed with an oath the wish that he might never hear of the United States again.

"The court sentenced him to have his wish fulfilled.

"For the present, the execution of the order is intrusted by the President to this department.

"You will take the prisoner on board your ship, and keep him there with such precautions as shall prevent his escape.

"You will provide him with such quarters, rations, and clothing as would be proper for an officer of his late rank, if he were a passenger on your vessel on the business of his Government.

"The gentlemen on board will make any arrangements agreeable to themselves regarding his society. He is to be exposed to no indignity of any kind, nor is he ever unnecessarily to be reminded that he is a prisoner.

"But under no circumstances is he ever to hear of his country or to see any information regarding it; and you will especially caution all the officers under your command to take care that, in the various indulgences which may be granted, this rule, in which his punishment is involved, shall not be broken.

"It is the intention of the Government that he shall never again see the country which he has disowned. Before the end of your cruise you will receive orders which will give effect to this intention.

"Resp'y yours,
"W. SOUTHARD, for the
"Sec'y of the Navy."

If I had only preserved the whole of this paper, there would be no break in the beginning of my sketch of this story. For Captain Shaw, if it was he, handed it to his successor in the charge, and he to his, and I suppose the commander of the Levant has it today as his authority for keeping this man in his mild custody.

The rule adopted on board the ships on which I have met "The Man Without a Country" was, I think, transmitted from the beginning. No mess liked to have him permanently, because his presence cut off all talk of home or of the prospect of return, of politics or letters, of peace or of war,—cut off more than half the talk men like to have at sea. But it was always thought too hard that he should never meet the rest of us, except to touch hats, and we finally sank into one system. He was not permitted to talk with the men unless an officer was by. With officers he had unrestrained intercourse, as far as they and he chose. But he grew shy, though he had favorites: I was one. Then the captain always asked him to dinner on Monday. Every mess in succession took up the invitation in its turn. According to the size of the ship, you had him at your mess more or less often at dinner. His breakfast he ate in his own stateroom,—he always had a stateroom,—which was where a sentinel, or somebody on the watch, could see the door. And whatever else he ate or drank he ate or drank alone. Sometimes, when the marines or sailors had any special jollification, they were permitted to invite "Plain-Buttons," as they called him. Then Nolan was sent with some officer, and the men were forbidden to speak of home while he was there. I believe the theory was, that the sight of his punishment did them good. They called him "Plain-Buttons," because, while he always chose to wear a regulation army uniform, he was not permitted to wear the army button, for the reason that it bore either the initials or the insignia of the country he had disowned.

I remember, soon after I joined the navy, I was on shore with some of the older officers from our ship and from the *Brandywine*, which we had met at Alexandria. We had leave to make a party and go up to Cairo and the Pyramids. As we jogged along (you went on donkeys then) some of the gentlemen (we boys called them "Dons," but the phrase was long since changed) fell to talking about Nolan, and some one told the system which was adopted from the first about his books and other reading. As he was almost never permitted to go on shore, even though the vessel lay in port for months, his time, at the best, hung heavy; and everybody was permitted to lend him books, if they were not published in America and made no allusion to it. These were common enough in the old days, when people in the other hemisphere talked of the United States as little as we do of Paraguay. He had almost all the foreign papers that came into the ship, sooner or later; only somebody must go over them first, and cut out any advertisement or stray paragraph that alluded to America. This was a little cruel sometimes, when the back of what was cut out might be as innocent as Hesiod. Right in the midst of one of Napoleon's battles, or one of Canning's speeches, poor Nolan would find a great hole, because on the back of the page of that paper there had been an advertisement of a packet for New York, or a scrap from the President's message. I say this was the first time I ever heard of this plan, which afterwards I had enough, and more than enough, to do with. I remember it because poor Phillips, who was of the party, as soon as the allusion to reading was made, told a story of something which happened at the Cape of Good Hope on Nolan's first voyage; and it is the only thing I ever knew of that voyage. They had touched at the Cape, and had done the civil thing with the English Admiral and the fleet, and then, leaving for a long cruise up the Indian Ocean, Phillips had borrowed a lot of English books from an officer, which, in those days, as indeed in these, was quite a windfall. Among them, as the Devil would order, was the "Lay of the Last Minstrel," which they had all of them heard of, but which most of them had never seen. I think it could not have been published long. Well, nobody thought there could be any risk of anything national in that, though Phillips swore old Shaw had cut out the "Tempest" from Shakespeare before he let

Nolan have it because he said "the Bermudas ought to be ours and, by Jove, should be one day." So Nolan was permitted to join the circle one afternoon when a lot of them sat on deck smoking and reading aloud. People do not do such things so often now, but when I was young we got rid of a great deal of time so. Well, so it happened that in his turn Nolan took the book and read to the others; and he read very well, as I know. Nobody in the circle knew a line of the poem, only it was all magic and Border chivalry, and was ten thousand years ago. Poor Nolan read steadily through the fifth canto, stopped a minute and drank something, and then began, without a thought of what was coming,–

"Breathes there the man, with soul so dead,
Who never to himself hath said"–

It seems impossible to us that anybody ever heard this for the first time; but all these fellows did then, and poor Nolan himself went on, still unconsciously or mechanically,–

"This is my own, my native land!"

Then they all saw something was to pay; but he expected to get through, I suppose, turned a little pale, but plunged on,–

"Whose heart hath ne'er within him burned,
As home his footsteps he hath turned
  From wandering on a foreign strand ?–
If such there breathe, go, mark him well."

By this time the men were all beside themselves, wishing there was any way to make him turn over two pages; but he had not quite presence of mind for that; he gagged a little, colored crimson, and staggered on,–

"For him no minstrel raptures swell;
High though his titles, proud his name,
Boundless his wealth as wish can claim,
Despite these titles, power and pelf,
The wretch, concentered all in self,"–

and here the poor fellow choked, could not go on, but started up, swung the book into the sea, vanished into his stateroom, "and by Jove," said Phillips, "we did not see him for two months again. And I had to make up some beggarly story to that English surgeon why I did not return his Walter Scott to him."

That story shows about the time when Nolan's braggadocio must have broken down. At first, they said, he took a very high tone, considered his imprisonment a mere farce, affected to enjoy the voyage, and all that; but Phillips said that after he came out of his state-room he never was the same man again. He never read aloud again, unless it was the Bible or Shakespeare, or something else he was sure of. But it was not that merely. He never entered in with the other young men exactly as a companion again. He was always shy afterwards, when I knew him,—very seldom spoke, unless he was spoken to, except to a very few friends. He lighted up occasionally,—I remember late in his life hearing him fairly eloquent on something which had been suggested to him by one of Fléchier's sermons,—but generally he had the nervous, tired look of a heart-wounded man.

When Captain Shaw was coming home,—if, as I say, it was Shaw,—rather to the surprise of everybody they made one of the Windward Islands, and lay off and on for nearly a week. The boys said the officers were sick of salt-junk, and meant to have turtle soup before they came home. But after several days the *Warren* came to the same rendezvous; they exchanged signals; she sent to Phillips and these homeward-bound men letters and papers, and told them she was outward bound, perhaps to the Mediterranean, and took poor Nolan and his traps on the boat back to try his second cruise. He looked very blank when he was told to get ready to join her. He had known enough of the signs of the sky to know that till that moment he was going "home." But this was a distinct evidence of something he had not thought of, perhaps,—that there was no going home for him, even to a prison. And this was the first of some twenty such transfers, which brought him sooner or later into half our best vessels, but which kept him all his life at least some hundred miles from the country he had hoped he might never hear of again.

It may have been on that second cruise—it was once when he was up the Mediterranean—that Mrs. Graff, the celebrated Southern beauty of those days, danced with him. They had been lying a long time in the Bay of Naples, and the officers were very intimate in the English fleet, and there had been great festivities, and our men thought they must give a great ball on board the ship. How they ever did it on board the *Warren* I am sure I do not know. Perhaps it was not the *Warren*, or perhaps ladies did not take up so much room as they do now. They wanted to use Nolan's state-room for something, and they hated to do it without asking him to the ball; so the captain said they might ask him, if they would be responsible that he did not talk with the wrong people, "who would give him intelligence." So the dance went on, the finest party that had ever been known, I dare say; for I never heard of a man-of-war ball that was not. For ladies they had the family of the American consul, one or two travelers who had adventured so far, and a nice bevy of English girls and matrons, perhaps Lady Hamilton herself.

Well, different officers relieved each other in standing and talking with

Nolan in a friendly way, so as to be sure that nobody else spoke to him. The dancing went on with spirit, and after a while even the fellows who took this honorary guard of Nolan ceased to fear any *contretemps*. Only when some English lady—Lady Hamilton, as I said, perhaps—called for a set of "American dances," an odd thing happened. Everybody then danced contra-dances. The black band, nothing loath, conferred as to what "American dances" were, and started off with "Virginia Reel," which they followed with "Money-Musk," which, in its turn in those days, should have been followed by "The Old Thirteen." But just as Dick, the leader, tapped for his fiddlers to begin, and bent forward, about to say, in true Negro state. "'The Old Thirteen,' gentlemen and ladies!" as he had said, "'Virginny Reel, if you please!" "'Money-Musk,' if you please!" the captain's boy tapped him on the shoulder, whispered to him, and he did not announce the name of the dance; he merely bowed, began on the air, and they all fell to,—the officers teaching the English girls the figure, but not telling them why it had no name.

But that is not the story I started to tell.—As the dancing went on, Nolan and our fellows all got at ease, as I said,—so much so that it seemed quite natural for him to bow to that splendid Mrs. Graff, and say,—

"I hope you have not forgotten me, Miss Rutledge. Shall I have the honor of dancing?"

He did it so quickly, that Shubrick, who was by him, could not hinder him. She laughed and said,—

"I am not Miss Rutledge any longer, Mr. Nolan; but I will dance all the same," just nodded to Shubrick, as if to say he must leave Mr. Nolan to her, and led him off to the place where the dance was forming.

Nolan thought he had got his chance. He had known her in Philadelphia, and at other places had met her, and this was a godsend. You could not talk in contra-dances, as you do in cotillions, or even in the pauses of waltzing; but there were chances for tongues and sounds, as well as for eyes and blushes. He began with her travels, and Europe, and Vesuvius, and the French; and then, when they had worked down, and had that long talking-time at the bottom of the set, he said boldly,—a little pale, she said, as she told me the story, years after,—

"And what do you hear from home, Mrs. Graff?"

And that splendid creature looked through him. Jove! how she must have looked through him! "Home!! Mr. Nolan!!! I thought you were the man who never wanted to hear of home again!"—and she walked directly up the deck to her husband, and left poor Nolan alone, as he always was.—He did not dance again.

I cannot give any history of him in order; nobody can now; and, indeed, I am not trying to. These are the traditions, which I sort out, as I believe them, from the myths which have been told about this man for forty years. The lies that have been told about him are legion. The fellows used to say he was the "Iron Mask"; and poor George Pons went to his grave in the belief that this was the author of "Junius," who was being punished for his celebrated libel on Thomas Jefferson. Pons was not very strong in the historical line. A happier story than either of these I have told is of the War. That came along soon after. I have heard this affair told in three or four ways,–and, indeed, it may have happened more than once. But which ship it was on I cannot tell. However, in one, at least, of the great frigate-duels with the English, in which the navy was really baptized, it happened that a round shot from the enemy entered one of our ports square, and took right down the officer of the gun himself, and almost every man of the gun's crew. Now you may say what you choose about courage, but that is not a nice thing to see. But as the men who were not killed picked themselves up, and the surgeon's people were carrying off the bodies, there appeared Nolan, in his shirt-sleeves, with the rammer in his hand, and, just as if he had been the officer, told them off with authority,–who should go to the cockpit with the wounded men, who should stay with him,–perfectly cheery, and with that way which makes men feel sure all is right and is going to be right. And he finished loading the gun with his own hands, aimed it, and bade the men fire. And there he stayed, captain of that gun, keeping those fellows in spirits, till the enemy struck,–sitting on the carriage while the gun was cooling, though he was exposed all the time–showing them easier ways to handle heavy shot,–making the raw hands laugh at their own blunders,–and when the gun cooled again, getting it loaded and fired twice as often as any other gun on the ship. The captain walked forward, by way of encouraging the men, and Nolan touched his hat and said,—

"I am showing them how we do this in the artillery, sir."

And this is a part of the story where all the legends agree: that the Commodore said,–

"I see you do, and I thank you, sir; and I shall never forget this day, sir, and you never shall, sir."

And after the whole thing was over, and he had the Englishman's sword, in the midst of the state and ceremony of the quarter-deck, he said,—

"Where is Mr. Nolan? Ask Mr. Nolan to come here."

And when Nolan came, the captain said,—

"Mr. Nolan, we are all very grateful to you today; you are one of us today; you will be named in the dispatches."

And then the old man took off his own sword of ceremony, and gave it to Nolan, and made him put it on. The man told me this who saw it. Nolan cried like a baby, and well he might. He had not worn a sword since that infernal day at Fort Adams. But always afterwards on occasions of ceremony, he wore that quaint old French sword of the Commodore's.

The captain did mention him in the dispatches. It was always said he asked that he might be pardoned. He wrote a special letter to the Secretary of

War. But nothing ever came of it. As I said, that was about the time when they began to ignore the whole transaction at Washington, and when Nolan's imprisonment began to carry itself on because there was nobody to stop it without any new orders from home.

I have heard it said that he was with Porter when he took possession of the Nukahiwa Islands. Not this Porter, you know, but old Porter, his father, Essex Porter,—that is, the old Essex Porter, not this Essex. As an artillery officer, who had seen service in the West, Nolan knew more about fortifications, embrasures, ravelins, stockades, and all that, than any of them did; and he worked with a right good will in fixing that battery all right. I have always thought it was a pity Porter did not leave him in command there with Gamble. That would have settled all the question about his punishment. We should have kept the islands, and at this moment we should have one station in the Pacific Ocean. Our French friends, too, when they wanted this little watering place, would have found it was preoccupied. But Madison and the Virginians, of course, flung all that away.

All that was near fifty years ago. If Nolan was thirty then, he must have been near eighty when he died. He looked sixty when he was forty. But he never seemed to me to change a hair afterwards. As I imagine his life, from what I have seen and heard of it, he must have been in every sea, and yet almost never on land. He must have known, in a formal way, more officers in our service than any man living knows. He told me once, with a grave smile, that no man in the world lived so methodical a life as he. "You know the boys say I am the Iron Mask, and you know how busy he was." He said it did not do for anyone to try to read all the time, more than to do anything else all the time; but that he read just five hours a day. "Then," he said, "I keep up my notebooks, writing in them at such and such hours from what I have been reading; and I include in them my scrap-books." Those were very curious indeed. He had six or eight, of different subjects. There was one of History, one of Natural Science, one which he called "Odds and Ends." But they were not merely books of extracts from newspapers. They had bits of plants and ribbons, shells tied on, and carved scraps of bone and wood, which he had taught the men to cut for him, and they were beautifully illustrated. He drew admirably. He had some of the funniest drawings there, and some of the most pathetic, that I have ever seen in my life. I wonder who will have Nolan's scrap-books.

Well, he said his reading and his notes were his profession, and that they took five hours and two hours respectively of each day. "Then," said he, "every man should have a diversion as well as a profession. My Natural History is my diversion." That took two hours a day more. The men used to bring him birds and fish, but on a long cruise he had to satisfy himself with centipedes and cockroaches and such small game. He was the only naturalist I ever met who knew anything about the habits of the house-fly and the mosquito. All those people can tell you whether they are *Leipidoptera* or *Steptopotera*; but as for telling how you can get rid of them, or how they get away from you when you strike them,—why Linnaeus knew as little of that as John Foy, the idiot, did. These nine hours made Nolan's regular daily "occupation." The rest of the time he talked or walked. Till he grew very old, he went aloft a great deal. He always kept up his exercise and I never heard that he was ill. If any other man was ill, he was the kindest nurse in the world; and he knew more than half the surgeons do. Then if anybody was sick or died, or if the captain wanted him to on any other occasion, he was always ready to read prayers. I have remarked that he read beautifully.

My own acquaintance with Philip Nolan began six or eight years after the War, on my first voyage after I was appointed a midshipman. It was in the first days after our Slave-Trade treaty, while the Reigning House, which was still the house of Virginia, had still a sort of sentimentalism about the suppression of the horrors of the Middle Passage, and something was sometimes done that way. We were in the South Atlantic on that business. From the time I joined, I believe I thought Nolan was a sort of lay chaplain,—a chaplain with a blue coat. I never asked about him. Everything in the ship was strange to me. I knew it was green to ask questions, and I suppose I thought there was a "Plain-Buttons" on every ship. We had him to dine in our mess once a week, and the caution was given that on that day nothing was to be said about home. But if they had told us not to say anything about the planet Mars or the Book of Deuteronomy, I should not have asked why; there were a great many things which seemed to me to have as little reason. I first came to understand anything about "the man without a country" one day when we overhauled a dirty little schooner which had slaves on board. An officer was sent to take charge of her, and after a few minutes he sent back his boat to ask that some one might be sent him who could speak Portuguese. We were all looking over the rail when the message came, and we all wished we could interpret, when the captain asked who spoke Portuguese. But none of the officers did; and just as the captain was sending forward to ask if any of the people could, Nolan stepped out and said he should be glad to interpret, if the captain wished, as he understood the language. The captain thanked him, fitted out another boat with him, and in this boat it was my luck to go.

When we got there, it was such a scene as you seldom see, and never want to. Nastiness beyond account, and chaos run loose in the midst of the nastiness. There were not a great many of the Negroes; but by way of making what there were understand that they were free, Vaughan had had their handcuffs and ankle-cuffs knocked off, and, for convenience sake, was putting them upon the rascals of the schooner's crew. The Negroes were, most of them, out of the hold, and swarming all round the dirty deck, with a central throng surrounding Vaughan and addressing him in every dialect and *patois* of a dialect, from the Zulu click up to the Parisian of Beledeljereed.

As we came on deck, Vaughan looked down from a hogshead, on which he had mounted in desperation, and said,—

"For God's love, is there anybody who can make these wretches understand something? The men gave them rum, and that did not quiet them. I knocked that big fellow down twice, and that did not soothe him. And then I talked Choctaw to all of them together; and I'll be hanged if they understood that as well as they understood the English."

Nolan said he could speak Portuguese, and one or two fine-looking Kroomen were dragged out, who, as it had been found already, had worked for the Portuguese on the coast at Fernando Po.

"Tell them they are free," said Vaughan; "and tell them that these rascals are to be hanged as soon as we can get rope enough."

Nolan "put that into Spanish,"* that is, he explained it in such Portuguese as the Kroomen could understand, and they in turn to such of the Negroes as could understand them. Then there was such a yell of delight, clinching of fists, leaping and dancing, kissing of Nolan's feet, and a general rush made to the hogshead by way of spontaneous worship of Vaughan as the *deus ex machina* of the occasion.

"Tell them," said Vaughan, well pleased, "that I will take them all to Cape Palmas."

This did not answer so well. Cape Palmas was practically as far from the homes of most of them as New Orleans or Rio Janeiro was; that is, they would be eternally separated from home there. And their interpreters, as we could understand, instantly said, "*Ah, non Palmas,*" and began to propose infinite other expedients in most voluble language. Vaughan was rather disappointed at this result of his liberality, and asked Nolan eagerly what they said. The drops stood on poor Nolan's white forehead as he hushed the men down, and said,—

"He says, 'Not Palmas.' He says, 'Take us home, take us to our own country, take us to our own house, take us to our own pickaninnies and our own women.' He says he has an old father and mother, who will die, if they do not see him. And this one says he left his people all sick, and paddled down to Fernando to beg the white doctor to come and help them, and that these devils caught him in the bay just in sight of home, and that he has never seen anybody from home since then. And this one says," choked out Nolan,

*The phrase is General Taylor's. When Santa Ana brought up his immense army at Buena Vista, he sent a flag of truce to invite Taylor to surrender. "Tell him to go to hell," said old Rough-and-Ready. "Bliss, put that into Spanish." "Perfect Bliss," as this accomplished officer, too early lost, was called, interpreted liberally, replying to the flag, in exquisite Castilian, "Say to General Santa Ana that, if he wants us, he must come and take us." And this is the answer which has gone into history.

"that he has not heard a word from his home in six months, while he has been locked up in an infernal barracoon."

Vaughan always said he grew gray himself while Nolan struggled through his interpretation. I, who did not understand anything of the passion involved in it, saw that the very elements were melting with fervent heat, and that something was to pay somewhere. Even the Negroes themselves stopped howling as they saw Nolan's agony, and Vaughan's almost equal agony of sympathy. As quick as he could get words, he said,—

"Tell them yes, yes; tell them they shall go to the Mountains of the Moon, if they will. If I sail the schooner through the Great White Desert, they shall go home!"

And after some fashion Nolan said so. And then they all fell to kissing him again and wanted to rub his nose with theirs.

But he could not stand it long; and getting Vaughan to say he might go back, he beckoned me down into our boat. As we lay back in the stern-sheets and the men gave way, he said to me: "Youngster, let that show you what it is to be without a family, without a home, and without a country. And if you are ever tempted to say a word or to do a thing that shall put a bar between you and your family, your home, and your country, pray God in His mercy to take you that instant home to His own heaven. Stick by your family, boy; forget you have a self, while you do everything for them. Think of your home, boy; write and send, and talk about it. Let it be nearer and nearer to your thought, the farther you have to travel from it; and rush back to it, when you are free, as that poor black slave is doing now. And for your country, boy," and the words rattled in his throat, "and for that flag," and he pointed to the ship, "never dream a dream but of serving her as she bids you, though the service carry you through a thousand hells. No matter what happens to you, no matter who flatters you or who abuses you, never look at another flag, never let a night pass but you pray God to bless that flag. Remember, boy, that behind all these men you have to do with, behind officers and government, and people even, there is the Country Herself, your Country, and that you belong to her as you belong to your own mother. Stand by Her, boy, as you would stand by your mother, if those devils there had got held of her today!"

I was frightened to death by his calm, hard passion; but I blundered out that I would, by all that was holy, and that I had never thought of doing anything else. He hardly seemed to hear me; but he did, almost in a whisper say, "Oh, if anybody had said so to me when I was of your age!"

I think it was this half-confidence of his, which I never abused, for I never told this story till now, which afterward made us great friends. He was very kind to me. Often he sat up, or even got up, at night to walk the deck with me when it was my watch. He explained to me a great deal of my mathematics, and I owe to him my taste for mathematics. He lent me books, and helped me about my reading. He never alluded so directly to his story again; but from one and another officer I have learned, in thirty years, what I am telling. When we parted from him in St. Thomas harbor, at the end of our cruise, I was more sorry than I can tell. I was very glad to meet him again in 1830; and later in life, when I thought I had some influence in Washington, I moved heaven and earth to have him discharged. But it was like getting a ghost out of prison. They pretended there was no such man, and never was such a man. They will say so at the Department now! Perhaps they do not know. It will not be the first thing in the service of which the Department appears to know nothing!

There is a story that Nolan met Burr once on one of our vessels, when a party of Americans came on board in the Mediterranean. But this I believe to be a lie; or rather, it is a myth, *ben trovato,* involving a tremendous blowing-up with which he sunk Burr,–asking him how he liked to be "without a country." But it is clear, from Burr's life, that nothing of the sort could have happened; and I mention this only as an illustration of the stories which get a-going where there is the least mystery at bottom.

So poor Philip Nolan had his wish fulfilled. I know but one fate more dreadful; it is the fate reserved for those men who shall have one day to exile themselves from their country because they have attempted her ruin, and shall have at the same time to see the prosperity and honor to which she rises when she has rid herself of them and their iniquities. The wish of poor Nolan, as we all learned to call him, not because his punishment was too great, but because his repentance was so clear, was precisely the wish of every Bragg and Beauregard who broke a soldier's oath two years ago, and of every Maury and Barron who broke a sailor's. I do not know how often they have repented. I do know that they have done all that in them lay that they might have no country,–that all the honors, associations, memories, and hopes which belong to "country" might be broken up into little shreds and distributed to the winds. I know, too, that their punishment, as they vegetate through what is left of life to them in wretched Boulognes and Leicester Squares, where they are destined to upbraid each other till they die, will have all the agony of Nolan's, with the added pang that every one who sees them will see them to despise and to execrate them. They will have their wish, like him.

For him, poor fellow, he repented of his folly, and then, like a man, submitted to the fate he had asked for. He never intentionally added to the difficulty or delicacy of the charge of those who had him in hold. Accidents would happen; but they never happened from his fault. Lieutenant Truxton told me that when Texas was annexed, there was a careful discussion among the officers, whether they should get hold of Nolan's handsome set of maps, and cut Texas out of it,–from the map of the world and the map of Mexico. The United States had been cut out when the atlas was bought for him. But

It was voted, rightly enough, that to do this would be virtually to reveal to him what had happened, or, as Harry Cole said, to make him think Old Burr had succeeded. So it was from no fault of Nolan's that a great botch happened at my own table, when, for a short time, I was in command of the *George Washington* corvette, on the South American Station. We were lying in the La Plata, and some of the officers, who had been on shore, and had just joined again, were entertaining us with accounts of their misadventures in riding the half-wild horses of Buenos Aires. Nolan was at table, and was in an unusually bright and talkative mood. Some story of a tumble reminded him of an adventure of his own, when he was catching wild horses in Texas with his brother Stephen, at a time when he must have been quite a boy. He told the story with a good deal of spirit,–so much so, that the silence which often follows a good story hung over the table for an instant, to be broken by Nolan himself. For he asked, perfectly unconsciously,–

"Pray, what has become of Texas? After the Mexicans got their independence, I thought that province of Texas would come forward very fast. It is really one of the finest regions on earth; it is the Italy of this continent. But I have not seen or heard a word of Texas for near twenty years."

There were two Texan officers at the table. The reason he had never heard of Texas was that Texas and her affairs had been painfully out of his newspapers since Austin began his settlements; so that, while he read of Honduras and Tamaulipas, and, till quite lately, of California, this virgin province, in which his brother had traveled so far and, I believe, had died, had ceased to be with him. Waters and Williams, the two Texas men, looked grimly at each other, and tried not to laugh. Edward Morris had his attention attracted by the third link in the chain of the captain's chandelier. Watrous was seized with a convulsion of sneezing. Nolan himself saw that something was to pay, he did not know what. And I, as master of the feast, had to say,–

"Texas is out of the map, Mr. Nolan. Have you seen Captain Back's curious account of Sir Thomas Roe's Welcome?"

After that cruise I never saw Nolan again. I wrote to him at least twice a year, for in that voyage we became even confidentially intimate; but he never wrote to me. The other men tell me that in those fifteen years he aged very fast, as well he might indeed, but that he was still the same gentle, uncomplaining, silent sufferer that he ever was, bearing as best he could his self-appointed punishment,–rather less social, perhaps, with new men whom he did not know, but more anxious, apparently, than ever to serve and befriend and teach the boys, some of them fairly seemed to worship him. And now the dear old fellow is dead. He had found a home at last, and a country.

Since writing this, and while considering whether or no I would print it, as a warning to the young Nolans and Vallandighams and Tatnalls of today of what it is to throw away a country, I have received from Danforth, who is on board the *Levant*, a letter which gives an account of Nolan's last hours. It removes all my doubts about telling this story.

To understand the first words of the letter, the non-professional reader should remember that after 1817 the position of every officer who had Nolan in charge was one of the greatest delicacy. The government had failed to renew the order of 1807 regarding him. What was a man to do? Should he let him' go? What, then, if he were called to account by the Department for violating the order of 1807? Should he keep him? What, then, if Nolan should be liberated some day, and should bring an action for false imprisonment or kidnapping against every man who had had him in charge? I urged and pressed this upon Southard, and I have reason to think that other officers did the same thing. But the Secretary always said, as they so often do at Washington, that there were no special orders to give, and that we must act on our own judgment. That means, "If you succeed, you will be sustained; if you fail, you will be disavowed." Well, as Danforth says, all that is over now, though I do not know but I expose myself to a criminal prosecution on the evidence of the very revelation I am making.

Here is the letter:

"*Levant*, 2° 2" S. @ I3I° W.

"Dear Fred,—I try to find heart and life to tell you that it is all over with dear old Nolan. I have been with him on this voyage more than I ever was, and I can understand wholly now the way in which you used to speak of the dear old fellow. I could see that he was not strong, but I had no idea that the end was so near. The doctor had been watching him very carefully, and yesterday morning came to me and told me that Nolan was not so well, and had not left his state-room,—a thing I never remember before. He had let the doctor come and see him as he lay there,—the first time the doctor had been in the state-room, and he said he should like to see me. Oh, dear! do you remember the mysteries we boys used to invent about his room, in the old *Intrepid* days? Well, I went in, and there, to be sure, the poor fellow lay in his berth, smiling pleasantly as he gave me his hand, but looking very frail. I could not help a glance round, which showed me what a little shrine he had made of the box he was lying in. The stars and stripes were triced up above and around a picture of Washington and he had painted a majestic eagle, with lightnings blazing from his beak and his foot just clasping the whole globe, which his wings overshadowed. The dear old boy saw my glance, and, said, with a sad smile, 'Here, you see, I have a country!' And then he pointed to the foot of his bed, where I had not seen before a great map of the United States, as he had drawn it from memory, and which he had there to look upon as he lay. Quaint, queer old names were on it, in large letters: 'Indiana Territory,' 'Mississippi Territory,' and 'Louisiana,' as I supposed our fathers learned such things; but the old fellow had patched in Texas, too; he had carried his western boundary all the way to the Pacific, but on that shore he had defined nothing.

"'Oh, Danforth,' he said, 'I know I am dying. I cannot get home. Surely you will tell me something now?—Stop! stop! Do not speak till I say what I am sure you know, that there is not in this ship, that there is not in America,—God bless her!—a more loyal man than I. There cannot be a man who loves the old flag as I do, or prays for it as I do, or hopes for it as I do. There are thirty-four stars in it now, Danforth. I thank God for that, though I do not know what their names are. There has never been one taken away; I thank God for that. I know by that, that there has never been any successful Burr. Oh, Danforth, Danforth,' he sighed out, 'how like a wretched night's dream a boy's idea of personal fame or of separate sovereignty seems, when one looks back on it after such a life as mine! But tell me,—tell me something,—tell me everything, Danforth, before I die!'

"Ingham, I swear to you that I felt like a monster that I had not told him everything before. Danger or no danger, delicacy or no delicacy, who was I that I should have been acting the tyrant all this time over this dear, sainted old man, who had years ago expiated, in his whole manhood's life the madness of a boy's treason? 'Mr. Nolan,' said I, 'I will tell you everything you ask about. Only, where shall I begin?'

"Oh, the blessed smile that crept over his white face! and he pressed my hand and said, 'God bless you! Tell me their names,' he said, and he pointed to the stars on the flag. 'The last I know is Ohio. My father lived in Kentucky. But I have guessed Michigan and Indiana and Mississippi,—that was where Fort Adams is,—they make twenty. But where are your other fourteen? You have not cut up any of the old ones, I hope?'

"Well, that was not a bad text, and I told him the names, in as good order as I could. and he bade me take down his beautiful map and draw them in as I best could with my pencil. He was wild with delight about Texas, told me how his brother died there; he had marked a gold cross where he supposed his brother's grave was; and he had guessed at Texas. Then he was delighted as he saw California and Oregon;—that, he said, he had suspected partly, because he had never been permitted lo land on that shore, though the ships were there so much. 'And the men,' said he, laughing, 'brought off a good deal besides furs.' Then he went back—heavens, how far!—to ask about the Chesapeake, and what was done to Barron for surrendering her to the Leopard, and whether Burr ever tried again,—and he ground his teeth with the only passion he showed. But in a moment that was over, and he said, 'God forgive me, for I am sure I forgive him.' Then he asked about the old war,—told me the true story of his serving the gun the day we took the *Java*,—asked about dear old David Porter, as he called him. Then he settled down more quietly and very happily, to hear me tell in an hour the history of fifty years.

"How I wished it had been somebody who knew something! But I did as well as I could. I told him of the English war. I told him about Fulton and the steamboat beginning. I told him about old Scott and Jackson; told him all I could think about the Mississippi, and New Orleans, and Texas, and his own old Kentucky. And do you think he asked who was in command of the 'Legion of the West.' I told him it was a very gallant officer, named Grant and that, by our last news, he was about to establish his headquarters at Vicksburg. Then, 'Where was Vicksburg?' I worked that out on the map; it was about a hundred miles, more or less, above his old Fort Adams; and I thought Fort Adams must be a ruin now. 'It must be at old Vick's plantation,' said he; 'well that is a change!'

"I tell you, Ingham, it was a hard thing to condense the history of half a century into that talk with a sick man. And I do not now know what I told him,—of emigration, and the means of it,—of steamboats and rail-roads and telegraphs,—of inventions and books and literature,—of the colleges and West Point and the Naval School,—but with the queerest interruptions that ever you heard. You see it was Robinson Crusoe asking all the accumulated questions of fifty-six years!

"I remember he asked, all of a sudden, who was President now; and when I told him, he asked if Old Abe was General Benjamin Lincoln's son. He said he met old General Lincoln, when he was quite a boy himself, at some Indian treaty. I said no, that Old Abe was a Kentuckian like himself, but I could not tell him of what family; he had worked up from the ranks. 'Good for him!' cried Nolan; 'I am glad of that. As I have brooded and wondered, I have thought our danger was in keeping up those regular successions in the first families.' Then I got talking about my visit to Washington. I told him of meeting the Oregon Congressman, Harding; I told him about Smithsonian and the exploring Expedition; I told him about the Capitol,—and the statues for the pediment,—and Crawford's Liberty,—and Greenough's Washington: Ingham, I told him everything I could think of that would show the grandeur of his country and its prosperity; but I could not make up my mouth to tell him a word about this infernal Rebellion!*

"And he drank it in, and enjoyed it as I cannot tell you. He grew more and more silent, yet I never thought he was tired or faint. I gave him a glass of water, but he just wet his lips, and told me not to go away. Then he asked me to bring the Presbyterian 'Book of Public Prayer,' which lay there, and said, with a smile, that it would open at the right place,—and so it did. There was his double red mark down the page; and I knelt down and read, and he repeated with me, 'For ourselves and our country, O gracious God, we thank Thee, that, notwithstanding our manifold transgressions of Thy holy laws, Thou hast continued to us Thy marvelous kindness,'—and so to the end of

*This story was written in 1863.—EDITOR.

that thanksgiving. Then he turned to the end of the same book, and I read the words more familiar to me: 'Most heartily we beseech Thee with Thy favor to behold and bless Thy servant, the President of the United States, and all others in authority,'—and the rest of the Episcopal collect. 'Danforth,' said he, 'I have repeated those prayers night and morning, it is now fifty-five years.' And then he said he would go to sleep. He bent me down over him and kissed me; and he said, 'Look in my Bible, Danforth, when I am gone.' And I went away.

"But I had no thought it was the end. I thought he was tired and would sleep. I knew he was happy, and I wanted him to be alone.

"But in an hour, when the doctor went in gently, he found Nolan had breathed his life away with a smile. He had something pressed close to his lips. It was his father's badge of the Order of Cincinnati.

"We looked in his Bible, and there was a slip of paper, at the place where he had marked the text,—

"'They desire a country, even a heavenly: wherefore God is not ashamed to be called their God: for he hath prepared for them a city.'

"On this slip of paper he had written,—

"'Bury me in the sea; it has been my home, and I love it. But will not someone set up a stone for my memory at Fort Adams or at Orleans, that my disgrace, may not be more than I ought to bear? Say on it;—

IN MEMORY OF
PHILIP NOLAN,
LIEUTENANT
IN THE ARMY OF
THE UNITED STATES.
He loved his country as no other man has loved
her; but no man deserved less at her hands.'"

FRANK R. STOCKTON

[1834–1902]

The Lady, or the Tiger?

(First published in *Century Magazine*,
November, 1882; first book publication in 1884.)

IN THE VERY olden time, there lived a semi-barbaric king, whose ideas, though somewhat polished and sharpened by the progressiveness of distant Latin neighbors, were still large, florid, and untrammelled, as became the half of him which was barbaric. He was a man of exuberant fancy, and, withal, of an authority so irresistible that, at his will, he turned his varied fancies into facts. He was greatly given to self-communing; and, when he and himself agreed upon anything, the thing was done. When every member of his domestic and political systems moved smoothly in its appointed course, his nature was bland and genial; but whenever there was a little hitch, and some of his orbs got out of their orbits, he was blander and more genial still, for nothing pleased him so much as to make the crooked straight, and crush down uneven places.

Among the borrowed notions by which his barbarism had become semified was that of the public arena, in which, by exhibitions of manly and beastly valor, the minds of his subjects were refined and cultured.

But even here the exuberant and barbaric fancy asserted itself. The arena of the king was built, not to give the people an opportunity of hearing the rhapsodies of dying gladiators, nor to enable them to view the inevitable conclusion of a conflict between religious opinions and hungry jaws, but for purposes far better adapted to widen and develop the mental energies of the people. This vast amphitheater, with its encircling galleries, its mysterious vaults, and its unseen passages, was an agent of poetic justice, in which crime was punished, or virtue rewarded, by the decrees of an impartial and incorruptible chance.

When a subject was accused of a crime of sufficient importance to interest the king, public notice was given that on an appointed day the fate of the accused person would be decided in the king's arena,—a structure which well deserved its name; for, although its form and plan were borrowed from afar, its purpose emanated solely from the brain of this man, who, every barleycorn a king, knew no tradition to which he owed more allegiance than pleased his fancy, and who ingrafted on every adopted form of human thought and action the rich growth of his barbaric idealism.

When all the people had assembled in the galleries, and the king, surrounded by his court, sat high up on his throne of royal state on one side of the arena, he gave a signal, a door beneath him opened, and the accused subject stepped out into the amphitheater. Directly opposite him, on the other side of the enclosed space, were two doors, exactly alike and side by side. It was the duty and the privilege of the person on trial, to walk directly to these doors and open one of them. He could open either door he pleased: he was subject to no guidance or influence but that of the aforementioned impartial and incorruptible chance. If he opened the one, there came out of it a hungry tiger, the fiercest and most cruel that could be procured, which immediately sprang upon him, and tore him to pieces, as a punishment for his guilt. The moment that the case of the criminal was thus decided, doleful iron bells were clanged, great wails went up from the hired mourners posted on the outer rim of the arena, and the vast audience, with bowed heads and downcast hearts, wended slowly their homeward way, mourning greatly that one so young and fair, or so old and respected, should have merited so dire a fate.

But, if the accused person opened the other door, there came forth from it a lady, the most suitable to his years and station that his majesty could select among his fair subjects; and to this lady he was immediately married, as a reward of his innocence. It mattered not that he might already possess a wife and family, or that his affections might he engaged upon an object of his own selection: the king allowed no such subordinate arrangements to interfere with his great scheme of retribution and reward. The exercises, as in the other instance, took place immediately, and in the arena. Another door opened beneath the king, and a priest, followed by a band of choristers, and dancing maidens blowing joyous airs on golden horns and treading an epithalamic measure, advanced to where the pair stood, side by side; and the wedding was promptly and cheerily solemnized. Then the gay brass bells rang forth their merry peals, the people shouted glad hurrahs, and the innocent man, preceded by children strewing flowers on his path, led his bride to his home.

This was the king's semi-barbaric method of administering justice. Its perfect fairness is obvious. The criminal could not know out of which door would come the lady: he opened either he pleased, without having the slightest idea whether in the next instant, he was to be devoured or married. On some occasions the tiger came out of one door, and on some out of the other. The decisions of this tribunal were not only fair, they were positively determinate: the accused person was instantly punished if he found himself guilty; and, if innocent, he was rewarded on the spot, whether he liked it or not. There was no escape from the judgments of the king's arena.

The institution was a very popular one. When the people gathered together on one of the great trial days, they never knew whether they were to witness a bloody slaughter or a hilarious wedding. This element of uncertainty lent an interest to the occasion which it could not otherwise have attained. Thus, the masses were entertained and pleased, and the thinking part of the community could bring no charge of unfairness against this plan; for did not the accused person have the whole matter in his own hands?

This semi-barbaric king had a daughter as blooming as his most florid fancies, and with a soul as fervent and imperious as his own. As is usual in such cases, she was the apple of his eye, and was loved by him above all humanity. Among his courtiers was a young man of that fineness of blood and lowness of station common to the conventional heroes of romance who love royal maidens. This royal maiden was well satisfied with her lover, for he was handsome and brave to a degree unsurpassed in all this kingdom; and she loved him with an ardor that had enough of barbarism in it to make it exceedingly warm and strong. This love affair moved on happily for many months, until one day the king happened to discover its existence. He did not hesitate nor waver in regard to his duty in the premises. The youth was immediately cast into prison, and a day was appointed for his trial in the king's arena. This, of course, was an especially important occasion; and his majesty, as well as all the people, was greatly interested in the workings and development of this trial. Never before had such a case occurred; never before had a subject dared to love the daughter of a king. In after-years such things became commonplace enough; but then they were, in no slight degree, novel and startling.

The tiger-cages of the kingdom were searched for the most savage and relentless beasts, from which the fiercest monster might be selected for the arena; and the ranks of maiden youth and beauty throughout the land were carefully surveyed by competent judges, in order that the young man might have a fitting bride in case fate did not determine for him a different destiny. Of course, everybody knew that the deed with which the accused was charged had been done. He had loved the princess, and neither he, she, nor any one else thought of denying the fact; but the king would not think of allowing any fact of this kind to interfere with the workings of the tribunal, in which he took such great delight and satisfaction. No matter how the affair turned out, the youth would be disposed of; and the king would take an aesthetic pleasure in watching the course of events, which would determine whether or not the young man had done wrong in allowing himself to love the princess.

The appointed day arrived. From far and near the people gathered, and thronged the great galleries of the arena; and crowds, unable to gain admittance, massed themselves against its outside walls. The king and his court were in their places, opposite the twin doors,—those fateful portals, so terrible in their similarity.

All was ready. The signal was given. A door beneath the royal party opened, and the lover of the princess walked into the arena. Tall, beautiful, fair, his appearance was greeted with a low hum of admiration and anxiety. Half the audience had not known so grand a youth had lived among them. No wonder the princess loved him! What a terrible thing for him to be there!

As the youth advanced into the arena, he turned, as the custom was, to bow to the king: but he did not think at all of that royal personage; his eyes were fixed upon the princess, who sat to the right of her father. Had it not been for the moiety of barbarism in her nature, it is probable that lady would not have been there; but her intense and fervid soul would not allow her to be absent on an occasion in which she was so terribly interested. From the moment that the decree had gone forth, that her lover should decide his fate in the king's arena, she had thought of nothing, night or day, but this great event and the various subjects connected with it. Possessed of more power, influence, and force of character than any one who had ever before been interested in such a case, she had done what no other person had done,—she had possessed herself of the secret of the doors. She knew in which of the two rooms, that lay behind those doors, stood the cage of the tiger, with its open front, and in which waited the lady. Through these thick doors, heavily curtained with skins on the inside, it was impossible that any noise or suggestion should come from within to the person who should approach to raise the latch of one of them; but gold, and the power of a woman's will, had brought the secret to the princess.

And not only did she know in which room stood the lady ready to emerge, all blushing and radiant, should her door be opened, but she knew who the lady was. It was one of the fairest and loveliest of the damsels of the court who had been selected as the reward of the accused youth, should he be proved innocent of the crime of aspiring to one so far above him; and the princess hated her. Often had she seen, or imagined that she had seen, this fair creature throwing glances of admiration upon the person of her lover, and sometimes she thought these glances were perceived and even returned. Now and then she had seen them talking together; it was but for a moment or two, but much can be said in a brief space; it may have been on most unimportant topics, but how could she know that? The girl was lovely, but she had dared to raise her eyes to the loved one of the princess; and, with all the intensity of the savage blood transmitted to her through long lines of wholly barbaric ancestors, she hated the woman who blushed and trembled behind that silent door.

When her lover turned and looked at her, and his eye met hers as she sat there paler and whiter than any one in the vast ocean of anxious faces about her, he saw, by that power of quick perception which is given to those whose souls are one, that she knew behind which door crouched the tiger, and behind which stood the lady. He had expected her to know it. He understood her nature, and his soul was assured that she would never rest until she had made plain to herself this thing, hidden to all other lookers-on, even to the king. The only hope for the youth in which there was any element of certainty was based upon the success of the princess in discovering this mystery; and the moment he looked upon her, he saw she had succeeded, as in his soul he knew she would succeed.

Then it was that his quick and anxious glance asked the question: "Which?" It was as plain to her as if he shouted it from where he stood. There was not an instant to be lost. The question was asked in a flash: it must be answered in another.

Her right arm lay on the cushioned parapet before her. She raised her hand, and made a slight, quick movement toward the right. No one but her lover saw her. Every eye but his was fixed on the man in the arena.

He turned, and with a firm and rapid step he walked across the empty space. Every heart stopped beating, every breath was held, every eye was fixed immovably upon that man. Without the slightest hesitation, he went to the door on the right, and opened it.

Now, the point of the story is this: Did the tiger come out of that door, or did the lady?

The more we reflect upon this question, the harder it is to answer. It involves a study of the human heart which leads us through devious mazes of passion, out of which it is difficult to find our way. Think of it, fair reader, not as if the decision of the question depended upon yourself, but upon that hot-blooded, semi-barbaric princess, her soul at a white heat beneath the combined fires of despair and jealousy. She had lost him, but who should have him?

How often, in her waking hours and in her dreams, had she started in wild horror, and covered her face with her hands as she thought of her lover opening the door on the other side of which waited the cruel fangs of the tiger!

But how much oftener had she seen him at the other door! How in her grievous reveries had she gnashed her teeth, and torn her hair, when she saw his start of rapturous delight as he opened the door of the lady! How her soul had burned in agony when she had seen him rush to meet that woman, with her flushing cheek and sparkling eye of triumph; when she had seen him lead her forth, his whole frame kindled with the joy of recovered life; when she had heard the glad shouts from the multitude, and the wild ringing of the happy bells; when she had seen the priest, with his joyous followers, advance to the couple, and make them man and wife before her very eyes; and when she had seen them walk away together upon their path of flowers, followed by the tremendous shouts of the hilarious multitude, in which her one despairing shriek was lost and drowned!

Would it not be better for him to die at once, and go to wait for her in the blessed regions of semi-barbaric futurity?

And yet, that awful tiger, those shrieks, that blood!

Her decision had been indicated in an instant, but it had been made after days and nights of anguished deliberation. She had known she would be asked, she had decided what she would answer, and, without the slightest hesitation, she had moved her hand to the right.

The question of her decision is one not to be lightly considered, and it is not for me to presume to set myself up as the one person able to answer it. And so I leave it with all of you: Which came out of the opened door,—the lady, or the tiger?

MARK TWAIN

[1835–1910]

The Celebrated Jumping Frog of Calaveras County

(First published in *New York Saturday Press*, November 18, 1865; first book publication in 1867.)

IN COMPLIANCE WITH the request of a friend of mine, who wrote me from the East, I called on good-natured, garrulous old Sirnon Wheeler, and inquired after my friend's friend, *Leonidas W.* Smiley, as requested to do, and I hereunto append the result. I have a lurking suspicion that *Leonidas W.* Smiley is a myth; that my friend never knew such a personage; and that he only conjectured that, if I asked old Wheeler about him, it would remind him of his infamous Jim Smiley, and he would go to work and bore me nearly to death with some infernal reminiscence of him as long and tedious as it should be useless to me. If that was the design, it certainly succeeded.

I found Simon Wheeler dozing comfortably by the bar-room stove of the old, dilapidated tavern in the ancient mining camp of Angel's, and I noticed that he was fat and bald-headed, and had an expression of winning gentleness and simplicity upon his tranquil countenance. He roused up and gave me good-day. I told him a friend of mine had commissioned me to make some inquiries about a cherished companion of his boyhood named *Leonidas W.* Smiley—*Rev. Leonidas W.* Smiley—a young minister of the Gospel, who he had heard was at one time a resident of Angel's Camp. I added, that, if Mr. Wheeler could tell me anything about this Rev. Leonidas W. Smiley, I would feel under many obligations to him.

Simon Wheeler backed me into a corner and blockaded me there with his chair, and then sat me down and reeled off the monotonous narrative which follows this paragraph. He never smiled, he never frowned, he never changed his voice from the gentle-flowing key to which he tuned the initial sentence, he never betrayed the slightest suspicion of enthusiasm; but all through the interminable narrative there ran a vein of impressive earnestness and sincerity, which showed me plainly that, so far from his imagining that there was anything ridiculous or funny about his story, he regarded it as a really important matter, and admitted its two heroes as men of transcendent genius in *finesse*. To me, the spectacle of a man drifting serenely along through such a queer yarn without ever smiling, was exquisitely absurd. As I said before, I asked him to tell me what he knew of Rev. Leonidas W. Smiley, and he replied as follows. I let him go on in his own way, and never interrupted him once:

There was a feller here once by the name of *Jim* Smiley, in the winter of '49–maybe it was the spring of '50–I don't recollect exactly, somehow, though what makes me think it was one or the other is because I remember the big flume wasn't finished when he first came to the camp; but anyway, he was the curiousest man about always betting on anything that turned up you ever see, if he could get anybody to bet on the other side; and if he couldn't, he'd change sides. Any way that suited the other man would suit him–any way just so's he got a bet, *he* was satisfied. But still he was lucky, uncommon lucky–he most always come out winner. He was always ready and laying for a chance; there couldn't be no solit'ry thing mentioned but that feller'd offer to bet on it, and take any side you please, as I was just telling you. If there was a horse-race, you'd find him flush, or you'd find him busted at the end of it; if there was a dog-fight, he'd bet on it; if there was a cat-fight, he'd bet on it; if there was a chicken-fight, he'd bet on it; why, if there was two birds setting on a fence, he would bet you which one would fly first; or if there was a camp meeting, he would be there reg'lar, to bet on Parson Walker, which he judged to be the best exhorter about here, and so he was, too, and a good man. If he even seen a straddle-bug start to go anywheres, he would bet you how long it would take him to get wherever he was going to, and if you took him up, he would foller that straddle-bug to Mexico but what he would find out where he was bound for and how long he was on the road. Lots of the boys here has seen that Smiley, and can tell you about him. Why, it never made no difference to *him*–he would bet on *any*thing–the dangdest feller. Parson Walker's wife laid very sick once, for a good while, and it seemed as if they warn't going to save her; but one morning he came in, and Smiley asked how she was, and he said she was considerable better–thank the Lord for his inf'nit mercy–and coming on so smart that, with the blessing of Prov'dence, she'd get well yet; and Smiley, before he thought, says, "Well, I'll risk two-and-a-half that she don't, anyway."

Thish-yer Smiley had a mare–the boys called her the fifteen-minute nag, but that was only in fun, you know, because, of course, she was faster than that–and he used to win money on that horse, for all she was so slow and always had the asthma, or the distemper, or the consumption, or something of that kind. They used to give her two or three hundred yards start, and then pass her under way; but always at the fag-end of the race she'd get excited and desperate-like, and come cavorting and straddling up, and scattering her legs around limber, sometimes in the air, and sometimes out to one side amongst the fences, and kicking up m-o-r-e dust, and raising m-o-r-e racket with her coughing and sneezing and blowing her nose—and always fetch up at the stand just about a neck ahead, as near as you could cipher it down.

And he had a little small bull pup, that to look at him you'd think he wan't worth a cent but to set around and look ornery and lay for a chance to steal something. But as soon as money was up on him, he was a different dog; his under-jaw'd begin to stick out like the fo'castle of a steamboat, and his teeth would uncover, and shine savage like the furnaces. And a dog might tackle him, and bully-rag him, and bite him, and throw him over his shoulder two or three times, and Andrew Jackson—which was the name of the pup—Andrew Jackson would never let on but what *he* was satisfied, and hadn't expected nothing else—and the bets being doubled and doubled on the other side all the time, till the money was all up; and then all of a sudden he would grab that other dog jest by the j'int of his hind leg and freeze to it—not claw, you understand, but only jest grip and hang on till they throwed up the sponge, if it was a year. Smiley always come out winner on that pup, till he harnessed a dog once that didn't have no hind legs, because they'd been sawed off by a circular saw, and when the thing had gone along far enough, and the money was all up, and he come to make a snatch for his pet holt, he saw in a minute how he'd been imposed on, and how the other dog had him in the door, so to speak, and he 'peared surprised, and then he looked sorter discouraged-like, and didn't try no more to win the fight, and so he got shucked out bad. He give Smiley a look, as much to say his heart was broke and it was *his* fault for putting up a dog that hadn't no hind legs for him to take holt of, which was his main dependence in a fight, and then he limped off a piece and laid down and died. It was a good pup, was that Andrew Jackson, and would have made a name for hisself if he'd lived, for the stuff was in him, and he had genius—I know it, because he hadn't no opportunities to speak of, and it don't stand to reason that a dog could make such a fight as he could under them circumstances, if he hadn't no talent. It always makes me feel sorry when I think of that last fight of his'n, and the way it turned out.

Well, thish-yer Smiley had rat-tarriers, and chicken-cocks, and tomcats. and all them kind of things, till you couldn't rest, and you couldn't fetch nothing for him to bet on but he'd match you. He ketched a frog one day, and took him home, and said he cal'klated to edercate him; and so he never done nothing for these three months but set in his back yard and learn that frog to jump. And you bet you he *did* learn him, too. He'd give him a little punch behind, and the next minute you'd see that frog whirling in the air like a doughnut—see him turn one summerset, or maybe a couple, if he got a good start, and come down flat-footed and all right, like a cat. He got him up so in the matter of catching flies, and kept him in practice so constant, that he'd nail a fly every time as far as he could see him. Smiley said all a frog wanted was education, and he could do most anything—and I believe him. Why, I've seen him set Dan'l Webster down here on this floor—Dan'l Webster was the name of the frog—and sing out, "Flies, Dan'l, flies!" and quicker'n you could wink, he'd spring straight up, and snake a fly off'n the counter there, and flop down on the floor again as solid as a gob of mud, and fall to scratching the side of his head with his hind foot as indifferent as if he hadn't no idea he's been doin' any more'n any frog might do. You never see a frog so modest and straight-for'ard as he was, for all he was so gifted. And when it come to fair and square jumping on the dead level, he could get over more ground at one straddle than any animal of his breed you ever see. Jumping on a dead level was his strong suit, you understand; and when it come to that, Smiley would ante up money on him as long as he had a red. Smiley was monstrous proud of his frog, and well he might be, for fellers that had traveled and been everywhere all said he laid over any frog that ever *they* see.

Well, Smiley kept the beast in a little lattice box, and he used to fetch him downtown sometimes and lay for a bet. One day a feller—a stranger in the camp, he was—come across him with his box, and says:

"What might it be that you've got in the box?"

And Smiley says, sorter indifferent like, "It might be a parrot, or it might be a canary, maybe, but it ain't—it's only just a frog."

An' the feller took it, and looked at it careful, and turned it round this way and that, and says, "H'm—so 'tis. Well, what's *he* good for?"

"Well," Smiley says, easy and careless, "He's good enough for *one* thing, I should judge—he can outjump any frog in Calaveras county."

The feller took the box again, and took another long, particular look, and give it back to Smiley, and says, very deliberate, "Well, I don't see no p'ints about that frog that's any better'n any other frog."

"Maybe you don't," Smiley says. "Maybe you understand frogs, and maybe you don't understand 'em; maybe you've had experience, and maybe you ain't only a amature, as it were. Anyways, I've got *my* opinion, and I'll risk forty dollars that he can outjump any frog in Calaveras county."

And the feller studied a minute, and then says, kinder sad like, "Well, I'm only a stranger here, and I ain't got no frog; but if I had a frog, I'd bet you."

And then Smiley says, "That's all right—that's all right—if you'll hold my box a minute, I'll go and get you a frog." And so the feller took the box, and put up his forty dollars along with Smiley's, and set down to wait.

So he set there a good while thinking and thinking to hisself, and then he got the frog out and prized his mouth open and took a teaspoon and filled him full of quail shot—filled him pretty near up to his chin—and set him on the floor. Smiley he went to the swamp and slopped around in the mud for a long time, and finally he ketched a frog, and fetched him in, and give him to this feller, and says:

"Now, if you're ready, set him alongside of Dan'l, with his forepaws just even with Dan'l, and I'll give the word." Then he says. "One–two–three–jump!" and him and the feller touched up the frogs from behind, and the new frog hopped off, but Dan'l give a heave, and hysted up his shoulders–so–like a Frenchman, but it wasn't no use–he couldn't budge; he was planted as solid as an anvil, and he couldn't no more stir than if he was anchored out. Smiley was a good deal surprised, and he was disgusted too, but he didn't have no idea what the matter was, of course.

The feller took the money and started away; and when he was going out at the door, he sorter jerked his thumb over his shoulder–this way–at Dan'l, and says again, very deliberate, "Well, *I* don't see no p'ints about that frog that's any better'n any other frog."

Smiley he stood scratching his head and looking down at Dan'l a long time, and at last he says, "I do wonder what in the nation that frog throw'd off for–I wonder if there ain't something the matter with him–he 'pears to look mighty baggy, somehow." And he ketched Dan'l by the nap of the neck, and lifted him up and says, "Why, blame my cats, if he don't weigh five pounds!" and turned him upside down, and he belched out a double handful of shot. And then he see how it was, and he was the maddest man–he set the frog down and took out after that feller, but he never ketched him. And—

(Here Simon Wheeler heard his name called from the front yard, andgot up to see what was wanted.) And turning to me as he moved away, he said: "Just set where you are, stranger, and rest easy–I ain't going to be gone a second."

But, by your leave, I did not think that a continuation of the history of the enterprising vagabond *Jim* Smiley would be likely to afford me much information concerning the Rev. *Leonidas W.* Smiley, and so I started away.

At the door I met the sociable Wheeler returning, and he buttonholed me and recommenced:

"Well, thish-yer Smiley had a yeller one-eyed cow that didn't have no tail, only jest a short stump like a bannanner, and–"

"Oh, hang Smiley and his afflicted cow!" I muttered, good-naturedly, and bidding the old gentleman good-day, I departed.

The Man that Corrupted Hadleyburg

(First published in *Harper's Magazine*,
December, 1899; first book publication in 1900.)

IT WAS MANY years ago. Hadleyburg was the most honest and upright town in all the region round about. It had kept that reputation unsmirched during three generations, and was prouder of it than of any other of its possessions. It was so proud of it, and so anxious to insure its perpetuation, that it began to teach the principles of honest dealing to its babies in the cradle, and made the like teachings the staple of their culture thenceforward through all the years devoted to their education. Also, throughout the formative years temptations were kept out of the way of the young people, so that their honesty could have every chance to harden and solidify, and become a part of their very bone. The neighboring towns were jealous of this honorable supremacy, and affected to sneer at Hadleyburg's pride in it and call it vanity; but all the same they were obliged to acknowledge that Hadleyburg was in reality an incorruptible town; and if pressed they would also acknowledge that the mere fact that a young man hailed from Hadleyburg was all the recommendation he needed when he went forth from his natal town to seek for responsible employment.

But at last, in the drift of time, Hadleyburg had the ill luck to offend a passing stranger—possibly without knowing it, certainly without caring, for Hadleyburg was sufficient unto itself, and cared not a rap for strangers or their opinions. Still, it would have been well to make an exception in this one's case, for he was a bitter man and revengeful. All through his wanderings during a whole year he kept his injury in mind, and gave all his leisure moments to trying to invent a compensating satisfaction for it. He contrived many plans, and all of them were good, but none of them was quite sweeping enough; the poorest of them would hurt a great many individuals, but what he wanted was a plan which would comprehend the entire town, and not let so much as one person escape unhurt. At last he had a fortunate idea, and when it fell into his brain it lit up his whole head with an evil joy. He began to form a plan at once, saying to himself, "That is the thing to do—I will corrupt the town."

Six months later he went to Hadleyburg, and arrived in a buggy at the house of the old cashier of the bank about ten at night. He got a sack out of the buggy, shouldered it, and staggered with it through the cottage yard, and knocked at the door. A woman's voice said "Come in," and he entered, and set his sack behind the stove in the parlor, saying politely to the old lady who sat reading the *Missionary Herald* by the lamp:

"Pray keep your seat, madam, I will not disturb you. There—now it is pretty well concealed; one would hardly know it was there. Can I see your husband a moment, madam?"

No, he was gone to Brixton, and might not return before morning.

"Very well, madam, it is no matter. I merely wanted to leave that sack in his care, to be delivered to the rightful owner when he shall be found. I am a stranger; he does not know me; I am merely passing through the town tonight to discharge a matter which has been long in my mind. My errand is now completed, and I go pleased and a little proud, and you will never see me again. There is a paper attached to the sack which will explain everything. Good night, madam."

The old lady was afraid of the mysterious big stranger, and was glad to see him go. But her curiosity was roused, and she went straight to the sack and brought away the paper. It began as follows:

"TO BE PUBLISHED; or, the right man sought out by private inquiry—either will answer. This sack contains gold coin weighing a hundred and sixty pounds four ounces–"

"Mercy on us, and the door not locked!"

Mrs. Richards flew to it all in a tremble and locked it, then pulled down the window-shades and stood frightened, worried, and wondering if there was anything else she could do toward making herself and the money more safe. She listened awhile for burglars, then surrendered to curiosity and went back to the lamp and finished reading the paper:

"I am a foreigner, and am presently going back to my own country, to remain there permanently. I am grateful to America for what I have received at her hands during my long stay under her flag; and to one of her citizens—a citizen of Hadleyburg–I am especially grateful for a great kindness done me a year or two ago. Two great kindnesses, in fact. I will explain. I was a gambler. I say I was. I was a ruined gambler. I arrived in this village at night, hungry and without a penny. I asked for help–in the dark; I was ashamed to beg in the light. I begged of the right man. He gave me twenty dollars–that is to say, he gave me life, as I considered it. He also gave me fortune; for out of that money I have made myself rich at the gaming-table. And finally, a remark which he made to me has remained with me to this day, and has at last conquered me; and in conquering has saved the remnant of my morals: I shall gamble no more. Now I have no idea who that man was, but I want him found, and I want him to have this money, to give away, throw away, or keep, as he pleases. It is merely my way of testifying my gratitude to him. If I could stay, I would find him myself; but no matter, he will be found. This is an honest town, an incorruptible town, and I know I can trust it without fear. This man can be identified by the remark which he made to me; I feel persuaded that he will remember it.

"And now my plan is this: If you prefer to conduct the inquiry privately, do so. Tell the contents of this present writing to any one who is likely to be the right man. If he shall answer, 'I am the man; the remark I made was so-and-so', apply the test–to wit: open the sack, and in it you will find a sealed envelope containing that remark. If the remark mentioned by the candidate tallies with it, give him the money, and ask no further questions, for he is certainly the right man.

"But if you shall prefer a public inquiry, then publish this present writing in the local paper–with these instructions added, to wit: Thirty days from now, let the candidate appear at the town-hall at eight in the evening (Friday), and hand his remark, in a sealed envelope, to the Rev. Mr. Burgess (if he will be kind enough to act); and let Mr. Burgess there and then destroy the seals of the sack, open it, and see if the remark is correct; if correct, let the money be delivered, with my sincere gratitude, to my benefactor thus identified."

Mrs. Richards sat down, gently quivering with excitement, and was soon lost in thinkings–after this pattern: "What a strange thing it is! . . . And what a fortune for that kind man who set his bread afloat upon the waters! . . . If it had only been my husband that did it!–for we are so poor, so old and poor! . . ." Then, with a sigh–"But it was not my Edward; no, it was not he that gave a stranger twenty dollars. It is a pity, too; I see it now. . . ." Then, with a shudder–"But it is *gambler's* money! the wages of sin: we couldn't take it; we couldn't touch it. I don't like to be near it; it seems a defilement." She moved to a farther chair. . . . "I wish Edward would come, and take it to the bank; a burglar might come at any moment; it is dreadful to be here all alone with it."

At eleven Mr. Richards arrived, and while his wife was saying, "I am *so* glad you've come!" he was saying, "I'm so tired–tired clear out; it is dreadful to be poor, and have to make these dismal journeys at my time of life. Always at the grind, grind, grind, on a salary–another man's slave, and he sitting at home in his slippers, rich and comfortable."

"I am so sorry for you, Edward, you know that; but be comforted: we have our livelihood; we have our good name–"

"Yes, Mary, and that is everything. Don't mind my talk–it's just a moment's irritation and doesn't mean anything. Kiss me–there, it's all gone now, and I am not complaining any more. What have you been getting? What's in the sack?"

Then his wife told him the great secret. It dazed him for a moment; then he said:

"It weighs a hundred and sixty pounds? Why, Mary, it's forty thousand dollars–think of it–a whole fortune! Not ten men in this village are worth that much. Give me the paper."

He skimmed through it and said:

"Isn't it an adventure! Why, it's a romance; it's like the impossible things one reads about in books, and never sees in life." He was well stirred up now; cheerful, even gleeful. He tapped his old wife on the cheek, and said, humorously, "Why, we're rich, Mary, rich; all we've got to do is to bury the money and burn the papers. If the gambler ever comes to inquire, we'll merely look coldly upon him and say: 'What is this nonsense you are talking? We have never heard of you and your sack of gold before'; and then he would look foolish, and—"

"And in the meantime, while you are running on with your jokes, the money is still here, and it is fast getting along toward burglar-time."

"True. Very well, what shall we do—make the inquiry private? No, not that: it would spoil the romance. The public method is better. Think what a noise it will make! And it will make all the other towns jealous; for no stranger would trust such a thing to any town but Hadleyburg, and they know it. It's a great card for us. I must get to the printing-office now, or I shall be too late."

"But stop—stop—don't leave me here alone with it, Edward!"

But he was gone. For only a little while, however. Not far from his own house he met the editor-proprietor of the paper, and gave him the document, and said, "Here is a good thing for you, Cox—put it in."

"It may be too late, Mr. Richards, but I'll see."

At home again he and his wife sat down to talk the charming mystery over; they were in no condition for sleep. The first question was, Who could the citizen have been who gave the stranger the twenty dollars? It seemed a simple one; both answered it in the same breath—

"Barclay Goodson."

"Yes," said Richards, "he could have done it, and it would have been like him, but there's not another in the town."

"Everybody will grant that, Edward—grant it privately, anyway. For six months, now, the village has been its own proper self once more—honest, narrow, self-righteous, and stingy."

"It is what he always called it, to the day of his death—said it right out publicly, too."

"Yes, and he was hated for it."

"Oh, of course; but he didn't care. I reckon he was the best-hated man among us, except the Reverend Burgess."

"Well, Burgess deserves it—he will never get another congregation here. Mean as the town is, it knows how to estimate *him*. Edward, doesn't it seem odd that the stranger should appoint Burgess to deliver the money?"

"Well, yes—it does. That is—that is—"

"Why so much that-*is*-ing? Would *you* select him?"

"Mary, maybe the stranger knows him better than this village does."

"Much *that* would help Burgess!"

The husband seemed perplexed for an answer; the wife kept a steady eye upon him, and waited. Finally Richards said, with the hesitancy of one who is making a statement which is likely to encounter doubt.

"Mary, Burgess is not a bad man."

His wife was certainly surprised.

"Nonsense!" she exclaimed.

"He is not a bad man. I know. The whole of his unpopularity had its foundation in that one thing—the thing that made so much noise."

"That 'one thing,' indeed! As if that 'one thing' wasn't enough, all by itself."

"Plenty. Plenty. Only he wasn't guilty of it."

"How you talk! Not guilty of it! Everybody knows he *was* guilty."

"Mary, I give you my word—he was innocent."

"I can't believe it, and I don't. How do you know?"

"It is a confession. I am ashamed, but I will make it. I was the only man who knew he was innocent. I could have saved him, and—and—well, you know how the town was wrought up—I hadn't the pluck to do it. It would have turned everybody against me. I felt mean, ever so mean; but I didn't dare; I hadn't the manliness to face that."

Mary looked troubled, and for a while was silent. Then she said, stammeringly:

"I—I don't think it would have done for you to—to—One mustn't—er—public opinion—one has to be so careful—so—" It was a difficult road, and she got mired; but after a little she got started again. "It was a great pity, but—Why, we couldn't afford it, Edward—we couldn't indeed. Oh, I wouldn't have had you do it for anything!"

"It would have lost us the good will of so many people, Mary; and then—and then—"

"What troubles me now is, what *he* thinks of us, Edward."

"He? *He* doesn't suspect that I could have saved him."

"Oh," exclaimed the wife, in a tone of relief, "I am glad of that. As long as he doesn't know that you could have saved him, he—he—well, that makes it a great deal better. Why, I might have known he didn't know, because he is always trying to be friendly with us, as little encouragement as we give him. More than once people have twitted me with it. There's the Wilsons, and the Wilcoxes, and the Harknesses, they take a mean pleasure in saying, '*Your friend* Burgess,' because they know it pesters me. I wish he wouldn't persist in liking us so; I can't think why he keeps it up."

"I can explain it. It's another confession. When the thing was new and hot, and the town made a plan to ride him on a rail, my conscience hurt me so that I couldn't stand it, and I went privately and gave him notice, and he got out of the town and stayed out till it was safe to come back."

"Edward! If the town had found it out—"

"*Don't*! It scares me yet, to think of it. I repented of it the minute it was done; and I was even afraid to tell you, lest your face might betray it to somebody. I didn't sleep any that night, for worrying. But after a few days I saw that no one was going to suspect me, and after that I got to feeling glad I did it. And I feel glad yet, Mary—glad through and through."

"So do I, now, for it would have been a dreadful way to treat him. Yes, I'm glad; for really you did owe him that, you know. But, Edward, suppose it should come out yet, some day!"

"It won't."

"Why?"

"Because everybody thinks it was Goodson."

"Of course they would!"

"Certainly. And of course *he* didn't care. They persuaded poor old Sawlsberry to go and charge it on him, and he went blustering over there and did it. Goodson looked him over, like as if he was hunting for a place on him that he could despise the most, then he says, 'So you are the Committee of Inquiry, are you?' Sawlsberry said that was about what he was. 'Hm. Do they require particulars, or do you reckon a kind of a *general* answer will do?' 'If they require particulars, I will come back, Mr. Goodson; I will take the general answer first.' 'Very well, then, tell them to go to hell—I reckon that's general enough. And I'll give you some advice, Sawlsberry; when you come back for the particulars, fetch a basket to carry the relics of yourself home in.'"

"Just like Goodson; it's got all the marks. He had only one vanity: he thought he could give advice better than any other person."

"It settled the business, and saved us, Mary. The subject was dropped."

"Bless you, I'm not doubting *that*."

Then they took up the gold-sack mystery again, with strong interest. Soon the conversation began to suffer breaks—interruptions caused by absorbed thinkings. The breaks grew more and more frequent. At last Richards lost himself wholly in thought. He sat long, gazing vacantly at the floor, and by and by he began to punctuate his thoughts with little nervous movements of his hands that seemed to indicate vexation. Meantime his wife too had relapsed into a thoughtful silence, and her movements were beginning to show a troubled discomfort. Finally Richards got up and strode aimlessly about the room, plowing his hands through his hair, much as a somnambulist might do who was having a bad dream. Then he seemed to arrive at a definite purpose; and without a word he put on his hat and passed quickly out of the house. His wife sat brooding, with a drawn face, and did not seem to be aware that she was alone. Now and then she murmured, "Lead us not into t—. . . but—but—we are so poor, so poor! . . . Lead us not into. . . . Ah, who would be hurt by it?—and no one would ever know. . . . Lead us. . . ."

The voice died out in mumblings. After a little she glanced up and muttered in a half-frightened, half-glad way—

"He is gone! But, oh dear, he may be too late—too late. . . . Maybe not—maybe there is still time." She rose and stood thinking, nervously clasping and unclasping her hands. A slight shudder shook her frame, and she said, out of a dry throat, "God forgive me—it's awful to think such things—but . . . Lord, how we are made—how strangely we are made!"

She turned the light low, and slipped stealthily over and kneeled down by the sack and felt of its ridgy sides with her hands, and fondled them lovingly; and there was a gloating light in her poor old eyes. She fell into fits of absence; and came half out of them at times to mutter, "If we had only waited!—oh, if we had only waited a little, and not been in such a hurry!"

Meantime Cox had gone home from his office and told his wife all about the strange thing that had happened, and they had talked it over eagerly, and guessed that the late Goodson was the only man in the town who could have helped a suffering stranger with so noble a sum as twenty dollars. Then there was a pause, and the two became thoughtful and silent. And by and by nervous and fidgety. At last the wife said, as if to herself:

"Nobody knows this secret but the Richardses . . . and us . . . nobody."

The husband came out of his thinkings with a slight start, ant gazed wistfully at his wife, whose face was become very pale; then he hesitatingly rose, and glanced furtively at his hat, then at his wife—a sort of mute inquiry. Mrs. Cox swallowed once or twice, with her hand at her throat, then in place of speech she nodded her head. In a moment she was alone, and mumbling to herself.

And now Richards and Cox were hurrying through the deserted streets, from opposite directions. They met, panting, at the foot of the printing-office stairs; by the night-light there they read each other's face. Cox whispered,

"Nobody knows about this but us?"

The whispered answer was,

"Not a soul—on honor, not a soul!"

"If it isn't too late to—"

The men were starting upstairs; at this moment they were overtaken by a boy, and Cox asked,

"Is that you, Johnny?"

"Yes, sir."

"You needn't ship the early mail—nor *any* mail: wait till I tell you."

"It's already gone, sir."

"*Gone?*" It had the sound of an unspeakable disappointment in it.

"Yes, sir. Time-table for Brixton and all the towns beyond changed today, sir—had to get the papers in twenty minutes earlier than common. I had to rush; if I had been two minutes later—"

The men turned and walked slowly away, not waiting to hear the rest. Neither of them spoke during ten minutes; then Cox said, in a vexed tone,

"What possessed you to be in such a hurry, *I* can't make out."

The answer was humble enough:

"I see it now, but somehow I never thought, you know, until it was too late. But the next time–"

"Next time be hanged! It won't come in a thousand years."

Then the friends separated without a good-night, and dragged themselves home with the gait of mortally stricken men. At their homes their wives sprang up with an eager "Well?"–then saw the answer with their eyes and sank down sorrowing, without waiting for it to come in words. In both houses a discussion followed of a heated sort–a new thing; there had been discussions before, but not heated ones, not ungentle ones. The discussions tonight were a sort of seeming plagiarisms of each other. Mrs. Richards said,

"If you had only waited, Edward–if you had only stopped to think; but no, you must run straight to the printing-office and spread it all over the world."

"It *said* publish it."

"That is nothing; it also said do it privately, if you liked. There, now–is that true, or not?"

"Why, yes–yes, it is true; but when I thought what a stir it would make, and what a compliment it was to Hadleyburg that a stranger should trust it so–"

"Oh, certainly, I know all that; but if you had only stopped to think, you would have seen that you *couldn't* find the right man, because he is in his grave, and hasn't left chick nor child nor relation behind him; and as long as the money went to somebody that awfully needed it, and nobody would be hurt by it, and–and–"

She broke down, crying. Her husband tried to think of some comforting thing to say, and presently came out with this:

"But after all, Mary, it must be for the best–it *must* be; we know that. And we must remember that it was so ordered–"

"Ordered! Oh, everything's *ordered*, when a person has to find some way out when he has been stupid. Just the same, it was *ordered* that the money should come to us in this special way, and it was you that must take it on yourself to go meddling with the designs of Providence–and who gave you the right? It was wicked, that is what it was–just blasphemous presumption, and no more becoming to a meek and humble professor of–"

"But, Mary, you know how we have been trained all our lives long, like the whole village, till it is absolutely second nature to us to stop not a single moment to think when there's an honest thing to be done–"

"Oh, I know it, I know it–it's been one everlasting training and training and training in honesty—honesty shielded, from the very cradle, against every possible temptation, and so it's *artificial* honesty, and weak as water when temptation comes, as we have seen this night. God knows I never had shade nor shadow of a doubt of my petrified and indestructible honesty until now—and now, under the very first big and real temptation, I—Edward, it is my belief that this town's honesty is as rotten as mine is; as rotten as yours is. It is a mean town, a hard, stingy town, and hasn't a virtue in the world but this honesty it is so celebrated for and so conceited about; and so help me, I do believe that if ever the day comes that its honesty falls under great temptation, its grand reputation will go to ruin like a house of cards. There, now, I've made confession, and I feel better; I am a humbug, and I've been one all my life, without knowing it. Let no man call me honest again—I will not have it."

"I—well, Mary, I feel a good deal as you do; I certainly do. It seems strange, too, so strange. I never could have believed it—never."

A long silence followed; both were sunk in thought. At last the wife looked up and said,

"I know what you are thinking, Edward."

Richards had the embarrassed look of a person who is caught.

"I am ashamed to confess it, Mary, but—"

"It's no matter, Edward, I was thinking the same question myself."

"I hope so. State it."

"You were thinking, if a body could only guess out *what the remark was* that Goodson made to the stranger."

"It's perfectly true. I feel guilty and ashamed. And you?"

"I'm past it. Let us make a pallet here; we've got to stand watch till the bank vault opens in the morning and admits the sack. . . . Oh dear, oh dear—if we hadn't made the mistake!"

The pallet was made, and Mary said:

"The open sesame—what could it have been? I do wonder what that remark could have been? But come; we will go to bed now."

"And sleep?"

"No, think."

"Yes, think."

By this time the Coxes too had completed their spat and their reconciliation, and were turning in—to think, to think, and toss, and fret, and worry over what the remark could possibly have been which Goodson made to the stranded derelict; that golden remark; that remark worth forty thousand dollars, cash.

The reason that the village telegraph office was open later than usual that night was this: The foreman of Cox's paper was the local representative of the Associated Press. One might say its honorary representative, for it wasn't four times a year that he could furnish thirty words that would be accepted. But this time it was different. His dispatch stating what he had caught got an instant answer:

"Send the whole thing–all the details–twelve hundred words."

A colossal order! The foreman filled the bill; and he was the proudest man in the State. By breakfast-time the next morning the name of Hadleyburg the Incorruptible was on every lip in America, from Montreal to the Gulf, from the glaciers of Alaska to the orange-groves of Florida; and millions and millions of people were discussing the stranger and his money-sack, and wondering if the right man would be found, and hoping some more news about the matter would come soon–right away.

II

Hadleyburg village woke up world-celebrated–astonished–happy–vain. Vain beyond imagination. Its nineteen principal citizens and their wives went about shaking hands with each other, and beaming, and smiling, and congratulating, and saying *this* thing adds a new word to the dictionary–*Hadleyburg*, synonym for *incorruptible*–destined to live in dictionaries forever! And the minor and unimportant citizens and their wives went around acting in much the same way. Everybody ran to the bank to see the gold-sack; and before noon grieved and envious crowds began to flock in from Brixton and all neighboring towns; and that afternoon and next day reporters began to arrive from everywhere to verify the sack and its history and write the whole thing up anew, and make dashing free-hand pictures of the sack, and of Richards's house, and the bank, and the Presbyterian church, and the Baptist church, and the public square, and the town hall where the test would be applied and the money delivered; and damnable portraits of the Richardses, and Pinkerton the banker, and Cox, and the foreman, and Reverend Burgess, and the postmaster–and even of Jack Halliday, who was the loafing, good-natured, no-account, irreverent fisherman, hunter, boys' friend, stray-dogs' friend, typical "Sam Lawson" of the town. The little mean, smirking, oily Pinkerton showed the sack to all comers, and rubbed his sleek palms together pleasantly, and enlarged upon the town's fine old reputation for honesty and upon this wonderful endorsement of it, and hoped and believed that the example would now spread far and wide over the American world, and be epoch-making in the matter of moral regeneration. And so on, and so on.

By the end of a week things had quieted down again; the wild intoxication of pride and joy had sobered to a soft, sweet, silent delight–a sort of deep, nameless, unutterable content. All faces bore a look of peaceful, holy happiness.

Then a change came. It was a gradual change: so gradual that its beginnings were hardly noticed; maybe were not noticed at all, except by Jack Halliday, who always noticed everything; and always made fun of it, too, no matter what it was. He began to throw out chaffing remarks about people not looking quite so happy as they did a day or two ago; and next he claimed that the new aspect was deepening to positive sadness; next, that it was taking on a sick look; and finally he said that everybody was become so moody, thoughtful, and absent-minded that he could rob the meanest man in town of a cent out of the bottom of his breeches pocket and not disturb his reverie.

At this stage—or at about this stage—a saying like this was dropped at bedtime—with a sigh, usually—by the head of each of the nineteen principal households: "Ah, what *could* have been the remark that Goodson made?"

And straightway—with a shudder—came this, from the man's wife:

"Oh, *don't*! What horrible thing are you mulling in your mind? Put it away from you, for God's sake!"

But that question was wrung from those men again the next night—and got the same retort. But weaker.

And the third night the men uttered the question yet again—with anguish, and absently. This time—and the following night—the wives fidgeted feebly, and tried to say something. But didn't.

And the night after that they found their tongues and responded—longingly:

"Oh, if we *could* only guess!"

Halliday's comments grew daily more and more sparklingly disagreeable and disparaging. He went diligently about, laughing at the town, individually and in mass. But his laugh was the only one left in the village: it fell upon a hollow and mournful vacancy and emptiness. Not even a smile was findable anywhere. Halliday carried a cigar-box around on a tripod, playing that it was a camera, and halted all passers and aimed the thing and said, "Ready!—now look pleasant, please," but not even this capital joke could surprise the dreary faces into any softening.

So three weeks passed—one week was left. It was Saturday evening—after supper. Instead of the aforetime Saturday-evening flutter and bustle and shopping and larking, the streets were empty and desolate. Richards and his old wife sat apart in their little parlor—miserable and thinking. This was become their evening habit now: the lifelong habit which had preceded it, of reading, knitting, and contented chat, of receiving or paying neighborly calls, was dead and gone and forgotten, ages ago—two or three weeks ago; nobody talked now, nobody read, nobody visited—the whole village sat at home, sighing, worrying, silent. Trying to guess out that remark.

The postman left a letter. Richards glanced listlessly at the superscription and the postmark—unfamiliar, both—and tossed the letter on the table and resumed his might-have-beens and his hopeless dull miseries where he had left them off. Two or three hours later his wife got wearily up and was going away to bed without a good-night—custom now—but she stopped near the letter and eyed it awhile with a dead interest, then broke it open, and began to skim it over. Richards, sitting there with his chair tilted back against the wall and his chin between his knees, heard something fall. It was his wife. He sprang to her side, but she cried out:

"Leave me alone, I am too happy. Read the letter—read it!"

He did. He devoured it, his brain reeling. The letter was from a distant State, and it said:

"I am a stranger to you, but no matter: I have something to tell. I have just arrived home from Mexico, and learned about that episode. Of course you do not know who made that remark, but I know, and I am the only person living who does know. It was GOODSON. *I knew him well, many years ago. I passed through your village that very night, and was his guest till the midnight train came along. I overheard him make that remark to the stranger in the dark—it was in Hale Alley. He and I talked of it the rest of the way home, and while smoking in his house. He mentioned many of your villagers in the course of his talk—most of them in a very uncomplimentary way, but two or three favorably; among these latter yourself. I say 'favorably'—nothing stronger. I remember his saying he did not actually* LIKE *any person in the town—not one; but that you—*I THINK *he said you—am almost sure—had done him a very great service once, possibly without knowing the full value of it, and he wished he had a fortune, he would leave it to you when he died, and a curse apiece for the rest of the citizens. Now, then, if it was you that did him that service, you are his legitimate heir, and entitled to the sack of gold. I know that I can trust to your honor and honesty, for in a citizen of Hadleyburg these virtues are an unfailing inheritance, and so I am going to reveal to you the remark, well satisfied that if you are not the right man you will seek and find the right one and see that poor Goodson's debt of gratitude for the service referred to is paid. This is the remark:* 'YOU ARE FAR FROM BEING A BAD MAN: GO, AND REFORM.'

"HOWARD L. STEPHENSON."

"Oh, Edward, the money is ours, and I am so grateful, *oh*, so grateful—kiss me, dear, it's forever since we kissed—and we needed it so—the money—and now you are free of Pinkerton and his bank, and nobody's slave any more; it seems to me I could fly for joy."

It was a happy half-hour that the couple spent there on the settee caressing each other; it was the old days come again—days that had begun with their courtship and lasted without a break till the stranger brought the deadly money. By and by the wife said:

"Oh, Edward, how lucky it was you did him that grand service, poor Goodson! I never liked him, but I love him now. And it was fine and beautiful of you never to mention it or brag about it." Then, with a touch of reproach, "But you ought to have told *me*, Edward, you ought to have told your wife, you know."

"Well, I–er–well, Mary, you see–"

"Now stop hemming and hawing, and tell me about it, Edward. I always loved you, and now I'm proud of you. Everybody believes there was only one good generous soul in this village, and now it turns out that you–Edward, why don't you tell me?"

"Well–er–er– Why, Mary, I can't!"

"You *can't*? *Why* can't you?"

"You see, he–well, he–he made me promise I wouldn't."

The wife looked him over, and said, very slowly,

"Made–you–promise? Edward, what do you tell me that for?"

"Mary, do you think I would lie?"

She was troubled and silent for a moment, then she laid her hand within his and said:

"No . . . no. We have wandered far enough from our bearings–God spare us that! In all your life you have never uttered a lie. But now–now that the foundations of things seem to be crumbling from under us, we–we–" She lost her voice for a moment. then said, brokenly, "Lead us not into temptation. . . . I think you made the promise, Edward. Let it rest so. Let us keep away from that ground. Now–that is all gone by; let us be happy again; it is no time for clouds."

Edward found it something of an effort to comply, for his mind kept wandering–trying to remember what the service was that he had done Goodson.

The couple lay awake the most of the night, Mary happy and busy, Edward busy but not so happy. Mary was planning what she would do with the money. Edward was trying to recall that service. At first his conscience was sore on account of the lie he had told Mary–if it was a lie. After much reflection–suppose it *was* a lie? What then? Was it such a great matter? Aren't we always *acting* lies? Then why not *tell* them? Look at Mary–look what she had done. While he was hurrying off on his honest errand, what was she doing? Lamenting because the papers hadn't been destroyed and the money kept! Is theft better than lying?

That point lost its sting–the lie dropped into the background and left comfort behind it. The next point came to the front: *Had* he rendered that service? Well, here was Goodson's own evidence as reported in Stephenson's letter; there could be no better evidence than that–it was even *proof* that he had rendered it. Of course. So that point was settled. . . . No, not quite. He recalled with a wince that this unknown Mr. Stephenson was just a trifle unsure as to whether the performer of it was Richards or some other–and, oh dear, he had put Richards on his honor! He must himself decide whither that money must go—and Mr. Stephenson was not doubting that if he was the wrong man he would go honorably and find the right one. Oh, it was odious to put a man in such a situation—ah, why couldn't Stephenson have left out that doubt! What did he want to intrude that for?

Further reflection. How did it happen that *Richards's* name remained in Stephenson's mind as indicating the right man, and not some other man's name? That looked good. Yes, that looked very good. In fact, it went on looking better and better, straight along—until by and by it grew into positive *proof*. And then Richards put the matter at once out of his mind, for he had a private instinct that a proof once established is better left so.

He was feeling reasonably comfortable now, but there was still one other detail that kept pushing itself on his notice: of course he had done that service that was settled; but what *was* that service? He must recall it—he would not go to sleep till he had recalled it; it would make his peace of mind perfect. And so he thought and thought. He thought of a dozen things—possible services, even probable services—but none of them seemed adequate, none of them seemed large enough, none of them seemed worth the money—worth the fortune Goodson had wished he could leave in his will. And besides, he couldn't remember having done them, anyway. Now, then—now, then—what *kind* of a service would it be that would make a man so inordinately grateful? Ah—the saving of his soul! That must be it. Yes, he could remember, now, how he once set himself the task of converting Goodson, and labored at it as much as—he was going to say three months; but upon closer examination it shrunk to a month, then to a week, then to a day, then to nothing. Yes, he remembered now, and with unwelcome vividness, that Goodson had told him to go to thunder and mind his own business—*he* wasn't hankering to follow Hadleyburg to heaven!

So that solution was a failure—he hadn't saved Goodson's soul. Richards was discouraged. Then after a little came another idea: had he saved Goodson's property? No, that wouldn't do—he hadn't any. His life? That is it! Of course. Why, he might have thought of it before. This time he was on the right track, sure. His imagination-mill was hard at work in a minute, now.

Thereafter during a stretch of two exhausting hours he was busy saving Goodson's life. He saved it in all kinds of difficult and perilous ways. In every case he got it saved satisfactorily up to a certain point; then, just as he was beginning to get well persuaded that it had really happened, a troublesome detail would turn up which made the whole thing impossible. As in the matter of drowning, for instance. In that case he had swum out and tugged Goodson ashore in an unconscious state with a great crowd looking on and applauding, but when he had got it all thought out and was just beginning to remember all about it, a whole swarm of disqualifying details arrived on the ground: the town would have known of the circumstance, Mary would have known of it, it would glare like a limelight in his own memory instead of being an inconspicuous service which he had possibly rendered "without knowing its full value." And at this point he remembered that he couldn't swim, anyway.

Ah—*there* was a point which he had been overlooking from the start: it had to be a service which he had rendered "possibly without knowing the full value of it." Why, really, that ought to be an easy hunt—much easier than those others. And sure enough, by and by he found it. Goodson, years and years ago, came near marrying a very sweet and pretty girl, named Nancy Hewitt, but in some way or other the match had been broken off; the girl died, Goodson remained a bachelor, and by and by became a soured one and a frank despiser of the human species. Soon after the girl's death the village found out, or thought it had found out, that she carried a spoonful of Negro blood in her veins. Richards worked at these details a good while, and in the end he thought he remembered things concerning them which must have gotten mislaid in his memory through long neglect. He seemed dimly to remember that it was *he* that found out about the Negro blood; that it was he that told the village; that the village told Goodson where they got it; that he thus saved Goodson from marrying the tainted girl; that he had done him this great service "without knowing the full value of it," in fact without knowing that he *was* doing it; but that Goodson knew the value of it, and what a narrow escape he had had, and so went to his grave grateful to his benefactor and wishing he had a fortune to leave him. It was all clear and simple now, and the more he went over it the more luminous and certain it grew; and at last, when he nestled to sleep satisfied and happy, he remembered the whole thing just as if it had been yesterday. In fact, he dimly remembered Goodson's *telling* him his gratitude once. Meantime Mary had spent six thousand dollars on a new house for herself and a pair of slippers for her pastor, and then had fallen peacefully to rest.

That same Saturday evening the postman had delivered a letter to each of the other principal citizens—nineteen letters in all. No two of the envelopes were alike, and no two of the superscriptions were in the same hand, but the letters inside were just like each other in every detail but one. They were exact copies of the letter received by Richards—handwriting and all—and were all signed by Stephenson, but in place of Richards's name each receiver's own name appeared.

All night long eighteen principal citizens did what their caste-brother Richards was doing at the same time—they put in their energies trying to remember what notable service it was that they had unconsciously done Barclay Goodson. In no case was it a holiday job; still they succeeded.

And while they were at this work, which was difficult, their wives put in the night spending the money, which was easy. During that one night the nineteen wives spent an average of seven thousand dollars each out of the forty thousand in the sack—a hundred and thirty-three thousand altogether.

Next day there was a surprise for Jack Halliday. He noticed that the faces of the nineteen chief citizens and their wives bore that expression of peaceful and holy happiness again. He could not understand it, neither was he able to invent any remarks about it that could damage it or disturb it. And so it was his turn to be dissatisfied with life. His private guesses at the reasons for the happiness failed in all instances, upon examination. When he met Mrs. Wilcox and noticed the placid ecstasy in her face, he said to himself, "Her cat has had kittens"—and went and asked the cook: it was not so; the cook had detected the happiness, but did not know the cause. When Halliday found the duplicate ecstasy in the face of "Shadbelly" Billson (village nickname), he was sure some neighbor of Billson's had broken his leg, but inquiry showed that this had not happened. The subdued ecstasy in Gregory Yates's face could mean but one thing—he was a mother-in-law short: it was another mistake. "And Pinkerton—Pinkerton—he has collected ten cents that he thought he was going to lose." And so on, and so on. In some cases the guesses had to remain in doubt, in the others they proved distinct errors. In the end Halliday said to himself, "Anyway it foots up that there's nineteen Hadleyburg families temporarily in heaven: I don't know how it happened; I only know Providence is off duty today."

An architect and builder from the next State had lately ventured to set up a small business in this unpromising village, and his sign had now been hanging out a week. Not a customer yet; he was a discouraged man, and sorry he had come. But his weather changed suddenly now. First one and then another chief citizen's wife said to him privately:

"Come to my house Monday week—but say nothing about it for the present. We think of building."

He got eleven invitations that day. That night he wrote his daughter and broke off her match with her student. He said she could marry a mile higher than that.

Pinkerton the banker and two or three other well-to-do men planned country-seats—but waited. That kind don't count their chickens until they are hatched.

The Wilsons devised a grand new thing—a fancy-dress ball. They made no actual promises, but told all their acquaintanceship in confidence that they were thinking the matter over and thought they should give it—"and if we do, you will be invited, of course." People were surprised, and said, one to another, "Why, they are crazy, those poor Wilsons, they can't afford it." Several among the nineteen said privately to their husbands, "It is a good idea: we will keep still till their cheap thing is over, then *we* will give one that will make it sick."

The days drifted along, and the bill of future squanderings rose higher and higher, wilder and wilder, more and more foolish and reckless. It began to look as if every member of the nineteen would not only spend his whole forty thousand dollars before receiving-day, but be actually in debt by the time he got the money. In some cases light-headed people did not stop with planning to spend, they really spent—on credit. They bought land, mortgages, farms, speculative stock, fine clothes, horses, and various other things, paid down the bonus, and made themselves liable for the rest—at ten days. Presently the sober second thought came, and Halliday noticed that a ghastly anxiety was beginning to show up in a good many faces. Again he was puzzled, and didn't know what to make of it. "The Wilcox kittens aren't dead, for they weren't born; nobody's broken a leg; there's no shrinkage in mother-in-laws; *nothing* has happened—it is an unsolvable mystery."

There was another puzzled man, too—the Rev. Mr. Burgess. For days, wherever he went, people seemed to follow him or to be watching out for him; and if he ever found himself in a retired spot, a member of the nineteen would be sure to appear, thrust an envelope privately into his hand, whisper "To be opened at the town hall Friday evening," then vanish away like a guilty thing. He was expecting that there might be one claimant for the sack,—doubtful, however, Goodson being dead,—but it never occurred to him that all this crowd might be claimants. When the great Friday came at last, he found that he had nineteen envelopes.

III

The town hall had never looked finer. The platform at the end of it was backed by a showy draping of flags; at intervals along the walls were festoons of flags; the gallery fronts were clothed in flags; the supporting columns were swathed in flags; all this was to impress the stranger, for he would be there in considerable force, and in a large degree he would be connected with the press. The house was full. The 412 fixed seats were occupied; also the 68 extra chairs which had been packed into the aisles; the steps of the platform were occupied; some distinguished strangers were given seats on the platform; at the horseshoe of tables which fenced the front and sides of the platform sat a strong force of special correspondents who had come from everywhere. It was the best-dressed house the town had ever produced. There were some tolerably expensive toilets there, and in several cases the ladies who wore them had the look of being unfamiliar with that kind of clothes. At least the town thought they had that look, but the notion could have arisen from the town's knowledge of the fact that these ladies had never inhabited such clothes before.

The gold-sack stood on a little table at the front of the platform where all the house could see it. The bulk of the house gazed at it with a burning interest, a mouth-watering interest, a wistful and pathetic interest; a minority of nineteen couples gazed at it tenderly, lovingly, proprietarily, and the male half of this minority kept saying over to themselves the moving little impromptu speeches of thankfulness for the audience's applause and congratulations which they were presently going to get up and deliver. Every now and then one of these got a piece of paper out of his vest pocket and privately glanced at it to refresh his memory.

Of course there was a buzz of conversation going on—there always is; but at last when the Rev. Mr. Burgess rose and laid his hand on the sack he could hear his microbes gnaw, the place was so still. He related the curious history of the sack, then went on to speak in warm terms of Hadleyburg's old and well-earned reputation for spotless honesty, and of the town's just pride in this reputation. He said that this reputation was a treasure of priceless value; that under Providence its value had now become inestimably enhanced, for the recent episode had spread this fame far and wide, and thus had focused the eyes of the American world upon this village, and made its name for all time, as he hoped and believed, a synonym for commercial incorruptibility. [*Applause.*] "And who is to be the guardian of this noble treasure—the community as a whole? No! The responsibility is individual, not communal. From this day forth each and every one of you is in his own person its special guardian, and individually responsible that no harm shall come to it. Do you—does each of you—accept this great trust? [*Tumultuous assent.*] Then all is well. Transmit it to your children and to your children's children. Today your purity is beyond reproach—see to it that it shall remain so. Today there is not a person in your community who could be beguiled to touch a penny not his own—see to it that you abide in this grace. ["*We will! we will!*"] This is not the place to make comparisons between ourselves and other communities—some of them ungracious toward us; they have their ways, we have ours; let us be content. [*Applause.*] I am done. Under my hand, my friends, rests a stranger's eloquent recognition of what we are; through him the world will always henceforth know what we are. We do not know who he is, but in your name I utter your gratitude, and ask you to raise your voices in endorsement."

The house rose in a body and made the walls quake with the thunders of its thankfulness for the space of a long minute. Then it sat down, and Mr. Burgess took an envelope out of his pocket. The house held its breath while he slit the envelope open and took from it a slip of paper. He read its contents—slowly and impressively—the audience listening with tranced attention to this magic document, each of whose words stood for an ingot of gold:

"'*The remark which I made to the distressed stranger was this: "You are very far from being a bad man: go, and reform.*"'" Then he continued:

"We shall know in a moment now whether the remark here quoted corresponds with the one concealed in the sack; and if that shall prove to be so—and it undoubtedly will—this sack of gold belongs to a fellow-citizen who will henceforth stand before the nation as the symbol of the special virtue which has made our town famous throughout the land—Mr. Billson!"

The house had gotten itself all ready to burst into the proper tornado of applause; but instead of doing it, it seemed stricken with a paralysis: there was a deep hush for a moment or two, then a wave of whispered murmurs swept the place—of about this tenor: "*Billson*! oh, come, this is *too* thin! Twenty dollars to a stranger—or *anybody*—*Billson*! tell it to the marines!" And now at this point the house caught its breath all of a sudden in a new access of astonishment, for it discovered that whereas in one part of the hall Deacon Billson was standing up with his head meekly bowed, in another part of it Lawyer Wilson was doing the same. There was a wondering silence now for a while.

Everybody was puzzled, and nineteen couples were surprised and indignant.

Billson and Wilson turned and stared at each other. Billson asked, bitingly,

"Why do *you* rise, Mr. Wilson?"

"Because I have a right to. Perhaps you will be good enough to explain to the house why *you* rise?"

"With great pleasure. Because I wrote that paper."

"It is an impudent falsity! I wrote it myself."

It was Burgess's turn to be paralyzed. He stood looking vacantly at first one of the men and then the other, and did not seem to know what to do. The house was stupefied. Lawyer Wilson spoke up, now, and said,

"I ask the Chair to read the name signed to that paper."

That brought the Chair to itself, and it read out the name,

"'John Wharton *Billson*.'"

"There!" shouted Billson, "what have you got to say for yourself, now? And what kind of apology are you going to make to me and to this insulted house for the imposture which you have attempted to play here?"

"No apologies are due, sir; and as for the rest of it, I publicly charge you with pilfering my note from Mr. Burgess and substituting a copy of it signed with your own name. There is no other way by which you could have gotten hold of the test-remark; I alone, of living men, possessed the secret of its wording."

There was likely to be a scandalous state of things if this went on; everybody noticed with distress that the short-hand scribes were scribbling like mad; many people were crying "Chair, Chair! Order! Order!" Burgess rapped with his gavel, and said:

"Let us not forget the proprieties due. There has evidently been a mistake somewhere, but surely that is all. If Mr. Wilson gave me an envelope—and I remember now that he did—I still have it."

He took one out of his pocket, opened it, glanced at it, looked surprised and worried, and stood silent a few moments. Then he waved his hand in a wandering and mechanical way, and made an effort or two to say something, then gave it up, despondently. Several voices cried out:

"Read it! read it! What is it?"

So he began in a dazed and sleep-walker fashion:

"'*The remark which I made to the unhappy stranger was this: "You are far from being a bad man.* [The house gazed at him, marveling.] *Go, and reform.*"' [*Murmurs*: "Amazing! What can this mean?"] This one," said the Chair, "is signed Thurlow G. Wilson."

"There!" cried Wilson, "I reckon that settles it! I knew perfectly well my note was purloined."

"Purloined!" retorted Billson. "I'll let you know that neither you nor any man of your kidney must venture to–"

The Chair. "Order, gentlemen, order! Take your seats, both of you, please."

They obeyed, shaking their heads and grumbling angrily. The house was profoundly puzzled; it did not know what to do with this curious emergency. Presently Thompson got up. Thompson was the hatter. He would have liked to be a Nineteener; but such was not for him: his stock of hats was not considerable enough for the position. He said:

"Mr. Chairman, if I may be permitted to make a suggestion, can both of these gentlemen be right? I put it to you, sir, can both have happened to say the very same words to the stranger? It seems to me–"

The tanner got up and interrupted him. The tanner was a disgruntled man; he believed himself entitled to be a Nineteener, but he couldn't get recognition. It made him a little unpleasant in his ways and speech. Said he:

"Sho, *that's* not the point! That could happen–twice in a hundred years–but not the other thing. *Neither* of them gave the twenty dollars!"

[*A ripple of applause.*]

Billson. "*I* did!"

Wilson. "*I* did!"

Then each accused the other of pilfering.

The Chair. "Order! Sit down, if you please–both of you. Neither of the notes has been out of my possession at any moment."

A Voice. "Good–that settles *that*!"

The Tanner. "Mr. Chairman, one thing is now plain: one of these men has been eavesdropping under the other one's bed, and filching family secrets. If it is not unparliamentary to suggest it, I will remark that both are equal to it. [*The Chair.* "Order! Order!"] I withdraw the remark, sir, and will confine myself to suggesting that *if* one of them has overheard the other reveal the test-remark to his wife, we shall catch him now."

A Voice. "How?"

The Tanner. "Easily. The two have not quoted the remark in exactly the same words. You would have noticed that, if there hadn't been a considerable stretch of time and an exciting quarrel inserted between the two readings."

A Voice. "Name the difference."

The Tanner. "The word *very* is in Billson's note, and not in the other.

Many Voices. "That's so—he's right!"

The Tanner. "And so, if the Chair will examine the test-remark in the sack, we shall know which of these two frauds—[*The Chair.* "Order!"]—which of these two adventurers—[*The Chair.* "Order! Order!"]—which of these two gentlemen—[*laughter and applause*]—is entitled to wear the belt as being the first dishonest blatherskite ever bred in this town—which he has dishonored, and which will be a sultry place for him from now out!" [*Vigorous applause.*]

Many Voices. "Open it!—open the sack!"

Mr. Burgess made a slit in the sack, slid his hand in and brought out an envelope. In it were a couple of folded notes. He said:

"One of these is marked, 'Not to be examined until all written communications which have been addressed to the Chair—if any—shall have been read.' The other is marked '*The Test.*' Allow me. It is worded—to wit:

"'I do not require that the first half of the remark which was made to me by my benefactor shall be quoted with exactness, for it was not striking, and could be forgotten; but its closing fifteen words are quite striking, and I think easily rememberable; unless *these* shall be accurately reproduced, let the applicant be regarded as an impostor. My benefactor began by saying he seldom gave advice to anyone, but that it always bore the hall-mark of high value when he did give it. Then he said this—and it has never faded from my memory: "*You are far from being a bad man—*"'"

Fifty Voices. "That settles it—the money's Wilson's! Wilson! Wilson! Speech! Speech!"

People jumped up and crowded around Wilson, wringing his hand and congratulating fervently—meantime the Chair was hammering with the gavel and shouting:

"Order, gentlemen! Order! Order! Let me finish reading, please." When quiet was restored, the reading was resumed—as follows:

"'"*Go, and reform—or, mark my words—some day, for your sins, you will die and go to hell or Hadleyburg—*TRY AND MAKE IT THE FORMER."'"

A ghastly silence followed. First an angry cloud began to settle darkly upon the faces of the citizenship; after a pause the cloud began to rise, and a tickled expression tried to take its place; tried so hard that it was only kept under with great and painful difficulty; the reporters, the Brixtonites, and other strangers bent their heads down and shielded their faces with their hands, and managed to hold in by main strength and heroic courtesy. At this most inopportune time burst upon the stillness the roar of a solitary voice—Jack Halliday's:

"*That's* got the hall-mark on it!"

Then the house let go, strangers and all. Even Mr. Burgess's gravity broke down presently, then the audience considered itself officially absolved from all restraint, and it made the most of its privilege. It was a good long laugh, and a tempestuously wholehearted one, but it ceased at last—long enough for Mr. Burgess to try to resume, and for the people to get their eyes partially wiped; then it broke out again; and afterward yet again; then at last Burgess was able to get out these serious words:

"It is useless to try to disguise the fact—we find ourselves in the presence of a matter of grave import. It involves the honor of your town, it strikes at the town's good name. The difference of a single word between the test-remarks offered by Mr. Wilson and Mr. Billson was itself a serious thing, since it indicated that one or the other of these gentlemen had committed a theft—"

The two men were sitting limp, nerveless, crushed; but at these words both were electrified into movement, and started to get up—

"Sit down!" said the Chair, sharply, and they obeyed. "That, as I have said, was a serious thing. And it was—but for only one of them. But the matter has become graver; for the honor of *both* is now in formidable peril. Shall I go even further, and say in inextricable peril? *Both* left out the crucial fifteen words." He paused. During several moments he allowed the pervading stillness to gather and deepen its impressive effects, then added: "There would seem to be but one way whereby this could happen. I ask these gentlemen— Was there *collusion?—agreement?*"

A low murmur sifted through the house; its import was, "He's got them both."

Billson was not used to emergencies; he sat in a helpless collapse. But Wilson was a lawyer. He struggled to his feet, pale and worried, and said:

"I ask the indulgence of the house while I explain this most painful matter. I am sorry to say what I am about to say, since it must inflict irreparable injury upon Mr. Billson, whom I have always esteemed and respected until now, and in whose invulnerability to temptation I entirely believed—as did you all. But for the preservation of my own honor I must speak—and with frankness. I confess with shame—and I now beseech your pardon for it—that I said to the ruined stranger all of the words contained in the test-remark, including the disparaging fifteen. [*Sensation.*] When the late publication was made I recalled them, and I resolved to claim the sack of coin, for by every right I was entitled to it. Now I will ask you to consider this point, and weigh it well: that stranger's gratitude to me that night knew no bounds; he said himself that he could find no words for it that were adequate, and that if he should ever be able he would repay me a thousand fold. Now, then, I ask you this: Could I expect—could I believe—could I even remotely imagine—that, feeling as he did, he would do so ungrateful a thing as to add those quite unnecessary fifteen words to his test?—set a trap for me?—expose me as a slanderer of my own town before my own people assembled in a public hall? It was preposterous; it was impossible. His test would contain only the kindly opening clause of my remark. Of that I had no shadow of doubt. You would have thought as I did. You would not have expected a base betrayal from one whom you had befriended and against whom you had committed no offense. And so, with perfect confidence, perfect trust, I wrote on a piece of paper the opening words—ending with 'Go, and reform,'—and signed it. When I was about to put it in an envelope I was called into my back office, and without thinking I left the paper lying open on my desk." He stopped, turned his head slowly toward Billson, waited a moment, then added: "I ask you to note this: when I returned, a little later, Mr. Billson was retiring by my street door." [*Sensation.*]

In a moment Billson was on his feet and shouting:

"It's a lie! It's an infamous lie!"

The Chair. "Be seated, sir! Mr. Wilson has the floor."

Billson's friends pulled him into his seat and quieted him, and Wilson went on:

"Those are the simple facts. My note was now lying in a different place on the table from where I had left it. I noticed that, but attached no importance to it, thinking a draught had blown it there. That Mr. Billson would read a private paper was a thing which could not occur to me; he was an honorable man, and he would be above that. If you will allow me to say it, I think his extra word '*very*' stands explained; it is attributable to a defect of memory. I was the only man in the world who could furnish here any detail of the test-remark—by *honorable* means. I have finished."

There is nothing in the world like a persuasive speech to fuddle the mental apparatus and upset the convictions and debauch the emotions of an audience not practiced in the tricks and delusions of oratory. Wilson sat down victorious. The house submerged him in tides of approving applause; friends swarmed to him and shook him by the hand and congratulated him, and Billson was shouted down and not allowed to say a word. The Chair hammered and hammered with its gavel, and kept shouting,

"But let us proceed, gentlemen, let us proceed!"

At last there was a measurable degree of quiet, and the hatter said:

"But what is there to proceed with, sir, but to deliver the money?"

Voices. "That's it! That's it! Come forward, Wilson!"

The Hatter. "I move three cheers for Mr. Wilson, Symbol of the special virtue which—"

The cheers burst forth before he could finish; and in the midst of them—and in the midst of the clamor of the gavel also—some enthusiasts mounted Wilson on a big friend's shoulder and were going to fetch him in triumph to the platform. The Chair's voice now rose above the noise—

"Order! To your places! You forget that there is still a document to be read." When quiet had been restored he took up the document, and was going to read it, but laid it down again, saying, "I forgot; this is not to be read until all written communications received by me have first been read." He took an envelope out of his pocket, removed its enclosure, glanced at it–seemed astonished–held it out and gazed at it–stared at it.

Twenty or thirty voices cried out:

"What is it? Read it! read it!"

And he did–slowly, and wondering:

"'The remark which I made to the stranger–[*Voices.* "Hello! how's this?"]– was this: "You are far from being a bad man. [*Voices.* "Great Scott!"] Go, and reform."' [*Voice.* "Oh, saw my leg off!"] Signed by Mr. Pinkerton the banker."

The pandemonium of delight which turned itself loose now was of a sort to make the judicious weep. Those whose withers were unwrung laughed till the tears ran down; the reporters, in throes of laughter, set down disordered pot-hooks which would never in the world be decipherable; and a sleeping dog jumped up, scared out of its wits, and barked itself crazy at the turmoil. All manner of cries were scattered through the din: "We're getting rich–*two* Symbols of Incorruptibility!–without counting Billson!" "*Three*!–count Shadbelly in–we can't have too many!" "All right–Billson's elected!" "Alas, poor Wilson–victim of *two* thieves!"

A Powerful Voice. "Silence! The Chair's fished up something more out of its pocket."

Voices. "Hurrah! Is it something fresh? Read it! read! read!"

The Chair [*reading.*] "'The remark which I made,' etc.: 'You are far from being a bad man. Go,' etc. Signed, 'Gregory Yates.'"

Tornado of Voices. "Four Symbols!" "'Rah for Yates!" "Fish again."

The house was in a roaring humor now, and ready to get all the fun out of the occasion that might be in it. Several Nineteeners, looking pale and distressed, got up and began to work their way toward the aisles, but a score of shouts went up:

"The doors, the doors–close the doors; no Incorruptible shall leave this place! Sit down, everybody!"

The mandate was obeyed.

"Fish again! Read! read!"

The Chair fished again, and once more the familiar words began to fall from its lips– "'You are far from being a bad man–'"

"Name! name! What's his name?"

"'L. Ingoldsby Sargent.'"

"Five elected! Pile up the Symbols! Go on, go on!"

"'You are far from being a bad–'"

"Name! name!"

"'Nicholas Whitworth.'"

"Hooray! hooray! it's a symbolical day!"

Somebody wailed in, and began to sing this rhyme (leaving out "it's") to the lovely "Mikado" tune of "When a man's afraid, a beautiful maid–"; the audience joined in, with joy; then, just in time, somebody contributed another line–

"And don't you this forget–"

The house roared it out. A third line was at once furnished–

"Corruptibles far from Hadleyburg are–"

The house roared that one too. As the last note died, Jack Halliday's voice rose high and clear, freighted with a final line–

"But the Symbols are here, you bet!"

That was sung, with booming enthusiasm. Then the happy house started in at the beginning and sang the four lines through twice, with immense swing and dash, and finished up with a crashing three-times-three and a tiger for "Hadleyburg the Incorruptible and all Symbols of it which we shall find worthy to receive the hall-mark tonight."

Then the shoutings at the Chair began again, all over the place:

"Go on! go on! Read! read some more! Read all you've got!"

"That's it–go on! We are winning eternal celebrity!"

A dozen men got up now and began to protest. They said that this farce was the work of some abandoned joker, and was an insult to the whole community. Without a doubt these signatures were all forgeries–"Sit down! sit down! Shut up! You are confessing. We'll find *your* names in the lot."

"Mr. Chairman, how many of those envelopes have you got?"

The Chair counted.

"Together with those that have been already examined, there are nineteen."

A storm of derisive applause broke out.

"Perhaps they all contain the secret. I move that you open them all and read every signature that is attached to a note of that sort–and read also the first eight words of the note."

"Second the motion!"

It was put and carried–uproariously. Then poor old Richards got up, and his wife rose and stood at his side. Her head was bent down, so that none might see that she was crying. Her husband gave her his arm, and so supporting her, he began to speak in a quavering voice:

"My friends, you have known us two–Mary and me–all our lives, and I think you have liked us and respected us–"

The Chair interrupted him:

"Allow me. It is quite true—that which you are saying, Mr. Richards: this town *does* know you two; it *does* like you; it *does* respect you; more—it honors you and *loves* you—"

Halliday's voice rang out:

"That's the hall-marked truth, too! If the Chair is right, let the house speak up and say it. Rise! Now, then—hip! hip! hip!—all together!"

The house rose in mass, faced toward the old couple eagerly, filled the air with a snowstorm of waving handkerchiefs, and delivered the cheers with all its affectionate heart.

The Chair then continued:

"What I was going to say is this: We know your good heart, Mr. Richards, but this is not a time for the exercise of charity toward offenders. [*Shouts of "Right! right!"*] I see your generous purpose in your face, but I cannot allow you to plead for these men—"

"But I was going to—"

"Please take your seat, Mr. Richards. We must examine the rest of these notes—simple fairness to the men who have already been exposed requires this. As soon as that has been done—I give you my word for this—you shall be heard."

Many Voices. "Right!—the Chair is right—no interruption can be permitted at this stage! Go on!—the names! the names!—according to the terms of the motion!"

The old couple sat reluctantly down, and the husband whispered to the wife, "It is pitifully hard to have to wait; the shame will be greater than ever when they find we were only going to plead for *ourselves*."

Straightway the jollity broke loose again with the reading of the names.

"'You are far from being a bad man—' Signature, 'Robert J. Titmarsh.'

"'You are far from being a bad man—' Signature, 'Eliphalet Weeks.'

"'You are far from being a bad man—' Signature, 'Oscar B. Wilder.'"

At this point the house lit upon the idea of taking the eight words out of the Chairman's hands. He was not unthankful for that. Thence-forward he held up each note in its turn, and waited. The house droned out the eight words in a massed and measured and musical deep volume of sound (with a daringly close resemblance to a well-known church chant)— "'You are f-a-r from being a b-a-a-a-d man.'" Then the Chair said, "Signature, 'Archibald Wilcox.'" And so on, and so on, name after name, and everybody had an increasingly and gloriously good time except the wretched Nineteen. Now and then, when a particularly shining name was called, the house made the Chair wait while it chanted the whole of the test-remark from the beginning to the closing words, "And go to hell or Hadleyburg—try and make it the for-or-m-e-r!" and in these special cases they added a grand and agonized and imposing "A-a-a-a-*men*!"

The list dwindled, dwindled, dwindled, poor old Richards keeping tally of the count, wincing when a name resembling his own was pronounced, and waiting in miserable suspense for the time to come when it would be his humiliating privilege to rise with Mary and finish his plea, which he was intending to word thus: ". . . for until now we have never done any wrong thing, but have gone our humble way unreproached. We are very poor, we are old, and have no chick nor child to help us; we were sorely tempted, and we fell. It was my purpose when I got up before to make a confession and beg that my name might not be read out in this public place, for it seemed to us that we could not bear it; but I was prevented. It was just; it was our place to suffer with the rest. It has been hard for us. It is the first time we have ever heard our name fall from any one's lips–sullied. Be merciful–for the sake of the better days; make our shame as light to bear as in your charity you can." At this point in his reverie Mary nudged him, perceiving that his mind was absent. The house was chanting, "You are f-a-r," etc.

"Be ready," Mary whispered. "Your name comes now; he has read eighteen."

The chant ended.

"Next! next! next!" came volleying from all over the house.

Burgess put his hand into his pocket. The old couple, trembling, began to rise. Burgess fumbled a moment, then said,

"I find I have read them all."

Faint with joy and surprise, the couple sank into their seats, and Mary whispered,

"Oh, bless God, we are saved!–he has lost ours–I wouldn't give this for a hundred of those sacks!"

The house burst out with its "Mikado" travesty, and sang it three times with ever-increasing enthusiasm, rising to its feet when it reached for the third time the closing line–

"But the Symbols are here, you bet!"

And finishing up with cheers and a tiger for "Hadleyburg purity and our eighteen immortal representatives of it."

Then Wingate, the saddler, got up and proposed cheers "for the cleanest man in town, the one solitary important citizen in it who didn't try to steal that money–Edward Richards."

They were given with great and moving heartiness; then somebody proposed that Richards be elected sole guardian and Symbol of the now Sacred Hadleyburg Tradition, with power and right to stand up and look the whole sarcastic world in the face.

Passed, by acclamation; then they sang the "Mikado" again, and ended it with,

"And there's *one* Symbol left, you bet!"

There was a pause; then—

A Voice. "Now, then, who's to get the sack?"

The Tanner (*with bitter sarcasm*). "That's easy. The money has to be divided among the eighteen Incorruptibles. They gave the suffering stranger twenty dollars apiece—and that remark—each in his turn—it took twenty-two minutes for the procession to move past. Staked the stranger—total contribution, $360. All they want is just the loan back—and interest—forty thousand dollars altogether."

Many Voices [*derisively.*] "That's it! Divvy! divvy! Be kind to the poor—don't keep them waiting!"

The Chair. "Order! I now offer the stranger's remaining document. It says: 'If no claimant shall appear [*grand chorus of groans*], I desire that you open the sack and count out the money to the principal citizens of your town, they to take it in trust [*cries of "Oh! Oh! Oh!"*], and use it in such ways as to them shall seem best for the propagation and preservation of your community's noble reputation for incorruptible honesty [*more cries*]—a reputation to which their names and their efforts will add a new and far-reaching luster.' [*Enthusiastic outburst of sarcastic applause.*] That seems to be all. No—here is a postscript:

"'P. S.—Citizens of Hadleyburg: There *is* no test-remark—nobody made one. [*Great sensation.*] There wasn't any pauper stranger, nor any twenty-dollar contribution, nor any accompanying benediction and compliment—these are all inventions. [*General buzz and hum of astonishment and delight.*] Allow me to tell my story—it will take but a word or two. I passed through your town at a certain time, and received a deep offense which I had not earned. Any other man would have been content to kill one or two of you and call it square, but to me that would have been a trivial revenge, and inadequate; for the dead do not *suffer*. Besides, I could not kill you all—and, anyway, mad as I am, even that would not have satisfied me. I wanted to damage every man in the place, and every woman—and not in their bodies or in their estate, but in their vanity—the place where feeble and foolish people are most vulnerable. So I disguised myself and came back and studied you. You were easy game. You had an old and lofty reputation for honesty, and naturally you were proud of it—it was your treasure of treasures, the very apple of your eye. As soon as I found out that you carefully and vigilantly kept yourselves and your children *out of temptation*, I knew how to proceed. Why, you simple creatures, the weakest of all weak things is a virtue which has not been tested in the fire. I laid a plan, and gathered a list of names. My project was to corrupt Hadleyburg the Incorruptible. My idea was to make liars and thieves of nearly half a hundred smirchless men and women who had never in their lives uttered a lie or stolen a penny. I was afraid of Goodson. He was neither born nor reared in Hadleyburg. I was afraid that if I started to operate my scheme by getting my letter laid before you, you would say to yourselves, "Goodson is the only man among us who would give away twenty dollars to a poor devil"—and then you might not bite at my bait. But Heaven took Goodson; then I knew I was safe, and I set my trap and baited it. It may be that I shall not catch all the men to whom I mailed the pretended test secret, but I shall catch the most of them, if I know Hadleyburg nature. [*Voices.* "Right—he got every last one of them."] I believe they will even steal ostensible *gamble*-money rather than miss, poor, tempted, and mistrained fellows. I am hoping to eternally and everlastingly squelch your vanity and give Hadleyburg a new renown—one that will *stick*—and spread far. If I have succeeded, open the sack and summon the Committee on Propagation and Preservation of the Hadleyburg Reputation.'"

A Cyclone of Voices. "Open it! Open it! The Eighteen to the front! Committee on Propagation of the Tradition! Forward—the Incorruptibles!"

The Chair ripped the sack wide, and gathered up a handful of bright, broad, yellow coins, shook them together, then examined them—

"Friends, they are only gilded disks of lead!"

There was a crashing outbreak of delight over this news, and when the noise had subsided, the tanner called out:

"By right of apparent seniority in this business, Mr. Wilson is Chairman of the Committee on Propagation of the Tradition. I suggest that he step forward on behalf of his pals, and receive in trust the money."

A Hundred Voices. "Wilson! Wilson! Wilson! Speech! Speech!"

Wilson [*in a voice trembling with anger.*] "You will allow me to say, and without apologies for my language, *damn* the money!"

A Voice. "Oh, and him a Baptist!"

A Voice. "Seventeen Symbols left! Step up, gentlemen, and assume your trust!"

There was a pause—no response.

The Saddler. "Mr. Chairman, we've got *one* clean man left, anyway, out of the late aristocracy; and he needs money, and deserves it. I move that you appoint Jack Halliday to get up there and auction off that sack of gilt twenty-dollar pieces, and give the result to the right man—the man whom Hadleyburg delights to honor—Edward Richards."

This was received with great enthusiasm, the dog taking a hand again; the saddler started the bids at a dollar, the Brixton folk and Barnum's representative fought hard for it, the people cheered every jump that the bids made, the excitement climbed moment by moment higher and higher, the bidders got on their mettle and grew steadily more and more daring, more and more determined, the jumps went from a dollar up to five, then to ten, then to twenty, then fifty, then to a hundred, then—

At the beginning of the auction Richards whispered in distress to his wife:

"Oh, Mary, can we allow it? It–it–you see, it is an honor-reward, a testimonial to purity of character, and–and–can we allow it? Hadn't I better get up and–Oh, Mary, what ought we to do?–what do you think we–[*Halliday's voice. "Fifteen I'm bid!–fifteen for the sack!–twenty!–ah, thanks!–thirty–thanks again! Thirty, thirty, thirty!–do I hear forty?–forty it is! Keep the ball rolling, gentlemen, keep it rolling!–fifty!–thanks, noble Roman! going at fifty, fifty, fifty!–seventy! –ninety!–splendid!–a hundred!–pile it up, pile it up!–hundred and twenty–forty!–just in time!–hundred and fifty!–*TWO *hundred!–superb! Do I hear two h–thanks!–two hundred and fifty!–"*]

"It is another temptation, Edward–I'm all in a tremble–but, oh, we've escaped *one* temptation, and that ought to warn us to–[*"Six did I hear?–thanks!–six fifty, six f–*SEVEN *hundred!"*] And yet Edward, when you think–nobody susp–[*"Eight hundred dollars!–hurrah!–make it nine!–Mr. Parsons, did I hear you say–thanks–nine!–this noble sack–of virgin lead going at only nine hundred dollars, gilding and all–come! do I hear–a thousand!–gratefully yours!–did some one say eleven?–a sack which is going to be the most celebrated in the whole Uni–"*] Oh, Edward" (beginning to sob), "we are *so* poor!–but–but–do as you think best–do as you think best."

Edward fell–that is, he sat still; sat with a conscience which was not satisfied, but which was overpowered by circumstances.

Meantime a stranger, who looked like an amateur detective gotten up as an impossible English earl, had been watching the evening's proceedings with manifest interest, and with a contented expression in his face; and he had been privately commenting to himself. He was now soliloquizing somewhat like this: "None of the Eighteen are bidding; that is not satisfactory; I must change that–the dramatic unities require it; they must buy the sack they tried to steal; they must pay a heavy price, too–some of them are rich. And another thing, when I make a mistake in Hadleyburg nature the man that puts that error upon me is entitled to a high honorarium, and some one must pay it. This poor old Richards has brought my judgment to shame; he is an honest man:–I don't understand it, but I acknowledge it. Yes, he saw my deuces *and* with a straight flush, and by rights the pot is his. And it shall be a jack-pot, too, if I can manage it. He disappointed me, but let that pass."

He was watching the bidding. At a thousand, the market broke; the prices tumbled swiftly. He waited–and still watched. One competitor dropped out; then another, and another. He put in a bid or two, now. When the bids had sunk to ten dollars, he added a five; some one raised him a three; he waited a moment, then flung in a fifty-dollar jump, and the sack was his–at S1,282. The house broke out in cheers–then stopped; for he was on his feet, and had lifted his hand. He began to speak.

"I desire to say a word, and ask a favor. I am a speculator in rarities, and I have dealings with persons interested in numismatics all over the world. I can make a profit on this purchase, just as it stands; but there is a way, if I can get your approval, whereby I can make every one of these leaden twenty-dollar pieces worth its face in gold, and perhaps more. Grant me that approval, and I will give part of my gains to your Mr. Richards, whose invulnerable probity you have so justly and cordially recognized tonight; his share shall be ten thousand dollars, and I will hand him the money tomorrow. [*Great applause from the house.* But the "invulnerable probity" made the Richardses blush prettily; however, it went for modesty, and did no harm.] If you will pass my proposition by a good majority—I would like a two-thirds vote—I will regard that as the town's consent, and that is all I ask. Rarities are always helped by any device which will rouse curiosity and compel remark. Now if I may have your permission to stamp upon the faces of each of these ostensible coins the names of the eighteen gentlemen who—"

Nine-tenths of the audience were on their feet in a moment—dog and all—and the proposition was carried with a whirlwind of approving applause and laughter.

They sat down, and all the Symbols except "Dr." Clay Harkness got up, violently protesting against the proposed outrage, and threatening to—

"I beg you not to threaten me," said the stranger, calmly. "I know my legal rights, and am not accustomed to being frightened at bluster." [*Applause.*] He sat down. "Dr." Harkness saw an opportunity here. He was one of the two very rich men of the place, and Pinkerton was the other. Harkness was proprietor of a mint; that is to say, a popular patent medicine. He was running for the Legislature on one ticket, and Pinkerton on the other. It was a close race and a hot one, and getting hotter every day. Both had strong appetites for money; each had bought a great tract of land, with a purpose; there was going to be a new railway, and each wanted to be in the Legislature and help locate the route to his own advantage; a single vote might make the decision, and with it two or three fortunes. The stake was large, and Harkness was a daring speculator. He was sitting close to the stranger. He leaned over while one or another of the other Symbols was entertaining the house with protests and appeals, and asked, in a whisper,

"What is your price for the sack?"

"Forty thousand dollars."

"I'll give you twenty." '

"No."

"Twenty-five."

"No."

"Say thirty."

"The price is forty thousand dollars; not a penny less."

"All right, I'll give it. I will come to the hotel at ten in the morning. I don't want it known; will see you privately."

"Very good." Then the stranger got up and said to the house:

"I find it late. The speeches of these gentlemen are not without merit, not without interest, not without grace; yet if I may be excused I will take my leave. I thank you for the great favor which you have shown me in granting my petition. I ask the Chair to keep the sack for me until tomorrow, and to hand these three five-hundred-dollar notes to Mr. Richards." They were passed up to the Chair. "At nine I will call for the sack, and at eleven will deliver the rest of the ten thousand to Mr. Richards in person, at his home. Good night."

Then he slipped out, and left the audience making a vast noise, which was composed of a mixture of cheers, the "Mikado" song, dog-disapproval, and the chant, "You are f-a-r from being a b-a-a-d man-a-a-a a-men!"

IV

At home the Richardses had to endure congratulations and compliments until midnight. Then they were left to themselves. They looked a little sad, and they sat silent and thinking. Finally Mary sighed and said,

"Do you think we are to blame, Edward—*much* to blame?" and her eyes wandered to the accusing triplet of big bank notes lying on the table, where the congratulators had been gloating over them and reverently fingering them. Edward did not answer at once; then he brought out a sigh and said, hesitatingly:

"We—we couldn't help it, Mary. It—well, it was ordered. *All* things are."

Mary glanced up and looked at him steadily, but he didn't return the look. Presently she said:

"I thought congratulations and praises always tasted good. But—it seems to me, now—Edward?"

"Well?"

"Are you going to stay in the bank?"

"N-no."

"Resign?"

"In the morning—by note."

"It does seem best."

Richards bowed his head in his hands and muttered:

"Before, I was not afraid to let oceans of people's money pour through my hands, but—Mary, I am so tired, so tired—"

"We will go to bed."

At nine in the morning the stranger called for the sack and took it to the hotel in a cab. At ten Harkness had a talk with him privately. The stranger asked for and got five checks on a metropolitan bank—drawn to "Bearer,"—four for $1,500 each, and one for $34,000. He put one of the former in his pocketbook, and the remainder, representing $38,500, he put in an envelope, and with these he added a note, which he wrote after Harkness was gone. At eleven he called at the Richards house and knocked. Mrs. Richards peeped through the shutters, then went and received the envelope, and the stranger disappeared without a word. She came back flushed and a little unsteady on her legs, and gasped out:

"I am sure I recognized him! Last night it seemed to me that maybe I had seen him somewhere before."

"He is the man that brought the sack here?"

"I am almost sure of it." .

"Then he is the ostensible Stephenson, too, and sold every important citizen in this town with his bogus secret. Now if he has sent checks instead of money, we are sold, too, after we thought we had escaped. 1 was beginning to feel fairly comfortable once more, after my night's rest, but the look of that envelope makes me sick. It isn't fat enough; $8,500 in even the largest bank notes makes more bulk than that."

"Edward, why do you object to checks?"

"Checks signed by Stephenson! I am resigned to take the $8,500 if it could come in bank notes—for it does seem that it was so ordered, Mary—but I have never had much courage, and I have not the pluck to try to market a check signed with that disastrous name. It would be a trap. That man tried to catch me; we escaped somehow or other; and now he is trying a new way. If it is checks—"

"Oh, Edward, it is too bad!" and she held up the checks and began to cry.

"Put them in the fire! quick! we mustn't be tempted. It is a trick to make the world laugh at us, along with the rest, and—Give them to *me*, since you can't do it!" He snatched them and tried to hold his grip till he could get to the stove; but he was human, he was a cashier, and he stopped a moment to make sure of the signature. Then he came near to fainting.

"Fan me, Mary, fan me! They are the same as gold!"

"Oh, how lovely, Edward! Why?"

"Signed by Harkness. What can the mystery of that be, Mary?"

"Edward, do you think—"

"Look here—look at this! Fifteen—fifteen—fifteen—thirty-four. Thirty-eight thousand five hundred! Mary, the sack isn't worth twelve dollars, and Harkness—apparently—has paid about par for it."

"And does it all come to us, do you think—instead of the ten thousand?"

"Why, it looks like it. And the checks are made to 'Bearer,' too."

"Is that good, Edward? What is it for?"

"A hint to collect them at some distant bank, I reckon. Perhaps Harkness doesn't want the matter known. What is that—a note?"

"Yes. It was with the checks."

It was in the "Stephenson" handwriting, but there was no signature. It said:

"I am a disappointed man. Your honesty is beyond the reach of temptation. I had a different idea about it, but I wronged you in that, and I beg pardon, and do it sincerely. I honor you–and that is sincere too. This town is not worthy to kiss the hem of your garment. Dear sir, I made a square bet with myself that there were nineteen debauchable men in your self-righteous community. I have lost. Take the whole pot, you are entitled to it."

Richards drew a deep sigh, and said:

"It seems written with fire–it burns so. Mary–I am miserable again."

"I, too. Ah, dear, I wish–"

"To think, Mary–he *believes* in me."

"Oh, don't, Edward–I can't bear it."

"If those beautiful words were deserved, Mary–and God knows I believed I deserved them once–I think I could give the forty thousand dollars for them. And I would put that paper away, as representing more than gold and jewels, and keep it always. But now–We could not live in the shadow of its accusing presence, Mary."

He put it in the fire.

A messenger arrived and delivered an envelope.

Richards took from it a note and read it; it was from Burgess.

"You saved me, in a difficult time. I saved you last night. It was at cost of a lie, but I made the sacrifice freely, and out of a grateful heart. None in this village knows so well as I know how brave and good and noble you are. At bottom you cannot respect me, knowing as you do of that matter of which I am accused, and by the general voice condemned; but I beg that you will at least believe that I am a grateful man; it will help me to bear my burden.

[*Signed*] "BURGESS."

"Saved, once more. And on such terms!" He put the note in the fire. "I–I wish I were dead, Mary, I wish I were out of it all."

"Oh, these are bitter, bitter days, Edward. The stabs, through their very generosity, are so deep–and they come so fast!"

Three days before the election each of two thousand voters suddenly found himself in possession of a prized memento–one of the renowned bogus double-eagles. Around one of its faces was stamped these words: "THE REMARK I MADE TO THE POOR STRANGER WAS–" Around the other face was stamped these: "GO, AND REFORM. [SIGNED] PINKERTON." Thus the entire remaining refuse of the renowned joke was emptied upon a single head, and with calamitous effect. It revived the recent vast laugh and concentrated it upon Pinkerton; and Harkness's election was a walk over.

Within twenty-four hours after the Richardses had received their checks their consciences were quieting down, discouraged; the old couple were learning to reconcile themselves to the sin which they had committed. But they were to learn, now, that a sin takes on new and real terrors when there seems a chance that it is going to be found out. This gives it a fresh and most substantial and important aspect. At church the morning sermon was of the usual pattern; it was the same old things said in the same old way; they had heard them a thousand times and found them innocuous, next to meaningless, and easy to sleep under; but now it was different: the sermon seemed to bristle with accusations; it seemed aimed straight and specially at people who were concealing deadly sins. After church they got away from the mob of congratulators as soon as they could, and hurried homeward, chilled to the bone at they did not know what—vague, shadowy, indefinite fears. And by chance they caught a glimpse of Mr. Burgess as he turned a corner. He paid no attention to their nod of recognition! He hadn't seen it; but they did not know that. What could his conduct mean? It might mean—it might mean—oh, a dozen dreadful things. Was it possible that he knew that Richards could have cleared him of guilt in that bygone time, and had been silently waiting for a chance to even up accounts? At home, in their distress they got to imagining that their servant might have been in the next room listening when Richards revealed the secret to his wife that he knew of Burgess's innocence; next, Richards began to imagine that he had heard the swish of a gown in there at that time; next, he was sure he *had* heard it. They would call Sarah in, on a pretext, and watch her face: if she had been betraying them to Mr. Burgess, it would show in her manner. They asked her some questions—questions which were so random and incoherent and seemingly purposeless that the girl felt sure that the old people's minds had been affected by their sudden good fortune; the sharp and watchful gaze which they bent upon her frightened her, and that completed the business. She blushed, she became nervous and confused, and to the old people these were plain signs of guilt—guilt of some fearful sort or other—without doubt she was a spy and a traitor. When they were alone again they began to piece many unrelated things together and get horrible results out of the combination. When things had got about to the worst, Richards was delivered of a sudden gasp, and his wife asked,

"Oh, what is it?—what is it?"

"The note—Burgess's note! Its language was sarcastic, I see it now." He quoted: "'At bottom you cannot respect me, *knowing*, as you do, of *that matter* of which I am accused'—oh, it is perfectly plain, now, God help me! He knows that I know! You see the ingenuity of the phrasing. It was a trap—and like a fool, I walked into it. And Mary—?"

"Oh, it is dreadful—I know what you are going to say—he didn't return your transcript of the pretended test-remark."

"No—kept it to destroy us with. Mary, he has exposed us to some already. I know it—I know it well. I saw it in a dozen faces after church. Ah, he wouldn't answer our nod of recognition—*he* knew what he had been doing!"

In the night the doctor was called. The news went around in the morning that the old couple were rather seriously ill—prostrated by the exhausting excitement growing out of their great windfall, the congratulations, and the late hours, the doctor said. The town was sincerely distressed; for these old people were about all it had left to be proud of, now.

Two days later the news was worse. The old couple were delirious, and were doing strange things. By witness of the nurses, Richards had exhibited checks—for $8,500? No—for an amazing sum—$38,500! What could be the explanation of this gigantic piece of luck?

The following day the nurses had more news—and wonderful. They had concluded to hide the checks, lest harm come to them; but when they searched they were gone from under the patient's pillow—vanished away. The patient said:

"Let the pillow alone; what do you want?"

"We thought it best that the checks—"

"You will never see them again—they are destroyed. They came from Satan. I saw the hell-brand on them, and I knew they were sent to betray me to sin." Then he fell to gabbling strange and dreadful things which were not clearly understandable, and which the doctor admonished them to keep to themselves.

Richards was right; the checks were never seen again.

A nurse must have talked in her sleep, for within two days the forbidden gabblings were the property of the town; and they were of a surprising sort. They seemed to indicate that Richards had been a claimant for the sack himself, and that Burgess had concealed that fact and then maliciously betrayed it.

Burgess was taxed with this and stoutly denied it. And he said it was not fair to attach weight to the chatter of a sick old man who was out of his mind. Still, suspicion was in the air, and there was much talk.

After a day or two it was reported that Mrs. Richards's delirious deliveries were getting to be duplicates of her husband's. Suspicion flamed up into conviction, now, and the town's pride in the purity of its one undiscredited important citizen began to dim down and flicker toward extinction.

Six days passed, then came more news. The old couple were dying. Richards's mind cleared in his latest hour, and he sent for Burgess. Burgess said:

"Let the room be cleared. I think he wishes to say something in privacy."

"No!" said Richards: "I want witnesses. I want you all to hear my confession, so that I may die a man, and not a dog. I was clean—artificially—like the rest; and like the rest I fell when temptation came. I signed a lie, and claimed the miserable sack. Mr. Burgess remembered that I had done him a service, and in gratitude (and ignorance) he suppressed my claim and saved me. You know the thing that was charged against Burgess years ago. My testimony, and mine alone, could have cleared him, and I was a coward, and left him to suffer disgrace—"

"No—no—Mr. Richards, you—"

"My servant betrayed my secret to him—"

"No one has betrayed anything to me—"

—"and then he did a natural and justifiable thing, he repented of the saving kindness which he had done me, and he *exposed* me—as I deserved—"

"Never!—I make oath—"

"Out of my heart I forgive him."

Burgess's impassioned protestations fell upon deaf ears; the dying man passed away without knowing that once more he had done poor Burgess a wrong. The old wife died that night.

The last of the sacred Nineteen had fallen a prey to the fiendish sack; the town was stripped of the last rag of its ancient glory. Its mourning was not showy, but it was deep.

By act of the Legislature—upon prayer and petition—Hadleyburg was allowed to change its name to (never mind what—I will not give it away), and leave one word out of the motto that for many generations had graced the town's official seal.

It is an honest town once more, and the man will have to rise early that catches it napping again.

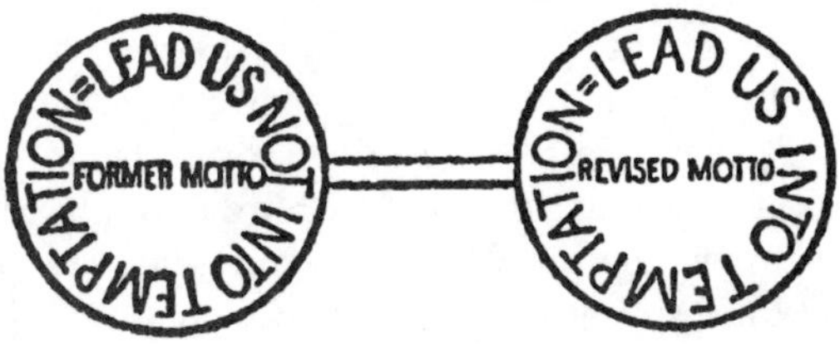

BRET HARTE

[1836–1902]

The Luck of Roaring Camp

(First published in *Overland Monthly*, August, 1868; first book publication in 1870.)

THERE WAS COMMOTION in Roaring Camp. It could not have been a fight, for in 1850 that was not novel enough to have called together the entire settlement. The ditches and claims were not only deserted, but 'Tuttle's grocery' had contributed its gamblers, who, it will be remembered, calmly continued their game the day that French Pete and Kanaka Joe shot each other to death over the bar in the front room. The whole camp was collected before a rude cabin on the outer edge of the clearing. Conversation was carried on in a low tone, but the name of a woman was frequently repeated. It was a name familiar enough to the camp–'Cherokee Sal.'

Perhaps the less said of her the better. She was a coarse and, it is to be feared, a very sinful woman. But at that time she was the only woman in Roaring Camp, and was just then lying in sore extremity, when she most needed the ministration of her own sex. Dissolute, abandoned, and irreclaimable, she was yet suffering a martyrdom hard enough to bear even when veiled by sympathizing womanhood, but now terrible in her loneliness. The primal curse had come to her in that original isolation which must have made the punishment of the first transgression so dreadful. It was, perhaps, part of the expiation of her sin that, at a moment when she most lacked her sex's intuitive tenderness and care, she met only the half-contemptuous faces of her masculine associates. Yet a few of the spectators were, I think, touched by her sufferings. Sandy Tipton thought it was 'rough on Sal,' and in the contemplation of her condition, for a moment rose superior to the fact that he had an ace and two bowers in his sleeve.

It will be seen also that the situation was novel. Deaths were by no means uncommon in Roaring Camp, but a birth was a new thing. People had been dismissed the camp effectively, finally, and with no possibility of return; but this was the first time that anybody had been introduced *ab initio*. Hence the excitement.

'You go in there, Stumpy,' said a prominent citizen known as 'Kentuck,' addressing one of the loungers. 'Go in there, and see what you kin do. You've had experience in them things.'

Perhaps there was a fitness in the selection. Stumpy, in other climes, had been the putative head of two families; in fact, it was owing to some legal informality in these proceedings that Roaring Camp—a city of refuge—was indebted to his company. The crowd approved the choice, and Stumpy was wise enough to bow to the majority. The door closed on the extempore surgeon and midwife, and Roaring Camp sat down outside, smoked its pipe, and awaited the issue.

The assemblage numbered about a hundred men. One or two of these were actual fugitives from justice, some were criminal, and all were reckless. Physically they exhibited no indication of their past lives and character. The greatest scamp had a Raphael face, with a profusion of blond hair; Oakhurst, a gambler, had the melancholy air and intellectual abstraction of a Hamlet; the coolest and most courageous man was scarcely over five feet in height, with a soft voice and an embarrassed, timid manner. The term 'roughs' applied to them was a distinction rather than a definition. Perhaps in the minor details of fingers, toes, ears, etc., the camp may have been deficient, but these slight omissions did not detract from their aggregate force. The strongest man had but three fingers on his right hand; the best shot had but one eye.

Such was the physical aspect of the men that were dispersed around the cabin. The camp lay in a triangular valley between two hills and a river. The only outlet was a steep trail over the summit of a hill that faced the cabin, now illuminated by the rising moon. The suffering woman might have seen it from the rude bunk whereon she lay—seen it winding like a silver thread until it was lost in the stars above.

A fire of withered pine boughs added sociability to the gathering. By degrees the natural levity of Roaring Camp returned. Bets were freely offered and taken regarding the result. Three to five that 'Sal would get through with it'; even that the child would survive; side bets as to the sex and complexion of the coming stranger. In the midst of an excited discussion an exclamation came from those nearest the door, and the camp stopped to listen. Above the swaying and moaning of the pines, the swift rush of the river, and the crackling of the fire rose a sharp, querulous cry—a cry unlike anything heard before in the camp. The pines stopped moaning, the river ceased to rush, and the fire to crackle. It seemed as if Nature had stopped to listen too.

The camp rose to its feet as one man! It was proposed to explode a barrel of gunpowder; but in consideration of the situation of the mother, better counsels prevailed, and only a few revolvers were discharged; for whether owing to the rude surgery of the camp, or some other reason, Cherokee Sal was sinking fast. Within an hour she had climbed, as it were, that rugged road that led to the stars, and so passed out of Roaring Camp, its sin and shame, forever. I do not think that the announcement disturbed them much, except in speculation as to the fate of the child. 'Can he live now?' was asked of Stumpy. The answer was doubtful. The only other being of Cherokee Sal's sex and maternal condition in the settlement was an ass. There was some conjecture as to fitness, but the experiment was tried. It was less problematical than the ancient treatment of Romulus and Remus, and apparently as successful.

When these details were completed, which exhausted another hour, the door was opened, and the anxious crowd of men, who had already formed themselves into a queue, entered in single file. Beside the low bunk or shelf, on which the figure of the mother was starkly outlined below the blankets, stood a pine table. On this a candlebox was placed, and within it, swathed in staring red flannel, lay the last arrival at Roaring Camp. Beside the candlebox was placed a hat. Its use was soon indicated. 'Gentlemen,' said Stumpy, with a singular mixture of authority and *ex officio* complacency—'gentlemen will please pass in at the front door, round the table, and out at the back door. Them as wishes to contribute anything toward the orphan will find a hat handy.' The first man entered with his hat on; he uncovered, however, as he looked about him, and so unconsciously set an example to the next. In such communities good and bad actions are catching. As the procession filed in comments were audible—criticisms addressed perhaps rather to Stumpy in the character of showman: 'Is that him?' 'Mighty small specimen;' 'Hasn't more'n got the color;' 'Ain't bigger nor a derringer.' The contributions were as characteristic: A silver tobacco box; a doubloon; a navy revolver, silver mounted; a gold specimen; a very beautifully embroidered lady's handkerchief (from Oakhurst the gambler); a diamond breastpin; a diamond ring (suggested by the pin, with the remark from the giver that he 'saw that pin and went two diamonds better'); a slung shot; a Bible (contributor not detected); a golden spur; a silver teaspoon (the initials, I regret to say, were not the giver's); a pair of surgeon's shears; a lancet; a Bank of England note for £5; and about $200 in loose gold and silver coin. During these proceedings Stumpy maintained a silence as impassive as the dead on his left, a gravity as inscrutable as that of the newly born on his right. Only one incident occurred to break the monotony of the curious procession. As Kentuck bent over the candlebox half curiously, the child turned, and, in a spasm of pain, caught at his groping finger and held it fast for a moment. Kentuck looked foolish and embarrassed. Something like a blush tried to assert itself in his weather-beaten cheek. 'The d—d little cuss!' he said, as he extricated his finger, with perhaps more tenderness and care than he might have been deemed capable of showing. He held that finger a little apart from its fellows as he went out, and examined it curiously. The examination provoked the same original remark in regard to the child. In fact, he seemed to enjoy repeating it. 'He rastled with my finger,' he remarked to Tipton, holding up the member, 'the d–d little cuss!'

It was four o'clock before the camp sought repose. A light burnt in the cabin where the watchers sat, for Stumpy did not go to bed that night. Nor did Kentuck. He drank quite freely, and related with great gusto his experience, invariably ending with his characteristic condemnation of the newcomer. It seemed to relieve him of any unjust implication of sentiment, and Kentuck had the weaknesses of the nobler sex. When everybody else had gone to bed, he walked down to the river and whistled reflectingly. Then he walked up the gulch past the cabin, still whistling with demonstrative unconcern. At a large redwood tree he paused and retraced his steps, and again passed the cabin. Halfway down to the river's bank he again paused, and then returned and knocked at the door. It was opened by Stumpy. 'How goes it?' said Kentuck, looking past Stumpy toward the candlebox. 'All serene!' replied Stumpy. 'Anything up?' 'Nothing.' There was a pause–an embarrassing one–Stumpy still holding the door. Then Kentuck had recourse to his finger, which he held up to Stumpy. 'Rastled with it–the d–d little cuss,' he said, and retired.

The next day Cherokee Sal had such rude sepulture as Roaring Camp afforded. After her body had been committed to the hillside, there was a formal meeting of the camp to discuss what should be done with her infant. A resolution to adopt it was unanimous and enthusiastic. But an animated discussion in regard to the manner and feasibility of providing for its wants at once sprang up. It was remarkable that the argument partook of none of those fierce personalities with which discussions were usually conducted at Roaring Camp. Tipton proposed that they should send the child to Red Dog–a distance of forty miles–where female attention could be procured. But the unlucky suggestion met with fierce and unanimous opposition. It was evident that no plan which entailed parting from their new acquisition would for a moment be entertained. 'Besides,' said Tom Ryder, 'them fellows at Red Dog would swap it, and ring in somebody else on us.' A disbelief in the honesty of other camps prevailed at Roaring Camp, as in other places.

The introduction of a female nurse in the camp also met with objection. It was argued that no decent woman could be prevailed to accept Roaring Camp as her home, and the speaker urged that 'they didn't want any more of the other kind.' This unkind allusion to the defunct mother, harsh as it may seem, was the first spasm of propriety–the first symptom of the camp's regeneration. Stumpy advanced nothing. Perhaps he felt a certain delicacy in interfering with the selection of a possible successor in office. But when questioned, he averred stoutly that he and 'Jinny'–the mammal before alluded to–could manage to rear the child. There was something original, independent, and heroic about the plan that pleased the camp. Stumpy was retained. Certain articles were sent for to Sacramento. 'Mind,' said the treasurer, as he pressed a bag of gold dust into the expressman's hand, 'the best that can be got–lace, you know, and filigree work and frills–d–n the cost!'

Strange to say, the child thrived. Perhaps the invigorating climate of the mountain camp was compensation for material deficiencies. Nature took the foundling to her broader breast. In that rare atmosphere of the Sierra foothills–that air pungent with balsamic odor, that ethereal cordial at once bracing and exhilarating–he may have found food and nourishment, or a subtle chemistry that transmuted ass's milk to lime and phosphorus. Stumpy inclined to the belief that it was the latter and good nursing. 'Me and that ass,' he would say, 'has been father and mother to him! Don't you,' he would add, apostrophizing the helpless bundle before him, 'never go back on us.'

By the time he was a month old the necessity of giving him a name became apparent. He had generally been known as 'The Kid,' 'Stumpy's Boy,' 'The Coyote' (an allusion of his vocal powers), and even by Kentuck's endearing diminutive of 'The d–d little cuss.' But these were felt to be vague and unsatisfactory, and were at last dismissed under another influence. Gamblers and adventurers are generally superstitious, and Oakhurst one day declared that the baby had brought 'the luck' to Roaring Camp. It was certain that of late they had been successful. 'Luck' was the name agreed upon, with the prefix of Tommy for greater convenience. No allusion was made to the mother, and the father was unknown. 'It's better,' said the philosophical Oakhurst, 'to take a fresh deal all round. Call him Luck, and start him fair.' A day was accordingly set apart for the christening. What was meant by this ceremony the reader may imagine who has already gathered some idea of the reckless irreverence of Roaring Camp. The master of ceremonies was one 'Boston,' a noted wag, and the occasion seemed to promise the greatest facetiousness. This ingenious satirist had spent two days in preparing a burlesque of the Chureh service, with pointed local allusions. The choir was properly trained, and Sandy Tipton was to stand godfather. But after the procession had marched to the grove with music and banners, and the child had been deposited before a mock altar, Stumpy stepped before the expectant crowd. 'It ain't my style to spoil fun, boys,' said the little man, stoutly eying the races around him, 'but it strikes me that this thing ain't exactly on the squar. It's playing it pretty low down on this yer baby to ring in fun on him that he ain't goin' to understand. And ef there's goin' to be any godfathers round, I'd like to see who's got any better rights than me.' A silence followed Stumpy's speech. To the credit of all humorists be it said that the first man to acknowledge its justice was the satirist thus stopped of his fun. 'But,' said Stumpy, quickly following up his advantage, 'we're here for a christening, and we'll have it. I proclaim you

Thomas Luck, according to the laws of the United States and the State of California, so help me God.' It was the first time that the name of the Deity had been otherwise uttered than profanely in the camp. The form of christening was perhaps ever more ludicrous than the satirist had conceived; but strangely enough, nobody saw it and nobody laughed. 'Tommy' was christened as seriously as he would have been under a Christian roof, and cried and was comforted in as orthodox fashion.

And so the work of regeneration began in Roaring Camp. Almost imperceptibly a change came over the settlement. The cabin assigned to 'Tommy Luck'–or 'The Luck,' as he was more frequently called–first showed signs of improvement. It was kept scrupulously clean and whitewashed. Then it was boarded, clothed, and papered. The rosewood cradle, packed eighty miles by mule, had, in Stumpy's way of putting it, 'sorter killed the rest of the furniture.' So the rehabilitation of the camp became a necessity. The men who were in the habit of lounging in at Stumpy's to see 'how "The Luck" got on' seemed to appreciate the change, and in self-defense the rival establishment of 'Tuttle's grocery' bestirred itself and imported a carpet and mirrors. The reelections of the latter on the appearance of Roaring Camp tended to produce stricter habits of personal cleanliness. Again Stumpy imposed a kind of quarantine upon those who aspired to the honor and privilege of holding The Luck. It was a cruel mortification to Kentuck–who, in the carelessness of a large nature and the habits of frontier life, had begun to regard all garments as a second cuticle, which, like a snake's, only sloughed off through decay–to be debarred this privilege from certain prudential reasons. Yet such was the subtle influence of innovation that he thereafter appeared regularly every afternoon in a clean shirt and face still shining from his ablutions. Nor were moral and social sanitary laws neglected. 'Tommy,' who was supposed to spend his whole existence in a persistent attempt to repose, must not be disturbed by noise. The shouting and yelling, which had gained the camp its infelicitous title, were not permitted within hearing distance of Stumpy's. The men conversed in whispers or smoked with Indian gravity. Profanity was tacitly given up in these sacred precincts, and throughout the camp a popular form of expletive, known as 'D–n the luck!' and 'Curse the luck!' was abandoned, as having a new personal bearing. Vocal music was not interdicted, being supposed to have a soothing, tranquilizing quality; and one song, sung by 'Man-o'-War Jack,' an English sailor from her Majesty's Australian colonies, was quite popular as a lullaby. It was a lugubrious recital of the exploits of 'the Arethusa, Seventy-four,' in a muffled minor, ending with a prolonged dying fall at the burden of each verse, 'On b-oo-o-ard of the Arethusa.' It was a fine sight to see Jack holding The Luck, rocking from side to side as if with the motion of a ship, and crooning forth this naval ditty. Either through the peculiar rocking of Jack or the length of his song–it contained ninety stanzas, and was continued with conscientious deliberation to the bitter end–the lullaby generally had the desired effect. At such times the men would lie at full length under the trees in the soft summer twilight, smoking their pipes and drinking in the melodious utterances. An indistinct idea that this was pastoral happiness pervaded the camp. 'This 'ere kind o' think,' said the Cockney Simmons, meditatively reclining on his elbow, 'is 'evingly.' It reminded him of Greenwich.

On the long summer days The Luck was usually carried to the gulch from whence the golden store of Roaring Camp was taken. There, on a blanket spread over pine boughs, he would lie while the men were working in the ditches below. Latterly there was a rude attempt to decorate this bower with flowers and sweet-smelling shrubs, and generally some one would bring him a cluster of wild honeysuckles, azaleas, or the painted blossoms of Las Mariposas. The men had suddenly awakened to the fact that there were beauty and significance in these trifles, which they had so long trodden carelessly beneath their feet. A flake of glittering mica, a fragment of variegated quartz, a bright pebble from the bed of the creek, became beautiful to eyes thus cleared and strengthened, and were invariably put aside for The Luck. It was wonderful how many treasures the woods and hillsides yielded that 'would do for Tommy.' Surrounded by playthings such as never child out of fairyland had before, it is to be hoped that Tommy was content. He appeared to be serenely happy, albeit there was an infantine gravity about him, a contemplative light in his round gray eyes, that sometimes worried Stumpy. He was always tractable and quiet, and it is recorded that once, having crept beyond his 'corral' – a hedge of tessellated pine boughs, which surrounded his bed–he dropped over the bank on his head in the soft earth, and remained with his mottled legs in the air in that position for at least five minutes with unflinching gravity. He was extricated without a murmur. I hesitate to record the many other instances of his sagacity, which rest, unfortunately, upon the statements of prejudiced friends. Some of them were not without a tinge of superstition. 'I crep' up the bank just now,' said Kentuck one day, in a breathless state of excitement, 'and dern my skin if he wasn't a-talking to a jay bird as was a-sittin' on his lap. There they was, just as free and sociable as anything you please, ajawin' at each other just like two cherrybums.' Howbeit, whether creeping over the pine boughs or lying lazily on his back blinking at the leaves above him, to him the birds sang, the squirrels chattered, and the flowers bloomed. Nature was his nurse and playfellow. For him she would let slip between the leaves golden shafts of sunlight that fell just within his grasp; she would send wandering breezes to visit him with the balm of bay and resinous gum; to him the tall redwoods nodded familiarly and sleepily, the bumblebees buzzed, and the rooks cawed a slumberous accompaniment.

Such was the golden summer of Roaring Camp. They were 'flush times,' and the luck was with them. The claims had yielded enormously. The camp was jealous of its privileges and looked suspiciously on strangers. No encouragement was given to immigration, and, to make their seclusion more perfect, the land on either side of the mountain wall that surrounded the camp they duly pre-empted. This, and a reputation for singular proficiency with the revolver, kept the reserve of Roaring Camp inviolate. The expressman—their only connecting link with the surrounding world—sometimes told wonderful stories of the camp. He would say, 'They've a street up there in "Roaring" that would lay over any street in Red Dog. They've got vines and flowers round their houses, and they wash themselves twice a day. But they're mighty rough on strangers, and they worship an Ingin baby.'

With the prosperity of the camp came a desire for further improvement. It was proposed to build a hotel in the following spring, and to invite one or two decent families to reside there for the sake of The Luck, who might perhaps profit by female companionship. The sacrifice that this concession to the sex cost these men, who were fiercely skeptical in regard to its general virtue and usefulness, can only be accounted for by their affection for Tommy. A few still held out. But the resolve could not be carried into effect for three months, and the minority meekly yielded in the hope that something might turn up to prevent it. And it did.

The winter of 1851 will long be remembered in the foothills. The snow lay deep on the Sierras, and every mountain creek became a river, and every river a lake. Each gorge and gulch was transformed into a tumultuous watercourse that descended the hillsides, tearing down giant trees and scattering its drift and debris along the plain. Red Dog had been twice under water, and Roaring Camp had been forewarned. 'Water put the gold into them gulches,' said Stumpy. 'It's been here once and will be here again!' And that night the North Fork suddenly leaped over its banks and swept up the triangular valley of Roaring Camp.

In the confusion of rushing water, crashing trees, and crackling timber, and the darkness which seemed to flow with the water and blot out the fair valley, but little could be done to collect the scattered camp. When the morning broke, the cabin of Stumpy, nearest the river-bank, was gone. Higher up the gulch they found the body of its unlucky owner; but the pride, the hope, the joy, The Luck, of Roaring Camp had disappeared. They were returning with sad hearts when a shout from the bank recalled them.

It was a relief-boat from down the river. They had picked up, they said, a man and an infant, nearly exhausted, about two miles below. Did anybody know them, and did they belong here?

It needed but a glance to show them Kentuck lying there, cruelly crushed and bruised, but still holding The Luck of Roaring Camp in his arms. As they bent over the strangely assorted pair, they saw that the child was cold and pulseless. 'He is dead,' said one. Kentuck opened his eyes. 'Dead?' he repeated feebly. 'Yes, my man, and you are dying too.' A smile lit the eyes of the expiring Kentuck. 'Dying!' he repeated; 'he's a-taking me with him. Tell the boys I've got The Luck with me now;' and the strong man, clinging to the frail babe as a drowning man is said to cling to a straw, drifted away into the shadowy river that flows forever to the unknown sea.

The Outcasts of Poker Flat

(First published in *Overland Monthly*,
January, 1869; first book publication in 1870.)

As MR. JOHN Oakhurst, gambler, stepped into the main street of Poker Flat on the morning of the twenty-third of November, 1850, he was conscious of a change in its moral atmosphere since the preceding night. Two or three men, conversing earnestly together, ceased as he approached, and exchanged significant glances. There was a Sabbath lull in the air, which, in a settlement unused to Sabbath influences, looked ominous.

Mr. Oakhurst's calm, handsome face betrayed small concern of these indications. Whether he was conscious of any predisposing cause, was another question. "I reckon they're after somebody," he reflected; "likely it's me." He returned to his pocket the handkerchief with which he had been whipping away the red dust of Poker Flat from his neat boots, and quietly discharged his mind of any further conjecture.

In point of fact, Poker Flat was "after somebody." It had lately suffered the loss of several thousand dollars, two valuable horses, and a prominent citizen. It was experiencing a spasm of virtuous reaction, quite as lawless and ungovernable as any of the acts that had provoked it. A secret committee had determined to rid the town of all improper persons. This was done permanently in regard of two men who were then hanging from the boughs of a sycamore in the gulch, and temporarily in the banishment of certain other objectionable characters. I regret to say that some of these were ladies. It is but due to the sex, however, to state that their impropriety was professional, and it was only in such easily established standards of evil that Poker Flat ventured to sit in judgment.

Mr. Oakhurst was right in supposing that he was included in this category. A few of the committee had urged hanging him as a possible example, and a sure method of reimbursing themselves from his pockets of the sums he had won from them. "It's agin justice," said Jim Wheeler, "to let this yer young man from Roaring Camp—an entire stranger—carry away our money." But a crude sentiment of equity residing in the breasts of those who had been fortunate enough to win from Mr. Oakhurst overruled this narrower local prejudice.

Mr. Oakhurst received his sentence with philosophic calmness, none the less coolly that he was aware of the hesitation of his judges. He was too much of a gambler not to accept Fate. With him life was at best an uncertain game, and he recognized the usual percentage in favor of the dealer.

A body of armed men accompanied the deported wickedness of Poker Flat to the outskirts of the settlement. Besides Mr. Oakhurst, who was known to be a coolly desperate man, and for those intimidation the armed escort was intended, the expatriated party consisted of a young woman familiarly known as "The Duchess"; another, who had gained the infelicitous title of "Mother Shipton"; and "Uncle Billy," a suspected sluice-robber and confirmed drunkard. The cavalcade provoked no comments from the spectators, nor was any word uttered by the escort. Only, when the gulch which marked the uttermost limit of Poker Flat was reached, the leader spoke briefly and to the point. The exiles were forbidden to return at the peril of their lives.

As the escort disappeared, their pent-up feelings found vent in a few hysterical tears from the Duchess, some bad language from Mother Shipton, and a Parthian volley of expletives from Uncle Billy. The philosophic Oakhurst alone remained still. He listened calmly to Mother Shipton's desire to cut somebody's heart out, to the repeated statements of the Duchess that she would die on the road, and to the alarming oaths that seemed to be bumped out of Uncle Billy as he rode forward. With the easy good humor characteristic of his class, he insisted upon exchanging his own riding-horse, Five Spot, for the sorry mule which the Duchess rode. But even this act did not draw the party into any closer sympathy. The young woman readjusted her somewhat draggled plumes with a feeble, faded coquetry; Mother Shipton eyed the possessor of Five Spot with malevolence, and Uncle Billy included the whole party in one sweeping anathema.

The road to Sandy Bar—a camp that, not having as yet experienced the regenerating influences of Poker Flat, consequently seemed to offer some invitation to the emigrants—lay over a steep mountain range. It was distant a day's severe journey. In that advanced season, the party soon passed out of the moist, temperate regions of the foothills into the dry, cold, bracing air of the Sierras. The trail was narrow and difficult. At noon the Duchess, rolling out of her saddle upon the ground, declared her intention of going no farther, and the party halted.

The spot was singularly wild and impressive. A wooded amphitheater, surrounded on three sides by precipitous cliffs of naked granite, sloped gently toward the crest of another precipice that overlooked the valley. It was undoubtedly the most suitable spot for a camp, had camping been advisable. But Mr. Oakhurst knew that scarcely half the journey to Sandy Bar was accomplished, and the party were not equipped or provisioned for delay. This fact he pointed out to his companions curtly, with a philosophic commentary on the folly of "throwing up their hand before the game was played out." But they were furnished with liquor, which in this emergency stood them in place of food, fuel, rest, and prescience. In spite of his remonstrances, it was not long before they were more or less under its influence. Uncle Billy passed rapidly from a bellicose state into one of stupor, the Duchess became maudlin, and Mother Shipton snored. Mr. Oakhurst alone remained erect, leaning against a rock, calmly surveying them.

Mr. Oakhurst did not drink. It interfered with a profession which required coolness, impassiveness, and presence of mind, and, in his own language, he "couldn't afford it." As he gazed at his recumbent fellow-exiles, the loneliness begotten of his pariah-trade, his habits of life, his very vices, for the first time seriously oppressed him. He bestirred himself in dusting his black clothes, washing his hands and face, and other acts characteristic of his studiously neat habits, and for a moment forgot his annoyance. The thought of deserting his weaker and more pitiable companions never perhaps occurred to him. Yet he could not help feeling the want of that excitement which, singularly enough, was most conducive to that calm equanimity for which he was notorious. He looked at the gloomy walls that rose a thousand feet sheer above the circling pines around him; at the sky, ominously clouded; at the valley below, already deepening into shadow. And, doing so, suddenly he heard his own name called.

A horseman slowly ascended the trail. In the fresh, open face of the newcomer Mr. Oakhurst recognized Tom Simson, otherwise known as "The Innocent" of Sandy Bar. He had met him some months before over a "little game," and had, with perfect equanimity, won the entire fortune–amounting to some forty dollars–of that guileless youth. After the game was finished, Mr. Oakhurst drew the youthful speculator behind the door and thus addressed him: "Tommy, you're a good little man, but you can't gamble worth a cent. Don't try it over again." He then handed him his money back, pushed him gently from the room, and so made a devoted slave of Tom Simson.

There was a remembrance of this in his boyish and enthusiastic greeting of Mr. Oakhurst. He had started, he said, to go to Poker Flat to seek his fortune. "Alone?" No, not exactly alone; in fact–a giggle–he had run away with Piney Woods. Didn't Mr. Oakhurst remember Piney? She that used to wait on the table at the Temperance House? They had been engaged a long time, but old Jake Woods had objected, and so they had run away, and were going to Poker Flat to be married, and here they were. And they were tired out, and how lucky it was they had found a place to camp and company. All this the Innocent delivered rapidly, while Piney–a stout, comely damsel of fifteen–emerged from behind the pine-tree, where she had been blushing unseen, and rode to the side of her lover.

Mr. Oakhurst seldom troubled himself with sentiment, still less with propriety; but he had a vague idea that the situation was not felicitous. He retained, however, his presence of mind sufficiently to kick Uncle Billy, who was about to say something, and Uncle Billy was sober enough to recognize in Mr. Oakhurst's kick a superior power that would not bear trifling.

He then endeavored to dissuade Tom Simson from delaying further, but in vain. He even pointed out the fact that there was no provision, nor means of making a camp. But, unluckily, the Innocent met this objection by assuring the party that he was provided with an extra mule loaded with provisions, and by the discovery of a rude attempt at a log-house near the trail. "Piney can stay with Mrs. Oakhurst," said the Innocent, pointing to the Duchess, "and I can shift for myself."

Nothing but Mr. Oakhurst's admonishing foot saved Uncle Billy from bursting into a roar of laughter. As it was, he felt compelled to retire up the canyon until he could recover his gravity. There he confided the joke to the tall pine trees, with many slaps of his leg, contortions of his face, and the usual profanity. But when he returned to the party, he found them seated by a fire—for the air had grown strangely chill and the sky overcast—in apparently amicable conversation. Piney was actually talking in an impulsive, girlish fashion to the Duchess, who was listening with an interest and animation she had not shown for many days. The Innocent was holding forth, apparently with equal effect, to Mr. Oakhurst and Mother Shipton, who was actually relaxing into amiability. "Is this yer a d—d picnic?" said Uncle Billy, with inward scorn, as he surveyed the sylvan group, the glancing fire-light, and the tethered animals in the foreground. Suddenly an idea mingled with the alcoholic fumes that disturbed his brain. It was apparently of a jocular nature, for he felt impelled to slap his leg again and cram his fist into his mouth.

As the shadows crept slowly up the mountain, a slight breeze rocked the tops of the pine-trees, and moaned through their long and gloomy aisles. The ruined cabin, patched and covered with pine boughs, was set apart for the ladies. As the lovers parted, they unaffectedly exchanged a kiss, so honest and sincere that it might have been heard above the swaying pines. The frail Duchess and the malevolent Mother Shipton were probably too stunned to remark upon this last evidence of simplicity, and so turned without a word to the hut. The fire was replenished, the men lay down before the door, and in a few minutes were asleep.

Mr. Oakhurst was a light sleeper. Toward morning he awoke benumbed and cold. As he stirred the dying fire, the wind, which was now blowing strongly, brought to his cheek that which caused the blood to leave it—snow!

He started to his feet with the intention of awakening the sleepers, for there was no time to lose. But turning to where Uncle Billy had been lying, he found him gone. A suspicion leaped to his brain and a curse to his lips. He ran to the spot where the mules had been tethered; they were no longer there. The tracks were already rapidly disappearing in the snow.

The momentary excitement brought Mr. Oakhurst back to the fire with his usual calm. He did not waken the sleepers. The Innocent slumbered peacefully, with a smile on his good humored, freckled face; the virgin Piney slept beside her frailer sisters as sweetly as though attended by celestial guardians, and Mr. Oakhurst, drawing his blanket over his shoulders, stroked his mustachios and waited for the dawn. It came slowly in the whirling mist of snowflakes, that dazzled and confused the eye. What could be seen of the landscape appeared magically changed. He looked over the valley, and summed up the present and future in two words–"Snowed in!"

A careful inventory of the provisions, which, fortunately for the party, had been stored within the hut, and so escaped the felonious fingers of Uncle Billy, disclosed the fact that with care and prudence they might last ten days longer. "That is," said Mr. Oakhurst, *sotto voce* to the Innocent, "if you're willing to board us. If you ain't–and perhaps you'd better not–you can wait till Uncle Billy gets back with provisions." For some occult reason, Mr. Oakhurst could not bring himself to disclose Uncle Billy's rascality, and so offered the hypothesis that he had wandered from the camp and had accidentally stampeded the animals. He dropped a warning to the Duchess and Mother Shipton, who of course knew the facts of their associate's defection. "They'll find out the truth about us *all*, when they find out anything," he added, significantly, "and there's no good frightening them now."

Tom Simson not only put all his worldly store at the disposal of Mr. Oakhurst, but seemed to enjoy the prospect of their enforced seclusion. We'll have a good camp for a week, and then the snow'll melt, and we'll all go back together." The cheerful gayety of the young man and Mr. Oakhurst's calm infected the others. The Innocent, with the aid of pine boughs, extemporized a thatch for the roofless cabin, and the Duchess directed Piney in the rearrangement of the interior with a taste and tact that opened the blue eyes of that provincial maiden to their fullest extent.

"I reckon now you're used to fine things at Poker Flat," said Piney. The Duchess turned away sharply to conceal something that reddened her cheek through its professional tint, and Mother Shipton requested Piney not to "chatter." But when Mr. Oakhurst returned from a weary search for the trail, he heard the sound of happy laughter echoed from the rocks. He stopped in some alarm, and his thoughts first naturally reverted to the whisky, which he had prudently *cached*. "And yet it don't somehow sound like whisky," said the gambler. It was not until he caught sight of the blazing fire through the still blinding storm, and the group around it, that he settled to the conviction that it was "square fun."

Whether Mr. Oakhurst had *cached* his cards with the whisky as something debarred the free access of the community, I cannot say. It was certain that, in Mother Shipton's words, he "didn't say cards once" during the evening. Haply the time was beguiled by an accordion, produced somewhat ostentatiously by Tom Simson, from his pack. Notwithstanding some difficulties attending the manipulation of this instrument, Piney Woods managed to pluck several reluctant melodies from its keys, to an accompaniment by the

Innocent on a pair of bone castinets. But the crowning festivity of the evening was reached in a rude camp-meeting hymn, which the lovers, joining hands, sang with great earnestness and vociferation. I fear that a certain defiant tone and Covenanter's swing to its chorus, rather than any devotional quality, caused it speedily to infect the others, who at last joined in the refrain:

> I'm proud to live in the service of the Lord,
> And I'm bound to die in His army.

The pines rocked, the storm eddied and whirled above the miserable group, and the flames of their altar leaped heavenward, as if in token of the vow.

At midnight the storm abated, the rolling clouds parted, and the stars glittered keenly above the sleeping camp. Mr. Oakhurst, whose professional habits had enabled him to live on the smallest possible amount of sleep, in dividing the watch with Tom Simson, somehow managed to take upon himself the greater part of that duty. He excused himself to the Innocent, by saying that he had "often been a week without sleep." "Doing what?" asked Tom. "Poker!" replied Oakhurst, sententiously, "when a man gets a streak of luck—nigger-luck—he don't get tired. The luck gives in first. Luck," continued the gambler, reflectively, "is a mighty queer thing. All you know about it for certain is that it's bound to change. And it's finding out when it's going to change that makes you. We've had a streak of bad luck since we left Poker Flat—you come along, and slap you get into it, too. If you can hold your cards right along you're all right. For," added the gambler, with cheerful irrelevance,

> "I'm proud to live in the service of the Lord,
> And I'm bound to die in His army."

The third day came, and the sun, looking through the white-curtained valley, saw the outcasts divide their slowly decreasing store of provisions for the morning meal. It was one of the peculiarities of that mountain climate that its rays diffused a kindly warmth over the wintry landscape, as if in regretful commiseration of the past. But it revealed drift on drift of snow piled high around the hut; a hopeless, uncharted, trackless sea of white lying below the rocky shores to which the castaways still clung. Through the marvelously clear air, the smoke of the pastoral village of Poker Flat rose miles away. Mother Shipton saw it, and from a remote pinnacle of her rocky fastness, hurled in that direction a final malediction. It was her last vituperative attempt, and perhaps for that reason was invested with a certain degree of sublimity. It did her good. she privately informed the Duchess.

"Just to go out there and cuss, and see." She then set herself to the task of amusing "the child," as she and the Duchess were pleased to call Piney. Piney was no chicken, but it was a soothing and ingenious theory of the pair thus to account for the fact that she didn't swear and wasn't improper.

When night crept up again through the gorges, the reedy notes of the accordion rose and fell in fitful spasms and long-drawn gasps by the flickering camp-fire. But music failed to fill entirely the aching void left by insufficient food, and a new diversion was proposed by Piney—storytelling. Neither Mr. Oakhurst nor his female companions caring to relate their personal experiences, this plan would have failed, too, but for the Innocent. Some months before he had chanced upon a stray copy of Mr. Pope's ingenious translation of the Iliad. He now proposed to narrate the principal incidents of that poem—having thoroughly mastered the argument and fairly forgotten the words—in the current vernacular of Sandy Bar. And so for the rest of that night the Homeric demigods again walked the earth. Trojan bully and wily Greek wrestled in the winds, and the great pines in the canyon seemed to bow to the wrath of the son of Peleus. Mr. Oakhurst listened with quiet satisfaction. Most especially was he interested in the fate of "Ash-heels," as the Innocent persisted in denominating the "swift-footed Achilles."

So with small food and much of Homer and the accordion, a week passed over the heads of the outcasts. The sun again forsook them, and again from leaden skies the snowflakes were sifted over the land. Day by day closer around them drew the snowy circle, until at last they looked from their prison over drifted walls of dazzling white, that towered twenty feet above their heads. It became more and more difficult to replenish their fires, even from the fallen trees beside them, now half-hidden in the drifts. And yet no one complained. The lovers turned from the dreary prospect and looked into each other's eyes, and were happy. Mr. Oakhurst settled himself coolly to the losing game before him. The Duchess, more cheerful than she had been, assumed the care of Piney. Only Mother Shipton—once the strongest of the party—seemed to sicken and fade. At midnight on the tenth day she called Oakhurst to her side. "I'm going," she said, in a voice of querulous weakness, "but don't say anything about it. Don't waken the kids. Take the bundle from under my head and open it." Mr. Oakhurst did so. It contained Mother Shipton's rations for the last week, untouched. "Give 'em to the child," she said, pointing to the sleeping Piney. "You've starved yourself," said the gambler. "That's what they call it," said the woman, querulously, as she lay down again, and, turning her face to the wall, passed quietly away.

The accordion and the bones were put aside that day, and Homer was forgotten. When the body of Mother Shipton had been committed to the snow, Mr. Oakhurst took the Innocent aside, and showed him a pair of snowshoes, which he had fashioned from the old pack-saddle. "There's one chance in a hundred to save her yet," he said, pointing to Piney; "but it's there," he added, pointing toward Poker Flat. "If you can reach there in two days she's safe." "And you?" asked Tom Simson. "I'll stay here," was the curt reply.

The lovers parted with a long embrace. "You are not going, too?" said the Duchess, as she saw Mr. Oakhurst apparently waiting to accompany him. "As far as the canyon," he replied. He turned suddenly, and kissed the Duchess, leaving her pallid face aflame, and her trembling limbs rigid with amazement.

Night came, but not Mr. Oakhurst. It brought the storm again and the whirling snow. Then the Duchess, feeding the fire, found that some one had quietly piled beside the hut enough fuel to last a few days longer. The tears rose to her eyes, but she hid them from Piney.

The women slept but little. In the morning, looking into each other's faces, they read their fate. Neither spoke; but Piney, accepting the position of the stronger, drew near and placed her arm around the Duchess's waist. They kept this attitude for the rest of the day. That night the storm reached its greatest fury, and, rending asunder the protecting pines, invaded the very hut.

Toward morning they found themselves unable to feed the fire, which gradually died away. As the embers slowly blackened, the Duchess crept closer to Piney, and broke the silence of many hours: "Piney, can you pray?" "No, dear," said Piney, simply. The Duchess without knowing exactly why, felt relieved, and, putting her head upon Piney's shoulder, spoke no more. And so reclining, the younger and purer pillowing the head of her soiled sister upon her virgin breast, they fell asleep.

The wind lulled as if it feared to waken them. Feathery drifts of snow, shaken from the long pine boughs, flew like white-winged birds, and settled about them as they slept. The moon through the rifted clouds looked down upon what had been the camp. But all human stain, all trace of earthly travail, was hidden beneath the spotless mantle mercifully flung from above.

They slept all that day and the next, nor did they waken when voices and footsteps broke the silence of the camp. And when pitying fingers brushed the snow from their wan faces, you could scarcely have told from the equal peace that dwelt upon them, which was she that had sinned. Even the Law of Poker Flat recognized this, and turned away, leaving them still locked in each other's arms.

But at the head of the gulch, on one of the largest pine trees, they found the deuce of clubs pinned to the bark with a bowie knife. It bore the following, written in pencil, in a firm hand:

†

BENEATH THIS TREE

LIES THE BODY

OF

JOHN OAKHURST,

WHO STRUCK A STREAK OF BAD LUCK

ON THE 23D OF NOVEMBER, 1850,

AND

HANDED IN HIS CHECKS

ON THE 7TH OF DECEMBER, 1850.

†

And pulseless and cold, with a Derringer by his side and a bullet in his heart, though still calm as in life, beneath the snow lay he who was at once the strongest and yet the weakest of the outcasts of Poker Flat.

THOMAS BAILEY ALDRICH

[1836–1907]

Marjorie Daw

(First published in *Atlantic Monthly*, 1873; first book publication in 1873.)

I

DR. DILLON TO EDWARD DELANEY, ESQ., AT THE PINES, NEAR RYE, N. H.

August 8, 187-.

MY DEAR SIR: I am happy to assure you that your anxiety is without reason. Flemming will be confined to the sofa for three or four weeks, and will have to be careful at first how he uses his leg. A fracture of this kind is always a tedious affair. Fortunately, the bone was very skillfully set by the surgeon who chanced to be in the drug-store where Flemming was brought after his fall, and I apprehend no permanent inconvenience from the accident. *Flemming is doing perfectly well physically;* but I must confess that the irritable and morbid state of mind into which he has fallen causes me a great deal of uneasiness. He is the last man in the world who ought to break his leg. You know how impetuous our friend is ordinarily, what a soul of restlessness and energy, never content unless he is rushing at some object, like a sportive bull at a red shawl; but amiable withal. He is no longer amiable. His temper has become something frightful. Miss Fanny Flemming came up from Newport, where the family are staying for the summer, to nurse him; but he packed her off the next morning in tears. He has a complete set of Balzac's works, twenty-seven volumes, piled up near his sofa, to throw at Watkins whenever that exemplary serving-man appears with his meals. Yesterday I very innocently brought Flemming a small basket of lemons. You know it was a strip of lemon-peel on the curbstone that caused our friend's mischance. Well, he no sooner set his eyes upon these lemons than he fell into such a rage as I cannot adequately describe. This is only one of his moods, and the least distressing. At other times he sits with bowed head regarding his splintered limb, silent, sullen, despairing. When this fit is on him—and it sometimes lasts all day—nothing can distract his melancholy.

He refuses to eat, does not even read the newspapers; books, except as projectiles for Watkins, have no charms for him. His state is truly pitiable.

Now, if he were a poor man, with a family depending on his daily labor, this irritability and despondency would be natural enough. But in a young fellow of twenty-four, with plenty of money and seemingly not a care in the world, the thing is monstrous. If he continues to give way to his vagaries in this manner, he will end by bringing on an inflammation of the fibula. It was the fibula he broke. I am at my wits' end to know what to prescribe for him. I have anæsthetics and lotions, to make people sleep and to soothe pain; but I've no medicine that will make a man have a little common sense. That is beyond my skill, but maybe it is not beyond yours. You are Flemming's intimate friend, his *fidus Achates*. Write to him, write to him frequently, distract his mind, cheer him up, and prevent him from becoming a confirmed case of melancholia. Perhaps he has some important plans disarranged by his present confinement. If he has you will know, and will know how to advise him judiciously. I trust your father finds the change beneficial? I am, my dear sir, with great respect, etc.

II
EDWARD DELANEY TO JOHN FLEMMING, WEST 38TH STREET, NEW YORK.

August 9,–.

MY DEAR JACK: I had a line from Dillon this morning, and was rejoiced to learn that your hurt is not so bad as reported. Like a certain personage, you are not so black and blue as you are painted. Dillon will put you on your pins again in two or three weeks, if you will only have patience and follow his counsels. Did you get my note of last Wednesday? I was greatly troubled when I heard of the accident.

I can imagine how tranquil and saintly you are with your leg in a trough! It is deuced awkward, to be sure, just as we had promised ourselves a glorious month together at the seaside; but we must make the best of it. It is unfortunate, too, that my father's health renders it impossible for me to leave him. I think he has much improved; the sea air is his native element; but he still needs my arm to lean upon in his walks, and requires someone more careful than a servant to look after him. I cannot come to you, dear Jack, but I have hours of unemployed time on hand, and I will write you a whole post-office full of letters if that will divert you. Heaven knows, I haven't anything to write about. It isn't as if we were living at one of the beach houses; then I could do you some character studies, and fill your imagination with groups of sea-goddesses, with their (or somebody else's) raven and blond manes hanging down their shoulders. You should have Aphrodite in morning wrapper, in evening costume, and in her prettiest bathing suit.

But we are far from all that here. We have rooms in a farmhouse, on a cross-road, two miles from the hotels, and lead the quietest of lives.

I wish I were a novelist. This old house, with its sanded floors and high wainscots, and its narrow windows looking out upon a cluster of pines that turn themselves into Æolian-harps every time the wind blows, would be the place in which to write a summer romance. It should be a story with the odors of the forest and the breath of the sea in it. It should be a novel like one of that Russian fellow's,–what's his name?–Tourguénieff, Turguenef, Turgenif, Toorguniff, Turgénjew–nobody knows how to spell him. Yet I wonder if even a Liza or an Alexandra Paulovna could stir the heart of a man who has constant twinges in his leg. I wonder if one of our own Yankee girls of the best type, haughty and *spirituelle*, would be of any comfort to you in your present deplorable condition. If I thought so, I would hasten down to the Surf House and catch one for you; or, better still, I would find you one over the way.

Picture to yourself a large white house just across the road, nearly opposite our cottage. It is not a house, but a mansion, built, perhaps, in the colonial period, with rambling extensions, and gambrel roof, and a wide piazza on three sides–a self-possessed, high-bred piece of architecture, with its nose in the air. It stands back from the road, and has an obsequious retinue of fringed elms and oaks and weeping willows. Sometimes in the morning, and oftener in the afternoon, when the sun has withdrawn from that part of the mansion, a young woman appears on the piazza with some mysterious Penelope web of embroidery in her hand, or a book. There is a hammock over there–of pineapple fiber, it looks from here. A hammock is very becoming when one is eighteen, and has golden hair, and dark eyes, and an emerald-colored illusion dress looped up after the fashion of a Dresden china shepherdess, and is *chaussée* like a belle of the time of Louis Quatorze. All this splendor goes into that hammock, and sways there like a pond-lily in the golden afternoon. The window of my bedroom looks down on that piazza—and so do I.

But enough of this nonsense, which ill becomes a sedate young attorney taking his vacation with an invalid father. Drop me a line, deaf Jack, and tell me how you really are. State your case. Write me a long, quiet letter. If you are violent or abusive, I'll take the law to you.

III

JOHN FLEMMING TO EDWARD DELANEY

August 11,–.

YOUR LETTER, DEAR Ned, was a godsend. Fancy what a fix I am in–I, who never had a day's sickness since I was born. My left leg weighs three tons. It is embalmed in spices and smothered in layers of fine linen, like a mummy. I can't move. I haven't moved for five thousand years. I'm of the time of Pharaoh.

I lie from morning till night on a lounge, staring into the hot street. Everybody is out of town enjoying himself. The brown-stone-front houses across the street resemble a row of particularly ugly coffins set up on end. A green mold is settling on the names of the deceased, carved on the silver door-plates. Sardonic spiders have sewed up the keyholes. All is silence and dust and desolation.—I interrupt this a moment, to take a shy at Watkins with the second volume of César Birotteau. Missed him! I think I could bring him down with a copy of Sainte-Beuve or the Dictionnaire Universel, if I had it. These small Balzac books somehow don't quite fit my hand; but I shall fetch him yet. I've an idea Watkins is tapping the old gentleman's Château Yquem. Duplicate key of the wine-cellar. Hibernian soirées in the front basement. Young Cheops upstairs, snug in his cerements. Watkins glides into my chamber, with that colorless, hypocritical face of his drawn out long like an accordion; but I know he grins all the way downstairs, and is glad I have broken my leg. Was not my evil star in the very zenith when I ran up to town to attend that dinner at Delmonico's? I didn't come up altogether for that. It was partly to buy Frank Livingstone's roan mare Margot. And now I shall not be able to sit in the saddle these two months. I'll send the mare down to you at The Pines—is that the name of the place?

Old Dillon fancies that I have something on my mind. He drives me wild with lemons. Lemons for a mind diseased! Nonsense. I am only as restless as the devil under this confinement—a thing I'm not used to. Take a man who has never had so much as a headache or a toothache in his life, strap one of his legs in a section of water-spout, keep him in a room in the city for weeks, with the hot weather turned on, and then expect him to smile and purr and be happy! It is preposterous. I can't be cheerful or calm.

Your letter is the first consoling thing I have had since my disaster, ten days ago. It really cheered me up for half an hour. Send me a screed, Ned, as often as you can, if you love me. Anything will do. Write me more about that little girl in the hammock. That was very pretty, all that about the Dresden china shepherdess and the pond-lily; the imagery a little mixed, perhaps, but very pretty. I didn't suppose you had so much sentimental furniture in your upper story. It shows how one may be familiar for years with the reception-room of his neighbor, and never suspect what is directly under his mansard. I supposed your loft stuffed with dry legal parchments, mortgages and affidavits; you take down a package of manuscript, and lo! there are lyrics and sonnets and canzonettas. You really have a graphic descriptive touch, Edward Delaney, and I suspect you of anonymous love-tales in the magazines.

I shall be a bear until I hear from you again. Tell me all about your pretty *inconnue* across the road. What is her name? Who is she? Who's her father?

Where's her mother? Who's her lover? You cannot imagine how this will occupy me. The more trifling the better. My imprisonment has weakened me intellectually to such a degree that I find your epistolary gifts quite considerable. I am passing into my second childhood. In a week or two I shall take to India-rubber rings and prongs of coral. A silver cup, with an appropriate inscription, would be a delicate attention on your part. In the meantime, write!

IV
EDWARD DELANEY TO JOHN FLEMMING

August 12, –.

THE SICK PASHA shall be amused. *Bismillah!* He wills it so. If the story-teller becomes prolix and tedious—the bow-string and the sack, and two Nubians to drop him into the Piscataqua! But, truly, Jack, I have a hard task. There is literally nothing here except the little girl over the way. She is swinging in the hammock at this moment. It is to me compensation for many of the ills of life to see her now and then put out a small kid boot, which fits like a glove, and set herself going. Who is she, and what is her name? Her name is Daw. Only daughter of Mr. Richard W. Daw, ex-colonel and banker. Mother dead. One brother at Harvard, elder brother killed at the battle of Fair Oaks, nine years ago. Old, rich family, the Daws. This is the homestead, where father and daughter pass eight months of the twelve; the rest of the year in Baltimore and Washington. The New England winter too many for the old gentleman. The daughter is called Marjorie—Marjorie Daw. Sounds odd at first, doesn't it? But after you say it over to yourself half a dozen times, you like it. There's a pleasing quaintness to it, something prim and violet-like. Must be a nice sort of girl to be called Marjorie Daw.

I had mine host of The Pines in the witness-box last night, and drew the foregoing testimony from him. He has charge of Mr. Daw's vegetable garden, and has known the family these thirty years. Of course I shall make the acquaintance of my neighbors before many days. It will be next to impossible for me not to meet Mr. Daw or Miss Daw in some of my walks. The young lady has a favorite path to the sea beach. I shall intercept her some morning, and touch my hat to her. Then the princess will bend her fair head to me with courteous surprise not unmixed with haughtiness. Will snub me, in fact. All this for thy sake, O Pasha of the Snapt Axle-tree! . . . How oddly things fall out! Ten minutes ago I was called down to the parlor—you know the kind of parlors in farmhouses on the coast, a sort of amphibious parlor, with seashells on the mantel-piece and spruce branches in the chimneyplace—where I found my father and Mr. Daw doing the antique polite to each other. He had come to pay his respects to his new neighbors. Mr. Daw is a tall, slim gentleman of about fifty-five, with a florid face and snow-white mustache and side-whiskers. Looks like Mr. Dombey, or as Mr. Dombey would have looked if he had served a few years in the British Army. Mr. Daw was a colonel in the late war, commanding the regiment in which his son was a lieutenant. Plucky old boy, backbone of New Hampshire granite. Before taking his leave, the colonel delivered himself of an invitation as if he were issuing a general order. Miss Daw has a few friends coming, at 4 P.M., to play croquet on the lawn (parade-ground) and have tea (cold rations) on the piazza. Will we honor them with our company? (or be sent to the guardhouse.) My father declines on the plea of ill-health. My father's son bows with as much suavity as he knows, and accepts.

In my next I shall have something to tell you. I shall have seen the little beauty face to face. I have a presentiment, Jack, that this Daw is a *rara avis!* Keep up your spirits, my boy, until I write you another letter—and send me along word how's your leg.

V

EDWARD DELANEY TO JOHN FLEMMING

August 13, –.

THE PARTY, MY dear Jack, was as dreary as possible. A lieutenant of the navy, the rector of the Episcopal church at Stillwater, and a society swell from Nahant. The lieutenant looked as if he had swallowed a couple of his buttons, and found the bullion rather indigestible; the rector was a pensive youth, of the daffydowndilly sort; and the swell from Nahant was a very weak tidal wave indeed. The women were much better, as they always are; the two Miss Kingsburys of Philadelphia, staying at the Sea-shell House, two bright and engaging girls. But Marjorie Daw!

The company broke up soon after tea, and I remained to smoke a cigar with the colonel on the piazza. It was like seeing a picture to see Miss Marjorie hovering around the old soldier, and doing a hundred gracious little things for him. She brought the cigars and lighted the tapers with her own delicate fingers, in the most enchanting fashion. As we sat there, she came and went in the summer twilight, and seemed, with her white dress and pale gold hair, like some lovely phantom that had sprung into existence out of the smoke-wreaths. If she had melted into air, like the statue of Galatea in the play, I should have been more sorry than surprised.

It was easy to perceive that the old colonel worshipped her, and she him. I think the relation between an elderly father and a daughter just blooming into womanhood the most beautiful possible. There is in it a subtle sentiment that cannot exist in the case of mother and daughter, or that of son and mother. But this is getting into deep water.

I sat with the Daws until half past ten, and saw the moon rise on the sea. The ocean, that had stretched motionless and black against the horizon, was changed by magic into a broken field of glittering ice, interspersed with marvelous silvery fjords. In the far distance the Isles of Shoals loomed up like a group of huge bergs drifting down on us. The Polar regions in a June thaw! It was exceedingly fine. What did we talk about? We talked about the weather–and *you!* The weather has been disagreeable for several days past–and so have you. I glided from one topic to the other very naturally. I told my friends of your accident; how it had frustrated all our summer plans, and what our plans were. I played quite a spirited solo on the fibula. Then I described you; or, rather, I didn't. I spoke of your amiability, of your patience under this severe affliction; of your touching gratitude when Dillon brings you little presents of fruit; of your tenderness to your sister Fanny, whom you would not allow to stay in town to nurse you, and how you heroically sent her back to Newport; preferring to remain alone with Mary, the cook, and your man Watkins, to whom, by the way, you were devotedly attached. If you had been there, Jack, you wouldn't have known yourself. I should have excelled as a criminal lawyer, if I had not turned my attention to a different branch of jurisprudence.

Miss Marjorie asked all manner of leading questions concerning you. It did not occur to me then, but it struck me forcibly afterwards, that she evinced a singular interest in the conversation. When I got back to my room, I recalled how eagerly she leaned forward, with her full, snowy throat in strong moonlight, listening to what I said. Positively, I think I made her like you!

Miss Daw is a girl whom you would like immensely, I can tell you that. A beauty without affectation, a high and tender nature–if one can read the soul in the face. And the old colonel is a noble character, too.

I am glad the Daws are such pleasant people. The Pines is an isolated spot, and my resources are few. I fear I should have found life here somewhat monotonous before long, with no other society than that of my excellent sire. It is true, I might have made a target of the defenseless invalid; but I haven't a taste for artillery, *moi.*

VI

JOHN FLEMMING TO EDWARD DELANEY

August 17, –.

FOR A MAN who hasn't a taste for artillery, it occurs to me, my friend, you are keeping up a pretty lively fire on my inner works. But go on. Cynicism is a small brass field-piece that eventually bursts and kills the artilleryman.

You may abuse me as much as you like, and I'll not complain; for I don't know what I should do without your letters. They are curing me. I haven't hurled anything at Watkins since last Sunday, partly because I have grown more amiable under your teaching, and partly because Watkins captured my ammunition one night, and carried it off to the library. He is rapidly losing the habit he had acquired of dodging whenever I rub my ear, or make any slight motion with my right arm. He is still suggestive of the wine-cellar, however. You may break, you may shatter Watkins, if you will, but the scent of the Roederer will hang round him still.

Ned, that Miss Daw must be a charming person. I should certainly like her. I like her already. When you spoke in your first letter of seeing a young girl swinging in a hammock under your chamber window, I was somehow strangely drawn to her. I cannot account for it in the least. What you have subsequently written of Miss Daw has strengthened the impression. You seem to be describing a woman I have known in some previous state of existence, or dreamed of in this. Upon my word, if you were to send me her photograph, I believe I should recognize her at a glance. Her manner, that listening attitude, her traits of character, as you indicate them, the light hair and the dark eyes—they are all familiar things to me. Asked a lot of questions, did she? Curious about me? That is strange.

You would laugh in your sleeve, you wretched old cynic, if you knew how I lie awake nights, with my gas turned down to a star, thinking of The Pines and the house across the road. How cool it must be down there! I long for the salt smell in the air. I picture the colonel smoking his cheroot on the piazza. I send you and Miss Daw off on afternoon rambles along the beach. Sometimes I let you stroll with her under the elms in the moonlight, for you are great friends by this time, I take it, and see each other every day. I know your ways and your manners! Then I fall into a truculent mood, and would like to destroy somebody. Have you noticed anything in the shape of a lover hanging around the colonial Lares and Penates? Does that lieutenant of the horse marines or that young Stillwater parson visit the house much? Not that I am pining for news of them, but any gossip of the kind would be in order. I wonder, Ned, you don't fall in love with Miss Daw. I am ripe to do it myself. Speaking of photographs, couldn't you manage to slip one of her *cartesde-visite* from her album—she must have an album, you know—and send it to me? I will return it before it could be missed. That's a good fellow! Did the mare arrive safe and sound? It will be a capital animal this autumn for Central Park.

O—my leg? I forgot about my leg. It's better.

VII

EDWARD DELANEY TO JOHN FLEMMING

August 20, —.

YOU ARE CORRECT in your surmises. I am on the most friendly terms with our neighbors. The colonel and my father smoke their afternoon cigar together in our sitting-room or on the piazza opposite, and I pass an hour or two of the day or the evening with the daughter. I am more and more struck by the beauty, modesty, and intelligence of Miss Daw.

You ask me why I do not fall in love with her. I will be frank, Jack: I have thought of that. She is young, rich, accomplished, uniting in herself more attractions, mental and personal, than I can recall in any girl of my acquaintance; but she lacks the something that would be necessary to inspire in me that kind of interest. Possessing this unknown quantity, a woman neither beautiful nor wealthy nor very young could bring me to her feet. But not Miss Daw. If we were shipwrecked together on an uninhabited island—let me suggest a tropical island, for it costs no more to be picturesque—I would build her a bamboo hut, I would fetch her breadfruit and cocoanuts, I would fry yams for her, I would lure the ingenuous turtle and make her nourishing soups, but I wouldn't make love to her—not under eighteen months. I would like to have her for a sister, that I might shield her and counsel her, and spend half my income on thread-laces and camel's-hair shawls. (We are off the island now.) If such were not my feeling, there would still be an obstacle to my loving Miss Daw. A greater misfortune could scarcely befall me than to love her. Flemming, I am about to make a revelation that will astonish you. I may be all wrong in my premises and consequently in my conclusions; but you shall judge.

That night when I returned to my room after the croquet party at the Daws', and was thinking over the trivial events of the evening, I was suddenly impressed by the air of eager attention with which Miss Daw had followed my account of your accident. I think I mentioned this to you. Well, the next morning, as I went to mail my letter, I overtook Miss Daw on the road to Rye, where the post-office is, and accompanied her thither and back, an hour's walk. The conversation again turned on you, and again I remarked that inexplicable look of interest which had lighted up her face the previous evening. Since then, I have seen Miss Daw perhaps ten times, perhaps oftener, and on each occasion I found that when I was not speaking of you or your sister, or some person or place associated with you, I was not holding her attention. She would be absent-minded, her eyes would wander away from me to the sea, or to some distant object in the landscape; her fingers would play with the leaves of a book in a way that convinced me she was not listening. At these moments if I abruptly changed the theme—I did it several times as an experiment—and dropped some remark about my friend Flemming, then the somber blue eyes would come back to me instantly.

Now, is not this the oddest thing in the world? No, not the oddest. The effect which you tell me was produced on you by my casual mention of an unknown girl swinging in a hammock is certainly as strange. You can conjecture how that passage in your letter of Friday startled me. Is it possible, then, that two people who have never met, and who are hundreds of miles apart, can exert a magnetic influence on each other? I have read of such psychological phenomena, but never credited them. I leave the solution of the problem to you. As for myself, all other things being favorable, it would be impossible for me to fall in love with a woman who listens to me only when I am talking of my friend!

I am not aware that any one is paying marked attention to my fair neighbor. The lieutenant of the navy—he is stationed at Rivermouth—sometimes drops in of an evening, and sometimes the rector from Stillwater; the lieutenant the oftener. He was there last night. I would not be surprised if he had an eye to the heiress; but he is not formidable. Mistress Daw carries a neat little spear of irony, and the honest lieutenant seems to have a particular facility for impaling himself on the point of it. He is not dangerous, I should say; though I have known a woman to satirize a man for years, and marry him after all. Decidedly, the lowly rector is not dangerous; yet, again, who has not seen Cloth of Frieze victorious in the lists where Cloth of Gold went down?

As to the photograph. There is an exquisite ivorytype of Marjorie, in passe-partout, on the drawing-room mantelpiece. It would be missed at once, if taken. I would do anything reasonable for you, Jack; but I've no burning desire to be hauled up before the local justice of the peace, on a charge of petty larceny.

P. S.—Enclosed is a spray of mignonette, which I advise you to treat tenderly. Yes, we talked of you again last night, as usual. It is becoming a little dreary for me.

VIII

EDWARD DELANEY TO JOHN FLEMMING

August 22, —.

YOUR LETTER IN reply to my last has occupied my thoughts all the morning. I do not know what to think. Do you mean to say that you are seriously half in love with a woman whom you have never seen—with a shadow, a chimera? for what else can Miss Daw be to you? I do not understand it at all. I understand neither you nor her. You are a couple of ethereal beings moving in finer air than I can breathe with my commonplace lungs. Such delicacy of sentiment is something I admire without comprehending. I am bewildered. I am of the earth earthy, and I find myself in the incongruous position of having to do with mere souls, with natures so finely tempered that I run some risk of shattering them in my awkwardness. I am as Caliban among the spirits!

Reflecting on your letter, I am not sure it is wise in me to continue this correspondence. But no, Jack; I do wrong to doubt the good sense that forms the basis of your character. You are deeply interested in Miss Daw; you feel that she is a person whom you may perhaps greatly admire when you know her: at the same time you bear in mind that the chances are ten to five that, when you do come to know her, she will fall far short of your ideal, and you will not care for her in the least. Look at it in this sensible light, and I will hold back nothing from you.

Yesterday afternoon my father and myself rode over to Rivermouth with the Daws. A heavy rain in the morning had cooled the atmosphere and laid the dust. To Rivermouth is a drive of eight miles, along a winding road lined all the way with wild barberry-bushes. I never saw anything more brilliant than these bushes, the green of the foliage and the pink of the coral berries intensified by the rain. The colonel drove, with my father in front, Miss Daw and I on the back seat. I resolved that for the first five miles your name should not pass my lips. I was amused by the artful attempts she made, at the start, to break through my reticence. Then a silence fell upon her; and then she became suddenly gay. That keenness which I enjoyed so much when it was exercised on the lieutenant was not so satisfactory directed against myself. Miss Daw has great sweetness of disposition, but she can be disagreeable. She is like the young lady in the rhyme, with the curl on her forehead,

"When she is good,
She is very, very good,
And when she is bad, she is horrid!"

I kept to my resolution, however; but on the return home I relented, and talked of your mare! Miss Daw is going to try a side-saddle on Margot some morning. The animal is a trifle too light for my weight. By the by, I nearly forgot to say Miss Daw sat for a picture yesterday to a River-mouth artist. If the negative turns out well, I am to have a copy. So our ends will be accomplished without crime. I wish, though, I could send you the ivorytype in the drawing-room; it is cleverly colored, and would give you an idea of her hair and eyes, which of course the other will not.

No, Jack, the spray of mignonette did not come from me. A man of twenty-eight doesn't enclose flowers in his letters–to another man. But don't attach too much significance to the circumstance. She gives sprays of mignonette to the rector, sprays to the lieutenant. She has even given a rose from her bosom to your slave. It is her jocund nature to scatter flowers, like Spring.

If my letters sometimes read disjointedly, you must understand that I never finish one at a sitting, but write at intervals. when the mood is on me.

The mood is not on me now.

IX

EDWARD DELANEY TO JOHN FLEMMING

August 23, –.

I HAVE JUST returned from the strangest interview with Marjorie. She has all but confessed to me her interest in you. But with what modesty and dignity! Her words elude my pen as I attempt to put them on paper; and, indeed, it was not so much what she said as her manner; and that I cannot reproduce. Perhaps it was of a piece with the strangeness of this whole business. That she should tacitly acknowledge to a third party the love she feels for a man she has never beheld! But I have lost, through your aid, the faculty of being surprised. I accept things as people do in dreams. Now that I am again in my room, it all appears like an illusion—the black masses of Rembrandtish shadow under the trees, the fireflies whirling in Pyrrhic dances among the shrubbery, the sea over there, Mariorie sitting on the hammock!

It is past midnight, and I am too sleepy to write more.

Thursday Morning.

My father has suddenly taken it into his head to spend a few days at the Shoals. In the meanwhile you will not hear from me. I see Marjorie walking in the garden with the colonel. I wish I could speak to her alone, but shall probably not have an opportunity before we leave.

X

EDWARD DELANEY TO JOHN FLEMMING

August 28, —.

YOU WERE PASSING into your second childhood, were you? Your intellect was so reduced that my epistolary gifts seemed quite considerable to you, did they? I rise superior to the sarcasm in your favor of the 11th instant, when I notice that five days' silence on my part is sufficient to throw you into the depths of despondency.

We returned only this morning from Appledore, that enchanted island —at four dollars per day. I find on my desk three letters from you! Evidently there is no lingering doubt in your mind as to the pleasure I derive from your correspondence. These letters are undated, but in what I take to be the latest are two passages that require my consideration. You will pardon my candor, dear Flemming, but the conviction forces itself upon me that as your leg grows stronger your head becomes weaker. You ask my advice on a certain point. I will give it. In my opinion you could do nothing more unwise than to address a note to Miss Daw, thanking her for the flower. It would, I am sure, offend her delicacy beyond pardon. She knows you only through me; you are to her an abstraction, a figure in a dream—a dream from which the faintest shock would awaken her. Of course, if you enclose a note to me and insist on its delivery, I shall deliver it; but I advise you not to do so.

You say you are able, with the aid of a cane, to walk about your chamber, and that you purpose to come to The Pines the instant Dillon thinks you strong enough to stand the journey. Again I advise you not to. Do you not see that, every hour you remain away, Marjorie's glamor deepens, and your influence over her increases? You will ruin everything by precipitancy. Wait until you are entirely recovered; in any case, do not come without giving me warning. I fear the effect of your abrupt advent here—under the circumstances.

Miss Daw was evidently glad to see us back again, and gave me both hands in the frankest way. She stopped at the door a moment, this afternoon, in the carriage; she had been over to Rivermouth for her pictures. Unluckily the photographer had spilt some acid on the plate, and she was obliged to give him another sitting. I have an intuition that something is troubling Marjorie. She had an abstracted air not usual with her. However, it may be only my fancy. . . . I end this, leaving several things unsaid, to accompany my father on one of those long walks which are now his chief medicine—and mine!

XI

EDWARD DELANEY TO JOHN FLEMMING

August 29, —.

I WRITE IN great haste to tell you what has taken place here since my letter of last night. I am in the utmost perplexity. Only one thing is plain—*you* must not dream of coming to The Pines. Marjorie has told her father everything! I saw her for a few minutes, an hour ago, in the garden; and, as near as I could gather from her confused statement, the facts are these: Lieutenant Bradly—that's the naval officer stationed at Rivermouth—has been paying court to Miss Daw for some time past, but not so much to her liking as to that of the colonel, who it seems is an old friend of the young gentleman's father. Yesterday (I knew she was in some trouble when she drove up to our gate) the colonel spoke to Marjorie of Bradly—urged his suit, I infer. Marjorie expressed her dislike for the lieutenant with characteristic frankness, and finally confessed to her father—well, I really do not know what she confessed. It must have been the vaguest of confessions, and must have sufficiently puzzled the colonel. At any rate, it exasperated him. I suppose I am implicated in the matter, and that the colonel feels bitterly toward me. I do not see why: I have carried no messages between you and Miss Daw; I have behaved with the greatest discretion. I can find no flaw anywhere in my proceeding. I do not see that anybody has done anything—except the colonel himself.

It is probable, nevertheless, that the friendly relations between the two houses will be broken off. "A plague o' both your houses," say you. I will keep you informed, as well as I can, of what occurs over the way. We shall remain here until the second week in September. Stay where you are, or, at all events, do not dream of joining me. . . . Colonel Daw is sitting on the piazza looking rather wicked. I have not seen Marjorie since I parted with her in the garden.

XII
EDWARD DELANEY TO THOMAS DILLON, M. D., MADISON SQUARE, NEW YORK.

August 30, –.

MY DEAR DOCTOR: If you have any influence over Flemming, I beg of you to exert it to prevent his coming to this place at present. There are circumstances, which I will explain to you before long, that make it of the first importance that he should not come into this neighborhood. His appearance here, I speak advisedly, would be disastrous to him. In urging him to remain in New York, or to go to some inland resort, you will be doing him and me a real service. Of course you will not mention my name in this connection. You know me well enough, my dear doctor, to be assured that, in begging your secret co-operation, I have reasons that will meet your entire approval when they are made plain to you. We shall return to town on the 15th of next month, and my first duty will be to present myself at your hospitable door and satisfy your curiosity, if I have excited it. My father, I am glad to state, has so greatly improved that he can no longer be regarded as an invalid. With great esteem, I am, etc., etc.

XIII
EDWARD DELANEY TO JOHN FLEMMING

August 31, –.

YOUR LETTER, ANNOUNCING your mad determination to come here, has just reached me. I beseech you to reflect a moment. The step would be fatal to your interests and hers. You would furnish just cause for irritation to R. W. D.; and, though he loves Marjorie tenderly, he is capable of going to any lengths if opposed. You would not like, I am convinced, to be the means of causing him to treat *her* with severity. That would be the result of your presence at The Pines at this juncture. I am annoyed to be obliged to point out these things to you. We are on very delicate ground, Jack; the situation is critical, and the slightest mistake in a move would cost us the game. If you consider it worth the winning, be patient. Trust a little to my sagacity. Wait and see what happens. Moreover, I understand from Dillon that you are in no condition to take so long a journey. He thinks the air of the coast would be the worst thing possible for you; that you ought to go inland if anywhere. Be advised by me. Be advised by Dillon.

XIV
TELEGRAMS

September 1, –.

I.—TO EDWARD DELANEY

Letter received. Dillon be hanged. I think I ought to be on the ground.

J. F.

2.—TO JOHN FLEMMING

Stay where you are. You would only complicate matters. Do not move until you hear from me.

E. D.

3.—TO EDWARD DELANEY

My being at The Pines could be kept secret. I must see her.

J. F.

4.—TO JOHN FLEMMING

Do not think of it. It would be useless. R. W. D. has locked M. in her room. You would not be able to effect an interview.

E. D.

5.—TO EDWARD DELANEY

Locked her in her room. Good God. That settles the question. I shall leave by the twelve-fifteen express.

J. F.

XV
THE ARRIVAL

ON THE SECOND of September, 187–, as the down express due at 3.40 left the station at Hampton, a young man, leaning on the shoulder of a servant, whom he addressed as Watkins, stepped from the platform into a hack, and requested to be driven to "The Pines." On arriving at the gate of a modest farmhouse, a few miles from the station, the young man descended with difficulty from the carriage, and, casting a hasty glance across the road, seemed much impressed by some peculiarity in the landscape. Again leaning on the shoulder of the person Watkins, he walked to the door of the farmhouse and inquired for Mr. Edward Delaney. He was informed by the aged man who answered his knock, that Mr. Edward Delaney had gone to Boston the day before, but that Mr. Jonas Delaney was within. This information did not appear satisfactory to the stranger, who inquired if Mr. Edward Delaney had left any message for Mr. John Flemming. There *was* a letter for Mr. Flemming, if he were that person. After a brief absence the aged man reappeared with a letter.

XVI

EDWARD DELANEY TO JOHN FLEMMING

September 1, –.

I AM HORROR-STRICKEN at what I have done! When I began this correspondence I had no other purpose than to relieve the tedium of your sick-chamber. Dillon told me to cheer you up. I tried to. I thought you entered into the spirit of the thing. I had no idea, until within a few days that you were taking matters *au sérieux.*

What can I say? I am in sackcloth and ashes. I am a pariah, a dog of an outcast. I tried to make a little romance to interest you, something soothing and idyllic, and, by Jove! I have done it only too well! My father doesn't know a word of this, so don't jar the old gentleman any more than you can help. I fly from the wrath to come–when you arrive! For O, dear Jack, there isn't any colonial mansion on the other side of the road, there isn't any piazza, there isn't any hammock–there isn't any Marjorie Daw!!

AMBROSE BIERCE

[1842–1914?]

The Damned Thing

(First book publication in 1893.)

1 ONE DOES NOT ALWAYS EAT WHAT IS ON THE TABLE

By the light of a tallow candle which had been placed on one end of a rough table a man was reading something written in a book. It was an old account book, greatly worn; and the writing was not, apparently, very legible, for the man sometimes held the page close to the flame of the candle to get a stronger light on it. The shadow of the book would then throw into obscurity a half of the room, darkening a number of faces and figures; for besides the reader, eight other men were present. Seven of them sat against the rough log walls, silent, motionless, and the room being small, not very far from the table. By extending an arm any one of them could have touched the eighth man, who lay on the table, face upward, partly covered by a sheet, his arms at his sides. He was dead.

The man with the book was not reading aloud, and no one spoke. All seemed to be waiting for something to occur; the dead man only was without expectation. From the blank darkness outside came in, through the aperture that served for a window, all the ever unfamiliar noises of night in the wilderness—the long nameless note of a distant coyote; the stilly pulsing trill of tireless insects in trees; strange cries of night birds, so different from those of the birds of the day; the drone of great blundering beetles, and all that mysterious chorus of small sounds that seem always to have been but half heard when they have suddenly ceased, as if conscious of an indiscretion. But nothing of all this was noted in that company; its members were not overmuch addicted to idle interest in matters of no practical importance; that was obvious in every line of their rugged faces—obvious even in the dim light of the single candle. They were evidently men of the vicinity—farmers and woodsmen.

The person reading was a trifle different; one would have said of him that he was of the world, worldly, albeit there was that in his attire which attested a certain fellowship with the organisms of his environment. His coat would hardly have passed muster in San Francisco; his footgear was not of urban origin, and the hat that lay by him on the floor (he was the only one uncovered) was such that if one had considered it as an article of mere personal adornment he would have missed its meaning. In countenance the man was rather prepossessing, with just a hint of sternness; though that he may have assumed or cultivated, as appropriate to one in authority. For he was a coroner. It was by virtue of his office that he had possession of the book in which he was reading. It had been found among the dead man's effects–in his cabin, where the inquest was now taking place.

When the coroner had finished reading he put the book into his breast pocket. At that moment the door was pushed open and a young man entered. He, clearly, was not of mountain birth and breeding: he was clad as those who dwelt in cities. His clothing was dusty, however, as from travel. He had, in fact, been riding hard to attend the inquest.

The coroner nodded. No one else greeted him.

'We have waited for you,' said the coroner. 'It is necessary to have done with this business tonight.'

The young man smiled. 'I am sorry to have kept you,' he said. 'I went away, not to evade your summons, but to post to my newspaper an account of what I suppose I am called back to relate.'

The coroner smiled.

'The account that you posted to your newspaper,' he said, 'differs, probably, from that which you will give here under oath.'

'That,' replied the other, rather hotly and with a visible flush, 'is as you please. I used manifold paper and have a copy of what I sent. It was not written as news, for it is incredible, but as fiction. It may go as a part of my testimony under oath.'

'But you say it is incredible.'

'That is nothing to you, sir, if I also swear that it is true.'

The coroner was silent for a time, his eyes upon the floor. The men about the sides of the cabin talked in whispers, but seldom withdrew their gaze from the face of the corpse. Presently the coroner lifted his eyes and said, 'We will resume the inquest.'

The men removed their hats. The witness was sworn.

'What is your name?' the coroner asked.

'William Harker.'

'Age?'

'Twenty-seven.'

'You knew the deceased, Hugh Morgan?'

'Yes.'

'You were with him when he died?'

'Near him.'

'How did that happen–your presence, I mean?'

'I was visiting him at this place to shoot and fish. A part of my purpose, however, was to study him and his odd, solitary way of life. He seemed a good model for a character in fiction. I sometimes write stories.'

'I sometimes read them.'

'Thank you.'

'Stories in general–not yours.'

Some of the jurors laughed. Against a somber background humor shows high lights. Soldiers in the intervals of battle laugh easily, and a jest in the death chamber conquers by surprise.

'Relate the circumstances of this man's death,' said the coroner. 'You may use any notes or memoranda that you please.'

The witness understood. Pulling a manuscript from his breast pocket he held it near the candle and turning the leaves until he found the passage that he wanted began to read.

2 WHAT MAY HAPPEN IN A FIELD OF WILD OATS

'. . . The sun had hardly risen when we left the house. We were looking for quail, each with a shotgun, but we had only one dog. Morgan said our best ground was beyond a certain ridge that he pointed out, and we crossed it by a trail through the chaparral. On the other side was comparatively level ground, thickly covered with wild oats. As we emerged from the chaparral Morgan was but a few yards in advance. Suddenly we heard, at a little distance to our right and partly in front, a noise as of some animal thrashing about in the bushes, which we could see were violently agitated.

'"We've started a deer," I said. "I wish we had brought a rifle."

'Morgan, who had stopped and was intently watching the agitated chaparral, said nothing, but had cocked both barrels of his gun and was holding it in readiness to aim. I thought him a trifle excited, which surprised me, for he had a reputation for exceptional coolness, even in moments of sudden and imminent peril.

'"O, come," I said. "You are not going to fill up a deer with quail-shot, are you?"

'Still he did not reply, but catching a sight of his face as he turned it slightly toward me I was struck by the intensity of his look. Then I understood that we had serious business in hand, and my first conjecture was that we had jumped a grizzly. I advanced to Morgan's side, cocking my piece as I moved.

'The bushes were now quiet and the sounds had ceased, but Morgan was as attentive to the place as before.

'"What is it? What the devil is it?" I asked.

'"That Damned Thing!" he replied, without turning his head. His voice was husky and unnatural. He trembled visibly.

'I was about to speak further, when I observed the wild oats near the place of the disturbance moving in the most inexplicable way. I can hardly describe it. It seemed as if stirred by a streak of wind, which not only bent it, but pressed it down–crushed it so that it did not rise–and this movement was slowly prolonging itself directly toward us.

'Nothing that I had ever seen had affected me so strangely as this unfamiliar and unaccountable phenomenon, yet I am unable to recall any sense of fear. I remember–and tell it here because, singularly enough, I recollected it then–that once in looking carelessly out of an open window I momentarily mistook a small tree close at hand for one of a group of larger trees at a little distance away. It looked the same size as the others, but being more distinctly and sharply defined in mass and detail seemed out of harmony with them. It was a mere falsification of the law of aerial perspective, but it startled, almost terrified me. We so rely upon the orderly operation of familiar natural laws that any seeming suspension of them is noted as a menace to our safety, a warning of unthinkable calamity. So now the apparently causeless movement of the herbage and the slow, undeviating approach of the line of disturbance were distinctly disquieting. My companion appeared actually frightened, and I could hardly credit my senses when I saw him suddenly throw his gun to his shoulder and fire both barrels at the agitated grain! Before the smoke of the discharge had cleared away I heard a loud savage cry–a scream like that of a wild animal–and flinging his gun upon the ground Morgan sprang away and ran swiftly from the spot. At the same instant I was thrown violently to the ground by the impact of something unseen in the smoke–some soft, heavy substance that seemed thrown against me with great force.

'Before I could get upon my feet and recover my gun, which seemed to have been struck from my hands, I heard Morgan crying out as if in mortal agony, and mingling with his cries were such hoarse, savage sounds as one hears from fighting dogs. Inexpressibly terrified, I struggled to my feet and looked in the direction of Morgan's retreat–and may Heaven in mercy spare me from another sight like that! At a distance of less than thirty yards was my friend, down upon one knee, his head thrown back at a frightful angle, hatless, his long hair in disorder and his whole body in violent movement from side to side, backward and forward. His right arm was lifted and seemed to lack the hand–at least, I could see none. The other arm was invisible. At times, as my memory now reports this extraordinary scene, I could discern but a part of his body. It was as if he had been partly blotted out–I cannot otherwise express it–then a shifting of his position would bring it all into view again.

'All this must have occurred within a few seconds, yet in that time Morgan assumed all the postures of a determined wrestler vanquished by superior weight and strength. I saw nothing but him, and him not always distinctly. During the entire incident his shouts and curses were heard, as if through an enveloping uproar of such sounds of rage and fury as I had never heard from the throat of man or brute!

'For a moment only I stood irresolute, then throwing down my gun I ran forward to my friend's assistance. I had a vague belief that he was suffering from a fit, or some form of convulsion. Before I could reach his side he was down and quiet. All sounds had ceased, but with a feeling of such terror as even these awful events had not inspired I now saw again the mysterious movement of the wild oats, prolonging itself from the trampled area about the prostrate man toward the edge of a wood. It was only when it had reached the wood that I was able to withdraw my eyes and look at my companion. He was dead.'

3 A MAN THOUGH NAKED MAY BE IN RAGS

The coroner rose from his seat and stood beside the dead man. Lifting an edge of the sheet he pulled it away, exposing the entire body, altogether naked and showing in the candlelight a claylike yellow. It had, however, broad maculations of bluish black, obviously caused by extravasated blood from contusions. The chest and sides looked as if they had been beaten with a bludgeon. There were dreadful lacerations; the skin was torn in strips and shreds.

The coroner moved round to the end of the table and undid a silk handkerchief which had been passed under the chin and knotted on the top of the head. When the handkerchief was drawn away it exposed what had been the throat. Some of the jurors who had risen to get a better view repented their curiosity and turned away their faces. Witness Harker went to the open window and leaned out across the sill, faint and sick. Dropping the handkerchief upon the dead man's neck the coroner stepped to an angle of the room and from a pile of clothing produced one garment after another, each of which he held up a moment for inspection. All were torn, and stiff with blood. The jurors did not make a closer inspection. They seemed rather uninterested. They had, in truth, seen all this before, the only thing that was new to them being Harker's testimony.

'Gentlemen,' the coroner said, 'we have no more evidence, I think. Your duty has been already explained to you. If there is nothing you wish to ask you may go outside and consider your verdict.'

The foreman rose—a tall, bearded man of sixty, coarsely clad.

'I should like to ask one question, Mr Coroner,' he said. 'What asylum did this yer witness escape from?'

'Mr Harker,' said the coroner, gravely and tranquilly, 'from what asylum did you last escape?'

Harker flushed crimson again, but said nothing, and the seven jurors rose and solemnly filed out of the cabin.

'If you have done insulting me, sir,' said Harker, as soon as he and the officer were left alone with the dead man, 'I suppose I am at liberty to go?'

'Yes.'

Harker started to leave, but paused, with his hand on the door latch. The habit of his profession was strong in him—stronger than his sense of personal dignity. He turned about and said:

'The book that you have there—I recognize it as Morgan's diary. You seemed greatly interested in it; you read in it while I was testifying. May I see it? The public would like—'

'The book will cut no figure in this matter,' replied the official, slipping it into his coat pocket. 'All the entries in it were made before the writer's death.'

As Harker passed out of the house the jury reentered and stood about the table, on which the now covered corpse showed under the sheet with sharp definition. The foreman seated himself near the candle, produced from his breast pocket a pencil and scrap of paper and wrote rather laboriously the following verdict, which with various degrees of effort all signed:

'We, the jury, do find that the remains come to their death at the hands of a mountain lion, but some of us thinks, all the same, they had fits.'

4 AN EXPLANATION FROM THE TOMB

In the diary of the late Hugh Morgan are certain interesting entries having, possibly, a scientific value as suggestions. At the inquest upon his body the book was not put in evidence; possibly the coroner thought it not worthwhile to confuse the jury. The date of the first entries mentioned cannot be ascertained; the upper part of the leaf is torn away. The part of the entry remaining follows:

'. . . would run in a half-circle, keeping his head turned always toward the center, and again he would stand still, barking furiously. At last he ran away into the brush as fast as he could go. I thought at first that he had gone mad, but on returning to the house found no other alteration in his manner than what was obviously due to fear of punishment.

'Can a dog see with his nose? Do odors impress some cerebral center with images of the thing that emitted them? . . .

'Sept. 2—Looking at the stars last night as they rose above the crest of the ridge east of the house, I observed them successively disappear—from left to right. Each was eclipsed but an instant, and only a few at the same time, but along the entire length of the ridge all that were within a degree or two of the crest were blotted out. It was as if something had passed along between me and them; but I could not see it, and the stars were not thick enough to define its outline. Ugh! I don't like this.'

Several weeks' entries are missing, three leaves being torn from the book.

'Sept. 27–It has been about here again–I find evidences of its presence every day. I watched again all last night in the same cover, gun in hand, double-charged with buckshot. In the morning the fresh footprints were there, as before. Yet I would have sworn that I did not sleep–indeed, I hardly sleep at all. It is terrible, insupportable! If these amazing experiences are real I shall go mad; if they are fanciful I am mad already.

'Oct. 3–I shall not go–it shall not drive me away. No, this is *my* house, *my* land. God hates a coward. . . .

'Oct. 5–I can stand it no longer; I have invited Harker to pass a few weeks with me–he has a level head. I can judge from his manner if he thinks me mad.

'Oct. 7–I have the solution of the mystery; it came to me last night–suddenly, as by revelation. How simple–how terribly simple!

'There are sounds that we cannot hear. At either end of the scale are notes that stir no chord of that imperfect instrument, the human ear. They are too high or too grave. I have observed a flock of blackbirds occupying an entire treetop–the tops of several trees–and all in full song. Suddenly–in a moment–at absolutely the same instant–all spring into the air and fly away. How? They could not all see one another – whole treetops intervened. At no point could a leader have been visible to all. There must have been a signal of warning or command, high and shrill above the din, but by me unheard. I have observed, too, the same simultaneous flight when all were silent, among not only blackbirds, but other birds–quail, for example, widely separated by bushes–even on opposite sides of a hill.

'It is known to seamen that a school of whales basking or sporting on the surface of the ocean, miles apart, with the convexity of the earth between, will sometimes dive at the same instant–all gone out of sight in a moment. The signal has been sounded–too grave for the ear of the sailor at the masthead and his comrades on the deck–who nevertheless feel its vibrations in the ship as the stones of a cathedral are stirred by the bass of the organ.

'As with sounds, so with colors. At each end of the solar spectrum the chemist can detect the presence of what are known as actinic rays. They represent colors–integral colors in the composition of light–which we are unable to discern. The human eye is an imperfect instrument; its range is but a few octaves of the real chromatic scale. I am not mad; there are colors that we cannot see.

'And, God help me! the Damned Thing is of such a color!'

An Occurrence at Owl Creek Bridge

(First published in *The San Francisco Examiner*, June, 1890; first book publication in 1891.)

A MAN STOOD upon a railroad bridge in northern Alabama, looking down into the swift water twenty feet below. The man's hands were behind his back, the wrists bound with a cord. A rope closely encircled his neck. It was attached to a stout cross-timber above his head and the slack fell to the level of his knees. Some loose boards laid upon the sleepers supporting the metals of the railway supplied a footing for him and his executioners–two private soldiers of the Federal army, directed by a sergeant who in civil life may have been a deputy sheriff. At a short remove upon the same temporary platform was an officer in the uniform of his rank, armed. He was a captain. A sentinel at each end of the bridge stood with his rifle in the position known as "support," that is to say, vertical in front of the left shoulder, the hammer resting on the forearm thrown straight across the chest–a formal and unnatural position, enforcing an erect carriage of the body. It did not appear to be the duty of these two men to know what was occurring at the center of the bridge; they merely blockaded the two ends of the foot planking that traversed it.

Beyond one of the sentinels nobody was in sight; the railroad ran straight away into a forest for a hundred yards, then, curving, was lost to view. Doubtless there was an outpost farther along. The other bank of the stream was open ground–a gentle acclivity topped with a stockade of vertical tree trunks, loopholed for rifles, with a single embrasure through which protruded the muzzle of a brass cannon commanding the bridge. Midway of the slope between the bridge and fort were the spectators–a single company of infantry in line, at "parade rest," the butts of the rifles on the ground, the barrels inclining slightly backward against the right shoulder, the hands crossed upon the stock. A lieutenant stood at the right of the line, the point of his sword upon the ground, his left hand resting upon his right. Excepting the group of four at the center of the bridge, not a man moved. The company faced the bridge, staring stonily, motionless. The sentinels, facing the banks of the stream, might have been statues to adorn the bridge. The captain stood with folded arms, silent, observing the work of his subordinates, but making no sign. Death is a dignitary who when he comes announced is to be received with formal manifestations of respect, even by those most familiar with him. In the code of military etiquette silence and fixity are forms of deference.

The man who was engaged in being hanged was apparently about thirty-five years of age. He was a civilian, if one might judge from his habit, which was that of a planter. His features were good—a straight nose, firm mouth, broad forehead, from which his long, dark hair was combed straight back, falling behind his ears to the collar of his well-fitting frock coat. He wore a mustache and pointed beard, but no whiskers; his eyes were large and dark gray, and had a kindly expression which one would hardly have expected in one whose neck was in the hemp. Evidently this was no vulgar assassin. The liberal military code makes provision for hanging many kinds of persons, and gentlemen are not excluded.

The preparations being complete, the two private soldiers stepped aside and each drew away the plank upon which he had been standing. The sergeant turned to the captain, saluted and placed himself immediately behind that officer, who in turn moved apart one pace. These movements left the condemned man and the sergeant standing on the two ends of the same plank, which spanned three of the cross-ties of the bridge. The end upon which the civilian stood almost, but not quite, reached a fourth. This plank had been held in place by the weight of the captain; it was now held by that of the sergeant. At a signal from the former the latter would step aside, the plank would tilt and the condemned man go down between two ties. The arrangement commended itself to his judgment as simple and effective. His face had not been covered nor his eyes bandaged. He looked a moment at his "unsteadfast footing," then let his gaze wander to the swirling water of the stream racing madly beneath his feet. A piece of dancing driftwood caught his attention and his eyes followed it down the current. How slowly it appeared to move! What a sluggish stream!

He closed his eyes in order to fix his last thoughts upon his wife and children. The water, touched to gold by the early sun, the brooding mists under the banks at some distance down the stream, the fort, the soldiers, the piece of drift—all had distracted him. And now he became conscious of a new disturbance. Striking through the thought of his dear ones was a sound which he could neither ignore nor understand, a sharp, distinct, metallic percussion like the stroke of a blacksmith's hammer upon the anvil; it had the same ringing quality. He wondered what it was, and whether immeasurably distant or near by—it seemed both. Its recurrence was regular, but as slow as the tolling of a death knell. He awaited each stroke with impatience and—he knew not why—apprehension. The intervals of silence grew progressively longer; the delays became maddening. With their greater infrequency the sounds increased in strength and sharpness. They hurt his ear like the thrust of a knife; he feared he would shriek. What he heard was the ticking of his watch.

He unclosed his eyes and saw again the water below him. "If I could free my hands," he thought, "I might throw off the noose and spring into the stream. By diving I could evade the bullets and, swimming vigorously, reach the bank, take to the woods and get away home. My home, thank God, is as yet outside their lines; my wife and little ones are still beyond the invader's farthest advance."

As these thoughts, which have here to be set down in words, were flashed into the doomed man's brain rather than evolved from it the captain nodded to the sergeant. The sergeant stepped aside.

II

Peyton Farquhar was a well-to-do planter, of an old and highly respected Alabama family. Being a slave owner and like other slave owners a politician he was naturally an original secessionist and ardently devoted to the Southern cause. Circumstances of an imperious nature, which it is unnecessary to relate here, had prevented him from taking service with the gallant army that had fought the disastrous campaigns ending with the fall of Corinth, and he chafed under the inglorious restraint, longing for the release of his energies, the larger life of the soldier, the opportunity for distinction. That opportunity, he felt, would come, as it comes to all in war time. Meanwhile he did what he could. No service was too humble for him to perform in aid of the South, no adventure too perilous for him to undertake if consistent with the character of a civilian who was at heart a soldier, and who in good faith and without too much qualification assented to at least a part of the frankly villainous dictum that all is fair in love and war.

One evening while Farquhar and his wife were sitting on a rustic bench near the entrance to his grounds, a gray-clad soldier rode up to the gate and asked for a drink of water. Mrs. Farquhar was only too happy to serve him with her own white hands. While she was fetching the water her husband approached the dusty horseman and inquired eagerly for news from the front.

"The Yanks are repairing the railroads," said the man, "and are getting ready for another advance. They have reached the Owl Creek bridge, put it in order and built a stockade on the north bank. The commandant has issued an order, which is posted everywhere, declaring that any civilian caught interfering with the railroad, its bridges, tunnels or trains will be summarily hanged. I saw the order."

"How far is it to the Owl Creek bridge?" Farquhar asked.

"About thirty miles."

"Is there no force on this side the creek?"

"Only a picket post half a mile out, on the railroad, and a single sentinel at this end of the bridge."

"Suppose a man—a civilian and student of hanging—should elude the picket post and perhaps get the better of the sentinel," said Farquhar, smiling, "what could he accomplish?"

The soldier reflected. "I was there a month ago," he replied. "I observed that the flood of last winter had lodged a great quantity of driftwood against the wooden pier at this end of the bridge. It is now dry and would burn like tow."

The lady had now brought the water, which the soldier drank. He thanked her ceremoniously, bowed to her husband and rode away. An hour later, after nightfall, he repassed the plantation, going northward in the direction from which he had come. He was a Federal scout.

III

As Peyton Farquhar fell straight downward through the bridge he lost consciousness and was as one already dead. From this state he was awakened—ages later, it seemed to him—by the pain of a sharp pressure upon his throat, followed by a sense of suffocation. Keen, poignant agonies seemed to shoot from his neck downward through every fiber of his body and limbs. These pains appeared to flash along well-defined lines of ramification and to beat with an inconceivably rapid periodicity. They seemed like streams of pulsating fire heating him to an intolerable temperature. As to his head, he was conscious of nothing but a feeling of fulness—of congestion. These sensations were unaccompanied by thought. The intellectual part of his nature was already effaced; he had power only to feel, and feeling was torment. He was conscious of motion. Encompassed in a luminous cloud, of which he was now merely the fiery heart, without material substance, he swung through unthinkable arcs of oscillation, like a vast pendulum. Then all at once, with terrible suddenness, the light about him shot upward with the noise of a loud plash; a frightful roaring was in his ears, and all was cold and dark. The power of thought was restored; he knew that the rope had broken and he had fallen into the stream. There was no additional strangulation; the noose about his neck was already suffocating him and kept the water from his lungs. To die of hanging at the bottom of a river!—the idea seemed to him ludicrous. He opened his eyes in the darkness and saw above him a gleam of light, but how distant, how inaccessible! He was still sinking, for the light became fainter and fainter until it was a mere glimmer. Then it began to grow and brighten, and he knew that he was rising toward the surface—knew it with reluctance, for he was now very comfortable. "To be hanged and drowned," he thought, "that is not so bad; but I do not wish to be shot. No; I will not be shot; that is not fair."

He was not conscious of an effort, but a sharp pain in his wrist apprised him that he was trying to free his hands. He gave the struggle his attention, as an idler might observe the feat of a juggler, without interest in the outcome. What splendid effort!—what magnificent, what superhuman strength! Ah, that was a fine endeavor! Bravo! The cord fell away; his arms parted and floated upward, the hands dimly seen on each side in the growing light. He watched them with a new interest as first one and then the other pounced upon the noose at his neck. They tore it away and thrust it fiercely aside, its undulations resembling those of a water snake. "Put it back, put it back!" He thought he shouted these words to his hands, for the undoing of the noose had been succeeded by the direst pang that he had yet experienced. His neck ached horribly; his brain was on fire; his heart, which had been fluttering faintly, gave a great leap, trying to force itself out at his mouth. His whole body was racked and wrenched with an insupportable anguish! But his disobedient hands gave no heed to the command. They beat the water vigorously with quick, downward strokes, forcing him to the surface. He felt his head emerge; his eyes were blinded by the sunlight; his chest expanded convulsively, and with a supreme and crowning agony his lungs engulfed a great draught of air, which instantly he expelled in a shriek!

He was now in full possession of his physical senses. They were, indeed, preternaturally keen and alert. Something in the awful disturbance of his organic system had so exalted and refined them that they made record of things never before perceived. He felt the ripples upon his face and heard their separate sounds as they struck. He looked at the forest on the bank of the stream, saw the individual trees, the leaves and the veining of each leaf—saw the very insects upon them: the locusts, the brilliant-bodied flies, the gray spiders stretching their webs from twig to twig. He noted the prismatic colors in all the dewdrops upon a million blades of grass. The humming of the gnats that danced above the eddies of the stream, the beating of the dragon flies' wings, the strokes of the water-spiders' legs, like oars which had lifted their boat—all these made audible music. A fish slid along beneath his eyes and he heard the rush of its body parting the water.

He had come to the surface facing down the stream; in a moment the visible world seemed to wheel slowly round, himself the pivotal point, and he saw the bridge, the fort, the soldiers upon the bridge, the captain, the sergeant, the two privates, his executioners. They were in silhouette against the blue sky. They shouted and gesticulated, pointing at him. The captain had drawn his pistol, but did not fire; the others were unarmed. Their movements were grotesque and horrible, their forms gigantic.

Suddenly he heard a sharp report and something struck the water smartly within a few inches of his head, spattering his face with spray. He heard a second report, and saw one of the sentinels with his rifle at his shoulder, a light cloud of blue smoke rising from the muzzle. The man in the water saw the eye of the man on the bridge gazing into his own through the sights of the rifle. He observed that it was a gray eye and remembered having read that gray eyes were keenest, and that all famous marksmen had them. Nevertheless, this one had missed.

A counter-swirl had caught Farquhar and turned him half round; he was again looking into the forest on the bank opposite the fort. The sound of a clear, high voice in a monotonous singsong now rang out behind him and came across the water with a distinctness that pierced and subdued all other sounds, even the beating of the ripples in his ears. Although no soldier, he had frequented camps enough to know the dread significance of that deliberate, drawling, aspirated chant; the lieutenant on shore was taking a part in the morning's work. How coldly and pitilessly—with what an even, calm intonation, presaging, and enforcing tranquillity in the men—with what accurately measured intervals fell those cruel words:

"Attention, company! . . . Shoulder arms! . . . Ready! . . . Aim! . . . Fire!"

Farquhar dived—dived as deeply as he could. The water roared in his ears like the voice of Niagara, yet he heard the dulled thunder of the volley and, rising again toward the surface, met shining bits of metal, singularly flattened, oscillating slowly downward. Some of them touched him on the face and hands, then fell away, continuing their descent. One lodged between his collar and neck; it was uncomfortably warm and he snatched it out.

As he rose to the surface, gasping for breath, he saw that he had been a long time under water; he was perceptibly farther down stream—nearer to safety. The soldiers had almost finished reloading; the metal ramrods flashed all at once in the sunshine as they were drawn from the barrels, turned in the air, and thrust into their sockets. The two sentinels fired again, independently and ineffectually.

The hunted man saw all this over his shoulder; he was now swimming vigorously with the current. His brain was as energetic as his arms and legs; he thought with the rapidity of lightning.

"The officer," he reasoned, "will not make that martinet's error a second time. It is as easy to dodge a volley as a single shot. He has probably already given the command to fire at will. God help me, I cannot dodge them all!"

An appalling plash within two yards of him was followed by a loud, rushing sound, *diminuendo*, which seemed to travel back through the air to the fort and died in an explosion which stirred the very river to its deeps! A rising sheet of water curved over him, fell down upon him, blinded him, strangled him! The cannon had taken a hand in the game. As he shook his head free from the commotion of the smitten water he heard the deflected shot humming through the air ahead, and in an instant it was cracking and smashing the branches in the forest beyond.

"They will not do that again," he thought; "the next time they will use a charge of grape. I must keep my eye upon the gun; the smoke will apprise me—the report arrives too late; it lags behind the missile. That is a good gun."

Suddenly he felt himself whirled round and round—spinning like a top. The water, the banks, the forests, the now distant bridge, fort and men—all were commingled and blurred. Objects were represented by their colors only; circular horizontal streaks of color—that was all he saw. He had been caught in a vortex and was being whirled on with a velocity of advance and gyration that made him giddy and sick. In a few moments he was flung upon the gravel at the foot of the left bank of the stream—the southern bank—and behind a projecting point which concealed him from his enemies. The sudden arrest of his motion, the abrasion of one of his hands on the gravel, restored him, and he wept with delight. He dug his fingers into the sand, threw it over himself in handfuls and audibly blessed it. It looked like diamonds, rubies, emeralds; he could think of nothing beautiful which it did not resemble. The trees upon the bank were giant garden plants; he noted a definite order in their arrangement, inhaled the fragrance of their blooms. A strange, roseate light shone through the spaces among their trunks and the wind made in their branches the music of Æolian harps. He had no wish to perfect his escape—was content to remain in that enchanting spot until retaken.

A whiz and rattle of grapeshot among the branches high above his head roused him from his dream. The baffled cannoneer had fired him a random farewell. He sprang to his feet, rushed up the sloping bank, and plunged into the forest.

All that day he traveled, laying his course by the rounding sun. The forest seemed interminable; nowhere did he discover a break in it, not even a woodman's road. He had not known that he lived in so wild a region. There was something uncanny in the revelation.

By nightfall he was fatigued, footsore, famishing. The thought of his wife and children urged him on. At last he found a road which led him in what he knew to be the right direction. It was as wide and straight as a city street, yet it seemed untraveled. No fields bordered it, no dwelling anywhere. Not so much as the barking of a dog suggested human habitation. The black bodies of the trees formed a straight wall on both sides, terminating on the horizon in a point, like a diagram in a lesson in perspective. Overhead, as he looked up through this rift in the wood, shone great golden stars looking unfamiliar and grouped in strange constellations. He was sure they were arranged in some order which had a secret and malign significance. The wood on either side was full of singular noises, among which—once, twice, and again—he distinctly heard whispers in an unknown tongue.

His neck was in pain and lifting his hand to it found it horribly swollen. He knew that it had a circle of black where the rope had bruised it. His eyes felt congested; he could no longer close them. His tongue was swollen with thirst; he relieved its fever by thrusting it forward from between his teeth into the cold air. How softly the turf had carpeted the untraveled avenue—he could no longer feel the roadway beneath his feet!

Doubtless, despite his suffering, he had fallen asleep while walking, for now he sees another scene—perhaps he has merely recovered from a delirium. He stands at the gate of his own home. All is as he left it, and all bright and beautiful in the morning sunshine. He must have traveled the entire night. As he pushes open the gate and passes up the wide white walk, he sees a flutter of female garments; his wife, looking fresh and cool and sweet, steps down from the veranda to meet him. At the bottom of the steps she stands waiting, with a smile of ineffable joy, an attitude of matchless grace and dignity. Ah, how beautiful she is! He springs forward with extended arms. As he is about to clasp her he feels a stunning blow upon the back of the neck; a blinding white light blazes all about him with a sound like the shock of a cannon—then all is darkness and silence!

Peyton Farquhar was dead; his body, with a broken neck, swung gently from side to side beneath the timbers of the Owl Creek bridge.

HENRY JAMES

[1843–1916]

The Turn of the Screw

(First published in *Collier's*, January-April, 1898;
first book publication in 1898.)

THE STORY HAD held us, round the fire, sufficiently breathless, but except the obvious remark that it was gruesome, as, on Christmas eve in an old house, a strange tale should essentially be, I remember no comment uttered till somebody happened to say that it was the only case he had met in which such a visitation had fallen on a child. The case, I may mention, was that of an apparition in just such an old house as had gathered us for the occasion of an appearance, of a dreadful kind, to a little boy sleeping in the room with his mother and waking her up in the terror of it; waking her not to dissipate his dread and soothe him to sleep again, but to encounter also, herself, before she had succeeded in doing so, the same sight that had shaken him. It was this observation that drew from Douglas–not immediately, but later in the evening–a reply that had the interesting consequence to which I call attention. Someone else told a story not particularly effective, which I saw he was not following. This I took for a sign that he had himself something to produce and that we should only have to wait. We waited in fact till two nights later; but that same evening, before we scattered, he brought out what was in his mind.

'I quite agree–in regard to Griffin's ghost, or whatever it was–that its appearing first to the little boy, at so tender an age, adds a particular touch. But it's not the first occurrence of its charming kind that I know to have involved a child. If the child gives the effect another turn of the screw, what do you say to *two* children–?'

'We say, of course,' somebody exclaimed, 'that they give two turns! Also that we want to hear about them.'

I can see Douglas there before the fire, to which he had got up to present his back, looking down at his interlocutor with his hands in his pockets. 'Nobody but me, till now, has ever heard. It's quite too horrible.' This, naturally, was declared by several voices to give the thing the utmost price, and our friend, with quiet art, prepared his triumph by turning his eyes over the rest of us and going on: 'It's beyond everything. Nothing at all that I know touches it.'

'For sheer terror?' I remember asking.

He seemed to say it was not so simple as that; to be really at a loss how to qualify it. He pased his hand over his eyes, made a little wincing grimace. 'For dreadful–dreadfulness!'

'Oh, how delicious!' cried one of the women.

He took no notice of her; he looked at me, but as if, instead of me, he saw what he spoke of. 'For general uncanny ugliness and horror and pain.'

'Well then,' I said, 'just sit right down and begin.'

He turned round to the fire, gave a kick to a log, watched it an instant. Then as he faced us again: 'I can't begin. I shall have to send to town.' There was a unanimous groan at this, and much reproach; after which, in his preoccupied way, he explained. 'The story's written. It's in a locked drawer–it has not been out for years. I could write to my man and enclose the key; he could send down the packet as he finds it.' It was to me in particular that he appeared to propound this–appeared almost to appeal for aid not to hesitate. He had broken a thickness of ice, the formation of many a winter; had had his reasons for a long silence. The others resented postponement, but it was just his scruples that charmed me. I adjured him to write by the first post and to agree with us for an early hearing; then I asked him if the experience in question had been his own. To this his answer was prompt. 'Oh, thank God, no!'

'And is the record yours? You took the thing down?'

'Nothing but the impression. I took that *here*'–he tapped his heart. 'I've never lost it.'

'Then your manuscript–?'

'Is in old, faded ink, and in the most beautiful hand.' He hung fire again. 'A woman's. She has been dead these twenty years. She sent me the pages in question before she died.' They were all listening now, and of course there was somebody to be arch, or at any rate to draw the inference. But if he put the inference by without a smile it was also without irritation. 'She was a most charming person, but she was ten years older than I. She was my sister's governess,' he quietly said. 'She was the most agreeable woman I've ever known in her position; she would have been worthy of any whatever. It was long ago, and this episode was long before. I was at Trinity, and I found her at home on my coming down the second summer. I was much there that year–it was a beautiful one; and we had, in her off-hours, some strolls and talks in the garden–talks in which she struck me as awfully clever and nice. Oh yes; don't grin: I liked her extremely and am glad to this day to think she liked me too. If she hadn't she wouldn't have told me. She had never told anyone. It wasn't simply that she said so, but that I knew she hadn't. I was sure; I could see. You'll easily judge why when you hear.'

'Because the thing had been such a scare?'

He continued to fix me. 'You'll easily judge,' he repeated: '*you* will.'

I fixed him too. 'I see. She was in love.'

He laughed for the first time. 'You *are* acute. Yes, she was in love. That is she had been. That came out—she couldn't tell her story without it's coming out. I saw it, and she saw I saw it; but neither of us spoke of it. I remember the time and the place—the corner of the lawn, the shade of the great beeches and the long, hot summer afternoon. It wasn't a scene for a shudder; but oh—!' He quitted the fire and dropped back into his chair.

'You'll receive the packet Thursday morning?' I inquired.

'Probably not till the second post.'

'Well then; after dinner—'

'You'll all meet me here?' He looked us round again. 'Isn't anybody going?' It was almost the tone of hope.

'Everybody will stay!'

'*I* will—and *I* will!' cried the ladies whose departure had been fixed. Mrs Griffin, however, expressed the need for a little more light. 'Who was it she was in love with?'

'The story will tell,' I took upon myself to reply.

'Oh, I can't wait for the story!'

'The story *won't* tell,' said Douglas; 'not in any literal, vulgar way.'

'More's the pity then. That's the only way I ever understand.'

'Won't *you* tell, Douglas?' Somebody else inquired.

He sprang to his feet again. 'Yes—tomorrow. Now I must go to bed. Good night.' And, quickly, catching up a candlestick, he left us slightly bewildered. From our end of the great brown hall we heard his step on the stair; whereupon Mrs Griffin spoke. 'Well, if I don't know who she was in love with, I know who *he* was.'

'She was ten years older,' said her husband.

'*Raison de plus*—at that age! But it's rather nice, his long reticence.'

'Forty years!' Griffin put in.

'With this outbreak at last.'

'The outbreak,' I returned, 'will make a tremendous occasion of Thursday night'; and everyone so agreed with me that, in the light of it, we lost all attention for everything else. The last story, however incomplete and like the mere opening of a serial, had been told; we handshook and 'candlestuck', as somebody said, and went to bed.

I knew the next day that a letter containing the key had, by the first post, gone off to his London apartments; but in spite of—or perhaps just on account of—the eventual diffusion of this knowledge we quite let him alone till after dinner, till such an hour of the evening, in fact, as might best accord with the kind of emotion on which our hopes were fixed. Then he became as communicative as we could desire and indeed gave us his best reason for being so. We had it from him again before the fire in the hall, as we had had our mild wonders of the previous night. It appeared that the narrative he had promised to read us really required for a proper intelligence a few words of prologue. Let me say here distinctly, to have done with it, that this narrative, from an exact transcript of my own made much later, is what I shall presently give. Poor Douglas, before his death–when it was in sight–committed to me the manuscript that reached him on the third of these days and that, on the same spot, with immense effect, he began to read to our hushed little circle on the night of the fourth. The departing ladies who had said they would stay didn't, of course, thank heaven, stay: they departed, in consequence of arrangements made, in a rage of curiosity, as they professed, produced by the touches with which he had already worked us up. But that only made his little final auditory more compact and select, kept it, round the hearth, subject to a common thrill.

The first of these touches conveyed that the written statement took up the tale at a point after it had, in a manner, begun. The fact to be in possession of was therefore that his old friend, the youngest of several daughters of a poor country parson, had, at the age of twenty, on taking service for the first time in the schoolroom, come up to London, in trepidation, to answer in person an advertisement that had already placed her in brief correspondence with the advertiser. This person proved, on her presenting herself, for judgement, at a house, in Harley Street, that impressed her as vast and imposing–this prospective patron proved a gentleman, a bachelor in the prime of life, such a figure as had never risen, save in a dream or an old novel, before a fluttered, anxious girl out of a Hampshire vicarage. One could easily fix his type; it never, happily, dies out. He was handsome and bold and pleasant, off-hand and gay and kind. He struck her, inevitably, as gallant and splendid, but what took her most of all and gave her the courage she afterwards showed was that he put the whole thing to her as a kind of favour, an obligation he should gratefully incur. She conceived him as rich, but as fearfully extravagant–saw him all in a glow of high fashion, of good looks, of expensive habits, of charming ways with women. He had for his town residence a big house filled with the spoils of travel and the trophies of the chase; but it was to his country home, an old family place in Essex, that he wished her immediately to proceed.

He had been left, by the death of their parents in India, guardian to a small nephew and a small niece, children of a younger, a military brother, whom he had lost two years before. These children were, by the strangest of chances for a man in his position–a lone man without the right sort of experience or a grain of patience–very heavily on his hands. It had all been a great worry and, on his own part doubtless, a series of blunders, but he immensely pitied the poor chicks and had done all he could; had in particular sent them down to his other house, the proper place for them being of course the country, and kept them there, from the first, with the best people he could find to look after them, parting even with his own servants to wait on them and going down himself, whenever he might, to see how they were doing. The awkward thing was that they had practically no other relations and that his own affairs took up all his time. He had put them in possession of Bly, which was healthy and secure, and had placed at the head of their little establishment—but below stairs only—an excellent woman, Mrs Grose, whom he was sure his visitor would like and who had formerly been maid to his mother. She was now housekeeper and was also acting for the time as superintendent to the little girl, of whom, without children of her own, she was, by good luck, extremely fond. There were plenty of people to help, but of course the young lady who should go down as governess would be in supreme authority. She would also have, in holidays, to look after the small boy, who had been for a term at school—young as he was to be sent, but what else could be done?—and who, as the holidays were about to begin, would be back from one day to the other. There had been for the two children at first a young lady whom they had had the misfortune to lose. She had done for them quite beautifully—she was a most respectable person—till her death, the great awkwardness of which had, precisely, left no alternative but the school for little Miles. Mrs Grose, since then, in the way of manners and things, had done as she could for Flora; and there were further, a cook, a housemaid, a dairywoman, an old pony, an old groom and an old gardener, all likewise thoroughly respectable.

So far had Douglas presented his picture when someone put a question. 'And what did the former governess die of?—of so much respectability.'

Our friend's answer was prompt. 'That will come out. I don't anticipate.'

'Excuse me—I thought that was just what you *are* doing.'

'In her successor's place,' I suggested, 'I should have wished to learn that the office brought with it—'

'Necessary danger to life?' Douglas completed my thought. 'She did wish to learn, and she did learn. You shall hear tomorrow what she learnt. Meanwhile, of course, the prospect struck her as slightly grim. She was young, untried, nervous: it was a vision of serious duties and little company, of really great loneliness. She hesitated—took a couple of days to consult and consider. But the salary offered much exceeded her modest measure, and on a second interview she faced the music, she engaged.' And Douglas, with this, made a pause that, for the benefit of the company, moved me to throw in—

'The moral of which was of course the seduction exercised by the splendid young man. She succumbed to it.'

He got up and, as he had done the night before, went to the fire, gave a stir to a log with his foot, then stood a moment with his back to us. 'She saw him only twice.'

'Yes, but that's just the beauty of her passion.'

A little to my surprise, on this, Douglas turned round to me. 'It *was* the beauty of it. There were others,' he went on, 'who hadn't succumbed. He told her frankly all his difficulty—that for several applicants the conditions had been prohibitive. They were, somehow, simply afraid. It sounded dull—it sounded strange; and all the more so because of his main condition.'

'Which was—?'

'That she should never trouble him—but never, never: neither appeal nor complain nor write about anything; only meet all questions herself, receive all moneys from his solicitor, take the whole thing over and let him alone. She promised to do this, and she mentioned to me that when, for a moment, disburdened, delighted, he held her hand, thanking her for the sacrifice, she already felt rewarded.'

'But was that all her reward?' one of the ladies asked.

'She never saw him again.'

'Oh!' said the lady; which, as our friend immediately left us again, was the only other word of importance contributed to the subject till, the next night, by the corner of the hearth, in the best chair, he opened the faded red cover of a thin old-fashioned gilt-edged album. The whole thing took indeed more nights than one, but on the first occasion the same lady put another question. 'What is your title?'

'I haven't one.'

'Oh, *I* have!' I said. But Douglas, without heeding me, had begun to read with a fine clearness that was like a rendering to the ear of the beauty of his author's hand.

1

I remember the whole beginning as a succession of flights and drops, a little see-saw of the right throbs and the wrong. After rising, in town, to meet his appeal, I had at all events a couple of very bad days—found myself doubtful again, felt indeed sure I had made a mistake. In this state of mind I spent the long hours of bumping, swinging coach that carried me to the stopping place at which I was to be met by a vehicle from the house. This convenience I was told, had been ordered, and I found, towards the close of the June afternoon, a commodious fly in waiting for me. Driving at that hour, on a lovely day, through a country to which the summer sweetness seemed to offer me a friendly welcome, my fortitude mounted afresh and, as we turned into the avenue, encountered a reprieve that was probably but a proof of the point to which it had sunk. I suppose I had expected, or had dreaded, something so melancholy that what greeted me was a good surprise. I remember as a most pleasant impression the broad, clear front, its open windows and fresh curtains and the pair of maids looking out; I remember the lawn and the bright flowers and the crunch of my wheels on the gravel and the clustered tree-tops over which the rooks circled and cawed in the golden sky. The scene had a greatness that made it a different affair from my own scant home, and there immediately appeared at the door, with a little girl in her hand, a civil person who dropped me as decent a curtsey as if I had been the mistress or a distinguished visitor. I had received in Harley Street a narrower notion of the place, and that, as I recalled it, made me think the proprietor still more of a gentleman, suggested that what I was to enjoy might be something beyond his promise.

I had no drop again till the next day, for I was carried triumphantly through the following hours by my introduction to the younger of my pupils. The little girl who had accompanied Mrs Grose appeared to me on the spot a creature so charming as to make it a great fortune to have to do with her. She was the most beautiful child I had ever seen, and I afterwards wondered that my employer had not told me more of her. I slept little that night. I was too much excited; and this astonished me too, I recollect, remained with me, adding to my sense of the liberality with which I was treated. The large impressive room, one of the best in the house, the great state bed, as I almost felt it, the full, figured draperies, the long glasses in which, for the first time I could see myself from head to foot, all struck me–like the extraordinary charm of my small charge–as so many things thrown in. It was thrown in as well, from the first moment, that I should get on with Mrs Grose in a relation over which, on my way, in the coach, I fear I had rather brooded. The only thing indeed that in this early outlook might have made me shrink again was the clear circumstance of her being so glad to see me. I perceived within half an hour that she was so glad–stout, simple, plain, clean wholesome woman–as to be positively on her guard against showing it too much. I wondered even then a little why she should wish not to show it and that, with reflection, with suspicion, might of course have made me uneasy.

But it was a comfort that there could be no uneasiness in a connexion with anything so beatific as the radiant image of my little girl, the vision of whose angelic beauty had probably more than anything else to do with the restlessness that, before morning, made me several times rise and wander about my room to take in the whole picture and prospect; to watch, from my open window, the faint summer dawn, to look at such portions of the rear of the house as I could catch, and to listen, while, in the fading dusk, the first birds began to twitter, for the possible recurrence of a sound or two, less natural and not without, but within, that I fancied I heard. There had been a moment when I believed I recognized, faint and far, the cry of a child; there had been another when I found myself just consciously starting up at the passage, before my door, of a light footstep. But these fancies were not marked enough not to be thrown off, and it is only in the light, or the gloom, I should rather say, of other and subsequent matters that they now come back to me. To watch, teach, 'form' little Flora would too evidently be the making of a happy and useful life. It had been agreed between us downstairs that after this first occasion I should have her as a matter of course at night, her small white bed being already arranged, to that end, in my room. What I had undertaken was the whole care of her, and she had remained, just this last time, with Mrs Grose only as an effect of our consideration for my inevitable strangeness and her natural timidity. In spite of this timidity–which the child herself, in the oddest way in the world, had been perfectly frank and brave about, allowing it, without a sign of uncomfortable consciousness, with the deep, sweet serenity indeed of one of Raphael's holy infants, to be discussed, to be imputed to her and to determine us. I felt quite sure she would presently like me. It was part of what I already liked Mrs Grose herself for, the pleasure I could see her feel in my admiration and wonder as I sat at supper with four tall candles and with my pupil, in a high chair and bib, brightly facing me, between them, over bread and milk. There were naturally things that in Flora's presence could pass between us only as prodigious and gratified looks, obscure and roundabout allusions.

'And the little boy–does he look like her? Is he too so very remarkable?'

One wouldn't flatter a child. 'Oh Miss, *most* remarkable. If you think well of this one!'–and she stood there with a plate in her hand, beaming at our companion, who looked from one of us to the other with placid heavenly eyes that contained nothing to check us.

'Yes; if I do–?'

'You *will* be carried away by the little gentleman!'

'Well, that, I think, is what I came for–to be carried away. I'm afraid, however,' I remember feeling the impulse to add, 'I'm rather easily carried away. I was carried away in London!'

I can still see Mrs Grose's broad face as she took this in. 'In Harley Street?'

'In Harley Street.'

'Well, Miss, you're not the first–and you won't be the last.'

'Oh, I've no pretension,' I could laugh, 'to being the only one. My other pupil, at any rate, as I understand, comes back tomorrow?'

'Not tomorrow–Friday, Miss. He arrives, as you did, by the coach, under care of the guard, and is to be met by the same carriage.'

I forthwith expressed that the proper as well as the pleasant and friendly thing would be therefore that on the arrival of the public conveyance I should be waiting for him with his little sister; an idea in which Mrs Grose concurred so heartily that I somehow took her manner as a kind of comforting pledge–never falsified, thank heaven!–that we should on every question be quite at one. Oh, she was glad I was there!

What I felt the next day was, I suppose, nothing that could be fairly called a reaction from the cheer of my arrival; it was probably at the most only a slight oppression produced by a fuller measure of the scale, as I walked round them, gazed up at them, took them in, of my new circumstances. They had, as it were, an extent and mass for which I had not been prepared and in the presence of which I found myself, freshly, a little scared as well as a little proud. Lessons, in this agitation, certainly suffered some delay; I reflected that my first duty was, by the gentlest arts I could contrive, to win the child into the sense of knowing me. I spent the day with her out of doors; I arranged with her, to her great satisfaction, that it should be she, she only, who might show me the place. She showed it step by step and room by room and secret by secret, with droll, delightful, childish talk about it and with the result, in half an hour, of our becoming immense friends. Young as she was, I was struck, throughout our little tour, with her confidence and courage with the way, in empty chambers and dull corridors, on crooked staircases that made me pause and even on the summit of an old machicolated square tower that made me dizzy, her morning music, her disposition to tell me so many more things than she asked, rang out and led me on. I have not seen Bly since the day I left it, and I dare say that to my older and more informed eyes it would now appear sufficiently contracted. But as my little conductress with her hair of gold and her frock of blue, danced before me round corners and pattered down passages, I had the view of a castle of romance inhabited by a rosy sprite, such a place as would somehow, for diversion of the young idea, take all colour out of storybooks and fairy-tales. Wasn't it just a storybook over which I had fallen a-doze and a-dream? No; it was a big ugly, antique, but convenient house, embodying a few features of a building still older, half replaced and half utilized, in which I had the fancy of our being almost as lost as a handful of passengers in a great drifting ship. Well, I was, strangely, at the helm!

2

This came home to me when, two days later, I drove over with Flora to meet, as Mrs Grose said, the little gentleman; and all the more for an incident that, presenting itself the second evening, had deeply disconcerted me. The first day had been, on the whole, as I have expressed, reassuring, but I was to see it wind up in keen apprehension. The postbag, that evening–it came late–contained a letter for me, which, however, in the hand of my employer, I found to be composed but of a few words enclosing another, addressed to himself, with a seal still unbroken. 'This, I recognize, is from the head-master, and the head-master's an awful bore. Read him, please; deal with him; but mind you don't report. Not a word. I'm off!' I broke the seal with a great effort–so great a one that I was a long time coming to it; took the unopened missive at last up to my room and only attacked it just before going to bed. I had better have let it wait till morning, for it gave me a second sleepless night. With no counsel to take, the next day, I was full of distress; and it finally got so the better of me that I determined to open myself at least to Mrs Grose.

'What does it mean? The child's dismissed his school.'

She gave me a look that I remarked at the moment; then, visibly, with a quick blankness, seemed to try to take it back. 'But aren't they all–?'

'Sent home–yes. But only for the holidays. Miles may never go back at all.'

Consciously, under my attention, she reddened. 'They won't take him?'

'They absolutely decline.'

At this she raised her eyes, which she had turned to me; I saw them fill with good tears. 'What has he done?'

I hesitated; then I judged best simply to hand her my letter–which, however, had the effect of making her, without taking it, simply put her hands behind her. She shook her head sadly. 'Such things are not for me, Miss.'

My counsellor couldn't read! I winced at my mistake, which I attenuated as I could, and opened my letter again to repeat it to her; then, faltering in the act and folding it up once more, I put it back in my pocket. 'Is he really *bad*?'

The tears were still in her eyes. 'Do the gentlemen say so?'

'They go into no particulars. They simply express their regret that it should be impossible to keep him. That can have only one meaning.' Mrs Grose listened with dumb emotion; she forbore to ask me what this meaning might be; so that, presently, to put the thing with some coherence and with the mere aid of her presence to my own mind, I went on: 'That he's an injury to the others.'

At this, with one of the quick turns of simple folk, she suddenly flamed up. 'Master Miles!–*him* an injury?'

There was such a flood of good faith in it that, though I had not yet seen the child, my very fears made me jump to the absurdity of the idea. I found myself, to meet my friend the better, offering it, on the spot, sarcastically. 'To his poor little innocent mates!'

'It's too dreadful,' cried Mrs Grose, 'to say such cruel things! Why, he's scarce ten years old.'

'Yes, yes; it would be incredible.'

She was evidently grateful for such a profession. 'See him, Miss, first. *Then* believe it!' I felt forthwith a new impatience to see him; it was the beginning of a curiosity that, for all the next hours, was to deepen almost to pain. Mrs Grose was aware, I could judge, of what she had produced in me, and she followed it up with assurance. 'You might as well believe it of the little lady. Bless her,' she added the next moment–'*look* at her!'

I turned and saw Flora, whom, ten minutes before, I had established in the school room with a sheet of white paper, a pencil and a copy of nice 'round O's', now presented herself to view at the open door. She expressed in her little way an extraordinary detachment from disagreeable duties, looking at me, however, with a great childish light that seemed to offer it as a mere result of the affection she had conceived for my person, which had rendered necessary that she should follow me. I needed nothing more than this to feel the full force of Mrs Grose's comparison, and, catching my pupil in my arms, covered her with kisses in which there was a sob of atonement.

None the less, the rest of the day, I watched for further occasion to approach my colleague, especially as, towards evening, I began to fancy she rather sought to avoid me. I overtook her, I remember, on the staircase, we went down together, and at the bottom I detained her, holding her there with a hand on her arm. 'I take what you said to me at noon as a declaration that *you've* never known him to be bad.'

She threw back her head; she had clearly, by this time, and very honestly adopted an attitude. 'Oh, never known him–I don't pretend *that*!'

I was upset again. 'Then you *have* known him–?'

'Yes indeed, Miss, thank God!'

On reflection I accepted this. 'You mean that a boy who never is–?'

'Is no boy for *me*!'

I held her tighter. 'You like them with the spirit to be naughty?' Then keeping pace with her answer. 'So do I!' I eagerly brought out. 'But not to the degree to contaminate–'

'To contaminate?'–my big word left her at a loss.

I explained it. 'To corrupt.'

She stared, taking my meaning in; but it produced in her an odd laugh. 'Are you afraid he'll corrupt *you*?' She put the question with such a fine bold humour that, with a laugh, a little silly doubtless, to match her own I gave way for the time to the apprehension of ridicule.

But the next day, as the hour for my drive approached, I cropped up in another place. 'What was the lady who was here before?'

'The last governess? She was also young and pretty–almost as young and almost as pretty, Miss, even as you.'

'Ah, then, I hope her youth and her beauty helped her!' I recollect throwing off. 'He seems to like us young and pretty!'

'Oh, he *did*,' Mrs Grose assented: 'it was the way he liked everyone!' She had no sooner spoken indeed than she caught herself up. 'I mean that's *his* way–the master's.'

I was struck. 'But of whom did you speak first?'

She looked blank, but she coloured. 'Why, of *him*.'

'Of the master?'

'Of who else?'

There was so obviously no one else that the next moment I had lost my impression of her having accidentally said more than she meant; and I merely asked what I wanted to know. 'Did *she* see anything in the boy–?'

'That wasn't right? she never told me.'

I had a scruple, but I overcame it. 'Was she careful–particular?'

Mrs Grose appeared to try to be conscientious. 'About some things–yes.'

'But not about all?'

Again she considered. 'Well, Miss–she's gone. I won't tell tales.'

'I quite understand your feeling,' I hastened to reply; but I thought it, after an instant, not opposed to this concession to pursue 'Did she die here?'

'No–she went off.'

I don't know what there was in this brevity of Mrs Grose's that struck me as ambiguous. 'Went off to die?' Mrs Grose looked straight out of the window, but I felt that, hypothetically, I had a right to know what young persons engaged for Bly were expected to do. 'She was taken ill, you mean, and went home?'

'She was not taken ill, so far as appeared, in this house. She left it, at the end of the year, to go home, as she said, for a short holiday, to which the time she had put in had certainly given her a right. We had then a young woman–a nursemaid who had stayed on and who was a good girl and clever; and *she* took the children altogether for the interval. But our young lady never came back, and at the very moment I was expecting her I heard from the master that she was dead.'

I turned this over. 'But of what?'

'He never told me! But please, Miss,' said Mrs Grose, 'I must get to my work.'

3

Her thus turning her back on me was fortunately not, for my just preoccupations, a snub that could check the growth of our mutual esteem. We met, after I had brought home little Miles, more intimately than ever on the ground of my stupefaction, my general emotion: so monstrous was I then ready to pronounce it that such a child as had now been revealed to me should be under an interdict. I was a little late on the scene, and I felt, as he stood wistfully looking out for me before the door of the inn at which the coach had put him down, that I had seen him, on the instant, without and within, in the great glow of freshness, the same positive fragrance of purity, in which I had, from the first moment, seen his little sister. He was incredibly beautiful, and Mrs Grose had put her finger on it: everything but a sort of passion of tenderness for him was swept away by his presence. What I then and there took him to my heart for was something divine that I have never found to the same degree in any child–his indescribable little air of knowing nothing in the world but love. It would have been impossible to carry a bad name with a greater sweetness of innocence, and by the time I had got back to Bly with him I remained merely bewildered—so far, that is, as I was not outraged—by the sense of the horrible letter locked up in my room, in a drawer. As soon as I could compass a private word with Mrs Grose I declared to her that it was grotesque.

She promptly understood me. 'You mean the cruel charge—?'

'It doesn't live an instant. My dear woman, *look* at him!'

She smiled at my pretension to have discovered his charm. 'I assure you, Miss, I do nothing else! What will you say, then?' she immediately added.

'In answer to the letter?' I had made up my mind. 'Nothing.'

'And to his uncle?'

I was incisive. 'Nothing.'

'And to the boy himself?'

I was wonderful. 'Nothing.'

She gave with her apron a great wipe to her mouth. 'Then I'll stand by you. We'll see it out.'

'We'll see it out!' I ardently echoed, giving her my hand to make it a vow.

She held me there a moment, then whisked up her apron again with her detached hand. 'Would you mind, Miss, if I used the freedom—'

'To kiss me? No!' I took the good creature in my arms and, after we had embraced like sisters, felt still more fortified and indignant.

This, at all events, was for the time: a time so full that, as I recall the way it went, it reminds me of all the art I now need to make it a little distinct. What I look back at with amazement is the situation I accepted. I had undertaken, with my companion, to see it out, and I was under a charm, apparently, that could smooth away the extent and the far and difficult connexions of such an effort. I was lifted aloft on a great wave of infatuation and pity. I found it simple, in my ignorance, my confusion, and perhaps my conceit, to assume that I could deal with the boy whose education for the world was all on the point of beginning. I am unable even to remember at this day what proposal I framed for the end of his holidays and the resumption of his studies. Lessons with me indeed, that charming summer, we all had a theory that he was to have; but I now reel that, for weeks, the lessons must have been rather my own. I learnt something—at first certainly—that had not been one of the teachings of my small, smothered life; learnt to be amused, and even amusing, and not to think for the morrow. It was the first time, in a manner, that I had known space and air and freedom, all the music of summer and all the mystery of nature. And then there was consideration—and consideration was sweet. Oh, it was a trap—not designed, but deep—to my imagination, to my delicacy, perhaps to my vanity; to whatever, in me, was most excitable. The best way to picture it all is to say that I was off my guard. They gave me so little trouble—they were of a gentleness so extraordinary. I used to speculate—but even this with a dim disconnectedness—as to how the rough future (for all futures are rough!) would handle them and might bruise them. They had the bloom of health and happiness; and yet, as if I had been in charge of a pair of little grandees, of princes of the blood, for whom everything, to be right, would have to be enclosed and protected, the only form that, in my fancy, the after-years could take for them was that of a romantic, a really royal extension of the garden and the park. It may be, of course, above all, that what suddenly broke into this gives the previous time a charm of stillness—that hush in which something gathers or crouches. The change was actually like the spring of a beast.

In the first weeks the days were long; they often, at their finest, gave me what I used to call my own hour, the hour when, for my pupils, tea-time and bed-time having come and gone, I had, before my final retirement, a small interval alone. Much as I liked my companions, this hour was the thing in the day I liked most; and I liked it best of all when, as the light faded—or rather, I should say, the day lingered and the last calls of the last birds sounded, in a flushed sky, from the old trees—I could take a turn into the grounds and enjoy, almost with a sense of property that amused and flattered me, the beauty and dignity of the place. It was a pleasure at these moments to feel myself tranquil and justified; doubtless, perhaps, also to reflect that by my discretion, my quiet good sense and general high propriety, I was giving pleasure—if he ever thought of it!—to the person to whose pressure I had responded. What I was doing was what he had earnestly hoped and directly asked of me, and that I *could*, after all, do it proved even a greater joy than I had expected. I dare say I fancied myself, in short, a remarkable young woman and took comfort in the faith that this would more publicly appear. Well, I needed to be remarkable to offer a front to the remarkable things that presently gave their first sign.

It was plump, one afternoon, in the middle of my very hour: the children were tucked away and I had come out for my stroll. One of the thoughts that, as I don't in the least shrink now from noting, used to be with me in these wanderings was that it would be as charming as a charming story suddenly to meet someone. Someone would appear there at the turn of a path and would stand before me and smile and approve. I didn't ask more than that—I only asked that he should *know*; and the only way to be sure he knew would be to see it, and the kind light of it, in his handsome face. That was exactly present to me—by which I mean the face was—when, on the first of these occasions, at the end of a long June day, I stopped short on emerging from one of the plantations and coming into view of the house. What arrested me on the spot—and with a shock much greater than any vision had allowed for—was the sense that my imagination had, in a flash turned real. He did stand there!—but high up, beyond the lawn and at the very top of the tower to which, on that first morning, little Flora had conducted me. This tower was one of a pair—square, incongruous, crenelated structures—

that were distinguished, for some reason, though I could see little difference, as the new and the old. They flanked opposite ends of the house and were probably architectural absurdities, redeemed in a measure indeed by not being wholly disengaged nor of a height too pretentious, dating, in their gingerbread antiquity, from a romantic revival that was already a respectable past. I admired them, had fancies about them, for we could all profit in a degree, especially when they loomed through the dusk, by the grandeur of their actual battlements; yet it was not at such an elevation that the figure I had so often invoked seemed most in place.

It produced in me, this figure, in the clear twilight, I remember, two distinct gasps of emotion, which were, sharply, the shock of my first and that of my second surprise. My second was a violent perception of the mistake of my first: the man who met my eyes was not the person I had precipitately supposed. There came to me thus a bewilderment of vision of which, after these years, there is no living view that I can hope to give. An unknown man in a lonely place is a permitted object of fear to a young woman privately bred; and the figure that faced me was—a few more seconds assured me—as little anyone else I knew as it was the image that had been in my mind. I had not seen it in Harley Street—I had not seen it anywhere. The place, moreover, in the strangest way in the world, had, on the instant, and by the very fact of its appearance, become a solitude. To me at least, making my statement here with a deliberation with which I have never made it, the whole feeling of the moment returns. It was as if, while I took in—what I did take in—all the rest of the scene had been stricken with death. I can hear again, as I write, the intense hush in which the sounds of evening dropped. The rooks stopped cawing in the golden sky and the friendly hour lost, for a minute, all its voice. But there was no other change in nature, unless indeed it were a change that I saw with a stranger sharpness. The gold was still in the sky, the clearness in the air, and the man who looked at me over the battlements was as definite as a picture in a frame. That's how I thought, with extraordinary quickness, of each person that he might have been and that he was not. We were confronted across our distance quite long enough for me to ask myself with intensity who then he was and to feel, as an effect of my inability to say, a wonder that in a few instants more became intense.

The great question, or one of these, is, afterwards, I know, with regard to certain matters, the question of how long they have lasted. Well, this matter of mine, think what you will of it, lasted while I caught at a dozen possibilities, none of which made a difference for the better, that I could see in there having been in the house—and for how long, above all?—a person of whom I was in ignorance. It lasted while I just bridled a little with the sense that my office demanded that there should be no such ignorance and no such person. It lasted while this visitant, at all events—and there was a touch of the strange freedom, as I remember, in the sign of familiarity of his wearing no hat—seemed to fix me, from his position, with just the question, just the scrutiny through the fading light, that his own presence provoked. We were too far apart to call to each other, but there was a moment at which, at shorter range, some challenge between us, breaking the hush, would have been the right result of our straight mutual stare. He was in one of the angles, the one away from the house, very erect, as it struck me, and with both hands on the ledge. So I saw him as I see the letters I form on this page; then, exactly, after a minute, as if to add to the spectacle, he slowly changed his place—passed, looking at me hard all the while, to the opposite corner of the platform. Yes, I had the sharpest sense that during this transit he never took his eyes from me, and I can see at this moment the way his hand, as he went, passed from one of the crenelations to the next. He stopped at the other corner, but less long, and even as he turned away still markedly fixed me. He turned away; that was all I knew.

4

It was not that I didn't wait, on this occasion, for more, for I was rooted as deeply as I was shaken. Was there a 'secret' at Bly—a mystery of Udolpho or an insane, an unmentionable relative kept in unsuspected confinement? I can't say how long I turned it over, or how long, in a confusion of curiosity and dread, I remained where I had had my collision; I only recall that when I re-entered the house darkness had quite closed in. Agitation, in the interval, certainly had held me and driven me, for I must, in circling about the place, have walked three miles; but I was to be, later on, so much more overwhelmed that this mere dawn of alarm was a comparatively human chill. The most singular part of it in fact—singular as the rest had been—was the part I became, in the hall, aware of in meeting Mrs Grose. This picture comes back to me in the general train—the impression, as I received it on my return, of the wide white panelled space, bright in the lamplight and with its portraits and red carpet, and of the good surprised look of my friend, which immediately told me she had missed me. It came to me straightway, under her contact, that, with plain heartiness, mere relieved anxiety at my appearance, she knew nothing whatever that could bear upon the incident I had there ready for her. I had not suspected in advance that her comfortable face would pull me up, and I somehow measured the importance of what I had seen by my thus finding myself hesitate to mention it. Scarce anything in the whole history seems to me so odd as this fact that my real beginning of fear was one, as I may say, with the instinct of sparing my companion. On the spot, accordingly, in the pleasant hall and with her eyes on me, I, for a reason that I couldn't then have phrased, achieved an inward revolution—offered a vague pretext for my lateness and, with the plea of the beauty of the night and of the heavy dew and wet feet, went as soon as possible to my room.

Here it was another affair; here, for many days after, it was a queer affair enough. There were hours, from day to day—or at least there were moments, snatched even from clear duties—when I had to shut myself up to think. It was not so much yet that I was more nervous than I could bear to be as that I was remarkably afraid of becoming so; for the trust I had now to turn over was, simply and clearly, the truth that I could arrive at no account whatever of the visitor with whom I had been so inexplicably and yet, as it seemed to me, so intimately concerned. It took little time to see that I could sound without forms of inquiry and without exciting remark any domestic complication. The shock I had suffered must have sharpened all my senses; I felt sure, at the end of three days and as the result of mere closer attention, that I had not been practised upon by the servants nor made the object of any 'game'. Of whatever it was that I knew nothing was known around me. There was but one sane inference: someone had taken a liberty rather gross. That was what, repeatedly, I dipped into my room and locked the door to say to myself. We had been, collectively, subject to an intrusion; some unscrupulous traveller, curious in old houses, had made his way in unobserved, enjoyed the prospect from the best point of view and then stolen out as he came. If he had given me such a bold hard stare, that was but a part of his indiscretion. The good thing, after all, was that we should surely see no more of him.

This was not so good a thing, I admit, as not to leave me to judge that what, essentially, made nothing else much signify was simply my charming work. My charming work was just my life with Miles and Flora, and through nothing could I so like it as through feeling that I could throw myself into it in trouble. The attraction of my small charges was a constant joy, leading me to wonder afresh at the vanity of my original fears, the distaste I had begun by entertaining for the probable grey prose of my office. There was to be no grey prose, it appeared, and no long grind; so how could work not be charming that presented itself as daily beauty? It was all the romance of the nursery and the poetry of the schoolroom. I don't mean by this, of course, that we studied only fiction and verse; I mean I can express no otherwise the sort of interest my companions inspired. How can I describe that except by saying that instead of growing used to them—and it's a marvel for a governess: I call the sisterhood to witness!—I made constant fresh discoveries. There was one direction, assuredly, in which these discoveries stopped: deep obscurity continued to cover the region of the boy's conduct at school. It had been promptly given me, I have noted, to face that mystery without a pang. Perhaps even it would be nearer the truth to say that—without a word—he himself had cleared it up. He had made the whole charge absurd.

My conclusion bloomed there with the real rose-flush of his innocence: he was only too fine and fair for the little horrid, unclean school world, and he had paid a price for it. I reflected acutely that the sense of such differences, such superiorities of quality, always, on the part of the majority–which could include even stupid, sordid head-masters–turns infallibly to the vindictive.

Both the children had a gentleness (it was their only fault, and it never made Miles a muff) that kept them–how shall I express it?–almost impersonal and certainly quite unpunishable. They were like cherubs of the anecdote, who had–morally at any rate–nothing to whack! I remember feeling with Miles in especial as if he had had, as it were, no history. We expect of a small child a scant one, but there was in this beautiful little boy something extraordinarily sensitive, yet extraordinarily happy, that, more than in any creature of his age I have seen, struck me as beginning anew each day. He had never for a second suffered. I took this as a direct disproof of his having really been chastised. If he had been wicked he would have 'caught' it, and I should have caught it by the rebound–I should have found the trace. I found nothing at all, and he was therefore an angel. He never spoke of his school, never mentioned a comrade or a master; and I, for my part, was quite too much disgusted to allude to them. Of course I was under the spell, and the wonderful part is that, even at the time, I perfectly knew I was. But I gave myself up to it; it was an antidote to any pain, and I had more pains than one. I was in receipt in these days of disturbing letters from home, where things were not going well. But with my children, what things in the world mattered? That was the question I used to put to my scrappy retirements. I was dazzled by their loveliness.

There was a Sunday–to get on–when it rained with such force and for so many hours that there could be no procession to church; in consequence of which, as the day declined, I had arranged with Mrs Grose that, should the evening show improvement, we would attend together the late service. The rain happily stopped, and I prepared for our walk, which, through the park and by the good road to the village, would be a matter of twenty minutes. Coming down stairs to meet my colleague in the hall, I remembered a pair of gloves that had required three stitches and that had received them–with a publicity perhaps not edifying–while I sat with the children at their tea, served on Sundays, by exception, in that cold, clean temple of mahogany and brass, the 'grown-up' dining-room. The gloves had been dropped there, and I turned to recover them. The day was grey enough, but the afternoon light still lingered, and it enabled me, on crossing the threshold, not only to recognize, on a chair near the wide window, then closed, the articles I wanted, but to become aware of a person on the other side of the window and looking straight in. One step into the room had sufficed; my vision was instantaneous; it was all there. The person looking straight in was the person who had already appeared to me. He appeared thus again with I won't say greater distinctness, for that was impossible, but with a nearness that represented a forward stride in our intercourse and made me, as I met him, catch my breath and turn cold. He was the same—he was the same, and seen, this time, as he had been seen before, from the waist up, the window, though the dining-room was on the ground floor, not going down to the terrace on which he stood. His face was close to the glass, yet the effect of this better view was, strangely, only to show me how intense the former had been. He remained but a few seconds—long enough to convince me he also saw and recognized; but it was as if I had been looking at him for years and had known him always. Something, however, happened this time that had not happened before; his stare into my face, through the glass and across the room, was as deep and hard as then, but it quitted me for a moment during which I could still watch it, see it fix successively several other things. On the spot there came to me the added shock of a certitude that it was not for me he had come there. He had come for someone else.

The flash of this knowledge—for it was knowledge in the midst of dread—produced in me the most extraordinary effect, started, as I stood there, a sudden vibration of duty and courage. I say courage because I was beyond all doubt already far gone. I bounded straight out of the door again, reached that of the house, got, in an instant, upon the drive, and, passing along the terrace as fast as I could rush, turned a corner and came full in sight. But it was in sight of nothing now—my visitor had vanished. I stopped, I almost dropped, with the real relief of this; but I took in the whole scene—I gave him time to reappear. I call it time, but how long was it? I can't speak to the purpose today of the duration of these things. That kind of measure must have left me: they couldn't have lasted as they actually appeared to me to last. The terrace and the whole place, the lawn and the garden beyond it, all I could see of the park, were empty with a great emptiness. There were shrubberies and big trees, but I remember the clear assurance I felt that none of them concealed him. He was there or was not there: not there if I didn't see him. I got hold of this; then, instinctively, instead of returning as I had come, went to the window. It was confusedly present to me that I ought to place myself where he had stood. I did so; I applied my face to the pane and looked, as he had looked, into the room. As if, at this moment, to show me exactly what his range had been, Mrs Grose, as I had done for himself just before, came in from the hall. With this I had the full image of a repetition of what had already occurred. She saw me as I had seen my own visitant; she pulled up short as I had done; I gave her something of the shock that I had received. She turned white, and this made me ask myself if I had blanched as much. She stared, in short, and retreated on just *my* lines, and I knew she had then passed out and come round to me and that I should presently meet her. I remained where I was, and while I waited I thought of more things than one. But there's only one I take space to mention. I wondered why *she* should be scared.

5

Oh, she let me know as soon as, round the corner of the house, she loomed again into view. 'What in the name of goodness is the matter–?' She was now flushed and out of breath.

I said nothing till she came quite near. 'With me?' I must have made a wonderful face. 'Do I show it?'

'You're as white as a sheet. You look awful.'

I considered; I could meet on this, without scruple, any innocence. My need to respect the bloom of Mrs Grose's had dropped, without a rustle from my shoulders, and if I wavered for the instant it was not with what I kept back. I put out my hand to her and she took it; I held her hard a little, liking to feel her close to me. There was a kind of support in the shy heave of her surprise. 'You came for me for church, of course, but I can't go.'

'Has anything happened?'

'Yes. You must know now. Did I look very queer?'

'Through this window? Dreadful!'

'Well,' I said, 'I've been frightened.' Mrs Grose's eyes expressed plainly that *she* had no wish to be, yet also that she knew too well her place not to be ready to share with me any marked inconvenience. Oh, it was quite settled that she *must* share! 'Just what you saw from the dining-room a minute ago was the effect of that. What *I* saw–just before–was much worse.'

Her hand tightened. 'What was it?'

'An extraordinary man. Looking in.'

'What extraordinary man?'

'I haven't the least idea.'

Mrs Grose gazed round us in vain. 'Then where is he gone?'

'I know still less.'

'Have you seen him before?'

'Yes–once. On the old tower.'

She could only look at me harder. 'Do you mean he's a stranger?'

'Oh, very much!'

'Yet you didn't tell me?'

'No–for reasons. But now that you've guessed–'

Mrs Grose's round eyes encountered this charge. 'Ah, I haven't guessed!' she said very simply. 'How can I if *you* don't imagine?'

'I don't in the very least.'

'You've seen him nowhere but on the tower?'

'And on this spot just now.'

Mrs Grose looked round again. 'What was he doing on the tower?'

'Only standing there and looking down at me'.

She thought a minute. 'Was he a gentleman?'

I found I had no need to think. 'No.' She gazed in deeper wonder. 'No.'

'Then nobody about the place? Nobody from the village?'

'Nobody–nobody. I didn't tell you, but I made sure.'

She breathed a vague relief: this was, oddly, so much to the good. It only went indeed a little way. 'But if he isn't a gentleman–'

'What *is* he? He's a horror.'

'A horror?'

'He's–God help me if I know *what* he is!'

Mrs Grose looked round once more; she fixed her eyes on the duskier distance, then, pulling herself together, turned to me with abrupt inconsequence. 'It's time we should be at church.'

'Oh, I'm not fit for church.'

'Won't it do you good?'

'It won't do *them*–!' I nodded at the house.

'The children?'

'I can't leave them now.'

'You're afraid–?'

I spoke boldly, 'I'm afraid of *him*.'

Mrs Grose's large face showed me, at this, for the first time, the far-away faint glimmer of a consciousness more acute: I somehow made out in it the delayed dawn of an idea I myself had not given her and that was as yet quite obscure to me. It comes back to me that I thought instantly of this as something I could get from her; and I felt it to be connected with the desire she presently showed to know more. 'When was it–on the tower?'

'About the middle of the month. At this same hour.'

'Almost at dark,' said Mrs Grose.

'Oh no, not nearly. I saw him as I see you.'

'Then how did he get in?'

'And how did he get out?' I laughed. 'I had no opportunity to ask him! This evening, you see,' I pursued, 'he has not been able to get in.'

'He only peeps?'

'I hope it will be confined to that!' She had now let go my hand; she turned away a little. I waited an instant; then I brought out: 'Go to church. Goodbye. I must watch.'

Slowly she faced me again. 'Do you fear for them?'

We met in another long look. 'Don't *you*?' Instead of answering she came nearer to the window and, for a minute, applied her face to the glass. 'You see how he could see,' I meanwhile went on.

She didn't move. 'How long was he here?'

'Till I came out. I came to meet him.'

Mrs Grose at last turned round, and there was still more in her face. '*I* couldn't have come out.'

'Neither could I!' I laughed again. 'But I did come. I have my duty.'

'So have I mine,' she replied; after, which she added: 'What is he like?'

'I've been dying to tell you. But he's like nobody.'

'Nobody?' she echoed.

'He has no hat.' Then seeing in her face that she already, in this, with a deeper dismay, found a touch of picture, I quickly added stroke to stroke. 'He has red hair, very red, close-curling, and a pale face, long in shape, with straight, good features and little, rather queer whiskers that are as red as his hair. His eyebrows are, somehow, darker; they look particularly arched and as if they might move a good deal. His eyes are sharp, strange–awfully, but I only know clearly that they're rather small and very fixed. His mouth's wide, and his lips are thin, and except for his little whiskers he's quite clean-shaven. He gives me a sort of sense of looking like an actor.'

'An actor!' It was impossible to resemble one less, at least, than Mrs Grose at that moment.

'I've never seen one, but so I suppose them. He's tall, active, erect,' I continued, 'but never–no, never!–a gentleman.'

My companion's face had blanched as I went on; her round eyes started and her mild mouth gaped. 'A gentleman?' she gasped, confounded, stupefied, 'a gentleman *he*?'

'You know him then?'

She visibly tried to hold herself. 'But he *is* handsome?'

I saw the way to help her. 'Remarkably!'

'And dressed–?'

'In somebody's clothes. They're smart, but they're not his own.'

She broke into a breathless affirmative groan. 'They're the master's!'

I caught it up. 'You *do* know him?'

She faltered but a second. 'Quint!' she cried.

'Quint?'

'Peter Quint–his own man, his valet, when he was here!'

'When the master was?'

Gaping still, but meeting me, she pieced it all together. 'He never wore his hat, but he did wear–well, there were waistcoats missed! They were both here–last year. Then the master went, and Quint was alone.'

I followed, but halting a little. 'Alone?'

'Alone with *us*.' Then, as from a deeper depth, 'In charge,' she added.

'And what became of him?'

She hung fire so long that I was still more mystified. 'He went too,' she brought out at last.

'Went where?'

Her expression, at this, became extraordinary. 'God knows where! He died.'

'Died?' I almost shrieked.

She seemed fairly to square herself, plant herself more firmly to utter the wonder of it. 'Yes. Mr Quint is dead.'

6

It took of course more than that particular passage to place us together in presence of what we had now to live with as we could–my dreadful liability to impressions of the order so vividly exemplified, and my companion's knowledge, henceforth–a knowledge half consternation and half compassion–of that liability. There had been, this evening, after the revelation that left me, for an hour, so prostrate–there had been, for either of us, no attendance on any service but a little service of tears and vows, of prayers and promises, a climax to the series of mutual challenges and pledges that had straightway ensued on our retreating together to the schoolroom and shutting ourselves up there to have everything out. The result of our having everything out was simply to reduce our situation to the last rigour of its elements. She herself had seen nothing, not the shadow of a shadow, and nobody in the house but the governess was in the governess's plight; yet she accepted without directly impugning my sanity the truth as I gave it to her, and ended by showing me, on this ground, an awe-stricken tenderness, an expression of the sense of my more than questionable privilege, of which the very breath has remained with me as that of the sweetest of human charities.

What was settled between us, accordingly, that night, was that we thought we might bear things together; and I was not even sure that, in spite of her exemption, it was she who had the best of the burden. I knew at this hour, I think, as well as I knew later what I was capable of meeting to shelter my pupils; but it took me some time to be wholly sure of what my honest ally was prepared for to keep terms with so compromising a contract. I was queer company enough–quite as queer as the company I received; but as I trace over what we went through I see how much common ground we must have found in the one idea that, by good fortune, *could* steady us. It was the idea, the second movement, that led me straight out, as I may say, of the inner chamber of my dread. I could take the air in the court, at least, and there Mrs Grose could join me. Perfectly can I recall now the particular way strength came to me before we separated for the night. We had gone over and over every feature of what I had seen.

'He was looking for someone else, you say–someone who was not you?'

'He was looking for little Miles.' A portentous clearness now possessed me. '*That's* whom he was looking for.'

'But how do you know?'

'I know, I know, I know!' My exaltation grew. 'And *you* know, my dear!'

She didn't deny this, but I required, I felt, not even so much telling as that. She resumed in a moment, at any rate: 'What if *he* should see him?'

'Little Miles? That's what he wants!'

She looked immensely scared again. 'The child?'

'Heaven forbid! The man. He wants to appear to *them*.' That he might was an awful conception, and yet, somehow, I could keep at bay; which, moreover, as we lingered there, was what I succeeded in practically proving. I had an absolute certainty that I should see again what I had already seen, but something within me said that by offering myself bravely as the sole subject of such experience, by accepting, by inviting, by surmounting it all, I should serve as an expiatory victim and guard the tranquillity of my companions. The children, in especial, I should thus fence about and absolutely save. I recall one of the last things I said that night to Mrs Grose.

'It does strike me that my pupils have never mentioned–'

She looked at me hard as I musingly pulled up. 'His having been here and the time they were with him?'

'The time they were with him, and his name, his presence, his history, in any way.'

'Oh, the little lady doesn't remember. She never heard or knew.'

'The circumstances of his death?' I thought with some intensity. 'Perhaps not. But Miles would remember–Miles would know.'

'Ah, don't try him!' broke from Mrs Grose.

I returned her the look she had given me. 'Don't be afraid.' I continued to think. 'It *is* rather odd.'

'That he has never spoken of him?'

'Never by the least allusion. And you tell me they were "great friends"?'

'Oh, it wasn't *him*!' Mrs Grose with emphasis declared. 'It was Quint's own fancy. To play with him, I mean–to spoil him.' She paused a moment, then she added: 'Quint was much too free.'

This gave me, straight from my vision of his face–*such* a face!–a sudden sickness of disgust. 'Too free with *my* boy?'

'Too free with everyone!'

I forebore, for the moment, to analyse this description further than by the reflection that a part of it applied to several of the members of the household, of the half-dozen maids and men who were still of our small colony. But there was everything, for our apprehension, in the lucky fact that no discomfortable legend, no perturbation of scullions, had ever, within anyone's memory, attached to the kind old place. It had neither bad name nor ill fame, and Mrs Grose, most apparently, only desired to cling to me and to quake in silence. I even put her, the very last thing of all, to the test. It was when, at midnight, she had her hand on the schoolroom door to take her leave. 'I have it from you then—for it's of great importance—that he was definitely and admittedly bad?'

'Oh, not admittedly. *I* knew it—but the master didn't.'

'And you never told him?'

'Well, he didn't like tale-bearing—he hated complaints. He was terribly short with anything of that kind, and if people were all right to *him*—'

'He wouldn't be bothered with more?' This squared well enough with my impression of him: he was not a trouble-loving gentleman, nor so very particular perhaps about some of the company *he* kept. All the same, I pressed my interlocutress. 'I promise you *I* would have told!'

She felt my discrimination. 'I dare say I was wrong. But, really, I was afraid.

'Afraid of what?'

'Of things that man could do. Quint was so clever—he was so deep.'

I took this in still more than, probably, I showed. 'You weren't afraid of anything else? Not of his effect—?'

'His effect?' she repeated with a face of anguish and waiting while I faltered.

'On innocent little precious lives. They were in your charge.'

'No, they were not in mine!' she roundly and distressfully returned. 'The master believed in him and placed him here because he was supposed not to be well and the country air so good for him. So he had everything to say. Yes'—she let me have it—'even about *them*.'

'Them—that creature?' I had to smother a kind of howl. 'And you could bear it?'

'No. I couldn't—and I can't now!' And the poor woman burst into tears.

A rigid control, from the next day, was, as I have said, to follow them; yet how often and how passionately, for a week, we came back together to the subject! Much as we had discussed it that Sunday night, I was, in the immediate later hours in especial—for it may be imagined whether I slept—still haunted with the shadow of something she had not told me. I myself had kept back nothing, but there was a word Mrs Grose had kept back. I was sure, moreover, by morning, that this was not from a failure of frankness, but because on every side there were fears. It seems to me indeed, in retrospect, that by the time the morrow's sun was high I had restlessly read into the facts before us almost all the meaning they were to receive from subsequent and more cruel occurrences. What they gave me above all was just the sinister figure of the living man—the dead one would keep a while!—and of the months he had continuously passed at Bly, which, added up, made a formidable stretch. The limit of this evil time had arrived only when, on the dawn of a winter's morning, Peter Quint was found, by a labourer going to early work, stone dead on the road from the village—a catastrophe explained—superficially at least—by a visible wound to his head; such a wound as might have been produced—and as, on the final evidence, *had* been—by a fatal slip, in the dark and after leaving the public-house, on the steepish icy slope, a wrong path altogether, at the bottom of which he lay. The icy slope, the turn mistaken at night and in liquor, accounted for much—practically, in the end and after the inquest and boundless chatter, for everything; but there had been matters in his life—strange passages and perils, secret disorders, vices more than suspected—that would have accounted for a good deal more.

I scarce know how to put my story into words that shall be a credible picture of my state of mind; but I was in these days literally able to find a joy in the extraordinary flight of heroism the occasion demanded of me. I now saw that I had been asked for a service admirable and difficult; and there would be a greatness in letting it be seen—oh, in the right quarter!—that I could succeed where many another girl might have failed. It was an immense help to me—I confess I rather applaud myself as I look back!—that I saw my service so strongly and so simply. I was there to protect and defend the little creatures in the world the most bereaved and the most lovable, the appeal of whose helplessness had suddenly become only too explicit, a deep, constant ache of one's own committed heart. We were cut off, really, together; we were united in our danger. They had nothing but me, and I—well, I had *them*. It was in short a magnificent chance. This chance presented itself to me in an image richly material. I was a screen—I was to stand before them. The more I saw, the less they would. I began to watch them in a stifled suspense, a disguised excitement that might well, had it continued too long, have turned to something like madness. What saved me, as I now see, was that it turned to something else altogether. It didn't last as suspense—it was superseded by horrible proofs. Proofs, I say, yes—from the moment I really took hold.

This moment dated from an afternoon hour that I happened to spend in the grounds with the younger of my pupils alone. We had left Miles indoors, on the red cushion of a deep window-seat; he had wished to finish a book, and I had been glad to encourage a purpose so laudable in a young man whose only defect was an occasional excess of the restless. His sister, on the contrary, had been alert to come out, and I strolled with her half an hour, seeking the shade, for the sun was still high and the day exceptionally warm. I was aware afresh, with her, as we went, of how, like her brother, she contrived—it was the charming thing in both children—to let me alone without appearing to drop me and to accompany me without appearing to surround. They were never importunate and yet never listless. My attention to them all really went to seeing them amuse themselves immensely without me: this was a spectacle they seemed actively to prepare and that engaged me as an active admirer. I walked in a world of their invention—they had no occasion whatever to draw upon mine; so that my time was taken only with being, for them, some remarkable person or thing that the game of the moment required and that was merely, thanks to my superior, my exalted stamp, a happy and highly distinguished sinecure. I forget what I was on the present occasion; I only remember that I was something very important and very quiet and that Flora was playing very hard. We were on the edge of the lake, and, as we had lately begun geography, the lake was the Sea of Azof.

Suddenly, in these circumstances, I became aware that, on the other side of the Sea of Azof, we had an interested spectator. The way this knowledge gathered in me was the strangest thing in the world—the strangest, that is, except the very much stranger in which it quickly merged itself. I had sat down with a piece of work—for I was something or other that could sit—on the old stone bench which overlooked the pond; and in this position I began to take in with certitude, and yet without direct vision, the presence, at a distance, of a third person. The old trees, the thick shrubbery, made a great and pleasant shade, but it was all suffused with the brightness of the hot, still hour. There was no ambiguity in anything; none whatever, at least in the conviction I from one moment to another found myself forming as to what I should see straight before me and across the lake as a consequence of raising my eyes. They were attached at this juncture to the stitching in which I was engaged, and I can feel once more the spasm of my effort not to move them till I should so have steadied myself as to be able to make up my mind what to do. There was an alien object in view—a figure whose right of presence I instantly, passionately questioned. I recollect counting over perfectly the possibilities, reminding myself that nothing was more natural, for instance, than the appearance of one of the men about the place, or even of a messenger, a postman or a tradesman's boy, from the village. That reminder had as little effect on my practical certitude as I was conscious—still even without looking—of its having upon the character and attitude of our visitor. Nothing was more natural than that these things should be the other things that they absolutely were not.

Of the positive identity of the apparition I would assure myself as soon as the small clock of my courage should have ticked out the right second; meanwhile, with an effort that was already sharp enough, I transferred my eyes straight to little Flora, who, at the moment, was about ten yards away. My heart had stood still for an instant with the wonder and terror of the question whether she too would see; and I held my breath while I waited for what a cry from her, what some sudden innocent sign either of interest or of alarm, would tell me. I waited, but nothing came; then, in the first place—and there is something more dire in this, I feel, than in anything I have to relate—I was determined by a sense that, within a minute, all sounds from her had previously dropped; and, in the second, by the circumstance that, also within the minute, she had, in her play, turned her back to the water. This was her attitude when I at last looked at her–looked with the confirmed conviction that we were still, together, under direct personal notice. She had picked up a small flat piece of wood, which happened to have in it a little hole that had evidently suggested to her the idea of sticking in another fragment that might figure as a mast and make the thing a boat. This second morsel, as I watched her, she was very markedly and intently attempting to tighten in its place. My apprehension of what she was doing sustained me so that after some seconds I felt I was ready for more. Then I again shifted my eyes–I faced what I had to face.

7

I got hold of Mrs Grose as soon after this as I could; and I can give no intelligible account of how I fought out the interval. Yet I still hear myself cry as I fairly threw myself into her arms: 'They *know*–it's too monstrous: they know, they know!'

'And what on earth–?' I felt her incredulity as she held me.

'Why, all that *we* know–and heaven knows what else besides!' Then, as she released me, I made it out to her, made it out perhaps only now with full coherency even to myself. 'Two hours ago, in the garden'–I could scarce articulate–'Flora *saw*!'

Mrs Grose took it as she might have taken a blow to the stomach. 'She has told you?' she panted.

'Not a word–that's the horror. She kept it to herself! the child of eight, *that* child!' Unutterable still, for me, was the stupefaction of it.

Mrs Grose, of course, could only gape the wider. 'Then how do you know?'

'I was there–I saw with my eyes: saw that she was perfectly aware.'

'Do you mean aware of *him*?'

'No–of *her*.' I was conscious as I spoke that I looked prodigious things for I got the slow reflection of them in my companion's face. 'Another person–this time; but a figure of quite unmistakable horror and evil: a woman in black, pale and dreadful–with such an air also, and such a face!–on the other side of the lake. I was there with the child–quiet for the hour, and in the midst of it she came.'

'Came how–from where?'

'From where they come from! she just appeared and stood there–but not so near.'

'And without coming nearer?'

'Oh, for the effect and the feeling, she might have been as close as you!'

My friend, with an odd impulse, fell back a step. 'Was she someone you've never seen?'

'Yes. But someone the child has. Someone you have.' Then, to show how I had thought it all out: 'My predecessor–the one who died.'

'Miss Jessel?'

'Miss Jessel. You don't believe me?' I pressed.

She turned right and left in her distress. 'How can you be sure?'

This drew from me, in the state of my nerves, a flash of impatience. 'Then ask Flora–*she's* sure!' But I had no sooner spoken than I caught myself up. 'No, for God's sake, *don't*! She'll say she isn't–she'll lie!'

Mrs Grose was not too bewildered instinctively to protest. 'Ah, how *can* you?'

'Because I'm clear. Flora doesn't want me to know.'

'It's only then to spare you.'

'No, no–there are depths, depths! The more I go over it, the more I see in it, and the more I see in it the more I fear. I don't know what I *don't* see–what I *don't* fear!'

Mrs Grose tried to keep up with me. 'You mean you're afraid of seeing her again?'

'Oh no; that's nothing–now!' Then I explained. 'It's of *not* seeing her.'

But my companion only looked wan. 'I don't understand you.'

'Why, it's that the child may keep it up–and that the child assuredly *will*–without my knowing it.'

At the image of this possibility Mrs Grose for a moment collapsed, yet presently to pull herself together again, as if from the positive force of the sense of what, should we yield an inch, there would really be to give way to. 'Dear, dear–we must keep our heads! And after all, if she doesn't mind it–!' She even tried a grim joke. 'Perhaps she likes it!'

'Likes *such* things–a scrap of an infant!'

'Isn't it just a proof of her blessed innocence?' my friend bravely inquired.

She brought me, for the instant, almost round. 'Oh, we must clutch at *that*–we must cling to it! If it isn't a proof of what you say, it's a proof of–God knows what! For the woman's a horror of horrors.'

Mrs Grose, at this, fixed her eyes a minute on the ground; then at last raising them, 'Tell me how you know,' she said.

'Then you admit it's what she was?' I cried.

'Tell me how you know,' my friend simply repeated.

'Know? By seeing her! By the way she looked.'

'At you, do you mean–so wickedly?'

'Dear me, no–I could have borne that. She gave me never a glance. She only fixed the child.'

Mrs Grose tried to see it. 'Fixed her?'

'Ah, with such awful eyes!'

She stared at mine as if they might really have resembled them. 'Do you mean of dislike?'

'God help us, no. Of something much worse.'

'Worse than dislike?'—this left her indeed at a loss.

'With a determination—indescribable. With a kind of fury of intention.'

I made her turn pale. 'Intention?'

'To get hold of her.' Mrs Grose—her eyes just lingering on mine—gave a shudder and walked to the window; and while she stood there looking out I completed my statement. '*That's* what Flora knows.'

After a little she turned round. 'The person was in black, you say?'

'In mourning—rather poor, almost shabby. But—yes—with extraordinary beauty.' I now recognized to what I had at last, stroke by stroke, brought the victim of my confidence, for she quite visibly weighed this. 'Oh, handsome—very, very,' I insisted; 'wonderfully handsome. But infamous.'

She slowly came back to me. 'Miss Jessel—*was* infamous.' She once more took my hand in both her own, holding it as tight as if to fortify me against the increase of alarm I might draw from this disclosure. 'They were both infamous,' she finally said.

So, for a little, we faced it once more together; and I found absolutely a degree of help in seeing it now so straight. 'I appreciate,' I said, 'the great decency of your not having hitherto spoken; but the time has certainly come to give me the whole thing.' She appeared to assent to this, but still only in silence; seeing which I went on: 'I must have it now. Of what did she die? Come, there was something between them.'

'There was everything.'

'In spite of the difference—?'

'Oh, of their rank, their condition'—she brought it woefully out. '*She* was a lady.'

I turned it over; I again saw. 'Yes—she was a lady.'

'And he so dreadfully below,' said Mrs Grose.

I felt that I doubtless needn't press too hard, in such company, on the place of a servant in the scale; but there was nothing to prevent an acceptance of my companion's own measure of my predecessor's abasement. There was a way to deal with that, and I dealt; the more readily for my full vision—on the evidence—of our employer's late clever, good-looking 'own' man; impudent, assured, spoiled, depraved. 'The fellow was a hound.'

Mrs Grose considered as if it were perhaps a little a case for a sense of shades. 'I've never seen one like him. He did what he wished.'

'With *her*?'

'With them all.'

It was as if now in my friend's own eyes Miss Jessel had again appeared. I seemed at any rate, for an instant, to see their evocation of her as distinctly as I had seen her by the pond; and I brought out with decision: 'It must have been also what *she* wished!'

Mrs Grose's face signified that it had been indeed, but she said at the same time: 'Poor woman–she paid for it!'

'Then you do know what she died of?' I asked.

'No–I know nothing. I wanted not to know; I was glad enough I didn't and I thanked heaven she was well out of this!'

'Yet you had, then, your idea–'

'Of her real reason for leaving? Oh yes–as to that. She couldn't have stayed. Fancy it here–for a governess! And afterwards I imagined–and I still imagine. And what I imagine is dreadful.'

'Not so dreadful as what I do,' I replied; on which I must have shown her–as I was indeed but too conscious–a front of miserable defeat. It brought out again all her compassion for me, and at the renewed touch of her kindness my power to resist broke down. I burst, as I had, the other time, made her burst, into tears; she took me to her motherly breast, and my lamentation overflowed. 'I don't do it!' I sobbed in despair; 'I don't save or shield them! It's far worse than I dreamed–they're lost!'

8

What I had said to Mrs Grose was true enough: there were in the matter I had put before her depths and possibilities that I lacked resolution to sound; so that when we met once more in the wonder of it we were of a common mind about the duty of resistance to extravagant fancies. We were to keep our heads if we should keep nothing else–difficult indeed as that might be in the face of what, in our prodigious experience, was least to be questioned. Late that night, while the house slept, we had another talk in my room; when she went all the way with me as to its being beyond doubt that I had seen exactly what I had seen. To hold her perfectly in the pinch of that, I found, I had only to ask her how, if I had 'made it up', I came to be able to give, of each of the persons appearing to me, a picture disclosing, to the last detail, their special marks–a portrait on the exhibition of which she had instantly recognized and named them. She wished, of course–small blame to her!–to sink the whole subject; and I was quick to assure her that my own interest in it had now violently taken the form of a search for the way to escape from it. I encountered her on the ground of a probability that with recurrence–for recurrence we took for granted–I should get used to my danger; distinctly professing that my personal exposure had suddenly become the least of my discomforts. It was my new suspicion that was intolerable; and yet even to this complication the later hours of the day had brought a little ease.

On leaving her, after my first outbreak, I had of course returned to my pupils, associating the right remedy for my dismay with the sense of their charm which I had already found to be a thing I could positively cultivate and which had never failed me yet. I had simply, in other words, plunged afresh into Flora's special society and there become aware–it was almost a luxury!–that she could put her little conscious hand straight upon the spot that ached. She had looked at me in sweet speculation and then had accused me to my face of having 'cried'. I had supposed I had brushed away the ugly signs; but I could literally–for the time, at all events–rejoice, under this fathomless charity, that they had not entirely disappeared. To gaze into the depths of blue of the child's eyes and pronounce their loveliness a trick of premature cunning was to be guilty of a cynicism in preference to which I naturally preferred to abjure my judgement and, so far as might be, my agitation. I couldn't abjure for merely wanting to, but I could repeat to Mrs Grose–as I did there, over and over, in the small hours–that with their voices in the air, their pressure on one's heart and their fragrant faces against one's cheek, everything fell to the ground but their incapacity and their beauty. It was a pity that, somehow, to settle this once for all, I had equally to re-enumerate the signs of subtlety that, in the afternoon, by the lake, had made a miracle of my show of self-possession. It was a pity to be obliged to re-investigate the certitude of the moment itself and repeat how it had come to me as a revelation that the inconceivable communion I then surprised was a matter, for either party, of habit. It was a pity that I should have had to quaver out again the reasons for my not having, in my delusion, so much as questioned that the little girl saw our visitant even as I actually saw Mrs Grose herself, and that she wanted, by just so much as she did thus see, to make me suppose she didn't, and at the same time, without showing anything, arrive at a guess as to whether I myself did! It was a pity that I needed once more to describe the portentous little activity by which she sought to divert my attention–the perceptible increase of movement, the greater intensity of play, the singing, the gabbling, of nonsense and the invitation to romp.

Yet if I had not indulged, to prove there was nothing in it, in this review, I should have missed the two or three dim elements of comfort that still remained to me. I should not for instance have been able to asseverate to my friend that I was certain–which was so much to the good–that *I* at least had not betrayed myself. I should not have been prompted, by stress of need, by desperation of mind–I scarce know what to call it–to invoke such further aid to intelligence as might spring from pushing my colleague fairly to the wall. She had told me, bit by bit, under pressure, a great deal; but a small shifty spot on the wrong side of it all still sometimes brushed my brow like the wing of a bat; and I remember how on this occasion–for the sleeping house and the concentration alike of our danger and our watch seemed to help–I felt the importance of giving the last jerk to the curtain. 'I don't believe anything so horrible,' I recollect saying; 'no, let us put it definitely, my dear, that I don't. But if I did, you know, there's a thing I should require now, just without sparing you the least bit more–oh, not a scrap, come!–to get out of you. What was it you had in mind when, in our distress, before Miles came back, over the letter from his school, you said, under my insistence, that you didn't pretend for him that he had not literally *ever* been "bad"? He has *not* literally "ever", in these weeks that I myself have lived with him and so closely watched him; he has been an imperturbable little prodigy of delightful, loveable goodness. Therefore you might perfectly have made the claim for him if you had not, as it happened, seen an exception to take. What was your exception, and to what passage in your personal observation of him did you refer?'

It was a dreadfully austere inquiry, but levity was not our note, and, at any rate, before the grey dawn admonished us to separate I had got my answer. What my friend had had in mind proved to be immensely to the purpose. It was neither more nor less than the circumstance that for a period of several months Quint and the boy had been perpetually together. It was in fact the very appropriate truth that she had ventured to criticize the propriety, to hint at the incongruity, of so close an alliance, and even to go so far on the subject as a frank overture to Miss Jessel. Miss Jessel had, with a most strange manner, requested her to mind her business, and the good woman had, on this, directly approached little Miles. What she had said to him, since I pressed, was that she liked to see young gentlemen not forget their station.

I pressed again, of course, at this. 'You reminded him that Quint was only a base menial?'

'As you might say! And it was his answer, for one thing, that was bad.'

'And for another thing?' I waited. 'He repeated your words to Quint?'

'No, not that. It's just that he *wouldn't*!' she could still impress upon me. 'I was sure, at any rate,' she added, 'that he didn't. But he denied certain occasions.

'What occasions?'

'When they had been about together quite as if Quint were his tutor–and a very grand one–and Miss Jessel only for the little lady. When he had gone off with the fellow, I mean, and spent hours with him.'

'He then prevaricated about it–he said he hadn't?' Her assent was clear enough to cause me to add in a moment: 'I see. He lied.'

'Oh!' Mrs Grose mumbled. This was a suggestion that it didn't matter, which indeed she backed up by a further remark. 'You see, after all, Miss Jessel didn't mind. She didn't forbid him.'

I considered. 'Did he put that to you as a justification?'

At this she dropped again. 'No, he never spoke of it.'

'Never mentioned her in connexion with Quint?'

She saw, visibly flushing, where I was coming out. 'Well, he didn't show anything. He denied,' she repeated; 'he denied.'

Lord, how I pressed her now! 'So that you could see he knew what was between the two wretches?'

'I don't know–I don't know!' the poor woman groaned.

'You do know, you dear thing,' I replied; 'only you haven't my dreadful boldness of mind, and you keep back, out of timidity and modesty and delicacy, even the impression that, in the past, when you had, without my aid, to flounder about in silence, most of all made you miserable. But I shall get it out of you yet! There was something in the boy that suggested to you,' I continued, 'that he covered and concealed their relation.'

'Oh, he couldn't prevent–'

'Your learning the truth? I dare say! But, heavens,' I fell, with vehemence, a-thinking, 'what it shows that they must, to that extent, have succeeded in making of him!'

'Ah, nothing that's not nice *now*!' Mrs Grose lugubriously pleaded.

'I don't wonder you looked queer,' I persisted, 'when I mentioned to you the letter from his school!'

'I doubt if I looked as queer as you!' she retorted with homely force. 'And if he was so bad then as that comes to, how is he such an angel now?'

'Yes indeed–and if he was a fiend at school! How, how, how? Well,' I said in my torment, 'you must put it to me again, but I shall not be able to tell you for some days. Only, put it to me again!' I cried in a way that made my friend stare. 'There are directions in which I must not for the present let myself go.' Meanwhile I returned to her first example–the one to which she had just previously referred–of the boy's happy capacity for an occasional slip. 'If Quint–on your remonstrance at the time you speak of–was a base menial, one of the things Miles said to you, I find myself guessing, was that you were another.' Again her admission was so adequate that I continued: 'And you forgave him that?'

'Wouldn't *you*?'

'Oh yes!' And we exchanged there, in the stillness, a sound of the oddest amusement. Then I went on: 'At all events, while he was with the man–'

'Miss Flora was with the woman. It suited them all!'

It suited me too, I felt, only too well; by which I mean that it suited exactly the particular deadly view I was in the very act of forbidding myself to entertain. But I so far succeeded in checking the expression of this view that I will throw, just here, no further light on it than may be offered by the mention of my final observation to Mrs Grose. 'His having lied and been impudent are, I confess, less engaging specimens than I had hoped to have from you of the outbreak in him of the little natural man. Still,' I mused, 'they must do, for they make me feel more than ever that I must watch.'

It made me blush, the next minute, to see in my friend's face how much more unreservedly she had forgiven him than her anecdote struck me as presenting to my own tenderness an occasion for doing. This came out when, at the schoolroom door, she quitted me. 'Surely you don't accuse *him*–'

'Of carrying on an intercourse that he conceals from me? Ah, remember that, until further evidence, I now accuse nobody.' Then, before shutting her out to go, by another passage, to her own place, 'I must just wait,' I wound up.

9

I waited and waited, and the days, as they elapsed, took something from my consternation. A very few of them, in fact, passing, in constant sight of my pupils, without a fresh incident, sufficed to give to grievous fancies and even to odious memories a kind of brush of the sponge. I have spoken of the surrender to their extraordinary childish grace as a thing I could actively cultivate, and it may be imagined if I neglected now to address myself to this source for whatever it would yield. Stranger than I can express, certainly, was the effort to struggle against my new lights; it would doubtless have been, however, a greater tension still had it not been so frequently successful. I used to wonder how my little charges could help guessing that I thought strange things about them; and the circumstances that these things only made them more interesting was not by itself a direct aid to keeping them in the dark. I trembled lest they should see that they *were* so immensely more interesting. Putting things at the worst, at all events, as in meditation I so often did, any clouding of their innocence could only be–blameless and foredoomed as they were–a reason the more for taking risks. There were moments when, by an irresistible impulse, I found myself catching them up and pressing them to my heart. As soon as I had done so I used to say to myself: 'What will they think of that? Doesn't it betray too much?' It would have been easy to get into a sad, wild tangle about how much I might betray, but the real account, I feel, of the hours of peace that I could still enjoy was that the immediate charm of my companions was a beguilement still effective even under the shadow of the possibility that it was studied. For if it occurred to me that I might occasionally excite suspicion by the little outbreaks of my sharper passion for them, so too I remember wondering if I mightn't see a queerness in the traceable increase of their own demonstrations.

They were at this period extravagantly and preternaturally fond of me, which, after all, I could reflect, was no more than a graceful response in children perpetually bowed over and hugged. The homage of which they were so lavish succeeded, in truth, for my nerves, quite as well as if I never appeared to myself, as I may say, literally to catch them at a purpose in it.

They had never, I think, wanted to do so many things for their poor protectress; I mean–though they got their lessons better and better, which was naturally what would please her most–in the way of diverting, entertaining, surprising her; reading her passages, telling her stories, acting her charades, pouncing out at her, in disguises, as animals and historical characters, and above all astonishing her by the 'pieces' they had secretly got by heart and could interminably recite. I should never get to the bottom–were I to let myself go even now–of the prodigious private commentary, all under still more private correction, with which, in these days, I overscored their full hours. They had shown me from the first a facility for everything, a general faculty which, taking a fresh start, achieved remarkable flights. They got their little tasks as if they loved them, and indulged, from the mere exuberance of the gift, in the most unimposed little miracles of memory. They not only popped out at me as tigers and as Romans, but as Shakespeareans, astronomers and navigators. This was so singularly the case that it had presumably much to do with the fact as to which, at the present day, I am at a loss for a different explanation: I allude to my unnatural composure on the subject of another school for Miles. What I remember is that I was content not, for the time, to open the question, and that contentment must have sprung from the sense of his perpetually striking show of cleverness. He was too clever for a bad governess, for a parson's daughter, to spoil; and the strangest if not the brightest thread in the pensive embroidery I just spoke of was the impression I might have got, if I had dared to work it out, that he was under some influence operating in his small intellectual life as a tremendous incitement.

If it was easy to reflect, however, that such a boy could postpone school, it was at least as marked that for such a boy to have been 'kicked out' by a schoolmaster was a mystification without end. Let me add that in their company now–and I was careful almost never to be out of it–I could follow no scent very far. We lived in a cloud of music and love and success and private theatricals. The musical sense in each of the children was of the quickest, but the elder in especial had a marvellous knack of catching and repeating. The schoolroom piano broke into all gruesome fancies; and when that failed there were confabulations in corners with a sequel of one of them going out in the highest spirits in order to 'come in' as something new. I had had brothers myself, and it was no revelation to me that little girls could be slavish idolaters of little boys. What surpassed everything was that there was a little boy in the world who could have for the inferior age, sex and intelligence so fine a consideration. They were extraordinarily at one, and to say that they never either quarrelled or complained is to make the note of praise coarse for their quality of sweetness. Sometimes indeed, when I dropped into coarseness, I perhaps came across traces of little understandings between them by which one of them should keep me occupied while the other slipped away. There is a *naïf* side, I suppose, in all diplomacy; but if my pupils practised upon me it was surely with the minimum of grossness. It was all in the other quarter that, after a lull, the grossness broke out.

I find that I really hang back; but I must take my plunge. In going on with the record of what was hideous at Bly I not only challenge the most liberal faith—for which I little care; but—and this is another matter—I renew what I myself suffered, I again push my way through it to the end. There came suddenly an hour after which, as I look back, the affair seems to me to have been all pure suffering; but I have at least reached the heart of it, and the straightest road out is doubtless to advance. One evening—with nothing to lead up or to prepare it—I felt the cold touch of the impression that had breathed on me the night of my arrival and which, much lighter then, as I have mentioned, I should probably have made little of in memory had my subsequent sojourn been less agitated. I had not gone to bed; I sat reading by a couple of candles. There was a roomful of old books at Bly—last-century fiction, some of it, which, to the extent of a distinctly deprecated renown, but never to so much as that of a stray specimen, had reached the sequestered home and appealed to the unavowed curiosity of my youth. I remember that the book I had in my hand was Fielding's *Amelia*; also that I was wholly awake. I recall further both a general conviction that it was horribly late and a particular objection to looking at my watch. I figure, finally, that the white curtain draping, in the fashion of those days, the head of Flora's little bed, shrouded, as I had assured myself long before, the perfection of childish rest. I recollect in short that, though I was deeply interested in my author, I found myself, at the turn of a page and with his spell all scattered, looking straight up from him and hard at the door of my room. There was a moment during which I listened, reminded of the faint sense I had had, the first night, of there being something undefinably astir in the house, and noted the soft breath of the open casement just move the half-drawn blind. Then, with all the marks of a deliberation that must have seemed magnificent had there been anyone to admire it, I laid down my book, rose to my feet and, taking a candle, went straight out of the room and, from the passage, on which my light made little impression, noiselessly closed and locked the door.

I can say now neither what determined nor what guided me, but I went straight along the lobby, holding my candle high, till I came within sight of the tall window that presided over the great turn of the staircase. At this point I precipitately found myself aware of three things. They were practically simultaneous, yet they had flashes of succession. My candle, under a bold flourish, went out, and I perceived, by the uncovered window, that the yielding dusk of earliest morning rendered it unnecessary. Without it, the next instant, I saw that there was someone on the stair. I speak of sequences, but I required no lapse of seconds to stiffen myself for a third encounter with Quint. The apparition had reached the landing half way up and was therefore on the spot nearest the window, where, at sight of me, it stopped short and fixed me exactly as it had fixed me from the tower and from the garden. He knew me as well as I knew him; and so, in the cold, faint twilight, with a glimmer in the high glass and another on the polish of the oak stair below, we faced each other in our common intensity. He was absolutely, on this occasion, a living, detestable, dangerous presence. But that was not the wonder of wonders; I reserve this distinction for quite another circumstance: the circumstance that dread had unmistakably quitted me and that there was nothing in me there that didn't meet and measure him.

I had plenty of anguish after that extraordinary moment, but I had, thank God, no terror. And he knew I had not—I found myself at the end of an instant magnificently aware of this. I felt, in a fierce rigour of confidence, that if I stood my ground a minute I should cease—for the time, at least—to have him to reckon with; and during the minute, accordingly, the thing was as human and hideous as a real interview; hideous just because it *was* human, as human as to have met alone, in the small hours, in a sleeping house, some enemy, some adventurer, some criminal. It was the dead silence of our long gaze at such close quarters that gave the whole horror, huge as it was, its only note of the unnatural. If I had met a murderer in such a place and at such an hour we still at least would have spoken. Something would have passed, in life, between us; if nothing had passed one of us would have moved. The moment was so prolonged that it would have taken but little more to make me doubt if even *I* were in life. I can't express what followed it save by saying that the silence itself—which was indeed in a manner an attestation of my strength—became the element into which I saw the figure disappear; in which I definitely saw it turn, as I might have seen the low wretch to which it had once belonged turn on receipt of an order, and pass, with my eyes on the villainous back that no hunch could have more disfigured, straight down the staircase and into the darkness in which the next bend was lost.

10

I remained a while at the top of the stair, but with the effect presently of understanding that when my visitor had gone, he had gone: then I returned to my room. The foremost thing I saw there by the light of the candle I had left burning was that Flora's little bed was empty; and on this I caught my breath with all the terror that, five minutes before, I had been able to resist. I dashed at the place in which I had left her lying and over which (for the small silk counterpane and the sheets were disarranged), the white curtains had been deceivingly pulled forward; then my step, to my unutterable relief, produced an answering sound: I perceived an agitation of the window-blind, and the child, ducking down, emerged rosily from the other side of it. She stood there in so much of her candour and so little of her nightgown, with her pink bare feet and golden glow of her curls. She looked intensely grave, and I had never had such a sense of losing an advantage acquired (the thrill of which had just been prodigious), as on my consciousness that she addressed me with reproach. 'You naughty: where *have* you been?'–instead of challenging her own irregularity I found myself arraigned and explaining. She herself explained, for that matter, with the loveliest, eagerest simplicity. She had known suddenly, as she lay there, that I was out of the room, and had jumped up to see what had become of me. I had dropped, with the joy of her reappearance, back into my chair–feeling then, and then only, a little faint; and she had pattered straight over to me, thrown herself upon my knee, given herself to be held with the flame of the candle full in the wonderful little face that was still flushed with sleep. I remember closing my eyes an instant, yieldingly, consciously, as before the excess of something beautiful that shone out of the blue of her own. 'You were looking for me out of the window?' I said. 'You thought I might be walking in the grounds?'

'Well, you know, I thought someone was'–she never blanched as she smiled out that at me.

O, how I looked at her now! 'And did you see anyone?'

'Ah, *no*!' she returned, almost, with the full privilege of childish inconsequence, resentfully, though with a long sweetness in her little drawl of the negative.

At that moment, in the state of my nerves, I absolutely believed she lied; and if I once more closed my eyes it was before the dazzle of the three or four possible ways in which I might take this up. One of these, for a moment, tempted me with such singular intensity that, to withstand it, I must have gripped my little girl with a spasm that, wonderfully, she submitted to without a cry or a sign of fright. Why not break out at her on the spot and have it all over?–give it to her straight in her lovely little lighted face? 'You see, you see, you *know* that you do and that you already quite suspect I believe it; therefore why not frankly confess it to me, so that we may at least live with it together and learn perhaps, in the strangeness of our fate, where we are and what it means?' This solicitation dropped, alas, as it came: if I could immediately have succumbed to it I might have spared myself–well, you'll see what. Instead of succumbing I sprang again to my feet, looked at her bed and took a helpless middle way. 'Why did you pull the curtain over the place to make me think you were still there?'

Flora luminously considered; after which, with her little divine smile: 'Because I don't like to frighten you!'

'But if I had, by your idea, gone out–?'

She absolutely declined to be puzzled; she turned her eyes to the flame of the candle as if the question were as irrelevant, or at any rate as impersonal, as Mrs Marcet or nine-times-nine. 'Oh, but you know,' she quite adequately answered, 'that you might come back, you dear, and that you *have*!' And after a little, when she had got into bed, I had, for a long time, by almost sitting on her to hold her hand, to prove that I recognized the pertinence of my return.

You may imagine the general complexion, from that moment, of my nights. I repeatedly sat up till I didn't know when; I selected moments when my room-mate unmistakably slept, and, stealing out, took noiseless turns in the passage and even pushed as far as to where I had last met Quint. But I never met him there again; and I may as well say at once that I on no other occasion saw him in the house. I just missed, on the staricase, on the other hand, a different adventure. Looking down it from the top I once recognized the presence of a woman seated on one of the lower steps with her back presented to me, her body half bowed and her head, in an attitude of woe, in her hands. I had been there but an instant, however, when she vanished without looking round at me. I knew, none the less, exactly what dreadful face she had to show; and I wondered whether, if instead of being above I had been below, I should have had, for going up, the same nerve I had lately shown Quint. Well, there continued to be plenty of chance for nerve. On the eleventh night after my latest encounter with that gentleman–they were all numbered now–I had an alarm that perilously skirted it and that indeed, from the particular quality of its unexpectedness, proved quite my sharpest shock. It was precisely the first night during this series that, weary with watching, I had felt that I might again without laxity lay myself down at my old hour. I slept immediately, and, as I afterwards knew, till about one o'clock; but when I woke it was to sit straight up, as completely roused as if a hand had shook me. I had left a light burning but it was now out, and I felt an instant certainty that Flora had extinguished it. This brought me to my feet and straight, in the darkness, to her bed, which I found she had left. A glance at the window enlightened me further, and the striking of a match completed the picture.

The child had again got up–this time blowing out the taper, and had again, for some purpose of observation or response, squeezed in behind the blind and was peering out into the night. That she now saw–as she had not, I had satisfied myself, the previous time–was proved to me by the fact that she was disturbed neither by my re-illumination nor by the haste I made to get into slippers and into a wrap. Hidden, protected, absorbed, she evidently rested on the sill–the casement opened forward–and gave herself up. There was a great still moon to help her, and this fact had counted in my quick decision. She was face to face with the apparition we had met at the lake, and could now communicate with it as she had not then been able to do. What I, on my side, had to care for was, without disturbing her, to reach, from the corridor, some other window in the same quarter. I got to the door without her hearing me; I got out of it, closed it and listened, from the other side, for some sound from her. While I stood in the passage I had my eyes on her brother's door, which was but ten steps off and which, indescribably, produced in me a renewal of the strange impulse that I lately spoke of as my temptation. What if I should go straight in and march to *his* window?—what if, by risking to his boyish bewilderment a revelation of my motive, I should throw across the rest of the mystery the long halter of my boldness?

This thought held me sufficiently to make me cross to his threshold and pause again. I preternaturally listened; I figured to myself what might portentously be; I wondered if his bed were also empty and he too were secretly at watch. It was a deep, soundless minute, at the end of which my impulse failed. He was quiet; he might be innocent; the risk was hideous; I turned away. There was a figure in the grounds—a figure prowling for a sight, the visitor with whom Flora was engaged; but it was not the visitor most concerned with my boy. I hesitated afresh, but on other grounds and only a few seconds; then I had made my choice. There were empty rooms at Bly, and it was only a question of choosing the right one. The right one suddenly presented itself to me as the lower one—though high above the gardens—in the solid corner of the house that I have spoken of as the old tower. This was a large, square chamber, arranged with some state as a bedroom, the extravagant size of which made it so inconvenient that it had not for years, though kept by Mrs Grose in exemplary order, been occupied. I had often admired it and I knew my way about in it; I had only, after just faltering at the first chill gloom of its disuse, to pass across it and unbolt as quietly as I could one of the shutters. Achieving this transit, I uncovered the glass without a sound and, applying my face to the pane, was able, the darkness without being much less than within, to see that I commanded the right direction. Then I saw something more. The moon made the night extraordinarily penetrable and showed me on the lawn a person, diminished by distance, who stood there motionless and as if fascinated, looking up to where I had appeared—looking, that is, not so much straight at me as at something that was apparently above me. There was clearly another person above me—there was a person on the tower; but the presence on the lawn was not in the least what I had conceived and had confidently hurried to meet. The presence on the lawn—I felt sick as I made it out—was poor little Miles himself.

11

It was not till late next day that I spoke to Mrs Grose; the rigour with which I kept my pupils in sight making it often difficult to meet her privately, and the more as we each felt the importance of not provoking—on the part of the servants quite as much as on that of the children—any suspicion of a secret flurry or of a discussion of mysteries. I drew a great security in this particular from her mere smooth aspect. There was nothing in her fresh face to pass on to others my horrible confidences. She believed me, I was sure, absolutely: if she hadn't I don't know what would have become of me, for I couldn't have borne the business alone. But she was a magnificent monument to the blessing of a want of imagination, and if she could see in our little charges nothing but their beauty and amiability, their happiness and cleverness, she had no direct communication with the sources of my trouble. If they had been at all visibly blighted or battered she would doubtless have grown, on tracing it back, haggard enough to match them, as matters stood, however, I could feel her, when she surveyed them with her large white arms folded and the habit of serenity in all her look, thank the Lord's mercy that if they were ruined the pieces would still serve. Flights of fancy gave place, in her mind, to a steady fireside glow, and I had already begun to perceive how, with the development of the conviction that—as time went on without a public accident—our young things could, after all, look out for themselves, she addressed her greatest solicitude to the sad case presented by their instructress. That, for myself, was a sound simplification: I could engage that, to the world, my face should tell no tales, but it would have been, in the conditions, an immense added strain to find myself anxious about hers.

At the hour I now speak of she had joined me, under pressure, on the terrace, where, with the lapse of the season, the afternoon sun was now agreeable; and we sat there together while, before us, at a distance, but within call if we wished, the children strolled to and fro in one of their most manageable moods. They moved slowly, in unison, below us, over the lawn, the boy, as they went, reading aloud from a storybook and passing his arm round his sister to keep her quite in touch. Mrs Grose watched them with positive placidity; then I caught the supressed intellectual creak with which she conscientiously turned to take from me a view of the back of the tapestry. I had made her a receptacle of lurid things, but there was an odd recognition of my superiority—my accomplishments and my function—in her patience under my pain. She offered her mind to my disclosures as, had I wished to mix a witch's broth and proposed it with assurance, she would have held out a large clean saucepan. This had become thoroughly her attitude by the time that, in my recital of the events of the night, I reached the point of what Miles had said to me when, after seeing him, at such a monstrous hour, almost on the very spot where he happened now to be, I had gone down to bring him in; choosing then, at the window, with a concentrated need of not alarming the house, rather that method than a signal more resonant. I had left her meanwhile in little doubt of my small hope of representing with success even to her actual sympathy my sense of the real splendour of the little inspiration with which, after I had got him into the house, the boy met my final articulate challenge. As soon as I appeared in the moonlight on the terrace he had come to me as straight as possible; on which I had taken his hand without a word and led him, through the dark spaces, up the staircase where Quint had so hungrily hovered for him, along the lobby where I had listened and trembled, and so to his forsaken room.

Not a sound, on the way, had passed between us, and I had wondered–oh, *how* I had wondered!–if he were groping about in his little mind for something plausible and not too grotesque. It would tax his invention, certainly, and I felt, this time, over his real embarrassment, a curious thrill of triumph. It was a sharp trap for the inscrutable! He couldn't play any longer at innocence; so how the deuce would he get out of it? There beat in me indeed, with the passionate throb of this question, an equal dumb appeal as to how the deuce *I* should. I was confronted at last, as never yet, with all the risk attached even now to sounding my own horrid note. I remember in fact that as we pushed into his little chamber, where the bed had not been slept in at all and the window, uncovered to the moonlight, made the place so clear that there was no need of striking a match–I remember how I suddenly dropped, sank upon the edge of the bed from the force of the idea that he must know how he really, as they say, 'had' me. He could do what he liked, with all his cleverness to help him, so long as I should continue to defer to the old tradition of the criminality of those caretakers of the young who minister to superstitions and fears. He 'had' me indeed, and in a cleft stick; for who would ever absolve me, who would consent that I should go unhung, if, by the faintest tremor of an overture, I were the first to introduce into our perfect intercourse an element so dire? No, no: it was useless to attempt to convey to Mrs Grose, just as it is scarcely less so to attempt to suggest here, how, in our short, stiff brush in the dark, he fairly shook me with admiration. I was of course thoroughly kind and merciful; never, never yet had I placed on his little shoulders hands of such tenderness as those with which, while I rested against the bed, I held him there well under fire. I had no alternative but, in form at least, to put it to him.

'You must tell me now–and all the truth. What did you go out for? What were you doing there?'

I can still see his wonderful smile, the whites of his beautiful eyes and the uncovering of his little teeth, shine to me in the dusk. 'If I tell you why, will you understand?' My heart, at this, leaped into my mouth. *Would* he tell me why? I found no sound on my lips to press it, and I was aware of replying only with a vague, repeated, grimacing nod. He was gentleness itself, and while I wagged my head at him he stood there more than ever a little fairy prince. It was his brightness indeed that gave me a respite. Would it be so great if he were really going to tell me? 'Well,' he said at last, 'just exactly in order that you should do this.'

'Do what?'

'Think me–for a change–*bad*!' I shall never forget the sweetness and gaiety with which he brought out the word, nor how, on top of it, he bent forward and kissed me. It was practically the end of everything. I met his kiss and I had to make, while I folded him for a minute in my arms, the most stupendous effort not to cry. He had given exactly the account of himself that permitted least of my going behind it, and it was only with the effect of confirming my acceptance of it that, as I presently glanced about the room, I could say–

'Then you didn't undress at all?'

He fairly glittered in the gloom. 'Not at all. I sat up and read.'

'And when did you go down?'

'At midnight. When I'm bad I *am* bad!'

'I see, I see–it's charming. But how could you be sure I would know it?'

'Oh, I arranged it with Flora.' His answers rang out with a readiness! 'She was to get up and look out.'

'Which is what she did do.' It was I who fell into the trap!

'So she disturbed you, and, to see what she was looking at, you also looked–you saw.'

'While you,' I concurred, 'caught your death in the night air!'

He literally bloomed so from his exploit that he could afford radiantly to assent. 'How otherwise should I have been bad enough?' he asked. Then, after another embrace, the incident and our interview closed on my recognition of all the reserves of goodness that, for his joke, he had been able to draw upon.

12

The particular impression I had received proved in the morning light, I repeat, not quite successfully presentable to Mrs Grose, though I reinforced it with the mention of still another remark that he had made before we separated. 'It all lies in half-a-dozen words,' I said to her, 'words that really settle the matter. "Think, you know, what I *might* do!" He threw that off to show me how good he is. He knows down to the ground what he "might" do. That's what he gave them a taste of at school.'

'Lord, you do change!' cried my friend.

'I don't change–I simply make it out. The four, depend upon it, perpetually meet. If on either of these last nights you had been with either child you would clearly have understood. The more I've watched and waited the more I've felt that if there were nothing else to make it sure it would be made so by the systematic silence of each. *Never*, by a slip of the tongue, have they so much as alluded to either of their old friends, any more than Miles has alluded to his expulsion. Oh yes, we may sit here and look at them, and they may show off to us there to their fill; but even while they pretend to be lost in their fairy-tale they're steeped in their vision of the dead restored. He's not reading to her,' I declared; 'they're talking of *them*–they're talking horrors! I go on, I know, as if I were crazy; and it's a wonder I'm not. What I've seen would have made *you* so; but it has only made me more lucid, made me get hold of still other things.'

My lucidity must have seemed awful, but the charming creatures who were victims of it, passing and repassing in their interlocked sweetness, gave my colleague something to hold on by; and I felt how tight she held as, without stirring in the breath of my passion, she covered them still with her eyes. 'Of what other things have you got hold?'

'Why, of the very things that have delighted, fascinated and yet, at bottom, as I now so strangely see, mystified and troubled me. Their more than earthly beauty, the absolutely unnatural goodness. It's a game.' I went on; 'it's a policy and a fraud!'

'On the part of little darlings–?'

'As yet mere lovely babies? Yes, mad as that seems!' The very act of bringing it out really helped me to trace it–follow it all up and piece it all together. 'They haven't been good–they've only been absent. It has been easy to live with them, because they're simply leading a life of their own. They're not mine–they're not ours. They're his and they're hers!'

'Quint's and that woman's?'

'Quint's and that woman's. They want to get to them.'

Oh, how, at this, poor Mrs Grose appeared to study them! 'But for what?'

'For the love of all the evil that, in those dreadful days, the pair put into them. And to ply them with that evil still, to keep up the work of demons, is what brings the others back.'

'Laws!' said my friend under her breath. The exclamation was homely, but it revealed a real acceptance of my further proof of what, in the bad time–for there had been a worse even than this!–must have occurred. There could have been no justification for me as the plain assent of her experience to whatever depth of depravity I found credible in our brace of scoundrels. It was in obvious submission of memory that she brought out after a moment: 'They *were* rascals! But what can they now do?' she pursued.

'Do?' I echoed so loud that Miles and Flora, as they passed at their distance, paused an instant in their walk and looked at us. 'Don't they do enough?' I demanded in a lower tone, while the children, having smiled and nodded and kissed hands to us, resumed their exhibition. We were held by it a minute; then I answered: 'They can destroy them!' At this my companion did turn, but the inquiry she launched was a silent one, the effect of which was to make me more explicit. 'They don't know, as yet, quite how—but they're trying hard. They're seen only across, as it were, and beyond—in strange places and on high places, the top of towers, the roof of houses, the outside of windows, the further edge of pools; but there's a deep design, on either side, to shorten the distance and overcome the obstacle; and the success of the tempters is only a question of time. They've only to keep to their suggestions of danger.'

'For the children to come?'

'And perish in the attempt!' Mrs Grose slowly got up, and I scrupulously added: 'Unless, of course, we can prevent!'

Standing there before me while I kept my seat, she visibly turned things over. 'Their uncle must do the preventing. He must take them away.'

'And who's to make him?'

She had been scanning the distance, but she now dropped on me a foolish face. 'You, Miss.'

'By writing to him that his house is poisoned and his little nephew and niece mad?'

'But if they *are*, Miss?'

'And if I am myself, you mean? That's charming news to be sent him by a governess whose prime undertaking was to give him no worry.'

Mrs Grose considered, following the children again. 'Yes, he do hate worry. That was the great reason—'

'Why those fiends took him in so long? No doubt, though his indifference must have been awful. As I'm not a fiend, at any rate, I shouldn't take him in.'

My companion after an instant and for all answer, sat down again and grasped my arm. 'Make him at any rate come to you.'

I stared. 'To *me*?' I had a sudden fear of what she might do. "'Him"?'

'He ought to *be* here—he ought to help.'

I quickly rose, and I think I must have shown her a queerer face than ever yet. 'You see me asking him for a visit?' No, with her eyes on my face she evidently couldn't. Instead of it even—as a woman reads another—she could see what I myself saw: his derision, his amusement, his contempt for the breakdown of my resignation at being left alone and for the fine machinery I had set in motion to attract his attention to my slighted charms. She didn't know—no one knew—how proud I had been to serve him and to stick to our terms; yet she none the less took the measure, I think, of the warning I now gave her. 'If you should so lose your head as to appeal to him for me—'

She was really frightened. 'Yes, Miss?'

'I would leave, on the spot, both him and you.'

13

It was all very well to join them, but speaking to them proved as much as ever an effort beyond my strength—offered, in close quarters, difficulties as insurmountable as before. This situation continued a month, and with new aggravations and particular notes, the note above all, sharper and sharper, of the small ironic consciousness on the part of my pupils. It was not, I am as sure today as I was sure then, my mere infernal imagination: it was absolutely traceable that they were aware of my predicament and that this strange relation made, in a manner, for a long time, the air in which we moved. I don't mean that they had their tongues in their cheeks or did anything vulgar, for that was not one of their dangers: I do mean, on the other hand, that the element of the unnamed and untouched became, between us, greater than any other, and that so much avoidance could not have been so successfully effected without a great deal of tacit arrangement. It was as if, at moments, we were perpetually coming into sight of subjects before which we must stop short, turning suddenly out of alleys that we perceived to be blind, closing with a little bang that made us look at each other—for, like all bangs, it was something louder than we had intended—the doors we had indiscreetly opened. All roads lead to Rome, and there were times when it might have struck us that almost every branch of study or subject of conversation skirted forbidden ground. Forbidden ground was the question of the return of the dead in general and of whatever, in especial, might survive, in memory, of the friends little children had lost. There were days when I could have sworn that one of them had, with a small invisible nudge, said to the other: 'She thinks she'll do it this time—but she *won't*!' To 'do it' would have been to indulge for instance—and for once in a way—in some direct reference to the lady who had prepared them for my discipline. They had a delightful endless appetite for passages in my own history, to which I had again and again treated them; they were in possession of everything that had ever happened to me, had had, with every circumstance, the story of my smallest adventures and of those of my brothers and sisters and of the cat and the dog at home, as well as many particulars of the eccentric nature of my father, of the furniture and arrangement of our house and of the conversation of the old women of our village. There were things enough, taking one with another, to chatter about, if one went very fast and knew by instinct when to go round. They pulled with an art of their own the strings of my invention and my memory; and nothing else perhaps, when I thought of such occasions afterwards, gave me so the suspicion of being watched from under cover. It was in any case over *my* life, *my* past and *my* friends alone that we could take anything like our ease; a state of affairs that led them sometimes without the least pertinence to break out into sociable reminders. I was invited—with no visible connexion—to repeat afresh Goody Gosling's celebrated *mot* or to confirm the details already supplied as to the cleverness of the vicarage pony.

It was partly at such junctures as these and partly at quite different ones that, with the turn my matters had now taken, my predicament, as I have called it, grew more sensible. The fact that the days passed for me without another encounter ought, it would have appeared, to have done something towards soothing my nerves. Since the light brush, that second night on the upper landing, of the presence of a woman at the foot of the stair, I had seen nothing, whether in or out of the house, that one had better not have seen. There was many a corner round which I expected to come upon Quint, and many a situation that, in a merely sinister way, would have favoured the appearance of Miss Jessel. The summer had turned, the summer had gone; the autumn had dropped upon Bly and had blown out half our lights. The place, with its grey sky and withered garlands, its bared spaces and scattered dead leaves, was like a theatre after the performance–all strewn with crumpled playbills. They were exactly states of the air, conditions of sound and of stillness, unspeakable impressions of the *kind* of ministering moment, that brought back to me, long enough to catch it, the feeling of the medium in which, that June evening out-of-doors, I had had my first sight of Quint, and in which, too, at those other instants, I had, after seeing him through the window, looked for him in vain in the circle of shrubbery. I recognized the signs, the portents–I recognized the moment, the spot. But they remained unaccompanied and empty, and I continued unmolested; if unmolested one could call a young woman whose sensibility had, in the most extraordinary fashion, not declined but deepened. I had said in my talk with Mrs Grose on that horrid scene of Flora's by the lake–and had perplexed her by so saying–that it would from that moment distress me much more to lose my power than to keep it. I had then expressed what was vividly in my mind the truth that, whether the children really saw or not–since, that is, it was not yet definitely proved–I greatly preferred, as a safeguard, the fullness of my own exposure. I was ready to know the very worst that was to be known. What I had then had an ugly glimpse of was that my eyes might be sealed just while theirs were most opened. Well, my eyes *were* sealed, it appeared, at present–a consummation for which it seemed blasphemous not to thank God. There was, alas, a difficulty about that: I would have thanked him with all my soul had I not had in a proportionate measure this conviction of the secret of my pupils.

How can I retrace today the strange steps of my obsession? There were times of our being together when I would have been ready to swear that, literally, in my presence, but with my direct sense of it closed, they had visitors who were known and were welcome. Then it was that, had I not been deterred by the very chance that such an injury might prove greater than the injury to be averted, my exaltation would have broken out. 'They're here, they're here, you little wretches,' I would have cried, 'and you can't deny it now!' The little wretches denied it with all the added volume of their sociability and their tenderness, in just the crystal depths of which—like the flash of a fish in a stream—the mockery of their advantage peeped up. The shock, in truth, had sunk into me still deeper than I knew on the night when, looking out to see either Quint or Miss Jessel under the stars, I had beheld the boy over whose rest I watched and who had immediately brought in with him—had straightway, there, turned it on me—the lovely upward look with which, from the battlements above me, the hideous apparition of Quint had played. If it was a question of a scare, my discovery on this occasion had scared me more than any other, and it was in the condition of nerves produced by it that I made my actual inductions. They harassed me so that sometimes, at odd moments, I shut myself up audibly to rehearse—it was at once a fantastic relief and a renewed despair—the manner in which I might come to the point. I approached it from one side and the other while, in my room, I flung myself about, but I always broke down in the monstrous utterance of names. As they died away on my lips I said to myself that I should indeed help them to represent something infamous if, by pronouncing them, I should violate as rare a little case of instinctive delicacy as any schoolroom, probably, had ever known. When I said to myself: '*They* have the manners to be silent, and you, trusted as you are, the baseness to speak!' I felt myself crimson and I covered my face with my hands. After these secret scenes I chattered more than ever, going on volubly enough till one of our prodigious, palpable hushes occurred—I can call them nothing else—the strange, dizzy lift or swim (I try for terms!) into a stillness, a pause of all life, that had nothing to do with the more or less noise that at the moment we might be engaged in making and that I could hear through any deepened exhilaration or quickened recitation or louder strum of the piano. Then it was that the others, the outsiders, were there. Though they were not angels, they 'passed', as the French say, causing me, while they stayed, to tremble with the fear of their addressing to their younger victims some yet more infernal message or more vivid image than they had thought good enough for myself.

What it was most impossible to get rid of was the cruel idea that, whatever I had seen, Miles and Flora saw *more*—things terrible and unguessable and that sprang from dreadful passages of intercourse in the past. Such things naturally left on the surface, for the time, a chill which we vociferously denied that we felt; and we had, all three, with repetition, got into such splendid training that we went, each time, almost automatically, to mark the close of the incident, through the very same movements. It was striking of the children, at all events, to kiss me inveterately with a kind of wild irrelevance and never to fail—one or the other—of the precious question that has helped us through many a peril. 'When do you think he *will* come? Don't you think we *ought* to write?'–there was nothing like that inquiry, we found by experience, for carrying off an awkwardness. 'He' of course was their uncle in Harley Street; and we lived in much profusion of theory that he might at any moment arrive to mingle in our circle. It was impossible to have given less encouragement than he had done to such a doctrine, but if we had not had the doctrine to fall back upon we should have deprived each other of some of our finest exhibitions. He never wrote to them–that may have been selfish, but it was a part of the flattery of his trust of me; for the way in which a man pays his highest tribute to a woman is apt to be but by the more festal celebration of one of the sacred laws of his comfort; and I held that I carried out the spirit of the pledge given not to appeal to him when I let my charges understand that their own letters were but charming literary exercises. They were too beautiful to be posted; I kept them myself; I have them all to this hour. This was a rule indeed which only added to the satiric effect of my being plied with the supposition that he might at any moment be among us. It was exactly as if my charges knew how almost more awkward than anything else might be for me. There appears to me, moreover, as I look back, no note in all this more extraordinary than the mere fact that, in spite of my tension and of their triumph, I never lost patience with them. Adorable they must in truth have been, I now reflect, that I didn't in these days hate them! Would exasperation, however, if relief had longer been postponed, finally have betrayed me? It little matters, for relief arrived. I call it relief though it was only the relief that a snap brings to a strain or the burst of a thunderstorm to a day of suffocation. It was at least change, and it came with a rush.

14

Walking to church a certain Sunday morning, I had little Miles at my side and his sister, in advance of us and at Mrs Grose's, well in sight. It was a crisp, clear day, the first of its order for some time; the night had brought a touch of frost, and the autumn air, bright and sharp, made the church-bells almost gay. It was an odd accident of thought that I should have happened at such a moment to be particularly and very gratefully struck with the obedience of my little charges. Why did they never resent my inexorable, my perpetual society? Something or other had brought nearer home to me that I had all but pinned the boy to my shawl and that, in the way our companions were marshalled before me, I might have appeared to provide against some danger of rebellion. I was like a gaoler with an eye to possible surprises and escapes. But all this belonged–I mean their magnificent little surrender–just to the special array of the facts that were most abysmal. Turned out for Sunday by his uncle's tailor, who had had a free hand and a notion of pretty waistcoats and of his grand little air, Miles's whole title to independence, the rights of his sex and situation, were so stamped upon him that if he had suddenly struck for freedom I should have had nothing to say. I was by the strangest of chances wondering how I should meet him when the revolution unmistakably occurred. I call it a revolution because I now see how, with the word he spoke, the curtain rose on the last act of my dreadful drama and the catastrophe was precipitated. 'Look here, my dear, you know,' he charmingly said, 'when in the world, please, am I going back to school?'

Transcribed here the speech sounds harmless enough, particularly as uttered in the sweet, high, casual pipe with which, at all interlocutors, but above all at his eternal governess, he threw off intonations as if he were tossing roses. There was something in them that always made one 'catch', and I caught, at any rate, now so effectually that I stopped as short as if one of the trees of the park had fallen across the road. There was something new, on the spot, between us, and he was perfectly aware that I recognized it, though, to enable me to do so, he had no need to look a whit less candid and charming than usual. I could feel in him how he already, from my at first finding nothing to reply, perceived the advantage he had gained. I was so slow to find anything that he had plenty of time, after a minute, to continue with his suggestive but inconclusive smile: 'You know, my dear, that for a fellow to be with a lady *always*–!' His 'my dear' was constantly on his lips for me, and nothing could have expressed more the exact shade of the sentiment with which I desired to inspire my pupils than its fond familiarity. It was so respectfully easy.

But, oh, how I felt that at present I must pick my own phrases! I remember that, to gain time, I tried to laugh, and I seemed to see in the beautiful face with which he watched me how ugly and queer I looked. 'And always with the same lady?' I returned.

He neither blenched nor winked. The whole thing was virtually out between us. 'Ah, of course she's a jolly, "perfect" lady; but, after all, I'm a fellow, don't you see? that's–well, getting on.'

I lingered there with him an instant ever so kindly. 'Yes, you're getting on.' Oh, but I felt helpless!

I have kept to this day the heartbreaking little idea of how he seemed to know that and to play with it. 'And you can't say I've not been awfully good, can you?'

I laid my hand on his shoulder, for, though I felt how much better it would have been to walk on, I was not yet quite able. 'No, I can't say that, Miles.'

'Except just that one night, you know–!'

'That one night?' I couldn't look as straight as he.

'Why, when I went down–went out of the house.'

'Oh yes. But I forget what you did it for.'

'You forget?'—he spoke with the sweet extravagance of childish reproach. 'Why, it was to show you I could!'

'Oh yes, you could.'

'And I can again.'

I felt that I might, perhaps, after all, succeed in keeping my wits about me. 'Certainly. But you won't.'

'No, not *that* again. It was nothing.'

He resumed our walk with me, passing his hand into my arm. 'Then when *am* I going back?'

I wore, in turning it over, my most responsible air. 'Were you very happy at school?'

He just considered. 'Oh, I'm happy enough anywhere!'

'Well then,' I quavered, 'if you're just as happy here—!'

'Ah, but that isn't everything! Of course *you* know a lot—'

'But you hint that you know almost as much?' I risked as he paused.

'Not half I want to!' Miles honestly professed. 'But it isn't so much that.'

'What is it then?'

'Well—I want to see more life.'

'I see; I see.' We had arrived within sight of the church and of various persons, including several of the household of Bly, on their way to it and clustered about the door to see us go in. I quickened our step; I wanted to get there before the question between us opened up much further; I reflected hungrily that, for more than an hour, he would have to be silent; and I thought with envy of the comparative dusk of the pew and of the almost spiritual help of the hassock on which I might bend my knees. I seemed literally to be running a race with some confusion to which he was about to reduce me, but I felt that he had got in first when, before we even entered the churchyard, he threw out—

'I want my own sort!'

It literally made me bound forward. 'There are not many of your own sort, Miles!' I laughed. 'Unless perhaps dear little Flora!'

'You really compare me to a baby girl?'

This found me singularly weak. 'Don't you, then, *love* our sweet Flora?'

'If I didn't—and you too; if I didn't—!' he repeated as if retreating for a jump, yet leaving his thought so unfinished that, after we had come into the gate, another stop, which he imposed on me by the pressure of his arm, had become inevitable. Mrs Grose and Flora had passed into the church, the other worshippers had followed, and we were, for the minute, alone among the old, thick graves. We had paused, on the path from the gate, by a low, oblong, table-like tomb.

'Yes, if you didn't—?'

He looked, while I waited, about at the graves. 'Well, you know what!' But he didn't move, and he presently produced something that made me drop straight down on the stone slab, as if suddenly to rest. 'Does my uncle think what *you* think?'

I markedly rested. 'How do you know what I think?'

'Ah well, of course I don't; for it strikes me you never tell me. But I mean does *he* know?'

'Know what, Miles?'

'Why, the way I'm going on.'

I perceived quickly enough that I could make, to this inquiry, no answer that would not involve something of a sacrifice of my employer. Yet it appeared to me that we were all, at Bly, sufficiently sacrificed to make that venial. 'I don't think your uncle much cares.'

Miles, on this, stood looking at me. 'Then don't you think he can be made to?'

'In what way?'

'Why, by his coming down'

'But who'll get him to come down?'

'*I* will!' the boy said with extraordinary brightness and emphasis. He gave me another look charged with that expression and then marched off alone into church.

15

The business was practically settled from the moment I never followed him. It was a pitiful surrender to agitation, but my being aware of this had somehow no power to restore me. I only sat there on my tomb and read into what my little friend had said to me the fullness of its meaning; by the time I had grasped the whole of which I had also embraced, for absence, the pretext that I was ashamed to offer my pupils and the rest of the congregation such an example of delay. What I said to myself above all was that Miles had got something out of me and that the proof of it, for him, would be just this awkward collapse. He had got out of me that there was something I was much afraid of and that he should probably be able to make use of my fear to gain, for his own purpose, more freedom. My fear was of having to deal with the intolerable question of the grounds of his dismissal from school, for that was really but the question of the horrors gathered behind. That his uncle should arrive to treat with me of these things was a solution that, strictly speaking, I ought now to have desired to bring on; but I could so little face the ugliness and the pain of it that I simply procrastinated and lived from hand to mouth. The boy, to my deep discomposure, was immensely in the right, was in a position to say to me: 'Either you clear up with my guardian the mystery of this interruption of my studies, or you cease to expect me to lead with you a life that's so unnatural for a boy.' What was so unnatural for the particular boy I was concerned with was this sudden revelation of a consciousness and a plan.

That was what really overcame me, what prevented my going in. I walked round the church, hesitating, hovering; I reflected that I had already, with him, hurt myself beyond repair. Therefore I could patch up nothing, and it was too extreme an effort to squeeze beside him into the pew: he would be so much more sure than ever to pass his arm into mine and make me sit there for an hour in close, silent contact with his commentary on our talk. For the first minute since his arrival I wanted to get away from him. As I paused beneath the high east window and listened to the sounds of worship I was taken with an impulse that might master me, I felt, completely should I give it the least encouragement. I might easily put an end to my predicament by getting away altogether. Here was my chance; there was no one to stop me; I could give the whole thing up—turn my back and retreat. It was only a question of hurrying again, for a few preparations, to the house which the attendance at church of so many of the servants would practically have left unoccupied. No one, in short, could blame me if I should just drive desperately off. What was it to get away if I got away only till dinner? That would be in a couple of hours, at the end of which—I had the acute prevision—my little pupils would play at innocent wonder about my non-appearance in their train.

'What *did* you do, you naughty, bad thing? Why in the world, to worry us so—and take our thoughts off too, don't you know?—did you desert us at the very door?' I couldn't meet such questions nor, as they asked them, their false little lovely eyes; yet it was all so exactly what I should have to meet that, as the prospect grew sharp to me, I at last let myself go.

I got, so far as the immediate moment was concerned, away; I came straight out of the churchyard and, thinking hard, retraced my steps through the park. It seemed to me that by the time I reached the house I had made up my mind I would fly. The Sunday stillness both of the approaches and of the interior, in which I met no one, fairly excited me with a sense of opportunity. Were I to get off quickly, this way, I should get off without a scene, without a word. My quickness would have to be remarkable, however, and the question of a conveyance was the great one to settle. Tormented, in the hall, with difficulties and obstacles, I remember sinking down at the foot of the staircase—suddenly collapsing there on the lowest step and then, with a revulsion, recalling that it was exactly where, more than a month before, in the darkness of night and just so bowed with evil things, I had seen the spectre of the most horrible of women. At this I was able to straighten myself; I went the rest of the way up; I made, in my bewilderment, for the schoolroom, where there were objects belonging to me that I should have to take. But I opened the door to find again, in a flash, my eyes unsealed. In the presence of what I saw I reeled straight back upon my resistance.

Seated at my own table in the clear noonday light I saw a person whom, without my previous experience, I should have taken at the first blush for some housemaid who might have stayed at home to look after the place and who, availing herself of rare relief from observation and of the schoolroom table and my pens, ink and paper, had applied herself to the considerable effort of a letter to her sweetheart. There was an effort in the way that, while her arms rested on the table, her hands, with evident weariness, supported her head; but at the moment I took this in I had already become aware that, in spite of my entrance, her attitude strangely persisted. Then it was–with the very act of announcing itself–that her identity flared up in a change of posture. She rose, not as if she had heard me, but with an indescribable grand melancholy of indifference and detachment, and, within a dozen feet of me, stood there as my vile predecessor. Dishonoured and tragic, she was all before me; but even as I fixed and, for memory, secured it, the awful image passed away. Dark as midnight in her black dress, her haggard beauty and her unutterable woe, she had looked at me long enough to appear to say that her right to sit at my table was as good as mine to sit at hers. While these instants lasted indeed I had the extraordinary chill of a feeling that it was I who was the intruder. It was as a wild protest against it that, actually addressing her–'You terrible, miserable woman!'–I heard myself break into a sound that, by the open door, rang through the long passage and the empty house. She looked at me as if she heard me, but I had recovered myself and cleared the air. There was nothing in the room the next minute but the sunshine and a sense that I must stay.

16

I had so perfectly expected that the return of my pupils would be marked by a demonstration that I was freshly upset at having to take into account that they were dumb about my absence. Instead of gaily denouncing and caressing me they made no allusion to my having failed them, and I was left, for the time, on perceiving that she too said nothing, to study Mrs Grose's odd face. I did this to such purpose that I made sure they had in some way bribed her to silence; a silence that, however, I would engage to break down on the first private opportunity. This opportunity came before tea: I secured five minutes with her in the houskeeper's room, where, in the twilight, amid a smell of lately-baked bread, but with the place all swept and garnished, I found her sitting in pained placidity before the fire. So I see her still, so I see her best: facing the flame from her straight chair in the dusky, shining room, a large clean image of the 'put away'–of drawers closed and locked and rest without a remedy.

'Oh yes, they asked me to say nothing; and to please them–so long as they were there–of course I promised. But what had happened to you?'

'I only went with you for a walk,' I said. 'I had then to come back to meet a friend.'

She showed her surprise. 'A friend–*you?*'

'Oh yes, I have a couple!' I laughed. 'But did the children give you a reason?'

'For not alluding to your leaving us? Yes; they said you would like it better. Do you like it better?'

My face had made her rueful. 'No, I like it worse!' But after an instant I added: 'Did they say why I should like it better?'

'No; Master Miles only said "We must do nothing but what she likes!"'

'I wish indeed he would! And what did Flora say?'

'Miss Flora was too sweet. She said "Oh, of course, of course!"–and I said the same.'

I thought a moment. 'You were too sweet too–I can hear you all. But none the less, between Miles and me, it's now all out.'

'All out?' My companion stared. 'But what, Miss?'

'Everything. It doesn't matter. I've made up my mind. I came home, my dear,' I went on, 'for a talk with Miss Jessel.'

I had by this time formed the habit of having Mrs Grose literally well in hand in advance of my sounding that note; so that even now, as she bravely blinked under the signal of my word, I could keep her comparatively firm. 'A talk! Do you mean she spoke?'

'It came to that. I found her, on my return, in the schoolroom.'

'And what did she say?' I can hear the good woman still, and the candour of her stupefaction.

'That she suffers the torments–!'

It was this, of a truth, that made her, as she filled out my picture, gape. 'Do you mean,' she faltered, '–of the lost?'

'Of the lost. Of the damned. And that's why, to share them–' I faltered myself with the horror of it.

But my companion, with less imagination, kept me up. 'To share them–?'

'She wants Flora.' Mrs Grose might, as I gave it to her, fairly have fallen away from me had I not been prepared. I still held her there, to show I was. 'As I've told you, however, it doesn't matter.'

'Because you've made up your mind? But to what?'

'To everything.'

'And what do you call "everything"?'

'Why, sending for their uncle.'

'Oh Miss, in pity do,' my friend broke out.

'Ah, but I will, I *will!* I see it's the only way. What's "out", as I told you, with Miles is that if he thinks I'm afraid to–and has ideas of what he gains by that–he shall see he's mistaken. Yes, yes; his uncle shall have it here from me on the spot (and before the boy himself if necessary), that if I'm to be reproached with having done nothing again about more school–'

'Yes Miss–' my companion pressed me.

'Well, there's that awful reason.'

There were now clearly so many of these for my poor colleague that she was excusable for being vague. 'But–a–which?'

'Why, the letter from his old place.'

'You'll show it to the master?'

'I ought to have done so on the instant.'

'Oh no!' said Mrs Grose with decision.

'I'll put it before him,' I went on inexorably, 'that I can't undertake to work the question on behalf of a child who has been expelled–'

'For we've never in the least known what!' Mrs Grose declared.

'For wickedness. For what else–when he's so clever and beautiful and perfect? Is he stupid? Is he untidy? Is he infirm? Is he ill-natured? He's exquisite–so it can be only *that*; and that would open up the whole thing. After all,' I said, 'it's their uncle's fault. If he left here such people–!'

'He didn't really in the least know them. The fault's mine.' She had turned quite pale.

'Well, you shan't suffer,' I answered.

'The children shan't!' she emphatically returned.

I was silent a while; we looked at each other. 'Then what am I to tell him?'

'You needn't tell him anything. *I'll* tell him.'

I measured this. 'Do you mean you'll write–?' Remembering she couldn't, I caught myself up. 'How do you communicate?'

'I tell the bailiff. *He* writes.'

'And should you like him to write our story?'

My question had a sarcastic force that I had not fully intended, and it made her, after a moment, inconsequently break down. The tears were again in her eyes. 'Ah, Miss, *you* write!'

'Well–tonight,' I at last answered; and on this we separated.

17

I went so far, in the evening, as to make a beginning. The weather had changed back, a great wind was abroad, and beneath the lamp, in my room, with Flora at peace beside me, I sat for a long time before a blank sheet of paper and listened to the lash of the rain and the batter of the gusts. Finally I went out, taking a candle; I crossed the passage and listened a minute at Miles's door. What, under my endless obsession, I had been impelled to listen for was some betrayal of his not being at rest, and I presently caught one, but not in the form I had expected. His voice tinkled out. 'I say, you there–come in.' It was a gaiety in the gloom!

I went in with my light and found him, in bed, very wide awake, but very much at his ease. 'Well, what are *you* up to?' he asked with a grace of sociability in which it occurred to me that Mrs Grose, had she been present, might have looked in vain for proof that anything was 'out'.

I stood over him with my candle. 'How did you know I was there?'

'Why, of course I heard you. Did you fancy you made no noise? You're like a troop of cavalry!' he beautifully laughed.

'Then you weren't asleep?'

'Not much! I lie awake and think.'

I had put my candle, designedly, a short way off, and then, as he held out his friendly old hand to me, had sat down on the edge of his bed. 'What is it,' I asked, 'that you think of?'

'What in the world, my dear, but *you*?'

'Ah, the pride I take in your appreciation doesn't insist on that! I had so far rather you slept.'

'Well, I think also, you know, of this queer business of ours.'

I marked the coolness of his firm little hand. 'Of what queer business, Miles?'

'Why, the way you bring me up. And all the rest!'

I fairly held my breath a minute, and even from my glimmering taper there was light enough to show how he smiled up at me from his pillow. 'What do you mean by all the rest?'

'Oh, you know, you know!'

I could say nothing for a minute, though I felt, as I held his hand and our eyes continued to meet, that my silence had all the air of admitting his charge and that nothing in the whole world of reality was perhaps at that moment so fabulous as our actual relation. 'Certainly you shall go back to school,' I said, 'if it be that that troubles you. But not to the old place–we must find another, a better. How could I know it did trouble you, this question, when you never told me so, never spoke of it at all?' His clear, listening face, framed in its smooth whiteness, made him for the minute as appealing as some wistful patient in a children's hospital; and I would have given, as the resemblance came to me, all I possessed on earth really to be the nurse or the sister of charity who might have helped to cure him. Well, even as it was, I perhaps might help! 'Do you know you've never said a word to me about your school–I mean the old one; never mentioned it in any way?'

He seemed to wonder; he smiled with the same loveliness. But he clearly gained time; he waited, he called for guidance. 'Haven't I?' It wasn't for *me* to help him–it was for the thing I had met!

Something in his tone and the expression of his face, as I got this from him, set my heart aching with such a pang as it had never yet known; so unutterably touching was it to see his little brain puzzled and his little resources taxed to play, under the spell laid on him, a part of innocence and consistency. 'No, never–from the hour you came back. You've never mentioned to me one of your masters, one of your comrades, nor the least little thing that ever happened to you at school. Never, little Miles–no never–

have you given me an inkling of anything that *may* have happened there. Therefore you can fancy how much I'm in the dark. Until you came out, that way, this morning, you had, since the first hour I saw you, scarce even made a reference to anything in your previous life. You seemed so perfectly to accept the present.' It was extraordinary how my absolute conviction of his secret precocity (or whatever I might call the poison of an influence that I dared but half to phrase), made him, in spite of the faint breath of his inward trouble, appear as accessible as an older person—imposed him almost as an intellectual equal. 'I thought you wanted to go on as you are.'

It struck me that at this he just faintly coloured. He gave, at any rate, like a convalescent slightly fatigued, a languid shake of his head. 'I don't—I don't. I want to get away.'

'You're tired of Bly?'

'Oh no, I like Bly.'

'Well, then—?'

'Oh, *you* know what a boy wants!'

I felt that I didn't know so well as Miles, and I took temporary refuge. 'You want to go to your uncle?'

Again, at this, with his sweet ironic face, he made a movement on the pillow. 'Ah, you can't get off with that!'

I was silent a little, and it was I, now, I think, who changed colour. 'My dear, I don't want to get off!'

'You can't, even if you do. You can't, you can't!'—he lay beautifully staring. 'My uncle must come down, and you must completely settle things.'

'If we do,' I returned with some spirit, 'you may be sure it will be to take you quite away.'

'Well, don't you understand that that's exactly what I'm working for? You'll have to tell him—about the way you've let it all drop: you'll have to tell him a tremendous lot!'

The exultation with which he uttered this helped me somehow, for the instant, to meet him rather more. 'And how much will *you*, Miles, have to tell him? There are things he'll ask you!'

He turned it over. 'Very likely. But what things?'

'The things you've never told me. To make up his mind what to do with you. He can't send you back—'

'Oh, I don't want to go back!' he broke in. 'I want a new field.'

He said it with admirable serenity, with positive unimpeachable gaiety, and doubtless it was that very note that most evoked for me the poignancy, the unnatural childish tragedy, of his probable reappearance at the end of three months with all his bravado and still more dishonour. It overwhelmed me now that I should never be able to bear that, and it made me let myself go. I threw myself upon him and in the tenderness of my pity I embraced him. 'Dear little Miles, dear little Miles—!'

My face was close to his, and he let me kiss him, simply taking it with indulgent good humour. 'Well, old lady?'

'Is there nothing–nothing at all that you want to tell me?'

He turned off a little, facing round towards the wall and holding up his hand to look at as one had seen sick children look. 'I've told you–I told you this morning.'

Oh, I was sorry for him! 'That you just want me not to worry you?'

He looked round at me now, as if in recognition of my understanding him; then ever so gently, 'To let me alone,' he replied.

There was even a singular little dignity in it, something that made me release him, yet, when I had slowly risen, linger beside him. God knows I never wished to harass him, but I felt that merely, at this, to turn my back on him was to abandon or, to put it more truly, to lose him. 'I've just begun a letter to your uncle,' I said.

'Well then, finish it!'

I waited a minute. 'What happened before?'

He gazed up at me again. 'Before what?'

'Before you came back. And before you went away.'

For some time he was silent, but he continued to meet my eyes. 'What happened?'

It made me, the sound of the words, in which it seemed to me that I caught for the very first time a small faint quaver of consenting consciousness–it made me drop on my knees beside the bed and seize once more the chance of possessing him. 'Dear little Miles, dear little Miles, if you *knew* how I want to help you! It's only that, it's nothing but that, and I'd rather die than give you a pain or do you a wrong–I'd rather die than hurt a hair of you. Dear little Miles'–oh, I brought it out now even if I *should* go too far–'I just want you to help me to save you!' But I knew in a moment after this that I had gone too far. The answer to my appeal was instantaneous, but it came in the form of an extraordinary blast and chill, a gust of frozen air and a shake of the room as great as if, in the wild wind, the casement had crashed in. The boy gave a loud, high shriek which, lost in the rest of the shock of sound, might have seemed, indistinctly, though I was so close to him, a note either of jubilation or of terror. I jumped to my feet again and was conscious of darkness. So for a moment we remained, while I stared about me and saw that the drawn curtains were unstirred and the window tight. 'Why, the candle's out!' I then cried.

'It was I who blew it, dear!' said Miles.

18

The next day, after lessons, Mrs Grose found a moment to say to me quietly: 'Have you written, Miss?'

'Yes—I've written.' But I didn't add—for the hour—that my letter, sealed and directed, was still in my pocket. There would be time enough to send it before the messenger should go to the village. Meanwhile there had been, on the part of my pupils, no more brilliant, more exemplary morning. It was exactly as if they had both had at heart to gloss over any recent little friction. They performed the dizziest feats of arithmetic, soaring quite out of my feeble range, and perpetrated, in higher spirits than ever, geographical and historical jokes. It was conspicuous of course in Miles in particular that he appeared to wish to show how easily he could let me down. This child, to my memory, really lives in a setting of beauty and misery that no words can translate; there was a distinction all his own in every impulse he revealed; never was a small natural creature, to the uninitiated eye all frankness and freedom, a more ingenious, a more extraordinary little gentleman. I had perpetually to guard against the wonder of contemplation into which my initiated view betrayed me; to check the irrelevant gaze and discouraged sigh in which I constantly both attacked and renounced the enigma of what such a little gentleman could have done that deserved a penalty. Say that, by the dark prodigy I knew, the imagination of all evil *had* been opened up to him: all the justice within me ached for the proof that it could ever have flowered into an act.

He had never, at any rate, been such a little gentleman as when, after our early dinner on this dreadful day, he came round to me and asked if I shouldn't like him, for half an hour, to play to me. David playing to Saul could never have shown a finer sense of the occasion. It was literally a charming exhibition of tact, of magnanimity, and quite tantamount to his saying outright: 'The true knights we love to read about never push an advantage too far. I know what you mean now: you mean that—to be left alone yourself and not followed up—you'll cease to worry and spy upon me, won't keep me so close to you, will let me go and come. Well, I "come", you see—but I don't go! There'll be plenty of time for that. I do really delight in your society, and I only want to show you that I contended for a principle.' It may be imagined whether I resisted this appeal or failed to accompany him again, hand in hand, to the schoolroom. He sat down at the old piano and played as he had never played; and if there are those who think he had better have been kicking a football I can only say that I wholly agree with them. For at the end of a time that under his influence I had quite ceased to measure I started up with a strange sense of having literally slept at my post. It was after luncheon, and by the schoolroom fire, and yet I hadn't really, in the least, slept: I had only done something much worse—I had forgotten. Where, all this time, was Flora? When I put the question to Miles he played on a minute before answering, and then could only say: 'Why, my dear, how do *I* know?'—breaking moreover into a happy laugh which immediately after, as if it were a vocal accompaniment, he prolonged into incoherent, extravagant song

I went straight to my room, but his sister was not there; then, before going downstairs, I looked into several others. As she was nowhere about she would surely be with Mrs Grose, whom, in the comfort of that theory, I accordingly proceeded in the quest of. I found her where I had found her the evening before, but she met my quick challenge with blank, scared ignorance. She had only supposed that, after the repast, I had carried off both the children; as to which she was quite in her right, for it was the very first time I had allowed the little girl out of my sight without some special provision. Of course now indeed she might be with the maids, so that the immediate thing was to look for her without an air of alarm. This we promptly arranged between us; but when, ten minutes later and in pursuance of our arrangement, we met in the hall, it was only to report on either side that after guarded inquiries we had altogether failed to trace her. For a minute there, apart from observation, we exchanged mute alarms, and I could feel with what high interest my friend returned me all those I had from the first given her.

'She'll be above,' she presently said–'in one of the rooms you haven't searched.'

'No; she's at a distance.' I made up my mind. 'She has gone out.'

Mrs Grose started. 'Without a hat?'

I naturally also looked volumes. 'Isn't that woman always without one?'

'She's with *her*?'

'She's with *her*!' I declared. 'We must find them.'

My hand was on my friend's arm, but she failed for the moment, confronted with such an account of the matter, to respond to my pressure. She communed, on the contrary, on the spot, with her uneasiness. 'And where's Master Miles?'

'Oh, *he's* with Quint. They're in the schoolroom.'

'Lord, Miss!' My view, I was myself aware–and therefore I suppose my tone–had never yet reached so calm an assurance.

'The trick's played,' I went on; 'they've successfully worked their plan. He found the most divine little way to keep me quiet while she went off.'

'"Divine"?' Mrs Grose bewilderedly echoed.

'Infernal, then!' I almost cheerfully rejoined. 'He has provided for himself as well. But come!'

She had helplessly gloomed at the upper regions. 'You leave him–?'

'So long with Quint? Yes–I don't mind that now.'

She always ended, at these moments, by getting possession of my hand, and in this manner she could at present still stay me. But after grasping an instant at my sudden resignation, 'Because of your letter?' she eagerly brought out.

I quickly, by way of answer, felt for my letter, drew it forth, held it up, and then, freeing myself, went and laid it on the great hall-table. 'Luke will take it,' I said as I came back. I reached the house-door and opened it; I was already on the steps.

My companion still demurred: the storm of the night and the early morning had dropped, but the afternoon was damp and grey. I came down to the drive while she stood in the doorway. 'You go with nothing on?'

'What do I care when the child has nothing? I can't wait to dress,' I cried, 'and if you must do so I leave you. Try meanwhile, yourself, upstairs.'

'With *them*?' Oh, on this, the poor woman promptly joined me!

19

We went straight to the lake, as it was called at Bly, and I dare say rightly called, though I reflect that it may in fact have been a sheet of water less remarkable than it appeared to my untravelled eyes. My acquaintance with sheets of water was small, and the pool of Bly, at all events on the few occasions of my consenting, under the protection of my pupils, to affront its surface in the old flat-bottomed boat moored there for our use, had impressed me both with its extent and its agitation. The usual place of embarkation was half a mile from the house, but I had an intimate conviction that wherever Flora might be, she was not near home. She had not given me the slip for any small adventure, and, since the day of the very great one that I had shared with her by the pond, I had been aware, in our walks, of the quarter to which she most inclined. This was why I had now given to Mrs Grose's steps so marked a direction–a direction that made her, when she perceived it, oppose a resistance that showed me she was freshly mystified. 'You're going to the water, Miss?–you think she's *in*–?'

'She may be, though the depth is, I believe, nowhere very great. But what I judge most likely is that she's on the spot from which, the other day, we saw together when I told you.'

'When she pretended not to see–?'

'With that astounding self-possession! I've always been sure she wanted to go back alone. And now her brother has managed it for her.'

Mrs Grose still stood where she had stopped. 'You suppose they really *talk* of them?'

I could meet this with confidence! 'They say things that, if we heard them, would simply appal us.'

'And if she *is* there–?'

'Yes?'

'Then Miss Jessel is?'

'Beyond a doubt. You shall see.'

'Oh, thank you!' my friend cried, planted so firm that, taking it in, I went straight on without her. By the time I reached the pool, however, she was close behind me, and I knew that, whatever, to her apprehension, might befall me, the exposure of my society struck her as her least danger. She exhaled a moan of relief as we at last came in sight of the greater part of the water without a sight of the child. There was no trace of Flora on that nearer side of the bank where my observation of her had been most startling, and none on the opposite edge, where, save for a margin of some twenty yards, a thick copse came down to the water. The pond, oblong in shape, had a width so scant compared to its length that, with its ends out of view, it might have been taken for a scant river. We looked at the empty expanse, and then I felt the suggestion of my friend's eyes. I knew what she meant and I replied with a negative headshake.

'No, no; wait! she has taken the boat.'

My companion stared at the vacant mooring-place and then again across the lake. 'Then where is it?'

'Our not seeing it is the strongest of proofs. She has used it to go over, and then has managed to hide it.'

'All alone—that child?'

'She's not alone, and at such times she's not a child: she's an old, old woman.' I scanned all the visible shore while Mrs Grose took again, into the queer element I offered her, one of her plunges of submission; then I pointed out that the boat might perfectly be in a small refuge formed by one of the recesses of the pool, an indentation masked, for the hither side, by a projection of the bank and by a clump of trees growing close to the water.

'But if the boat's there, where on earth's *she*?' my colleague anxiously asked.

'That's exactly what we must learn.' And I started to walk further.

'By going all the way round?'

'Certainly, far as it is. It will take us but ten minutes, but it's far enough to have made the child prefer not to walk. She went straight over.'

'Laws!' cried my friend again; the chain of my logic was ever too much for her. It dragged her at my heels even now, and when we had got half way round—a devious, tiresome process, on ground much broken and by a path choked with overgrowth—I paused to give her breath. I sustained her with a grateful arm, assuring her that she might hugely help me; and this started us afresh, so that in the course of but few minutes more we reached a point from which we found the boat to be where I had supposed it. It had been intentionally left as much as possible out of sight and was tied to one of the stakes of a fence that came, just there, down to the brink and that had been an assistance to disembarking. I recognized, as I looked at the pair of short, thick oars, quite safely drawn up, the prodigious character of the feat for a little girl; but I had lived, by this time, too long among wonders and had panted to too many livelier measures. There was a gate in the fence, through which we passed, and that brought us, after a trifling interval, more in the open. Then 'There she is!' we both exclaimed at once.

Flora, a short way off, stood before us on the grass and smiled as if her performance was now complete. The next thing she did, however, was to stoop straight down and pluck–quite as if it were all she was there for–a big, ugly spray of withered fern. I instantly became sure she had just come out of the copse. She waited for us, not herself taking a step, and I was conscious of the rare solemnity with which we presently approached her. She smiled and smiled, and we met; but it was all done in a silence by this time flagrantly ominous. Mrs Grose was the first to break the spell: she threw herself on her knees and, drawing the child to her breast, clasped in a long embrace the little tender, yielding body. While this dumb convulsion lasted I could only watch it–which I did the more intently when I saw Flora's face peep at me over our companion's shoulder. It was serious now–the flicker had left it; but it strengthened the pang with which I at that moment envied Mrs Grose the simplicity of *her* relation. Still, all this while, nothing more passed between us save that Flora had let her foolish fern again drop to the ground. What she and I had virtually said to each other was that pretexts were useless now. When Mrs Grose finally got up she kept the child's hand, so that the two were still before me; and the singular reticence of our communion was even more marked in the frank look she launched me. 'I'll be hanged,' it said, 'if *I'll* speak!'

It was Flora who, gazing all over me in candid wonder, was the first. She was struck with our bareheaded aspect. 'Why, where are your things?'

'Where yours are, my dear!' I promptly returned.

She had already got back her gaiety and appeared to take this as an answer quite sufficient, 'And where's Miles?' she went on.

There was something in the small valour of it that quite finished me: these three words from her were, in a flash like the glitter of a drawn blade, the jostle of the cup that my hand, for weeks and weeks, had held high and full to the brim and that now, even before speaking, I felt overflow in a deluge. 'I'll tell you if you'll tell *me*–' I heard myself say, then heard the tremor in which it broke.

'Well, what?'

Mrs Grose's suspense blazed at me, hut it was too late now, and I brought the thing out handsomely. 'Where, my pet, is Miss Jessel?'

20

Just as in the churchyard with Miles, the whole thing was upon us. Much as I had made of the fact that this name had never once, between us, been sounded, the quick, smitten glare with which the child's face now received it fairly likened my breach of the silence to the smash of a pane of glass. It added to the interposing cry, as if to stay the blow, that Mrs Grose, at the same instant, uttered over my violence–the shriek of a creature scared, or rather wounded, which, in turn, within a few seconds, was completed by a gasp of my own. I seized my colleague's arm. 'She's there, she's there!'

Miss Jessel stood before us on the opposite bank exactly as she had stood the other time, and I remember, strangely, as the first feeling now produced in me, my thrill of joy of having brought on a proof. She was there, and I was justified; she was there, and I was neither cruel nor mad. She was there for poor scared Mrs Grose, but she was there most for Flora; and no moment of my monstrous time was perhaps so extraordinary as that in which I consciously threw out to her, with the sense that–pale and ravenous demon as she was, she would catch and understand it–an inarticulate message of gratitude. She rose erect on the spot my friend and I had lately quitted, and there was not, in all the long reach of her desire, an inch of her evil that fell short. This first vividness of vision and emotion were things of a few seconds during which Mrs Grose's dazed blink across to where I pointed struck me as a sovereign sign that she too at last saw, just as it carried my own eyes precipitately to the child. The revelation then of the manner in which Flora was affected startled me, in truth, far more that it would have done to find her also merely agitated, for direct dismay was of course not what I had expected. Prepared and on our guard as our pursuit had actually made her, she would repress every betrayal; and I was therefore shaken, on the spot, by my first glimpse of the particular one for which I had not allowed. To see her, without a convulsion of her small pink face, not even feign to glance in the direction of the prodigy I announced, but only, instead of that, turn at *me* an expression of hard, still gravity, an expression absolutely new and unprecedented and that appeared to read and accuse and judge me–this was a stroke that somehow converted the little girl herself into the very presence that could make me quail. I quailed even though my certitude that she thoroughly saw was never greater than at that instant, and in the immediate need to defend myself I called it passionately to witness. 'She's there, you little unhappy thing–there, there, *there*, and you see her as well as you see me!' I had said shortly before to Mrs Grose that she was not at these times a child, but an old, old woman, and that description of her could not have been more strikingly confirmed than in the way in which, for all answer to this, she simply showed me, without a concession, an admission, of her eyes, a countenance of deeper and deeper, of indeed suddenly quite fixed reprobation. I was by this time–if I can put the whole thing at all together–more appalled at what I may properly call her manner than at anything else, though it was simultaneously with this that I became aware of having Mrs Grose also, and very formidably, to reckon with. My elder companion, the next moment, at any rate, blotted out everything but her own flushed face and her loud, shocked protest, a burst of high disapproval.

'What a dreadful turn, to be sure, Miss! Where on earth do you see anything?'

I could only grasp her more quickly yet, for even while she spoke the hideous plain presence stood undimmed and undaunted. It had already lasted a minute, and it lasted while I continued, seizing my colleague, quite thrusting her at it and presenting her to it, to insist with my pointing hand. 'You don't see her exactly as *we* see?–you mean to say you don't now–*now*? She's as big as a blazing fire! Only look, dearest woman, *look*–!' She looked, even as I did, and gave me, with her deep groan of negation, repulsion, compassion–the mixture with her pity of her relief at her exemption–a sense, touching to me even then, that she would have backed me up if she could. I might well have needed that, for with this hard blow of the proof that her eyes were hopelessly sealed I felt my own situation horribly crumble, I felt–I saw–my livid predecessor press, from her position, on my defeat, and I was conscious, more than all, of what I should have from this instant to deal with in the astounding little attitude of Flora. Into this attitude Mrs Grose immediately and violently entered, breaking, even while there pierced through my sense of ruin a prodigious private triumph, into breathless reassurance.

'She isn't there, little lady, and nobody's there–and you never see nothing, my sweet! How can poor Miss Jessel–when poor Miss Jessel's dead and buried? *We* know, don't we, love?'–and she appealed, blundering in, to the child. 'It's all a mere mistake and a worry and a joke–and we'll go home as fast as we can!'

Our companion, on this, had responded with a strange, quick primness of propriety, and they were again, with Mrs Gross on her feet, united, as it were, in pained opposition to me. Flora continued to fix me with her small mask of reprobation, and even at that minute I prayed God to forgive me for seeming to see that, as she stood there holding tight to our friend's dress, her incomparable childish beauty had suddenly failed, had quite vanished. I've said it already–she was literally, she was hideously hard; she had turned common and almost ugly. 'I don't know what you mean. I see nobody. I see nothing. I never *have*. I think you're cruel. I don't like you!' Then, after this deliverance, which might have been that of a vulgarly pert little girl in the street, she hugged Mrs Grose more closely and buried in her skirts the dreadful little face. In this position she produced an almost furious wail. 'Take me away, take me away–oh, take me away from *her*!'

'From *me*?' I panted.

'From *you*–from you!' she cried.

Even Mrs Grose looked across at me dismayed; while I had nothing to do but communicate again with the figure that, on the opposite bank, without a movement, as rigidly still as if catching, beyond the interval, our voices, was as vividly there for my disaster as it was not there for my service. The wretched child had spoken exactly as if she had got from some outside source each of her stabbing little words, and I could therefore, in the full despair of all I had to accept, but sadly shake my head at her. 'If I had ever doubted all my doubt would at present have gone, I've been living with the miserable truth, and now it has only too much closed round me. Of course I've lost you: I've interfered, and you've seen—under *her* dictation'—with which I faced, over the pool again, our infernal witness—'the easy and perfect way to meet it. I've done my best, but I've lost you. Good-bye.' For Mrs Grose I had an imperative, an almost frantic 'Go, go!' before which, in infinite distress, but mutely possessed of the little girl and clearly convinced, in spite of her blindness, that something awful had occurred and some collapse engulfed us, she retreated, by the way we had come, as fast as she could move.

Of what first happened when I was left alone I had no subsequent memory. I only knew that at the end of, I suppose, a quarter of an hour, an odorous dampness and roughness, chilling and piercing my trouble, had made me understand that I must have thrown myself, on my face, on the ground and given way to a wildness of grief. I must have lain there long and cried and sobbed, for when I raised my head the day was almost done. I got up and looked a moment, through the twilight, at the grey pool and its blank, haunted edge, and then I took, back to the house, my dreary and difficult course. When I reached the gate in the fence the boat, to my surprise, was gone, so that I had a fresh reflection to make on Flora's extraordinary command of the situation. She passed that night, by the most tacit, and I should add, were not the word so grotesque a false note, the happiest of arrangements, with Mrs Grose. I saw neither of them on my return, but, on the other hand, as by an ambiguous compensation, I saw a great deal of Miles. I saw—I can use no other phrase—so much of him that it was as if it were more than it had ever been. No evening I had passed at Bly had the portentous quality of this one; in spite of which—and in spite also of the deeper depths of consternation that had opened beneath my feet—there was literally, in the ebbing actual, an extraordinarily sweet sadness. On reaching the house I had never so much as looked for the boy; I had simply gone straight to my room to change what I was wearing and to take in, at a glance, much material testimony to Flora's rupture. Her little belongings had all been removed. When later, by the schoolroom fire, I was served with tea by the usual maid, I indulged, on the article of my other pupil, in no inquiry whatever. He had his freedom now—he might have it to the end! Well, he did have it; and it consisted—in part at least—of his coming in at about eight o'clock and sitting down with me in silence. On the removal of the tea-things I had blown out the candles and drawn my chair closer: I was conscious of a mortal coldness and felt as if I should never again be warm. So, when he appeared, I was sitting in the glow with my thoughts. He paused a moment by the door as if to look at me; then—as if to share them—came to the other side of the hearth and sank into a chair. We sat there in absolute stillness; yet he wanted, I felt, to be with me.

21

Before a new day, in my room, had fully broken, my eyes opened to Mrs Grose, who had come to my bedside with worse news. Flora was so markedly feverish that an illness was perhaps at hand; she had passed a night of extreme unrest, a night agitated above all by fears that had for their subject not in the least her former, but wholly her present governess. It was not against the possible re-entrance of Miss Jessel on the scene that she protested—it was conspicuously and passionately against mine. I was promptly on my feet of course, and with an immense deal to ask; the more that my friend had discernibly now girded her loins to meet me once more. This I felt as soon as I had put to her the question of her sense of the child's sincerity as against my own. 'She persists in denying to you that she saw, or has ever seen, anything?'

My visitor's trouble, truly, was great. 'Ah, Miss, it isn't a matter on which I can push her! Yet it isn't either, I must say, as if I much needed to. It has made her, every inch of her, quite old.'

'Oh, I see her perfectly from here. She resents, for all the world like some high little personage, the imputation on her truthfulness and, as it were, her respectability. "Miss Jessel indeed—*she*!" Ah, she's "respectable", the chit! The impression she gave me there yesterday was, I assure you, the very strangest of all; it was quite beyond any of the others. I *did* put my foot in it! She'll never speak to me again.'

Hideous and obscure as it all was, it held Mrs Grose briefly silent; then she granted my point with a frankness which, I made sure, had more behind it. 'I think indeed, Miss, she never will. She do have a grand manner about it!'

'And that manner'—I summed it up—'is practically what's the matter with her now.'

Oh, that manner, I could see in my visitor's face, and not a little else besides! 'She asks me every three minutes if I think you're coming in.'

'I see—I see.' I too, on my side, had so much more than worked it out. 'Has she said to you since yesterday—except to repudiate her familiarity with anything so dreadful—a single word about Miss Jessel?'

'Not one, Miss. And of course you know,' my friend added, 'I took it from her, by the lake that, just then and there at least, there *was* nobody.'

'Rather! and, naturally, you take it from her still.'

'I don't contradict her. What else can I do?'

'Nothing in the world! You've the cleverest little person to deal with. They've made them—their two friends, I mean—still cleverer even than nature did; for it was wondrous material to play on! Flora has now her grievance, and she'll work it to the end.'

'Yes, Miss; but to *what* end?'

'Why, that of dealing with me to her uncle. She'll make me out to him the lowest creature—!'

I winced at the fair show of the scene in Mrs Grose's face; she looked for a minute as if she sharply saw them together. 'And him who thinks so well of you!'

'He has an odd way—it comes over me now,' I laughed, '—of proving it! But that doesn't matter. What Flora wants, of course, is to get rid of me!'

My companion bravely concurred. 'Never again to so much as look at you.'

'So that what you've come to me now for,' I asked, 'is to speed me on my way?' Before she had time to reply, however, I had her in check. 'I've a better idea—the result of my reflections. My going *would* seem the right thing, and on Sunday I was terribly near it. Yet that won't do. It's *you* who must go. You must take Flora.'

My visitor, at this, did speculate. 'But where in the world—?'

'Away from here. Away from *them*. Away, even most of all, now, from me. Straight to her uncle.'

'Only to tell on you—?'

'No, not "only!" to leave me, in addition, with my remedy.'

She was still vague. 'And what *is* your remedy?'

'Your loyalty, to begin with. And then Miles's.'

She looked at me hard. 'Do you think he—?'

'Won't, if he has the chance, turn on me? Yes, I venture still to think it. At all events, I want to try. Get off with his sister as soon as possible and leave me with him alone.' I was amazed, myself, at the spirit I had still in reserve, and therefore perhaps a trifle the more disconcerted at the way in which, in spite of this fine example of it, she hesitated. 'There's one thing, of course,' I went on: 'they mustn't, before she goes, see each other for three seconds.' Then it came over me that, in spite of Flora's presumable sequestration from the instant of her return from the pool, it might already be too late. 'Do you mean,' I anxiously asked, 'that they *have* met?'

At this she quite flushed. 'Ah, Miss, I'm not such a fool as that! If I've been obliged to leave her three or four times, it has been each time with one of the maids, and at present, though she's alone, she's locked in safe. And yet—and yet!' There were too many things.

'And yet what?'

'Well, are you so sure of the little gentleman?'

'I'm not sure of anything but *you*. But I have, since last evening, a new hope. I think he wants to give me an opening. I do believe that–poor little exquisite wretch!–he wants to speak. Last evening, in the firelight and the silence, he sat with me for two hours as if it were just coming.'

Mrs Grose looked hard, through the window, at the grey, gathering day. 'And did it come?'

'No, though I waited and waited, I confess it didn't, and it was without a breach of the silence or so much as a faint allusion to his sister's condition and absence that we at last kissed for good night. All the same,' I continued, 'I can't, if her uncle sees her, consent to his seeing her brother without my having given the boy–and most of all because things have got so bad–a little more time.'

My friend appeared on this ground more reluctant than I could quite understand. 'What do you mean by more time?'

'Well, a day or two–really to bring it out. He'll then be on *my* side–of which you see the importance. If nothing comes, I shall only fail, and you will, at the worst, have helped me by doing, on your arrival in town, whatever you may have found possible.' So I put it before her, but she continued for a little so inscrutably embarrassed that I came again to her aid. 'Unless indeed,' I wound up, 'You really want *not* to go.'

I could see it, in her face, at last clear itself; she put out her hand to me as a pledge. 'I'll go–I'll go. I'll go this morning.'

I wanted to be very just. 'If you *should* wish still to wait, I would engage she shouldn't see me.'

'No, no: it's the place itself. She must leave it.' She held me a moment with heavy eyes, then brought out the rest. 'Your idea's the right one. I myself, Miss–'

'Well?'

'I can't stay.'

The look she gave me with it made me jump at possibilities. 'You mean that, since yesterday, you *have* seen–?'

She shook her head with dignity. 'I've *heard*–!'

'Heard?'

'From that child–horrors! There!' she sighed with tragic relief. 'On my honour, Miss, she says things–!' But at this evocation she broke down; she dropped, with a sudden sob, upon my sofa and, as I had seen her do before, gave way to all the grief of it.

It was quite in another manner that I, for my part, let myself go. 'Oh, thank God!'

She sprang up again at this, drying her eyes with a groan. '"Thank God?"'

'It so justifies me!'

'It does that, Miss!'

I couldn't have desired more emphasis, but I just hesitated, 'She's so horrible?'

I saw my colleague scarce knew how to put it. 'Really shocking.'

'And about me?'

'About you, Miss–since you must have it. It's beyond everything, for a young lady; and I can't think wherever she must have picked up–'

'The appalling language she applied to me? I can, then!' I broke in with a laugh that was doubtless significant enough.

It only, in truth, left my friend still more grave. 'Well, perhaps I ought to also–since I've heard some of it before! Yet I can't bear it,' the poor woman went on while, with the same movement, she glanced, on my dressing-table, at the face of my watch. 'But I must go back.'

I kept her, however. 'Ah, if you can't bear it–!'

'How can I stop with her, you mean? Why, just *for* that: to get her away. Far from this,' she pursued, 'far from *them*–'

'She may be different? she may be free?' I seized her almost with joy. 'Then, in spite of yesterday, you *believe*–'

'In such doings?' Her simple description of them required, in the light of her expression, to be carried no further, and she gave me the whole thing as she had never done. 'I believe.'

Yes, it was a joy, and we were still shoulder to shoulder: if I might continue sure of that I should care but little what else happened. My support in the presence of disaster would be the same as it had been in my early need of confidence, and if my friend would answer for my honesty I would answer for all the rest. On the point of taking leave of her, none the less, I was to some extent embarrassed. 'There's one thing of course–it occurs to me–to remember. My letter, giving the alarm, will have reached town before you.'

I now perceived still more how she had been beating about the bush and how weary at last it had made her. 'Your letter won't have got there. Your letter never went.'

'What then became of it?'

'Goodness knows! Master Miles–'

'Do you mean *he* took it?' I gasped.

She hung fire, but she overcame her reluctance. 'I mean that I saw yesterday, when I came back with Miss Flora, that it wasn't where you had put it. Later in the evening I had the chance to question Luke, and he declared that he had neither noticed nor touched it.' We could only exchange on this, one of our deeper mutual soundings, and it was Mrs Grose who first brought up the plumb with an almost elate 'You see!'

'Yes, I see that if Miles took it instead he probably will have read it and destroyed it.'

'And don't you see anything else?'

I faced her a moment with a sad smile. 'It strikes me that by this time your eyes are open even wider than mine.'

They proved to be so indeed, but she could still blush, almost, to show it. 'I make out now what he must have done at school.' And she gave, in her simple sharpness, an almost droll disillusioned nod. 'He stole!'

I turned it over–I tried to be more judicial. 'Well–perhaps.'

She looked as if she found me unexpectedly calm. 'He stole *letters*!'

She couldn't know my reasons for a calmness after all pretty shallow; so I showed them off as I might. 'I hope then it was to more purpose than in this case! The note, at any rate, that I put on the table yesterday,' I pursued, 'will have given him so scant an advantage–for it contained only the bare demand for an interview–that he is already much ashamed of having gone so far for so little, and that what he had on his mind last evening was precisely the need of confession.' I seemed to myself, for the instant, to have mastered it, to see it all. 'Leave us, leave us'–I was already, at the door, hurrying her off. 'I'll get it out of him. He'll meet me–he'll confess. If he confesses, he's saved. And if he's saved–'

'Then *you* are?' The dear woman kissed me on this, and I took her farewell. 'I'll save you without him!' she cried as she went.

22

Yet it was when she had got off–and I missed her on the spot–that the great pinch really came. If I had counted on what it would give me to find myself alone with Miles I speedily perceived, at least, that it would give me a measure. No hour of my stay in fact was so assailed with apprehensions as that of my coming down to learn that the carriage containing Mrs Grose and my younger pupil had already rolled out of the gates. Now I *was*, I said to myself, face to face with the elements, and for much of the rest of the day, while I fought my weakness, I could consider that I had been supremely rash. It was a tighter place still than I had yet turned round in; all the more that, for the first time, I could see in the aspect of others a confused reflection of the crisis. What had happened naturally caused them all to stare; there was too little of the explained, throw out whatever we might, in the suddenness of my colleague's act. The maids and the men looked blank; the effect of which on my nerves was an aggravation until I saw the necessity of making it a positive aid. It was precisely, in short, by just clutching the helm that I avoided total wreck; and I daresay that, to bear up at all, I became, that morning, very grand and very dry. I welcomed the consciousness that I was charged with much to do, and I caused it to be known as well that, left thus to myself, I was quite remarkably firm. I wandered with that manner, for the next hour or two, all over the place and looked, I have no doubt, as if I were ready for any onset. So, for the benefit of whom it might concern, I paraded with a sick heart.

The person it appeared least to concern proved to be, till dinner, little

Miles himself. My perambulations had given me, meanwhile, no glimpse of him, but they had tended to make more public the change taking place in our relation as a consequence of his having at the piano, the day before, kept me, in Flora's interest, so beguiled and befooled. The stamp of publicity had of course been fully given by her confinement and departure, and the change itself was now ushered in by our non-observance of the regular custom of the schoolroom. He had already disappeared when, on my way down, I pushed open his door, and I learned below that he had breakfasted—in the presence of a couple of maids—with Mrs Grose and his sister. He had then gone out, as he said, for a stroll; than which nothing, I reflected, could better have expressed his frank view of the abrupt transformation of my office. What he would now permit this office to consist of was yet to be settled: there was a queer relief, at all events—I mean for myself in especial—in the renouncement of one pretension. If so much had sprung to the surface I scarce put it too strongly in saying that what had perhaps sprung highest was the absurdity of our prolonging the fiction that I had anything more to teach him. It sufficiently stuck out that, by tacit little tricks in which even more than myself he carried out the care of my dignity, I had had to appeal to him to let me off straining to meet him on the ground of his true capacity. He had at any rate his freedom now; I was never to touch it again, as I had amply shown, moreover, when, on his joining me in the schoolroom the previous night, I had uttered, on the subject of the interval just concluded, neither challenge nor hint. I had too much, from this moment, my other ideas. Yet when he at last arrived the difficulty of applying them, the accumulations of my problem, were brought straight home to me by the beautiful little presence on which what had occurred had as yet, for the eye, dropped neither stain nor shadow.

To mark, for the house, the high state I cultivated I decreed that my meals with the boy should be served, as we called it, downstairs; so that I had been awaiting him in the ponderous pomp of the room outside of the window of which I had had from Mrs Grose, that first scared Sunday, my flash of something it would scarce have done to call light. Here at present I felt afresh—for I had felt it again and again—how my equilibrium depended on the success of my rigid will, the will to shut my eyes as tight as possible to the truth that what I had to deal with was, revoltingly, against nature. I could only get on at all by taking 'nature' into my confidence and my account, by treating my monstrous ordeal as a push in a direction unusual, of course, and unpleasant, but demanding, after all, for a fair front, only another turn of the screw of ordinary human virtue. No attempt, none the less, could well require more tact than just this attempt to supply, one's self, *all* the nature. How could I put even a little of that article into a suppression of reference to what had occurred? How, on the other hand, could I make a reference without a new plunge into the hideous obscure? Well, a sort of answer, after a time, had come to me, and it was so far confirmed as that I was met, incontestably, by the quickened vision of what was rare in my little companion. It was indeed as if he had found even now—as he had so often found at lessons—still some other delicate way to ease me off. Wasn't there light in the fact which, as we shared our solitude, broke out with a specious glitter it had never yet quite worn?—the fact that (opportunity aiding, precious opportunity which had now come), it would be preposterous, with a child so endowed, to forego the help one might wrest from absolute intelligence? What had his intelligence been given him for but to save him? Mightn't one, to reach his mind, risk the stretch of an angular arm over his character? It was as if, when we were face to face in the dining-room, he had literally shown me the way. The roast mutton was on the table, and I had dispensed with attendance. Miles, before he sat down, stood a moment with his hands in his pockets and looked at the joint, on which he seemed on the point of passing some humorous judgement. But what he presently produced was 'I say, my dear, is she really very awfully ill?'

'Little Flora? Not so bad but that she'll presently be better. London will set her up. Bly had ceased to agree with her. Come here and take your mutton.'

He alertly obeyed me, carried the plate carefully to his seat and, when he was established, went on. 'Did Bly disagree with her so terribly suddenly?'

'Not so suddenly as you might think. One had seen it coming on.'

'Then why didn't you get her off before?'

'Before what?'

'Before she became too ill to travel.'

I found myself prompt. 'She's *not* too ill to travel: she only might have become so if she had stayed. This was just the moment to seize. The journey will dissipate the influence'—oh, I was grand!—'and carry it off.'

'I see, I see'—Miles, for that matter, was grand too. He settled to his repast with the charming little 'table manner' that, from the day of his arrival, had relieved me of all grossness of admonition. Whatever he had been driven from school for, it was not for ugly feeding. He was irreproachable, as always, today; but he was unmistakably more conscious. He was discernibly trying to take for granted more things than he found, without assistance, quite easy; and he dropped into peaceful silence while he felt his situation. Our meal was of the briefest—mine a vain pretence, and I had the things immediately removed. While this was done Miles stood again with his hands in his little pockets and his back to me—stood and looked out of the wide window through which, that other day, I had seen what pulled me up. We continued silent while the maid was with us—as silent, it whimsically occurred to me, as some young couple who, on their wedding-journey, at the inn, feel shy in the presence of the waiter. He turned round only when the waiter had left us. 'Well—so we're alone!'

23

'Oh, more or less.' I fancy my smile was pale. 'Not absolutely. We shouldn't like that!' I went on.

'No–I suppose we shouldn't. Of course we have the others.'

'We have the others–we have indeed the others,' I concurred.

'Yet even though we have them,' he returned, still with his hands in his pockets and planted there in front of me, 'they don't much count, do they?'

I made the best of it, but I felt wan. 'It depends on what you call "much"!'

'Yes'–with all accommodation–'everything depends!' On this, however, he faced to the window again and presently reached it with his vague, restless, cogitating step. He remained there a while, with his forehead against the glass, in contemplation of the stupid shrubs I knew and the dull things of November. I had always my hypocrisy of 'work', behind which, now, I gained the sofa. Steadying myself with it there as I had repeatedly done at those moments of torment that I have described as the moments of my knowing the children to be given to something from which I was barred, I sufficiently obeyed my habit of being prepared for the worst. But an extraordinary impression dropped on me as I extracted a meaning from the boy's embarrassed back–none other than the impression that I was not barred now. This inference grew in a few minutes to sharp intensity and seemed bound up with the direct perception that it was positively *he* who was. The frames and squares of the great window were a kind of image, for him, of a kind of failure. I felt that I saw him, at any rate, shut in or shut out. He was admirable, but not comfortable: I took it in with a throb of hope. Wasn't he looking, through the haunted pane, for something he couldn't see?–and wasn't it the first time in the whole business that he had known such a lapse? The first, the very first: I found it a splendid portent. It made him anxious, though he watched himself; he had been anxious all day and, even while in his usual sweet little manner he sat at table, had needed all his small strange genius to give it a gloss. When he at last turned round to meet me it was almost as if this genius had succumbed. 'Well, I think I'm glad Bly agrees with *me*!'

'You would certainly seem to have seen, these twenty-four hours, a good deal more of it than for some time before. I hope,' I went on bravely, 'that you've been enjoying yourself.'

'Oh yes, I've been ever so far; all round about–miles and miles away. I've never been so free.'

He had really a manner of his own, and I could only try to keep up with him. 'Well, do you like it?'

He stood there smiling; then at last he put into two words–'Do *you*?'–more discrimination than I had ever heard two words contain. Before I had time to deal with that, however, he continued as if with the sense that this was an impertinence to be softened. 'Nothing could be more charming than the way you take it, for of course if we're alone together now it's you that are alone most. But I hope,' he threw in, 'you don't particularly mind!'

'Having to do with you?' I asked. 'My dear child, how can I help minding? Though I've renounced all claim to your company—you're so beyond me—I at least greatly enjoy it. What else should I stay on for?'

He looked at me more directly, and the expression of his face, graver now, struck me as the most beautiful I had ever found in it. 'You stay on just for *that*?'

'Certainly. I stay on as your friend and from the tremendous interest I take in you till something can be done for you that may be more worth your while. That needn't surprise you.' My voice trembled so that I felt it impossible to suppress the shake. 'Don't you remember how I told you, when I came and sat on your bed the night of the storm, that there was nothing in the world I wouldn't do for you?'

'Yes, yes!' He, on his side, more and more visibly nervous, had a tone to master; but he was so much more successful than I that, laughing out through his gravity, he could pretend we were pleasantly jesting. 'Only that, I think, was to get me to do something for *you*!'

'It was partly to get you to do something,' I conceded. 'But, you know, you didn't do it.'

'Oh yes,' he said with the brightest superficial eagerness, 'you wanted me to tell you something.'

'That's it. Out, straight out. What you have on your mind, you know.'

'Ah then, is *that* what you've stayed over for?'

He spoke with a gaiety through which I could still catch the finest little quiver of resentful passion; but I can't begin to express the effect upon me of an implication of surrender even so faint. It was as if what I had yearned for had come at last only to astonish me. 'Well, yes—I may as well make a clean breast of it. It was precisely for that.'

He waited so long that I supposed it for the purpose of repudiating the assumption on which my action had been founded; but what he finally said was: 'Do you mean now—here?'

'There couldn't be a better place or time.' He looked round him uneasily, and I had the rare—oh, the queer!—impression of the very first symptom I had seen in him of the approach of immediate fear. It was as if he were suddenly afraid of me—which struck me indeed as perhaps the best thing to make him. Yet in the very pang of the effort I felt it vain to try sternness, and I heard myself the next instant so gentle as to be almost grotesque. 'You want so to go out again?'

'Awfully!' He smiled at me heroically, and the touching little bravery of it was enhanced by his actually flushing with pain. He had picked up his hat, which he had brought in, and stood twirling it in a way that gave me, even as I was just nearly reaching port, a perverse horror of what I was doing. To do it in *any* way was an act of violence, for what did it consist of but the obtrusion of the idea of grossness and guilt on a small helpless creature who had been for me a revelation of the possibilities of beautiful intercourse? Wasn't it base to create for a being so exquisite a mere alien awkwardness? I suppose I now read into our situation a clearness it couldn't have had at the time, for I seem to see our poor eyes already lighted with some spark of a prevision of the anguish that was to come. So we circled about, with terrors and scruples, like fighters not daring to close. But it was for each other we feared! That kept us a little longer suspended and unbruised. 'I'll tell you everything,' Miles said–'I mean I'll tell you anything you like. You'll stay on with me, and we shall both be all right and I *will* tell you–I *will*. But not now.'

'Why not now?'

My insistence turned him from me and kept him once more at his window in a silence during which, between us, you might have heard a pin drop. Then he was before me again with the air of a person for whom, outside, someone who had frankly to be reckoned with was waiting. 'I have to see Luke.'

I had not yet reduced him to quite so vulgar a lie, and I felt proportionately ashamed. But, horrible as it was, his lies made up my truth. I achieved thoughtfully a few loops of my knitting. 'Well then, go to Luke, and I'll wait for what you promise. Only, in return for that, satisfy, before you leave me, one very much smaller request.'

He looked as if he felt he had succeeded enough to be able still a little to bargain. 'Very much smaller–?'

'Yes, a mere fraction of the whole. Tell me'–oh, my work preoccupied me, and I was off-hand!–'if, yesterday afternoon, from the table in the hall, you took, you know, my letter.'

24

My sense of how he received this suffered for a minute from something that I can describe only as a fierce split of my attention–a stroke that at first, as I sprang straight up, reduced me to the mere blind movement of getting hold of him, drawing him close and, while I just fell for support against the nearest piece of furniture, instinctively keeping him with his back to the window. The appearance was full upon us that I had already had to deal with here: Peter Quint had come into view like a sentinel before a prison. The next thing I saw was that, from outside, he had reached the window, and then I knew that, close to the glass and glaring in through it, he offered once more to the room his white face of damnation. It represents but grossly what took place within me at the sight to say that on the second my decision was made; yet I believe that no woman so overwhelmed ever in so short a time recovered her grasp of the *act*. It came to me in the very horror of the immediate presence that the act would be, seeing and facing what I saw and faced, to keep the boy himself unaware. The inspiration—I can call it by no other name—was that I felt how voluntarily, how transcendently, I *might*. It was like fighting with a demon for a human soul, and when I had fairly so appraised it I saw how the human soul—held out, in the tremor of my hands, at arms' length—had a perfect dew of sweat on a lovely childish forehead. The face that was close to mine was as white as the face against the glass, and out of it presently came a sound, not low nor weak, but as if from much farther away, that I drank like a waft of fragrance.

'Yes—I took it.'

At this, with a moan of joy, I enfolded, I drew him close; and while I held him to my breast, where I could feel in the sudden fever of his little body the tremendous pulse of his little heart, I kept my eyes on the thing at the window and saw it move and shift its posture. I have likened it to a sentinel, but its slow wheel, for a moment, was rather the prowl of a baffled beast. My present quickened courage, however, was such that, not too much to let it through, I had to shade, as it were, my flame. Meanwhile the glare of the face was again at the window, the scoundrel fixed as if to watch and wait. It was the very confidence that I might now defy him, as well as the positive certitude, by this time, of the child's unconsciousness, that made me go on. 'What did you take it for?'

'To see what you said about me.'

'You opened the letter?'

'I opened it.'

My eyes were now, as I held him off a little again, on Miles's own face, in which the collapse of mockery showed me how complete was the ravage of uneasiness. What was prodigious was that at last, by my success, his sense was sealed and his communication stopped: he knew that he was in presence, but knew not of what, and knew still less that I also was and that I did know. And what did this strain of trouble matter when my eyes went back to the window only to see that the air was clear again and—by my personal triumph—the influence quenched? There was nothing there. I felt that the cause was mine and that I should surely get *all*. 'And you found nothing!'—I let my elation out.

He gave the most mournful, thoughtful little headshake. 'Nothing.'

'Nothing, nothing!' I almost shouted in my joy.

'Nothing, nothing,' he sadly repeated.

I kissed his forehead; it was drenched. 'So what have you done with it?'

'I've burnt it.'

'Burnt it?' It was now or never. 'Is that what you did at school?'

Oh, what this brought up! 'At school?'

'Did you take letters?—or other things?'

'Other things?' He appeared now to be thinking of something far off and that reached him only through the pressure of his anxiety. Yet it did reach him. 'Did I *steal*?'

I felt myself redden to the roots of my hair as well as wonder if it were more strange to put to a gentleman such a question or to see him take it with allowances that gave the very distance of his fall in the world. 'Was it for that you mightn't go back?'

The only thing he felt was rather a dreary little surprise. 'Did you know I mightn't go back?'

'I know everything.'

He gave me at this the longest and strangest look. 'Everything?'

'Everything. Therefore *did* you—?' But I couldn't say it again.

Miles could, very simply. 'No. I didn't steal.'

My face must have shown him I believed him utterly; yet my hands—but it was for pure tenderness—shook him as if to ask him why, if it was all for nothing, he had condemned me to months of torment. 'What then did you do?'

He looked in vague pain all round the top of the room and drew his breath, two or three times over, as if with difficulty. He might have been standing at the bottom of the sea and raising his eyes to some faint green twilight. 'Well—I said things.'

'Only that?'

'They thought it was enough!'

'To turn you out for?'

Never, truly, had a person 'turned out' shown so little to explain it as this little person! He appeared to weigh my question, but in a manner quite detached and almost helpless. 'Well, I suppose I oughtn't.'

'But to whom did you say them?'

He evidently tried to remember, but it dropped—he had lost it. 'I don't know!'

He almost smiled at me in the desolation of his surrender, which was indeed practically, by this time, so complete that I ought to have left it there. But I was infatuated—I was blind with victory, though even then the very effect that was to have brought him so much nearer was already that of added separation. 'Was it to everyone?' I asked.

'No; it was only to—' But he gave a sick little headshake. 'I don't remember their names.'

'Were they then so many?'

'No—only a few. Those I liked.'

Those he liked? I seemed to float not into clearness, but into a darker obscure, and within a minute there had come to me out of my very pity the appalling alarm of his being perhaps innocent. It was for the instant confounding and bottomless, for if he *were* innocent, what then on earth was *I*?

Paralysed, while it lasted, by the mere brush of the question, I let him go a little, so that, with a deep-drawn sigh, he turned away from me again; which, as he faced towards the clear window, I suffered, feeling that I had nothing now there to keep him from. 'And did they repeat what you said?' I went on after a moment.

He was soon at some distance from me, still breathing hard and again with the air, though now without anger for it, of being confined against his will. Once more, as he had done before, he looked up at the dim day as if, of what had hitherto sustained him, nothing was left but an unspeakable anxiety. 'Oh yes,' he nevertheless replied–'they must have repeated them. To those *they* liked,' he added.

There was, somehow, less of it than I had expected; but I turned it over. 'And these things came round–?

'To the masters? Oh yes!' he answered very simply. 'But I didn't know they'd tell.'

'The masters? They didn't–they've never told. That's why I ask you.'

He turned to me again his little beautiful fevered face. 'Yes, it was too bad.'

'Too bad?'

'What I suppose I sometimes said. To write home.'

I can't name the exquisite pathos of the contradiction given to such a speech by such a speaker; I only know that the next instant I heard myself throw off with homely force: 'Stuff and nonsense!' But the next after that I must have sounded stern enough. 'What *were* these things?'

My sternness was all for his judge, his executioner; yet it made him avert himself again, and that movement made *me*, with a single bound and an irrepressible cry, spring straight upon him. For there again, against the glass, as if to blight his confession and stay his answer, was the hideous author of our woe–the white face of damnation. I felt a sick swim at the drop of my victory and all the return of my battle, so that the wildness of my veritable leap only served as a great betrayal. I saw him, from the midst of my act, meet it with a divination, and on the perception that even now he only guessed, and that the window was still to his own eyes free, I let the impulse flame up to convert the climax of his dismay into the very proof of his liberation. 'No more, no more, no more!' I shrieked, as I tried to press him against me, to my visitant.

'Is she *here*?' Miles panted as he caught with his sealed eyes the direction of my words. Then as his strange 'she' staggered me and, with a gasp, I echoed it, 'Miss Jessel, Miss Jessel!' he with a sudden fury gave me back.

I seized, stupefied, his supposition–some sequel to what we had done to Flora, but this made me only want to show him that it was better still than that. 'It's not Miss Jessel! But it's at the window–straight before us. It's *there*–the coward horror, there for the last time!'

At this, after a second in which his head made the movement of a baffled dog's on a scent and then gave a frantic little shake for air and light, he was at me in a white rage, bewildered, glaring vainly over the place and missing wholly, though it now, to my sense, filled the room like the taste of poison, the wide, overwhelming presence. 'It's *he*?'

I was so determined to have all my proof that I flashed into ice to challenge him. 'Whom do you mean by "he"?'

'Peter Quint–you devil!' His face gave again, round the room, its convulsed supplication. '*Where*?'

They are in my ears still, his supreme surrender of the name and his tribute to my devotion. 'What does he matter now, my own?–what will he ever matter? *I* have you,' I launched at the beast, 'but he has lost you for ever!' Then, for the demonstration of my work, 'There, *there*!' I said to Miles.

But he had already jerked straight round, stared, glared again, and seen but the quiet day. With the stroke of the loss I was so proud of he uttered the cry of a creature hurled over an abyss, and the grasp with which I recovered him might have been that of catching him in his fall. I caught him, yes, I held him–it may be imagined with what a passion; but at the end of a minute I began to feel what it truly was that I held. We were alone with the quiet day, and his little heart, dispossessed, had stopped.

JOEL CHANDLER HARRIS

[1848–1908]

Brer Rabbit, Brer Fox, and the Tar Baby

(AN UNCLE REMUS STORY)

(First published in *Constitution,* July, 1879; first book publication in 1881.)

One evening recently, the lady whom Uncle Remus calls "Miss Sally" missed her little seven-year-old boy. Making search for him through the house and through the yard, she heard the sound of voices in the old man's cabin, and, looking through the window, saw the child sitting by Uncle Remus. His head rested against the old man's arm, and he was gazing with an expression of the most intense interest into the rough, weather-beaten face, that beamed so kindly upon him. This is what "Miss Sally" heard:

"Bimeby, one day, arter Brer Fox bin doin' all dat he could fer ter ketch Brer Rabbit, en Brer Rabbit bin doin' all he could fer to keep 'im fum it, Brer Fox say to hisse'f dat he'd put up a game on Brer Rabbit, en he ain't mo'n got de wuds out'n his mouf twel Brer Rabbit come a lopin' up de big road, lookin' des ez plump, en ez fat, en ez sassy ez a Moggin hoss in a barley-patch.

"'Hol' on dar, Brer Rabbit,' sez Brer Fox, sezee.

"'I ain't got time, Brer Fox,' sez Brer Rabbit, sezee, sorter mendin' his licks.

"'I wanter have some confab wid you, Brer Rabbit,' sez Brer Fox, sezee.

"'All right, Brer Fox, but you better holler fum whar you stan'. I'm monstus full er fleas dis mawnin',' sez Brer Rabbit, sezee.

"'I seed Brer B'ar yistiddy,' sez Brer Fox, sezee, 'en he sorter rake me over de coals kaze you en me ain't make frens en live naberly, en I told 'im dat I'd see you.'

"Den Brer Rabbit scratch one year wid his off hinefoot sorter jub'usly, en den he ups en sez, sezee:

"'All a settin', Brer Fox. Spose'n you drap roun' ter-morrer en take dinner wid me. We ain't got no great doin's at our house, but I speck de old 'oman en de chilluns kin sorter scramble roun' en git up sump'n fer ter stay yo' stummuck.'

"'I'm 'gree'ble, Brer Rabbit,' sez Brer Fox, sezee.

"'Den I'll 'pen' on you,' sez Brer Rabbit, sezee.

"Nex' day, Mr. Rabbit an' Miss Rabbit got up soon, 'fo' day, en raided on a gyarden like Miss Sally's out dar, en got some cabbiges, en some roas'n years, en some sparrer-grass, en dey fix up a smashin' dinner. Bimeby one er de little Rabbits, playin' out in de backyard, come runnin' in hollerin', 'Oh, ma! oh, ma! I seed Mr. Fox a comin'!' En den Brer Rabbit he tuck de chilluns by der years en make um set down, en den him and Miss Rabbit sorter dally roun' waitin' for Brer Fox. En dey keep on waitin', but no Brer Fox ain't come. Atter 'while Brer Rabbit goes to de do', easy like, en peep out, en dar, stickin' fum behime de cornder, wuz de tip-een' er Brer Fox tail. Den Brer Rabbit shot de do' en sot down, en put his paws behime his years en begin fer ter sing:

"'De Place wharbouts you spill de grease,
Right dar youer boun' ter slide,
An' whar you fine a bunch er ha'r,
You'll sholy fine de hide.'

"Nex' day, Brer Fox sont word by Mr. Mink, en skuze hisse'f kaze he wuz too sick fer ter come, en he ax Brer Rabbit fer to come en take dinner wid him, en Brer Rabbit say he wuz 'gree'ble.

"Bimeby, w'en de shadders wuz at der shortes', Brer Rabbit he sorter brush up en santer down ter Brer Fox's house, en w'en he got dar, he hear somebody groanin, en he look in de do' en dar he see Brer Fox settin' up in a rockin' cheer all wrop up wid flannil, en he look mighty weak. Brer Rabbit look all 'roun', he did, but he ain't see no dinner, De dish-pan wuz settin' on de table, en close by wuz a kyarvin' knife.

"'Look like you gwineter have chicken fer dinner, Brer Fox,' sez Brer Rabbit, sezee.

"'Yes, Brer Rabbit, deyer nice, en fresh, en tender,' sez Brer Fox, sezee.

"Den Brer Rabbit sorter pull his mustarsh, en say: 'You ain't got no calamus root, is you, Brer Fox? I done got so now dat I can't eat no chicken 'ceppin she's seasoned up wid calamus root.' En wid dat Brer Rabbit lipt out er de do' and dodge 'mong de bushes, en sot dar watchin' fer Brer Fox; en he ain't watch long, nudder, kaze Brer Fox flung off de flannil en crope out er de house en got whar he could cloze in on Brer Rabbit, en bimeby Brer Rabbit holler out: 'Oh, Brer Fox! I'll des put yo' calamus root out yer on dish yer stump. Better come git it while hit's fresh,' and wid dat Brer Rabbit gallop off home. En Brer Fox ain't never kotch 'im yet, en w'at's mo', honey, he ain't gwineter."

"Didn't the fox *never* catch the rabbit, Uncle Remus?" asked the little boy the next evening.

"He come mighty nigh it' honey, sho's you born—Brer Fox did. One day atter Brer Rabbit fool 'im wid dat calamus root, Brer Fox went ter wuk en got 'im some tar, en mix it wid some turkentime, en fix up a contrapshun wat he call a Tar-Baby, en he tuck dish yer Tar-Baby en he sot 'er in de big road, en den he lay off in de bushes fer to see wat de news wuz gwineter be. En he didn't hatter wait long, nudder, kaze bimeby here come Brer Rabbit pacin' down de road—lippity-clippity, clippity-lippity—dez ez sassy ez a jay-bird. Brer Fox, he lay low. Brer Rabbit come prancin' 'long twel he spy de Tar-Baby, en den he fotch up on his behime legs like he wuz 'stonished. De Tar-Baby, she sot dar, she did, en Brer Fox, he lay low.

"'Mawnin'!' sez Brer Rabbit, sezee—'nice wedder dis mawnin',' sezee.

"Tar-Baby ain't sayin' nothin', en Brer Fox, he lay low.

"'How duz yo' sym'tums seem ter segashuate?' sez Brer Rabbit, sezee.

"Brer Fox, he wink his eye slow, en lay low, en de Tar-Baby, she ain't sayin' nothin'.

"'How you come on, den? Is you deaf?' sez Brer Rabbit, sezee. 'Kaze if you is, I kin holler louder,' sezee.

"Tar-Baby stay still, en Brer Fox, he lay low.

"'Youer stuck up, dat's w'at you is,' says Brer Rabbit, sezee, 'en I'm gwineter kyore you, dat's w'at I'm a gwineter do,' sezee.

"Brer Fox, he sorter chuckle in his stummuck, he did, but Tar-Baby ain't sayin' nothin'.

"'I'm gwineter larn you howter talk ter 'specttubble fokes ef hit's de las' ack,' sez Brer Rabbit, sezee. 'Ef you don't take off dat hat en tell me howdy, I'm gwineter bus' you wide open,' sezee.

"Tar-Baby stay still, en Brer Fox, he lay low.

"Brer Rabbit keep on axin' 'im, en de Tar-Baby, she keep on sayin' nothin', twel present'y Brer Rabbit draw back wid his fis', he did, en blip he tuck 'er side er de head. Right dar's whar he broke his merlasses jug. His fis' stuck, en he can't pull loose. De tar hilt 'im. But Tar-Baby, she stay still, en Brer Fox, he lay low.

"'Ef you don't lemme loose, I'll knock you agin,' sez Brer Rabbit, sezee, en wid dat he fotch 'en a wipe wid de udder han', en dat stuck. Tar-Baby, she ain't sayin' nothin', en Brer Fox, he lay low.

"'Tu'n me loose, fo' I kick de natal stuffin' outen you,' sez Brer Rabbit, sezee, but de Tar-Baby, she ain't sayin' nothin'. She des hilt on, en den Brer Rabbit lose de use er his feet in de same way. Brer Fox, he lay low. Den Brer Rabbit squall out dat ef de Tar-Baby don't tu'n 'im loose he butt'er cranksided. En den he butted, en his head got stuck. Den Brer Fox, he sa'ntered fort', lookin' des ez innercent ez one er yo' mammy's mockin'-birds.

"'Howdy, Brer Rabbit,' sez Brer Fox, sezee. 'You look sorter stuck up dis mawnin',' sezee, en den he rolled on de groun', en laughed en laughed twel he couldn't laugh no mo'. 'I speck you'll take dinner wid me dis time, Brer Rabbit. I done laid in some calamus root, en I ain't gwineter take no skuse,' sez Brer Fox, sezee."

Here Uncle Remus paused, and drew a two-pound yam out of the ashes.

"Did the fox eat the rabbit?" asked the little boy to whom the story had been told.

"Dat's all de fur de tale goes," replied the old man. "He mout, en den agin he moutent. Some say Jedge B'ar come 'long en loosed 'im—some say he didn't. I hear Miss Sally callin'. You better run 'long."

SARAH ORNE JEWETT

[1849–1909]

A White Heron

(1886)

I

THE WOODS WERE already filled with shadows one June evening, just before eight o'clock, though a bright sunset still glimmered faintly among the trunks of the trees. A little girl was driving home her cow, a plodding, dilatory, provoking creature in her behavior, but a valued companion for all that. They were going away from whatever light there was, and striking deep into the woods, but their feet were familiar with the path, and it was no matter whether their eyes could see it or not.

There was hardly a night the summer through when the old cow could be found waiting at the pasture bars; on the contrary, it was her greatest pleasure to hide herself away among the huckleberry bushes, and though she wore a loud bell she had made the discovery that if one stood perfectly still it would not ring. So Sylvia had to hunt for her until she found her, and call Co'! Co'! with never an answering Moo, until her childish patience was quite spent. If the creature had not given good milk and plenty of it, the case would have seemed very different to her owners. Besides, Sylvia had all the time there was, and very little use to make of it. Sometimes in pleasant weather it was a consolation to look upon the cow's pranks as an intelligent attempt to play hide and seek, and as the child had no playmates she lent herself to this amusement with a good deal of zest. Though this chase had been so long that the wary animal herself had given an unusual signal of her whereabouts, Sylvia had only laughed when she came upon Mistress Moolly at the swamp-side, and urged her affectionately homeward with a twig of birch leaves. The old cow was not inclined to wander farther, she even turned in the right direction for once as they left the pasture, and stepped along the road at a good pace. She was quite ready to be milked now, and seldom stopped to browse. Sylvia wondered what her grandmother would say because they were so late. It was a great while since she had left home at half-past five o'clock, but everybody knew the difficulty of making this errand a short one. Mrs. Tilley had chased the hornéd torment too many summer evenings herself to blame any one else for lingering, and was only thankful as she waited that she had Sylvia, nowadays, to give such valuable assistance. The good woman suspected that Sylvia loitered occasionally on her own account; there never was such a child for straying about out-of-doors since the world was made! Everybody said that it was a good change for a little maid who had tried to grow for eight years in a crowded manufacturing town, but, as for Sylvia herself, it seemed as if she never had been alive at all before she came to live at the farm. She thought often with wistful compassion of a wretched geranium that belonged to a town neighbor.

"'Afraid of folks,'" old Mrs. Tilley said to herself, with a smile, after she had made the unlikely choice of Sylvia from her daughter's houseful of children, and was returning to the farm, "'Afraid of folks,' they said! I guess she won't be troubled no great with 'em up to the old place!" When they reached the door of the lonely house and stopped to unlock it, and the cat came to purr loudly, and rub against them, a deserted pussy, indeed, but fat with young robins, Sylvia whispered that this was a beautiful place to live in, and she never should wish to go home.

The companions followed the shady wood-road, the cow taking slow steps and the child very fast ones. The cow stopped long at the brook to drink, as if the pasture were not half a swamp, and Sylvia stood still and waited, letting her bare feet cool themselves in the shoal water, while the great twilight moths struck softly against her. She waded on through the brook as the cow moved away, and listened to the thrushes with a heart that beat fast with pleasure. There was a stirring in the great boughs overhead. They were full of little birds and beasts that seemed to be wide awake, and going about their world, or else saying good-night to each other in sleepy twitters. Sylvia herself felt sleepy as she walked along. However, it was not much farther to the house, and the air was soft and sweet. She was not often in the woods so late as this, and it made her feel as if she were a part of the gray shadows and the moving leaves. She was just thinking how long it seemed since she first came to the farm a year ago, and wondering if everything went on in the noisy town just the same as when she was there; the thought of the great red-faced boy who used to chase and frighten her made her hurry along the path to escape from the shadow of the trees.

Suddenly this little woods-girl is horror-stricken to hear a clear whistle not very far away. Not a bird's-whistle, which would have a sort of friendliness, but a boy's whistle, determined, and somewhat aggressive. Sylvia left the cow to whatever sad fate might await her, and stepped discreetly aside into the brushes, but she was just too late. The enemy had discovered her, and called out in a very cheerful and persuasive tone, "Halloa, little girl, how far is it to the road?" and trembling Sylvia answered almost inaudibly, "A good ways."

She did not dare to look boldly at the tall young man, who carried a gun over his shoulder, but she came out of her bush and again followed the cow, while he walked alongside.

"I have been hunting for some birds," the stranger said kindly, "and I have lost my way, and need a friend very much. Don't be afraid," he added gallantly. "Speak up and tell me what your name is, and whether you think I can spend the night at your house, and go out gunning early in the morning."

Sylvia was more alarmed than before. Would not her grandmother consider her much to blame? But who could have foreseen such an accident as this? It did not seem to be her fault, and she hung her head as if the stem of it were broken, but managed to answer "Sylvy," with much effort when her companion again asked her name.

Mrs. Tilley was standing in the doorway when the trio came into view. The cow gave a loud moo by way of explanation.

"Yes, you'd better speak up for yourself, you old trial! Where'd she tucked herself away this time, Sylvy?" But Sylvia kept an awed silence; she knew by instinct that her grandmother did not comprehend the gravity of the situation. She must be mistaking the stranger for one of the farmer-lads of the region.

The young man stood his gun beside the door, and dropped a lumpy game-bag beside it; then he bade Mrs. Tilley good-evening, and repeated his wayfarer's story, and asked if he could have a night's lodging.

"Put me anywhere you like," he said. "I must be off early in the morning, before day; but I am very hungry, indeed. You can give me some milk at any rate, that's plain."

"Dear sakes, yes," responded the hostess, whose long slumbering hospitality seemed to be easily awakened. "You might fare better if you went out to the main road a mile or so, but you're welcome to what we've got. I'll milk right off, and you make yourself at home. You can sleep on husks or feathers," she proffered graciously. "I raised them all myself. There's good pasturing for geese just below here towards the ma'sh. Now step round and set a plate for the gentleman, Sylvy!" And Sylvia promptly stepped. She was glad to have something to do, and she was hungry herself.

It was a surprise to find so clean and comfortable a little dwelling in this New England wilderness. The young man had known the horrors of its most primitive housekeeping, and the dreary squalor of that level of society which does not rebel at the companionship of hens. This was the best thrift of an old-fashioned farmstead, though on such a small scale that it seemed like a hermitage. He listened eagerly to the old woman's quaint talk, he watched Sylvia's pale face and shining gray eyes with ever growing enthusiasm, and insisted that this was the best supper he had eaten for a month, and afterward the new-made friends sat down in the doorway together while the moon came up.

Soon it would be berry-time, and Sylvia was a great help at picking. The cow was a good milker, though a plaguy thing to keep track of, the hostess gossiped frankly, adding presently that she had buried four children, so Sylvia's mother, and a son (who might be dead) in California were all the children she had left. "Dan, my boy, was a great hand to go gunning," she explained sadly. "I never wanted for pa'tridges or gray squer'ls while he was to home. He's been a great wand'rer, I expect, and he's no hand to write letters. There. I don't blame him, I'd ha' seen the world myself if it had been so I could."

"Sylvy takes after him," the grandmother continued affectionately, after a minute's pause. "There ain't a foot o' ground she don't know her way over, and the wild creaturs counts her one o' themselves. Squer'ls she'll tame to come an' feed right out o' her hands, and all sorts o' birds. Last winter she got the jaybirds to bangeing here, and I believe she'd 'a' scanted herself of her own meals to have plenty to throw out amongst 'em, if I had n't kep' watch. Anything but crows, I tell her, I'm willin' to help support–though Dan he had a tamed one o' them that did seem to have reason same as folks. It was round here a good spell after he went away. Dan an' his father they did n't hitch,–but he never held up his head ag'in after Dan had dared him an' gone off."

The guest did not notice this hint of family sorrows in his eager interest in something else.

"So Sylvy knows all about birds, does she?" he exclaimed, as he looked round at the little girl who sat, very demure but increasingly sleepy, in the moonlight. "I am making a collection of birds myself. I have been at it ever since I was a boy." (Mrs. Tilley smiled.) "There are two or three very rare ones I have been hunting for these five years. I mean to get them on my own ground if they can be found."

"Do you cage 'em up?" asked Mrs. Tilley doubtfully, in response to this enthusiastic announcement.

"Oh no, they 're stuffed and preserved, dozens and dozens of them," said the ornithologist, "and I have shot or snared every one myself. I caught a glimpse of a white heron a few miles from here on Saturday, and I have followed it in this direction. They have never been found in this district at all. The little white heron, it is," and he turned again to look at Sylvia with the hope of discovering that the rare bird was one of her acquaintances.

But Sylvia was watching a hop-toad in the narrow footpath.

"You would know the heron if you saw it," the stranger continued eagerly. "A queer tall white bird with soft feathers and long thin legs. And it would have a nest perhaps in the top of a high tree, made of sticks, something like a hawk's nest."

Sylvia's heart gave a wild beat; she knew that strange white bird, and had once stolen softly near where it stood in some bright green swamp grass, away over at the other side of the woods. There was an open place where the sunshine always seemed strangely yellow and hot, where tall, nodding rushes grew, and her grandmother had warned her that she might sink in the soft black mud underneath and never be heard of more. Not far beyond were the salt marshes just this side the sea itself, which Sylvia wondered and dreamed much about, but never had seen, whose great voice could sometimes be heard above the noise of the woods on stormy nights.

"I can't think of anything I should like so much as to find that heron's nest," the handsome stranger was saying. "I would give ten dollars to anybody who could show it to me," he added desperately, "and I mean to spend my whole vacation hunting for it if need be. Perhaps it was only migrating, or had been chased out of its own region by some bird of prey."

Mrs. Tilley gave amazed attention to all this, but Sylvia still watched the toad, not divining, as she might have done at some calmer time, that the creature wished to get to its hole under the door-step, and was much hindered by the unusual spectators at that hour of the evening. No amount of thought, that night, could decide how many wished-for treasures the ten dollars, so lightly spoken of, would buy.

The next day the young sportsman hovered about the woods, and Sylvia kept him company, having lost her first fear of the friendly lad, who proved to be most kind and sympathetic. He told her many things about the birds and what they knew and where they lived and what they did with themselves. And he gave her a jack knife, which she thought as great a treasure as if she were a desert-islander. All day long he did not once make her troubled or afraid except when he brought down some unsuspecting singing creature from its bough. Sylvia would have liked him vastly better without his gun; she could not understand why he killed the very birds he seemed to like so much. But as the day waned, Sylvia still watched the young man with loving admiration. She had never seen anybody so charming and delightful; the woman's heart, asleep in the child, was vaguely thrilled by a dream of love. Some premonition of that great power stirred and swayed these young creatures who traversed the solemn woodlands with soft-footed silent care. They stopped to listen to a bird's song; they pressed forward again eagerly, parting the branches—speaking to each other rarely and in whispers; the young man going first and Sylvia following, fascinated, a few steps behind, with her gray eyes dark with excitement.

She grieved because the longed-for white heron was elusive, but she did not lead the guest, she only followed, and there was no such thing as speaking first. The sound of her own unquestioned voice would have terrified her—it was hard enough to answer yes or no when there was need of that. At last evening began to fall, and they drove the cow home together, and Sylvia smiled with pleasure when they came to the place where she heard the whistle and was afraid only the night before.

II

Half a mile from home, at the farther edge of the woods, where the land was highest, a great pine-tree stood, the last of its generation. Whether it was left for a boundary mark, or for what reason, no one could say; the wood-choppers who had felled its mates were dead and gone long ago, and a whole forest of sturdy trees, pines and oaks and maples, had grown again. But the stately head of this old pine towered above them all and made a landmark for sea and shore miles and miles away. Sylvia knew it well. She had always believed that whoever climbed to the top of it could see the ocean; and the little girl had often laid her hand on the great rough trunk and looked up wistfully at those dark boughs that the wind always stirred, no matter how hot and still the air might be below. Now she thought of the tree with a new excitement, for why, if one climbed it at break of day could not one see all the world, and easily discover from whence the white heron flew, and mark the place, and find the hidden nest?

What a spirit of adventure, what wild ambition! What fancied triumph and delight and glory for the later morning when she could make known the secret! It was almost too real and too great for the childish heart to bear.

All night the door of the little house stood open and the whippoorwills came and sang upon the very step. The young sportsman and his old hostess were sound asleep, but Sylvia's great design kept her broad awake and watching. She forgot to think of sleep. The short summer night seemed as long as the winter darkness, and at last when the whippoorwills ceased, and she was afraid the morning would after all come too soon, she stole out of the house and followed the pasture path through the woods, hastening toward the open ground beyond, listening with a sense of comfort and companionship to the drowsy twitter of a half-awakened bird, whose perch she had jarred in passing. Alas, if the great wave of human interest which flooded for the first time this dull little life should sweep away the satisfactions of an existence heart to heart with nature and the dumb life of the forest!

There was the huge tree asleep yet in the paling moonlight, and small and silly Sylvia began with utmost bravery to mount to the top of it, with tingling, eager blood coursing the channels of her whole frame, with her bare feet and fingers, that pinched and held like bird's claws to the monstrous ladder reaching up, up, almost to the sky itself. First she must mount the white oak tree that grew alongside, where she was almost lost among the dark branches and the green leaves heavy and wet with dew; a bird fluttered off its nest, and a red squirrel ran to and fro and scolded pettishly at the harmless housebreaker. Sylvia felt her way easily. She had often climbed there, and knew that higher still one of the oak's upper branches chafed against the pine trunk, just where its lower boughs were set close together. There, when she made the dangerous pass from one tree to the other, the great enterprise would really begin.

She crept out along the swaying oak limb at last, and took the daring step across into the old pine-tree. The way was harder than she thought; she must reach far and hold fast, the sharp dry twigs caught and held her and scratched her like angry talons, the pitch made her thin little fingers clumsy and stiff as she went round and round the tree's great stem, higher and higher upward. The sparrows and robins in the woods below were beginning to wake and twitter to the dawn, yet it seemed much lighter there aloft in the pine-tree, and the child knew she must hurry if her project were to be of any use.

The tree seemed to lengthen itself out as she went up, and to reach farther and farther upward. It was like a great main-mast to the voyaging earth; it must truly have been amazed that morning through all its ponderous frame as it felt this determined spark of human spirit wending its way from higher branch to branch. Who knows how steadily the least twigs held themselves to advantage this light, weak creature on her way! The old pine must have loved his new dependent. More than all the hawks, and bats, and moths, and even the sweet voiced thrushes, was the brave, beating heart of the solitary gray-eyed child. And the tree stood still and frowned away the winds that June morning while the dawn grew bright in the east.

Sylvia's face was like a pale star, if one had seen it from the ground, when the last thorny bough was past, and she stood trembling and tired but wholly triumphant, high in the treetop. Yes, there was the sea with the dawning sun making a golden dazzle over it, and toward that glorious east flew two hawks with slow-moving pinions. How low they looked in the air from that height when one had only seen them before far up, and dark against the blue sky. Their gray feathers were as soft as moths; they seemed only a little way from the tree, and Sylvia felt as if she too could go flying away among the clouds. Westward, the woodlands and farms reached miles and miles into the distance; here and there were church steeples, and white villages, truly it was a vast and awesome world!

The birds sang louder and louder. At last the sun came up bewilderingly bright. Sylvia could see the white sails of ships out at sea, and the clouds that were purple and rose-colored and yellow at first began to fade away. Where was the white heron's nest in the sea of green branches, and was this wonderful sight and pageant of the world the only reward for having climbed to such a giddy height? Now look down again, Sylvia, where the green marsh is set among the shining birches and dark hemlocks; there where you saw the white heron once you will see him again; look, look! a white spot of him like a single floating feather comes up from the dead hemlock and grows larger, and rises, and comes close at last, and goes by the landmark pine with steady sweep of wing and outstretched slender neck and crested head. And wait! wait! do not move a foot or a finger, little girl, do not send an arrow of light and consciousness from your two eager eyes, for the heron has perched on a pine bough not far beyond yours, and cries back to his mate on the nest and plumes his feathers for the new day!

The child gives a long sigh a minute later when a company of shouting cat-birds comes also to the tree, and vexed by their fluttering and lawlessness the solemn heron goes away. She knows his secret now, the wild, light, slender bird that floats and wavers, and goes back like an arrow presently to his home in the green world beneath. Then Sylvia, well satisfied, makes her perilous way down again, not daring to look far below the branch she stands on, ready to cry sometimes because her fingers ache and her lamed feet slip. Wondering over and over again what the stranger would say to her, and what he would think when she told him how to find his way straight to the heron's nest.

"Sylvy, Sylvy!" called the busy old grandmother again and again, but nobody answered, and the small husk bed was empty and Sylvia had disappeared.

The guest waked from a dream, and remembering his day's pleasure hurried to dress himself that might it sooner begin. He was sure from the way the shy little girl looked once or twice yesterday that she had at least seen the white heron, and now she must really be made to tell. Here she comes now, paler than ever, and her worn old frock is torn and tattered, and smeared with pine pitch. The grandmother and the sportsman stand in the door together and question her, and the splendid moment has come to speak of the dead hemlock-tree by the green marsh.

But Sylvia does not speak after all, though the old grandmother fretfully rebukes her, and the young man's kind, appealing eyes are looking straight in her own. He can make them rich with money; he has promised it, and they are poor now. He is so well worth making happy, and he waits to hear the story she can tell.

No, she must keep silence! What is it that suddenly forbids her and makes her dumb? Has she been nine years growing and now, when the great world for the first time puts out a hand to her, must she thrust it aside for a bird's sake? The murmur of the pine's green branches is in her ears, she remembers how the white heron came flying through the golden air and how they watched the sea and the morning together, and Sylvia cannot speak; she cannot tell the heron's secret and give its life away.

Dear loyalty, that suffered a sharp pang as the guest went away disappointed later in the day, that could have served and followed him and loved him as a dog loves! Many a night Sylvia heard the echo of his whistle haunting the pasture path as she came home with the loitering cow. She forgot even her sorrow at the sharp report of his gun and the piteous sight of thrushes and sparrows dropping silent to the ground, their songs hushed and their pretty feathers stained and wet with blood. Were the birds better friends than their hunter might have been,–who can tell? Whatever treasures were lost to her, woodlands and summer time, remember! Bring your gifts and graces and tell your secrets to this lonely country child!

HENRY VAN DYKE

[1852–1933]

The Story of the Other Wise Man

(1895)

THE SIGN IN THE SKY

IN THE DAYS when Augustus Cæsar was master of many kings and Herod reigned in Jerusalem, there lived in the city of Ecbatana, among the mountains of Persia, a certain man named Artaban, the Median. His house stood close to the outermost of the seven walls which encircled the royal treasury. From his roof he could look over the rising battlements of black and white and crimson and blue and red and silver and gold, to the hill where the summer palace of the Parthian emperors glittered like a jewel in a sevenfold crown.

Around the dwelling of Artaban spread a fair garden, a tangle of flowers and fruit trees, watered by a score of streams descending from the slopes of Mount Orontes, and made musical by innumerable birds. But all color was lost in the soft and odorous darkness of the late September night, and all sounds were hushed in the deep charm of its silence, save the plashing of the water, like a voice half sobbing and half laughing under the shadows. High above the trees a dim glow of light shone through the curtained arches of the upper chamber, where the master of the house was holding council with his friends.

He stood by the doorway to greet his guests—a tall, dark man of about forty years, with brilliant eyes set near together under his broad brow, and firm lines graven around his fine, thin lips; the brow of a dreamer and the mouth of a soldier, a man of sensitive feeling but inflexible will—one of those who, in whatever age they may live, are born for inward conflict and a life of quest.

His robe was of pure white wool, thrown over a tunic of silk; and a white pointed cap, with long lapels at the sides, rested on his flowing black hair. It was the dress of the ancient priesthood of the Magi, called the fire-worshipers.

"Welcome!" he said, in his low, pleasant voice, as one after another entered the room—"welcome, Abdus; peace be with you, Rhodaspes and

Tigranes, and with you my father, Abgarus. You are all welcome, and this house grows bright with the joy of your presence."

There were nine of the men, differing widely in age, but alike in the richness of their dress of many-colored silks, and in the massive golden collars around their necks, marking them as Parthian nobles, and the winged circles of gold resting upon their breasts, the sign of the followers of Zoroaster.

They took their places around a small black altar at the end of the room, where a tiny flame was burning. Artaban, standing beside it, and waving a barsom of thin tamarisk branches above the fire, fed it with dry sticks of pine and fragrant oils. Then he began the ancient chant of the Yasna, and the voices of his companions joined in the beautiful hymn to Ahura-Mazda:

We worship the Spirit Divine, all wisdom and goodness possessing,
Surrounded by Holy Immortals, the givers of bounty and blessing,
We joy in the works of His hands, His truth and His power confessing.

We praise all the things that are pure, for these are His only Creation;
The thoughts that are true, and the words and deeds that have won approbation;
These are supported by Him and for these we make adoration.

Hear us, O Mazda! Thou livest in truth and in heavenly gladness;
Cleanse us from falsehood, and keep us from evil and bondage to badness;
Pour out the light and the joy of Thy life on our darkness and sadness.

Shine on our gardens and fields, Shine on our working and weaving;
Shine on the whole race of man, Believing and unbelieving;
  Shine on us now through the night,
  Shine on us now in Thy might,
The flame of our holy love and the song of our worship receiving.

The fire rose with the chant, throbbing as if it were made of musical flame, until it cast a bright illumination through the whole apartment, revealing its simplicity and splendor.

The floor was laid with tiles of dark blue veined with white; pilasters of twisted silver stood out against the blue walls; the clear-story of round-arched windows above them was hung with azure silk; the vaulted ceiling was a pavement of sapphires, like the body of heaven in its clearness, sown with silver stars. From the four corners of the roof hung four golden magic-wheels, called the tongues of the gods. At the eastern end, behind the altar, there were two dark-red pillars of porphyry; above them a lintel of the same stone, on which was carved the figure of a winged archer, with his arrow set to the string and his bow drawn.

The doorway between the pillars, which opened upon the terrace of the roof, was covered with a heavy curtain of the color of a ripe pomegranate, embroidered with innumerable golden rays shooting upward from the floor. In effect the room was like a quiet, starry night, all azure and silver, flushed in the east with rosy promise of the dawn. It was, as the house of a man should be, an expression of the character and spirit of the master.

He turned to his friends when the song was ended, and invited them to be seated on the divan at the western end of the room.

"You have come to-night," said he, looking around the circle, "at my call, as the faithful scholars of Zoroaster, to renew your worship and rekindle your faith in the God of Purity, even as this fire has been rekindled on the altar. We worship not the fire, but Him of whom it is the chosen symbol, because it is the purest of all created things. It speaks to us of one who is Light and Truth. Is it not so, my father?"

"It is well said, my son," answered the venerable Abgarus. "The enlightened are never idolaters. They lift the veil of the form and go into the shrine of the reality, and new light and truth are coming to them continually through the old symbols."

"Hear me, then, my father and my friends," said Artaban, very quietly, "while I tell you of the new light and truth that have come to me through the most ancient of all signs. We have searched the secrets of nature together, and studied the healing virtues of water and fire and the plants. We have read also the books of prophecy in which the future is dimly foretold in words that are hard to understand. But the highest of all learning is the knowledge of the stars. To trace their courses is to untangle the threads of mystery of life from the beginning to the end. If we could follow them perfectly, nothing would be hidden from us. But is not our knowledge of them still incomplete? Are there not many stars still beyond our horizon—lights that are known only to the dwellers in the far southland, among the spice-trees of Punt and the gold-mines of Ophir?"

There was a murmur of assent among the listeners.

"The stars," said Tigranes, "are the thoughts of the Eternal. They are numberless. But the thoughts of man can be counted, like the years of his life. The wisdom of the Magi is the greatest of all wisdoms on earth, because it knows its own ignorance. And that is the secret of power. We keep men always looking and waiting for a new sunrise. But we ourselves know that the darkness is equal to the light, and that the conflict between them will never be ended."

"That does not satisfy me," answered Artaban, "for, if the waiting must be endless, if there could be no fulfilment of it, then it would not be wisdom to look and wait. We should become like those new teachers of the Greeks, who say that there is no truth, and that the only wise men are those who spend their lives in discovering and exposing the lies that have been believed in the world. But the new sunrise will certainly dawn in the appointed time. Do not our own books tell us that this will come to pass, and that men will see the brightness of a great light?"

"That is true," said the voice of Abgarus; "every faithful disciple of

Zoroaster knows the prophecy of the Avesta and carries the word in his heart. 'In that day Sosiosh the Victorious shall arise out of the number of the prophets in the east country. Around him shall shine a mighty brightness, and he shall make life everlasting, incorruptible, and immortal, and the dead shall rise again."'

"This is a dark saying," said Tigranes, "and it may be that we shall never understand it. It is better to consider the things that are near at hand, and to increase the influence of the Magi in their own country, rather than to look for one who may be a stranger, and to whom we must resign our power."

The others seemed to approve these words. There was a silent feeling of agreement manifest among them; their looks responded with that indefinable expression which always follows when a speaker has uttered the thought that has been slumbering in the hearts of his listeners. But Artaban turned to Abgarus with a glow on his face, and said:

"My father, I have kept this prophecy in the secret place of my soul. Religion without a great hope would be like an altar without a living fire. And now the flame has burned more brightly, and by the light of it I have read other words which also have come from the fountain of Truth, and speak yet more clearly of the rising of the Victorious One in his brightness."

He drew from the breast of his tunic two small rolls of fine linen, with writing upon them, and unfolded them carefully upon his knee.

"In the years that are lost in the past, long before our fathers came into the land of Babylon, there were wise men in Chaldea, from whom the first of the Magi learned the secret of the heavens. And of these Balaam the son of Beor was one of the mightiest. Hear the words of his prophecy: 'There shall come a star out of Jacob, and a scepter shall arise out of Israel.'"

The lips of Tigranes drew downward with contempt, as he said:

"Judah was a captive by the waters of Babylon, and the sons of Jacob were in bondage to our kings. The tribes of Israel are scattered through the mountains like lost sheep, and from the remnant that dwells in Judea under the yoke of Rome neither star nor scepter shall arise."

"And yet," answered Artaban, "it was the Hebrew Daniel, the mighty searcher of dreams, the counselor of kings, the wise Belteshazzar, who was most honored and beloved of our great King Cyrus. A prophet of sure things and a reader of the thoughts of God, Daniel proved himself to our people. And these are the words that he wrote." (Artaban read from the second roll:) "'Know, therefore, and understand that from the going forth of the commandment to restore Jerusalem, unto the Anointed One, the Prince, the time shall be seven and threescore and two weeks.'"

"But, my son," said Abgarus, doubtfully, "these are mystical numbers. Who can interpret them, or who can find the key that shall unlock their meaning?"

Artaban answered: "It has been shown to me and to my three companions among the Magi—Caspar, Melchior, and Balthazar. We have searched the ancient tablets of Chaldea and computed the time. It falls in this year. We have studied the sky, and in the spring of the year we saw two of the greatest stars draw near together in the sign of the Fish, which is the house of the Hebrews. We also saw a new star there, which shone for one night and then vanished. Now again the two great planets are meeting. This night is their conjunction. My three brothers are watching at the ancient Temple of the Seven Spheres, at Borsippa, in Babylonia, and I am watching here. If the star shines again, they will wait ten days for me at the temple, and then we will set out together for Jerusalem, to see and worship the promised one who shall be born King of Israel. I believe the sign will come. I have made ready for the journey. I have sold my house and my possessions, and bought these three jewels—a sapphire, a ruby, and a pearl—to carry them as tribute to the King. And I ask you to go with me on the pilgrimage, that we may have joy together in finding the Prince who is worthy to be served."

While he was speaking he thrust his hand into the inmost fold of his girdle and drew out three great gems—one blue as a fragment of the night sky, one redder than a ray of sunrise, and one as pure as the peak of a snow mountain at twilight—and laid them on the outspread linen scrolls before him.

But his friends looked on with strange and alien eyes. A veil of doubt and mistrust came over their faces, like a fog creeping up from the marshes to hide the hills. They glanced at each other with looks of wonder and pity, as those who have listened to incredible sayings, the story of a wild vision, or the proposal of an impossible enterprise.

At last Tigranes said: "Artaban, this is a vain dream. It comes from too much looking upon the stars and the cherishing of lofty thoughts. It would be wiser to spend the time in gathering money for the new fire-temple at Chala. No king will ever rise from the broken race of Israel, and no end will ever come to the eternal strife of light and darkness. He who looks for it is a chaser of shadows. Farewell."

And another said: "Artaban, I have no knowledge of these things, and my office as guardian of the royal treasure binds me here. The quest is not for me. But if thou must follow it, fare thee well."

And another said: "In my house there sleeps a new bride, and I cannot leave her nor take her with me on this strange journey. This quest is not for me. But may thy steps be prospered wherever thou goest. So farewell."

And another said: "I am ill and unfit for hardship, but there is a man among my servants whom I will send with thee when thou goest, to bring me word how thou farest."

But Abgarus, the oldest and the one who loved Artaban the best, lingered after the others had gone, and said, gravely: "My son, it may be that the light of truth is in this sign that has appeared in the skies, and then it will surely lead to the Prince and the mighty brightness. Or it may be that it is only a shadow of the light, as Tigranes has said, and then he who follows it will have only a long pilgrimage and an empty search. But it is better to follow even the shadow of the best than to remain content with the worst. And those who would see wonderful things must often be ready to travel alone. I am too old for this journey, but my heart shall be a companion of the pilgrimage day and night, and I shall know the end of thy quest. Go in peace."

So one by one they went out of the azure chamber with its silver stars, and Artaban was left in solitude.

He gathered up the jewels and replaced them in his girdle. For a long time he stood and watched the flame that flickered and sank upon the altar. Then he crossed the hall, lifted the heavy curtain, and passed out between the dull red pillars of porphyry to the terrace on the roof.

The shiver that thrills through the earth ere she rouses from her night sleep had already begun, and the cool wind that heralds the daybreak was drawing downward from the lofty snow-traced ravines of Mount Orontes. Birds, half awakened, crept and chirped among the rustling leaves and the smell of ripened grapes came in brief wafts from the arbors.

Far over the eastern plain a white mist stretched like a lake. But where the distant peak of Zagros serrated the western horizon the sky was clear. Jupiter and Saturn rolled together like drops of lambent flame about to blend in one.

As Artaban watched them, behold ! an azure spark was born out of the darkness beneath, rounding itself with purple splendors to a crimson sphere, and spiring upward through rays of saffron and orange into a point of white radiance. Tiny and infinitely remote, yet perfect in every part, it pulsated in the enormous vault as if the three jewels in the Magian's breast had mingled and been transformed into a living heart of light.

He bowed his head. He covered his brow with his hands.

"It is the sign," he said. "The King is coming, and I will go to meet him."

BY THE WATERS OF BABYLON

All night long Vasda, the swiftest of Artaban's horses, had been waiting, saddled and bridled, in her stall, pawing the ground impatiently and shaking her bit as if she shared the eagerness of her master's purpose, though she knew not its meaning.

Before the birds had fully roused to their strong, high, joyful chant of morning song, before the white mist had begun to lift lazily from the plain, the other wise man was in the saddle, riding swiftly along the highroad, which skirted the base of Mount Orontes, westward.

How close, how intimate is the comradeship between a man and his favorite horse on a long journey. It is a silent, comprehensive friendship, an intercourse beyond the need of words.

They drink at the same wayside spring, and sleep under the same guardian stars. They are conscious together of the subduing spell of nightfall and the quickening joy of daybreak. The master shares his evening meal with his hungry companion, and feels the soft, moist lips caressing the palm of his hand as they close over the morsel of bread. In the gray dawn he is roused from his bivouac by the gentle stir of a warm, sweet breath over his sleeping face, and looks up into the eyes of his faithful fellow-traveler, ready and waiting for the toil of the day. Surely, unless he is a pagan and an unbeliever, by whatever name he calls upon his God, he will thank Him for this voiceless sympathy, this dumb affection, and his morning prayer will embrace a double blessing—God bless us both, and keep our feet from falling and our souls from death!

And then, through the keen morning air, the swift hoofs beat their spirited music along the road, keeping time to the pulsing of two hearts that are moved with the same eager desire—to conquer space, to devour the distance, to attain the goal of the journey.

Artaban must, indeed, ride wisely and well if he would keep the appointed hour with the other Magi; for the route was a hundred and fifty parasangs, and fifteen was the utmost that he could travel in a day. But he knew Vasda's strength, and pushed forward without anxiety, making the fixed distance every day, though he must travel late into the night, and in the morning long before sunrise.

He passed along the brown slopes of Mount Orontes, furrowed by the rocky courses of a hundred torrents.

He crossed the level plains of the Nisæans, where the famous herds of horses, feeding in the wide pastures, tossed their heads at Vasda's approach and galloped away with a thunder of many hoofs, and flocks of wild birds rose suddenly from the swampy meadows, wheeling in great circles with a shining flutter of innumerable wings and shrill cries of surprise.

He traversed the fertile fields of Concabar, where the dust from the threshing-floors filled the air with a golden mist, half hiding the huge Temple of Astarte with its four hundred pillars.

At Baghistan, among the rich gardens watered by fountains from the rock, he looked up at the mountain thrusting its immense rugged brow out over the road, and saw the figure of King Darius trampling upon his fallen foes, and the proud list of his wars and conquests graven high upon the face of the eternal cliff.

Over many a cold and desolate pass, crawling painfully across the windswept shoulders of the hills; down many a black mountain gorge, where the river roared and raced before him like a savage guide; across many a smiling vale, with terraces of yellow limestone full of vines and fruit trees; through the oak groves of Carine and the dark Gates of Zagros, walled in by precipices; into the ancient city of Chala, where the people of Samaria had been kept in captivity long ago; and out again by the mighty portal, riven through the encircling hills, where he saw the image of the High Priest of the Magi sculptured on the wall of rock, with hand uplifted as if to bless the centuries of pilgrims; past the entrance of the narrow defile, filled from end to end with orchards of peaches and figs, through which the river Gyndes foamed down to meet him; over the broad rice-fields, where the autumnal vapors spread their deathly mists; following along the course of the river, under tremulous shadows of poplar and tamarind, among the lower hills; and out upon the flat plain, where the road ran straight as an arrow through the stubble-fields and parched meadows; past the city of Ctesiphon, where the Parthian emperors reigned, and the vast metropolis of Seleucia which Alexander built; across the swirling floods of Tigris and the many channels of Euphrates, flowing yellow through the corn-lands—Artaban pressed onward until he arrived, at nightfall of the tenth day, beneath the shattered walls of populous Babylon.

Vasda was almost spent, and he would gladly have turned into the city to find rest and refreshment for himself and for her. But he knew that it was three hours' journey yet to the Temple of the Seven Spheres, and he must reach the place by midnight if he would find his comrades waiting. So he did not halt, but rode steadily across the stubble-fields.

A grove of date-palms made an island of glooms in the pale yellow sea. As she passed into the shadow Vasda slackened her pace, and began to pick her way more carefully.

Near the farther end of the darkness an access of caution seemed to fall upon her. She scented some danger or difficulty; it was not in her heart to fly from it—only to be prepared for it, and to meet it wisely as a good horse should do. The grove was close and silent as the tomb; not a leaf rustled, not a bird sang.

She felt her steps before her delicately, carrying her head low, and sighing now and then with apprehension. At last she gave a quick breath of anxiety and dismay, and stood stock-still, quivering in every muscle, before a dark object in the shadow of the last palm-tree.

Artaban dismounted. The dim starlight revealed the form of a man lying across the road. His humble dress and the outline of his haggard face showed that he was probably one of the poor Hebrew exiles who still dwelt in great numbers in the vicinity. His pallid skin, dry and yellow as parchment, bore the mark of the deadly fever which ravaged the marshlands in autumn. The chill of death was in his lean hand, and, as Artaban released it, the arm fell back inertly upon the motionless breast.

He turned away with a thought of pity, consigning the body to that strange burial which the Magians deemed most fitting—the funeral of the desert, from which the kites and vultures rise on dark wings, and the beasts of prey slink furtively away, leaving only a heap of white bones in the sand.

But, as he turned, a long, faint, ghostly sigh came from the man's lips. The brown, bony fingers closed convulsively on the hem of the Magian's robe and held him fast.

Artaban's heart leaped to his throat, not with fear, but with a dumb resentment at the importunity of this blind delay.

How could he stay here in the darkness to minister to a dying stranger? What claim had this unknown fragment of human life upon his compassion or his service? If he lingered but for an hour he could hardly reach Borsippa at the appointed time. His companions would think he had given up the journey. They would go without him. He would lose his quest.

But if he went on now, the man would surely die. If he stayed, life might be restored. His spirit throbbed and fluttered with the urgency of the crisis. Should he risk the great reward of his divine faith for the sake of a single deed of human love? Should he turn aside, if only for a moment, from the following of the star, to give a cup of cold water to a poor, perishing Hebrew?

"God of truth and purity," he prayed, "direct me in the holy path, the way of wisdom which only Thou knowest."

Then he turned back to the sick man. Loosening the grasp of his hand, he carried him to a little mound at the foot of the palm-tree.

He unbound the thick folds of the turban and opened the garment above the sunken breast. He brought water from one of the small canals near by, and moistened the sufferer's brow and mouth. He mingled a draught of one of those simple but potent remedies which he carried always in his girdle—for the Magians were physicians as well as astrologers—and poured it slowly between the colorless lips. Hour after hour he labored as only a skilful healer of disease can do; and, at last, the man's strength returned; he sat up and looked about him.

"Who art thou?" he said, in the rude dialect of the country, "and why hast thou sought me here to bring back my life?"

"I am Artaban the Magian, of the city of Ecbatana, and I am going to Jerusalem in search of one who is to be born King of the Jews, a great Prince and Deliverer of all men. I dare not delay any longer upon my journey, for the caravan that has waited for me may depart without me. But see, here is all that I have left of bread and wine, and here is a potion of healing herbs. When thy strength is restored thou canst find the dwellings of the Hebrews among the houses of Babylon."

The Jew raised his trembling hand solemnly to heaven.

"Now may the God of Abraham and Isaac and Jacob bless and prosper the journey of the merciful, and bring him in peace to his desired haven.

But stay; I have nothing to give thee in return—only this: that I can tell thee where the Messiah must be sought. For our prophets have said that he should be born not in Jerusalem, but in Bethlehem of Judah. May the Lord bring thee in safety to that place, because thou hast had pity upon the sick."

It was already long past midnight. Artaban rode in haste, and Vasda, restored by the brief rest, ran eagerly through the silent plain and swam the channels of the river. She put forth the remnant of her strength, and fled over the ground like a gazelle.

But the first beam of the sun sent her shadow before her as she entered upon the final stadium of the journey, and the eyes of Artaban, anxiously scanning the great mound of Nimrod and the Temple of the Seven Spheres, could discern no trace of his friends.

The many-colored terraces of black and orange and red and yellow and green and blue and white, shattered by the convulsions of nature, and crumbling under the repeated blows of human violence, still glittered like a ruined rainbow in the morning light.

Artaban rode swiftly around the hill. He dismounted and climbed to the highest terrace, looking out toward the west.

The huge desolation of the marshes stretched away to the horizon and the border of the desert. Bitterns stood by the stagnant pools and jackals skulked through the low bushes; but there was no sign of the caravan of the wise men, far or near.

At the edge of the terrace he saw a little cairn of broken bricks, and under them a piece of parchment. He caught it up and read: "We have waited past the midnight and can delay no longer. We go to find the King. Follow us across the desert."

Artaban sat down upon the ground and covered his head in despair.

"How can I cross the desert," said he, "with no food and with a spent horse? I must return to Babylon, sell my sapphire, and buy a train of camels, and provision for the journey. I may never overtake my friends. Only God the merciful knows whether I shall not lose the sight of the King because I tarried to show mercy."

FOR THE SAKE OF A LITTLE CHILD

There was a silence in the Hall of Dreams, where I was listening to the story of the Other Wise Man. And through this silence I saw, but very dimly, his figure passing over the dreary undulations of the desert, high upon the back of his camel, rocking steadily onward like a ship over the waves.

The land of death spread its cruel net around him. The stony wastes bore no fruit but briers and thorns. The dark ledges of rock thrust themselves above the surface here and there, like the bones of perished monsters. Arid and inhospitable mountain ranges rose before him, furrowed with dry channels of ancient torrents, white and ghastly as scars on the face of nature. Shifting hills of treacherous sand were heaped like tombs along the horizon. By day, the fierce heat pressed its intolerable burden on the quivering air; and no living creature moved on the dumb, swooning earth but tiny jerboas scuttling through the parched bushes, or lizards vanishing in the clefts of the rock. By night the jackals prowled and barked in the distance, and the lion made the black ravines echo with his hollow roaring, while a bitter, blighting chill followed the fever of the day. Through heat and cold, the Magian moved steadily onward.

Then I saw the gardens and orchards of Damascus, watered by the streams of Aldana and Pharpar, with their sloping swards inlaid with bloom, and their thickets of myrrh and roses. I saw also the long, snowy ridge of Hermon, and the dark groves of cedars, and the valley of the Jordan, and the blue waters of the Lake of Galilee, and the fertile plain of Esdraelon and the hills of Ephraim, and the highlands of Judah. Through all these I followed the figure of Artaban moving steadily onward, until he arrived at Bethlehem. And it was the third day after the three wise men had come to that place and had found Mary and Joseph, with the young child, Jesus, and had lain their gifts of gold and frankincense and myrrh at his feet.

Then the other wise man drew near, weary, but full of hope, bearing his ruby and his pearl to offer to the King. "For now at last," he said, "I shall surely find him, though it be alone, and later than my brethren. This is the place of which the Hebrew exile told me that the prophets had spoken, and here I shall behold the rising of the great light. But I must inquire about the visit of my brethren, and to what house the star directed them, and to whom they presented their tribute."

The streets of the village seemed to be deserted, and Artaban wondered whether the men had all gone up to the hill-pastures to bring down their sheep. From the open door of a low stone cottage he heard the sound of a woman's voice singing softly. He entered and found a young mother hushing her baby to rest. She told him of the strangers from the Far East who had appeared in the village three days ago, and how they said that a star had guided them to the place where Joseph of Nazareth was lodging with his wife and her new-born child, and how they had paid reverence to the child and given him many rich gifts.

"But the travelers disappeared again," she continued, "as suddenly as they had come. We were afraid at the strangeness of their visit. We could not understand it. The man of Nazareth took the babe and his mother and fled away that same night secretly, and it was whispered that they were going far away to Egypt. Ever since there has been a spell upon the village; something evil hangs over it. They say that the Roman soldiers are coming from Jerusalem to force a new tax from us, and the men have driven the flocks and herds far back among the hills, and hidden themselves to escape it."

Artaban listened to her gentle, timid speech and the child in her arms looked up in his face and smiled, stretching out its rosy hands to grasp at the winged circle of gold on his breast. His heart warmed to the touch. It seemed like a greeting of love and trust to one who had journeyed long in loneliness and perplexity, fighting with his own doubts and fears, and following a light that was veiled in clouds.

"Might not this child have been the promised Prince?" he asked within himself, as he touched its soft cheek. "Kings have been born ere now in lowlier houses than this, and the favorite of the stars may rise even from a cottage. But it has not seemed good to the God of wisdom to reward my search so soon and so easily. The one whom I seek has gone before me; and now I must follow the King to Egypt."

The young mother laid the babe in its cradle, and rose to minister to the wants of the strange guest that fate had brought into her house. She set food before him, the plain fare of peasants, but willingly offered, and therefore full of refreshment for the soul as well as for the body. Artaban accepted it gratefully; and, as he ate, the child fell into a happy slumber, and murmured sweetly in its dreams, and a great peace filled the quiet room.

But suddenly there came the noise of a wild confusion and uproar in the streets of the village, a shrieking and wailing of women's voices, a clangor of swords, and a desperate cry: "The soldiers! the soldiers of Herod! They are killing our children."

The young mother's face grew white with terror. She clasped her child to her bosom, and crouched motionless in the darkest corner of the room, covering him with the folds of her robe, lest he should wake and cry.

But Artaban went quickly and stood in the doorway of the house. His broad shoulders filled the portal from side to side, and the peak of his white cap all but touched the lintel.

The soldiers came hurrying down the street with bloody hands and dripping swords. At the sight of the stranger in his imposing dress they hesitated with surprise. The captain of the band approached the threshold to thrust him aside. But Artaban did not stir. His face was as calm as though he were watching the stars, and in his eyes there burned that steady radiance before which even the half-tamed hunting-leopard shrinks and the fierce bloodhound pauses in his leap. He held the soldier silently for an instant, and then said, in a low voice:

"I am all alone in this place, and I am waiting to give this jewel to the prudent captain who will leave me in peace."

He showed the ruby, glistening in the hollow of his hand like a great drop of blood.

The captain was amazed at the splendor of the gem. The pupils of his eyes expanded with desire, and the hard lines of greed wrinkled around his lips. He stretched out his hand and took the ruby.

"March on!" he cried to his men. "There is no child here. The house is still."

The clamor and the clang of arms passed down the street as the headlong fury of the chase sweeps by the secret covert where the trembling deer is hidden. Artaban re-entered the cottage. He turned his face to the east and prayed:

"God of truth, forgive my sin! I have said the thing that is not, to save the life of a child. And two of my gifts are gone. I have spent for man that which was meant for God. Shall I ever be worthy to see the face of the King?"

But the voice of the woman, weeping for joy in the shadow behind him, said, very gently:

"Because thou hast saved the life of my little one, may the Lord bless thee and keep thee; the Lord make His face to shine upon thee and be gracious unto thee; the Lord lift up His countenance upon thee and give thee peace."

IN THE HIDDEN WAY OF SORROW

Then again there was a silence in the Hall of Dreams, deeper and more mysterious than the first interval, and I understood that the years of Artaban were flowing very swiftly under the stillness of that clinging fog, and I caught only a glimpse, here and there, of the river of his life shining through the shadows that concealed its course.

I saw him moving among the throngs of men in populous Egypt, seeking everywhere for traces of the household that had come down from Bethlehem, and finding them under the spreading sycamore-trees of Heliopolis, and beneath the walls of the Roman fortress of New Babylon beside the Nile—traces so faint and dim that they vanished before him continually, as footprints on the hard river-sand glisten for a moment with moisture and then disappear.

I saw him again at the foot of the pyramids, which lifted their sharp points into the intense saffron glow of the sunset sky, changeless monuments of the perishable glory and the imperishable hope of man. He looked up into the vast countenance of the crouching Sphinx and vainly tried to read the meaning of the calm eyes and smiling mouth. Was it, indeed, the mockery of all effort and all aspiration, as Tigranes had said—the cruel jest of a riddle that has no answer, a search that never can succeed? Or was there a touch of pity and encouragement in that inscrutable smile—a promise that even the defeated should attain a victory, and the disappointed should discover a prize, and the ignorant should be made wise, and the blind should see, and the wandering should come into the haven at last?

I saw him again in an obscure house of Alexandria, taking counsel with a Hebrew rabbi. The venerable man, bending over the rolls of parchment on which the prophecies of Israel were written, read aloud the pathetic words which foretold the sufferings of the promised Messiah—the despised and rejected of men, the man of sorrows and the acquaintance of grief.

"And remember, my son," said he, fixing his deep-set eyes upon the face of Artaban, "the King whom you are seeking is not to be found in a palace, nor among the rich and powerful. If the light of the world and the glory of Israel had been appointed to come with the greatness of earthly splendor, it must have appeared long ago. For no son of Abraham will ever again rival the power which Joseph had in the palaces of Egypt, or the magnificence of Solomon throned between the lions in Jerusalem. But the light for which the world is waiting is a new light, the glory that shall rise out of patient and triumphant suffering. And the kingdom which is to be established forever is a new kingdom, the royalty of perfect and unconquerable love.

"I do not know how this shall come to pass, nor how the turbulent kings and peoples of earth shall be brought to acknowledge the Messiah and pay homage to Him. But this I know. Those who seek Him will do well to look among the poor and the lowly, the sorrowful and the oppressed."

So I saw the other wise man again and again, traveling from place to place, and searching among the people of the dispersion, with whom the little family from Bethlehem might, perhaps, have found a refuge. He passed through countries where famine lay heavy upon the land, and the poor were crying for bread. He made his dwelling in plague-stricken cities where the sick were languishing in the bitter companionship of helpless misery. He visited the oppressed and the afflicted in the gloom of subterranean prisons, and the crowded wretchedness of slave-markets, and the weary toil of galley-ships. In all this populous and intricate world of anguish, though he found none to worship, he found many to help. He fed the hungry, and clothed the naked, and healed the sick, and comforted the captive; and his years went by more swiftly than the weaver's shuttle that flashes back and forth through the loom while the web grows and the invisible pattern is completed.

It seemed almost as if he had forgotten his quest. But once I saw him for a moment as he stood alone at sunrise, waiting at the gate of a Roman prison. He had taken from a secret resting-place in his bosom the pearl, the last of his jewels. As he looked at it, a mellower luster, a soft and iridescent light, full of shifting gleams of azure and rose, trembled upon its surface. It seemed to have absorbed some reflection of the colors of the lost sapphire and ruby. So the profound, secret purpose of a noble life draws into itself the memories of past joy and past sorrow. All that has helped it, all that has hindered it, is transfused by a subtle magic into its very essence. It becomes more luminous and precious the longer it is carried close to the warmth of the beating heart.

Then, at last, while I was thinking of this pearl, and of its meaning, I heard the end of the story of the Other Wise Man.

A PEARL OF GREAT PRICE

Three-and-thirty years of the life of Artaban had passed away, and he was still a pilgrim, and a seeker after light. His hair, once darker than the cliffs of Zagros, was now white as the wintry snow that covered them. His eyes, that once flashed like flames of fire, were dull as embers smoldering among the ashes.

Worn and weary and ready to die, but still looking for the King, he had come for the last time to Jerusalem. He had often visited the holy city before, and had searched through all its lanes and crowded hovels and black prisons without finding any trace of the family of Nazarenes who had fled from Bethlehem long ago. But now it seemed as if he must make one more effort, and something whispered in his heart that, at last, he might succeed.

It was the season of the Passover. The city was thronged with strangers. The children of Israel, scattered in far lands all over the world, had returned to the Temple for the great feast, and there had been a confusion of tongues in the narrow streets for many days.

But on this day there was a singular agitation visible in the multitude. The sky was veiled with a portentous gloom, and currents of excitement seemed to flash through the crowd like the thrill which shakes the forest on the eve of a storm. A secret tide was sweeping them all one way. The clatter of sandals, and the soft, thick sound of thousands of bare feet shuffling over the stones, flowed unceasingly along the street that leads to the Damascus gate.

Artaban joined company with a group of people from his own country, Parthian Jews who had come up to keep the Passover, and inquired of them the cause of the tumult, and where they were going.

"We are going," they answered, "to the place called Golgotha, outside the city walls, where there is to be an execution. Have you not heard what has happened? Two famous robbers are to be crucified, and with them another, called Jesus of Nazareth, a man who has done many wonderful works among the people, so that they love him greatly. But the priests and elders have said that he must die, because he gave himself out to be the Son of God. And Pilate has sent him to the cross because he said that he was the 'King of the Jews.'"

How strangely these familiar words fell upon the tired heart of Artaban! They had led him for a lifetime over land and sea. And now they came to him darkly and mysteriously like a message of despair. The King had arisen, but He had been denied and cast out. He was about to perish. Perhaps He was already dying. Could it be the same who had been born in Bethlehem thirty-three years ago, at whose birth the star had appeared in heaven, and of whose coming the prophets had spoken?

Artaban's heart beat unsteadily with that troubled, doubtful apprehension which is the excitement of old age. But he said within himself: "The ways of God are stranger than the thoughts of men, and it may be that I shall find the King, at last, in the hands of His enemies, and shall come in time to offer my pearl for His ransom before He dies."

So the old man followed the multitude with slow and painful steps toward the Damascus gate of the city. Just beyond the entrance of the guard-house a troop of Macedonian soldiers came down the street, dragging a young girl with torn dress and disheveled hair. As the Magian paused to look at her with compassion she broke suddenly from the hands of her tormentors and threw herself at his feet, clasping him around the knees. She had seen his white cap and the winged circle on his breast.

"Have pity on me," she cried, "and save me, for the sake of the God of Purity! I also am a daughter of the true religion which is taught by the Magi. My father was a merchant of Parthia, but he is dead, and I am seized for his debts to be sold as a slave. Save me from worse than death."

Artaban trembled.

It was the old conflict in his soul, which had come to him in the palm-grove of Babylon and in the cottage at Bethlehem–the conflict between the expectation of faith and the impulse of love. Twice the gift which he had consecrated to the worship of religion had been drawn from his hand to the service of humanity. This was the third trial, the ultimate probation, the final and irrevocable choice.

Was it his great opportunity, or his last temptation? He could not tell. One thing only was clear in the darkness of his mind–it was inevitable. And does not the inevitable come from God?

One thing only was sure to his divided heart–to rescue this helpless girl would be a true deed of love. And is not love the light of the soul?

He took the pearl from his bosom. Never had it seemed so luminous, so radiant, so full of tender, living luster. He laid it in the hand of the slave.

"This is thy ransom, daughter! It is the last of my treasures which I kept for the King."

While he spoke, the darkness of the sky thickened, and shuddering tremors ran through the earth, heaving convulsively like the breast of one who struggles with mighty grief.

The walls of the houses rocked to and fro. Stones were loosened and crashed into the street. Dust-clouds filled the air. The soldiers fled in terror, reeling like drunken men. But Artaban and the girl whom he had ransomed crouched helpless beneath the wall of the Prætorium.

What had he to fear? What had he to live for? He had given away the last remnant of his tribute for the King. He had parted with the last hope of finding Him. The quest was over, and it had failed. But, even in that thought, accepted and embraced, there was peace. It was not resignation. It was not submission. It was something more profound and searching. He knew that all was well, because he had done the best that he could, from day to day. He had been true to the light that had been given to him. He had looked for more. And if he had not found it, if a failure was all that came out of his life, doubtless that was the best that was possible. He had not seen the revelation of "life everlasting, incorruptible, and immortal." But he knew that even if he could live his earthly life over again, it could not be otherwise than it had been.

One more lingering pulsation of the earthquake quivered through the ground. A heavy tile, shaken from the roof, fell and struck the old man on the temple. He lay breathless and pale, with his gray head resting on the young girl's shoulder, and the blood trickling from the wound. As she bent over him, fearing that he was dead, there came a voice through the twilight, very small and still, like music sounding from a distance, in which the notes are clear but the words are lost. The girl turned to see if some one had spoken from the window above them, but she saw no one.

Then the old man's lips began to move, as if in answer, and she heard him say in the Parthian tongue:

"Not so, my Lord: For when saw I thee an-hungered and fed thee? Or thirsty, and gave thee drink? When saw I thee a stranger, and took thee in? Or naked, and clothed thee? When saw I thee sick or in prison, and came unto thee? Three-and-thirty years have I looked for thee; but I have never seen thy face, nor ministered to thee, my King."

He ceased, and the sweet voice came again. And again the maid heard it, very faintly and far away. But now it seemed as though she understood the words:

"*Verily I say unto thee, Inasmuch as thou hast done it unto one of the least of these my brethren, thou hast done it unto me.*"

A calm radiance of wonder and joy lighted the pale face of Artaban like the first ray of dawn on a snowy mountain-peak. One long, last breath of relief exhaled gently from his lips.

His journey was ended. His treasures were accepted. The Other Wise Man had found the King.

THE END

HAMLIN GARLAND

[1860–1940]

The Return of a Private

(First published in *Arena*, 1891;
first book publication in 1891.)

THE NEARER THE train drew toward La Crosse, the soberer the little group of "vets" became. On the long way from New Orleans they had beguiled tedium with jokes and friendly chaff; or with planning with elaborate detail what they were going to do now, after the war. A long journey, slowly, irregularly, yet persistently pushing northward. When they entered on Wisconsin territory they gave a cheer, and another when they reached Madison, but after that they sank into a dumb expectancy. Comrades dropped off at one or two points beyond, until there were only four or five left who were bound for La Crosse County.

Three of them were gaunt and brown, the fourth was gaunt and pale, with signs of fever and ague upon him. One had a great scar down his temple, one limped, and they all had unnaturally large, bright eyes, showing emaciation. There were no bands greeting them at the station, no banks of gayly dressed ladies waving handkerchiefs and shouting "Bravo!" as they came in on the caboose of a freight train into the towns that had cheered and blared at them on their way to war. As they looked out or stepped upon the platform for a moment, while the train stood at the station, the loafers looked at them indifferently. Their blue coats, dusty and grimy, were too familiar now to excite notice, much less a friendly word. They were the last of the army to return, and the loafers were surfeited with such sights.

The train jogged forward so slowly that it seemed likely to be midnight before they should reach La Crosse. The little squad grumbled and swore, but it was no use; the train would not hurry, and, as a matter of fact, it was nearly two o'clock when the engine whistled "down brakes."

All of the group were farmers, living in districts several miles out of the town and all were poor.

"Now, boys," said Private Smith, he of the fever and ague, "we are landed in La Crosse in the night. We've got to stay somewhere till mornin'. Now I ain't got no two dollars to waste on a hotel. I've got a wife and children, so I'm goin' to roost on a bench and take the cost of a bed out of my hide."

"Same here," put in one of the other men. "Hide'll grow on again, dollars'll come hard. It's goin' to be mighty hot skirmishin' to find a dollar these days."

"Don't think they'll be a deputation of citizens waitin' to 'scort us to a hotel, eh?" said another. His sarcasm was too obvious to require an answer.

Smith went on, "Then at daybreak we'll start for home—at least, I will."

"Well, I'll be dummed if I'll take two dollars out o' *my* hide," one of the younger men said. "I'm goin' to a hotel, ef I don't never lay up a cent."

"That'll do f'r you," said Smith; "but if you had a wife an' three young uns dependin' on yeh—"

"Which I ain't, thank the Lord! and don't intend havin' while the court knows itself."

The station was deserted, chill and dark, as they came into it at exactly a quarter to two in the morning. Lit by the oil lamps that flared a dull red light over the dingy benches, the waiting room was not an inviting place. The younger man went off to look up a hotel, while the rest remained and prepared to camp down on the floor and benches. Smith was attended to tenderly by the other men, who spread their blankets on the bench for him, and, by robbing themselves, made quite a comfortable bed, though the narrowness of the bench made his sleeping precarious.

It was chill, though August, and the two men, sitting with bowed heads, grew stiff with cold and weariness, and were forced to rise now and again and walk about to warm their stiffened limbs. It did not occur to them, probably, to contrast their coming home with their going forth, or with the coming home of the generals, colonels, or even captains—but to Private Smith, at any rate, there came a sickness at heart almost deadly as he lay there on his hard bed and went over his situation.

In the deep of the night, lying on a board in the town where he had enlisted three years ago, all elation and enthusiasm gone out of him, he faced the fact that with the joy of home-coming was already mingled the bitter juice of care. He saw himself sick, worn out, taking up the work on his half-cleared farm, the inevitable mortgage standing ready with open jaw to swallow half his earnings. He had given three years of his life for a mere pittance of pay, and now—!

Morning dawned at last, slowly, with a pale yellow dome of light rising silently above the bluffs, which stand like some huge storm-devastated castle, just east of the city. Out to the left the great river swept on its massive yet silent way to the south. Bluejays called across the water from hillside to hillside through the clear, beautiful air, and hawks began to skim the tops of the hills. The older men were astir early, but Private Smith had fallen at last into a sleep, and they went out without waking him. He lay on his knapsack, his gaunt face turned toward the ceiling, his hands clasped on his breast, with a curious pathetic effect of weakness and appeal.

An engine switching near woke him at last, and he slowly sat up and stared about. He looked out of the window and saw that the sun was lightening the hills across the river. He rose and brushed his hair as well as he could, folded his blankets up, and went out to find his companions. They stood gazing silently at the river and at the hills.

"Looks natcher'l, don't it?" they said, as he came out.

"That's what it does," he replied. "An' it looks good. D'yeh see that peak?" He pointed at a beautiful symmetrical peak, rising like a slightly truncated cone, so high that it seemed the very highest of them all. It was touched by that morning sun and it glowed like a beacon, and a light scarf of gray morning fog was rolling up its shadowed side.

"My farm's just beyond that. Now, if I can only ketch a ride, we'll be home by dinner-time."

"I'm talkin' about breakfast," said one of the others.

"I guess it's one more meal o' hardtack f'r me," said Smith.

They foraged around, and finally found a restaurant with a sleepy old German behind the counter, and procured some coffee, which they drank to wash down their hardtack.

"Time'll come," said Smith, holding up a piece by the corner, "when this'll be a curiosity."

"I hope to God it will! I bet I've chawed hardtack enough to shingle every house in the coolly. I've chawed it when my lampers was down, and when they wasn't. I've took it dry, soaked, and mashed. I've had it wormy, musty, sour, and blue-moldy. I've had it in little bits and big bits; 'fore coffee an' after coffee. I'm ready f'r a change. I'd like t' git holt jest about now o' some of the hot biscuits my wife c'n make when she lays herself out f'r company."

"Well, if you set there gabblin', you'll never *see* yer wife."

"Come on," said Private Smith. "Wait a moment, boys; le's take suthin'. It's on me." He led them to the rusty tin dipper which hung on a nail beside the wooden water-pail, and they grinned and drank. Then shouldering their blankets and muskets, which they were "takin' home to the boys," they struck out on their last march.

"They called that coffee Jayvy," grumbled one of them, "but it never went by the road where government Jayvy resides. I reckon I know coffee from peas."

They kept together on the road along the turnpike, and up the winding road by the river, which they followed for some miles. The river was very lovely, curving down along its sandy beds, pausing now and then under broad basswood trees, or running in dark, swift, silent currents under tangles of wild grape vines, and drooping alders, and haw trees. At one of these lovely spots the three vets sat down on the thick green sward to rest, "on Smith's account." The leaves of the trees were as fresh and green as in June, the jays called cheery greetings to them, and kingfishers darted to and fro with swooping, noiseless flight.

"I tell yeh, boys, this knocks the swamps of Loueesiana into kingdom come."

"You bet. All they c'n raise down there is snakes, niggers, and p'rticler hell."

"An' fightin' men," put in the older man.

"An' fightin' men. If I had a good hook an' line I'd sneak a pick'rel out o' that pond. Say, remember that time I shot that alligator—"

"I guess we'd better be crawlin' along," interrupted Smith, rising and shouldering his knapsack, with considerable effort, which he tried to hide.

"Say, Smith, lemme give you a lift on that."

"I guess I c'n manage," said Smith grimly.

"Course. But, yo' see, I may not have a chance right off to pay yeh back for the times you've carried my gun and hull caboodle. Say, now, gimme that gun, anyway."

"All right, if yeh feel like it, Jim." Smith replied, and they trudged along doggedly in the sun, which was getting higher and hotter each half-mile.

"Ain't it queer there ain't no teams comin' along," said Smith, after a long silence.

"Well, no, seein's it's Sunday."

"By jinks, that's a fact. It *is* Sunday. I'll git home in time f'r dinner, sure!" he exulted. "She don't hev dinner usially till about *one* on Sundays." And he fell into a muse, in which he smiled.

"Well, I'll git home jest about six o'clock, jest about when the boys are milkin' the cows," said old Jim Cranby. "I'll step into the barn, an' then I'll say, 'He*ah*! why ain't this milkin' done before this time o' day?' An' then won't they yell!" he added, slapping his thigh in great glee.

Smith went on. "I'll jest go up the path. Old Rover'll come down the road to meet me. He won't bark—he'll know me—an' he'll come down waggin' his tail an' showin' his teeth. That's his way of laughin'. An' so I'll walk up to the kitchen door, an' I'll say, '*Dinner* f'r a hungry man!' An' then she'll jump up, an'—"

He couldn't go on. His voice choked at the thought of it. Saunders, the third man, hardly uttered a word, but walked silently behind the others. He had lost his wife the first year he was in the army. She died of pneumonia, caught in the autumn rains while working in the fields in his place.

They plodded along till at last they came to a parting of the ways. To the right the road continued up the main valley; to the left it went over the big ridge.

"Well, boys," began Smith, as they grounded their muskets and looked away up the valley, "here's where we shake hands. We've marched together a good many miles, an' now I s'pose we're done."

"Yes, I don't think we'll do any more of it f'r a while. I don't want to, I know."

"I hope I'll see yeh once in a while, boys, to talk over old times."

"Of course," said Saunders, whose voice trembled a little, too. "It ain't *exactly* like dyin'." They all found it hard to look at each other.

"But we'd ought'r go home with you," said Cranby. "You'll never climb that ridge with all them things on yer back."

"Oh, I'm all right! Don't worry about me. Every step takes me nearer home, yeh see. Well, good-by, boys."

They shook hands. "Good-by. Good luck!"

"Same to you. Lemme know how you find things at home."

"Good-by."

"Good-by."

He turned once before they passed out of sight, and waved his cap, and they did the same, and all yelled. Then all marched away with their long, steady, loping, veteran step. The solitary climber in blue walked on for a time, with his mind filled with the kindness of his comrades, and musing upon the many wonderful days they had had together in camp and field.

He thought of his chum, Billy Tripp. Poor Billy! A "minie" ball fell into his breast one day, fell wailing like a cat, and tore a great ragged hole in his heart. He looked forward to a sad scene with Billy's mother and sweetheart. They would want to know all about it. He tried to recall all that Billy had said, and the particulars of it, but there was little to remember, just that wild wailing sound high in the air, a dull slap, a short, quick, expulsive groan, and the boy lay with his face in the dirt in the plowed field they were marching across.

That was all. But all the scenes he had since been through had not dimmed the horror, the terror of that moment, when his boy comrade fell, with only a breath between a laugh and a death-groan. Poor handsome Billy! Worth millions of dollars was his young life.

These somber recollections gave way at length to more cheerful feelings as he began to approach his home coolly. The fields and houses grew familiar, and in one or two he was greeted by people seated in the doorways. But he was in no mood to talk, and pushed on steadily, though he stopped and accepted a drink of milk once at the well-side of a neighbor.

The sun was burning hot on that slope, and his step grew slower, in spite of his iron resolution. He sat down several times to rest. Slowly he crawled up the rough, reddish-brown road, which wound along the hillside, under great trees, through dense groves of jack oaks, with treetops far below him on his left hand, and the hills far above him on his right. He crawled along like some minute, wingless variety of fly.

He ate some hardtack, sauced with wild berries, when he reached the summit of the ridge, and sat there for some time, looked down into his home coolly.

Somber, pathetic figure! His wide, round, gray eyes gazing down into the beautiful valley, seeing and not seeing, the splendid cloud-shadows sweeping over the western hills and across the green and yellow wheat far below. His head dropped forward on his palm, his shoulders took on a tired stoop, his cheek-bones showed painfully. An observer might have said, "He is looking down upon his own grave."

II

Sunday comes in a Western wheat harvest with such sweet and sudden relaxation to man and beast that it would be holy for that reason, if for no other, and Sundays are usually fair in harvest-time. As one goes out into the field in the hot morning sunshine, with no sound abroad save the crickets and the indescribably pleasant silken rustling of the ripened grain, the reaper and the very sheaves in the stubble seem to be resting, dreaming.

Around the house, in the shade of the trees, the men sit, smoking, dozing, or reading the papers, while the women, never resting, move about at the housework. The men eat on Sundays about the same as on other days, and breakfast is no sooner over and out of the way than dinner begins.

But at the Smith farm there were no men dozing or reading. Mrs. Smith was alone with her three children, Mary, nine, Tommy, six, and little Ted, just past four. Her farm, rented to a neighbor, lay at the head of a coolly or narrow gully, made at some far-off post-glacial period by the vast and angry floods of water which gullied these tremendous furrows in the level prairie—furrows so deep that undisturbed portions of the original level rose like hills on either side, rose to quite considerable mountains.

The chickens wakened her as usual that Sabbath morning from dreams of her absent husband, from whom she had not heard for weeks. The shadows drifted over the hills, down the slopes, across the wheat, and up the opposite wall in leisurely way, as if, being Sunday, they could take it easy also. The fowls clustered about the housewife as she went out into the yard. Fuzzy little chickens swarmed out from the coops where their clucking and perpetually disgruntled mothers tramped about, petulantly thrusting their heads through the spaces between the slats.

A cow called in a deep, musical bass, and a calf answered from a little pen near by, and a pig scurried guiltily out of the cabbages. Seeing all this, seeing the pig in the cabbages, the tangle of grass in the garden, the broken fence which she had mended again and again—the little woman, hardly more than a girl, sat down and cried. The bright Sabbath morning was only a mockery without him!

A few years ago they had bought this farm, paying part, mortgaging the rest in the usual way. Edward Smith was a man of terrible energy. He worked "nights and Sundays," as the saying goes, to clear the farm of its brush and of its insatiate mortgage! In the midst of his Herculean struggle came the call for volunteers, and with the grim and unselfish devotion to his country which made the Eagle Brigade able to "whip its weight in wildcats," he threw down his scythe and grub-axe, turned his cattle loose, and became a blue-coated cog in a vast machine for killing men, and not thistles. While the millionaire sent his money to England for safekeeping, this man, with his girl-wife and three babies, left them on a mortgaged farm, and went away to fight for an idea. It was foolish but it was sublime for all that.

That was three years before, and the young wife, sitting on the well curb on this bright Sabbath harvest morning, was righteously rebellious. It seemed to her that she had borne her share of the country's sorrow. Two brothers had been killed, the renter in whose hands her husband had left the farm had proved a villain; one year the farm had been without crops, and now the over-ripe grain was waiting the tardy hand of the neighbor who had rented it, and who was cutting his own grain first.

About six weeks before, she had received a letter saying, "We'll be discharged in a little while." But no other word had come from him. She had seen by the papers that his army was being discharged, and from day to day other soldiers slowly percolated in blue streams back into the state and country, but still her hero did not return.

Each week she had told the children that he was coming, and she had watched the road so long that it had become unconscious; and as she stood at the well, or by the kitchen door, her eyes were fixed unthinkingly on the road that wound down the coolly.

Nothing wears on the human soul like waiting. If the stranded mariner, searching the sun-bright seas, could once give up hope of a ship, that horrible grinding on his brain would cease. It was this waiting, hoping, on the edge of despair, that gave Emma Smith no rest.

Neighbors said, with kind intentions: "He's sick, maybe, an' can't start north just yet. He'll come along one o' these days."

"Why don't he write?" was her question, which silenced them all. This Sunday morning it seemed to her as if she could not stand it longer. The house seemed intolerably lonely. So she dressed the little ones in their best calico dresses and home-made jackets, and, closing up the house, set off down the coolly to old Mother Gray's.

"Old Widder Gray" lived at the "mouth of the coolly." She was a widow woman with a large family of stalwart boys and laughing girls. She was the visible incarnation of hospitality and optimistic poverty. With Western open-heartedness she fed every mouth that asked food of her, and worked herself to death as cheerfully as her girls danced in the neighborhood harvest dances.

She waddled down the path to meet Mrs. Smith with a broad smile on her face.

"Oh, you little dears! Come right to your granny. Gimme a kiss! Come right in, Mis' Smith. How are yeh, anyway? Nice mornin', ain't it? Come in an' set down. Everything's in a clutter, but that won't scare you any."

She led the way into the best room, a sunny, square room, carpeted with a faded and patched rag carpet, and papered with white and green-striped wall-paper, where a few faded effigies of dead members of the family hung in variously sized oval walnut frames. The house resounded with singing, laughter, whistling, tramping of heavy boots, and riotous scufflings. Half-grown boys came to the door and crooked their fingers at the children, who ran out, and were soon heard in the midst of the fun.

"Don't s'pose you've heard from Ed?" Mrs. Smith shook her head. "He'll turn up some day, when you ain't lookin' for 'm." The good old soul had said that so many times that poor Mrs. Smith derived no comfort from it any longer.

"Liz heard from Al the other day. He's comin' some day this week. Anyhow, they expect him."

"Did he say anything of–"

"No, he didn't," Mrs. Gray admitted. "But then it was only a short letter, anyhow. Al ain't much for writin', anyhow. But come out and see my new cheese. I tell yeh, I don't believe I ever had better luck in my life. If Ed should come, I want you should take him up a piece of this cheese."

It was beyond human nature to resist the influence of that noisy, hearty, loving household, and in the midst of the singing and laughing the wife forgot her anxiety, for the time at least, and laughed and sang with the rest.

About eleven o'clock a wagon-load more drove up to the door, and Bill Gray, the widow's oldest son, and his whole family from Sand Lake Coolly piled out amid a good-natured uproar. Every one talked at once, except Bill, who sat in the wagon with his wrists on his knees, a straw in his mouth, and an amused twinkle in his blue eyes.

"Ain't heard nothin' o' Ed, I s'pose?" he asked in a kind of bellow. Mrs. Smith shook her head. Bill, with a delicacy very striking in such a great giant, rolled his quid in his mouth, and said:

"Didn't know but you had. I hear two or three of the Sand Lake boys are comin'. Left New Orleens some time this week. Didn't write nothin' about Ed, but no news is good news in such cases, mother always says."

"Well, go put out yer team," said Mrs. Gray, "an' go'n bring me in some taters, an', Sim, you go see if you c'n find some corn. Sadie, you put on the water to bile. Come now, hustle yer boots, all o' yeh. If I feed this yer crowd, we've got to have some raw materials. If y' think I'm goin' to feed yeh on pie–you're jest mightily mistaken."

The children went off into the fields, the girls put dinner on to boil, and then went to change their dresses and fix their hair. "Somebody might come," they said.

"Land sakes, I *hope* not! I don't know where in time I'd set 'em, 'less they'd eat at the second table," Mrs Gray laughed, in pretended dismay.

The two older boys, who had served their time in the army, lay out on the grass before the house, and whittled and talked desultorily about the war and the crops, and planned buying a threshing-machine. The older girls and Mrs. Smith helped enlarge the table and put on the dishes, talking all the time in that cheery, incoherent, and meaningful way a group of such women have—a conversation to be taken for its spirit rather than for its letter, though Mrs. Gray at last got the ear of them all and dissertated at length on girls.

"Girls in love ain't no use in the whole blessed week," she said. "Sundays they're a-lookin, down the road, expectin' he'll come. Sunday afternoons they can't think o' nothin' else, 'cause he's *here*. Monday mornin's they're sleepy and kind o' dreamy and slimpsy, and good f'r nothin' on Tuesday and Wednesday. Thursday they git absent-minded, an' begin to look off toward Sunday again, an' mope aroun' and let the dishwater git cold, right under their noses. Friday they break dishes, an' go off in the best room an' snivel, an' look out o' the winder. Saturdays they have queer spurts o' workin' like all p'ssessed, an' spurts o' frizzin' their hair. An' Sunday they begin it all over again."

The girls giggled and blushed all through this tirade from their mother, their broad faces and powerful frames anything but suggestive of lackadaisical sentiment. But Mrs. Smith said:

"Now, Mrs. Gray, I hadn't ought to stay to dinner. You've got—"

"Now you set right down! If any of them girls' beaux comes, they'll have to take what's left, that's all. They ain't s'posed to have much appetite, nohow. No, you're goin' to stay if they starve, an' they ain't no danger o' that."

At one o'clock the long table was piled with boiled potatoes, cords of boiled corn on the cob; squash and pumpkin pies, hot biscuits, sweet pickles, bread and butter, and honey. Then one of the girls took down a conch-shell from a nail, and going to the door, blew a long, fine, free blast, that showed there was no weakness of lungs in her ample chest.

Then the children came out of the forest of corn, out of the creek, out of the loft of the barn, and out of the garden.

"They come to their feed f'r all the world jest like the pigs when y' holler 'poo-ee!' See 'em scoot!" laughed Mrs. Gray, every wrinkle on her face shining with delight.

The men shut up their jack-knives, and surrounded the horse-trough to souse their faces in the cold, hard water, and in a few moments the table was filled with a merry crowd, and a row of wistful-eyed youngsters circled the kitchen wall, where they stood first on one leg and then on the other, in impatient hunger.

"Now pitch in, Mrs. Smith," said Mrs. Gray, presiding over the table. "You know these men critters. They'll eat every grain of it, if yeh give 'em a chance. I swan, they're made o' India-rubber, their stomachs is, I know it."

"Haf to eat to work," said Bill, gnawing a cob with a swift, circular motion that rivalled a corn-sheller in results.

"More like workin' to eat," put in one of the girls, with a giggle. "More eat 'n work with *you*."

"You needn't say anything, Net. Anyone that'll eat seven ears—"

"I didn't no such thing. You piled your cobs on my plate."

"That'll do to tell Ed Varney. It won't go down here where we know yeh."

"Good land! Eat all yeh want! They's plenty more in the fiel's, but I can't afford to give you young uns tea. The tea is for us womenfolks, and 'specially f'r Mis' Smith an' Bill's wife. We're a-goin' to tell fortunes by it."

One by one the men filled up and shoved back, and one by one the children slipped into their places, and by two o'clock the women alone remained around the débris-covered table, sipping their tea and telling fortunes.

As they got well down to the grounds in the cup, they shook them with a circular motion in the hand, and then turned them bottom-side up quickly in the saucer, then twirled them three or four times one way, and three or four times the other, during a breathless pause. Then Mrs. Gray lifted the cup, and, gazing into it with profound gravity, pronounced the impending fate.

It must be admitted that, to a critical observer, she had abundant preparation for hitting close to the mark, as when she told the girls that "somebody was comin'." "It's a man," she went on gravely. "He is cross-eyed—"

"Oh, you hush!" cried Nettie.

"He has red hair, and is death on b'iled corn and hot biscuit."

The others shrieked with delight.

"But he's goin' to get the mitten, that red-headed feller is, for I see another feller comin' up behind him."

"Oh, lemme see, lemme see!" cried Nettie.

"Keep off," said the priestess, with a lofty gesture. "His hair is black. He don't eat so much, and he works more."

The girls exploded in a shriek of laughter, and pounded their sister on the back.

At last came Mrs. Smith's turn, and she was trembling with excitement as Mrs. Gray again composed her jolly face to what she considered a proper solemnity of expression.

"Somebody is comin' to *you*," she said, after a long pause. "He's got a musket on his back. He's a soldier. He's almost here. See?"

She pointed at two little tea-stems, which really formed a faint suggestion of a man with a musket on his back. He had climbed nearly to the edge of the cup. Mrs. Smith grew pale with excitement. She trembled so she could hardly hold the cup in her hand as she gazed into it.

"It's Ed," cried the old woman. "He's on the way home. Heavens an' earth! There he is now!" She turned and waved her hand out toward the road. They rushed to the door to look where she pointed.

A man in a blue coat, with a musket on his back, was toiling slowly up the hill on the sun-bright, dusty road, toiling slowly, with bent head half hidden by a heavy knapsack. So tired it seemed that walking was indeed a process of falling. So eager to get home he would not stop, would not look aside, but plodded on, amid the cries of the locusts, the welcome of the crickets, and the rustle of the yellow wheat. Getting hack to God's country, and his wife and babies!

Laughing, crying, trying to call him and the children at the same time, the little wife, almost hysterical, snatched her hat and ran out into the yard. But the soldier had disappeared over the hill into the hollow beyond, and, by the time she had found the children, he was too far away for her voice to reach him. And, besides, she was not sure it was her husband, for he had not turned his head at their shouts. This seemed so strange. Why didn't he stop to rest at his old neighbor's house? Tortured by hope and doubt, she hurried up the coolly as fast as she could push the baby wagon, the blue-coated figure just ahead pushing steadily, silently forward up the coolly.

When the excited, panting little group came in sight of the gate they saw the blue-coated figure standing, leaning upon the rough rail fence, his chin on his palms, gazing at the empty house. His knapsack, canteen, blankets, and musket lay upon the dusty grass at his feet.

He was like a man lost in a dream. His wide, hungry eyes devoured the scene. The rough lawn, the little unpainted house, the field of clear yellow wheat behind it, down across which streamed the sun, now almost ready to touch the high hill to the west, the crickets crying merrily, a cat on the fence near by, dreaming, unmindful of the stranger in blue—

How peaceful it all was. O God! How far removed from all camps, hospitals, battle lines. A little cabin in a Wisconsin coolly, but it was majestic in its peace. How did he ever leave it for those years of tramping, thirsting, killing?

Trembling, weak with emotion, her eyes on the silent figure, Mrs. Smith hurried up to the fence. Her feet made no noise in the dust and grass, and they were close upon him before he knew of them. The oldest boy ran a little ahead. He will never forget that figure, that face. It will always remain as something epic, that return of the private. He fixed his eyes on the pale face covered with a ragged beard.

"Who *are* you, sir?" asked the wife, or, rather, started to ask, for he turned, stood a moment, and then cried:

"Emma!"

"Edward!"

The children stood in a curious row to see their mother kiss this bearded, strange man, the elder girl sobbing sympathetically with her mother. Illness had left the soldier partly deaf, and this added to the strangeness of his manner.

But the youngest child stood away, even after the girl had recognized her father and kissed him. The man turned then to the baby, and said in a curiously unpaternal tone:

"Come here, my little man; don't you know me?" But the baby backed away under the fence and stood peering at him critically.

"My little man!" What meaning in those words! This baby seemed like some other woman's child, and not the infant he had left in his wife's arms. The war had come between him and his baby—he was only a strange man to him, with big eyes; a soldier, with mother hanging to his arm, and talking in a loud voice.

"And this is Tom," the private said, drawing the oldest boy to him. "*He'll* come and see me. *He* knows his poor old pap when he comes home from the war."

The mother heard the pain and reproach in his voice and hastened to apologize.

"You've changed so, Ed. He can't know yeh. This is papa, Teddy; come and kiss him—Tom and Mary do. Come, won't you ?" But Teddy still peered through the fence with solemn eyes, well out of reach. He resembled a half-wild kitten that hesitates, studying the tones of one's voice.

"I'll fix him," said the soldier, and sat down to undo his knapsack, out of which he drew three enormous and very red apples. After giving one to each of the older children, he said:

"*Now* I guess he'll come. Eh, my little man? Now come see your pap."

Teddy crept slowly under the fence, assisted by the over-zealous Tommy, and a moment later was kicking and squalling in his father's arms. Then they entered the house, into the sitting room, poor, bare, art-forsaken little room, too, with its rag carpet, its square clock, and its two or three chromos and pictures from *Harper's Weekly* pinned about.

"Emma, I'm all tired out," said Private Smith, as he flung himself down on the carpet as he used to do, while his wife brought a pillow to put under his head, and the children stood about munching their apples.

"Tommy, you run and get me a pan of chips, and Mary, you get the tea-kettle on, and I'll go and make some biscuit."

And the soldier talked. Question after question he poured forth about the crops, the cattle, the renter, the neighbor. He slipped his heavy government brogan shoes off his poor, tired, blistered feet, and lay out with utter, sweet relaxation. He was a free man again, no longer a soldier under command. At supper he stopped once, listened and smiled "That's old Spot. I know her voice. I s'pose that's her calf out there in the pen. I can't milk her tonight, though. I'm too tired. But I tell you I'd like a drink o' her milk. What's become of old Rove?"

"He died last winter. Poisoned, I guess." There was a moment of sadness for them all. It was some time before the husband spoke again, in a voice that trembled a little.

"Poor old feller! He'd 'a' known me half a mile away. I expected him to come down the hill to meet me. It 'ud 'a' been more like comin' home if I could 'a' seen him comin' down the road an' waggin' his tail, an' laughin' that way he had. I tell yeh, it kind o' took hold o' me to see the blinds down an' the house shut up."

"But, yeh see, we–we expected you'd write again 'fore you started. And then we thought we'd see you if you *did* come," she hastened to explain.

"Well, I ain't worth a cent on writin'. Besides, it's just as well yeh didn't know when I was comin'. I tell you, it sounds good to hear them chickens out there, an' turkeys, an' the crickets. Do you know they don't have just the same kind o' crickets down South? Who's Sam hired t' help cut yer grain?"

"The Ramsey boys."

"Looks like a good crop; but I'm afraid I won't do much gettin' it cut. This cussed fever an' ague has got me down pretty low. I don't know when I'll get rid of it. I'll bet I've took twenty-five pounds of quinine if I've taken a bit. Gimme another biscuit. I tell yeh, they taste good, Emma. I ain't had anything like it–say, if you'd 'a' hear'd me braggin' to th' boys about your butter 'n' biscuits I'll bet your ears 'ud a' burnt."

The private's wife colored with pleasure. "Oh, you're always a-braggin' about your things. Everybody makes good butter."

"Yes; old lady Snyder, for instance."

"Oh, well, she ain't to be mentioned. She's Dutch."

"Or old Mis' Snively. One more cup o' tea, Mary. That's my girl! I'm feeling better already. I just b'lieve the matter with me is, I'm *starved*."

This was a delicious hour, one long to be remembered. They were like lovers again. But their tenderness, like that of a typical American family, found utterance in tones, rather than in words. He was praising her when praising her biscuit, and she knew it. They grew soberer when he showed where he had been struck, one ball burning the back of his hand, one cutting away a lock of hair from his temple, and one passing through the calf of his leg. The wife shuddered to think how near she had come to being a soldier's widow. Her waiting no longer seemed hard. This sweet, glorious hour effaced it all.

Then they rose, and all went out into the garden and down to the barn. He stood beside her while she milked old Spot. They began to plan fields and crops for next year.

His farm was weedy and encumbered, a rascally renter had run away with his machinery (departing between two days), his children needed clothing, the years were coming upon him, he was sick and emaciated, but his heroic soul did not quail. With the same courage with which he had faced his Southern march he entered upon a still more hazardous future.

Oh, that mystic hour! The pale man with big eyes standing there by the well, with his young wife by his side. The vast moon swinging above the eastern peaks, the cattle winding down the pasture slopes with jangling bells, the crickets singing, the stars blooming out sweet and far and serene; the katydids rhythmically calling, the little turkeys crying querulously, as they settle to roost in the poplar tree near the open gate. The voices at the well drop lower, the little ones nestle in their father's arms at last, and Teddy falls asleep there.

The common soldier of the American volunteer army had returned. His war with the South was over, and his fight, his daily running fight with Nature and against the injustice of his fellow-men, was begun again.

EDITH WHARTON

[1862–1937]

*The Mission of Jane**

(First published in *Harper's Magazine*, December, 1902; first book publication in 1904.)

I

LETHBURY, SURVEYING HIS wife across the dinner table, found his transient glance arrested by an indefinable change in her appearance.

"How smart you look! Is that a new gown?" he asked.

Her answering look seemed to deprecate his charging her with the extravagance of wasting a new gown on him, and he now perceived that the change lay deeper than any accident of dress. At the same time, he noticed that she betrayed her consciousness of it by a delicate, almost frightened blush. It was one of the compensations of Mrs. Lethbury's protracted childishness that she still blushed as prettily as at eighteen. Her body had been privileged not to outstrip her mind, and the two, as it seemed to Lethbury, were destined to travel together through an eternity of girlishness.

"I don't know what you mean," she said.

Since she never did, he always wondered at her bringing this out as a fresh grievance against him; but his wonder was unresentful, and he said good-humoredly: "You sparkle so that I thought you had on your diamonds."

She sighed and blushed again.

"It must be," he continued, "that you've been to a dressmaker's opening. You're absolutely brimming with illicit enjoyment."

She stared again, this time at the adjective. His adjectives always embarrassed her: their unintelligibleness savoured of impropriety.

"In short," he summed up, "you've been doing something that you're thoroughly ashamed of."

To his surprise she retorted: "I don't see why I should be ashamed of it!"

Lethbury leaned back with a smile of enjoyment. When there was nothing better going he always liked to listen to her explanations.

"Well–?" he said.

She was becoming breathless and ejaculatory. "Of course you'll laugh–you laugh at everything!"

"That rather blunts the point of my derision, doesn't it?" he interjected; but she pushed on without noticing:

"It's so easy to laugh at things."

"Ah," murmured Lethbury with relish, "that's Aunt Sophronia's, isn't it?"

Most of his wife's opinions were heirlooms, and he took a quaint pleasure in tracing their descent. She was proud of their age, and saw no reason for discarding them while they were still serviceable. Some, of course, were so fine that she kept them for state occasions, like her great-grandmother's Crown Derby; but from the lady known as Aunt Sophronia she had inherited a stout set of every-day prejudices that were practically as good as new; whereas her husband's, as she noticed, were always having to be replaced. In the early days she had fancied there might be a certain satisfaction in taxing him with the fact; but she had long since been silenced by the reply: "My dear, I'm not a rich man, but I never use an opinion twice if I can help it."

She was reduced, therefore, to dwelling on his moral deficiencies; and one of the most obvious of these was his refusal to take things seriously. On this occasion, however, some ulterior purpose kept her from taking up his taunt.

"I'm not in the least ashamed!" she repeated, with the air of shaking a banner to the wind; but the domestic atmosphere being calm, the banner drooped unheroically.

"That," said Lethbury judicially, "encourages me to infer that you ought to be, and that, consequently, you've been giving yourself the unusual pleasure of doing something I shouldn't approve of."

She met this with an almost solemn directness. "No," she said. "You won't approve of it. I've allowed for that."

"Ah," he exclaimed, setting down his liqueur-glass. "You've worked out the whole problem, eh?"

"I believe so."

"That's uncommonly interesting. And what is it?"

She looked at him quietly. "A baby."

If it was seldom given her to surprise him, she had attained the distinction for once.

"A baby?"

"Yes."

"A–human baby?"

"Of course!" she cried, with the virtuous resentment of the woman who has never allowed dogs in the house.

Lethbury's puzzled stare broke into a fresh smile. "A baby I shan't approve of? Well, in the abstract I don't think much of them, I admit. Is this an abstract baby?"

Again she frowned at the adjective; but she had reached a pitch of exaltation at which such obstacles could not deter her.

"It's the loveliest baby—" she murmured.

"Ah, then it's concrete. It exists. In this harsh world it draws its breath in pain—"

"It's the healthiest child I ever saw!" she indignantly corrected.

"You've seen it, then?"

Again the accusing blush suffused her. "Yes—I've seen it."

"And to whom does the paragon belong?"

And here indeed she confounded him. "To me—I hope," she declared.

He pushed his chair back with an articulate murmur. "To *you*—?"

"To *us*," she corrected.

"Good Lord!" he said. If there had been the least hint of hallucination in her transparent gaze—but no; it was as clear, as shallow, as easily fathomable as when he had first suffered the sharp surprise of striking bottom in it.

It occurred to him that perhaps she was trying to be funny: he knew that there is nothing more cryptic than the humor of the unhumorous.

"Is it a joke?" he faltered.

"Oh, I hope not. I want it so much to be a reality—"

He paused to smile at the limitations of a world in which jokes were not realities, and continued gently: "But since it is one already—"

"To us, I mean: to you and me. I want—" her voice wavered, and her eyes with it. "I have always wanted so dreadfully . . . it has been such a disappointment . . . not to . . . "

"I see," said Lethbury slowly.

But he had not seen before. It seemed curious now that he had never thought of her taking it in that way, had never surmised any hidden depths beneath her outspread obviousness. He felt as though he had touched a secret spring in her mind.

There was a moment's silence, moist and tremulous on her part, awkward and slightly irritated on his.

"You've been lonely, I suppose?" he began. It was odd, having suddenly to reckon with the stranger who gazed at him out of her trivial eyes.

"At times," she said.

"I'm sorry."

"It was not your fault. A man has so many occupations; and women who are clever—or very handsome—I suppose that's an occupation too. Sometimes I've felt that when dinner was ordered I had nothing to do till the next day."

"Oh," he groaned.

"It wasn't your fault," she insisted. "I never told you—but when I chose that rose-bud paper for the front-room upstairs, I always thought—"

"Well—?"

"It would be such a pretty paper—for a baby—to wake up in. That was years ago, of course; but it was rather an expensive paper. . . and it hasn't faded in the least . . ." she broke off incoherently.

"It hasn't faded?"

"No—and so I thought . . . as we don't use the room for anything . . . now that Aunt Sophronia is dead . . . I thought I might . . . you might . . . oh, Julian, if you could only have seen it just waking up in its crib!"

"Seen what—where? You haven't got a baby upstairs?"

"Oh, no—not yet," she said, with her rare laugh—the girlish bubbling of merriment that had seemed one of her chief graces in the early days. It occurred to him that he had not given her enough things to laugh about lately. But then she needed such very elementary things: she was as difficult to amuse as a savage. He concluded that he was not sufficiently simple.

"Alice," he said almost solemnly, "what *do* you mean?"

She hesitated a moment: he saw her gather her courage for a supreme effort. Then she said slowly, gravely, as though she were pronouncing a sacramental phrase:

"I'm so lonely without a little child—and I thought perhaps you'd let me adopt one . . . It's at the hospital . . . its mother is dead . . . and I could . . . pet it, and dress it, and do things for it . . . and it's such a good baby . . . you can ask any of the nurses . . . it would never, never bother you by crying . . ."

II

Lethbury accompanied his wife to the hospital in a mood of chastened wonder. It did not occur to him to oppose her wish. He knew, of course, that he would have to bear the brunt of the situation: the jokes at the club, the enquiries, the explanations. He saw himself in the comic role of the adopted father and welcomed it as an expiation. For in his rapid reconstruction of the past he found himself cutting a shabbier figure than he cared to admit. He had always been intolerant of stupid people, and it was his punishment to be convicted of stupidity. As his mind traversed the years between his marriage and this unexpected assumption of paternity, he saw, in the light of an overheated imagination, many signs of unwonted crassness. It was not that he had ceased to think his wife stupid: she *was* stupid, limited, inflexible; but there was a pathos in the struggles of her swaddled mind, in its blind reachings toward the primal emotions. He had always thought she would have been happier with a child; but he had thought it mechanically, because it had so often been thought before, because it was in the nature of things to think it of every woman, because his wife was so eminently one of a species that she fitted into all the generalizations of the sex. But he had regarded this generalization as merely typical of the triumph of tradition over experience. Maternity was no doubt the supreme function of primitive woman, the one end to which her whole organism tended; but the law of increasing complexity had operated in both sexes, and he had not seriously supposed that, outside the world of Christmas fiction and anecdotic art, such truisms had any special hold on the feminine imagination. Now he saw that the arts in question were kept alive by the vitality of the sentiments they appealed to.

Lethbury was in fact going through a rapid process of readjustment. His marriage had been a failure, but he had preserved toward his wife the exact fidelity of act that is sometimes supposed to excuse any divagation of feeling; so that, for years, the tie between them had consisted mainly in his abstaining from making love to other women. The abstention had not always been easy, for the world is surprisingly well-stocked with the kind of woman one ought to have married but did not; and Lethbury had not escaped the solicitation of such alternatives. His immunity had been purchased at the cost of taking refuge in the somewhat rarefied atmosphere of his perceptions; and his world being thus limited, he had given unusual care to its details, compensating himself for the narrowness of his horizon by the minute finish of his foreground. It was a world of fine shadings and the nicest proportions, where impulse seldom set a blundering foot, and the feast of reason was undisturbed by an intemperate flow of soul. To such a banquet his wife naturally remained uninvited. The diet would have disagreed with her, and she would probably have objected to the other guests. But Lethbury, miscalculating her needs, had hitherto supposed that he had made ample provision for them, and was consequently at liberty to enjoy his own fare without any reproach of mendicancy at his gates. Now he beheld her pressing a starved face against the windows of his life, and in his imaginative reaction he invested her with a pathos borrowed from the sense of his own shortcomings.

In the hospital the imaginative process continued with increasing force. He looked at his wife with new eyes. Formerly she had been to him a mere bundle of negations, a labyrinth of dead walls and bolted doors. There was nothing behind the walls, and the doors led no whither: he had sounded and listened often enough to be sure of that. Now he felt like a traveler who, exploring some ancient ruin, comes on an inner cell, intact amid the general dilapidation, and painted with images which reveal the forgotten uses of the building.

His wife stood by a white crib in one of the wards. In the crib lay a child, a year old, the nurse affirmed, but to Lethbury's eye a mere dateless fragment of humanity projected against a background of conjecture. Over this anonymous particle of life Mrs. Lethbury leaned, such ecstasy reflected in her face as strikes up, in Correggio's *Night-piece*, from the child's body to the mother's countenance. It was a light that irradiated and dazzled her. She looked up at an enquiry of Lethbury's, but as their glances met he perceived that she no longer saw him, that he had become as invisible to her as she had long been to him. He had to transfer his question to the nurse.

"What is the child's name?" he asked.

"We call her Jane," said the nurse.

III

Lethbury, at first, had resisted the idea of a legal adoption; but when he found that his wife could not be brought to regard the child as hers till it had been made so by process of law, he promptly withdrew his objection. On one point only he remained inflexible; and that was the changing of the waif's name. Mrs. Lethbury, almost at once, had expressed a wish to rechristen it: she fluctuated between Muriel and Gladys, deferring the moment of decision like a lady wavering between two bonnets. But Lethbury was unyielding. In the general surrender of his prejudices this one alone held out.

"But Jane is so dreadful," Mrs. Lethbury protested.

"Well, we don't know that *she* won't be dreadful. She may grow up a Jane."

His wife exclaimed reproachfully. "The nurse says she's the loveliest—"

"Don't they always say that?" asked Lethbury patiently. He was prepared to be inexhaustibly patient now that he had reached a firm foothold of opposition.

"It's cruel to call her Jane," Mrs. Lethbury pleaded.

"It's ridiculous to call her Muriel."

"The nurse is *sure* she must be a lady's child."

Lethbury winced: he had tried, all along, to keep his mind off the question of antecedents.

"Well, let her prove it," he said, with a rising sense of exasperation. He wondered how he could ever have allowed himself to be drawn into such a ridiculous business; for the first time he felt the fully irony of it. He had visions of coming home in the afternoon to a house smelling of linseed and paregoric, and of being greeted by a chronic howl as he went up-stairs to dress for dinner. He had never been a club-man, but he saw himself becoming one now.

The worst of his anticipations were unfulfilled. The baby was surprisingly well and surprisingly quiet. Such infantile remedies as she absorbed were not potent enough to be perceived beyond the nursery; and when Lethbury could be induced to enter that sanctuary, there was nothing to jar his nerves in the mild pink presence of his adopted daughter. Jars there were, indeed: they were probably inevitable in the disturbed routine of the household; but they occurred between Mrs. Lethbury and the nurses, and Jane contributed to them only a placid stare which might have served as a rebuke to the combatants.

In the reaction from his first impulse of atonement, Lethbury noted with sharpened perceptions the effect of the change on his wife's character. He saw already the error of supposing that it could work any transformation in her. It simply magnified her existing qualities. She was like a dried sponge put in water: she expanded, but she did not change her shape. From the stand-point of scientific observation it was curious to see how her stored instincts responded to the pseudo-maternal call. She overflowed with the petty maxims of the occasion. One felt in her the epitome, the consummation, of centuries of animal maternity, so that this little woman, who screamed at a mouse and was nervous about burglars, came to typify the cave-mother rending her prey for her young.

It was less easy to regard philosophically the practical effects of her borrowed motherhood. Lethbury found with surprise that she was becoming assertive and definite. She no longer represented the negative side of his life; she showed, indeed, a tendency to inconvenient affirmations. She had gradually expanded her assumption of motherhood till it included his own share in the relation, and he suddenly found himself regarded as the father of Jane. This was a contingency he had not foreseen, and it took all his philosophy to accept it; but there were moments of compensation. For Mrs. Lethbury was undoubtedly happy for the first time in years; and the thought that he had tardily contributed to this end reconciled him to the irony of the means.

At first he was inclined to reproach himself for still viewing the situation from the outside, for remaining a spectator instead of a participant. He had been allured, for a moment, by the vision of several hands meeting over a cradle, as the whole body of domestic fiction bears witness to their doing; and the fact that no such conjunction took place he could explain only on the ground that it was a borrowed cradle. He did not dislike the little girl. She still remained to him a hypothetical presence, a query rather than a fact; but her nearness was not unpleasant, and there were moments when her tentative utterances, her groping steps, seemed to loosen the dry accretions enveloping his inner self. But even at such moments–moments which he invited and caressed–she did not bring him nearer to his wife. He now perceived that he had made a certain place in his life for Mrs. Lethbury, and that she no longer fitted into it. It was too late to enlarge the space, and so she overflowed and encroached. Lethbury struggled against the sense of submergence. He let down barrier after barrier, yielding privacy after privacy; but his wife's personality continued to dilate. She was no longer herself alone: she was herself and Jane. Gradually, in a monstrous fusion of identity, she became herself, himself and Jane; and instead of trying to adapt her to a spare crevice of his character, he found himself carelessly squeezed into the smallest compartment of the domestic economy.

IV

He continued to tell himself that he was satisfied if his wife was happy; and it was not till the child's tenth year that he felt a doubt of her happiness.

Jane had been a preternaturally good child. During the eight years of her adoption she had caused her foster-parents no anxiety beyond those connected with the usual succession of youthful diseases. But her unknown progenitors had given her a robust constitution, and she passed unperturbed through measles, chicken-pox and whooping-cough. If there was any suffering it was endured vicariously by Mrs. Lethbury, whose temperature rose and fell with the patient's, and who could not hear Jane sneeze without visions of a marble angel weeping over a broken column. But though Jane's prompt recoveries continued to belie such premonitions, though her existence continued to move forward on an even keel of good health and good conduct, Mrs. Lethbury's satisfaction showed no corresponding advance. Lethbury, at first, was disposed to add her disappointment to the long list of feminine inconsistencies with which the sententious observer of life builds up his favorable induction; but circumstances presently led him to take a kindlier view of the case.

Hitherto his wife had regarded him as a negligible factor in Jane's evolution. Beyond providing for his adopted daughter, and effacing himself before her, he was not expected to contribute to her well-being. But as time passed he appeared to his wife in a new light. It was he who was to educate Jane. In matters of the intellect, Mrs. Lethbury was the first to declare her deficiencies—to proclaim them, even, with a certain virtuous superiority. She said she did not pretend to be clever, and there was no denying the truth of the assertion. Now, however, she seemed less ready, not to own her limitations, but to glory in them. Confronted with the problem of Jane's instruction she stood in awe of the child.

"I have always been stupid, you know," she said to Lethbury with a new humility, "and I'm afraid I shan't know what is best for Jane. I'm sure she has a wonderfully good mind, and I should reproach myself if I didn't give her every opportunity." She looked at him helplessly. "You must tell me what ought to be done."

Lethbury was not unwilling to oblige her. Somewhere in his mental lumber-room there rusted a theory of education such as usually lingers among the impedimenta of the childless. He brought this out, refurbished it, and applied it to Jane. At first he thought his wife had not overrated the quality of the child's mind. Jane seemed extraordinarily intelligent. Her precocious definiteness of mind was encouraging to her inexperienced preceptor. She had no difficulty in fixing her attention, and he felt that every fact he imparted was being etched in metal. He helped his wife to engage the best teachers, and for a while continued to take an ex-official interest in his adopted daughter's studies. But gradually his interest waned. Jane's ideas did not increase with her acquisitions. Her young mind remained a mere receptacle for facts: a kind of cold-storage from which anything which had been put there could be taken out at a moment's notice, intact but congealed. She developed, moreover, an inordinate pride in the capacity of her mental storehouse, and a tendency to pelt her public with its contents. She was overheard to jeer at her nurse for not knowing when the Saxon Heptarchy had fallen, and she alternately dazzled and depressed Mrs. Lethbury by the wealth of her chronological allusions. She showed no interest in the significance of the facts she amassed: she simply collected dates as another child might have collected stamps or marbles. To her foster-mother she seemed a prodigy of wisdom; but Lethbury saw, with a secret movement of sympathy, how the aptitudes in which Mrs. Lethbury gloried were slowly estranging her from her child.

"She is getting too clever for me," his wife said to him, after one of Jane's historical flights, "but I am so glad that she will be a companion to you."

Lethbury groaned in spirit. He did not look forward to Jane's companionship. She was still a good little girl; but there was something automatic and formal in her goodness, as though it were a kind of moral calisthenics which she went through for the sake of showing her agility. An early consciousness of virtue had moreover constituted her the natural guardian and adviser of her elders. Before she was fifteen she had set about reforming the household. She took Mrs. Lethbury in hand first; then she extended her efforts to the servants, with consequences more disastrous to the domestic harmony; and lastly she applied herself to Lethbury. She proved to him by statistics that he smoked too much, and that it was injurious to the optic nerve to read in bed. She took him to task for not going to church more regularly, and pointed out to him the evils of desultory reading. She suggested that a regular course of study encourages mental concentration, and hinted that inconsecutiveness of thought is a sign of approaching age.

To her adopted mother her suggestions were equally pertinent. She instructed Mrs. Lethbury in an improved way of making beef stock, and called her attention to the unhygienic qualities of carpets. She poured out distracting facts about bacilli and vegetable mould, and demonstrated that curtains and picture-frames are a hot-bed of animal organisms. She learned by heart the nutritive ingredients of the principal articles of diet, and revolutionized the cuisine by an attempt to establish a scientific average between starch and phosphates. Four cooks left during this experiment, and Lethbury fell into the habit of dining at his club.

Once or twice, at the outset, he had tried to check Jane's ardor; but his efforts resulted only in hurting his wife's feelings. Jane remained impervious, and Mrs. Lethbury resented any attempt to protect her from her daughter. Lethbury saw that she was consoled for the sense of her own inferiority by the thought of what Jane's intellectual companionship must be to him; and he tried to keep up the illusion by enduring with what grace he might the blighting edification of Jane's discourse.

V

As Jane grew up he sometimes avenged himself by wondering if his wife was still sorry that they had not called her Muriel. Jane was not ugly; she developed, indeed, a kind of categorical prettiness which might have been a projection of her mind. She had a creditable collection of features, but one had to take an inventory of them to find out that she was good-looking. The fusing grace had been omitted.

Mrs. Lethbury took a touching pride in her daughter's first steps in the world. She expected Jane to take by her complexion those whom she did not capture by her learning. But Jane's rosy freshness did not work any perceptible ravages. Whether the young men guessed the axioms on her lips and detected the encyclopædia in her eye, or whether they simply found no intrinsic interest in these features, certain it is, that, in spite of her mother's heroic efforts, and of incessant calls on Lethbury's purse, Jane, at the end of her first season, had dropped hopelessly out of the running. A few duller girls found her interesting, and one or two young men came to the house with the object of meeting other young women; but she was rapidly becoming one of the social supernumeraries who are asked out only because they are on people's lists.

The blow was bitter to Mrs. Lethbury; but she consoled herself with the idea that Jane had failed because she was too clever. Jane probably shared this conviction; at all events she betrayed no consciousness of failure. She had developed a pronounced taste for society, and went out, unweariedly and obstinately, winter after winter, while Mrs. Lethbury toiled in her wake, showering attentions on oblivious hostesses. To Lethbury there was something at once tragic and exasperating in the sight of their two figures, the one conciliatory, the other dogged, both pursuing with unabated zeal the elusive prize of popularity. He even began to feel a personal stake in the pursuit, not as it concerned Jane but as it affected his wife. He saw that the latter was the victim of Jane's disappointment: that Jane was not above the crude satisfaction of "taking it out" of her mother. Experience checked the impulse to come to his wife's defence; and when his resentment was at its height, Jane disarmed him by giving up the struggle.

Nothing was said to mark her capitulation; but Lethbury noticed that the visiting ceased and that the dressmaker's bills diminished. At the same time Mrs. Lethbury made it known that Jane had taken up charities; and before long Jane's conversation confirmed this announcement. At first Lethbury congratulated himself on the change; but Jane's domesticity soon began to weigh on him. During the day she was sometimes absent on errands of mercy; but in the evening she was always there. At first she and Mrs. Lethbury sat in the drawing-room together, and Lethbury smoked in the library; but presently Jane formed the habit of joining him there, and he began to suspect that he was included among the objects of her philanthropy.

Mrs. Lethbury confirmed the suspicion. "Jane has grown very serious-minded lately," she said. "She imagines that she used to neglect you and she is trying to make up for it. Don't discourage her," she added innocently.

Such a plea delivered Lethbury helpless to his daughter's ministrations; and he found himself measuring the hours he spent with her by the amount of relief they must be affording her mother. There were even moments when he read a furtive gratitude in Mrs. Lethbury's eye.

But Lethbury was no hero, and he had nearly reached the limit of vicarious endurance when something wonderful happened. They never quite knew afterward how it had come about, or who first perceived it; but Mrs. Lethbury one day gave tremulous voice to their discovery.

"Of course," she said, "he comes here because of Elise." The young lady in question, a friend of Jane's, was possessed of attractions which had already been found to explain the presence of masculine visitors.

Lethbury risked a denial. "I don't thing he does," he declared.

"But Elise is thought very pretty," Mrs. Lethbury insisted.

"I can't help that," said Lethbury doggedly.

He saw a faint light in his wife's eyes, but she remarked carelessly: "Mr. Budd would be a very good match for Elise."

Lethbury could hardly repress a chuckle: he was so exquisitely aware that she was trying to propitiate the gods.

For a few weeks neither said a word; then Mrs. Lethbury once more reverted to the subject.

"It is a month since Elise went abroad," she said.

"Is it?"

"And Mr. Budd seems to come here just as often—"

"Ah," said Lethbury with heroic indifference; and his wife hastily changed the subject.

Mr. Winstanley Budd was a young man who suffered from an excess of manner. Politeness gushed from him in the driest season. He was always performing feats of drawingroom chivalry, and the approach of the most unobtrusive female threw him into attitudes which endangered the furniture. His features, being of the cherubic order, did not lend themselves to this role; but there were moments when he appeared to dominate them, to force them into compliance with an aquiline ideal. The range of Mr. Budd's social benevolence made its object hard to distinguish. He spread his cloak so indiscriminately that one could not always interpret the gesture, and Jane's impassive manner had the effect of increasing his demonstrations: she threw him into paroxysms of politeness.

At first he filled the house with his amenities; but gradually it became apparent that his most dazzling effects were directed exclusively to Jane. Lethbury and his wife held their breath and looked away from each other. They pretended not to notice the frequency of Mr. Budd's visits, they struggled against an imprudent inclination to leave the young people too much alone. Their conclusions were the result of indirect observation, for neither of them dared to be caught watching Mr. Budd: they behaved like naturalists on the trail of a rare butterfly.

In his efforts not to notice Mr. Budd, Lethbury centred his attentions on Jane; and Jane, at this crucial moment, wrung from him a reluctant admiration. While her parents went about dissembling their emotions, she seemed to have none to conceal. She betrayed neither eagerness nor surprise; so complete was her unconcern that there were moments when Lethbury feared it was obtuseness, when he could hardly help whispering to her that now was the moment to lower the net.

Meanwhile the velocity of Mr. Budd's gyrations increased with the ardor of courtship; his politeness became incandescent, and Jane found herself the centre of a pyrotechnical display culminating in the "set piece" of an offer of marriage.

Mrs. Lethbury imparted the news to her husband one evening after their daughter had gone to bed. The announcement was made and received with an air of detachment, as though both feared to be betrayed into unseemly exultation; but Lethbury, as his wife ended, could not repress the inquiry, "Have they decided on a day?"

Mrs. Lethbury's superior command of her features enabled her to look shocked. "What can you be thinking of? He only offered himself at five!"

"Of course—of course—" stammered Lethbury—"but nowadays people marry after such short engagements—"

"Engagement!" said his wife solemnly. "There is no engagement."

Lethbury dropped his cigar. "What on earth do you mean ?"

"Jane is thinking it over."

"*Thinking it over?*"

"She has asked for a month before deciding."

Lethbury sank back with a gasp. Was it genius or was it madness? He felt incompetent to decide; and Mrs. Lethbury's next words showed that she shared his difficulty.

"Of course I don't want to hurry Jane–"

"Of course not," he acquiesced.

"But I pointed out to her that a young man of Mr. Budd's impulsive temperament might–might be easily discouraged–"

"Yes; and what did she say?"

"She said that if she was worth winning she was worth waiting for."

VI

The period of Mr. Budd's probation could scarcely have cost him as much mental anguish as it caused his would-be parents-in-law.

Mrs. Lethbury, by various ruses, tried to shorten the ordeal, but Jane remained inexorable; and each morning Lethbury came down to breakfast with the certainty of finding a letter of withdrawal from her discouraged suitor.

When at length the decisive day came, and Mrs. Lethbury, at its close, stole into the library with an air of chastened joy, they stood for a moment without speaking; then Mrs. Lethbury paid a fitting tribute to the proprieties by faltering out: "It will be dreadful to have to give her up–"

Lethbury could not repress a warning gesture; but even as it escaped him he realized that his wife's grief was genuine.

"Of course, of course," he said, vainly sounding his own emotional shallows for an answering regret. And yet it was his wife who had suffered most from Jane!

He had fancied that these sufferings would be effaced by the milder atmosphere of their last weeks together; but felicity did not soften Jane. Not for a moment did she relax her dominion: she simply widened it to include a new subject. Mr. Budd found himself under orders with the others; and a new fear assailed Lethbury as he saw Jane assume prenuptial control of her betrothed. Lethbury had never felt any strong personal interest in Mr. Budd; but as Jane's prospective husband the young man excited his sympathy. To his surprise he found that Mrs. Lethbury shared the feeling.

"I'm afraid he may find Jane a little exacting," she said, after an evening dedicated to a stormy discussion of the wedding arrangements. "She really ought to make some concessions. If he *wants* to be married in a black frock-coat instead of a dark gray one–" She paused and looked doubtfully at Lethbury.

"What can I do about it?" he said.

"You might explain to him–tell him that Jane isn't always–"

Lethbury made an impatient gesture. "What are you afraid of ? His finding her out or his not finding her out?"

Mrs. Lethbury flushed. "You put it so dreadfully!"

Her husband mused for a moment; then he said with an air of cheerful hypocrisy: "After all, Budd is old enough to take care of himself."

But the next day Mrs. Lethbury surprised him. Late in the afternoon she entered the library, so breathless and inarticulate that he scented a catastrophe.

"I've done it!" she cried.

"Done what?"

"Told him." She nodded toward the door. "He's just gone. Jane is out, and I had a chance to talk to him alone."

Lethbury pushed a chair forward and she sank into it.

"What did you tell him? That she is *not* always—"

Mrs. Lethbury lifted a tragic eye. "No; I told him that she always *is*—"

"Always *is*—?"

"Yes."

There was a pause. Lethbury made a call on his hoarded philosophy. He saw Jane suddenly reinstated in her evening sent by the library fire; but an answering chord in him thrilled at his wife's heroism.

"Well—what did he say?"

Mrs. Lethbury's agitation deepened. It was clear that the blow had fallen.

"He . . . he said . . . that we . . . had never understood Jane . . . or appreciated her . . . " The final syllables were lost in her handkerchief, and she left him marvelling at the mechanism of woman.

After that, Lethbury faced the future with an undaunted eye. They had done their duty—at least his wife had done hers—and they were reaping the usual harvest of ingratitude with a zest seldom accorded to such reaping. There was a marked change in Mr. Budd's manner, and his increasing coldness sent a genial glow through Lethbury's system. It was easy to bear with Jane in the light of Mr. Budd's disapproval.

There was a good deal to be borne in the last days, and the brunt of it fell on Mrs. Lethbury. Jane marked her transition to the married state by a seasonable but incongruous display of nerves. She became sentimental, hysterical and reluctant. She quarrelled with her betrothed and threatened to return the ring. Mrs. Lethbury had to intervene, and Lethbury felt the hovering sword of destiny. But the blow was suspended. Mr. Budd's chivalry was proof against all his bride's caprices and his devotion throve on her cruelty. Lethbury feared that he was too faithful, too enduring, and longed to urge him to vary his tactics. Jane presently reappeared with the ring on her finger, and consented to try on the wedding-dress; but her uncertainties, her reactions, were prolonged till the final day.

When it dawned, Lethbury was still in an ecstasy of apprehension. Feeling reasonably sure of the principal actors he had centered his fears on incidental possibilities. The clergyman might have a stroke, or the church might burn down, or there might be something wrong with the license. He did all that was humanly possible to avert such contingencies, but there remained that incalcuable factor known as the hand of God. Lethbury seemed to feel it groping for him.

At the altar it almost had him by the nape. Mr. Budd was late; and for five immeasurable minutes Lethbury and Jane faced a churchful of conjecture. Then the bridegroom appeared, flushed but chivalrous, and explaining to his father-in-law under cover of the ritual that he had torn his glove and had to go back for another.

"You'll be losing the ring next," muttered Lethbury; but Mr. Budd produced this article punctually, and a moment or two later was bearing its wearer captive down the aisle.

At the wedding-breakfast Lethbury caught his wife's eye fixed on him in mild disapproval, and understood that his hilarity was exceeding the bounds of fitness. He pulled himself together and tried to subdue his tone; but his jubilation bubbled over like a champagne-glass perpetually refilled. The deeper his draughts the higher it rose.

It was at the brim when, in the wake of the dispersing guests, Jane came down in her travelling-dress and fell on her mother's neck.

"I can't leave you!" she wailed, and Lethbury felt as suddenly sobered as a man under a douche. But if the bride was reluctant her captor was relentless. Never had Mr. Budd been more dominant, more aquiline. Lethbury's last fears were dissipated as the young man snatched Jane from her mother's bosom and bore her off to the brougham.

The brougham rolled away, the last milliner's girl forsook her post by the awning, the red carpet was folded up, and the house door closed. Lethbury stood alone in the hall with his wife. As he turned toward her, he noticed the look of tired heroism in her eyes, the deepened lines of her face. They reflected his own symptoms too accurately not to appeal to him. The nervous tension had been horrible. He went up to her, and an answering impulse made her lay a hand on his arm. He held it there a moment.

"Let us go off and have a jolly little dinner at a restaurant," he proposed.

There had been a time when such a suggestion would have surprised her to the verge of disapproval; but now she agreed to it at once.

"Oh, that would be so nice," she murmured with a great sigh of relief and assuagement.

Jane had fulfilled her mission after all: she had drawn them together at last.

O. HENRY

[1862–1910]

The Gift of the Magi

(First published in *New York Sunday World*, December, 1905; first book publication in 1906.)

ONE DOLLAR AND eighty-seven cents. That was all. And sixty cents of it was in pennies. Pennies saved one and two at a time by bulldozing the grocer and the vegetable man and the butcher until one's cheeks burned with the silent imputation of parsimony that such close dealing implied. Three times Della counted it. One dollar and eighty-seven cents. And the next day would be Christmas.

There was clearly nothing to do but flop down on the shabby little couch and howl. So Della did it. Which instigates the moral reflection that life is made up of sobs, sniffles, and smiles, with sniffles predominating.

While the mistress of the home is gradually subsiding from the first stage to the second, take a look at the home. A furnished flat at $8 per week. It did not exactly beggar description, but it certainly had that word on the lookout for the mendicancy squad.

In the vestibule below was a letter-box into which no letter would go, and an electric button from which no mortal finger could coax a ring. Also appertaining thereunto was a card bearing the name 'Mr James Dillingham Young.'

The 'Dillingham' had been flung to the breeze during a former period of prosperity when its possessor was being paid $30 per week. Now, when the income was shrunk to $20, the letters of 'Dillingham' looked blurred, as though they were thinking seriously of contracting to a modest and unassuming D. But whenever Mr James Dillingham Young came home and reached his flat above he was called 'Jim' and greatly hugged by Mrs James Dillingham Young, already introduced to you as Della. Which is all very good.

Della finished her cry and attended to her cheeks with the powder rag. She stood by the window and looked out dully at a gray cat walking a gray fence in a gray backyard. Tomorrow would be Christmas Day, and she had only $1.87 with which to buy Jim a present. Her Jim. She had been saving every penny she could for months, with this result. Twenty dollars a week doesn't go far. Expenses had been greater than she had calculated. They always are. Only $1.87 to buy a present for Jim. Many a happy hour she had spent planning for something nice for him. Something fine and rare and sterling–something just a little bit near to being worthy of the honor of being owned by Jim.

There was a pier-glass between the windows of the room. Perhaps you have seen a pier-glass in an $8 flat. A very thin and very agile person may, by observing his reflection in a rapid sequence of longitudinal strips, obtain a fairly accurate conception of his looks. Della, being slender, had mastered the art.

Suddenly she whirled from the window and stood before the glass. Her eyes were shining brilliantly, but her face had lost its color within twenty seconds. Rapidly she pulled down her hair and let it fall to its full length.

Now, there were two possessions of the James Dillingham Youngs in which they both took a mighty pride. One was Jim's gold watch that had been his father's and his grandfather's. The other was Della's hair. Had the Queen of Sheba lived in the flat across the airshaft, Della would have let her hair hang out the window some day to dry just to depreciate Her Majesty's jewels and gifts. Had King Solomon been the janitor, with all his treasures piled up in the basement, Jim would have pulled out his watch every time he passed, just to see him pluck at his beard from envy.

So now Della's beautiful hair fell about her rippling and shining like a cascade of brown waves. It reached below her knee and made itself almost a garment for her. And then she did it up again nervously and quickly. Once she faltered for a minute and stood still while a tear or two splashed on the worn red carpet.

On went her old brown jacket; on went her old brown hat. With a whirl of skirts and with the brilliant sparkle still in her eyes, she fluttered out the door and down the stairs to the street.

Where she stopped the sign read: 'Mme. Sofronie. Hair Goods of All Kinds.' One flight up Della ran, and collected herself, panting. Madame, large, too white, chilly, hardly looked the 'Sofronie.'

'Will you buy my hair?' asked Della.

'I buy hair,' said Madame. 'Take yer hat off and let's have a sight at the looks of it.'

Down rippled the brown cascade.

'Twenty dollars,' said Madame, lifting the mass with a practised hand.

'Give it to me quick,' said Della.

Oh, and the next two hours tripped by on rosy wings. Forget the hashed metaphor. She was ransacking the stores for Jim's present.

She found it at last. It surely had been made for Jim and no one else. There was no other like it in any of the stores, and she had turned all of them inside out. It was a platinum fob chain simple and chaste in design, properly proclaiming its value by substance alone and not by meretricious ornamentation—as all good things should do. It was even worthy of The Watch. As soon as she saw it she knew that it must be Jim's. It was like him. Quietness and value—the description applied to both. Twenty-one dollars they took from her for it, and she hurried home with the 87 cents. With that chain on his watch Jim might be properly anxious about the time in any company. Grand as the watch was, he sometimes looked at it on the sly on account of the old leather strap that he used in place of a chain.

When Della reached home her intoxication gave way a little to prudence and reason. She got out her curling irons and lighted the gas and went to work repairing the ravages made by generosity added to love. Which is always a tremendous task, dear friends—a mammoth task.

Within forty minutes her head was covered with tiny, close-lying curls that made her look wonderfully like a truant schoolboy. She looked at her reflection in the mirror long, carefully, and critically.

'If Jim doesn't kill me,' she said to herself, 'before he takes a second look at me, he'll say I look like a Coney Island chorus girl. But what could I do—oh! what could I do with a dollar and eighty-seven cents?'

At 7 o'clock the coffee was made and the frying-pan was on the back of the stove hot and ready to cook the chops.

Jim was never late. Delta doubled the fob chain in her hand and sat on the corner of the table near the door that he always ectered. Then she heard his step on the stair away down on the first flight, and she turned white for just a moment. She had a habit of saying little silent prayers about the simplest everyday things, and now she whispered: 'Please God, make him think I am still pretty.'

The door opened and Jim stepped in and closed it. He looked thin and very serious. Poor fellow, he was only twenty-two—and to be burdened with a family! He needed a new overcoat and he was without gloves.

Jim stopped inside the door, as immovable as a setter at the scent of quail. His eyes were fixed upon Della, and there was an expression in them that she could not read, and it terrified her. It was not anger, nor surprise, nor disapproval, nor horror, nor any of the sentiments that she had been prepared for. He simply stared at her fixedly with that peculiar expression on his face.

Della wriggled off the table and went for him.

'Jim, darling,' she cried, 'don't look at me that way. I had my hair cut off and sold it because I couldn't have lived through Christmas without giving you a present. It'll grow out again—you won't mind, will you? I just had to do it. My hair grows awfully fast. "Merry Christmas!" Jim, and let's be happy. You don't know what a nice—what a beautiful, nice gift I've got for you.'

'You've cut off your hair?' asked Jim, laboriously, as if he had not arrived at that patent fact yet even after the hardest mental labor.

'Cut it off and sold it,' said Della. 'Don't you like me just as well, anyhow? I'm me without my hair, ain't I?'

Jim looked about the room curiously.

'You say your hair is gone?' he said, with an air almost of idiocy.

'You needn't look for it,' said Della. 'It's sold, I tell you–sold and gone, too. It's Christmas Eve, boy. Be good to me, for it went for you. Maybe the hairs on my head were numbered,' she went on with a sudden serious sweetness, 'but nobody could ever count my love for you. Shall I put the chops on, Jim?'

Out of his trance Jim seemed quickly to wake. He enfolded his Della. For ten seconds let us regard with discreet scrutiny some inconsequential object in the other direction. Eight dollars a week or a million a year–what is the difference? A mathematician or a wit would give you the wrong answer. The Magi brought valuable gifts, but that was not among them. This dark assertion will be illuminated later on.

Jim drew a package from his overcoat pocket and threw it upon the table.

'Don't make any mistake, Dell,' he said, 'about me. I don't think there's anything in the way of a haircut or a shave or a shampoo that could make me like my girl any less. But if you'll unwrap that package you may see why you had me going a while at first.'

White fingers and nimble tore at the string and paper. And then an ecstatic scream of joy; and then, alas! a quick feminine charge to hysterical tears and wails, necessitating the immediate employment of all the comforting powers of the lord of the flat.

For there lay The Combs–the set of combs, side and back, that Della had worshipped for long in a Broadway window. Beautiful combs, pure tortoise shell, with jewelled rims–just the shade to wear in the beautiful vanished hair. They were expensive combs, she knew, and her heart had simply craved and yearned over them without the least hope of possession. And now, they were hers, but the tresses that should have adorned the coveted adornments were gone.

But she hugged them to her bosom, and at length she was able to look up with dim eyes and smile and say: 'My hair grows so fast, Jim!'

And then Della leaped up like a little singed cat and cried, 'Oh, oh!'

Jim had not yet seen his beautiful present. She held it out to him eagerly upon her open palm. The dull precious metal seemed to flash with a reflection of her bright and ardent spirit.

'Isn't it a dandy, Jim? I hunted all over town to find it. You'll have to look at the time a hundred times a day now. Give me your watch. I want to see how it looks on it.'

Instead of obeying, Jim tumbled down on the couch and put his hands under the back of his head and smiled.

'Dell,' said he, 'let's put our Christmas presents away and keep 'em a while.

They're too nice to use just at present. I sold the watch to get the money to buy your combs. And now suppose you put the chops on.'

The Magi, as you know, were wise men–wonderfully wise men–who brought gifts to the Babe in the manger. They invented the art of giving Christmas presents. Being wise, their gifts were no doubt wise ones, possibly bearing the privilege of exchange in case of duplication. And here I have lamely related to you the uneventful chronicle of two foolish children in a flat who most unwisely sacrificed for each other the greatest treasures of their house. But in a last word to the wise of these days let it be said that of all who give gifts these two were the wisest. Of all who give and receive gifts, such as they are wisest. Everywhere they are wisest. They are the Magi.

The Furnished Room

(First published in the *New York Sunday World Magazine*,
August, 1904; first book publication in 1906.)

RESTLESS, SHIFTING, FUGACIOUS as time itself is a certain vast bulk of the population of the red brick district of the lower West Side. Homeless, they have a hundred homes. They flit from furnished room to furnished room, transients forever—transients in abode, transients in heart and mind. They sing "Home, Sweet Home" in ragtime; they carry their *lares et penates* in a bandbox; their vine is entwined about a picture hat; a rubber plant is their fig tree.

Hence the houses of this district, having had a thousand dwellers, should have a thousand tales to tell, mostly dull ones, no doubt; but it would be strange if there could not be found a ghost or two in the wake of all these vagrant guests.

One evening after dark a young man prowled among these crumbling red mansions, ringing their bells. At the twelfth he rested his lean hand-baggage upon the step and wiped the dust from his hatband and forehead. The bell sounded faint and far away in some remote, hollow depths.

To the door of this, the twelfth house whose bell he had rung, came a housekeeper who made him think of an unwholesome, surfeited worm that had eaten its nut to a hollow shell and now sought to fill the vacancy with edible lodgers.

He asked if there was a room to let.

"Come in," said the housekeeper. Her voice came from her throat; her throat seemed lined with fur. "I have the third-floor-back, vacant since a week back. Should you wish to look at it?"

The young man followed her up the stairs. A faint light from no particular source mitigated the shadows of the halls. They trod noiselessly upon a stair carpet that its own loom would have forsworn. It seemed to have become vegetable; to have degenerated in that rank, sunless air to lush lichen or spreading moss that grew in patches to the staircase and was viscid under the foot like organic matter. At each turn of the stairs were vacant niches in the wall. Perhaps plants had once been set within them. If so they had died in that foul and tainted air. It may be that statues of the saints had stood there, but it was not difficult to conceive that imps and devils had dragged them forth in the darkness and down to the unholy depths of some furnished pit below.

"This is the room," said the housekeeper, from her furry throat. "It's a nice room. It ain't often vacant. I had some most elegant people in it last summer—no trouble at all, and paid in advance to the minute. The water's at the end of the hall. Sprowls and Mooney kept it three months. They done a vaudeville sketch. Miss B'retta Sprowls—you may have heard of her—oh, that was just the stage names—right there over the dresser is where the marriage certificate hung, framed. The gas is here, and you see there is plenty of closet room. It's a room everybody likes. It never stays idle long."

"Do you have many theatrical people rooming here?" asked the young man.

"They comes and goes. A good proportion of my lodgers is connected with the theaters. Yes, sir, this is the theatrical district. Actor people never stays long anywhere. I get my share. Yes, they comes and they goes."

He engaged the room, paying for a week in advance. He was tired, he said, and would take possession at once. He counted out the money. The room had been made ready, she said, even to towels and water. As the housekeeper moved away he put, for the thousandth time, the question that he carried at the end of his tongue.

"A young girl—Miss Vashner—Miss Eloise Vashner—do you remember such a one among your lodgers? She would be singing on the stage, most likely. A fair girl, of medium height and slender, with reddish, gold hair and dark mole near her left eyebrow."

"No, I don't remember the name. Them stage people has names they change as often as their rooms. They comes and they goes. No, I don't call that one to mind."

No. Always no. Five months of ceaseless interrogation and the inevitable negative. So much time spent by days in questioning managers, agents, schools and choruses; by night among the audiences of theaters from all-star casts down to music halls so low that he dreaded to find what he most hoped for. He who had loved her best had tried to find her. He was sure that since her disappearance from home this great, water-girt city held her somewhere, but it was like a monstrous quicksand, shifting its particles constantly, with no foundation, its upper granules of today buried tomorrow in ooze and slime.

The furnished room received its latest guest with a first glow of pseudo-hospitality, a hectic, haggard, perfunctory welcome like the specious smile of a demirep. The sophistical comfort came in reflected gleams from the decayed furniture, the ragged brocade upholstery of a couch and two chairs, a foot-wide cheap pier glass between the two windows, from one or two gilt picture frames and a brass bedstead in a corner.

The guest reclined, inert, upon a chair, while the room, confused in speech as though it were an apartment in Babel, tried to discourse to him of its divers tenantry.

A polychromatic rug like some brilliant-flowered rectangular, tropical islet lay surrounded by a billowy sea of soiled matting. Upon the gay-papered wall were those pictures that pursue the homeless one from house to house—The Huguenot Lovers, The First Quarrel, The Wedding Breakfast, Psyche at the Fountain. The mantel's chastely severe outline was ingloriously veiled behind some pert drapery drawn rakishly askew like the sashes of the Amazonian ballet. Upon it was some desolate flotsam cast aside by the room's marooned when a lucky sail had borne them to a fresh port—a trifling vase or two, pictures of actresses, a medicine bottle, some stray cards out of a deck.

One by one, as the characters of a cryptograph became explicit, the little signs left by the furnished room's procession of guests developed a significance. The threadbare space in the rug in front of the dresser told that lovely woman had marched in the throng. The tiny fingerprints on the wall spoke of little prisoners trying to feel their way to sun and air. A splattered stain, raying like the shadow of a bursting bomb, witnessed where a hurled glass or bottle had splintered with its contents against the wall. Across the pier glass had been scrawled with a diamond in staggering letters the name "Marie." It seemed that the succession of dwellers in the furnished room had turned in fury—perhaps tempted beyond forebearance by its garish coldness—and wreaked upon it their passions. The furniture was chipped and bruised; the couch, distorted by bursting springs, seemed a horrible monster that had been slain during the strcss of some grotesque convulsion. Some more potent upheaval had cloven a great slice from the marble mantel. Each plank in the floor owned its particular cant and shriek as from a separate and individual agony. It seemed incredible that all this malice and injury had been wrought upon the room by those who had called it for a time their home; and yet it may have been the cheated home instinct surviving blindly, the resentful rage at false household gods that had kindled their wrath. A hut that is our own we can sweep and adorn and cherish.

The young tenant in the chair allowed these thoughts to file, soft-shod, through his mind, while there drifted into the room furnished sounds and furnished scents. He heard in one room a tittering and incontinent, slack laughter; in others the monologue of a scold, the rattling of dice, a lullaby, and one crying dully; above him a banjo tinkled with spirit. Doors banged somewhere; the elevated trains roared intermittently; a cat yowled miserably upon a back fence. And he breathed the breath of the house—a dank savor rather than a smell—a cold, musty effluviam as from underground vaults mingled with the reeking exhalations of linoleum and mildewed and rotten woodwork.

Then suddenly, as he rested there, the room was filled with the strong, sweet odor of mignonette. It came as upon a single buffet of wind with such sureness and fragrance and emphasis that it almost seemed a living visitant. And the man cried aloud: "What, dear?" as if he had been called, and sprang up and faced about. The rich odor clung to him and wrapped him around.

He reached out his arms for it, all his senses for the time confused and commingled. How could one be peremptorily called by an odor? Surely it must have been a sound. But, was it not the sound that had touched, that had caressed him?

"She has been in this room," he cried, and he sprang to wrest from it a token, for he knew he would recognize the smallest thing that had belonged to her or that she had touched. This enveloping scent of mignonette, the odor that she had loved and made her own—whence came it?

The room had been but carelessly set in order. Scattered upon the flimsy dresser scarf were half a dozen hairpins—those discreet, indistinguishable friends of womankind, feminine of gender, infinite mood and uncommunicative of tense. These he ignored, conscious of their triumphant lack of identity. Ransacking the drawers of the dresser he came upon a discarded, tiny, ragged handkerchief. He pressed it to his face. It was racy and insolent with heliotrope; he hurled it to the floor. In another drawer he found odd buttons, a theater program, a pawnbroker's card, two lost marshmallows, a book on the divination of dreams. In the last was a woman's black satin hair bow, which halted him, poised between ice and fire. But the black satin hair bow also is femininity's demure, impersonal common ornament and tells no tales.

And then he traversed the room like a hound on the scent, skimming the walls, considering the corners of the bulging matting on his hands and knees, rummaging mantel and tables, the curtains and hangings, the drunken cabinet in the corner, for a visible sign, unable to perceive that she was there beside, around, against, within, above him, clinging to him, wooing him, calling him so poignantly through the finer senses that even his grosser ones became cognizant of the call. Once again he answered loudly: "Yes, dear!" and turned, wild-eyed, to gaze on vacancy, for he could not yet discern form and color and love and outstretched arms in the odor of mignonette. Oh, God! whence that odor, and since when have odors had a voice to call? Thus he groped.

He burrowed in crevices and corners, and found corks and cigarettes. These he passed in passive contempt. But once he found in a fold of the matting a half-smoked cigar, and this he ground beneath his heel with a green and trenchant oath. He sifted the room from end to end. He found dreary and ignoble small records of many a peripatetic tenant; but of her whom he sought, and who may have lodged there, and whose spirit seemed to hover there, he found no trace.

And then he thought of the housekeeper.

He ran from the haunted room downstairs and to a door that showed a crack of light. She came out to his knock. He smothered his excitement as best he could.

"Will you tell me, madam," he besought her, "who occupied the room I have before I came ?"

"Yes, sir. I can tell you again. 'Twas Sprowls and Mooney, as I said Miss B'retta Sprowls it was in the theaters, but Missis Mooney she was. My house is well known for respectability. The marriage certificate hung, framed, on a nail over–"

"What kind of a lady was Miss Sprowls–in looks, I mean?"

"Why, black-haired, sir, short, and stout, with a comical face. They left a week ago Tuesday."

"And before they occupied it?"

"Why, there was a single gentleman connected with the draying business. He left owing me a week. Before him was Missis Crowder and her two children, that stayed four months; and back of them was old Mr. Doyle, whose sons paid for him. He kept the room six months. That goes back a year, sir, and further I do not remember."

He thanked her and crept back to his room. The room was dead. The essence that had vivified it was gone. The perfume of mignonette had departed. In its place was the old, stale odor of moldy house furniture, of atmosphere in storage.

The ebbing of his hope drained his faith. He sat staring at the yellow, singing gaslight. Soon he walked to the bed and began to tear the sheets into strips. With the blade of his knife he drove them tightly into every crevice around windows and door. When all was snug and taut he turned out the light, turned the gas full on again and laid himself gratefully upon the bed.

It was Mrs. McCool's night to go with the can for beer. So she fetched it and sat with Mrs. Purdy in one of those subterranean retreats where housekeepers foregather and the worm dieth seldom.

"I rented out my third-floor-back this evening," said Mrs. Purdy, across a fine circle of foam. "A young man took it. He went up to bed two hours ago."

"Now, did ye, Mrs. Purdy, ma'am?" said Mrs. McCool, with intense admiration. "You do be a wonder for rentin' rooms of that kind. And did ye tell him, then?" she concluded in a husky whisper laden with mystery.

"Rooms," said Mrs. Purdy, in her furriest tones, "are furnished for to rent. I did not tell him, Mrs. McCool."

"'Tis right ye are, ma'am; 'tis by renting rooms we kape alive. Ye have the rale sense for business, ma'am. There be many people will rayjict the rentin' of a room if they be tould a suicide has been after dyin' in the bed of it."

"As you say, we has our living to be making," remarked Mrs. Purdy.

"Yis, ma'am; 'tis true. 'Tis just one wake ago this day I helped ye lay out the third-floor-back. A pretty slip of a colleen she was to be killin' herself wid the gas—a swate little face she had, Mrs. Purdy ma'am."

"She'd a-been called handsome, as you say," said Mrs. Purdy, assenting but critical, "but for that mole she had a-growin' by her left eyebrow. Do fill up your glass again, Mrs. McCool."

FRANK NORRIS

[1870–1902]

A Deal in Wheat

(1903)

I. THE BEAR—WHEAT AT SIXTY-TWO

As Sam Lewiston backed the horse into the shafts of his buckboard and began hitching the tugs to the whiffletree, his wife came out from the kitchen door of the house and drew near, and stood for some time at the horse's head, her arms folded and her apron rolled around them. For a long moment neither spoke. They had talked over the situation so long and so comprehensively the night before that there seemed to be nothing more to say.

The time was late in the summer, the place a ranch in South-Western Kansas, and Lewiston and his wife were two of a vast population of farmers, wheat growers, who at that moment were passing through a crisis—a crisis that at any moment might culminate in tragedy. Wheat was down to sixty-six.

At length Emma Lewiston spoke.

"Well," she hazarded, looking vaguely out across the ranch toward the horizon, leagues distant; "well, Sam, there's always that offer of brother Joe's. We can quit—and go to Chicago—if the worst comes."

"And give up!" exclaimed Lewiston, running the lines through the torets. "Leave the ranch! Give up! After all these years!"

His wife made no reply for the moment. Lewiston climbed into the buckboard and gathered up the lines. "Well, here goes for the last try, Emmie," he said. "Good-by, girl. Maybe things will look better in town today."

"Maybe," she said gravely. She kissed her husband good-by and stood for some time looking after the buckboard traveling toward the town in a moving pillar of dust.

"I don't know," she murmured at length; "I don't know just how we're going to make out."

When he reached town, Lewiston tied the horse to the iron railing in front of the Odd-Fellows Hall, the ground floor of which was occupied by the post-office, and went across the street and up the stairway of a building of brick and granite—quite the most pretentious structure of the town—and knocked at a door upon the first landing. The door was furnished with a pane of frosted glass, on which, in gold letters, was inscribed, "Bridges & Co., Grain Dealers."

Bridges himself, a middle-aged man who wore a velvet skull-cap and who was smoking a Pittsburgh stogy, met the farmer at the counter and the two exchanged perfunctory greetings.

"Well," said Lewiston, tentatively, after a while.

"Well, Lewiston," said the other, "I can't take that wheat of yours at any better than sixty-two."

"Sixty-*two*!"

"It's the Chicago price that does it, Lewiston. Truslow is bearing the stuff for all he's worth. It's Truslow and the bear clique that stick the knife into us. The price broke again this morning. We've just got a wire."

"Good heavens," murmured Lewiston, looking vaguely from side to side. "That—that ruins me. I *can't* carry my grain any longer—what with storage charges and—and—Bridges, I don't see just how I'm going to make out. Sixty-two cents a bushel! Why, man, what with this and with that it's cost me nearly a dollar a bushel to raise that wheat, and now Truslow—"

He turned away abruptly with a quick gesture of infinite discouragement.

He went down the stairs, and making his way to where his buckboard was hitched, got in, and, with eyes vacant, the reins slipping and sliding in his limp, half-open hands, drove slowly back to the ranch. His wife had seen him coming, and met him as he drew up before the barn.

"Well?" she demanded.

"Emmie," he said as he got out of the buckboard, laying his arm across her shoulder, "Emmie, I guess we'll take up with Joe's offer. We'll go to Chicago. We're cleaned out!"

II. THE BULL—WHEAT AT A DOLLAR-TEN

. . . .—and said Party of the Second Part further covenants and agrees, to merchandise such wheat in foreign ports, it being understood and agreed between the Party of the First Part and the Party of the Second Part that the wheat hereinbefore mentioned is released and sold to the Party of the Second Part for export purposes only, and not for consumption or distribution within the boundaries of the United States of America or of Canada.

"Now, Mr. Gates, if you will sign for Mr. Truslow I guess that'll be all," remarked Hornung when he had finished reading.

Hornung affixed his signature to the two documents and passed them over to Gates, who signed for his principal and client, Truslow—or, as he has been called ever since he had gone into the fight against Hornung's corner—the Great Bear. Hornung's secretary was called in and witnessed the signatures, and Gates thrust the contract into his Gladstone bag and stood up, smoothing his hat.

"You will deliver the warehouse receipts for the grain," began Gates.

"I'll send a messenger to Truslow's office before noon," interrupted Hornung. "You can pay by certified check through the Illinois Trust people."

When the other had taken himself off, Hornung sat for some moments gazing abstractedly toward his office windows, thinking over the whole matter. He had just agreed to release to Truslow, at the rate of one dollar and ten cents per bushel, one hundred thousand out of the two million and odd bushels of wheat that he, Hornung, controlled, or actually owned. And for the moment he was wondering if, after all, he had done wisely in not goring the Great Bear to actual financial death. He had made him pay one hundred thousand dollars. Truslow was good for this amount. Would it not have been better to have put a prohibitive figure on the grain and forced the bear into bankruptcy? True, Hornung would then be without his enemy's money, but Truslow would have been eliminated from the situation, and that—so Hornung told himself—was always a consummation most devoutly, strenuously, and diligently to be striven for. Truslow once dead was dead, but the Bear was never more dangerous than when desperate.

"But so long as he can't get *wheat*," muttered Hornung at the end of his reflections, "he can't hurt me. And he can't get it. That I *know*."

For Hornung controlled the situation. So far back as the February of that year an "unknown bull" had been making his presence felt on the floor of the Board of Trade. By the middle of March the commercial reports of the daily press had begun to speak of "the powerful bull clique"; a few weeks later that legendary condition of affairs implied and epitomized in the magic words "Dollar Wheat" had been attained, and by the first of April, when the price had been boosted to one dollar and ten cents a bushel, Hornung had disclosed his hand, and in place of mere rumors, the definite and authoritative news that May wheat had been cornered in the Chicago pit went flashing around the world from Liverpool to Odessa and from Duluth to Buenos Aires.

It was—so the veteran operators were persuaded—Truslow himself who had made Hornung's corner possible. The Great Bear had for once overreached himself, and, believing himself all-powerful, had hammered the price just the fatal fraction too far down. Wheat had gone to sixty-two—for the time, and under the circumstances, an abnormal price. When the reaction came it was tremendous. Hornung saw his chance, seized it, and in a few months had turned the tables, had cornered the product, and virtually driven the bear clique out of the pit.

On the same day that the delivery of the hundred thousand bushels was made to Truslow, Hornung met his broker at his lunch club.

"Well," said the latter, "I see you let go that line of stuff to Truslow."

Hornung nodded; but the broker added:

"Remember, I was against it from the very beginning. I know we've cleared up over a hundred thou'. I would have fifty times preferred to have lost twice that and *smashed Truslow dead*. Bet you what you like he makes us pay for it somehow."

"Huh!" grunted his principal. "How about insurance, and warehouse charges, and carrying expenses on that lot? Guess we'd have had to pay those, too, if we'd held on."

But the other put up his chin, unwilling to be persuaded. "I won't sleep easy," he declared, "till Truslow is busted."

III. THE PIT

Just as Going mounted the steps on the edge of the pit the great gong struck, a roar of a hundred voices developed with the swiftness of successive explosions, the rush of a hundred men surging downward to the center of the pit filled the air with the stamp and grind of feet, a hundred hands in eager, strenuous gestures tossed upward from out the brown of the crowd, the official reporter in his cage on the margin of the pit leaned far forward with straining ear to catch the opening bid, and another day of battle was begun.

Since the sale of the hundred thousand bushels of wheat to Truslow, the "Hornung crowd" had steadily shouldered the price higher until on this particular morning it stood at one dollar and a half. That was Hornung's price. No one else had any grain to sell.

But not ten minutes after the opening, Going was surprised out of all countenance to hear shouted from the other side of the pit these words:

"Sell May at one-fifty."

Going was for the moment touching elbows with Kimbark on one side and with Merriam on the other, all three belonging to the "Hornung crowd." Their answering challenge of "Sold" was as the voice of one man. They did not pause to reflect upon the strangeness of the circumstance. (That was for afterward.) Their response to the offer was as unconscious as reflex action and almost as rapid, and before the pit was well aware of what had happened the transaction of one thousand bushels was down upon Going's trading-card and fifteen hundred dollars had changed hands. But here was a marvel—the whole available supply of wheat cornered, Hornung master of the situation, invincible, unassailable; yet behold a man willing to sell, a bear bold enough to raise his head.

"That was Kennedy, wasn't it, who made that offer?" asked Kimbark, as Going noted down the trade—"Kennedy, that new man?"

"Yes; who do you suppose he's selling for; who's willing to go short at this stage of the game?"

"Maybe he ain't short."

"Short! Great heavens, man, where'd he get the stuff?"

"Blamed if I know. We can account for every handful of May. Steady! Oh, there he goes again.

"Sell a thousand May at one-fifty," vociferated the bear-broker, throwing out his hand, one finger raised to indicate the number of "contracts" offered. This time it was evident that he was attacking the Hornung crowd deliberately, for, ignoring the jam of traders that swept toward him, he looked across the pit to where Going and Kimbark were shouting "*Sold! Sold!*" and nodded his head.

A second time Going made memoranda of the trade, and either the Hornung holdings were increased by two thousands bushels of May wheat or the Hornung bank account swelled by at least three thousand dollars of some unknown short's money.

Of late—so sure was the bull crowd of its position—no one had even thought of glancing at the inspection sheet on the bulletin board. But now one of Going's messengers hurried up to him with the announcement that this sheet showed receipts at Chicago for that morning of twenty-five thousand bushels, and not credited to Hornung. Someone had got hold of a line of wheat overlooked by the "clique" and was dumping it upon them.

Wire the Chief, said Going over his shoulder to Merriam. This one struggled out of the crowd, and on a telegraph blank scribbled:

"Strong bear movement—New man—Kennedy—Selling in lots of five contracts—Chicago receipts twenty-five thousand."

The message was despatched, and in a few moments the answer came back, laconic, of military terseness:

"Support the market."

And Going obeyed, Merriam and Kimbark following, the new broker fairly throwing the wheat at them in thousand-bushel lots.

"Sell May at 'fifty; sell May; sell May." A moment's indecision, an instant's hesitation, the first faint suggestion of weakness, and the market would have broken under them. But for the better part of four hours they stood their ground, taking all that was offered, in constant communication with the Chief, and from time to time stimulated and steadied by his brief, unvarying command:

"Support the market."

At the close of the session they had brought in the twenty-five thousand bushels of May. Hornung's position was as stable as a rock, and the price closed even with the opening figure—one dollar and a half.

But the morning's work was the talk of all La Salle Street. Who was back of the raid? What was the meaning of this unexpected selling? For weeks the pit trading had been merely nominal. Truslow, the Great Bear, from whom the most serious attack might have been expected, had gone to his country seat at Geneva Lake, in Wisconsin, declaring himself to be out of the market entirely. He went bass-fishing every day.

IV. THE BELT LINE

On a certain day toward the middle of the month, at a time when the mysterious Bear had unloaded some eighty thousand bushels upon Hornung, a conference was held in the library of Hornung's home. His broker attended it, and also a clean-faced, bright-eyed individual whose name of Cyrus Ryder might have been found upon the pay-roll of a rather well-known detective agency. For upward of half an hour after the conference began the detective spoke, the other two listening attentively, gravely.

"Then, last of all," concluded Ryder, "I made out I was a hobo, and began stealing rides on the Belt Line Railroad. Know that road? It just circles Chicago. Truslow owns it. Yes? Well, then I began to catch on. I noticed that cars of certain numbers–thirty-one nought thirty-four, thirty-two one ninety–well, the numbers don't matter, but anyhow, these cars were always switched onto the sidings by Mr. Truslow's main elevator D soon as they came in. The wheat was shunted in, and they were pulled out again. Well, I spotted one car and stole a ride on her. Say, look here, *that car went right around the city on the Belt, and came back to D again, and the same wheat in her all the time.* The grain was re-inspected–it was raw, I tell you–and the warehouse receipts made out just as though the stuff had come in from Kansas or Iowa.

"The same wheat all the time!" interrupted Hornung.

"The same wheat–your wheat, that you sold to Truslow."

"Great snakes!" ejaculated Hornung's broker. "Truslow never took it abroad at all."

"Took it abroad! Say, he's just been running it around Chicago, like the supers in 'Shenandoah,' round an' round, so you'd think it was a new lot, an' selling it back to you again."

"No wonder we couldn't account for so much wheat."

"Bought it from us at one-ten, and made us buy it back–our own wheat–at one-fifty."

Hornung and his broker looked at each other in silence for a moment. Then all at once Hornung struck the arm of his chair with his fist and exploded in a roar of laughter. The broker stared for one bewildered moment, then followed his example.

"Sold! Sold!" shouted Hornung almost gleefully. "Upon my soul it's as good as a Gilbert and Sullivan show. And we– Oh, Lord! Billy, shake on it, and hats off to my distinguished friend, Truslow. He'll be President some day. Hey! What? Prosecute him? Not I."

"He's done us out of a neat hatful of dollars for all that," observed the broker, suddenly grave.

"Billy, it's worth the price."

"Well, tell you what. We were going to boost the price to one seventy-five next week, and make that our settlement figure."

"Can't do it now. Can't afford it."

"No. Here; we'll let out a big link; we'll put wheat at two dollars, and let it go at that."

"Two it is, then," said the broker.

V. THE BREAD LINE

The street was very dark and absolutely deserted. It was a district on the "South Side," not far from the Chicago River, given up largely to wholesale stores, and after nightfall was empty of all life. The echoes slept but lightly hereabouts, and the slightest footfall, the faintest noise, woke them upon the instant and sent them clamoring up and down the length of the pavement between the iron-shuttered fronts. The only light visible came from the side door of a certain "Vienna" bakery, where at one o'clock in the morning loaves of bread were given away to any who should ask. Every evening about nine o'clock the outcasts began to gather about the side door. The stragglers came in rapidly, and the line–the "bread line," as it was called–began to form. By midnight it was usually some hundred yards in length, stretching almost the entire length of the block.

Toward ten in the evening, his collar turned up against the fine drizzle that pervaded the air, his hands in his pockets, his elbows gripping his sides, Sam Lewiston came up and silently took his place at the end of the line.

Unable to conduct his farm upon a paying basis at the time when Truslow, the "Great Bear," had sent the price of grain down to sixty-two cents a bushel, Lewiston had turned over the entire property to his creditors, and, leaving Kansas for good, had abandoned farming, and had left his wife at her sister's boarding house in Topeka with the understanding that she was to join him in Chicago as soon as he had found a steady job. Then he had come to Chicago and had turned workman. His brother Joe conducted a small hat factory on Archer Avenue, and for a time he found there a meager employment. But difficulties had occurred, times were bad, the hat factory was involved in debts, the repealing of a certain import duty on manufactured felt overcrowded the home market with cheap Belgian and French products, and in the end his brother had assigned and gone to Milwaukee.

Thrown out of work, Lewiston drifted aimlessly about Chicago, from pillar to post, working a little, earning here a dollar, there a dime, but always sinking, sinking, till at last the ooze of the lowest bottom dragged at his feet and the rush of the great ebb went over him and engulfed him and shut him out from the light, and a park bench became his home and the "bread line" his chief makeshift of subsistence.

He stood now in the enfolding drizzle, sodden, stupefied with fatigue. Before and behind stretched the line. There was no talking. There was no sound. The street was empty. It was so still that the passing of a cable car in the adjoining thoroughfare grated like prolonged rolling explosions, beginning and ending at immeasurable distances. The drizzle descended incessantly. After a long time midnight struck.

There was something ominous and gravely impressive in this interminable line of dark figures, close-pressed, soundless; a crowd, yet absolutely still; a close-packed, silent file, waiting, waiting in the vast deserted night-ridden street; waiting without a word, without a movement, there under the night and under the slow-moving mists of rain.

Few in the crowd were professional beggars. Most of them were workmen, long since out of work, forced into idleness by long-continued "hard times," by ill luck, by sickness. To them the "bread line" was a godsend. At least they could not starve. Between jobs here in the end was something to hold them up–a small platform, as it were, above the sweep of black water, where for a moment they might pause and take breath before the plunge.

The period of waiting on this night of rain seemed endless to those silent, hungry men; but at length there was a stir. The line moved. The side door opened. Ah, at last! They were going to hand out the bread.

But instead of the usual white aproned undercook with his crowded hampers there now appeared in the doorway a new man–a young fellow who looked like a bookkeeper's assistant. He bore in his hand a placard, which he tacked to the outside of the door. Then he disappeared within the bakery, locking the door after him.

A shudder of poignant despair, an unformed, inarticulate sense of calamity, seemed to run from end to end of the line. What had happened? Those in the rear, unable to read the placard, surged forward, a sense of bitter disappointment clutching at their hearts.

The line broke up, disintegrated into a shapeless throng–a throng that crowded forward and collected in front of the shut door whereon the placard was affixed. Lewiston, with the others, pushed forward. On the placard he read these words:

"Owing to the fact that the price of grain has been increased to two dollars a bushel, there will be no distribution of bread from this bakery until further notice."

Lewiston turned away, dumb, bewildered. Till morning he walked the streets, going on without purpose, without direction. But now at last his luck had turned. Overnight the wheel of his fortunes had creaked and swung upon its axis, and before noon he had found a job in the street-cleaning brigade. In the course of time he rose to be first shift boss, then deputy inspector, then inspector, promoted to the dignity of driving in a red wagon with rubber tires and drawing a salary instead of mere wages. The wife was sent for and a new start made.

But Lewiston never forgot. Dimly he began to see the significance of things. Caught once in the cogs and wheels of a great and terrible engine, he had seen—none better—its workings. Of all the men who had vainly stood in the "bread line" on that rainy night in early summer, he, perhaps, had been the only one who had struggled up to the surface again. How many others had gone down in the great ebb? Grim question; he dared not think how many.

He had seen the two ends of a great wheat operation—a battle between Bear and Bull. The stories (subsequently published in the city's press) of Truslow's countermove in selling Hornung his own wheat, supplied the unseen section. The farmer—he who raised the wheat—was ruined upon one hand; the working man—he who consumed it—was ruined upon the other. But between the two, the great operators, who never saw the wheat they traded in, bought and sold the world's food, gambled in the nourishment of entire nations, practiced their tricks, their chicanery and oblique shifty "deals," were reconciled in their differences, and went on through their appointed way, jovial, contented, enthroned and unassailable.

STEPHEN CRANE

[1871–1900]

The Open Boat

A TALE INTENDED TO BE AFTER THE FACT. BEING THE EXPERIENCE OF FOUR MEN FROM THE SUNK STEAMER "COMMODORE"

(First published in *Scribner's Magazine*, June, 1897; first book publication in 1898.)

NONE OF THEM knew the color of the sky. Their eyes glanced level, and were fastened upon the waves that swept toward them. These waves were of the hue of slate, save for the tops, which were of foaming white, and all of the men knew the colors of the sea. The horizon narrowed and widened, and dipped and rose, and at all times its edge was jagged with waves that seemed thrust up in points like rocks. Many a man ought to have a bath-tub larger than the boat which here rode upon the sea. These waves were most wrongfully and barbarously abrupt and tall, and each froth top was a problem in small boat navigation.

The cook squatted in the bottom and looked with both eyes at the six inches of gunwale which separated him from the ocean. His sleeves were rolled over his fat forearms, and two flaps of his unbuttoned vest dangled as he bent to bail out the boat. Often he said: "Gawd! That was a narrow clip." As he remarked it he invariably gazed eastward over the broken sea.

The oiler, steering with one of the two oars in the boat, sometimes raised himself suddenly to keep clear of water that swirled in over the stern. It was a thin little oar and it seemed often ready to snap.

The correspondent, pulling at the other oar, watched the waves and wondered why he was there.

The injured captain, lying in the bow, was at this time buried in that profound dejection and indifference which comes, temporarily at least, to even the bravest and most enduring when, willy-nilly, the firm fails, the army loses, the ship goes down. The mind of the master of a vessel is rooted deep in the timbers of her, though he commanded for a day or a decade, and this captain had on him the stern impression of a scene in the grays of dawn of seven turned faces, and later a stump of a top mast with a white ball on it that slashed to and fro at the waves, went low and lower, and down. Thereafter there was something strange in his voice. Although steady, it was deep with mourning, and of a quality beyond oration or tears.

"Keep 'er a little more south, Billie," said he.

"'A little more south,' sir," said the oiler in the stern.

A seat in this boat was not unlike a seat upon a bucking broncho, and by the same token, a broncho is not much smaller. The craft pranced and reared, and plunged like an animal. As each wave came, and she rose for it, she seemed like a horse making at a fence outrageously high. The manner of her scramble over these walls of water is a mystic thing, and, moreover, at the top of them were ordinarily these problems in white water, the foam racing down from the summit of each wave, requiring a new leap, and a leap from the air. Then, after scornfully bumping a crest, she would slide, and race, and splash down a long incline, and arrive bobbing and nodding in front of the next menace.

A singular disadvantage of the sea lies in the fact that after successfully surmounting one wave you discover that there is another behind it just as important and just as nervously anxious to do something effective in the way of swamping boats. In a ten-foot dingey one can get an idea of the resources of the sea in the line of waves that is not probable to the average experience which is never at sea in a dingey. As each slatey wall of water approached, it shut all else from the view of the men in the boat, and it was not difficult to imagine that this particular wave was the final outburst of the ocean, the last effort of the grim water. There was a terrible grace in the move of the waves, and they came in silence, save for the snarling of the crests.

In the wan light, the faces of the men must have been gray. Their eyes must have glinted in strange ways as they gazed steadily astern. Viewed from a balcony, the whole thing would doubtless have been weirdly picturesque. But the men in the boat had no time to see it, and if they had had leisure there were other things to occupy their minds. The sun swung steadily up the sky, and they knew it was broad day because the color of the sea changed from slate to emerald green, streaked with amber lights, and the foam was like tumbling snow. The process of the breaking day was unknown to them. They were aware only of this effect upon the color of the waves that rolled toward them.

In disjointed sentences the cook and the correspondent argued as to the difference between a life-saving station and a house of refuge. The cook had said: "There's a house of refuge just north of the Mosquito Inlet Light, and as soon as they see us, they'll come off in their boat and pick us up."

"As soon as who see us?" said the correspondent.

"The crew," said the cook.

"Houses of refuge don't have crews," said the correspondent. "As I understand them, they are only places where clothes and grub are stored for the benefit of shipwrecked people. They don't carry crews."

"Oh, yes, they do," said the cook.

"No, they don't," said the correspondent.

"Well, we're not there yet, anyhow," said the oiler, in the stern.

"Well," said the cook, "perhaps it's not a house of refuge that I'm thinking of as being near Mosquito Inlet Light. Perhaps it's a life-saving station."

"We're not there yet," said the oiler, in the stern.

II

As the boat bounced from the top of each wave, the wind tore through the hair of the hatless men, and as the craft plopped her stern down again the spray splashed past them. The crest of each of these waves was a hill, from the top of which the men surveyed, for a moment, a broad tumultuous expanse, shining and wind-riven. It was probably splendid. It was probably glorious, this play of the free sea, wild with lights of emerald and white and amber.

"Bully good thing it's an on-shore wind," said the cook. "If not, where would we be? Wouldn't have a show."

"That's right," said the correspondent.

The busy oiler nodded his assent.

Then the captain, in the bow, chuckled in a way that expressed humor, contempt, tragedy, all in one. "Do you think we've got much of a show now, boys?" said he.

Whereupon the three were silent, save for a trifle of hemming and hawing. To express any particular optimism at this time they felt to be childish and stupid, but they all doubtless possessed this sense of the situation in their mind. A young man thinks doggedly at such times. On the other hand, the ethics of their condition was decidedly against any open suggestion of hopelessness. So they were silent.

"Oh, well," said the captain, soothing his children, "We'll get ashore all right."

But there was that in his tone which made them think, so the oiler quoth: "Yes! If this wind holds!"

The cook was bailing: "Yes! If we don't catch hell in the surf."

Canton flannel gulls flew near and far. Sometimes they sat down on the sea, near patches of brown seaweed that rolled on the waves with a movement like carpets on a line in a gale. The birds sat comfortably in groups, and they were envied by some in the dingey, for the wrath of the sea was no more to them than it was to a covey of prairie chickens a thousand miles inland. Often they came very close and stared at the men with black bead-like eyes. At these times they were uncanny and sinister in their unblinking scrutiny, and the men hooted angrily at them, telling them to be gone. One came, and evidently decided to alight on the top of the captain's head. The bird flew parallel to the boat and did not circle, but made short sidelong jumps in the air in chicken fashion. His black eyes were wistfully fixed upon the captain's head. "Ugly brute," said the oiler to the bird. "You look as if you were made with a jack-knife." The cook and the correspondent swore darkly at the creature. The captain naturally wished to knock it away with the end of the heavy painter; but he did not dare do it, because anything resembling an emphatic gesture would have capsized this freighted boat, and so with his open hand, the captain gently and carefully waved the gull away. After it had been discouraged from the pursuit the captain breathed easier on account of his hair, and others breathed easier because the bird struck their minds at this time as being somehow gruesome and ominous.

In the meantime the oiler and the correspondent rowed. And also they rowed.

They sat together in the same seat, and each rowed an oar. Then the oiler took both oars; then the correspondent took both oars; then the oiler; then the correspondent. They rowed and they rowed. The very ticklish part of the business was when the time came for the reclining one in the stern to take his turn at the oars. By the very last star of truth, it is easier to steal eggs from under a hen than it was to change seats in the dingey. First the man in the stern slid his hand along the thwart and moved with care, as if he were of Sèvres. Then the man in the rowing seat slid his hand along the other thwart. It was all done with the most extraordinary care. As the two sidled past each other, the whole party kept watchful eyes on the coming wave, and the captain cried: "Look out now! Steady there!"

The brown mats of seaweed that appeared from time to time were like islands, bits of earth. They were traveling, apparently, neither one way nor the other. They were, to all intents, stationary. They informed the men in the boat that it was making progress slowly toward the land.

The captain, rearing cautiously in the bow, after the dingey soared on a great swell, said that he had seen the lighthouse at Mosquito Inlet. Presently the cook remarked that he had seen it. The correspondent was at the oars then, and for some reason he too wished to look at the lighthouse, but his back was toward the far shore and the waves were important, and for some time he could not seize an opportunity to turn his head. But at last there came a wave more gentle than the others, and when at the crest of it he swiftly scoured the western horizon.

"See it?" said the captain.

"No," said the correspondent slowly, "I didn't see anything."

"Look again," said the captain. He pointed. "It's exactly in that direction."

At the top of another wave, the correspondent did as he was bid, and this time his eyes chanced on a small still thing on the edge of the swaying horizon. It was precisely like the point of a pin. It took an anxious eye to find a lighthouse so tiny.

"Think we'll make it, captain?"

"If this wind holds and the boat don't swamp, we can't do much else," said the captain.

The little boat, lifted by each towering sea, and splashed viciously by the crests, made progress that in the absence of seaweed was not apparent to those in her. She seemed just a wee thing wallowing, miraculously top up, at the mercy of five oceans. Occasionally, a great spread of water, like white flames, swarmed into her.

"Bail her, cook," said the captain serenely.

"All right, captain," said the cheerful cook.

III

It would be difficult to describe the subtle brotherhood of men that was here established on the seas. No one said that it was so. No one mentioned it. But it dwelt in the boat, and each man felt it warm him. They were a captain, an oiler, a cook and a correspondent, and they were friends, friends in a more curiously iron-bound degree than may be common. The hurt captain, lying against the water jar in the bow, spoke always in a low voice and calmly, but he could never command a more ready and swiftly obedient crew than the motley three of the dingey. It was more than a mere recognition of what was best for the common safety. There was surely in it a quality that was personal and heartfelt. And after this devotion to the commander of the boat there was this comradeship that the correspondent, for instance, who had been taught to be cynical of men, knew even at the time was the best experience of his life. But no one said that it was so. No one mentioned it.

"I wish we had a sail," remarked the captain. "We might try my overcoat on the end of an oar and give you two boys a chance to rest." So the cook and the correspondent held the mast and spread wide the overcoat. The oiler steered, and the little boat made good way with her new rig. Sometimes the oiler had to scull sharply to keep a sea from breaking into the boat, but otherwise sailing was a success.

Meanwhile the lighthouse had been growing slowly larger. It had now almost assumed color, and appeared like a little gray shadow on the sky. The man at the oars could not be prevented from turning his head rather often to try for a glimpse of this little gray shadow.

At last, from the top of each wave the men in the tossing boat could see land. Even as the lighthouse was an upright shadow on the sky, this land seemed but a long black shadow on the sea. It certainly was thinner than paper. "We must be about opposite New Smyrna," said the cook, who had coasted this shore often in schooners. "Captain, by the way, I believe they abandoned that life-saving station there about a year ago."

"Did they?" said the captain.

The wind slowly died away. The cook and the correspondent were not now obliged to slave in order to hold high the oar. But the waves continued their old impetuous swooping at the dingey, and the little craft, no longer under way, struggled woundily over them. The oiler or the correspondent took the oars again.

Shipwrecks are *à propos* of nothing. If men could only train for them and have them occur when the men had reached pink condition, there would be less drowning at sea. Of the four in the dingey none had slept any time worth mentioning for two days and two nights previous to embarking in the dingey, and in the excitement of clambering about the deck of a foundering ship they had also forgotten to eat heartily.

For these reasons, and for others, neither the oiler nor the correspondent was fond of rowing at this time. The correspondent wondered ingenuously how in the name of all that was sane could there be people who thought it amusing to row a boat. It was not an amusement; it was a diabolical punishment, and even a genius of mental aberrations could never conclude that it was anything but a horror to the muscles and a crime against the back. He mentioned to the boat in general how the amusement of rowing struck him, and the weary-faced oiler smiled in full sympathy. Previously to the foundering, by the way, the oiler had worked double-watch in the engine-room of the ship.

"Take her easy, now, boys," said the captain. "Don't spend yourselves. If we have to run a surf you'll need all your strength, because we'll sure have to swim for it. Take your time."

Slowly the land arose from the sea. From a black line it became a line of black and a line of white, trees and sand. Finally, the captain said that he could make out a house on the shore. "That's the house of refuge, sure," said the cook. "They'll see us before long, and come out after us."

The distant lighthouse reared high. "The keeper ought to be able to make us out now, if he's looking through a glass," said the captain "He'll notify the life-saving people."

"None of those other boats could have got ashore to give word of the wreck," said the oiler, in a low voice. "Else the lifeboat would be out hunting us."

Slowly and beautifully the land loomed out of the sea. The wind came again. It had veered from the northeast to the southeast. Finally, a new sound struck the ears of the men in the boat. It was the low thunder of the surf on the shore. "We'll never be able to make the lighthouse now," said the captain. "Swing her head a little more north, Billie," said he.

"'A little more north,' sir," said the oiler.

Whereupon the little boat turned her nose once more down the wind, and all but the oarsman watched the shore grow. Under the influence of this expansion doubt and direful apprehension was leaving the minds of the men. The management of the boat was still most absorbing, but it could not prevent a quiet cheerfulness. In an hour, perhaps, they would be ashore.

Their backbones had become thoroughly used to balancing in the boat, and they now rode this wild colt of a dingey like circus men. The correspondent thought that he had been drenched to the skin, but happening to feel in the top pocket of his coat, he found therein eight cigars. Four of them were soaked with sea water; four were perfectly scatheless. After a search, somebody produced three dry matches, and thereupon the four waifs rode impudently in their little boat, and with an assurance of an impending rescue shining in their eyes, puffed at the big cigars and judged well and ill of all men. Everybody took a drink of water.

IV

"Cook," remarked the captain, "there don't seem to be any signs of life about your house of refuge."

"No," replied the cook. "Funny they don't see us!"

A broad stretch of lowly coast lay before the eyes of the men. It was of dunes topped with dark vegetation. The roar of the surf was plain, and sometimes they could see the white lip of a wave as it spun up the beach. A tiny house was blocked out black upon the sky. Southward, the slim lighthouse lifted its little gray length.

Tide, wind, and waves were swinging the dingey northward. "Funny they don't see us," said the men.

The surf's roar was here dulled, but its tone was, nevertheless, thunderous and mighty. As the boat swam over the great roilers, the men sat listening to this roar. "We'll swamp sure," said everybody.

It is fair to say here that there was not a life-saving station within twenty miles in either direction, but the men did not know this fact, and in consequence they made dark and opprobrious remarks concerning the eyesight of the nation's life-savers. Four scowling men sat in the dingey and surpassed records in the invention of epithets.

"Funny they don't see us."

The lightheartedness of a former time had completely faded. To their sharpened minds it was easy to conjure pictures of all kinds of incompetency and blindness and, indeed, cowardice. There was the shore of the populous land, and it was bitter and bitter to them that from it came no sign.

"Well," said the captain, ultimately, "I suppose we'll have to make a try for ourselves. If we stay out here too long, we'll none of us have strength left to swim after the boat swamps."

And so the oiler, who was at the oars, turned the boat straight for the shore. There was a sudden tightening of muscle. There was some thinking.

"If we don't all get ashore—" said the captain. "If we don't all get ashore, I suppose you fellows know where to send news of my finish?"

They then briefly exchanged some addresses and admonitions. As for the reflections of the men, there was a great deal of rage in them. Perchance they might be formulated thus: "If I am going to be drowned—if I am going to be drowned—if I am going to be drowned, why, in the name of the seven mad gods who rule the sea, was I allowed to come thus far and contemplate sand and trees? Was I brought here merely to have my nose dragged away as I was about to nibble the sacred cheese of life? It is preposterous. If this old ninny woman, Fate, cannot do better than this, she should be deprived of the management of men's fortunes. She is an old hen who knows not her intention. If she has decided to drown me, why did she not do it in the beginning and save me all this trouble? The whole affair is absurd. . . . But no, she cannot mean to drown me. She dare not drown me. She cannot drown me. Not after all this work." Afterward the man might have had an impulse to shake his fist at the clouds: "Just you drown me, now, and then hear what I call you!"

The billows that came at this time were more formidable. They seemed always just about to break and roll over the little boat in a turmoil of foam. There was a preparatory and long growl in the speech of them. No mind unused to the sea would have concluded that the dingey could ascend these sheer heights in time. The shore was still afar. The oiler was a wily surfman. "Boys," he said swiftly, "she won't live three minutes more, and we're too far out to swim. Shall I take her to sea again, captain?"

"Yes! Go ahead!" said the captain.

This oiler, by a series of quick miracles, and fast and steady oarsmanship, turned the boat in the middle of the surf and took her safely to sea again.

There was a considerable silence as the boat bumped over the furrowed sea to deeper water. Then somebody in gloom spoke. "Well, anyhow, they must have seen us from the shore by now."

The gulls went in slanting flight up the wind toward the gray desolate east. A squall, marked by dingy clouds, and clouds brick red, like smoke from a burning building, appeared from the southeast.

"What do you think of those life-saving people? Ain't they peaches?"

"Funny they haven't seen us."

"Maybe they think we're out here for sport! Maybe they think we're fishin'. Maybe they think we're damned fools."

It was a long afternoon. A changed tide tried to force them southward, but the wind and wave said northward. Far ahead, where coastline, sea, and sky formed their mighty angle, there were little dots which seemed to indicate a city on the shore.

"St. Augustine?"

The captain shook his head. "Too near Mosquito Inlet."

And the oiler rowed, and then the correspondent rowed. Then the oiler rowed. It was a weary business. The human back can become the seat of more aches and pains than are registered in books for the composite anatomy of a regiment. It is a limited area, but it can become the theater of innumerable muscular conflicts, tangles, wrenches, knots, and other comforts.

"Did you ever like to row, Billie?" asked the correspondent.

"No," said the oiler. "Hang it!"

When one exchanged the rowing seat for a place in the bottom of the boat, he suffered a bodily depression that caused him to be careless of everything save an obligation to wiggle one finger. There was cold sea water swashing to and fro in the boat, and he lay in it. His head, pillowed on a thwart, was within an inch of the swirl of a wave crest, and sometimes a particularly obstreperous sea came in-board and drenched him once more. But these matters did not annoy him. It is almost certain that if the boat had capsized he would have tumbled comfortably out upon the ocean as if he felt sure that it was a great soft mattress.

"Look! There's a man on the shore!"

"Where?"

"There! See 'im? See 'im?"

"Yes, sure! He's walking along."

"Now he's stopped. Look! He's facing us!"

"He's waving at us!"

"So he is! By thunder!"

"Ah, now we're all right! Now we're all right! There'll be a boat out here for us in half an hour."

"He's going on. He's running. He's going up to that house there."

The remote beach seemed lower than the sea, and it required a searching glance to discern the little black figure. The captain saw a floating stick and they rowed to it. A bath towel was by some weird chance in the boat, and, tying this on the stick, the captain waved it. The oarsman did not dare turn his head, so he was obliged to ask questions.

"What's he doing now?"

"He's standing still again. He's looking, I think. . . . There he goes again. Toward the house. . . . Now he's stopped again."

"Is he waving at us?"

"No, not now! he was, though."

"Look! There comes another man!"

"He's running."

"Look at him go, would you."

"Why, he's on a bicycle. Now he's met the other man. They're both waving at us. Look!"

"There comes something up the beach."

"What the devil is that thing?"

"Why it looks like a boat."

"Why, certainly it's a boat."

"No, it's on wheels."

"Yes, so it is. Well, that must be the life-boat. They drag them along shore on a wagon."

"That's the life-boat, sure."

"No, by–, it's–it's an omnibus."

"I tell you it's a life-boat."

"It is not! It's an omnibus. I can see it plain. See? One of these big hotel omnibuses."

"By thunder, you're right. It's an omnibus, sure as fate. What do you suppose they are doing with an omnibus? Maybe they are going around collecting the life-crew, hey?"

"That's it, likely. Look! There's a fellow waving a little black flag. He's standing on the steps of the omnibus. There come those other two fellows. Now they're all talking together. Look at the fellow with the flag. Maybe he ain't waving it."

"That ain't a flag, is it? That's his coat. Why, certainly, that's his coat."

"So it is. It's his coat. He's taken it off and is waving it around his head. But would you look at him swing it."

"Oh, say, there isn't any life-saving station there. That's just a winter resort hotel omnibus that has brought over some of the boarders to see us drown."

"What's that idiot with the coat mean? What's he signaling, anyhow?"

"It looks as if he were trying to tell us to go north. There must be a life-saving station up there."

"No! He thinks we're fishing. Just giving us a merry hand. See? Ah, there, Willie!"

"Well, I wish I could make something out of those signals. What do you suppose he means?"

"He don't mean anything. He's just playing."

"Well, if he'd just signal us to try the surf again, or to go to sea and wait, or go north, or go south, or go to hell–there would be some reason in it. But look at him. He just stands there and keeps his coat revolving like a wheel. The ass!"

"There come more people."

"Now there's quite a mob. Look! Isn't that a boat?"

"Where? Oh, I see where you mean. No, that's no boat."

"That fellow is still waving his coat."

"He must think we like to see him do that. Why don't he quit it? It don't mean anything."

"I don't know. I think he is trying to make us go north. It must be that there's a life-saving station there somewhere."

"Say, he ain't tired yet. Look at 'im wave."

"Wonder how long he can keep that up. He's been revolving his coat ever since he caught sight of us. He's an idiot. Why aren't they getting men to bring a boat out? A fishing boat—one of those big yawls—could come out here all right. Why don't he do something?"

"Oh, it's all right, now."

"They'll have a boat out here for us in less than no time, now that they've seen us."

A faint yellow tone came into the sky over the low land. The shadows on the sea slowly deepened. The wind bore coldness with it, and the men began to shiver.

"Holy smoke!" said one, allowing his voice to express his impious mood, "if we keep on monkeying out here! If we've got to flounder out here all night!"

"Oh, we'll never have to stay here all night! Don't you worry. They've seen us now, and it won't be long before they'll come chasing out after us."

The shore grew dusky. The man waving a coat blended gradually into this gloom, and it swallowed in the same manner the omnibus and the group of people. The spray, when it dashed uproariously over the side, made the voyagers shrink and swear like men who were being branded.

"I'd like to catch the chump who waved the coat. I feel like soaking him one, just for luck."

"Why? What did he do?"

"Oh, nothing, but then he seemed so damned cheerful."

In the meantime the oiler rowed, and then the correspondent rowed, and then the oiler rowed. Gray-faced and bowed forward, they mechanically, turn by turn, plied the leaden oars. The form of the lighthouse had vanished from the southern horizon, but finally a pale star appeared, just lifting from the sea. The streaked saffron in the west passed before the all-merging darkness, and the sea to the east was black. The land had vanished, and was expressed only by the low and drear thunder of the surf.

"If I am going to be drowned—if I am going to be drowned—if I am going to be drowned, why, in the name of the seven mad gods who rule the sea, was I allowed to come thus far and contemplate sand and trees? Was I brought here merely to have my nose dragged away as I was about to nibble the sacred cheese of life?"

The patient captain, drooped over the water jar, was sometimes obliged to speak to the oarsman.

"Keep her head up! Keep her head up!"

"'Keep her head up,' sir." The voices were weary and low.

This was surely a quiet evening. All save the oarsman lay heavily and listlessly in the boat's bottom. As for him, his eyes were just capable of noting the tall black waves that swept forward in a most sinister silence, save for an occasional subdued growl of a crest.

The cook's head was on a thwart, and he looked without interest at the water under his nose. He was deep in other scenes. Finally he spoke. "Billie," he murmured, dreamily, "what kind of pie do you like best?"

V

"Pie," said the oiler and the correspondent, agitatedly. "Don't talk about those things, blast you!"

"Well," said the cook, "I was just thinking about ham sandwiches, and—"

A night on the sea in an open boat is a long night. As darkness settled finally, the shine of the light, lifting from the sea in the south, changed to full gold. On the northern horizon a new light appeared, a small bluish gleam on the edge of the waters. These two lights were the furniture of the world. Otherwise there was nothing but waves.

Two men huddled in the stern, and distances were so magnificent in the dingey that the rower was enabled to keep his feet partly warmed by thrusting them under his companions. Their legs indeed extended far under the rowing seat until they touched the feet of the captain forward. Sometimes, despite the efforts of the tired oarsman, a wave came piling into the boat, an icy wave of the night, and the chilling water soaked them anew. They would twist their bodies for a moment and groan, and sleep the dead sleep once more, while the water in the boat gurgled about them as the craft rocked.

The plan of the oiler and the correspondent was for one to row until he lost the ability, and then arouse the other from his sea water couch in the bottom of the boat.

The oiler plied the oars until his head drooped forward, and the overpowering sleep blinded him. And he rowed yet afterward. Then he touched a man in the bottom of the boat and called his name. "Will you spell me for a little while?" he said, meekly.

"Sure, Billie," said the correspondent, awakening and dragging himself to a sitting position. They exchanged places carefully, and the oiler, cuddling down in the sea water at the cook's side, seemed to go to sleep instantly.

The particular violence of the sea had ceased. The waves came without snarling. The obligation of the man at the oars was to keep the boat headed so that the tilt of the rollers would not capsize her, and to preserve her from filling when the crests rushed past. The black waves were silent and hard to be seen in the darkness. Often one was almost upon the boat before the oarsman was aware.

In a low voice the correspondent addressed the captain. He was not sure that the captain was awake, although this iron man seemed to be always awake. "Captain, shall I keep her making for that light north, sir?"

The same steady voice answered him. "Yes. Keep it about two points off the port bow."

The cook had tied a life belt around himself in order to get even the warmth which this clumsy cork contrivance could donate, and he seemed almost stove-like when a rower, whose teeth invariably chattered wildly as soon as he ceased his labor, dropped down to sleep.

The correspondent, as he rowed, looked down at the two men sleeping under foot. The cook's arm was around the oiler's shoulders, and, with their fragmentary clothing and haggard faces, they were the babes of the sea, a grotesque rendering of the old babes in the wood.

Later he must have grown stupid at his work, for suddenly there was a growling of water, and a crest came with a roar and a swash into the boat, and it was a wonder that it did not set the cook afloat in his life belt. The cook continued to sleep, but the oiler sat up, blinking his eyes and shaking with the new cold.

"Oh, I'm awful sorry, Billie," said the correspondent contritely.

"That's all right, old boy," said the oiler, and lay down again and was asleep.

Presently it seemed that even the captain dozed, and the correspondent thought that he was the one man afloat on all the oceans. The wind had a voice as it came over the waves, and it was sadder than the end.

There was a long, loud swishing astern of the boat, and a gleaming trail of phosphorescence, like blue flame, was furrowed on the black waters. It might have been made by a monstrous knife.

Then there came a stillness, while the correspondent breathed with the open mouth and looked at the sea.

Suddenly there was another swish and another long flash of bluish light, and this time it was alongside the boat, and might almost have been reached with an oar. The correspondent saw an enormous fin speed like a shadow through the water, hurling the crystalline spray and leaving the long glowing trail.

The correspondent looked over his shoulder at the captain. His face was hidden, and he seemed to be asleep. He looked at the babes of the sea. They certainly were asleep. So, being bereft of sympathy, he leaned a little way to one side and swore softly into the sea.

But the thing did not then leave the vicinity of the boat. Ahead or astern, on one side or the other, at intervals long or short, fled the long sparkling streak, and there was to be heard the whirroo of the dark fin. The speed and power of the thing was greatly to be admired. It cut the water like a gigantic and keen projectile.

The presence of this biding thing did not affect the man with the same horror that it would if he had been a picnicker. He simply looked at the sea dully and swore in an undertone.

Nevertheless, it is true that he did not wish to be alone. He wished one of his companions to awaken by chance and keep him company with it. But the captain hung motionless over the water jar, and the oiler and the cook in the bottom of the boat were plunged in slumber.

VI

"If I am going to be drowned–if I am going to be drowned–if I am going to be drowned, why, in the name of the seven mad gods who rule the sea, was I allowed to come thus far and contemplate sand and trees?"

During this dismal night, it may be remarked that a man would conclude that it was really the intention of the seven mad gods to drown him, despite the abominable injustice of it. For it was certainly an abominable injustice to drown a man who had worked so hard, so hard. The man felt it would be a crime most unnatural. Other people had drowned at sea since galleys swarmed with painted sails, but still–

When it occurs to a man that nature does not regard him as important, and that she feels she would not maim the universe by disposing of him, he at first wishes to throw bricks at the temple, and he hates deeply the fact that there are no bricks and no temples. Any visible expression of nature would surely be pelleted with his jeers.

Then, if there be no tangible thing to hoot he feels, perhaps, the desire to confront a personification and indulge in pleas, bowed to one knee, and with hands supplicant, saying: "Yes, but I love myself."

A high cold star on a winter's night is the word he feels that she says to him. Thereafter he knows the pathos of his situation.

The men in the dingey had not discussed these matters, but each had, no doubt, reflected upon them in silence and according to his mind. There was seldom any expression upon their faces save the general one of complete weariness. Speech was devoted to the business of the boat.

To chime the notes of his emotion, a verse mysteriously entered the correspondent's head. He had even forgotten that he had forgotten this verse, but it suddenly was in his mind.

"A soldier of the Legion lay dying in Algiers,
There was a lack of woman's nursing, there was dearth of woman's tears;
But a comrade stood beside him, and he took that comrade's hand,
And he said: 'I shall never see my own, my native land.'"

In his childhood, the correspondent had been made acquainted with the fact that a soldier of the Legion lay dying in Algiers, but he had never regarded the fact as important. Myriads of his school fellows had informed him of the soldier's plight, but the dinning had naturally ended by making him perfectly indifferent. He had never considered it his affair that a soldier of the Legion lay dying in Algiers, nor had it appeared to him as a matter for sorrow. It was less to him than the breaking of a pencil's point.

Now, however, it quaintly came to him as a human, living thing. It was no longer merely a picture of a few throes in the breast of a poet, meanwhile drinking tea and warming his feet at the grate; it was an actuality—stern, mournful, and fine.

The correspondent plainly saw the soldier. He lay on the sand with his feet out straight and still. While his pale left hand was upon his chest in an attempt to thwart the going of his life, the blood came between his fingers. In the far Algerian distance, a city of low square forms was set against a sky that was faint with the last sunset hues. The correspondent, plying the oars and dreaming of the slow and slower movements of the lips of the soldier, was moved by a profound and perfectly impersonal comprehension. He was sorry for the soldier of the Legion who lay dying in Algiers.

The thing which had followed the boat and waited, had evidently grown bored at the delay. There was no longer to be heard the slash of the cut water, and there was no longer the flame of the long trail. The light in the north still glimmered, but it was apparently no nearer to the boat. Sometimes the boom of the surf rang in the correspondent's ears, and he turned the craft seaward then and rowed harder. Southward, someone had evidently built a watch fire on the beach. It was too low and too far to be seen, but it made a shimmering, roseate reflection upon the bluff back of it, and this could be discerned from the boat. The wind came stronger, and sometimes a wave suddenly raged out like a mountain cat, and there was to be seen the sheen and sparkle of a broken crest.

The captain, in the bow, moved on his water jar and sat erect. "Pretty long night," he observed to the correspondent. He looked at the shore. "Those life-saving people take their time."

"Did you see that shark playing around?"

"Yes, I saw him. He was a big fellow, all right."

"Wish I had known you were awake."

Later the correspondent spoke into the bottom of the boat.

"Billie!" There was a slow and gradual disentanglement. "Billie, will you spell me?"

"Sure," said the oiler.

As soon as the correspondent touched the cold comfortable sea water in the bottom of the boat, and had huddled close to the cook's life belt he was deep in sleep, despite the fact that his teeth played all the popular airs. This sleep was so good to him that it was but a moment before he heard a voice call his name in a tone that demonstrated the last stages of exhaustion. "Will you spell me?"

"Sure, Billie."

The light in the north had mysteriously vanished, but the correspondent took his course from the wide-awake captain.

Later in the night they took the boat farther out to sea, and the captain directed the cook to take one oar at the stern and keep the boat facing the seas. He was to call out if he should hear the thunder of the surf. This plan enabled the oiler and the correspondent to get respite together. "We'll give those boys a chance to get into shape again," said the captain. They curled down and, after a few preliminary chatterings and trembles, slept once more the dead sleep. Neither knew they had bequeathed to the cook the company of another shark, or perhaps the same shark.

As the boat caroused on the waves, spray occasionally bumped over the side and gave them a fresh soaking, but this had no power to break their repose. The ominous slash of the wind and the water affected them as it would have affected mummies.

"Boys," said the cook, with the notes of every reluctance in his voice, "she's drifted in pretty close. I guess one of you had better take her to sea again." The correspondent, aroused, heard the crash of the toppled crests.

As he was rowing, the captain gave him some whisky and water, and this steadied the chills out of him. "If I ever get ashore and anybody shows me even a photograph of an oar—"

At last there was a short conversation.

"Billie. . . . Billie, will you spell me?"

"Sure," said the oiler.

VII

When the correspondent again opened his eyes, the sea and the sky were each of the gray hue of the dawning. Later, carmine and gold was painted upon the waters. The morning appeared finally, in its splendor, with a sky of pure blue, and the sunlight flamed on the tips of the waves.

On the distant dunes were set many little black cottages, and a tall white windmill reared above them. No man, nor dog, nor bicycle appeared on the beach. The cottages might have formed a deserted village.

The voyagers scanned the shore. A conference was held in the boat. "Well," said the captain, "if no help is coming we might better try a run through the surf right away. If we stay out here much longer we will be too weak to do anything for ourselves at all." The others silently acquiesced in this reasoning. The boat was headed for the beach. The correspondent wondered if none ever ascended the tall wind tower, and if then they never looked seaward. This tower was a giant, standing with its back to the plight of the ants. It represented in a degree, to the correspondent, the serenity of nature amid the struggles of the individual—nature in the wind, and nature in the vision of men. She did not seem cruel to him then, nor beneficent, nor treacherous, nor wise. But she was indifferent, flatly indifferent. It is, perhaps, plausible that a man in this situation, impressed with the unconcern of the universe, should see the innumerable flaws of his life, and have them taste wickedly in his mind and wish for another chance. A distinction between right and wrong seems absurdly clear to him, then, in this new ignorance of the grave edge, and he understands that if he were given another opportunity he would mend his conduct and his words, and be better and brighter during an introduction or at a tea.

"Now, boys," said the captain, "she is going to swamp, sure. All we can do is to work her in as far as possible, and then when she swamps, pile out and scramble for the beach. Keep cool now, and don't jump until she swamps sure."

The oiler took the oars. Over his shoulders he scanned the surf. "Captain," he said, "I think I'd better bring her about, and keep her head-on to the seas and back her in."

"All right, Billie," said the captain. "Back her in." The oiler swung the boat then and, seated in the stern, the cook and the correspondent were obliged to look over their shoulders to contemplate the lonely and indifferent shore.

The monstrous in-shore rollers heaved the boat high until the men were again enabled to see the white sheets of water scudding up the slanted beach. "We won't get in very close," said the captain. Each time a man could wrest his attention from the rollers, he turned his glance toward the shore, and in the expression of the eyes during this contemplation there was a singular quality. The correspondent, observing the others, knew that they were not afraid, but the full meaning of their glances was shrouded.

As for himself, he was too tired to grapple fundamentally with the fact. He tried to coerce his mind into thinking of it, but the mind was dominated at this time by the muscles, and the muscles said they did not care. It merely occurred to him that if he should drown it would be a shame.

There were no hurried words, no pallor, no plain agitation. The men simply looked at the shore. "Now, remember to get well clear of the boat when you jump," said the captain.

Seaward the crest of a roller suddenly fell with a thunderous crash, and the long white comber came roaring down upon the boat.

"Steady now," said the captain. The men were silent. They turned their eyes from the shore to the comber and waited. The boat slid up the incline, leaped at the furious top, bounced over it, and swung down the long back of the wave. Some water had been shipped and the cook bailed it out.

But the next crashed also. The tumbling, boiling flood of white water caught the boat and whirled it almost perpendicular. Water swarmed in from all sides. The correspondent had his hands on the gunwale at this time, and when the water entered at that place he swiftly withdrew his fingers, as if he objected to wetting them.

The little boat, drunken with this weight of water, reeled and snuggled deeper into the sea.

"Bail her out, cook! Bail her out," said the captain.

"All right, captain," said the cook.

"Now, boys, the next one will do for us, sure," said the oiler. "Mind to jump clear of the boat."

The third wave moved forward, huge, furious, implacable. It fairly swallowed the dingey, and almost simultaneously the men tumbled into the sea. A piece of life belt had lain in the bottom of the boat, and as the correspondent went overboard he held this to his chest with his left hand.

The January water was icy, and he reflected immediately that it was colder than he had expected to find it on the coast of Florida. This appeared to his dazed mind as a fact important enough to be noted at the time. The coldness of the water was sad; it was tragic. This fact was somehow so mixed and confused with his opinion of his own situation that it seemed almost a proper reason for tears. The water was cold.

When he came to the surface he was conscious of little but the noisy water. Afterward he saw his companions in the sea. The oiler was ahead in the race. He was swimming strongly and rapidly. Off to the correspondent's left, the cook's great white and corked back bulged out of the water, and in the rear the captain was hanging with his one good hand to the keel of the overturned dingey.

There is a certain immovable quality to a shore, and the correspondent wondered at it amid the confusion of the sea.

It seemed also very attractive, but the correspondent knew that it was a long journey, and he paddled leisurely. The piece of life preserver lay under him, and sometimes he whirled down the incline of a wave as if he were on a hand-sled.

But finally he arrived at a place in the sea where travel was beset with difficulty. He did not pause swimming to inquire what manner of current had caught him, but there his progress ceased. The shore was set before him like a bit of scenery on a stage, and he looked at it and understood with his eyes each detail of it.

As the cook passed, much farther to the left, the captain was calling to him, "Turn over on your back, cook! Turn over on your back and use the oar."

"All right, sir." The cook turned on his back, and, paddling with an oar, went ahead as if he were a canoe.

Presently the boat also passed to the left of the correspondent with the captain clinging with one hand to the keel. He would have appeared like a man raising himself to look over a board fence, if it were not for the extraordinary gymnastics of the boat. The correspondent marveled that the captain could still hold to it.

They passed on, nearer to shore—the oiler, the cook, the captain—and following them went the water jar, bouncing gayly over the seas.

The correspondent remained in the grip of this strange new enemy—a current. The shore, with its white slope of sand and its green bluff, topped with little silent cottages, was spread like a picture before him. It was very near to him then, but he was impressed as one who in a gallery looks at a scene from Brittany or Holland.

He thought: "I am going to drown? Can it be possible? Can it be possible? Can it be possible?" Perhaps an individual must consider his own death to be the final phenomenon of nature.

But later a wave perhaps whirled him out of this small, deadly current, for he found suddenly that he could again make progress toward the shore. Later still, he was aware that the captain, clinging with one hand to the keel of the dingey, had his face turned away from the shore and toward him, and was calling his name. "Come to the boat! Come to the boat!"

In his struggle to reach the captain and the boat, he reflected that when one gets properly wearied, drowning must really be a comfortable arrangement, a cessation of hostilities accompanied by a large degree of relief, and he was glad of it, for the main thing in his mind for some months had been horror of the temporary agony. He did not wish to be hurt.

Presently he saw a man running along the shore. He was undressing with most remarkable speed. Coat, trousers, shirt, everything flew magically off him.

"Come to the boat," called the captain.

"All right, captain." As the correspondent paddled, he saw the captain let himself down to bottom and leave the boat. Then the correspondent performed his one little marvel of the voyage. A large wave caught him and flung him with ease and supreme speed completely over the boat and far beyond it. It struck him even then as an event in gymnastics, and a true miracle of the sea. An overturned boat in the surf is not a plaything to a swimming man.

The correspondent arrived in water that reached only to his waist, but his condition did not enable him to stand for more than a moment. Each wave knocked him into a heap, and the undertow pulled at him.

Then he saw the man who had been running and undressing, and undressing and running, come bounding into the water. He dragged ashore the cook, and then waded towards the captain, but the captain waved him away, and sent him to the correspondent. He was naked, naked as a tree in winter, but a halo was about his head, and he shone like a saint. He gave a strong pull, and a long drag, and a bully heave at the correspondent's hand. The correspondent, schooled in the minor formulae, said: "Thanks, old man." But suddenly the man cried: "What's that?" He pointed a swift finger. The correspondent said: "Go."

In the shallows, face downward, lay the oiler. His forehead touched sand that was periodically, between each wave, clear of the sea.

The correspondent did not know all that transpired afterward. When he achieved safe ground he fell, striking the sand with each particular part of his body. It was as if he had dropped from a roof, but the thud was grateful to him.

It seems that instantly the beach was populated with men with blankets, clothes, and flasks, and women with coffee pots and all the remedies sacred to their minds. The welcome of the land to the men from the sea was warm and generous, but a still and dripping shape was carried slowly up the beach, and the land's welcome for it could only be the different and sinister hospitality of the grave.

When it came night, the white waves paced to and fro in the moonlight, and the wind brought the sound of the sea's great voice to the men on shore, and they felt that they could then be interpreters.

THEODORE DREISER

[1871–1945]

The Lost Phœbe

(First published in *Century Magazine*, April, 1916; first book publication in 1918.)

THEY LIVED TOGETHER in a part of the country which was not so prosperous as it had once been, about three miles from one of those towns that, instead of increasing in population, is steadily decreasing. The territory was not very thickly settled; perhaps a house every other mile or so, with large areas of corn- and wheat-land and fallow fields that at odd seasons had been sown to timothy and clover. Their particular house was part log and part frame, the log portion being the old original home of Henry's grandfather. The new portion, of now rain-beaten, time-worn slabs, through which the wind squeaked in the chinks at times, and which several overshadowing elms and a butternut tree made picturesque and reminiscently pathetic, but a little damp, was erected by Henry when he was twenty-one and just married.

That was forty-eight years before. The furniture inside, like the house outside, was old and mildewy and reminiscent of an earlier day. You have seen the what-not of cherry wood, perhaps, with spiral legs and fluted top. It was there. The old-fashioned four-poster bed, with its ball-like protuberances and deep curving incisions, was there also, a sadly alienated descendant of an early Jacobean ancestor. The bureau of cherry was also high and wide and solidly built, but faded-looking, and with a musty odor. The rag carpet that underlay all these sturdy examples of enduring furniture was a weak, faded, lead and pink colored affair woven by Phœbe Ann's own hands, when she was fifteen years younger than she was when she died. The creaky wooden loom on which it had been done now stood like a dusty, bony skeleton, along with a broken rocking-chair, a worm-eaten clothes press—Heavens knows how old—a lime-stained bench that had once been used to keep flowers on outside the door, and other decrepit factors of household utility in an east room that was a lean-to against this so-called main portion. All sorts of other broken-down furniture were about this place; an antiquated clothes-horse, cracked in two of its ribs; a broken mirror in an old cherry frame, which had fallen from a nail and cracked itself three days before their youngest son, Jerry, died; an extension hat-rack, which once had had porcelain knobs on the ends of its pegs; and a sewing machine, long since outdone in its clumsy mechanism by rivals of a newer generation.

The orchard to the east of the house was full of gnarled old apple trees, worm eaten as to trunks and branches, and fully ornamented with green and white lichens, so that it had a sad, greenish-white, silvery effect in moonlight. The low outhouses, which had once housed chickens, a horse or two, a cow, and several pigs, were covered with patches of moss as to their roof, and the sides had been free of paint for so long that they were blackish-gray as to color, and a little spongy. The picket fence in front, with its gate squeaky and askew, and the side fences of the stake-and-rider type were in an equally run-down condition. As a matter of fact, they had aged synchronously with the persons who lived here, old Henry Reifsneider and his wife Phœbe Ann.

They had lived here, these two, ever since their marriage, forty-eight years before, and Henry had lived here before that from his childhood up. His father and mother, well along in years when he was a boy, had invited him to bring his wife here when he had first fallen in love and decided to marry; and he had done so. His father and mother were the companions of himself and his wife for ten years after they were married, when both died; and then Henry and Phœbe were left with their five children growing lustily apace. But all sorts of things had happened since then. Of the seven children, all told, that had been born to them, three had died; one girl had gone to Kansas; one boy had gone to Sioux Falls, never even to be heard of after; another boy had gone to Washington; and the last girl lived five counties away in the same State, but was so burdened with cares of her own that she rarely gave them a thought. Time and a commonplace home life that had never been attractive had weaned them thoroughly, so that, wherever they were, they gave little thought as to how it might be with their father and mother.

Old Henry Reifsneider and his wife Phœbe were a loving couple. You perhaps know how it is with simple natures that fasten themselves like lichens on the stones of circumstance and weather their days to a crumbling conclusion. The great world sounds widely, but it has no call for them. They have no soaring intellect. The orchard, the meadow, the cornfield, the pig-pen, and the chicken-lot measure the range of their human activities. When the wheat is headed it is reaped and threshed; when the corn is browned and frosted it is cut and shocked; when the timothy is in full head it is cut, and the hay-cock erected. After that comes winter, with the hauling of grain to market, the sawing and splitting of wood, the simple chores of fire-building, meal-getting, occasional repairing, and visiting. Beyond these and the changes of weather—the snows, the rains, and the fair days—there are no immediate, significant things. All the rest of life is a far-off, clamorous phantasmagoria, flickering like Northern lights in the night, and sounding as faintly as cow-bells tinkling in the distance.

Old Henry and his wife Phœbe were as fond of each other as it is possible for two old people to be who have nothing else in this life to be fond of. He was a thin old man, seventy when she died, a queer, crotchety person with coarse gray-black hair and beard, quite straggly and unkempt. He looked at you out of dull, fishy, watery eyes that had deep-brown crow's-feet at the sides. His clothes, like the clothes of many farmers, were aged and angular and baggy, standing out at the pockets, not fitting about the neck, protuberant and worn at elbow and knee. Phœbe Ann was thin and shapeless, a very umbrella of a woman, clad in shabby black, and with a black bonnet for her best wear. As time had passed, and they had only themselves to look after, their movements had become slower and slower, their activities fewer and fewer. The annual keep of pigs had been reduced from five to one grunting porker, and the single horse which Henry now retained was a sleepy animal, not over-nourished and not very clean. The chickens, of which formerly there was a large flock, had almost disappeared, owing to ferrets, foxes, and the lack of proper care, which produces disease. The former healthy garden was now a straggling memory of itself, and the vines and flowerbeds that formerly ornamented the windows and dooryard had now become choking thickets. A will had been made which divided the small tax-eaten property equally among the remaining four, so that it was really of no interest to any of them. Yet these two lived together in peace and sympathy, only that now and then old Henry would become unduly cranky, complaining almost invariably that something had been neglected or mislaid which was of no importance at all.

"Phœbe, where's my corn knife? You ain't never minded to let my things alone no more."

"Now you hush, Henry," his wife would caution him in a cracked and squeaky voice. "If you don't, I'll leave yuh. I'll git up and walk out of here some day, and then where would y' be? Y' ain't got anybody but me to look after yuh, so yuh just behave yourself. Your corn knife's on the mantel where it's allus been unless you've gone an' put it summers else."

Old Henry, who knew his wife would never leave him under any circumstances, used to speculate at times as to what he would do if she were to die. That was the one leaving that he really feared. As he climbed on the chair at night to wind the old, long-pendulumed, double-weighted clock, or went finally to the front and the back door to see that they were safely shut in, it was a comfort to know that Phœbe was there, properly ensconsed on her side of the bed, and that if he stirred restlessly in the night, she would be there to ask what he wanted.

"Now, Henry, do lie still! You're as restless as a chicken."

"Well, I can't sleep, Phœbe."

"Well, yuh needn't roll so, anyhow. Yuh kin let me sleep."

This usually reduced him to a state of somnolent ease. If she wanted a pail of water, it was a grumbling pleasure for him to get it; and if she did rise first to build the fires, he saw that the wood was cut and placed within easy reach. They divided this simple world nicely between them.

As the years had gone on, however, fewer and fewer people had called. They were well-known for a distance of as much as ten square miles as old Mr. and Mrs. Reifsneider, honest, moderately Christian, but too old to be really interesting any longer. The writing of letters had become an almost impossible burden too difficult to continue or even negotiate via others, although an occasional letter still did arrive from the daughter in Pemberton County. Now and then some old friend stopped with a pie or cake or a roasted chicken or duck, or merely to see that they were well; but even these kindly minded visits were no longer frequent.

One day in the early spring of her sixty-fourth year Mrs. Reifsneider took sick, and from a low fever passed into some indefinable ailment which, because of her age, was no longer curable. Old Henry drove to Swinnerton, the neighboring town, and procured a doctor. Some friends called, and the immediate care of her was taken off his hands. Then one chill spring night she died, and old Henry, in a fog of sorrow and uncertainty, followed her body to the nearest graveyard, an unattractive space with a few pines growing in it. Although he might have gone to the daughter in Pemberton or sent for her, it was really too much trouble and he was too weary and fixed. It was suggested to him at once by one friend and another that he come to stay with them awhile, but he did not see fit. He was so old and so fixed in his notions and so accustomed to the exact surroundings he had known all his days, that he could not think of leaving. He wanted to remain near where they had put his Phœbe; and the fact that he would have to live alone did not trouble him in the least. The living children were notified and the care of him offered if he would leave, but he would not.

"I kin make a shift for myself," he continually announced to old Dr. Morrow, who had attended his wife in this case. "I kin cook a little, and, besides, it don't take much more'n coffee an' bread in the mornin's to satisfy me. I'll get along now well enough. Yuh just let me be." And after many pleadings and proffers of advice, with supplies of coffee and bacon and baked bread duly offered and accepted, he was left to himself. For a while he sat idly outside his door brooding in the spring sun. He tried to revive his interest in farming, and to keep himself busy and free from thought by looking after the fields, which of late had been much neglected. It was a gloomy thing to come in of an evening, however, or in the afternoon, and find no shadow of Phœbe where everything suggested her. By degrees he put a few of her things away. At night he sat beside his lamp and read in the papers that were left him occasionally or in a Bible that he had neglected for years, but he could get little solace from these things. Mostly he held his hand over his mouth and looked at the floor as he sat and thought of what had become of her, and how soon he himself would die. He made a great business of making his coffee in the morning and frying himself a little bacon at night; but his appetite was gone. The shell in which he had been housed so long seemed vacant, and its shadows were suggestive of immedicable griefs. So he lived quite dolefully for five long months, and then a change began.

It was one night, after he had looked after the front and the back door, wound the clock, blown out the light, and gone through all the selfsame motions that he had indulged in for years, that he went to bed not so much to sleep as to think. It was a moonlight night. The green-lichen-covered orchard just outside and to be seen from his bed where he now lay was a silvery affair, sweetly spectral. The moon shone through the east windows, throwing the pattern of the panes on the wooden floor, and making the old furniture, to which he was accustomed, stand out dimly in the room. As usual he had been thinking of Phœbe and the years when they had been young together, and of the children who had gone, and the poor shift he was making of his present days. The house was coming to be in a very bad state indeed. The bedclothes were in disorder and not clean, for he made a wretched shift of washing. It was a terror to him. The roof leaked, causing things, some of them, to remain damp for weeks at a time, but he was getting into that brooding state where he would accept anything rather than exert himself. He preferred to pace slowly to and fro or to sit and think.

By twelve o'clock of this particular night he was asleep, however, and by two had waked again. The moon by this time had shifted to a position on the western side of the house, and it now shone in through the windows of the living-room and those of the kitchen beyond. A certain combination of furniture—a chair near a table with his coat on it, the half-open kitchen door casting a shadow, and the position of a lamp near a paper—gave him an exact representation of Phœbe leaning over the table as he had often seen her do in life. It gave him a great start. Could it be she—or her ghost? He had scarcely ever believed in spirits; and still—. He looked at her fixedly in the feeble half-light, his old hair tingling oddly at the roots, and then sat up. The figure did not move. He put his thin legs out of the bed and sat looking at her, wondering if this could really be Phœbe. They had talked of ghosts often in their lifetime, of apparitions and omens; but they had never agreed that such things could be. It had never been a part of his wife's creed that she could have a spirit that could return to walk the earth. Her afterworld was quite a different affair, a vague heaven, no less, from which the righteous did not trouble to return. Yet here she was now, bending over the table in her black skirt and gray shawl, her pale profile outlined against the moonlight.

"Phœbe," he called, thrilling from head to toe, and putting out one bony hand, "have yuh come back?"

The figure did not stir, and he arose and walked uncertainly to the door, looking at it fixedly the while. As he drew near, however, the apparition resolved itself into its primal content—his old coat over the high backed chair, the lamp by the paper, the half-open door.

"Well," he said to himself, his mouth open, "I thought shore I saw her." And he ran his hand strangely and vaguely through his hair, the while his nervous tension relaxed. Vanished as it had, it gave him the idea that she might return.

Another night, because of this first illusion, and because his mind was now constantly on her and he was old, he looked out of the window that was nearest his bed and commanded a hen-coop and pig-pen and a part of the wagon-shed, and there, a faint mist exuding from the damp of the ground, he thought he saw her again. It was one of those little wisps of mist, one of those faint exhalations of the earth that rise in a cool night after a warm day, and flicker like small white cypresses of fog before they disappear. In life it had been a custom of hers to cross this lot from her kitchen door to the pig-pen to throw in any scrap that was left from her cooking, and here she was again. He sat up and watched it strangely, doubtfully, because of his previous experience, but inclined, because of the nervous titillation that passed over his body, to believe that spirits really were, and that Phœbe, who would be concerned because of his lonely state, must be thinking about him, and hence returning. What other way would she have? How otherwise could she express herself? It would be within the province of her charity so to do, and like her loving interest in him. He quivered and watched it eagerly; but, a faint breath of air stirring, it wound away toward the fence and disappeared.

A third night, as he was actually dreaming, some ten days later, she came to his bedside and put her hand on his head.

"Poor Henry!" she said. "It's too bad."

He roused out of his sleep, actually to see her, he thought, moving from his bedroom into the one living room, her figure a shadowy mass of black. The weak straining of his eyes caused little points of light to flicker about the outlines of her form. He arose, greatly astonished, walked the floor in the cool room, convinced that Phœbe was coming back to him. If he only thought sufficiently, if he made it perfectly clear by his feeling that he needed her greatly, she would come back, this kindly wife, and tell him what to do. She would perhaps be with him much of the time, in the night, anyhow; and that would make him less lonely, this state more endurable.

In age and with the feeble it is not such a far cry from the subtleties of illusion to actual hallucination, and in due time this transition was made for Henry. Night after night he waited, expecting her return. Once in his weird mood he thought he saw a pale light moving about the room, and another time he thought he saw her walking in the orchard after dark. It was one morning when the details of his lonely state were virtually unendurable that he woke with the thought that she was not dead. How he had arrived at this conclusion it is hard to say. His mind had gone. In its place was a fixed illusion. He and Phœbe had had a senseless quarrel. He had reproached her for not leaving his pipe where he was accustomed to find it, and she had left. It was an aberrated fulfillment of her old jesting threat that if he did not behave himself she would leave him.

"I guess I could find yuh ag'in," he had always said. But her cackling threat had always been:

"Yuh'll not find me if I ever leave yuh. I guess I kin git some place where yuh can't find me."

This morning when he arose he did not think to build the fire in the customary way or to grind his coffee and cut his bread, as was his wont, but solely to meditate as to where he should search for her and how he should induce her to come back. Recently the one horse had been dispensed with because he found it cumbersome and beyond his needs. He took down his soft crush hat after he had dressed himself, a new glint of interest and determination in his eye, and taking his black crook cane from behind the door, where he had always placed it, started out briskly to look for her among the nearest neighbors. His old shoes clumped soundly in the dust as he walked, and his gray-black locks, now grown rather long, straggled out in a dramatic fringe or halo from under his hat. His short coat stirred busily as he walked, and his hands and face were peaked and pale.

"Why, hello, Henry! Where're yuh goin' this mornin'?" inquired Farmer Dodge, who, hauling a load of wheat to market, encountered him on the public road. He had not seen the aged farmer in months, not since his wife's death, and he wondered now, seeing him looking so spry.

"Yuh ain't seen Phœbe, have yuh?" inquired the old man, looking up quizzically.

"Phœbe who?" inquired Farmer Dodge, not for the moment connecting the name with Henry's dead wife.

"Why, my wife Phœbe, o' course. Who do yuh s'pose I mean?" He stared up with a pathetic sharpness of glance from under his shaggy, gray eyebrows.

"Wall, I'll swan, Henry, yuh ain't jokin', are yuh?" said the solid Dodge, a pursy man, with a smooth, hard, red face. "It can't be your wife yuh're talkin' about. She's dead."

"Dead! Shucks!" retorted the demented Reifsneider. "She left me early this mornin', while I was sleepin'. She allus got up to build the fire, but she's gone now. We had a little spat last night, an' I guess that's the reason. But I guess I kin find her. She's gone over to Matilda Race's, that's where she's gone."

He started briskly up the road, leaving the amazed Dodge to stare in wonder after him.

"Well, I'll be switched!" he said aloud to himself. "He's clean out'n his head. That poor old feller's been livin' down there till he's gone outen his mind. I'll have to notify the authorities." And he flicked his whip with great enthusiasm. "Geddap!" he said, and was off.

Reifsneider met no one else in this poorly populated region until he reached the whitewashed fence of Matilda Race and her husband three miles away. He had passed several other houses en route, but these not being within the range of his illusion were not considered. His wife, who had known Matilda well, must be here. He opened the picket-gate which guarded the walk, and stamped briskly up to the door.

"Why, Mr. Reifsneider," exclaimed old Matilda herself, a stout woman, looking out of the door in answer to his knock, "what brings yuh here this mornin'?"

"Is Phœbe here?" he demanded eagerly.

"Phœbe who? What Phœbe?" replied Mrs. Race, curious as to this sudden development of energy on his part.

"Why, my Phœbe, o' course. My wife Phœbe. Who do yuh s'pose? Ain't she here now?"

"Lawsy me!" exclaimed Mrs. Race, opening her mouth. "Yuh pore man! So you're clean out'n your mind now. Yuh come right in and sit down. I'll git yuh a cup o' coffee. O' course your wife ain't here; but yuh come in an' sit down. I'll find her fer yuh after a while. I know where she is."

The old farmer's eyes softened, and he entered. He was so thin and pale a specimen, pantalooned and patriarchal, that he aroused Mrs. Race's extremest sympathy as he took off his hat and laid it on his knees quite softly and mildly.

"We had a quarrel last night, an' she left me," he volunteered.

"Laws! laws!" sighed Mrs. Race, there being no one present with whom to share her astonishment as she went to her kitchen. "The pore man! Now somebody's just got to look after him. He can't be allowed to run around the country this way lookin' for his dead wife. It's turrible."

She boiled him a pot of coffee and brought in some of her new-baked bread and fresh butter. She set out some of her best jam and put a couple of eggs to boil, lying whole-heartedly the while.

"Now yuh stay right there, Uncle Henry, till Jake comes in, an' I'll send him to look for Phœbe. I think it's more'n likely she's over to Swinnerton with some o' her friends. Anyhow, we'll find out. Now yuh just drink this coffee an' eat this bread. Yuh must be tired. Yuh've had a long walk this mornin'." Her idea was to take counsel with Jake, "her man," and perhaps have him notify the authorities.

She bustled about, meditating on the uncertainties of life, while old

Reifsneider thrummed on the rim of his hat with his pale fingers and later ate abstractedly of what she offered. His mind was on his wife, however, and since she was not here, or did not appear, it wandered vaguely away to a family by the name of Murray, miles away in another direction. He decided after a time that he would not wait for Jack Race to hunt his wife but would seek her for himself. He must be on, and urge her to come back.

"Well, I'll be goin'," he said, getting up and looking strangely about him. "I guess she didn't come here after all. She went over to the Murrays, I guess. I'll not wait any longer, Mis' Race. There's a lot to do over to the house today." And out he marched in the face of her protests taking to the dusty road again in the warm spring sun, his cane striking the earth as he went.

It was two hours later that this pale figure of a man appeared in the Murrays' doorway, dusty, perspiring, eager. He had tramped all of five miles, and it was noon. An amazed husband and wife of sixty heard his strange query, and realized also that he was mad. They begged him to stay to dinner, intending to notify the authorities later and see what could be done; but though he stayed to partake of a little something, he did not stay long, and was off again to another distant farmhouse, his idea of many things to do and his need of Phœbe impelling him. So it went for that day and the next and the next, the circle of his inquiry ever widening.

The process by which a character assumes the significance of being peculiar, his antics weird, yet harmless, in such a community is often involute and pathetic. This day, as has been said, saw Reifsneider at other doors, eagerly asking his unnatural question, and leaving a trail of amazement, sympathy, and pity in his wake. Although the authorities were informed—the county sheriff, no less—it was not deemed advisable to take him into custody; for when those who knew old Henry, and had for so long, reflected on the condition of the county insane asylum, a place which, because of the poverty of the district, was of staggering aberration and sickening environment, it was decided to let him remain at large; for, strange to relate, it was found on investigation that at night he returned peaceably enough to his lonesome domicile there to discover whether his wife had returned, and to brood in loneliness until the morning. Who would lock up a thin, eager, seeking old man with iron-gray hair and an attitude of kindly, innocent inquiry, particularly when he was well known for a past of only kindly servitude and reliability? Those who had known him best rather agreed that he should be allowed to roam at large. He could do no harm. There were many who were willing to help him as to food, old clothes, the odds and ends of his daily life—at least at first. His figure after a time became not so much a commonplace as an accepted curiosity, and the replies, "Why, no, Henry; I ain't see her," or "No, Henry; she ain't been here today," more customary.

For several years thereafter then he was an odd figure in the sun and rain, on dusty roads and muddy ones, encountered occasionally in strange and unexpected places, pursuing his endless search. Undernourishment, after a time, although the neighbors and those who knew his history gladly contributed from their store, affected his body; for he walked much and ate little. The longer he roamed the public highway in this manner, the deeper became his strange hallucination; and finding it harder and harder to return from his more and more distant pilgrimages, he finally began taking a few utensils with him from his home, making a small package of them, in order that he might not be compelled to return. In an old tin coffee-pot of large size he placed a small tin cup, a knife, fork, and spoon, some salt and pepper, and to the outside of it, by a string forced through a pierced hole, he fastened a plate, which could be released, and which was his woodland table. It was no trouble for him to secure the little food that he needed, and with a strange, almost religious dignity, he had no hesitation in asking for that much. By degrees his hair became longer and longer, his once black hat became an earthen brown, and his clothes threadbare and dusty.

For all of three years he walked, and none knew how wide were his perambulations, nor how he survived the storms and cold. They could not see him, with homely rural understanding and forethought, sheltering himself in haycocks, or by the sides of cattle, whose warm bodies protected him from the cold, and whose dull understandings were not opposed to his harmless presence. Overhanging rocks and trees kept him at times from the rain, and a friendly hay-loft or corn-crib was not above his humble consideration.

The involute progression of hallucination is strange. From asking at doors and being constantly rebuffed or denied, he finally came to the conclusion that although his Phœbe might not be in any of the houses at the doors of which he inquired, she might nevertheless be within the sound of his voice. And so, from patient inquiry, he began to call sad, occasional cries, that ever and anon waked the quiet landscapes and ragged hill regions, and set to echoing his thin "O-o-o Phœbe! O-o-o Phœbe!" It had a pathetic, albeit insane, ring, and many a farmer or plowboy came to know it even from afar and say, "There goes old Reifsneider."

Another thing that puzzled him greatly after a time and after many hundreds of inquiries was, when he no longer had any particular dooryard in view and no special inquiry to make, which way to go. These cross-roads, which occasionally led in four or even six directions, came after a time to puzzle him. But to solve this knotty problem, which became more and more of a puzzle, there came to his aid another hallucination. Phœbe's spirit or some power of the air or wind or nature would tell him. If he stood at the center of the parting of the ways, closed his eyes, turned thrice about, and called "O-o-o Phœbe!" twice, and then threw his cane straight before him, that would surely indicate which way to go, for Phœbe, or one of these mystic powers would surely govern its direction and fall! In whichever direction it went, even though, as was not infrequently the case, it took him back along the path he had already come, or across fields, he was not so far gone in his mind but that he gave himself ample time to search before he called again. Also the hallucination seemed to persist that at some time he would surely find her. There were hours when his feet were sore, and his limbs weary, when he would stop in the heat to wipe his seamed brow, or in the cold to beat his arms. Sometimes, after throwing away his cane, and finding it indicating the direction from which he had just come, he would shake his head wearily and philosophically, as if contemplating the unbelievable or an untoward fate, and then start briskly off. His strange figure came finally to be known in the farthest reaches of three or four counties. Old Reifsneider was a pathetic character. His fame was wide.

Near a little town called Watersville, in Green County, perhaps four miles from that minor center of human activity, there was a place or precipice locally known as the Red Cliff, a sheer wall of red sandstone, perhaps a hundred feet high, which raised its sharp face for half a mile or more above the fruitful cornfields and orchards that lay beneath, and which was surmounted by a thick grove of trees. The slope that slowly led up to it from the opposite side was covered by a rank growth of beech, hickory, and ash, through which threaded a number of wagon-tracks crossing at various angles. In fair weather it had become old Reifsneider's habit, so inured was he by now to the open, to make his bed in some such patch of trees as this, to fry his bacon or boil his eggs at the foot of some tree, before laying himself down for the night. Occasionally, so light and inconsequential was his sleep, he would walk at night. More often, the moonlight or some sudden wind stirring in the trees or a reconnoitering animal arousing him, he would sit up and think, or pursue his quest in the moonlight or the dark, a strange, unnatural, half wild, half savage-looking but utterly harmless creature, calling at lonely road crossings, staring at dark and shuttered houses, and wondering where, where Phœbe could really be.

That particular lull that comes in the systole-diastole of this earthly ball at two o'clock in the morning invariably aroused him, and though he might not go any farther he would sit up and contemplate the darkness or the stars, wondering. Sometimes in the strange processes of his mind he would fancy that he saw moving among the trees the figure of his lost wife, and then he would get up to follow, taking his utensils, always on a string, and his cane. If she seemed to evade him too easily he would run, or plead, or, suddenly losing track of the fancied figure, stand awed or disappointed, grieving for the moment over the almost insurmountable difficulties of his search.

It was in the seventh year of these hopeless peregrinations, in the dawn of a similar springtime to that in which his wife had died, that he came at last one night to the vicinity of this selfsame patch that crowned the rise to the Red Cliff. His far-flung cane, used as a divining-rod at the last cross-roads, had brought him hither. He had walked many, many miles. It was after ten o'clock at night, and he was very weary. Long wandering and little eating had left him but a shadow of his former self. It was a question now not so much of physical strength but of spiritual endurance which kept him up. He had scarcely eaten this day, and now, exhausted, he set himself down in the dark to rest and possibly to sleep.

Curiously on this occasion a strange suggestion of the presence of his wife surrounded him. It would not be long now, he counseled with himself, although the long months had brought him nothing, until he should see her, talk to her. He fell asleep after a time, his head on his knees. At midnight the moon began to rise, and at two in the morning, his wakeful hour, was a large silver disk shining through the trees to the east. He opened his eyes when the radiance became strong, making a silver pattern at his feet and lighting the woods with strange lusters and silvery, shadowy forms. As usual, his old notion that his wife must be near occurred to him on this occasion, and he looked about him with a speculative, anticipatory eye. What was it that moved in the distant shadows along the path by which he had entered—a pale, flickering will-o'-the-wisp that bobbed gracefully among the trees and riveted his expectant gaze? Moonlight and shadows combined to give it a strange form and a stranger reality, this fluttering of bog-fire or dancing of wandering fireflies. Was it truly his lost Phœbe? By a circuitous route it passed about him, and in his fevered state he fancied that he could see the very eyes of her, not as she was when he last saw her in the black dress and shawl, but now a strangely younger Phœbe, gayer, sweeter, the one whom he had known years before as a girl. Old Reifsneider got up. He had been expecting and dreaming of this hour all these years, and now as he saw the feeble light dancing lightly before him he peered at it questioningly, one thin hand in his gray hair.

Of a sudden there came to him now for the first time in many years the full charm of her girlish figure as he had known it in boyhood, the pleasing, sympathetic smile, the brown hair, the blue sash she had once worn about her waist at a picnic, her gay, graceful movements. He walked around the base of the tree, straining with his eyes, forgetting for once his cane and utensils, and following eagerly after. On she moved before him, a will-o'-the-wisp of the spring, a little flame above her head, and it seemed as though among the small saplings of ash and beech and the thick trunks of hickory and elm that she signaled with a young, a lightsome hand.

"Oh, Phœbe! Phœbe!" he called. "Have yuh really come? Have yuh really answered me?" And hurrying faster, he fell once, scrambling lamely to his feet, only to see the light in the distance dancing illusively on. On and on he hurried until he was fairly running, brushing his ragged arms against the trees striking his hands and face against impeding twigs. His hat was gone, his lungs were breathless, his reason quite astray, when coming to the edge of the cliff he saw her below among a silvery bed of apple trees now blooming in the spring.

"Oh, Phœbe!" he called. "Oh, Phœbe! Oh, no, don't leave me!" And feeling the lure of a world where love was young and Phœbe, as this vision presented her, a delightful epitome of their quondam youth, he gave a gay cry of "Oh, wait, Phœbe!" and leaped.

Some farmer-boys, reconnoitering this region of bounty and prospect some few days afterward, found first the tin utensils tied together under the tree where he had left them, and then later at the foot of the cliff, pale, broken, but elate, a molded smile of peace and delight upon his lips, his body. His old hat was discovered lying under some low-growing saplings, the twigs of which had held it back. No one of all the simple population knew how eagerly and joyously he had found his lost mate.

WILLA CATHER

[1873–1947]

Paul's Case

(First published in *McClure's Magazine*, 1905; first book publication in 1905.)

It was Paul's afternoon to appear before the faculty of the Pittsburgh High School to account for his various misdemeanors. He had been suspended a week ago, and his father had called at the Principal's office and confessed his perplexity about his son. Paul entered the faculty room suave and smiling. His clothes were a trifle outgrown, and the tan velvet on the collar of his open overcoat was frayed and worn; but for all that there was something of the dandy about him, and he wore an opal pin in his neatly knotted black four-in-hand, and a red carnation in his buttonhole. This latter adornment the faculty somehow felt was not properly significant of the contrite spirit befitting a boy under the ban of suspension.

Paul was tall for his age and very thin, with high, cramped shoulders and a narrow chest. His eyes were remarkable for a certain hysterical brilliancy, and he continually used them in a conscious, theatrical sort of way, peculiarly offensive in a boy. The pupils were abnormally large, as though he were addicted to belladonna, but there was a glassy glitter about them which that drug does not produce.

When questioned by the Principal as to why he was there, Paul stated, politely enough, that he wanted to come back to school. This was a lie, but Paul was quite accustomed to lying; found it, indeed, indispensable for overcoming friction. His teachers were asked to state their respective charges against him, which they did with such a rancor and aggrievedness as evinced that this was not a usual case. Disorder and impertinence were among the offenses named, yet each of his instructors felt that it was scarcely possible to put into words the real cause of the trouble which lay in a sort of hysterically defiant manner of the boy's; in the contempt which they all knew he felt for them, and which he seemingly made not the least effort to conceal. Once, when he had been making a synopsis of a paragraph at the blackboard, his English teacher had stepped to his side and attempted to guide his hand. Paul had started back with a shudder and thrust his hands violently behind him. The astonished woman could scarcely have been more hurt and embarrassed had he struck at her. The insult was so involuntary and definitely personal as to be unforgettable. In one way and another, he had made all his teachers, men and women alike, conscious of the same feeling of physical aversion. In one class he habitually sat with his hand shading his eyes; in another he always looked out of the window during the recitation; in another he made a running commentary on the lecture, with humorous intent.

His teachers felt this afternoon that his whole attitude was symbolized by his shrug and his flippantly red carnation flower, and they fell upon him without mercy, his English teacher leading the pack. He stood through it smiling, his pale lips parted over his white teeth. (His lips were continually twitching, and he had a habit of raising his eyebrows that was contemptuous and irritating to the last degree.) Older boys than Paul had broken down and shed tears under that ordeal, but his set smile did not once desert him, and his only sign of discomfort was the nervous trembling of the fingers that toyed with the buttons of his overcoat, and an occasional jerking of the other hand which held his hat. Paul was always smiling, always glancing about him, seeming to feel that people might be watching him and trying to detect something. This conscious expression, since it was as far as possible from boyish mirthfulness, was usually attributed to insolence or "smartness."

As the inquisition proceeded, one of his instructors repeated an impertinent remark of the boy's, and the Principal asked him whether he thought that a courteous speech to make to a woman. Paul shrugged his shoulders slightly and his eyebrows twitched.

"I don't know," he replied. "I didn't mean to be polite or impolite, either. I guess it's a sort of way I have, of saying things regardless."

The Principal asked him whether he didn't think that a way it would be well to get rid of. Paul grinned and said he guessed so. When he was told that he could go, he bowed gracefully and went out. His bow was like a repetition of the scandalous red carnation.

His teachers were in despair, and his drawing master voiced the feeling of them all when he declared there was something about the boy which none of them understood. He added: "I don't really believe that smile of his comes altogether from insolence; there's something sort of haunted about it. The boy is not strong, for one thing. There is something wrong about the fellow."

The drawing master had come to realize that, in looking at Paul, one saw only his white teeth and the forced animation of his eyes. One warm afternoon the boy had gone to sleep at his drawing board, and his master had noted with amazement what a white, blue-veined face it was; drawn and wrinkled like an old man's about the eyes, the lips twitching even in his sleep.

His teachers left the building dissatisfied and unhappy; humiliated to have felt so vindictive toward a mere boy, to have uttered this feeling in cutting terms, and to have set each other on, as it were, in the gruesome game of intemperate reproach. One of them remembered having seen a miserable street cat set at bay by a ring of tormentors.

As for Paul, he ran down the hill whistling the Soldiers' Chorus from *Faust*, looking wildly behind him now and then to see whether some of his teachers were not there to witness his light-heartedness. As it was now late in the afternoon and Paul was on duty that evening as usher at Carnegie Hall, he decided that he would not go home to supper.

When he reached the concert hall the doors were not yet open. It was chilly outside, and he decided to go up into the picture gallery—always deserted at this hour—where there were some of Raffelli's gay studies of Paris streets and an airy blue Venetian scene or two that always exhilarated him. He was delighted to find no one in the gallery but the old guard, who sat in the corner, a newspaper on his knee, a black patch over one eye and the other closed. Paul possessed himself of the place and walked confidently up and down, whistling under his breath. After a while he sat down before a blue Rico and lost himself. When he bethought him to look at his watch, it was after seven o'clock, and he rose with a start and ran downstairs, making a face at Augustus Cæsar, peering out from the cast-room, and an evil gesture at the Venus of Milo as he passed her on the stairway.

When Paul reached the ushers' dressing-room half a dozen boys were there already, and he began excitedly to tumble into his uniform. It was one of the few that at all approached fitting, and Paul thought it very becoming—though he knew the tight, straight coat accentuated his narrow chest, about which he was exceedingly sensitive. He was always excited while he dressed, twanging all over to the tuning of the strings and the preliminary flourishes of the horns in the music-room; but tonight he seemed quite beside himself, and he teased and plagued the boys until, telling him that he was crazy, they put him down on the floor and sat on him.

Somewhat calmed by his suppression, Paul dashed out to the front of the house to seat the early comers. He was a model usher. Gracious and smiling he ran up and down the aisles. Nothing was too much trouble for him; he carried messages and brought programs as though it were his greatest pleasure in life, and all the people in his section thought him a charming boy, feeling that he remembered and admired them. As the house filled, he grew more and more vivacious and animated, and the color came to his cheeks and lips. It was very much as though this were a great reception and Paul were the host. Just as the musicians came out to take their places, his English teacher arrived with checks for the seats which a prominent manufacturer had taken for the season. She betrayed some embarrassment when she handed Paul the tickets, and a *hauteur* which subsequently made her feel very foolish. Paul was startled for a moment, and had the feeling of wanting to put her out; what business had she here among all these fine people and gay colors? He looked her over and decided that she was not appropriately dressed and must be a fool to sit downstairs in such togs. The tickets had probably been sent her out of kindness, he reflected, as he put down a seat for her, and she had about as much right to sit there as he had.

When the symphony began Paul sank into one of the rear seats with a long sigh of relief, and lost himself as he had done before the Rico. It was not that symphonies, as such, meant anything in particular to Paul, but the first sigh of the instruments seemed to free some hilarious spirit within him; something that struggled there like the Genius in the bottle found by the Arab fisherman. He felt a sudden zest of life; the lights danced before his eyes and the concert hall blazed into unimaginable splendor. When the soprano soloist came on, Paul forgot even the nastiness of his teacher's being there, and gave himself up to the peculiar intoxication such personages always had for him. The soloist chanced to be a German woman, by no means in her first youth, and the mother of many children; but she wore a satin gown and a tiara, and she had that indefinable air of achievement, that world-shine upon her, which always blinded Paul to any possible defects.

After a concert was over, Paul was often irritable and wretched until he got to sleep,—and tonight he was even more than usually restless. He had the feeling of not being able to let down; of its being impossible to give up this delicious excitement which was the only thing that could be called living at all. During the last number he withdrew and, after hastily changing his clothes in the dressing-room, slipped out to the side door where the singer's carriage stood. Here he began pacing rapidly up and down the walk, waiting to see her come out.

Over yonder the Schenley, in its vacant stretch, loomed big and square through the fine rain, the windows of its twelve stories glowing like those of a lighted cardboard house under a Christmas tree. All the actors and singers of any importance stayed there when they were in the city, and a number of the big manufacturers of the place lived there in the winter. Paul had often hung about the hotel, watching the people go in and out, longing to enter and leave schoolmasters and dull care behind him forever.

At last the singer came out, accompanied by the conductor, who helped her into her carriage and closed the door with a cordial *auf wiedersehen*,—which set Paul to wondering whether she were not an old sweetheart of his. Paul followed the carriage over to the hotel, walking so rapidly as not to be far from the entrance when the singer alighted and disappeared behind the swinging glass doors which were opened by a Negro in a tall hat and a long coat. In the moment that the door was ajar, it seemed to Paul that he, too, entered. He seemed to feel himself go after her up the steps, into the warm, lighted building, into an exotic, a tropical world of shiny, glistening surfaces and basking ease. He reflected upon the mysterious dishes that were brought into the dining-room, the green bottles in buckets of ice, as he had seen them in the supper party pictures of the Sunday supplement. A quick gust of wind brought the rain down with sudden vehemence, and Paul was startled to find that he was still outside in the slush of the gravel driveway; that his boots were letting in the water and his scanty overcoat was clinging wet about him; that the lights in front of the concert hall were out, and that the rain was driving in sheets between him and the orange glow of the windows above him. There it was, what he wanted—tangibly before him, like the fairy world of a Christmas pantomime; as the rain beat in his face, Paul wondered whether he were destined always to shiver in the black night outside, looking up at it.

He turned and walked reluctantly toward the car tracks. The end had to come some time; his father in his night-clothes at the top of the stairs, explanations that did not explain, hastily improvised fictions that were forever tripping him up, his upstairs room and its horrible yellow wall-paper, the creaking bureau with the greasy plush collar-box, and over his painted wooden bed the pictures of George Washington and John Calvin, and the framed motto, "Feed my Lambs," which had been worked in red worsted by his mother, whom Paul could not remember.

Half an hour later, Paul alighted from the Negley Avenue car and went slowly down one of the side streets off the main thoroughfare. It was a highly respectable street, where all the houses were exactly alike, and where business men of moderate means begot and reared large families of children, all of whom went to Sabbath-school and learned the shorter catechism, and were interested in arithmetic; all of whom were as exactly alike as their homes, and of a piece with the monotony in which they lived. Paul never went up Cordelia Street without a shudder of loathing. His home was next the house of the Cumberland minister. He approached it tonight with the nerveless sense of defeat, the hopeless feeling of sinking back forever into ugliness and commonness that he had always had when he came home. The moment he turned into Cordelia Street he felt the waters close above his head. After each of these orgies of living, he experienced all the physical depression which follows a debauch; the loathing of respectable beds, of common food, of a house permeated by kitchen odors; a shuddering repulsion for the flavorless, colorless mass of everyday existence; a morbid desire for cool things and soft lights and fresh flowers.

The nearer he approached the house, the more absolutely unequal Paul felt to the sight of it all; his ugly sleeping chamber; the cold bathroom with the grimy zinc tub, the cracked mirror, the dripping spiggots; his father, at the top of the stairs, his hairy legs sticking out from his nightshirt, his feet thrust into carpet slippers. He was so much later than usual that there would certainly be inquiries and reproaches. Paul stopped short before the door. He felt that he could not be accosted by his father tonight; that he could not toss again on that miserable bed. He would not go in. He would tell his father that he had no car fare, and it was raining so hard he had gone home with one of the boys and stayed all night.

Meanwhile, he was wet and cold. He went around to the back of the house and tried one of the basement windows, found it open, raised it cautiously, and scrambled down the cellar wall to the floor. There he stood, holding his breath, terrified by the noise he had made; but the floor above him was silent, and there was no creak on the stairs. He found a soap-box, and carried it over to the soft ring of light that streamed from the furnace door, and sat down. He was horribly afraid of rats, so he did not try to sleep, but sat looking distrustfully at the dark, still terrified lest he might have awakened his father. In such reactions, after one of the experiences which made days and nights out of the dreary blanks of the calendar, when his senses were deadened, Paul's head was always singularly clear. Suppose his father had heard him getting in at the window and had come down and shot him for a burglar? Then, again, suppose his father had come down, pistol in hand, and he had cried out in time to save himself, and his father had been horrified to think how nearly he had killed him? Then, again, suppose a day should come when his father would remember that night, and wish there had been no warning cry to stay his hand? With this last supposition Paul entertained himself until daybreak.

The following Sunday was fine; the sodden November chill was broken by the last flash of autumnal summer. In the morning Paul had to go to church and Sabbath-school, as always. On seasonable Sunday afternoons the burghers of Cordelia Street usually sat out on their front "stoops," and talked to their neighbors on the next stoop, or called to those across the street in neighborly fashion. The men sat placidly on gay cushions placed upon the steps that led down to the sidewalk, while the women, in their Sunday "waists," sat in rockers on the cramped porches, pretending to be greatly at their ease. The children played in the streets; there were so many of them that the place resembled the recreation grounds of a kindergarten. The men on the steps—all in their shirt sleeves, their vests unbuttoned—sat with their legs well apart, their stomachs comfortably protruding, and talked of the prices of things, or told anecdotes of the sagacity of their various chiefs and overlords. They occasionally looked over the multitude of squabbling children, listened affectionately to their high-pitched, nasal voices, smiling to see their own proclivities reproduced in their offspring, and interspersed their legends of the iron kings with remarks about their sons' progress at school, their grades in arithmetic, and the amounts they had saved in their toy banks. On this last Sunday of November, Paul sat all the afternoon on the lowest step of his "stoop," staring into the street, while his sisters, in their rockers, were talking to the minister's daughters next door about how many shirtwaists they had made in the last week, and how many waffles someone had eaten at the last church supper. When the weather was warm, and his father was in a particularly jovial frame of mind, the girls made lemonade, which was always brought out in a red-glass pitcher, ornamented with forget-me-nots in blue enamel. This the girls thought very fine, and the neighbors joked about the suspicious color of the pitcher.

Today Paul's father, on the top step, was talking to a young man who shifted a restless baby from knee to knee. He happened to be the young man who was daily held up to Paul as a model, and after whom it was his father's dearest hope that he would pattern. This young man was of a ruddy complexion, with a compressed, red mouth, and faded, near-sighted eyes, over which he wore thick spectacles, with gold bows that curved about his ears. He was clerk to one of the magnates of a great steel corporation, and was looked upon in Cordelia Street as a young man with a future. There was a story that, some five years ago—he was now barely twenty-six—he had been a trifle 'dissipated,' but in order to curb his appetites and save the loss of time and strength that a sowing of wild oats might have entailed, he had taken his chief's advice, oft reiterated to his employees, and at twenty-one had married the first woman whom he could persuade to share his fortunes. She happened to be an angular school mistress, much older than he, who also wore thick glasses, and who had now borne him four children, all near-sighted, like herself.

The young man was relating how his chief, now cruising in the Mediterranean, kept in touch with all the details of the business, arranging his office hours on his yacht just as though he were at home, and "knocking off work enough to keep two stenographers busy." His father told, in turn, the plan his corporation was considering, of putting in an electric railway plant at Cairo. Paul snapped his teeth; he had an awful apprehension that they might spoil it all before he got there. Yet he rather liked to hear these legends of the iron kings, that were told and retold on Sundays and holidays; these stories of palaces in Venice, yachts on the Mediterranean, and high play at Monte Carlo appealed to his fancy, and he was interested in the triumphs of cash boys who had become famous, though he had no mind for the cash-boy stage.

After supper was over, and he had helped to dry the dishes, Paul nervously asked his father whether he could go to George's to get some help in his geometry, and still more nervously asked for car fare. This latter request he had to repeat, as his father, on principle, did not like to hear requests for money, whether much or little. He asked Paul whether he could not go to some boy who lived nearer, and told him that he ought not to leave his school work until Sunday; but he gave him the dime. He was not a poor man, but he had a worthy ambition to come up in the world. His only reason for allowing Paul to usher was that he thought a boy ought to be earning a little.

Paul bounded upstairs, scrubbed the greasy odor of the dishwater from his hands with the ill-smelling soap he hated, and then shook over his fingers a few drops of violet water from the bottle he kept hidden in his drawer. He left the house with his geometry conspicuously under his arm, and the moment he got out of Cordelia Street and boarded a downtown car, he shook off the lethargy of two deadening days, and began to live again.

The leading juvenile of the permanent stock company which played at one of the downtown theaters was an acquaintance of Paul's, and the boy had been invited to drop in at the Sunday night rehearsals whenever he could. For more than a year Paul had spent every available moment loitering about Charley Edwards's dressing-room. He had won a place among Edwards's following not only because the young actor, who could not afford to employ a dresser, often found him useful, but because he recognized in Paul something akin to what churchmen term "vocation."

It was at the theater and at Carnegie Hall that Paul really lived; the rest was but a sleep and a forgetting. This was Paul's fairy tale, and it had for him all the allurement of a secret love. The moment he inhaled, the gassy, painty, dusty odor behind the scenes, he breathed like a prisoner set free, and felt within him the possibility of doing or saying splendid, brilliant things. The moment the cracked orchestra beat out the overture from *Martha*, or jerked at the serenade from *Rigoletto*, all stupid and ugly things slid from him, and his senses were deliciously, yet delicately fired.

Perhaps it was because, in Paul's world, the natural nearly always wore the guise of ugliness, that a certain element of artificiality seemed to him necessary in beauty. Perhaps it was because his experience of life elsewhere was so full of Sabbath-school picnics, petty economies, wholesome advice as to how to succeed in life, and the unescapable odors of cooking, that he found this existence so alluring, these smartly-clad men and women so attractive, that he was so moved by these starry apple orchards that bloomed perennially under the limelight.

It would be difficult to put it strongly enough how convincingly the stage entrance of that theater was for Paul the actual portal of Romance. Certainly none of the company ever suspected it, least of all Charley Edwards. It was very like the old stories that used to float about London of fabulously rich Jews, who had subterranean halls, with palms, and fountains, and soft lamps and richly apparelled women who never saw the disenchanting light of London day. So, in the midst of that smoke-palled city, enamored of figures and grimy toil, Paul had his secret temple, his wishing-carpet, his bit of blue-and-white Mediterranean shore bathed in perpetual sunshine.

Several of Paul's teachers had a theory that his imagination had been perverted by garish fiction; but the truth was, he scarcely ever read at all.

The books at home were not such as would either tempt or corrupt a youthful mind, and as for reading the novels that some of his friends urged upon him—well, he got what he wanted much more quickly from music; any sort of music, from an orchestra to a barrel organ. He needed only the spark, the indescribable thrill that made his imagination master of his senses, and he could make plots and pictures enough of his own. It was equally true that he was not stage-struck—not, at any rate, in the usual acceptation of that expression. He had no desire to become an actor, any more than he had to become a musician. He felt no necessity to do any of these things; what he wanted was to see, to be in the atmosphere, float on the wave of it, to be carried out, blue league after blue league, away from everything.

After a night behind the scenes, Paul found the school-room more than ever repulsive; the bare floors and naked walls; the prosy men who never wore frock coats, or violets in their buttonholes; the women with their dull gowns, shrill voices, and pitiful seriousness about prepositions that govern the dative. He could not bear to have the other pupils think, for a moment, that he took these people seriously; he must convey to them that he considered it all trivial, and was there only by way of a joke, anyway. He had autograph pictures of all the members of the stock company which he showed his classmates, telling them the most incredible stories of his familiarity with these people, of his acquaintance with the soloists who came to Carnegie Hall, his suppers with them and the flowers he sent them. When these stories lost their effect, and his audience grew listless, he would bid all the boys good-by, announcing that he was going to travel for a while; going to Naples, to California, to Egypt. Then, next Monday, he would slip back, conscious and nervously smiling; his sister was ill, and he would have to defer his voyage until spring.

Matters went steadily worse with Paul at school. In the itch to let his instructors know how heartily he despised them, and how thoroughly he was appreciated elsewhere, he mentioned once or twice that he had no time to fool with theorems; adding—with a twitch of the eyebrows and a touch of that nervous bravado which so perplexed them—that he was helping the people down at the stock company; they were old friends of his.

The upshot of the matter was, that the Principal went to Paul's father, and Paul was taken out of school and put to work. The manager at Carnegie Hall was told to get another usher in his stead; the doorkeeper at the theater was warned not to admit him to the house; and Charley Edwards remorsefully promised the boy's father not to see him again.

The members of the stock company were vastly amused when some of Paul's stories reached them—especially the women. They were hardworking women, most of them supporting indolent husbands or brothers, and they laughed rather bitterly at having stirred the boy to such fervid and florid inventions. They agreed with the faculty and with his father, that Paul's was a bad case.

The east-bound train was plowing through a January snowstorm; the dull dawn was beginning to show gray when the engine whistled a mile out of Newark. Paul started up from the seat where he had lain curled in uneasy slumber, rubbed the breath-misted window glass with his hand, and peered out. The snow was whirling in curling eddies above the white bottom lands, and the drifts lay already deep in the fields and along the fences, while here and there the long dead grass and dried weed stalks protruded black above it. Lights shone from the scattered houses, and a gang of laborers who stood beside the track waved their lanterns.

Paul had slept very little, and he felt grimy and uncomfortable. He had made the all-night journey in a day coach because he was afraid if he took a Pullman he might be seen by some Pittsburgh business man who had noticed him in Denny & Carson's office. When the whistle woke him, he clutched quickly at his breast pocket, glancing about him with an uncertain smile. But the little, clay-bespattered Italians were still sleeping, the slatternly women across the aisle were in open-mouthed oblivion, and even the crumby, crying babies were for the nonce stilled. Paul settled back to struggle with his impatience as best he could.

When he arrived at the Jersey City station, he hurried through his breakfast, manifestly ill at ease and keeping a sharp eye about him. After he reached the Twenty-third Street station, he consulted a cabman, and had himself driven to a men's furnishing establishment which was just opening for the day. He spent upward of two hours there, buying with endless reconsidering and great care. His new street suit he put on in the fitting-room; the frock coat and dress clothes he had bundled into the cab with his new shirts. Then he drove to a hatter's and a shoe house. His next errand was at Tiffany's, where he selected silver-mounted brushes and a scarf-pin. He would not wait to have his silver marked, he said. Lastly, he stopped at a trunk shop on Broadway, and had his purchases packed into various traveling bags.

It was a little after one o'clock when he drove up to the Waldorf, and, after settling with the cabman, went into the office. He registered from Washington; said his mother and father had been abroad, and that he had come down to await the arrival of their steamer. He told his story plausibly and had no trouble, since he offered to pay for them in advance, in engaging his rooms; a sleeping-room, sitting room and bath.

Not once, but a hundred times Paul had planned this entry into New York. He had gone over every detail of it with Charley Edwards, and in his scrap book at home there were pages of description about New York hotels, cut from the Sunday papers.

When he was shown to his sitting room on the eighth floor, he saw at a glance that everything was as it should be; there was but one detail in his mental picture that the place did not realize, so he rang for the bell boy and sent him down for flowers. He moved about nervously until the boy returned, putting away his new linen and fingering it delightedly as he did so. When the flowers came, he put them hastily into water, and then tumbled into a hot bath. Presently he came out of his white bathroom, resplendent in his new silk underwear, and playing with the tassels of his red robe. The snow was whirling so fiercely outside his windows that he could scarcely see across the street; but within, the air was deliciously soft and fragrant. He put the violets and jonquils on the tabouret beside the couch, and threw himself down with a long sigh, covering himself with a Roman blanket. He was thoroughly tired; he had been in such haste, he had stood up to such a strain, covered so much ground in the last twenty-four hours, that he wanted to think how it had all come about. Lulled by the sound of the wind, the warm air, and the cool fragrance of the flowers, he sank into deep, drowsy retrospection.

It had been wonderfully simple; when they had shut him out of the theater and concert hall, when they had taken away his bone, the whole thing was virtually determined. The rest was a mere matter of opportunity. The only thing that at all surprised him was his own courage—for he realized well enough that he had always been tormented by fear, a sort of apprehensive dread that, of late years, as the meshes of the lies he had told closed about him, had been pulling the muscles of his body tighter and tighter. Until now, he could not remember a time when he had not been dreading something. Even when he was a little boy, it was always there—behind him, or before, or on either side. There had always been the shadowed corner, the dark place into which he dared not look, but from which something seemed always to be watching him—and Paul had done things that were not pretty to watch, he knew.

But now he had a curious sense of relief, as though he had at last thrown down the gauntlet to the thing in the corner.

Yet it was but a day since he had been sulking in the traces; but yesterday afternoon that he had been sent to the bank with Denny & Carson's deposit, as usual—but this time he was instructed to leave the book to be balanced. There was above two thousand dollars in checks, and nearly a thousand in the bank notes which he had taken from the book and quietly transferred to his pocket. At the bank he had made out a new deposit slip. His nerves had been steady enough to permit of his returning to the office, where he had finished his work and asked for a full day's holiday tomorrow, Saturday, giving a perfectly reasonable pretext. The bank book, he knew, would not be returned before Monday or Tuesday, and his father would be out of town for the next week. From the time he slipped the bank notes into his pocket until he boarded the night train for New York, he had not known a moment's hesitation.

How astonishingly easy it had all been; here he was, the thing done; and this time there would be no awakening, no figure at the top of the stairs. He watched the snowflakes whirling by his window until he fell asleep.

When he awoke, it was four o'clock in the afternoon. He bounded up with a start; one of his precious days gone already! He spent nearly an hour in dressing, watching every stage of his toilet carefully in the mirror. Everything was quite perfect; he was exactly the kind of boy he had always wanted to be.

When he went downstairs, Paul took a carriage and drove up Fifth avenue toward the Park. The snow had somewhat abated; carriages and tradesmen's wagons were hurrying soundlessly to and fro in the winter twilight; boys in woolen mufflers were shoveling off the doorsteps; the avenue stages made fine spots of color against the white street. Here and there on the corners whole flower gardens blooming behind glass windows, against which the snow flakes stuck and melted; violets, roses, carnations, lilies of the valley—somehow vastly more lovely and alluring that they blossomed thus unnaturally in the snow. The Park itself was a wonderful stage winter-piece.

When he returned, the pause of the twilight had ceased, and the tune of the streets had changed. The snow was falling faster, lights streamed from the hotels that reared their many stories fearlessly up into the storm, defying the raging Atlantic winds. A long, black stream of carriages poured down the avenue, intersected here and there by other streams, tending horizontally. There were a score of cabs about the entrance of his hotel, and his driver had to wait. Boys in livery were running in and out of the awning stretched across the sidewalk, up and down the red velvet carpet laid from the door to the street. Above, about, within it all, was the rumble and roar, the hurry and toss of thousands of human beings as hot for pleasure as himself, and on every side of him towered the glaring affirmation of the omnipotence of wealth.

The boy set his teeth and drew his shoulders together in a spasm of realization; the plot of all dramas, the text of all romances, the nerve-stuff of all sensations was whirling about him like the snowflakes. He burnt like a faggot in a tempest.

When Paul came down to dinner, the music of the orchestra floated up the elevator shaft to greet him. As he stepped into the thronged corridor, he sank back into one of the chairs against the wall to get his breath. The lights, the chatter, the perfumes, the bewildering medley of color—he had, for a moment, the feeling of not being able to stand it. But only for a moment; these were his own people, he told himself. He went slowly about the corridors, through the writing-rooms, smoking-rooms, reception-rooms, as though he were exploring the chambers of an enchanted palace, built and peopled for him alone.

When he reached the dining room he sat down at a table near a window. The flowers, the white linen, the many-colored wine glasses, the gay toilettes of the women, the low popping of corks, the undulating repetitions of the *Blue Danube* from the orchestra, all flooded Paul's dream with bewildering radiance. When the roseate tinge of his champagne was added—that cold, precious, bubbling stuff that creamed and foamed in his glass—Paul wondered that there were honest men in the world at all. This was what all the world was fighting for, he reflected; this was what all the struggle was about. He doubted the reality of his past. Had he ever known a place called Cordelia Street, a place where fagged-looking business men boarded the early car? Mere rivets in a machine they seemed to Paul,—sickening men, with combings of children's hair always hanging to their coats, and the smell of cooking in their clothes. Cordelia Street—Ah, that belonged to another time and country! Had he not always been thus, had he not sat here night after night, from as far back as he could remember, looking pensively over just such shimmering textures, and slowly twirling the stem of a glass like this one between his thumb and middle finger? He rather thought he had.

He was not in the least abashed or lonely. He had no especial desire to meet or to know any of these people; all he demanded was the right to look on and conjecture, to watch the pageant. The mere stage properties were all he contended for. Nor was he lonely later in the evening, in his loge at the Opera. He was entirely rid of his nervous misgivings, of his forced aggressiveness, of the imperative desire to show himself different from his surroundings. He felt now that his surroundings explained him. Nobody questioned the purple; he had only to wear it passively. He had only to glance down at his dress coat to reassure himself that here it would be impossible for anyone to humiliate him.

He found it hard to leave his beautiful sitting room to go to bed that night, and sat long watching the raging storm from his turret window. When he went to sleep, it was with the lights turned on in his bedroom; partly because of his old timidity, and partly so that, if he should wake in the night, there would be no wretched moment of doubt, no horrible suspicion of yellow wall-paper, or of Washington and Calvin above his bed.

On Sunday morning the city was practically snow-bound. Paul breakfasted late, and in the afternoon he fell in with a wild San Francisco boy, a freshman at Yale, who said he had run down for a "little flyer" over Sunday. The young man offered to show Paul the night side of the town, and the two boys went off together after dinner, not returning to the hotel until seven o'clock the next morning. They had started out in the confiding warmth of a champagne friendship, but their parting in the elevator was singularly cool. The freshman pulled himself together to make his train, and Paul went to bed. He awoke at two o'clock in the afternoon, very thirsty and dizzy, and rang for ice water, coffee, and the Pittsburgh papers.

On the part of the hotel management, Paul excited no suspicion. There was this to be said for him, that he wore his spoils with dignity and in no way made himself conspicuous. His chief greediness lay in his ears and eyes, and his excesses were not offensive ones. His dearest pleasures were the gray winter twilights in his sitting room; his quiet enjoyment of his flowers, his clothes, his wide divan, his cigarette and his sense of power. He could not remember a time when he had felt so at peace with himself. The mere release from the necessity of petty lying, lying every day and every day, restored his self-respect. He had never lied for pleasure, even at school; but to make himself noticed and admired, to assert his difference from other Cordelia Street boys; and he felt a good deal more manly, more honest, even, now that he had no need for boastful pretensions, now that he could, as his actor friends used to say, "dress the part." It was characteristic that remorse did not occur to him. His golden days went by without a shadow, and he made each as perfect as he could.

On the eighth day after his arrival in New York, he found the whole affair exploited in the Pittsburgh papers, exploited with a wealth of detail which indicated that local news of a sensational nature was at a low ebb. The firm of Denny & Carson announced that the boy's father had refunded the full amount of his theft, and that they had no intention of prosecuting. The Cumberland minister had been interviewed, and expressed his hope of yet reclaiming the motherless lad, and Paul's Sabbath-school teacher declared that she would spare no effort to that end. The rumor had reached Pittsburgh that the boy had been seen in a New York hotel, and his father had gone East to find him and bring him home.

Paul had just come in to dress for dinner; he sank into a chair, weak in the knees, and clasped his head in his hands. It was to be worse than jail, even; the tepid waters of Cordelia Street were to close over him finally and forever. The gray monotony stretched before him in hopeless, unrelieved years; Sabbath-school, Young People's Meeting, the yellow-papered room, the damp dish-towels; it all rushed back upon him with sickening vividness. He had the old feeling that the orchestra had suddenly stopped, the sinking sensation that the play was over. The sweat broke out on his face, and he sprang to his feet, looked about him with his white, conscious smile, and winked at himself in the mirror. With something of the childish belief in miracles with which he had so often gone to class, all his lessons unlearned, Paul dressed and dashed whistling down the corridor to the elevator.

He had no sooner entered the dining room and caught the measure of the music, than his remembrance was lightened by his old elastic power of claiming the moment, mounting with it, and finding it all sufficient. The glare and glitter about him, the mere scenic accessories had again, and for the last time, their old potency. He would show himself that he was game, he would finish the thing splendidly. He doubted, more than ever, the existence of Cordelia Street, and for the first time he drank his wine recklessly.

Was he not, after all, one of these fortunate beings? Was he not still himself, and in his own place? He drummed a nervous accompaniment to the music and looked about him, telling himself over and over that it had paid.

He reflected drowsily, to the swell of the violin and the chill sweetness of his wine, that he might have done it more wisely. He might have caught an outbound steamer and been well out of their clutches before now. But the other side of the world had seemed too far away and too uncertain then; he could not have waited for it; his need had been too sharp. If he had to choose over again, he would do the same thing tomorrow. He looked affectionately about the dining room, now gilded with a soft mist. Ah, it had paid indeed!

Paul was awakened next morning by a painful throbbing in his head and feet. He had thrown himself across the bed without undressing, and had slept with his shoes on. His limbs and hands were lead heavy, and his tongue and throat were parched. There came upon him one of those fateful attacks of clear-headedness that never occurred except when he was physically exhausted and his nerves hung loose. He lay still and closed his eyes and let the tide of realities wash over him.

His father was in New York; "stopping at some joint or other," he told himself. The memory of successive summers on the front stoop fell upon him like a weight of black water. He had not a hundred dollars left; and he knew now, more than ever, that money was everything, the wall that stood between all he loathed and all he wanted. The thing was winding itself up; he had thought of that on his first glorious day in New York, and had even provided a way to snap the thread. It lay on his dressing-table now; he had got it out last night when he came blindly up from dinner,—but the shiny metal hurt his eyes, and he disliked the look of it, anyway.

He rose and moved about with a painful effort, succumbing now and again to attacks of nausea. It was the old depression exaggerated; all the world had become Cordelia Street. Yet somehow he was not afraid of anything, was absolutely calm; perhaps because he had looked into the dark corner at last, and knew. It was bad enough, what he saw there; but somehow not so bad as his long fear of it had been. He saw everything clearly now. He had a feeling that he had made the best of it, that he had lived the sort of life he was meant to live, and for half an hour he sat staring at the revolver. But he told himself that was not the way, so he went downstairs and took a cab to the ferry.

When Paul arrived at Newark, he got off the train and took another cab, directing the driver to follow the Pennsylvania tracks out of the town. The snow lay heavy on the roadways and had drifted deep in the open fields. Only here and there the dead grass or dried weed stalks projected, singularly black, above it. Once well into the country, Paul dismissed the carriage and walked, floundering along the tracks, his mind a medley of irrelevant things. He seemed to hold in his brain an actual picture of everything he had seen that morning. He remembered every feature of both his drivers, the toothless old woman from whom he had bought the red flowers in his coat, the agent from whom he had got his ticket. and all of his fellow-passengers on the ferry. His mind, unable to cope with vital matters near at hand, worked feverishly and deftly at sorting and grouping these images. They made for him a part of the ugliness of the world, of the ache in his head, and the bitter burning on his tongue. He stooped and put a handful of snow into his mouth as he walked, but that, too, seemed hot. When he reached a little hillside, where the tracks ran through a cut some twenty feet below him, he stopped and sat down.

The carnations in his coat were drooping with the cold, he noticed; all their red glory over. It occurred to him that all the flowers he had seen in the show windows that first night must have gone the same way, long before this. It was only one splendid breath they had, in spite of their brave mockery at the winter outside the glass. It was a losing game in the end, it seemed, this revolt against the homilies by which the world is run. Paul took one of the blossoms carefully from his coat and scooped a little hole in the snow, where he covered it up. Then he dozed a while, from his weak condition, seeming insensible to the cold.

The sound of an approaching train woke him, and he started to his feet, remembering only his resolution, and afraid lest he should be too late. He stood watching the approaching locomotive, his teeth chattering, his lips drawn away from them in a frightened smile; once or twice he glanced nervously sidewise, as though he were being watched. When the right moment came, he jumped. As he fell, the folly of his haste occurred to him with merciless clearness, the vastness of what he had left undone. There flashed through his brain, clearer than ever before, the blue of Adriatic water, the yellow of Algerian sands.

He felt something strike his chest,—his body was being thrown swiftly through the air, on and on, immeasurably far and fast, while his limbs gently relaxed. Then, because the picture-making mechanism was crushed, the disturbing visions flashed into black, and Paul dropped back into the immense design of things.

JACK LONDON

[1876–1916]

To Build a Fire

(First published in *Century Magazine*, August, 1908; first book publication in 1910.)

DAY HAD BROKEN cold and gray, exceedingly cold and gray, when the man turned aside from the main Yukon trail and climbed the high earth-bank, where a dim and little-traveled trail led eastward through the fat spruce timberland. It was a steep bank, and he paused for breath at the top, excusing the act to himself by looking at his watch. It was nine o'clock. There was no sun nor hint of sun, though there was not a cloud in the sky. It was a clear day, and yet there seemed an intangible pall over the face of things, a subtle gloom that made the day dark, and that was due to the absence of sun. This fact did not worry the man. He was used to the lack of sun. It had been days since he had seen the sun, and he knew that a few more days must pass before that cheerful orb, due south, would just peep above the sky-line and dip immediately from view.

The man flung a look back along the way he had come. The Yukon lay a mile wide and hidden under three feet of ice. On top of this ice were as many feet of snow. It was all pure white, rolling in gentle, undulations where the ice-jams of the freeze-up had formed. North and south, as far as his eye could see, it was unbroken white, save for a dark hairline that curved and twisted from around the spruce-covered island to the south, and that curved and twisted away into the north, where it disappeared behind another spruce-covered island. This dark hair-line was the trail—the main trail—that led south five hundred miles to the Chilcoot Pass, Dyea, and salt water; and that led north seventy miles to Dawson, and still on to the north a thousand miles to Nulato, and finally to St. Michael on Bering Sea, a thousand miles and half a thousand more.

But all this—the mysterious, far-reaching hair-line trail, the absence of sun from the sky, the tremendous cold, and the strangeness and weirdness of it all—made no impression on the man. It was not because he was long used to it. He was a newcomer in the land, a *chechaquo*, and this was his first winter. The trouble with him was that he was without imagination. He was quick and alert in the things of life, but only in the things, and not in the significances. Fifty degrees below zero meant eighty-odd degrees of frost. Such fact impressed him as being cold and uncomfortable, and that was all. It did not lead him to meditate upon his frailty as a creature of temperature, and upon man's frailty in general, able only to live within certain narrow limits of heat and cold; and from there on it did not lead him to the conjectural field of immortality and man's place in the universe. Fifty degrees below zero stood for a bite of frost that hurt and that must be guarded against by the use of mittens, ear-flaps, warm moccasins, and thick socks. Fifty degrees below zero was to him just precisely fifty degrees below zero. That there should be anything more to it than that was a thought that never entered his head.

As he turned to go on, he spat speculatively. There was a sharp, explosive crackle that startled him. He spat again. And again, in the air, before it could fall to the snow, the spittle crackled. He knew that at fifty below spittle crackled on the snow, but this spittle had crackled in the air. Undoubtedly it was colder than fifty below—how much colder he did not know. But the temperature did not matter. He was bound for the old claim on the left fork of Henderson Creek, where the boys were already. They had come over across the divide from the Indian Creek country, while he had come the roundabout way to take a look at the possibilities of getting out logs in the spring from the islands in the Yukon. He would be in to camp by six o'clock; a bit after dark, it was true, but the boys would be there, a fire would be going, and a hot supper would he ready. As for lunch, he pressed his hand against the protruding bundle under his jacket. It was also under his shirt, wrapped up in a handkerchief and lying against the naked skin. It was the only way to keep the biscuits from freezing. He smiled agreeably to himself as he thought of those biscuits, each cut open and sopped in bacon grease, and each enclosing a generous slice of fried bacon.

He plunged in among the big spruce trees. The trail was faint. A foot of snow had fallen since the last sled had passed over, and he was glad he was without a sled, traveling light. In fact, he carried nothing but the lunch wrapped in the handkerchief. He was surprised, however, at the cold. It certainly was cold, he concluded, as he rubbed his numb nose and cheekbones with his mittened hand. He was a warm-whiskered man, but the hair on his face did not protect the high cheek-bones and the eager nose that thrust itself aggressively into the frosty air.

At the man's heels trotted a dog, a big native husky, the proper wolf-dog, gray-coated and without any visible or temperamental difference from its brother, the wild wolf. The animal was depressed by the tremendous cold. It knew that it was no time for traveling. Its instinct told it a truer tale than was told to the man by the man's judgment. In reality, it was not merely colder than fifty below zero; it was colder than sixty below, than seventy below. It was seventy-five below zero. Since the freezing point is thirty-two above zero, it meant that one hundred and seven degrees of frost obtained. The dog did not know anything about thermometers. Possibly in its brain there was no sharp consciousness of a condition of very cold such as was in the man's brain. But the brute had its instinct. It experienced a vague but menacing apprehension that subdued it and made it slink along at the man's heels, and that made it question eagerly every unwonted movement of the man as if expecting him to go into camp or to seek shelter somewhere and build a fire. The dog had learned fire, and it wanted fire, or else to burrow under the snow and cuddle its warmth away from the air.

The frozen moisture of its breathing had settled on its fur in a fine powder of frost, and especially were its jowls, muzzle, and eyelashes whitened by its crystalled breath. The man's red beard and mustache were likewise frosted, but more solidly, the deposit taking the form of ice and increasing with every warm, moist breath he exhaled. Also, the man was chewing tobacco, and the muzzle of ice held his lips so rigidly that he was unable to clear his chin when he expelled the juice. The result was that a crystal beard of the color and solidity of amber was increasing its length on his chin. If he fell down it would shatter itself, like glass, into brittle fragments. But he did not mind the appendage. It was the penalty all tobacco-chewers paid in that country, and he had been out before in two cold snaps. They had not been so cold as this, he knew, but by the spirit thermometer at Sixty Mile he knew they had been registered at fifty below and at fifty-five.

He held on through the level stretch of woods for several miles, crossed a wide flat of nigger-heads, and dropped down a bank to the frozen bed of a small stream. This was Henderson Creek, and he knew he was ten miles from the forks. He looked at his watch. It was ten o'clock. He was making four miles an hour, and he calculated that he would arrive at the forks at half-past twelve. He decided to celebrate that event by eating his lunch there.

The dog dropped in again at his heels, with a tail drooping discouragement, as the man swung along the creek-bed. The furrow of the old sled-trail was plainly visible, but a dozen inches of snow covered the marks of the last runners. In a month no man had come up or down that silent creek. The man held steadily on. He was not much given to thinking, and just then particularly he had nothing to think about save that he would eat lunch at the forks and that at six o'clock he would be in camp with the boys. There was nobody to talk to; and, had there been, speech would have been impossible because of the ice-muzzle on his mouth. So he continued monotonously to chew tobacco and to increase the length of his amber beard.

Once in a while the thought reiterated itself that it was very cold and that he had never experienced such cold. As he walked along he rubbed his check-bones and nose with the back of his mittened hand. He did this automatically, now and again changing hands. But rub as he would, the instant he stopped his cheek-bones went numb, and the following instant the end of his nose went numb. He was sure to frost his cheeks; he knew that, and experienced a pang of regret that he had not devised a nose-strap of the sort Bud wore in cold snaps. Such a strap passed across the cheeks, as well, and saved them. But it didn't matter much, after all. What were frosted cheeks? A bit painful, that was all; they were never serious.

Empty as the man's mind was of thoughts, he was keenly observant, and he noticed the changes in the creek, the curves and bends and timber-jams, and always he sharply noted where he placed his feet. Once, coming around a bend, he shied abruptly, like a startled horse, curved away from the place where he had been walking, and retreated several paces back along the trail. The creek he knew was frozen clear to the bottom,—no creek could contain water in that arctic winter,—but he knew also that there were springs that bubbled out from the hillsides and ran along under the snow and on top the ice of the creek. He knew that the coldest snaps never froze these springs, and he knew likewise their danger. They were traps. They hid pools of water under the snow that might be three inches deep, or three feet. Sometimes a skin of ice half an inch thick covered them, and in turn was covered by the snow. Sometimes there were alternate layers of water and ice-skin, so that when one broke through he kept on breaking through for a while, sometimes wetting himself to the waist.

That was why he had shied in such panic. He had felt the give under his feet and heard the crackle of a snow-hidden ice-skin. And to get his feet wet in such a temperature meant trouble and danger. At the very least it meant delay, for he would be forced to stop and build a fire, and under its protection to bare his feet while he dried his socks and moccasins. He stood and studied the creek-bed and its banks, and decided that the flow of water came from the right. He reflected a while, rubbing his nose and cheeks, then skirted to the left, stepping gingerly and testing the footing for each step. Once clear of the danger, he took a fresh chew of tobacco and swung along at his four-mile gait.

In the course of the next two hours he came upon several similar traps. Usually the snow above the hidden pools had a sunken, candied appearance that advertised the danger. Once again, however, he had a close call; and once, suspecting danger, he compelled the dog to go on in front. The dog did not want to go. It hung back until the man shoved it forward, and then it went quickly across the white, unbroken surface. Suddenly it broke through, floundered to one side, and got away to firmer footing. It had wet its forefeet and legs, and almost immediately the water that clung to it turned to ice. It made quick efforts to lick the ice off its legs, then dropped down in the snow and began to bite out the ice that had formed between the toes. This was a matter of instinct. To permit the ice to remain would mean sore feet. It did not know this. It merely obeyed the mysterious prompting that arose from the deep crypts of its being. But the man knew, having achieved a judgment on the subject, and he removed the mitten from his right hand and helped tear out the ice-particles. He did not expose his fingers more than a minute, and was astonished at the swift numbness that smote them. It certainly was cold. He pulled on the mitten hastily, and beat the hand savagely across his chest.

At twelve o'clock the day was at its brightest. Yet the sun was too far south on its winter journey to clear the horizon. The bulge of the earth intervened between it and Henderson Creek, where the man walked under a clear sky at noon and cast no shadow. At half-past twelve, to the minute, he arrived at the forks of the creek. He was pleased at the speed he had made. If he kept it up, he would certainly be with the boys by six. He unbuttoned his jacket and shirt and drew forth his lunch. The action consumed no more than a quarter of a minute, yet in that brief moment the numbness laid hold of the exposed fingers. He did not put the mitten on, but, instead, struck the fingers a dozen sharp smashes against his leg. Then he sat down on a snow-covered log to eat. The sting that followed upon the striking of his fingers against his leg ceased so quickly that he was startled. He had had no chance to take a bite of biscuit. He struck the fingers repeatedly and returned them to the mitten, baring the other hand for the purpose of eating. He tried to take a mouthful, but the ice-muzzle prevented. He had forgotten to build a fire and thaw out. He chuckled at his foolishness, and as he chuckled he noted the numbness creeping into the exposed fingers. Also, he noted that the stinging which had first come to his toes when he sat down was already passing away. He wondered whether the toes were warm or numb. He moved them inside the moccasins and decided that they were numb.

He pulled the mitten on hurriedly and stood up. He was a bit frightened. He stamped up and down until the stinging returned into the feet. It certainly was cold, was his thought. That man from Sulphur Creek had spoken the truth when telling how cold it sometimes got in the country. And he had laughed at him at the time! That showed one must not be too sure of things. There was no mistake about it, it *was* cold. He strode up and down, stamping his feet and threshing his arms, until reassured by the returning warmth. Then he got out matches and proceeded to make a fire. From the undergrowth, where high water of the previous spring had lodged a supply of seasoned twigs, he got his firewood. Working carefully from a small beginning, he soon had a roaring fire, over which he thawed the ice from his face and in the protection of which he ate his biscuits. For the moment the cold of space was outwitted. The dog took satisfaction in the fire, stretching out close enough for warmth and far enough away to escape being singed.

When the man had finished, he filled his pipe and took his comfortable time over a smoke. Then he pulled on his mittens, settled the earflaps of his cap firmly about his ears, and took the creek trail up the left fork. The dog was disappointed and yearned back toward the fire. This man did not know cold. Possibly all the generations of his ancestry had been ignorant of cold, of real cold, of cold one hundred and seven degrees below freezing point. But the dog knew; all its ancestry knew, and it had inherited the knowledge. And it knew that it was not good to walk abroad in such fearful cold. It was the time to lie snug in a hole in the snow and wait for a curtain of cloud to be drawn across the face of outer space whence this cold came. On the other hand, there was no keen intimacy between the dog and the man. The one was the toil-slave of the other, and the only caresses it had ever received were the caresses of the whiplash and of harsh and menacing throat-sounds that threatened the whiplash. So the dog made no effort to communicate its apprehension to the man. It was not concerned in the welfare of the man; it was for its own sake that it yearned back toward the fire. But the man whistled, and spoke to it with the sound of whiplashes, and the dog swung in at the man's heel and followed after.

The man took a chew of tobacco and proceeded to start a new amber beard. Also, his moist breath quickly powdered with white his mustache, eyebrows, and lashes. There did not seem to be so many springs on the left fork of the Henderson, and for half an hour the man saw no signs of any. And then it happened. At a place where there were no signs, where the soft, unbroken snow seemed to advertise solidity beneath, the man broke through. It was not deep. He wet himself halfway to the knees before he floundered out to the firm crust.

He was angry, and cursed his luck aloud. He had hoped to get into camp with the boys at six o'clock, and this would delay him an hour, for he would have to build a fire and dry out his foot-gear. This was imperative at that low temperature—he knew that much; and he turned aside to the bank, which he climbed. On top, tangled in the underbrush about the trunks of several small spruce trees, was a high-water deposit of dry firewood—sticks and twigs, principally, but also larger portions of seasoned branches and fine, dry, last-year's grasses. He threw down several large pieces on top of the snow. This served for a foundation and prevented the young flame from drowning itself in the snow it otherwise would melt. The flame he got by touching a match to a small shred of birch bark that he took from his pocket. This burned even more readily than paper. Placing it on the foundation, he fed the young flame with wisps of dry grass and with the tiniest dry twigs.

He worked slowly and carefully, keenly aware of his danger. Gradually, as the flame grew stronger, he increased the size of the twigs with which he fed it. He squatted in the snow, pulling the twigs out from their entanglement in the brush and feeding directly to the flame. He knew there must be no failure. When it is seventy-five below zero, a man must not fail in his first attempt to build a fire—that is, if his feet are wet. If his feet are dry, and he fails, he can run along the trail for half a mile and restore his circulation. But the circulation of wet and freezing feet cannot be restored by running when it is seventy-five below. No matter how fast he runs, the wet feet will freeze the harder.

All this the man knew. The old-timer on Sulphur Creek had told him about it the previous fall, and now he was appreciating the advice. Already all sensation had gone out of his feet. To build the fire he had been forced to remove his mittens, and the fingers had quickly gone numb. His pace of four miles an hour had kept his heart pumping blood to the surface of his body and to all the extremities. But the instant he stopped, the action of the pump eased down. The cold of space smote the unprotected tip of the planet, and he, being on that unprotected tip, received the full force of the blow. The blood of his body recoiled before it. The blood was alive, like the dog, and like the dog it wanted to hide away and cover itself up from the fearful cold. So long as he walked four miles an hour, he pumped that blood, willy-nilly, to the surface; but now it ebbed away and sank down into the recesses of his body. The extremities were the first to feel its absence. His wet feet froze the faster, and his exposed fingers numbed the faster, though they had not yet begun to freeze. Nose and cheeks were already freezing, while the skin of all his body chilled as it lost its blood.

But he was safe. Toes and nose and cheeks would be only touched by the frost, for the fire was beginning to burn with strength. He was feeding it with twigs the size of his finger. In another minute he would be able to feed it with branches the size of his wrist, and then he could remove his wet foot-gear, and, while it dried, he could keep his naked feet warm by the fire, rubbing them at first, of course, with snow. The fire was a success. He was safe. He remembered the advice of the old-timer on Sulphur Creek, and smiled. The old-timer had been very serious in laying down the law that no man must travel alone in the Klondike after fifty below. Well, here he was; he had had the accident; he was alone; and he had saved himself. Those old-timers were rather womanish, some of them, he thought. All a man had to do was to keep his head, and he was all right. Any man who was a man could travel alone. But it was surprising, the rapidity with which his cheeks and nose were freezing. And he had not thought his fingers could go lifeless in so short a time. Lifeless they were, for he could scarcely make them move together to grip a twig, and they seemed remote from his body and from him. When he touched a twig, he had to look and see whether or not he had hold of it. The wires were pretty well down between him and his finger-ends.

All of which counted for little. There was the fire, snapping and crackling and promising life with every dancing flame. He started to untie his moccasins. They were coated with ice; the thick German socks were like sheaths of iron halfway to the knees; and the moccasin strings were like rods of steel all twisted and knotted as by some conflagration. For a moment he tugged with his numb fingers, then, realizing the folly of it, he drew his sheath-knife.

But before he could cut the strings, it happened. It was his own fault or, rather, his mistake. He should not have built the fire under the spruce tree. He should have built it in the open. But it had been easier to pull the twigs from the brush and drop them directly on the fire. Now the tree under which he had done this carried a weight of snow on its boughs. No wind had blown for weeks, and each bough was fully freighted. Each time he had pulled a twig he had communicated a slight agitation to the tree—an imperceptible agitation, so far as he was concerned, but an agitation sufficient to bring about the disaster. High up in the tree one bough capsized its load of snow. This fell on the boughs beneath, capsizing them. This process continued, spreading out and involving the whole tree. It grew like an avalanche, and it descended without warning upon the man and the fire, and the fire was blotted out! Where it had burned was a mantle of fresh and disordered snow.

The man was shocked. It was as though he had just heard his own sentence of death. For a moment he sat and stared at the spot where the fire had been. Then he grew very calm. Perhaps the old-timer on Sulphur Creek was right. If he had only had a trail-mate he would have been in no danger now. The trail-mate could have built the fire. Well, it was up to him to build the fire over again, and this second tune there must be no failure. Even if he succeeded, he would most likely lose some toes. His feet must be badly frozen by now, and there would be some time before the second fire was ready.

Such were his thoughts, but he did not sit and think them. He was busy all the time they were passing through his mind. He made a new foundation for a fire, this time in the open, where no treacherous tree could blot it out. Next, he gathered dry grasses and tiny twigs from the high-water flotsam. He could not bring his fingers together to pull them out, but he was able to gather them by the handful. In this way he got many rotten twigs and bits of green moss that were undesirable, but it was the best he could do. He worked methodically, even collecting an armful of the larger branches to be used later when the fire gathered strength. And all the while the dog sat and watched him, a certain yearning wistfulness in its eyes, for it looked upon him as the fire-provider, and the fire was slow in coming.

When all was ready, the man reached in his pocket for a second piece of birch bark. He knew the bark was there, and, though he could not feel it with his fingers, he could hear its crisp rustling as he fumbled for it. Try as he would, he could not clutch hold of it. And all the time, in his consciousness, was the knowledge that each instant his feet were freezing. This thought tended to put him in a panic, but he fought against it and kept calm. He pulled on his mittens with his teeth, and threshed his arms back and forth, beating his hands with all his might against his sides. He did this sitting down, and he stood up to do it; and all the while the dog sat in the snow, its wolf-brush of a tail curled around warmly over its forefeet, its sharp wolf-ears pricked forward intently as it watched the man. And the man, as he beat and threshed with his arms and hands, felt a great surge of envy as he regarded the creature that was warm and secure in its natural covering.

After a time he was aware of the first far-away signals of sensation in his beaten fingers. The faint tingling grew stronger till it evolved into a stinging ache that was excruciating, but which the man hailed with satisfaction. He stripped the mitten from his right hand and fetched forth the birch bark. The exposed fingers were quickly going numb again. Next he brought out his bunch of sulphur matches. But the tremendous cold had already driven the life out of his fingers. In his effort to separate one match from the others, the whole bunch fell in the snow. He tried to pick it out of the snow, but failed. The dead fingers could neither touch nor clutch. He was very careful. He drove the thought of his freezing feet, and nose, and cheeks, out of his mind, devoting his whole soul to the matches. He watched, using the sense of vision in place of that of touch, and when he saw his fingers on each side the bunch, he closed them—that is, he willed to close them, for the wires were down, and the fingers did not obey. He pulled the mitten on the right hand, and beat it fiercely against his knee. Then, with both mittened hands, he scooped the bunch of matches, along with much snow, into his lap. Yet he was no better off.

After some manipulation he managed to get the bunch between the heels of his mittened hands. In this fashion he carried it to his mouth. The ice crackled and snapped when by a violent effort he opened his mouth. He drew the lower jaw in, curled the upper lip out of the way, and scraped the bunch with his upper teeth in order to separate a match. He succeeded in getting one, which he dropped on his lap. He was no better off. He could not pick it up. Then he devised a way. He picked it up in his teeth and scratched it on his leg. Twenty times he scratched before he succeeded in lighting it. As it flamed he held it with his teeth to the birch bark. But the burning brimstone went up his nostrils and into his lungs, causing him to cough spasmodically. The match fell into the snow and went out.

The old-timer on Sulphur Creek was right, he thought in the moment of controlled despair that ensued: after fifty below, a man should travel with a partner. He beat his hands, but failed in exciting any sensation. Suddenly he bared both hands, removing the mittens with his teeth. He caught the whole bunch between the heels of his hands. His arm-muscles not being frozen enabled him to press the hand-heels tightly against the matches. Then he scratched the bunch along his leg. It flared into flame, seventy sulphur matches at once! There was no wind to blow them out. He kept his head to one side to escape the strangling fumes, and held the blazing bunch to the birch bark. As he so held it, he became aware of sensation in his hand. His flesh was burning. He could smell it. Deep down below the surface he could feel it. The sensation developed into pain that grew acute. And still he endured it, holding the flame of the matches clumsily to the bark that would not light readily because his own burning hands were in the way, absorbing most of the flame.

At last, when he could endure no more, he jerked his hands apart. The blazing matches fell sizzling into the snow, but the birch bark was alight. He began laying dry grasses and the tiniest twigs on the flame. He could not pick and choose, for he had to lift the fuel between the heels of his hands. Small pieces of rotten wood and green moss clung to the twigs, and he bit them off as well as he could with his teeth. He cherished the flame carefully and awkwardly. It meant life, and it must not perish. The withdrawal of blood from the surface of his body now made him begin to shiver, and he grew more awkward. A large piece of green moss fell squarely on the little fire. He tried to poke it out with his fingers, but his shivering frame made him poke too far, and he disrupted the nucleus of the little fire, the burning grasses and tiny twigs separating and scattering. He tried to poke them together again, but in spite of the tenseness of the effort, his shivering got away with him, and the twigs were hopelessly scattered. Each twig gushed a puff of smoke and went out. The fire-provider had failed. As he looked apathetically about him, his eyes chanced on the dog, sitting across the ruins of the fire from him, in the snow, making restless, hunching movements, slightly lifting one forefoot and then the other, shifting its weight back and forth on them with wistful eagerness.

The sight of the dog put a wild idea into his head. He remembered the tale of the man, caught in a blizzard, who killed a steer and crawled inside the carcass, and so was saved. He would kill the dog and bury his hands in the warm body until the numbness went out of them. Then he could build another fire. He spoke to the dog, calling it to him; but in his voice was a strange note of fear that frightened the animal, who had never known the man to speak in such way before. Something was the matter, and its suspicious nature sensed danger–it knew not what danger, but somewhere, somehow, in its brain arose an apprehension of the man. It flattened its ears down at the sound of the man's voice, and its restless, hunching movements and the liftings and shiftings of its forefeet became more pronounced; but it would not come to the man. He got on his hands and knees and crawled toward the dog. This unusual posture again excited suspicion, and the animal sidled mincingly away.

The man sat up in the snow for a moment and struggled for calmness. Then he pulled on his mittens, by means of his teeth, and got upon his feet. He glanced down at first in order to assure himself that he was really standing up, for the absence of sensation in his feet left him unrelated to the earth. His erect position in itself started to drive the webs of suspicion from the dog's mind; and when he spoke peremptorily, with the sound of whip-lashes in his voice, the dog rendered its customary allegiance and came to him. As it came within reaching distance, the man lost his control. His arms flashed out to the dog, and he experienced genuine surprise when he discovered that his hands could not clutch, that there was neither bend nor feeling in the fingers. He had forgotten for the moment that they were frozen and that they were freezing more and more. All this happened quickly, and before the animal could get away, he encircled its body with his arms. He sat down in the snow, and in this fashion held the dog, while it snarled and whined and struggled.

But it was all he could do, hold its body encircled in his arms and sit there. He realized that he could not kill the dog. There was no way to do it. With his helpless hands he could neither draw nor hold his sheath-knife nor throttle the animal. He released it, and it plunged wildly away, with tail between its legs, and still snarling. It halted forty feet away and surveyed him curiously, with ears sharply pricked forward. The man looked down at his hands in order to locate them, and found them hanging on the ends of his arms. It struck him as curious that one should have to use his eyes in order to find out where his hands were. He began threshing his arms back and forth, beating the mittened hands against his sides. He did this for five minutes, violently, and his heart pumped enough blood up to the surface to put a stop to his shivering. But no sensation was aroused in the hands. He had an impression that they hung like weights on the ends of his arms, but when he tried to run the impression down, he could not find it.

A certain fear of death, dull and oppressive, came to him. This fear quickly became poignant as he realized that it was no longer a mere matter of freezing his fingers and toes, or of losing his hands and feet, but that it was a matter of life and death with the chances against him. This threw him into a panic, and he turned and ran up the creek-bed along the old, dim trail. The dog joined in behind and kept up with him. He ran blindly, without intention, in fear such as he had never known in his life. Slowly, as he plowed and floundered through the snow, he began to see things again,—the banks of the creek, the old timber-jams, the leafless aspens, and the sky. The running made him feel better. He did not shiver. Maybe, if he ran on, his feet would thaw out; and, anyway, if he ran far enough, he would reach camp and the boys. Without doubt he would lose some fingers and toes and some of his face; but the boys would take care of him, and save the rest of him when he got there. And at the same time there was another thought in his mind that said he would never get to the camp and the boys; that it was too many miles away, that the freezing had too great a start on him, and that he would soon be stiff and dead. This thought he kept in the background and refused to consider. Sometimes it pushed itself forward and demanded to be heard, but he thrust it back and strove to think of other things.

It struck him as curious that he could run at all on feet so frozen that he could not feel them when they struck the earth and took the weight of his body. He seemed to himself to skim along above the surface, and to have no connection with the earth. Somewhere he had once seen a winged Mercury, and he wondered if Mercury felt as he felt when skimming over the earth.

His theory of running until he reached camp and the boys had one flaw in it: he lacked the endurance. Several times he stumbled, and finally he tottered, crumpled up, and fell. When he tried to rise, he failed. He must sit and rest, he decided, and next time he would merely walk and keep on going. As he sat and regained his breath, he noted that he was feeling quite warm and comfortable. He was not shivering, and it even seemed that a warm glow had come to his chest and trunk. And yet, when he touched his nose or cheeks, there was no sensation. Running would not thaw them out. Nor would it thaw out his hands and feet. Then the thought came to him that the frozen portions of his body must be extending. He tried to keep this thought down, to forget it, to think of something else; he was aware of the panicky feeling that it caused, and he was afraid of the panic. But the thought asserted itself, and persisted, until it produced a vision of his body totally frozen. This was too much, and he made another wild run along the trail. Once he slowed down to a walk, but the thought of the freezing extending itself made him run again.

And all the time the dog ran with him, at his heels. When he fell down a second time, it curled its tail over its forefeet and sat in front of him, facing him, curiously eager and intent. The warmth and security of the animal angered him, and he cursed it till it flattened down its ears appeasingly. This time the shivering came more quickly upon the man. He was losing in his battle with the frost. It was creeping into his body from all sides. The thought of it drove him on, but he ran no more than a hundred feet, when he staggered and pitched headlong. It was his last panic. When he had recovered his breath and control, he sat up and entertained in his mind the conception of meeting death with dignity. However, the conception did not come to him in such terms. His idea of it was that he had been making a fool of himself, running around like a chicken with its head cut off—such was the simile that occurred to him. Well, he was bound to freeze anyway, and he might as well take it decently. With this new-foound peace of mind came the first glimmerings of drowsiness. A good idea, he thought, to sleep off to death. It was like taking an anæsthetic. Freezing was not so bad as people thought. There were lots worse ways to die.

He pictured the boys finding his body next day. Suddenly he found himself with them, coming along the trail and looking for himself. And, still with them, he came around a turn in the trail and found himself lying in the snow. He did not belong with himself any more, for even then he was out of himself, standing with the boys and looking at himself in the snow. It certainly was cold, was his thought. When he got back to the States he could tell the folks what real cold was. He drifted on from this to a vision of the old-timer on Sulphur Creek. He could see him quite clearly, warm and comfortable, and smoking a pipe.

"You were right, old hoss; you were right," the man mumbled to the old-timer of Sulphur Creek.

Then the man drowsed off into what seemed to him the most comfortable and satisfying sleep he had ever known. The dog sat facing him and waiting. The brief day drew to a close in a long, slow twilight. There were no signs of a fire to be made, and, besides, never in the dog's experience had it known a man to sit like that in the snow and make no fire. As the twilight drew on, its eager yearning for the fire mastered it, and with a great lifting and shifting of forefeet, it whined softly, then flattened its ears down in anticipation of being chidden by the man. But the man remained silent. Later, the dog whined loudly. And still later it crept close to the man and caught the scent of death. This made the animal bristle and back away. A little longer it delayed, howling under the stars that leaped and danced and shone brightly in the cold sky. Then it turned and trotted up the trail in the direction of the camp it knew, where were the other food-providers and fire-providers.

SHERWOOD ANDERSON

[1876–1941]

I'm a Fool

(First published in the *Dial*, 1922;
first book publication in 1924.)

IT WAS A hard jolt for me, one of the most bitterest I ever had to face. And it all came about through my own foolishness too. Even yet, sometimes, I want to cry or swear or kick myself. Perhaps, even now, after all this time, there will be a kind of satisfaction in making myself look cheap by telling of it.

It began at three o'clock one October afternoon as I sat in the grandstand at the fall trotting and pacing meet at Sandusky, Ohio.

To tell the truth, I felt a little foolish that I should be sitting in the grandstand at all. During the summer before I had left my home town with Harry Whitehead and, with a nigger named Burt, had taken a job as swipe with one of the two horses Harry was campaigning through the fall race meets that year. Mother cried and my sister Mildred, who wanted to get a job as school teacher in our town that fall, stormed and scolded about the house all during the week before I left. They both thought it something disgraceful that one of our family should take a place as a swipe with race horses. I've an idea Mildred thought my taking the place would stand in the way of her getting the job she'd been working so long for.

But after all I had to work and there was no other work to be got. A big lumbering fellow of nineteen couldn't just hang around the house and I had got too big to mow people's lawns and sell newspapers. Little chaps who could get next to people's sympathies by their sizes were always getting jobs away from me. There was one fellow who kept saying to everyone who wanted a lawn mowed or a cistern cleaned that he was saving money to work his way through college, and I used to lie awake nights thinking up ways to injure him without being found out. I kept thinking of wagons running over him and bricks falling on his head as he walked along the street. But never mind him.

I got the place with Harry and I liked Burt fine. We got along splendid together. He was a big nigger with a lazy sprawling body and soft kind eyes, and when it came to a fight he could hit like Jack Johnson. He had Bucephalus, a big black pacing stallion that could do 2.09 or 2.10 if he had to, and I had a little gelding named Doctor Fritz that never lost a race all fall when Harry wanted him to win.

We set out from home late in July in a box car with the two horses, and after that, until late November, we kept moving along to the race meets and the fairs. It was a peachy time for me, I'll say that. Sometimes, now, I think that boys who are raised regular in houses, and never have a fine nigger like Burt for best friend, and go to high school, and college, and never steal anything or get drunk a little, or learn to swear from fellows who know how, or come walking up in front of a grandstand in their shirt sleeves and with dirty horsey pants on when the races are going on and the grandstand is full of people all dressed up—What's the use talking about it? Such fellows don't know nothing at all. They've never had no opportunity.

But I did. Burt taught me how to rub down a horse and put the bandages on after a race and steam a horse out and a lot of valuable things for any man to know. He could wrap a bandage on a horse's leg so smooth that if it had been the same color you would think it was his skin, and I guess he'd have been a big driver, too, and got to the top like Murphy and Walter Cox and the others if he hadn't been black.

Gee whizz, it was fun. You got to a county seat town maybe, say, on a Saturday or Sunday, and the fair began the next Tuesday and lasted until Friday afternoon. Doctor Fritz would be, say, in the 2.25 trot on Tuesday afternoon and on Thursday afternoon Bucephalus would knock 'em cold in the "free-for-all" pace. It left you a lot of time to hang around and listen to horse talk, and see Burt knock some yap cold that got too gay, and you'd find out about horses and men and pick up a lot of stuff you could use all the rest of your life if you had some sense and salted down what you heard and felt and saw.

And then at the end of the week when the race meet was over, and Harry had run home to tend up to his livery stable business, you and Burt hitched the two horses to carts and drove slow and steady across country to the place for the next meeting so as not to overheat the horses, etc., etc., you know.

Gee whizz, gosh amighty, the nice hickorynut and beechnut and oaks and other kinds of trees along the roads, all brown and red, and the good smells, and Burt singing a song that was called Deep River, and the country girls at the windows of houses and everything. You can stick your colleges up your nose for all me. I guess I know where I got my education.

Why, one of those little burgs of towns you come to on the way, say now, on a Saturday afternoon, and Burt says, "let's lay up here." And you did.

And you took the horses to a livery stable and fed them and you got your good clothes out of a box and put them on.

And the town was full of farmers, gaping, because they could see you were race horse people, and the kids maybe never see a nigger before and was afraid and run away when the two of us walked down their main street.

And that was before prohibition and all that foolishness, and so you went into a saloon, the two of you, and all the yaps come and stood around, and there was always someone pretended he was horsey and knew things and spoke up and began asking questions, and all you did was to lie and lie all you could about what horses you had, and I said I owned them, and then some fellow said, "Will you have a drink of whisky?" and Burt knocked his eye out the way he could say, offhand like, "Oh, well, all, all right, I'm agreeable to a little nip. I'll split a quart with you." Gee whizz.

But that isn't what I want to tell my story about. We got home late in November and I promised mother I'd quit the race horses for good. There's a lot of things you've got to promise a mother because she don't know any better.

And so, there not being any work in our town any more than when I left there to go to the races, I went off to Sandusky and got a pretty good place taking care of the horses for a man who owned a teaming and delivery and storage business there. It was a pretty good place with good eats and a day off each week and sleeping on a cot in the big barn, and mostly just shoveling in hay and oats to a lot of big good-enough skates of horses that couldn't have trotted a race with a toad. I wasn't dissatisfied and I could send money home.

And then, as I started to tell you, the fall races come to Sandusky and I got the day off and I went. I left the job at noon and had on my good clothes and my new brown derby hat I'd just bought the Saturday before, and a stand-up collar.

First of all I went downtown and walked about with the dudes. I've always thought to myself, "put up a good front," and so I did it. I had forty dollars in my pocket and so I went into the West House, a big hotel, and walked up to the cigar stand. "Give me three twenty-five cent cigars," I said. There was a lot of horse men and strangers and dressed-up people from other towns standing around in the lobby and in the bar, and I mingled amongst them. In the bar there was a fellow with a cane and a Windsor tie on, that it made me sick to look at him. I like a man to be a man and dress up, but not to go put on that kind of airs. So I pushed him aside, kind of rough, and had me a drink of whisky. And then he looked at me as though he thought he'd get gay, but he changed his mind and didn't say anything. And then I had another drink of whisky, just to show him something, and went out and had a hack out to the races all to myself, and when I got there I bought myself the best seat I could get up in the grandstand, but didn't go in for any of these boxes. That's putting on too many airs.

And so there I was, sitting up in the grandstand as gay as you please and looking down on the swipes coming out with their horses and with their dirty horsey pants on and the horse blankets swung over their shoulders same as I had been doing all the year before. I liked one thing about the same as the other, sitting up there and feeling grand and being down there and looking up at the yaps and feeling grander and more important too. One thing's about as good as another if you take it just right. I've often said that.

Well, right in front of me, in the grandstand that day, there was a fellow with a couple of girls and they was about my age. The young fellow was a nice guy all right. He was the kind maybe that goes to college and then comes to be a lawyer or maybe a newspaper editor or something like that, but he wasn't stuck on himself. There are some of that kind are all right and he was one of the ones.

He had his sister with him and another girl and the sister looked around over his shoulder, accidental at first, not intending to start anything–she wasn't that kind–and her eyes and mine happened to meet.

You know how it is. Gee, she was a peach. She had on a soft dress kind of a blue stuff, and it looked carelessly made, but was well sewed and made and everything. I knew that much. I blushed when she looked right at me and so did she. She was the nicest girl I've ever seen in my life. She wasn't stuck on herself and she could talk proper grammar without being like a school teacher or something like that. What I mean is, she was O.K. I think maybe her father was well-to-do, but not rich to make her chesty because she was his daughter, as some are. Maybe he owned a drug store or a dry goods store in their home town, or something like that. She never told me and I never asked.

My own people are all O.K. too, when you come to that. My grandfather was Welsh and over in the old country, in Wales, he was–but never mind that.

The first heat of the first race come off and the young fellow setting there with the two girls left them and went down to make a bet. I knew what he was up to, but he didn't talk big and noisy and let everyone around know he was a sport, as some do. He wasn't that kind. Well, he come back and I heard him tell the two girls what horse he'd bet on, and when the heat was trotted they all half got to their feet and acted in the excited, sweaty way people do when they've got money down on a race, and the horse they bet on is up there pretty close at the end, and they think maybe he'll come on with a rush, but he never does because he hasn't got the old juice in him, come right down to it.

And, then, pretty soon, the horses came out for the 2.18 pace and there was a horse in it I knew. He was a horse Bob French had in his string, but Bob didn't own him. He was a horse owned by a Mr. Mathers down at Marietta, Ohio.

This Mr. Mathers had a lot of money and owned a coal mine or something, and he had a swell place out in the country, and he was stuck on race horses, but was a Presbyterian or something, and I think more than likely his wife was one, too, maybe a stiffer one than himself. So he never raced his horses hisself, and the story round the Ohio race tracks was that when one of his horses got ready to go to the races he turned him over to Bob French and pretended to his wife he was sold.

So Bob had the horses and he did pretty much as he pleased and you can't blame Bob; at least, I never did. Sometimes he was out to win and sometimes he wasn't. I never cared much about that when I was swiping a horse. What I did want to know was that my horse had the speed and could go out in front if you wanted him to.

And, as I'm telling you, there was Bob in this race with one of Mr. Mathers' horses, was named "About Ben Ahem" or something like that, and was fast as a streak. He was a gelding and had a mark of 2.21, but could step in .08 or .09.

Because when Burt and I were out, as I've told you, the year before, there was a nigger Burt knew, worked for Mr. Mathers, and we went out there one day when we didn't have no race on at the Marietta Fair and our boss Harry had gone home.

And so everyone was gone to the fair but just this one nigger, and he took us all through Mr. Mathers' swell house and he and Burt tapped a bottle of wine Mr. Mathers had hid in his bedroom, back in a closet, without his wife knowing, and he showed us this Ahem horse. Burt was always stuck on being a driver, but didn't have much chance to get to the top, being a nigger, and he and the other nigger gulped that whole bottle of wine and Burt got a little lit up.

So the nigger let Burt take this About Ben Ahem and step him a mile in a track Mr. Mathers had all to himself, right there on the farm. And Mr. Mathers had one child, a daughter, kinda sick and not very goodlooking, and she came home and we had to hustle and get About Ben Ahem stuck back in the barn.

I'm only telling you to get everything straight. At Sandusky, that afternoon I was at the fair, this young fellow with the two girls was fussed, being with the girls and losing his bet. You know how a fellow is that way. One of them was his girl and the other his sister. I had figured that out.

"Gee whizz," I says to myself, "I'm going to give him the dope."

He was mighty nice when I touched him on the shoulder. He and the girls were nice to me right from the start and clear to the end. I'm not blaming them.

And so he leaned back and I gave him the dope on About Ben Ahem. "Don't bet a cent on this first heat because he'll go like an oxen hitched to a plough, but when the first heat is over go right down and lay on your pile." That's what I told him.

Well, I never saw a fellow treat any one sweller. There was a fat man sitting beside the little girl that had looked at me twice by this time, and I at her, and both blushing, and what did he do but have the nerve to turn and ask the fat man to get up and change places with me so I could set with his crowd.

Gee whizz, amighty. There I was. What a chump I was to go and get gay up there in the West House bar, and just because that dude was standing there with a cane and that kind of a necktie on, to go and get all balled up and drink that whisky, just to show off.

Of course, she would know, me setting right beside her and letting her smell of my breath. I could have kicked myself right down out of that grandstand and all around that race track and made a faster record than most of the skates of horses they had there that year.

Because that girl wasn't any mutt of a girl. What wouldn't I have given right then for a stick of chewing gum to chew, or a lozenger, or some licorice, or most anything. I was glad I had those twenty-five cent cigars in my pocket, and right away I give that fellow one and lit one myself. Then that fat man got up and we changed places and there I was plunked down beside her.

They introduced themselves, and the fellow's best girl he had with him, was named Miss Elinor Woodbury, and her father was a manufacturer of barrels from a place called Tiffin, Ohio. And the fellow himself was named Wilbur Wessen and his sister was Miss Lucy Wessen.

I suppose it was their having such swell names got me off my trolley. A fellow, just because he has been a swipe with a race horse, and works taking care of horses for a man in the teaming, delivery and storage business, isn't any better or worse than anyone else. I've often thought that, and said it, too.

But you know how a fellow is. There's something in that kind of nice clothes, and the kind of nice eyes she had, and the way she looked at me, awhile before, over her brother's shoulder, and me looking back at her, and both of us blushing.

I couldn't show her up for a boob, could I?

I made a fool of myself, that's what I did. I said my name was Walter Mathers from Marietta, Ohio, and then I told all three of them the smashingest lie you ever heard. What I said was that my father owned the horse About Ben Ahem, and that he had let him out to this Bob French for racing purposes, because our family was proud and had never gone into racing that way, in our own name, I mean. Then I had got started, and they were all leaning over and listening, and Miss Lucy Wessen's eyes were shining, and I went the whole hog.

I told about our place down at Marietta, and about the big stables and the grand brick house we had on a hill, up above the Ohio River, but I knew enough not to do it in no bragging way. What I did was to start things and then let them drag the rest out of me. I acted just as reluctant to tell as I could. Our family hasn't got any barrel factory, and, since I've known us, we've always been pretty poor, but not asking anything of anyone at that, and my grandfather, over in Wales—but never mind that.

We set there talking like we had known each other for years and years, and I went and told them that my father had been expecting maybe this Bob French wasn't on the square, and had sent me up to Sandusky on the sly to find out what I could.

And I bluffed it through I had found out all about the 2.18 pace in which About Ben Ahem was to start.

I said he would lose the first heat by pacing like a lame cow and then he would come back and skin 'em alive after that. And to back up what I said I took thirty dollars out of my pocket and handed it to Mr. Wilbur Wessen and asked him would he mind, after the first heat, to go down and place it on About Ben Ahem for whatever odds he could get. What I said was that I didn't want Bob French to see me and none of the swipes.

Sure enough the first heat come off and About Ben Ahem went off his stride, up the back stretch, and looked like a wooden horse or a sick one, and come in to be last. Then this Wilbur Wessen went down to the betting place under the grandstand and there I was with the two girls, and when that Miss Woodbury was looking the other way once, Lucy Wessen kinda, with her shoulder you know, kinda touched me. You know how a woman can do. They get close, but not getting gay either. You know what they do. Gee whizz.

And then they give me a jolt. What they had done when I didn't know, was to get together, and they had decided Wilbur Wessen would bet fifty dollars, and the two girls had gone and put in ten dollars each of their own money, too. I was sick then, but I was sicker later.

About the gelding, About Ben Ahem, and their winning their money I wasn't worried a lot about that. It come out O.K. Ahem stepped the next three heats like a bushel of spoiled eggs going to market before they could be found out, and Wilbur Wessen had got nine to two for the money. There was something else eating at me.

Because Wilbur come back after he had bet the money, and after that he spent most of his time talking to that Miss Woodbury, and Lucy Wessen and I was left alone together like on a desert island. Gee, if I'd only been on the square or if there had been any way of getting myself on the square. There ain't any Walter Mathers, like I said to her and them, and there hasn't ever been one, but if there was, I bet I'd go to Marietta, Ohio, and shoot him tomorrow.

There I was, big boob that I am. Pretty soon the race was over, and Wilbur had gone down and collected our money, and we had a hack downtown, and he stood us a swell dinner at the West House, and a bottle of champagne beside.

And I was with that girl and she wasn't saying much, and I wasn't saying much either. One thing I know. She wasn't stuck on me because of the lie about my father being rich and all that. There's a way you know. . . . Craps amighty. There's a kind of girl you see just once in your life, and if you don't get busy and make hay then you're gone for good and all and might as well go jump off a bridge. They give you a look from inside of them somewhere, and it ain't no vamping, and what it means is—you want that girl to be your wife, and you want nice things around her like flowers and swell clothes, and you want her to have the kids you're going to have, and you want good music played and no ragtime. Gee whizz.

There's a place over near Sandusky, across a kind of bay, and it's called Cedar Point. And when we had had that dinner we went over to it in a launch, all by ourselves. Wilbur and Miss Lucy and that Miss Woodbury had to catch a ten o'clock train back to Tiffin, Ohio, because when you're out with girls like that you can't get careless and miss any trains and stay out all night like you can with some kinds of Janes.

And Wilbur blowed himself to the launch and it cost him fifteen cold plunks, but I wouldn't ever have knew it if I hadn't listened. He wasn't no tin horn kind of a sport.

Over at the Cedar Point place we didn't stay around where there was a gang of common kind of cattle at all.

There was big dance halls and dining places for yaps, and there was a beach you could walk along and get where it was dark, and we went there.

She didn't talk hardly at all and neither did I, and I was thinking how glad I was my mother was all right, and always made us kids learn to eat with a fork at table and not swill soup and not be noisy and rough like a gang you see around a race track that way.

Then Wilbur and his girl went away up the beach and Lucy and I set down in a dark place where there was some roots of old trees the water had washed up, and after that, the time, till we had to go back in the launch and they had to catch their trains, wasn't nothing at all. It went like winking your eye.

Here's how it was. The place we were setting in was dark, like I said, and there was the roots from that old stump sticking up like arms, and there was a watery smell, and the night was like—as if you could put your hand out and feel it—so warm and soft and dark and sweet like a orange.

I most cried and I most swore and I most jumped up and danced, I was so mad and happy and sad.

When Wilbur come back from being alone with his girl and she saw him coming, Lucy she says, "We got to go to the train now," and she was most crying, too, but she never knew nothing I knew, and she couldn't be so all busted up. And then, before Wilbur and Miss Woodbury got up to where she was, she put her face up and kissed me quick and put her head up against me and she was all quivering and—Gee whizz.

Sometimes I hope I have cancer and die. I guess you know what I mean. We went in the launch across the bay to the train like that, and it was dark too. She whispered and said it was like she and I could get out of the boat and walk on the water, and it sounded foolish, but I knew what she meant.

And then quick, we were right at the depot, and there was a big gang of yaps, the kind that goes to the fairs, and crowded and milling around like cattle, and how could I tell her? "It won't be long because you'll write and I'll write to you." That's all she said.

I got a chance like a hay barn afire. A swell chance I got.

And maybe she would write me, down at Marietta that way, and the letter would come back, and stamped on the front of it by the U.S.A. "There ain't any such guy," or something like that, whatever they stamp on a letter that way.

And me trying to pass myself off for a bigbug and a swell—to her, as decent a little body as God ever made. Craps amighty. A swell chance I got.

And then the train come in and she got on, and Wilbur Wessen come and shook hands with me and that Miss Woodbury was nice and bowed to me and I at her and the train went and I busted out and cried like a kid.

Gee, I could have run after that train and made Dan Patch look like a freight train after a wreck, but socks amighty, what was the use? Did you ever see such a fool?

I'll bet you what—if I had an arm broke right now or a train had run over my foot—I wouldn't go to no doctor at all. I'd go set down and let her hurt and hurt—that's what I'd do.

I'll bet you what—if I hadn't a drunk that booze I'd never been such a boob as to go tell such a lie—that couldn't never be made straight to a lady like her.

I wish I had that fellow right here that had on a Windsor tie and carried a cane. I'd smash him for fair. Gosh darn his eyes. He's a big fool—that's what he is.

And if I'm not another you just go find me one and I'll quit working and be a bum and give him my job. I don't care nothing for working and earning money and saving it for no such boob as myself.

RING LARDNER

[1885–1933]

The Golden Honeymoon

(First published in *Cosmopolitan*, July, 1922; first book publication in 1924.)

MOTHER SAYS THAT when I start talking I never know when to stop. But I tell her the only time I get a chance is when she ain't around, so I have to make the most of it. I guess the fact is neither one of us would be welcome in a Quaker meeting, but as I tell Mother, what did God give us tongues for if He didn't want we should use them? Only she says He didn't give them to us to say the same thing over and over again, like I do, and repeat myself. But I say:

"Well, Mother," I say, "when people is like you and I and been married fifty years, do you expect everything I say will be something you ain't heard me say before? But it may be new to others, as they ain't nobody else lived with me as long as you have."

So she says:

"You can bet they ain't, as they couldn't nobody else stand you that long."

"Well," I tell her, "you look pretty healthy."

"Maybe I do," she will say, "but I looked even healthier before I married you."

You can't get ahead of Mother.

Yes, sir, we was married just fifty years ago the seventeenth day of last December and my daughter and son-in-law was over from Trenton to help us celebrate the Golden Wedding. My son-in-law is John H. Kramer, the real estate man. He made $12,000 one year and is pretty well thought of around Trenton; a good, steady, hard worker. The Rotarians was after him a long time to join, but he kept telling them his home was his club. But Edie finally made him join. That's my daughter.

Well, anyway, they come over to help us celebrate the Golden Wedding and it was pretty crimpy weather and the furnace don't seem to heat up no more like it used to and Mother made the remark that she hoped this winter wouldn't be as cold as the last, referring to the winter previous. So Edie said if she was us, and nothing to keep us home, she certainly wouldn't spend no more winters up here and why didn't we just shut off the water and close up the house and go down to Tampa, Florida? You know we was there four winters ago and stayed five weeks, but it cost us over three hundred and fifty dollars for hotel bill alone. So Mother said we wasn't going no place to be robbed. So my son-in-law spoke up and said that Tampa wasn't the only place in the South, and besides we didn't have to stop at no high price hotel but could rent us a couple rooms and board out somewheres, and he had heard that St. Petersburg, Florida, was *the* spot and if we said the word he would write down there and make inquiries.

Well, to make a long story short, we decided to do it and Edie said it would be our Golden Honeymoon and for a present my son-in-law paid the difference between a section and a compartment so as we could have a compartment and have more privacy. In a compartment you have an upper and lower berth just like the regular sleeper, but it is a shut in room by itself and got a wash bowl. The car we went in was all compartments and no regular berths at all. It was all compartments.

We went to Trenton the night before and stayed at my daughter and son-in-law and we left Trenton the next afternoon at 3.23 P.M.

This was the twelfth day of January. Mother set facing the front of the train, as it makes her giddy to ride backwards. I set facing her, which does not affect me. We reached North Philadelphia at 4.03 P.M. and we reached West Philadelphia at 4.14, but did not go into Broad Street. We reached Baltimore at 6.30 and Washington, D.C, at 7.25. Our train laid over in Washington two hours till another train come along to pick us up and I got out and strolled up the platform and into the Union Station. When I come back, our car had been switched on to another track, but I remembered the name of it, the La Belle, as I had once visited my aunt out in Oconomowoc, Wisconsin, where there was a lake of that name, so I had no difficulty in getting located. But Mother had nearly fretted herself sick for fear I would be left.

"Well," I said, "I would of followed you on the next train."

"You could of," said Mother, and she pointed out that she had the money.

"Well," I said, "we are in Washington and I could of borrowed from the United States Treasury. I would of pretended I was an Englishman."

Mother caught the point and laughed heartily.

Our train pulled out of Washington at 9.40 P.M. and Mother and I turned in early, I taking the upper. During the night we passed through the green fields of old Virginia, though it was too dark to tell if they was green or what color. When we got up in the morning, we was at Fayetteville, North Carolina. We had breakfast in the dining car and after breakfast I got in conversation with the man in the next compartment to ours. He was from Lebanon, New Hampshire, and a man about eighty years of age. His wife was with him, and two unmarried daughters and I made the remark that I should think the four of them would be crowded in one compartment, but he said they had made the trip every winter for fifteen years and knowed how to keep out of each other's way. He said they was bound for Tarpon Springs.

We reached Charleston, South Carolina, at 12.50 P.M. and arrived at Savannah, Georgia, at 4.20. We reached Jacksonville, Florida, at 8.45 P.M. and had an hour and a quarter to lay over there, but Mother made a fuss about me getting off the train, so we had the darky make up our berths and retired before we left Jacksonville. I didn't sleep good as the train done a lot of hemming and hawing, and Mother never sleeps good on a train as she says she is always worrying that I will fall out. She says she would rather have the upper herself, as then she would not have to worry about me, but I tell her I can't take the risk of having it get out that I allowed my wife to sleep in an upper berth. It would make talk.

We was up in the morning in time to see our friends from New Hampshire get off at Tarpon Springs, which we reached at 6.53 A.M.

Several of our fellow passengers got off at Clearwater and some at Belleair, where the train backs right up to the door of the mammoth hotel. Belleair is the winter headquarters for the golf dudes and everybody that got off there had their bag of sticks, as many as ten and twelve in a bag. Women and all. When I was a young man we called it shinny and only needed one club to play with and about one game of it would of been a-plenty for some of these dudes, the way we played it.

The train pulled into St. Petersburg at 8.20 and when we got off the train you would think they was a riot, what with all the darkies barking for the different hotels.

I said to Mother, I said:

"It is a good thing we have got a place picked out to go to and don't have to choose a hotel, as it would be hard to choose amongst them if every one of them is the best."

She laughed.

We found a jitney and I give him the address of the room my son-in-law had got for us and soon we was there and introduced ourselves to the lady that owns the house, a young widow about forty-eight years of age. She showed us our room, which was light and airy with a comfortable bed and bureau and washstand. It was twelve dollars a week, but the location was good, only three blocks from Williams Park.

St. Pete is what folks calls the town, though they also call it the Sunshine City, as they claim they's no other place in the country where they's fewer days when Old Sol don't smile down on Mother Earth, and one of the newspapers gives away all their copies free every day when the sun don't shine. They claim to of only give them away some sixty-odd times in the last eleven years. Another nickname they have got for the town is "the Poor Man's Palm

Beach," but I guess they's men that comes there that could borrow as much from the bank as some of the Willie boys over to the other Palm Beach.

During our stay we paid a visit to the Lewis Tent City, which is the headquarters for the Tin Can Tourists. But may be you ain't heard about them. Well, they are an organization that takes their vacation trips by auto and carries everything with them. That is, they bring along their tents to sleep in and cook in and they don't patronize no hotels or cafeterias, but they have got to be bona fide auto campers or they can't belong to the organization.

They tell me they's over 200,000 members to it and they call themselves the Tin Canners on account of most of their food being put up in tin cans. One couple we seen in the Tent City was a couple from Brady, Texas, named Mr. and Mrs. Pence, which the old man is over eighty years of age and they had come in their auto all the way from home, a distance of 1,641 miles. They took five weeks for the trip, Mr. Pence driving the entire distance.

The Tin Canners hails from every State in the Union and in the summer time they visit places like New England and the Great Lakes region, but in the winter the most of them comes to Florida and scatters all over the State. While we was down there, they was a national convention of them at Gainesville, Florida, and they elected a Fredonia, New York, man as their president. His title is Royal Tin Can Opener of the World. The have got a song wrote up which everybody has got to learn it before they are a member:

"The tin can forever! Hurrah, boys! Hurrah!
Up with the tin can! Down with the foe!
We will rally round the campfire, we'll rally once again,
Shouting, 'We auto camp forever!'"

That is something like it. And the members has also got to have a tin can fastened on to the front of their machine.

I asked Mother how she would like to travel around that way and she said:

"Fine, but not with an old rattle brain like you driving."

"Well," I said, "I am eight years younger than this Mr. Pence who drove here from Texas."

"Yes," she said, "but he is old enough to not be skittish."

You can't get ahead of Mother.

Well, one of the first things we done in St. Petersburg was to go to the Chamber of Commerce and register our names and where we was from as they's great rivalry amongst the different States in regards to the number of their citizens visiting in town and of course our little State don't stand much of a show, but still every little bit helps, as the fella says. All and all, the man told us, they was eleven thousand names registered, Ohio leading with some fifteen hundred-odd and New York State next with twelve hundred. Then come Michigan, Pennsylvania and so on down, with one man each from Cuba and Nevada.

The first night we was there, they was a meeting of the New York-New Jersey Society at the Congregational Church and a man from Ogdensburg, New York State, made the talk. His subject was Rainbow Chasing. He is a Rotarian and a very convicting speaker, though I forget his name.

Our first business, of course, was to find a place to eat and after trying several places we run on to a cafeteria on Central Avenue that suited us up and down. We eat pretty near all our meals there and it averaged about two dollars per day for the two of us, but the food was well cooked and everything nice and clean. A man don't mind paying the price if things is clean and well cooked.

On the third day of February, which is Mother's birthday, we spread ourselves and eat supper at the Poinsettia Hotel and they charged us seventy-five cents for a sirloin steak that wasn't hardly big enough for one.

I said to Mother: "Well," I said, "I guess it's a good thing every day ain't your birthday or we would be in the poorhouse."

"No," says Mother, "because if every day was my birthday, I would be old enough by this time to of been in my grave long ago."

You can't get ahead of Mother.

In the hotel they had a card-room where they was several men and ladies playing five hundred and this new fangled whist bridge. We also seen a place where they was dancing, so I asked Mother would she like to trip the light fantastic toe and she said no, she was too old to squirm like you have got to do now days. We watched some of the young folks at it awhile till Mother got disgusted and said we would have to see a good movie to take the taste out of our mouth. Mother is a great movie heroyne and we go twice a week here at home.

But I want to tell you about the Park. The second day we was there we visited the Park, which is a good deal like the one in Tampa, only bigger, and they's more fun goes on here every day than you could shake a stick at. In the middle they's a big bandstand and chairs for the folks to set and listen to the concerts, which they give you music for all tastes, from Dixie up to classical pieces like Hearts and Flowers.

Then all around they's places marked off for different sports and games—chess and checkers and dominoes for folks that enjoys those kind of games, and roque and horse-shoes for the nimbler ones. I used to pitch a pretty fair shoe myself, but ain't done much of it in the last twenty years.

Well, anyway, we bought a membership ticket in the club which costs one dollar for the season, and they tell me that up to a couple years ago it was fifty cents, but they had to raise it to keep out the riffraff.

Well, Mother and I put in a great day watching the pitchers and she wanted I should get in the game, but I told her I was all out of practice and would make a fool of myself, though I seen several men pitching who I guess I could take their measure without no practice. However, they was some good pitchers, too, and one boy from Akron, Ohio, who could certainly throw a pretty shoe. They told me it looked like he would win the championship of the United States in the February tournament. We come away a few days before they held that and I never did hear if he win. I forget his name, but he was a clean cut young fella and he has got a brother in Cleveland that's a Rotarian.

Well, we just stood around and watched the different games for two or three days and finally I set down in a checker game with a man named Weaver from Danville, Illinois. He was a pretty fair checker player, but he wasn't no match for me, and I hope that don't sound like bragging. But I always could hold my own on a checker-board and the folks around here will tell you the same thing. I played with this Weaver pretty near all morning for two or three mornings and he beat me one game and the only other time it looked like he had a chance, the noon whistle blowed and we had to quit and go to dinner.

While I was playing checkers, Mother would set and listen to the band, as she loves music, classical or no matter what kind, but anyway she was setting there one day and between selections the woman next to her opened up a conversation. She was a woman about Mother's own age, seventy or seventy-one, and finally she asked Mother's name and Mother told her her name and where she was from and Mother asked her the same question, and who do you think the woman was?

Well, sir, it was the wife of Frank M. Hartsell, the man who was engaged to Mother till I stepped in and cut him out, fifty-two years ago!

Yes, sir!

You can imagine Mother's surprise! And Mrs. Hartsell was surprised, too, when Mother told her she had once been friends with her husband, though Mother didn't say how close friends they had been, or that Mother and I was the cause of Hartsell going out West. But that's what we was. Hartsell left his town a month after the engagement was broke off and ain't never been back since. He had went out to Michigan and become a veterinary, and that is where he had settled down, in Hillsdale, Michigan, and finally married his wife.

Well, Mother screwed up her courage to ask if Frank was still living and Mrs. Hartsell took her over to where they was pitching horse-shoes and there was old Frank, waiting his turn. And he knowed Mother as soon as he seen her, though it was over fifty years. He said he knowed her by her eyes.

"Why, it's Lucy Frost!" he says, and he throwed down his shoes and quit the game.

Then they come over and hunted me up and I will confess I wouldn't of knowed him. Him and I is the same age to the month, but he seems to show it more, some way. He is balder for one thing. And his beard is all white, where mine has still got a streak of brown in it. The very first thing I said to him, I said:

"Well, Frank, that beard of yours makes me feel like I was back north. It looks like a regular blizzard."

"Well," he said, "I guess yourn would be just as white if you had it dry cleaned."

But Mother wouldn't stand that.

"Is that so!" she said to Frank. "Well, Charley ain't had no tobacco in his mouth for over ten years!"

And I ain't!

Well, I excused myself from the checker game and it was pretty close to noon, so we decided to all have dinner together and they was nothing for it only we must try their cafeteria on Third Avenue. It was a little more expensive than ours and not near as good, I thought. I and Mother had about the same dinner we had been having every day and our bill was $1.10. Frank's check was $1.20 for he and his wife. The same meal wouldn't of cost them more than a dollar at our place.

After dinner we made them come up to our house and we all set in the parlor, which the young woman had give us the use of to entertain company. We begun talking over old times and Mother said she was a-scared Mrs. Hartsell would find it tiresome listening to we three talk over old times, but as it turned out they wasn't much chance for nobody else to talk with Mrs. Hartsell in the company. I have heard lots of women that could go it, but Hartsell's wife takes the cake of all the women I ever seen. She told us the family history of everybody in the State of Michigan and bragged for a half hour about her son, who she said is in the drug business in Grand Rapids, and a Rotarian.

When I and Hartsell could get a word in edgeways we joked one another back and forth and I chafed him about being a horse doctor.

"Well, Frank," I said, "you look pretty prosperous, so I suppose they's been plenty of glanders around Hillsdale."

"Well," he said, "I've managed to make more than a fair living. But I've worked pretty hard."

"Yes," I said, "and I suppose you get called out all hours of the night to attend births and so on."

Mother made me shut up.

Well, I thought they wouldn't never go home and I and Mother was in misery trying to keep awake, as the both of us generally always takes a nap after dinner. Finally they went, after we had made an engagement to meet them in the Park the next morning, and Mrs. Hartsell also invited us to come to their place the next night and play five hundred. But she had forgot that they was a meeting of the Michigan Society that evening, so it was not till two evenings later that we had our first card game.

Hartsell and his wife lived in a house on Third Avenue North and had a private setting room besides their bedroom. Mrs. Hartsell couldn't quit talking about their private setting room like it was something wonderful. We played cards with them, with Mother and Hartsell partners against his wife and I. Mrs. Hartsell is a miserable card player and we certainly got the worst of it.

After the game she brought out a dish of oranges and we had to pretend it was just what we wanted, though oranges down there is like a young man's whiskers; you enjoy them at first, but they get to be a pesky nuisance.

We played cards again the next night at our place with the same partners and I and Mrs. Hartsell was beat again. Mother and Hartsell was full of compliments for each other on what a good team they made, but the both of them knowed well enough where the secret of their success laid. I guess all and all we must of played ten different evenings and they was only one night when Mrs. Hartsell and I come out ahead. And that one night wasn't no fault of hern.

When we had been down there about two weeks, we spent one evening as their guest in the Congregational Church, at a social give by the Michigan Society. A talk was made by a man named Bitting of Detroit, Michigan, on How I was Cured of Story Telling. He is a big man in the Rotarians and give a witty talk.

A woman named Mrs. Oxford rendered some selections which Mrs Hartsell said was grand opera music, but whatever they was my daughter Edie could of give her cards and spades and not made such a hullabaloo about it neither.

Then they was a ventriloquist from Grand Rapids and a young woman about forty-five years of age that mimicked different kinds of birds. I whispered to Mother that they all sounded like a chicken, but she nudged me to shut up.

After the show we stopped in a drug store and I set up the refreshments and it was pretty close to ten o'clock before we finally turned in. Mother and I would of preferred tending the movies, but Mother said we mustn't offend Mrs. Hartsell, though I asked her had we came to Florida to enjoy ourselves or to just not offend an old chatter-box from Michigan.

I felt sorry for Hartsell one morning. The women folks both had an engagement down to the chiropodist's and I run across Hartsell in the Park and he foolishly offered to play me checkers.

It was him that suggested it, not me, and I guess he repented himself before we had played one game. But he was too stubborn to give up and set there while I beat him game after game and the worst part of it was that a crowd of folks had got in the habit of watching me play and there they all was, looking on, and finally they seen what a fool Frank was making of himself, and they began to chafe him and pass remarks. Like one of them said:

"Who ever told you you was a checker player!"

And:

"You might maybe be good for tiddle-de-winks, but not checkers!"

I almost felt like letting him beat me a couple games. But the crowd would of knowed it was a put up job.

Well, the women folks joined us in the Park and I wasn't going to mention our little game, but Hartsell told about it himself and admitted he wasn't no match for me.

"Well," said Mrs. Hartsell, "checkers ain't much of a game anyway, is it?" She said: "It's more of a children's game, ain't it? At least, I know my boy's children used to play it a good deal."

"Yes, ma'am," I said. "It's a children's game the way your husband plays it, too."

Mother wanted to smooth things over, so she said:

"Maybe they's other games where Frank can beat you."

"Yes," said Mrs. Hartsell, "and I bet he could beat you pitching horseshoes."

"Well," I said, "I would give him a chance to try, only I ain't pitched a shoe in over sixteen years."

"Well," said Hartsell, "I ain't played checkers in twenty years."

"You ain't never played it," I said.

"Anyway," says Frank, "Lucy and I is your master at five hundred."

Well, I could of told him why that was, but had decency enough to hold my tongue.

It had got so now that he wanted to play cards every night and when I or Mother wanted to go to a movie, any one of us would have to pretend we had a headache and then trust to goodness that they wouldn't see us sneak into the theater. I don't mind playing cards when my partner keeps their mind on the game, but you take a woman like Hartsell's wife and how can they play cards when they have got to stop every couple seconds and brag about their son in Grand Rapids?

Well, the New York-New Jersey Society announced that they was goin' to give a social evening too and I said to Mother, I said:

"Well, that is one evening when we will have an excuse not to play five hundred."

"Yes," she said, "but we will have to ask Frank and his wife to go to the social with us as they asked us to go to the Michigan social."

"Well," I said, "I had rather stay home than drag that chatter-box everywheres we go."

So Mother said:

"You are getting too cranky. Maybe she does talk a little too much but she is good hearted. And Frank is always good company."

So I said:

"I suppose if he is such good company you wished you had of married him."

Mother laughed and said I sounded like I was jealous. Jealous of a cow doctor!

Anyway we had to drag them along to the social and I will say that we give them a much better entertainment than they had given us.

Judge Lane of Paterson made a fine talk on business conditions and a Mrs. Newell of Westfield imitated birds, only you could really tell what they was the way she done it. Two young women from Red Bank sung a choral selection and we clapped them back and they gave us Home to Our Mountains and Mother and Mrs. Hartsell both had tears in their eyes. And Hartsell, too.

Well, some way or another the chairman got wind that I was there and asked me to make a talk and I wasn't even going to get up, but Mother made me, so I got up and said:

"Ladies and gentlemen," I said. "I didn't expect to be called on for a speech on an occasion like this or no other occasion as I do not set myself up as a speech maker, so will have to do the best I can, which I often say is the best anybody can do."

Then I told them the story about Pat and the motorcycle, using the brogue, and it seemed to tickle them and I told them one or two other stories, but altogether I wasn't on my feet more than twenty or twenty-five minutes and you ought to of heard the clapping and hollering when I set down. Even Mrs. Hartsell admitted that I am quite a speechifier and said if I ever went to Grand Rapids, Michigan, her son would make me talk to the Rotarians.

When it was over, Hartsell wanted we should go to their house and play cards, but his wife reminded him that it was after 9.30 P.M., rather a late hour to start a card game, but he had went crazy on the subject of cards, probably because he didn't have to play partners with his wife. Anyway, we got rid of them and went home to bed.

It was the next morning, when we met over to the Park, that Mrs. Hartsell made the remark that she wasn't getting no exercise so I suggested that why didn't she take part in the roque game.

She said she had not played a game of roque in twenty years, but if Mother would play she would play. Well, at first Mother wouldn't hear of it, but finally consented, more to please Mrs. Hartsell than anything else.

Well, they had a game with a Mrs. Ryan from Eagle, Nebraska, and a young Mrs. Morse from Rutland, Vermont, who Mother had met down to the chiropodist's. Well, Mother couldn't hit a flea and they all laughed at her and I couldn't help from laughing at her myself and finally she quit and said her back was too lame to stoop over. So they got another lady and kept on playing and soon Mrs. Hartsell was the one everybody was laughing at, as she had a long shot to hit the black ball, and as she made the effort her teeth fell out on to the court. I never seen a woman so flustered in my life. And I never heard so much laughing, only Mrs. Hartsell didn't join in and she was madder than a hornet and wouldn't play no more, so the game broke up.

Mrs. Hartsell went home without speaking to nobody, but Hartsell stayed around and finally he said to me, he said:

"Well, I played you checkers the other day and you beat me bad and now what do you say if you and me play a game of horse-shoes?"

I told him I hadn't pitched a shoe in sixteen years, but Mother said:

"Go ahead and play. You used to be good at it and maybe it will come back to you."

Well, to make a long story short, I give in. I oughtn't to of never tried it, as I hadn't pitched a shoe in sixteen years, and I only done it to humor Hartsell.

Before we started, Mother patted me on the back and told me to do my best, so we started in and I seen right off that I was in for it, as I hadn't pitched a shoe in sixteen years and didn't have my distance. And besides, the plating had wore off the shoes so that they was points right where they stuck into my thumb and I hadn't throwed more than two or three times when my thumb was raw and it pretty near killed me to hang on to the shoe, let alone pitch it.

Well, Hartsell throws the awkwardest shoe I ever seen pitched and to see him pitch you wouldn't think he would ever come nowheres near, but he is also the luckiest pitcher I ever seen and he made some pitches where the shoe lit five and six feet short and then schoonered up and was a ringer. They's no use trying to beat that kind of luck.

They was a pretty fair size crowd watching us and four or five other ladies besides Mother, and it seems like, when Hartsell pitches, he has got to chew and it kept the ladies on the anxious seat as he don't seem to care which way he is facing when he leaves go.

You would think a man as old as him would of learnt more manners.

Well, to make a long story short, I was just beginning to get my distance when I had to give up on account of my thumb, which I showed it to Hartsell and he seen I couldn't go on, as it was raw and bleeding. Even if I could of stood it to go on myself, Mother wouldn't of allowed it after she seen my thumb. So anyway I quit and Hartsell said the score was nineteen to six, but I don't know what it was. Or don't care, neither.

Well, Mother and I went home and I said I hoped we was through with the Hartsells as I was sick and tired of them, but it seemed like she had promised we would go over to their house that evening for another game of their everlasting cards.

Well, my thumb was giving me considerable pain and I felt kind of out of sorts and I guess maybe I forgot myself, but anyway, when we was about through playing Hartsell made the remark that he wouldn't never lose a game of cards if he could always have Mother for a partner.

So I said:

"Well, you had a chance fifty years ago to always have her for a partner, but you wasn't man enough to keep her."

I was sorry the minute I had said it and Hartsell didn't know what to say and for once his wife couldn't say nothing. Mother tried to smooth things over by making the remark that I must of had something stronger than tea or I wouldn't talk so silly. But Mrs. Hartsell had froze up like an iceberg and hardly said good night to us and I bet her and Frank put in a pleasant hour after we was gone.

As we was leaving, Mother said to him: 'Never mind Charley's nonsense, Frank. He is just mad because you beat him all hollow pitching horse-shoes and playing cards."

She said that to make up for my slip, but at the same time she certainly riled me. I tried to keep ahold of myself, but as soon as we was out of the house she had to open up the subject and began to scold me for the break I had made.

Well, I wasn't in no mood to be scolded. So I said:

"I guess he is such a wonderful pitcher and card player that you wished you had married him."

"Well," she said, "at least he ain't a baby to give up pitching because his thumb has got a few scratches."

"And how about you," I said, "making a fool of yourself on the roque court and then pretending your back is lame and you can't play no more!"

"Yes," she said, "but when you hurt your thumb I didn't laugh at you, and why did you laugh at me when I sprained my back?"

"Who could help from laughing!" I said.

"Well," she said, "Frank Hartsell didn't laugh."

"Well," I said, "why didn't you marry him?"

"Well," said Mother, "I almost wished I had!"

"And I wished so, too!" I said.

"I'll remember that!" said Mother, and that's the last word she said to me for two days.

We seen the Hartsells the next day in the Park and I was willing to apologize, but they just nodded to us. And a couple days later we heard they had left for Orlando, where they have got relatives.

I wished they had went there in the first place.

Mother and I made it up setting on a bench.

"Listen, Charley," she said. "This is our Golden Honeymoon and we don't want the whole thing spoilt with a silly old quarrel."

"Well," I said, "did you mean that about wishing you had married Hartsell?"

"Of course not," she said, "that is, if you didn't mean that you wished I had, too."

So I said:

"I was just tired and all wrought up. I thank God you chose me instead of him as they's no other woman in the world who I could of lived with all these years."

"How about Mrs. Hartsell?" says Mother.

"Good gracious!" I said. "Imagine being married to a woman that plays five hundred like she does and drops her teeth on the roque court!"

"Well," said Mother, "it wouldn't be no worse than being married to a man that expectorates towards ladies and is such a fool in a checker game."

So I put my arm around her shoulder and she stroked my hand and I guess we got kind of spoony.

They was two days left of our stay in St. Petersburg and the next to the last day Mother introduced me to a Mrs. Kendall from Kingston, Rhode Island, who she had met at the chiropodist's.

Mrs. Kendall made us acquainted with her husband, who is in the grocery business. They have got two sons and five grandchildren and one great-grandchild. One of their sons lives in Providence and is way up in the Elks as well as a Rotarian.

We found them very congenial people and we played cards with them the last two nights we was there. They was both experts and I only wished we had met them sooner instead of running into the Hartsells. But the Kendalls will be there again next winter and we will see more of them, that is, if we decide to make the trip again.

We left the Sunshine City on the eleventh day of February, at 11 A.M. This give us a day trip through Florida and we seen all the country we had passed through at night on the way down.

We reached Jacksonville at 7 P.M. and pulled out of there at 8.10 P.M. We reached Fayetteville, North Carolina, at nine o'clock the following morning, and reached Washington, D. C., at 6.30 P.M., laying over there half an hour.

We reached Trenton at 11.01 P.M. and had wired ahead to my daughter and son-in-law and they met us at the train and we went to their house and they put us up for the night. John would of made us stay up all night, telling about our trip, but Edie said we must be tired and made us go to bed. That's my daughter.

The next day we took our train for home and arrived safe and sound, having been gone just one month and a day.

Here comes Mother, so I guess I better shut up.

EDNA FERBER

[1887–1968]

The Afternoon of a Faun

(1922)

THOUGH HE RARELY heeded its summons—cagy boy that he was—the telephone rang oftenest for Nick. Because of the many native noises of the place, the telephone had a special bell that was a combination buzz and ring. It sounded above the roar of outgoing cars, the splash of the hose, the sputter and hum of the electric battery in the rear. Nick heard it, unheeding. A voice—Smitty's or Mike's or Elmer's—answering its call. Then, echoing through the gray, vaulted spaces of the big garage: "Nick! Oh, Ni-ick!"

From the other side of the great cement-floored enclosure, or in muffled tones from beneath a car: "Whatcha want?"

"Dame on the wire."

"I ain't in."

The obliging voice again, dutifully repeating the message: "He ain't in. . . . Well, it's hard to say. He might be in in a couple hours and then again he might not be back till late. I guess he's went to Hammond on a job—" (Warming to his task now.) "Say, won't I do? . . . Who's fresh ! Aw, say, *lady*!"

You'd think, after repeated rebuffs of this sort, she could not possibly be so lacking in decent pride as to leave her name for Smitty or Mike or Elmer to bandy about. But she invariably did, baffled by Nick's elusiveness. She was likely to be any one of a number. Miss Bauers phoned: Will you tell him, please? (A nasal voice, and haughty, with the hauteur that seeks to conceal secret fright.) Tell him it's important. Miss Ahearn phoned: Will you tell him, please? Just say Miss Ahearn. A-h-e-a-r-n. Miss Olson: Just Gertie. But oftenest Miss Bauers.

Cupid's messenger, wearing grease-grimed overalls and the fatuous grin of the dalliant male, would transmit his communication to the uneager Nick.

"'S wonder you wouldn't answer the phone onct yourself. Says you was to call Miss Bauers any time you come in between one and six at Hyde Park—wait a min't'—yeh—Hyde Park 6079, and any time after six at—"

"Wha'd she want?"

"Well, how the hell should *I* know! Says call Miss Bauers any time between one and six at Hyde Park 6—"

"Swell chanst. *Swell* chanst!"

Which explains why the calls came oftenest for Nick. He was so indifferent to them. You pictured the patient and persistent Miss Bauers, or the oxlike Miss Olson, or Miss Ahearn, or just Gertie hovering within hearing distance of the telephone listening, listening—while one o'clock deepened to six—for the call that never came; plucking up fresh courage at six until six o'clock dragged on to bedtime. When next they met: "I bet you was there all the time. Pity you wouldn't answer a call when a person leaves their name. You could of give me a ring. I bet you was there all the time."

"Well, maybe I was."

Bewildered, she tried to retaliate with the boomerang of vituperation.

How could she know? How could she know that this slim, slick young garage mechanic was a woodland creature in disguise—a satyr in store clothes—a wild thing who perversely preferred to do his own pursuing? How could Miss Bauers know—she who cashiered in the Green Front Grocery and Market on Fifty-third Street? Or Miss Olson, at the Rialto ticket window? Or the Celtic, emotional Miss Ahearn, the manicure? Or Gertie the goof? They knew nothing of mythology; of pointed ears and pug noses and goat's feet. Nick's ears, to their fond gaze, presented an honest red surface protruding from either side of his head. His feet, in tan laced shoes, were ordinary feet, a little more than ordinarily expert, perhaps, in the convolutions of the dance at Englewood Masonic Hall, which is part of Chicago's vast South Side. No; a faun, to Miss Bauers, Miss Olson, Miss Ahearn, and just Gertie, was one of those things in the Lincoln Park Zoo.

Perhaps, sometimes, they realized, vaguely, that Nick was different. When, for example, they tried—and failed—to picture him looking interestedly at one of those three-piece bedroom sets glistening like pulled taffy in the window of the instalment furniture store, while they, shy yet proprietary, clung to his arm and eyed the price ticket. Now $98.50. You couldn't see Nick interested in bedroom sets, in price tickets, in any of those settled, fixed, everyday things. He was fluid, evasive, like quicksilver, though they did not put it thus.

Miss Bauers, goaded to revolt, would say pettishly: "You're like a mosquito, that's what. Person never knows from one minute to the other where you're at."

"Yeh," Nick would retort. "When you know where a mosquito's at, what do you do to him? Plenty. I ain't looking to be squashed."

Miss Ahearn, whose public position (the Hygienic Barber Shop. Gent's manicure, 50c.) offered unlimited social opportunities, would assume a gay indifference. "They's plenty boys begging to take me out every hour in the day. Swell lads, too. I ain't waiting round for any greasy mechanic like you.

Don't think it. Say, lookit your nails! They'd queer you with me, let alone what else all is wrong with you."

In answer Nick would put one hand—one broad, brown, steel-strong hand with its broken discolored nails—on Miss Ahearn's arm, in its flimsy georgette sleeve. Miss Ahearn's eyelids would flutter and close, and a little shiver would run with icy-hot feet all over Miss Ahearn.

Nick was like that.

Nick's real name wasn't Nick at all—or scarcely at all. His last name was Nicholas, and his parents, long before they became his parents, traced their origin to some obscure Czechoslovakian province—long before we became so glib with our Czechoslovakia. His first name was Dewey, knowing which you automatically know the date of his birth. It was a patriotic but unfortunate choice on the part of his parents. The name did not fit him; was too mealy; not debonair enough. Nick. Nicky in tenderer moments (Miss Bauers, Miss Olson, Miss Ahearn, just Gertie, et al.).

His method with women was firm and somewhat stern, but never brutal. He never waited for them if they were late. Any girl who assumed that her value was enhanced in direct proportion to her tardiness in keeping an engagement with Nick found herself standing disconsolate on the corner of Fifty-third and Lake trying to look as if she were merely waiting for the Lake Park car and not peering wistfully up and down the street in search of a slim, graceful, hurrying figure that never came.

It is difficult to convey in words the charm that Nick possessed. Seeing him, you beheld merely a medium-sized young mechanic in reasonably grimed garage clothes when working; and in tight pants, tight coat, silk shirt, long-visored green cap when at leisure. A rather pallid skin due to the nature of his work. Large deft hands, a good deal like the hands of a surgeon, square, blunt-fingered, spatulate. Indeed, as you saw him at work, a wire-netted electric bulb held in one hand, the other plunged deep into the vitals of the car on which he was engaged, you thought of a surgeon performing a major operation. He wore one of those round skullcaps characteristic of his craft (the brimless crown of an old felt hat). He would deftly remove the transmission case and plunge his hand deep into the car's guts, feeling expertly about with his engine-wise fingers as a surgeon feels for liver, stomach, gall bladder, intestines, appendix. When he brought up his hands, all dripping with grease (which is the warm blood of the car), he invariably had put his finger on the sore spot.

All this, of course, could not serve to endear him to the girls. On the contrary, you would have thought that his hands alone, from which he could never quite free the grease and grit, would have caused some feeling of repugnance among the lily-fingered. But they, somehow, seemed always to be finding an excuse to touch him: his tie, his hair, his coat sleeve. They seemed even to derive a vicarious thrill from holding his hat or cap when on an outing. They brushed imaginary bits of lint from his coat lapel. They tried on his seal ring, crying: "Oo, lookit, how big it is. for me, even my thumb!" He called this "pawing a guy over"; and the lint ladies he designated as "thread pickers."

No; it can't be classified, this powerful draw he had for them. His conversation furnished no clue. It was commonplace conversation, limited, even dull. When astonished, or impressed, or horrified, or amused, he said: "Ken yuh feature that!" When emphatic or confirmatory, he said: "You *tell* 'em!"

It wasn't his car and the opportunities it furnished for drives, both country and city. That motley piece of mechanism represented such an assemblage of unrelated parts as could only have been made to coordinate under Nick's expert guidance. It was out of commission more than half the time, and could never be relied upon to furnish a holiday. Both Miss Bauers and Miss Ahearn had twelve-cylinder opportunities that should have rendered them forever unfit for travel in Nick's one-lung vehicle of locomotion.

It wasn't money. Though he was generous enough with what he had, Nick couldn't be generous with what he hadn't. And his wage at the garage was $40 a week. Miss Ahearn's silk stockings cost $4.50.

His unconcern should have infuriated them, but it served to pique. He wasn't actually as unconcerned as he appeared, but he had early learned that effort in their direction was unnecessary. Nick had little imagination; a gorgeous selfishness; a tolerantly contemptuous liking for the sex. Naturally, however, his attitude toward them had been somewhat embittered by being obliged to watch their method of driving a car in and out of the Ideal Garage doorway. His own manipulation of the wheel was nothing short of wizardry.

He played the harmonica.

Each Thursday afternoon was Nick's half day off. From twelve until seven-thirty he was free to range the bosky highways of Chicago. When his car—he called it "the bus"—was agreeable, he went awheel in search of amusement. The bus being indisposed, he went afoot. He rarely made plans in advance; usually was accompanied by some successful telephonee. He rather liked to have a silken skirt beside him fluttering and flirting in the breeze as he broke the speed regulations.

On this Thursday afternoon in July he had timed his morning job to a miraculous nicety so that at the stroke of twelve his workaday garments dropped from him magically, as though he were a male (and reversed) Cinderella. There was a wash room and a rough sort of sleeping room containing two cots situated in the second story of the Ideal Garage. Here Nick shed the loose garments of labor for the fashionably tight habiliments of leisure. Private chauffeurs whose employers housed their cars in the Ideal Garage used this nook for a lounge and smoker. Smitty, Mike, Elmer, and Nick snatched stolen siestas there in the rare absences of the manager.

Sometimes Nick spent the night there when forced to work overtime. His home life, at best, was a sketchy affair. Here chauffeurs, mechanics, washers lolled at ease exchanging soft-spoken gossip, motor chat, speculation, comment, and occasional verbal obscenity. Each possessed a formidable knowledge of that neighborhood section of Chicago known as Hyde Park. This knowledge was not confined to car costs and such impersonal items, but included meals, scandals, relationships, finances, love affairs, quarrels, peccadillos. Here Nick often played his harmonica, his lips sweeping the metal length of it in throbbing rendition of such sure-fire sentimentality as The Long, Long Trail, or Mammy, while the others talked, joked, kept time with tapping feet or wagging heads.

Today the hot little room was empty except for Nick, shaving before the cracked mirror on the wall, and old Elmer, reading a scrap of yesterday's newspaper as he lounged his noon hour away. Old Elmer was thirty-seven, and Nicky regarded him as an octogenarian. Also, old Elmer's conversation bored Nick to the point of almost sullen resentment. Old Elmer was a family man. His talk was all of his family—the wife, the kids, the flat. A garrulous person, lank, pasty, dish-faced, and amiable. His half day off was invariably spent tinkering about the stuffy little flat—painting, nailing up shelves, mending a broken window shade, puttying a window, playing with his pasty little boy, aged sixteen months, and his pasty little girl, aged three years. Next day he regaled his fellow workers with elaborate recitals of his holiday hours.

"Believe me, that kid's a caution. Sixteen months old, and what does he do yesterday? He unfastens the ketch on the back-porch gate. We got a gate on the back porch, see." (This frequent "see" which interlarded Elmer's verbiage was not used in an interrogatory way, but as a period, and by way of emphasis. His voice did not take the rising inflection as he uttered it.) "What does he do, he opens it. I come home, and the wife says to me: 'Say, you better get busy and fix a new ketch on that gate to the back porch. Little Elmer, first thing I know, he'd got it open today and was crawling out almost.' Say, can you beat that for a kid sixteen months—"

Nick had finished shaving, had donned his clean white soft shirt. His soft collar fitted to a miracle about his strong throat. Nick's sartorial effects were a triumph—on forty a week. "Say, can't you talk about nothing but that kid of yours? I bet he's a bum specimen at that. Runt, like his pa."

Elmer flung down his newspaper in honest indignation as Nick had wickedly meant he should. "Is that so! Why, we was wrastling round—me and him, see—last night on the floor, and what does he do, he raises his mitt and hands me a wallop in the stomick it like to knock the wind out of me. That's all. Sixteen months—"

"Yeh. I suppose this time next year he'll be boxing for money."

Elmer resumed his paper. "What do *you* know." His tone mingled pity with contempt.

Nick took a last critical survey of the cracked mirror's reflection and found it good. "Nothing, only this: you make me sick with your kids and your missus and your place. Say, don't you never have no fun?"

"Fun! Why, say, last Sunday we was out to the beach, and the kid swum out first thing you know—"

"Oh, shut up!" He was dressed now. He slapped his pockets. Harmonica. Cigarettes. Matches. Money. He was off, his long-visored cloth cap pulled jauntily over his eyes.

Elmer, bearing no rancor, flung a last idle query: "Where you going?"

"How should I know? Just bumming around. Bus is outa commission, and I'm outa luck."

He clattered down the stairs, whistling.

Next door for a shine at the Greek bootblack's. Enthroned on the dais, a minion at his feet, he was momentarily monarchial. How's the boy? Good? Same here. Down, his brief reign ended. Out into the bright noon-day glare of Fifty-third Street.

A fried-egg sandwich. Two blocks down and into the white-tiled lunchroom. He took his place in the row perched on stools in front of the white slab, his feet on the railing, his elbows on the counter. Four white-aproned vestals with blotchy skins performed rites over the steaming nickel urns, slid dishes deftly along the slick surface of the white slab, mopped up moisture with a sly gray rag. No nonsense about them. This was the rush hour. Hungry men from the shops and offices and garages of the district were bent on food (not badinage). They ate silently, making a dull business of it. Coffee? What kinda pie do you want? No fooling here. "Hello, Jessie."

As she mopped the slab in front of him you noticed a slight softening of her features, intent so grimly on her task. "What's yours?"

"Bacon-and-egg sandwich. Glass of milk. Piece of pie. Blueberry."

Ordinarily she would not have bothered. But with him: "The blueberry ain't so good today, I noticed. Try the peach?"

"All right." He looked at her. She smiled. Incredibly, the dishes ordered seemed to leap out at her from nowhere. She crashed them down on the glazed white surface in front of him. The bacon-and-egg sandwich was served open-faced, an elaborate confection. Two slices of white bread, side by side. On one reposed a fried egg, hard, golden, delectable, indigestible. On the other three crisp curls of bacon. The ordinary order held two curls only. A dish so rich in calories as to make it food sufficient for a day. Jessie knew nothing of calories, nor did Nick. She placed a double order of butter before him—two yellow pats, moisture-beaded. As she scooped up his milk from the can you saw that the glass was but three-quarters filled. From a deep crock she ladled a smaller scoop and filled the glass to the top. The deep crock held cream. Nick glanced up at her again. Again Jessie smiled. A plain damsel, Jessie, and capable. She went on about her business. What's yours? Coffee with? White or rye? No nonsense about her. And yet: "Pie all right?"

"Yeh. It's good."

She actually blushed.

He finished, swung himself off the stool, nodded to Jessie. She stacked his dishes with one lean, capable hand, mopped the slab with the other, but as she made for the kitchen she flung a glance at him over her shoulder.

"Day off?"

"Yeh."

"Some folks has all the luck."

He grinned. His teeth were strong and white and even. He walked toward the door with his light quick step, paused for a toothpick as he paid his check, was out again into the July sunlight. Her face became dull again.

Well, not one o'clock. Guessed he'd shoot a little pool. He dropped into Moriarty's cigar store. It was called a cigar store because it dealt in magazines, newspapers, soft drinks, golf balls, cigarettes, pool, billiards, chocolates, chewing gum, and cigars. In the rear of the store were four green-topped tables, three for pool and one for billiards. He hung about aimlessly, watching the game at the one occupied table. The players were slim young men like himself, their clothes replicas of his own, their faces lean and somewhat hard. Two of them dropped out. Nick took a cue from the rack, shed his tight coat. They played under a glaring electric light in the heat of the day, yet they seemed cool, aloof, immune from bodily discomfort. It was a strangely silent game and as mirthless as that of the elfin bowlers in Rip Van Winkle. The slim-waisted shirted figures bent plastically over the table in the graceful postures of the game. You heard only the click of the balls, an occasional low-voiced exclamation. A solemn crew, and unemotional.

Now and then: "What's all the shootin' fur?"

"In she goes."

Nick, winner, tired of it in less than an hour. He bought a bottle of some acidulous drink just off the ice and refreshed himself with it, drinking from the bottle's mouth. He was vaguely restless, dissatisfied. Out again into the glare of two o'clock Fifty-third Street. He strolled up a block toward Lake Park Avenue. It was hot. He wished the bus wasn't sick. Might go in swimming, though. He considered this idly. Hurried steps behind him. A familiar perfume wafted to his senses. A voice nasal yet cooing. Miss Bauers. Miss Bauers on a pleasure bent, palpably, being attired in the briefest of silks, white-strapped slippers, white silk stockings, scarlet hat. The Green Front Grocery and Market closed for a half day each Thursday afternoon during July and August. Nicky had not availed himself of the knowledge.

"Well, if it ain't Nicky! I just seen you come out of Moriarty's as I was passing." (She had seen him go in an hour before and had waited a patient hour in the drug store across the street.) "What you doing around loose this hour the day, anyway?"

"I'm off 'safternoon."

"Are yuh? So'm I." Nicky said nothing. Miss Bauers shifted from one plump silken leg to the other. "What you doing?"

"Oh, nothing much."

"So'm I. Let's do it together." Miss Bauers employed the direct method.

"Well," said Nick, vaguely. He didn't object particularly. And yet he was conscious of some formless program forming mistily in his mind—a program that did not include the berouged, bepowdered, plump, and silken Miss Bauers.

"I phoned you this morning, Nicky. Twice."

"Yeh?"

"They said you wasn't in."

"Yeh?"

A hard young woman, Miss Bauers, yet simple: powerfully drawn toward this magnetic and careless boy; powerless to forge chains strong enough to hold him. "Well, how about Riverview? I ain't been this summer."

"Oh, that's so darn far. Take all day getting there, pretty near."

"Not driving, it wouldn't."

"I ain't got the bus. Busted."

His apathy was getting on her nerves. "How about a movie, then?" Her feet hurt. It was hot.

His glance went up the street toward the Harper, down the street toward the Hyde Park. The sign above the Harper offered Mother o' Mine. The lettering above the Hyde Park announced Love's Sacrifice.

"Gawd, no," he made decisive answer.

Miss Bauers's frazzled nerves snapped. "You make me sick! Standing there. Nothing don't suit you. Say, I ain't so crazy to go round with you. Cheap guy! Prob'ly you'd like to go over to Wooded Island or something, in Jackson Park, and set on the grass and feed the squirrels. That'd be a treat for me, that would." She laughed a high, scornful tear-near laugh.

"Why—say—" Nick stared at her, and yet she felt he did not see her. A sudden peace came into his face—the peace of a longing fulfilled. He turned his head. A Lake Park Avenue street car was roaring its way toward them. He took a step toward the roadway. "I got to be going."

Fear flashed its flame into Miss Bauers's pale blue eyes. "Going! How do you mean, going? Going where?"

"I got to be going." The car had stopped opposite them. His young face was stern, implacable. Miss Bauers knew she was beaten, but she clung to hope tenaciously, piteously. "I got to see a party, see?"

"You never said anything about it in the first place. Pity you wouldn't say so in the first place. Who you got to see, anyway?" She knew it was useless to ask. She knew she was beating her fists against a stone wall, but she must needs ask notwithstanding: "Who you got to see?"

"I got to see a party. I forgot." He made the car step in two long strides; had swung himself up. "So long!" The car door slammed after him. Miss Bauers, in her unavailing silks, stood disconsolate on the hot street corner.

He swayed on the car platform until Sixty-third Street was reached. There he alighted and stood a moment at the curb surveying idly the populous corner. He purchased a paper bag of hot peanuts from a vender's glittering scarlet and nickel stand, and crossed the street into the pathway that led to Jackson Park, munching as he went. In an open space reserved for games some boys were playing baseball with much hoarse hooting and frenzied action. He drew near to watch. The ball, misdirected, sailed suddenly toward him. He ran backward at its swift approach, leaped high, caught it, and with a long curving swing, so easy as to appear almost effortless, sent it hurtling back. The lad on the pitcher's mound made as if to catch it, changed his mind, dodged, started after it.

The boy at bat called to Nick: "Heh, you! Wanna come on and pitch?"

Nick shook his head and went on.

He wandered leisurely along the gravel path that led to the park golf shelter. The wide porch was crowded with golfers and idlers. A foursome was teed up at the first tee. Nick leaned against a porch pillar waiting for them to drive. That old boy had pretty good practise swing. . . . Stiff, though. . . . Lookit that dame. Je's! I bet she takes fifteen shots before she ever gets on to the green. . . . There, that kid had pretty good drive. Must of been hundred and fifty, anyway. Pretty good for a kid.

Nick, in the course of his kaleidoscopic career, had been a caddie at thirteen in torn shirt and flapping knickers. He had played the smooth, expert, scornful game of the caddie with a natural swing from the lithe waist and a follow-through that was the envy of the muscle-bound men who watched him. He hadn't played in years. The game no longer interested him. He entered the shelter lunchroom. The counters were lined with lean, brown, hungry men and lean, brown, hungry women. They were eating incredible dishes considering that the hour was 3 P.M. and the day a hot one. Corned-beef hash with a poached egg on top; wieners and potato salad; meat pies; hot roast beef sandwiches; steaming cups of coffee in thick white ware; watermelon. Nick slid a leg over a stool as he had done earlier in the afternoon. Here, too, the Hebes were of stern stuff, as they needs must be to serve these ravenous hordes of club swingers who swarmed upon them from dawn to dusk. Their task it was to wait upon the golfing male, which is man at his simplest—reduced to the least common denominator and shorn of all attraction for the female eye and heart. They represented merely hungry mouths, weary muscles, reaching fists. The waitresses served them as a capable attendant serves another woman's child—efficiently and without emotion.

"Blueberry pie à la mode," said Nick—"with strawberry ice cream."

Inured as she was to the horrors of gastronomic miscegenation, the waitress—an old girl—recoiled at this.

"Say, I don't think you'd like that. They don't mix so very good. Why don't you try the peach pie instead with the strawberry ice cream—if you want strawberry?" He looked so young and cool and fresh.

"Blueberry," repeated Nick sternly, and looked her in the eye. The old waitress laughed a little and was surprised to find herself laughing. "'S for you to say." She brought him the monstrous mixture, and he devoured it to the last chromatic crumb.

"Nothing the matter with that," he remarked as she passed, dishladen.

She laughed again tolerantly, almost tenderly. "Good thing you're young." Her busy glance lingered a brief moment on his face. He sauntered out.

Now he took the path to the right of the shelter, crossed the road, struck the path again, came to a rustic bridge that humped high in the middle, spanning a cool green stream, willow-bordered. The cool green stream was an emerald chain that threaded its way in a complete circlet about the sylvan spot known as Wooded Island, relic of World's Fair days.

The little island lay, like a thing under enchantment, silent, fragrant, golden, green, exquisite. Squirrels and blackbirds, rabbits and pigeons mingled in Æsopian accord. The air was warm and still, held by the encircling trees and shrubbery. There was not a soul to be seen. At the far north end the two Japanese model houses, survivors of the exposition, gleamed white among the trees.

Nick stood a moment. His eyelids closed, languorously. He stretched his arms out and up deliciously, bringing his stomach in and his chest out. He took off his cap and stuffed it into his pocket. He strolled across the thick cool nap of the grass, deserting the pebble path. At the west edge of the island a sign said: "No One Allowed in the Shrubbery." Ignoring it, Nick parted the branches, stopped and crept, reached the bank that sloped down to the cool green stream, took off his coat, and lay relaxed upon the ground. Above him the tree branches made a pattern against the sky. Little ripples lipped the shore. Scampering velvet-footed things, feathered things, winged things made pleasant stir among the leaves. Nick slept.

He awoke in half an hour refreshed. He lay there, thinking of nothing—a charming gift. He found a stray peanut in his pocket and fed it to a friendly squirrel. His hand encountered the cool metal of his harmonica. He drew out the instrument, placed his coat, folded, under his head, crossed his knees, one leg swinging idly, and began to play rapturously. He was perfectly happy. He played Gimme Love, whose jazz measures are stolen from

Mendelssohn's Spring Song. He did not know this. The leaves rustled. He did not turn his head.

"Hello, Pan!" said a voice. A girl came down the slope and seated herself beside him. She was not smiling.

Nick removed the harmonica from his lips and wiped his mouth with the back of his hand. "Hello who?"

"Hello, Pan."

"Wrong number, lady," Nick said, and again applied his lips to the mouth organ. The girl laughed then, throwing back her head. Her throat was long and slim and brown. She clasped her knees with her arms and looked at Nick amusedly. Nick thought she was a kind of homely little thing.

"Pan," she explained, "was a pagan deity. He played pipes in the woods.

"'S all right with me," Nick ventured, bewildered but amiable. He wished she'd go away. But she didn't. She began to take off her shoes and stockings. She went down to the water's edge, then, and paddled her feet. Nick sat up, outraged. "Say, you can't do that."

She glanced back at him over her shoulder. "Oh, yes, I can. It's so hot." She wriggled her toes ecstatically.

The leaves rustled again, briskly, unmistakably this time. A heavy tread. A rough voice. 'Say, looka here! Get out of there, you! What the–" A policeman, red-faced, wroth. "You can't do that! Get outa here!"

It was like a movie, Nick thought.

The girl turned her head. "Oh, now, Mr. Elwood," she said.

"Oh, it's you, miss," said the policeman. You would not have believed it was the same policeman. He even giggled. "Thought you was away."

"I was. In fact, I am, really. I just got sick of it and ran away for a day. Drove. Alone. The family'll be wild."

"All the way?" said the policeman, incredulously. "Say, I thought that looked like your car standing out there by the road; but I says no, she ain't in town." He looked sharply at Nick, whose face had an Indian composure, though his feelings were mixed. "Who's this?"

"He's a friend of mine. His name's Pan." She was drying her feet with an inadequate rose-colored handkerchief. She crept crabwise up the bank, and put on her stockings and slippers.

"Why'n't you come out and set on a bench?" suggested the policeman, worriedly.

The girl shook her head. "In Arcadia we don't sit on benches. I should think you'd know that. Go on away, there's a dear. I want to talk to this–to Pan."

He persisted. "What'd your pa say, I'd like to know!" The girl shrugged her shoulders. Nick made as though to rise. He was worried. A nut, that's what. She pressed him down with a hard brown hand.

"Now it's all right. He's going. Old Fuss!" The policeman stood a brief moment longer. Then the foliage rustled again. He was gone. The girl sighed, happily. "Play that thing some more, will you? You're a wiz at it, aren't you?"

"I'm pretty good," said Nick, modestly. Then the outrageousness of her conduct struck him afresh. "Say, who're you, anyway?"

"My name's Berry—short for Bernice. . . . What's yours, Pan?"

"Nick—that is—Nick."

"Ugh, terrible! I'll stick to Pan. What d'you do when you're not Panning?" Then, at the bewilderment in his face: "What's your job?"

"I work in the Ideal Garage. Say, you're pretty nosey, ain't you?"

"Yes, pretty. . . . That accounts for your nails, h'm?" She looked at her own brown paws. "'Bout as bad as mine. I drove one hundred and fifty miles today."

"Ya-as, you did!"

"I did! Started at six. And I'll probably drive back tonight."

"You're crazy!"

"I know it," she agreed, "and it's wonderful. . . . Can you play the Tommy Toddle?"

"Yeh. It's kind of hard, though, where the runs are. I don't get the runs so very good." He played it. She kept time with head and feet. When he had finished and wiped his lips:

"Elegant!" She took the harmonica from him, wiped it brazenly on the much-abused, rose-colored handkerchief and began to play, her cheeks puffed out, her eyes round with effort. She played the Tommy Toddle, and her runs were perfect. Nick's chagrin was swallowed by his admiration and envy.

"Say, kid, you got more wind than a factory whistle. Who learned you to play?"

She struck her chest with a hard brown fist. "Tennis. . . . Tim taught me."

"Who's Tim?"

"The—a chauffeur."

Nick leaned closer. "Say, do you ever go to the dances at Englewood Masonic Hall?"

"I never have."

"'Jah like to go some time?"

"I'd love it." She grinned up at him, her teeth flashing white in her brown face.

"It's swell here," he said, dreamily. "Like the woods?"

"Yes."

"Winter, when it's cold and dirty, I think about how it's here summers. It's like you could take it out of your head and look at it whenever you wanted to."

"Endymion."

"Huh?"

"A man said practically the same thing the other day. Name of Keats."

"Yeh?"

"He said: 'A thing of beauty is a joy forever.'"

"That's one way putting it," he agreed, graciously.

Unsmilingly she reached over with one slim forefinger, as if compelled, and touched the blond hairs on Nick's wrist. Just touched them. Nick remained motionless. The girl shivered a little, deliciously. She glanced at him shyly. Her lips were provocative. Thoughtlessly, blindly, Nick suddenly flung an arm about her, kissed her. He kissed her as he had never kissed Miss Bauers—as he had never kissed Miss Ahearn, Miss Olson, or just Gertie. The girl did not scream, or push him away, or slap him, or protest, or giggle as would have the above-mentioned young ladies. She sat breathing rather fast, a tinge of scarlet showing beneath the tan.

"Well, Pan," she said, low-voiced, "you're running true to form, anyway." She eyed him appraisingly. "Your appeal is in your virility, I suppose. Yes."

"My what?"

She rose. "I've got to go."

Panic seized him. "Say, don't drive back tonight, huh? Wherever it is you've got to go. You ain't driving back tonight?"

She made no answer; parted the bushes, was out on the gravel path in the sunlight, a slim, short-skirted, almost childish figure. He followed. They crossed the bridge, left the island, reached the roadway almost in silence. At the side of the road was a roadster. Its hood was the kind that conceals power. Its lamps were two giant eyes rimmed in precious metal. Its line spelled strength. Its body was foreign. Nick's engine-wise eyes saw these things at a glance.

"That your car?"

"Yes."

"Gosh!"

She unlocked it, threw in the clutch, shifted, moved. "Say!" was wrung from Nick helplessly. She waved at him. "Good-by, Pan." He stared, stricken. She was off swiftly, silently; flashed around a corner; was hidden by the trees and shrubs.

He stood a moment. He felt bereaved, cheated. Then a little wave of exaltation shook him. He wanted to talk to someone. "Gosh!" he said again. He glanced at his wrist. Five-thirty. He guessed he'd go home. He guessed he'd go home and get one of Ma's dinners. One of Ma's dinners and talk to Ma. The Sixty-third Street car. He could make it and back in plenty time.

Nick lived in that section of Chicago known as Englewood, which is not so sylvan as it sounds, but appropriate enough for a faun. Not only that; he lived in S. Green Street, Englewood. S. Green Street, near Seventieth, is almost rural with its great elms and poplars, its frame cottages, its back gardens. A neighborhood of thrifty, foreign-born fathers and mothers, many children, tree-lined streets badly paved. Nick turned in at a two-story brown frame cottage. He went around to the back. Ma was in the kitchen.

Nick's presence at the evening meal was an uncertain thing. Sometimes he did not eat at home for a week, excepting only his hurried early breakfast. He rarely spent an evening at home, and when he did used the opportunity for making up lost sleep. Pa never got home from work until after six. Nick liked his dinner early and hot. On his rare visits his mother welcomed him like one of the Gracchi. Mother and son understood each other wordlessly, having much in common. You would not have thought it of her (forty-six bust, forty waist, measureless hips), but Ma was a nymph at heart. Hence Nick.

"Hello, Ma!" She was slamming expertly about the kitchen.

"Hello, yourself," said Ma. Ma had a line of slang gleaned from her numerous brood. It fell strangely from her lips. Ma had never quite lost a tinge of foreign accent, though she had come to America when a girl, A hearty, zestful woman, savoring life with gusto, undiminished by child-bearing and hard work. Eating home, Dewey?" She alone used his given name.

"Yeh, but I gotta be back by seven-thirty. Got anything ready?"

"Dinner ain't, but I'll get you something. Plenty. Platter ham and eggs and a quick fry. Cherry cobbler's done. I'll fix you some." (Cherry cobbler is shortcake with a soul.)

He ate enormously at the kitchen table, she hovering over him.

"What's the news, Dewey?"

"Ain't none." He ate in silence. Then: "How old was you when you married Pa?"

"Me? Say, I wasn't no more'n a kid. I gotta laugh when I think of it."

"What was Pa earning?"

She laughed a great hearty laugh, dipping a piece of bread sociably in the ham fat on the platter as she stood by the table, just to bear him company.

"Say, earn! If he'd of earned what you was earning now, we'd of thought we was millionaires. Time Etty was born he was pulling down thirteen a week, and we saved on it." She looked at him suddenly, sharply. "Why?"

"Oh, I was just wondering."

"Look what good money he's getting now! If I was you, I wouldn't stick around no old garage for what they give you. You could get a good job in the works with Pa; first thing you know you'd be pulling down big money. You're smart like that with engines. . . . Takes a lot of money nowadays for feller to get married."

"You *tell* 'em," agreed Nick. He looked up at her, having finished eating. His glance was almost tender. "How'd you come to marry Pa, anyway? You and him's so different."

The nymph in Ma leaped to the surface and stayed there a moment, sparkling, laughing, dimpling. "Oh, I dunno. I kept running away and he kept running after. Like that."

He looked up again quickly at that. "Yeh. That's it. Fella don't like to have no girl chasing him all the time. Say, he likes to do the chasing himself. Ain't that the truth?"

"You *tell* 'em!" agreed Ma. A great jovial laugh shook her. Heavy-footed now, but light of heart.

Suddenly: "I'm thinking; of going to night school. Learn something. I don't know nothing."

"You do, too, Dewey!"

"Aw, wha'd I know? I never had enough schooling. Wished I had."

"Who's doings was it? You wouldn't stay. Wouldn't go no more than sixth reader and quit. Nothing wouldn't get you to go."

He agreed gloomily. "I know it. I don't know what nothing is. Uh—Arcadia—or—now—vitality or nothing."

"Oh, that comes easy," she encouraged him, "when you begin once."

He reached for her hand gratefully. "You're a swell cook, Ma." He had a sudden burst of generosity, of tenderness. "Soon's the bus is fixed I'll take you joy-riding over to the lake."

Ma always wore a boudoir cap of draggled lace and ribbon for motoring. Nick almost never offered her a ride. She did not expect him to.

She pushed him playfully. "Go on! You got plenty young girls to take riding, not your ma."

"Oh, girls!" he said, scornfully. Then in another tone: "Girls."

He was off. It was almost seven. Pa was late. He caught a car back to Fifty-third Street. Elmer was lounging in the cool doorway of the garage. Nick, in sheer exuberance of spirits, squared off, doubled his fists, and danced about Elmer in a semicircle, working his arms as a prizefighter does, warily. He jabbed at Elmer's jaw playfully.

"What you been doing," inquired that long-suffering gentleman, "makes you feel so good? Where you been?"

"Oh, nowheres. Bumming round. Park."

He turned in the direction of the stairway. Elmer lounged after him. "Oh, say, dame's been calling you for the last hour and a half. Like to busted the phone. Makes me sick."

"Aw, Bauers."

"No, that wasn't the name. Name's Mary or Berry, or something like that. A dozen times, I betcha. Says you was to call her as soon as you come in. Drexel 47—wait a min't'—yeh—that's right—Drexel 473—"

"Swell chanst," said Nick. Suddenly his buoyancy was gone. His shoulders drooped. His cigarette dangled limp. Disappointment curved his lips, burdened his eyes. "*Swell* chanst!"

FANNIE HURST

[1889–1968]

Humoresque

(First published in *Cosmopolitan*, March, 1919; first book publication in 1919.)

ON EITHER SIDE of the Bowery, which cuts through like a drain to catch its sewage, Every Man's Land, a reeking march of humanity and humidity, steams with the excrement of seventeen languages, flung in patois from tenement windows, fire-escapes, curbs, stoops, and cellars whose walls are terrible and spongy with fungi.

By that impregnable chemistry of race whereby the red blood of the Mongolian and the red blood of the Caucasian become as oil and water in the mingling, Mulberry Street, bounded by sixteen languages, runs its intact Latin length of push-carts, clothes-lines, naked babies, drying vermicelli; black-eyed women in rhinestone combs and perennially big with child; whole families of buttonhole-makers who first saw the blue-and-gold light of Sorrento, bent at home work round a single gas flare; pomaded barbers of a thousand Neapolitan amours. And then, just as suddenly, almost without osmosis and by the mere stepping down from the curb, Mulberry becomes Mott Street, hung in grill-work balconies, the moldy smell of poverty touched up with incense. Orientals whose feet shuffle and whose faces are carved out of satinwood. Forbidden women, their white, drugged faces behind upper windows. Yellow children, incongruous enough in Western clothing. A draughty areaway with an oblique of gaslight and a black well of descending staircase. Show-windows of jade and tea and Chinese porcelains.

More streets emanating out from Mott like a hand-ful of crooked rheumatic fingers, then suddenly the Bowery again, cowering beneath Elevated trains, where men burned down to the butt end of soiled lives pass in and out and out and in of the knee-high swinging doors, a veiny-nosed, acid-eaten race in themselves.

Allen Street, too, still more easterly, and half as wide, is straddled its entire width by the steely, long-legged skeleton of Elevated traffic, so that its third-floor windows no sooner shudder into silence from the rushing shock of one train than they are shaken into chatter by the passage of another. Indeed, third-floor dwellers of Allen Street, reaching out, can almost touch the serrated edges of the Elevated structure, and in summer the smell of its hot rails becomes an actual taste in the mouth. Passengers, in turn, look in upon this horizontal of life as they whiz by. Once, in fact, the blurry figure of what might have been a woman leaned out, as she passed, to toss into one Abrahm Kantor's apartment a short-stemmed pink carnation. It hit softly on little Leon Kantor's crib, brushing him fragrantly across the mouth and causing him to pucker up.

Beneath, where even in August noonday, the sun cannot find its way by a chink, and babies lie stark naked in the cavernous shade, Allen Street presents a sort of submarine and greenish gloom, as if its humanity were actually moving through a sea of aqueous shadows, faces rather bleached and shrunk from sunlessness as water can bleach and shrink. And then, like a shimmering background of orange-finned and copper-flanked marine life, the brass-shops of Allen Street, whole rows of them, burn flamelessly and without benefit of fuel.

To enter Abrahm Kantor's—Brasses, was three steps down, so that his casement show-window, at best filmed over with the constant rain of dust ground down from the rails above, was obscure enough, but crammed with copied loot of khedive and of czar. The seven-branch candlestick so biblical and supplicating of arms. An urn, shaped like Rebecca's, of brass, all beaten over with little pocks. Things—cups, trays, knockers, ikons, gargoyles, bowls, and teapots. A symphony of bells in graduated sizes. Jardinières with fat sides. A potbellied samovar. A swinging-lamp for the dead, star-shaped. Against the door, an octave of tubular chimes, prisms of voiceless harmony and of heatless light.

Opening this door, they rang gently, like melody heard through water and behind glass. Another bell rang, too, in tilted singsong from a pulley operating somewhere in the catacomb rear of this lambent vale of things and things and things. In turn, this pulley set in toll still another bell, two flights up in Abrahm Kantor's tenement, which overlooked the front of whizzing rails and a rear wilderness of gibbet-looking clothes-lines, dangling perpetual specters of flapping union suits in a mid-air flaky with soot.

Often at lunch, or even the evening meal, this bell would ring in on Abrahm Kantor's digestive wellbeing, and while he hurried down, napkin often bib-fashion still about his neck, and into the smouldering lanes of copper, would leave an eloquent void at the head of his well-surrounded table.

This bell was ringing now, jingling in upon the slumber of a still newer Kantor, snuggling peacefully enough within the ammoniac depths of a cradle recently evacuated by Leon, heretofore impinged upon you.

On her knees before an oven that billowed forth hotly into her face, Mrs. Kantor, fairly fat and not yet forty, and at the immemorial task of plumbing a delicately swelling layer-cake with broomstraw, raised her face, reddened and faintly moist.

"Isadore, run down and say your papa is out until six. If it's a customer, remember the first asking-price is the two middle figures on the tag, and the last asking-price is the two outside figures. See once, with your papa out to buy your little brother his birthday present, and your mother in a cake, if you can't make a sale for first price."

Isadore Kantor, aged eleven and hunched with a younger Kantor over an oilcloth-covered table, hunched himself still deeper in a barter for a large crystal marble with a candy stripe down its center.

"Izzie, did you hear me?"

"Yes 'm."

"Go down this minute—do you hear? Rudolph, stop always letting your big brother get the best of you in marbles. Iz-zie!"

"In-a-minute."

"Don't let me have to ask you again, Isadore Kantor!"

"Aw, ma, I got some 'rithmetic to do. Let Esther go!"

"Always Esther! Your sister stays right in the front room with her spelling."

"Aw, ma, I got spelling, too."

"Every time I ask that boy he should do me one thing, right away he gets lessons! With me, that lessons-talk don't go no more. Every time you get put down in school, I'm surprised there's a place left lower where they can put you. Working-papers for such a boy like you!"

"I'll woik—"

"How I worried myself! Violin lessons yet—thirty cents a lesson out of your papa's pants while he slept! That's how I wanted to have in the family a profession—maybe a musician on the violin! Lessons for you out of money I had to lie to your papa about! Honest, when I think of it—my own husband—it's a wonder I don't potch you just for remembering it. Rudolph, will you stop licking that cake-pan? It's saved for your little brother Leon. Ain't you ashamed even on your little brother's birthday to steal from him?"

"Ma, gimme the spoon?"

"I'll give you the spoon, Isadore Kantor, where you don't want it. If you don't hurry down, the way that bell is ringing, not one bite do you get out of your little brother's birthday cake to-night!"

"I'm goin', ain't I?"

"Always on my children's birthdays a meanness sets into this house! Rudolph, will you put down that bowl! Iz-zie—for the last time I ask you—for the last time—"

Erect now, Mrs. Kantor lifted an expressive hand, letting it hover.

"I'm goin', ma; for golly sakes, I'm goin'!" said her recalcitrant one, shuffling off toward the staircase, shuffling, shuffling.

Then Mrs. Kantor resumed her plumbing, and through the little apartment, its middle and only bedroom of three beds and a crib lighted vicariously by the front room and kitchen, began to wind the warm, the golden-brown fragrance of cake in the rising.

By six o'clock the shades were drawn against the dirty dusk of Allen Street and the oilcloth-covered table dragged out center and spread by Esther Kantor, nine in years, in the sturdy little legs bulging over shoe-tops, in the pink cheeks that sagged slightly of plumpness, and in the utter roundness of face and gaze, but mysteriously older in the little-mother lore of crib and knee-dangling ditties and in the ropy length and thickness of the two brown plaits down her back.

There was an eloquence to that waiting, laid-out table, the print of the family already gathered about it; the dynastic high chair, throne of each succeeding Kantor; an armchair drawn up before the paternal mustache-cup; the ordinary kitchen chair of Mannie Kantor, who spilled things, an oil cloth sort of bib dangling from its back; the little chair of Leon Kantor, cushioned in an old family album that raised his chin above the table. Even in cutlery the Kantor family was not lacking in variety. Surrounding a centerpiece of thick Russian lace were Russian spoons washed in washed-off gilt; forks of one, two, and three tines; steel knives with black handles; a hartshorn carving-knife. A round four pound loaf of black bread waiting to be torn, and to-night, on the festive mat of cotton lace, a cake of pinkly gleaming icing, encircled with five pink little candles.

At slightly after six Abrahm Kantor returned, leading by a resisting wrist Leon Kantor, his stemlike little legs, hit midship, as it were, by not sufficiently cut-down trousers and so narrow and birdlike of face that his eyes quite obliterated the remaining map of his features, like those of a still wet nestling. All except his ears. They poised at the sides of Leon's shaved head of black bristles, as if butterflies had just lighted there, whispering, with very spread wings, their message, and presently would fly off again. By some sort of muscular contraction he could wiggle these ears at will, and would do so for a penny or a whistle, and upon one occasion for his brother Rudolph's dead rat, so devised as to dangle from string and window before the unhappy passerby. They were quivering now, these ears, but because the entire little face was twitching back tears and gulp of sobs.

"Abrahm–Leon–what is it?" Her hands and her forearms instantly out from the business of kneading something meaty and floury, Mrs. Kantor rushed forward, her glance quick from one to the other of them. "Abrahm, what's wrong?"

"I'll feedle him! I'll feedle him!"

The little pulling wrist still in clutch, Mr. Kantor regarded his wife, the lower half of his face, well covered with reddish bristles, undershot, his free hand and even his eyes violently lifted. To those who see in a man a perpetual kinship to that animal kingdom of which he is supreme, there was something undeniably anthropoidal about Abrahm Kantor, a certain simian width between the eyes and long, rather agile hands with hairy backs.

"Hush it!" cried Mr. Kantor, his free hand raised in threat of descent, and cowering his small son to still more undersized proportions. "Hush it or, by golly! I'll—"

"Abrahm—Abrahm—what is it?"

Then Mr. Kantor gave vent in acridity of word and feature.

"*Schlemmil*!" he cried. "*Momser*! *Ganef*! *Nebich*!" by which, in smiting mother tongue, he branded his offspring with attributes of apostate and ne'er-do-well, of idiot and thief.

"Abrahm!"

"*Schlemmil*!" repeated Mr. Kantor, swinging Leon so that he described a large semicircle that landed him into the meaty and waiting embrace of his mother. "Take him! You should be proud of such a little *momser* for a son! Take him, and here you got back his birthday dollar. A feedle! Honest —when I think on it—a feedle!"

Such a rush of outrage seemed fairly to strangle Mr. Kantor that he stood, hand still upraised, choking and inarticulate above the now frankly howling huddle of his son.

"Abrahm, you should just once touch this child! How he trembles! Leon—mamma's baby—what is it? Is this how you come back when papa takes you out to buy your birthday present? Ain't you ashamed?"

Mouth distended to a large and blackly hollow O, Leon, between terrifying spells of breath-holding, continued to howl.

"All the way to Naftel's toy-store I drag him. A birthday present for a dollar his mother wants he should have, all right, a birthday present! I give you my word till I'm ashamed for Naftel, every toy in his shelves is pulled down. Such a cow—that shakes with his head—"

"No—no—no!" This from young Leon, beating at his mother's skirts.

Again the upraised but never quite descending hand of his father.

"By golly! I'll 'no—no' you!"

"Abrahm—go 'way! Baby, what did papa do?"

Then Mr. Kantor broke into an actual tarantella of rage, his hands palms up and dancing.

"'What did papa do?' she asks. She's got easy asking. 'What did papa do?' The whole shop, I tell you. A sheep with a baa inside when you squeeze on him—games—a horn so he can holler my head off—such a knife like Izzie's with a scissors in it. 'Leon,' I said, ashamed for Naftel, 'that's a fine knife, like Izzie's so you can cut up with. All right then'—when I see how he hollers—'such a box full of soldiers to have war with,' 'Dollar seventy-five,' says Naftel. 'All right, then,' I says, when I seen how he keeps hollering. 'Give you a dollar fifteen for 'em.' I should make myself small for fifteen cents more.

'Dollar fifteen,' I says - anything so he should shut up with his hollering for what he seen in the window."

"He seen something in the window he wanted Abrahm?"

"Didn't I tell you? A feedle! A four-dollar feedle! A moosicer, so we should have another feedler in the family for some thirty-cents lessons."

"Abrahm—you mean—he—our Leon—wanted a violin?"

"'Wanted,' she says. I could potch him again this minute for how he wanted it! Du—you little bum you—chammer—momser—I'll feedle you!"—

Across Mrs. Kantor's face, as she knelt there in the shapeless cotton-stuff uniform of poverty through the very tenement of her body, a light had flashed up into her eyes. She drew her son closer, crushing his puny cheek up against hers, cupping his bristly little head in her by no means immaculate palms.

"He wanted a violin! It's come, Abrahm! The dream of all my life—my prayers—it's come. I knew it must be one of my children if I waited long enough—and prayed enough. A musician! He wants a violin! He cried for a violin! My baby! Why, darlink, mama'll sell her clothes off her back to get you a violin. He's a musician, Abrahm! I should have known it the way he's fooling always around the chimes and the bells in the store!"

Then Mr. Kantor took to rocking his head between his palms.

"Oi-oi! The mother is crazier as her son. A moosician! A *fresser*, you mean. Such an eater, it's a wonder he ain't twice too big instead of twice too little for his age."

"That's a sign, Abrahm; geniuses, they all eat big. For all we know, he's a genius. I swear to you, Abrahm, all the months before he was born I prayed for it. Each one before they came, I prayed it should be the one. I thought that time the way our Isadore ran after the organ grinder he would be the one. How could I know it was the monkey he wanted? When Isadore wouldn't take to it I prayed my next one, and then my next one, should have the talent. I've prayed for it, Abrahm. If he wants a violin, please, he should have it."

"Not with my money."

"With mine! I got enough saved, Abrahm. Them three extra dollars right here inside my own waist. Just that much for that cape down on Grand Street. I wouldn't have it now, the way they say the wind blows up them—"

"I tell you the woman's crazy—"

I feel it! I know he's got talent! I know my children so well. A—a father don't understand. I'm so next to them. It's like I can tell always everything that will happen to them—it's like a pain—somewheres here—like in back of my heart."

"A pain in the heart she gets."

"For my own children I'm always a prophet, I tell you! You think I didn't know that—that terrible night after the pogrom after we got out of Kief to across the border! You remember, Abrahm, how I predicted it to you then—how our Mannie would be born too soon and—and not right from my suffering! Did it happen on the ship to America just the way I said it would? Did it happen just exactly how I predicted our Izzie wold break his leg that time playing on the fire-escape? I tell you, Abrahm, I get a real pain here under my heart that tells me what comes to my children. Didn't I tell you how Esther would be the first in her confirmation-class and our baby Boris would be red-headed? At only five years, our Leon all by himself cries for a fiddle—get it for him, Abrahm—get it for him!"

"I tell you, Sarah, I got a crazy woman for a wife! It ain't enough we celebrate eight birthdays a year with one-dollar presents each time and copper goods every day higher. It ain't enough that right to-morrow I got a fifty-dollar note over me from Sol Ginsberg; a four-dollar present she wants for a child that don't even know the name of a feedle."

"Leon, baby, stop hollering. Papa will go back and get the fiddle for you now before supper. See, mamma's got money here in her waist—"

"Papa will go back for the feedle *not*—three dollars she's saved for herself he can holler out of her for a feedle!"

"Abrahm, he's screaming so he—he'll have a fit."

"He should have two fits."

"Darlink—"

"I tell you the way you spoil your children it will some day come back on us."

"It's his birthday night, Abrahm—five years since his little head first lay on the pillow next to me."

"All right—all right—drive me crazy because he's got a birthday."

"Leon baby—if you don't stop hollering you'll make yourself sick. Abrahm, I never saw him like this—he's green—"

"I'll green him. Where is that old feedle from Isadore—that seventy-five-cents one?"

"I never thought of that! You broke it that time you got mad at Isadore's lessons. I'll run down. Maybe it's with the junk behind the store. I never thought of that fiddle. Leon darlink—wait! Mamma'll run down and look. Wait, Leon, till mamma finds you a fiddle."

The raucous screams stopped then, suddenly, and on their very lustiest crest, leaving an echoing gash across silence. On willing feet of haste Mrs. Kantor wound down backward the high, ladder-like staircase that led to the brass-shop.

Meanwhile to a gnawing consciousness of dinner-hour had assembled the house of Kantor. Attuned to the intimate atmosphere of the tenement which is so constantly rent with cry of child, child-bearing, delirium, delirium tremens, Leon Kantor had howled no impression into the motley din of things. There were Isadore, already astride his chair, leaning well into center table, for first vociferous tear at the four-pound loaf; Esther, old at chores, settling an infant into the high chair, careful of tiny fingers in lowering the wooden bib.

"Papa, Izzie's eating first again."

"Put down that loaf and wait until your mother dishes up, or you'll get a potch you won't soon forget."

"Say, pop–"

"Don't 'say, pop' me! I don't want no streetbum freshness from you!"

"I mean, papa, there was an up-town swell in, and she bought one of them seventy-five-cent candlesticks for the first price."

"*Schlemmil*! *Chammer*!" said Mr. Kantor, rinsing his hands at the sink. "Didn't I always tell you it's the first price, times two, when you see up-town business come in? Haven't I learned it to you often enough a slummer must pay for her nosiness?"

There entered then, on poor, shuffling feet, Mannie Kantor, so marred in the mysterious and ceramic process of life that the brain and the soul had stayed back sooner than inhabit him. Seventeen in years, in the down upon his face and in growth unretarded by any great nervosity of system, his vacuity of face was not that of childhood, but rather as if his light eyes were peering out from some hinterland and wanting so terribly and so dumbly to communicate what they beheld to brain-cells closed against himself.

At sight of Mannie, Leon Kantor, the tears still wetly and dirtily down his cheeks, left off his black, fierce-eyed stare of waiting long enough to smile, darkly, it is true, but sweetly.

"Giddy-app!" he cried. "Giddy-app!"

And then Mannie, true to habit, would scamper and scamper.

Up out of the traplike stair-opening came the head of Mrs. Kantor, disheveled and a smudge of soot across her face, but beneath her arm, triumphant, a violin of one string and a broken back.

"See, Leon–what mamma got! A violin! A fiddle! Look! The bow, too, I found. It ain't much, baby, but it's a fiddle."

"Aw, ma–that's my old violin. Gimme. I want it. Where'd you find–"

"Hush up, Izzie! This ain't yours no more. See, Leon, what mamma brought you. A violin!"

"Now, you little *chammer*, you got a feedle, and if you ever let me hear you holler again for a feedle, by golly! if I don't–"

From his corner, Leon Kantor reached out, taking the instrument and fitting it beneath his chin, the bow immediately feeling, surely and lightly, for string.

"Look, Abrahm, he knows how to hold it! What did I tell you? A child that never in his life seen a fiddle, except a beggar's on the street!"

Little Esther suddenly cantered down-floor, clapping her chubby hands.

"Lookie–lookie–Leon!"

The baby ceased clattering his spoon against the wooden bib. A silence seemed to shape itself.

So black and so bristly of head, his little clawlike hands hovering over the bow, Leon Kantor withdrew a note, strangely round and given up almost sobbingly from the single string. A note of warm twining quality, like a baby's finger.

"Leon–darlink!"

Fumbling for string and for notes the instrument could not yield up to him, the birdlike mouth began once more to open widely and terribly into the orificial O.

It was then Abrahm Kantor came down with a large hollow resonance of palm against that aperture, lifting his small son and depositing him plop upon the family album.

"Take that! By golly! One more whimper out of you and if I don't make you black-and-blue, birthday or no birthday! Dish up, Sarah, quick, or I'll give him something to cry about."

The five pink candles had been lighted, burning pointedly and with slender little smoke wisps. Regarding them owlishly, the tears dried on Leon's face, his little tongue licking up at them.

"Look how solemn he is, like he was thinking of something a million miles away except how lucky he is he should have a pink birthday-cake. Uh—uh–uh! Don't you begin to holler again. Here, I'm putting the feedle next to you. Uh–uh–uh!"

To a meal plentifully ladled out directly from stove to table, the Kantor family drew up, dipping first into the rich black soup of the occasion. All except Mrs. Kantor.

"Esther, you dish up. I'm going somewhere. I'll be back in a minute."

"Where you going, Sarah? Won't it keep until–"

But even in the face of query, Sarah Kantor was two flights down and well through the lambent aisles of the copper-shop. Outside, she broke into a run, along two blocks of the indescribable bazaar atmosphere of Grand Street, then one block to the right.

Before Naftel's show-window, a jet of bright gas burned into a jibberwock land of toys. There was that in Sarah Kantor's face that was actually lyrical as, fumbling at the bosom of her dress, she entered.

To Leon Kantor, by who knows what symphonic scheme of things, life was a chromatic scale, yielding up to him, through throbbing, living nerves of sheep-gut, the sheerest semitones of man's emotions.

When he tucked his Stradivarius beneath his chin the book of life seemed suddenly translated to him in melody. Even Sarah Kantor, who still brewed for him, on a small portable stove carried from city to city and surreptitiously unpacked in hotel suites, the blackest of soups, and, despite his protestation, would incase his ears of nights in an old home-made device against their flightiness, would oftentimes bleed inwardly at this sense of his isolation.

There was a realm into which he went alone, leaving her as detached as the merest ticket purchaser at the box-office.

At seventeen Leon Kantor had played before the crowned heads of Europe, the aching heads of American capital, and even the shaved head of a South Sea prince. There was a layout of anecdotal gifts, from the molar tooth of the South Sea prince set in a South Sea pearl to a blue-enameled snuff-box incrusted with the rearing-lion coat-of-arms of a very royal house.

At eighteen came the purchase of a king's Stradivarius for a king's ransom, and acclaimed by Sunday supplements to repose of nights in an ivory cradle.

At nineteen, under careful auspices of press agent, the ten singing digits of the son of Abrahm Kantor were insured at ten thousand dollars the finger.

At twenty he had emerged surely and safely from the perilous quicksands which have sucked down whole Lilliputian worlds of infant prodigies.

At twenty-one, when Leon Kantor played a Sunday-night concert, there was a human queue curling entirely around the square block of the opera-house, waiting its one, two, even three and four hours for the privilege of standing room only.

Usually these were Leon Kantor's own people pouring up from the lowly lands of the East Side to the white lands of Broadway, parched for music, these burning brethren of his—old men in that line, frequently carrying their own little folding camp-chairs, not against weariness of the spirit, but of the flesh; youth with Slavic eyes and cheek-bones. These were the six-deep human phalanx which would presently slant down at him from tiers of steepest balconies and stand frankly emotional and jammed in the unreserved space behind the railing which shut them off from the three dollar seats of the reserved.

At a very special one of these concerts, dedicated to the meager purses of just these, and held in New York's super opera-house, the Amphitheater, a great bowl of humanity, the metaphor made perfect by tiers of seats placed upon the stage, rose from orchestra to dome. A gigantic cup of a Colosseum lined in stacks and stacks of faces. From the door of his dressing-room, leaning out, Leon Kantor could see a great segment of it, buzzing down into adjustment, orchestra twitting and tuning into it.

In the bare little room, illuminated by a sheaf of roses, just arrived, Mrs. Kantor drew him back by the elbow.

"Leon, you're in a draught."

The amazing years had dealt kindly with Mrs. Kantor. Stouter, softer, apparently even taller, she was full of small new authorities that could shut out cranks, newspaper reporters, and autograph fiends. A fitted-over-corsets black taffeta and a high comb in the graying hair had done their best with her. Pride, too, had left its flush upon her cheeks, like two round spots of fever.

"Leon, it's thirty minutes till your first number. Close that door. Do you want to let your papa and his excitement in on you?"

The son of Sarah Kantor obeyed, leaning his short, rather narrow form in silhouette against the closed door. In spite of slimly dark evening clothes worked out by an astute manager to the last detail in boyish effects, there was that about him which defied long-haired precedent. Slimly and straightly he had shot up into an unmannered, a short, even a bristly-haired young manhood, disqualifying by a close shave for the older school of hirsute virtuosity.

But his nerves did not spare him. On concert nights they seemed to emerge almost to the surface of him and shriek their exposure.

"Just feel my hands, ma. Like ice."

She dived down into her large silk what-not of a reticule.

"I've got your fleece-lined gloves here, son."

"No–no! For God's sake–not those things! No!"

He was back at the door again, opening it to a slit, peering through.

"They're bringing more seats on the stage. If they crowd me in I won't go on. I can't play if I hear them breathe. Hi–out there–no more chairs! Pa! Hancock–"

"Leon, Leon, ain't you ashamed to get so worked up? Close that door. Have you got a manager who is paid just to see to your comfort? When papa comes, I'll have him go out and tell Hancock you don't want chairs so close to you. Leon, will you mind mamma and sit down?"

"It's a bigger house than the royal concert in Madrid, ma. Why, I never saw anything like it! It's a stampede. God! this is real–this is what gets me, playing for my own! I should have given a concert like this three years ago. I'll do it every year now. I'd rather play before them than all the crowned heads on earth. It's the biggest night of my life. They're rioting out there, ma–rioting to get in."

"Leon, Leon, won't you sit down, if mamma begs you to?"

He sat then, strumming with all ten fingers upon his knees.

"Try to get quiet, son. Count–like you always do. One–two–three–"

"Please, ma–for God's sake–please–please!"

"Look–such beautiful roses! From Sol Ginsberg, an old friend of papa's he used to buy brasses from eighteen years ago. Six years he's been away with his daughter in Munich. Such a beautiful mezzo they say, engaged already for Metropolitan next season.

"I hate it, ma, if they breathe on my neck."

"Leon darlink, did mamma promise to fix it? Have I ever let you play a concert when you wouldn't be comfortable?"

His long, slim hands suddenly prehensile and cutting a streak of upward gesture, Leon Kantor rose to his feet, face whitening.

"Do it now! Now, I tell you. I won't have them breathe on me. Do you hear me? Now! Now! Now!"

Risen also, her face soft and tremulous for him, Mrs. Kantor put out a gentle, a sedative hand upon his sleeve.

"Son," she said, with an edge of authority even behind her smile, "don't holler at me!"

He grasped her hand with his two and, immediately quiet, lay a close string of kisses along it.

"Mamma," he said, kissing again and again into the palm, "mamma—mamma."

"I know, son; it's nerves!"

"They eat me, ma. Feel—I'm like ice! I didn't mean it; you know I didn't mean it!"

"My baby," she said, "my wonderful boy, it's like I can never get used to the wonder of having you. The greatest one of them all should be mine—a plain woman's like mine!"

He teased her, eager to conciliate and to ride down his own state of quivering.

"Now, ma—now—now—don't forget Rimsky!"

"Rimsky! A man three times your age who was playing concerts before you was born! Is that a comparison? From your clippings-books I can show Rimsky who the world considers the greatest violinist. Rimsky he rubs into me!"

"All right, then, the press-clippings, but did Elsass, the greatest manager of them all, bring me a contract for thirty concerts at two thousand a concert? Now I've got you! Now!"

She would not meet his laughter. "Elsass! Believe me, he'll come to you yet! My boy should worry if he makes fifty thousand a year more or less. Rimsky should have that honor—for so long as he can hold it. But he won't hold it long. Believe me, I don't rest easy in my bed till Elsass comes after you. Not for so big a contract like Rimsky's, but bigger—not for thirty concerts, but for fifty!"

"*Brava! Brava!* There's a woman for you. More money than she knows what to do with, and then not satisfied!"

She was still too tremulous for banter. "'Not satisfied'? Why, Leon, I never stop praying my thanks for you!"

"All right, then," he cried, laying his icy fingers on her cheek; " to-morrow we'll call a *mignon*—a regular old-fashioned Allen Street prayer-party."

"Leon, you mustn't make fun."

"Make fun of the sweetest girl in this room!"

"'Girl'! Ah, if I could only hold you by me this way, Leon. Always a boy—with me—your poor old mother—your only girl. That's a fear I suffer with, Leon—to lose you to a—girl. That's how selfish the mother of such a wonder-child like mine can get to be."

"All right! Trying to get me married off again. Nice! Fine!"

"Is it any wonder I suffer, son? Twenty-one years to have kept you by me a child. A boy that never in his life was out after midnight except to catch trains. A boy that never has so much as looked at a girl and could have looked at princesses. To have kept you all these years—mine—is it any wonder, son, I never stop praying my thanks for you? You don't believe Hancock, son, the way he keeps always teasing you that you should have a—what he calls—affair—a love-affair? Such talk is not nice, Leon—an affair!"

"Love-affair poppycock!" said Leon Kantor, lifting his mother's face and kissing her on eyes about ready to tear. "Why, I've got something, ma, right here in my heart for you that—"

"Leon, be careful your shirt-front!"

"That's so—so what you call 'tender,' for my best sweetheart that I— Oh, love-affair—poppycock!"

She would not let her tears come.

"My boy—my wonder-boy!"

"There goes the overture, ma."

"Here, darlink—your glass of water."

"I can't stand it in here; I'm suffocating!"

"Got your mute in your pocket, son?"

"Yes, ma; for God's sake, yes! Yes! Don't keep asking things!"

"Ain't you ashamed, Leon, to be in such an excitement! For every concert you get worse."

"The chairs—they'll breathe on my neck."

" Leon, did mamma promise you those chairs would be moved?"

" Where's Hancock ?"

"Say—I'm grateful if he stays out. It took me enough work to get this room cleared. You know your papa how he likes to drag in the whole world to show you off—always just before you play. The minute he walks in the room right away he gets everybody to trembling just from his own excitements. I dare him this time he should bring people. No dignity has that man got, the way he brings every one."

Even upon her words came a rattling of door, of door-knob, and a voice through the clamor.

"Open—quick—Sarah! Leon!"

A stiffening raced over Mrs. Kantor, so that she sat rigid on her chair-edge, lips compressed, eye darkly upon the shivering door.

"Open—Sarah!"

With a narrowing glance, Mrs. Kantor laid to her lips a forefinger of silence.

"Sarah, it's me! Quick, I say!"

Then Leon Kantor sprang up, the old prehensile gesture of curving fingers shooting up.

"For God's sake, ma, let him in! I can't stand that infernal battering."

"Abrahm, go away! Leon's got to have quiet before his concert."

"Just a minute, Sarah. Open quick!"

With a spring his son was at the door, unlocking and flinging it back.

"Come in, pa."

The years had weighed heavily upon Abrahm Kantor in avoirdupois only. He was himself plus eighteen years, fifty pounds, and a new sleek pomposity that was absolutely oleaginous. It shone roundly in his face, doubling of chin, in the bulge of waistcoat, heavily gold-chained, and in eyes that behind the gold-rimmed glasses gave sparklingly forth his estate of well-being.

"Abrahm, didn't I tell you not to dare to—"

On excited balls of feet that fairly bounced him, Abrahm Kantor burst in.

"Leon—mamma—I got out here an old friend—Sol Ginsberg. You remember, mamma, from brasses—"

"Abrahm—not now—"

"Go 'way with your 'not now'! I want Leon should meet him. Sol, this is him—a little grown up from such a *nebich* like you remember him—*nu*? Sarah, you remember Sol Ginsberg? Say—I should ask you if you remember your right hand! Ginsberg & Esel, the firm. This is his girl, a five years' contract signed yesterday—five hundred dollars an opera for a beginner—six rôles—not bad—*nu*?"

"Abrahm, you must ask Mr. Ginsberg please to excuse Leon until after his concert—"

"Shake hands with him, Ginsberg. He's had his hand shook enough in his life, and by kings, to shake it once more with an old bouncer like you!"

Mr. Ginsberg, not unlike his colleague in rotundities, held out a short, a dimpled hand.

"It's a proud day," he said, "for me to shake the hands from mine old friend's son and the finest violinist livink to-day. My little daughter—"

"Yes, yes, Gina. Here, shake hands with him. Leon, they say a voice like a fountain. Gina Berg—eh, Ginsberg—is how you stage-named her? You hear, mamma, how fancy—Gina Berg? We go hear her, eh?"

There was about Miss Gina Berg, whose voice could soar to the tirra-lirra of a lark and then deepen to mezzo, something of the actual slimness of the poor, maligned Elsa so long buried beneath the buxomness of divas. She was like a little flower that in its crannied nook keeps dewy longest.

"How do you do, Leon Kantor?"

There was a whir through her English of three acquired languages.

"How do *you* do?"

"We—father and I—traveled once all the way from Brussels to Dresden to hear you. It was worth it. I shall never forget how you played the 'Humoresque.' It made me laugh and cry."

"You like Brussels?"

She laid her little hand to her heart, half closing her eyes.

"I will never be so happy again as with the sweet little people of Brussels."

"I, too, love Brussels. I studied there four years with Ahrenfest."

"I know you did. My teacher, Lyndahl, in Berlin, was his brother-in-law."

"You have studied with Lyndahl?"

"He is my master."

"I— Will I some time hear you sing?"

"I am not yet great. When I am foremost like you, yes."

"Gina—Gina Berg; that is a beautiful name to make famous."

"You see how it is done? Gins—berg. Gina Berg."

"Clev—er!"

They stood then smiling across a chasm of the diffidence of youth, she fumbling at the great fur pelt out of which her face flowered so dewily.

"I— Well—we—we—are in the fourth box— I guess we had better be going— Fourth box, left."

He wanted to find words, but for consciousness of self, could not.

"It's a wonderful house out there waiting for you, Leon Kantor, and you—you're wonderful, too!"

"The—flowers—thanks!"

"My father, he sent them. Come, father—quick!"

Suddenly there was a tight tensity seemed to crowd up the little room.

"Abrahm—quick—get Hancock. That first row of chairs—has got to be moved. There he is, in the wings. See that the piano ain't dragged down too far! Leon, got your mute in your pocket? Please, Mr. Ginsberg—you must excuse— Here, Leon, is your glass of water; drink it, I say. Shut that door out there, boy, so there ain't a draught in the wings. Here, Leon, your violin. Got your neckerchief? Listen how they're shouting! It's for you—Leon—darlink— Go!"

The center of that vast human bowl which had shouted itself out, slim, boylike, and in his supreme isolation, Leon Kantor drew bow and a first thin, pellucid, and perfect note into a silence breathless to receive it.

Throughout the arduous flexuosities of the Mendelssohn E minor concerto, singing, winding from tonal to tonal climax, and out of the slow movement which is like a tourniquet twisting the heart into the spirited *allegro molto vivace*, it was as if beneath Leon Kantor's fingers the strings were living veincords, youth, vitality, and the very foam of exuberance racing through them.

That was the power of him. The vichy and the sparkle of youth, so that, playing, the melody poured round him like wine and went down seething and singing into the hearts of his hearers.

Later, and because these were his people and because they were dark and Slavic with his Slavic darkness, he played, as if his very blood were weeping, the "Kol Nidre," which is the prayer of his race for atonement.

And then the super-amphitheater, filled with those whose emotions lie next to the surface and whose pores have not been closed over with a water-tight veneer, burst into its cheers and its tears.

There were fifteen recalls from the wings, Abrahm Kantor standing counting them off on his fingers and trembling to receive the Stradivarius. Then, finally, and against the frantic negative pantomime of his manager, a scherzo, played so lacily that it swept the house in lightest laughter.

When Leon Kantor finally completed his program they were loath to let him go, crowding down the aisles upon him, applauding up, down, around him until the great disheveled house was like the roaring of a sea, and he would laugh and throw out his arm in widespread helplessness, and always his manager in the background gesticulating against too much of his precious product for the money, ushers already slamming up chairs, his father's arms out for the Stradivarius, and, deepest in the gloom of the wings, Sarah Kantor, in a rocker especially dragged out for her, and from the depths of the black-silk reticule, darning his socks.

"Bravo–bravo! Give us the 'Humoresque'–Chopin Nocturne–Polonaise –'Humoresque.' Bravo–bravo!"

And even as they stood, hatted and coated, importuning and pressing in upon him, and with a wisp of a smile to the fourth left box, Leon Kantor played them the "Humoresque" of Dvorák, skedaddling, plucking, quirking–that laugh on life with a tear behind it. Then suddenly, because he could escape no other way, rushed straight back for his dressing-room, bursting in upon a flood of family already there: Isadore Kantor, blue-shaved, aquiline, and already graying at the temples; his five-year-old son, Leon; a soft little pouter-pigeon of a wife, too, enormous of bust, in glittering ear-drops and a wrist watch of diamonds half buried in chubby wrist; Miss Esther Kantor, pink and pretty; Rudolph; Boris, not yet done with growing-pains.

At the door Miss Kantor met her brother, her eyes as sweetly moist as her kiss.

"Leon darling, you surpassed even yourself!"

"Quit crowding, children. Let him sit down. Here, Leon, let mamma give you a fresh collar. Look how the child's perspired. Pull down that window, Boris. Rudolph, don't let no one in. I give you my word if to-night wasn't as near as I ever came to seeing a house go crazy. Not even that time in Milan, darlink, when they broke down the doors, was it like to-night–"

"Ought to seen, ma, the row of police outside–"

"Hush up, Roody! Don't you see your brother is trying to get his breath?"

From Mrs. Isadore Kantor: "You should have seen the balconies, mother. Isadore and I went up just to see the jam."

"Six thousand dollars in the house to-night, if there was a cent," said Isadore Kantor.

"Hand me my violin, please, Esther. I must have scratched it, the way they pushed."

"No, son, you didn't. I've already rubbed it up. Sit quiet, darlink!"

He was limply white, as if the vitality had flowed out of him.

"God! wasn't it—tremendous?"

"Six thousand, if there was a cent," repeated Isadore Kantor. "More than Rimsky ever played to in his life!"

"Oh, Izzie, you make me sick, always counting-counting!"

"Your sister's right, Isadore. You got nothing to complain of if there was only six hundred in the house. A boy whose fiddle has made already enough to set you up in such a fine business, his brother Boris in such a fine college, automobiles—style—and now because Vladimir Rimsky, three times his age, gets signed up with Elsass for a few thousand more a year, right away the family gets a long face—"

"Ma, please! Isadore didn't mean it that way!"

"Pa's knocking, ma! Shall I let him in?"

"Let him in, Roody. I'd like to know what good it will do to try to keep him out."

In an actual rain of perspiration, his tie slid well under one ear, Abrahm Kantor burst in, mouthing the words before his acute state of strangulation would let them out.

"Elsass—it's Elsass outside! He—wants—to sign—Leon—fifty concerts—coast to coast—two thousand—next season! He's got the papers—already drawn up—the pen outside waiting—"

"Abrahm!"

"Pa!"

In the silence that followed, Isadore Kantor, a poppiness of stare and a violent redness set in, suddenly turned to his five-year-old son, sticky with lollipop, and came down soundly and with smack against the infantile, the slightly outstanding and unsuspecting ear.

"*Momser!*" he cried. "*Chammer! Lump! Ganef!* You hear that? Two thousand! Two thousand! Didn't I tell you—didn't I tell you to practise?"

Even as Leon Kantor put pen to this princely document, Franz Ferdinand of Serbia, the assassin's bullet cold, lay dead in state, and let slip were the dogs of war.

In the next years, men, forty deep, were to die in piles; hayricks of fields to become human hayricks of battle-fields; Belgium disemboweled, her very entrails dragging, to find all the civilized world her champion, and between the poppies of Flanders, crosses, thousand upon thousand of them, to mark the places where the youth of her allies fell, avenging outrage. Seas, even when calmest, were to become terrible, and men's heart-beats, a bit sluggish with the fatty degeneration of a sluggard peace, to quicken and then to throb with the rat-a-tat-tat, the rat-a-tat-tat of the most peremptory, the most reverberating call to arms in the history of the world.

In June, 1917, Leon Kantor, answering that rat-a-tat-tat, enlisted.

In November, honed by the interim of training to even a new leanness, and sailing-orders heavy and light in his heart, Lieutenant Kantor, on two days' home-leave, took leave of home, which can be cruelest when it is tenderest.

Standing there in the expensive, the formal, the enormous French parlor of his up-town apartment de luxe, from not one of whose chairs would his mother's feet touch floor, a wall of living flesh, mortared in blood, was throbbing and hedging him in.

He would pace up and down the long room, heavy with the faces of those who mourn, with a laugh too ready, too facetious, in his fear for them.

"Well, well, what is this, anyway, a wake? Where's the coffin? Who's dead?"

His sister-in-law shot out her plump, watch-encrusted wrist. "Don't, Leon!" she cried. "Such talk is a sin! It might come true."

"Rosie-posy-butter-ball," he said, pausing beside her chair to pinch her deeply soft cheek. "Cry-baby-roly-poly, you can't shove me off in a wooden kimono that way."

From his place before the white-and-gold mantel, staring steadfastly at the floor tiling, Isadore Kantor turned suddenly, a bit whiter and older at the temples.

"I don't get your comedy, Leon."

"'Wooden kimono'—Leon?"

"That's the way the fellows at camp joke about coffins, ma. I didn't mean anything but fun! Great Scott! Can't any one take a joke!"

"O God! O God!" His mother fell to swaying softly, hugging herself against shivering.

"Did you sign over power of attorney to pa, Leon?"

"All fixed, Izzie."

"I'm so afraid, son, you don't take with you enough money in your pockets. You know how you lose it. If only you would let mamma sew that little bag inside your uniform with a little place for bills and a little place for the asafoetida!"

"Now, please, ma—please! If I needed more, wouldn't I take it? Wouldn't I be a pretty joke among the fellows, tied up in that smelling stuff! Orders are orders, ma. I know what to take and what not to take."

"Please, Leon, don't get mad at me, but if you will let me put in your suit-case just one little box of that salve, for your finger-tips, so they don't crack–"

Pausing as he paced to lay cheek to her hair, he patted her. "Three boxes, if you want. Now, how's that?"

"And you won't take it out so soon as my back is turned?"

"Cross my heart."

His touch seemed to set her trembling again, all her illy concealed emotions rushing up. "I can't stand it! Can't! Can't! Take my life–take my blood, but don't take my boy–don't take my boy–"

"Mamma, mamma, is that the way you're going to begin all over again, after your promise?"

She clung to him, heaving against the rising storm of sobs. " I can't help it–can't! Cut out my heart from me, but let me keep my boy–my wonder boy–"

"Oughtn't she be ashamed of herself? Just listen to her, Esther! What will we do with her? Talks like she had a guarantee I wasn't coming back. Why, I wouldn't be surprised if by spring I wasn't tuning up again for a coast-to-coast tour–"

"Spring! That talk don't fool me. Without my boy, the springs in my life are over–"

"Why, ma, you talk like every soldier who goes to war was killed! There's only the smallest percentage of them die in battle–"

"'Spring,' he says; 'spring'! Crossing the seas from me! To live through months with that sea between us–my boy maybe shot–my–"

"Mamma, please!"

"I can't help it, Leon; I'm not one of those fine mothers that can be so brave. Cut out my heart, but leave my boy! My wonder-boy–my child I prayed for!"

"There's other mothers, ma, with sons!"

"Yes, but not wonder-sons! A genius like you could so easy get excused, Leon. Give it up. Genius it should be the last to be sent to–the slaughter-pen. Leon darlink–don't go!"

"Ma, ma–you don't mean what you're saying. You wouldn't want me to reason that way! You wouldn't want me to hide behind my–violin."

"I would! Would! You should wait for the draft. With my Roody and even my baby Boris enlisted, ain't it enough for one mother? Since they got to be in camp, all right, I say, let them be there, if my heart breaks for it, but not my wonder-child! You can get exemption, Leon, right away for the asking. Stay with me, Leon! Don't go away! The people at home got to be kept happy with music. That's being a soldier, too, playing their troubles away. Stay with me, Leon! Don't go leave me–don't–don't–"

He suffered her to lie, tear-drenched, back into his arms, holding her close in his compassion for her, his own face twisting.

"God! ma, this—this is awful! Please—you make us ashamed—all of us! I don't know what to say. Esther, come quiet her—for God's sake quiet her!"

From her place in that sobbing circle Esther Kantor crossed to kneel beside her mother.

"Mamma darling, you're killing yourself. What if every family went on this way? You want papa to come in and find us all crying? Is this the way you want Leon to spend his last hour with us—"

"Oh, God—God!"

"I mean his last hour until he comes back, darling. Didn't you just hear him say, darling, it may be by spring?"

"'Spring'—'spring'—never no more springs for me—"

"Just think, darling, how proud we should be! Our Leon, who could so easily have been excused, not even to wait for the draft."

"It's not too late yet—please—Leon—"

"Our Roody and Boris both in camp, too, training to serve their country. Why, mamma, we ought to be crying for happiness. As Leon says, surely the Kantor family, who fled out of Russia to escape massacre, should know how terrible slavery can be. That's why we must help our boys, mamma, in their fight to make the world free! Right, Leon?" trying to smile with her red-rimmed eyes.

"We've got no fight with no one! Not a child of mine was ever raised to so much as lift a finger against no one. We've got no fight with no one!"

"We have got a fight with some one! With autocracy! Only this time it happens to be Hunnish autocracy. You should know it, mamma—oh, you should know it deeper down in you than any of us, the fight our family right here has got with autocracy! We should be the first to want to avenge Belgium!"

"Leon's right, mamma darling, the way you and papa were beaten out of your country—"

"There's not a day in your life you don't curse it without knowing it! Every time we three boys look at your son and our brother Mannie, born an—an imbecile—because of autocracy, we know what we're fighting for. We know. You know, too. Look at him over there, even before he was born, ruined by autocracy! Know what I'm fighting for? Why, this whole family knows! What's music, what's art, what's life itself in a world without freedom? Every time, ma, you get to thinking we've got a fight with no one, all you have to do is look at our poor Mannie. He's the answer. He's the answer."

In a foaming sort of silence, Mannie Kantor smiled softly from his chair beneath the pink-and-gold shade of the piano-lamp. The heterogeneous sounds of women weeping had ceased. Straight in her chair, her great shelf of bust heaving, sat Rosa Kantor, suddenly dry of eye; Isadore Kantor head up. Erect now, and out from the embrace of her daughter, Sarah looked up at her son.

"What time do you leave, Leon?" she asked, actually firm of lip.

"Any minute, ma. Getting late."

This time she pulled her lips to a smile, waggling her forefinger.

"Don't let them little devils of French girls fall in love with my dude in his uniform."

Her pretense at pleasantry was almost more than he could bear.

"Hear! Hear! Our mother thinks I'm a regular lady-killer! Hear that, Esther?" pinching her cheek.

"You are, Leon—only—only, you don't know it!"

"Don't you bring down too many beaux while I'm gone, either, Miss Kantor!"

"I—won't, Leon."

Sotto voce to her: "Remember, Esther, while I'm gone, the royalties from the discaphone records are yours. I want you to have them for pin-money and—maybe a dowry?"

She turned from him. "Don't, Leon—don't—"

"I like him! Nice fellow, but too slow! Why, if I were in his shoes I'd have popped long ago."

She smiled with her lashes dewy.

There entered then, in a violet-scented little whirl, Miss Gina Berg, rosy with the sting of a winter's night, and, as usual, swathed in the high-napped furs.

"Gina!"

She was for greeting every one, a wasted kiss to Mrs. Kantor, and then, arms wide, a great bunch of violets in one outstretched hand, her glance straight, sure, and sparkling for Leon Kantor.

"Surprise—everybody—surprise!"

"Why, Gina—we read—we thought you were singing in Philadelphia to-night!"

"So did I, Esther darling, until a little bird whispered to me that Lieutenant Kantor was home on farewell leave."

He advanced to her down the great length of room, lowering his head over her hand, his puttee-clad legs clicking together. "You mean, Miss Gina—Gina—you didn't sing?"

"Of course I didn't! Hasn't every prima donna a larynx to hide behind?" She lifted off her fur cap, spilling curls.

"Well, I—I'll be hanged!" said Lieutenant Kantor, his eyes lakes of her reflected loveliness.

She let her hand linger in his. " Leon—you—really going? How—terrible! How—how—wonderful!"

"How wonderful—your coming!"

"I— You think it was not nice of me—to come?"

"I think it was the nicest thing that ever happened in the world."

"All the way here in the train I kept saying, 'Crazy—crazy—running to tell Leon—Lieutenant—Kantor good-by—when you haven't even seen him three times in three years—'"

"But each—each of those three times we—we've remembered, Gina."

"But that's how I feel toward all the boys, Leon—our fighting boys—just like flying to them to kiss them each one good-by."

"Come over, Gina. You'll be a treat to our mother. I— Well, I'm hanged! All the way from Philadelphia!"

There was even a sparkle to talk, then, and a let-up of pressure. After a while Sarah Kantor looked up at her son, tremulous, but smiling.

"Well, son, you going to play—for your old mother before—you go? It'll be many a month—spring—maybe longer, before I hear my boy again except on the discaphone."

He shot a quick glance to his sister. "Why, I—I don't know. I—I'd love it, ma, if—if you think, Esther, I'd better."

"You don't need to be afraid of me, darlink. There's nothing can give me the strength to bear—what's before me like—like my boy's music. That's my life, his music."

"Why, yes; if mamma is sure she feels that way, play for us, Leon."

He was already at the instrument, where it lay, swathed, atop the grand piano. "What'll it be, folks?"

"Something to make ma laugh, Leon—something light, something funny."

"'Humoresque,'" he said, with a quick glance for Miss Berg.

"'Humoresque,'" she said, smiling back at him.

He capered through, cutting and playful of bow, the melody of Dvorak's, which is as ironic as a grinning mask.

Finished, he smiled at his parent, her face still untearful.

"How's that?"

She nodded. "It's like life, son, that piece. Crying to hide its laughing and laughing to hide its crying."

"Play that new piece, Leon—the one you set to music. You know. The words by that young boy in the war who wrote such grand poetry before he was killed. The one that always makes poor Mannie laugh. Play it for him, Leon."

Her plump little unlined face innocent of fault, Mrs. Isadore Kantor ventured her request, her smile tired with tears.

"No, no—Rosa—not now! Ma wouldn't want that!"

"I do, son; I do! Even Mannie should have his share of good-by."

To Gina Berg: "They want me to play that little arrangement of mine from Allan Seegar's poem. 'I Have a Rendezvous. . . .'"

"It—it's beautiful, Leon. I was to have sung it on my program to-night—only, I'm afraid you had better not—here—now—"

"Please, Leon! Nothing you play can ever make me as sad as it makes me glad. Mannie should have, too, his good-by."

"All right, then, ma, if—if you're sure you want it. Will you sing it, Gina?"

She had risen. "Why, yes, Leon."

She sang it then, quite purely, her hands clasped simply together and her glance mistily off, the beautiful, the heroic, the lyrical prophecy of a soldier-poet and a poet-soldier:

"But I've a rendezvous with Death
On some scarred slope of battered hill,
When spring comes round again this year
And the first meadow-flowers appear."

In the silence that followed, a sob burst out, stifled, from Esther Kantor, this time her mother holding her in arms that were strong.

"That, Leon, is the most beautiful of all your compositions. What does it mean, son, that word, 'rondy-voo'?"

"Why, I—I don't exactly know. A rendezvous—it's a sort of meeting, an engagement, isn't it, Miss Gina? Gina? You're up on languages. As if I had an appointment to meet you some place—at the opera-house, for instance."

"That's it, Leon—an engagement."

"Have I an engagement with you, Gina?"

She let her lids droop. "Oh, how—how I hope you have, Leon."

"When?"

"In the spring?"

"That's it—in the spring."

Then they smiled, these two, who had never felt more than the merest butterfly wings of love brushing them, light as lashes. No word between them, only an unfinished sweetness, waiting to be linked up.

Suddenly there burst in Abrahm Kantor, in a carefully rehearsed gale of bluster.

"Quick, Leon! I got the car down-stairs. Just fifteen minutes to make the ferry. Quick! The sooner we get him over there the sooner we get him back! I'm right, mamma? Now, now! No waterworks! Get your brother's suit-case, Isadore. Now, now! No nonsense! Quick—quick—"

With a deftly manoeuvered round of good-bys, a grip-laden dash for the door, a throbbing moment of turning back when it seemed as though Sarah Kantor's arms could not unlock their deadlock of him, Leon Kantor was out and gone, the group of faces point-etched into the silence behind him.

The poor, mute face of Mannie, laughing softly. Rosa Kantor crying into her hands. Esther, grief-crumpled, but rich in the enormous hope of youth. The sweet Gina, to whom the waiting months had already begun their reality.

Not so Sarah Kantor. In a bedroom adjoining, its high-ceilinged vastness as cold as a cathedral to her lowness of stature, sobs dry and terrible were rumbling up from her, only to dash against lips tightly restraining them.

On her knees beside a chest of drawers, and unwrapping it from swaddling-clothes, she withdrew what at best had been a sorry sort of fiddle.

Cracked of back and solitary of string, it was as if her trembling arms, raising it above her head, would make of themselves and her swaying body the tripod of an altar.

The old twisting and prophetic pain was behind her heart. Like the painted billows of music that the old Italian masters loved to do, there wound and wreathed about her clouds of song:

But I've a rendezvous with Death
On some scarred slope of battered hill,
When spring comes round again this year
And the first meadow-flowers appear.

CONRAD AIKEN

[1889–1973]

Silent Snow, Secret Snow

(1934)

JUST WHY IT should have happened, or why it should have happened just when it did, he could not, of course, possibly have said; nor perhaps could it even have occurred to him to ask. The thing was above all a secret, something to be preciously concealed from Mother and Father; and to that very fact it owed an enormous part of its deliciousness. It was like a peculiarly beautiful trinket to be carried unmentioned in one's trouser-pocket—a rare stamp, an old coin, a few tiny gold links found trodden out of shape on the path in the park, a pebble of carnelian, a sea shell distinguishable from all others by an unusual spot or stripe—and, as if it were anyone of these, he carried around with him everywhere a warm and persistent and increasingly beautiful sense of possession. Nor was it only a sense of possession—it was also a sense of protection. It was as if, in some delightful way, his secret gave him a fortress, a wall behind which he could retreat into heavenly seclusion. This was almost the first thing he had noticed about it—apart from the oddness of the thing itself—and it was this that now again, for the fiftieth time, occurred to him, as he sat in the little schoolroom. It was the half hour for geography. Miss Buell was revolving with one finger, slowly, a huge terrestrial globe which had been placed on her desk. The green and yellow continents passed and repassed, questions were asked and answered, and now the little girl in front of him, Deirdre, who had a funny little constellation of freckles on the back of her neck, exactly like the Big Dipper, was standing up and telling Miss Buell that the equator was the line that ran round the middle.

Miss Buell's face, which was old and grayish and kindly, with gray stiff curls beside the cheeks, and eyes that swam very brightly, like little minnows, behind thick glasses, wrinkled itself into a complication of amusements.

"Ah! I see. The earth is wearing a belt, or a sash. Or someone drew a line round it!"

"Oh, no—not that—I mean—"

In the general laughter, he did not share, or only a very little. He was thinking about the Arctic and Antarctic regions, which of course, on the globe, were white. Miss Buell was now telling them about the tropics, the jungles, the steamy heat of equatorial swamps, where the birds and butterflies, and even the snakes, were like living jewels. As he listened to these things, he was already, with a pleasant sense of half-effort, putting his secret between himself and the words. Was it really an effort at all? For effort implied something voluntary, and perhaps even something one did not especially want; whereas this was distinctly pleasant, and came almost of its own accord. All he needed to do was to think of that morning, the first one, and then of all the others—

But it was all so absurdly simple! It had amounted to so little. It was nothing, just an idea—and just why it should have become so wonderful, so permanent, was a mystery—a very pleasant one, to be sure, but also, in an amusing way, foolish. However, without ceasing to listen to Miss Buell, who had now moved up to the north temperate zones, he deliberately invited his memory of the first morning. It was only a moment or two after he had waked up—or perhaps the moment itself. But was there, to be exact, an exact moment? Was one awake all at once? or was it gradual? Anyway, it was after he had stretched a lazy hand up towards the headrail, and yawned, and then relaxed again among his warm covers, all the more grateful on a December morning, that the thing had happened. Suddenly, for no reason, he had thought of the postman, he remembered the postman. Perhaps there was nothing so odd in that. After all, he heard the postman almost every morning in his life—his heavy boots could be heard clumping round the corner at the top of the little cobbled hill-street, and then, progressively nearer, progressively louder, the double knock at each door, the crossings and re-crossings of the street, till finally the clumsy steps came stumbling across to the very door, and the tremendous knock came which shook the house itself.

(Miss Buell was saying "Vast wheat-growing areas in North America and Siberia."

Dierdre had for the moment placed her left hand across the back of her neck.)

But on this particular morning, the first morning, as he lay there with his eyes closed, he had for some reason *waited* for the postman. He wanted to hear him come round the corner. And that was precisely the joke—he never did. He never came. He never had come—*round the corner*—again. For when at last the steps *were* heard, they had already, he was quite sure, come a little down the hill, to the first house; and even so, the steps were curiously different—they were softer, they had a new secrecy about them, they were muffled and indistinct; and while the rhythm of them was the same, it now said a new thing—it said peace, it said remoteness, it said cold, it said sleep. And he had understood the situation at once—nothing could have seemed simpler—there had been snow in the night, such as all winter he had been longing for; and it was this which had rendered the postman's first footsteps inaudible, and the later ones faint. Of course! How lovely! And even now it must be snowing—it was going to be a snowy day—the long white ragged lines were drifting and sifting across the street, across the faces of the old houses whispering and hushing, making little triangles of white in the corners between cobblestones, seething a little when the wind blew them over the ground to a drifted corner; and so it would be all day, getting deeper and deeper and silenter and silenter.

(Miss Buell was saying "Land of perpetual snow.")

All this time, of course (while he lay in bed), he had kept his eyes closed, listening to the nearer progress of the postman, the muffled footsteps thumping and slipping on the snow-sheathed cobbles; and all the other sounds—the double knocks, a frosty far-off voice or two, a bell ringing thinly and softly as if under a sheet of ice—had the same slightly abstracted quality, as if removed by one degree from actuality—as if everything in the world had been insulated by snow. But when at last, pleased, he opened his eyes, and turned them towards the window, to see for himself this long-desired and now so clearly imagined miracle—what he saw instead was brilliant sunlight on a roof; and when, astonished, he jumped out of bed and stared down into the street, expecting to see the cobbles obliterated by the snow, he saw nothing but the bare bright cobbles themselves.

Queer, the effect this extraordinary surprise had had upon him—all the following morning he had kept with him a sense as of snow falling about him, a secret screen of new snow between himself and the world. If he had not dreamed such a thing—and how could he have dreamed it while awake?—how else could one explain it? In any case, the delusion had been so vivid as to affect his entire behavior. He could not now remember whether it was on the first or the second morning—or was it even the third?—that his mother had drawn attention to some oddness in his manner.

"But my darling—" she had said at the breakfast table—"what has come over you? You don't seem to be listening. . . ."

And how often that very thing had happened since!

(Miss Buell was now asking if anyone knew the difference between the North Pole and the Magnetic Pole. Deirdre was holding up her flickering brown hand, and he could see the four white dimples that marked the knuckles.)

Perhaps it hadn't been either the second or third morning—or even the fourth or fifth. How could he be sure? How could he be sure just when the delicious *progress* had become clear? Just when it had really *begun*? The intervals weren't very precise. . . . All he now knew was, that at some point or other—perhaps the second day, perhaps the sixth—he had noticed that the presence of the snow was a little more insistent, the sound of it clearer; and, conversely, the sound of the postman's footsteps more indistinct. Not only could he not hear the steps come round the corner, he could not even hear them at the first house. It was below the first house that he heard them; and then, a few days later, it was below the second house that he heard them; and a few days later again, below the third. Gradually, gradually, the snow was becoming heavier, the sound of its seething louder, the cobblestones more and more muffled. When he found, each morning, on going to the window, after the ritual of listening, that the roofs and cobbles were as bare as ever, it made no difference. This was, after all, only what he had expected. It was even what pleased him, what rewarded him: the thing was his own, belonged to no one else. No one else knew about it, not even his mother and father. There, outside, were the bare cobbles; and here, inside, was the snow. Snow growing heavier each day, muffling the world, hiding the ugly, and deadening increasingly—above all—the steps of the postman.

"But my darling—" she had said at the luncheon table—"what has come over you? You don't seem to listen when people speak to you. That's the third time I've asked you to pass your plate. . . ."

How was one to explain this to Mother? or to Father? There was, of course, nothing to be done about it: nothing. All one could do was to laugh embarrassedly, pretend to be a little ashamed, apologize, and take a sudden and somewhat disingenuous interest in what was being done or said. The cat had stayed out all night. He had a curious swelling on his left cheek—perhaps somebody had kicked him, or a stone had struck him. Mrs. Kempton was or was not coming to tea. The house was going to be house cleaned, or "turned out," on Wednesday instead of Friday. A new lamp was provided for his evening work—perhaps it was eyestrain which accounted for this new and so peculiar vagueness of his—Mother was looking at him with amusement as she said this, but with something else as well. A new lamp? A new lamp. Yes Mother, No Mother, Yes Mother. School is going very well. The geometry is very easy. The history is very dull. The geography is very interesting—particularly when it takes one to the North Pole. Why the North Pole? Oh, well, it would be fun to be an explorer. Another Peary or Scott or Shackleton. And then abruptly he found his interest in the talk at an end, stared at the pudding on his plate, listened, waited, and began once more—ah how heavenly, too, the first beginnings—to hear or feel—for could he actually hear it?—the silent snow, the secret snow.

(Miss Buell was telling them about the search for the Northwest Passage, about Hendrik Hudson, the Half Moon.)

This had been, indeed, the only distressing feature of the new experience: the fact that it so increasingly had brought him into a kind of mute misunderstanding, or even conflict, with his father and mother. It was as if he were trying to lead a double life. On the one hand he had to be Paul

Hasleman, and keep up the appearance of being that person—dress, wash, and answer intelligently when spoken to—; on the other, he had to explore this new world which had been opened to him. Nor could there be the slightest doubt—not the slightest—that the new world was the profounder and more wonderful of the two. It was irresistible. It was miraculous. Its beauty was simply beyond anything—beyond speech as beyond thought—utterly incommunicable. But how then, between the two worlds, of which he was thus constantly aware, was he to keep a balance? One must get up, one must go to breakfast, one must talk with Mother, go to school, do one's lessons—and, in all this, try not to appear too much of a fool. But if all the while one was also trying to extract the full deliciousness of another and quite separate existence, one which could not easily (if at all) be spoken of—how was one to manage? How was one to explain? Would it be safe to explain? Would it be absurd ? Would it merely mean that he would get into some obscure kind of trouble?

These thoughts came and went, came and went, as softly and secretly as the snow; they were not precisely a disturbance, perhaps they were even a pleasure; he liked to have them; their presence was something almost palpable, something he could stroke with his hand, without closing his eyes, and without ceasing to see Miss Buell and the schoolroom and the globe and the freckles on Deirdre's neck; nevertheless he did in a sense cease to see, or to see the obvious external world, and substituted for this vision the vision of snow, the sound of snow, and the slow, almost soundless, approach of the postman. Yesterday, it had been only at the sixth house that the postman had become audible; the snow was much deeper now, it was falling more swiftly and heavily, the sound of its seething was more distinct, more soothing, more persistent. And this morning, it had been—as nearly as he could figure—just above the seventh house—perhaps only a step or two above: at most, he had heard two or three footsteps before the knock had sounded. . . . And with each such narrowing of the sphere, each nearer approach of the limit at which the postman was first audible, it was odd how sharply was increased the amount of illusion which had to be carried into the ordinary business of daily life. Each day, it was harder to get out of bed, to go to the window, to look out at the—as always—perfectly empty and snowless street. Each day it was more difficult to go through the perfunctory motions of greeting Mother and Father at breakfast, to reply to their questions, to put his books together and go to school. And at school, how extraordinarily hard to conduct with success simultaneously the public life and the life that was secret. There were times when he longed—positively ached—to tell everyone about it—to burst out with it—only to be checked almost at once by a far-off feeling as of some faint absurdity which was inherent in it—but *was* it absurd?—and more importantly by a sense of mysterious power in his very secrecy. Yes: it must be kept secret. That, more and more, became clear. At whatever cost to himself, whatever pain to others–

(Miss Buell looked straight at him, smiling, and said, "Perhaps we'll ask Paul. I'm sure Paul will come out of his day-dream long enough to be able to tell us. Won't you, Paul." He rose slowly from his chair, resting one hand on the brightly varnished desk, and deliberately stared through the snow towards the blackboard. It was an effort, but it was amusing to make it. "Yes," he said slowly, "it was what we now call the Hudson River. This he thought to be the Northwest Passage. He was disappointed." He sat down again, and as he did so Deirdre half turned in her chair and gave him a shy smile, of approval and admiration.)

At whatever pain to others.

This part of it was very puzzling, very puzzling. Mother was very nice, and so was Father. Yes, that was all true enough. He wanted to be nice to them, to tell them everything–and yet, was it really wrong of him to want to have a secret place of his own?

At bedtime, the night before, Mother had said, "If this goes on, my lad, we'll have to see a doctor, we will! We can't have our boy–" But what was it she had said? "Live in another world"? "Live so far away"? The word "far" had been in it, he was sure, and then Mother had taken up a magazine again and laughed a little, but with an expression which wasn't mirthful. He had felt sorry for her. . . .

The bell rang for dismissal. The sound came to him through long curved parallels of falling snow. He saw Deirdre rise, and had himself risen almost as soon–but not quite as soon–as she.

II

On the walk homeward, which was timeless, it pleased him to see through the accompaniment, or counterpoint, of snow, the items of mere externality on his way. There were many kinds of bricks in the sidewalks, and laid in many kinds of pattern. The garden walls too were various, some of wooden palings, some of plaster, some of stone. Twigs of bushes leaned over the walls; the little hard green winter-buds of lilac, on gray stems, sheathed and fat; other branches very thin and fine and black and dessicated. Dirty sparrows huddled in the bushes, as dull in color as dead fruit left in leafless trees. A single starling creaked on a weather vane. In the gutter, beside a drain, was a scrap of torn and dirty newspaper, caught in a little delta of filth: the word ECZEMA appeared in large capitals, and below it was a letter from Mrs. Amelia D. Cravath, 2100 Pine Street, Fort Worth, Texas, to the effect that after being a sufferer for years she had been cured by Caley's Ointment. In the little delta, beside the fan-shaped and deeply runneled continent of brown mud, were lost twigs, descended from their parent trees, dead matches, a rusty horse-chestnut burr, a small concentration of sparkling gravel on the lip of the sewer, a fragment of eggshell, a streak of yellow sawdust which had been wet and was now dry and congealed, a brown pebble, and a broken feather. Further on was a cement sidewalk, ruled into geometrical parallelograms, with a brass inlay at one end commemorating the contractors who had laid it, and, halfway across, an irregular and random series of dog-tracks, immortalized in synthetic stone. He knew these well, and always stepped on them; to cover the little hollows with his own foot had always been a queer pleasure; today he did it once more, but perfunctorily and detachedly, all the while thinking of something else. That was a dog, a long time ago, who had made a mistake and walked on the cement while it was still wet. He had probably wagged his tail, but that hadn't been recorded. Now, Paul Hasleman, aged twelve, on his way home from school, crossed the same river, which in the meantime had frozen into rock. Homeward through the snow, the snow falling in bright sunshine. Homeward?

Then came the gateway with the two posts surmounted by eggshaped stones which had been cunningly balanced on their ends, as if by Columbus, and mortared in the very act of balance: a source of perpetual wonder. On the brick wall just beyond, the letter H had been stenciled, presumably for some purpose. H? H.

The green hydrant, with a little green-painted chain attached to the brass screw-cap.

The elm tree, with the great gray wound in the bark, kidney-shaped, into which he always put his hand—to feel the cold but living wood. The injury, he had been sure, was due to the gnawings of a tethered horse. But now it deserved only a passing palm, a merely tolerant eye. There were more important things. Miracles. Beyond the thoughts of trees, mere elms. Beyond the thoughts of sidewalks, mere stone, mere brick, mere cement. Beyond the thoughts even of his own shoes, which trod these sidewalks obediently, bearing a burden—far above—of elaborate mystery. He watched them. They were not very well polished; he had neglected them, for a very good reason: they were one of the many parts of the increasing difficulty of the daily return to daily life, the morning struggle. To get up, having at last opened one's eyes, to go to the window, and discover no snow, to wash, to dress, to descend the curving stairs to breakfast—

At whatever pain to others, nevertheless, one must persevere in severance, since the incommunicability of the experience demanded it. It was desirable of course to be kind to Mother and Father, especially as they seemed to be worried, but it was also desirable to be resolute. If they should decide—as appeared likely—to consult the doctor, Doctor Howells, and have Paul inspected, his heart listened to through a kind of dictaphone, his lungs, his stomach—well, that was all right. He would go through with it. He would give them answer for question, too—perhaps such answers as they hadn't expected? No. That would never do. For the secret world must, at all costs, be preserved.

The bird-house in the apple-tree was empty—it was the wrong time of year for wrens. The little round black door had lost its pleasure. The wrens were enjoying other houses, other nests, remoter trees. But this too was a notion which he only vaguely and grazingly entertained—as if, for the moment, he merely touched an edge of it; there was something further on, which was already assuming a sharper importance; something which already teased at the corners of his eyes, teasing also at the corner of his mind. It was funny to think that he so wanted this, so awaited it—and yet found himself enjoying this momentary dalliance with the bird-house, as if for a quite deliberate postponement and enhancement of the approaching pleasure. He was aware of his delay, of his smiling and detached and now almost uncomprehending gaze at the little bird-house; he knew what he was going to look at next: it was his own little cobbled hill-street, his own house, the little river at the bottom of the hill, the grocer's shop with the cardboard man in the window—and now, thinking of all this, he turned his head, still smiling, and looking quickly right and left through the snow-laden sunlight.

And the mist of snow, as he had foreseen, was still on it—a ghost of snow falling in the bright sunlight, softly and steadily floating and turning and pausing, soundlessly meeting the snow that covered, as with a transparent mirage, the bare bright cobbles. He loved it—he stood still and loved it. Its beauty was paralyzing—beyond all words, all experience, all dream. No fairy-story he had ever read could be compared with it—none had ever given him this extraordinary combination of ethereal loveliness with a something else, unnameable, which was just faintly and deliciously terrifying. What was this thing? As he thought of it, he looked upward toward his own bedroom window, which was open—and it was as if he looked straight into the room and saw himself lying half awake in his bed. There he was—at this very instant he was still perhaps actually there—more truly there than standing here at the edge of the cobbled hill-street, with one hand lifted to shade his eyes against the snow-sun. Had he indeed ever left his room, in all this time? since that very first morning? Was the whole progress still being enacted there, was it still the same morning, and himself not yet wholly awake? And even now, had the postman not yet come round the corner?. . .

This idea amused him, and automatically, as he thought of it, he turned his head and looked toward the top of the hill. There was, of course, nothing there—nothing and no one. The street was empty and quiet. And all the more because of its emptiness it occurred to him to count the houses—a thing which, oddly enough, he hadn't before thought of doing. Of course, he had known there weren't many—many, that is, on his own side of the street, which were the ones that figured in the postman's progress—but nevertheless it came to him as something of a shock to find that there were precisely *six*, above his own house—his own house was the seventh.

Six!

Astonished, he looked at his own house—looked at the door, on which was the number thirteen—and then realized that the whole thing was exactly and logically and absurdly what he ought to have known. Just the same, the realization gave him abruptly, and even a little frighteningly, a sense of hurry. He was being hurried—he was being rushed. For—he knit his brows—he couldn't be mistaken—it was just above the *seventh* house, his *own* house, that the postman had first been audible this very morning. But in that case—in that case—did it mean that tomorrow he would hear nothing? The knock he had heard must have been the knock of their own door. Did it mean—and this was an idea which gave him a really extraordinary feeling of surprise—that he would never hear the postman again?—that tomorrow morning the postman would already have passed the house, in a snow by then so deep as to render his footsteps completely inaudible? That he would have made his approach down the snow-filled street so soundlessly, so secretly, that he, Paul Hasleman, there lying in bed, would not have waked in time, or, waking, would have heard nothing?

But how could that be? Unless even the knocker should be muffled in the snow—frozen tight, perhaps?. . . But in that case—

A vague feeling of disappointment came over him; a vague sadness, as if he felt himself deprived of something which he had long looked forward to, something much prized. After all this, all this beautiful progress, the slow delicious advance of the postman through the silent and secret snow, the knock creeping closer each day, and the footsteps nearer, the audible compass of the world thus daily narrowed, narrowed, narrowed, as the snow soothingly and beautifully encroached and deepened, after all this, was he to be defrauded of the one thing he had so wanted—to be able to count, as it were, the last two or three solemn footsteps, as they finally approached his own door? Was it all going to happen, at the end, so suddenly? or indeed, had it already happened? with no slow and subtle gradations of menace, in which he could luxuriate?

He gazed upward again, toward his own window which flashed in the sun: and this time almost with a feeling that it would be better if he *were* still in bed, in that room; for in that case this must still be the first morning, and there would be six more mornings to come—or, for that matter, seven or eight or nine—how could he be sure?—or even more.

III

After supper, the inquisition began. He stood before the doctor, under the lamp, and submitted silently to the usual thumpings and tappings.

"Now will you please say 'Ah!'?"

"Ah!"

"Now again please, if you don't mind."

"Ah."

"Say it slowly, and hold it if you can–"

"Ah-h-h-h-h-h–"

"Good."

How silly all this was. As if it had anything to do with his throat! Or his heart or lungs!

Relaxing his mouth, of which the corners, after all this absurd stretching, felt uncomfortable, he avoided the doctor's eyes, and stared towards the fireplace, past his mother's feet (in gray slippers) which projected from the green chair, and his father's feet (in brown slippers) which stood neatly side by side on the hearth rug.

"Hm. There is certainly nothing wrong there. . ."

He felt the doctor's eyes fixed upon him, and, as if merely to be polite, returned the look, but with a feeling of justifiable evasiveness.

"Now, young man, tell me,–do you feel all right?"

"Yes, sir, quite all right."

"No headaches? no dizziness?"

"No, I don't think so."

"Let me see. Let's get a book, if you don't mind–yes, thank you, that will do splendidly–and now, Paul, if you'll just read it, holding it as you would normally hold it–"

He took the book and read:

"And another praise have I to tell for this the city our mother, the gift of a great god, a glory of the land most high; the might of horses, the might of young horses, the might of the sea. . . . For thou, son of Cronus, our lord Poseidon, hast throned herein this pride, since in these roads first thou didst show forth the curb that cures the rage of steeds. And the shapely oar, apt to men's hands, hath a wondrous speed on the brine, following the hundred-footed Nereids. . . . O land that art praised above all lands, now is it for thee to make those bright praises seen in deeds."

He stopped, tentatively, and lowered the heavy book.

"No–as I thought–there is certainly no superficial sign of eye-strain."

Silence thronged the room, and he was aware of the focused scrutiny of the three people who confronted him. . . .

"We could have his eyes examined–but I believe it is something else."

"What could it be?" This was his father's voice.

"It's only this curious absent-minded–" This was his mother's voice.

In the presence of the doctor, they both seemed irritatingly apologetic.

"I believe it is something else. Now Paul–I would like very much to ask you a question or two. You will answer them, won't you–you know I'm an old, old friend of yours, eh? That's right!. . ."

His back was thumped twice by the doctor's fat fist,—then the doctor was grinning at him with false amiability, while with one finger-nail he was scratching the top button of his waistcoat. Beyond the doctor's shoulder was the fire, the fingers of flame making light prestidigitation against the sooty fireback, the soft sound of their random flutter the only sound.

"I would like to know—is there anything that worries you?"

The doctor was again smiling, his eyelids low against the little black pupils, in each of which was a tiny white bead of light. Why answer him? why answer him at all? "At whatever pain to others"—but it was all a nuisance, this necessity for resistance, this necessity for attention: it was as if one had been stood up on a brilliantly lighted stage, under a great round blaze of spotlight; as if one were merely a trained seal, or a performing dog, or a fish, dipped out of an aquarium and held up by the tail. It would serve them right if he were merely to bark or growl. And meanwhile, to miss these last few precious hours, these hours of which every minute was more beautiful than the last, more menacing—? He still looked, as if from a great distance, at the beads of light in the doctor's eyes, at the fixed false smile, and then, beyond, once more at his mother's slippers, his father's slippers, the soft flutter of the fire. Even here, even amongst these hostile presences, and in this arranged light, he could see the snow, he could hear it—it was in the corners of the room, where the shadow was deepest, under the sofa, behind the half-opened door which led to the dining room. It was gentler here, softer, its seethe the quietest of whispers, as if, in deference to a drawing room, it had quite deliberately put on its "manners"; it kept itself out of sight, obliterated itself, but distinctly with an air of saying, "Ah, but just wait! Wait till we are alone together! Then I will begin to tell you something new! Something white! something cold! something sleepy! something of cease, and peace, and the long bright curve of space! Tell them to go away. Banish them. Refuse to speak. Leave them, go upstairs to your room, turn out the light and get into bed—I will go with you, I will be waiting for you, I will tell you a better story than Little Kay of the Skates, or The Snow Ghost—I will surround your bed, I will close the windows, pile a deep drift against the door, so that none will ever again be able to enter. Speak to them! . . ." It seemed as if the little hissing voice came from a slow white spiral of falling flakes in the corner by the front window—but he could not be sure. He felt himself smiling, then, and said to the doctor, but without looking at him, looking beyond him still—

"Oh, no, I think not—"

"But are you sure, my boy?"

His father's voice came softly and coldly then—the familiar voice of silken warning. . . .

"You needn't answer at once, Paul—remember we're trying to help you—think it over and be quite sure, won't you?"

He felt himself smiling again, at the notion of being quite sure. What a joke! As if he weren't so sure that reassurance was no longer necessary, and all this cross-examination a ridiculous farce, a grotesque parody! What could they know about it? These gross intelligences, these humdrum minds so bound to the usual, the ordinary? Impossible to tell them about it! Why, even now, even now, with the proof so abundant, so formidable, so imminent, so appallingly present here in this very room, could they believe it?—could even his mother believe it? No—it was only too plain that if anything were said about it, the merest hint given, they would be incredulous—they would laugh—they would say "Absurd!"—think things about him which weren't true. . . .

"Why no, I'm not worried—why should I be?"

He looked then straight at the doctor's low-lidded eyes, looked from one of them to the other, from one bead of light to the other, and gave a little laugh.

The doctor seemed to be disconcerted by this. He drew back in his chair, resting a fat white hand on either knee. The smile faded slowly from his face.

"Well, Paul!" he said, and paused gravely, "I'm afraid you don't take this quite seriously enough. I think you perhaps don't quite realize—don't quite realize—" He took a deep quick breath, and turned, as if helplessly, at a loss for words, to the others. But Mother and Father were both silent—no help was forthcoming.

"You must surely know, be aware, that you have not been quite yourself, of late? don't you know that?. . ."

It was amusing to watch the doctor's renewed attempt at a smile, a queer disorganized look, as of confidential embarrassment.

"I feel all right, sir," he said, and again gave the little laugh.

"And we're trying to help you." The doctor's tone sharpened.

"Yes sir, I know. But why? I'm all right. I'm just *thinking*, that's all."

His mother made a quick movement forward, resting a hand on the back of the doctor's chair.

"Thinking?" she said. "But my dear, about what?"

This was a direct challenge—and would have to be directly met. But before he met it, he looked again into the corner by the door, as if for reassurance. He smiled again at what he saw, at what he heard. The little spiral was still there, still softly whirling, like the ghost of a white kitten chasing the ghost of a white tail, and making as it did so the faintest of whispers. It was all right! If only he could remain firm, everything was going to be all right.

"Oh, about anything, about nothing,—*you* know the way you do!"

"You mean—day-dreaming?"

"Oh, no—thinking!"

"But thinking about *what*?"

"Anything."

He laughed a third time—but this time, happening to glance upward towards his mother's face, he was appalled at the effect his laughter seemed to have upon her. Her mouth had opened in an expression of horror. . . . This was too bad! Unfortunate! He had known it would cause pain, of course—but he hadn't expected it to be quite so bad as this. Perhaps—perhaps if he just gave them a tiny gleaming hint—?

"About the snow," he said.

"What on earth!" This was his father's voice. The brown slippers came a step nearer on the hearth-rug.

"But my dear, what do you mean!" This was his mother's voice.

The doctor merely stared.

"Just *snow*, that's all. I like to think about it."

"Tell us about it, my boy."

"But that's all it is. There's nothing to tell. *You* know what snow is?"

This he said almost angrily, for he felt that they were trying to corner him. He turned sideways so as no longer to face the doctor, and the better to see the inch of blackness between the window-sill and the lowered curtain,—the cold inch of beckoning and delicious night. At once he felt better, more assured.

"Mother—can I go to bed, now, please? I've got a headache."

"But I thought you said—"

"It's just come. It's all these questions—! Can I, mother?"

"You can go as soon as the doctor has finished."

"Don't you think this thing ought to be gone into thoroughly, and *now*?" This was Father's voice. The brown slippers again came a step nearer, the voice was the well-known "punishment" voice, resonant and cruel.

"Oh, what's the use, Norman—"

Quite suddenly, everyone was silent. And without precisely facing them, nevertheless he was aware that all three of them were watching him with an extraordinary intensity—staring hard at him—as if he had done something monstrous, or was himself some kind of monster. He could hear the soft irregular flutter of the flames; the cluck-click-cluck-click of the clock; far and faint, two sudden spurts of laughter from the kitchen, as quickly cut off as begun; a murmur of water in the pipes; and then, the silence seemed to deepen, to spread out, to become worldlong and worldwide, to become timeless and shapeless, and to center inevitably and rightly, with a slow and sleepy but enormous concentration of all power, on the beginning of a new sound. What this new sound was going to be, he knew perfectly well. It might begin with a hiss, but it would end with a roar—there was no time to lose—he must escape. It mustn't happen here—

Without another word, he turned and ran up the stairs.

IV

Not a moment too soon. The darkness was coming in long white waves. A prolonged sibilance filled the night—a great seamless seethe of wild influence went abruptly across it—a cold low humming shook the windows. He shut the door and flung off his clothes in the dark. The bare black floor was like a little raft tossed in waves of snow, almost overwhelmed, washed under whitely, up again, smothered in curled billows of feather. The snow was laughing: it spoke from all sides at once: it pressed closer to him as he ran and jumped exulting into his bed.

"Listen to us!" it said. "Listen! We have come to tell you the story we told you about. You remember? Lie down. Shut your eyes, now—you will no longer see much—in this white darkness who could see, or want to see? We will take the place of everything. . . . Listen—"

A beautiful varying dance of snow began at the front of the room, came forward and then retreated, flattened out toward the floor, then rose fountain-like to the ceiling, swayed, recruited itself from a new stream of flakes which poured laughing in through the humming window, advanced again, lifted long white arms. It said peace, it said remoteness, it said cold—it said—

But then a gash of horrible light fell brutally across the room from the opening door—the snow drew back hissing—something alien had come into the room—something hostile. This thing rushed at him, clutched at him, shook him—and he was not merely horrified, he was filled with such a loathing as he had never known. What was this? this cruel disturbance? this act of anger and hate? It was as if he had to reach up a hand toward another world for any understanding of it,—an effort of which he was only barely capable. But of that other world he still remembered just enough to know the exorcising words. They tore themselves from his other life suddenly—

"Mother! Mother! Go away! I hate you!"

And with that effort, everything was solved, everything became all right: the seamless hiss advanced once more, the long white wavering lines rose and fell like enormous whispering sea-waves, the whisper becoming louder, the laughter more numerous.

"Listen!" it said. "We'll tell you the last, the most beautiful and secret story—shut your eyes—it is a very small story—a story that gets smaller and smaller—it comes inward instead of opening like a flower—it is a flower becoming a seed—a little cold seed—do you hear? we are leaning closer to you—"

The hiss was now becoming a roar—the whole world was a vast moving screen of snow—but even now it said peace, it said remoteness, it said cold, it said sleep.

KATHERINE ANNE PORTER

[1890–1980]

Flowering Judas

(First published in *Hound and Horn,* Spring, 1930; first book publication in 1930.)

BRAGGIONI SITS HEAPED upon the edge of a straight-backed chair much too small for him, and sings to Laura in a furry, mournful voice. Laura has begun to find reasons for avoiding her own house until the latest possible moment, for Braggioni is there almost every night. No matter how late she is, he will be sitting there with a surly, waiting expression, pulling at his kinky yellow hair, thumbing the strings of his guitar, snarling a tune under his breath. Lupe the Indian maid meets Laura at the door, and says with a flicker of a glance towards the upper room, "He waits."

Laura wishes to lie down, she is tired of her hairpins and the feel of her long tight sleeves, but she says to him, "Have you a new song for me this evening?" If he says yes, she asks him to sing it. If he says no, she remembers his favorite one, and asks him to sing it again. Lupe brings her a cup of chocolate and a plate of rice, and Laura eats at the small table under the lamp, first inviting Braggioni, whose answer is always the same: "I have eaten, and besides, chocolate thickens the voice."

Laura says, "Sing, then," and Braggioni heaves himself into song. He scratches the guitar familiarly as though it were a pet animal, and sings passionately off key, taking the high notes in a prolonged painful squeal. Laura, who haunts the markets listening to the ballad singers, and stops every day to hear the blind boy playing his reed-flute in Sixteenth of September Street, listens to Braggioni with pitiless courtesy, because she dares not smile at his miserable performance. Nobody dares to smile at him. Braggioni is cruel to everyone, with a kind of specialized insolence, but he is so vain of his talents, and so sensitive to slights, it would require a cruelty and vanity greater than his own to lay a finger on the vast cureless wound of his self-esteem. It would require courage, too, for it is dangerous to offend him, and nobody has this courage.

Braggioni loves himself with such tenderness and amplitude and eternal charity that his followers—for he is a leader of men, a skilled revolutionist, and his skin has been punctured in honorable warfare—warm themselves in the reflected glow, and say to each other: "He has a real nobility, a love of humanity raised above mere personal affections." The excess of this self-love has flowed out, inconveniently for her, over Laura, who with so many others, owes her comfortable situation and her salary to him. When he is in a very good humor, he tells her, "I am tempted to forgive you for being a *gringa. Gringita*!"* and Laura, burning, imagines herself leaning forward suddenly, and with a sound back-handed slap wiping the suety smile from his face. If he notices her eyes at these moments he gives no sign.

She knows what Braggioni would offer her, and she must resist tenaciously without appearing to resist, and if she could avoid it she would not admit even to herself the slow drift of his intention. During these long evenings which have spoiled a long month for her, she sits in her deep chair with an open book on her knees, resting her eyes on the consoling rigidity of the printed page when the sight and sound of Braggioni singing threaten to identify themselves with all her remembered afflictions and to add their weight to her uneasy premonitions of the future. The gluttonous bulk of Braggioni has become a symbol of her many disillusions, for a revolutionist should be lean, animated by heroic faith, a vessel of abstract virtues. This is nonsense, she knows it now and is ashamed of it. Revolution must have leaders, and leadership is a career for energetic men. She is, her comrades tell her, full of romantic error, for what she defines as cynicism in them is merely "a developed sense of reality." She is almost too willing to say, "I am wrong, I suppose I don't really understand the principles," and afterward she makes a secret truce with herself, determined not to surrender her will to such expedient logic. But she cannot help feeling that she has been betrayed irreparably by the disunion between her way of living and her feeling of what life should be, and at times she is almost contented to rest in this sense of grievance as a private store of consolation. Sometimes she wishes to run away, but she stays. Now she longs to fly out of this room, down the narrow stairs, and into the street where the houses lean together like conspirators under a single mottled lamp, and leave Braggioni singing to himself.

Instead she looks at Braggioni, frankly and clearly, like a good child who understands the rules of behavior. Her knees cling together under sound blue serge, and her round white collar is not purposely nun-like. She wears the uniform of an idea, and has renounced vanities. She was born Roman Catholic, and in spite of her fear of being seen by someone who might make a scandal of it, she slips now and again into some crumbling little church, kneels on the chilly stone, and says a Hail Mary on the gold rosary she bought in Tehuantepec. It is no good and she ends by examining the altar with its

*Yankee. Little Yankee!

tinsel flowers and ragged brocades, and feels tender about the battered doll-shape of some male saint whose white, lace-trimmed drawers hang limply around his ankles below the hieratic dignity of his velvet robe. She has encased herself in a set of principles derived from her early training, leaving no detail of gesture or of personal taste untouched, and for this reason she will not wear lace made on machines. This is her private heresy, for in her special group the machine is sacred, and will be the salvation of the workers. She loves fine lace, and there is a tiny edge of fluted cobweb on this collar, which is one of twenty precisely alike, folded in blue tissue paper in the upper drawer of her clothes chest.

Braggioni catches her glance solidly as if he had been waiting for it, leans forward, balancing his paunch between his spread knees, and sings with tremendous emphasis, weighing his words. He has, the song relates, no father and no mother, nor even a friend to console him; lonely as a wave of the sea he comes and goes, lonely as a wave. His mouth opens round and yearns sideways, his balloon cheeks grow oily with the labor of song. He bulges marvelously in his expensive garments. Over his lavender collar, crushed upon a purple necktie, held by a diamond hoop: over his ammunition belt of tooled leather worked in silver, buckled cruelly around his gasping middle: over the tops of his glossy yellow shoes Braggioni swells with ominous ripeness, his mauve silk hose stretched taut, his ankles bound with the stout leather thongs of his shoes.

When he stretches his eyelids at Laura she notes again that his eyes are the true tawny yellow cat's eyes. He is rich, not in money, he tells her, but in power, and this power brings with it the blameless ownership of things, and the right to indulge his love of small luxuries. "I have a taste for the elegant refinements," he said once, flourishing a yellow silk handkerchief before her nose. "Smell that? It is Jockey Club, imported from New York." Nonetheless he is wounded by life. He will say so presently. "It is true everything turns to dust in the hand, to gall on the tongue." He sighs and his leather belt creaks like a saddle girth. "I am disappointed in everything as it comes. Everything." He shakes his head. "You, poor thing, you will be disappointed too. You are born for it. We are more alike than you realize in some things. Wait and see. Some day you will remember what I have told you, you will know that Braggioni was your friend."

Laura feels a slow chill, a purely physical sense of danger, a warning in her blood that violence, mutilation, a shocking death, wait for her with lessening patience. She had translated this fear into something homely, immediate, and sometimes hesitates before crossing the street. "My personal fate is nothing, except as the testimony of a mental attitude," she reminds herself, quoting from some forgotten philosophic primer, and is sensible enough to add, "Anyhow, I shall not be killed by an automobile if I can help it."

"It may be true I am as corrupt, in another way, as Braggioni," she thinks in spite of herself, "as callous, as incomplete," and if this is so, any kind of death seems preferable. Still she sits quietly, she does not run. Where could she go? Uninvited she has promised herself to this place; she can no longer imagine herself as living in another country, and there is no pleasure in remembering her life before she came here.

Precisely what is the nature of this devotion, its true motives, and what are its obligations? Laura cannot say. She spends part of her days in Xochimilco, near by, teaching Indian children to say in English, "The cat is on the mat." When she appears in the classroom they crowd about her with smiles on their wise, innocent, clay-colored faces, crying, "Good morning, my titcher!" in immaculate voices, and they make of her desk a fresh garden of flowers every day.

During her leisure she goes to union meetings and listens to busy important voices quarreling over tactics, methods, internal politics. She visits the prisoners of her own political faith in their cells, where they entertain themselves with counting cockroaches, repenting of their indiscretions, composing their memoirs, writing out manifestoes and plans for their comrades who are still walking about free, hands in pockets, sniffing fresh air. Laura brings them food and cigarettes and a little money, and she brings messages disguised in equivocal phrases from the men outside who dare not set foot in the prison for fear of disappearing into the cells kept empty for them. If the prisoners confuse night and day, and complain, "Dear little Laura, time doesn't pass in this infernal hole, and I won't know when it is time to sleep unless I have a reminder," she brings them their favorite narcotics, and says in a tone that does not wound them with pity, "Tonight will really be night for you," and though her Spanish amuses them, they find her comforting, useful. If they lose patience and all faith, and curse the slowness of their friends in coming to their rescue with money and influence, they trust her not to repeat everything, and if she inquires, "Where do you think we can find money, or influence?" they are certain to answer, "Well, there is Braggioni, why doesn't he do something?"

She smuggles letters from headquarters to men hiding from firing squads in back streets in mildewed houses, where they sit in tumbled beds and talk bitterly as if all Mexico were at their heels, when Laura knows positively they might appear at the band concert in the Alameda on Sunday morning, and no one would notice them. But Braggioni says, "Let them sweat a little. The next time they may be careful. It is very restful to have them out of the way for a while." She is not afraid to knock on any door in any street after midnight, and enter in the darkness, and say to one of these men who is really in danger: "They will be looking for you—seriously—tomorrow morning after six. Here is some money from Vicente. Go to Vera Cruz and wait."

She borrows money from the Roumanian agitator to give to his bitter enemy the Polish agitator. The favor of Braggioni is their disputed territory, and Braggioni holds the balance nicely, for he can use them both. The Polish agitator talks love to her over café tables, hoping to exploit what he believes is her secret sentimental preference for him, and he gives her misinformation which he begs her to repeat as the solemn truth to certain persons. The Roumanian is more adroit. He is generous with his money in all good causes, and lies to her with an air of ingenuous candor, as if he were her good friend and confidant. She never repeats anything they may say. Braggioni never asks questions. He has other ways to discover all that he wishes to know about them.

Nobody touches her, but all praise her gray eyes, and the soft, round under lip which promises gaiety, yet is always grave, nearly always firmly closed: and they cannot understand why she is in Mexico. She walks back and forth on her errands, with puzzled eyebrows, carrying her little folder of drawings and music and school papers. No dancer dances more beautifully than Laura walks, and she inspires some amusing, unexpected ardors, which cause little gossip, because nothing comes of them. A young captain who had been a soldier in Zapata's army* attempted, during a horseback ride near Cuernavaca, to express his desire for her with the noble simplicity befitting a rude folk-hero; but gently, because he was gentle. This gentleness was his defeat, for when he alighted, and removed her foot from the stirrup, and essayed to draw her down into his arms, her horse, ordinarily a tame one, shied fiercely, reared and plunged away. The young hero's horse careered blindly after his stable-mate, and the hero did not return to the hotel until rather late that evening. At breakfast he came to her table in full charro dress, gray buckskin jacket and trousers with strings of silver buttons down the leg, and he was in a humorous, careless mood. "May I sit with you?" and "You are a wonderful rider. I was terrified that you might be thrown and dragged. I should never have forgiven myself. But I cannot admire you enough for your riding!"

"I learned to ride in Arizona," said Laura.

"If you will ride with me again this morning, I promise you a horse that will not shy with you," he said. But Laura remembered that she must return to Mexico City at noon.

Next morning the children made a celebration and spent their playtime writing on the blackboard, "We lov ar ticher," and with tinted chalks they drew wreaths of flowers around the words. The young hero wrote her a letter: "I am a very foolish, wasteful, impulsive man. I should have first said I love you, and then you would not have run away. But you shall see me again." Laura thought, "I must send him a box of colored crayons," but she

*Emiliano Zapata led an agrarian uprising in the south of Mexico against the ineffective reformist presidency of Francisco Madero in 1911 and 1912.

was trying to forgive herself for having spurred her horse at the wrong moment.

A brown, shock-haired youth came and stood in her patio one night and sang like a lost soul for two hours, but Laura could think of nothing to do about it. The moonlight spread a wash of gauzy silver over the clear spaces of the garden, and the shadows were cobalt blue. The scarlet blossoms of the Judas tree were dull purple, and the names of the colors repeated themselves automatically in her mind, while she watched not the boy, but his shadow, fallen like a dark garment across the fountain rim, trailing in the water. Lupe came silently and whispered expert counsel in her ear: "If you will throw him one little flower, he will sing another song or two and go away." Laura threw the flower, and he sang a last song and went away with the flower tucked in the band of his hat. Lupe said, "He is one of the organizers of the Typographers Union, and before that he sold corridos* in the Merced market, and before that, he came from Guanajuato, where I was born. I would not trust any man, but I trust least those from Guanajuato."

She did not tell Laura that he would be back again the next night, and the next, nor that he would follow her at a certain fixed distance around the Merced market, through the Zócolo, up Francisco I. Madero Avenue, and so along the Paseo de la Reforma to Chapultepec Park, and into the Philosopher's Footpath, still with that flower withering in his hat, and an indivisible attention in his eyes.

Now Laura is accustomed to him, it means nothing except that he is nineteen years old and is observing a convention with all propriety, as though it were founded on a law of nature, which in the end it might well prove to be. He is beginning to write poems which he prints on a wooden press, and he leaves them stuck like handbills in her door. She is pleasantly disturbed by the abstract, unhurried watchfulness of his black eyes which will in time turn easily towards another object. She tells herself that throwing the flower was a mistake, for she is twenty-two years old and knows better; but she refuses to regret it, and persuades herself that her negation of all external events as they occur is a sign that she is gradually perfecting herself in the stoicism she strives to cultivate against that disaster she fears, though she cannot name it.

She is not at home in the world. Every day she teaches children who remain strangers to her, though she loves their tender round hands and their charming opportunist savagery. She knocks at unfamiliar doors not knowing whether a friend or a stranger shall answer, and even if a known face emerges from the sour gloom of that unknown interior, still it is the face of a stranger. No matter what this stranger says to her, nor what her message to him, the very cells of her flesh reject knowledge and kinship in

*ballads

one monotonous word. No. No. No. She draws her strength from this one holy talismanic word which does not suffer her to be led into evil. Denying everything, she may walk anywhere in safety, she looks at everything without amazement.

No, repeats this firm unchanging voice of her blood; and she looks at Braggioni without amazement. He is a great man, he wishes to impress this simple girl who covers her great round breasts with thick dark cloth, and who hides long, invaluably beautiful legs under a heavy skirt. She is almost thin except for the incomprehensible fullness of her breasts, like a nursing mother's, and Braggioni, who considers himself a judge of women, speculates again on the puzzle of her notorious virginity, and takes the liberty of speech which she permits without a sign of modesty, indeed, without any sort of sign, which is disconcerting.

"You think you are so cold, *gringita*! Wait and see. You will surprise yourself some day! May I be there to advise you!" He stretches his eyelids at her, and his ill-humored cat's eyes waver in a separate glance for the two points of light marking the opposite ends of a smoothly drawn path between the swollen curve of her breasts. He is not put off by that blue serge, nor by her resolutely fixed gaze. There is all the time in the world. His cheeks are bellying with the wind of song. "O girl with the dark eyes," he sings, and reconsiders. "But yours are not dark. I can change all that. O girl with the green eyes, you have stolen my heart away!" then his mind wanders to the song, and Laura feels the weight of his attention being shifted elsewhere. Singing thus, he seems harmless, he is quite harmless, there is nothing to do but sit patiently and say "No," when the moment comes. She draws a full breath, and her mind wanders also, but not far. She dares not wander too far.

Not for nothing has Braggioni taken pains to be a good revolutionist and a professional lover of humanity. He will never die of it. He has the malice, the cleverness, the wickedness, the sharpness of wit, the hardness of heart, stipulated for loving the world profitably. *He will never die of it.* He will live to see himself kicked out from his feeding trough by other hungry world-saviors. Traditionally he must sing in spite of his life which drives him to bloodshed, he tells Laura, for his father was a Tuscany peasant who drifted to Yucatan and married a Maya woman: a woman of race, an aristocrat. They gave him the love and knowledge of music, thus: and under the rip of his thumbnail, the strings of the instrument complain like exposed nerves.

Once he was called Delgadito* by all the girls and married women who ran after him; he was so scrawny all his bones showed under his thin cotton clothing, and he could squeeze his emptiness to the very backbone with his two hands. He was a poet and the revolution was only a dream then; too many women loved him and sapped away his youth, and he could never

*little slender one

find enough to eat anywhere, anywhere! Now he is a leader of men, crafty men who whisper in his ear, hungry men who wait for hours outside his office for a word with him, emaciated men with wild faces who waylay him at the street gate with a timid, "Comrade, let me tell you. . ." and they blow the foul breath from their empty stomachs in his face.

He is always sympathetic. He gives them handfuls of small coins from his own pocket, he promises them work, there will be demonstrations, they must join the unions and attend the meetings, above all they must be on the watch for spies. They are closer to him than his own brothers, without them he can do nothing—until tomorrow, comrade!

Until tomorrow. "They are stupid, they are lazy, they are treacherous, they would cut my throat for nothing," he says to Laura. He has good food and abundant drink, he hires an automobile and drives in the Paseo on Sunday morning, and enjoys plenty of sleep in a soft bed beside a wife who dares not disturb him; and he sits pampering his bones in easy billows of fat, singing to Laura, who knows and thinks these things about him. When he was fifteen, he tried to drown himself because he loved a girl, his first love, and she laughed at him. "A thousand women have paid for that," and his tight little mouth turns down at the corners. Now he perfumes his hair with Jockey Club, and confides to Laura: "One woman is really as good as another for me, in the dark. I prefer them all."

His wife organizes unions among the girls in the cigarette factories, and walks in picket lines, and even speaks at meetings in the evening. But she cannot be brought to acknowledge the benefits of true liberty. "I tell her I must have my freedom, net. She does not understand my point of view." Laura has heard this many times. Braggioni scratches the guitar and meditates. "She is an instinctively virtuous woman, pure gold, no doubt of that. If she were not, I should lock her up, and she knows it."

His wife, who works so hard for the good of the factory girls, employs part of her leisure lying on the floor weeping because there are so many women in the world, and only one husband for her, and she never knows where nor when to look for him. He told her: "Unless you can learn to cry when I am not here, I must go away for good." That day he went away and took a room at the Hotel Madrid.

It is this month of separation for the sake of higher principles that has been spoiled not only for Mrs. Braggioni, whose sense of reality is beyond criticism, but for Laura, who feels herself bogged in a nightmare. Tonight Laura envies Mrs. Braggioni, who is alone, and free to weep as much as she pleases about a concrete wrong. Laura has just come from a visit to the prison, and she is waiting for tomorrow with a bitter anxiety as if tomorrow may not come, but time may be caught immovably in this hour, with herself transfixed, Braggioni singing on forever, and Eugenio's body not yet discovered by the guard.

Braggioni says: "Are you going to sleep?" Almost before she can shake her head, he begins telling her about the May-day disturbances coming on in Morelia, for the Catholics hold a festival in honor of the Blessed Virgin, and the Socialists celebrate their martyrs on that day. "There will be two independent processions, starting from either end of town, and they will march until they meet, and the rest depends . . ." He asks her to oil and load his pistols. Standing up, he unbuckles his ammunition belt, and spreads it laden across her knees. Laura sits with the shells slipping through the cleaning cloth dipped in oil, and he says again he cannot understand why she works so hard for the revolutionary idea unless she loves some man who is in it. "Are you not in love with someone?" "No," says Laura. "And no one is in love with you?" "No." "Then it is your own fault. No woman need go begging. Why, what is the matter with you? The legless begger woman in the Alameda has a perfectly faithful lover. Did you know that?"

Laura peers down the pistol barrel and says nothing, but a long, slow faintness rises and subsides in her; Braggioni curves his swollen fingers around the throat of the guitar and softly smothers the music out of it, and when she hears him again he seems to have forgotten her, and is speaking in the hypnotic voice he uses when talking in small rooms to a listening, close-gathered crowd. Some day this world, now seemingly so composed and eternal, to the edges of every sea shall be merely a tangle of gaping trenches, of crashing walls and broken bodies. Everything must be torn from its accustomed place where it has rotted for centuries, hurled skyward and distributed, cast down again clean as rain, without separate identity. Nothing shall survive that the stiffened hands of poverty have created for the rich and no one shall be left alive except the elect spirits destined to procreate a new world cleansed of cruelty and injustice, ruled by benevolent anarchy. "Pistols are good, I love them, cannon are even better, but in the end I pin my faith to good dynamite," he concludes, and strokes the pistol lying in her hands. "Once I dreamed of destroying this city, in case it offered resistance to General Ortiz,* but it fell into his hands like an overripe pear."

He is made restless by his own words, rises and stands waiting. Laura holds up the belt to him: "Put that on, and go kill somebody in Morelia, and you will be happier," she says softly. The presence of death in the room makes her bold. "Today I found Eugenio going into a stupor. He refused to allow me to call the prison doctor. He had taken all the tablets I brought him yesterday. He said he took them because he was bored."

"He is a fool, and his death is his own business," says Braggioni, fastening his belt carefully.

*Pascual Ortiz Rubio (1877–1963) led revolutionary troops in the 1920s and was later President of Mexico.

"I told him if he had waited only a little while longer, you would have got him set free," says Laura. "He said he did not want to wait."

"He is a fool and we are well rid of him," says Braggioni, reaching for his hat.

He goes away. Laura knows his mood has changed, she will not see him any more for a while. He will send word when he needs her to go on errands into strange streets, to speak to the strange faces that will appear, like clay masks with the power of human speech, to mutter their thanks to Braggioni for his help. Now she is free, and she thinks, I must run while there is time. But she does not go.

Braggioni enters his own house where for a month his wife has spent many hours every night weeping and tangling her hair upon her pillow. She is weeping now, and she weeps more at the sight of him, the cause of all her sorrows. He looks about the room. Nothing is changed, the smells are good and familiar, he is well acquainted with the woman who comes toward him with no reproach except grief on her face. He says to her tenderly: "You are so good, please don't cry any more, you dear good creature." She says, "Are you tired, my angel? Sit here and I will wash your feet." She brings a bowl of water, and kneeling, unlaces his shoes, and when from her knees she raises her sad eyes under her blackened lids, he is sorry for everything, and bursts into tears. "Ah, yes, I am hungry, I am tired, let us eat something together," he says, between sobs. His wife leans her head on his arm and says, "Forgive me!" and this time he is refreshed by the solemn, endless rain of her tears.

Laura takes off her serge dress and puts on a white linen nightgown and goes to bed. She turns her head a little to one side, and lying still, reminds herself that it is time to sleep. Numbers tick in her brain like little clocks, soundless doors close of themselves around her. If you would sleep, you must not remember anything, the children will say tomorrow, good morning, my teacher, the poor prisoners who come every day bringing flowers to their jailor. 1–2–3–4–5–it is monstrous to confuse love with revolution, night with day, life with death–ah, Eugenio!

The tolling of the midnight bell is a signal, but what does it mean? Get up, Laura, and follow me: come out of your sleep, out of your bed, out of this strange house. What are you doing in this house? Without a word, without fear she rose and reached for Eugenio's hand, but he eluded her with a sharp, sly smile and drifted away. This is not all, you shall see—Murderer, he said, follow me, I will show you a new country, but it is far away and we must hurry. No, said Laura, not unless you take my hand, no; and she clung first to the stair rail, and then to the topmost branch of the Judas tree that bent down slowly and set her upon the earth, and then to the rocky ledge of a cliff, and then to the jagged wave of a sea that was not water but a desert of crumbling stone. Where are you taking me, she asked in wonder but without fear. To death, and it is a long way off, and we must hurry, said Eugenio. No, said Laura, not unless you take my hand. Then eat these flowers, poor prisoner, said Eugenio in a voice of pity, take and eat: and from the Judas tree he stripped the warm bleeding flowers, and held them to her lips. She saw that his hand was fleshless, a cluster of small white petrified branches, and his eye sockets were without light, but she ate the flowers greedily for they satisfied both hunger and thirst. Murderer! said Eugenio, and Cannibal! This is my body and my blood. Laura cried No! and at the sound of her own voice, she awoke trembling, and was afraid to sleep again.

DOROTHY PARKER

[1893–1967]

Big Blonde

(First published in *Bookman*, February, 1929;
first book publication in 1933.)

HAZEL MORSE WAS a large, fair woman of the type that incites some men when they use the word "blonde" to click their tongues and wag their heads roguishly. She prided herself upon her small feet and suffered for her vanity, boxing them in snub-toed, high-heeled slippers of the shortest bearable size. The curious things about her were her hands, strange terminations to the flabby white arms splattered with pale tan spots—long, quivering hands with deep and convex nails. She should not have disfigured them with little jewels.

She was not a woman given to recollections. At her middle thirties, her old days were a blurred and flickering sequence, an imperfect film, dealing with the actions of strangers.

In her twenties, after the deferred death of a hazy widowed mother, she had been employed as a model in a wholesale dress establishment—it was still the day of the big woman, and she was then prettily colored and erect and high-breasted. Her job was not onerous, and she met numbers of men and spent numbers of evenings with them, laughing at their jokes and telling them she loved their neckties. Men liked her, and she took it for granted that the liking of many men was a desirable thing. Popularity seemed to her to be worth all the work that had to be put into its achievement. Men liked you because you were fun, and when they liked you they took you out, and there you were. So, and successfully, she was fun. She was a good sport. Men like a good sport.

No other form of diversion, simpler or more complicated, drew her attention. She never pondered if she might not be better occupied doing something else. Her ideas, or, better, her acceptances, ran right along with those of the other substantially built blondes in whom she found her friends.

When she had been working in the dress establishment some years she met Herbie Morse. He was thin, quick, attractive, with shifting lines about his shiny, brown eyes and a habit of fiercely biting at the skin around his finger nails. He drank largely; she found that entertaining. Her habitual greeting to him was an allusion to his state of the previous night.

"Oh, what a peach you had," she used to say, through her easy laugh. "I thought I'd die, the way you kept asking the waiter to dance with you."

She liked him immediately upon their meeting. She was enormously amused at his fast, slurred sentences, his interpolations of apt phrases from vaudeville acts and comic strips; she thrilled at the feel of his lean arm tucked firm beneath the sleeve of her coat; she wanted to touch the wet, flat surface of his hair. He was as promptly drawn to her. They were married six weeks after they had met.

She was delighted at the idea of being a bride; coquetted with it, played upon it. Other offers of marriage she had had, and not a few of them, but it happened that they were all from stout, serious men who had visited the dress establishment as buyers; men from Des Moines and Houston and Chicago and, in her phrase, even funnier places. There was always something immensely comic to her in the thought of living elsewhere than New York. She could not regard as serious proposals that she share a western residence.

She wanted to be married. She was nearing thirty now, and she did not take the years well. She spread and softened, and her darkening hair turned her to inexpert dabblings with peroxide. There were times when she had little flashes of fear about her job. And she had had a couple of thousand evenings of being a good sport among her male acquaintances. She had come to be more conscientious than spontaneous about it.

Herbie earned enough, and they took a little apartment far uptown. There was a Mission-furnished dining room with a hanging central light globed in liver-colored glass; in the living room were an "overstuffed suite," a Boston fern and a reproduction of the Henner "Magdalene" with the red hair and the blue draperies; the bedroom was in gray enamel and old rose, with Herbie's photograph on Hazel's dressing table and Hazel's likeness on Herbie's chest of drawers.

She cooked—and she was a good cook—and marketed and chatted with the delivery boys and the colored laundress. She loved the flat, she loved her life, she loved Herbie. In the first months of their marriage, she gave him all the passion she was ever to know.

She had not realized how tired she was. It was a delight, a new game, a holiday, to give up being a good sport. If her head ached or her arches throbbed, she complained piteously, babyishly. If her mood was quiet, she did not talk. If tears came to her eyes, she let them fall.

She fell readily into the habit of tears during the first year of her marriage. Even in her good sport days, she had been known to weep lavishly and disinterestedly on occasion. Her behavior at the theater was a standing joke. She could weep at anything in a play—tiny garments, love both unrequited and mutual, seduction, purity, faithful servitors, wedlock, the triangle.

"There goes Haze," her friends would say, watching her. "She's off again."

Wedded and relaxed, she poured her tears freely. To her who had laughed so much, crying was delicious. All sorrows became her sorrows; she was Tenderness. She would cry long and softly over newspaper accounts of kidnapped babies, deserted wives, unemployed men, strayed cats, heroic dogs. Even when the paper was no longer before her, her mind revolved upon these things and the drops slipped rhythmically over her plump cheeks.

"Honestly," she would say to Herbie, "all the sadness there is in the world when you stop to think about it!"

"Yeah," Herbie would say.

She missed nobody. The old crowd, the people who had brought her and Herbie together, dropped from their lives, lingeringly at first. When she thought of this at all, it was only to consider it fitting. This was marriage. This was peace.

But the thing was that Herbie was not amused.

For a time, he had enjoyed being alone with her. He found the voluntary isolation novel and sweet. Then it palled with a ferocious suddenness. It was as if one night, sitting with her in the steam-heated living room, he would ask no more; and the next night he was through and done with the whole thing.

He became annoyed by her misty melancholies. At first, when he came home to find her softly tired and moody, he kissed her neck and patted her shoulder and begged her to tell her Herbie what was wrong. She loved that. But time slid by, and he found that there was never anything really, personally, the matter.

"Ah, for God's sake," he would say, "Crabbing again. All right, sit here and crab your head off. I'm going out."

And he would slam out of the flat and come back late and drunk.

She was completely bewildered by what happened to their marriage. First they were lovers; and then, it seemed without transition, they were enemies. She never understood it.

There were longer and longer intervals between his leaving his office and his arrival at the apartment. She went through agonies of picturing him run over and bleeding, dead and covered with a sheet. Then she lost her fears for his safety and grew sullen and wounded. When a person wanted to be with a person, he came as soon as possible. She desperately wanted him to want to be with her; her own hours only marked the time till he would come. It was often nearly nine o'clock before he came home to dinner. Always he had had many drinks, and their effect would die in him, leaving him loud and querulous and bristling for affronts.

He was too nervous, he said, to sit and do nothing for an evening. He boasted, probably not in all truth, that he had never read a book in his life.

"What am I expected to do—sit around this dump on my tail all night?" he would ask, rhetorically. And again he would slam out.

She did not know what to do. She could not manage him. She could not meet him.

She fought him furiously. A terrific domesticity had come upon her, and she would bite and scratch to guard it. She wanted what she called "a nice home." She wanted a sober, tender husband, prompt at dinner, punctual at work. She wanted sweet, comforting evenings. The idea of intimacy with other men was terrible to her; the thought that Herbie might be seeking entertainment in other women set her frantic.

It seemed to her that almost everything she read—novels from the drug-store lending library, magazine stories, women's pages in the papers—dealt with wives who lost their husbands' love. She could bear those, at that, better than accounts of neat, companionable marriage and living happily ever after.

She was frightened. Several times when Herbie came home in the evening, he found her determinedly dressed—she had had to alter those of her clothes that were not new, to make them fasten—and rouged.

"Let's go wild tonight, what do you say?" she would hail him. "A person's got lots of time to hang around and do nothing when they're dead."

So they would go out, to chop houses and the less expensive cabarets. But it turned out badly. She could no longer find amusement in watching Herbie drink. She could not laugh at his whimsicalities, she was so tensely counting his indulgences. And she was unable to keep back her remonstrances—"Ah, come on, Herb, you've had enough, haven't you? You'll feel something terrible in the morning."

He would be immediately enraged. All right, crab; crab, crab, crab, crab, that was all she ever did. What a lousy sport *she* was! There would be scenes, and one or the other of them would rise and stalk out in fury.

She could not recall the definite day that she started drinking, herself. There was nothing separate about her days. Like drops upon a window-pane, they ran together and trickled away. She had been married six-months; then a year; then three years.

She had never needed to drink, formerly. She could sit for most of a night at a table where the others were imbibing earnestly and never droop in looks or spirits, nor be bored by the doings of those about her. If she took a cocktail, it was so unusual as to cause twenty minutes or so of jocular comment. But now anguish was in her. Frequently, after a quarrel, Herbie would stay out for the night, and she could not learn from him where the time had been spent. Her heart felt tight and sore in her breast, and her mind turned like an electric fan.

She hated the taste of liquor. Gin, plain or in mixtures, made her promptly sick. After experiment, she found that Scotch whisky was best for her. She took it without water, because that was the quickest way to its effect.

Herbie pressed it on her. He was glad to see her drink. They both felt it might restore her high spirits, and their good times together might again be possible.

"'Atta girl," he would approve her. "Let's see you get boiled, baby."

But it brought them no nearer. When she drank with him, there would be a little while of gayety and then, strangely without beginning, they would be in a wild quarrel. They would wake in the morning not sure what it had all been about, foggy as to what had been said and done, but each deeply injured and bitterly resentful. There would be days of vengeful silence.

There had been a time when they had made up their quarrels, usually in bed. There would be kisses and little names and assurances of fresh starts . . ."Oh, it's going to be great now, Herb. We'll have swell times. I was a crab. I guess I must have been tired. But everything's going to be swell. You'll see."

Now there were no gentle reconciliations. They resumed friendly relations only in the brief magnanimity caused by liquor, before more liquor drew them into new battles. The scenes became more violent. There were shouted invectives and pushes, and sometimes sharp slaps. Once she had a black eye. Herbie was horrified next day at sight of it. He did not go to work; he followed her about, suggesting remedies and heaping dark blame on himself. But after they had had a few drinks—"to pull themselves together"—she made so many wistful references to her bruise that he shouted at her and rushed out and was gone for two days.

Each time he left the place in a rage, he threatened never to come back. She did not believe him, nor did she consider separation. Somewhere in her head or her heart was the lazy, nebulous hope that things would change and she and Herbie settle suddenly into soothing married life. Here were her home, her furniture, her husband, her station. She summoned no alternatives.

She could no longer bustle and potter. She had no more vicarious tears; the hot drops she shed were for herself. She walked ceaselessly about the rooms, her thoughts running mechanically round and round Herbie. In those days began the hatred of being alone that she was never to overcome. You could be by yourself when things were all right, but when you were blue you got the howling horrors.

She commenced drinking alone, little, short, drinks all through the day. It was only with Herbie that alcohol made her nervous and quick in offense. Alone, it blurred sharp things for her. She lived in a haze of it. Her life took on a dream-like quality. Nothing was astonishing.

A Mrs. Martin moved into the flat across the hall. She was a great blonde woman of forty, a promise in looks of what Mrs. Morse was to be. They made acquaintance, quickly became inseparable. Mrs. Morse spent her days in the opposite apartment. They drank together, to brace themselves after the drinks of the nights before.

She never confided her troubles about Herbie to Mrs. Martin. The subject was too bewildering to her to find comfort in talk. She let it be assumed that her husband's business kept him much away. It was not regarded as important; husbands, as such, played but shadowy parts in Mrs. Martin's circle.

Mrs. Martin had no visible spouse; you were left to decide for yourself whether he was or was not dead. She had an admirer, Joe, who came to see her almost nightly. Often he brought several friends with him—"The Boys," they were called. The Boys were big, red, good-humored men, perhaps forty-five, perhaps fifty. Mrs. Morse was glad of invitations to join the parties—Herbie was scarcely ever at home at night now. If he did come home, she did not visit Mrs. Martin. An evening alone with Herbie meant inevitably a quarrel, yet she would stay with him. There was always her thin and wordless idea that, maybe, this night, things would begin to be all right.

The Boys brought plenty of liquor along with them whenever they came to Mrs. Martin's. Drinking with them, Mrs. Morse became lively and good-natured and audacious. She was quickly popular. When she had drunk enough to cloud her most recent battle with Herbie, she was excited by their approbation. Crab, was she? Rotten sport, was she? Well, there were some that thought different.

Ed was one of The Boys. He lived in Utica—had "his own business" there, was the awed report—but he came to New York almost every week. He was married. He showed Mrs. Morse the then current photographs of Junior and Sister, and she praised them abundantly and sincerely. Soon it was accepted by the others that Ed was her particular friend.

He staked her when they all played poker; sat next to her and occasionally rubbed his knee against hers during the game. She was rather lucky. Frequently she went home with a twenty-dollar bill or a ten-dollar bill or a handful of crumpled dollars. She was glad of them. Herbie was getting, in her words, something awful about money. To ask him for it brought an instant row.

"What the hell do you do with it?" he would say. "Shoot it all on Scotch?"

"I try to run this house half-way decent," she would retort. "Never thought of that, did you? Oh, no, his lordship couldn't be bothered with that."

Again, she could not find a definite day, to fix the beginning of Ed's proprietorship. It became his custom to kiss her on the mouth when he came in, as well as for farewell, and he gave her little quick kisses of approval all through the evening. She liked this rather more than she disliked it. She never thought of his kisses when she was not with him.

He would run his hand lingeringly over her back and shoulders.

"Some dizzy blonde, eh?" he would say. "Some doll."

One afternoon she came home from Mrs. Martin's to find Herbie in the bedroom. He had been away for several nights, evidently on a prolonged drinking bout. His face was gray, his hands jerked as if they were on wires. On the bed were two old suitcases, packed high. Only her photograph remained on his bureau, and the wide doors of his closet disclosed nothing but coat-hangers.

"I'm blowing," he said. "I'm through with the whole works. I got a job in Detroit."

She sat down on the edge of the bed. She had drunk much the night before, and the four Scotches she had had with Mrs. Martin had only increased her fogginess.

"Good job?" she said.

"Oh, yeah," he said. "Looks all right."

He closed a suitcase with difficulty, swearing at it in whispers.

"There's some dough in the bank," he said. "The bank book's in your top drawer. You can have the furniture and stuff."

He looked at her, and his forehead twitched.

"God damn it, I'm through, I'm telling you," he cried. "I'm through."

"All right, all right," she said. "I heard you, didn't I?"

She saw him as if he were at one end of a canyon and she at the other. Her head was beginning to ache bumpingly, and her voice had a dreary, tiresome tone. She could not have raised it.

"Like a drink before you go?" she asked.

Again he looked at her, and a corner of his mouth jerked up.

"Cockeyed again for a change, aren't you?" he said. "That's nice. Sure, get a couple of shots, will you?"

She went to the pantry, mixed him a stiff highball, poured herself a couple of inches of whisky and drank it. Then she gave herself another portion and brought the glasses into the bedroom. He had strapped both suitcases and had put on his hat and overcoat.

He took his highball.

"Well," he said, and he gave a sudden, uncertain laugh. "Here's mud in your eye."

"Mud in your eye," she said.

They drank. He put down his glass and took up the heavy suitcases.

"Got to get a train around six," he said.

She followed him down the hall. There was a song, a song that Mrs. Martin played doggedly on the phonograph, running loudly through her mind. She had never liked the thing.

"Night and daytime,
Always playtime.
Ain't we got fun?"

At the door he put down the bags and faced her.

"Well," he said. "Well, take care of yourself. You'll be all right, will you?"

"Oh, sure," she said.

He opened the door, then came back to her, holding out his hand.

"'By, Haze," he said. "Good luck to you."

She took his hand and shook it.

"Pardon my wet glove," she said.

When the door had closed behind him, she went back to the pantry.

She was flushed and lively when she went in to Mrs. Martin's that evening. The Boys were there, Ed among them. He was glad to be in town, frisky and loud and full of jokes. But she spoke quietly to him for a minute.

"Herbie blew today," she said. "Going to live out West."

"That so?" he said. He looked at her and played with the fountain pen clipped to his waistcoat pocket.

"Think he's gone for good, do you?" he asked.

"Yeah," she said. "I know he is. I know. Yeah."

"You going to live on across the hall just the same?" he said. "Know what you're going to do?"

"Gee, I don't know," she said. "I don't give much of a damn."

"Oh, come on, that's no way to talk," he told her. "What you need–you need a little snifter. How about it?"

"Yeah," she said. "Just straight."

She won forty-three dollars at poker. When the game broke up, Ed took her back to her apartment.

"Got a little kiss for me?" he asked.

He wrapped her in his big arms and kissed her violently. She was entirely passive. He held her away and looked at her.

"Little tight, honey?" he asked, anxiously. "Not going to be sick, are you?"

"Me?" she said. "I'm swell."

II

When Ed left in the morning, he took her photograph with him. He said he wanted her picture to look at, up in Utica. "You can have that one on the bureau," she said.

She put Herbie's picture in a drawer, out of her sight. When she could look at it, she meant to tear it up. She was fairly successful in keeping her mind from racing around him. Whisky slowed it for her. She was almost peaceful, in her mist.

She accepted her relationship with Ed without question or enthusiasm. When he was away, she seldom thought definitely of him. He was good to her; he gave her frequent presents and a regular allowance. She was even able to save. She did not plan ahead of any day, but her wants were few, and you might as well put money in the bank as have it lying around.

When the lease of her apartment neared its end, it was Ed who suggested moving. His friendship with Mrs. Martin and Joe had become strained over a dispute at poker; a feud was impending.

"Let's get the hell out of here," Ed said. "What I want you to have is a place near the Grand Central. Make it easier for me."

So she took a little flat in the Forties. A colored maid came in every day to clean and to make coffee for her—she was "through with that housekeeping stuff," she said, and Ed, twenty years married to a passionately domestic woman, admired this romantic uselessness and felt doubly a man of the world in abetting it.

The coffee was all she had until she went out to dinner, but alcohol kept her fat. Prohibition she regarded only as a basis for jokes. You could always get all you wanted. She was never noticeably drunk and seldom nearly sober. It required a larger daily allowance to keep her misty-minded. Too little, and she was achingly melancholy.

Ed brought her to Jimmy's. He was proud, with the pride of the transient who would be mistaken for a native, in his knowledge of small, recent restaurants occupying the lower floors of shabby brown-stone houses; places where, upon mentioning the name of an habitué friend, might be obtained strange whisky and fresh gin in many of their ramifications. Jimmy's place was the favorite of his acquaintances.

There, through Ed, Mrs. Morse met many men and women, formed quick friendships. The men often took her out when Ed was in Utica. He was proud of her popularity.

She fell into the habit of going to Jimmy's alone when she had no engagement. She was certain to meet some people she knew, and join them. It was a club for her friends, both men and women.

The women at Jimmy's looked remarkably alike, and this was curious, for, through feuds, removals and opportunities of more profitable contacts, the personnel of the group changed constantly. Yet always the newcomers resembled those whom they replaced. They were all big women and stout, broad of shoulder and abundantly breasted, with faces thickly clothed in soft, high-colored flesh. They laughed loud and often, showing opaque and lusterless teeth like squares of crockery. There was about them the health of the big, yet a slight, unwholesome suggestion of stubborn preservation. They might have been thirty-six or forty-five or anywhere between.

They composed their titles of their own first names with their husbands' surnames—Mrs. Florence Miller, Mrs. Vera Riley, Mrs. Lilian Block. This gave at the same time the solidity of marriage and the glamour of freedom. Yet only one or two were actually divorced. Most of them never referred to their dimmed spouses; some, a shorter time separate, described them in terms of great biological interest. Several were mothers, each of an only child—a boy at school somewhere, or a girl being cared for by a grandmother. Often, well on towards morning, there would be displays of kodak portraits and of tears.

They were comfortable women, cordial and friendly and irrepressibly matronly. Theirs was the quality of ease. Become fatalistic, especially about money matters, they were unworried. Whenever their funds dropped alarmingly, a new donor appeared; this had always happened. The aim of each was to have one man, permanently, to pay all her bills, in return for which she would have immediately given up other admirers and probably would have become exceedingly fond of him; for the affections of all of them were, by now, unexacting, tranquil, and easily arranged. This end, however, grew increasingly difficult yearly. Mrs. Morse was regarded as fortunate.

Ed had a good year, increased her allowance and gave her a sealskin coat. But she had to be careful of her moods with him. He insisted upon gayety. He would not listen to admissions of aches or weariness.

"Hey, listen." he would say, "I got worries of my own, and plenty. Nobody wants to hear other people's troubles, sweetie. What you got to do, you got to be a sport and forget it. See? Well, slip us a little smile, then. That's my girl."

She never had enough interest to quarrel with him as she had with Herbie, but she wanted the privilege of occasional admitted sadness. It was strange. The other women she saw did not have to fight their moods. There was Mrs. Florence Miller who got regular crying jags. and the men sought only to cheer and comfort her. The others spent whole evenings in grieved recitals of worries and ills; their escorts paid them deep sympathy. But she was instantly undesirable when she was low in spirits. Once, at Jimmy's, when she could not make herself lively, Ed had walked out and left her.

"Why the hell don't you stay home and not go spoiling everybody's evening?" he had roared.

Even her slightest acquaintances seemed irritated if she were not conspicuously light-hearted.

"What's the matter with you, anyway?" they would say. "Be your age, why don't you? Have a little drink and snap out of it."

When her relationship with Ed had continued nearly three years, he moved to Florida to live. He hated leaving her; he gave her a large check and some shares of a sound stock, and his pale eyes were wet when he said good-by. She did not miss him. He came to New York infrequently, perhaps two or three times a year, and hurried directly from the train to see her. She was always pleased to have him come and never sorry to see him go.

Charley, an acquaintance of Ed's that she had met at Jimmy's, had long admired her. He had always made opportunities of touching her and leaning close to talk to her. He asked repeatedly of all their friends if they had ever heard such a fine laugh as she had. After Ed left, Charley became the main figure in her life. She classified him and spoke of him as "not so bad." There was nearly a year of Charley; then she divided her time between him and Sydney, another frequenter of Jimmy's; then Charley slipped away altogether.

Sydney was a little, brightly dressed, clever Jew. She was perhaps nearest contentment with him. He amused her always; her laughter was not forced.

He admired her completely. Her softness and size delighted him. And he thought she was great, he often told her, because she kept gay and lively when she was drunk.

"Once I had a gal," he said, "used to try and throw herself out of the window every time she got a can on. Jee-*zuss*," he added, feelingly.

Then Sydney married a rich and watchful bride, and then there was Billy. No—after Sydney came Ferd, then Billy. In her haze, she never recalled how men entered her life and left it. There were no surprises. She had no thrill at their advent, nor woe at their departure. She seemed to be always able to attract men. There was never another as rich as Ed, but they were all generous to her, in their means.

Once she had news of Herbie. She met Mrs. Martin dining at Jimmy's, and the old friendship was vigorously renewed. The still admiring Joe, while on a business trip, had seen Herbie. He had settled in Chicago, he looked fine, he was living with some woman—seemed to be crazy about her. Mrs. Morse had been drinking vastly that day. She took the news with mild interest, as one hearing of the sex peccadilloes of somebody whose name is, after a moment's groping, familiar.

"Must be damn near seven years since I saw him," she commented. "Gee. Seven years."

More and more, her days lost their individuality. She never knew dates, nor was sure of the day of the week.

"My God, was that a year ago!" she would exclaim, when an event was recalled in conversation.

She was tired much of the time. Tired and blue. Almost everything could give her the blues. Those old horses she saw on Sixth Avenue—struggling and slipping along the car-tracks, or standing at the curb, their heads dropped level with their worn knees. The tightly stored tears would squeeze from her eyes as she teetered past on her aching feet in the stubby, champagne-colored slippers.

The thought of death came and stayed with her and lent her a sort of drowsy cheer. It would be nice, nice and restful, to be dead.

There was no settled, shocked moment when she first thought of killing herself; it seemed to her as if the idea had always been with her. She pounced upon all the accounts of suicides in the newspapers. There was an epidemic of self-killings—or maybe it was just that she searched for the stories of them so eagerly that she found many. To read of them roused reassurance in her; she felt a cozy solidarity with the big company of the voluntary dead.

She slept, aided by whisky, till deep into the afternoons, then lay abed, a bottle and a glass at her hand, until it was time to dress to go out for dinner. She was beginning to feel toward alcohol a little puzzled distrust, as toward an old friend who has refused a simple favor. Whisky could still soothe her for most of the time, but there were sudden, inexplicable moments when the cloud fell treacherously away from her, and she was sawn by the sorrow and bewilderment and nuisance of all living. She played voluptuously with the thought of cool, sleepy retreat. She had never been troubled by religious belief and no vision of an after-life intimidated her. She dreamed by day of never again putting on tight shoes, of never having to laugh and listen and admire, of never more being a good sport. Never.

But how would you do it? It made her sick to think of jumping from heights. She could not stand a gun. At the theater, if one of the actors drew a revolver, she crammed her fingers into her ears and could not even look at the stage until after the shot had been fired. There was no gas in her flat. She looked long at the bright blue veins in her slim wrists—a cut with a razor blade, and there you'd be. But it would hurt, hurt like hell, and there would be blood to see. Poison—something tasteless and quick and painless—was the thing. But they wouldn't sell it to you in drug-stores, because of the law.

She had few other thoughts.

There was a new man now—Art. He was short and fat and exacting and hard on her patience when he was drunk. But there had been only occasionals for some time before him, and she was glad of a little stability. Too, Art must be away for weeks at a stretch, selling silks, and that was restful. She was convincingly gay with him, though the effort shook her.

"The best sport in the world," he would murmur, deep in her neck. "The best sport in the world."

One night, when he had taken her to Jimmy's, she went into the dressing-room with Mrs. Florence Miller. There, while designing curly mouths on their faces with lip-rouge, they compared experiences of insomnia.

"Honestly," Mrs. Morse said, "I wouldn't close an eye if I didn't go to bed full of Scotch. I lie there and toss and turn and toss and turn. Blue! Does a person get blue lying awake that way!"

"Say, listen, Hazel," Mrs. Miller said, impressively, "I'm telling you I'd be awake for a year if I didn't take veronal. That stuff makes you sleep like a fool."

"Isn't it poison, or something?" Mrs. Morse asked.

"Oh, you take too much and you're out for the count," said Mrs. Miller. "I just take five grains—they come in tablets. I'd be scared to fool around with it. But five grains, and you cork off pretty."

"Can you get it anywhere?" Mrs. Morse felt superbly Machiavellian.

"Get all you want in Jersey," said Mrs. Miller. "They won't give it to you here without you have a doctor's prescription. Finished? We'd better go back and see what the boys are doing."

That night, Art left Mrs. Morse at the door of her apartment; his mother was in town. Mrs. Morse was still sober, and it happened that there was no whisky left in her cupboard. She lay in bed, looking up at the black ceiling.

She rose early, for her, and went to New Jersey. She had never taken the tube, and did not understand it. So she went to the Pennsylvania Station and bought a railroad ticket to Newark. She thought of nothing in particular on the trip out. She looked at the uninspired hats of the women about her and gazed through the smeared window at the flat, gritty scene.

In Newark, in the first drug-store she came to, she asked for a tin of talcum powder, a nail-brush and a box of veronal tablets. The powder and the brush were to make the hypnotic seem also a casual need. The clerk was entirely unconcerned. "We only keep them in bottles," he said, and wrapped up for her a little glass vial containing ten white tablets, stacked one on another.

She went to another drug-store and bought a face-cloth, an orange-wood stick and a bottle of veronal tablets. The clerk was also uninterested.

"Well, I guess I got enough to kill an ox," she thought, and went back to the station.

At home. she put the little vials in the drawer of her dressing-table and stood looking at them with a dreamy tenderness.

"There they are, God bless them," she said, and she kissed her finger-tip and touched each bottle.

The colored maid was busy in the living room.

"Hey, Nettie," Mrs. Morse called. "Be an angel, will you? Run around to Jimmy's and get me a quart of Scotch."

She hummed while she awaited the girl's return.

During the next few days, whisky ministered to her as tenderly as it had done when she first turned to its aid. Alone, she was soothed and vague, at Jimmy's she was the gayest of the groups. Art was delighted with her.

Then, one night, she had an appointment to meet Art at Jimmy's for an early dinner. He was to leave afterward on a business excursion, to be away for a week. Mrs. Morse had been drinking all the afternoon; while she dressed to go out, she felt herself rising pleasurably from drowsiness to high spirits. But as she came out into the street the effects of the whisky deserted her completely, and she was filled with a slow, grinding wretchedness so horrible that she stood swaying on the pavement, unable for a moment to move forward. It was a gray night with spurts of mean, thin snow, and the streets shone with dark ice. As she slowly crossed Sixth Avenue, consciously dragging one foot past the other, a big, scarred horse pulling a rickety express-wagon crashed to his knees before her. The driver swore and screamed and lashed the beast insanely, bringing the whip back over his shoulder for every blow, while the horse struggled to get a footing on the slippery asphalt. A group gathered and watched with interest.

Art was waiting when Mrs. Morse reached Jimmy's.

"What's the matter with you, for God's sake?" was his greeting to her.

"I saw a horse," she said. "Gee, I—a person feels sorry for horses. I—it isn't just horses. Everything's kind of terrible, isn't it? I can't help getting sunk."

"Ah, sunk, me eye," he said. "What's the idea of all the bellyaching? What have you got to be sunk about?"

"I can't help it," she said.

"Ah, help it, me eye," he said. "Pull yourself together, will you? Come on and sit down, and take that face off you."

She drank industriously and she tried hard, but she could not overcome her melancholy. Others joined them and commented on her gloom, and she could do no more for them than smile weakly. She made little dabs at her eyes with her handkerchief, trying to time her movements so they would be unnoticed, but several times Art caught her and scowled and shifted impatiently in his chair.

When it was time for him to go to his train, she said she would leave, too, and go home.

"And not a bad idea, either," he said. "See if you can't sleep yourself out of it. I'll see you Thursday. For God's sake, try and cheer up by then, will you?"

"Yeah," she said. "I will."

In her bedroom, she undressed with a tense speed wholly unlike her usual slow uncertainty. She put on her nightgown, took off her hair-net and passed the comb quickly through her dry, vari-colored hair. Then she took the two little vials from the drawer and carried them into the bathroom. The splintering misery had gone from her, and she felt the quick excitement of one who is about to receive an anticipated gift.

She uncorked the vials, filled a glass with water and stood before the mirror, a tablet between her fingers. Suddenly she bowed graciously to her reflection, and raised the glass to it.

"Well, here's mud in your eye," she said.

The tablets were unpleasant to take, dry and powdery and sticking obstinately half-way down her throat. It took her a long time to swallow all twenty of them. She stood watching her reflection with deep, impersonal interest, studying the movements of the gulping throat. Once more she spoke aloud.

"For God's sake, try and cheer up by Thursday, will you?" she said. "Well, you know what he can do. He and the whole lot of them."

She had no idea how quickly to expect effect from the veronal. When she had taken the last tablet, she stood uncertainly, wondering, still with a courteous, vicarious interest, if death would strike her down then and there. She felt in no way strange, save for a slight stirring of sickness from the effort of swallowing the tablets, nor did her reflected face look at all different. It would not be immediate, then; it might even take an hour or so.

She stretched her arms high and gave a vast yawn.

"Guess I'll go to bed," she said. "Gee, I'm nearly dead."

That struck her as comic, and she turned out the bathroom light and went in and laid herself down in her bed, chuckling softly all the time.

"Gee, I'm nearly dead," she quoted. "That's a hot one!"

III

Nettie, the colored maid, came in late the next afternoon to clean the apartment, and found Mrs. Morse in her bed. But then, that was not unusual. Usually, though, the sounds of cleaning waked her, and she did not like to wake up. Nettie, an agreeable girl, had learned to move softly about her work.

But when she had done the living room and stolen in to tidy the little square bedroom, she could not avoid a tiny clatter as she arranged the objects on the dressing-table. Instinctively, she glanced over her shoulder at the sleeper, and without warning a sickly uneasiness crept over her. She came to the bed and stared down at the woman lying there.

Mrs. Morse lay on her back, one flabby, white arm flung up, the wrist against her forehead. Her stiff hair hung untenderly along her face. The bed covers were pushed down, exposing a deep square of soft neck and a pink nightgown, its fabric worn uneven by many launderings; her great breasts, freed from their tight confiner, sagged beneath her arm-pits. Now and then she made knotted, snoring sounds, and from the corner of her opened mouth to the blurred turn of her jaw ran a lane of crusted spittle.

"Mis' Morse," Nettie called. "Oh, Mis' Morse! It's terrible late."

Mrs. Morse made no move.

"Mis' Morse," said Nettie. "Look, Mis' Morse. How'm I goin' get this bed made?"

Panic sprang upon the girl. She shook the woman's hot shoulder.

"Ah, wake up, will yuh?" she whined. "Ah, please wake up."

Suddenly the girl turned and ran out in the hall to the elevator door, keeping her thumb firm on the black, shiny button until the elderly car and its Negro attendant stood before her. She poured a jumble of words over the boy, and led him back to the apartment. He tiptoed creakingly in to the bedside; first gingerly, then so lustily that he left marks on the soft flesh, he prodded the unconscious woman.

"Hey, there!" he cried, and listened intently, as for an echo.

"Jeez. Out like a light," he commented.

At his interest in the spectacle, Nettie's panic left her. Importance was big in both of them. They talked in quick, unfinished whispers, and it was the boy's suggestion that he fetch the young doctor who lived on the ground floor. Nettie hurried along with him. They looked forward to the limelit moment of breaking their news of something untoward, something pleasurably unpleasant. Mrs. Morse had become the medium of drama. With no ill wish to her, they hoped that her state was serious, that she would not let them down by being awake and normal on their return. A little fear of this determined them to make the most, to the doctor, of her present condition. "Matter of life and death," returned to Nettie from her thin store of reading. She considered startling the doctor with the phrase.

The doctor was in and none too pleased at interruption. He wore a yellow and blue striped dressing-gown, and he was lying on his sofa, laughing with a dark girl, her face scaly with inexpensive powder, who perched on the arm. Half-emptied highball glasses stood beside them, and her coat and hat were neatly hung up with the comfortable implication of a long stay.

Always something, the doctor grumbled. Couldn't let anybody alone after a hard day. But he put some bottles and instruments into a case, changed his dressing-gown for his coat and started out with the Negroes.

"Snap it up there, big boy," the girl called after him. "Don't be all night."

The doctor strode loudly into Mrs. Morse's flat and on to the bedroom, Nettie and the boy right behind him. Mrs. Morse had not moved; her sleep was as deep, but soundless, now. The doctor looked sharply at her, then plunged his thumbs into the lidded pits above her eyeballs and threw his weight upon them. A high, sickened cry broke from Nettie.

"Look like he tryin' to push her right on th'ough the bed," said the boy. He chuckled.

Mrs. Morse gave no sign under the pressure. Abruptly the doctor abandoned it, and with one quick movement swept the covers down to the foot of the bed. With another he flung her nightgown back and lifted the thick, white legs, cross-hatched with blocks of tiny, iris-colored veins. He pinched them repeatedly, with long, cruel nips, back of the knees. She did not awaken.

"What's she been drinking?" he asked Nettie, over his shoulder.

With the certain celerity of one who knows just where to lay hands on a thing, Nettie went into the bathroom, bound for the cupboard where Mrs. Morse kept her whisky. But she stopped at the sight of the two vials, with their red and white labels, lying before the mirror. She brought them to the doctor.

"Oh, for the Lord Almighty's sweet sake!" he said. He dropped Mrs. Morse's legs, and pushed them impatiently across the bed. "What did she want to go taking that tripe for? Rotten yellow trick, that's what a thing like that is. Now we'll have to pump her out, and all that stuff. Nuisance, a thing like that is; that's what it amounts to. Here, George, take me down in the elevator. You wait here, maid. She won't do anything."

"She won' die on me, will she?" cried Nettie.

"No," said the doctor. "God, no. You couldn't kill her with an ax."

IV

After two days, Mrs. Morse came back to consciousness, dazed at first, then with a comprehension that brought with it the slow, saturating wretchedness.

"Oh, Lord, oh, Lord," she moaned, and tears for herself and for life striped her cheeks.

Nettie came in at the sound. For two days she had done the ugly, incessant tasks in the nursing of the unconscious, for two nights she had caught broken bits of sleep on the living-room couch. She looked coldly at the big, blown woman in the bed.

"What you been tryin' to do, Mis' Morse?" she said. "What kine o' work is that, takin' all that stuff?"

"Oh, Lord," moaned Mrs. Morse, again, and she tried to cover her eyes with her arms. But the joints felt stiff and brittle, and she cried out at their ache.

"Tha's no way to ack, takin' them pills," said Nettie. "You can thank you' stars you heah at all. How you feel now?"

"Oh, I feel great," said Mrs. Morse. "Swell, I feel."

Her hot, painful tears fell as if they would never stop.

"Tha's no way to take on, cryin' like that," Nettie said. "After what you done. The doctor, he says he could have you arrested, doin' a thing like that. He was fit to be tied, here."

"Why couldn't he let me alone?" wailed Mrs. Morse. "Why the hell couldn't he have?"

"Tha's terr'ble, Mis' Morse, swearin' an' talkin' like that," said Nettie, "after what people done for you. Here I ain' had no sleep at all for two nights, an' I had to give up goin' out to my other ladies!"

"Oh, I'm sorry, Nettie," she said. "You're a peach. I'm sorry I've given you so much trouble. I couldn't help it. I just got sunk. Didn't you ever feel like doing it? When everything looks just lousy to you?"

"I wouldn' think o' no such thing," declared Nettie. "You got to cheer up. Tha's what you got to do. Everybody's got their troubles."

"Yeah," said Mrs. Morse. "I know."

"Come a pretty picture card for you," Nettie said. "Maybe that will cheer you up."

She handed Mrs. Morse a post-card. Mrs. Morse had to cover one eye with her hand, in order to read the message; her eyes were not yet focusing correctly.

It was from Art. On the back of a view of the Detroit Athletic Club he had written: "Greeting and salutations. Hope you have lost that gloom. Cheer up and don't take any rubber nickels. See you on Thursday."

She dropped the card to the floor. Misery crushed her as if she were between great smooth stones. There passed before her a slow, slow pageant of days spent lying in her flat, of evenings at Jimmy's being a good sport, making herself laugh and coo at Art and other Arts; she saw a long parade of weary horses and shivering beggars and all beaten, driven, stumbling things. Her feet throbbed as if she had crammed them into the stubby champagne-colored slippers. Her heart seemed to swell and harden.

"Nettie," she cried, "for heaven's sake pour me a drink, will you?"

The maid looked doubtful.

"Now you know, Mis' Morse," she said, "you been near daid. I don' know if the doctor he let you drink nothin' yet."

"Oh, never mind him," she said. "You get me one, and bring in the bottle. Take one yourself."

"Well," said Nettie.

She poured them each a drink, deferentially leaving hers in the bathroom to be taken in solitude, and brought Mrs. Morse's glass in to her.

Mrs. Morse looked into the liquor and shuddered back from its odor. Maybe it would help. Maybe, when you had been knocked cold for a few days, your very first drink would give you a lift. Maybe whisky would be her friend again. She prayed without addressing a God, without knowing a God. Oh, please, please, let her be able to get drunk, please keep her always drunk.

She lifted the glass.

"Thanks, Nettie," she said. "Here's mud in your eye."

The maid giggled. "Tha's the way, Mis' Morse," she said. "You cheer up, now."

"Yeah," said Mrs. Morse. "Sure."

JAMES THURBER

[1894–1961]

The Secret Life of Walter Mitty

(First published in *The New Yorker*, 1939; first book publication in 1942.)

WE'RE GOING THROUGH!" The Commander's voice was like thin ice breaking. He wore his full-dress uniform, with the heavily braided white cap pulled down rakishly over one cold gray eye. "We can't make it, sir. It's spoiling for a hurricane, if you ask me." "I'm not asking you, Lieutenant Berg," said the Commander. "Throw on the power light! Rev her up to 8,500! We're going through!" The pounding of the cylinders increased: ta-pocketa-pocketa-pocketa-*pocketa-pocketa*. The Commander stared at the ice forming on the pilot window. He walked over and twisted a row of complicated dials. "Switch on No. 8 auxiliary!" he shouted. "Switch on No. 8 auxiliary!" repeated Lieutenant Berg. "Full strength in No. 3 turret!" shouted the Commander. "Full strength in No. 3 turret!" The crew, bending to their various tasks in the huge, hurtling eight-engined Navy hydroplane, looked at each other and grinned. "The Old Man'll get us through," they said to one another. "The Old Man ain't afraid of Hell!" . . .

"Not so fast! You're driving too fast!" said Mrs. Mitty. "What are you driving so fast for?"

"Hmm?" said Walter Mitty. He looked at his wife, in the seat beside him, with shocked astonishment. She seemed grossly unfamiliar, like a strange woman who had yelled at him in a crowd. "You were up to fifty-five," she said. "You know I don't like to go more than forty. You were up to fifty-five." Walter Mitty drove on toward Waterbury in silence, the roaring of the SN202 through the worst storm in twenty years of Navy flying fading in the remote, intimate airways of his mind. "You're tensed up again," said Mrs. Mitty. "It's one of your days. I wish you'd let Dr. Renshaw look you over."

Walter Mitty stopped the car in front of the building where his wife went to have her hair done. "Remember to get those overshoes while I'm having my hair done," she said. "I don't need overshoes," said Mitty. She put her mirror back into her bag. "We've been all through that," she said, getting out of the car. "You're not a young man any longer." He raced the engine a little. "Why don't you wear your gloves? Have you lost your gloves?" Walter

Mitty reached in a pocket and brought out the gloves. He put them on, but after she had turned and gone into the building and he had driven on to a red light, he took them off again. "Pick it up, brother!" snapped a cop as the light changed, and Mitty hastily pulled on his gloves and lurched ahead. He drove around the streets aimlessly for a time, and then he drove past the hospital on his way to the parking lot.

. . . "It's the millionaire banker, Wellington McMillan," said the pretty nurse. "Yes?" said Walter Mitty, removing his gloves slowly. "Who has the case?" "Dr. Renshaw and Dr. Benbow, but there are two specialists here, Dr. Remington from New York and Mr. Pritchard-Mitford from London. He flew over." A door opened down a long, cool corridor and Dr. Renshaw came out. He looked distraught and haggard. "Hello, Mitty," he said. "We're having the devil's own time with McMillan, the millionaire banker and close personal friend of Roosevelt. Obstreosis of the ductal tract. Tertiary. Wish you'd take a look at him." "Glad to," said Mitty.

In the operating room there were whispered introductions: "Dr. Remington, Dr. Mitty. Mr. Pritchard-Mitford, Dr. Mitty." "I've read your book on streptothricosis," said Pritchard-Mitford, shaking hands. "A brilliant performance, sir." "Thank you," said Walter Mitty. "Didn't know you were in the States, Mitty," grumbled Remington. "Coals to Newcastle, bringing Mitford and me up here for a tertiary." "You are very kind," said Mitty. A huge, complicated machine, connected to the operating table, with many tubes and wires, began at this moment to go pocketa-pocketa-pocketa. "The new anesthetizer is giving way!" shouted an interne. "There is no one in the East who knows how to fix it!" "Quiet, man!" said Mitty, in a low, cool voice. He sprang to the machine, which was now going pocketa-pocketa-queep-pocketa-queep. He began fingering delicately a row of glistening dials. "Give me a fountain pen!" he snapped. Someone handed him a fountain pen. He pulled a faulty piston out of the machine and inserted the pen in its place. "That will hold for ten minutes," he said. "Get on with the operation." A nurse hurried over and whispered to Renshaw, and Mitty saw the man turn pale. "Coreopsis has set in," said Renshaw nervously. "If you would take over, Mitty?" Mitty looked at him and at the craven figure of Benbow, who drank, and at the grave, uncertain faces of the two great specialists. "If you wish," he said. They slipped a white gown on him; he adjusted a mask and drew on thin gloves; nurses handed him shining . . .

"Back it up, Mac! Look out for that Buick!" Walter Mitty jammed on the brakes. "Wrong lane, Mac," said the parking-lot attendant, looking at Mitty closely. "Gee. Yeh," muttered Mitty. He began cautiously to back out of the lane marked "Exit Only." "Leave her sit there," said the attendant. "I'll put her away." Mitty got out of the car. "Hey, better leave the key." "Oh," said Mitty, handing the man the ignition key. The attendant vaulted into the car, backed it up with insolent skill, and put it where it belonged.

They're so damn cocky, thought Walter Mitty, walking along Main Street; they think they know everything. Once he had tried to take his chains off, outside New Milford, and he had got them wound around the axles. A man had had to come out in a wrecking car and unwind them, a young, grinning garageman. Since then Mrs. Mitty always made him drive to a garage to have the chains taken off. The next time, he thought, I'll wear my right arm in a sling; they won't grin at me then. I'll have my right arm in a sling and they'll see I couldn't possibly take the chains off myself. He kicked at the slush on the sidewalk. "Overshoes," he said to himself, and he began looking for a shoe store.

When he came out into the street again, with the overshoes in a box under his arm, Walter Mitty began to wonder what the other thing was his wife had told him to get. She had told him twice, before they set out from their house for Waterbury. In a way he hated these weekly trips to town—he was always getting something wrong. Kleenex, he thought, Squibb's, razor blades? No. Toothpaste, toothbrush, bicarbonate, carborundum, initiative and referendum? He gave it up. But she would remember it. "Where's the what's-its-name?" she would ask. "Don't tell me you forgot the what's-its-name." A newsboy went by shouting something about the Waterbury trial.

. . . "Perhaps this will refresh your memory." The District Attorney suddenly thrust a heavy automatic at the quiet figure on the witness stand. "Have you ever seen this before?" Walter Mitty took the gun and examined it expertly. "This is my Webley-Vickers 50.80," he said calmly. An excited buzz ran around the courtroom. The judge rapped for order. "You are a crack shot with any sort of firearms, I believe?" said the District Attorney, insinuatingly. "Objection!" shouted Mitty's attorney. "We have shown that the defendant could not have fired the shot. We have shown that he wore his right arm in a sling on the night of the fourteenth of July." Walter Mitty raised his hand briefly and the bickering attorneys were stilled. "With any known make of gun," he said evenly, "I could have killed Gregory Fitzhurst at three hundred feet *with my left hand.*" Pandemonium broke loose in the courtroom. A woman's scream rose above the bedlam and suddenly a lovely, dark-haired girl was in Walter Mitty's arms. The District Attorney struck at her savagely. Without rising from his chair, Mitty let the man have it on the point of the chin. "You miserable cur!" . . .

"Puppy biscuit," said Walter Mitty. He stopped walking and the buildings of Waterbury rose up out of the misty courtroom and surrounded him again. A woman who was passing laughed. "He said 'Puppy biscuit,'" she said to her companion. "That man said 'Puppy biscuit' to himself." Walter Mitty hurried on. He went into an A. & P., not the first one he came to but a smaller one farther up the street. "I want some biscuit for small, young dogs," he said to the clerk. "Any special brand, sir?" The greatest pistol shot in the world thought a moment. "It says 'Puppies Bark for It' on the box," said Walter Mitty.

His wife would be through at the hairdresser's in fifteen minutes, Mitty saw in looking at his watch, unless they had trouble drying it; sometimes they had trouble drying it. She didn't like to get to the hotel first; she would want him to be there waiting for her as usual. He found a big leather chair in the lobby, facing a window, and he put the overshoes and the puppy biscuit on the floor beside it. He picked up an old copy of *Liberty* and sank down into the chair. "Can Germany Conquer the World Through the Air?" Walter Mitty looked at the pictures of bombing planes and of ruined streets.

. . . "The cannonading has got the wind up in young Raleigh, sir," said the sergeant. Captain Mitty looked up at him through tousled hair. "Get him to bed," he said wearily. "With the others. I'll fly alone." "But you can't, sir," said the sergeant anxiously. "It takes two men to handle that bomber and the Archies are pounding hell out of the air. Von Kichtman's circus is between here and Saulier." "Somebody's got to get that ammunition dump," said Mitty. "I'm going over. Spot of brandy?" He poured a drink for the sergeant and one for himself. War thundered and whined around the dugout and battered at the door. There was a rending of wood and splinters flew through the room. "A bit of a near thing," said Captain Mitty carelessly. "The box barrage is closing in," said the sergeant. "We only live once, Sergeant," said Mitty, with his faint, fleeting smile. "Or do we?" He poured another brandy and tossed it off. "I never see a man could hold his brandy like you, sir," said the sergeant. "Begging your pardon, sir." Captain Mitty stood up and strapped on his huge Webley-Vickers automatic. "It's forty kilometers through hell, sir," said the sergeant. Mitty finished one last brandy. "After all," he said softly, "what isn't?" The pounding of the cannon increased; there was the rat-tat-tatting of machine guns, and from somewhere came the menacing pocketa-pocketa-pocketa of the new flame-throwers. Walter Mitty walked to the door of the dugout humming "Auprès de Ma Blonde." He turned and waved to the sergeant. "Cheerio!" he said. . . .

Something struck his shoulder. "I've been looking all over this hotel for you," said Mrs. Mitty. "Why do you have to hide in this old chair? How did you expect me to find you?" "Things close in," said Walter Mitty vaguely. "What?" Mrs. Mitty said. "Did you get the what's-its-name? The puppy biscuit? What's in that box?" "Overshoes," said Mitty. "Couldn't you have put them on in the store?" "I was thinking," said Walter Mitty. "Does it ever occur to you that I am sometimes thinking?" She looked at him. "I'm going to take your temperature when I get you home," she said.

They went out through the revolving doors that made a faintly derisive whistling sound when you pushed them. It was two blocks to the parking lot. At the drugstore on the corner she said, "Wait here for me. I forgot something. I won't be a minute." She was more than a minute. Walter Mitty lighted a cigarette. It began to rain, rain with sleet in it. He stood up against the wall of the drugstore, smoking. . . . He put his shoulders back and his heels together. "To hell with the handkerchief," said Walter Mitty scornfully. He took one last drag on his cigarette and snapped it away. Then, with that faint, fleeting smile playing about his lips, he faced the firing squad; erect and motionless, proud and disdainful, Walter Mitty the Undefeated, inscrutable to the last.

F. SCOTT FITZGERALD

[1896–1940]

Babylon Revisited

(First published in The *Saturday Evening Post*, February, 1931; first book publication in 1935.)

"AND WHERE'S MR. Campbell?" Charlie asked.

"Gone to Switzerland. Mr. Campbell's a pretty sick man, Mr. Wales."

"I'm sorry to hear that. And George Hardt?" Charlie inquired.

"Back in America, gone to work."

"And where is the Snow Bird?"

"He was in here last week. Anyway, his friend, Mr. Schaeffer, is in Paris."

Two familiar names from the long list of a year and a half ago. Charlie scribbled an address in his notebook and tore out the page.

"If you see Mr. Schaeffer, give him this," he said. "It's my brother-in-law's address. I haven't settled on a hotel yet."

He was not really disappointed to find Paris was so empty. But the stillness in the Ritz bar was strange and portentous. It was not an American bar any more—he felt polite in it, and not as if he owned it. It had gone back into France. He felt the stillness from the moment he got out of the taxi and saw the doorman, usually in a frenzy of activity at this hour, gossiping with a *chasseur* by the servants' entrance.

Passing through the corridor, he heard only a single, bored voice in the once-clamorous women's room. When he turned into the bar he traveled the twenty feet of green carpet with his eyes fixed straight ahead by old habit; and then, with his foot firmly on the rail, he turned and surveyed the room, encountering only a single pair of eyes that fluttered up from a newspaper in the corner. Charlie asked for the head barman, Paul, who in the latter days of the bull market had come to work in his own custom-built car—disembarking, however, with due nicety at the nearest corner. But Paul was at his country house today and Alix giving him information.

"No, no more," Charlie said, "I'm going slow these days."

Alix congratulated him: "You were going pretty strong a couple of years ago."

"I'll stick to it all right," Charlie assured him. "I've stuck to it for over a year and a half now."

"How do you find conditions in America?"

"I haven't been to America for months. I'm in business in Prague, representing a couple of concerns there. They don't know about me down there."

Alix smiled.

"Remember the night of George Hardt's bachelor dinner here?" said Charlie. "By the way, what's become of Claude Fessenden?"

Alix lowered his voice confidentially: "He's in Paris, but he doesn't come here any more. Paul doesn't allow it. He ran up a bill of thirty thousand francs, charging all his drinks and his lunches, and usually his dinner, for more than a year. And when Paul finally told him he had to pay, he gave him a bad check."

Alix shook his head sadly.

"I don't understand it, such a dandy fellow. Now he's all bloated up—" He made a plump apple of his hands.

Charlie watched a group of strident queens installing themselves in a corner.

"Nothing affects them," he thought. "Stocks rise and fall, people loaf or work, but they go on forever." The place oppressed him. He called for the dice and shook with Alix for the drink.

"Here for long, Mr. Wales?"

"I'm here for four or five days to see my little girl."

"Oh-h! You have a little girl?"

Outside, the fire-red, gas-blue, ghost-green signs shone smokily through the tranquil rain. It was late afternoon and the streets were in movement; the *bistros* gleamed. At the corner of the Boulevard des Capucines he took a taxi. The Place de la Concorde moved by in pink majesty; they crossed the logical Seine, and Charlie felt the sudden provincial quality of the Left Bank.

Charlie directed his taxi to the Avenue de l'Opera, which was out of his way. But he wanted to see the blue hour spread over the magnificent façade, and imagine that the cab horns, playing endlessly the first few bars of *Le Plus que Lent*, were the trumpets of the Second Empire. They were closing the iron grill in front of Brentano's Bookstore, and people were already at dinner behind the trim little bourgeois hedge of Duval's. He had never eaten at a really cheap restaurant in Paris. Five-course dinner, four francs fifty, eighteen cents, wine included. For some odd reason he wished that he had.

As they rolled on to the Left Bank and he felt its sudden provincialism, he thought, "I spoiled this city for myself. I didn't realize it, but the days came along one after another, and then two years were gone, and everything was gone, and I was gone."

He was thirty-five, and good to look at. The Irish mobility of his face was sobered by a deep wrinkle between his eyes. As he rang his brother-in-law's bell in the Rue Palatine, the wrinkle deepened till it pulled down his brows;

he felt a cramping sensation in his belly. From behind the maid who opened the door darted a lovely little girl of nine who shrieked "Daddy"! and flew up, struggling like a fish, into his arms. She pulled his head around by one ear and set her cheek against his.

"My old pie," he said.

"Oh, daddy, daddy, daddy, daddy, dads, dads, dads!"

She drew him into the salon, where the family waited, a boy and girl his daughter's age, his sister-in-law and her husband. He greeted Marion with his voice pitched carefully to avoid either feigned enthusiasm or dislike, but her response was more frankly tepid, though she minimized her expression of unalterable distrust by directing her regard toward his child. The two men clasped hands in a friendly way and Lincoln Peters rested his for a moment on Charlie's shoulder.

The room was warm and comfortably American. The three children moved intimately about, playing through the yellow oblongs that led to other rooms; the cheer of six o'clock spoke in the eager smacks of the fire and the sounds of French activity in the kitchen. But Charlie did not relax; his heart sat up rigidly in his body and he drew confidence from his daughter, who from time to time came close to him, holding in her arms the doll he had brought.

"Really extremely well," he declared in answer to Lincoln's question. "There's a lot of business there that isn't moving at all, but we're doing even better than ever. In fact, damn well. I'm bringing my sister over from America next month to keep house for me. My income last year was bigger than it was when I had money. You see, the Czechs–"

His boasting was for a specific purpose; but after a moment, seeing a faint restiveness in Lincoln's eye, he changed the subject: "Those are fine children of yours, well brought up, good manners."

"We think Honoria's a great little girl too."

Marion Peters came back from the kitchen. She was a tall woman with worried eyes, who had once possessed a fresh American loveliness. Charlie had never been sensitive to it and was always surprised when people spoke of how pretty she had been. From the first there had been an instinctive antipathy between them.

"Well, how do you find Honoria?" she asked.

"Wonderful. I was astonished how much she's grown in ten months. All the children are looking well."

"We haven't had a doctor for a year. How do you like being back in Paris?"

"It seems very funny to see so few Americans around."

"I'm delighted," Marion said vehemently. "Now at least you can go into a store without their assuming you're a millionaire. We've suffered like everybody, but on the whole it's a good deal pleasanter."

"But it was nice while it lasted," Charlie said. "We were a sort of royalty, almost infallible, with a sort of magic around us. In the bar this afternoon"—he stumbled, seeing his mistake—"there wasn't a man I knew."

She looked at him keenly. "I should think you'd have had enough of bars."

"I only stayed a minute. I take one drink every afternoon, and no more."

"Don't you want a cocktail before dinner?" Lincoln asked.

"I take only one drink every afternoon, and I've had that."

"I hope you keep to it," said Marion.

Her dislike was evident in the coldness with which she spoke, but Charlie only smiled; he had larger plans. Her very aggressiveness gave him an advantage, and he knew enough to wait. He wanted them to initiate the discussion of what they knew had brought him to Paris.

At dinner he couldn't decide whether Honoria was most like him or her mother. Fortunate if she didn't combine the traits of both that had brought them to disaster. A great wave of protectiveness went over him. He thought he knew what to do for her. He believed in character; he wanted to jump back a whole generation and trust in character again as the eternally valuable element. Everything wore out.

He left soon after dinner, but not to go home. He was curious to see Paris by night with clearer and more judicious eyes than those of other days. He bought a *strapontin* for the Casino and watched Josephine Baker go through her chocolate arabesques.

After an hour he left and strolled toward Montmartre, up the Rue Pigalle into the Place Blanche. The rain had stopped and there were a few people in evening clothes disembarking from taxis in front of cabarets, and *cocottes* prowling singly or in pairs, and many Negroes. He passed a lighted door from which issued music, and stopped with the sense of familiarity; it was Bricktop's, where he had parted with so many hours and so much money. A few doors farther on he found another ancient rendezvous and incautiously put his head inside. Immediately an eager orchestra burst into sound, a pair of professional dancers leaped to their feet and a maître d'hôtel swooped toward him, crying, "Crowd just arriving, sir!" But he withdrew quickly.

"You have to be damn drunk," he thought.

Zelli's was closed, the bleak and sinister cheap hotels surrounding it were dark; up in the Rue Blanche there was more light and a local, colloquial French crowd. The Poet's Cave had disappeared, but the two great mouths of the Café of Heaven and the Café of Hell still yawned—even devoured, as he watched, the meagre contents of a tourist bus—a German, a Japanese, and an American couple who glanced at him with frightened eyes.

So much for the effort and ingenuity of Montmartre. All the catering to vice and waste was on an utterly childish scale, and he suddenly realized the meaning of the word "dissipate"—to dissipate into thin air; to make nothing out of something. In the little hours of the night every move from place to place was an enormous human jump, an increase of paying for the privilege of slower and slower motion.

He remembered thousand-franc notes given to an orchestra for playing a single number, hundred-franc notes tossed to a doorman for calling a cab.

But it hadn't been given for nothing.

It had been given, even the most wildly squandered sum, as an offering to destiny that he might not remember the things most worth remembering, the things that now he would always remember—his child taken from his control, his wife escaped to a grave in Vermont.

In the glare of a *brasserie* a woman spoke to him. He bought her some eggs and coffee, and then, eluding her encouraging stare, gave her a twenty-franc note and took a taxi to his hotel.

II

He woke upon a fine fall day—football weather. The depression of yesterday was gone and he liked the people on the streets. At noon he sat opposite Honoria at Le Grand Vatel, the only restaurant he could think of not reminiscent of champagne dinners and long luncheons that began at two and ended in a blurred and vague twilight.

"Now, how about vegetables? Oughtn't you to have some vegetables?"

"Well, yes."

"Here's *épinards* and *chou-fleur* and carrots and *haricots*."

"I'd like *chou-fleur*."

"Wouldn't you like to have two vegetables?"

"I usually only have one at lunch."

The waiter was pretending to be inordinately fond of children. "*Qu'elle est mignonne la petite? Elle parle exactement comme une française*."

"How about dessert? Shall we wait and see?"

The waiter disappeared. Honoria looked at her father expectantly.

"What are we going to do?"

"First, we're going to that toy store in the Rue Saint-Honoré and buy you anything you like. And then we're going to the vaudeville at the Empire."

She hesitated. "I like it about the vaudeville, but not the toy store."

"Why not ?"

"Well, you brought me this doll." She had it with her. "And I've got lots of things. And we're not rich any more, are we?"

"We never were. But today you are to have anything you want."

"All right," she agreed resignedly.

When there had been her mother and a French nurse he had been inclined to be strict; now he extended himself, reached out for a new tolerance; he must be both parents to her and not shut any of her out of communication.

"I want to get to know you," he said gravely. "First let me introduce myself. My name is Charles J. Wales, of Prague."

"Oh, daddy!" her voice cracked with laughter.

"And who are you, please?" he persisted, and she accepted a rôle immediately: "Honoria Wales, Rue Palatine, Paris."

"Married or single?"

"No, not married. Single."

He indicated the doll. "But I see you have a child, madame."

Unwilling to disinherit it, she took it to her heart and thought quickly: "Yes, I've been married, but I'm not married now. My husband is dead."

He went on quickly, "And the child's name?"

"Simone. That's after my best friend at school."

"I'm very pleased that you're doing so well at school."

"I'm third this month," she boasted. "Elsie"—that was her cousin—"is only about eighteenth, and Richard is about at the bottom."

"You like Richard and Elsie, don't you?"

"Oh, yes. I like Richard quite well and I like her all right."

Cautiously and casually he asked, "And Aunt Marion and Uncle Lincoln—which do you like best?"

"Oh, Uncle Lincoln, I guess."

He was increasingly aware of her presence. As they came in, a murmur of " . . . adorable" followed them, and now the people at the next table bent all their silences upon her, staring as if she were something no more conscious than a flower.

"Why don't I live with you?" she asked suddenly. "Because mamma's dead?"

"You must stay here and learn more French. It would have been hard for daddy to take care of you so well."

"I don't really need much taking care of any more. I do everything for myself."

Going out of the restaurant, a man and a woman unexpectedly hailed him!

"Well, the old Wales!"

"Hello there, Lorraine . . . Dunc."

Sudden ghosts out of the past: Duncan Schaeffer, a friend from college. Lorraine Quarrles, a lovely, pale blonde of thirty; one of a crowd who had helped them make months into days in the lavish times of three years ago.

"My husband couldn't come this year," she said, in answer to his question. "We're poor as hell. So he gave me two hundred a month and told me I could do my worst on that. . . . This your little girl?"

"What about coming back and sitting down?" Duncan asked.

"Can't do it." He was glad for an excuse. As always he felt Lorraine's passionate, provocative attraction, but his own rhythm was different now.

"Well, how about dinner?" she asked.

"I'm not free. Give me your address and let me call you."

"Charlie, I believe you're sober," she said judicially. "I honestly believe he's sober, Dunc. Pinch him and see if he's sober."

Charlie indicated Honoria with his head. They both laughed.

"What's your address?" said Duncan skeptically.

He hesitated, unwilling to give the name of his hotel.

"I'm not settled yet. I'd better call you. We're going to see the vaudeville at the Empire."

"There! That's what I want to do," Lorraine said. "I want to see some clowns and acrobats and jugglers. That's just what we'll do, Dunc."

"We've got to do an errand first," said Charlie. "Perhaps we'll see you there."

"All right, you snob. . . . Good-bye, beautiful little girl."

"Good-bye."

Honoria bobbed politely.

Somehow, an unwelcome encounter. They liked him because he was functioning, because he was serious; they wanted to see him, because he was stronger than they were now, because they wanted to draw a certain sustenance from his strength.

At the Empire, Honoria proudly refused to sit upon her father's folded coat. She was already an individual with a code of her own, and Charlie was more and more absorbed by the desire of putting a little of himself into her before she crystallized utterly. It was hopeless to try to know her in so short a time.

Between the acts they came upon Duncan and Lorraine in the lobby where the band was playing.

"Have a drink?"

"All right, but not up at the bar. We'll take a table."

"The perfect father."

Listening abstractedly to Lorraine, Charlie watched Honoria's eyes leave their table, and he followed them wistfully about the room, wondering what they saw. He met her glance and she smiled.

"I liked that lemonade," she said.

What had she said? What had he expected? Going home in a taxi afterward, he pulled her over until her head rested against his chest.

"Darling, do you ever think about your mother?"

"Yes, sometimes," she answered vaguely.

"I don't want you to forget her. Have you got a picture of her?"

"Yes, I think so. Anyhow, Aunt Marion has. Why don't you want me to forget her?"

"She loved you very much."

"I loved her too."

They were silent for a moment.

"Daddy, I want to come and live with you," she said suddenly.

His heart leaped; he had wanted it to come like this.

"Aren't you perfectly happy?"

"Yes, but I love you better than anybody. And you love me better than anybody, don't you, now that mummy's dead?"

"Of course I do. But you won't always like me best, honey. You'll grow up and meet somebody your own age and go marry him and forget you ever had a daddy."

"Yes, that's true," she agreed tranquilly.

He didn't go in. He was coming back at nine o'clock and he wanted to keep himself fresh and new for the thing he must say then.

"When you're safe inside, just show yourself in that window."

"All right. Good-bye, dads, dads, dads, dads."

He waited in the dark street until she appeared, all warm and glowing, in the window above and kissed her fingers out into the night.

III

They were waiting. Marion sat behind the coffee service in a dignified black dinner dress that just faintly suggested mourning. Lincoln was walking up and down with the animation of one who had already been talking. They were as anxious as he was to get into the question. He opened it almost immediately: "I suppose you know what I want to see you about—why I really came to Paris."

Marion played with the black stars on her necklace and frowned.

"I'm awfully anxious to have a home," he continued. "And I'm awfully anxious to have Honoria in it. I appreciate your taking in Honoria for her mother's sake, but things have changed now"—he hesitated and then continued more forcibly—"changed radically with me, and I want to ask you to reconsider the matter. It would be silly for me to deny that about three years ago I was acting badly—"

Marion looked up at him with hard eyes.

"—but all that's over. As I told you, I haven't had more than a drink a day for over a year, and I take that drink deliberately, so that the idea of alcohol won't get too big in my imagination. You see the idea?"

"No," said Marion succinctly.

"It's a sort of stunt I set myself. It keeps the matter in proportion."

"I get you," said Lincoln. "You don't want to admit it's got any attraction for you."

"Something like that. Sometimes I forget and don't take it. But I try to take it. Anyhow, I couldn't afford to drink in my position. The people I represent are more than satisfied with what I've done, and I'm bringing my sister over from Burlington to keep house for me, and I want awfully to have Honoria too. You know that even when her mother and I weren't getting along well we never let anything that happened touch Honoria. I know she's fond of me and I know I'm able to take care of her and—well, there you are. How do you feel about it?"

He knew that now he would have to take a beating. It would last an hour or two hours, and it would be difficult, but if he modulated his inevitable resentment to the chastened attitude of the reformed sinner, he might win his point in the end.

Keep your temper, he told himself. You don't want to be justified. You want Honoria.

Lincoln spoke first: "We've been talking it over ever since we got your letter last month. We're happy to have Honoria here. She's a dear little thing, and we're glad to be able to help her, but of course that isn't the question—"

Marion interrupted suddenly. "How long are you going to stay sober, Charlie?" she asked.

"Permanently, I hope."

"How can anybody count on that?"

"You know I never did drink heavily until I gave up business and came over here with nothing to do. Then Helen and I began to run around with—"

"Please leave Helen out of it. I can't bear to hear you talk about her like that."

He stared at her grimly; he had never been certain how fond of each other the sisters were in life.

"My drinking only lasted about a year and a half—from the time we came over until I—collapsed."

"It was time enough."

"It was time enough," he agreed.

"My duty is entirely to Helen," she said. "I try to think what she would have wanted me to do. Frankly, from the night you did that terrible thing you haven't really existed for me. I can't help that. She was my sister."

"Yes."

"When she was dying she asked me to look out for Honoria. If you hadn't been in a sanitarium then, it might have helped matters."

He had no answer.

"I'll never in my life be able to forget the morning when Helen knocked at my door, soaked to the skin and shivering, and said you'd locked her out."

Charlie gripped the sides of the chair. This was more difficult than he expected; he wanted to launch out into a long expostulation and explanation, but he only said, "The night I locked her out—" and she interrupted, "I don't feel up to going over that again."

After a moment's silence Lincoln said, "We're getting off the subject.

You want Marion to set aside her legal guardianship and give you Honoria. I think the main point for her is whether she has confidence in you or not."

"I don't blame Marion," Charlie said slowly, "but I think she can have entire confidence in me. I had a good record up to three years ago. Of course, it's within human possibilities I might go wrong any time. But if we wait much longer I'll lose Honoria's childhood and my chance for a home." He shook his head, "I'll simply lose her, don't you see?"

"Yes, I see," said Lincoln.

"Why didn't you think of all this before?" Marion asked.

"I suppose I did, from time to time, but Helen and I were getting along badly. When I consented to the guardianship, I was flat on my back in a sanitarium and the market had cleaned me out. I knew I'd acted badly, and I thought if it would bring any peace to Helen, I'd agree to anything. But now it's different. I'm functioning, I'm behaving damn well, so far as—"

"Please don't swear at me," Marion said.

He looked at her, startled. With each remark the force of her dislike became more and more apparent. She had built up all her fear of life into one wall and faced it toward him. This trivial reproof was possibly the result of some trouble with the cook several hours before. Charlie became increasingly alarmed at leaving Honoria in this atmosphere of hostility against himself; sooner or later it would come out, in a word here, a shake of the head there, and some of that distrust would be irrevocably implanted in Honoria. But he pulled his temper down out of his face and shut it up inside him; he had won a point, for Lincoln realized the absurdity of Marion's remark and asked her lightly since when she had objected to the word "damn."

"Another thing," Charlie said, "I'm able to give her certain advantages now. I'm going to take a French governess to Prague with me. I've got a lease on a new apartment—"

He stopped, realizing that he was blundering. They couldn't be expected to accept with equanimity the fact that his income was again twice as large as their own.

"I suppose you can give her more luxuries than we can," said Marion. "When you were throwing away money we were living along watching every ten francs. . . . I suppose you'll start doing it again."

"Oh, no," he said. "I've learned. I worked hard for ten years, you know—until I got lucky in the market, like so many people. Terribly lucky. It didn't seem any use working any more, so I quit. It won't happen again."

There was a long silence. All of them felt their nerves straining, and for the first time in a year Charlie wanted a drink. He was sure now that Lincoln Peters wanted him to have his child.

Marion shuddered suddenly; part of her saw that Charlie's feet were planted on the earth now, and her own maternal feeling recognized the naturalness of his desire; but she had lived for a long time with a prejudice—a prejudice founded on a curious disbelief in her sister's happiness, and which, in the shock of one terrible night, had turned to hatred for him. It had all happened at a point in her life where the discouragement of ill health and adverse circumstances made it necessary for her to believe in tangible villainy and a tangible villain.

"I can't help what I think!" she cried out suddenly. "How much you were responsible for Helen's death, I don't know. It's something you'll have to square with your own conscience."

An electric current of agony surged through him; for a moment he was almost on his feet, an unuttered sound echoing in his throat. He hung on to himself for a moment, another moment.

"Hold on there," said Lincoln uncomfortably. "I never thought you were responsible for that."

"Helen died of heart trouble," Charlie said dully.

"Yes, heart trouble." Marion spoke as if the phrase had another meaning for her.

Then, in the flatness that followed her outburst, she saw him plainly and she knew he had somehow arrived at control over the situation. Glancing at her husband, she found no help from him, and as abruptly as if it were a matter of no importance, she threw up the sponge.

"Do what you like!" she cried, springing up from her chair. "She's your child. I'm not the person to stand in your way. I think if it were my child I'd rather see her—" She managed to check herself. "You two decide it. I can't stand this. I'm sick. I'm going to bed."

She hurried from the room; after a moment Lincoln said, "This has been a hard day for her. You know how strongly she feels—" His voice was almost apologetic: "When a woman gets an idea in her head."

"Of course."

"It's going to be all right. I think she sees now that you—can provide for the child, and so we can't very well stand in your way or Honoria's way."

"Thank you, Lincoln."

"I'd better go along and see how she is."

"I'm going."

He was still trembling when he reached the street, but a walk down the Rue Bonaparte to the quais set him up, and as he crossed the Seine, fresh and new by the quai lamps, he felt exultant. But back in his room he couldn't sleep. The image of Helen haunted him. Helen whom he had loved so until they had senselessly begun to abuse each other's love, tear it into shreds. On that terrible February night that Marion remembered so vividly, a slow quarrel had gone on for hours. There was a scene at the Florida, and then he attempted to take her home, and then she kissed young Webb at a table; after that there was what she had hysterically said. When he arrived home alone he turned the key in the lock in wild anger. How could he know she would arrive an hour later alone, that there would be a snowstorm in which she wandered about in slippers, too confused to find a taxi? Then the aftermath, her escaping pneumonia by a miracle, and all the attendant horror. They were "reconciled," but that was the beginning of the end, and Marion, who had seen with her own eyes and who imagined it to be one of many scenes from her sister's martyrdom, never forgot.

Going over it again brought Helen nearer, and in the white, soft light that steals upon half sleep near morning he found himself talking to her again. She said that he was perfectly right about Honoria and that she wanted Honoria to be with him. She said she was glad he was being good and doing better. She said a lot of other things—very friendly things—but she was in a swing in a white dress, and swinging faster and faster all the time, so that at the end he could not hear clearly all that she said.

IV

He woke up feeling happy. The door of the world was open again. He made plans, vistas, futures for Honoria and himself, but suddenly he grew sad, remembering all the plans he and Helen had made. She had not planned to die. The present was the thing—work to do and someone to love. But not to love too much, for he knew the injury that a father can do to a daughter or a mother to a son by attaching them too closely: afterward, out in the world, the child would seek in the marriage partner the same blind tenderness and, failing probably to find it, turn against love and life.

It was another bright, crisp day. He called Lincoln Peters at the bank where he worked and asked if he could count on taking Honoria when he left for Prague. Lincoln agreed that there was no reason for delay. One thing—the legal guardianship. Marion wanted to retain that a while longer. She was upset by the whole matter, and it would oil things if she felt that the situation was still in her control for another year. Charlie agreed, wanting only the tangible, visible child.

Then the question of a governess. Charlie sat in a gloomy agency and talked to a cross Bernaise and to a buxom Breton peasant, neither of whom he could have endured. There were others whom he would see tomorrow.

He lunched with Lincoln Peters at Griffons, trying to keep down his exultation.

"There's nothing quite like your own child," Lincoln said. "But you understand how Marion feels too."

"She's forgotten how hard I worked for seven years there," Charlie said. "She just remembers one night."

"There's another thing." Lincoln hesitated. "While you and Helen were tearing around Europe throwing money away, we were just getting along.

I didn't touch any of the prosperity because I never got ahead enough to carry anything but my insurance. I think Marion felt there was some kind of injustice in it—you not even working toward the end, and getting richer and richer."

"It went just as quick as it came," said Charlie.

"Yes, a lot of it stayed in the hands of *chasseurs* and saxophone players and maîtres d'hôtel—well, the big party's over now. I just said that to explain Marion's feeling about those crazy years. If you drop in about six o'clock tonight before Marion's too tired, we'll settle the details on the spot."

Back at his hotel, Charlie found a *pneumatique* that had been redirected from the Ritz bar where Charlie had left his address for the purpose of finding a certain man.

DEAR CHARLIE: You were so strange when we saw you the other day that I wondered if I did something to offend you. If so, I'm not conscious of it. In fact, I have thought about you too much for the last year, and it's always been in the back of my mind that I might see you if I came over here. We *did* have such good times that crazy spring, like the night you and I stole the butcher's tricycle, and the time we tried to call on the president and you had the old derby rim and the wire cane. Everybody seems so old lately, but I don't feel old a bit. Couldn't we get together some time today for old time's sake? I've got a vile hangover for the moment, but will be feeling better this afternoon and will look for you about five in the sweet-shop at the Ritz.

Always devotedly,

LORRAINE

His first feeling was one of awe that he had actually, in his mature years, stolen a tricycle and pedaled Lorraine all over the Étoile between the small hours and dawn. In retrospect it was a nightmare. Locking out Helen didn't fit in with any other act of his life, but the tricycle incident did—it was one of many. How many weeks or months of dissipation to arrive at that condition of utter irresponsibility?

He tried to picture how Lorraine had appeared to him then—very attractive; Helen was unhappy about it, though she said nothing. Yesterday, in the restaurant, Lorraine had seemed trite, blurred, worn away. He emphatically did not want to see her, and he was glad Alix had not given away his hotel address. It was a relief to think, instead, of Honoria, to think of Sundays spent with her and of saying good morning to her and of knowing she was there in his house at night, drawing her breath in the darkness.

At five he took a taxi and bought presents for all the Peters—a piquant cloth doll, a box of Roman soldiers, flowers for Marion, big linen handkerchiefs for Lincoln.

He saw, when he arrived in the apartment, that Marion had accepted the inevitable. She greeted him now as though he were a recalcitrant member of the family, rather than a menacing outsider. Honoria had been told she was going; Charlie was glad to see that her tact made her conceal her excessive happiness. Only on his lap did she whisper her delight and the question "When?" before she slipped away with the other children.

He and Marion were alone for a minute in the room, and on an impulse he spoke out boldly: "Family quarrels are bitter things. They don't go according to any rules. They're not like aches or wounds; they're more like splits in the skin that won't heal because there's not enough material. I wish you and I could be on better terms."

"Some things are hard to forget," she answered. "It's a question of confidence." There was no answer to this and presently she asked, "When do you propose to take her?"

"As soon as I can get a governess. I hoped the day after tomorrow."

"That's impossible. I've got to get her things in shape. Not before Saturday."

He yielded. Coming back into the room, Lincoln offered him a drink.

"I'll take my daily whisky," he said.

It was warm here, it was a home, people together by a fire. The children felt very safe and important; the mother and father were serious, watchful. They had things to do for the children more important than his visit here. A spoonful of medicine was, after all, more important than the strained relations between Marion and himself. They were not dull people, but they were very much in the grip of life and circumstances. He wondered if he couldn't do something to get Lincoln out of his rut at the bank.

A long peal at the doorbell; the *bonne de toute faire* passed through and went down the corridor. The door opened upon another long ring, and then voices, and the three in the salon looked up expectantly; Richard moved to bring the corridor within his range of vision, and Marion rose. Then the maid came back along the corridor, closely followed by the voices, which developed under the light into Duncan Schaeffer and Lorraine Quarrles.

They were gay, they were hilarious, they were roaring with laughter. For a moment Charlie was astounded; unable to understand how they ferreted out the Peters' address.

"Ah-h-h!" Duncan wagged his finger roguishly at Charlie. "Ah-h-h!"

They both slid down another cascade of laughter. Anxious and at a loss, Charlie shook hands with them quickly and presented them to Lincoln and Marion. Marion nodded, scarcely speaking. She had drawn back a step toward the fire; her little girl stood beside her, and Marion put an arm about her shoulder.

With growing annoyance at the intrusion, Charlie waited for them to explain themselves. After some concentration Duncan said, "We came to invite you out to dinner. Lorraine and I insist that all this shishi, cagy business 'bout your address got to stop."

Charlie came closer to them, as if to force them backward down the corridor.

"Sorry, but I can't. Tell me where you'll be and I'll phone you in half an hour."

This made no impression. Lorraine sat down suddenly on the side of a chair, and focusing her eyes on Richard, cried, "Oh, what a nice little boy! Come here, little boy." Richard glanced at his mother, but did not move. With a perceptible shrug of her shoulders, Lorraine turned back to Charlie, "Come and dine. Sure your cousins won' mine. See you so sel'om. Or solemn."

"I can't," said Charlie sharply. "You two have dinner and I'll phone you."

Her voice became suddenly unpleasant. "All right, we'll go. But I remember once when you hammered on my door at four A.M. I was enough of a good sport to give you a drink. Come on, Dunc."

Still in slow motion, with blurred, angry faces, with uncertain feet, they retired along the corridor.

"Good night," Charlie said.

"Good night!" responded Lorraine emphatically.

When he went back into the salon Marion had not moved, only now her son was standing in the circle of her other arm. Lincoln was still swinging Honoria back and forth like a pendulum from side to side.

"What an outrage!" Charlie broke out. "What an absolute outrage!"

Neither of them answered. Charlie dropped into an armchair, picked up his drink, set it down again and said, "People I haven't seen for two years having the colossal nerve–"

He broke off. Marion had made the sound "Oh!" in one swift, furious breath, turned her body from him with a jerk and left the room.

Lincoln set down Honoria carefully.

"You children go in and start your soup," he said, and when they obeyed, he said to Charlie, "Marion's not well and she can't stand shocks. That kind of people make her really physically sick."

"I didn't tell them to come here. They wormed your name out of somebody. They deliberately–"

"Well, it's too bad. It doesn't help matters. Excuse me a minute."

Left alone, Charlie sat tense in his chair. In the next room he could hear the children eating, talking in monosyllables, already oblivious to the scene between their elders. He heard a murmur of conversation from a farther room and then the ticking bell of a telephone receiver picked up, and in a panic he moved to the other side of the room and out of earshot.

In a minute Lincoln came back. "Look here, Charlie. I think we'd better call off dinner for tonight. Marion's in bad shape."

"Is she angry with me?"

"Sort of," he said, almost roughly. "She's not strong and–"

"You mean she's changed her mind about Honoria?"

"She's pretty bitter right now. I don't know. You phone me at the bank tomorrow."

"I wish you'd explain to her I never dreamed these people would come here. I'm just as sore as you are."

"I couldn't explain anything to her now."

Charlie got up. He took his coat and hat and started down the corridor. Then he opened the door of the dining room and said in a strange voice, "Good night, children."

Honoria rose and ran around the table to hug him.

"Good night, sweetheart," he said vaguely, and then trying to make his voice more tender, trying to conciliate something, "Good night, dear children."

V

Charlie went directly to the Ritz bar with the furious idea of finding Lorraine and Duncan, but they were not there, and he realized that in any case there was nothing he could do. He had not touched his drink at the Peters', and now he ordered a whisky and soda. Paul came over to say hello.

"It's a great change," he said sadly. "We do about half the business we did. So many fellows I hear about back in the States lost everything, maybe not in the first crash, but then in the second. Your friend George Hardt lost every cent, I hear. Are you back in the States?"

"No, I'm in business in Prague."

"I heard that you lost a lot in the crash."

"I did," and he added grimly, "but I lost everything I wanted in the boom."

"Selling short."

"Something like that."

Again the memory of those days swept over him like a nightmare—the people they had met traveling; then people who couldn't add a row of figures or speak a coherent sentence. The little man Helen had consented to dance with at the ship's party, who had insulted her ten feet from the table; the women and girls carried screaming with drink or drugs out of public places–

–The men who locked their wives out in the snow, because the snow of twenty-nine wasn't real snow. If you didn't want it to be snow, you just paid some money.

He went to the phone and called the Peters' apartment; Lincoln answered.

"I called up because this thing is on my mind. Has Marion said anything definite?"

"Marion's sick," Lincoln answered shortly. "I know this thing isn't altogether your fault, but I can't have her go to pieces about it. I'm afraid we'll have to let it slide for six months; I can't take the chance of working her up to this state again."

"I see."

"I'm sorry, Charlie."

He went back to his table. His whisky glass was empty, but he shook his head when Alix looked at it questioningly. There wasn't much he could do now except send Honoria some things; he would send her a lot of things tomorrow. He thought rather angrily that this was just money—he had given so many people money. . . .

"No, no more," he said to another waiter. "What do I owe you?"

He would come back some day; they couldn't make him pay forever. But he wanted his child, and nothing was much good now, beside that fact. He wasn't young any more, with a lot of nice thoughts and dreams to have by himself. He was absolutely sure Helen wouldn't have wanted him to be so alone.

WILLIAM FAULKNER

[1897–1962]

A Rose for Emily

(First published in *Forum*, 1930;
first book publication in 1931.)

When Miss Emily Grierson died, our whole town went to her funeral: the men through a sort of respectful affection for a fallen monument, the women mostly out of curiosity to see the inside of her house, which no one save an old manservant—a combined gardener and cook—had seen in at least ten years.

It was a big, squarish frame house that had once been white, decorated with cupolas and spires and scrolled balconies in the heavily lightsome style of the Seventies, set on what had once been our most select street. But garages and cotton gins had encroached and obliterated even the august names of that neighborhood; only Miss Emily's house was left, lifting its stubborn and coquettish decay above the cotton wagons and the gasoline pumps—an eyesore among eyesores. And now Miss Emily had gone to join the representatives of those august names where they lay in the cedar-bemused cemetery among the ranked and anonymous graves of Union and Confederate soldiers who fell at the battle of Jefferson.

Alive, Miss Emily had been a tradition, a duty, and a care; a sort of hereditary obligation upon the town, dating from that day in 1894 when Colonel Sartoris, the mayor—he who fathered the edict that no Negro woman should appear on the streets without an apron—remitted her taxes, the dispensation dating from the death of her father on into perpetuity. Not that Miss Emily would have accepted charity. Colonel Sartoris invented an involved tale to the effect that Miss Emily's father had loaned money to the town, which the town, as a matter of business, preferred this way of repaying. Only a man of Colonel Sartoris' generation and thought could have invented it, and only a woman could have believed it.

When the next generation, with its more modern ideas, became mayors and aldermen, this arrangement created some little dissatisfaction. On the first of the year they mailed her a tax notice. February came, and there was no reply. They wrote her a formal letter, asking her to call at the sheriff's office at her convenience. A week later the mayor wrote her himself, offering to call or to send his car for her, and received in reply a note on paper of an archaic shape, in a thin, flowing calligraphy in faded ink, to the effect that she no longer went out at all. The tax notice was also enclosed, without comment.

They called a special meeting of the Board of Aldermen. A deputation waited upon her, knocked at the door through which no visitor had passed since she ceased giving china-painting lessons eight or ten years earlier. They were admitted by the old Negro into a dim hall from which a stairway mounted into still more shadow. It smelled of dust and disuse—a close, dank smell. The Negro led them into the parlor. It was furnished in heavy, leather-covered furniture. When the Negro opened the blinds of one window, they could see that the leather was cracked; and when they sat down, a faint dust rose sluggishly about their thighs, spinning with slow motes in the single sun-ray. On a tarnished gilt easel before the fireplace stood a crayon portrait of Miss Emily's father.

They rose when she entered—a small, fat woman in black, with a thin gold chain descending to her waist and vanishing into her belt, leaning on an ebony cane with a tarnished gold head. Her skeleton was small and spare; perhaps that was why what would have been merely plumpness in another was obesity in her. She looked bloated, like a body long submerged in motionless water, and of that pallid hue. Her eyes, lost in the fatty ridges of her face, looked like two small pieces of coal pressed into a lump of dough as they moved from one face to another while the visitors stated their errand.

She did not ask them to sit. She just stood in the door and listened quietly until the spokesman came to a stumbling halt. Then they could hear the invisible watch ticking at the end of the gold chain.

Her voice was dry and cold. "I have no taxes in Jefferson. Colonel Sartoris explained it to me. Perhaps one of you can gain access to the city records and satisfy yourselves."

"But we have. We are the city authorities, Miss Emily. Didn't you get a notice from the sheriff, signed by him?"

"I received a paper, yes," Miss Emily said. "Perhaps he considers himself the sheriff . . . I have no taxes in Jefferson."

"But there is nothing on the books to show that, you see. We must go by the—"

"See Colonel Sartoris. I have no taxes in Jefferson."

"But, Miss Emily—"

"See Colonel Sartoris." (Colonel Sartoris had been dead almost ten years.) "I have no taxes in Jefferson. Tobe!" The Negro appeared. "Show these gentlemen out."

II

So she vanquished them, horse and foot, just as she had vanquished their fathers thirty years before about the smell. That was two years after her father's death and a short time after her sweetheart—the one we believed would marry her—had deserted her. After her father's death she went out very little; after her sweetheart went away, people hardly saw her at all. A few of the ladies had the temerity to call, but were not received, and the only sign of life about the place was the Negro man—a young man then—going in and out with a market basket.

"Just as if a man—any man—could keep a kitchen properly," the ladies said; so they were not surprised when the smell developed. It was another link between the gross, teeming world and the high and mighty Griersons.

A neighbor, a woman, complained to the mayor, Judge Stevens eighty years old.

"But what will you have me do about it, madam?" he said.

"Why, send her word to stop it," the woman said. "Isn't there a law?"

"I'm sure that won't be necessary," Judge Stevens said. "It's probably just a snake or a rat that nigger of hers killed in the yard. I'll speak to him about it."

The next day he received two more complaints, one from a man who came in diffident deprecation. "We really must do something about it, Judge. I'd be the last one in the world to bother Miss Emily, but we've got to do something." That night the Board of Aldermen met—three graybeards and one younger man, a member of the rising generation.

"It's simple enough," he said. "Send her word to have her place cleaned up. Give her a certain time to do it in, and if she don't . . ."

"Dammit, sir," Judge Stevens said, "will you accuse a lady to her face of smelling bad?"

So the next night, after midnight, four men crossed Miss Emily's lawn and slunk about the house like burglars, sniffing along the base of the brickwork and at the cellar openings while one of them performed a regular sowing motion with his hand out of a sack slung from his shoulder. They broke open the cellar door and sprinkled lime there, and in all the outbuildings. As they recrossed the lawn, a window that had been dark was lighted and Miss Emily sat in it, the light behind her, and her upright torso motionless as that of an idol. They crept quietly across the lawn and into the shadow of the locusts that lined the street. After a week or two the smell went away.

That was when people had begun to feel really sorry for her. People in our town, remembering how Old Lady Wyatt, her great-aunt, had gone completely crazy at last, believed that the Griersons held themselves a little too high for what they really were. None of the young men was quite good enough to Miss Emily and such. We had long thought of them as a tableau:

Miss Emily a slender figure in white in the background, her father a spraddled silhouette in the foreground, his back to her and clutching a horsewhip, the two of them framed by the back-flung front door. So when she got to be thirty and was still single, we were not pleased exactly, but vindicated; even with insanity in the family she wouldn't have turned down all of her chances if they had really materialized.

When her father died, it got about that the house was all that was left to her; and in a way, people were glad. At last they could pity Miss Emily. Being left alone, and a pauper, she had become humanized. Now she too would know the old thrill and the old despair of a penny more or less.

The day after his death all the ladies prepared to call at the house and offer condolence and aid, as is our custom. Miss Emily met them at the door, dressed as usual and with no trace of grief on her face. She told them that her father was not dead. She did that for three days, with the ministers calling on her, and the doctors, trying to persuade her to let them dispose of the body. Just as they were about to resort to law and force, she broke down, and they buried her father quickly.

We did not say she was crazy then. We believed she had to do that. We remembered all the young men her father had driven away, and we knew that with nothing left, she would have to cling to that which had robbed her, as people will.

III

She was sick for a long time. When we saw her again, her hair was cut short, making her look like a girl, with a vague resemblance to those angels in colored church windows–sort of tragic and serene.

The town had just let the contracts for paving the sidewalks, and in the summer after her father's death they began the work. The construction company came with niggers and mules and machinery, and a foreman named Homer Barron, a Yankee–a big, dark, ready man, with a big voice and eyes lighter than his face. The little boys would follow in groups to hear him cuss the niggers, and the niggers singing in time to the rise and fall of picks. Pretty soon he knew everybody in town. Whenever you heard a lot of laughing anywhere about the square, Homer Barron would be in the center of the group. Presently we began to see him and Miss Emily on Sunday afternoons driving in the yellow-wheeled buggy and the matched team of bays from the livery stable.

At first we were glad that Miss Emily would have an interest, because the ladies all said, "Of course a Grierson would not think seriously of a Northerner, a day laborer." But there were still others, older people, who said that even grief could not cause a real lady to forget *noblesse oblige*–without calling it *noblesse oblige*. They just said, "Poor Emily. Her kinsfolk should come to her." She had some kin in Alabama; but years ago her father had fallen out with them over the estate of Old Lady Wyatt, the crazy woman, and there was no communication between the two families. They had not even been represented at the funeral.

And as soon as the old people said, "Poor Emily," the whispering began. "Do you suppose it's really so?" they said to one another "Of course it is. What else could . . ." This behind their hands; rustling of craned silk and satin behind jalousies closed upon the sun of Sunday afternoon as the thin, swift clop-clop-clop of the matched team passed: "Poor Emily."

She carried her head high enough—even when we believed that she was fallen. It was as if she demanded more than ever the recognition of her dignity as the last Grierson; as if it had wanted that touch of earthiness to reaffirm her imperviousness. Like when she bought the rat poison, the arsenic. That was over a year after they had begun to say "Poor Emily," and while the two female cousins were visiting her.

"I want some poison," she said to the druggist. She was over thirty then, still a slight woman, though thinner than usual, with cold, haughty black eyes in a face the flesh of which was strained across the temples and about the eye-sockets as you imagine a lighthouse-keeper's face ought to look. "I want some poison," she said

"Yes, Miss Emily. What kind? For rats and such? I'd recom—"

"I want the best you have. I don't care what kind."

The druggist named several. "They'll kill anything up to an elephant. But what you want is—"

"Arsenic," Miss Emily said. "Is that a good one?"

"Is . . . arsenic? Yes, ma'am. But what you want—"

"I want arsenic."

The druggist looked down at her. She looked back at him, erect, her face like a strained flag. "Why, of course," the druggist said. "If that's what you want. But the law requires you to tell what you are going to use it for."

Miss Emily just stared at him, her head tilted back in order to look him eye for eye, until he looked away and went and got the arsenic and wrapped it up. The Negro delivery boy brought her the package; the druggist didn't come back. When she opened the package at home there was written on the box, under the skull and bones: "For rats."

IV

So the next day we all said, "She will kill herself"; and we said it would be the best thing. When she had first begun to be seen with Homer Barron, we had said, "She will marry him." Then we said, "She will persuade him yet," because Homer himself had remarked—he liked men, and it was known that he drank with the younger men in the Elks' Club—he was not a marrying man. Later we said, "Poor Emily" behind the jalousies as they passed on Sunday afternoon in the glittering buggy, Miss Emily with her head high and Homer Barron with his hat cocked and a cigar in his teeth, reins and whip in a yellow glove.

Then some of the ladies began to say that it was a disgrace to the town and a bad example to the young people. The men did not want to interfere, but at last the ladies forced the Baptist minister—Miss Emily's people were Episcopal—to call upon her. He would never divulge what happened during that interview, but he refused to go back again. The next Sunday they again drove about the streets, and the following day the minister's wife wrote to Miss Emily's relations in Alabama.

So she had blood-kin under her roof again and we sat back to watch developments. At first nothing happened. Then we were sure that they were to be married. We learned that Miss Emily had been to the jeweler's and ordered a man's toilet set in silver, with the letter H. B. on each piece. Two days later we learned that she had bought a complete outfit of men's clothing, including a nightshirt, and we said, "They are married." We were really glad. We were glad because the two female cousins were even more Grierson than Miss Emily had ever been.

So we were not surprised when Homer Barron—the streets had been finished some time since—was gone. We were a little disappointed that there was not a public blowing-off, but we believed that he had gone on to prepare for Miss Emily's coming, or to give her a chance to get rid of the cousins. (By that time it was a cabal, and we were all Miss Emily's allies to help circumvent the cousins.) Sure enough, after another week they departed. And, as we had expected all along, within three days Homer Barron was back in town. A neighbor saw the Negro man admit him at the kitchen door at dusk one evening.

And that was the last we saw of Homer Barron. And of Miss Emily for some time. The Negro man went in and out with the market basket, but the front door remained closed. Now and then we would see her at a window for a moment, as the men did that night when they sprinkled the lime, but for almost six months she did not appear on the streets. Then we knew that this was to be expected too; as if that quality of her father which had thwarted her woman's life so many times had been too virulent and too furious to die.

When we next saw Miss Emily, she had grown fat and her hair was turning gray. During the next few years it grew grayer and grayer until it attained an even pepper-and-salt iron-gray, when it ceased turning. Up to the day of her death at seventy-four it was still that vigorous iron-gray, like the hair of an active man.

From that time on her front door remained closed, save for a period of six or seven years, when she was about forty, during which she gave lessons in china-painting. She fitted up a studio in one of the downstairs rooms, where the daughters and granddaughters of Colonel Sartoris' contemporaries were sent to her with the same regularity and in the same spirit that they were sent to church on Sundays with a twenty-five-cent piece for the collection plate. Meanwhile her taxes had been remitted.

Then the newer generation became the backbone and the spirit of the town, and the painting pupils grew up and fell away and did not send their children to her with boxes of color and tedious brushes and pictures cut from the ladies' magazines. The front door closed upon the last one and remained closed for good. When the town got free postal delivery, Miss Emily alone refused to let them fasten the metal numbers above her door and attach a mailbox to it. She would not listen to them.

Daily, monthly, yearly we watched the Negro grow grayer and more stooped, going in and out with the market basket. Each December we sent her a tax notice, which would be returned by the post office a week later, unclaimed. Now and then we would see her in one of the downstairs windows—she had evidently shut up the top floor of the house—like the carven torso of an idol in a niche, looking or not looking at us, we could never tell which. Thus she passed from generation to generation—dear, inescapable, impervious, tranquil, and perverse.

And so she died. Fell ill in the house filled with dust and shadows, with only a doddering Negro man to wait on her. We did not even know she was sick; we had long since given up trying to get any information from the Negro. He talked to no one, probably not even to her, for his voice had grown harsh and rusty, as if from disuse.

She died in one of the downstairs rooms, in a heavy walnut bed with a curtain, her gray head propped on a pillow yellow and moldy with age and lack of sunlight.

V

The Negro met the first of the ladies at the front door and let them in, with their hushed, sibilant voices and their quick, curious glances, and then he disappeared. He walked right through the house and out the back and was not seen again.

The two female cousins came at once. They held the funeral on the second day, with the town coming to look at Miss Emily beneath a mass of bought flowers, with the crayon face of her father musing profoundly above the bier and the ladies sibilant and macabre; and the very old men—some in their brushed Confederate uniforms—on the porch and the lawn, talking of Miss Emily as if she had been a contemporary of theirs, believing that they had danced with her and courted her perhaps, confusing time with its mathematical progression, as the old do, to whom all the past is not a diminishing road but, instead, a huge meadow which no winter ever quite touches, divided from them now by the narrow bottle-neck of the most recent decade of years.

Already we knew that there was one room in that region above stairs which no one had seen in forty years, and which would have to be forced. They waited until Miss Emily was decently in the ground before they opened it.

The violence of breaking down the door seemed to fill this room with pervading dust. A thin, acrid pall as of the tomb seemed to lie everywhere upon this room decked and furnished as for a bridal: upon the valence curtains of faded rose color, upon the rose-shaded lights, upon the dressing table, upon the delicate array of crystal and the man's toilet things backed with tarnished silver, silver so tarnished that the monogram was obscured. Among them lay a collar and tie, as if they had just been removed, which, lifted, left upon the surface a pale crescent in the dust. Upon a chair hung the suit, carefully folded; beneath it the two mute shoes and the discarded socks.

The man himself lay in the bed.

For a long while we just stood there, looking down at the profound and fleshless grin. The body had apparently once lain in the attitude of an embrace, but now the long sleep that outlasts love, that conquers even the grimace of love, had cuckolded him. What was left of him, rotted beneath what was left of the nightshirt, had become inextricable from the bed in which he lay; and upon him and upon the pillow beside him lay that even coating of the patient and biding dust.

Then we noticed that in the second pillow was the indentation of a head. One of us lifted something from it, and leaning forward, that faint and invisible dust dry and acrid in the nostrils, we saw a long strand of iron-gray hair.

STEPHEN VINCENT BENET

[1898–1943]

The Devil and Daniel Webster

(First published in the *Saturday Evening Post*, October, 1936; first book publication in 1936.)

I

It's a story they tell in the border country, where Massachusetts joins Vermont and New Hampshire.

Yes, Dan'l Webster's dead—or, at least, they buried him. But every time there's a thunderstorm around Marshfield, they say you can hear his rolling voice in the hollows of the sky. And they say that if you go to his grave and speak loud and clear, "Dan'l Webster—Dan'l Webster!" the ground'll begin to shiver and the trees begin to shake. And after a while you'll hear a deep voice saying, "Neighbor, how stands the Union?" Then you better answer the Union stands as she stood, rock-bottomed and copper-sheathed, one and indivisible, or he's liable to rear right out of the ground. At least, that's what I was told when I was a youngster.

You see, for a while, he was the biggest man in the country. He never got to be President, but he was the biggest man. There were thousands that trusted in him right next to God Almighty, and they told stories about him and all the things that belonged to him that were like the stories of patriarchs and such. They said, when he stood up to speak, stars and stripes came right out in the sky, and once he spoke against a river and made it sink into the ground. They said, when he walked the woods with his fishing rod, Killall, the trout would jump out of the streams right into his pockets, for they knew it was no use putting up a fight against him; and, when he argued a case, he could turn on the harps of the blessed and the shaking of the earth underground. That was the kind of man he was, and his big farm up at Marshfield was suitable to him. The chickens he raised were all white meat down through the drumsticks, the cows were tended like children, and the big ram he called Goliath had horns with a curl like a morning-glory vine and could butt through an iron door. But Dan'l wasn't one of your gentlemen farmers; he knew all the ways of the land, and he'd be up by candlelight to see that the chores got done. A man with a mouth like a mastiff, a brow like a mountain and eyes like burning anthracite—that was Dan'l Webster in his prime. And the biggest case he argued never got written down in the books, for he argued it against the devil, nip and tuck and no holds barred. And this is the way I used to hear it told.

There was a man named Jabez Stone, lived at Cross Corners, New Hampshire. He wasn't a bad man to start with, but he was an unlucky man. If he planted corn, he got borers; if he planted potatoes, he got blight. He had good-enough land, but it didn't prosper him; he had a decent wife and children, but the more children he had, the less there was to feed them. If stones cropped up in his neighbor's field, boulders boiled up in his; if he had a horse with the spavins, he'd trade it for one with the staggers and give something extra. There's some folks bound to be like that, apparently. But one day Jabez Stone got sick of the whole business.

He'd been plowing that morning and he'd just broke the plowshare on a rock that he could have sworn hadn't been there yesterday. And, as he stood looking at the plowshare, the off horse began to cough—that ropy kind of cough that means sickness and horse doctors. There were two children down with the measles, his wife was ailing, and he had a whitlow on his thumb. It was about the last straw for Jabez Stone. "I vow," he said, and he looked around him kind of desperate—"I vow it's enough to make a man want to sell his soul to the devil! And I would, too, for two cents!"

Then he felt a kind of queerness come over him at having said what he'd said; though, naturally, being a New Hampshireman he wouldn't take it back. But, all the same, when it got to be evening and, as far as he could see, no notice had been taken, he felt relieved in his mind, for he was a religious man. But notice is always taken, sooner or later, just like the Good Book says. And, sure enough, next day, about suppertime, a soft-spoken, dark-dressed stranger drove up in a handsome buggy and asked for Jabez Stone.

Well, Jabez told his family it was a lawyer, come to see him about a legacy. But he knew who it was. He didn't like the looks of the stranger, nor the way he smiled with his teeth. They were white teeth, and plentiful—some say they were filed to a point, but I wouldn't vouch for that. And he didn't like it when the dog took one look at the stranger and ran away howling, with his tail between his legs. But having passed his word, more or less, he stuck to it, and they went out behind the barn and made their bargain. Jabez Stone had to prick his finger to sign, and the stranger lent him a silver pin. The wound healed clean, but it left a little white scar.

II

After that, all of a sudden, things began to pick up and prosper for Jabez Stone. His cows got fat and his horses sleek, his crops were the envy of the neighborhood, and lightning might strike all over the valley, but it wouldn't strike his barn. Pretty soon, he was one of the prosperous people of the county; they asked him to stand for selectman, and he stood for it; there began to be talk of running him for state senate. All in all, you might say the Stone family was as happy and contented as cats in a dairy. And so they were, except for Jabez Stone.

He'd been contented enough, the first few years. It's a great thing when bad luck turns; it drives most other things out of your head. True, every now and then, especially in rainy weather, the little white scar on his finger would give him a twinge. And once a year, punctual as clockwork, the stranger with the handsome buggy would come driving by. But the sixth year, the stranger lighted, and, after that, his peace was over for Jabez Stone.

The stranger came up through the lower field, switching his boots with a cane—they were handsome black boots, but Jabez Stone never liked the look of them, particularly the toes. And, after he'd passed the time of day, he said, "Well, Mr. Stone, you're a hummer! It's a very pretty property you've got here, Mr. Stone."

"Well, some might favor it and others might not," said Jabez Stone, for he was a New Hampshireman.

"Oh, no need to decry your industry!" said the stranger, very easy, showing his teeth in a smile. "After all, we know what's been done, and it's been according to contract and specifications. So when—ahem—the mortgage falls due next year, you shouldn't have any regrets."

"Speaking of that mortgage, mister," said Jabez Stone, and he looked around for help to the earth and the sky, "I'm beginning to have one or two doubts about it."

"Doubts?" said the stranger, not quite so pleasantly.

"Why, yes," said Jabez Stone. "This being the U. S. A. and me always having been a religious man." He cleared his throat and got bolder. "Yes, sir," he said, "I'm beginning to have considerable doubts as to that mortgage holding in court."

"There's courts and courts," said the stranger, clicking his teeth. "Still, we might as well have a look at the original document." And he hauled out a big black pocketbook, full of papers. "Sherwin, Slater, Stevens, Stone," he muttered. "I, Jabez Stone, for a term of seven years—Oh, it's quite in order, I think."

But Jabez Stone wasn't listening, for he saw something else flutter out of the black pocketbook. It was something that looked like a moth, but it wasn't a moth. And as Jabez Stone stared at it, it seemed to speak to him in a small sort of piping voice, terrible small and thin, but terrible human.

"Neighbor Stone!" it squeaked. "Neighbor Stone! Help me! For God's sake, help me!"

But before Jabez Stone could stir hand or foot, the stranger whipped out a big bandanna handkerchief, caught the creature in it, just like a butterfly, and started tying up the ends of the bandanna.

"Sorry for the interruption," he said. "As I was saying—"

But Jabez Stone was shaking all over like a scared horse.

"That's Miser Stevens' voice!" he said, in a croak. "And you've got him in your handkerchief!"

The stranger looked a little embarrassed.

"Yes, I really should have transferred him to the collecting box," he said with a simper, "but there were some rather unusual specimens there and I didn't want them crowded. Well, well, these little contretemps will occur."

"I don't know what you mean by contertan," said Jabez Stone, "but that was Miser Stevens' voice! And he ain't dead! You can't tell me he is! He was just as spry and mean as a woodchuck, Tuesday!"

"In the midst of life—" said the stranger, kind of pious. "Listen!" Then a bell began to toll in the valley and Jabez Stone listened, with the sweat running down his face. For he knew it was tolled for Miser Stevens and that he was dead.

"These long-standing accounts," said the stranger with a sigh; "one really hates to close them. But business is business."

He still had the bandanna in his hand, and Jabez Stone felt sick as he saw the cloth struggle and flutter.

"Are they all as small as that?" he asked hoarsely.

"Small?" said the stranger. "Oh, I see what you mean. Why, they vary." He measured Jabez Stone with his eyes, and his teeth showed. 'Don't worry, Mr. Stone," he said. "You'll go with a very good grade. I wouldn't trust you outside the collecting box. Now, a man like Dan'l Webster, of course—well, we'd have to build a special box for him, and even at that, I imagine the wing spread would astonish you. He'd certainly be a prize. I wish we could see our way clear to him. But, in your case, as I was saying—"

"Put that handkerchief away!" said Jabez Stone, and he began to beg and to pray. But the best he could get at the end was a three years' extension, with conditions.

But till you make a bargain like that, you've got no idea of how fast four years can run. By the last months of those years, Jabez Stone's known all over the state and there's talk of running him for governor—and it's dust and ashes in his mouth. For every day, when he gets up, he thinks, "There's one more night gone," and every night when he lies down, he thinks of the black pocketbook and the soul of Miser Stevens, and it makes him sick at heart. Till, finally, he can't bear it any longer, and, in the last days of the last year, he hitches up his horse and drives off to seek Dan'l Webster. For Dan'l was born in New Hampshire, only a few miles from Cross Corners, and it's well known that he has a particular soft spot for old neighbors.

III

It was early in the morning when he got to Marshfield, but Dan'l was up already, talking Latin to the farm hands and wrestling with the ram, Goliath, and trying out a new trotter and working up speeches to make against John C. Calhoun. But when he heard a New Hampshireman had come to see him, he dropped everything else he was doing, for that was Dan'l's way. He gave Jabez Stone a breakfast that five men couldn't eat, went into the living history of every man and woman in Cross Corners, and finally asked him how he could serve him.

Jabez Stone allowed that it was a kind of mortgage case.

"Well, I haven't pleaded a mortgage case in a long time, and I don't generally plead now, except before the Supreme Court," said Dan'l, "but if I can, I'll help you."

"Then I've got hope for the first time in ten years," said Jabez Stone, and told him the details.

Dan'l walked up and down as he listened, hands behind his back, now and then asking a question, now and then plunging his eyes at the floor, as if they'd bore through it like gimlets. When Jabez Stone had finished, Dan'l puffed out his cheeks and blew. Then he turned to Jabez Stone and a smile broke over his face like the sunrise over Monadnock.

"You've certainly given yourself the devil's own row to hoe, Neighbor Stone," he said. "but I'll take your case."

"You'll take it?" said Jabez Stone, hardly daring to believe.

"Yes," said Dan'l Webster. "I've got about seventy-five other things to do and the Missouri Compromise to straighten out, but I'll take your case. For if two New Hampshiremen aren't a match for the devil, we might as well give the country back to the Indians."

Then he shook Jabez Stone by the hand and said, "Did you come down here in a hurry?"

"Well, I admit I made time," said Jabez Stone.

"You'll go back faster," said Dan'l Webster, and he told 'em to hitch up Constitution and Constellation to the carriage. They were matched grays with one white forefoot, and they stepped like greased lightning.

Well, I won't describe how excited and pleased the whole Stone family was to have the great Dan'l Webster for a guest, when they finally got there. Jabez Stone had lost his hat on the way, blown off when they overtook a wind, but he didn't take much account of that. But after supper he sent the family off to bed, for he had most particular business with Mr. Webster. Mrs. Stone wanted them to sit in the front parlor, but Dan'l Webster knew front parlors and said he preferred the kitchen. So it was there they sat, waiting for the stranger, with a jug on the table between them and a bright fire on the hearth—the stranger being scheduled to show up on the stroke of midnight, according to specification.

Well, most men wouldn't have asked for better company than Dan'l Webster and a jug. But with every tick of the clock Jabez Stone got sadder and sadder. His eyes roved round, and though he sampled the jug you could see he couldn't taste it. Finally, on the stroke of 11:30 he reached over and grabbed Dan'l Webster by the arm.

"Mr. Webster, Mr. Webster!" he said, and his voice was shaking with fear and a desperate courage. "For God's sake, Mr. Webster, harness your horses and get away from this place while you can!"

"You've brought me a long way, neighbor, to tell me you don't like my company," said Dan'l Webster, quite peaceable, pulling at the jug.

"Miserable wretch that I am!" groaned Jabez Stone. "I've brought you a devilish way, and now I see my folly. Let him take me if he wills. I don't hanker after it, I must say, but I can stand it. But you're the Union's stay and New Hampshire's pride! He mustn't get you, Mr. Webster! He mustn't get you!"

Dan'l Webster looked at the distracted man, all gray and shaking in the firelight, and laid a hand on his shoulder.

"I'm obliged to you, Neighbor Stone," he said gently. "It's kindly thought of. But there's a jug on the table and a case in hand. And I never left a jug or a case half finished in my life."

And just at that moment there was a sharp rap on the door.

"Ah," said Dan'l Webster, very coolly, "I thought your clock was a trifle slow, Neighbor Stone." He stepped to the door and opened it. "Come in!" he said.

The stranger came in—very dark and tall he looked in the firelight. He was carrying a box under his arm—a black, japanned box with little air holes in the lid. At the sight of the box, Jabez Stone gave a low cry and shrank into a corner of the room.

"Mr. Webster, I presume," said the stranger, very polite, but with his eyes glowing like a fox's deep in the woods.

"Attorney of record for Jabez Stone," said Dan'l Webster, but his eyes were glowing too. "Might I ask your name?"

"I've gone by a good many," said the stranger carelessly. "Perhaps Scratch will do for the evening. I'm often called that in these regions."

Then he sat down at the table and poured himself a drink from the jug. The liquor was cold in the jug, but it came steaming into the glass.

"And now," said the stranger, smiling and showing his teeth, "I shall call upon you, as a law-abiding citizen, to assist me in taking possession of my property."

Well, with that the argument began—and it went hot and heavy. At first,

Jabez Stone had a flicker of hope, but when he saw Dan'l Webster being forced back at point after point, he just sat scrunched in his corner, with his eyes on that japanned box. For there wasn't any doubt as to the deed or the signature—that was the worst of it. Dan'l Webster twisted and turned and thumped his fist on the table, but he couldn't get away from that. He offered to compromise the case; the stranger wouldn't hear of it. He pointed out the property had increased in value, and state senators ought to be worth more; the stranger stuck to the letter of the law. He was a great lawyer, Dan'l Webster, but we know who's the King of Lawyers, as the Good Book tells us, and it seemed as if, for the first time, Dan'l Webster had met his match.

Finally, the stranger yawned a little. "Your spirited efforts on behalf of your client do you credit, Mr. Webster," he said, "but if you have no more arguments to adduce, I'm rather pressed for time—" and Jabez Stone shuddered.

Dan'l Webster's brow looked dark as a thundercloud. "Pressed or not, you shall not have this man!" he thundered. "Mr. Stone is an American citizen, and no American citizen may be forced into the service of a foreign prince. We fought England for that in '12 and we'll fight all hell for it again!"

"Foreign?" said the stranger. "And who calls me a foreigner?"

"Well, I never yet heard of the dev—of your claiming American citizenship," said Dan'l Webster with surprise.

"And who with better right?" said the stranger, with one of his terrible smiles. "When the first wrong was done to the first Indian, I was there. When the first slaver put out for the Congo, I stood on her deck. Am I not in your books and stories and beliefs, from the first settlements on? Am I not spoken of, still, in every church in New England? 'Tis true the North claims me for a Southerner, and the South for a Northerner, but I am neither. I am merely an honest American like yourself—and of the best descent—for, to tell the truth, Mr. Webster, though I don't like to boast of it, my name is older in this country than yours."

"Aha!" said Dan'l Webster, with the veins standing out in his forehead. "Then I stand on the Constitution! I demand a trial for my client!"

"The case is hardly one for an ordinary court," said the stranger, his eyes flickering. "And, indeed, the lateness of the hour—"

"Let it be any court you choose, so it is an American judge and an American jury!" said Dan'l Webster in his pride. "Let it be the quick or the dead; I'll abide the issue!"

"You have said it," said the stranger, and pointed his finger at the door. And with that, and all of a sudden, there was a rushing of wind outside and a noise of footsteps. They came, clear and distinct, through the night. And yet, they were not like the footsteps of living men.

"In God's name, who comes by so late?" cried Jabez Stone, in an ague of fear.

"The jury Mr. Webster demands," said the stranger, sipping at his boiling glass. "You must pardon the rough appearance of one or two; they will have come a long way."

IV

And with that the fire burned blue and the door blew open and twelve men entered, one by one.

If Jabez Stone had been sick with terror before, he was blind with terror now. For there was Walter Butler, the loyalist, who spread fire and horror through the Mohawk Valley in the times of the Revolution; and there was Simon Girty, the renegade, who saw white men burned at the stake and whooped with the Indians to see them burn. His eyes were green, like a catamount's, and the stains on his hunting shirt did not come from the blood of the deer. King Philip was there, wild and proud as he had been in life, with the great gash in his head that gave him his death wound, and cruel Governor Dale, who broke men on the wheel. There was Morton of Merry Mount, who so vexed the Plymouth Colony, with his flushed, loose, handsome face and his hate of the godly. There was Teach, the bloody pirate, with his black beard curling on his breast. The Reverend John Smeet, with his strangler's hands and his Geneva gown, walked as daintily as he had to the gallows. The red print of the rope was still around his neck, but he carried a perfumed handkerchief in one hand. One and all, they came into the room with the fires of hell still upon them, and the stranger named their names and their deeds as they came, till the tale of twelve was told. Yet the stranger had told the truth—they had all played a part in America.

"Are you satisfied with the jury, Mr. Webster?" said the stranger mockingly, when they had taken their places.

The sweat stood upon Dan'l Webster's brow, but his voice was clear.

"Quite satisfied," he said. "Though I miss General Arnold from the company."

"Benedict Arnold is engaged upon other business," said the stranger, with a glower. "Ah, you asked for a justice, I believe."

He pointed his finger once more, and a tall man, soberly clad in Puritan garb, with the burning gaze of the fanatic, stalked into the room and took his judge's place.

"Justice Hathorne is a jurist of experience," said the stranger. "He presided at certain witch trials once held in Salem. There were others who repented of the business later, but not he."

"Repent of such notable wonders and undertakings?" said the stern old justice. "Nay, hang them—hang them all!" And he muttered to himself in a way that struck ice into the soul of Jabez Stone.

Then the trial began, and, as you might expect, it didn't look anyways good for the defense. And Jabez Stone didn't make much of a witness in his own behalf. He took one look at Simon Girty and screeched, and they had to put him back in his corner in a kind of swoon.

It didn't halt the trial, though; the trial went on, as trials do. Dan'l Webster had faced some hard juries and hanging judges in his time, but this was the hardest he'd ever faced, and he knew it. They sat there with a kind of glitter in their eyes, and the stranger's smooth voice went on and on. Every time he'd raise an objection, it'd be "Objection sustained," but whenever Dan'l objected, it'd be "Objection denied." Well, you couldn't expect fair play from a fellow like this Mr. Scratch.

It got to Dan'l in the end, and he began to heat, like iron in the forge. When he got up to speak he was going to flay that stranger with every trick known to the law, and the judge and jury too. He didn't care if it was contempt of court or what would happen to him for it. He didn't care any more what happened to Jabez Stone. He just got madder and madder, thinking of what he'd say. And yet, curiously enough, the more he thought about it, the less he was able to arrange his speech in his mind.

Till, finally, it was time for him to get up on his feet, and he did so, all ready to bust out with lightnings and denunciations. But before he started he looked over the judge and jury for a moment, such being his custom. And he noticed the glitter in their eyes was twice as strong as before, and they all leaned forward. Like hounds just before they get the fox, they looked, and the blue mist of evil in the room thickened as he watched them. Then he saw what he'd been about to do, and he wiped his forehead, as a man might who's just escaped falling into a pit in the dark.

For it was him they'd come for, not only Jabez Stone. He read it in the glitter of their eyes and in the way the stranger hid his mouth with one hand. And if he fought them with their own weapons, he'd fall into their power; he knew that, though he couldn't have told you how. It was his own anger and horror that burned in their eyes; and he'd have to wipe that out or the case was lost. He stood there for a moment, his black eyes burning like anthracite. And then he began to speak.

He started off in a low voice, though you could hear every word. They say he could call on the harps of the blessed when he chose. And this was just as simple and easy as a man could talk. But he didn't start out by condemning or reviling. He was talking about the things that make a country a country, and a man a man.

And he began with the simple things that everybody's known and felt—the freshness of a fine morning when you're young, and the taste of food when you're hungry, and the new day that's every day when you're a child. He took them up and he turned them in his hands. They were good things for any man. But without freedom, they sickened. And when he talked of those enslaved, and the sorrows of slavery, his voice got like a big bell. He talked of the early days of America and the men who had made those days. It wasn't a spread-eagle speech, but he made you see it. He admitted all the wrong that had ever been done. But he showed how, out of the wrong and the right, the suffering and the starvations, something new had come. And everybody had played a part in it, even the traitors.

Then he turned to Jabez Stone and showed him as he was—an ordinary man who'd had hard luck and wanted to change it. And, because he'd wanted to change it, now he was going to be punished for all eternity. And yet there was good in Jabez Stone, and he showed that good. He was hard and mean, in some ways, but he was a man. There was sadness in being a man, but it was a proud thing too. And he showed what the pride of it was till you couldn't help feeling it. Yes, even in hell, if a man was a man, you'd know it. And he wasn't pleading for any one person any more, though his voice rang like an organ. He was telling the story and the failures and the endless journey of mankind. They got tricked and trapped and bamboozled, but it was a great journey. And no demon that was ever foaled could know the inwardness of it—it took a man to do that.

V

The fire began to die on the hearth and the wind before morning to blow. The light was getting gray in the room when Dan'l Webster finished. And his words came back at the end to New Hampshire ground, and the one spot of land that each man loves and clings to. He painted a picture of that, and to each one of that jury he spoke of things long forgotten. For his voice could search the heart, and that was his gift and his strength. And to one, his voice was like the forest and its secrecy, and to another like the sea and the storms of the sea; and one heard the cry of his lost nation in it, and another saw a little harmless scene he hadn't remembered for years. But each saw something. And when Dan'l Webster finished he didn't know whether or not he'd saved Jabez Stone. But he knew he'd done a miracle. For the glitter was gone from the eyes of judge and jury, and, for the moment, they were men again, and knew they were men.

"The defense rests," said Dan'l Webster, and stood there like a mountain. His ears were still ringing with his speech, and he didn't hear anything else till he heard Judge Hathorne say, "The jury will retire to consider its verdict."

Walter Butler rose in his place and his face had a dark, gay pride on it.

"The jury has considered its verdict," he said, and looked the stranger full in the eye. "We find for the defendant, Jabez Stone."

With that, the smile left the stranger's face, but Walter Butler did not flinch.

"Perhaps 'tis not strictly in accordance with the evidence," he said, "but even the damned may salute the eloquence of Mr. Webster."

With that, the long crow of a rooster split the gray morning sky, and judge and jury were gone from the room like a puff of smoke and as if they had never been there. The stranger turned to Dan'l Webster, smiling wryly. "Major Butler was always a bold man," he said. "I had not thought him quite so bold. Nevertheless, my congratulations, as between two gentlemen."

"I'll have that paper first, if you please," said Dan'l Webster, and he took it and tore it into four pieces. It was queerly warm to the touch. "And now," he said, "I'll have you!" and his hand came down like a bear trap on the stranger's arm. For he knew that once you bested anybody like Mr. Scratch in fair fight, his power on you was gone. And he could see that Mr. Scratch knew it too.

The stranger twisted and wriggled, but he couldn't get out of that grip. "Come, come, Mr. Webster," he said, smiling palely. "This sort of thing is ridic—ouch!—is ridiculous. If you're worried about the costs of the case, naturally, I'd be glad to pay—"

"And so you shall!" said Dan'l Webster, shaking him till his teeth rattled. "For you'll sit right down at that table and draw up a document, promising never to bother Jabez Stone nor his heirs or assigns nor any other New Hampshireman till doomsday! For any hades we want to raise in this state, we can raise ourselves, without assistance from strangers."

"Ouch!" said the stranger. "Ouch! Well, they never did run very big to the barrel, but—ouch!—I agree!"

So he sat down and drew up the document. But Dan'l Webster kept his hand on his coat collar all the time.

"And, now, may I go?" said the stranger, quite humble, when Dan'l'd seen the document was in proper and legal form.

"Go?" said Dan'l, giving him another shake. "I'm still trying to figure out what I'll do with you. For you've settled the costs of the case, but you haven't settled with me. I think I'll take you back to Marshfield," he said, kind of reflective. "I've got a ram there named Goliath that can butt through an iron door. I'd kind of like to turn you loose in his field and see what he'd do."

Well, with that the stranger began to beg and to plead. And he begged and he pled so humble that finally Dan'l, who was naturally kindhearted, agreed to let him go. The stranger seemed terrible grateful for that and said, just to show they were friends, he'd tell Dan'l's fortune before leaving. So Dan'l agreed to that, though he didn't take much stock in fortunetellers ordinarily.

But, naturally, the stranger was a little different. Well, he pried and he peered at the lines in Dan'l's hands. And he told him one thing and another that was quite remarkable. But they were all in the past.

"Yes, all that's true, and it happened," said Dan'l Webster. "But what's to come in the future?"

The stranger grinned, kind of happily, and shook his head. "The future's not as you think it," he said. "It's dark. You have a great ambition, Mr. Webster."

"I have," said Dan'l firmly, for everybody knew he wanted to be President.

"It seems almost within your grasp," said the stranger, "but you will not attain it. Lesser men will be made President and you will be passed over."

"And, if I am, I'll still be Daniel Webster," said Dan'l. "Say on."

"You have two strong sons," said the stranger, shaking his head. "You look to found a line. But each will die in war and neither reach greatness."

"Live or die, they are still my sons," said Dan'l Webster. "Say on."

"You have made great speeches," said the stranger. "You will make more."

"Ah," said Dan'l Webster.

"But the last great speech you make will turn many of your own against you," said the stranger. "They will call you Ichabod; they will call you by other names. Even in New England some will say you have turned your coat and sold your country, and their voices will be loud against you till you die."

"So it is an honest speech, it does not matter what men say," said Dan'l Webster. Then he looked at the stranger and their glances locked.

"One question," he said. "I have fought for the Union all my life. Will I see that fight won against those who would tear it apart?"

"Not while you live," said the stranger, grimly, "but it will be won. And after you are dead, there are thousands who will fight for your cause, because of words that you spoke."

"Why, then, you long-barreled, slab-sided, lantern-jawed, fortune-telling note shaver!" said Dan'l Webster, with a great roar of laughter, "be off with you to your own place before I put my mark on you! For, by the thirteen original colonies, I'd go to the Pit itself to save the Union!"

And with that he drew back his foot for a kick that would have stunned a horse. It was only the tip of his shoe that caught the stranger, but he went flying out of the door with his collecting box under his arm.

"And now," said Dan'l Webster, seeing Jabez Stone beginning to rouse from his swoon, "let's see what's left in the jug, for it's dry work talking all night. I hope there's pie for breakfast, Neighbor Stone."

But they say that whenever the devil comes near Marshfield, even now, he gives it a wide berth. And he hasn't been seen in the state of New Hampshire from that day to this. I'm not talking about Massachusetts or Vermont.

ERNEST HEMINGWAY

[1899–1961]

The Snows of Kilimanjaro

(First published in *Esquire*, 1936;
first book publication in 1938.)

"THE MARVELLOUS THING is that it's painless," he said. "That's how you know when it starts."

"Is it really?"

"Absolutely. I'm awfully sorry about the odor though. That must bother you."

"Don't! Please don't."

"Look at them," he said. "Now is it sight or is it scent that brings them like that?"

The cot the man lay on was in the wide shade of a mimosa tree and as he looked out past the shade onto the glare of the plain there were three of the big birds squalled obscenely, while in the sky a dozen more sailed, making quick-moving shadows as they passed.

"They've been there since the truck broke down," he said. "Today's the first time any have lit on the ground. I watched the way they sailed very carefully at first in case I ever wanted to use them in a story. That's funny now."

"I wish you wouldn't," she said.

"I'm only talking," he said. "It's much easier if I talk. But I don't want to bother you."

"You know it doesn't bother me," she said. "It's that I've gotten so very nervous not being able to do anything. I think we might make it as easy as we can until the plane comes."

"Or until the plane doesn't come."

"Please tell me what I can do. There must be something I can do."

"You can take the leg off and that might stop it, though I doubt it. Or you can shoot me. You're a good shot now. I taught you to shoot didn't I."

"Please don't talk that way. Couldn't I read to you?"

"Read what?"

"Anything in the book bag that we haven't read."

"I can't listen to it," he said. "Talking is the easiest. We quarrel and that makes the time pass."

"I don't quarrel. I never want to quarrel. Let's not quarrel any more. No matter how nervous we get. Maybe they will be back with another truck today. Maybe the plane will come."

"I don't want to move," the man said. "There is no sense in moving now except to make it easier for you."

"That's cowardly."

"Can't you let a man die as comfortably as he can without calling him names? What's the use of slanging me?"

"You're not going to die."

"Don't be silly. I'm dying now. Ask those bastards." He looked over to where the huge, filthy birds sat, their naked heads sunk in the hunched feathers. A fourth planed down, to run quick-legged and then waddle slowly toward the others.

"They are around every camp. You never notice them. You can't die if you don't give up."

"Where did you read that? You're such a bloody fool."

"You might think about someone else."

"For Christ's sake," he said, "that's been my trade." He lay then and was quiet for a while and looked across the heat shimmer of the plain to the edge of the bush. There were a few Tommies that showed minute and white against the yellow and, far off, he saw a herd of zebra, white against the green of the bush. This was a pleasant camp under big trees against a hill, with good water, and, close by, a nearly dry water hole where sand grouse flighted in the mornings.

"Wouldn't you like me to read?" she asked. She was sitting on a canvas chair beside his cot. "There's a breeze coming up."

"No thanks."

"Maybe the truck will come."

"I don't give a damn about the truck."

"I do."

"You give a damn about so many things that I don't."

"Not so many, Harry."

"What about a drink?"

"It's supposed to be bad for you. It said in Black's to avoid all alcohol. You shouldn't drink."

"Molo!" he shouted.

"Yes Bwana."

"Bring whiskey-soda."

"Yes Bwana."

"You shouldn't," she said. "That's what I mean by giving up. It says it's bad for you. I know it's bad for you."

"No," he said. "It's good for me."

So now it was all over, he thought. So now he would never have a chance to finish it. So this was the way it ended in a bickering over a drink. Since the gangrene started in his right leg he had no pain and with the pain the horror had gone and all he felt now was a great tiredness and anger that this was the end of it. For this, that now was coming, he had very little curiosity. For years it had obsessed him; but now it meant nothing in itself. It was strange how easy being tired enough made it.

Now he would never write the things that he had saved to write until he knew enough to write about them well. Well, he would not have to fail at trying to write them either. Maybe you could never write them, and that was why you put them off and delayed the starting. Well he would never know, now.

"I wish we'd never come," the woman said. She was looking at him holding the glass and biting her lip. "You never would have gotten anything like this in Paris. You always said you loved Paris. We could have stayed in Paris or gone anywhere. I'd have gone anywhere. I said I'd go anywhere you wanted. If you wanted to shoot we could have gone shooting in Hungary and been comfortable."

"Your bloody money," he said.

"That's not fair," she said. "It was always yours as much as mine. I left everything and I went wherever you wanted to go and I've done what you wanted to do. But I wish we'd never come here."

"You said you loved it."

"I did when you were all right. But now I hate it. I don't see why that had to happen to your leg. What have we done to have that happen to us?"

"I suppose what I did was to forget to put iodine on it when I first scratched it. Then I didn't pay any attention to it because I never infect. Then, later, when it got bad, it was probably using that weak carbolic solution when the other antiseptics ran out that paralyzed the minute blood vessels and started the gangrene." He looked at her, "What else?"

"I don't mean that."

"If we would have hired a good mechanic instead of a half baked kikuyu driver, he would have checked the oil and never burned out that bearing in the truck."

"I don't mean that."

"If you hadn't left your own people, your goddamned old Westbury, Saratoga, Palm Beach people to take me on—"

"Why I loved you. That's not fair. I love you now. I'll always love you. Don't you love me?"

"No," said the man. "I don't think so. I never have."

"Harry, what are you saying? You're out of your head."

"No. I haven't any head to go out of."

"Don't drink that," she said. "Darling, please don't drink that. We have to do everything we can."

"You do it," he said. "I'm tired."

Now in his mind he saw a railway station at Karagatch and he was standing with his pack and that was the headlight of the Simplon-Orient cutting the dark now and he was leaving Thrace then after the retreat. That was one of the things he had saved to write, with, in the morning at breakfast, looking out the window and seeing snow on the mountains in Bulgaria and Nansen's Secretary asking the old man if it were snow and the old man looking at it and saying, No, that's not snow. It's too early for snow. And the Secretary repeating to the other girls, No, you see. It's not snow and them all saying, It's not snow we were mistaken. But it was the snow all right and he sent them on into it when he evolved exchange of populations. And it was snow they tramped along in until they died that winter.

It was snow too that fell all Christmas week that year up in the Gauertal, that year they lived in the woodcutter's house with the big square porcelain stove that filled half the room, and they slept on mattresses filled with beech leaves, the time the deserter came with his feet bloody in the snow. He said the police were right behind him and they gave him woolen socks and held the gendarmes talking until the tracks had drifted over. In Schruns, on Christmas day, the snow was so bright it hurt your eyes when you looked out from the weinstube and saw everyone coming home from church. That was where they walked up the sleigh-smoothed urine-yellowed road along the river with the steep pine hills, skis heavy on the shoulder, and where they ran that great run down the glacier above the Madlener-haus, the snow as smooth to see as cake frosting and as light as powder and he remembered the noiseless rush the speed made as you dropped down like a bird. They were snowbound a week in the Madlener-haus that time in the blizzard playing cards in the smoke by the lantern light and the stakes were higher all the time as Herr Lent lost more. Finally he lost it all. Everything, the ski-schule money and all the season's profit and then his capital. He could see him with his long nose, picking up the cards and then opening, "Sans Voir." There was always gambling then. When there was no snow you gambled and when there was too much you gambled. He thought of all the time in his life he had spent gambling. But he had never written a line of that, nor of that cold, bright Christmas day with the mountains showing across the plain that Barker had flown across the lines to bomb the Austrian officers' leave train, maching-gunning them as they scattered and ran. He remembered Barker afterwards coming into the mess and starting to tell about it. And how quiet it got and then somebody saying, "You bloody, murderous bastard." Those were the same Austrians they killed then that he skied with later. No not the same. Hans, that he skied with all that year, had been in the Kaiser-Jagers and when they went hunting hares together up the little valley above the saw-mill they had talked of the fighting on Pasubio and of the attack on Pertica and Asalone and he had never written a word of that. Nor of Monte Corno, nor the Siete Communi, nor of Arsiero. How many winters had he lived in the Vorarlberg and the Arlberg? It was four and then he remem-

bered the man who had the fox to sell when they had walked into Bludenz, that time to buy presents, and the cherry pit taste of good kirsch, the fast-slipping rush of running powder-snow on crust, singing "Hi Ho said Rolly!" as you ran down the last stretch to the steep drop, taking it straight, then running the orchard in three turns and out across the ditch and onto the icy road behind the inn. Knocking your bindings loose, kicking the skis free and leaning them up against the wooden wall of the inn, the lamplight coming from the window where inside, in the smoky, new-wine smelling warmth, they were playing the accordion.

"Where did we stay in Paris?" he asked the woman who was sitting by him in a canvas chair, now, in Africa.

"At the Crillon. You know that."

"Why do I know that?"

"That's where we always stayed."

"No. Not always."

"There and at the Pavillion Henri-Quatre in St. Germain. You said you loved it there."

"Love is a dunghill," said Harry. "And I'm the cock that gets on it to crow."

"If you have to go away," she said, "is it absolutely necessary to kill everything you leave behind? I mean do you have to take away everything? Do you have to kill your horse, and your wife and burn your saddle and your armour?"

"Yes," he said. "Your damned money was my armour. My Swift and my Armour."

"Don't."

"All right. I'll stop that. I don't want to hurt you."

"It's a little bit late now."

"All right then. I'll go on hurting you. It's more amusing. The only thing I ever really liked to do with you I can't do now."

"No, that's not true. You liked to do many things and everything you wanted to do I did."

"Oh for Christ's sake stop bragging will you?"

He looked at her and saw her crying.

"Listen," he said. "Do you think that it is fun to do this? I don't know why I'm doing it. It's trying to kill to keep yourself alive I imagine. I was all right when we started talking. I didn't mean to start this, and now I'm crazy as a coot and being as cruel to you as I can be. Don't pay any attention, darling, to what I say. I love you, really. You know I love you. I've never loved anyone else the way I love you." He slipped into the familiar lie he made his bread and butter by.

"You're sweet to me."

"You bitch," he said. "You rich bitch. That's poetry. I'm full of poetry now. Rot and poetry. Rotten poetry."

"Stop it. Harry, why do you have to turn into a devil now?"

"I don't like to leave anything," the man said. "I don't like to leave things behind."

It was evening now and he had been asleep. The sun was gone behind the hill and there was a shadow all across the plain and the small animals were feeding close to camp; quick dropping heads and switching tails, he watched them keeping well out away from the bush now. The birds no longer waited on the ground. They were all perched heavily in a tree. There were many more of them. His personal boy was sitting by the bed.

"Memsahib's gone to shoot," the boy said. "Does Bwana want?"

"Nothing."

She had gone to kill a piece of meat and, knowing how he liked to watch the game, she had gone well away so she would not disturb this little pocket of the plain that he could see. She was always thoughtful, he thought. On anything she knew about, or had read, or that she had ever heard.

It was not her fault that when he went to her he was already over. How could a woman know that you meant nothing that you said; that you spoke only from habit and to be comfortable. After he no longer meant what he said, his lies were more successful with women than when he had told them the truth.

It was not that he lied as that there was no truth to tell. He had had his life and it was over and then he went on living it again with different people and more money, with the best of the same places, and some new ones. You kept from thinking and it was all marvellous. You were equipped with good insides so that you did not go to pieces that way, the way most of them had, and you made an attitude that you cared nothing for the work you used to do, now that you could no longer do it. But, in yourself, you said that you would write about these people; about the very rich; that you were really not of them but a spy in their country; that you would leave it and write of it and for once it would be written by someone who knew what he was writing of. But he would never do it, because each day of not writing, of comfort, of being that which he despised, dulled his ability and softened his will to work so that, finally, he did no work at all. The people he knew now were all much more comfortable when he did not work. Africa was where he had been happiest in the good time of his life so he had come out here to start again. They had made this safari with the minimum of comfort. There was no hardship; but there was no luxury and he had thought that he could get back into training that way. That in some way he could work the fat off his soul the way a fighter went into the mountains to work and train in order to burn it out of his body.

She had liked it. She said she loved it. She loved anything that was exciting, that involved a change of scene, where there were new people and where things were pleasant. And he had felt the illusion of returning strength of will to work. Now if this was how it ended, and he knew it was, he must not turn like some snake biting itself because its back was broken. It wasn't this woman's fault. If it had not been she it would have been another. If he lived by a lie he should try to die by it. He heard a shot beyond the hill.

She shot very well this good, this rich bitch, this kindly caretaker and destroyer of his talent. Nonsense. He had destroyed his talent himself. Why should he blame this woman because she kept him well? He had destroyed his talent by not using it, by betrayals of himself and what he believed in, by drinking so much that he blunted the edge of his perceptions, by laziness, by sloth, and by snobbery, by pride and by prejudice, by hook and by crook. What was this? A catalogue of old books? What was his talent anyway? It was a talent all right but instead of using it, he had traded on it. It was never what he had done, but always what he could do. And he had chosen to make his living with something else instead of a pen or a pencil. It was strange too, wasn't it, that when he fell in love with another woman, that woman should always have more money than the last one? But when he no longer was in love, when he was only lying, as to this woman, now, who had the most money of all, who had all the money there was, who had had a husband and children, who had taken lovers and been dissatisfied with them, and who loved him dearly as a writer, as a man, as a companion and as a proud possession; it was strange that when he did not love her at all and was lying, that he should be able to give her more for her money than when he had really loved. We must all be cut out for what we do, he thought. However you make your living is where your talent lies. He had sold vitality, in one form or another, all his life and when your affections are not too involved you give much better value for the money. He had found that out but he would never write that, now, either. No, he would not write that, although it was well worth writing.

Now she came in sight, walking across the open toward the camp. She was wearing jodhpurs and carrying her rifle. The two boys had a Tommy slung and they were coming along behind her. She was still a good looking woman, he thought, and she had a pleasant body. She had a great talent and appreciation for the bed, she was not pretty, but he liked her face, she read enormously, liked to ride and shoot and, certainly, she drank too much. Her husband had died when she was still a comparatively young woman and for a while she had devoted herself to her two just-grown children, who did not need her and were embarrassed at having her about, to her stable of horses, to books, and to bottles. She liked to read in the evening before dinner and she drank scotch and soda while she read. By dinner she was fairly drunk and after a bottle of wine at dinner she was usually drunk enough to sleep.

That was before the lovers. After she had the lovers she did not drink so much because she did not have to be drunk to sleep. But the lovers bored her. She had been married to a man who had never bored her and these people bored her very much.

Then one of her two children was killed in a plane crash and after that was over she did not want the lovers, and drink being so anaesthetic she had to make another life. Suddenly she had been acutely frightened of being alone. But she wanted someone that she respected with her.

It had begun very simply. She liked what he wrote and she had always envied the life he led. She thought he did exactly what he wanted to. The steps by which she had acquired him and the way in which she had finally fallen in love with him were all part of a regular progression in which she had built herself a new life and he had traded away what remained of his old life. He had traded it for security, for comfort too, there was no denying that, and for what else? He did not know. She would have brought him anything he wanted. He knew that. She was a damned nice woman too. He would as soon be in bed with her as anyone; rather with her, because she was richer, because she was very pleasant and appreciative and because she never made scenes. And now this life that she had built again was coming to a term because he had not used iodine two weeks ago when a thorn had scratched his knee as they moved forward trying to photograph a herd of waterbuck standing, their heads up, peering while their nostrils searched the air, their ears spread wide to hear the first noise that would send them rushing into the bush. They had bolted, too, before he got the picture.

Here she came now.

He turned his head on the cot to look toward her. "Hello," he said.

"I shot a Tommy ram," she told him. "He'll make you good broth and I'll have them mash some potatoes with the Klim. How do you feel?"

"Much better."

"Isn't that lovely. You know I thought perhaps you would. You were sleeping when I left."

"I had a good sleep. Did you walk far?"

"No. Just around behind the hill. I made quite a good shot on the Tommy."

"You shoot marvellously you know."

"I love it. I've loved Africa. Really. If *you're* all right it's the most fun that I've ever had. You don't know the fun it's been to shoot with you. I've loved the country."

"I love it too."

"Darling you don't know how marvellous it is to see you feeling better. I couldn't stand it when you felt that way. You won't talk to me like that again, will you? Promise me?"

"No," he said. "I don't remember what I said."

"You don't have to destroy me. Do you? I'm only a middle-aged woman who loves you and wants to do what you want to do. I've been destroyed two or three times already. You wouldn't want to destroy me again, would you?"

"I'd like to destroy you a few times in bed," he said.

"Yes. That's the good destruction. That's the way we're made to be destroyed. The plane will be here tomorrow."

"How do you know?"

"I'm sure. It's bound to come. The boys have the wood all ready and the grass to make the smudge. I went down and looked at it again today. There's plenty of room to land and we have the smudges ready at both ends."

"What makes you think it will come tomorrow?"

"I'm sure it will. It's overdue now. Then, in town, they will fix up your leg and then we will have some good destruction. Not that dreadful talking kind."

"Should we have a drink? The sun is down."

"Do you think you should?"

"I'm having one."

"We'll have one together. *Molo, letti dui whiskey-soda!*" she called.

"You'd better put on your mosquito boots," he told her.

"I'll wait till I bathe . . ."

While it grew dark they drank and just before it was dark and there was no longer enough light to shoot, a hyena crossed the open on his way around the hill.

"That bastard comes there every night," the man said. "Every night for two weeks."

"He's the one makes the noise at night. I don't mind it. They're a filthy animal though."

Drinking together, with no pain now except the discomfort of lying in the one position, the boys lighting a fire, its shadow jumping on the tents, he could feel the return of acquiescence of this life of pleasant surrender. She *was* very good to him. He had been cruel and unjust in the afternoon. She was a fine woman, marvellous really. And just then it occurred to him that he was going to die.

It came with a rush; not as a rush of water nor of wind; but of a sudden evil smelling emptiness and the odd thing was that the hyena slipped lightly along the edge of it.

"What is it, Harry?" she asked him.

"Nothing," he said. "You had better move over to the other side. To windward."

"Did Molo change the dressing?"

"Yes. I'm just using the boric now."

"How do you feel?"

"A little wobbly."

"I'm going in to bathe," she said. "I'll be right out. I'll eat with you and then we'll put the cot in."

So, he said to himself, we did well to stop the quarreling. He had never quarreled much with this woman, while with the women that he loved he had quarreled so much they had finally, always, with the corrosion of the quarreling, killed what they had together. He had loved too much, demanded too much, and he wore it all out.

He thought about alone in Constantinople that time, having quarreled in Paris before he had gone out. He had whored the whole time and then, when that was over, and he had failed to kill his loneliness, but only made it worse, he had written her, the first one, the one who left him, a letter telling her how he had never been able to kill it . . . How when he thought he saw her outside the Regence *one time it made him go all faint and sick inside, and that he would follow a woman who looked like her in some way, along the Boulevard, afraid to see it was not she, afraid to lose the feeling it gave him. How everyone he had slept with had only made him miss her more. How what she had done could never matter since he knew he could not cure himself of loving her. He wrote this letter at the Club, cold sober, and mailed it to New York asking her to write him at the office in Paris. That seemed safe. And that night missing her so much it made him feel hollow sick inside, he wandered up past Taxim's, picked a girl up and took her out to supper. He had gone to a place to dance with her afterward, she danced badly, and left her for a hot Armenian slut, that swung her belly against him so it almost scalded. He took her away from a British gunner subaltern after a row. The gunner asked him outside and they fought in the street on the cobbles in the dark. He'd hit him twice, hard, on the side of the jaw and when he didn't go down he knew he was in for a fight. The gunner hit him in the body, then beside his eye. He swung with his left again and landed and the gunner fell on him and grabbed his coat and tore the sleeve off and he clubbed him twice behind the ear and then smashed him with his right as he pushed him away. When the gunner went down his head hit first and he ran with the girl because they heard the M.P.'s coming. They got into a taxi and drove out to Rimmily Hissa along the Bosphorus, and around, and back in the cool night and went to bed and she felt as overripe as she looked but smooth, rose-petal, syrupy, smooth-bellied, big-breasted and needed no pillow under her, and he left her before she was awake looking blowzy enough in the first daylight and turned up at the Pera Palace with a black eye, carrying his coat because one sleeve was missing. That same night he left for Anatolia and he remembered, later on that trip, riding all day through fields of the poppies that they raised for opium and how strange it made you feel finally and all the distances seemed wrong, to where they had made the attack with the newly arrived Constantine officers, that did not know a goddamned thing, and the artillery had fired into the troops and the British observer had cried like a child. That was the day he'd first seen dead men wearing white ballet skirts and upturned shoes with pompons on them. The Turks had come steadily and lumpily and he had seen the skirted men running and the officers shooting into them and running then themselves and he and the British observer had run too until his lungs ached and his mouth was full of the taste of pennies and they stopped behind some rocks and there were the Turks coming as lumpily as ever. Later he had seen the things that he could never think of and later still he had seen much worse. So when he got back to Paris that time he could not talk about it or stand to have it mentioned. And there in the café as he passed was that American poet with a pile of saucers in front of him and a stupid look on his potato face talking about the Dada movement with a Roumanian who said his name was Tristan Tzara, who always wore a monocle and had a headache, and, back at the apartment with his wife that now he loved again, the quarrel all over, the madness all over, glad to be home, the office sent his mail up to the flat. So when the letter in answer to the one he'd written came in on a platter one morning and when he saw the handwriting he went cold all over and tried to slip the letter underneath another. But his wife said, "Who is that letter from, dear?" and that was the end of the beginning of that. He remembered the good times with them all, and the quarrels. They always picked the finest places to have the quarrels. And why had they always quarreled when he was feeling best? He had never written any of that because, at first, he never wanted to hurt anyone and then it seemed as though there was enough to write without it. But he had always thought that he would write it finally. There was so much to write. He had seen the world change; not just the events; although he had seen many of them and had watched the people, but he had seen the subtler change and he could remember how the people were at different times. He had been in it and he had watched it and it was his duty to write of it; but now he never would.*

"How do you feel?" she said. She had come out from the tent now after her bath.

"All right."

"Could you eat now?" He saw Molo behind her with the folding table and the other boy with the dishes.

"I want to write," he said.

"You ought to take some broth to keep your strength up."

"I'm going to die tonight." he said. "I don't need my strength up."

"Don't be melodramatic, Harry, please," she said.

"Why don't you use your nose? I'm rotted half way up my thigh now. What the hell should I fool with broth for? Molo bring whisky-soda."

"Please take the broth," she said gently.

"All right."

The broth was too hot. He had to hold it in the cup until it cooled enough to take it and then he just got it down without gagging.

"You're a fine woman," he said. "Don't pay any attention to me."

She looked at him with her well known, well loved face from *Spur* and *Town and Country*, only a little the worse for drink, only a little the worse for bed, but *Town and Country* never showed those good breasts and those useful thighs and those lightly small-of-back caressing hands, and as he looked and saw her well known pleasant smile, he felt death come again.

This time there was no rush. It was a puff, as of a wind that makes a candle flicker and the flame go tall.

"They can bring my net out later and hang it from the tree and build the fire up. I'm not going in the tent tonight. It's not worth moving. It's a clear night. There won't be any rain."

So this was how you died, in whispers that you did not hear. Well, there would be no more quarreling. He could promise that. The one experience that he had never had he was not going to spoil now. He probably would. You spoiled everything. But perhaps he wouldn't.

"You can't take dictation, can you?"

"I never learned," she told him.

"That's all right."

There wasn't time, of course, although it seemed as though it telescoped so that you might put it all into one paragraph if you could get it right.

There was a log house, chinked white with mortar, on a hill above the lake. There was a bell on a pole by the door to call the people to meals. Behind the house were fields and behind the fields was the timber. A line of lombardy poplars ran from the house to the dock. Other poplars ran along the point. A road went up to the hills along the edge of the timber and along that road he picked blackberries. Then that log house was burned down and all the guns that had been on deer foot racks above the open fire place were burned and afterwards their barrels, with the lead melted in the magazines, and the stocks burned away, lay out on the heap of ashes that were used to make lye for the big iron soap kettles, and you asked Grandfather if you could have them to play with, and he said, no. You see they were his guns still and he never bought any others. Nor did he hunt any more. The house was rebuilt in the same place out of lumber now and painted white and from its porch you saw the poplars and the lake beyond; but there were never any more guns. The barrels of the guns that had hung on the deer feet on the wall of the log house lay out there on the heap of ashes and no one ever touched them.

In the Black Forest, after the war, we rented a trout stream and there were two ways to walk to it. One was down the valley from Triberg and around the valley road in the shade of the trees that bordered the white road, and then up a side road that went up through the hills past many small farms, with the big Schwartzwald houses, until that road crossed the stream. That was where our fishing began. The other way was to climb steeply up to the edge of the woods and then go across the top of the hills through the pine woods, and then out to the edge of a meadow and down across this meadow to the bridge. There were birches along the stream and it was not big, but narrow, clear and fast, with pools where it had cut under the roots of the birches. At the Hotel in Triberg the proprietor had a fine season. It was very pleasant and we were all great friends. The next year came the inflation and the money he had made the year before was not enough to buy supplies to open the hotel and he hanged himself.

You could dictate that, but you could not dictate the Place Contrescarpe where the flower sellers dyed their flowers in the street and the dye ran over the paving where the autobus started and the old men and the women, always drunk on wine and bad marc; and the children with their noses running in the cold; the smell of dirty sweat and poverty and drunkenness at the Café des Amateurs and the whores at the Bal Musette they lived above. The Concierge who entertained the trooper of the Garde Republicaine in her loge, his horsehair plumed helmet on a chair. The locataire across the hall whose husband was a bicycle racer and her joy that morning at the Cremerie when she had opened L'Auto and seen where he placed third in Paris-Tours, his first big race. She had blushed and laughed and then gone upstairs crying with the yellow sporting paper in her hand. The husband of the woman who ran the Bal Musette drove a taxi and when he, Harry, had to take an early plane the husband knocked upon the door to wake him and they each drank a glass of white wine at the Zinc of the bar before they started. He knew his neighbors in that quarter then because they were all poor. Around that Place *there were two kinds; the drunkards and the sportifs. The drunkards killed their poverty that way; the sportifs took it out in exercise. They were the descendants of the Communards and it was no struggle for them to know their politics. They knew who had shot their fathers, their relatives, their brothers, and their friends when the Versailles troops came in and took the town after the Commune and executed anyone they could catch with calloused hands, or who wore a cap, or carried any other sign he was a working man. And in that poverty, and in that quarter across the street from Boucherie Chevaline and a wine co-operative he had written the start of all he was to do. There never was another part of Paris that he loved like that, the sprawling trees, the old white plastered houses painted brown below, the long green of the autobus in that round square, the purple flower dye upon the paving, the sudden drop down the hill of the rue Cardinal Lemoine to the River, and the other way the narrow crowded world of the rue Mouffetard. The street that ran up toward the Pantheon and the other that he always took with the bicycle, the only asphalted street in all that quarter, smooth under the tires, with the high narrow houses and the cheap tall hotel where Paul Verlaine had died. There were only two rooms in the apartment where they lived and he had a room on the top floor of that hotel that cost him sixty francs a month where he did his writing, and from it he could see the roofs and chimney pots and all the hills of Paris.*

From the apartment you could only see the wood and coal man's place. He sold wine too, bad wine. The golden horse's head outside the Boucherie Chevaline where the carcasses hung yellow gold and red in the open window, and the green painted co-operative where they bought their wine; good wine and cheap. The rest was plaster walls and the windows of the neighbors. The neighbors who, at night, when someone lay drunk in the street, moaning and groaning in that typical French ivresse *that you were propaganded to believe did not exist, would open their windows and then the murmur of talk.*

"Where is the policeman? When you don't want him the bugger is always there.

He's sleeping with some concierge. Get the Agent.*" Till someone threw a bucket of water from a window and the moaning stopped. "What's that? Water. Ah, that's intelligent." And the windows shutting. Marie, his femme de ménage, protesting against the eight hour day saying, "If a husband works until six he gets only a little drunk on the way home and does not waste too much. If he works only until five he is drunk every night and one has no money. It is the wife of the working man who suffers from this shortening of hours."*

"Wouldn't you like some more broth?" the woman asked him now.

"No thank you very much. It is awfully good."

"Try just a little."

"I would like a whiskey-soda."

"It's not good for you."

"No. It's bad for me. Cole Porter wrote the words and the music. This knowledge that you're going mad for me."

"You know I like you to drink."

"Oh yes. Only it's bad for me."

When she goes, he thought. I'll have all I want. Not all I want but all there is. Ayee he was tired. Too tired. He was going to sleep a little while. He lay still and death was not there. It must have gone around another street. It went in pairs, on bicycles, and moved absolutely silently on the pavements.

No, he had never written about Paris. Not the Paris that he cared about. But what about the rest that he had never written.

What about the ranch and the silvered gray of the sage brush, the quick, clear water in the irrigation ditches, and the heavy green of the alfalfa. The trail went up into the hills and the cattle in the summer were shy as deer. The bawling and the steady noise and slow moving mass raising a dust as you brought them down in the fall. And behind the mountains, the clear sharpness of the peak in the evening light and riding down along the trail in the moonlight, bright across the valley. Now he remembered coming down through the timber in the dark holding the horse's tail when you could not see and all the stories that he meant to write.

About the half-wit chore boy who was left at the ranch that time and told not to let anyone get any hay, and that old bastard from the Forks who had beaten the boy when he had worked for him stopping to get some feed. The boy refusing and the old man saying he would beat him again. The boy got the rifle from the kitchen and shot him when he tried to come into the barn and when they came back to the ranch he'd been dead a week, frozen in the corral, and the dogs had eaten a big part of him. But what was left you packed on a sled wrapped in a blanket and roped on and you got the boy to help you haul it, and the two of you took it out over the road on skis, and sixty miles down to town to turn the boy over. He having no idea he would be arrested. Thinking he had done his duty and that you were his friend and he would be rewarded. He'd helped to haul the old man in so everybody could know how bad the old man had been and how he'd tried to steal some feed that didn't belong to him, and when the sheriff put the handcuffs on the boy he couldn't believe it. Then he'd started to cry. That was one story he had saved to write. He knew at least twenty good stories from out there and he had never written one. Why?

"You tell them why," he said.

"Why what, dear?"

"Why nothing."

She didn't drink so much, now, since she had him. But if he lived he would never write about her, he knew that now. Nor about any of them. The rich were dull and they drank too much, or they played too much backgammon. They were dull and they were repetitious. He remembered poor Scott Fitzgerald and his romantic awe of them and how he had started a story once that began, "The very rich are different from you and me." And how someone had said to Scott, Yes they have more money. But that was not humorous to Scott. He thought they were a special glamorous race and when he found they weren't it wrecked him just as much as any other thing that wrecked him.

He had been contemptuous of those who wrecked. You did not have to like it because you understood it. He could beat anything, he thought, because no thing could hurt him if he did not care.

All right. Now he would not care for death. One thing he had always dreaded was the pain. He could stand pain as well as any man, until it went on too long, and wore him out, but here he had something that had hurt frightfully and just when he had felt it breaking him, the pain had stopped.

He remembered long ago when Williamson, the bombing officer, had been hit by a stick bomb someone in a German patrol had thrown as he was coming in through the wire that night and, screaming, had begged everyone to kill him. He was a fat man, very brave, and a good officer, although addicted to fantastic shows. But that night he was caught in the wire, with a flare lighting him up and his bowels spilled out into the wire, so when they brought him in, alive, they had to cut him loose. Shoot me, Harry. For Christ's sake shoot me. They had had an argument one time about our Lord never sending you anything you could not bear and someone's theory had been that meant that at a certain time the pain passed you out automatically. But he had always remembered Williamson that night. Nothing passed out Williamson until he gave him all his morphine tablets that he had always saved to use himself and then they did not work right away.

Still this now, that he had, was very easy; and if it was no worse as it went on there was nothing to worry about. Except that he would rather be in better company.

He thought a little about the company that he would like to have.

No, he thought, when everything you do, you do too long, and do too late, you can't expect to find the people still there. The people all are gone. The party's over and you are with your hostess now.

I'm getting as bored with dying as with everything else, he thought.

"It's a bore," he said out loud.

"What is, my dear?"

"Anything you do too bloody long."

He looked at her face between him and the fire. She was leaning back in the chair and the firelight shone on her pleasantly lined face and he could see that she was sleepy. He heard the hyena make a noise just outside the range of the fire.

"I've been writing," he said. "But I got tired."

"Do you think you will be able to sleep?"

"Pretty sure. Why don't you turn in?"

"I like to sit here with you."

"Do you feel anything strange?" he asked her.

"No. Just a little sleepy."

"I do," he said.

He had just felt death come by again.

"You know the only thing I've never lost is curiosity," he said to her.

"You've never lost anything. You're the most complete man I've ever known."

"Christ," he said. "How little a woman knows. What is that? Your intuition?"

Because, just then, death had come and rested its head on the foot of the cot and he could smell its breath.

"Never believe any of that about a scythe and a skull," he told her. "It can be two bicycle policemen as easily, or be a bird. Or it can have a wide snout like a hyena."

It had moved up on him now, but it had no shape any more. It simply occupied space.

"Tell it to go away."

It did not go away but moved a little closer.

"You've got a hell of a breath," he told it. "You stinking bastard."

It moved up closer to him still and now he could not speak to it, and when it saw he could not speak it came a little closer, and now he tried to send it away without speaking, but it moved in on him so its weight was all upon his chest, and while it crouched there and he could not move, or speak, he heard the woman say, "Bwana is asleep now. Take the cot up very gently and carry it into the tent."

He could not speak to tell her to make it go away and it crouched now, heavier, so he could not breathe. And then, while they lifted the cot, suddenly it was all right and the weight went from his chest.

It was morning and had been morning for some time and he heard the plane. It showed very tiny and then made a wide circle and the boys ran out and lit the fires, using kerosene, and piled on grass so there were two big smudges at each end of the level place and the morning breeze blew them toward the camp and the plane circled twice more, low this time, and then glided down and levelled off and landed smoothly and, coming walking toward him, was old Compton in slacks, a tweed jacket and a brown felt hat.

"What's the matter, old cock?" Compton said.

"Bad leg," he told him. "Will you have some breakfast?"

"Thanks. I'll just have some tea. It's the Puss Moth you know. I won't be able to take the Memsahib. There's only room for one. Your lorry is on the way."

Helen had taken Compton aside and was speaking to him. Compton came back more cheery than ever.

"We'll get you right in," he said. "I'll be back for the Mem. Now I'm afraid I'll have to stop at Arusha to refuel. We'd better get going."

"What about the tea?"

"I don't really care about it you know."

The boys had picked up the cot and carried it around the green tents and down along the rock and out onto the plain and along past the smudges that were burning brightly now, the grass all consumed, and the wind fanning the fire, to the little plane. It was difficult getting him in, but once in he lay back in the leather seat, and the leg was stuck straight out to one side of the seat where Compton sat. Compton started the motor and got in. He waved to Helen and to the boys and, as the clatter moved into the old familiar roar, they swung around with Compie watching for warthog holes and roared, bumping, along the stretch between the fires and with the last bump rose and he saw them all standing below, waving, and the camp beside the hill, flattening now, and the plain spreading, clumps of trees, and the bush flattening, while the game trails ran now smoothly to the dry waterholes, and there was a new water that he had never known of. The zebra, small rounded backs now, and the wildebeeste, big headed dots seeming to climb as they moved in long fingers across the plain, now scattering as the shadow came toward them, they were tiny now, and the movement had no gallop, and the plain as far as you could see, gray-yellow now and ahead old Compie's tweed back and the brown felt hat. Then they were over the first hills and the wildebeeste were trailing up them, and then they were over mountains with sudden depths of green-rising forest and the solid bamboo slopes, and then the heavy forest again, sculptured into peaks and hollows until they crossed, and hills sloped down and then another plain, hot now, and purple brown, bumpy, with heat and Compie looking back to see how he was riding. Then there were other mountains dark ahead. And then instead of going on to Arusha they turned left, he evidently figured that they had the gas, and looking down he saw a pink sifting cloud, moving over the ground, and in the air, like the first snow in a blizzard, that comes from nowhere, and he knew the locusts were coming up from the South.

Then they began to climb and they were going to the East it seemed, and then it darkened and they were in a storm, the rain so thick it seemed like flying through a waterfall, and then they were out and Compie turned his head and grinned and pointed and there, ahead, all he could see, as wide as all the world, great, high, and unbelievably white in the sun, was the square top of Kilimanjaro. And then he knew that there was where he was going.

Just then the hyena stopped whimpering in the night and started to make a strange, human, almost crying sound. The woman heard it and stirred uneasily. She did not wake. In her dream she was at the house on Long Island and it was the night before her daughter's début. Somehow her father was there and he had been very rude. Then the noise the hyena made was so loud she woke and for a moment she did not know where she was and she was very afraid. Then she took the flashlight and shone it on the other cot that they had carried in after Harry had gone to sleep. She could see his bulk under the mosquito bar but somehow he had gotten his leg out and it hung down alongside the cot. The dressings had all come down and she could not look at it.

"Molo," she called. "Molo! Molo!"

Then she said, "Harry, Harry!" Then her voice rising, "Harry! Please, Oh Harry!"

There was no answer and she could not hear him breathing.

Outside the tent the hyena made the same strange noise that had awakened her. But she did not hear him for the beating of her heart.

THOMAS WOLFE

[1900–1938]

The Lost Boy

(First published in *Redbook Magazine*,
November, 1937; first book publication in 1941.)

THE LIGHT CAME and went, the booming strokes of three o'clock beat out across the town in thronging bronze, light winds of April blew the fountain out in rainbow sheets, until the plume returned and pulsed, as Robert turned into the Square. He was a child dark-eyed and grave, birthmarked upon his neck—a berry of warm brown—and with a gentle face, perhaps too quiet and listening for his years. The scuffed boy's shoes, the thick-ribbed stockings gartered at the knees, the short knee pants cut straight with three small useless buttons at the side, the sailor blouse, the old cap battered out of shape, perched sideways up on top the raven head—these friendly shabby garments, shaped by Robert, uttered him. He turned and passed along the north side of the Square, and in that moment felt the union of Forever and Now.

Light came and went and came again; the great plume of the fountain pulsed, and the winds of April sheeted it across the Square in rainbow gossamer of spray. The street-cars ground into the Square from every portion of the town's small compass and halted briefly like wound toys in their old quarter-hourly formula of assembled Eight. The courthouse bell boomed out its solemn warning of immediate Three, and everything was just the same as it had always been.

He saw with quiet eyes that haggis of vexed shapes, that hodge-podge of ill-sorted masonries, and he did not feel lost. For "Here," thought Robert, "here's the Square as it has always been—and Papa's shop, the fire department and the city hall, the fountain pulsing with its plume, the drug-store on the corner there, the row of old brick buildings on this side, the people passing and the cars that come and go, the light that comes and changes and that always will come back again, and everything that comes and goes and changes in the Square, and yet will be the same—here," Robert thought, "here is the Square that never changes; here is Robert almost twelve—and here is Time."

For so it seemed to him: small center of his little universe, itself the accidental masonry of twenty years, the chance agglomerate of time and of disrupted strivings, it was for him earth's pivot and the granite core of changelessness, the eternal Place where all things came and passed, the Place that would abide forever and would never change.

The Square walked past him then with steady steps—plume, pulse, and fountain, and the sheeting spray, the open arches of the fire department doors, the wooden stomp of the great hoofs, the casual whiskings of the dry coarse tails. He passed the firetrap of a wiener stand; and the Singer shop, the steel-bright smartness of the new machines, with their swift evocations of the house, the whir, the treadle, and the mounting hum—the vague monotony of women's work. He passed the music-store, the coffined splendor of piano shapes, the deep-toned richness, and the smell of proud dark wood, the stale yet pleasant memory of parlors.

He passed the grocery store then, the gaunt gray horse, the old head leaning to its hitching block; within, the pickle-barrels, the fans, the sultry coffee and the cloven cheese, the musty compost of cool plenty, the delicious All-Smell, and the buttered unction of the grocer with his strawcuffed sleeves.

He was going past the hardware store now. He always had to stop by places that had shining perfect things in them, and windows full of geometric tools, of hammers, saws, and planing-boards, and strong new rakes and hoes with unworn handles of white perfect wood, stamped hard and vivid with the maker's seal. Ah, how he loved such things as these, strong perfect shapes and pungent smells, the great integrities of use and need, the certitude of this unchanging pattern, set to the grand assurance of the everlasting Square. He turned a corner, and he *was* caught, held. A waft of air, warm, chocolate-laden, filled his nostrils. He tried to pass the white front of the little eight-foot shop; he paused, struggling with conscience; he could not go on. It was the little candy-shop run by old Crocker and his wife. And Robert could not pass.

"Old stingy Crockers!" he thought scornfully. "I'll not go there again. They're so stingy they stop the clocks at night. But—" The maddening fragrance of rich cooking chocolate touched him once again. "I'll just look in the window and see what they've got." He paused a moment, looking with his dark and quiet eyes into the window of the candy shop. His dark eyes rested for a moment on a tray of chocolate drops. Unconsciously he licked his lips. Put one of them upon your tongue and it just melted there like honey. And then the trays full of rich home-made fudge. He looked longingly at the deep body of the chocolate fudge, reflectively at the maple walnut, more critically, yet with longing, at the mints, the nougatines, and all the other tempters.

"Old stingy Crockers!" Robert muttered once again, and turned to go. "I wouldn't go in *there* again."

And yet—he did not go away. "Old stingy Crockers," it was true; still, they did make the best candy in town, the best, in fact, that he had ever tasted.

He looked through the window back into the little shop and saw Mrs. Crocker there. A customer had made a purchase, and as Robert looked, he saw Mrs. Crocker, with her little wrenny face, lean over and peer primly at the scales. She had a piece of fudge in her clean bony fingers—and now she broke it, primly, in her little bony hands. She dropped a morsel down into the scales. They weighted down alarmingly, and her thin lips tightened. She snatched a piece of fudge out of the scales and broke it carefully once again. This time the scale wavered, went down very slowly, and came back again. Mrs. Crocker carefully put the reclaimed piece of fudge back in the tray, put the remainder in a paper bag, folded it and gave it to the customer, counted the money carefully, and doled it out into the till.

Robert stood there, looking scornfully. "Old stingy Crocker—afraid that she might give a crumb away."

He grunted, and again he turned to go. But now Mr. Crocker came out from the little partitioned place behind, bearing a tray of fresh-made candy in his skinny hands. Old man Crocker rocked along the counter to the front and put it down. He was a cripple. One leg was inches shorter than the other, and on this leg there was an enormous thick-soled boot, with a kind of wooden rocker-like arrangement, six inches high at least, to make up for the deficiency of his game right leg. And on this wooden cradle Mr. Crocker rocked along. He was a little pinched and skinny figure of a man with bony hands and meager features, and when he walked, he really rocked along, with a kind of prim and apprehensive little smile, as if he was afraid he was going to lose something.

"Old stingy Crocker," muttered Robert. "Humph! He wouldn't give you *anything.*"

And yet he did not go away. He hung there curiously, peering through the window, with his dark and gentle face now focused and intent, flattening his nose against the glass. Unconsciously he scratched the thick-ribbed fabric of one stockinged leg with the scuffed toe of his old shoe. The fresh warm odor of the new-made fudge had reached him. It was delicious. It was a little maddening. Half-consciously, he began to fumble in one trouser pocket and pulled out his purse, a shabby worn old black one with a twisted clasp. He opened it and prowled about inside.

What he found was not inspiring: a nickel and two pennies and—he had forgotten them—the stamps. He took the stamps out and unfolded them. There were five twos, eight ones, all that remained of the dollar and sixty cents' worth which Reed, the pharmacist, had given him for running errands a week or two before.

"Old Crocker," Robert thought, looked somberly at the grotesque little form and—"Well—" indefinitely—"He's had all the rest of them. He might as well take these."

So, soothing conscience with this Sop of scorn, he went into the shop, and pointing with a slightly grimy finger at the fresh-made tray of chocolate fudge, he said: "I'll take fifteen cents' worth of this, Mr. Crocker."

He paused a moment, fighting with embarrassment; then he lifted his dark face and said quietly: "And please, I'll have to give you stamps again."

Mr. Crocker made no answer. He pressed his tips together. Then he got the candy scoop, slid open the door of the glass case, put fudge into the scoop, and rocking to the scales, began to weigh the candy out. Robert watched him as he peered and squinted, watched him purse his lips together, saw him take a piece of fudge and break it into two parts. And then old Crocker broke two parts in two. He weighed, he squinted, he hovered, until it seemed to Robert that by calling *Mrs.* Crocker stingy he had been guilty of a rank injustice. But finally the scales hung there, quivering apprehensively, upon the very hairline of nervous balance, as if even the scales were afraid that one more move from old man Crocker and they would be undone.

Mr. Crocker took the candy, dumped it into a paper bag, and rocking back along the counter toward the boy, he said: "Where are the stamps?" Robert gave them to him. Mr. Crocker relinquished his claw-like hold on the bag and set it down upon the counter. Robert took the bag and then remembered. "Mr. Crocker,"–again he felt the old embarrassment that was almost like strong pain,–"I gave you too much," Robert said. "There were eighteen cents in stamps. You–you can just give me three ones back."

Mr. Crocker did not answer for a moment. He was busy unfolding the stamps and flattening them out on top of the glass counter. When he had done so, he peered at them sharply, for a moment, thrusting his scrawny neck forward and running his eye up and down, as a bookkeeper who tots up rows of figures.

Then he said tartly: "I don't like this kind of business. I'm not a post office. The next time you come in here and want anything, you'll have to have the money for it."

Hot anger rose in Robert's throat. His olive face suffused with angry color. His tarry eyes got black and bright. For a moment he was on the verge of saying: "Then why did you take my other stamps? Why do you tell me now, when you have taken all the stamps I had, that you don't want them?"

But he was a quiet, gentle, gravely thoughtful boy, and he had been taught how to respect his elders. So he just stood there looking with his tar-black eyes. Old Man Crocker took the stamps up in his thin, parched fingers, and turning, rocked away down to the till.

He took the twos and laid them in one rounded scallop, then took the ones and folded them and put them in the one next to it. Then he closed the till and started to rock off, down toward the other end. Robert kept looking at him, but Mr. Crocker did not look at Robert. Instead, he began to take some cardboard shapes and fold them into boxes.

In a moment Robert said: "Mr. Crocker, will you give me the three ones, please?"

Mr. Crocker did not answer. But Mrs. Crocker, also folding boxes with her parsley hands, muttered tartly: "Hm! *I'd* give him nothing!"

Mr. Crocker looked at Robert: "What are you waiting for?"

"Will you give me the three ones, please?" Robert said.

"I'll give you nothing," Mr. Crocker said. "Now you get out of here! And don't you come here with any more of those stamps."

"I should like to know where he gets them, that's what *I* should like to know," said Mrs. Crocker.

"You get out of here," said Mr. Crocker. "And don't you come back here with any stamps. . . . Where did you get those stamps?" he said.

"That's just what *I've* been thinking," Mrs. Crocker said.

"You've been coming in here for the last two weeks with stamps," said Mr. Crocker. "I don't like the look of it. Where did you get those stamps?" he said.

"That's what *I've* been thinking all along," said Mrs. Crocker.

Robert had got white underneath his olive skin. His eyes had lost their luster. They looked like dull, stunned balls of tar. "From Mr. Reed," he said. "I got the stamps from Mr. Reed." He burst out desperately: "Mr. Crocker, Mr. Reed will tell you how I got the stamps. I did some work for Mr. Reed; he gave me those stamps two weeks ago."

"Mr. *Reed*," said Mrs. Crocker acidly. "I call it mighty funny."

"Mr. Crocker," Robert said, "if you'll just let me have the three ones—"

"You get out of here, boy!" cried Mr. Crocker. "Now don't you come in here again! There's something funny about this whole business! If you can't pay as other people do, then I don't want your trade."

"Mr. Crocker," Robert said again, and underneath the olive skin his face was gray, "if you'll just let me have those three—"

"You get out of here," Mr. Crocker cried, and began to rock forward toward the boy. "If you don't get out—"

"*I'd* call a policeman, that's what I'd do," Mrs. Crocker said.

Mr. Crocker came rocking up to Robert, took the boy and pushed him with his bony little hands. Robert felt sick and gray down to the hollow pit of his stomach.

"You've got to give me those three ones," he said.

"You get out of here!" shrilled Mr. Crocker. He seized the screen door, pulled it open, and pushed Robert out. "Don't you come back in here," he said, pausing for a moment, working thinly at the lips. Then he turned and rocked back in the shop again. Robert stood there on the pavement. And light came and went and came again.

The boy stood there for a moment, and a wagon rattled past. There were some people passing by, but Robert did not notice them. He stood there blindly, in the watches of the sun, but something had gone out of the day.

He felt the soul-sickening guilt that all the children, all the good men of the earth, have felt since time began. And even anger had been drowned out, in the swelling tide of guilt. "There is the square," thought Robert as before. "This is Now. There is my father's shop. And all of it is as it has always been—save I."

And the Square reeled drunkenly around him, light went in blind gray motes before his eyes, the fountain sheeted out to rainbow iridescence and returned to its proud pulsing plume again. But all the brightness had gone out of day.

The scuffed boots of the lost boy moved and stumbled blindly over. The numb feet crossed the pavement—reached the sidewalk, crossed the plotted central Square—the grass plots, the flower-beds, so soon with red and packed geraniums.

"I want to be alone," thought Robert, "where I can not go near him. Oh, God, I hope he never hears, that no one ever tells him—"

The plume blew out; the iridescent sheet of spray blew over him. He passed through, found the other side and crossed the street. "Oh, God, if Papa ever hears," thought Robert, as his numb feet started up the steps into his father's shop.

He found and felt the steps—the thickness of old lumber twenty feet in length. He saw it all: the iron columns on his father's porch, painted with the dull anomalous black-green that all such columns in this land and weather come to; two angels, fly-specked, and the waiting stones. Beyond and all around, in the stonecutter's shop, cold shapes of white and marble, rounded stone, the limestone base, the languid angel with strong marble hands of love.

He went on down the aisle; the white shapes stood around him. He went on back into the workroom. This he knew—the little cast-iron stove in the left-hand corner, the high, dirty window, looking down across the market square, the rude old shelves, upon the shelves the chisels and a layer of stone dust; an emery wheel with pump tread, and two trestles of coarse wood upon which rested gravestones. At one trestle was a man, at work.

The boy looked numbly, saw the name was *Creasman*: the carved analysis of John, the symmetry of S, the fine finality of *Creasman—November, Nineteen-Three*.

The man looked up and then returned to work. He was a man of fifty-three, immensely long and tall and gaunt. He wore good dark clothes, save he had no coat. He worked in shirt-sleeves with his vest on, a strong watch-chain stretching across his vest; wing collar and black tie, Adam's apple, bony forehead, bony nose, light eyes, gray-green, undeep and cold, and somehow lonely-looking, a striped apron going up around his shoulders, and starched cuffs. And in one hand a tremendous rounded wooden mallet like a butcher's bole; and in his other hand, implacable and cold, the chisel.

"How are you, son?"

He did not look up as he spoke. He spoke quietly, absently. He worked upon the chisel and the wooden mallet as delicately as a jeweler might work upon a watch, except that in the man and the wooden mallet there was power, too.

"What is it, son?" he said.

He moved around the table from the head, and started up on it again.

"Papa, I never stole the stamps," said Robert.

The man put down the mallet, laid the chisel down. He came around the trestle.

"What?" he said. And Robert winked his tar-black eyes; they brightened; the hot tears shot out. "I never stole the stamps," he said.

"Hey? What is this?" the man said. "What stamps?"

"That Mr. Reed gave to me, when the other boy was sick and I worked there for three days . . . . And old man Crocker," Robert said, "he took all the stamps. And I told him Mr. Reed had given them to me. And now he owes me three ones—and old man Crocker says—he says—I must have taken them."

"The stamps that Reed gave to you—hey?" the stonecutter said. "The stamps you had—" He wet his great thumb briefly on his lips, strode from his workshop out into the storeroom aisle.

The man came back, cleared his throat, and as he passed the old gray board-partition of his office, he cleared his throat and wet his thumb, and said: "I tell you, now—"

Then he turned and strode up toward the front again and cleared his throat and said: "I tell you, now—" And coming back, along the aisle between the rows of marshaled gravestones, he muttered underneath his breath: "By God, now—"

He took Robert by the hand. They went out flying down along the aisle by all the gravestones, the fly-specked angels waiting there, the wooden steps, across the cobbles and the central plot—across the whole thing, but they did not notice it.

And the fountain pulsed, the plume blew out in sheeted spray and swept across them, and an old gray horse, with a peaceful look about its torn lips, swucked up the cool, the flowing mountain water from the trough as Robert and his father went across the Square.

They went across the Square through the sheeted iridescence of the spray and to the other street and to the candy-shop. The man was dressed in his striped apron still; he was still holding Robert by the hand. He opened the screen door and stepped inside. "Give him the stamps," he said.

Mr. Crocker came rocking forward behind the counter, with a prim and careful look that now was somewhat like a smile. "It was just—" he said.

"Give him the stamps," the man said, and threw some coins down on the counter.

Mr. Crocker rocked away and got the stamps. "I just didn't know—" he said.

The stonecutter took the stamps and gave them to the boy. And Mr. Crocker took the coins.

"It was just that—" Mr. Crocker said, and smiled.

The man in the apron cleared his throat: "You never were a father," the man said. "You never knew the feeling of a child. And that is why you acted as you did. But a judgment is upon you. God has cursed you. He has afflicted you. He has made you lame and childless—and miserable as you are, you will go lame and childless to your grave—and be forgotten!"

And Crocker's wife kept kneading her bony little hands and said imploringly: "Oh, no—oh, don't say that! Please don't say that!"

The stonecutter, the breath still hoarse in him, left the store. Light came again into the day.

"Well, son," he said, and laid his hand on the boy's back. "Now don't you mind."

They walked across the Square, the sheeted spray of iridescent light swept out on them; a horse swizzled at the water-trough.

"Well, son," the gaunt man said again, "now don't you mind."

And he trod his own steps then with his great stride and went back again into his shop.

The lost boy stood upon the Square, close by the porch of his father's shop: light came again into the Square. A car curved in, upon the billboard of the car-end was a poster and some words: "*St. Louis*" and "*Excursion*" and "*The Fair.*"

And light came and went into the Square, and Robert stood there thinking quietly: "Here is the Square that never changes; here is Time."

And light came and went and came again into the Square—but now not quite the same as it had done before. He saw that pattern of familiar shapes, and knew that they were just the same as they had always been. But something had gone out of the day, and something had come in again: out of the vision of those quiet eyes some brightness had been lost; into their vision some deeper color come. He could not say, he did not know through what transforming shadows life had passed within that quarter-hour. He only knew that something had been gained forever—something lost.

As we went down through Indiana—you were too young, child, to remember it, but I always think of all of you, the way you looked that morning, when we went down through Indiana, going to the Fair. All of the apple trees were coming out, and it was April; all of the trees were coming out; it was the beginning of the spring in Indiana, and everything was getting green.

Of course we don't have farms at home like those in Indiana. The children had never seen such farms as those, and I reckon, kid-like, had to take it in.

So all of them kept running up and down the aisle—well, no, except for you and *Robert–you* were too young; you were just three; I kept you with me. As for Robert: well, I'm going to tell you about that. But the rest of them kept running up and down the aisle and from one window to another. They kept calling out and hollering to each other every time they saw something new. They kept trying to look out on all sides in every way at once, as if they wished they had eyes in the back of their heads. It was the first time any of them had been in Indiana, and I reckon, that, kid-like, it all seemed strange and new.

And so it seemed they couldn't get enough. It seemed they never could be still.

You see, they were excited about going to St. Louis and so curious over everything they saw. They couldn't help it, and they wanted to see everything. But "I'll vow," I said, "if you children don't sit down and rest, you'll be worn to a frazzle before we ever get to see St. Louis and the Fair!"

Except for Robert! He—no sir, not him! Now, boy, I want to tell you—I've raised the lot of you, and if I do say so, there wasn't a numbskull in the lot. But *Robert*! Well, you've all grown up now, all of you have gone away, and none of you are children any more. . . . And of course, I hope that, as the fellow says, you have reached the dignity of man's estate. . . . I suppose you have the judgment of a grown man. . . . But Robert! *Robert* had it, even then!

Oh, even as a child, you know—at a time I was almost afraid to trust the rest of you out of my sight—I could depend on Robert. I could send him anywhere, and I'd always know he'd get back safe, and do exactly what I told him to!

Why, I didn't even have to tell him—you could send that child to market and tell him what you wanted, and he'd come home with *twice* as much as you could get yourself for the same money.

Now you know, I've always been considered a good trader, but *Robert*! Why, it got so finally that your papa said to me: "You'd be better off if you just tell him what you want and leave the rest to him. For," your papa says, "damned if I don't believe he's a better trader than you are. . . . He gets more for the money than anyone I ever saw."

Well, I had to admit it, you know. . . . I had to own up then. . . . Robert, even as a child, was a far better trader than I was. . . . Why, yes, they told it on him all over town, you know. . . . They said all of the market men, all of the farmers, would begin to laugh when they saw him coming. They'd say, "Look out! Here's Robert! Here's one trader you're not going to fool!"

And they were right! . . . *That* child! . . . I'd say: "Robert, suppose you run uptown and see if they've got anything good to *eat* today. Suppose you take this dollar and just see what you can do with it."

Well, sir, that was all that was needed. The minute that you told that child that you depended on his judgment, he'd have gone to the ends of the earth for you—and let me tell you something, he wouldn't *miss*, either!

His eyes would get black as coals—oh, the way that child would look at you, the intelligence and sense in his expression! He'd say, "Yes, *ma'am*! Now don't you worry, Mamma, you leave it all to me—and I'll do *good*!" said Robert.

And he'd be off like a streak of lightning and oh, Lord! As your father said to me, "I've been living in this town for almost thirty years," he said, "and I thought I knew everything there was to know about it—but that child," your papa says, "he knows places that I never heard of!" Oh, he'd go right down there to that place below your papa's shop where the draymen used to park their wagons—or he'd go down there to those old lots on Concord Street where the farmers used to keep their wagons. And child that he was, he'd go right in among them, *sir–Robert* would!—go right in and barter with them like a grown man!

And he'd come home with things he'd bought that would make your eyes stick out. . . . Here he comes one time with another boy, dragging a great bushel basket full of ripe termaters between them. "Why, Robert," I says, "how on earth are we ever going to use them? Why, they'll go bad on us before we're half-way through them." "Well, Mamma," he says, "I know,"—oh, just as solemn as a judge—"but they were the last the man had," he says, "and he wanted to go home, and so I got them for ten cents," he says. "I thought it was a shame to let 'em go, and I figgered what we couldn't eat—why," says Robert, "you could *put up*!" Well, the way he said it, so earnest and so serious, I had to laugh. "But I'll vow," I said, "if you don't beat all!" . . . But that was *Robert* the way he was in *those* days! As everyone said, boy that he was, he had the sense and judgment of a grown man. . . . Child, child, I've seen you all grow up, and all of you were bright enough, but for all-round intelligence, judgment, and general ability, Robert surpassed the whole crowd. . . . I've never seen his equal, and everyone who knew him as a child will say the same.

So that's what I tell them now, when they ask me about all of you. I have to tell the truth. I always said that you were smart enough—but when they come around and brag to me about you, and I reckon how you have got on and have a kind of name—I don't let on to them, I never say a word. Why, yes! Why, here, you know—oh, 'long about a month ago, this feller comes. He said he came from New Jersey, or somewhere up in that part of the country—and he began to ask me all sorts of questions, what you were like when you were a boy and all such stuff as that.

I just pretended to study it all over; then I said, "Well, yes," real seriouslike, you know. "Well, yes—I reckon I ought to know a little something about him: he was my child, just the same as all the others were; I brought him up just the the way I brought up all the others. And," I says—oh, just as solemn as you please, "he wasn't a *bad* sort of a boy. Why," I says, "up to the time that he was twelve years old he was just about the same as any other boy—a good average normal sort of fellow."

"Oh," he says. "But didn't you notice something? Didn't you notice how brilliant he was? He must have been more brilliant than the rest!"

"Well, now," I says, and pretended to study that all over, too. "Now let me see . . . Yes," I says—I just looked him in the eye, as solemn as you please. "I guess he was a fairly bright sort of a boy. I never had no complaints to make of him on that score. He was bright enough," I says. "The only trouble with him was that he was lazy."

"Lazy!" he says—oh, you should have seen the look upon his face, you know—he jumped like someone had stuck a pin in him. "Lazy!" he says, "Why, you don't mean to tell me—"

"Yes," I says, "I was telling him the same thing myself the last time that I saw him. I told him it was a mighty lucky thing for him that he had the gift of gab. Of course, he went off to college and read a lot of books, and I reckon that's where he got this flow of language they say he has. . . . But as I said to him, 'Now look a-here,' I said, 'if you can earn your living doing a light easy class of work like this you do,' I says, 'you're mighty lucky, because none of the rest of your people had any such luck as that. They had to work hard for a living.'"

Oh, I told him, you know. I made no bones about it. And I tell you what—I wish you could have seen his face. It was a study.

"Well," he says, at last, "you've got to admit this, haven't you—he was the brightest boy you had, now wasn't he?"

I just looked at him a moment. I had to tell the truth. I couldn't fool him any longer. "No," I says. "He was a good bright boy—I have no complaint to make about him on that score; but the brightest boy I had, the one that surpassed all the rest of them in sense, and in understanding, and in judgment—the best boy that I had, the smartest boy I ever saw, was—well, it wasn't him," I said. "It was another one."

He looked at me a moment; then he said: "Which boy was that?"

Well, I just looked at him, and smiled. I shook my head. I wouldn't tell him. "I never brag about my own," I said. "You'll have to find out for yourself."

But—I'll have to tell *you*: the best one of the whole lot was—*Robert*!

. . . And when I think of Robert as he was along about that time, I always see him sitting there, so grave and earnest-like, with his nose pressed to the window, as we went down through Indiana in the morning, to the Fair.

So Robert sat beside this gentleman and looked out the window. I never knew the man—I never asked his name—but I tell you what! He was certainly a fine-looking, well-dressed, good substantial sort of man, and I could see that he had taken a great liking to Robert, and Robert sat there looking out, and then turned to this gentleman, as grave and earnest as a grown-up man, and says: "What kind of crops grow here, sir?" Well, this gentleman threw his head back and just ha-ha-ed. "Well, I'll see if I can tell you," says this gentleman, and then, you know, he talked to him, and Robert took it all in, as solemn as you please, and asked this gentleman every sort of question—what the trees were, what was growing there, how big the farms were—all sorts of questions, which this gentleman would answer, until I said: "I'll vow, Robert! You'll bother the very life out of this gentleman "

The gentleman threw his head back and laughed right out. "Now you leave that boy alone. He's all right," he said. "He doesn't bother me a bit, and if I know the answers to his questions, I will answer him. And if I don't know, why, then, I'll tell him so. But he's *all right*," he said, and put his arm around Roberts's shoulders. "You leave him alone. He doesn't bother me a bit."

And I can still remember how he looked, that morning, with his black eyes, his black hair, and with the birthmark on his neck—so grave, so serious, so earnest-like—as he looked out the windows at the apple trees, the farms, the barns, the houses, and the orchards, taking it all in because it was, I reckon, strange and new to him.

It was so long ago, but when I think of it, it all comes back, as if it happened yesterday. And all of you have grown up and gone away, and nothing is the same as it was then. But all of you were there with me that morning, and I guess I should remember how the others looked, but every time I think of it, I still see Robert just the way he was, the way he looked that morning when we went down through Indiana, by the river, to the Fair.

Can you remember how Robert used to look? . . . I mean the birthmark, the black eyes, the olive skin—the birthmark always showed because of those open sailor blouses kids used to wear. . . . But I guess you must have been too young. . . . I was looking at that old photograph the other day—that picture showing all of us before the house in Orchard Street? . . . *You* weren't there. . . . *You* hadn't arrived. . . . You remember how mad you used to get when we used to tell you that you were only a dish-rag hanging out in Heaven, when something happened?

I was looking at that old picture just the other day. There we were. . . . And my God, what is it all about? . . . I mean, when you see the way you were—Mary and Dick and Robert, Bill and all of us—and then—look at us now! Do you ever get to feeling funny? You know what I mean—do you ever get to feeling *queer*?—when you try to figure these things out. . . . You've been to college, and you ought to know the answer. . . . And I wish you'd tell me if you know. . . .

My Lord, when I think sometimes of the way I used to be—the dreams I used to have. . . . Taking singing lessons from Aunt Nell because I felt that some day I was going to have a great career in opera. . . . Can you beat it now? . . . Can you imagine it? . . . *Me*! In grand opera! . . . Now I want to ask you. . . . I'd like to know. . . .

My Lord! When I go uptown and look at all these funny-looking little boys and girls hanging around the drug-store—do you suppose any of them have ambitions the way we did? . . . Do you suppose any of these funny-looking little girls are thinking about a big career in opera? . . . Didn't you ever see that picture of us? It was made before the old house down on Orchard Street, with Papa standing there in his swallow-tail, and Mamma there beside him—and Robert and Dick and Jim, and Mary, Bill, and me, with our feet up on our bicycles.

Well, there I was, and my poor old skinny legs and long white dress, and two pigtails hanging down my back. And all the funny-looking clothes we wore, with the doo-lolly business on them. . . . But I guess you can't remember. You weren't born.

But—well, we were a right nice-looking set of people, if I do say so. And there was *86* the way it used to be, with the front porch, the grape-vines, and the flower-beds before the house. And Miss Martha standing there by Papa with a watch-charm pinned to her waist. . . . I shouldn't laugh, but Miss Martha. . . . Well, Mamma was a pretty woman then—and Papa in his swallow-tail was a good-looking man. Do you remember how he used to get dressed up on Sunday? And how grand he thought he was? And how wonderful that dinky little shop on the Square looked to us! . . . Can you beat it, now? . . . Why, we thought that Papa was the biggest man in town and—oh, you can't tell me! You can't tell me! He had his faults, but Papa was a wonderful man. You know he was!

And there was Jim and Dick and Robert, Mary, Bill, and me lined up there before the house with one foot on our bicycles. . . . And I got to thinking back about it all. It all came back.

Do you remember anything about St. Louis? You were only three or four years old then, but you must remember something. . . . Do you remember how you used to bawl when I would scrub you? How you'd bawl for Robert? . . . Poor kid, you used to yell for Robert every time I'd get you in the tub. He was a sweet kid, and he was crazy about you: he almost brought you up.

That year Robert was working at the Inside Inn out on the Fair Grounds . . . Do you remember the old Inside Inn? That big old wooden thing inside the Fair? . . . And how I used to take you there to wait for Robert when he got through working? . . . And Billy Pelham at the news-stand, how he used to give you a stick of chewing-gum?

They were all crazy about Robert. . . . Everybody liked him. . . . And how proud Robert was of you! . . . Don't you remember how he used to show you off? . . . How he used to take you around and make you talk to Billy Pelham? . . . And Mr. Curtis at the desk? . . . And how Robert would try to make you talk and get you to say, "Robert"? And you couldn't pronounce the "*r*"—and you'd say "*Wobbut.*" Have you forgotten that? . . . You shouldn't forget *that,* because . . . you were a *cute* kid, then . . . Ho-ho-ho-ho-ho. . . . I don't know where it's gone to, but you were a big hit in those days. . . .

And I was thinking of it all the other day: how we used to go and meet Robert there and how he'd take us to the Midway. . . . Do you remember the Midway? The Snake-Eater and the Living Skeleton, the Fat Woman and the Shoot the Chute, the Scenic Railway and the Ferris Wheel? . . . How you bawled the night we took you up on the Ferris Wheel! You yelled your head off. . . . I tried to laugh it off, but I tell you, I was scared myself . . . And how Robert laughed at us and told us there was no danger. . . . My Lord, poor little Robert! He was only twelve years old at the time, but he seemed so grown-up to us. I was two years older, but I thought he knew it all.

It was always that way with him. . . . Looking back now, it sometimes seems that it was Robert who brought us up. He was always looking after us, telling us what to do, bringing us something—some ice-cream or some candy, something he had bought out of the poor little money he'd got at the Inn. . . .

Then I got to thinking of the afternoon we sneaked away from home. . . . Mamma had gone out somewhere. And Robert and I got on the street-car and came downtown. . . . And my Lord, in those days, that was what we called a *trip.* A ride on the street-car was something to write home about in those days. . . . I hear that it's all built up around there now.

So we got on the car and rode the whole way down into the business section of St. Louis. Robert took me into a drug-store and set me up to soda-water. Then we came out and walked around some, down to the Union Station and clear over to the river. . . . And both of us half scared to death at what we'd done and wondering what Mamma would say if she found out.

We stayed there till it was getting dark, and we passed by a lunch-room—an old joint with one-armed chairs and people eating at the counter. . . . We read all the signs to see what they had to eat and how much it cost, and I guess nothing on the menu was more than fifteen cents, but it couldn't have looked grander to us if it had been Delmonico's. . . . So we stood there with our noses pressed against the window, looking in. . . . Two skinny little kids, both of us scared half to death, getting the thrill of a lifetime out of it. . . . You know what I mean? . . . And smelling everything with all our might and thinking how good it all smelled. . . . Then Robert turned to me and whispered, "Come on, Sue. . . . Let's go in. . . . It says fifteen cents for pork and beans. And I've got money," Robert said. "I've got sixty cents."

I was so scared I couldn't speak. . . . I'd never been in a place like that before. . . . But I kept thinking, "Oh, Lord, if Mamma should find out!" . . . Don't you know how it is when you're a kid? It was the thrill of a lifetime. . . . I couldn't resist. So we both went in and ordered pork and beans and a cup of coffee. . . . I suppose we were too frightened at what we'd done really to enjoy anything. We just gobbled it all up in a hurry, and gulped our coffee down. And I don't know whether it was the excitement—I guess the poor kid was already sick when we came in there and didn't know it. But I turned and looked at him, and he was as white as death. . . . And when I asked him what was the matter, he wouldn't tell me. . . . He was too proud. He said he was all right, but I could see that he was sick as a dog. . . . So he paid the bill. . . . It came to forty cents; I'll never forget that as long as I live. . . . And sure enough, we no more than got out the door—he'd hardly time to reach the curb—before it all came up. . . .

And the poor kid was so scared and so ashamed. What scared him so was not that he had got sick but that he had spent all that money, and it had come to nothing. And Mamma would find out. . . . Poor kid, he just stood there looking at me and he whispered, "Oh, Sue, don't tell Mamma. She'll be mad if she finds out." Then we hurried home, and he was still white as a sheet when we got there.

Mamma was waiting for us. . . . She looked at us—you know how Miss Martha looks at you, when she thinks you've been doing something that you shouldn't? . . . Mamma said: "Why, where on earth have you two children been?" I guess she was all set to lay us out. Then she took one look at Robert's face. That was enough for her. She said: "Why, child, what in the world—" She was white as a sheet herself. . . . And all that Robert said was "Mamma, I feel sick."

He was sick as a dog. He fell over on the bed, and we undressed him, and Mamma put her hand upon his forehead and came out in the hall—she was so white you could have made a black mark on her face with chalk—and whispered to me:

"Go and get the doctor quick; he's burning up."

And I went running, my pigtails flying, to get Dr. Packer. I brought him back with me. When he came out of Robert's room, he told Mamma what to do, but I don't know if she even heard him.

Her face was white as a sheet. She looked at me and looked right through me. . . . And oh, my Lord, I'll never forget the way she looked, the way my heart stopped and came up in my throat. . . . I was only a skinny little kid of fourteen. But she looked as if she was dying right before my eyes. . . . And I knew that if anything happened to him, she'd never get over it, if she lived to be a hundred.

Poor old Mamma. You know, he always was her eyeballs—you know that, don't you?—Not the rest of us!—No, sir! I know what I'm talking about. It always has been Robert—she always thought more of him than she did of any of the others and—Poor kid! I can see him lying there white as a sheet and remember how sick he was, and how scared I was! . . . I don't know why—all we'd done had been to sneak away from home and go to a lunch-room—but I felt guilty about the whole thing, as if it was my fault. . . .

It all came back to me the other day when I was looking at that picture, and I thought, my God, we were two kids together, and I was only two years older than Robert was. . . . And now I'm forty-six. . . . Can you imagine that—the way we all grow up and change and go away? . . . And my Lord, Robert seemed so grown-up to me even then. He was only a kid; yet he seemed older than the rest of us.

I was thinking of it just the other day, and I wonder what Robert would say now if he could see that picture. For when you look at it, it all comes back—the boarding house, St. Louis and the Fair. . . . And all of it is just the same as it has always been, as if it happened yesterday. . . . And all of us have grown up and gone away. And nothing has turned out the way we thought it would. . . . And all my hopes and dreams and big ambitions have come to nothing.

It's all so long ago, as if it happened in another world. And then it all comes back, as if it happened yesterday. . . . And sometimes I will lie awake at night and think of all the people who have come and gone, and all the things that happened. And hear the trains down by the river, and the whistles and the bell. . . . And how we went to St. Louis back in 1904.

And then I go out into the street and see the faces of the people that I pass. . . . Don't you see something funny in their eyes, as if they were wondering what had happened to them since they were kids—what it was that they had lost? . . . Now am I crazy, or do they look that way to you?

My God, I'd like to find out what is wrong. . . . What has changed since then. . . . And if we have that same queer funny look in our eyes, too. . . . And if it happens to us all, to everyone. . . . Robert and Jim and Dick and me—all standing there before that house on Orchard Street—and then you see the way we were—and how it all gets lost. . . .

The way it all turns out is nothing like the way we thought that it would be. . . . And how it all gets lost, until it seems that it has never happened—that it is something that we dreamed somewhere. . . . You see what I mean now? . . . That it is something that we hear somewhere, that it happened to someone else. . . . And then it all comes back again.

And there you are, two funny, frightened, skinny little kids with their noses pressed against a dirty window thirty years ago. . . . The way it felt, the way it smelled, even the funny smell in that old pantry of our house. And the steps before the house, the way the rooms looked. Those two little boys in sailor suits who used to ride up and down before the house on their tricycles. . . . And the birthmark on Robert's neck. . . . The Inside Inn. . . . St. Louis and the Fair. . . . It all comes back as if it happened yesterday. And then it goes away and seems farther off and stranger than if it happened in a dream.

"This is King's Highway," a man said. I looked and saw that it was just a street. There were some new buildings, and a big hotel; some restaurants, "bar-grill" places of the modern kind, the livid monotone of neon lights, the ceaseless traffic of the motorcars—all this was new, but it was just a street. And I knew that it had always been a street and nothing more. But somehow—I stood there looking at it, wondering what else I had expected to find.

The man kept looking at me, and I asked him if the Fair had been out this way.

"Sure, the Fair was out beyond here," the man said. "Where the park is now. But this street you're looking for? Don't you remember the name of the street or nothing?"

I said I thought the name was Edgemont Street, but that I was not sure. And I said the house was on the corner of this street and another street. And then the man said, "What street was that?" I said I did not know, but that King's Highway was a block or so away and that an interurban line ran past about a block or so from where we lived.

"What line was this?" the man said, and stared at me.

"The interurban line," I said.

Then he stared at me again and finally, "I don't know no interurban line," he said.

I said it was a line that ran behind some houses and that there were board fences there and grass beside the tracks. But somehow I could not say that it was summer in those days and that you could smell the ties, a kind of wooden tarry smell, and feel a kind of absence in the afternoon, after the car had gone. I could not say that King's Highway had not been a street in those days but a kind of road that wound from magic out of some dim land, and that along the way it had got mixed with Tom the Piper's son, with hot cross buns, with all the light that came and went, and with cloud shadows passing on the mountains, with coming down through Indiana in the morning, and the smell of engine smoke, the Union Station, and most of all with voices lost and far and long ago that said, "King's Highway."

I didn't say those things about King's Highway because I looked about me and I saw what King's Highway was. I left him then and went on till I found the place. And again, again, I turned into the street, finding the place where the two corners meet, the huddled block, the turret, and the steps, and paused a moment, looking back, as if the street was Time.

So I waited for a moment for a word, for a door to open, for the child to come. I waited, but no words were spoken; no one came.

Yet all of it was just as it had always been except the steps were lower and the porch less high, the strip of grass less wide than I had thought. A graystone front, St. Louis style, three-storied, with a slant slate roof, the side red brick and windowed, still with the old arched entrance in the center for the doctor's use.

There was a tree in front, a lamp-post, and behind and to the side more trees than I had known there would be. And all the slaty turret gables, all the slaty window gables going into points, the two arched windows, in strong stone, in the front room.

It was all so strong, so solid and so ugly—and so enduring and good, the way I had remembered it, except I did not smell the tar, the hot and caulky dryness of the old cracked ties, the boards of backyard fences and the coarse and sultry grass, and absence in the afternoon when the street-car had gone, and the feel of the hot afternoon, and that everyone was absent at the Fair.

It was a hot day. Darkness had come; the heat hung and sweltered like a sodden blanket in St. Louis. The heat soaked down, and the people sweltered in it; the faces of the people were pale and greasy with the heat. And in their faces was a kind of patient wretchedness, and one felt the kind of desolation that one feels at the end of a hot day in a great city in America—when one's home is far away across the continent, and he thinks of all that distance, all that heat, and feels: "Oh, God, but it's a big country!"

Then he hears the engine and the wheel again, the wailing whistle and the bell, the sound of shifting in the sweltering yard, and walks the street, and walks the street, beneath the clusters of hard lights, and by the people with sagged faces, and is drowned in desolation and no belief.

He feels the way one feels when one comes back, and knows that he should not have come, and when he sees that, after all, King's Highway is—a street; and St. Louis—the enchanted name—a big hot common town upon the river, sweltering in wet dreary heat, and not quite South, and nothing else enough to make it better.

It had not been like this before. I could remember how it got hot in the afternoons, and how I would feel a sense of absence and vague sadness when everyone had gone away. The house would seem so lonely, and sometimes I would sit inside, on the second step of the hall stairs, and listen to the sound of silence and absence in the afternoon. I could smell the oil upon the floor and on the stairs, and see the sliding doors with their brown varnish and the beady chains across the door, and thrust my hand among the beady chains, and gather them together in my arms, and let them clash, and swish with light beady swishings all round me. I could feel darkness, absence, and stained light, within the house, through the stained glass of the window on the stairs, through the small stained glasses by the door, stained light and absence, and vague sadness in the house in a hot mid-afternoon. And all these things themselves would have a kind of life: would seem to wait attentively, to be most living and most still.

Then I would long for evening and return, the slant of light, and feet along the street, the sharp-faced twins in sailor-suits upon their tricycles, the smell of supper and the sound of voices in the house again, and Robert coming from the Fair.

And again, again, I turned into the street, finding the place where two corners meet, turning at last to see if Time was there. I passed the house; some lights were burning in the house; the door was open, and a woman sat upon the porch. And presently I turned and stopped before the house again. I stood looking at it for a moment, and I put my foot upon the step.

Then I said to the woman who was sitting on the porch: "This house—excuse me, but could you tell me, please, who lives here?"

I knew my words were strange and hollow and I had not said what I wished to say. She stared at me a moment, puzzled.

Then she said: "I live here. Who are you looking for?"

I said, "Why, I am looking for–There used to be a house–" I said.

The woman was now staring hard at me.

"I used to live here in this house," I said.

She was silent for a moment; then she said: "When was it that you lived here?"

"In 1904."

Again she was silent, looking at me for a moment. Then presently: "Oh. . . . That was the year of the Fair. You were here then?"

"Yes." I now spoke rapidly, with more confidence: "My mother had the house, and we were here for seven months. . . . And the house belonged to Dr. Packer," I went on. "We rented it from him."

"Yes," the woman said, and nodded now. "This was Dr. Packer's house. He's been dead for many years. But this was the Packer house, all right."

"That entrance on the side," I said, "where the steps go up–that was for Dr. Packer's patients. That was the entrance to his office."

"Oh," the woman said, "I didn't know that. I've often wondered what it was. I didn't know what it was for."

"And this big room here in front," I said, "that was the office. And there were sliding doors, and next to it a kind of alcove for his patients."

"Yes, the alcove is still there, only all of it has been made into one room now–and I never knew just what the alcove was for."

"And there were sliding doors on this side, too, that opened on the hall–

and a stairway going up upon this side. And halfway up the stairway, at the landing, a little window of stained glass—and across the sliding doors here in the hall a kind of curtain made of strings of beads."

She nodded, smiling. "Yes, it's just the same—we still have the sliding doors and the stained glass window on the stairs. There's no bead curtain any more," she said, "but I remember when people had them. I know what you mean."

"When we were here," I said, "we used the Doctor's office for a parlor—except later on, the last month or two; and then we used it for a bedroom."

"It is a bedroom now," she said. "I rent rooms—all of the rooms upstairs are rented—but I have two brothers and they sleep in this front room."

And we were silent for a moment; then I said, "My brother stayed there, too."

"In the front room?" the woman said.

I answered: "Yes."

She paused a moment; then she said: "Won't you come in? I don't believe it's changed much. Would you like to see?"

I thanked her and said I would, and I went up the steps. She opened the screen door, and I went in.

And it was just the same—the stairs, the hallway, and the sliding doors, the window of stained glass upon the stairs. All of it was just the same except the stained light of absence in the afternoon, and the child who sat there, waiting on the stairs, and something fading like a dream, something coming like a light, something going, passing, fading like the shadows of a wood. And then it would be gone again, fading like cloud shadows in the hills, coming like the vast, the drowsy rumors of the distant enchanted Fair, and coming, going, coming, being found and lost, possessed and held and never captured, like lost voices in the mountains, long ago, like the dark eyes and the quiet face, the dark lost boy, my brother, who himself like shadows, or like absence in the house, would come, would go, and would return again.

The woman took me into the house and through the hall. I told her of the pantry, and I told her where it was and pointed to the place, but now it was no longer there. And I told her of the back yard, and the old board fence around the yard. But the old board fence was gone. And I told her of the carriage-house, and told her it was painted red. But now there was a small garage. And the back yard was still there, but smaller than I thought, and now there was a tree.

"I did not know there was a tree," I said. "I do not remember any tree."

"Perhaps it wasn't there," she said. "A tree could grow in thirty years." And then we came back through the house and paused a moment at the sliding doors.

"And could I see this room?" I said.

She slid the doors back. They slid open smoothly, with a kind of rolling heaviness, as they used to do. And then I saw the room again. It was the same.

There was a window to the side, the two arched windows to the front, the alcove and the sliding doors, the fireplace with the tiles of mottled green, the mantel of dark mission wood, a dresser and a bed, just where the dresser and the bed had been so long ago.

"Is this the room?" the woman said. "It hasn't changed?"

I told her it was the same.

"And your brother slept here where my brothers sleep?"

"This was his room," I said.

And we were silent for a moment. Then I turned to go, and said: "Well, thank you. I appreciate your showing me."

The woman said that she was glad and that it was no trouble. And she said, "And when you see your family, you can tell them that you saw the house," she said. "And my name is Mrs. Bell. You can tell your mother that a Mrs. Bell has got the house. And when you see your brother, you can tell him that you saw the room he slept in, and that you found it just the same."

I told her then that he was dead.

The woman was silent for a moment. Then she looked at me and said: "He died here, didn't he? In this room?"

I told her that he did.

"Well, then," she said, "I knew it. I don't know how. But when you told me he was here, I knew it."

I said nothing. In a moment the woman said: "What did he die of?"

"Typhoid."

She looked shocked and troubled, and began involuntarily:

"My two brothers–"

"That was so long ago," I said. "I don't think you need to worry now."

"Oh, I wasn't thinking about that," she said. . . . "It was just hearing that a little boy–your brother–was–was in this room that my two brothers sleep in now–"

"Well, maybe I shouldn't have told you then. But he was a good boy and if you'd known him, you wouldn't mind."

She said nothing, and I added quickly: "Besides, he didn't stay here long. This wasn't really his room–but the night he came back with my sister, he was so sick–they didn't move him."

"Oh," the woman said, "I see." And in a moment; "Are you going to tell your mother you were here?"

"I don't think so."

"I–I wonder how she feels about this room."

"I don't know. She never speaks of it."

"Oh. . . . How old was he?'

"He was twelve."

"You must have been pretty young yourself."

"I was four."

"And—you just wanted to see the room, didn't you? Is that why you came back?"

"Yes."

"Well"—indefinitely—"I guess you've seen it now."

"Yes, thank you."

"I guess you don't remember much about him, do you? I shouldn't think you would."

"No, not much."

The years dropped off like fallen leaves: the face came back again—the soft dark oval, the dark eyes, the soft brown berry on the neck, the raven hair, all bending down, approaching—the whole ghost-wise, intent and instant, like faces from a haunted wood.

"Now say it: *Robert*!"

"Wobbut."

"No, not *Wobbut: Robert*. . . . Say it."

"Wobbut."

"Ah-h—you *didn't* say it. . . . You said Wobbut: *Robert*! . . . Now say it."

"Wobbut."

"Look, I'll tell you what I'll do if you say it right. . . . Would you like to go down to King's Highway? Would you like Robert to set you up? All right, then. . . . If you say Robert right, I'll take you to King's Highway and set you up to ice-cream. . . . Now say it right: say *Robert*."

"Wobbut."

"Ah-h you-u! . . . Old tongue-tie, that's what you are. Some day I'm going to. . . . Well, come on, then. I'll set you up, anyway."

It all came back and faded and was lost again. I turned to go, and thanked the woman, and I said: "Good-bye."

"Well, then, good-bye," the woman said, and we shook hands. "I'm glad if I could show you. I'm glad if—" She did not finish, and at length she said: "Well, then, that was a long time ago. You'll find it all changed now, I guess. It's all built up around here now—way out beyond here, out beyond where the Fair grounds used to be. I guess you'll find it changed," she said.

We could find no more to say. We stood there for a moment on the steps, and shook hands once more.

"Well, then, good-bye."

And again, again, I turned into the street, finding the place where corners meet, turning to look again to see where Time had gone. And all of it was just the same, it seemed that it had never changed since then, except all had been found and caught and captured for forever. And so, finding all, I knew all had been lost.

I knew that I would never come again, and that lost magic would not come again, and that the light that came, that passed and went and that returned again, the memory of lost voices in the hills, cloud shadows passing in the mountains, the voices of our kinsmen long ago, the street, the heat, King's Highway, and the piper's son, the vast and drowsy murmur of the distant Fair—oh, strange and bitter miracle of Time—come back again.

But I knew that it could not come back—the cry of absence in the afternoon, the house that waited and the child that dreamed; and through the thicket of man's memory, from the enchanted wood, the dark eye and the quiet face,—poor child, life's stranger and life's exile, lost, like all of us, a cipher in blind mazes, long ago—my parent, friend, and brother, the lost boy, was gone forever and would not return.

JOHN STEINBECK

[1902–1963]

The Red Pony

(First published in *North American Review*, November, 1933; first book publication in 1945.)

I. THE GIFT

AT DAYBREAK BILLY Buck emerged from the bunkhouse and stood for a moment on the porch looking up at the sky. He was a broad, bandy-legged little man with a walrus mustache, with square hands, puffed and muscled on the palms. His eyes were a contemplative, watery gray and the hair which protruded from under his Stetson hat was spiky and weathered. Billy was still stuffing his shirt into his blue jeans as he stood on the porch. He unbuckled his belt and tightened it again. The belt showed, by the worn shiny places opposite each hole, the gradual increase of Billy's middle over a period of years. When he had seen to the weather, Billy cleared each nostril by holding its mate closed with his forefinger and blowing fiercely. Then he walked down to the barn, rubbing his hands together. He curried and brushed two saddle horses in the stalls, talking quietly to them all the time; and he had hardly finished when the iron triangle started ringing at the ranch house. Billy stuck the brush and currycomb together and laid them on the rail, and went up to breakfast. His action had been so deliberate and yet so wasteless of time that he came to the house while Mrs. Tiflin was still ringing the triangle. She nodded her gray head to him and withdrew into the kitchen. Billy Buck sat down on the steps, because he was a cow-hand, and it wouldn't be fitting that he should go first into the dining room. He heard Mr. Tiflin in the house, stamping his feet into his boots.

The high jangling note of the triangle put the boy Jody in motion. He was only a little boy, ten years old, with hair like dusty yellow grass and with shy polite gray eyes, and with a mouth that worked when he thought. The triangle picked him up out of sleep. It didn't occur to him to disobey the harsh note. He never had: no one he knew ever had. He brushed the tangled hair out of his eyes and skinned his nightgown off. In a moment he was dressed—blue chambray shirt and overalls. It was late in the summer, so of course there were no shoes to bother with. In the kitchen he waited until his mother got from in front of the sink and went back to the stove. Then he washed himself and brushed back his wet hair with his fingers. His mother turned sharply on him as he left the sink. Jody looked shyly away.

"I've got to cut your hair before long," his mother said. "Breakfast's on the table. Go on in, so Billy can come."

Jody sat at the long table which was covered with white oilcloth washed through to the fabric in some places. The fried eggs lay in rows on their platter. Jody took three eggs on his plate and followed with three thick slices of crisp bacon. He carefully scraped a spot of blood from one of the egg yolks.

Billy Buck clumped in. "That won't hurt you," Billy explained. "That's only a sign the rooster leaves."

Jody's tall stern father came in then and Jody knew from the noise on the floor that he was wearing boots, but he looked under the table anyway, to make sure. His father turned off the oil lamp over the table, for plenty of morning light now came through the windows.

Jody did not ask where his father and Billy Buck were riding that day, but he wished he might go along. His father was a disciplinarian. Jody obeyed him in everything without questions of any kind. Now, Carl Tiflin sat down and reached for the egg platter.

"Got the cows ready to go, Billy?" he asked.

"In the lower corral," Billy said. "I could just as well take them in alone."

"Sure you could. But a man needs company. Besides your throat gets pretty dry." Carl Tiflin was jovial this morning.

Jody's mother put her head in the door. "What time do you think to be back, Carl?"

"I can't tell. I've got to see some men in Salinas. Might be gone till dark."

The eggs and coffee and big biscuits disappeared rapidly. Jody followed the two men out of the house. He watched them mount their horses and drive six old milk cows out of the corral and start over the hill toward Salinas. They were going to sell the old cows to the butcher.

When they had disappeared over the crown of the ridge Jody walked up the hill in back of the house. The dogs trotted around the house corner hunching their shoulders and grinning horribly with pleasure. Jody patted their heads—Doubletree Mutt with the big thick tail and yellow eyes, and Smasher, the shepherd, who had killed a coyote and lost an ear in doing it. Smasher's one good ear stood up higher than a collie's ear should. Billy Buck said that always happened. After the frenzied greeting the dogs lowered their noses to the ground in a businesslike way and went ahead, looking back now and then to make sure that the boy was coming. They walked up through the chicken yard and saw the quail eating with the chickens. Smasher chased the chickens a little to keep in practice in case there should ever be sheep to herd. Jody continued on through the large vegetable patch where the green corn was higher than his head. The cow-pumpkins were green and small yet. He went on to the sagebrush line where the cold spring ran out of its pipe and fell into a round wooden tub. He leaned over and drank close to the green mossy wood where the water tasted best. Then he turned and looked back on the ranch, on the low, whitewashed house girded with red geraniums, and on the long bunkhouse by the cypress tree where Billy Buck lived alone. Jody could see the great black kettle under the cypress tree. That was where the pigs were scalded. The sun was coming over the ridge now, glaring on the whitewash of the houses and barns, making the wet grass blaze softly. Behind him, in the tall sagebrush, the birds were scampering on the ground, making a great noise among the dry leaves; the squirrels piped shrilly on the side-hills. Jody looked along at the farm buildings. He felt an uncertainty in the air, a feeling of change and of loss and of the gain of new and unfamiliar things. Over the hillside two big black buzzards sailed low to the ground and their shadows slipped smoothly and quickly ahead of them. Some animal had died in the vicinity. Jody knew it. It might be a cow or it might be the remains of a rabbit. The buzzards overlooked nothing. Jody hated them as all decent things hate them; but they could not be hurt because they made away with carrion.

After a while the boy sauntered down hill again. The dogs had long ago given him up and gone into the brush to do things in their own way. Back through the vegetable garden he went, and he paused for a moment to smash a green muskmelon with his heel, but he was not happy about it. It was a bad thing to do, he knew perfectly well. He kicked dirt over the ruined melon to conceal it.

Back at the house his mother bent over his rough hands, inspecting his fingers and nails. It did little good to start him clean to school, for too many things could happen on the way. She sighed over the black cracks on his fingers, and then gave him his books and his lunch and started him on the mile walk to school. She noticed that his mouth was working a good deal this morning.

Jody started his journey. He filled his pockets with little pieces of white quartz that lay in the road, and every so often he took a shot at a bird or at some rabbit that had stayed sunning itself in the road too long. At the crossroads over the bridge he met two friends and the three of them walked to school together, making ridiculous strides and being rather silly. School had just opened two weeks before. There was still a spirit of revolt among the pupils.

It was four o'clock in the afternoon when Jody topped the hill and looked down on the ranch again. He looked for the saddle horses, but the corral was empty. His father was not back yet. He went slowly, then, toward the afternoon chores. At the ranch house, he found his mother sitting on the porch, mending socks.

"There's two doughnuts in the kitchen for you," she said. Jody slid to the kitchen, and returned with half of one of the doughnuts already eaten and his mouth full. His mother asked him what he had learned in school that day, but she didn't listen to his doughnut-muffled answer. She interrupted, "Jody, tonight see you fill the wood-box clear full. Last night you crossed the sticks and it wasn't only about half full. Lay the sticks flat tonight. And Jody, some of the hens are hiding eggs, or else the dogs are eating them. Look about in the grass and see if you can find any nests."

Jody, still eating, went out and did his chores. He saw the quail come down to eat with the chickens when he threw out the grain. For some reason his father was proud to have them come. He never allowed any shooting near the house for fear the quail might go away.

When the wood-box was full, Jody took his twenty-two rifle up to the cold spring at the brush line. He drank again and then aimed the gun at all manner of things, at rocks, at birds on the wing, at the big black pig kettle under the cypress tree, but he didn't shoot, for he had no cartridges and wouldn't have until he was twelve. If his father had seen him aim the rifle in the direction of the house he would have put the cartridges off another year. Jody remembered this and did not point the rifle down the hill again. Two years was enough to wait for cartridges. Nearly all of his father's presents were given with reservations which hampered their value somewhat. It was good discipline.

The supper waited until dark for his father to return. When at last he came in with Billy Buck, Jody could smell the delicious brandy on their breaths. Inwardly he rejoiced, for his father sometimes talked to him when he smelled of brandy, sometimes even told things he had done in the wild days when he was a boy.

After supper, Jody sat by the fireplace and his shy polite eyes sought the room corners, and he waited for his father to tell what it was he contained, for Jody knew he had news of some sort. But he was disappointed. His father pointed a stern finger at him.

"You'd better go to bed, Jody I'm going to need you in the morning."

That wasn't so bad. Jody liked to do things he had to do as long as they weren't routine things. He looked at the floor and his mouth worked out a question before he spoke it. "What are we going to do in the morning, kill a pig?" he asked softly.

"Never you mind. You better get to bed."

When the door was closed behind him, Jody heard his father and Billy Buck chuckling and he knew it was a joke of some kind. And later, when he lay in bed, trying to make words out of the murmurs in the other room, he heard his father protest, "But, Ruth, I didn't give much for him."

Jody heard the hoot-owls hunting mice down by the barn, and he heard a fruit tree limb tap-tapping against the house. A cow was lowing when he went to sleep.

When the triangle sounded in the morning, Jody dressed more quickly even than usual. In the kitchen, while he washed his face and combed back his hair, his mother addressed him irritably. "Don't you go out until you get a good breakfast in you."

He went into the dining room and sat at the long white table. He took a steaming hotcake from the platter, arranged two fried eggs on it, covered them with another hotcake and squashed the whole thing with his fork.

His father and Billy Buck came in. Jody knew from the sound on the floor that both of them were wearing flat-heeled shoes, but he peered under the table to make sure. His father turned off the oil lamp, for the day had arrived, and he looked stern and disciplinary, but Billy Buck didn't look at Jody at all. He avoided the shy questioning eyes of the boy and soaked a whole piece of toast in his coffee.

Carl Tiflin said crossly, "You come with us after breakfast!"

Jody had trouble with his food then, for he felt a kind of doom in the air. After Billy had tilted his saucer and drained the coffee which had slopped into it, and had wiped his hands on his jeans, the two men stood up from the table and went out into the morning light together, and Jody respectfully followed a little behind them. He tried to keep his mind from running ahead, tried to keep it absolutely motionless.

His mother called, "Carl! Don't you let it keep him from school."

They marched past the cypress, where a singletree hung from a limb to butcher the pigs on, and past the black iron kettle, so it was not a pig killing. The sun shone over the hill and threw long, dark shadows of the trees and buildings. They crossed a stubble-field to shortcut to the barn. Jody's father unhooked the door and they went in. They had been walking toward the sun on the way down. The barn was black as night in contrast and warm from the hay and from the beasts. Jody's father moved over toward the one box stall. "Come here!" he ordered. Jody could begin to see things now. He looked into the box stall and then stepped back quickly.

A red pony colt was looking at him out of the stall. Its tense ears were forward and a light of disobedience was in its eyes. Its coat was rough and thick as an airedale's fur and its mane was long and tangled. Jody's throat collapsed in on itself and cut his breath short.

"He needs a good currying," his father said, "and if I ever hear of you not feeding him or leaving his stall dirty, I'll sell him off in a minute."

Jody couldn't bear to look at the pony's eyes any more. He gazed down at his hands for a moment, and he asked very shyly, "Mine?" No one answered him. He put his hand out toward the pony. Its gray nose came close, sniffling loudly, and then the lips drew back and the strong teeth closed on Jody's fingers. The pony shook its head up and down and seemed to laugh with amusement. Jody regarded his bruised fingers. "Well," he said with pride—"Well, I guess he can bite all right." The two men laughed, somewhat in relief. Carl Tiflin went out of the barn and walked up a side-hill to be by himself, for he was embarrassed, but Billy Buck stayed. It was easier to talk to Billy Buck. Jody asked again—"Mine?"

Billy became professional in tone. "Sure! That is, if you look out for him and break him right. I'll show you how. He's just a colt. You can't ride him for some time."

Jody put out his bruised hand again, and this time the red pony let his nose be rubbed. "I ought to have a carrot," Jody said. "Where'd we get him, Billy?"

"Bought him at a sheriff's auction," Billy explained. "A show went broke in Salinas and had debts. The sheriff was selling off their stuff."

The pony stretched out his nose and shook the forelock from his wild eyes. Jody stroked the nose a little. He said softly, "There isn't a—saddle?"

Billy Buck laughed. "I'd forgot. Come along."

In the harness room he lifted down a little saddle of red morocco leather. "It's just a show saddle," Billy Buck said disparagingly. "It isn't practical for the brush, but it was cheap at the sale."

Jody couldn't trust himself to look at the saddle either, and he couldn't speak at all. He brushed the shining red leather with his fingertips, and after a long time he said, "It'll look pretty on him though." He thought of the grandest and prettiest things he knew. "If he hasn't a name already, I think I'll call him Gabilan Mountains," he said.

Billy Buck knew how he felt. "It's a pretty long name. Why don't you just call him Gabilan? That means hawk. That would be a fine name for him." Billy felt glad. "If you will collect tail hair, I might be able to make a hair rope for you sometime. You could use it for a hackamore."

Jody wanted to go back to the box stall. "Could I lead him to school, do you think—to show the kids?"

But Billy shook his head. "He's not even halter-broke yet. We had a time getting him here. Had to almost drag him. You better be starting for school though."

"I'll bring the kids to see him here this afternoon," Jody said.

Six boys came over the hill half an hour early that afternoon, running hard, their heads down, their forearms working, their breath whistling. They swept by the house and cut across the stubble-field to the barn. And then they stood self-consciously before the pony, and then they looked at Jody with eyes in which there was a new admiration and a new respect. Before today Jody had been a boy, dressed in overalls and a blue shirt—quieter than most, even suspected of being a little cowardly. And now he was different. Out of a thousand centuries they drew the ancient admiration of the footman for the horseman. They knew instinctively that a man on a horse is spiritually as well as physically bigger than a man on foot. They knew that Jody had been miraculously lifted out of equality with them, and had been placed over them. Gabilan put his head out of the stall and sniffed them.

"Why'n't you ride him?" the boys cried. "Why'n't you braid his tail with ribbons like in the fair?" "When you going to ride him?"

Jody's courage was up. He too felt the superiority of the horseman. "He's not old enough. Nobody can ride him for a long time. I'm going to train him on the long halter. Billy Buck is going to show me how."

"Well, can't we even lead him around a little?"

"He isn't even halter-broke," Jody said. He wanted to be completely alone when he took the pony out the first time. "Come and see the saddle."

They were speechless at the red morocco saddle, completely shocked out of comment. "It isn't much use in the brush," Jody explained. "It'll look pretty on him though. Maybe I'll ride bareback when I go into the brush."

"How you going to rope a cow without a saddle horn?"

"Maybe I'll get another saddle for every day. My father might want me to help him with the stock." He let them feel the red saddle, and showed them the brass chain throat-latch on the bridle and the big brass buttons at each temple where the headstall and brow band crossed. The whole thing was too wonderful. They had to go away after a little while, and each boy, in his mind, searched among his possessions for a bribe worthy of offering in return for a ride on the red pony when the time should come.

Jody was glad when they had gone. He took brush and currycomb from the wall, took down the barrier of the box stall and stepped cautiously in. The pony's eyes glittered, and he edged around into kicking position. But Jody touched him on the shoulder and rubbed his high arched neck as he had always seen Billy Buck do, and he crooned, "So-o-o Boy," in a deep voice. The pony gradually relaxed his tenseness. Jody curried and brushed until a pile of dead hair lay in the stall and until the pony's coat had taken on a deep red shine. Each time he finished he thought it might have been done better. He braided the mane into a dozen little pigtails, and he braided the forelock, and then he undid them and brushed the hair out straight again.

Jody did not hear his mother enter the barn. She was angry when she came, but when she looked in at the pony and at Jody working over him, she felt a curious pride rise up in her. "Have you forgot the wood-box?" she asked gently. "It's not far off from dark and there's not a stick of wood in the house, and the chickens aren't fed."

Jody quickly put up his tools. "I forgot, ma'am."

"Well, after this do your chores first. Then you won't forget. I expect you'll forget lots of things now if I don't keep an eye on you."

"Can I have carrots from the garden for him, ma'am?"

She had to think about that. "Oh—I guess so, if you only take the big tough ones."

"Carrots keep the coat good," he said, and again she felt the curious rush of pride.

Jody never waited for the triangle to get him out of bed after the coming of the pony. It became his habit to creep out of bed even before his mother was awake, to slip into his clothes and to go quietly down to the barn to see Gabilan. In the gray quiet mornings when the land and the brush and the houses and the trees were silver-gray and black like a photograph negative, he stole toward the barn, past the sleeping stones and the sleeping cypress tree. The turkeys, roosting in the tree out of coyotes' reach, clicked drowsily. The fields glowed with a gray frost-like light and in the dew the tracks of rabbits and of field mice stood out sharply. The good dogs came stiffly out of their little houses, hackles up and deep growls in their throats. Then they caught Jody's scent, and their stiff tails rose up and waved a greeting—Doubletree Mutt with the big thick tail, and Smasher, the incipient shepherd—then went lazily back to their warm beds.

It was a strange time and a mysterious journey, to Jody—an extension of a dream. When he first had the pony he liked to torture himself during the trip by thinking Gabilan would not be in his stall, and worse, would never have been there. And he had other delicious little self-induced pains. He thought how the rats had gnawed ragged holes in the red saddle, and how the mice had nibbled Gabilan's tail until it was stringy and thin. He usually ran the last little way to the barn. He unlatched the rusty hasp of the barn door and stepped in, and no matter how quietly he opened the door, Gabilan was always looking at him over the barrier of the box stall and Gabilan whinnied softly and stamped his front foot, and his eyes had big sparks of red fire in them like oakwood embers.

Sometimes, if the work horses were to be used that day, Jody found Billy Buck in the barn harnessing and currying. Billy stood with him and looked long at Gabilan and he told Jody a great many things about horses. He explained that they were terribly afraid for their feet, so that one must make a practice of lifting the legs and patting the hoofs and ankles to remove their terror. He told Jody how horses love conversation. He must talk to the pony all the time, and tell him the reasons for everything. Billy wasn't sure a horse could understand everything that was said to him, but it was impossible to say how much was understood. A horse never kicked up a fuss if some one he liked explained things to him. Billy could give examples, too. He had known, for instance, a horse nearly dead beat with fatigue to perk up when told it was only a little farther to his destination. And he had known a horse paralyzed with fright to come out of it when his rider told him what it was that was frightening him. While he talked in the mornings, Billy Buck cut twenty or thirty straws into neat three-inch lengths and stuck them into his hatband. Then during the whole day, if he wanted to pick his teeth or merely to chew on something, he had only to reach up for one of them.

Jody listened carefully, for he knew and the whole country knew that Billy Buck was a fine hand with horses. Billy's own horse was a stringy cayuse with a hammer head, but he nearly always won the first prizes at the stock trials. Billy could rope a steer, take a double half-hitch about the horn with his riata, and dismount, and his horse would play the steer as an angler plays a fish, keeping a tight rope until the steer was down or beaten.

Every morning, after Jody had curried and brushed the pony, he let down the barrier of the stall, and Gabilan thrust past him and raced down the barn and into the corral. Around and around he galloped, and sometimes he jumped forward and landed on stiff legs. He stood quivering, stiff ears forward, eyes rolling so that the whites showed, pretending to be frightened. At last he walked snorting to the watertrough and buried his nose in the water up to the nostrils. Jody was proud then, for he knew that was the way to judge a horse. Poor horses only touched their lips to the water, but a fine spirited beast put his whole nose and mouth under, and only left room to breathe.

Then Jody stood and watched the pony, and he saw things he had never noticed about any other horse, the sleek, sliding flank muscles and the cords of the buttocks, which flexed like a closing fist, and the shine the sun put on the red coat. Having seen horses all his life, Jody had never looked at them very closely before. But now he noticed the moving ears which gave expression and even inflection of expression to the face. The pony talked with his ears. You could tell exactly how he felt about everything by the way his ears pointed. Sometimes they were stiff and upright and sometimes lax and sagging. They went back when he was angry or fearful, and forward when he was anxious and curious and pleased; and their exact position indicated which emotion he had.

Billy Buck kept his word. In the early fall the training began. First there was the halter-breaking, and that was the hardest because it was the first thing. Jody held a carrot and coaxed and promised and pulled on the rope. The pony set his feet like a burro when he felt the strain. But before long he learned. Jody walked all over the ranch leading him. Gradually he took to dropping the rope until the pony followed him unled wherever he went.

And then came the training on the long halter. That was slower work. Jody stood in the middle of a circle, holding the long halter. He clucked with his tongue and the pony started to walk in a big circle, held in by the long rope. He clucked again to make the pony trot, and again to make him gallop. Around and around Gabilan went thundering and enjoying it immensely. 'Then he called, "Whoa," and the pony stopped. It was not long until Gabilan was perfect at it. But in many ways he was a bad pony. He bit Jody in the pants and stomped on Jody's feet. Now and then his ears went back and he aimed a tremendous kick at the boy. Every time he did one of these bad things, Gabilan settled back and seemed to laugh to himself.

Billy Buck worked at the hair rope in the evenings before the fireplace. Jody collected tail hair in a bag, and he sat and watched Billy slowly constructing the rope, twisting a few hairs to make a string and rolling two strings together for a cord, and then braiding a number of cords to make the rope. Billy rolled the finished rope on the floor under his foot to make it round and hard.

The long halter work rapidly approached perfection. Jody's father, watching the pony stop and start and trot and gallop, was a little bothered by it.

"He's getting to be almost a trick pony," he complained. "I don't like trick horses. It takes all the—dignity out of a horse to make him do tricks. Why, a trick horse is kind of like an actor—no dignity, no character of his own." And his father said, "I guess you better be getting him used to the saddle pretty soon."

Jody rushed for the harness-room. For some time he had been riding the saddle on a sawhorse. He changed the stirrup length over and over, and could never get it just right. Sometimes, mounted on the sawhorse in the harness-room, with collars and hames and tugs hung all about him, Jody rode out beyond the room. He carried his rifle across the pommel. He saw the fields go flying by, and he heard the beat of the galloping hoofs.

It was a ticklish job, saddling the pony the first time. Gabilan hunched and reared and threw the saddle off before the cinch could be tightened. It had to be replaced again and again until at last the pony let it stay. And the cinching was difficult, too. Day by day Jody tightened the girth a little more until at last the pony didn't mind the saddle at all.

Then there was the bridle. Billy explained how to use a stick of licorice for a bit until Gabilan was used to having something in his mouth. Billy explained, "Of course we could force-break him to everything, but he wouldn't be as good a horse if we did. He'd always be a little bit afraid, and he wouldn't mind because he wanted to."

The first time the pony wore the bridle he whipped his head about and worked his tongue against the bit until the blood oozed from the corners of his mouth. He tried to rub the headstall off on the manger. His ears pivoted about and his eyes turned red with fear and with general rambunctiousness. Jody rejoiced, for he knew that only a mean-souled horse does not resent training.

And Jody trembled when he thought of the time when he would first sit in the saddle. The pony would probably throw him off. There was no disgrace in that. The disgrace would come if he did not get right up and mount again. Sometimes he dreamed that he lay in the dirt and cried and couldn't make himself mount again. The shame of the dream lasted until the middle of the day.

Gabilan was growing fast. Already he had lost the long-leggedness of the colt; his mane was getting longer and blacker. Under the constant currying and brushing his coat lay as smooth and gleaming as orange-red lacquer. Jody oiled the hoofs and kept them carefully trimmed so they would not crack.

The hair rope was nearly finished. Jody's father gave him an old pair of spurs and bent in the side bars and cut down the strap and took up the chainlets until they fitted. And then one day Carl Tiflin said:

"The pony's growing faster than I thought. I guess you can ride him by Thanksgiving. Think you can stick on?"

"I don't know," Jody said shyly. Thanksgiving was only three weeks off. He hoped it wouldn't rain, for rain would spot the red saddle.

Gabilan knew and liked Jody by now. He nickered when Jody came across the stubble-field, and in the pasture he came running when his master whistled for him. There was always a carrot for him every time.

Billy Buck gave him riding instructions over and over. "Now when you get up there, just grab tight with your knees and keep your hands away from the saddle, and if you get throwed, don't let that stop you. No matter how good a man is, there's always some horse can pitch him. You just climb up again before he gets to feeling smart about it. Pretty soon, he won't throw you no more, and pretty soon he *can't* throw you no more. That's the way to do it."

"I hope it don't rain before," Jody said.

"Why not? Don't want to get throwed in the mud?"

That was partly it, and also he was afraid that in the flurry of bucking Gabilan might slip and fall on him and break his leg or his hip. He had seen that happen to men before, had seen how they writhed on the ground like squashed bugs, and he was afraid of it.

He practiced on the sawhorse how he would hold the reins in his left hand and a hat in his right hand. If he kept his hands thus busy, he couldn't grab the horn if he felt himself going off. He didn't like to think of what would happen if he did grab the horn. Perhaps his father and Billy Buck would never speak to him again, they would be so ashamed. The news would get about and his mother would be ashamed too. And in the school yard—it was too awful to contemplate.

He began putting his weight in a stirrup when Gabilan was saddled, but he didn't throw his leg over the pony's back. That was forbidden until Thanksgiving.

Every afternoon he put the red saddle on the pony and cinched it tight. The pony was learning already to fill his stomach out unnaturally large while the cinching was going on, and then to let it down when the straps were fixed. Sometimes Jody led him up to the brush line and let him drink from the round green tub, and sometimes led him up through the stubble-field to the hilltop from which it was possible to see the white town of Salinas and the geometric fields of the great valley, and the oak trees clipped by the sheep. Now and then they broke through the brush and came to little cleared circles so hedged in that the world was gone and only the sky and the circle of brush were left from the old life. Gabilan liked these trips and showed it by keeping his head very high and by quivering his nostrils with interest. When the two came back from an expedition they smelled of the sweet sage they had forced through.

Time dragged on toward Thanksgiving, but winter came fast. The clouds swept down and hung all day over the land and brushed the hilltops, and the winds blew shrilly at night. All day the dry oak leaves drifted down from the trees until they covered the ground, and yet the trees were unchanged.

Jody had wished it might not rain before Thanksgiving, but it did. The brown earth turned dark and the trees glistened. The cut ends of the stubble turned black with mildew; the haystacks grayed from exposure to the damp, and on the roofs the moss, which had been all summer as gray as lizards, turned a brilliant yellow-green. During the week of rain, Jody kept the pony in the box stall out of the dampness, except for a little time after school when he took him out for exercise and to drink at the water-trough in the upper corral. Not once did Gabilan get wet.

The wet weather continued until little new grass appeared. Jody walked to school dressed in a slicker and short rubber boots. At length one morning the sun came out brightly. Jody, at his work in the box stall, said to Billy Buck, "Maybe I'll leave Gabilan in the corral when I go to school today."

"Be good for him to be out in the sun," Billy assured him. "No animal likes to be cooped up too long. Your father and me are going back on the hill to clean the leaves out of the spring." Billy nodded and picked his teeth with one of his little straws.

"If the rain comes, though—" Jody suggested.

"Not likely to rain today. She's rained herself out." Billy pulled up his sleeves and snapped his arm bands. "If it comes on to rain—why a little rain don't hurt a horse."

"Well, if it does come on to rain, you put him in, will you, Billy? I'm scared he might get cold so I couldn't ride him when the time comes."

"Oh sure! I'll watch out for him if we get back in time. But it won't rain today."

And so Jody, when he went to school, left Gabilan standing out in the corral.

Billy Buck wasn't wrong about many things. He couldn't be. But he was wrong about the weather that day, for a little after noon the clouds pushed over the hills and the rain began to pour down. Jody heard it start on the schoolhouse roof. He considered holding up one finger for permission to go to the outhouse and, once outside, running for home to put the pony in. Punishment would be prompt both at school and at home. He gave it up and took ease from Billy's assurance that rain couldn't hurt a horse. When school was finally out, he hurried home through the dark rain. The banks at the sides of the road spouted little jets of muddy water. The rain slanted and swirled under a cold and gusty wind. Jody dog-trotted home, slopping through the gravelly mud of the road.

From the top of the ridge he could see Gabilan standing miserably in the corral. The red coat was almost black, and streaked with water. He stood head down with his rump to the rain and wind. Jody arrived running and threw open the barn door and led the wet pony in by his forelock. Then he found a gunny sack and rubbed the soaked hair and rubbed the legs and ankles. Gabilan stood patiently, but he trembled in gusts like the wind.

When he had dried the pony as well as he could, Jody went up to the house and brought hot water down to the barn and soaked the grain in it. Gabilan was not very hungry. He nibbled at the hot mash, but he was not very much interested in it, and he still shivered now and then. A little steam rose from his damp back.

It was almost dark when Billy Buck and Carl Tiflin came home. "When the rain started we put up at Ben Herche's place, and the rain never let up all afternoon," Carl Tiflin explained. Jody looked reproachfully at Billy Buck and Billy felt guilty.

"You said it wouldn't rain," Jody accused him.

Billy looked away. "It's hard to tell, this time of year," he said, but his excuse was lame. He had no right to be fallible, and he knew it.

"The pony got wet, got soaked through."

"Did you dry him off?"

"I rubbed him with a sack and I gave him hot grain."

Billy nodded in agreement.

"Do you think he'll take cold, Billy?"

"A little rain never hurt anything," Billy assured him.

Jody's father joined the conversation then and lectured the boy a little. "A horse," he said, "isn't any lap-dog kind of thing." Carl Tiflin hated weakness and sickness, and he held a violent contempt for helplessness.

Jody's mother put a platter of steaks on the table and boiled potatoes and boiled squash, which clouded the room with their steam. They sat down to eat. Carl Tiflin still grumbled about weakness put into animals and men by too much coddling.

Billy Buck felt bad about his mistake. "Did you blanket him?" he asked.

"No. I couldn't find any blanket. I laid some sacks over his back."

"We'll go down and cover him up after we eat, then." Billy felt better about it then. When Jody's father had gone in to the fire and his mother was washing dishes, Billy found and lighted a lantern. He and Jody walked through the mud to the barn. The barn was dark and warm and sweet. The horses still munched their evening hay. "You hold the lantern!" Billy ordered. And he felt the pony's legs and tested the heat of the flanks. He put his cheek against the pony's gray muzzle and then he rolled up the eyelids to look at the eyeballs and he lifted the lips to see the gums, and he put his fingers inside the ears. "He don't seem so chipper," Billy said. "I'll give him a rub-down."

Then Billy found a sack and rubbed the pony's legs violently and he rubbed the chest and the withers. Gabilan was strangely spiritless. He submitted patiently to the rubbing. At last Billy brought an old cotton comforter from the saddle-room, and threw it over the pony's back and tied it at neck and chest with string.

"Now he'll be all right in the morning," Billy said.

Jody's mother looked up when he got back to the house. "You're late up from bed," she said. She held his chin in her hard hand and brushed the tangled hair out of his eyes and she said, "Don't worry about the pony. He'll be all right. Billy's as good as any horse doctor in the country."

Jody hadn't known she could see his worry. He pulled gently away from her and knelt down in front of the fireplace until it burned his stomach. He scorched himself through and then went in to bed, but it was a hard thing to go to sleep. He awakened after what seemed a long time. The room was dark but there was a grayness in the window like that which precedes the dawn. He got up and found his overalls and searched for the legs, and then the clock in the other room struck two. He laid his clothes down and got back into bed. It was broad daylight when he awakened again. For the first time he had slept through the ringing of the triangle. He leaped up, flung on his clothes and went out of the door still buttoning his shirt. His mother looked after him for a moment and then went quietly back to her work. Her eyes were brooding and kind. Now and then her mouth smiled a little but without changing her eyes at all.

Jody ran on toward the barn. Halfway there he heard the sound he dreaded, the hollow rasping cough of a horse. He broke into a sprint then. In the barn he found Billy Buck with the pony. Billy was rubbing its legs with his strong thick hands. He looked up and smiled gaily. "He just took a little cold," Billy said. "We'll have him out of it in a couple of days."

Jody looked at the pony's face. The eyes were half closed and the lids thick and dry. In the eye corners a crust of hard mucus stuck. Gabilan's ears hung loosely sideways and his head was low. Jody put out his hand, but the pony did not move close to it. He coughed again and his whole body constricted with the effort. A little stream of thin fluid ran from his nostrils.

Jody looked back at Billy Buck. "He's awful sick, Billy."

"Just a little cold, like I said," Billy insisted. "You go get some breakfast and then go back to school. I'll take care of him."

"But you might have to do something else. You might leave him."

"No, I won't. I won't leave him at all. Tomorrow's Saturday. Then you can stay with him all day." Billy had failed again, and he felt bad about it. He had to cure the pony now.

Jody walked up to the house and took his place listlessly at the table. The eggs and bacon were cold and greasy, but he didn't notice it. He ate his usual amount. He didn't even ask to stay home from school. His mother pushed his hair back when she took his plate. "Billy'll take care of the pony," she assured him.

He moped through the whole day at school. He couldn't answer any questions nor read any words. He couldn't even tell anyone the pony was sick, for that might make him sicker. And when school was finally out he started home in dread. He walked slowly and let the other boys leave him. He wished he might continue walking and never arrive at the ranch.

Billy was in the barn, as he had promised, and the pony was worse. His eyes were almost closed now, and his breath whistled shrilly past an obstruction in his nose. A film covered that part of the eyes that was visible at all. It was doubtful whether the pony could see any more. Now and then he snorted, to clear his nose, and by the action seemed to plug it tighter. Jody looked dispiritedly at the pony's coat. The hair lay rough and unkempt and seemed to have lost all of its old luster. Bill stood quietly beside the stall. Jody hated to ask, but he had to know.

"Billy, is he—is he going to get well?"

Billy put his fingers between the bars under the pony's jaw and felt about. "Feel here," he said and he guided Jody's fingers to a large lump under the jaw. "When that gets bigger, I'll open it up and then he'll get better."

Jody looked quickly away, for he had heard about that lump. "What is the matter with him?"

Billy didn't want to answer, but he had to. He couldn't be wrong three times. "Strangles," he said shortly, "but don't you worry about that. I'll pull him out of it. I've seen them get well when they were worse than Gabilan is. I'm going to steam him now. You can help."

"Yes," Jody said miserably. He followed Billy into the grain room and watched him make the steaming bag ready. It was a long canvas nose bag with straps to go over a horse's ears. Billy filled it one-third full of bran and then he added a couple of handfuls of dried hops. On top of the dry substance he poured a little carbolic acid and a little turpentine. "I'll be mixing it all up while you run to the house for a kettle of boiling water," Billy said.

When Jody came back with the steaming kettle, Billy buckled the straps over Gabilan's head and fitted the bag tightly around his nose. Then through a little hole in the side of the bag he poured the boiling water on the mixture. The pony started away as a cloud of strong steam rose up, but then the soothing fumes crept through his nose and into his lungs, and the sharp steam began to clear out the nasal passages. He breathed loudly. His legs trembled in an ague, and his eyes closed against the biting cloud. Billy poured in more water and kept the steam rising for fifteen minutes. At last he set down the kettle and took the bag from Gabilan's nose. The pony looked better. He breathed freely, and his eyes were open wider than they had been.

"See how good it makes him feel," Billy said. "Now we'll wrap him up in the blanket again. Maybe he'll be nearly well by morning."

"I'll stay with him tonight," Jody suggested.

"No. Don't you do it. I'll bring my blankets down here and put them in the hay. You can stay tomorrow and steam him if he needs it."

The evening was falling when they went to the house for their supper. Jody didn't even realize that someone else had fed the chickens and filled the wood-box. He walked up past the house to the dark brush line and took a drink of water from the tub. The spring water was so cold that it stung his mouth and drove a shiver through him. The sky above the hills was still light. He saw a hawk flying so high that it caught the sun on its breast and shone like a spark. Two blackbirds were driving him down the sky, glittering as they attacked their enemy. In the west, the clouds were moving in to rain again.

Jody's father didn't speak at all while the family ate supper, but after Billy Buck had taken his blankets and gone to sleep in the barn, Carl Tiflin built a high fire in the fireplace and told stories. He told about the wild man who ran naked through the country and had a tail and ears like a horse, and he told about the rabbit-cats of Moro Cojo that hopped into the trees for birds. He revived the famous Maxwell brothers who found a vein of gold and hid the traces of it so carefully that they could never find it again.

Jody sat with his chin in his hands; his mouth worked nervously, and his father gradually became aware that he wasn't listening very carefully. "Isn't that funny?' he asked.

Jody laughed politely and said, "Yes, sir." His father was angry and hurt, then. He didn't tell any more stories. After a while, Jody took a lantern and went down to the barn. Billy Buck was asleep in the hay, and, except that his breath rasped a little in his lungs, the pony seemed to be much better. Jody stayed a little while, running his fingers over the red rough coat, and then he took up the lantern and went back to the house. When he was in bed, his mother came into the room.

"Have you enough covers on? It's getting winter."

"Yes, ma'am."

"Well, get some rest tonight." She hesitated to go out, stood uncertainly. "The pony will be all right," she said.

Jody was tired. He went to sleep quickly and didn't awaken until dawn. The triangle sounded, and Billy Buck came up from the barn before Jody could get out of the house.

"How is he?" Jody demanded.

Billy always wolfed his breakfast. "Pretty good. I'm going to open that lump this morning. Then he'll be better maybe."

After breakfast, Billy got out his best knife, one with a needle point. He whetted the shining blade a long time on a little carborundum stone. He tried the point and the blade again and again on his calloused thumb-ball, and at last he tried it on his upper lip.

On the way to the barn, Jody noticed how the young grass was up and how the stubble was melting day by day into the new green crop of volunteer. It was a cold sunny morning.

As soon as he saw the pony, Jody knew he was worse. His eyes were closed and sealed shut with dried mucus. His head hung so low that his nose almost touched the straw of his bed. There was a little groan in each breath, a deep seated, patient groan.

Billy lifted the weak head and made a quick slash with the knife. Jody saw the yellow pus run out. He held up the head while Billy swabbed out the wound with weak carbolic acid salve.

"Now he'll feel better," Billy assured him. "That yellow poison is what makes him sick."

Jody looked unbelieving at Billy Buck. "He's awful sick."

Billy thought a long time what to say. He nearly tossed off a careless assurance, but he saved himself in time. "Yes, he's pretty sick," he said at last. "I've seen worse ones get well. If he doesn't get pneumonia, we'll pull him through. You stay with him. If he gets worse, you can come and get me."

For a long time after Billy went away, Jody stood beside the pony, stroking him behind the ears. The pony didn't flip his head the way he had done when he was well. The groaning in his breathing was becoming more hollow.

Doubletree Mutt looked into the barn, his big tail waving provocatively, and Jody was so incensed at his health that he found a hard black clod on the floor and deliberately threw it. Doubletree Mutt went yelping away to nurse a bruised paw.

In the middle of the morning, Billy Buck came back and made another steam bag. Jody watched to see whether the pony improved this time as he had before. His breathing eased a little, but he did not raise his head.

The Saturday dragged on. Late in the afternoon Jody went to the house and brought his bedding down and made up a place to sleep in the hay. He didn't ask permission. He knew from the way his mother looked at him that she would let him do almost anything. That night he left a lantern burning on a wire over the box stall. Billy had told him to rub the pony's legs every little while.

At nine o'clock the wind sprang up and howled around the barn. And in spite of his worry, Jody grew sleepy. He got into his blankets and went to sleep, but the breathy groans of the pony sounded in his dreams. And in his sleep he heard a crashing noise which went on and on until it awakened him. The wind was rushing through the barn. He sprang up and looked down the lane of stalls. The barn door had blown open, and the pony was gone.

He caught the lantern and ran outside into the gale, and he saw Gabilan weakly shambling away into the darkness, head down, legs working slowly and mechanically. When Jody ran up and caught him by the forelock, he allowed himself to be led back and put into his stall. His groans were louder, and a fierce whistling came from his nose. Jody didn't sleep any more then. The hissing of the pony's breath grew louder and sharper.

He was glad when Billy Buck came in at dawn. Billy looked for a time at the pony as though he had never seen him before. He felt the ears and flanks. "Jody," he said, "I've got to do something you won't want to see. You run up to the house for a while."

Jody grabbed him fiercely by the forearm. "You're not going to shoot him?"

Billy patted his hand. "No. I'm going to open a little hole in his windpipe so he can breathe. His nose is filled up. When he gets well, we'll put a little brass button in the hole for him to breath through."

Jody couldn't have gone away if he had wanted to. It was awful to see the red hide cut, but infinitely more terrible to know it was being cut and not to see it. "I'll stay right here," he said bitterly. "You sure you got to?"

"Yes. I'm sure. If you stay, you can hold his head. If it doesn't make you sick, that is."

The fine knife came out again and was whetted again just as carefully as it had been the first time. Jody held the pony's head up and the throat taut, while Billy felt up and down for the right place. Jody sobbed once as the bright knife point disappeared into the throat. The pony plunged weakly away and then stood still, trembling violently. The blood ran thickly out and up the knife and across Billy's hand and into his shirtsleeve. The sure square hand sawed out a round hole in the flesh, and the breath came bursting out of the hole, throwing a fine spray of blood. With the rush of oxygen, the pony took a sudden strength. He lashed out with his hind feet and tried to rear, but Jody held his head down while Billy mopped the new wound with carbolic salve. It was a good job. The blood stopped flowing and the air puffed out the hole and sucked it in regularly with a little bubbling noise.

The rain brought in by the night wind began to fall on the barn roof. Then the triangle rang for breakfast. "You go up and eat while I wait," Billy said. "We've got to keep this hole from plugging up."

Jody walked slowly out of the barn. He was too dispirited to tell Billy how the barn door had blown open and let the pony out. He emerged into the wet gray morning and sloshed up to the house, taking a perverse pleasure in splashing through all the puddles. His mother fed him and put dry clothes on. She didn't question him. She seemed to know he couldn't answer questions. But when he was ready to go back to the barn she brought him a pan of steaming meal. "Give him this," she said.

But Jody did not take the pan. He said, "He won't eat anything," and ran out of the house. At the barn, Billy showed him how to fix a ball of cotton on a stick, with which to swab out the breathing hole when it became clogged with mucus.

Jody's father walked into the barn and stood with them in front of the stall. At length he turned to the boy. "Hadn't you better come with me? I'm going to drive over the hill." Jody shook his head. "You better come on, out of this," his father insisted.

Billy turned on him angrily. "Let him alone. It's his pony, isn't it?"

Carl Tiflin walked away without saying another word. His feelings were badly hurt.

All morning Jody kept the wound open and the air passing in and out freely. At noon the pony lay wearily down on his side and stretched his nose out.

Billy came back. "If you're going to stay with him tonight, you better take a little nap," he said. Jody went absently out of the barn. The sky had cleared to a hard thin blue. Everywhere the birds were busy with worms that had come to the damp surface of the ground.

Jody walked to the brush line and sat on the edge of the mossy tub. He looked down at the house and at the old bunkhouse and at the dark cypress tree. The place was familiar, but curiously changed. It wasn't itself any more, but a frame for things that were happening. A cold wind blew out of the east now, signifying that the rain was over for a little while. At his feet Jody could see the little arms of new weeds spreading out over the ground. In the mud about the spring were thousands of quail tracks.

Doubletree Mutt came sideways and embarrassed up through the vegetable patch, and Jody, remembering how he had thrown the clod, put his arm about the dog's neck and kissed him on his wide black nose. Doubletree Mutt sat still, as though he knew some solemn thing was happening. His big tail slapped the ground gravely. Jody pulled a swollen tick out of Mutt's neck and popped it dead between his thumb-nails. It was a nasty thing. He washed his hands in the cold spring water.

Except for the steady swish of the wind, the farm was very quiet. Jody knew his mother wouldn't mind if he didn't go in to eat his lunch. After a little while he went slowly back to the barn. Mutt crept into his own little house and whined softly to himself for a long time.

Billy Buck stood up from the box and surrendered the cotton swab. The pony still lay on his side and the wound in his throat bellowsed in and out. When Jody saw how dry and dead the hair looked, he knew at last that there was no hope for the pony. He had seen the dead hair before on dogs and on cows, and it was a sure sign. He sat heavily on the box and let down the barrier of the box stall. For a long time he kept his eyes on the moving wound, and at last he dozed, and the afternoon passed quickly. Just before dark his mother brought a deep dish of stew and left it for him and went away. Jody ate a little of it, and, when it was dark, he set the lantern on the floor by the pony's head so he could watch the wound and keep it open. And he dozed again until the night chill awakened him The wind was blowing fiercely, bringing the north cold with it. Jody brought a blanket from his bed in the hay and wrapped himself in it. Gabilan's breathing was quiet at last; the hole in his throat moved gently. The owls flew through the hayloft, shrieking and looking for mice. Jody put his hands down on his head and slept. In his sleep he was aware that the wind had increased. He heard it slamming about the barn.

It was daylight when he awakened. The barn door had swung open. The pony was gone. He sprang up and ran out into the morning light.

The pony's tracks were plain enough, dragging through the frostlike dew on the young grass, tired tracks with little lines between them where the hoofs had dragged. They headed for the brush line halfway up the ridge. Jody broke into a run and followed them. The sun shone on the sharp white quartz that stuck through the ground here and there. As he followed the plain trail, a shadow cut across in front of him. He looked up and saw a high circle of black buzzards, and the slowly revolving circle dropped lower and lower. The solemn birds soon disappeared over the ridge. Jody ran faster then, forced on by panic and rage. The trail entered the brush at last and followed a winding route among the tall sage bushes.

At the top of the ridge Jody was winded. He paused, puffing noisily. The blood pounded in his ears. Then he saw what he was looking for. Below, in one of the little clearings in the brush, lay the red pony. In the distance, Jody could see the legs moving slowly and convulsively. And in a circle around him stood the buzzards, waiting for the moment of death they know so well.

Jody leaped forward and plunged down the hill. The wet ground muffled his steps and the brush hid him. When he arrived, it was all over. The first buzzard sat on the pony's head and its beak had just risen dripping with dark eye fluid. Jody plunged into the circle like a cat. The black brotherhood arose in a cloud, but the big one on the pony's head was too late. As it hopped along to take off, Jody caught its wing tip and pulled it down. It was nearly as big as he was. The free wing crashed into his face with the force of a club, but he hung on. The claws fastened on his leg and the wing elbows battered his head on either side. Jody groped blindly with his free hand. His fingers found the neck of the struggling bird. The red eyes looked into his face, calm and fearless and fierce; the naked head turned from side to side Then the beak opened and vomited a stream of putrefied fluid. Jody brought up his knee and fell on the great bird. He held the neck to the ground with one hand while his other found a piece of sharp white quartz. The first blow broke the beak sideways and black blood spurted from the twisted, leathery mouth corners. He struck again and missed. The red fearless eyes still looked at him, impersonal and unafraid and detached. He struck again and again, until the buzzard lay dead, until its head was a red pulp. He was still beating the dead bird when Billy Buck pulled him off and held him tightly to calm his shaking.

Carl Tiflin wiped the blood from the boy's face with a red bandana. Jody was limp and quiet now. His father moved the buzzard with his toe. "Jody," he explained, "the buzzard didn't kill the pony. Don't you know that?"

"I know it," Jody said wearily

It was Billy Buck who was angry. He had lifted Jody in his arms, and had turned to carry him home. But he turned back on Carl Tiflin. "'Course he knows it," Billy said furiously, "Jesus Christ! man, can't you see how he'd feel about it?"

II. THE GREAT MOUNTAINS

In the humming heat of a midsummer afternoon the little boy Jody listlessly looked about the ranch for something to do. He had been to the barn, had thrown rocks at the swallows' nests under the eaves until every one of the little mud houses broke open and dropped its lining of straw and dirty feathers. Then at the ranch house he baited a rat trap with stale cheese and set it where Doubletree Mutt, that good big dog, would get his nose snapped. Jody was not moved by an impulse of cruelty; he was bored with the long hot afternoon. Doubletree Mutt put his stupid nose in the trap and got it smacked, and shrieked with agony and limped away with blood on his nostrils. No matter where he was hurt, Mutt limped. It was just a way he had. Once when he was young, Mutt got caught in a coyote trap, and always after that he limped, even when he was scolded.

When Mutt yelped, Jody's mother called from inside the house, "Jody! Stop torturing that dog and find something to do."

Jody felt mean then, so he threw a rock at Mutt. Then he took his slingshot from the porch and walked up toward the brush line to try to kill a bird. It was a good slingshot, with store-bought rubbers, but while Jody had often shot at birds, he had never hit one. He walked up through the vegetable patch, kicking his bare toes into the dust. And on the way he found the perfect slingshot stone, round and slightly flattened and heavy enough to carry through the air. He fitted it into the leather pouch of his weapon and proceeded to the brush line. His eyes narrowed, his mouth worked strenuously; for the first time that afternoon he was intent. In the shade of the sagebrush the little birds were working, scratching in the leaves, flying restlessly a few feet and scratching again. Jody pulled back the rubbers of the sling and advanced cautiously. One little thrush paused and looked at him and crouched, ready to fly. Jody sidled nearer, moving one foot slowly after the other. When he was twenty feet away, he carefully raised the sling and aimed. The stone whizzed; the thrush started up and flew right into it. And down the little bird went with a broken head. Jody ran to it and picked it up.

"Well, I got you," he said.

The bird looked much smaller dead than it had alive. Jody felt a little mean pain in his stomach, so he took out his pocket-knife and cut off the bird's head. Then he disemboweled it, and took off its wings, and finally he threw all the pieces into the brush. He didn't care about the bird, or its life, but he knew what older people would say if they had seen him kill it; he was ashamed because of their potential opinion. He decided to forget the whole thing as quickly as he could, and never to mention it.

The hills were dry at this season, and the wild grass was golden, but where the spring-pipe filled the round tub and the tub spilled over, here lay a stretch of fine green grass, deep and sweet and moist. Jody drank from the mossy tub and washed the bird's blood from his hands in cold water. Then he lay on his back in the grass and looked up at the dumpling summer clouds. By closing one eye and destroying perspective he brought them down within reach so that he could put up his fingers and stroke them. He helped the gentle wind push them down the sky; it seemed to him that they went faster for his help. One fat white cloud he helped clear to the mountain rims and pressed it firmly over, out of sight. Jody wondered what it was seeing, then. He sat up, the better to look at the great mountains where they went piling back, growing darker and more savage until they finished with one jagged ridge, high up against the west. Curious secret mountains; he thought of the little he knew about them.

"What's on the either side?" he asked his father once.

"More mountains, I guess. Why?"

"And on the other side of them?"

"More mountains. Why?"

"More mountains on and on?"

"Well, no. At last you come to the ocean."

"But what's in the mountains?"

"Just cliffs and brush and rocks and dryness."

"Were you ever there?"

"No."

"Has anybody ever been there?"

"A few people, I guess. It's dangerous, with cliffs and things. Why, I've read there's more unexplored country in the mountains of Monterey County than any place in the United States." His father seemed proud that this should be so.

"And at last the ocean?"

"At last the ocean."

"But," the boy insisted, "but in between? No one knows?"

"Oh, a few people do, I guess. But there's nothing there to get. And not much water. Just rocks and cliffs and greasewood. Why?"

"It would be good to go."

"What for? There's nothing there."

Jody knew something was there, something very wonderful because it wasn't known, something secret and mysterious. He could feel within himself that this was so. He said to his mother, "Do you know what's in the big mountains?"

She looked at him and then back at the ferocious range, and she said, "Only the bear, I guess."

"What bear?"

"Why the one that went over the mountain to see what he could see."

Jody questioned Billy Buck, the ranch hand, about the possibility of ancient cities lost in the mountains, but Billy agreed with Jody's father.

"It ain't likely," Billy said. "There'd be nothing to eat unless a kind of people that can eat rocks live there."

That was all the information Jody ever got, and it made the mountains dear to him, and terrible. He thought often of the miles of ridge after ridge until at last there was the sea. When the peaks were pink in the morning they invited him among them: and when the sun had gone over the edge in the evening and the mountains were a purplelike despair, then Jody was afraid of them; then they were so impersonal and aloof that their very imperturbability was a threat.

Now he turned his head toward the mountains of the east, the Gabilans, and they were jolly mountains, with hill ranches in their creases, and with pine trees growing on the crests. People lived there, and battles had been fought against the Mexicans on the slopes. He looked back for an instant at the Great Ones and shivered a little at the contrast. The foothill cup of the home ranch below him was sunny and safe. The house gleamed with white light and the barn was brown and warm. The red cows on the farther hill ate their way slowly toward the north. Even the dark cypress tree by the bunkhouse was usual and safe. The chickens scratched about in the dust of the farmyard with quick waltzing steps.

Then a moving figure caught Jody's eye. A man walked slowly over the brow of the hill, on the road from Salinas, and he was headed toward the house. Jody stood up and moved down toward the house too, for if someone was coming, he wanted to be there to see. By the time the boy had got to the house the walking man was only halfway down the road, a lean man, very straight in the shoulders. Jody could tell he was old only because his heels struck the ground with hard jerks. As he approached nearer, Jody saw that he was dressed in blue jeans and in a coat of the same material. He wore clodhopper shoes and an old flat-brimmed Stetson hat. Over his shoulder he carried a gunny sack, lumpy and full. In a few moments he had trudged close enough so that his face could be seen. And his face was as dark as dried beef. A mustache, blue-white against the dark skin, hovered over his mouth, and his hair was white, too, where it showed at his neck. The skin of his face had shrunk back against the skull until it defined bone, not flesh, and made the nose and chin seem sharp and fragile. The eyes were large and deep and dark, with eyelids stretched tightly over them. Irises and pupils were one, and very black, but the eyeballs were brown. There were no wrinkles in the face at all. This old man wore a blue denim coat buttoned to the throat with brass buttons, as all men do who wear no shirts. Out of the sleeves came strong bony wrists and hands gnarled and knotted and hard as peach branches. The nails were flat and blunt and shiny.

The old man drew close to the gate and swung down his sack when he confronted Jody. His lips fluttered a little and a soft impersonal voice came from between them.

"Do you live here?"

Jody was embarrassed. He turned and looked at the house, and he turned back and looked toward the barn where his father and Billy Buck were. "Yes," he said, when no help came from either direction.

"I have come back," the old man said. "I am Gitano, and I have come back."

Jody could not take all this responsibility. He turned abruptly, and ran into the house for help, and the screen door banged after him. His mother was in the kitchen poking out the clogged holes of a colander with a hairpin, and biting her lower lip with concentration.

"It's an old man," Jody cried excitedly. "It's an old *paisano* man and he says he's come back."

His mother put down the colander and stuck the hairpin behind the sink board. "What's the matter now?" she asked patiently.

"It's an old man outside. Come on out."

"Well, what does he want?" She untied the strings of her apron and smoothed her hair with her fingers.

"I don't know. He came walking."

His mother smoothed down her dress and went out, and Jody followed her. Gitano had not moved.

"Yes?" Mrs. Tiflin asked.

Gitano took off his old black hat and held it with both hands in front of him. He repeated, "I am Gitano, and I have come back."

"Come back? Back where?"

Gitano's whole straight body leaned forward a little. His right hand described the circle of the hills, the sloping fields and the mountains, and ended at his hat again. "Back to the rancho. I was born here, and my father, too."

"Here?" she demanded. "This isn't an old place."

"No, there," he said, pointing to the western ridge. "On the other side there, in a house that is gone."

At last she understood. "The old 'dobe that's washed almost away, you mean?"

"Yes, *señora.* When the rancho broke up they put no more lime on the 'dobe, and the rains washed it down."

Jody's mother was silent for a little, and curious homesick thoughts ran through her mind, but quickly she cleared them out. "And what do you want here now, Gitano?"

"I will stay here," he said quietly, "until I die."

"But we don't need an extra man here."

"I cannot work hard any more, *señora*. I can milk a cow, feed chickens, cut a little wood; no more. I will stay here." He indicated the sack on the ground beside him. "Here are my things."

She turned to Jody. "Run down to the barn and call your father."

Jody dashed away, and he returned with Carl Tiflin and Billy Buck behind him. The old man was standing as he had been, but he was resting now. His whole body had sagged into a timeless repose.

"What is it?" Carl Tiflin asked. "What's Jody so excited about?"

Mrs. Tiflin motioned to the old man. "He wants to stay here. He wants to do a little work and stay here."

"Well, we can't have him. We don't need any more men. He's too old. Billy does everything we need."

They had been talking over him as though he did not exist, and now, suddenly, they both hesitated and looked at Gitano and were embarrassed.

He cleared his throat. "I am too old to work. I come back where I was born."

"You weren't born here," Carl said sharply.

"No. In the 'dobe house over the hill. It was all one rancho before you came."

"In the mud house that's all melted down?"

"Yes. I and my father. I will stay here now on the rancho."

"I tell you you won't stay," Carl said angrily. "I don't need an old man. This isn't a big ranch. I can't afford food and doctor bills for an old man. You must have relatives and friends. Go to them. It is like begging to come to strangers."

"I was born here," Gitano said patiently and inflexibly.

Carl Tiflin didn't like to be cruel, but he felt he must. "You can eat here tonight," he said. "You can sleep in the little room of the old bunkhouse. We'll give you your breakfast in the morning, and then you'll have to go along. Go to your friends. Don't come to die with strangers."

Gitano put on his black hat and stooped for the sack. "Here are my things," he said.

Carl turned away. "Come on, Billy, we'll finish down at the barn. Jody, show him the little room in the bunkhouse."

He and Billy turned back toward the barn. Mrs. Tiflin went into the house, saying over her shoulder, "I'll send some blankets down."

Gitano looked questioningly at Jody. "I'll show you where it is," Jody said.

There was a cot with a shuck mattress, an apple box holding a tin lantern, and a backless rocking-chair in the little room of the bunkhouse. Gitano laid his sack carefully on the floor and sat down on the bed. Jody stood shyly in the room, hesitating to go. At last he said,

"Did you come out of the big mountains?"

Gitano shook his head slowly. "No, I worked down the Salinas Valley."

The afternoon thought would not let Jody go. "Did you ever go into the big mountains back there?"

The old dark eyes grew fixed, and their light turned inward on the years that were living in Gitano's head. "Once—when I was a little boy I went with my father."

"Way back, clear into the mountains?"

"Yes."

"What was there?" Jody cried. "Did you see any people or any houses?"

"No."

"Well, what was there?"

Gitano's eyes remained inward. A little wrinkled strain came between his brows.

"What did you see in there?" Jody repeated.

"I don't know," Gitano said. "I don't remember."

"Was it terrible and dry?"

"I don't remember."

In his excitement, Jody had lost his shyness. "Don't you remember anything about it?"

Gitano's mouth opened for a word, and remained open while his brain sought the word. "I think it was quiet—I think it was nice."

Gitano's eyes seemed to have found something back in the years, for they grew soft and a little smile seemed to come and go in them.

"Didn't you ever go back in the mountains again?" Jody insisted.

"No."

"Didn't you ever want to?"

But now Gitano's face became impatient. "No," he said in a tone that told Jody he didn't want to talk about it any more. The boy was held by a curious fascination. He didn't want to go away from Gitano. His shyness returned.

"Would you like to come down to the barn and see the stock?" he asked.

Gitano stood up and put on his hat and prepared to follow.

It was almost evening now. They stood near the watering trough while the horses sauntered in from the hillsides for an evening drink. Gitano rested his big twisted hands on the top rail of the fence. Five horses came down and drank, and then stood about, nibbling at the dirt or rubbing their sides against the polished wood of the fence. Long after they had finished drinking an old horse appeared over the brow of the hill and came painfully down. It had long yellow teeth; its hoofs were flat and sharp as spades, and its ribs and hip-bones jutted out under its skin. It hobbled up to the trough and drank water with a loud sucking noise.

"That's old Easter," Jody explained. "That's the first horse my father ever had. He's thirty years old." He looked up into Gitano's old eyes for some response.

"No good any more," Gitano said.

Jody's father and Billy Buck came out of the barn and walked over.

"Too old to work," Gitano repeated. "Just eats and pretty soon dies."

Carl Tiflin caught the last words. He hated his brutality toward old Gitano, and so he became brutal again.

"It's a shame not to shoot Easter," he said. "It'd save him a lot of pains and rheumatism." He looked secretly at Gitano, to see whether he noticed the parallel, but the big bony hands did not move, nor did the dark eyes turn from the horse. "Old things ought to be put out of their misery," Jody's father went on. "One shot, a big noise, one big pain in the head maybe, and that's all. That's better than stiffness and sore teeth."

Billy Buck broke in. "They got a right to rest after they worked all of their life. Maybe they like to just walk around."

Carl had been looking steadily at the skinny horse. "You can't imagine now what Easter used to look like," he said softly. "High neck, deep chest, fine barrel. He could jump a five-bar gate in stride. I won a flat race on him when I was fifteen years old. I could of got two hundred dollars for him any time. You wouldn't think how pretty he was." He checked himself, for he hated softness. "But he ought to be shot now," he said.

"He's got a right to rest," Billy Buck insisted.

Jody's father had a humorous thought. He turned to Gitano. "If ham and eggs grew on a side-hill I'd turn you out to pasture too," he said. "But I can't afford to pasture you in my kitchen."

He laughed to Billy Buck about it as they went on toward the house. "Be a good thing for all of us if ham and eggs grew on the side-hills."

Jody knew how his father was probing for a place to hurt in Gitano. He had been probed often. His father knew every place in the boy where a word would fester.

"He's only talking," Jody said. "He didn't mean it about shooting Easter. He likes Easter. That was the first horse he ever owned."

The sun sank behind the high mountains as they stood there, and the ranch was hushed. Gitano seemed to be more at home in the evening. He made a curious sharp sound with his lips and stretched one of his hands over the fence. Old Easter moved stiffly to him, and Gitano rubbed the lean neck under the mane.

"You like him?" Jody asked softly.

"Yes—but he's no damn good."

The triangle sounded at the ranch house. "That's supper," Jody cried. "Come on up to supper."

As they walked up toward the house Jody noticed again that Gitano's body was as straight as that of a young man. Only by a jerkiness in his movements and by the scuffling of his heels could it be seen that he was old.

The turkeys were flying heavily into the lower branches of the cypress tree by the bunkhouse. A fat sleek ranch cat walked across the road carrying a rat so large that its tail dragged on the ground. The quail on the side-hills were still sounding the clear water call.

Jody and Gitano came to the back steps and Mrs. Tiflin looked out through the screen door at them.

"Come running, Jody. Come in to supper, Gitano."

Carl and Billy Buck had started to eat at the long oilcloth-covered table. Jody slipped into his chair without moving it, but Gitano stood holding his hat until Carl looked up and said, "Sit down, sit down. You might as well get your belly full before you go on." Carl was afraid he might relent and let the old man stay, and so he continued to remind himself that this couldn't be.

Gitano laid his hat on the floor and diffidently sat down. He wouldn't reach for food. Carl had to pass it to him. "Here, fill yourself up." Gitano ate very slowly, cutting tiny pieces of meat and arranging little pats of mashed potato on his plate.

The situation would not stop worrying Carl Tiflin. "Haven't you got any relatives in this part of the country?" he asked.

Gitano answered with some pride, "My brother-in-law is in Monterey. I have cousins there, too."

"Well, you can go and live there, then."

"I was born here," Gitano said in gentle rebuke.

Jody's mother came in from the kitchen, carrying a large bowl of tapioca pudding.

Carl chuckled to her, "Did I tell you what I said to him? I said if ham and eggs grew on the side-hills I'd put him out to pasture, like old Easter."

Gitano stared unmoved at his plate.

"It's too bad he can't stay," said Mrs. Tiflin.

"Now don't you start anything," Carl said crossly.

When they had finished eating, Carl and Billy Buck and Jody went into the living room to sit for a while, but Gitano, without a word of farewell or thanks, walked through the kitchen and out the back door. Jody sat and secretly watched his father. He knew how mean his father felt.

"This country's full of these old *paisanos*," Carl said to Billy Buck.

"They're damn good men," Billy defended them. "They can work older than white men. I saw one of them a hundred and five years old, and he could still ride a horse. You don't see any white men as old as Gitano walking twenty or thirty miles."

"Oh, they're tough, all right," Carl agreed. "Say, are you standing up for him too? Listen, Billy," he explained, "I'm having a hard enough time keeping this ranch out of the Bank of Italy without taking on anybody else to feed. You know that, Billy."

"Sure, I know," said Billy. "If you was rich, it'd be different."

"That's right, and it isn't like he didn't have relatives to go to. A brother-in-law and cousins right in Monterey. Why should I worry about him?"

Jody sat quietly listening, and he seemed to hear Gitano's gentle voice and its unanswerable, "But I was born here." Gitano was mysterious like the mountains. There were ranges back as far as you could see, but behind the last range piled up against the sky there was a great unknown country. And Gitano was an old man, until you got to the dull dark eyes. And in behind them was some unknown thing. He didn't ever say enough to let you guess what was inside, under the eyes. Jody felt himself irresistibly drawn toward the bunkhouse. He slipped from his chair while his father was talking and he went out the door without making a sound.

The night was very dark and far-off noises carried in clearly. The hamebells of a wood team sounded from way over the hill on the country road. Jody picked his way across the dark yard. He could see a light through the window of the little room of the bunkhouse. Because the night was secret he walked quietly up to the window and peered in. Gitano sat in the rocking-chair and his back was toward the window. His right arm moved slowly back and forth in front of him. Jody pushed the door open and walked in. Gitano jerked upright and, seizing a piece of deerskin, he tried to throw it over the thing in his lap, but the skin slipped away. Jody stood overwhelmed by the thing in Gitano's hand, a lean and lovely rapier with a golden basket hilt. The blade was like a thin ray of dark light. The hilt was pierced and intricately carved.

"What is it?" Jody demanded.

Gitano only looked at him with resentful eyes, and he picked up the fallen deerskin and firmly wrapped the beautiful blade in it.

Jody put out his hand. "Can't I see it?"

Gitano's eyes smoldered angrily and he shook his head.

"Where'd you get it? Where'd it come from?"

Now Gitano regarded him profoundly, as though he pondered. "I got it from my father."

"Well, where'd he get it?"

Gitano looked down at the long deerskin parcel in his hand. "I don't know."

"Didn't he ever tell you?"

"No."

"What do you do with it?"

Gitano looked slightly surprised. "Nothing. I just keep it."

"Can't I see it again?"

The old man slowly unwrapped the shining blade and let the lamp light slip along it for a moment. Then he wrapped it up again. "You go now. I want to go to bed." He blew out the lamp almost before Jody had closed the door.

As he went back toward the house, Jody knew one thing more sharply than he had ever known anything. He must never tell anyone about the rapier. It would be a dreadful thing to tell anyone about it, for it would destroy some fragile structure of truth. It was a truth that might be shattered by division.

On the way across the dark yard Jody passed Billy Buck. "They're wondering where you are," Billy said.

Jody slipped into the living room, and his father turned to him. "Where have you been?"

"I just went out to see if I caught any rats in my new trap."

"It's time you went to bed," his father said.

Jody was first at the breakfast table in the morning. Then his father came in, and last, Billy Buck. Mrs. Tiflin looked in from the kitchen.

"Where's the old man, Billy?" she asked.

"I guess he's out walking," Billy said. "I looked in his room and he wasn't there."

"Maybe he started early to Monterey," said Carl. "It's a long walk."

"No," Billy explained. "His sack is in the little room."

After breakfast Jody walked down to the bunkhouse. Flies were flashing about in the sunshine. The ranch seemed especially quiet this morning. When he was sure no one was watching him, Jody went into the little room, and looked into Gitano's sack. An extra pair of long cotton underwear was there, an extra pair of jeans and three pairs of worn socks. Nothing else was in the sack. A sharp loneliness fell on Jody. He walked slowly back toward the house. His father stood on the porch talking to Mrs. Tiflin.

"I guess old Easter's dead at last," he said. "I didn't see him come down to water with the other horses."

In the middle of the morning Jess Taylor from the ridge ranch rode down.

"You didn't sell that old gray crowbait of yours, did you, Carl?"

"No, of course not. Why?"

"Well," Jess said. "I was out this morning early, and I saw a funny thing. I saw an old man on an old horse, no saddle, only a piece of rope for a bridle. He wasn't on the road at all. He was cutting right up straight through the brush. I think he had a gun. At least I saw something shine in his hand."

"That's old Gitano," Carl Tiflin said. "I'll see if any of my guns are missing." He stepped into the house for a second. "Nope, all here. Which way was he heading, Jess?"

"Well, that's the funny thing. He was heading straight back into the mountains."

Carl laughed. "They never get too old to steal," he said. "I guess he just stole old Easter."

"Want to go after him, Carl?"

"Hell, no, just save me burying that horse. I wonder where he got the gun. I wonder what he wants back there."

Jody walked up through the vegetable patch, toward the brush line. He looked searchingly at the towering mountains–ridge after ridge after ridge until at last there was the ocean. For a moment he thought he could see a black speck crawling up the farthest ridge. Jody thought of the rapier and of Gitano. And he thought of the great mountains. A longing caressed him, and it was so sharp that he wanted to cry to get it out of his breast. He lay down in the green grass near the round tub at the brush line. He covered his eyes with his crossed arms and lay there a long time, and he was full of a nameless sorrow.

III. THE PROMISE

In a mid-afternoon of spring, the little boy Jody walked martially along the brush-lined road toward his home ranch. Banging his knee against the golden lard bucket he used for school lunch, he contrived a good bass drum, while his tongue fluttered sharply against his teeth to fill in snare drums and occasional trumpets. Some time back the other members of the squad that walked so smartly from the school had turned into the various little canyons and taken the wagon roads to their own home ranches. Now Jody marched seemingly alone, with high-lifted knees and pounding feet; but behind him there was a phantom army with great flags and swords, silent but deadly.

The afternoon was green and gold with spring. Underneath the spread branches of the oaks the plants grew pale and tall and on the hills the feed was smooth and thick. The sagebrushes shone with new silver leaves and the oaks wore hoods of golden green. Over the hills there hung such a green odor that the horses on the flats galloped madly, and then stopped, wondering; lambs, and even old sheep jumped in the air unexpectedly and landed on stiff legs, and went on eating; young clumsy calves butted their heads together and drew back and butted again.

As the gray and silent army marched past, led by Jody, the animals stopped their feeding and their play and watched it go by.

Suddenly Jody stopped. The gray army halted, bewildered and nervous. Jody went down on his knees. The army stood in long uneasy ranks for a moment, and then, with a soft sigh of sorrow, rose up in a faint gray mist and disappeared. Jody had seen the thorny crown of a horny-toad moving under the dust of the road. His grimy hand went out and grasped the spiked halo and held firmly while the little beast struggled. Then Jody turned the horny-toad over, exposing its pale gold stomach. With a gentle forefinger he stroked the throat and chest until the horny-toad relaxed, until its eyes closed and it lay languorous and asleep.

Jody opened his lunch pail and deposited the first game inside. He moved on now, his knees bent slightly, his shoulders crouched; his bare feet were wise and silent. In his right hand there was a long gray rifle. The brush along the road stirred restively under a new and unexpected population of gray tigers and gray bears. The hunting was very good, for by the time Jody reached the fork of the road where the mail box stood on a post, he had captured two more horny-toads, four little grass lizards, a blue snake, sixteen yellow-winged grasshoppers and a brown damp newt from under a rock. This assortment scrabbled unhappily against the tin of the lunch bucket.

At the road fork the rifle evaporated and the tigers and bears melted from the hillsides. Even the moist and uncomfortable creatures in the lunch pail ceased to exist, for the little red metal flag was up on the mail box, signifying that some postal matter was inside. Jody set his pail on the ground and opened the letter box. There was a Montgomery Ward catalogue and a copy of the *Salinas Weekly Journal*. He slammed the box, picked up his lunch pail and trotted over the ridge and down into the cup of the ranch. Past the barn he ran, and past the used-up haystack and the bunkhouse and the cypress tree. He banged through the front screen door of the ranch house calling, "Ma'am, ma'am, there's a catalogue."

Mrs. Tiflin was in the kitchen spooning clabbered milk into a cotton bag. She put down her work and rinsed her hands under the tap. "Here in the kitchen, Jody. Here I am."

He ran in and clattered his lunch pail on the sink. "Here it is. Can I open the catalogue, ma'am?"

Mrs. Tiflin took up the spoon again and went back to her cottage cheese. "Don't lose it, Jody. Your father will want to see it." She scraped the last of the milk into the bag. "Oh, Jody, your father wants to see you before you go to your chores." She waved a cruising fly from the cheese bag.

Jody closed the new catalogue in alarm. "Ma'am?"

"Why don't you ever listen? I say your father wants to see you."

The boy laid the catalogue gently on the sink board. "Do you—is it something I did?"

Mrs. Tiflin laughed. "Always a bad conscience. What did you do?"

"Nothing, ma'am," he said lamely. But he couldn't remember, and besides it was impossible to know what action might later be construed as a crime.

His mother hung the full bag on a nail where it could drip into the sink. "He just said he wanted to see you when you got home. He's somewhere down by the barn."

Jody turned and went out the back door. Hearing his mother open the lunch pail and then gasp with rage, a memory stabbed him and he trotted away toward the barn, conscientiously not hearing the angry voice that called him from the house.

Carl Tiflin and Billy Buck, the ranch hand, stood against the lower pasture fence. Each man rested one foot on the lowest bar and both elbows on the top bar. They were talking slowly and aimlessly. In the pasture half a dozen horses nibbled contentedly at the sweet grass. The mare, Nellie, stood backed up against the gate, rubbing her buttocks on the heavy post.

Jody sidled uneasily near. He dragged one foot to give an impression of great innocence and nonchalance. When he arrived beside the men he put one foot on the lowest fence rail, rested his elbows on the second bar and looked into the pasture too. The two men glanced sideways at him.

"I wanted to see you," Carl said in the stern tone he reserved for children and animals.

"Yes, sir," said Jody guiltily.

"Billy, here, says you took good care of the pony before it died."

No punishment was in the air. Jody grew bolder. "Yes, sir, I did."

"Billy says you have a good patient hand with horses."

Jody felt a sudden warm friendliness for the ranch hand.

Billy put in, "He trained that pony as good as anybody I ever seen."

Then Carl Tiflin came gradually to the point. "If you could have another horse would you work for it?"

Jody shivered. "Yes, sir."

"Well, look here, then. Billy says the best way for you to be a good hand with horses is to raise a colt."

"It's the *only* good way," Billy interrupted.

"Now, look here, Jody," continued Carl. "Jess Taylor, up to the ridge ranch, has a fair stallion, but it'll cost five dollars. I'll put up the money, but you'll have to work it out all summer. Will you do that?"

Jody felt that his insides were shriveling. "Yes, sir," he said softly.

"And no complaining? And no forgetting when you're told to do something?"

"Yes, sir."

"Well, all right, then. Tomorrow morning you take Nellie up to the ridge ranch and get her bred. You'll have to take care of her, too, till she throws the colt."

"Yes, sir."

"You better get to the chickens and the wood now."

Jody slid away. In passing behind Billy Buck he very nearly put out his hand to touch the blue-jeaned legs. His shoulders swayed a little with maturity and importance.

He went to his work with unprecedented seriousness. This night he did not dump the can of grain to the chickens so that they had to leap over each other and struggle to get it. No, he spread the wheat so far and so carefully that the hens couldn't find some of it at all. And in the house, after listening to his mother's despair over boys who filled their lunch pails with slimy, suffocated reptiles, and bugs, he promised never to do it again. Indeed, Jody felt that all such foolishness was lost in the past. He was far too grown up ever to put horny-toads in his lunch pail any more. He carried in so much wood and built such a high structure with it that his mother walked in fear of an avalanche of oak. When he was done, when he had gathered eggs that had remained hidden for weeks, Jody walked down again past the cypress tree, and past the bunkhouse toward the pasture. A fat warty toad that looked out at him from under the watering trough had no emotional effect on him at all.

Carl Tiflin and Billy Buck were not in sight, but from a metallic ringing on the other side of the barn Jody knew that Billy Buck was just starting to milk a cow.

The other horses were eating toward the upper end of the pasture, but Nellie continued to rub herself nervously against the post. Jody walked slowly near, saying, "So, girl, so-o, Nellie." The mare's ears went back naughtily and her lips drew away from her yellow teeth. She turned her head around;

her eyes were glazed and mad. Jody climbed to the top of the fence and hung his feet over and looked paternally down on the mare.

The evening hovered while he sat there. Bats and nighthawks flicked about. Billy Buck, walking toward the house carrying a full milk bucket, saw Jody and stopped. "It's a long time to wait," he said gently. "You'll get awful tired waiting."

"No, I won't, Billy. How long will it be?"

"Nearly a year."

"Well, I won't get tired."

The triangle at the house rang stridently. Jody climbed down from the fence and walked to supper beside Billy Buck. He even put out his hand and took hold of the milk bucket to help carry it.

The next morning after breakfast Carl Tiflin folded a five-dollar bill in a piece of newspaper and pinned the package in the bib pocket of Jody's overalls. Billy Buck haltered the mare Nellie and led her out of the pasture.

"Be careful now," he warned. "Hold her up short here so she can't bite you. She's crazy as a coot."

Jody took hold of the halter leather itself and started up the hill toward the ridge ranch with Nellie skittering and jerking behind him. In the pasturage along the road the wild oat heads were just clearing their scabbards. The warm morning sun shone on Jody's back so sweetly that he was forced to take a serious stiff-legged hop now and then in spite of his maturity. On the fences the shiny blackbirds with red epaulets clicked their dry call. The meadowlarks sang like water, and the wild doves, concealed among the bursting leaves of the oaks, made a sound of restrained grieving. In the fields the rabbits sat sunning themselves, with only their forked ears showing above the grass heads.

After an hour of steady uphill walking, Jody turned into a narrow road that led up a steeper hill to the ridge ranch. He could see the red roof of the barn sticking up above the oak trees, and he could hear a dog barking unemotionally near the house.

Suddenly Nellie jerked back and nearly freed herself. From the direction of the barn Jody heard a shrill whistling scream and a splintering of wood, and then a man's voice shouting. Nellie reared and whinnied. When Jody held to the halter rope she ran at him with bared teeth. He dropped his hold and scuttled out of the way, into the brush. The high scream came from the oaks again, and Nellie answered it. With hoofs battering the ground the stallion appeared and charged down the hill trailing a broken halter rope. His eyes glittered feverishly. His stiff, erected nostrils were as red as flame. His black, sleek hide shone in the sunlight. The stallion came on so fast that he couldn't stop when he reached the mare. Nellie's ears went back; she whirled and kicked at him as he went by. The stallion spun around and reared. He struck the mare with his front hoof, and while she staggered under the blow, his teeth raked her neck and drew an ooze of blood.

Instantly Nellie's mood changed. She became coquettishly feminine. She nibbled his arched neck with her lips. She edged around and rubbed her shoulder against his shoulder. Jody stood half-hidden in the brush and watched. He heard the step of a horse behind him, but before he could turn, a hand caught him by the overall straps and lifted him off the ground. Jess Taylor sat the boy behind him on the horse.

"You might have got killed," he said. "Sundog's a mean devil sometimes. He busted his rope and went right through a gate."

Jody sat quietly, but in a moment he cried, "He'll hurt her, he'll kill her. Get him away!"

Jess chuckled. "She'll be all right. Maybe you'd better climb off and go up to the house for a little. You could get maybe a piece of pie up there."

But Jody shook his head. "She's mine, and the colt's going to be mine. I'm going to raise it up."

Jess nodded. "Yes, that's a good thing. Carl has good sense some times."

In a little while the danger was over. Jess lifted Jody down and then caught the stallion by its broken halter rope. And he rode ahead, while Jody followed, leading Nellie.

It was only after he had unpinned and handed over the five dollars, and after he had eaten two pieces of pie, that Jody started for home again. And Nellie followed docilely after him. She was so quiet that Jody climbed on a stump and rode her most of the way home.

The five dollars his father had advanced reduced Jody to peonage for the whole late spring and summer. When the hay was cut he drove a rake. He led the horse that pulled on the Jackson-fork tackle, and when the baler came he drove the circling horse that put pressure on the bales. In addition, Carl Tiflin taught him to milk and put a cow under his care, so that a new chore was added night and morning.

The bay mare Nellie quickly grew complacent. As she walked about the yellowing hillsides or worked at easy tasks, her lips were curled in a perpetual fatuous smile. She moved slowly, with the calm importance of an empress. When she was put to a team, she pulled steadily and unemotionally. Jody went to see her every day. He studied her with critical eyes and saw no change whatever.

One afternoon Billy Buck leaned the many-tined manure fork against the barn wall. He loosened his belt and tucked in his shirt-tail and tightened the belt again. He picked one of the little straws from his hatband and put it in the corner of his mouth. Jody, who was helping Doubletree Mutt, the big serious dog, to dig out a gopher, straightened up as the ranch hand sauntered out of the barn.

"Let's go up and have a look at Nellie," Billy suggested.

Instantly Jody fell into step with him. Doubletree Mutt watched them over his shoulder; then he dug furiously, growled, sounded little sharp yelps to indicate that the gopher was practically caught. When he looked over his shoulder again, and saw that neither Jody nor Billy was interested, he climbed reluctantly out of the hole and followed them up the hill.

The wild oats were ripening. Every head bent sharply under its load of grain, and the grass was dry enough so that it made a swishing sound as Jody and Billy stepped through it. Halfway up the hill they could see Nellie and the iron-gray gelding, Pete, nibbling the heads from the wild oats. When they approached, Nellie looked at them and backed her ears and bobbed her head up and down rebelliously. Billy walked to her and put his hand under her mane and patted her neck, until her ears came forward again and she nibbled delicately at his shirt.

Jody asked, "Do you think she's really going to have a colt?"

Billy rolled the lids back from the mare's eyes with his thumb and forefinger. He felt the lower lip and fingered the black, leathery teats. "I wouldn't be surprised," he said.

"Well, she isn't changed at all. It's three months gone."

Billy rubbed the mare's flat forehead with his knuckle while she grunted with pleasure. "I told you you'd get tired waiting. It'll be five months more before you can even see a sign, and it'll be at least eight months more before she throws the colt, about next January."

Jody sighed deeply. "It's a long time, isn't it?"

"And then it'll be about two years more before you can ride."

Jody cried out in despair, "I'll be grown up."

"Yep, you'll be an old man," said Billy.

"What color do you think the colt'll be?"

"Why, you can't ever tell. The stud is black and the dam is bay. Colt might be black or bay or gray or dappled. You can't tell. Sometimes, a black dam might have a white colt."

"Well, I hope it's black, and a stallion."

"If it's a stallion, we'll have to geld it. Your father wouldn't let you have a stallion."

"Maybe he would," Jody said. "I could train him not to be mean."

Billy pursed his lips, and the little straw that had been in the corner of his mouth rolled down to the center. "You can't ever trust a stallion," he said critically. "They're mostly fighting and making trouble. Sometimes when they're feeling funny they won't work. They make the mares uneasy and kick hell out of the geldings. Your father wouldn't let you keep a stallion."

Nellie sauntered away, nibbling the drying grass. Jody skinned the grain from a grass stem and threw the handful into the air, so that each pointed, feathered seed sailed out like a dart. "Tell me how it'll be, Billy. Is it like when the cows have calves?"

"Just about. Mares are a little more sensitive. Sometimes you have to be there to help the mare. And sometimes if it's wrong you have to—" he paused.

"Have to what, Billy?"

"Have to tear the colt to pieces to get it out, or the mare'll die."

"But it won't be that way this time, will it, Billy?"

"Oh, no. Nellie's thrown good colts."

"Can I be there, Billy? Will you be certain to call me? It's my colt."

"Sure, I'll call you. Of course I will."

"Tell me how it'll be."

"Why, you've seen the cows calving. It's almost the same. The mare starts groaning and stretching, and then, if it's a good right birth, the head and forefeet come out, and the front hoofs kick a hole just the way the calves do. And the colt starts to breathe. It's good to be there, 'cause if its feet aren't right maybe he can't break the sac, and then he might smother."

Jody whipped his leg with a bunch of grass. "We'll have to be there, then, won't we?"

"Oh, we'll be there, all right."

They turned and walked slowly down the hill toward the barn. Jody was tortured with a thing he had to say, although he didn't want to. "Billy," he began miserably, "Billy, you won't let anything happen to the colt, will you?"

And Billy knew he was thinking of the red pony, Gabilan, and of how it died of strangles. Billy knew he had been infallible before that, and now he was capable of failure. This knowledge made Billy much less sure of himself than he had been. "I can't tell," he said roughly. "All sorts of things might happen, and they wouldn't be my fault. I can't do everything." He felt bad about his lost prestige, and so he said, meanly, "I'll do everything I know, but I won't promise anything. Nellie's a good mare. She's thrown good colts before. She ought to this time." And he walked away from Jody and went into the saddle-room beside the barn, for his feelings were hurt.

Jody traveled often to the brushline behind the house. A rusty iron pipe ran a thin stream of spring water into an old green tub. Where the water spilled over and sank into the ground there was a patch of perpetually green grass. Even when the hills were brown and baked in the summer that little patch was green. The water whined softly into the trough all the year round. This place had grown to be a centerpoint for Jody. When he had been punished the cool green grass and the singing water soothed him. When he had been mean the biting acid of meanness left him at the brushline. When he sat in the grass and listened to the purling stream, the barriers set up in his mind by the stern day went down to ruin.

On the other hand, the black cypress tree by the bunkhouse was as repulsive as the water-tub was dear; for to this tree all the pigs came, sooner or later, to be slaughtered. Pig killing was fascinating, with the screaming and the blood but it made Jody's heart beat so fast that it hurt him. After the pigs were scalded in the big iron tripod kettle and their skins were scraped and white, Jody had to go to the water-tub to sit in the grass until his heart grew quiet. The water-tub and the black cypress were opposites and enemies.

When Billy left him and walked angrily away, Jody turned up toward the house. He thought of Nellie as he walked, and of the little colt. Then suddenly he saw that he was under the black cypress, under the very singletree where the pigs were hung. He brushed his dry-grass hair off his forehead and hurried on. It seemed to him an unlucky thing to be thinking of his colt in the very slaughter place, especially after what Billy had said. To counteract any evil result of that bad conjunction he walked quickly past the ranch house, through the chicken yard, through the vegetable patch, until he came at last to the brushline.

He sat down in the green grass. The trilling water sounded in his ears. He looked over the farm buildings and across at the round hills, rich and yellow with grain. He could see Nellie feeding on the slope. As usual the water place eliminated time and distance. Jody saw a black, long-legged colt, butting against Nellie's flanks, demanding milk. And then he saw himself breaking a large colt to halter. All in a few moments the colt grew to be a magnificent animal, deep of chest, with a neck as high and arched as a seahorse's neck, with a tail that tongued and rippled like black flame. This horse was terrible to everyone but Jody. In the schoolyard the boys begged rides, and Jody smilingly agreed. But no sooner were they mounted than the black demon pitched them off. Why, that was his name, Black Demon! For a moment the trilling water and the grass and the sunshine came back, and then . . .

Sometimes in the night the ranch people, safe in their beds, heard a roar of hoofs go by. They said, "It's Jody, on Demon. He's helping out the sheriff again." And then . . .

The golden dust filled the air in the arena at the Salinas Rodeo. The announcer called the roping contests. When Jody rode the black horse to the starting chute the other contestants shrugged and gave up first place, for it was well known that Jody and Demon could rope and throw and tie a steer a great deal quicker than any roping team of two men could. Jody was not a boy any more, and Demon was not a horse. The two together were one glorious individual. And then . . .

The President wrote a letter and asked them to help catch a bandit in Washington. Jody settled himself comfortably in the grass. The little stream of water whined into the mossy tub.

The year passed slowly on. Time after time Jody gave up his colt for lost. No change had taken place in Nellie. Carl Tiflin still drove her to a light cart, and she pulled on a hay rake and worked the Jackson-fork tackle when the hay was being put into the barn.

The summer passed, and the warm bright autumn. And then the frantic morning winds began to twist along the ground, and a chill came into the air, and the poison oak turned red. One morning in September, when he had finished his breakfast, Jody's mother called him into the kitchen. She was pouring boiling water into a bucket full of dry midlings and stirring the materials to a steaming paste.

"Yes, ma'am?" Jody asked.

"Watch how I do it. You'll have to do it after this every other morning."

"Well, what is it?"

"Why, it's warm mash for Nellie. It'll keep her in good shape."

Jody rubbed his forehead with a knuckle. "Is she all right?" he asked timidly.

Mrs. Tiflin put down the kettle and stirred the mash with a wooden paddle. "Of course she's all right, only you've got to take better care of her from now on. Here, take this breakfast out to her!"

Jody seized the bucket and ran, down past the bunkhouse, past the barn, with the heavy bucket banging against his knees. He found Nellie playing with the water in the trough, pushing waves and tossing her head so that the water slopped out on the ground.

Jody climbed the fence and set the bucket of steaming mash beside her. Then he stepped back to look at her. And she was changed. Her stomach was swollen. When she moved, her feet touched the ground gently. She buried her nose in the bucket and gobbled the hot breakfast. And when she had finished and had pushed the bucket around the ground with her nose a little, she stepped quietly over to Jody and rubbed her cheek against him.

Billy Buck came out of the saddle-room and walked over. "Starts fast when it starts, doesn't it?"

"Did it come all at once?"

"Oh, no, you just stopped looking for a while." He pulled her head around toward Jody. "She's goin' to be nice, too. See how nice her eyes are! Some mares get mean, but when they turn nice, they just love everything." Nellie slipped her head under Billy's arm and rubbed her neck up and down between his arm and his side. "You better treat her awful nice now," Billy said.

"How long will it be?" Jody demanded breathlessly.

The man counted in whispers on his fingers. "About three months," he said aloud. "You can't tell exactly. Sometimes it's eleven months to the day, but it might be two weeks early, or a month late, without hurting anything."

Jody looked hard at the ground. "Billy," he began nervously, "Billy, you'll call me when it's getting born, won't you? You'll let me be there, won't you?"

Billy bit the tip of Nellie's ear with his front teeth. "Carl says he wants you to start right at the start. That's the only way to learn. Nobody can tell you anything. Like my old man did with me about the saddle blanket. He was a government packer when I was your size, and I helped him some. One day I left a wrinkle in my saddle blanket and made a saddle-sore. My old man didn't give me hell at all. But the next morning he saddled me up with a forty-pound stock saddle. I had to lead my horse and carry that saddle over a whole damn mountain in the sun. It darn near killed me, but I never left no wrinkles in a blanket again. I couldn't. I never in my life since then put on a blanket but I felt that saddle on my back."

Jody reached up a hand and took hold of Nellie's mane. "You'll tell me what to do about everything, won't you? I guess you know everything about horses, don't you?"

Billy laughed. "Why, I'm half horse myself, you see," he said. "My ma died when I was born, and being my old man was a government packer in the mountains, and no cows around most of the time, why he just gave me mostly mare's milk." He continued seriously, "And horses know that. Don't you know it, Nellie?"

The mare turned her head and looked full into his eyes for a moment, and this is a thing horses practically never do. Billy was proud and sure of himself now. He boasted a little. "I'll see you get a good colt. I'll start you right. And if you do like I say, you'll have the best horse in the county."

That made Jody feel warm and proud, too; so proud that when he went back to the house he bowed his legs and swayed his shoulders as horsemen do. And he whispered, "Whoa, you Black Demon, you! Steady down there and keep your feet on the ground."

The winter fell sharply. A few preliminary gusty showers, and then a strong steady rain. The hills lost their straw color and blackened under the water, and the winter streams scrambled noisily down the canyons. The mushrooms and puffballs popped up and the new grass started before Christmas.

But this year Christmas was not the central day to Jody. Some undetermined time in January had become the axis day around which the months swung. When the rains fell, he put Nellie in a box stall and fed her warm food every morning and curried her and brushed her.

The mare was swelling so greatly that Jody became alarmed. "She'll pop wide open," he said to Billy.

Billy laid his strong square hand against Nellie's swollen abdomen. "Feel here," he said quietly. "You can feel it move. I guess it would surprise you if there were twin colts."

"You don't think so?" Jody cried. "You don't think it will be twins, do you, Billy?"

"No, I don't, but it does happen, sometimes."

During the first two weeks of January it rained steadily. Jody spent most of his time, when he wasn't in school, in the box stall with Nellie. Twenty times a day he put his hand on her stomach to feel the colt move. Nellie became more and more gentle and friendly to him. She rubbed her nose on him. She whinnied softly when he walked into the barn.

Carl Tiflin came to the barn with Jody one day. He looked admiringly at the groomed bay coat, and he felt the firm flesh over ribs and shoulders. "You've done a good job," he said to Jody. And this was the greatest praise he knew how to give. Jody was tight with pride for hours afterward.

The fifteenth of January came, and the colt was not born. And the twentieth came; a lump of fear began to form in Jody's stomach. "Is it all right?" he demanded of Billy.

"Oh, sure."

And again, "Are you sure it's going to be all right?"

Billy stroked the mare's neck. She swayed her head uneasily. "I told you it wasn't always the same time, Jody. You just have to wait."

When the end of the month arrived with no birth, Jody grew frantic. Nellie was so big that her breath came heavily, and her ears were close together and straight up, as though her head ached. Jody's sleep grew restless, and his dreams confused.

On the night of the second of February he awakened crying. His mother called to him, "Jody, you're dreaming. Wake up and start over again."

But Jody was filled with terror and desolation. He lay quietly a few moments, waiting for his mother to go back to sleep, and then he slipped his clothes on, and crept out in his bare feet.

The night was black and thick. A little misting rain fell. The cypress tree and the bunkhouse loomed and then dropped back into the mist. The barn door screeched as he opened it, a thing it never did in the daytime. Jody went to the rack and found a lantern and a tin box of matches. He lighted the wick and walked down the long straw-covered aisle to Nellie's stall. She was standing up. Her whole body weaved from side to side. Jody called to her, "So, Nellie, so-o, Nellie," but she did not stop her swaying nor look around. When he stepped into the stall and touched her on the shoulder she shivered under his hand. Then Billy Buck's voice came from the hayloft right above the stall.

"Jody, what are you doing?"

Jody started back and turned miserable eyes up toward the nest where Billy was lying in the hay. "Is she all right, do you think?"

"Why, sure, I think so."

"You won't let anything happen, Billy, you're sure you won't?"

Billy growled down at him, "I told you I'd call you, and I will. Now you get back to bed and stop worrying that mare. She's got enough to do without you worrying her."

Jody cringed, for he had never heard Billy speak in such a tone. "I only thought I'd come and see," he said. "I woke up."

Billy softened a little then. "Well, you get to bed. I don't want you bothering her. I told you I'd get you a good colt. Get along now."

Jody walked slowly out of the barn. He blew out the lantern and set it in the rack. The blackness of the night, and the chilled mist struck him and enfolded him. He wished he believed everything Billy said as he had before the pony died. It was a moment before his eyes blinded by the feeble lantern-flame, could make any form of the darkness. The damp ground chilled his bare feet. At the cypress tree the roosting turkeys chattered a little in alarm, and the two good dogs responded to their duty and came charging out, barking to frighten away the coyotes they thought were prowling under the tree.

As he crept through the kitchen, Jody stumbled over a chair. Carl called from his bedroom, "Who's there? What's the matter there?"

And Mrs. Tiflin said sleepily, "What's the matter, Carl?"

The next second Carl came out of the bedroom carrying a candle, and found Jody before he could get into bed. "What are you doing out?"

Jody turned shyly away. "I was down to see the mare."

For a moment anger at being awakened fought with approval in Jody's father. "Listen," he said, finally, "there's not a man in this country that knows more about colts than Billy. You leave it to him."

Words burst out of Jody's mouth. "But the pony died—"

"Don't you go blaming that on him," Carl said sternly. "If Billy can't save a horse, it can't be saved."

Mrs. Tiflin called, "Make him clean his feet and go to bed, Carl. He'll be sleepy all day tomorrow."

It seemed to Jody that he had just closed his eyes to try to go to sleep when he was shaken violently by the shoulder. Billy Buck stood beside him, holding a lantern in his hand. "Get up," he said. "Hurry up." He turned and walked quickly out of the room.

Mrs. Tiflin called, "What's the matter? Is that you, Billy?"

"Yes, ma'am."

"Is Nellie ready?"

"Yes, ma'am."

"All right, I'll get up and heat some water in case you need it."

Jody jumped into his clothes so quickly that he was out the back door before Billy's swinging lantern was halfway to the barn. There was a rim of dawn on the mountain-tops, but no light had penetrated into the cup of the ranch yet. Jody ran frantically after the lantern and caught up to Billy just as he reached the barn. Billy hung the lantern to a nail on the stall-side and took off his blue denim coat. Jody saw that he wore only a sleeveless shirt under it.

Nellie was standing rigid and stiff. While they watched, she crouched. Her whole body was wrung with a spasm. The spasm passed. But in a few moments it started over again, and passed.

Billy muttered nervously, "There's something wrong." His bare hand disappeared. "Oh, Jesus," he said. "It's wrong."

The spasm came again, and this time Billy strained, and the muscles stood out on his arm and shoulder. He heaved strongly, his forehead beaded with perspiration. Nellie cried with pain. Billy was muttering, "It's wrong. I can't turn it. It's way wrong. It's turned all around wrong.

He glared wildly toward Jody. And then his fingers made a careful, careful diagnosis. His cheeks were growing tight and gray. He looked for a long questioning minute at Jody standing back of the stall. Then Billy stepped to the rack under the manure window and picked up horseshoe hammer with his wet right hand.

"Go outside, Jody," he said.

The boy stood still and stared dully at him.

"Go outside, I tell you. It'll be too late."

Jody didn't move.

Then Billy walked quickly to Nellie's head. He cried, "Turn your face away, damn you, turn your face."

This time Jody obeyed. His head turned sideways. He heard Billy whispering hoarsely in the stall. And then he heard a hollow crunch of bone. Nellie chuckled shrilly. Jody looked back in time to see the hammer rise and fall again on the flat forehead. Then Nellie fell heavily to her side and quivered for a moment.

Billy jumped to the swollen stomach; his big pocket-knife was in his hand. He lifted the skin and drove the knife in. He sawed and ripped at the tough belly. The air filled with the sick odor of warm living entrails. The other horses reared back against their halter chains and squealed and kicked.

Billy dropped the knife. Both of his arms plunged into the terrible ragged hole and dragged out a big, white, dripping bundle. His teeth tore a hole in the covering. A little black head appeared through the tear, and little slick, wet ears. A gurgling breath was drawn, and then another. Bill shucked off the sac and found his knife and cut the string. For a moment he held the little black colt in his arms and looked at it. And then he walked slowly over and laid it in the straw at Jody's feet.

Billy's face and arms and chest were dripping red. His body shivered and his teeth chattered. His voice was gone; he spoke in a throaty whisper. "There's your colt. I promised. And there it is. I had to do it—had to." He stopped and looked over his shoulder into the box stall. "Go get hot water and a sponge," he whispered. "Wash him and dry him the way his mother would. You'll have to feed him by hand. But there's your colt, the way I promised."

Jody stared stupidly at the wet, panting foal. It stretched out its chin and tried to raise its head. Its blank eyes were navy blue.

"God damn you," Billy shouted, "will you go now for the water? *Will you go?*"

Then Jody turned and trotted out of the barn into the dawn. He ached from his throat to his stomach. His legs were stiff and heavy. He tried to be glad because of the colt, but the bloody face, and the haunted, tired eyes of Billy Buck hung in the air ahead of him.

ISAAC BASHEVIS SINGER

[1904–1991]

Gimpel the Fool

(1957)

I

I AM GIMPEL the fool. I don't think myself a fool. On the contrary. But that's what folks call me. They gave me the name while I was still in school. I had seven names in all: imbecile, donkey, flax-head, dope, glump, ninny, and fool. The last name stuck. What did my foolishness consist of? I was easy to take in. They said, "Gimpel, you know the rabbi's wife has been brought to childbed?" So I skipped school. Well, it turned out to be a lie. How was I supposed to know? She hadn't had a big belly. But I never looked at her belly. Was that really so foolish? The gang laughed and hee-hawed, stomped and danced and chanted a good-night prayer. And instead of the raisins they give when a woman's lying in, they stuffed my hand full of goat turds. I was no weakling. If I slapped someone he'd see all the way to Cracow. But I'm really not a slugger by nature. I think to myself: Let it pass. So they take advantage of me.

I was coming home from school and heard a dog barking. I'm not afraid of dogs, but of course I never want to start up with them. One of them may be mad, and if he bites there's not a Tartar in the world who can help you. So I made tracks. Then I looked around and saw the whole market place wild with laughter. It was no dog at all but Wolf-Leib the Thief. How was I supposed to know it was he? It sounded like a howling bitch.

When the pranksters and leg-pullers found that I was easy to fool, every one of them tried his luck with me. "Gimpel, the Czar is coming to Frampol; Gimpel, the moon fell down in Turbeen; Gimpel, little Hodel Furpiece found a treasure behind the bathhouse." And I like a golem believed everyone. In the first place, everything is possible, as it is written in the Wisdom of the Fathers, I've forgotten just how. Second, I had to believe when the whole town came down on me! If I ever dared to say, "Ah, you're kidding!" there was trouble. People got angry. "What do you mean! You want to call everyone a liar?" What was I to do? I believed them, and I hope at least that did them some good.

I was an orphan. My grandfather who brought me up was already bent toward the grave. So they turned me over to a baker, and what a time they gave me there! Every woman or girl who came to bake a batch of noodles had to fool me at least once. "Gimpel, there's a fair in heaven; Gimpel, the rabbi gave birth to a calf in the seventh month; Gimpel, a cow flew over the roof and laid brass eggs." A student from the yeshiva came once to buy a roll, and he said, "You, Gimpel, while you stand here scraping with your baker's shovel the Messiah has come. The dead have arisen." "What do you mean?" I said. "I heard no one blowing the ram's horn!" He said, "Are you deaf?" And all began to cry, "We heard it, we heard!" Then in came Rietze the Candle-dipper and called out in her hoarse voice, "Gimpel, your father and mother have stood up from the grave. They're looking for you."

To tell the truth, I knew very well that nothing of the sort had happened, but all the same, as folks were talking, I threw on my wool vest and went out. Maybe something had happened. What did I stand to lose by looking? Well, what a cat music went up! And then I took a vow to believe nothing more. But that was no go either. They confused me so that I didn't know the big end from the small.

I went to the rabbi to get some advice. He said, "It is written, better to be a fool all your days than for one hour to be evil. You are not a fool. They are the fools. For he who causes his neighbor to feel shame loses Paradise himself." Nevertheless the rabbi's daughter took me in. As I left the rabbinical court she said, "Have you kissed the wall yet?" I said, "No; what for?" She answered, "It's the law; you've got to do it after every visit." Well, there didn't seem to be any harm in it. And she burst out laughing. It was a fine trick. She put one over on me, all right.

I wanted to go off to another town, but then everyone got busy matchmaking, and they were after me so they nearly tore my coat tails off. They talked at me and talked until I got water on the ear. She was no chaste maiden, but they told me she was virgin pure. She had a limp, and they said it was deliberate, from coyness. She had a bastard, and they told me the child was her little brother. I cried, "You're wasting your time. I'll never marry that whore." But they said indignantly, "What a way to talk! Aren't you ashamed of yourself? We can take you to the rabbi and have you fined for giving her a bad name." I saw then that I wouldn't escape them so easily and I thought: They're set on making me their butt. But when you're married the husband's the master, and if that's all right with her it's agreeable to me too. Besides, you can't pass through life unscathed, nor expect to.

I went to her clay house, which was built on the sand, and the whole gang, hollering and chorusing, came after me. They acted like bear-baiters. When we came to the well they stopped all the same. They were afraid to start anything with Elka. Her mouth would open as if it were on a hinge, and she had a fierce tongue. I entered the house. Lines were strung from wall to wall and clothes were drying. Barefoot she stood by the tub, doing the wash. She was dressed in a worn hand-me-down gown of plush. She had her hair put up in braids and pinned across her head. It took my breath away, almost, the reek of it all.

Evidently she knew who I was. She took a look at me and said, "Look who's here! He's come, the drip. Grab a seat."

I told her all; I denied nothing. "Tell me the truth," I said, "are you really a virgin, and is that mischievous Yechiel actually your little brother? Don't be deceitful with me, for I'm an orphan."

"I'm an orphan myself," she answered, "and whoever tries to twist you up, may the end of his nose take a twist. But don't let them think they can take advantage of me. I want a dowry of fifty guilders, and let them take up a collection besides. Otherwise they can kiss my you-know-what." She was very plainspoken. I said, "It's the bride and not the groom who gives a dowry." Then she said, "Don't bargain with me. Either a flat 'yes' or a flat 'no'—Go back where you came from."

I thought: No bread will ever be baked from *this* dough. But ours is not a poor town. They consented to everything and proceeded with the wedding. It so happened that there was a dysentery epidemic at the time. The ceremony was held at the cemetery gates, near the little corpse-washing hut. The fellows got drunk. While the marriage contract was being drawn up I heard the most pious high rabbi ask, "Is the bride a widow or a divorced woman?" And the sexton's wife answered for her, "Both a widow and divorced." It was a black moment for me. But what was I to do, run away from under the marriage canopy?

There was singing and dancing. An old granny danced opposite me, hugging a braided white *chalah*. The master of revels made a "God 'a mercy" in memory of the bride's parents. The schoolboys threw burrs, as on Tishe b'Av fast day. There were a lot of gifts after the sermon: a noodle board, a kneading trough, a bucket, brooms, ladles, household articles galore. Then I took a look and saw two strapping young men carrying a crib. "What do we need this for?" I asked. So they said, "Don't rack your brains about it. It's all right, it'll come in handy." I realized I was going to be rooked. Take it another way though, what did I stand to lose? I reflected: I'll see what comes of it. A whole town can't go altogether crazy.

II

At night I came where my wife lay, but she wouldn't let me in. "Say, look here, is this what they married us for?" I said. And she said, "My monthly has come." "But yesterday they took you to the ritual bath, and that's afterward, isn't it supposed to be?" "Today isn't yesterday," said she, "and yesterday's not today. You can beat it if you don't like it." In short, I waited.

Nor four months later she was in childbed. The townsfolk hid their laughter with their knuckles. But what could I do? She suffered intolerable pains and clawed at the walls. "Gimpel," she cried, "I'm going. Forgive me!" The house filled with women. They were boiling pans of water. The screams rose to the welkin.

The thing to do was to go to the House of Prayer to repeat Psalms, and that was what I did.

The townsfolk liked that, all right. I stood in a corner saying Psalms and prayers, and they shook their heads at me. "Pray, pray!" they told me. "Prayer never made any woman pregnant." One of the congregation put a straw to my mouth and said, "Hay for the cows." There was something to that too, by God!

She gave birth to a boy. Friday at the synagogue the sexton stood up before the Ark, pounded on the reading table, and announced, "The wealthy Reb Gimpel invites the congregation to a feast in honor of the birth of a son." The whole House of Prayer rang with laughter. My face was flaming. But there was nothing I could do. After all, I *was* the one responsible for the circumcision honors and rituals.

Half the town came running. You couldn't wedge another soul in. Women brought peppered chick-peas, and there was a keg of beer from the tavern. I ate and drank as much as anyone, and they all congratulated me. Then there was a circumcision, and I named the boy after my father, may he rest in peace. When all were gone and I was left with my wife alone, she thrust her head through the bed-curtain and called me to her.

"Gimpel," said she, "why are you silent? Has your ship gone and sunk?"

"What shall I say?" I answered. "A fine thing you've done to me! If my mother had known of it she'd have died a second time."

She said, "Are you crazy, or what?"

"How can you make such a fool," I said, "of one who should be the lord and master?"

"What's the matter with you?" she said. "What have you taken it into your head to imagine?"

I saw that I must speak bluntly and openly. "Do you think this is the way to use an orphan?" I said. "You have borne a bastard."

She answered, "Drive this foolishness out of your head. The child is yours."

"How can he be mine?" I argued. "He was born seventeen weeks after the wedding."

She told me then that he was premature. I said, "Isn't he a little too premature?" She said, she had had a grandmother who carried just as short a time and she resembled this grandmother of hers as one drop of water does another. She swore to it with such oaths that you would have believed a peasant at the fair if he had used them. To tell the plain truth, I didn't believe her; but when I talked it over next day with the schoolmaster he told me that the very same thing had happened to Adam and Eve. Two they went up to bed, and four they descended.

"There isn't a woman in the world who is not the granddaughter of Eve," he said.

That was how it was; they argued me dumb. But then, who really knows how such things are?

I began to forget my sorrow. I loved the child madly, and he loved me too. As soon as he saw me he'd wave his little hands and want me to pick him up, and when he was colicky I was the only one who could pacify him. I bought him a little bone teething ring and a little gilded cap. He was forever catching the evil eye from someone, and then I had to run to get one of those abracadabras for him that would get him out of it. I worked like an ox. You know how expenses go up when there's an infant in the house. I don't want to lie about it; I didn't dislike Elka either, for that matter. She swore at me and cursed, and I couldn't get enough of her. What strength she had! One of her looks could rob you of the power of speech. And her orations! Pitch and sulphur, that's what they were full of, and yet somehow also full of charm. I adored her every word. She gave me bloody wounds though.

In the evening I brought her a white loaf as well as a dark one, and also poppyseed rolls I baked myself. I thieved because of her and swiped everything I could lay hands on: macaroons, raisins, almonds, cakes. I hope I may be forgiven for stealing from the Saturday pots the women left to warm in the baker's oven. I would take out scraps of meat, a chunk of pudding, a chicken leg or head, a piece of tripe, whatever I could nip quickly. She ate and became fat and handsome.

I had to sleep away from home all during the week, at the bakery. On Friday nights when I got home she always made an excuse of some sort. Either she had heartburn, or a stitch in the side, or hiccups, or headaches. You know what women's excuses are. I had a bitter time of it. It was rough. To add to it, this little brother of hers, the bastard, was growing bigger. He'd put lumps on me, and when I wanted to hit back she'd open her mouth and curse so powerfully I saw a green haze floating before my eyes. Ten times a day she threatened to divorce me. Another man in my place would have taken French leave and disappeared. But I'm the type that bears it and says nothing. What's one to do? Shoulders are from God, and burdens too.

One night there was a calamity in the bakery; the oven burst, and we almost had a fire. There was nothing to do but go home, so I went home. Let me, I thought, also taste the joy of sleeping in bed in mid-week. I didn't want to wake the sleeping mite and tiptoed into the house. Coming in, it seemed to me that I heard not the snoring of one but, as it were, a double snore, one a thin enough snore and the other like the snoring of a slaughtered ox. Oh, I didn't like that! I didn't like it at all. I went up to the bed, and things suddenly turned black. Next to Elka lay a man's form. Another in my place would have made an uproar, and enough noise to rouse the whole town, but the thought occurred to me that I might wake the child. A little thing like that—why frighten a little swallow, I thought. All right then, I went back to the bakery and stretched out on a sack of flour and till morning I never shut an eye. I shivered as if I had had malaria. "Enough of being a donkey," I said to myself. "Gimpel isn't going to be a sucker all his life. There's a limit even to the foolishness of a fool like Gimpel."

In the morning I went to the rabbi to get advice, and it made a great commotion in the town. They sent the beadle for Elka right away. She came, carrying the child. And what do you think she did? She denied it, denied everything, bone and stone! "He's out of his head," she said. "I know nothing of dreams or divinations." They yelled at her, warned her, hammered on the table, but she stuck to her guns: it was a false accusation, she said.

The butchers and the horse-traders took her part. One of the lads from the slaughterhouse came by and said to me, "We've got our eye on you, you're a marked man." Meanwhile the child started to bear down and soiled itself. In the rabbinical court there was an Ark of the Covenant, and they couldn't allow that, so they sent Elka away.

I said to the rabbi, "What shall I do?"

"You must divorce her at once," said he.

"And what if she refuses?" I asked.

He said, "You must serve the divorce. That's all you'll have to do."

I said, "Well, all right, Rabbi. Let me think about it."

"There's nothing to think about," said he. "You mustn't remain under the same roof with her."

"And if I want to see the child?" I asked.

"Let her go, the harlot," said he, "and her brood of bastards with her."

The verdict he gave was that I mustn't even cross her threshold—never again, as long as I should live.

During the day it didn't bother me so much. I thought: It was bound to happen, the abscess had to burst. But at night when I stretched out upon the sacks I felt it all very bitterly. A longing took me, for her and for the child. I wanted to be angry, but that's my misfortune exactly, I don't have it in me to be really angry. In the first place—this was how my thoughts went—there's bound to be a slip sometimes. You can't live without errors. Probably that lad who was with her led her on and gave her presents and what not, and women are often long on hair and short on sense, and so he got around her. And then since she denies it so, maybe I was only seeing things? Hallucinations do happen. You see a figure or a mannikin or something, but when you come up closer it's nothing, there's not a thing there. And if that's so, I'm doing her an injustice. And when I got so far in my thoughts

I started to weep. I sobbed so that I wet the flour where I lay. In the morning I went to the rabbi and told him that I had made a mistake. The rabbi wrote on with his quill, and he said that if that were so he would have to reconsider the whole case. Until he had finished I wasn't to go near my wife, but I might send her bread and money by messenger.

III

Nine months passed before all the rabbis could come to an agreement. Letters went back and forth. I hadn't realized that there could be so much erudition about a matter like this.

Meanwhile Elka gave birth to still another child, a girl this time. On the Sabbath I went to the synagogue and invoked a blessing on her. They called me up to the Torah, and I named the child for my mother-in-law—may she rest in peace. The louts and loudmouths of the town who came into the bakery gave me a going over. All Frampol refreshed its spirits because of my trouble and grief. However, I resolved that I would always believe what I was told. What's the good of *not* believing? Today it's your wife you don't believe; tomorrow it's God Himself you won't take stock in.

By an apprentice who was her neighbor I sent her daily a corn or a wheat loaf, or a piece of pastry, rolls or bagels, or, when I got the chance, a slab of pudding, a slice of honeycake, or wedding strudel—whatever came my way. The apprentice was a goodhearted lad, and more than once he added something on his own. He had formerly annoyed me a lot, plucking my nose and digging me in the ribs, but when he started to be a visitor to my house he became kind and friendly. "Hey, you, Gimpel," he said to me, "you have a very decent little wife and two fine kids. You don't deserve them."

"But the things people say about her," I said.

"Well, they have long tongues," he said, "and nothing to do with them but babble. Ignore it as you ignore the cold of last winter."

One day the rabbi sent for me and said, "Are you certain, Gimpel, that you were wrong about your wife?"

I said, "I'm certain."

"Why, but look here! You yourself saw it."

"It must have been a shadow," I said.

"The shadow of what?"

"Just of one of the beams, I think."

"You can go home then. You owe thanks to the Yanover rabbi. He found an obscure reference in Maimonides that favored you."

I seized the rabbi's hand and kissed it.

I wanted to run home immediately. It's no small thing to be separated for so long a time from wife and child. Then I reflected: I'd better go back to work now, and go home in the evening. I said nothing to anyone, although as far as my heart was concerned it was like one of the Holy Days. The women teased and twitted me as they did every day, but my thought was: Go on, with your loose talk. The truth is out, like the oil upon the water. Maimonides says it's right, and therefore it is right!

At night, when I had covered the dough to let it rise, I took my share of bread and a little sack of flour and started homeward. The moon was full and the stars were glistening, something to terrify the soul. I hurried onward, and before me darted a long shadow. It was winter, and a fresh snow had fallen. I had a mind to sing, but it was growing late and I didn't want to wake the householders. Then I felt like whistling, but I remembered that you don't whistle at night because it brings the demons out. So I was silent and walked as fast as I could.

Dogs in the Christian yards barked at me when I passed, but I thought: Bark your teeth out! What are you but mere dogs? Whereas I am a man, the husband of a fine wife, the father of promising children.

As I approached the house my heart started to pound as though it were the heart of a criminal. I felt no fear, but my heart went thump! thump! Well, no drawing back. I quietly lifted the latch and went in. Elka was asleep. I looked at the infant's cradle. The shutter was closed, but the moon forced its way through the cracks. I saw the newborn child's face and loved it as soon as I saw it—immediately—each tiny bone.

Then I came nearer to the bed. And what did I see but the apprentice lying there beside Elka. The moon went out all at once. It was utterly black, and I trembled. My teeth chattered. The bread fell from my hands, and my wife waked and said, "Who is that, ah?"

I muttered, "It's me."

"Gimpel?" she asked. "How come you're here? I thought it was forbidden."

"The rabbi said," I answered and shook as with a fever.

"Listen to me, Gimpel," she said, "go out to the shed and see if the goat's all right. It seems she's been sick." I have forgotten to say that we had a goat. When I heard she was unwell I went into the yard. The nannygoat was a good little creature. I had a nearly human feeling for her.

With hesitant steps I went up to the shed and opened the door. The goat stood there on her four feet. I felt her everywhere, drew her by the horns, examined her udders, and found nothing wrong. She had probably eaten too much bark. "Good night, little goat," I said. "Keep well." And the little beast answered with a "Maa" as though to thank me for the good will.

I went back. The apprentice had vanished.

"Where," I asked, "is the lad?"

"What lad?" my wife answered.

"What do you mean?" I said. "The apprentice. You were sleeping with him."

"The things I have dreamed this night and the night before," she said, "may they come true and lay you low, body and soul! An evil spirit has taken root in you and dazzles your sight." She screamed out, "You hateful creature! You moon calf! You spook! You uncouth man! Get out, or I'll scream all Frampol out of bed!"

Before I could move, her brother sprang out from behind the oven and struck me a blow on the back of the head. I thought he had broken my neck. I felt that something about me was deeply wrong, and I said, "Don't make a scandal. All that's needed now is that people should accuse me of raising spooks and *dybbuks*." For that was what she had meant. "No one will touch bread of my baking."

In short, I somehow calmed her.

"Well," she said, "that's enough. Lie down, and be shattered by wheels."

Next morning I called the apprentice aside. "Listen here, brother!" I said. And so on and so forth. "What do you say?" He stared at me as though I had dropped from the roof or something.

"I swear," he said, "you'd better go to an herb doctor or some healer. I'm afraid you have a screw loose, but I'll hush it up for you." And that's how the thing stood.

To make a long story short, I lived twenty years with my wife. She bore me six children, four daughters and two sons. All kinds of things happened, but I neither saw nor heard. I believed, and that's all. The rabbi recently said to me, "Belief in itself is beneficial. It is written that a good man lives by his faith."

Suddenly my wife took sick. It began with a trifle, a little growth upon the breast. But she evidently was not destined to live long; she had no years. I spent a fortune on her. I have forgotten to say that by this time I had a bakery of my own and in Frampol was considered to be something of a rich man. Daily the healer came, and every witch doctor in the neighborhood was brought. They decided to use leeches, and after that to try cupping. They even called a doctor from Lublin, but it was too late. Before she died she called me to her bed and said, "Forgive me, Gimpel."

I said, "What is there to forgive? You have been a good and faithful wife."

"Woe, Gimpel!" she said. "It was ugly how I deceived you all these years. I want to go clean to my Maker, and so I have to tell you that the children are not yours."

If I had been clouted on the head with a piece of wood it couldn't have bewildered me more.

"Whose are they? " I asked.

"I don't know," she said. "There were a lot . . . but they're not yours." And as she spoke she tossed her head to the side, her eyes turned glassy, and it was all up with Elka. On her whitened lips there remained a smile.

I imagined that, dead as she was, she was saying, "I deceived Gimpel. That was the meaning of my brief life."

IV

One night, when the period of mourning was done, as I lay dreaming on the flour sacks, there came the Spirit of Evil himself and said to me, "Gimpel, why do you sleep?"

I said, "What should I be doing? Eating *kreplach*?"

"The whole world deceives you," he said, "and you ought to deceive the world in your turn."

"How can I deceive all the world?" I asked him.

He answered, "You might accumulate a bucket of urine every day and at night pour it into the dough. Let the sages of Frampol eat filth."

"What about the judgment in the world to come?" I said.

"There is no world to come," he said. "They've sold you a bill of goods and talked you into believing you carried a cat in your belly. What nonsense!"

"Well then," I said, "and is there a God?"

He answered, "There is no God either."

"What," I said, "*is* there, then?"

"A thick mire."

He stood before my eyes with a goatish beard and horn, long-toothed, and with a tail. Hearing such words, I wanted to snatch him by the tail, but I tumbled from the flour sacks and nearly broke a rib. Then it happened that I had to answer the call of nature, and, passing, I saw the risen dough, which seemed to say to me, "Do it! " In brief, I let myself be persuaded.

At dawn the apprentice came. We kneaded the bread, scattered caraway seeds on it, and set it to bake. Then the apprentice went away, and I was left sitting in the little trench by the oven, on a pile of rags. Well, Gimpel, I thought, you've revenged yourself on them for all the shame they've put on you. Outside the frost glittered, but it was warm beside the oven. The flames heated my face. I bent my head and fell into a doze.

I saw in a dream, at once, Elka in her shroud. She called to me, "What have you done, Gimpel?"

I said to her, "It's all your fault," and started to cry.

"You fool!" she said. "You fool! Because I was false is everything false too? I never deceived anyone but myself. I'm paying for it all, Gimpel. They spare you nothing here."

I looked at her face. It was black; I was startled and waked, and remained sitting dumb. I sensed that everything hung in the balance. A false step now and I'd lose Eternal Life. But God gave me His help. I seized the long shovel and took out the loaves, carried them into the yard, and started to dig a hole in the frozen earth.

My apprentice came back as I was doing it. "What are you doing boss?" he said, and grew pale as a corpse.

"I know what I'm doing," I said, and I buried it all before his very eyes.

Then I went home, took my hoard from its hiding place, and divided it among the children. "I saw your mother tonight," I said. "She's turning black, poor thing."

They were so astounded they couldn't speak a word.

"Be well," I said, "and forget that such a one as Gimpel ever existed." I put on my short coat, a pair of boots, took the bag that held my prayer shawl in one hand, my stock in the other, and kissed the *mezzuzah*. When people saw me in the street they were greatly surprised.

"Where are you going?" they said.

I answered, "Into the world." And so I departed from Frampol.

I wandered over the land, and good people did not neglect me. After many years I became old and white; I heard a great deal, many lies and falsehoods, but the longer I lived the more I understood that there were really no lies. Whatever doesn't really happen is dreamed at night. It happens to one if it doesn't happen to another, tomorrow if not today, or a century hence if not next year. What difference can it make? Often I heard tales of which I said, "Now this is a thing that cannot happen." But before a year had elapsed I heard that it actually had come to pass somewhere.

Going from place to place, eating at strange tables, it often happens that I spin yarns—improbable things that could never have happened—about devils, magicians, windmills, and the like. The children run after me, calling, "Grandfather, tell us a story." Sometimes they ask for particular stories, and I try to please them. A fat young boy once said to me, "Grandfather, it's the same story you told us before." The little rogue, he was right.

So it is with dreams too. It is many years since I left Frampol, but as soon as I shut my eyes I am there again. And whom do you think I see? Elka. She is standing by the washtub, as at our first encounter, but her face is shining and her eyes are as radiant as the eyes of a saint, and she speaks outlandish words to me, strange things. When I wake I have forgotten it all. But while the dream lasts I am comforted. She answers all my queries, and what comes out is that all is right. I weep and implore, "Let me be with you." And she consoles me and tells me to be patient. The time is nearer than it is far. Sometimes she strokes and kisses me and weeps upon my face. When I awaken I feel her lips and taste the salt of her tears.

No doubt the world is entirely an imaginary world, but it is only once removed from the true world. At the door of the hovel where I lie, there stands the plank on which the dead are taken away. The gravedigger Jew has his spade ready. The grave waits and the worms are hungry; the shrouds are prepared—I carry them in my beggar's sack. Another *shnorrer* is waiting to inherit my bed of straw. When the time comes I will go joyfully. Whatever may be there, it will be real, without complication, without ridicule, without deception. God be praised: there even Gimpel cannot be deceived.

Translated by Saul Bellow

JOHN O'HARA

[1905–1970]

Imagine Kissing Pete

(First published in the *New Yorker*, September, 1960; first book publication in 1960.)

TO THOSE WHO knew the bride and groom, the marriage of Bobbie Hammersmith and Pete McCrea was the surprise of the year. As late as April of '29 Bobbie was still engaged to a fellow who lived in Greenwich, Connecticut, and she had told friends that the wedding would take place in September. But the engagement was broken and in a matter of weeks the invitations went out for her June wedding to Pete. One of the most frequently uttered comments was that Bobbie was not giving herself much opportunity to change her mind again. The comment was doubly cruel, since it carried the implication that if she gave herself time to think, Pete McCrea would not be her ideal choice. It was not only that she was marrying Pete on the rebound; she seemed to be going out of her way to find someone who was so unlike her other beaus that the contrast was unavoidable. And it was.

I was working in New York and Pete wrote to ask me to be an usher. Pete and I had grown up together, played together as children, and gone to dancing school and to the same parties. But we had never been close friends and when Pete and I went away to our separate prep schools and, later, Pete to Princeton and I to work, we drifted into that relationship of young men who had known each other all their lives without creating anything that was enduring or warm. As a matter of fact, I had never in my life received a written communication from Pete McCrea, and his handwriting on the envelope was new to me, as mine in my reply was to him. He mentioned who the best man and the other ushers would be—all Gibbsville boys—and this somewhat pathetic commentary on his four years in prep school and four years in college made an appeal to home town and boyhood loyalty that I could not reject. I had some extra days coming to me at the office, and so I told Pete I would be honored to be one of his ushers. My next step was to talk to a Gibbsville girl who lived in New York, a friend of Bobbie Hammersmith's. I took her to dinner at an Italian speakeasy where my credit was good, and she gave me what information she had. She was to be a bridesmaid.

"Bobbie isn't saying a word," said Kitty Clark. "That is, nothing about the inner turmoil. Nothing *intime.* Whatever happened happened the last time she was in New York, four or five weeks ago. All she'd tell me was that Johnny White was impossible. Impossible. Well, he'd been very possible all last summer and fall."

"What kind of a guy was he?" I asked.

"Oh—*attractive,*" she said. "Sort of wild, I guess, but not a roué. Maybe he is a roué, but I'd say more just wild. I honestly don't know a thing about it, but it wouldn't surprise me if Bobbie was ready to settle down, and he wasn't. She was probably more in love with him than he was with her."

"I doubt that. She wouldn't turn around and marry Pete if she were still in love with this White guy."

"Oh, *wouldn't* she? Oh, are you ever wrong there. If she wanted to thumb her nose at Johnny, I can't think of a better way. Poor Pete. You know *Pete.* Ichabod McCrea. Remember when Mrs. McCrea made us stop calling him Ichabod? Lord and Taylor! She went to see my mother and I guess all the other mothers and said it just had to stop. Bad enough calling her little Angus by such a common nickname as Pete. But calling a boy Ichabod. I don't suppose Pete ever knew his mother went around like that."

"Yes he did. It embarrassed him. It always embarrassed him when Mrs. McCrea did those things."

"Yes, she was uncanny. I can remember when I was going to have a party, practically before I'd made out the list Mrs. McCrea would call Mother to be sure Pete wasn't left out. Not that I ever would have left him out. We all always had the same kids to our parties. But Mrs. McCrea wasn't leaving anything to chance. I'm dying to hear what she has to say about this marriage. I'll bet she doesn't like it, but I'll bet she's in fear and trembling in case Bobbie changes her mind again. Ichabod McCrea and Bobbie Hammersmith. Beauty and the beast. And actually he's not even a beast. It would be better if he were. She's the third of our old bunch to get married, but much as I hate to say it, I'll bet she'll be the first to get a divorce. Imagine *kissing* Pete, let alone any of the rest of it."

The wedding was on a Saturday afternoon; four o'clock in Trinity Church, and the reception at the country club. It had been two years since I last saw Bobbie Hammersmith and she was now twenty-two, but she could have passed for much more than that. She was the only girl in her crowd who had not bobbed her hair, which was jet-black and which she always wore with plaited buns over the ears. Except in the summer her skin was like Chinese white and it was always easy to pick her out first in group photographs; her eyes large dark dots, quite far apart, and her lips small but prominent in the whiteness of her face beneath the two small dots of her nose. In summer, with a tan, she reminded many non-operagoers of Carmen. She was a striking beauty, although it took two years' absence from her for me to realize it. In the theatre they have an expression, "walked through the part," which means that an actress played a role without giving it much of herself. Bobbie walked through the part of bride-to-be. A great deal of social activity was concentrated in the three days—Thursday, Friday, and Saturday—up to and including the wedding reception; but Bobbie walked through the part. Today, thirty years later, it would be assumed that she had been taking tranquilizers, but this was 1929.

Barbara Hammersmith had never been anything but a pretty child; if she had ever been homely it must have been when she was a small baby, when I was not bothering to look at her. We—Pete McCrea and the other boys—were two, three, four years older than Bobbie, but when she was fifteen or sixteen she began to pass among us, from boy to boy, trying one and then another, causing several fist fights, and half promising but never delivering anything more than the "soul kisses" that were all we really expected. By the time she was eighteen she had been in and out of love with all of us with the solitary exception of Pete McCrea. When she broke off with a boy, she would also make up with the girl he had temporarily deserted for Bobbie, and all the girls came to understand that every boy in the crowd had to go through a love affair with her. Consequently Bobbie was popular; the boys remembered her kisses, the girls forgave her because the boys had been returned virtually intact. We used the word hectic a lot in those days; Kitty Clark explained the short duration of Bobbie's love affairs by observing that being in love with Bobbie was too hectic for most boys. It was also true that it was not hectic enough. The boys agreed that Bobbie was a hot little number, but none of us could claim that she was not a virgin. At eighteen Bobbie entered a personal middle age, and for the big social occasions her beaus came from out-of-town. She was also busy at the college proms and football games, as far west as Ann Arbor, as far north as Brunswick, Maine. I was working on the Gibbsville paper during some of those years, the only boy in our crowd who was not away at college, and I remember Ann Arbor because Bobbie went there wearing a Delta Tau Delta pin and came back wearing the somewhat larger Psi U. "Now don't you say anything in front of Mother," she said. "She thinks they're both the same."

We played auction bridge, the social occupation in towns like ours, and Bobbie and I were assimilated into an older crowd: the younger married set and the youngest of the couples who were in their thirties. We played for prizes—flasks, cigarette lighters, vanity cases, cartons of cigarettes—and there was a party at someone's house every week. The hostess of the evening usually asked me to stop for Bobbie, and I saw her often. Her father and mother would be reading the evening paper and sewing when I arrived to pick up Bobbie. Philip Hammersmith was not a native of Gibbsville, but he had lived there long enough to have gone to the Mexican Border in 1916 with the Gibbsville company of mounted engineers, and he had gone to France with them, returning as a first lieutenant and with the Croix de Guerre with palm. He was one of the best golfers in the club, and everyone said he was making money hand-over-fist as an independent coal operator. He wore steel-rim glasses and he had almost completely gray hair, cut short. He inspired trust and confidence. He was slow-moving, taller than six feet, and always thought before speaking. His wife, a Gibbsville girl, was related, as she said, to half the town; a lively little woman who took her husband's arm even if they were walking only two doors away. I always used to feel that whatever he may have wanted out of life, yet unattained or unattainable, she had just what she wanted: a good husband, a nice home, and a pretty daughter who would not long remain unmarried. At home in the evening, and whenever I saw him on the street, Mr. Hammersmith was wearing a dark-gray worsted suit, cut loose and with a soft roll to the lapel; black knit four-in-hand necktie; white shirt; heavy gray woolen socks, and thick-soled brogues. This costume, completely unadorned—he wore a wrist watch—was what he always wore except for formal occasions, and the year-to-year sameness of his attire constituted his only known eccentricity. He was on the board of the second most conservative bank, the trustees of Gibbsville Hospital, the armory board, the Y.M.C.A., and the Gibbsville and Lantenengo country clubs. Nevertheless I sensed that that was not all there was to Philip Hammersmith, that the care he put into the creation of the general picture of himself—hard work, quiet clothes, thoughtful manner, conventional associations—was done with a purpose that was not necessarily sinister but was extraordinarily private. It delighted me to discover, one night while waiting for Bobbie, that he knew more about what was going on than most of us suspected he would know. "Jimmy, you know Ed Charney, of course," he said.

I knew Ed Charney, the principal bootlegger in the area. "Yes, I know him pretty well," I said.

"Then do you happen to know if there's any truth to what I heard? I heard that his wife is threatening to divorce him."

"I doubt it. They're Catholics."

"Do you know her?"

"Yes. I went to Sisters' school with her."

"Oh, then maybe you can tell me something else. I've heard that she's the real brains of those two."

"She quit school after eighth grade, so I don't know about that. I don't remember her being particularly bright. She's about my age but she was two grades behind me."

"I see. And you think their religion will keep them from getting a divorce?"

"Yes, I do. I don't often see Ed at Mass, but I know he carries rosary beads. And she's at the eleven o'clock Mass every Sunday, all dolled up."

This conversation was explained when Repeal came and with it public knowledge that Ed Charney had been quietly buying bank stock, one of several moves he had made in the direction of respectability. But the chief interest to me at the time Mr. Hammersmith and I talked was in the fact that he knew anything at all about the Charneys. It was so unlike him even to mention Ed Charney's name.

To get back to the weekend of Bobbie Hammersmith's wedding: it was throughout that weekend that I first saw Bobbie have what we called that faraway look, that another generation called Cloud 90. If you happened to catch her at the right moment, you would see her smiling up at Pete in a way that must have been reassuring to Mrs. McCrea and to Mrs. Hammersmith, but I also caught her at several wrong moments and I saw something I had never seen before: a resemblance to her father that was a subtler thing than the mere duplication of such features as mouth, nose, and set of the eyes. It was almost the same thing I have mentioned in describing Philip Hammersmith; the wish yet unattained or unattainable. However, the pre-nuptial parties and the wedding and reception went off without a hitch, or so I believed until the day after the wedding.

Kitty Clark and I were on the same train going back to New York and I made some comment about the exceptional sobriety of the ushers and how everything had gone according to plan. "Amazing, considering," said Kitty.

"Considering what?"

"That there was almost no wedding at all," she said. "You must promise word of honor, Jimmy, or I won't tell you."

"I promise. Word of honor."

"Well, after Mrs. McCrea's very-dull-I-must-say luncheon, when we all left to go to Bobbie's? A little after two o'clock?"

"Yes."

"Bobbie asked me if I'd go across the street to our house and put in a long-distance call to Johnny White. I said I couldn't do that, and what on earth was she thinking of. And Bobbie said, 'You're my oldest and best friend. The least you can do is make this one last effort, to keep me from ruining my life.' So I gave in and I dashed over to our house and called Johnny. He was out and they didn't know where he could be reached or what time he was coming home. So I left my name. *My* name, not Bobbie's. Six o'clock, at the reception, I was dancing with—I was dancing with *you*."

"When the waiter said you were wanted on the phone."

"It was Johnny. He'd been sailing and just got in. I made up some story about why I'd called him, but he didn't swallow it. '*You* didn't call me,' he said. '*Bobbie* did.' Well of course I wouldn't admit that. By that time she was married, and if her life was already ruined it would be a darned sight more ruined if I let him talk to her. Which he wanted to do. Then he tried to pump me. Where were they going on their wedding trip? I said nobody knew, which was a barefaced lie. I knew they were going to Bermuda. Known it since Thursday. But I wouldn't tell Johnny . . . I don't like him a bit after yesterday. I'd thought he was attractive, and he *is*, but he's got a mean streak that I never knew before. Feature this, if you will. When he realized I wasn't going to get Bobbie to come to the phone, or give him any information, he said, 'Well, no use wasting a long-distance call. What are you doing next weekend? How about coming out here?' 'I'm not that hard up,' I said, and banged down the receiver. I hope I shattered his eardrum."

I saw Pete and Bobbie McCrea when I went home the following Christmas. They were living in a small house on Twin Oaks Road, a recent real-estate development that had been instantly successful with the sons and daughters of the big two- and three-servant mansions. They were not going to any of the holiday dances; Bobbie was expecting a baby in April or early May.

"You're not losing any time," I said.

"I don't want to lose any time," said Bobbie. "I want to have a lot of children. Pete's an only child and so am I, and we don't think it's fair, if you can afford to have more."

"If we can afford it. The way that stock market is going, we'll be lucky to pay for this one," said Pete.

"Oh, don't start on that, Pete. That's all Father talks about," said Bobbie. "My father *was* hit pretty hard, but I wish he didn't have to keep talking about it all the time. Everybody's in the same boat."

"No they're not. *We're* on a *raft*."

"I asked you, please, Pete. Jimmy didn't come here to listen to our financial woes. Do you see much of Kitty? I've owed her a letter for ages."

"No, I haven't seen her since last summer, we went out a few times," I said.

"Kitty went to New York to try to rope in a millionaire. She isn't going to waste her time on Jim."

"That's not what she went to New York for at all. And as far as wasting her time on Jim, Jim may not want to waste his time on her." She smiled. "Have you got a girl, Jim?"

"Not really."

"Wise. Very wise," said Pete McCrea.

"I don't know how wise. It's just that I have a hell of a hard time supporting myself, without trying to support a wife, too," I said.

"Why I understood you were selling articles to magazines, and going around with all the big shots."

"I've had four jobs in two years, and the jobs didn't last very long. If things get any tougher I may have to come back here. At least I'll have a place to sleep and something to eat."

"But I see your name in magazines," said Pete. "I don't always read your articles, but they must pay you well."

"They don't. At least I can't live on the magazine pieces without a steady job. Excuse me, Bobbie. Now you're getting *my* financial woes."

"She'll listen to yours. It's mine she doesn't want to hear about."

"That's because I know about ours. I'm never allowed to forget them," said Bobbie. "Are you going to all the parties?"

"Yes, stag. I have to bum rides. I haven't got a car."

"We resigned from the club," said Pete.

"Well we didn't *have* to do that," said Bobbie. "Father was going to give it to us for a Christmas present. And you have your job."

"We'll see how much longer I have it. Is that the last of the gin?"

"Yes."

Pete rose. "I'll be back."

"Don't buy any more for me," I said.

"You flatter yourself," he said. "I wasn't only getting it for you." He put on his hat and coat. "No funny business while I'm gone. I remember you two."

He kept a silly grin on his face while saying the ugly things, but the grin was not genuine and the ugly things were.

"I don't know what's the matter with him," said Bobbie. "Oh, I do, but why talk about it?"

"He's only kidding."

"You know better than that. He says worse things, much worse, and I'm only hoping they don't get back to Father. Father has enough on his mind. I thought if I had this baby right away it would—you know—give Pete confidence. But it's had just the opposite effect. He says it isn't his child. *Isn't his child!* Oh, I married him out of spite. I'm sure Kitty must have told you that. But it *is* his child, I swear it, Jim. It couldn't be anybody else's."

"I guess it's the old inferiority complex," I said.

"The first month we were married—Pete was a virgin—and I admit it, I wasn't. I stayed with two boys before I was married. But I was certainly not pregnant when I married Pete, and the first few weeks he was loving and sweet, and grateful. But then something happened to him, and he made a pass at I-won't-say-who. It was more than a pass. It was quite a serious thing. I might as well tell you. It was Phyllis. We were all at a picnic at the Dam and several people got pretty tight, Pete among them. And there's no other word for it, he tried to rape Phyllis. Tore her bathing suit and slapped her and did other things. She got away from him and ran back to the cottage without anyone seeing her. Luckily Joe didn't see her or I'm sure he'd have killed Pete. You know, Joe's strong as an ox and terribly jealous. I found out about it from Phyllis herself. She came here the next day and told me. She said she wasn't going to say anything to Joe, but that we mustn't invite her to our house and she wasn't going to invite us to hers."

"I'm certainly glad Joe didn't hear about it. He would do something drastic," I said. "But didn't he notice that you two weren't going to his house, and they to yours? It's a pretty small group."

She looked at me steadily. "We haven't been going anywhere. My excuse is that I'm pregnant, but the truth is, we're not being asked. It didn't end with Phyllis, Jim. One night at a dinner party Mary Lander just slapped his face, in front of everybody. Everybody laughed and thought Pete must have said something, but it wasn't something he'd said. He'd taken her hand and put it—you know. This is *Pete*! *Ichabod*! Did you ever know any of this about him?"

"You mean have I heard any of this? No."

"No, I didn't mean that. I meant, did he go around making passes and I never happened to hear about it?"

"No. When we'd talk dirty he'd say, 'Why don't you fellows get your minds above your belts?'"

"I wish your father were still alive. I'd go see him and try to get some advice. I wouldn't think of going to Dr. English."

"Well, you're not the one that needs a doctor. Could you get Pete to go to one? He's a patient of Dr. English's, isn't he?"

"Yes, but so is Mrs. McCrea, and Pete would never confide in Dr. English."

"Or anyone else at this stage, I guess," I said. "I'm not much help, am I?"

"Oh, I didn't expect you to have a solution. You know, Jim, I wish you would come back to Gibbsville. Other girls in our crowd have often said it was nice to have you to talk to. Of course you were a very bad boy, too, but a lot of us miss you."

"That's nice to hear, Bobbie. Thank you. I may be back, if I don't soon make a go of it in New York. I won't have any choice."

During that Christmas visit I heard other stories about Pete McCrea. In general they were told as plain gossip, but two or three times there was a hint of a lack of sympathy for Bobbie. "She knew what she was doing . . . she made her bed . . ." And while there was no lack of righteous indignation over Pete's behavior, he had changed in six months from a semi-comic figure to an unpleasant man, but a man nevertheless. In half a year he had lost most of his old friends; they all said, "You've never seen such a change come over anybody in all your life," but when they remembered to call him Ichabod it was only to emphasize the change.

Bobbie's baby was born in April, but lived only a few weeks. "She was determined to have that baby," Kitty Clark told me. "She had to prove to Pete that it was anyway *conceived* after she married him. But it must have taken all her strength to hold on to it that long. All her strength *and* the baby's. Now would be a good time for her to divorce him. She can't go on like that."

But there was no divorce, and Bobbie was pregnant again when I saw her at Christmas, 1930. They no longer lived in the Twin Oaks Road house, and her father and mother had given up their house on Lantenengo Street. The Hammersmiths were living in an apartment on Market Street, and Bobbie and Pete were living with Mrs. McCrea. "Temporarily, till Pete decides whether to take this job in Tulsa, Oklahoma," said Bobbie.

"Who do you think you're kidding?" said Pete. "It isn't a question of me deciding. It's a cousin of mine deciding. It's a cousin of mine deciding if he'll take me on. And why the hell should he?"

"Well, you've had several years' banking experience," she said.

"Yes. And if I was so good, why did the bank let me go? Jim knows all this. What else have you heard about us, Jim? Did you hear Bobbie was divorcing me?"

"It doesn't look that way from here," I said.

"You mean because she's pregnant? That's elementary biology, and God knows you're acquainted with the facts of life. But if you want to be polite, all right. Pretend you didn't hear she was getting a divorce. You might as well pretend Mr. and Mrs. Hammersmith are still living on Lantenengo Street. If they were, Bobbie'd have got her divorce."

"Everybody tells me what I *was* going to do or *am* going to do," said Bobbie. "Nobody ever consults me."

"I suppose that's a crack at my mother."

"Oh, for Christ's sake, Pete, lay off, at least while I'm here," I said.

"Why? You like to think of yourself as an old friend of the family, so you might as well get a true picture. When you get married, if you ever do, I'll come and see you, and maybe your wife will cry on my shoulder." He got up and left the house.

"Well, it's just like a year ago," said Bobbie. "When you came to call on us last Christmas?"

"Where will he go now?"

"Oh, there are several places where he can charge drinks. They all think Mrs. McCrea has plenty of money, but they're due for a rude awakening. She's living on capital, but she's not going to sell any bonds to pay his liquor bills."

"Then maybe *he's* due for a rude awakening."

"Any awakening would be better than the last three months, since the bank fired him. He sits here all day long, then after Mrs. McCrea goes to bed he goes to one of his speakeasies." She sat up straighter. "He has a lady friend. Or have you heard?"

"No."

"Yes. He graduated from making passes at all my friends. He had to. We were never invited anywhere. Yes, he has a girl friend. Do you remember Muriel Nierhaus?"

"The chiropractor's wife. Sure. Big fat Murial Minzer till she married Nierhaus, then we used to say he gave her some adjustments. Where is Nierhaus?"

"Oh, he's opened several offices. Very prosperous. He divorced her but she gets alimony. She's Pete's girl friend. Murial Minzer is *Angus McCrea's* girl friend."

"You don't seem too displeased," I said.

"Would you be, if you were in my position?"

"I guess I know what you mean. But—well, nothing."

"But why don't I get a divorce?" She shook her head. "A spite marriage is a terrible thing to do to anybody. If I hadn't deliberately selected Pete out of all the boys I knew, he'd have gone on till Mrs. McCrea picked out somebody for him, and it would almost have had to be the female counterpart of Pete. A girl like—oh—Florence. Florence Temple."

"Florence Temple, with her cello. Exactly right."

"But I did that awful thing to Pete, and the first few weeks of marriage were just too much for him. He went haywire. I'd slept with two boys before I was married, so it wasn't as much of a shock to me. But Pete almost wore me out. And such adoration, I can't tell you. Then when we came back from Bermuda he began to see all the other girls he'd known all his life, and he'd ask me about them. It was as though he'd never seen them before, in a way. In other ways, it was as though he'd just been waiting all his life to start ripping their clothes off. He was dangerous, Jim. He really was. I could almost tell who would be next by the questions he'd ask. Before we'd go to a party, he'd say 'Who's going to be there tonight?' And I'd say I thought the usual crowd. Then he'd rattle off the list of names of our friends, and leave out one name. That was supposed to fool me, but it didn't for long. The name he left out, that girl was almost sure to be in for a bad time."

"And now it's all concentrated on Muriel Minzer?"

"As far as I know."

"Well, that's a break for you, *and* the other girls. Did you ever talk to him about the passes he made at the others?"

"Oh, how could we avoid it? Whoever it was, she was always 'that little whore.'"

"Did he ever get anywhere with any of them?"

She nodded. "One, but I won't tell you who. There was one girl that didn't stop him, and when that happened he wanted me to sleep with her husband."

"Swap, eh?"

"Yes. But I said I wasn't interested. Pete wanted to know why not? Why wouldn't I? And I almost told him. The boy was one of the two boys I'd stayed with before I was married—oh, when I was seventeen. And he never told anybody and neither have I, or ever will."

"You mean one of our old crowd actually did get somewhere with you, Bobbie?"

"One did. But don't try to guess. It won't do you any good to guess, because I'd never, never tell."

"Well, whichever one it was, he's the best liar I ever knew. And I guess the nicest guy in our whole crowd. You know, Bobbie, the whole damn bunch are going to get credit now for being as honorable as one guy."

"You were all nice, even if you all did talk too much. If it had been you, you would have lied, too."

"No, I don't think I would have."

"You lied about Kitty. Ha ha ha. You didn't know I knew about you and Kitty. I knew it the next day. The very next day. If you don't believe me, I'll tell you where it happened and how it happened, and all about it. That was the great bond we had in common. You and Kitty, and I and this other boy."

"Then Kitty's a gentleman, because she never told me a word about you."

"I kissed every boy in our crowd except Pete, and I necked, heavynecked two, as you well know, and stayed with one."

"The question is, did you stay with the other one that you heavynecked with?"

"You'll never know, Jim, and please don't try to find out."

"I won't, but I won't be able to stop theorizing," I said.

We knew everything, everything there was to know. We were so far removed from the technical innocence of eighteen, sixteen, nineteen. I was a man of the world, and Bobbie was indeed a woman, who had borne a child and lived with a husband who had come the most recently to the knowledge we had acquired, but was already the most intricately involved in the complications of sex. We—Bobbie and I—could discuss him and still remain outside the problems of Pete McCrea. We could almost remain outside our own problems. We knew so much, and since what we knew seemed to be all there was to know, we were shockproof. We had come to our maturity and our knowledgeability during the long decade of cynicism that was usually dismissed as "a cynical disregard of the law of the land," but that was something else, something deeper. The law had been passed with a "noble" but nevertheless cynical disregard of men's right to drink. It was a law that had been imposed on some who took pleasure in drinking by some who did not. And when the law was an instant failure, it was not admitted to be a failure by those who had imposed it. They fought to retain the law in spite of its immediate failure and its proliferating corruption, and they fought as hard as they would have for a law that had been an immediate success. They gained no recruits to their own way; they had only deserters, who were not brave deserters but furtive ones; there was no honest mutiny but only grumbling and small disobediences. And we grew up listening to the grumbling, watching the small disobediences; laughing along when the grumbling was intentionally funny, imitating the small disobediences in other ways besides the customs of drinking. It was not only a cynical disregard for a law of the land; the law was eventually changed. Prohibition, the zealots' attempt to force total abstinence on a temperate nation, made liars of a hundred million men and cheats of their children; the West Point cadets who cheated in examinations, the basketball players who connived with gamblers, the thousands of uncaught cheats in the high schools and colleges. We had grown up and away from our earlier esteem of God and country and valor, and had matured at a moment when riches were vanishing for reasons that we could not understand. We were the losing, not the lost, generation. We could not blame Pete McCrea's troubles—and Bobbie's—on the Southern Baptists and the Northern Methodists. Since we knew everything, we knew that Pete's sudden release from twenty years of frustrations had turned him loose in a world filled with women. But Bobbie and I sat there in her mother-in-law's house, breaking several laws of possession, purchase, transportation and consumption of liquor, and with great calmness discussing the destruction of two lives—one of them hers—and the loss of her father's fortune, the depletion of her mother-in-law's, the allure of a chiropractor's divorcée, and our own promiscuity. We knew everything, but we were incapable of recognizing the meaning of our complacency.

I was wearing my dinner jacket, and someone was going to pick me up and take me to a dinner dance at the club. "Who's stopping for you?" said Bobbie.

"It depends. Either Joe or Frank. Depends on whether they go in Joe's car or Frank's. I'm to be ready when they blow their horn."

"Do me a favor, Jim. Make them come in. Pretend you don't hear the horn."

"If it's Joe, he's liable to drive off without me. You know Joe if he's had a few too many."

In a few minutes there was a blast of a two-tone horn, repeated. "That's Joe's car," said Bobbie. "You'd better go." She went to the hall with me and I kissed her cheek. The front door swung open and it was Joe Whipple.

"Hello, Bobbie," he said.

"Hello, Joe. Won't you all come in? Haven't you got time for one drink?" She was trying not to sound suppliant, but Joe was not deceived.

"Just you and Jim here?" he said.

"Yes. Pete went out a little while ago."

"I'll see what the others say," said Joe. He left to speak to the three in the sedan, and obviously he was not immediately persuasive, but they came in with him. They would not let Bobbie take their coats, but they were nice to her and with the first sips of our drinks we were all six almost back in the days when Bobbie Hammersmith's house was where so many of our parties started from. Then we heard the front door thumping shut and Pete McCrea looked in.

There were sounds of hello, but he stared at us over his horn-rims and said to Bobbie: "You didn't have to invite me, but you could have told me." He turned and again the front door thumped.

"Get dressed and come with us," said Joe Whipple.

"I can't do that," said Bobbie.

"She can't, Joe," said Phyllis Whipple. "That would only make more trouble."

"What trouble? She's going to have to sit here alone till he comes home. She might as well be with us," said Joe.

"Anyway, I haven't got a dress that fits," said Bobbie. "But thanks for asking me."

"I won't have you sitting here–"

"Now don't make matters worse, Joe, for heaven's sake," said his wife.

"I could lend you a dress, Bobbie, but I think Phyllis is right," said Mary Lander. "Whatever *you* want to do."

"*Want* to do! That's not the question," said Bobbie. "Go on before I change my mind. Thanks, everybody. Frank, you haven't said a word."

"Nothing much for me to say," said Frank Lander. But as far as I was concerned he, and Bobbie herself, had said more than anyone else. I caught her looking at me quickly.

"Well, all right, then," said Joe. "I'm outnumbered. Or outpersuaded or something."

I was the last to say goodbye, and I whispered to Bobbie: "Frank, eh?"

"You're only guessing," she said. "Goodnight, Jim." Whatever they would be after we left, her eyes were brighter than they had been in years. She had very nearly gone to a party, and for a minute or two she had been part of it.

I sat in the back seat with Phyllis Whipple and Frank Lander. "If you'd had any sense you'd know there'd be a letdown," said Phyllis.

"Oh, drop it," said Joe.

"It might have been worth it, though, Phyllis," said Mary Lander. "How long is it since she's seen anybody but that old battle-ax, Mrs. McCrea? God, I hate to think what it must be like, living in that house with Mrs. McCrea."

"I'm sure it would have been a *lot* easier if Bobbie'd come with us," said Phyllis. "That would have fixed things just right with Mrs. McCrea. She's just the type that wants Bobbie to go out and have a good time. Especially without Pete. You forget how the old lady used to call up all the mothers as soon as she heard there was a party planned. What Joe did was cruel because it was so downright stupid. Thoughtless. Like getting her all excited and then leaving her hung up."

"You've had too much to drink," said Joe.

"*I* have?"

"Yes, you don't say things like that in front of a bachelor," said Joe.

"Who's—oh, Jim? It is to laugh. Did I shock you, Jim?"

"Not a bit. I didn't know what you meant. Did you say something risqué?"

"My husband thinks I did."

"Went right over my head," I said. "I'm innocent about such things."

"So's your old man," said Joe.

"Do you think she should have come with us, Frank?" I said.

"Why ask me? No. I'm with Phyllis. What's the percentage for Bobbie? You saw that son of a bitch in the doorway, and you know damn well when he gets home from Muriel Nierhaus's, he's going to raise hell with Bobbie."

"Then Bobbie had nothing to lose," said Joe. "If Pete's going to raise hell with her, anyway, she might as well have come with us."

"How does he raise hell with her?" I said.

No one said anything.

"Do you know, Phyllis?" I said.

"What?" said Phyllis.

"Oh, come on. You heard me," I said. "Mary?"

"I'm sure I don't know."

"Oh, nuts," I said.

"Go ahead, tell him," said Frank Lander.

"Nobody ever knew for sure," said Phyllis, quietly.

"That's not true. Caroline English, for one. She knew for sure."

Phyllis spoke: "A few weeks before Bobbie had her baby she rang Caroline's doorbell in the middle of the night and asked Caroline if she could stay there. Naturally Caroline said yes, and she saw that Bobbie had nothing but a coat over her nightgown and had bruises all over her arms and shoulders. Julian was away, a lucky break because he'd have gone over and had a fight with Pete. As it was, Caroline made Bobbie have Dr. English come out and have a look at her, and nothing more was said. I mean, it was kept secret from everybody, especially Mr. Hammersmith. But the story got out somehow. Not widespread, but we all heard about it."

"We don't want it to get back to Mr. Hammersmith," said Mary Lander.

"He knows," said Frank Lander.

"You keep saying that, but I don't believe he does," said Mary.

"I don't either," said Joe Whipple. "Pete wouldn't be alive today if Phil Hammersmith knew."

"That's where I think you're wrong," said Phyllis. "Mr. Hammersmith might want to kill Pete, but killing him is another matter. And what earthly good would it do? The Hammersmiths have lost every penny, so I'm told, and at least with Pete still alive, Mrs. McCrea supports Bobbie. Barely. But they have food and a roof over their heads."

"Phil Hammersmith knows the whole damn story, you can bet anything on that. And it's why he's an old man all of a sudden. Have you seen him this trip, Jim?" said Frank Lander.

"I haven't seen him since the wedding."

"Oh, well–" said Mary.

"You won't–" said Joe.

"You won't recognize him," said Frank Lander. "He's bent over–"

"They say he's had a stroke," said Phyllis Whipple.

"And on top of everything else he got a lot of people sore at him by selling his bank stock to Ed Charney," said Joe. "Well, not a lot of people, but some that could have helped him. My old man, to name one. And I don't think that was so hot. Phil Hammersmith was a carpetbagger himself, and damn lucky to be in the bank. Then to sell his stock to a lousy stinking bootlegger . . . You should hear Harry Reilly on the subject."

"I don't want to hear Harry Reilly on any subject," said Frank Lander. "Cheap Irish Mick."

"I don't like him any better than you do, Frank, but call him something else," I said.

"I'm sorry, Jim. I didn't mean that," said Frank Lander.

"No. It just slipped out," I said.

"I apologize," said Frank Lander.

"Oh, all right."

"Don't be sensitive, Jim," said Mary.

"Stay out of it, Mary," said Frank Lander.

"*Everybody* calm down," said Joe. "Everybody knows that Harry Reilly is a cheap Irish Mick, and nobody knows it better than Jim, an Irish Mick but not a cheap one. So shut the hell up, everybody."

"Another country heard from," said Phyllis.

"Now *you*, for Christ's sake," said Joe. "Who has the quart?"

"I have my quart," said Frank Lander.

"I have mine," I said.

"I asked who has mine. Phyllis?"

"When we get to the club, time enough," said Phyllis.

"Hand it over," said Joe.

"Three quarts of whiskey between five people. I'd like to know how we're going to get home tonight," said Mary Lander.

"Drunk as a monkey, if you really want to know," said Joe. "Tight as a nun's."

"Well, at least we're off the subject of Bobbie and Pete," said Phyllis.

"I'm not. I was coming back to it. Phyllis. The quart," said Joe.

"No," said Phyllis.

"Here," I said. "And remember where it came from." I handed him my bottle.

Joe took a swig in the corner of his mouth, swerving the car only slightly. "Thanks," he said, and returned the bottle. "Now, Mary, if you'll light me a cigarette like a dear little second cousin."

"Once removed," said Mary Lander.

"Once removed, and therefore related to Bobbie through her mother."

"No, *you* are but I'm not," said Mary Lander.

"Well, you're in it some way, through me. Now for the benefit of those who are not related to Bobbie or Mrs. Hammersmith, or Mary or me. Permit me to give you a little family history that will enlighten you on several points."

"Is this going to be about Mr. Hammersmith?" said Phyllis. "I don't think you'd better tell that."

"You're related only by marriage, so kindly keep your trap shut. If I want to tell it, I can."

"Everybody remember that I asked him not to," said Phyllis.

"Don't tell it, Joe, whatever it is," said Mary Lander.

"Yeah, what's the percentage?" said Frank Lander. "They have enough trouble without digging up past history."

"Oh, you're so noble, Lander," said Joe. "You fool nobody."

"If you're going to tell the story, go ahead, but stop insulting Frank," said Mary Lander.

"We'll be at the club before he gets started," said Phyllis.

"Then we'll sit there till I finish. Anyway, it doesn't take that long. So, to begin at the beginning. Phil Hammersmith. Phil Hammersmith came here before the war, just out of Lehigh."

"You're not even telling it right," said Phyllis.

"Phyllis is right. I'm screwing up my own story. Well, I'll begin again. Phil Hammersmith graduated from Lehigh, then a few years *later* he came to Gibbsville."

"That's better," said Phyllis.

"The local Lehigh contingent all knew him. He'd played lacrosse and he was a Sigma Nu around the time Mr. Chew was there. So he already had friends in Gibbsville."

"Now you're on the right track," said Phyllis.

"Thank you, love," said Joe.

"Where was he from originally?" I asked.

"Don't ask questions, Jim. It only throws me. He was from some place in New Jersey. So anyway he arrived in Gibbsville and got a job with the Coal & Iron Company. He was a civil engineer, and he had the job when he arrived. That is, he didn't come here looking for a job. He was hired before he got here."

"You've made that plain," said Phyllis.

"Well, it's important," said Joe.

"Yes, but you don't have to say the same thing over and over again," said Phyllis.

"Yes I do. Anyway, apparently the Coal & Iron people hired him on the strength of his record at Lehigh, plus asking a few questions of the local Lehigh contingent, that knew him, *plus* a very good recommendation he'd had from some firm in Bethlehem. Where he'd worked after getting out of college. But after he'd been here a while, and was getting along all right at the Coal & Iron, one day a construction engineer from New York arrived to talk business at the C. & I. Building. They took him down-cellar to the drafting-room and who should he see but Phil Hammersmith. But apparently Phil didn't see him. Well, the New York guy was a real wet smack, because he tattled on Phil.

"Old Mr. Duncan was general superintendent then and he sent for Phil. Was it true that Phil had once worked in South America, and if so, why hadn't he mentioned it when he applied for a job? Phil gave him the obvious answer. 'Because if I had, you wouldn't have hired me.' 'Not necessarily,' said Mr. Duncan. 'We might have accepted your explanation.' 'You say that now, but I tried telling the truth and I couldn't get a job.' 'Well, tell me the truth now,' said Mr. Duncan. 'All right,' said Phil. So he told Mr. Duncan what had happened.

"He was working in South America. Peru, I think. Or maybe Bolivia. In the jungle. And the one thing they didn't want the natives, the Indians, to get hold of was firearms. But one night he caught a native carrying an armful of rifles from the shanty, and when Phil yelled at him, the native ran, and Phil shot him. Killed him. The next day one of the other engineers was found with his throat cut. And the day after that the native chief came and called on the head man of the construction outfit. Either the Indians thought they'd killed the man that had killed their boy, or they didn't much care. But the chief told the white boss that the next time an Indian was killed, two white men would be killed. And not just killed. Tortured. Well, there were four or maybe five engineers, including Phil and the boss. The only white men in an area as big as Pennsylvania, and I guess they weighed their chances and being mathematicians, the odds didn't look so hot. So they quit. No hero stuff. They just quit. Except Phil. He was fired. The boss blamed Phil for everything and in his report to the New York office he put in a lot of stuff that just about fixed Phil for good. The boss, of course, was the same man that spotted Phil at the C. & I. drafting-room."

"You told it very well," said Phyllis.

"So any time you think of Phil Hammersmith killing Pete McCrea, it wouldn't be the first time," said Joe.

"And the war," I said. "He probably killed a few Germans."

"On the other hand, he never got over blaming himself for the other engineer's getting his throat cut," said Joe. "This is all the straight dope. Mr. Duncan to my old man."

We were used to engineers, their travels and adventures in far-off places, but engineers came and went and only a few became fixtures in our life.

Phil Hammersmith's story was all new to Mary and Frank and me, and in the cold moonlight, as we sat in a heated automobile in a snow-covered parking area of a Pennsylvania country club, Joe Whipple had taken us to a dark South American jungle, given us a touch of fear, and in a few minutes covered Phil Hammersmith in mystery and then removed the mystery.

"Tell us more about Mr. Hammersmith," said Mary Lander.

Mary Lander. I had not had time to realize the inference that must accompany my guess that Frank Lander was the one boy in our crowd who had stayed with Bobbie. Mary Lander was the only girl who had not fought off Pete McCrea. She was the last girl I would have suspected of staying with Pete, and yet the one that surprised me the least. She had always been the girl our mothers liked us to take out, a kind of mothers' ideal for their sons, and possibly even for themselves. Mary Morgan Lander was the third generation of a family that had always been in the grocery business, the only store in the county that sold caviar and English biscuits and Sportsmen's Bracer chocolate, as well as the most expensive domestic items of fruit, vegetables, and tinned goods. Her brother Llewellyn Morgan still scooped out dried prunes and operated the rotary ham slicer, but no one seriously believed that all the Morgan money came from the store. Lew Morgan taught Sunday School in the Methodist Episcopal Church and played basketball at the Y.M.C.A., but he had been to Blair Academy and Princeton, and his father had owned one of the first Pierce-Arrows in Gibbsville. Mary had been unfairly judged a teaser, in previous years. She was not a teaser, but a girl who would kiss a boy and allow him to wander all over her body so long as he did not touch bare skin. Nothing surprised me about Mary. It was in character for her to have slapped Pete McCrea at a dinner party, and then to have let him stay with her and to have discussed with him a swap of husbands and wives. No casual dirty remark ever passed unnoticed by Mary; when someone made a slip we would all turn to see how Mary was taking it, and without fail she had heard it, understood it, and taken a pious attitude. But in our crowd she was the one person most conscious of sex and scatology. She was the only one of whom I would say she had a dirty mind, but I kept that observation to myself along with my theory that she hated Frank Lander. My theory, based on no information whatever, was that marriage and Frank Lander had not been enough for her and that Pete McCrea had become attractive to her because he was so awful.

"There's no more to tell," said Joe Whipple. We got out of the car and Mary took Joe's arm, and her evening was predictable: fathers and uncles and older brothers would cut in on her, and older women would comment as they always did that Mary Lander was *such* a sensible girl, *so* considerate of her elders, a *wonderful* wife to Frank. And we of her own age would dance with her because under cover of the dancing crowd Mary would wrap both legs around our right legs with a promise that had fooled us for years. Quiet little Mary Lander, climbing up a boy's leg but never forgetting to smile her Dr. Lyons smile at old Mrs. Ginyan and old Mr. Heff. And yet through some mental process that I did not take time to scrutinize, I was less annoyed with Mary than I had been since we were children. I was determined not to dance with her, and I did not, but my special knowledge about her and Pete McCrea reduced her power to allure. Bobbie had married Pete McCrea and she was still attractive in spite of it; but Mary's seductiveness vanished with the revelation that she had picked Pete as her lover, if only for once, twice, or how many times. I had never laughed at Mary before, but now she was the fool, not we, not I.

I got quite plastered at the dance, and so did a lot of other people. On the way home we sang a little—"Body and Soul" was the song, but Phyllis was the only one who could sing the middle part truly—and Frank Lander tried to tell about an incident in the smoking-room, where Julian English apparently had thrown a drink in Harry Reilly's face. It did not seem worth making a fuss about, and Frank never finished his story. Mary Lander attacked me: "You never danced with me, not once," she said.

"I didn't?"

"No, you didn't, and you know you didn't," she said. "And you always do."

"Well, this time I guess I didn't."

"Well, *why* didn't you?"

"Because he didn't want to," said Frank Lander. "You're making a fool of yourself. I should think you'd have more pride."

"Yeah, why don't you have more pride, Mary?" said Joe Whipple. "You'd think it was an honor to dance with this Malloy guy."

"It is," I said.

"That's it. You're getting so conceited," said Mary. "Well, I'm sure I didn't have to sit any out."

"Then why all the fuss?" said Frank Lander.

"Such popularity must be deserved," I said, quoting an advertising slogan.

"Whose? Mary's or yours?" said Phyllis.

"Well, I was thinking of Mary's, but now that you mention it . . ." I said.

"How many times did he dance with *you*, Phyllis?" said Joe.

"Three or four," said Phyllis.

"In that case, Frank, Jim has insulted your wife. I don't see any other way out of it. You have to at least slap his face. Shall I stop the car?"

"My little trouble-maker," said Phyllis.

"Come on, let's have a fight," said Joe. "Go ahead, Frank. Give him a punch in the nose."

"Yeah, like you did at the Dam, Frank," I said.

"Oh, God. I remember that awful night," said Phyllis. "What did you fight over?"

"Bobbie," I said.

"Bobbie was the cause of *more* fights," said Mary Lander.

"Well, we don't need her to fight over now. We have you," said Joe. "Your honor's been attacked and your husband wants to defend it. The same as I would if Malloy hadn't danced with *my* wife. It's a good thing you danced with Phyllis, Malloy, or you and I'd get out of this car and start slugging."

"Why did you fight over Bobbie? I don't remember that," said Mary.

"Because she came to the picnic with Jim and then went off necking with Frank," said Phyllis. "I remember the whole thing."

"Stop *talking* about fighting and let's *fight*, " said Joe.

"All right, stop the car," I said.

"Now you're talking," said Joe.

"Don't be ridiculous," said Phyllis.

"Oh, shut up," said Joe. He pulled up on the side of the road. "I'll referee." He got out of the car, and so did Frank and I and Phyllis. "All right, put up your dukes." We did so, moved around a bit in the snow and slush. "Go on, mix it," said Joe, whereupon Frank rushed me and hit me on the left cheek. All blows were directed at the head, since all three of us were armored in coonskin coats. "That was a good one, Frank. Now go get him, Jim." I swung my right hand and caught Frank's left eye, and at that moment we were all splashed by slush, taken completely by surprise as Phyllis, whom we had forgotten, drove the car away.

"That bitch!" said Joe. He ran to the car and got hold of a door handle but she increased her speed and he fell in the snow. "God damn that bitch, I should have known she was up to something. Now what? Let's try to bum a ride." The fight, such as it was, was over, and we tried to flag down cars on their way home from the dance. We recognized many of them, but not one would stop.

"Well, thanks to you, we've got a nice three-mile walk to Swedish Haven," said Frank Lander.

"Oh, she'll be back," said Joe.

"I'll bet you five bucks she's not," I said.

"Well, I won't bet, but I'll be damned if I'm going to walk three miles. I'm just going to wait till we can bum a ride."

"If you don't keep moving you'll freeze," said Frank.

"We're nearer the club than we are Swedish Haven. Let's go back there," I said.

"And have my old man see me?" said Joe.

"Your old man went home hours ago," I said.

"Well, somebody'll see me," said Joe.

"Listen, half the club's seen you already, and they wouldn't even stop," I said.

"Who has a cigarette?" said Joe.

"Don't give him one," said Frank.

"I have no intention of giving him one," I said. "Let's go back to the club. My feet are soaking wet."

"So are mine," said Frank. We were wearing pumps, and our feet had been wet since we got out of the car.

"That damn Phyllis, she knows I just got over a cold," said Joe.

"Maybe that's why she did it," I said. "It'd serve you right if you got pneumonia."

We began to walk in the middle of the road, in the direction of the clubhouse, which we could see, warm and comfortable on top of a distant plateau. "That old place never looked so good," said Joe. "Let's spend the night there."

"The rooms are all taken. The orchestra's staying there," I said.

We walked about a mile, our feet getting sorer at every step, and the combination of exhaustion and the amount we had had to drink made even grumbling an effort. Then a Dodge touring car, becurtained, stopped about fifty yards from us and a spotlight was turned on each of our faces. A man in a short overcoat and fur-lined cap came toward us. He was a State Highway patrolman. "What happened to you fellows?" he said. "You have a wreck?"

"I married one," said Joe.

"Oh, a weisscrackah," said the patrolman, a Pennsylvania Dutchman. "Where's your car?"

"We got out to take a leak and my wife drove off with it," said Joe.

"You from the dance at the gulf club?"

"Yes," said Joe. "How about giving us a lift?"

"Let me see you' driwah's license," said the cop.

Joe took out his billfold and handed over the license. "So? From Lantenengo Street yet? All right, get in. Whereabouts you want to go to?"

"The country club," said Joe.

"The hell with that," said Frank. "Let's go on to Gibbsville."

"This ain't no taxi service," said the cop. "And I ain't taking you to no Gippsfille. I'm on my way to my substation. Swedish Haven. You can phone there for a taxi. Privileged characters, you think you are. A bunch of drunks, you ask me."

I had to go back to New York on the morning train and the events of the next few days, so far as they concerned Joe and Phyllis Whipple and Frank and Mary Lander, were obscured by the suicide, a day or two later, of Julian English, the man who had thrown a drink at Harry Reilly. The domestic crisis of the Whipples and the Landers and even the McCreas seemed very unimportant. And yet when I heard about English, who had not been getting along with his wife, I wondered about my own friends, people my own age but not so very much younger than Julian and Caroline English. English had danced with Phyllis and Mary that night, and now he was dead. I knew very little about the causes of the difficulties between him and Caroline, but they could have been no worse than the problems that existed in Bobbie's marriage and that threatened the marriage of Frank and Mary Lander. I was shocked and saddened by the English suicide; he was an attractive man whose shortcomings seemed out of proportion to the magnitude of killing himself. He had not been a friend of mine, only an acquaintance with whom I had had many drinks and played some golf; but friends of mine, my closest friends in the world, boys-now-men like myself, were at the beginning of the same kind of life and doing the same kind of thing that for Julian English ended in a sealed-up garage with a motor running. I hated what I thought those next few days and weeks. There is nothing young about killing oneself, no matter when it happens, and I hated this being deprived of the sweetness of youth. And that was what it was, that was what was happening to us. I, and I think the others, had looked upon our squabbles as unpleasant incidents but belonging to our youth. Now they were plainly recognizable as symptoms of life without youth, without youth's excuses or youth's recoverability. I wanted to love someone, and during the next year or two I confused the desperate need for love with love itself. I had put a hopeless love out of my life; but that is not part of this story, except to state it and thus to show that I knew what I was looking for.

II

When you have grown up with someone it is much easier to fill in gaps of five years, ten years, in which you do not see him, than to supply those early years in the life of a friend you meet in maturity. I do not know why this is so, unless it is a mere matter of insufficient time. With the friends of later life you may exchange boyhood stories that seem worth telling, but boyhood is not all stories. It is mostly not stories, but day-to-day, unepisodic living. And most of us are too polite to burden our later-life friends with unexciting anecdotes about people they will never meet. (Likewise we hope they will not burden us.) But it is easy to bring old friends up to date in your mental dossiers by the addition of a few vital facts. Have they stayed married? Have they had many more children? Have they made money or lost it? Usually the basic facts will do, and then you tell yourself that Joe Whipple is still Joe Whipple, plus two sons, a new house, a hundred thousand dollars, forty pounds, bifocals, fat in the neck, and a new concern for the state of the nation.

Such additions I made to my friends' dossiers as I heard about them from time to time; by letters from them, conversations with my mother, an occasional newspaper clipping. I received these facts with joy for the happy news, sorrow for the sad, and immediately went about my business, which was far removed from any business of theirs. I seldom went back to Gibbsville during the Thirties—mine and the century's—and when I did I stayed only long enough to stand at a grave, to toast a bride, to spend a few minutes beside a sickbed. In my brief encounters with my old friends I got no information about Bobbie and Pete McCrea, and only after I had returned to New York or California would I remember that I had intended to inquire about them.

There is, of course, some significance in the fact that no one volunteered information about Bobbie and Pete. It was that they had disappeared. They continued to live in Gibbsville, but in parts of the town that were out of the way for their old friends. There is no town so small that that cannot happen, and Gibbsville, a third-class city, was large enough to have all the grades of poverty and wealth and the many half grades in between, in which $10 a month in the husband's income could make a difference in the kind and location of the house in which he lived. No one had volunteered any information about Bobbie and Pete, and I had not remembered to inquire. In five years I had had no new facts about them, none whatever, and their disappearance from my ken might have continued but for a broken shoelace.

I was in Gibbsville for a funeral, and the year was 1938. I had broken a shoelace, it was evening and the stores were closed, and I was about to drive back to New York. The only place open that might have shoelaces was a poolroom that in my youth had had a two-chair bootblack stand. The poolroom was in a shabby section near the railroad stations and a couple of cheap hotels, four or five saloons, an automobile tire agency, a barber shop, and a quick-lunch counter. I opened the poolroom door, saw that the bootblack's chairs were still there, and said to the man behind the cigar counter: "Have you got any shoelaces?"

"Sorry I can't help you, Jim," said the man. He was wearing an eyeshade, but as soon as he spoke I recognized Pete McCrea.

"Pete, for God's sake," I said. We shook hands.

"I thought you might be in town for the funeral," he said. "I should have gone, too, I guess, but I decided I wouldn't. It was nice of you to make the trip."

"Well, you know. He was a friend of my father's. Do you own this place?"

"I run it. I have a silent partner, Bill Charney. You remember Ed Charney? His younger brother. I don't know where to send you to get a shoelace."

"The hell with the shoelace. How's Bobbie?"

"Oh, Bobbie's fine. *You* know. A lot of changes, but this is better than nothing. Why don't you call her up? She'd love to hear from you. We're living out on Mill Street, but we have a phone. Call her up and say hello. The number is 3385-J. If you have time maybe you could go see her. I have to stay here till I close up at one o'clock, but she's home."

"What number on Mill Street? You call her up and tell her I'm coming? Is that all right?"

"Hell, yes."

Someone thumped the butt of a cue on the floor and called out: "Rack 'em up, Pete?"

"I have to be here. You go on out and I'll call her up," he said. "Keep your shirt on," he said to the pool player, then, to me: "It's 402 Mill Street, across from the open hearth, second house from the corner. I guess I won't see you again, but I'm glad we had a minute. You're looking very well." I could not force a comment on his appearance. His nose was red and larger, his eyes watery, the dewlaps sagging, and he was wearing a blue denim work shirt with a dirty leather bow tie.

"Think I could get in the Ivy Club if I went back to Princeton?" he said. "I didn't make it the first time around, but now I'm a big shot. So long, Jim. Nice to've seen you."

The open hearth had long since gone the way of all the mill equipment; the mill itself had been inactive for years, and as a residential area the mill section was only about a grade and a half above the poorest Negro slums. But in front of most of the houses in the McCreas' row there were cared-for plots; there always had been, even when the mill was running and the air was full of smoke and acid. It was an Irish and Polish neighborhood, but knowledge of that fact did not keep me from locking all the doors of my car. The residents of the neighborhood would not have touched my father's car, but this was not his car and I was not he.

The door of Number 402 opened as soon as I closed my car door. Bobbie waited for me to lock up and when I got to the porch, she said: "*Jim.* Jim, Jim, Jim. How nice. I'm so glad to see you." She quickly closed the door behind me and then kissed me. "Give me a real kiss and a real hug. I didn't dare while the door was open." I kissed her and held her for a moment and then she said: "Hey, I guess we'd better cut this out."

"Yes," I said. "It's nice, though."

"Haven't done that since we were–God!" She stood away and looked at me. "You could lose some weight, but you're not so bad. How about a bottle of beer? Or would you rather have some cheap whiskey?"

"What are you drinking?"

"Cheap whiskey, but I'm used to it," she said.

"Let's both have some cheap whiskey," I said.

"Straight? With water? Or how?"

"Oh, a small slug of whiskey and a large slug of water in it. I'm driving back to New York tonight."

She went to the kitchen and prepared the drinks. I recognized some of the furniture from the Hammersmith and McCrea houses. "Brought together by a shoestring," she said. "Here's to it. How do I look?"

"If you want my frank and candid opinion, good enough to go right upstairs and make up for the time we lost. Pete won't be home till one o'clock."

"If then," she said. "Don't think I wouldn't, but it's too soon after my baby. Didn't Pete tell you I finally produced a healthy son?"

"No."

"You'll hear him in a little while. We have a daughter, two years old, and now a son. Angus McCrea, Junior. Seven pounds two ounces at birth."

"Good for you," I said.

"Not so damn good for me, but it's over, and he's healthy."

"And what about your mother and father?" I said.

"Oh, poor Jim. You didn't know? Obviously you didn't, and you're going to be so sorry you asked. Daddy committed suicide two years ago. He shot himself. And Mother's in Swedish Haven." Swedish Haven was local lore for the insane asylum. "I'm sorry I had to tell you."

"God, why won't they lay off you?" I said.

"Who is they? Oh, you mean just–life?"

"Yes."

"I don't know, Jim," she said. "I've had about as much as I can stand, or so I keep telling myself. But I must be awfully tough, because there's always something else, and I go right on. Will you let me complain for just a minute, and then I'll stop? The only one of the old crowd I ever see is Phyllis. She comes out and never forgets to bring a bottle, so we get tight together. But some things we don't discuss, Phyllis and I. Pete is a closed subject."

"What's he up to?"

"Oh, he has his women. I don't even know who they are any more, and couldn't care less. Just as long as he doesn't catch a disease. I told him that, so he's been careful about it." She sat up straight. "I haven't been the soul of purity, either, but it's Pete's son. Both children are Pete's. But I haven't been withering on the vine."

"Why should you?"

"That's what *I* said. Why should I have nothing? Nothing? The children are mine, and I love them, but I need more than that, Jim. Children don't love you back. All they do is depend on you to feed them and wash them and all the rest of it. But after they're in bed for the night–I never know whether Pete will be home at two o'clock or not at all. So I've had two tawdry romances, I guess you'd call them. Not you, but Mrs. McCrea would."

"Where is dear Mrs. McCrea?"

"She's living in Jenkintown, with an old maid sister. Thank heaven they can't afford carfare, so I'm spared that."

"Who are your gentlemen friends?"

"Well, the first was when we were living on the East Side. A gentleman by the name of Bill Charney. Yes, Ed's brother and Pete's partner. I was crazy about him. Not for one single minute in love with him, but I never even thought about love with him. He wanted to marry me, too, but I was a nasty little snob. I *couldn't* marry Bill Charney, Jim. I just couldn't. So he married a nice little Irish girl and they're living on Lantenengo Street in the house that used to belong to old Mr. Duncan. And I'm holding court on Mill Street, thirty dollars a month rent."

"Do you want some money?"

"Will you give me two hundred dollars?"

"More than that, if you want it."

"No, I'd just like to have two hundred dollars to hide, to keep in case of emergency."

"In case of emergency, you can always send me a telegram in care of my publisher." I gave her $200.

"Thank you. Now I have some money. For the last five or six years I haven't had any money of my own. You don't care how I spend this, do you?"

"As long as you spend it on yourself."

"I've gotten so stingy I probably won't spend any of it. But this is wonderful. Now I can read the ads and say to myself I could have some expensive lingerie. I think I will get a permanent, next month."

"Is that when you'll be back in circulation again?"

"Good guess. Yes, about a month," she said. "But not the same man. I didn't tell you about the second one. You don't know him. He came here after you left Gibbsville. His name is McCormick and he went to Princeton with Pete. They sat next to each other in a lot of classes, McC, McC, and he was sent here to do some kind of an advertising survey and ran into Pete. They'd never been exactly what you'd call pals, but they *knew* each other and Mac took one look and sized up the situation and—well, I thought, why not? He wasn't as exciting as Mr. Charney, but at one time I would have married him. *If* he'd asked me. He doesn't live here any more."

"But you've got the next one picked out?"

"No, but I know there will be a next one. Why lie to myself? And why lie to you? I don't think I ever have."

"Do you ever see Frank?"

"Frank? Frank Lander? What made you think of him?"

"Bobbie," I said.

"Oh, of course. That was a guess of yours, a long time ago," she said. "No, I never see Frank." She was smoking a cigarette, and sitting erect with her elbow on the arm of her chair, holding the cigarette high and with style. If her next words had been "Jeeves, have the black Rolls brought round at four o'clock" she would not have been more naturally grand. But her next words were: "I haven't even thought about Frank. There was another boy, Johnny White, the one I was engaged to. *Engaged* to. That close to spending the rest of my life with him—or at least part of it. But because he wanted me to go away with him before we were married, I broke the engagement and married Pete."

"Is that all it was? That he wanted you to go away with him?"

"That's really all it was. I got huffy and said he couldn't really love me if he wanted to take that risk. Not that we hadn't been taking risks, but a premarital trip, that was something else again. My five men, Jim. Frank. Johnny. Bill and Mac. And Pete."

"Why didn't you and Frank ever get engaged?"

"I wonder. I *have* thought about *that*, so I was wrong when I said I never think of Frank. But Frank in the old days, not Frank now. What may have happened was that Frank was the only boy I'd gone all the way with, and then I got scared because I didn't want to give up the fun, popularity, good times. Jim, I have a confession to make. About you."

"Oh?"

"I told Frank I'd stayed with you. He wouldn't believe he was my first and he kept harping on it, so I really got rid of Frank by telling him you were the first."

"Why me?"

"Because the first time I ever stayed with Frank, or anybody, it was at a picnic at the Dam, and I'd gone to the picnic with you. So you were the logical one."

"Did you tell him that night?"

"No. Later. Days later. But you had a fight with him that night, and the fight made it all the more convincing."

"Well, thanks, little pal," I said.

"Oh, you don't care, do you?"

"No, not really."

"You had Kitty, after all," she said. "Do you ever see Kitty?"

"No. Kitty lives in Cedarhurst and they keep to themselves, Cedarhurst people."

"What was your wife like?"

"She was nice. Pretty. Wanted to be an actress. I still see her once in a while. I like her, and always will, but if ever there were two people that shouldn't have got married . . ."

"I can name two others," said Bobbie.

"You and Pete. But you've stuck to him."

"Don't be polite. I'm stuck with him. Can you imagine what Pete would be like if I left him?"

"Well, to be brutally frank, what's he like anyway? You don't have to go on paying for a dirty trick the rest of your life."

"It wasn't just a dirty trick. It would have been a dirty trick if I'd walked out on him the day we were getting married. But I went through with it, and that made it more than a dirty trick. I *should have* walked out on him, the day we got married. I even tried. And he'd have recovered–then. Don't forget, Pete McCrea was used to dirty tricks being played on him, and he might have got over it if I'd left him at the church. But once I'd married him, he became a different person, took himself much more seriously, and so did everyone else. They began to dislike him, but that was better than being laughed at." She sipped her drink.

"Well, who did it? I did. Your little pal," she said. "How about some more cheap whiskey?"

"No thanks, but you go ahead," I said.

"The first time I ever knew there *was* a Mill Street was the day we rented this house," she said, as she poured herself a drink. "I'd never been out this way before."

"You couldn't have lived here when the mill was operating. The noise and the smoke."

"I can live anywhere," she said. "So can anyone else. And don't be too surprised if you find us back on Lantenengo. Do you know the big thing nowadays? Slot machines and the numbers racket. Pete wants to get into The Numbers, but he hasn't decided how to go about it. Bill Charney is the kingpin in the county, although not the real head. It's run by a syndicate in Jersey City."

"Don't let him do it, Bobbie," I said. "Really don't."

"Why not? He's practically in it already. He has slot machines in the poolroom, and that's where people call up to find out what number won today. He might as well be in it."

"No."

"It's the only way Pete will ever have any money, and if he ever gets his hands on some money, maybe he'll divorce me. Then I could take the children and go away somewhere. California."

"That's a different story. If you're planning it that way. But stay out of The Numbers if you ever have any idea of remaining respectable. You can't just go in for a few years and then quit."

"Respectable? Do you think my son's going to be able to get into Princeton? His father is the proprietor of a poolroom, and they're going to know that when Angus gets older. Pete will never be anything else. He's found his niche. But if I took the children to California they might have a chance. And *I* might have a chance, before it's too late. It's our only hope, Jim. Phyllis agrees with me."

I realized that I would be arguing against a hope and a dream, and if she had that much left, and only that much, I had no right to argue. She very nearly followed my thinking. "It's what I live on, Jim," she said. "That—and this." She held up her glass. "And a little admiration. A little—admiration. Phyllis wants to give me a trip to New York. Would you take us to '21' and those places?"

"Sure."

"Could you get someone for Phyllis?"

"I think so. Sure. Joe wouldn't go on this trip?"

"And give up a chance to be with Mary Lander?"

"So now it's Joe and Mary?"

"Oh, that's old hat in Gibbsville. They don't even pretend otherwise."

"And Frank? What about him?"

"Frank is the forgotten man. If there were any justice he ought to pair off with Phyllis, but they don't like each other. Phyllis calls Frank a wishy-washy namby-pamby, and Frank calls Phyllis a drunken trouble-maker. We've all grown up, Jim. Oh, haven't we just? Joe doesn't like Phyllis to visit me because Mary says all we do is gossip. Although how she'd know *what* we do . . ."

"They were all at the funeral, and I thought what a dull, stuffy little group they've become," I said.

"But that's what they are," said Bobbie. "Very stuffy and very dull. What else is there for them to do? If I were still back there with them I'd be just as bad. Maybe worse. In a way, you know, Pete McCrea has turned out to be the most interesting man in our old crowd, present company excepted. Joe was a very handsome young man and so was Frank, and their families had lots of money and all the rest of it. But you saw Joe and Frank today. I haven't seen them lately, but Joe looks like a professional wrestler and I remember how hairy he was, all over his chest and back and his arms and legs. And Frank just the opposite, skin like a girl's and slender, but now we could almost call *him* Ichabod. He looks like a cranky schoolteacher, and his glasses make him look like an owl. Mary, of course, beautifully dressed I'm sure, and not looking a day older."

"Several days older, but damn good-looking," I said.

A baby cried and Bobbie made no move. "That's my daughter. Teething. Now she'll wake up my son and you're in for a lot of howling." The son began to cry, and Bobbie excused herself. She came back in a few minutes with the infant in her arms. "It's against my rules to pick them up, but I wanted to show him to you. Isn't he an ugly little creature? The answer is yes." She took him away and returned with the daughter. "She's begun to have a face."

"Yes, I can see that. Your face, for which she can be thankful."

"Yes, I wouldn't want a girl to look like Pete. It doesn't matter so much with a boy." She took the girl away and when she rejoined me she refilled her glass.

"Are you sorry you didn't have children?" she said.

"Not the way it turned out, I'm not," I said.

"These two haven't had much of a start in life, the poor little things. They haven't even been christened. Do you know why? There was nobody we could ask to be their godfathers." Her eyes filled with tears. "That was when I really saw what we'd come to."

"Bobbie, I've got a four-hour drive ahead of me, so I think I'd better get started."

"Four hours to New York? In that car?"

"I'm going to stop and have a sandwich halfway."

"I could give you a sandwich and make some coffee."

"I don't want it now, thanks."

We looked at each other. "I'd like to show how much I appreciate your coming out to see me," she said. "But it's probably just as well I can't. But I'll be all right in New York, Jim. That is, if I ever get there. I won't believe that, either, till I'm on the train."

If she came to New York I did not know about it, and during the war years Bobbie and her problems receded from my interest. I heard that Pete was working in a defense plant, from which I inferred that he had not made the grade in the numbers racket. Frank Lander was in the Navy, Joe Whipple in the War Production Board, and by the time the war was over I discovered that so many other people and things had taken the place of Gibbsville in my thoughts that I had almost no active curiosity about the friends of my youth. I had even had a turnover in my New York friendships. I had married again, I was working hard, and most of my social life originated with my wife's friends. I was making, for me, quite a lot of money, and I was a middle-aged man whose physician had made some honest, unequivocal remarks about my life expectancy. It took a little time and one illness to make me realize that if I wanted to see my child grow to maturity, I had to retire from night life. It was not nearly so difficult as I had always anticipated it would be.

After I became reconciled to middle age and the quieter life I made another discovery: that the sweetness of my early youth was a persistent and enduring thing, so long as I kept it at the distance of years. Moments would come back to me, of love and excitement and music and laughter that filled my breast as they had thirty years earlier. It was not nostalgia, which only means homesickness, nor was it a wish to be living that excitement again. It was a splendid contentment with the knowledge that once I had felt those things so deeply and well that the throbbing urging of George Gershwin's "Do It Again" could evoke the original sensation and the pictures that went with it: a tea dance at the club and a girl in a long black satin dress and my furious jealousy of a fellow who wore a yellow foulard tie. I wanted none of it ever again, but all I had I wanted to keep. I could remember precisely the tone in which her brother had said to her: "Are you coming or aren't you?" and the sounds of his galoshes after she said: "I'm going home with Mr. Malloy." They were the things I knew before we knew everything, and, I suppose, before we began to learn. There was always a girl, and nearly always there was music; if the Gershwin tune belonged to that girl, a Romberg tune belonged to another and "When Hearts Are Young" became a personal anthem, enduringly sweet and safe from all harm, among the protected memories. In middle age I was proud to have lived according to my emotions at the right time, and content to live that way vicariously and at a distance. I had missed almost nothing, escaped very little, and at fifty I had begun to devote my energy and time to the last, simple but big task of putting it all down as well as I knew how.

In the midst of putting it all down, as novels and short stories and plays, I would sometimes think of Bobbie McCrea and the dinginess of her history. But as the reader will presently learn, the "they"—life—that had once made me cry out in anger, were not through with her yet. (Of course "they" are never through with anyone while he still lives, and we are not concerned here with the laws of compensation that seem to test us, giving us just enough strength to carry us in another trial.) I like to think that Bobbie got enough pleasure out of a pair of nylons, a permanent wave, a bottle of Phyllis Whipple's whiskey, to recharge the brightness in her. As we again take up her story I promise the reader a happy ending, if only because I want it that way. It happens also to be the true ending. . . .

Pete McCrea did not lose his job at the end of the war. His Princeton degree helped there. He had gone into the plant, which specialized in aluminum extrusion, as a manual laborer, but his IBM card revealed that he had taken psychology courses in college, and he was transferred to Personnel. It seemed an odd choice, but it is not hard to imagine that Pete was better fitted by his experience as a poolroom proprietor than as a two-year student of psychology. At least he spoke both languages, he liked the work, and in 1945 he was not bumped by a returning veteran.

Fair Grounds, the town in which the plant was situated, was only three miles from Gibbsville. For nearly a hundred years it had been the trading center for the Pennsylvania Dutch farmers in the area, and its attractions had been Becker's general store, the Fair Grounds Bank, the freight office of the Reading Railway, the Fair Grounds Hotel, and five Protestant churches. Clerks at Becker's and at the bank and the Reading, and bartenders at the hotel and the pastors of the churches, all had to speak Pennsylvania Dutch. English was desirable but not a requirement. The town was kept scrubbed, dusted and painted, and until the erection of the aluminum plant, jobs and trades were kept in the same families. An engineman's son worked as waterboy until he was old enough to take the examinations for brakeman; a master mechanic would give his boy calipers for Christmas. There were men and women in Fair Grounds who visited Gibbsville only to serve on juries or to undergo surgery at the Gibbsville Hospital. There were some men and women who had never been to Gibbsville at all and regarded Gibbsville as some Gibbsville citizens regarded Paris, France. That was the pre-aluminum Fair Grounds.

To this town in 1941 went Pete and Bobbie McCrea. They rented a house no larger than the house on Mill Street but cleaner and in better repair. Their landlord and his wife went to live with his mother-in-law, and collected the $50 legally frozen monthly rent and $50 side payment for the use of the radio and the gas stove. But in spite of under-the-table and black-market prices Peter and Bobbie McCrea were financially better off than they had been since their marriage, and nylons at black-market prices were preferable to the no nylons she had had on Mill Street. The job, and the fact that he continued to hold it, restored some respectability to Pete, and they discussed rejoining the club. "Don't try it, I warn you," said Phyllis Whipple. "The club isn't run by your friends any more. Now it's been taken over by people that couldn't have got in ten years ago."

"Well, we'd have needed all our old friends to go to bat for us, and I guess some would think twice about it," said Pete. "So we'll do our drinking at the Tavern."

The Dan Patch Tavern, which was a new name for the renovated Fair Grounds Hotel bar, was busy all day and all night, and it was one of the places where Pete could take pleasure in his revived respectability. It was also one of the places where Bobbie could count on getting that little admiration that she needed to live on. On the day of Pearl Harbor she was only thirty-four years old and at the time of the Japanese surrender she was only thirty-eight. She was accorded admiration in abundance. Some afternoons just before the shift changed she would walk the three blocks to the Tavern and wait for Pete. The bartender on duty would say "Hi, Bobbie," and bring her currently favorite drink to her booth. Sometimes there would be four men sitting with her when Pete arrived from the plant; she was never alone for long. If one man tried to persuade her to leave, and became annoyingly insistent, the bartenders came to her rescue. The bartenders and the proprietor knew that in her way Bobbie was as profitable as the juke box. She was an attraction. She was a good-looking broad who was not a whore or a falling-down lush, and all her drinks were paid for. She was the Tavern's favorite customer, male or female, and if she had given the matter any thought she could have been declared in. All she wanted in return was a steady supply of Camels and protection from being mauled. The owner of the Tavern, Rudy Schau, was the only one who was aware that Bobbie and Pete had once lived on Lantenengo Street in Gibbsville, but far from being impressed by their background, he had a German opinion of aristocrats who had lost standing. He was actively suspicious of Bobbie in the beginning, but in time he came to accept her as a wife whose independence he could not condone and a good-looking woman whose morals he had not been able to condemn. And she was good for business. Beer business was good, but at Bobbie's table nobody drank beer, and the real profit was in the hard stuff.

In the Fair Grounds of the pre-aluminum days Bobbie would have had few women friends. No decent woman would have gone to a saloon every day—or any day. She most likely would have received warnings from the Ku Klux Klan, which was concerned with personal conduct in a town that had only a dozen Catholic families, no Negroes and no Jews. But when the aluminum plant (which was called simply The Aluminum or The Loomy) went into war production the population of Fair Grounds immediately doubled and the solid Protestant character of the town was changed in a month. Eight hundred new people came to town and they lived in apartments in a town where there were no apartments: in rooms in private houses, in garages and old stables, in rented rooms and haylofts out in the farming area. The newcomers wasted no time with complaints of double-rent, inadequate heating, holes in the roof, insufficient sanitation. The town was no longer scrubbed, dusted or painted, and thousands of man-hours were lost while a new shift waited for the old to vacate parking space in the streets of the town. Bobbie and Pete were among the lucky early ones: they had a house. That fact of itself gave Bobbie some distinction. The house had two rooms and kitchen on the first floor, three rooms and bath on the second, and it had a cellar and an attic. In the identical houses on both sides there were a total of four families and six roomers. As a member of Personnel it was one of Pete's duties to find housing for workers, but Bobbie would have no roomers. "The money wouldn't do us much good, so let's live like human beings," she said.

"You mean there's nothing to buy with the money," said Pete. "But we could save it."

"If we had it, we'd spend it. You've never saved a cent in your life and neither have I. If you're thinking of the children's education, buy some more war bonds and have it taken out of your pay. But I'm not going to share my bathroom with a lot of dirty men. I'd have to do all the extra work, not you."

"You could make a lot of money doing their laundry. Fifty cents a shirt."

"Are you serious?"

"No."

"It's a good thing you're not, because I could tell you how else I could make a lot more money."

"Yes, a lot more," said Pete.

"Well, then, keep your ideas to yourself. I won't have boarders and I won't do laundry for fifty cents a shirt. That's final."

And so Bobbie had her house, she got the admiration she needed, and she achieved a moderate popularity among the women of her neighborhood by little friendly acts that came spontaneously out of her friendly nature. There was a dinginess to the new phase: the house was not much, the men who admired her and the women who welcomed her help were the ill-advantaged, the cheap, the vulgar, and sometimes the evil. But the next step down from Mill Street would have been hopeless degradation, and the next step up, Fair Grounds, was at least up. She was envied for her dingy house, and when Pete called her the Queen of the Klondike she was not altogether displeased. There was envy in the epithet, and in the envy was the first sign of respect he had shown her in ten years. He had never suspected her of an affair with Mac McCormick, and if he had suspected her during her infatuation with Bill Charney he had been afraid to make an accusation; afraid to anticipate his own feelings in the event that Charney would give him a job in The Numbers. When Charney brought in a Pole from Detroit for the job Pete had wanted, Pete accepted $1,000 for his share of the poolroom and felt only grateful relief. Charney did not always buy out his partners, and Pete refused to wonder if the money and the easy dissolution of the partnership had been paid for by Bobbie. It was not a question he wanted to raise, and when the war in Europe created jobs at Fair Grounds he believed that his luck had begun to change.

Whatever the state of Pete's luck, the pace of his marriage had begun to change. The pace of his marriage—and not his alone—was set by the time he spent at home and what he did during that time. For ten years he had spent little more time at home than was necessary for sleeping and eating. He could not sit still in the same room with Bobbie, and even after the children were born he did not like to have her present during the times he would play with them. He would arrive in a hurry to have his supper, and in a short time he would get out of the house, to be with a girl, to go back to work at the poolroom. He was most conscious of time when he was near Bobbie; everywhere else he moved slowly, spoke deliberately, answered hesitantly. But after the move to Fair Grounds he spent more time in the house, with the children, with Bobbie. He would sit in the front room, doing paper work from the plant, while Bobbie sewed. At the Tavern he would say to Bobbie: "It's time we were getting home." He no longer darted in and out of the house and ate his meals rapidly and in silence.

He had a new girl. Martha—"Martie"—Klinger was a typist at the plant, a Fair Grounds woman whose husband was in the Coast Guard at Lewes, Delaware. She was Bobbie's age and likewise had two children. She retained a young prettiness in the now round face and her figure had not quite reached the stage of plumpness. Sometimes when she moved an arm the flesh of her breast seemed to go all the way up to her neckline, and she had been one of the inspirations for a plant memo to women employees, suggesting that tight sweaters and tight slacks were out of place in wartime industry. Pete brought her to the Tavern one day after work, and she never took her eyes off Bobbie. She looked up and down, up and down, with her mouth half open as though she were listening to Bobbie through her lips. She showed no animosity of a defensive nature and was not openly possessive of Pete, but Bobbie knew on sight that she was Pete's new girl. After several sessions at the Tavern Bobbie could tell which of the men had already slept with Martie and which of them were likely to again. It was impossible to be jealous of Martie, but it was just as impossible not to feel superior to her. Pete, the somewhat changed Pete, kept up the absurd pretense that Martie was just a girl from the plant whom he happened to bring along for a drink, and there was no unpleasantness until one evening Martie said: "Jesus, I gotta go or I won't get any supper."

"Come on back to our house and have supper with us," said Pete. "That's okay by you, isn't it, Bobbie?"

"No, it isn't," said Bobbie.

"Rudy'll give us a steak and we can cook it at home," said Pete.

"I said no," said Bobbie, and offered no explanation.

"I'll see you all tomorrow," said Martie. "Goodnight, people."

"Why wouldn't you let her come home with us? I could have got a steak from Rudy. And Martie's a hell of a good cook."

"When we can afford a cook I may hire her," said Bobbie.

"Oh, that's what it is. The old snob department."

"That's exactly what it is."

"We're not in any position--"

"*You're* not."

"*We're* not. If I can't have my friends to my house," he said, but did not know how to finish.

"It's funny that she's the first one you ever asked. Don't forget what I told you about having boarders, and fifty cents a shirt. You keep your damn Marties out of my house. If you don't, I'll get a job and you'll be just another boarder yourself."

"Oh, why are you making such a stink about Martie?"

"Come *off* it, Pete, for heaven's *sake*."

The next statement, he knew, would have to be a stupidly transparent lie or an admission, so he made no statement. If there had to be a showdown he preferred to avert it until the woman in question was someone more entertaining than Martie Klinger. And he liked the status quo.

They both liked the status quo. They had hated each other, their house, the dinginess of their existence on Mill Street. When the fire whistle blew it was within the hearing of Mill Street and of Lantenengo Street; rain from the same shower fell on Mill Street and on Lantenengo Street; Mill Street and Lantenengo Street read the same Gibbsville newspaper at the same time every evening. And the items of their proximity only made the nearness worse, the remoteness of Mill Street from Lantenengo more vexatious. But Fair Grounds was a new town, where they had gone knowing literally nobody. They had spending money, a desirable house, the respectability of a white-collar job, and the restored confidence in a superiority to their neighbors that they had not allowed themselves to feel on Mill Street. In the Dan Patch Tavern they would let things slip out that would have been meaningless on Mill Street, where their neighbors' daily concern was a loaf of bread and a bottle of milk. "Pete, did you know Jimmy Stewart, the movie actor?" "No, he was several classes behind me, but he was in my club." "Bobbie, what's it like on one of them yachts?" "I've only been on one, but it was fun while it lasted." They could talk now about past pleasures and luxuries without being contradicted by their surroundings, and their new friends at the Tavern had no knowledge of the decade of dinginess that lay between that past and this present. If their new friends also guessed that Pete McCrea was carrying on with Martie Klinger, that very fact made Bobbie more credibly and genuinely the woman who had once cruised in a yacht. They would have approved Bobbie's reason for not wanting Martie Klinger as a guest at supper, as they would have fiercely resented Pete's reference to Bobbie as the Queen of the Klondike. Unintentionally they were creating a symbol of order that they wanted in their lives as much as Bobbie needed admiration, and if the symbol and the admiration were slightly ersatz, what, in war years, was not?

There was no one among the Tavern friends whom Bobbie desired to make love with. "I'd give a week's pay to get in bed with you, Bobbie," said one of them.

"Fifty-two weeks' pay, did you say?" said Bobbie.

"No dame is worth fifty-two weeks' pay," said the man, a foreman named Dick Hartenstein.

"Oh, I don't know. In fifty-two weeks you make what?"

"A little over nine thousand. Nine gees, about."

"A lot of women can get that, Dick. I've heard of women getting a diamond necklace for just one night, and they cost a lot more than nine thousand dollars."

"Well, I tell you, Bobby, if I ever hit the crap game for nine gees I'd seriously consider it, but not a year's pay that I worked for."

"You're not romantic enough for me. Sorry."

"Supposing I did hit the crap game and put nine gees on the table in front of you? Would you and me go to bed?"

"No."

"No, I guess not. If I asked you a question would you give me a truthful answer? No. You wouldn't."

"Why should I?"

"Yeah, why should you? I was gonna ask you, what does it take to get you in bed with a guy?"

"I'm a married woman."

"I skipped all that part, Bobbie. You'd go, if it was the right guy."

"You could get to be an awful nuisance, Dick. You're not far from it right this minute."

"I apologize."

"In fact, why don't you take your drink and stand at the bar?"

"What are you sore at? You get propositioned all the time."

"Yes, but you're too persistent, and you're a bore. The others don't keep asking questions when I tell them no. Go on, now, or I'll tell Rudy to keep you out of here."

"You know what you are?"

"Rudy! Will you come here, please?" she called. "All right, Dick. What am I? Say it in front of Rudy."

Rudy Schau made his way around from the bar. "What can I do for you, Bobbie?"

"I think Dick is getting ready to call me a nasty name."

"He won't," said Rudy Schau. He had the build of a man who had handled beer kegs all his life and he was now ready to squeeze the wind out of Hartenstein. "Apolochise to Bobbie and get the hell outa my place. And don't forget you got a forty-dollar tab here. You won't get a drink nowheres else in tahn."

"I'll pay my God damn tab," said Hartenstein.

"That you owe me. Bobbie you owe an apolochy."

"I apologize," said Hartenstein. He was immediately clipped behind the ear, and sunk to the floor.

"I never like that son of a bitch," said Rudy Schau. He looked down at the unconscious Hartenstein and very deliberately kicked him in the ribs.

"Oh, *don't*, Rudy," said Bobbie. "*Please* don't."

Others in the bar, which was now half filled, stood waiting for Rudy's next kick, and some of them looked at each other and then at Rudy, and they were ready to rush him. Bobbie stood up quickly. "Don't, Rudy," she said.

"All right. I learned him. Joe, throw the son of a bitch out," said Rudy. Then suddenly he wheeled and grabbed a man by the belt and lifted him off the floor, holding him tight against his body with one hand and making a hammer of his other hand. "You, you son of a bitch, you was gonna go after me, you was, yeah? Well, go ahead. Let's see you, you son of a bitch. You son of a bitch, I break you in pieces." He let go and the man retreated out of range of Rudy's fist. "Pay your bill and don't come back. Don't ever show your face in my place again. And any other son of a bitch was gonna gang me. You gonna gang Rudy, hey? I kill any two of you." Two of the men picked Hartenstein off the floor before the bartender got to him. "Them two, they paid up, Joe?"

"In the clear, Rudy," said the bartender.

"You two. Don't come back," said Rudy.

"Don't worry. We won't," they said.

Rudy stood at Bobbie's table. "Okay if I sit down with you, Bobbie?"

"Of course," said Bobbie.

"Joe, a beer, please, hey? Bobbie, you ready?"

"Not yet, thanks," she said.

Rudy mopped his forehead with a handkerchief. "You don't have to take it from these bums," said Rudy. "Any time any them get fresh, you tell me. You're what keeps this place decent, Bobbie. I know. As soon as you go home it's a pigpen. I get sick of hearing them, some of the women as bad as the men. Draft-dotchers. Essengial industry! Draft-dotchers. A bunch of 4-F draft-dotchers. I like to hear what your Daddy would say about them."

"Did you know him, my father?"

"Know him? I was in his platoon. Second platoon, C Company. I went over with him and come back with him. Phil Hammersmith."

"I never knew that."

Rudy chuckled. "Sure. Some of these 4-F draft-dotchers from outa town, they think I'm a Nazi because I never learn to speak good English, but my Daddy didn't speak no English at all and he was born out in the Walley. My old woman says put my dischartch papers up over the back-bar. I say what for? So's to make the good impression on a bunch of draft-dotchers? Corporal Rudolph W. Schau. Your Daddy was a good man and a good soldier."

"Why didn't you ever tell me you knew him?"

"Oh, I don't know, Bobbie. I wasn't gonna tell you now, but I did. It don't pay to be a talker in my business. A listener, not a talker."

"You didn't approve of me, did you?"

"I'm a saloonkeeper. A person comes to my—"

"You didn't approve of me. Don't dodge the issue."

"Well, your Daddy wouldn't of liked you coming to a saloon that often. But times change, and you're better off here than the other joints."

"I hope you don't *mind* my coming here."

"Listen, you come here as much as you want."

"Try and stop me," she said, smiling.

Pete joined them. "What happened to Dick Hartenstein?" he said.

"The same as will happen to anybody gets fresh with your wife," said Rudy, and got up and left them.

"There could be a hell of a stink about this. Rudy could lose his license if the Company wanted to press the point."

"Well, you just see that he doesn't," said Bobbie.

"Maybe it isn't such a good idea, your coming here so often."

"Maybe. On the other hand, maybe it's a wonderful idea. I happen to think it's a wonderful idea, so I'm going to keep on coming. If *you* want to go to one of the other places, that's all right. But I like Rudy's. I like it better than ever, now."

No action was taken against Rudy Schau, and Bobbie visited the Tavern as frequently as ever. Hartenstein was an unpopular foreman and the women said he got what had been coming to him for a long time. Bobbie's friends were pleased that their new symbol had such a forthright defender. It was even said that Bobbie had saved Hartenstein from a worse beating, a rumor that added to the respect she was given by the men and the women.

The McCrea children were not being brought up according to Lantenengo Street standards. On the three or four afternoons a week that Bobbie went to the Tavern she would take her son and daughter to a neighbor's yard. On the other afternoons the neighbors' children would play in her yard. During bad weather and the worst of the winter the McCreas' house was in more frequent service as a nursery, since some of the neighbors were living in one- or two-room apartments. But none of the children, the McCreas' or the neighbors', had individual supervision. Children who had learned to walk were separated from those who were still crawling, on the proven theory that the crawling children were still defenseless against the whimsical cruelties of the older ones. Otherwise there was no distinction, and all the children were toughened early in life, as most of their parents had been. "I guess it's all right," Pete once said to Bobbie. "But I hate to think what they'll be like when they get older. Little gangsters."

"Well, that was never your trouble, God knows," said Bobbie. "And I'm no shining example of having a nannie take care of me. Do you remember my nannie?"

"Vaguely."

"'Let's go and see the horsies,' she'd say. And we'd go to Mr. Duncan's stable and I'd come home covered with scratches from the stable cat. And I guess Patrick was covered with scratches from my nannie. Affectionate scratches, of course. Do you remember Mr. Duncan's Patrick?"

"Sure."

"He must have been quite a man. Phyllis used to go there with her nannie, too. But the cat liked Phyllis."

"I'm not suggesting that we have a nannie."

"No. You're suggesting that I stay away from the Tavern."

"In the afternoon."

"The afternoon is the only time the mothers will watch each other's children, except in rare cases. Our kids are all right. I'm with them all day most of the time, and we're home every evening, seven nights a week."

"What else is there to do?"

"Well, for instance once a month we could go to a movie."

"Where? Gibbsville?"

"Yes. Two gallons of gas at the most."

"Are you getting the itch to move back to Gibbsville?"

"Not at all. Are you?"

"Hell, no."

"We could get some high school kid to watch the children. I'd just like to have a change once in a while."

"All right. The next time there's something good at the Globe."

Their first trip to the Globe was their last. They saw no one they knew in the theatre or in the bar of the John Gibb Hotel, and when they came home the high school kid was naked in bed with a man Pete recognized from the plant. "Get out of here," said Pete.

"Is she your kid, McCrea?"

"No, she's not my kid. But did you ever hear of statutory rape?"

"Rape? This kid? I had to wait downstairs, for God's sake. She took on three other guys tonight. Ten bucks a crack."

The girl put on her clothes in sullen silence. She never spoke except to say to the man: "Do you have a room some place?"

"Well," said Pete, when they had gone. "Where did you get her from? The Junior League?"

"If you'd stared at her any more you'd have had to pay ten dollars too."

"For sixteen she had quite a shape."

"She won't have it much longer."

"You got an eyeful, too, don't pretend you didn't."

"Well, at least she won't get pregnant that way. And she *will* get *rich*," said Bobbie.

Pete laughed. "It was really quite funny. Where *did* you get her?"

"If you want her name and telephone number, I have it downstairs. I got her through one of the neighbors. She certainly got the word around quickly enough, where she'd be. There's the doorbell. Another customer?"

Pete went downstairs and informed the stranger at the door that he had the wrong address.

"Another customer, and I think he had two guys with him in the car. Seventy dollars she was going to make tonight. I guess I'm supposed to report this at the plant. We have a sort of a V-D file of known prostitutes. We sic the law on them before they infect the whole outfit, and I'll bet this little character—"

"Good heavens, yes. I must burn everything. Bed linen. Towels. Why that little bitch. Now I'm getting sore." She collected the linen and took it downstairs and to the trash burner in the yard. When she returned Pete was in bed, staring at the ceiling. "I'm going to sleep in the other room," she said.

"What's the matter?"

"I didn't like that tonight. I don't want to sleep with you."

"Oh, all right then, go to hell," said Pete.

She made up one of the beds in the adjoining room. He came and sat on the edge of her bed in the dark. "Go away, Pete," she said.

"Why?"

"Oh, all right, I'll *tell* you why. Tonight made me think of the time you wanted to exchange with Mary and Frank. That's all I've been able to think of."

"That's all passed, Bobbie. I'm not like that any more."

"You would have got in bed with that girl. I saw you."

"Then I'll tell you something. You would have got in bed with that man. I saw you, too. You were excited."

"How could I help being excited, to suddenly come upon something like that. But I was disgusted, too. And still am. Please go away and let me try to get some sleep."

She did not sleep until first light, and when the alarm clock sounded she prepared his and the children's breakfasts. She was tired and nervous throughout the day. She could not go to the Tavern because it was her turn to watch neighbors' children, and Pete telephoned and said bluntly that he would not be home for supper, offering no excuse. He got home after eleven that night, slightly drunk and with lipstick on his neck.

"Who was it? Martie?" said Bobbie.

"What difference does it make who it was? I've been trying to give up other women, but you're no help."

"I have no patience with that kind of an excuse. It's easy enough to blame me. Remember, Pete, I can pick up a man just as easily as you can make a date with Martie."

"I know you can, and you probably will."

It was the last year of the war, and she had remained faithful to Pete throughout the life of their son Angus. A week later she resumed her affair with Bill Charney. "You never forgot me," he said. "I never forgot you, either, Bobbie. I heard about you and Pete living in Fair Grounds. You know a couple times I took my car and dro' past your house to see which one it was. I didn't know, maybe you'd be sitting out on the front porch and if you saw me, you know. Maybe we just say hello and pass the time of day. But I didn't think no such thing, to tell you the God's honest truth. I got nothing against my wife, only she makes me weary. The house and the kids, she got me going to Mass every Sunday, all like that. But I ain't built that way, Bobbie. I'm the next thing to a hood, and you got that side of you, too. I'll make you any price you say, the other jerks you slept with, they never saw that side of you. You know, you hear a lot about love, Bobbie, but I guess I came closer to it with you than any other woman I ever knew. I never forgot you any more than you ever forgot me. It's what they call a mutual attraction. Like you know one person has it for another person."

"I know."

"I don't see how we stood it as long as we did. Be honest, now, didn't you often wish it was me instead of some other guy?"

"Yes."

"All right, I'll be honest with you. Many's the time in bed with my wife I used to say to myself, 'Peggy, you oughta take lessons from Bobbie McCrea.' But who can give lessons, huh? If you don't have the mutual attraction, you're nothin'. How do you think I look?" He slapped his belly. "You know I weigh the same as I used to weigh? You look good. You put on a little. What? Maybe six pounds?"

"Seven or eight."

"But you got it distributed. In another year Peggy's gonna weigh a hundred and fifty pounds, and I told her, I said either she took some of that off or I'd get another girl. Her heighth, you know. She can't get away with that much weight. I eat everything, but I do a lot of walking and standing. I guess I use up a lot of excess energy. Feel them muscles. Punch me in the belly. I got no fat on me anywhere, Bobbie. For my age I'm a perfect physical specimen. I could get any amount of insurance if I got out of The Numbers. But nobody's gonna knock me off so why do I want insurance? I may even give up The Numbers one of these days. I got a couple of things lined up, strictly, strictly legitimate, and when my kids are ready to go away to school, I may just give up The Numbers. For a price, naturally."

"That brings up a point."

"You need money? How much do you want? It's yours. I *mean* like ten, fifteen gees."

"No, no money. But everybody knows you now. Where can we meet?"

"What's the matter with here? I told you, I own this hotel."

"But I can't just come and go. People know me, too. I have an idea, though."

"What?"

"Buy a motel."

"Buy a motel. You know, that thought crossed me a year ago, but you know what I found out? They don't make money. You'd think they would, but those that come out ahead, you be surprised how little they make."

"There's one near Swedish Haven. It's only about a mile from my house."

"We want a big bed, not them twin beds. I tell you what I could do. I could rent one of the units by the month and move my own furniture in. How would that suit you?"

"I'd like it better if you owned the place."

"Blackmail? Is that what you're thinking about? Who'd blackmail me, Bobbie? Or my girl? I'm still a hood in the eyes of some people."

There was no set arrangement for their meetings. Bill Charney postponed the purchase of the motel until she understood he had no intention of buying it or of making any other arrangement that implied permanence. At first she resented his procrastination, but she discovered that she preferred his way; he would telephone her, she would telephone him whenever desire became urgent, and sometimes they would be together within an hour of the telephone call. They spaced out their meetings so that each one produced novelty and excitement, and a year passed and another and Bobbie passed the afternoon of her fortieth birthday with him.

It was characteristic of their relationship that she did not tell him it was her birthday. He always spoke of his wife and children and his business enterprises, but he did not notice that she never spoke of her home life. He was a completely egocentric man, equally admiring of his star sapphire ring on his strong shortfingered hand and of her slender waist, which in his egocentricity became his possession. Inevitably, because of the nature of his businesses, he had a reputation for being close-mouthed, but alone with Bobbie he talked freely. "You know, Bobbie, I laid a friend of yours?"

"Was it fun?"

"Aren't you gonna ask me who?"

"You'll tell me."

"At least I guess she's a friend of yours. Mary Lander."

"She used to be a friend of mine. I haven't seen her in years."

"Yeah. While her husband was in the service. Frank."

"You're so busy, with all your women."

"There's seven days in the week, honey, and it don't take up too much of your time. This didn't last very long, anyway. Five, maybe six times I slept with her. I took her to New York twice, that is I met her there. The other times in her house. You know, she's a neighbor of mine."

"And very neighborly."

"Yeah, that's how it started. She come to my house to collect for something, some war drive, and Peggy said I took care of all them things so when I got home I made out a cheque and took it over to the Landers' and inside of fifteen minutes—less than that—we were necking all over the parlor. Hell, I knew the minute she opened the door—"

"One of those mutual attractions?"

"Yeah, sure. I gave her the cheque and she said, 'I don't know how to thank you,' and I said if she had a couple minutes I'd show her how. 'Oh, Mr. Charney,' but she didn't tell me to get out, so I knew I was in."

"What ever broke up this romance?"

"Her. She had some guy in Washington, D.C., she was thinking of marrying, and when I finally got it out of her who the guy was, I powdered out. Joe Whipple. I gotta do business with Joe. We got a home-loan proposition that we're ready to go with any day, and this was three years ago when Joe and I were just talking about it, what they call the talking stage."

"So you're the one that broke it off, not Mary."

"If a guy's looking at you across a desk and thinking you're laying his girl, you stand to get a screwing from that guy. Not that I don't trust Joe, because I do."

"Do you trust Mary?"

"I wondered about that, if she'd blab to Joe. A dame like Mary Lander, is she gonna tell the guy she's thinking of marrying that she's been laying a hood like me? No. By the way, she's queer. She told me she'd go for a girl."

"I'm surprised she hasn't already."

"Maybe she has. I couldn't find out. I always try to find out."

"You never asked me."

"I knew you wouldn't. But a dame like Mary, as soon as she opened the door I knew I was in, but then the next thing is you find out what else she'll go for. In her case, the works, as long as it isn't gonna get around. I guess I always figured her right. I have to figure all angles, men *and* women. That's where my brother Ed was stupid. I used to say to him, find out what kind of a broad a guy goes for before you declare him in. Ed used to say all he had to do was play a game of cards with a guy. But according to my theory, everybody goes into a card game prepared. Both eyes open. But not a guy going after a broad. You find out more from broads, like take for instance Mary. Now I know Frank is married to a dame that is screwing his best friend, laid a hood like me, and will go for a girl. You think I'd ever depend on Frank Lander? No. And Joe Whipple. Married to a lush, and sleeping with his best friend's wife, Mary."

"Then you wouldn't depend on Joe, either?"

"Yes, I would. Women don't bother him. He don't care if his wife is a lush, he'll get his nooky from his best friend's wife, he *isn't* going to marry her because that was three-four years ago, and he's tough about everybody. His wife, his dame, his best friend, *and* the United States government. Because I tell you something, if we ever get going on the home-loan proposition, don't think Joe didn't use his job in Washington every chance he got. The partnership is gonna be me and Joe Whipple, because he's just as tough as I am. And one fine day he'll fall over dead from not taking care of himself, and I'll be the main guy. You know the only thing I don't like about you, Bobbie, is the booze. If you'd lay off the sauce for a year I'd get rid of Peggy, and you and I could get married. But booze is women's weakness like women are men's weakness."

"Men are women's weakness."

"No, you're wrong. Men don't make women talk, men don't make women lose their looks, and women can give up men for a hell of a long time, but a female lush is the worst kind of a lush."

"Am I a lush?"

"You have a couple drinks every day, don't you?"

"Yes."

"Then you're on the way. Maybe you only take three-four drinks a day now, but five years from now three or four drinks will get you stewed, so you'll be stewed every day. That's a lush. Peggy eats like a God damn pig, but if she ever started drinking, I'd kick her out. Fortunately her old man died with the D.T.'s, so she's afraid of it."

"Would you mind getting me a nice double Scotch with a little water?"

"Why should I mind?" He grinned from back molar to back molar. "When you got a little load on, you forget home and mother." He got her the drink, she took it in her right hand and slowly poured it down his furry chest. He jumped when the icy drink touched him.

"Thank you so much," she said. "Been a very pleasant afternoon, but the party's over."

"You sore at me?"

"Yes, I am. I don't like being called a lush, and I certainly don't like you to think I'd make a good substitute for Peggy."

"You *are* sore."

"Yes."

The children did not know it was her birthday, but when Pete came home he handed her two parcels. "For me?" she said.

"Not very much imagination, but I didn't have a chance to go to Gibbsville," he said.

One package contained half a dozen nylons, the other a bottle of Chanel Number 5. "Thank you. Just what I wanted. I really did."

He suddenly began to cry, and rushed out of the room.

"Why is Daddy crying?" said their daughter.

"Because it's my birthday and he did a very sweet thing."

"Why should he cry?" said their son. He was nine years old, the daughter eleven.

"Because he's sentimental," said the daughter.

"And it's a very nice thing to be," said Bobbie.

"Aren't you going to go to him?"

"Not quite yet. In a minute. Angus, will you go down to the drug store and get a quart of ice cream? Here's a dollar, and you and your sister may keep the change, divided."

"What flavor?" said the boy.

"Vanilla and strawberry, or whatever else they have."

Pete returned. "Kids gone to bed?"

"I sent them for some ice cream."

"Did they see me bawling?"

"Yes, and I think it did them good. Marjorie understood it. Angus was a little mystified. But it was good for both of them."

"Marjorie understood it? Did you?"

"She said it was because you were sentimental."

He shook his head. "I don't know if you'd call it sentimental. I just couldn't help thinking you were forty years old. Forty. You forty. Bobbie Hammersmith. And all we've been through, and what I've done to you. I know why you married me, Bobbie, but why did you stick it out?"

"Because I married you."

"Yes. Because you married Ichabod. You know, I wasn't in love with you when we were first married. You thought I was, but I wasn't. It was wonderful, being in bed with you and watching you walking around without any clothes on. Taking a bath. But it was too much for me and that's what started me making passes at everybody. And underneath it all I knew damn well why you married me and I hated you. You were making a fool of me and I kept waiting for you to say this farce was over. If you had, I'd have killed you."

"And I guess rightly."

"And all the later stuff. Running a poolroom and living on Mill Street. I blamed all of that on you. But things are better now since we moved here. Aren't they?"

"Yes, much better, as far as the way we live—"

"That's all I meant. If we didn't have Lantenengo Street and Princeton and those things to look back on, this wouldn't be a bad life for two ordinary people."

"It's not bad," she said.

"It's still pretty bad, but that's because we once had it better. Here's what I want to say. Any time you want to walk out on me, I won't make any fuss. You can have the children, and I won't fight about it. That's my birthday present to you, before it's too late. And I have no plans for myself. I'm not trying to get out of this marriage, but you're forty now and you're entitled to whatever is left."

"Thank you, Pete. I have nobody that wants to marry me."

"Well, maybe not. But you may have, sometime. I love you now, Bobbie, and I never used to. I guess you can't love anybody else while you have no self-respect. When the war was over I was sure I'd get the bounce at the plant, but they like me there, they've kept me on, and that one promotion. We'll never be back on Lantenengo Street, but I think I can count on a job here maybe the rest of my life. In a couple of years we can move to a nicer house."

"I'd rather buy this and fix it up a little. It's a better-built house than the ones they're putting up over on Fair Grounds Heights."

"Well, I'm glad you like it too," he said. "The other thing, that we hardly ever talk about. In fact never talk about. Only fight about sometimes. I'll try, Bobbie. I've been trying."

"I know you have."

"Well—how about you trying, too?"

"I did."

"But not lately. I'm not going to ask you who or when or any of that, but why is it you're faithful to me while I'm chasing after other women, and then when I'm faithful to you, you have somebody else? You're forty now and I'm forty-four. Let's see how long we can go without cheating?"

"You don't mean put a time limit on it, or put up a trophy, like an endurance contest? That's the way it sounds. We both have bad habits, Pete."

"Yes, and I'm the worst. But break it off, Bobbie, whoever it is. Will you please? If it's somebody you're not going to marry, and that's what you said, I've—well, it's a long time since I've cheated, and I like it much better this way. Will you stop seeing this other guy?"

"All right. As a matter of fact I *have* stopped, but don't ask me how long ago."

"I won't ask you anything. And if you fall in love with somebody and want to marry him—"

"And he wants to marry me."

"And he wants to marry you, I'll bow out." He leaned down and kissed her cheek. "I know you better than you think I do, Bobbie."

"That's an irritating statement to make to any woman."

"I guess it is, but not the way I meant it."

Now that is as far as I need go in the story of Pete and Bobbie McCrea. I promised a happy ending, which I shall come to in a moment. We have left Pete and Bobbie in 1947, on Bobbie's fortieth birthday. During the next thirteen years I saw them twice. On one occasion my wife and I spent the night with them in their house in Fair Grounds, which was painted, scrubbed and dusted like the Fair Grounds houses of old. My wife went to bed early, and Pete and Bobbie and I talked until past midnight, and then Pete retired and Bobbie and I continued our conversation until three in the morning. Twice she emptied our ash trays of cigarette butts, and we drank a drip-flask of coffee. It seemed to me that she was so thorough in her description of their life because she felt that the dinginess would vanish if she once succeeded in exposing it. But as we were leaving in the morning I was not so sure that it had vanished. My wife said to me: "Did she get it all out of her system?"

"Get what out of her system?"

"I don't know, but I don't think she did, entirely."

"That would be asking too much," I said. "But I guess she's happy."

"Content, but not happy," said my wife. "But the children are what interested me. The girl is going to be attractive in a few more years, but that boy! You didn't talk to him, but do you know about him? He's fourteen, and he's already passed his senior mathematics. He's *finished* the work that the high school seniors are supposed to be taking. The principal is trying to arrange correspondence courses for him. He's the brightest student they ever had in Fair Grounds High School, ever, and all the scientific men at the aluminum plant know about him. And he's a good-looking boy, too."

"Bobbie didn't tell me any of this."

"And I'll bet I know why. He's their future. With you she wanted to get rid of the past. She adores this boy, adores him. That part's almost terrifying."

"Not to me," I said. "It's the best thing that could have happened to her, and to Pete. The only thing that's terrifying is that they could have ruined it. And believe me, they could have."

In 1960, then, I saw Pete and Bobbie again. They invited me, of all their old friends, to go with them to the Princeton commencement. Angus McCrea, Junior, led his class, was awarded the mathematics prize, the physics prize, the Eubank Prize for scholarship, and some other honors that I am sure are listed in the program. I could not read the program because I was crying most of the time. Pete would lean forward in his chair, listening to the things that were being said about his son, but in an attitude that would have been more suitable to a man who was listening to a pronouncement of sentence. Bobbie sat erect and smiling, but every once in a while I could hear her whisper, "Oh, God. Oh, God."

There, I guess, is our happy ending.

WILLIAM SAROYAN

[1908–1981]

The Daring Young Man on the Flying Trapeze

(First published in *Story Magazine*, 1933; first book publication in 1934.)

I. SLEEP

HORIZONTALLY WAKEFUL AMID universal widths, practicing laughter and mirth, satire, the end of all, of Rome and yes of Babylon, clenched teeth, remembrance, much warmth volcanic, the streets of Paris, the plains of Jericho, much gliding as of reptile in abstraction, a gallery of watercolors, the sea and the fish with eyes, symphony, a table in the corner of the Eiffel Tower, jazz at the opera house, alarm clock and the tap-dancing of doom, conversation with a tree, the river Nile, Cadillac coupé to Kansas, the roar of Dostoyevsky, and the dark sun.

This earth, the face of one who lived, the form without the weight, weeping upon snow, white music, the magnified flower twice the size of the universe, black clouds, the caged panther staring, deathless space, Mr. Eliot with rolled sleeves baking bread, Flaubert and Guy de Maupassant, a wordless rhyme of early meaning, Finlandia, mathematics highly polished and slick as a green onion to the teeth, Jerusalem, the path to paradox.

The deep song of man, the sly whisper of someone unseen but vaguely known, hurricane in the cornfield, a game of chess, hush the queen, the king, Karl Franz, black Titanic, Mr. Chaplin weeping, Stalin, Hitler, a multitude of Jews, tomorrow is Monday, no dancing in the streets.

O swift moment of life: it is ended, the earth is again now.

II. WAKEFULNESS

He (the living) dressed and shaved, grinning at himself in the mirror. Very unhandsome, he said; where is my tie? (He had but one.) Coffee and a gray sky, Pacific Ocean fog, the drone of a passing streetcar, people going to the city, time again, the day, prose and poetry. He moved swiftly down the stairs to the street and began to walk, thinking suddenly, *It is only in sleep that we may know that we live. There only, in that living death, do we meet ourselves and the far earth, God and the saints, the names of our fathers, the substance of remote moments; it is there that the centuries merge in the moment that the vast becomes the tiny, tangible atom of eternity.*

He walked into the day as alertly as might be, making a definite noise with his heels, perceiving with his eyes the superficial truth of streets and structures, the trivial truth of reality. Helplessly his mind sang, *He flies through the air with the greatest of ease; the daring young man on the flying trapeze*; then laughed with all the might of his being. It was really a splendid morning: gray, cold, and cheerless, a morning for inward vigor; ah, Edgar Guest, he said, how I long for your music.

In the gutter he saw a coin which proved to be a penny dated 1923, and placing it in the palm of his hand he examined it closely, remembering that year and thinking of Lincoln whose profile was stamped upon the coin. There was almost nothing a man could do with a penny. I will purchase a motorcar, he thought. I will dress myself in the fashion of a fop, visit the hotel strumpets, drink and dine, and then return to the quiet. Or I will drop the coin into a slot and weigh myself.

It was good to be poor, and the Communists—but it was dreadful to be hungry. What appetites they had, how fond they were of food! Empty stomachs. He remembered how greatly he needed food. Every meal was bread and coffee and cigarettes, and now he had no more bread. Coffee without bread could never honestly serve as supper, and there were no weeds in the park that could be cooked as spinach is cooked.

If the truth were known, he was half starved, and yet there was still no end of books he ought to read before he died. He remembered the young Italian in a Brooklyn hospital, a small sick clerk named Mollica, who had said desperately, I would like to see California once before I die. And he thought earnestly, I ought at least to read Hamlet once again; or perhaps Huckleberry Finn.

It was then that he became thoroughly awake: at the thought of dying. Now wakefulness was a state in the nature of a sustained shock. A young man could perish rather unostentatiously, he thought; and already he was very nearly starved. Water and prose were fine, they filled much inorganic space, but they were inadequate. If there were only some work he might do for money, some trivial labor in the name of commerce. If they would only allow him to sit at a desk all day and add trade figures, subtract and multiply and divide, then perhaps he would not die. He would buy food, all sorts of it: untasted delicacies from Norway, Italy, and France; all manner of beef, lamb, fish, cheese; grapes, figs, pears, apples, melons, which he would worship when he had satisfied his hunger. He would place a bunch of red grapes on a dish beside two black figs, a large yellow pear, and a green apple. He would hold a cut melon to his nostrils for hours.

He would buy great brown loaves of French bread, vegetables of all sorts, meat; he would buy life.

From a hill he saw the city standing majestically in the east, great towers, dense with his kind, and there he was suddenly outside of it all, almost definitely certain that he should never gain admittance, almost positive that somehow he had ventured upon the wrong earth, or perhaps into the wrong age, and now a young man of twenty-two was to be permanently ejected from it. This thought was not saddening. He said to himself, sometime soon I must write *An Application For Permission To Live*. He accepted the thought of dying without pity for himself or for man, believing that he would at least sleep another night. His rent for another day was paid; there was yet another tomorrow. And after that he might go where other homeless men went. He might even visit the Salvation Army—sing to God and Jesus (unlover of my soul), be saved, eat and sleep. But he knew that he would not. His life was a private life. He did not wish to destroy this fact. Any other alternative would be better.

Through the air on the flying trapeze, his mind hummed. Amusing it was, astoundingly funny. A trapeze to God, or to nothing, a flying trapeze to some sort of eternity; he prayed objectively for the strength to make the flight with grace.

I have one cent, he said. It is an American coin. In the evening I shall polish it until it glows like a sun and I shall study the words.

He was now walking in the city itself, among living men. There were one or two places to go. He saw his reflection in the plate-glass windows of stores and was disappointed with his appearance. He seemed not at all as strong as he felt; he seemed, in fact, a trifle infirm in every part of his body, in his neck, his shoulders, arms, trunk, and knees. This will never do, he said, and with an effort he assembled all his disjointed parts and became tensely, artificially erect and solid.

He passed numerous restaurants with magnificent discipline, refusing even to glance into them, and at last reached a building, which he entered. He rose in an elevator to the seventh floor, moved down a hall, and, opening a door, walked into the office of an employment agency. Already there were two dozen young men in the place; he found a corner where he stood waiting his turn to be interviewed. At length he was granted this great privilege and was questioned by a thin, scatterbrained miss of fifty.

Now tell me, she said; what can you do?

He was embarrassed. I can write, he said pathetically.

You mean your penmanship is good? Is that it? said the elderly maiden.

Well, yes, he replied. But I mean that I can write.

Write what? said the miss, almost with anger.

Prose, he said simply.

There was a pause. At last the lady said:

Can you use a typewriter?

Of course, said the young man.

All right, went on the miss, we have your address; we will get in touch with you. There is nothing this morning, nothing at all.

It was much the same at the other agency, except that he was questioned by a conceited young man who closely resembled a pig. From the agencies he went to the large department stores: there was a good deal of pomposity, some humiliation on his part, and finally the report that work was not available. He did not feel displeased, and strangely did not even feel that he was personally involved in all the foolishness. He was a living young man who was in need of money with which to go on being one, and there was no way of getting it except by working for it; and there was no work. It was purely an abstract problem which he wished for the last time to attempt to solve. Now he was pleased that the matter was closed.

He began to perceive the definiteness of the course of his life. Except for moments, it had been largely artless, but now at the last minute he was determined that there should be as little imprecision as possible.

He passed countless stores and restaurants on his way to the Y. M. C. A., where he helped himself to paper and ink and began to compose his *Application*. For an hour he worked on this document, then suddenly, owing to the bad air in the place and to hunger, he became faint. He seemed to be swimming away from himself with great strokes, and hurriedly left the building. In the Civic Center Park, across from the Public Library Building, he drank almost a quart of water and felt himself refreshed. An old man was standing in the center of the brick boulevard surrounded by sea gulls, pigeons, and robins. He was taking handfuls of bread crumbs from a large paper sack and tossing them to the birds with a gallant gesture.

Dimly he felt impelled to ask the old man for a portion of the crumbs, but he did not allow the thought even nearly to reach consciousness; he entered the Public Library and for an hour read Proust, then, feeling himself to be swimming away again, he rushed outdoors. He drank more water at the fountain in the park and began the long walk to his room.

I'll go and sleep some more, he said; there is nothing else to do. He knew now that he was much too tired and weak to deceive himself about being all right, and yet his mind seemed somehow still lithe and alert. It, as if it were a separate entity, persisted in articulating impertinent pleasantries about his very real physical suffering. He reached his room early in the afternoon and immediately prepared coffee on the small gas range. There was no milk in the can and the half pound of sugar he had purchased a week before was all gone; he drank a cup of the hot black fluid, sitting on his bed and smiling.

From the Y. M. C. A. he had stolen a dozen sheets of letter paper upon which he hoped to complete his document, but now the very notion of writing was unpleasant to him. There was nothing to say. He began to polish the penny he had found in the morning, and this absurd act somehow afforded him great enjoyment. No American coin can be made to shine so brilliantly as a penny. How many pennies would he need to go on living? Wasn't there something more he might sell? He looked about the bare room. No. His watch was gone; also his books. All those fine books; nine of them for eighty-five cents. He felt ill and ashamed for having parted with his books. His best suit he had sold for two dollars, but that was all right. He didn't mind at all about clothes. But the books. That was different. It made him very angry to think that there was no respect for men who wrote.

He placed the shining penny on the table, looking upon it with the delight of a miser. How prettily it smiles, he said. Without reading them he looked at the words, *E Pluribus Unum One Cent United States Of America*, and turning the penny over, he saw Lincoln and the words, *In God We We Trust Liberty 1923*. How beautiful it is, he said.

He became drowsy and felt a ghastly illness coming over his blood, a feeling of nausea and disintegration. Bewildered, he stood beside his bed, thinking that there *is nothing to do but sleep*. Already he felt himself making great strides through the fluid of the earth, swimming away to the beginning. He fell face down upon the bed, saying, I ought first at least to give the coin to some child. A child could buy any number of things with a penny.

Then swiftly, neatly, with the grace of the young man on the trapeze, he was gone from his body. For an eternal moment he was all things at once: the bird, the fish, the rodent, the reptile, and man. An ocean of print undulated endlessly and darkly before him. The city burned. The herded crowd rioted. The earth circled away, and knowing that he did so, he turned his lost face to the empty sky and became dreamless, unalive, perfect.

EUDORA WELTY

[1909–2001]

Death of a Traveling Salesman

(First published in *Manuscript*,
June, 1936; first book publication in 1941.)

R. J. Bowman, who for fourteen years had traveled for a shoe company through Mississippi, drove his Ford along a rutted dirt path. It was a long day! The time did not seem to clear the noon hurdle and settle into soft afternoon. The sun, keeping its strength here even in winter, stayed at the top of the sky, and every time Bowman stuck his head out of the dusty car to stare up the road, it seemed to reach a long arm down and push against the top of his head, right through his hat—like the practical joke of an old drummer, long on the road. It made him feel all the more angry and helpless. He was feverish, and he was not quite sure of the way.

This was his first day back on the road after a long siege of influenza. He had had very high fever, and dreams, and had become weakened and pale, enough to tell the difference in the mirror, and he could not think clearly. . . . All afternoon, in the midst of his anger, and for no reason, he had thought of his dead grandmother. She had been a comfortable soul. Once more Bowman wished he could fall into the big feather bed that had been in her room. . . . Then he forgot her again.

This desolate hill country! And he seemed to be going the wrong way—it was as if he were going back, far back. There was not a house in sight. . . . There was no use wishing he were back in bed, though. By paying the hotel doctor his bill he had proved his recovery. He had not even been sorry when the pretty trained nurse said good-bye. He did not like illness, he distrusted it, as he distrusted the road without signposts. It angered him. He had given the nurse a really expensive bracelet, just because she was packing up her bag and leaving.

But now—what if in fourteen years on the road he had never been ill before and never had an accident? His record was broken, and he had even begun almost to question it. . . . He had gradually put up at better hotels, in the bigger towns, but weren't they all, eternally, stuffy in summer and drafty in winter? Women? He could only remember little rooms within little rooms, like a nest of Chinese paper boxes, and if he thought of one woman he saw the worn loneliness that the furniture of that room seemed built of. And he himself—he was a man who always wore rather wide-brimmed black hats, and in the wavy hotel mirrors had looked something like a bullfighter, as he paused for that inevitable instant on the landing, walking downstairs to supper. . . . He leaned out of the car again, and once more the sun pushed at his head.

Bowman had wanted to reach Beulah by dark, to go to bed and sleep off his fatigue. As he remembered, Beulah was fifty miles away from the last town, on a graveled road. This was only a cow trail. How had he ever come to such a place? One hand wiped the sweat from his face, and he drove on.

He had made the Beulah trip before. But he had never seen this hill or this petering-out path before—or that cloud, he thought shyly, looking up and then down quickly—any more than he had seen this day before. Why did he not admit he was simply lost and had been for miles?. . . He was not in the habit of asking the way of strangers, and these people never knew where the very roads they lived on went to; but then he had not even been close enough to anyone to call out. People standing in the fields now and then, or on top of the haystacks, had been too far away, looking like leaning sticks or weeds, turning a little at the solitary rattle of his car across their countryside, watching the pale sobered winter dust where it chunked out behind like big squashes down the road. The stares of these distant people had followed him solidly like a wall, impenetrable, behind which they turned back after he had passed.

The cloud floated there to one side like the bolster on his grandmother's bed. It went over a cabin on the edge of a hill, where two bare chinaberry trees clutched at the sky. He drove through a heap of dead oak leaves, his wheels stirring their weightless sides to make a silvery melancholy whistle as the car passed through their bed. No car had been along this way ahead of him. Then he saw that he was on the edge of a ravine that fell away, a red erosion, and that this was indeed the road's end.

He pulled the brake. But it did not hold, though he put all his strength into it. The car, tipped toward the edge, rolled a little. Without doubt, it was going over the bank.

He got out quietly, as though some mischief had been done him and he had his dignity to remember. He lifted his bag and sample case out, set them down, and stood back and watched the car roll over the edge. He heard something—not the crash he was listening for, but a slow, unuproarious crackle. Rather distastefully he went to look over, and he saw that his car had fallen into a tangle of immense grapevines as thick as his arm, which caught it and held it, rocked it like a grotesque child in a dark cradle, and then, as he watched, concerned somehow that he was not still inside it, released it gently to the ground.

He sighed.

Where am I? he wondered with a shock. Why didn't I do something? All his anger seemed to have drifted away from him. There was the house, back on the hill. He took a bag in each hand and with almost childlike willingness went toward it. But his breathing came with difficulty, and he had to stop to rest.

It was a shotgun house, two rooms and an open passage between, perched on the hill. The whole cabin slanted a little under the heavy heaped-up vine that covered the roof, light and green, as though forgotten from summer. A woman stood in the passage.

He stopped still. Then all of a sudden his heart began to behave strangely. Like a rocket set off, it began to leap and expand into uneven patterns of beats which showered into his brain, and he could not think. But in scattering and falling it made no noise. It shot up with great power, almost elation, and fell gently, like acrobats into nets. It began to pound profoundly, then waited irresponsibly, hitting in some sort of inward mockery first at his ribs, then against his eyes, then under his shoulder blades, and against the roof of his mouth when he tried to say, "Good afternoon, madam." But he could not hear his heart—it was as quiet as ashes falling. This was rather comforting; still, it was shocking to Bowman to feel his heart beating at all.

Stock-still in his confusion, he dropped his bags, which seemed to drift in slow bulks gracefully through the air and to cushion themselves on the gray prostrate grass near the doorstep.

As for the woman standing there, he saw at once that she was old. Since she could not possibly hear his heart, he ignored the pounding and now looked at her carefully, and yet in his distraction dreamily, with his mouth open.

She had been cleaning the lamp, and held it, half blackened, half clear, in front of her. He saw her with the dark passage behind her. She was a big woman with a weather-beaten but unwrinkled face; her lips were held tightly together, and her eyes looked with a curious dulled brightness into his. He looked at her shoes, which were like bundles. If it were summer she would be barefoot. . . . Bowman, who automatically judged a woman's age on sight, set her age at fifty. She wore a formless garment of some gray coarse material, rough-dried from a washing, from which her arms appeared pink and unexpectedly round. When she never said a word, and sustained her quiet pose of holding the lamp, he was convinced of the strength in her body.

"Good afternoon, madam," he said.

She stared on, whether at him or at the air around him he could not tell, but after a moment she lowered her eyes to show that she would listen to whatever he had to say.

"I wonder if you would be interested—" He tried once more. "An accident—my car . . ."

Her voice emerged low and remote, like a sound across a lake. "Sonny he ain't here."

"Sonny?"

"Sonny ain't here now."

Her son—a fellow able to bring my car up, he decided in blurred relief. He pointed down the hill. "My car's in the bottom of the ditch. I'll need help."

"Sonny ain't here, but he'll be here."

She was becoming clearer to him and her voice stronger, and Bowman saw that she was stupid.

He was hardly surprised at the deepening postponement and tedium of his journey. He took a breath, and heard his voice speaking over the silent blows of his heart. "I was sick. I am not strong yet. . . . May I come in?"

He stooped and laid his big black hat over the handle on his bag. It was a humble motion, almost a bow, that instantly struck him as absurd and betraying of all his weakness. He looked up at the woman, the wind blowing his hair. He might have continued for a long time in this unfamiliar attitude; he had never been a patient man, but when he was sick he had learned to sink submissively into the pillows, to wait for his medicine. He waited on the woman.

Then she, looking at him with blue eyes, turned and held open the door, and after a moment Bowman, as if convinced in his action, stood erect and followed her in.

Inside, the darkness of the house touched him like a professional hand, the doctor's. The woman set the half-cleaned lamp on a table in the center of the room and pointed, also like a professional person, a guide, to a chair with a yellow cowhide seat. She herself crouched on the hearth, drawing her knees up under the shapeless dress.

At first he felt hopefully secure. His heart was quieter. The room was enclosed in the gloom of yellow pine boards. He could see the other room, with the foot of an iron bed showing, across the passage. The bed had been made up with a red-and-yellow pieced quilt that looked like a map or a picture, a little like his grandmother's girlhood painting of Rome burning.

He had ached for coolness, but in this room it was cold. He stared at the hearth with dead coals lying on it and iron pots in the corners. The hearth and smoked chimney were of the stone he had seen ribbing the hills, mostly slate. Why is there no fire? he wondered.

And it was so still. The silence of the fields seemed to enter and move familiarly through the house. The wind used the open hall. He felt that he was in a mysterious, quiet, cool danger. It was necessary to do what?. . . To talk.

"I have a nice line of women's low-priced shoes . . ." he said.

But the woman answered, "Sonny'll be here. He's strong. Sonny'll move your car."

"Where is he now?"

"Farms for Mr. Redmond."

Mr. Redmond. Mr. Redmond. That was someone he would never have to encounter, and he was glad. Somehow the name did not appeal to him. . . . In a flare of touchiness and anxiety, Bowman wished to avoid even mention of unknown men and their unknown farms.

"Do you two live here alone?" He was surprised to hear his old voice, chatty, confidential, inflected for selling shoes, asking a question like that—a thing he did not even want to know.

"Yes. We are alone."

He was surprised at the way she answered. She had taken a long time to say that. She had nodded her head in a deep way too. Had she wished to affect him with some sort of premonition? he wondered unhappily. Or was it only that she would not help him, after all, by talking with him? For he was not strong enough to receive the impact of unfamiliar things without a little talk to break their fall. He had lived a month in which nothing had happened except in his head and his body—an almost inaudible life of heartbeats and dreams that came back, a life of fever and privacy, a delicate life which had left him weak to the point of—what? Of begging. The pulse in his palm leapt like a trout in a brook.

He wondered over and over why the woman did not go ahead with cleaning the lamp. What prompted her to stay there across the room, silently bestowing her presence upon him? He saw that with her it was not a time for doing little tasks. Her face was grave; she was feeling how right she was. Perhaps it was only politeness. In docility he held his eyes stiffly wide; they fixed themselves on the woman's clasped hands as though she held the cord they were strung on.

Then, "Sonny's coming," she said.

He himself had not heard anything, but there came a man passing the window and then plunging in at the door, with two hounds beside him. Sonny was a big enough man, with his belt slung low about his hips. He looked at least thirty. He had a hot, red face that was yet full of silence. He wore muddy blue pants and an old military coat stained and patched. World War? Bowman wondered. Great God, it was a Confederate coat. On the back of his light hair he had a wide filthy black hat which seemed to insult Bowman's own. He pushed down the dogs from his chest. He was strong, with dignity and heaviness in his way of moving. . . . There was the resemblance to his mother.

They stood side by side. . . . He must account again for his presence here.

"Sonny, this man, he had his car to run off over the prec'pice an' wants to know if you will git it out for him," the woman said after a few minutes.

Bowman could not even state his case.

Sonny's eyes lay upon him.

He knew he should offer explanations and show money—at least appear either penitent or authoritative. But all he could do was to shrug slightly.

Sonny brushed by him going to the window, followed by the eager dogs, and looked out. There was effort even in the way he was looking, as if he could throw his sight out like a rope. Without turning Bowman felt that his own eyes could have seen nothing: it was too far.

"Got me a mule out there an' got me a block an' tackle," said Sonny meaningfully. "I *could* catch me my mule an' git me my ropes, an' before long I'd git your car out the ravine."

He looked completely around the room, as if in meditation, his eyes roving in their own distance. Then he pressed his lips firmly and yet shyly together, and with the dogs ahead of him this time, he lowered his head and strode out. The hard earth sounded, cupping to his powerful way of walking—almost a stagger.

Mischievously, at the suggestion of those sounds, Bowman's heart leapt again. It seemed to walk about inside him.

"Sonny's goin' to do it," the woman said. She said it again, singing it almost, like a song. She was sitting in her place by the hearth.

Without looking out, he heard some shouts and the dogs barking and the pounding of hoofs in short runs on the hill. In a few minutes Sonny passed under the window with a rope, and there was a brown mule with quivering, shining, purple-looking ears. The mule actually looked in the window. Under its eyelashes it turned targetlike eyes into his. Bowman averted his head and saw the woman looking serenely back at the mule, with only satisfaction in her face.

She sang a little more, under her breath. It occurred to him, and it seemed quite marvelous, that she was not really talking to him, but rather following the thing that came about with words that were unconscious and part of her looking.

So he said nothing, and this time when he did not reply he felt a curious and strong emotion, not fear, rise up in him.

This time, when his heart leapt, something—his soul—seemed to leap too, like a little colt invited out of a pen. He stared at the woman while the frantic nimbleness of his feeling made his head sway. He could not move; there was nothing he could do, unless perhaps he might embrace this woman who sat there growing old and shapeless before him.

But he wanted to leap up, to say to her, I have been sick and I found out then, only then, how lonely I am. Is it too late? My heart puts up a struggle inside me, and you may have heard it, protesting against emptiness. . . .

It should be full, he would rush on to tell her, thinking of his heart now as a deep lake, it should be holding love like other hearts. It should be flooded with love. There would be a warm spring day . . . Come and stand in my heart, whoever you are, and a whole river would cover your feet and rise higher and take your knees in whirlpools, and draw you down to itself, your whole body, your heart too.

But he moved a trembling hand across his eyes, and looked at the placid crouching woman across the room. She was still as a statue. He felt ashamed and exhausted by the thought that he might, in one more moment, have tried by simple words and embraces to communicate some strange thing—something which seemed always to have just escaped him . . .

Sunlight touched the furthest pot on the hearth. It was late afternoon. This time tomorrow he would be somewhere on a good graveled road, driving his car past things that happened to people, quicker than their happening. Seeing ahead to the next day, he was glad, and knew that this was no time to embrace an old woman. He could feel in his pounding temples the readying of his blood for motion and for hurrying away.

"Sonny's hitched up your car by now," said the woman. "He'll git it out the ravine right shortly."

"Fine!" he cried with his customary enthusiasm.

Yet it seemed a long time that they waited. It began to get dark. Bowman was cramped in his chair. Any man should know enough to get up and walk around while he waited. There was something like guilt in such stillness and silence.

But instead of getting up, he listened. . . . His breathing restrained, his eyes powerless in the growing dark, he listened uneasily for a warning sound, forgetting in wariness what it would be. Before long he heard something—soft, continuous, insinuating.

"What's that noise?" he asked, his voice jumping into the dark. Then wildly he was afraid it would be his heart beating so plainly in the quiet room, and she would tell him so.

"You might hear the stream," she said grudgingly.

Her voice was closer. She was standing by the table. He wondered why she did not light the lamp. She stood there in the dark and did not light it.

Bowman would never speak to her now, for the time was past. I'll sleep in the dark, he thought, in his bewilderment pitying himself.

Heavily she moved on to the window. Her arm, vaguely white, rose straight from her full side and she pointed out into the darkness.

"That white speck's Sonny," she said, talking to herself.

He turned unwillingly and peered over her shoulder; he hesitated to rise and stand beside her. His eyes searched the dusky air. The white speck floated smoothly toward her finger, like a leaf on a river, growing whiter in the dark. It was as if she had shown him something secret, part of her life, but had offered no explanation. He looked away. He was moved almost to tears, feeling for no reason that she had made a silent declaration equivalent to his own. His hand waited upon his chest.

Then a step shook the house, and Sonny was in the room. Bowman felt how the woman left him there and went to the other man's side.

"I done got your car out, mister," said Sonny's voice in the dark. "She's settin' a-waitin' in the road, turned to go back where she come from."

"Fine!" said Bowman, projecting his own voice to loudness. "I'm surely much obliged—I could never have done it myself—I was sick. . . ."

"I could do it easy," said Sonny.

Bowman could feel them both waiting in the dark, and he could hear the dogs panting out in the yard, waiting to bark when he should go. He felt strangely helpless and resentful. Now that he could go, he longed to stay. From what was he being deprived? His chest was rudely shaken by the violence of his heart. These people cherished something here that he could not see, they withheld some ancient promise of food and warmth and light. Between them they had a conspiracy. He thought of the way she had moved away from him and gone to Sonny, she had flowed toward him. He was shaking with cold, he was tired, and it was not fair. Humbly and yet angrily he stuck his hand into his pocket.

"Of course I'm going to pay you for everything—"

"We don't take money for such," said Sonny's voice belligerently.

"I want to pay. But do something more . . . Let me stay—tonight. . . ." He took another step toward them. If only they could see him, they would know his sincerity, his real need! His voice went on, "I'm not very strong yet, I'm not able to walk far, even back to my car, maybe, I don't know—I don't know exactly where I am—"

He stopped. He felt as if he might burst into tears. What would they think of him!

Sonny came over and put his hands on him. Bowman felt them pass (they were professional too) across his chest, over his hips. He could feel Sonny's eyes upon him in the dark.

"You ain't no revenuer come sneakin' here, mister, ain't got no gun?"

To this end of nowhere! And yet *he* had come. He made a grave answer. "No."

"You can stay."

"Sonny," said the woman, "you'll have to borry some fire."

"I'll go git it from Redmond's," said Sonny.

"What?" Bowman strained to hear their words to each other.

"Our fire, it's out, and Sonny's got to borry some, because its dark an' cold," she said.

"But matches—I have matches—"

"We don't have no need for 'em," she said proudly. "Sonny's goin' after his own fire."

"I'm goin' to Redmond's," said Sonny with an air of importance, and he went out.

After they had waited a while, Bowman looked out the window and saw a light moving over the hill. It spread itself out like a little fan. It zigzagged along the field, darting and swift, not like Sonny at all. . . . Soon enough, Sonny staggered in, holding a burning stick behind him in tongs, fire flowing in his wake, blazing light into the corners of the room.

"We'll make a fire now," the woman said, taking the brand.

When that was done she lit the lamp. It showed its dark and light. The whole room turned golden-yellow like some sort of flower, and the walls smelled of it and seemed to tremble with the quiet rushing of the fire and the waving of the burning lampwick in its funnel of light.

The woman moved among the iron pots. With the tongs she dropped hot coals on top of the iron lids. They made a set of soft vibrations, like the sound of a bell far away.

She looked up and over at Bowman, but he could not answer. He was trembling. . . .

"Have a drink, mister?" Sonny asked. He had brought in a chair from the other room and sat astride it with his folded arms across the back. Now we are all visible to one another, Bowman thought, and cried, "Yes sir, you bet, thanks!"

"Come after me and do just what I do," said Sonny.

It was another excursion into the dark. They went through the hall, out to the back of the house, past a shed and a hooded well. They came to a wilderness of thicket.

"Down on your knees," said Sonny.

"What?" Sweat broke out on his forehead.

He understood when Sonny began to crawl through a sort of tunnel that the bushes made over the ground. He followed, startled in spite of himself when a twig or a thorn touched him gently without making a sound, clinging to him and finally letting him go.

Sonny stopped crawling and, crouched on his knees, began to dig with both his hands into the dirt. Bowman shyly struck matches and made a light. In a few minutes Sonny pulled up a jug. He poured out some of the whisky into a bottle from his coat pocket, and buried the jug again. "You never know who's liable to knock at your door," he said, and laughed. "Start back," he said, almost formally. "Ain't no need for us to drink outdoors, like hogs."

At the table by the fire, sitting opposite each other in their chairs, Sonny and Bowman took drinks out of the bottle, passing it across. The dogs slept; one of them was having a dream.

"This is good," said Bowman. "This is what I needed." It was just as though he were drinking the fire off the hearth.

"He makes it," said the woman with quiet pride.

She was pushing the coals off the pots, and the smells of corn bread and coffee circled the room. She set everything on the table before the men, with a bone-handled knife stuck into one of the potatoes, splitting out its golden fiber. Then she stood for a minute looking at them, tall and full above them where they sat. She leaned a little toward them.

"You all can eat now," she said, and suddenly smiled.

Bowman had just happened to be looking at her. He set his cup back on the table in unbelieving protest. A pain pressed at his eyes. He saw that she was not an old woman. She was young, still young. He could think of no number of years for her. She was the same age as Sonny, and she belonged to him. She stood with the deep dark corner of the room behind her, the shifting yellow light scattering over her head and her gray formless dress, trembling over her tall body when it bent over them in its sudden communication. She was young. Her teeth were shining and her eyes glowed. She turned and walked slowly and heavily out of the room, and he heard her sit down on the cot and then lie down. The pattern on the quilt moved.

"She's goin' to have a baby," said Sonny, popping a bite into his mouth.

Bowman could not speak. He was shocked with knowing what was really in this house. A marriage, a fruitful marriage. That simple thing. Anyone could have had that.

Somehow he felt unable to be indignant or protest, although some sort of joke had certainly been played upon him. There was nothing remote or mysterious here—only something private. The only secret was the ancient communication between two people. But the memory of the woman's waiting silently by the cold hearth, of the man's stubborn journey a mile away to get fire, and how they finally brought out their food and drink and filled the room proudly with all they had to show, was suddenly too clear and too enormous within him for response. . . .

"You ain't as hungry as you look," said Sonny.

The woman came out of the bedroom as soon as the men had finished, and ate her supper while her husband stared peacefully into the fire.

Then they put the dogs out, with the food that was left.

"I think I'd better sleep here by the fire, on the floor," said Bowman.

He felt that he had been cheated, and that he could afford now to be generous. Ill though he was, he was not going to ask them for their bed. He was through with asking favors in this house, now that he understood what was there.

"Sure, mister."

But he had not known yet how slowly he understood. They had not meant to give him their bed. After a little interval they both rose and looking at him gravely went into the other room.

He lay stretched by the fire until it grew low and dying. He watched every tongue of blaze lick out and vanish. "There will be special reduced prices on all footwear during the month of January," he found himself repeating quietly, and then he lay with his lips tight shut.

How many noises the night had! He heard the stream running, the fire dying, and he was sure now that he heard his heart beating, too, the sound it made under his ribs. He heard breathing, round and deep, of the man and his wife in the room across the passage. And that was all. But emotion swelled patiently within him, and he wished that the child were his.

He must get back to where he had been before. He stood weakly before the red coals and put on his overcoat. It felt too heavy on his shoulders. As he started out he looked and saw that the woman had never got through with cleaning the lamp. On some impulse he put all the money from his billfold under its fluted glass base, almost ostentatiously.

Ashamed, shrugging a little, and then shivering, he took his bags and went out. The cold of the air seemed to lift him bodily. The moon was in the sky.

On the slope he began to run, he could not help it. Just as he reached the road, where his car seemed to sit in the moonlight like a boat, his heart began to give off tremendous explosions like a rifle, bang bang bang.

He sank in fright onto the road, his bags falling about him. He felt as if all this had happened before. He covered his heart with both hands to keep anyone from hearing the noise it made.

But nobody heard it.

PIETRO DI DONATO

[1911–1992]

Christ in Concrete

(First published in *Esquire*,
March, 1937; first book publication to come.)

MARCH WHISTLED STINGING snow against the brick walls and up the gaunt girders. Geremio, the foreman, swung his arms about, and gaffed the men on.

Old Nick, the "Lean," stood up from over a dust-flying brick pile, and tapped the side of his nose.

"Master Geremio, the devil himself could not break his tail any harder than we here."

Burly Vincenzo of the walrus moustache, and known as the "Snoutnose," let fall the chute door of the concrete hopper and sang over in the Lean's direction: "Mari-Annina's belly and the burning night will make of me once more a milk-mouthed stripling lad . . ."

The Lean loaded his wheelbarrow and spat furiously. "Sons of two-legged dogs . . . despised of even the devil himself! Work! Sure! For America beautiful will eat you and spit your bones into the earth's hole! Work!" And with that his wiry frame pitched the barrow violently over the rough floor.

Snoutnose waved his head to and fro and with mock pathos wailed, "Sing on, oh guitar of mine . . ."

Short, cherry-faced Joe Chiappa, the scaffoldman, paused with hatchet in hand and tenpenny spike sticking out from small dice-like teeth to tell the Lean as he went by, in a voice that all could hear, "Ah, father of countless chicks, the old age is a carrion!"

Geremio chuckled and called to him: "Hey, little Joe, who are you to talk? You and big-titted Cola can't even hatch an egg, whereas the Lean has just to turn the doorknob of his bedroom and old Philomena becomes a balloon!"

Coarse throats tickled and mouths opened wide in laughter.

Mike, the "Barrel-mouth," pretended he was talking to himself and yelled out in his best English . . . he was always speaking English while the rest carried on in their native Italian: "I don't know myself, but somebodys whose gotta bigga buncha keeds and he alla times talka from somebodys elsa!"

Geremio knew it was meant for him and he laughed. "On the tomb of Saint Pimplelegs, this little boy my wife is giving me next week shall be the last! Eight hungry little Christians to feed is enough for any man."

Joe Chiappa nodded to the rest. "Sure, Master Geremio had a telephone call from the next bambino. Yes, it told him it had a little bell there instead of a rosebush . . . It even told him its name!"

"Laugh, laugh all of you," returned Geremio, "but I tell you that all my kids must be boys so that they someday will be big American builders. And then I'll help them to put the gold away in the basements for safe keeping!"

A great din of riveting shattered the talk among the fast-moving men. Geremio added a handful of "Honest" tobacco to his corncob, puffed strongly, and cupped his hands around the bowl for a bit of warmth. The chill day caused him to shiver, and he thought to himself, "Yes, the day is cold, cold . . . but who am I to complain when the good Christ himself was crucified?

"Pushing the job is all right (when has it been otherwise in my life?) but this job frightens me. I feel the building wants to tell me something; just as one Christian to another. I don't like this. Mr. Murdin tells me, 'Push it up!' That's all he knows. I keep telling him that the underpinning should be doubled and the old material removed from the floors, but he keeps the inspector drunk and . . . 'Hey, Ashes-ass! Get away from under that pilaster! Don't pull the old work. Push it away from you or you'll have a nice present for Easter if the wall falls on you!' . . . Well, with the help of God I'll see this job through. It's not my first, nor the . . . 'Hey, Patsy number two! Put more cement in that concrete; we're putting up a building, not an Easter cake!'"

Patsy hurled his shovel to the floor and gesticulated madly. "The padrone Murdin-sa tells me, 'Too much, too much! Lil' bit is plenty!' And you tell me I'm stingy! The rotten building can fall after I leave!"

Six floors below, the contractor called: "Hey Geremio! Is your gang of dagos dead?"

Geremio cautioned to the men: "On your toes, boys. If he writes out slips, someone won't have big eels on the Easter table."

The Lean cursed that "the padrone could take the job and shove it . . . !"

Curly-headed Sandino, the roguish, pigeon-toed scaffoldman, spat a clod of tobacco-juice and hummed to his own music.

"Yes, certainly yes to your face, master padrone . . . and behind, this to you and all your kind!"

The day, like all days, came to an end. Calloused and bruised bodies sighed, and numb legs shuffled towards shabby railroad flats. . . .

"Ah, *bella casa mia*. Where my little freshets of blood, and my good woman await me. Home where my broken back will not ache so. Home where midst the monkey chatter of my *piccolinos* I will float off to blessed slumber with my feet on the chair and the head on the wife's soft full breast."

These great child-hearted ones leave each other without words or ceremony, and as they ride and walk home, a great pride swells the breast. . . .

"Blessings to Thee, oh Jesus. I have fought winds and cold. Hand to hand I have locked dumb stones in place and the great building rises. I have earned a bit of bread for me and mine."

The mad day's brutal conflict is forgiven, and strained limbs prostrate themselves so that swollen veins can send the yearning blood coursing and pulsating deliciously as though the body mountained leaping streams.

The job alone remained behind . . . and yet, they too, having left the bigger part of their lives with it. The cold ghastly beast, the Job, stood stark, the eerie March wind wrapping it in sharp shadows of falling dusk.

That night was a crowning point in the life of Geremio. He bought a house! Twenty years he had helped to mould the New World. And now he was to have a house of his own! What mattered that it was no more than a wooden shack? It was his own!

He had proudly signed his name and helped Annunziata to make her **X** on the wonderful contract that proved them owners. And she was happy to think that her next child, soon to come, would be born under their own rooftree. She heard the church chimes, and cried to the children: "Children, to bed! It is near midnight. And remember, shut-mouth to the *paesanos*! Or they will send the evil eye to our new home even before we put foot."

The children scampered off to the icy yellow bedroom where three slept in one bed and three in the other. Coltishly and friskily they kicked about under the covers; their black iron-cotton stockings not removed . . . what! and freeze the peanut-little toes?

Said Annunziata, "The children are so happy, Geremio; let them be, for even I would a Tarantella dance." And with that she turned blushing. He wanted to take her on her word. She patted his hands, kissed them, and whispered, "Our children will dance for us . . . in the American style some day."

Geremio cleared his throat and wanted to sing. "Yes, with joy I could sing in a richer feeling than the great Caruso." He babbled little old country couplets and circled the room until the tenant below tapped the ceiling.

Annunziata whispered: "Geremio, to bed and rest. Tomorrow is a day for great things . . . and the day on which our Lord died for us."

The children were now hard asleep. Heads under the cover, over . . . moist noses whistling, and little damp legs entwined.

In bed Geremio and Annunziata clung closely to each other. They mumbled figures and dates until fatigue stilled their thoughts. And with chubby Johnnie clutching fast his bottle and warmed between them . . . life breathed heavily, and dreams entertained in far, far worlds, the nation-builder's brood.

But Geremio and Annunziata remained for a while staring into darkness, silently.

"Geremio?"

"Yes?"

"This job you are now working. . . ."

"So?"

"You used always to tell me about what happened on the jobs . . . who was jealous, and who praised. . . ."

"You should know by now that all work is the same. . . ."

"Geremio. The month you have been on this job, you have not spoken a word about the work . . . And I have felt that I am walking in a dream. Is the work dangerous? Why don't you answer . . . ?"

Job loomed up damp, shivery gray. Its giant members waiting.

Builders quietly donned their coarse robes, and waited.

Geremio's whistle rolled back into his pocket and the symphony of struggle began.

Trowel rang through brick and slashed mortar rivets were machinegunned fast with angry grind Patsy number one check Patsy number two check the Lean three check Vincenzo four steel bellowed back at hammer donkey engines coughed purple Ashes-ass Pietro fifteen chisel point intoned stone thin steel whirred and wailed through wood liquid stone flowed with dull rasp through iron veins and hoist screamed through space Carmine the Fat twenty-four and Giacomo Sangini check . . . The multitudinous voices of a civilization rose from the surroundings and welded with the efforts of the Job.

To the intent ear, Nation was voicing her growing pains, but, hands that create are attached to warm hearts and not to calculating minds. The Lean as he fought his burden on looked forward to only one goal, the end. The barrow he pushed, he did not love. The stones that brutalized his palms, he did not love. The great God Job, he did not love. He felt a searing bitterness and a fathomless consternation at the queer consciousness that inflicted the ever mounting weight of structure that he HAD TO! HAD TO! raise above his shoulders! When, when and where would the last stone be? Never . . . did he bear his toil with the rhythm of song! Never . . . did his gasping heart knead the heavy mortar with lilting melody! A voice within him spoke in wordless language.

The language of worn oppression and the despair of realizing that his life had been left on brick piles. And always, there had been hunger and her bastard, the fear of hunger.

Murdin bore down upon Geremio from behind and shouted:

"Goddamnit, Geremio, if you're givin' the men two hours off today with pay, why the hell are they draggin' their tails? And why don't you turn that skinny old Nick loose, and put a young wop in his place?"

"Now, listen-a to me, Mister Murdin—"

"Don't give me that! And bear in mind that there are plenty of good barefoot men in the streets who'll jump for a day's pay!"

"Padrone—padrone, the underpinning gotta be make safe and—"

"Lissenyawopbastard! If you don't like it, you know what you can do!"

And with that he swung swaggering away.

The men had heard, and those who hadn't knew instinctively.

The new home, the coming baby, and his whole background, kept the fire from Geremio's mouth and bowed his head. "Annunziata speaks of scouring the ashcans for the children's bread in case I didn't want to work on a job where . . . But am I not a man, to feed my own with these hands? Ah, but day will end and no boss in the world can then rob me of the joy of my home!"

Murdin paused for a moment before descending the ladder.

Geremio caught his meaning and jumped to, nervously directing the rush of work . . . No longer Geremio, but a machine-like entity.

The men were transformed into single, silent, beasts. Snoutnose steamed through ragged moustache whip-lashing sand into mixer Ashes-ass dragged under four by twelve beam Lean clawed wall knots jumping in jaws masonry crumbled dust billowed thundered choked. . . .

At noon, Geremio drank his wine from an old-fashioned magnesia bottle and munched a great pepper sandwich . . . no meat on Good Friday. Said one, "Are some of us to be laid off? Easter is upon us and communion dresses are needed and . . ."

That, while Geremio was dreaming of the new house and the joys he could almost taste. Said he: "Worry not. You should know Geremio." It then all came out. He regaled them with his wonderful joy of the new house. He praised his wife and children one by one. They listened respectfully and returned him well wishes and blessings. He went on and on. . . . "Paul made a radio—all by himself, mind you! One can hear Barney Google and many American songs! How proud he."

The ascent to labor was made, and as they trod the ladder, heads turned and eyes communed with the mute flames of the brazier whose warmth they were leaving, not with willing heart, and in that fleeting moment, the breast wanted so, so much to speak of hungers that never reached the tongue.

About an hour later, Geremio called over to Pietro: "Pietro, see if Mister Murdin is in the shanty and tell him I must see him! I will convince him that the work must not go on like this . . . just for the sake of a little more profit!"

Pietro came up soon. "The padrone is not coming up. He was drinking from a large bottle of whisky and cursed in American words that if you did not carry out his orders—"

Geremio turned away disconcerted, stared dumbly at the structure and mechanically listed in his mind's eye the various violations of construction safety. An uneasy sensation hollowed him. The Lean brought down an old piece of wall and the structure palsied. Geremio's heart broke loose and out-thumped the floor's vibrations, a rapid wave of heat swept him and left a chill touch in its wake. He looked about to the men, a bit frightened. They seemed usual, life-size, and moved about with the methodical deftness that made the moment then appear no different than the task of toil had ever been.

Snoutnose's voice boomed into him. "Master Geremio, the concrete is rea–dy!"

"Oh, yes, yes, Vincenz." And he walked gingerly towards the chute, but, not without leaving behind some part of his strength, sending out his soul to wrestle with the limbs of Job, who threatened in stiff silence. He talked and joked with Snoutnose. Nothing said anything, nor seemed wrong. Yet a vague uneasiness was to him as certain as the foggy murk that floated about Job's stone and steel.

"Shall I let the concrete down now, Master Geremio?"

"Well, let me see–no, hold it a minute. Hey, Sandino! tighten the chute cables!"

Snoutnose straightened, looked about, and instinctively rubbed the sore small of his spine. "Ah," sighed he, "all the men feel as I–yes, I can tell. They are tired but happy that today is Good Friday and we quit at three o'clock . . ." And he swelled in human ecstasy at the anticipation of food, drink, and the hairy flesh-tingling warmth of wife, and then, extravagant rest. In truth, they all felt as Snoutnose, although perhaps with variations on the theme.

It was the Lean only who had lived, and felt otherwise. His soul, accompanied with time, had shredded itself in the physical war to keep the physical alive. Perhaps he no longer had a soul, and the corpse continued from momentum. May he not be the Slave, working on from the birth of Man–He of whom it was said, "It was not for Him to reason"? And probably He who, never asking, taking, nor vaunting, created God and the creatable? Nevertheless, there existed in the Lean a sense of oppression suffered, so vast that the seas of time could never wash it away.

Geremio gazed about and was conscious of seeming to understand many things. He marveled at the strange feeling which permitted him to sense the familiarity of life. And yet–all appeared unreal, a dream pungent and nostalgic. Life, dream, reality, unreality, spiraling ever about each other. "Ha," he chuckled, "how and from where do these thoughts come?"

Snoutnose had his hand on the hopper latch and was awaiting the word from Geremio. "Did you say something, Master Geremio?"

"Why, yes, Vincenz, I was thinking–funny! A–yes, what is the time–yes, that is what I was thinking."

"My American can of tomatoes says ten minutes from two o'clock. It won't be long now, Master Geremio."

Geremio smiled. "No, about an hour . . . and then, home."

"Oh, but first we stop at Mulberry Street, to buy their biggest eels, and the other finger-licking stuffs."

Geremio was looking far off, and for a moment happiness came to his heart without words, a warm hand stealing over. Snoutnose's words sang to him pleasantly, and he nodded.

"And Master Geremio, we ought really to buy the seafruits with the shells–you know, for the much needed steam they put into the–"

He flushed despite himself and continued. "It is true, I know it—especially the juicy clams . . . uhmn, my mouth waters like a pump."

Geremio drew on his unlit pipe and smiled acquiescence. The men around him were moving to their tasks silently, feeling of their fatigue, but absorbed in contemplations the very same as Snoutnose's. The noise of labor seemed not to be noise, and as Geremio looked about, life settled over him a gray concert–gray forms, atmosphere, and gray notes . . . Yet his off-tone world felt so near, and familiar.

"Five minutes from two," swished through Snoutnose's moustache.

Geremio automatically took out his watch, rewound, and set it. Sandino had done with the cables. The tone and movement of the scene seemed to Geremio strange, differently strange, and yet, a dream familiar from a timeless date. His hand went up in motion to Vincenzo. The molten stone gurgled low, and then with heightening rasp. His eyes followed the stone-cementy pudding, and to his ears there was no other sound than its flow. From over the roofs somewhere, the tinny voice of *Barney Google* whined its way, hooked into his consciousness and kept itself a revolving record beneath his skull-plate.

"Ah, yes, Barney Google, my son's wonderful radio machine . . . wonderful Paul." His train of thought quickly took in his family, home and hopes. And with hope came fear. Something within asked, "Is it not possible to breathe God's air without fear dominating with the pall of unemployment? And the terror of production for Boss, Boss and Job? To rebel is to lose all of the very little. To be obedient is to choke. Oh, dear Lord, guide my path."

Just then, the floor lurched and swayed under his feet. The slipping of the underpinning below rumbled up through the undetermined floors.

Was he faint or dizzy? Was it part of the dreamy afternoon? He put his hands in front of him and stepped back, and looked up wildly. "No! No!"

The men poised stricken. Their throats wanted to cry out and scream but didn't dare. For a moment they were a petrified and straining pageant. Then the bottom of their world gave way. The building shuddered violently, her supports burst with the crackling slap of wooden gunfire. The floor vomited upward. Geremio clutched at the air and shrieked agonizingly. "Brothers, what have we done? Ahhh-h, children of ours!" With the speed of light, balance went sickeningly awry and frozen men went flying explosively. Job tore down upon them madly. Walls, floors, beams became whirling, solid, splintering waves crashing with detonations that ground man and material in bonds of death.

The strongly shaped body that slept with Annunziata nights and was perfect in all the limitless physical quantities, thudded as a worthless sack amongst the giant debris that crushed fragile flesh and bone with centrifugal intensity.

Darkness blotted out his terror and the resistless form twisted, catapulted insanely in its directionless flight, and shot down neatly and deliberately between the empty wooden forms of a foundation wall pilaster in upright position, his blue swollen face pressed against the form and his arms outstretched, caught securely through the meat by the thin round bars of reinforcing steel.

The huge concrete hopper that was sustained by an independent structure of thick timber, wavered a breath or so, its heavy concrete rolling uneasily until a great sixteen-inch wall caught it squarely with all the terrific verdict of its dead weight and impelled it downward through joists, beams and masonry, until it stopped short, arrested by two girders, an arm's length above Geremio's head; the gray concrete gushing from the hopper mouth, and sealing up the mute figure.

Giacomo had been thrown clear of the building and dropped six floors to the street gutter, where he lay writhing.

The Lean had evinced no emotion. When the walls descended, he did not move. He lowered his head. One minute later he was hanging in midair, his chin on his chest, his eyes tearing loose from their sockets, a green foam bubbling from his mouth and his body spasming, suspended by the shreds left of his mashed arms pinned between a wall and a girder.

A two-by-four hooked little Joe Chiappa up under the back of his jumper and swung him around in a circle to meet a careening I-beam. In the flash that he lifted his frozen cherubic face, its shearing edge sliced through the top of his skull.

When Snoutnose cried beseechingly, "Saint Michael!" blackness enveloped him. He came to in a world of horror. A steady stream, warm, thick, and sickening as hot wine bathed his face and clogged his nose, mouth, and eyes. The nauseous syrup that pumped over his face, clotted his moustache red and drained into his mouth. He gulped for air, and swallowed the rich liquid scarlet. As he breathed, the pain shocked him to oppressive semiconsciousness. The air was wormingly alive with cries, screams, moans and dust, and his crushed chest seared him with a thousand fires. He couldn't see, nor breathe enough to cry. His right hand moved to his face and wiped at the gelatinizing substance, but it kept coming on, and a heartbreaking moan wavered about him, not far. He wiped his eyes in subconscious despair. Where was he? What kind of a dream was he having? Perhaps he wouldn't wake up in time for work, and then what? But how queer; his stomach beating him, his chest on fire, he sees nothing but dull red, only one hand moving about, and a moaning in his face!

The sound and clamor of the rescue squads called to him from far off.

Ah, yes, he's dreaming in bed, and far out in the streets, engines are going to a fire. Oh poor devils! Suppose his house were on fire? With the children scattered about in the rooms he could not remember! He must do his utmost to break out of this dream! He's swimming under water, not able to raise his head and get to the air. He must get back to consciousness to save his children!

He swam frantically with his one right hand, and then felt a face beneath its touch. A face! It's Angelina alongside of him! Thank God, he's awake! He tapped her face. It moved. It felt cold, bristly, and wet. "It moves so. What is this?" His fingers slithered about grisly sharp bones and in a gluey, stringy, hollow mass, yielding as wet macaroni. Gray light brought sight, and hysteria punctured his heart. A girder lay across his chest his right hand clutched a grotesque human mask, and suspended almost on top of him was the twitching, faceless body of Joe Chiappa. Vincenzo fainted with an inarticulate sigh. His fingers loosed and the bodyless-headless face dropped and fitted to the side of his face while the drippings above came slower and slower.

The rescue men cleaved grimly with pick and axe.

Geremio came to with a start . . . far from their efforts. His brain told him instantly what had happened and where he was. He shouted wildly. "Save me! Save me! I'm being buried alive!"

He paused exhausted. His genitals convulsed. The cold steel rod upon which they were impaled froze his spine. He shouted louder and louder. "Save me! I am hurt badly! I can be saved, I can–save me before it's too late!" But the cries went no farther than his own ears. The icy wet concrete reached his chin. His heart was appalled. "In a few seconds I shall be entombed. If I can only breathe, they will reach me. Surely they will!" His face was quickly covered, its flesh yielding to the solid, sharpcut stones. "Air! Air!" screamed his lungs as he was completely sealed. Savagely, he bit into the wooden form pressing upon his mouth. An eighth of an inch of its surface splintered off. Oh, if he could only hold out long enough to bite even the smallest hole through to air! He must! There can be no other way! He is responsible for his family! He cannot leave them like this! He didn't want to die! This could not be the answer to life! He had bitten halfway through when his teeth snapped off to the gums in the uneven conflict. The pressure of the concrete was such, and its effectiveness so thorough, that the wooden splinters, stumps of teeth, and blood never left the choking mouth.

Why couldn't he go any farther?

Air! Quick! He dug his lower jaw into the little hollowed space and gnashed in choking agonized fury. "Why doesn't it go through? Mother of

Christ, why doesn't it give? Can there be a notch, or two-by-four stud behind it? Sweet Jesu! No! No! Make it give. . . . Air! Air!"

He pushed the bone-bare jaw maniacally; it splintered, cracked, and a jagged fleshless edge cut through the form, opening a small hole to air. With a desperate burst the lung-prisoned air blew an opening through the shredded mouth and whistled back greedily a gasp of fresh air. He tried to breathe, but it was impossible. The heavy concrete was settling immutably, and its rich cement-laden grout ran into his pierced face. His lungs would not expand, and were crushing in tighter and tighter under the settling concrete.

"Mother mine—mother of Jesu-Annunziata—children of mine—dear, dear, for mercy, Jesu-Giuseppe e 'Maria," his blue-foamed tongue called. It then distorted in a shuddering coil and mad blood vomited forth. Chills and fire played through him and his tortured tongue stuttered, "Mercy, blessed Father—salvation, most kind Father—Saviour —Saviour of His children help me—adored Saviour—I kiss your feet eternally—you are my Lord—there is but one God—you are my God of infinite mercy—Hail Mary divine Virgin—our Father who art in heaven hallowed by thy—name—our Father—my Father," and the agony excruciated with never-ending mount, "our Father—Jesu, Jesu, soon Jesu, hurry dear Jesu Jesu! Je-sssu . . . !" His mangled voice trebled hideously, and hung in jerky whimperings.

The unfeeling concrete was drying fast, and shrinking into monolithic density. The pressure temporarily de-sensitized sensation; leaving him petrified, numb, and substanceless. Only the brain remained miraculously alive.

"Can this be death? It is all too strangely clear. I see nothing nor feel nothing, my body and senses are no more, my mind speaks as it never did before. Am I or am I not Geremio? But I am Geremio! Can I be in the other world? I never was in any other world except the one I knew of; that of toil, hardship, prayer . . . of my wife who awaits with child for me, of my children and the first home I was to own. Where do I begin in this world? Where do I leave off? Why? I recall only a baffled life of cruelty from every direction. And hope was always as painful as fear, the fear of displeasing, displeasing the people and ideas whom I could never understand; laws, policemen, priests, bosses, and a rag with colors waving on a stick. I never did anything to these things. But what have I done with my life? Yes, my life! No one else's! Mine—mine—MINE—Geremio! It is clear. I was born hungry, and have always been hungry for freedom—life! I married and ran away to America so as not to kill and be killed in Tripoli for things they call 'God and Country.' I've never known the freedom I wanted in my heart. There was always an arm upraised to hit at me. What have I done to them? I did not want to make them toil for me. I did not raise my arm to them. In my life I could never breathe, and now without air, my mind breathes clearly for me. Wait! There has been a terrible mistake! A cruel crime! The world is not right! Murderers! Thieves! You have hurt me and my kind, and have taken my life from me! I have long felt it—yes, yes, yes, they have cheated me with flags, signs and fear . . . I say you can't take my life! I want to live! My life! To tell the cheated to rise and fight! Vincenz! Chiappa! Nick! Men! Do you hear me? We must follow the desires within us for the world has been taken from us; we, who made the world! Life!"

Feeling returned to the destroyed form.

"Ahhh-h, I am not dead yet. I knew it—you have not done with me. Torture away! I cannot believe you, God and Country, no longer!" His body was fast breaking under the concrete's closing wrack. Blood vessels burst like mashed flower stems. He screamed. "Show yourself now, Jesu! Now is the time! Save me! Why don't you come! Are you there! I cannot stand it—ohhh, why do you let it happen—it is bestial—where are you! Hurry, hurry, hurry! You do not come! You make me suffer, and what have I done! Come, come—come now—now save me, save me now! Now, now, now! If you are God, save me!"

The stricken blood surged through a weltering maze of useless pipes and exploded forth from his squelched eyes and formless nose, ears and mouth, seeking life in the indifferent stone.

"Aie—aie, aie—devils and Saints—beasts! Where are you—quick, quick, it is death and I am cheated—cheat—ed! Do you hear, you whoring bastards who own the world? Ohhh-ohhh aie-aie—hahahaha!" His bones cracked mutely and his sanity went sailing distorted in the limbo of the subconscious.

With the throbbing tones of an organ in the hollow background, the fighting brain disintegrated and the memories of a baffled lifetime sought outlet.

He moaned the simple songs of barefoot childhood, scenes flashed desperately on and off in disassociated reflex, and words and parts of words came pitifully high and low from his inaudible lips, the hysterical mind sang cringingly and breathlessly, "Jesu my Lord my God my all Jesu my Lord my God my all Jesu my Lord my God my all Jesu my Lord my God my all," and on as the whirling tempo screamed now far, now near, and came in soul-sickening waves as the concrete slowly contracted and squeezed his skull out of shape.

JOHN CHEEVER

[1912–1970]

The Country Husband

(First published in the *New Yorker*,
November, 1954; first book publication in 1956.)

TO BEGIN AT the beginning, the airplane from Minneapolis in which Francis Weed was travelling East ran into heavy weather. The sky had been a hazy blue, with the clouds below the plane lying so close together that nothing could be seen of the earth. Then mist began to form outside the windows, and they flew into a white cloud of such density that it reflected the exhaust fires. The color of the cloud darkened to gray, and the plane began to rock. Francis had been in heavy weather before, but he had never been shaken up so much. The man in the seat beside him pulled a flask out of his pocket and took a drink. Francis smiled at his neighbor, but the man looked away; he wasn't sharing his painkiller with anyone. The plane had begun to drop and flounder wildly. A child was crying. The air in the cabin was overheated and stale, and Francis' left foot went to sleep. He read a little from a paper book that he had bought at the airport, but the violence of the storm divided his attention. It was black outside the ports. The exhaust fires blazed and shed sparks in the dark, and, inside, the shaded lights, the stuffiness, and the window curtains gave the cabin an atmosphere of intense and misplaced domesticity. Then the lights flickered and went out. "You know what I've always wanted to do?" the man beside Francis said suddenly. "I've always wanted to buy a farm in New Hampshire and raise beef cattle." The stewardess announced that they were going to make an emergency landing. All but the child saw in their minds the spreading wings of the Angel of Death. The pilot could be heard singing faintly, "I've got sixpence, jolly, jolly sixpence. I've got sixpence to last me all my life. . ." There was no other sound.

The loud groaning of the hydraulic valves swallowed up the pilot's song, and there was a shrieking high in the air, like automobile brakes, and the plane hit flat on its belly in a cornfield and shook them so violently that an old man up forward howled, "Me kidneys! Me kidneys!" The stewardess flung open the door, and someone opened an emergency door at the back, letting in the sweet noise of their continuing mortality—the idle splash and smell of a heavy rain. Anxious for their lives, they filed out of the doors and scattered over the cornfield in all directions, praying that the thread would hold. It did. Nothing happened. When it was clear that the plane would not burn or explode, the crew and the stewardess gathered the passengers together and led them to the shelter of a barn. They were not far from Philadelphia, and in a little while a string of taxis took them into the city. "It's just like the Marne," someone said, but there was surprisingly little relaxation of that suspiciousness with which many Americans regard their fellow-travellers.

In Philadelphia, Francis Weed got a train to New York. At the end of that journey, he crossed the city and caught, just as it was about to pull out, the commuting train that he took five nights a week to his home in Shady Hill.

He sat with Trace Bearden. "You know, I was in that plane that just crashed outside Philadelphia," he said. "We came down in a field . . ." He had travelled faster than the newspapers or the rain, and the weather in New York was sunny and mild. It was a day in late September, as fragrant and shapely as an apple. Trace listened to the story, but how could he get excited? Francis had no powers that would let him re-create a brush with death—particularly in the atmosphere of a commuting train, journeying through a sunny countryside where already, in the slum gardens, there were signs of harvest. Trace picked up his newspaper, and Francis was left alone with his thoughts. He said good night to Trace on the platform at Shady Hill and drove in his second-hand Volkswagen up to the Blenhollow neighborhood, where he lived.

The Weeds' Dutch Colonial house was larger than it appeared to be from the driveway. The living room was spacious and divided like Gaul into three parts. Around an ell to the left as one entered from the vestibule was the long table, laid for six, with candles and a bowl of fruit in the center. The sounds and smells that came from the open kitchen door were appetizing, for Julia Weed was a good cook. The largest part of the living room centered around a fireplace. On the right were some bookshelves and a piano. The room was polished and tranquil, and from the windows that opened to the west there was some late-summer sunlight, brilliant and as clear as water. Nothing here was neglected; nothing had not been burnished. It was not the kind of household where, after prying open a stuck cigarette box, you would find an old shirt button and a tarnished nickel. The hearth was swept, the roses on the piano were reflected in the polish of the broad top, and there was an album of Schubert waltzes on the rack. Louisa Weed, a pretty girl of nine, was looking out the western windows. Her younger brother Henry was standing beside her. Her still younger brother, Toby, was studying the figures of some tonsured monks drinking beer on the polished brass of the wood box. Francis, taking off his hat and putting down his paper, was not consciously pleased with the scene; he was not that reflective. It was his element, his creation, and he returned to it with that sense of lightness and strength with which any creature returns to its home. "Hi, everybody," he said. "The plane from Minneapolis . . ."

Nine times out of ten, Francis would be greeted with affection, but tonight the children are absorbed in their own antagonisms. Francis has not finished his sentence about the plane crash before Henry plants a kick in Louisa's behind. Louisa swings around, saying, "*Damn* you!" Francis makes the mistake of scolding Louisa for bad language before he punishes Henry. Now Louisa turns on her father and accuses him of favoritism. Henry is always right; she is persecuted and lonely; her lot is hopeless. Francis turns to his son, but the boy has justification for the kick—she hit him first; she hit him on the ear, which is dangerous. Louisa agrees with this passionately. She hit him on the ear, and she *meant* to hit him on the ear, because he messed up her china collection. Henry says that this is a lie. Little Toby turns away from the wood box to throw in some evidence for Louisa. Henry claps his hand over little Toby's mouth. Francis separates the two boys but accidentally pushes Toby into the wood box. Toby begins to cry. Louisa is already crying. Just then, Julia Weed comes into that part of the room where the table is laid. She is a pretty, intelligent woman, and the white in her hair is premature. She does not seem to notice the fracas. "Hello, darling," she says serenely to Francis. "Wash your hands, everyone. Dinner is ready." She strikes a match and lights the six candles in this vale of tears.

This simple announcement, like the war cries of the Scottish chieftains, only refreshes the ferocity of the combatants. Louisa gives Henry a blow on the shoulder. Henry, although he seldom cries, has pitched nine innings and is tired. He bursts into tears. Little Toby discovers a splinter in his hand and begins to howl. Francis says loudly that he has been in a plane crash and that he is tired. Julia appears again, from the kitchen, and, still ignoring the chaos, asks Francis to go upstairs and tell Helen that everything is ready. Francis is happy to go; it is like getting back to headquarters company. He is planning to tell his oldest daughter about the airplane crash, but Helen is lying on her bed reading a *True Romance* magazine, and the first thing Francis does is to take the magazine from her hand and remind Helen that he has forbidden her to buy it. She did not buy it, Helen replies. It was given to her by her best friend, Bessie Black. Everybody reads *True Romance*. Bessie Black's father reads *True Romance*. There isn't a girl in Helen's class who doesn't read *True Romance*. Francis expresses his detestation of the magazine and then tells her dinner is ready—although from the sounds downstairs it doesn't seem so. Helen follows him down the stairs. Julia has sealed herself in the candlelight and spread a napkin over her lap. Neither Louisa nor Henry has come to the table. Little Toby is still howling, lying face down on the floor. Francis speaks to him gently: "Daddy was in a plane crash this afternoon, Toby. Don't you want to hear about it?" Toby goes on crying. "If you don't come to the table now, Toby," Francis says, "I'll have to send you to bed without any supper." The little boy rises, gives a cutting look, flies up the stairs to his bedroom, and slams the door. "Oh dear," Julia says, and starts to go after him. Francis says that she will spoil him. Julia says that Toby is ten pounds underweight and has to be encouraged to eat. Winter is coming, and he will spend the cold months in bed unless he has his dinner. Julia goes upstairs. Francis sits down at the table with Helen. Helen is suffering from the dismal feeling of having read too intently on a fine day, and she gives her father and the room a jaded look. She doesn't understand about the plane crash, because there wasn't a drop of rain in Shady Hill.

Julia returns with Toby, and they all sit down and are served. "Do I have to look at that big, fat slob?" Henry says, of Louisa. Everybody but Toby enters into this skirmish, and it rages up and down the table for five minutes. Toward the end, Henry puts his napkin over his head and, trying to eat that way, spills spinach all over his shirt. Francis asks Julia if the children couldn't have their dinner earlier. Julia's guns are loaded for this. She can't cook two dinners and lay two tables. She paints with lightning strokes that panorama of drudgery in which her youth, her beauty, and her wit have been lost. Francis says he must be understood; he was nearly killed in an airplane crash, and he doesn't like to come home every night to a battlefield. Now Julia is deeply committed. Her voice trembles. He doesn't come home every night to a battlefield. The accusation is stupid and mean. Everything was tranquil until he arrived. She stops speaking, puts down her knife and fork, and looks into her plate as if it is a gulf. She begins to cry. "Poor Mummy!" Toby says, and when Julia gets up from the table, drying her tears with a napkin, Toby goes to her side. "Poor Mummy," he says. "Poor Mummy!" And they climb the stairs together. The other children drift away from the battlefield, and Francis goes into the back garden for a cigarette and some air.

It was a pleasant garden, with walks and flower beds and places to sit. The sunset had nearly burned out, but there was still plenty of light. Put into a thoughtful mood by the crash and the battle, Francis listened to the evening sounds of Shady Hill. "Varmits! Rascals!" old Mr. Nixon shouted to the squirrels in his bird-feeding station. "Avaunt and quit my sight!" A door slammed. Someone was playing tennis on the Babcocks' court; someone was cutting grass. Then Donald Goslin, who lived at the corner, began to play the "Moonlight Sonata." He did this nearly every night. He threw tempo out the window and played it *rubato* from beginning to end, like an outpouring of tearful petulance, lonesomeness, and self-pity—of everything it was Beethoven's greatness not to know. The music rang up and down the street beneath the trees like an appeal for love, for tenderness, aimed at some lonely housemaid—some fresh-faced, homesick girl from Galway, looking at old snapshots in her third-floor room. "Here, Jupiter, here, Jupiter," Francis called to the Mercers' retriever. Jupiter crashed through the tomato vines with the remains of a felt hat in his mouth.

Jupiter was an anomaly. His retrieving instincts and his high spirits were out of place in Shady Hill. He was as black as coal, with a long, alert, intelligent, rakehell face. His eyes gleamed with mischief, and he held his head high. It was the fierce, heavily collared dog's head that appears in heraldry, in tapestry, and that used to appear on umbrella handles and walking sticks. Jupiter went where he pleased, ransacking wastebaskets, clotheslines, garbage pails, and shoebags. He broke up garden parties and tennis matches, and got mixed up in the processional at Christ's Church on Sunday, barking at the men in red dresses. He crashed through old Mr. Nixon's rose garden two or three times a day, cutting a wide swath through the Condesa de Sastagos, and as soon as Donald Goslin lighted his barbecue fire on Thursday nights, Jupiter would get the scent. Nothing the Goslins did could drive him away. Sticks and stones and rude commands only moved him to the edge of the terrace, where he remained, with his gallant and heraldic muzzle, waiting for Donald Goslin to turn his back and reach for the salt. Then he would spring onto the terrace, lift the steak lightly off the fire, and run away with the Goslins' dinner. Jupiter's days were numbered. The Wrightsons' German gardener or the Farquarsons' cook would soon poison him. Even old Mr. Nixon might put some arsenic in the garbage that Jupiter loved. "Here, Jupiter, Jupiter!" Francis called, but the dog pranced off, shaking the hat in his white teeth. Looking in at the windows of his house, Francis saw that Julia had come down and was blowing out the candles.

Julia and Francis Weed went out a great deal. Julia was well liked and gregarious, and her love of parties sprang from a most natural dread of chaos and loneliness. She went through her morning mail with real anxiety, looking for invitations, and she usually found some, but she was insatiable, and if she had gone out seven nights a week, it would not have cured her of a reflective look—the look of someone who hears distant music—for she would always suppose that there was a more brilliant party somewhere else. Francis limited her to two week-night parties, putting a flexible interpretation on Friday, and rode through the weekend like a dory in a gale. The day after the airplane crash, the Weeds were to have dinner with the Farquarsons.

Francis got home late from town, and Julia got the sitter while he dressed, and then hurried him out of the house. The party was small and pleasant, and Francis settled down to enjoy himself. A new maid passed the drinks. Her hair was dark, and her face was round and pale and seemed familiar to

Francis. He had not developed his memory as a sentimental faculty. Wood smoke, lilac, and other such perfumes did not stir him, and his memory was something like his appendix—a vestigial repository. It was not his limitation at all to be unable to escape the past; it was perhaps his limitation that he had escaped it so successfully. He might have seen the maid at other parties, he might have seen her taking a walk on Sunday afternoons, but in either case he would not be searching his memory now. Her face was, in a wonderful way, a moon face—Norman or Irish—but it was not beautiful enough to account for his feeling that he had seen her before, in circumstances that he ought to be able to remember. He asked Nellie Farquarson who she was. Nellie said that the maid had come through an agency, and that her home was Trénon, in Normandy—a small place with a church and a restaurant that Nellie had once visited. While Nellie talked on about her travels abroad, Francis realized where he had seen the woman before. It had been at the end of the war. He had left a replacement depot with some other men and taken a three-day pass in Trénon. On their second day, they had walked out to a crossroads to see the public chastisement of a young woman who had lived with the German commandant during the Occupation.

It was a cool morning in the fall. The sky was overcast, and poured down onto the dirt crossroads a very discouraging light. They were on high land and could see how like one another the shapes of the clouds and the hills were as they stretched off toward the sea. The prisoner arrived sitting on a three-legged stool in a farm cart. She stood by the cart while the mayor read the accusation and the sentence. Her head was bent and her face was set in that empty half smile behind which the whipped soul is suspended. When the mayor was finished, she undid her hair and let it fall across her back. A little man with a gray mustache cut off her hair with shears and dropped it on the ground. Then, with a bowl of soapy water and a straight razor, he shaved her skull clean. A woman approached and began to undo the fastenings of her clothes, but the prisoner pushed her aside and undressed herself. When she pulled her chemise over her head and threw it on the ground, she was naked. The women jeered; the men were still. There was no change in the falseness or the plaintiveness of the prisoner's smile. The cold wind made her white skin rough and hardened the nipples of her breasts. The jeering ended gradually, put down by the recognition of their common humanity. One woman spat on her, but some inviolable grandeur in her nakedness lasted through the ordeal. When the crowd was quiet, she turned—she had begun to cry—and, with nothing on but a pair of worn black shoes and stockings, walked down the dirt road alone away from the village. The round white face had aged a little, but there was no question but that the maid who passed his cocktails and later served Francis his dinner was the woman who had been punished at the crossroads.

The war seemed now so distant and that world where the cost of partisanship had been death or torture so long ago. Francis had lost track of the men who had been with him in Vésey. He could not count on Julia's discretion. He could not tell anyone. And if he had told the story now, at the dinner table, it would have been a social as well as a human error. The people in the Farquarsons' living room seemed united in their tacit claim that there had been no past, no war—that there was no danger or trouble in the world. In the recorded history of human arrangements, this extraordinary meeting would have fallen into place, but the atmosphere of Shady Hill made the memory unseemly and impolite. The prisoner withdrew after passing the coffee, but the encounter left Francis feeling languid; it had opened his memory and his senses, and left them dilated. He had Julia drove home when the party ended, and Julia went into the house. Francis stayed in the car to take the sitter home.

Expecting to see Mrs. Henlein, the old lady who usually stayed with the children, he was surprised when a young girl opened the door and came out onto the lighted stoop. She stayed in the light to count her textbooks. She was frowning and beautiful. Now, the world is full of beautiful young girls, but Francis saw here the difference between beauty and perfection. All those endearing flaws, moles, birthmarks, and healed wounds were missing, and he experienced in his consciousness that moment when music breaks glass, and felt a pang of recognition as strange, deep, and wonderful as anything in his life. It hung from her frown, from an impalpable darkness in her face—a look that impressed him as a direct appeal for love. When she had counted her books, she came down the steps and opened the car door. In the light, he saw that her cheeks were wet. She got in and shut the door.

"You're new," Francis said.

"Yes. Mrs. Henlein is sick. I'm Anne Murchison."

"Did the children give you any trouble?"

"Oh, no, no." She turned and smiled at him unhappily in the dim dashboard light. Her light hair caught on the collar of her jacket, and she shook her head to set it loose.

"You've been crying."

"Yes."

"I hope it was nothing that happened in our house."

"No, no, it was nothing that happened in your house." Her voice was bleak. "It's no secret. Everybody in the village knows. Daddy's an alcoholic, and he just called me from some saloon and gave me a piece of his mind. He thinks I'm immoral. He called just before Mrs. Weed came back."

"I'm sorry."

"Oh, *Lord*!" She gasped and began to cry. She turned toward Francis, and he took her in his arms and let her cry on his shoulder. She shook in his embrace, and this movement accentuated his sense of the fineness of her flesh and bone. The layers of their clothing felt thin, and when her shuddering began to diminish, it was so much like a paroxysm of love that Francis lost his head and pulled her roughly against him. She drew away. "I live on Belleview Avenue," she said. "You go down Lansing Street to the railroad bridge."

"All right." He started the car.

"You turn left at the traffic light . . . Now you turn right here and go straight on toward the tracks."

The road Francis took brought him out of his own neighborhood, across the tracks, and toward the river, to a street where the near-poor lived, in houses whose peaked gables and trimmings of wooden lace conveyed the purest feelings of pride and romance, although the houses themselves could not have offered much privacy or comfort, they were all so small. The street was dark, and, stirred by the grace and beauty of the troubled girl, he seemed, in turning in to it, to have come into the deepest part of some submerged memory. In the distance, he saw a porch light burning. It was the only one, and she said that the house with the light was where she lived. When he stopped the car, he could see beyond the porch light into a dimly lighted hallway with an old-fashioned clothes tree. "Well, here we are," he said, conscious that a young man would have said something different.

She did not move her hands from the books, where they were folded, and she turned and faced him. There were tears of lust in his eyes. Determinedly—not sadly—he opened the door on his side and walked around to open hers. He took her free hand, letting his fingers in between hers, climbed at her side the two concrete steps, and went up a narrow walk through a front garden where dahlias, marigolds, and roses—things that had withstood the light frosts—still bloomed, and made a bittersweet smell in the night air. At the steps, she freed her hand and then turned and kissed him swiftly. Then she crossed the porch and shut the door. The porch light went out, then the light in the hall. A second later, a light went on upstairs at the side of the house, shining into a tree that was still covered with leaves. It took her only a few minutes to undress and get into bed, and then the house was dark.

Julia was asleep when Francis got home. He opened a second window and got into bed to shut his eyes on that night, but as soon as they were shut—as soon as he had dropped off to sleep—the girl entered his mind, moving with perfect freedom through its shut doors and filling chamber after chamber with her light, her perfume, and the music of her voice. He was crossing the Atlantic with her on the old *Mauretania* and, later, living with her in Paris. When he woke from this dream, he got up and smoked a cigarette at the open window. Getting back into bed, he cast around in his mind for something he desired to do that would injure no one, and he thought of skiing. Up through the dimness in his mind rose the image of a mountain deep in snow. It was late in the day. Wherever his eyes looked, he saw broad and heartening things. Over his shoulder, there was a snow-filled valley, rising into wooded hills where the trees dimmed the whiteness like a sparse coat of hair. The cold deadened all sound but the loud, iron clanking of the lift machinery. The light on the trails was blue, and it was harder than it had been a minute or two earlier to pick the turns, harder to judge—now that the snow was all deep blue—the crust, the ice, the bare spots, and the deep piles of dry powder. Down the mountain he swung, matching his speed against the contours of a slope that had been formed in the first ice age, seeking with ardor some simplicity of feeling and circumstance. Night fell then, and he drank a Martini with some old friend in a dirty country bar.

In the morning, Francis' snow-covered mountain was gone, and he was left with his vivid memories of Paris and the *Mauretania*. He had been bitten gravely. He washed his body, shaved his jaws, drank his coffee, and missed the seven-thirty-one. The train pulled out just as he brought his car to the station, and the longing he felt for the coaches as they drew stubbornly away from him reminded him of the humors of love. He waited for the eight-two, on what was now an empty platform. It was a clear morning; the morning seemed thrown like a gleaming bridge of light over his mixed affairs. His spirits were feverish and high. The image of the girl seemed to put him into a relationship to the world that was mysterious and enthralling. Cars were beginning to fill up the parking lot, and he noticed that those that had driven down from the high land above Shady Hill were white with hoarfrost. This first clear sign of autumn thrilled him. An express train—a night train from Buffalo or Albany—came down the tracks between the platforms, and he saw that the roofs of the foremost cars were covered with a skin of ice. Struck by the miraculous physicalness of everything, he smiled at the passengers in the dining car, who could be seen eating eggs and wiping their mouths with napkins as they travelled. The sleeping-car compartments, with their soiled bed linen, trailed through the fresh morning like a string of rooming-house windows. Then he saw an extraordinary thing; at one of the bedroom windows sat an unclothed woman of exceptional beauty, combing her golden hair. She passed like an apparition through Shady Hill, combing and combing her hair, and Francis followed her with his eyes until she was out of sight. Then old Mrs. Wrightson joined him on the platform and began to talk.

"Well, I guess you must be surprised to see me here the third morning in a row," she said, "but because of my window curtains I'm becoming a regular commuter. The curtains I bought on Monday I returned on Tuesday, and the curtains I bought on Tuesday I'm returning today. On Monday, I got exactly what I wanted—it's a wool tapestry with roses and birds—

but when I got them home, I found they were the wrong length. Well, I exchanged them yesterday, and when I got them home, I found they were still the wrong length. Now I'm praying to high Heaven that the decorator will have them in the right length, because you know my house, you *know* my living-room windows, and you can imagine what a problem they present. I don't know what to do with them."

"I know what to do with them," Francis said.

"What?"

"Paint them black on the inside, and shut up."

There was a gasp from Mrs. Wrightson, and Francis looked down at her to be sure that she knew he meant to be rude. She turned and walked away from him, so damaged in spirit that she limped. A wonderful feeling enveloped him, as if light were being shaken about him, and he thought again of Venus combing and combing her hair as she drifted through the Bronx. The realization of how many years had passed since he had enjoyed being deliberately impolite sobered him. Among his friends and neighbors, there were brilliant and gifted people—he saw that—but many of them, also, were bores and fools, and he made the mistake of listening to them all with equal attention. He had confused a lack of discrimination with Christian love, and the confusion seemed general and destructive. He was grateful to the girl for this bracing sensation of independence. Birds were singing—cardinals and the last of the robins. The sky shone like enamel. Even the smell of ink from his morning paper honed his appetite for life, and the world that was spread out around him was plainly a paradise.

If Francis had believed in some hierarchy of love—in spirits armed with hunting bows, in the capriciousness of Venus and Eros—or even in magical potions, philtres, and stews, in scapulae and quarters of the moon, it might have explained his susceptibility and his feverish high spirits. The autumnal loves of middle age are well publicized, and he guessed that he was face to face with one of these, but there was not a trace of autumn in what he felt. He wanted to sport in the green woods, scratch where he itched, and drink from the same cup.

His secretary, Miss Rainey, was late that morning—she went to a psychiatrist three mornings a week—and when she came in, Francis wondered what advice a psychiatrist would have for him. But the girl promised to bring back into his life something like the sound of music. The realization that this music might lead him straight to a trial for statutory rape at the county courthouse collapsed his happiness. The photograph of his four children laughing into the camera on the beach at Gay Head reproached him. On the letterhead of his firm there was a drawing of the "Laocoön," and the figure of the priest and his sons in the coils of the snake appeared to him to have the deepest meaning.

He had lunch with Pinky Trabert, who told him a couple of dirty stories.

At a conversational level, the mores of his friends were robust and elastic, but he knew that the moral card house would come down on them all—on Julia and the children as well—if he got caught taking advantage of a babysitter. Looking back over the recent history of Shady Hill for some precedent, he found there was none. There was no turpitude; there had not been a divorce since he lived there; there had not even been a breath of scandal. Things seemed arranged with more propriety even than in the Kingdom of Heaven. After leaving Pinky, Francis went to a jeweller's and bought the girl a bracelet. How happy this clandestine purchase made him, how stuffy and comical the jeweller's clerks seemed, how sweet the women who passed at his back smelled! On Fifth Avenue, passing Atlas with his shoulders bent under the weight of the world, Francis thought of the strenuousness of containing his physicalness within the patterns he had chosen.

He did not know when he would see the girl next. He had the bracelet in his inside pocket when he got home. Opening the door of his house, he found her in the hall. Her back was to him, and she turned when she heard the door close. Her smile was open and loving. Her perfection stunned him like a fine day—a day after a thunderstorm. He seized her and covered her lips with his, and she struggled but she did not have to struggle for long, because just then little Gertrude Flannery appeared from somewhere and said, "Oh, Mr. Weed . . ."

Gertrude was a stray. She had been born with a taste for exploration, and she did not have it in her to center her life with her affectionate parents. People who did not know the Flannerys concluded from Gertrude's behavior that she was the child of a bitterly divided family, where drunken quarrels were the rule. This was not true. The fact that little Gertrude's clothing was ragged and thin was her own triumph over her mother's struggle to dress her warmly and neatly. Garrulous, skinny, and unwashed, she drifted from house to house around the Blenhollow neighborhood, forming and breaking alliances based on an attachment to babies, animals, children her own age, adolescents, and sometimes adults. Opening your front door in the morning, you would find Gertrude sitting on your stoop. Going into the bathroom to shave, you would find Gertrude using the toilet. Looking into your son's crib, you would find it empty, and, looking further, you would find that Gertrude had pushed him in his baby carriage into the next village. She was helpful, pervasive, honest, hungry, and loyal. She never went home of her own choice. When the time to go arrived, she was indifferent to all its signs. "Go home, Gertrude," people could be heard saying in one house or another, night after night. "Go home, Gertrude." "It's time for you to go home now, Gertrude." "You had better go home and get your supper, Gertrude." "I told you to go home twenty minutes ago, Gertrude." "You mother will be worrying about you, Gertrude." "Go home, Gertrude, go home."

There are times when the lines around the human eye seem like shelves of eroded stone and when the staring eye itself strikes us with such a wilderness of animal feeling that we are at a loss. The look Francis gave the little girl was ugly and queer, and it frightened her. He reached into his pocket—his hands were shaking—and took out a quarter. "Go home, Gertrude, go home, and don't tell anyone, Gertrude. Don't—" He choked and ran into the living room as Julia called down to him from upstairs to hurry and dress.

The thought that he would drive Anne Murchison home later that night ran like a golden thread through the events of the party that Francis and Julia went to, and he laughed uproariously at dull jokes, dried a tear when Mabel Mercer told him about the death of her kitten, and stretched, yawned, sighed, and grunted like any other man with a rendezvous at the back of his mind. The bracelet was in his pocket. As he sat talking, the smell of grass was in his nose, and he was wondering where he would park the car. Nobody lived in the old Parker mansion, and the driveway was used as a lover's lane. Townsend Street was a dead end, and he could park there, beyond the last house. The old lane that used to connect Elm Street to the riverbanks was overgrown, but he had walked there with his children, and he could drive his car deep enough into the brushwoods to be concealed.

The Weeds were the last to leave the party, and their host and hostess spoke of their own married happiness while they all four stood in the hallway saying good night. "She's my girl," their host said, squeezing his wife. "She's my blue sky. After sixteen years, I still bite her shoulders. She makes me feel like Hannibal crossing the Alps."

The Weeds drove home in silence. Francis brought his car up to the driveway and sat still, with the motor running. "You can put the car in the garage," Julia said as she got out. "I told the Murchison girl she could leave at eleven. Someone drove her home." She shut the door, and Francis sat in the dark. He would be spared nothing then, it seemed, that a fool was not spared: ravening, lewdness, jealousy, this hurt to his feelings that put tears in his eyes, even scorn—for he could see clearly the image he now presented, his arms spread over the steering wheel and his head buried in them for love. Francis had been a dedicated Boy Scout when he was young, and, remembering the precepts of his youth, he left his office early the next afternoon and played some round-robin squash, but, with his body toned up by exercise and a shower, he realized that he might better have stayed at his desk. It was a frosty night when he got home. The air smelled sharply of change. When he stepped into the house, he sensed an unusual stir. The children were in their best clothes, and when Julia came down she was wearing a lavender dress and her diamond sunburst. She explained the stir: Mr. Hubber was coming at seven to take their photograph for the Christmas card. She had put out Francis' blue suit and a tie with some color in it, because the picture was going to be in color this year. Julia was light-hearted at the thought of being photographed for Christmas. It was the kind of ceremony she enjoyed.

Francis went upstairs to change his clothes. He was tired from the day's work and tired with longing, and sitting on the edge of the bed had the effect of deepening his weariness. He thought of Anne Murchison, and the physical need to express himself, instead of being restrained by the pink lamps on Julia's dressing table, engulfed him. He went to Julia's desk, took a piece of writing paper, and began to write on it. "Dear Anne, I love you, I love you, I love you . . ." No one would see the letter, and he used no restraint. He used phrases like "Heavenly bliss," and "love nest." He salivated, sighed, and trembled. When Julia called him to come down, the abyss between his fantasy and the practical world opened so wide that he felt it affect the muscles of his heart.

Julia and the children were on the stoop, and the photographer and his assistant had set up a double battery of floodlights to show the family and architectural beauty of the entrance to their house. People who had come home on a late train slowed their cars to see the Weeds being photographed for their Christmas card. A few waved and called to the family. It took half an hour of smiling and wetting their lips before Mr. Hubber was satisfied. The heat of the lights made an unfresh smell in the frosty air, and when they were turned off, they lingered on the retina of Francis' eyes.

Later that night, while Francis and Julia were drinking their coffee in the living room, the doorbell rang. Julia answered the door and let in Clayton Thomas. He had come to pay her for some theatre tickets that she had given his mother some time ago, and that Helen Thomas had scrupulously insisted on paying for, though Julia had asked her not to. Julia invited him in to have a cup of coffee. "I won't have any coffee," Clayton said, "but I will come in for a minute." He followed her into the living room, said good evening to Francis, and sat down awkwardly in a chair.

Clayton's father had been killed in the war, and the young man's fatherlessness surrounded him like an element. This may have been conspicuous in Shady Hill because the Thomases were the only family that lacked a piece; all the other marriages were intact and productive. Clayton was in his second or third year of college, and he and his mother lived alone in a large house which she hoped to sell. Clayton had once made some trouble. Years ago, he had stolen some money and run away; he had got to California before they caught up with him. He was tall and homely, wore horn-rimmed glasses, and spoke in a deep voice.

"When do you go back to college, Clayton?" Francis asked.

"I'm not going back," Clayton said. "Mother doesn't have the money, and there's no sense in all this pretense. I'm going to get a job, and if we sell the house, we'll take an apartment in New York."

"Won't you miss Shady Hill?" Julia asked.

"No," Clayton said. "I don't like it."

"Why not?" Francis asked.

"Well, there's a lot here I don't approve of," Clayton said gravely. "Things like the club dances. Last Saturday night, I looked in toward the end and saw Mr. Granner trying to put Mrs. Minot into the trophy case. They were both drunk. I disapprove of so much drinking."

"It was Saturday night," Francis said.

"And all the dovecotes are phony," Clayton said. "And the way people clutter up their lives. I've thought about it a lot, and what seems to me to be really wrong with Shady Hill is that it doesn't have any future. So much energy is spent in perpetuating the place—in keeping out undesirables, and so forth—that the only idea of the future anyone has is just more and more commuting trains and more parties. I don't think that's healthy. I think people ought to be able to dream big dreams about the future. I think people ought to be able to dream great dreams."

"It's too bad you couldn't continue with college," Julia said.

"I wanted to go to divinity school," Clayton said.

"What's your church?" Francis asked.

"Unitarian, Theosophist, Transcendentalist, Humanist," Clayton said.

"Wasn't Emerson a transcendentalist?" Julia asked.

"I mean the English transcendentalists," Clayton said. "All the American transcendentalists were goops."

"What kind of a job do you expect to get?" Francis asked.

"Well, I'd like to work for a publisher," Clayton said, "but everyone tells me there's nothing doing. But it's the kind of thing I'm interested in. I'm writing a long verse play about good and evil. Uncle Charlie might get me into a bank, and that would be good for me. I need the discipline. I have a long way to go in forming my character. I have some terrible habits. I talk too much. I think I ought to take vows of silence. I ought to try not to speak for a week, and discipline myself. I've thought of making a retreat at one of the Episcopalian monasteries, but I don't like Trinitarianism."

"Do you have any girl friends?" Francis asked.

"I'm engaged to be married," Clayton said. "Of course, I'm not old enough or rich enough to have my engagement observed or respected or anything, but I bought a simulated emerald for Anne Murchison with the money I made cutting lawns this summer. We're going to be married as soon as she finishes school."

Francis recoiled at the mention of the girl's name. Then a dingy light seemed to emanate from his spirit, showing everything—Julia, the boy, the chairs—in their true colorlessness. It was like a bitter turn of the weather.

"We're going to have a large family," Clayton said. "Her father's a terrible rummy, and I've had my hard times, and we want to have lots of children. Oh, she's wonderful, Mr. and Mrs. Weed, and we have so much in common. We like all the same things. We sent out the same Christmas card last year without planning it, and we both have an allergy to tomatoes, and our eyebrows grow together in the middle. Well, good night."

Julia went to the door with him. When she returned, Francis said that Clayton was lazy, irresponsible, affected, and smelly. Julia said that Francis seemed to be getting intolerant; the Thomas boy was young and should be given a chance. Julia had noticed other cases where Francis had been short-tempered. "Mrs. Wrightson has asked everyone in Shady Hill to her anniversary party but us," she said.

"I'm sorry, Julia."

"Do you know why they didn't ask us?"

"Why?"

"Because you insulted Mrs. Wrightson."

"Then you know about it?"

"June Masterson told me. She was standing behind you."

Julia walked in front of the sofa with a small step that expressed, Francis knew, a feeling of anger.

"I did insult Mrs. Wrightson, Julia, and I meant to. I've never liked her parties, and I'm glad she's dropped us."

"What about Helen?"

"How does Helen come into this?"

"Mrs. Wrightson's the one who decides who goes to the assemblies."

"You mean she can keep Helen from going to the dances?"

"Yes."

"I hadn't thought of that."

"Oh, I knew you hadn't thought of it," Julia cried, thrusting hilt-deep into this chink of his armor. "And it makes me furious to see this kind of stupid thoughtlessness wreck everyone's happiness."

"I don't think I've wrecked anyone's happiness."

"Mrs. Wrightson runs Shady Hill and has run it for the last forty years. I don't know what makes you think that in a community like this you can indulge every impulse you have to be insulting, vulgar, and offensive."

"I have very good manners," Francis said, trying to give the evening a turn toward the light.

"Damn you, Francis Weed!" Julia cried, and the spit of her words struck him in the face. "I've worked hard for the social position we enjoy in this place, and I won't stand by and see you wreck it. You must have understood when you settled here that you couldn't expect to live like a bear in a cave."

"I've got to express my likes and dislikes."

"You can conceal your dislikes. You don't have to meet everything head-on, like a child. Unless you're anxious to be a social leper. It's no accident that we get asked out a great deal. It's no accident that Helen has so many friends. How would you like to spend your Saturday nights at the movies? How would you like to spend your Sundays raking up dead leaves? How would you like it if your daughter spent the assembly nights sitting at her window, listening to the music from the club? How would you like it—" He did something then that was, after all, not so unaccountable, since her words seemed to raise up between them a wall so deadening that he gagged: He struck her full in the face. She staggered and then, a moment later, seemed composed. She went up the stairs to their room. She didn't slam the door. When Francis followed, a few minutes later, he found her packing a suitcase.

"Julia, I'm very sorry."

"It doesn't matter," she said. She was crying.

"Where do you think you're going?"

"I don't know. I just looked at a timetable. There's an eleven-sixteen into New York. I'll take that."

"You can't go, Julia."

"I can't stay. I know that."

"I'm sorry about Mrs. Wrightson, Julia, and I'm—"

"It doesn't matter about Mrs. Wrightson. That isn't the trouble."

"What is the trouble?"

"You don't love me."

"I do love you, Julia."

"No, you don't."

"Julia, I do love you, and I would like to be as we were—sweet and bawdy and dark—but now there are so many people."

"You hate me."

"I don't hate you, Julia."

"You have no idea of how much you hate me. I think it's subconscious. You don't realize the cruel things you've done."

"What cruel things, Julia?"

"The cruel acts your subconscious drives you to in order to express your hatred of me."

"What, Julia?"

"I've never complained."

"Tell me."

"You don't know what you're doing."

"Tell me."

"Your clothes."

"What do you mean?"

"I mean the way you leave your dirty clothes around in order to express your subconscious hatred of me."

"I don't understand."

"I mean your dirty socks and your dirty pajamas and your dirty underwear and your dirty shirts!" She rose from kneeling by the suitcase and faced him, her eyes blazing and her voice ringing with emotion. "I'm talking about the fact that you've never learned to hang up anything. You just leave your clothes all over the floor where they drop, in order to humiliate me. You do it on purpose!" She fell on the bed, sobbing.

"Julia, darling!" he said, but when she felt his hand on her shoulder she got up.

"Leave me alone," she said. "I have to go." She brushed past him to the closet and came back with a dress. "I'm not taking any of the things you've given me," she said. "I'm leaving my pearls and the fur jacket."

"Oh, Julia!" Her figure, so helpless in its self-deceptions, bent over the suitcase made him nearly sick with pity. She did not understand how desolate her life would be without him. She didn't understand the hours that working women have to keep. She didn't understand that most of her friendships existed within the framework of their marriage, and that without this she would find herself alone. She didn't understand about travel, about hotels, about money. "Julia, I can't let you go! What you don't understand, Julia, is that you've come to be dependent on me."

She tossed her head back and covered her face with her hands. "Did you say that *I* was dependent on *you*?" she asked. "Is that what you said? And who is it that tells you what time to get up in the morning and when to go to bed at night? Who is it that prepares your meals and picks up your dirty closet and invites your friends to dinner? If it weren't for me, your neckties would be greasy and your clothing would be full of moth holes. You were alone when I met you, Francis Weed, and you'll be alone when I leave. When Mother asked you for a list to send out invitations to our wedding, how many names did you have to give her? Fourteen!"

"Cleveland wasn't my home, Julia."

"And how many of your friends came to the church? Two!"

"Cleveland wasn't my home, Julia."

"Since I'm not taking the fur jacket," she said quietly, "you'd better put it back into storage. There's an insurance policy on the pearls that comes due in January. The name of the laundry and the maid's telephone number—all those things are in my desk. I hope you won't drink too much, Francis. I hope that nothing bad will happen to you. If you do get into serious trouble, you can call me."

"Oh my darling, I can't let you go!" Francis said. "I can't let you go, Julia!" He took her in his arms.

"I guess I'd better stay and take care of you for a little while longer," she said.

Riding to work in the morning, Francis saw the girl walk down the aisle of the coach. He was surprised; he hadn't realized that the school she went to was in the city, but she was carrying books, she seemed to be going to school. His surprise delayed his reaction, but then he got up clumsily and stepped into the aisle. Several people had come between them, but he could see her ahead of him, waiting for someone to open the car door, and then, as the train swerved, putting out her hand to support herself as she crossed the platform into the next car. He followed her through that car and halfway through another before calling her name—"Anne! Anne!"—but she didn't turn. He followed her into still another car, and she sat down in an aisle seat. Coming up to her, all his feelings warm and bent in her direction, he put his hand on the back of her seat—even this touch warmed him—and, leaning down to speak to her, he saw that it was not Anne. It was an older woman wearing glasses. He went on deliberately into another car, his face red with embarrassment and the much deeper feeling of having his good sense challenged; for if he couldn't tell one person from another, what evidence was there that his life with Julia and the children had as much reality as his dreams of iniquity in Paris or the litter, the grass smell, and the cave-shaped trees in Lovers' Lane.

Late that afternoon, Julia called to remind Francis that they were going out for dinner. A few minutes later, Trace Bearden called. "Look, fellar," Trace said. "I'm calling for Mrs. Thomas. You know? Clayton, that boy of hers, doesn't seem able to get a job, and I wondered if you could help. If you'd call Charlie Bell—I know he's indebted to you—and say a good word for the kid, I think Charlie would—"

"Trace, I hate to say this," Francis said, "but I don't feel that I can do anything for that boy. The kid's worthless. I know it's a harsh thing to say, but it's a fact. Any kindness done for him would backfire in everybody's face. He's just a worthless kid, Trace, and there's nothing to be done about it. Even it we got him a job, he wouldn't be able to keep it for a week. I know that to be a fact. It's an awful thing, Trace, and I know it is, but instead of recommending that kid, I'd feel obliged to warn people against him—people who knew his father and would naturally want to step in and do something. I'd feel obliged to warn them. He's a thief . . ."

The moment this conversation was finished, Miss Rainey came in and stood by his desk. "I'm not going to be able to work for you any more, Mr. Weed," she said. "I can stay until the seventeenth if you need me, but I've been offered a whirlwind of a job, and I'd like to leave as soon as possible."

She went out, leaving him to face alone the wickedness of what he had done to the Thomas boy. His children in their photograph laughed and laughed, glazed with all the bright colors of summer, and he remembered that they had met a bagpiper on the beach that day and he had paid the piper a dollar to play them a battle song of The Black Watch. The girl would be at the house when he got home. He would spend another evening among his kind neighbors, picking and choosing dead-end streets, car tracks, and the driveways of abandoned houses. There was nothing to mitigate his feeling—nothing that laughter or a game of softball with the children would change—and, thinking back over the plane crash, the Farquarsons' new maid, and Anne Murchison's difficulties with her drunken father, he wondered how he could have avoided arriving at just where he was. He was in trouble. He had been lost once in his life, coming back from a trout stream in the north woods, and he had now the same bleak realization that no amount of cheerfulness or hopefulness or valor or perseverance could help him find, in the gathering dark, the path that he'd lost. He smelled the forest. The feeling of bleakness was intolerable, and he saw clearly that he had reached the point where he would have to make a choice.

He could go to a psychiatrist, like Miss Rainey; he could go to church and confess his lusts; he could go to a Danish massage parlor in the West Seventies that had been recommended by a salesman; he could rape the girl or trust that he would somehow be prevented from doing this; or he could get drunk. It was his life, his boat, and, like every other man, he was made to be the father of thousands, and what harm could there be in a tryst that would make them both feel more kindly toward the world? This was the wrong train of thought, and he came back to the first, the psychiatrist. He had the telephone number of Miss Rainey's doctor, and he called and asked for an immediate appointment. He was insistent with the doctor's secretary—it was his manner in business—and when she said that the doctor's schedule was full for the next few weeks, Francis demanded an appointment that day and was told to come at five.

The psychiatrist's office was in a building that was used mostly by doctors and dentists, and the hallways were filled with the candy smell of mouthwash and memories of pain. Francis' character had been formed upon a series of private resolves—resolves about cleanliness, about going off the high diving board or repeating any other feat that challenged his courage, about punctuality, honesty, and virtue. To abdicate the perfect loneliness in which he had made his most vital decisions shattered his concept of character and left him now in a condition that felt like shock. He was stupefied. The scene for his *miserere mei Deus* was, like the waiting room of so many doctors' offices, a crude token gesture toward the sweets of domestic bliss: a place arranged with antiques, coffee tables, potted plants, and etchings of snow-covered bridges and geese in flight, although there were no children, no marriage bed, no stove, even, in this travesty of a house, where no one had ever spent the night and where the curtained windows looked straight onto a dark air shaft. Francis gave his name and address to a secretary and then saw, at the side of the room, a policeman moving toward him. "Hold it, hold it," the policeman said. "Don't move. Keep your hands where they are."

"I think it's all right, Officer," the secretary began "I think it will be—"

"Let's make sure," the policeman said, and he began to slap Francis' clothes, looking for what—pistols, knives, an icepick? Finding nothing, he went off, and the secretary began a nervous apology: "When you called on the telephone, Mr. Weed, you seemed very excited, and one of the doctor's patients has been threatening his life, and we have to be careful. If you want to go in now?" Francis pushed open a door connected to an electrical chime, and in the doctor's lair sat down heavily, blew his nose into a handkerchief, searched in his pockets for cigarettes, for matches, for something, and said hoarsely, with tears in his eyes, "I'm in love, Dr. Herzog."

It is a week or ten days later in Shady Hill. The seven-fourteen has come and gone, and here and there dinner is finished and the dishes are in the dishwashing machine. The village hangs, morally and economically, from a thread; but it hangs by its thread in the evening light. Donald Goslin has begun to worry the "Moonlight Sonata" again. *Marcato ma sempre pianissimo!* He seems to be wringing out a wet bath towel, but the housemaid does not heed him. She is writing a letter to Arthur Godfrey. In the cellar of his house, Francis Weed is building a coffee table. Dr. Herzog recommended woodwork as a therapy, and Francis finds some true consolation in the simple arithmetic involved and in the holy smell of new wood. Francis is happy. Upstairs, little Toby is crying, because he is tired. He puts off his cowboy hat, gloves, and fringed jacket, unbuckles the belt studded with gold and rubies, the silver bullets and holsters, slips off his suspenders, his checked shirt, and Levis, and sits on the edge of his bed to pull off his high boots. Leaving this equipment in a heap, he goes to the closet and takes his space suit off a nail. It is a struggle for him to get into the long tights, but he succeeds. He loops the magic cape over his shoulders and, climbing onto the footboard of his bed, he spreads his arms and flies the short distance to the floor, landing with a thump that is audible to everyone in the house but himself.

"Go home, Gertrude, go home," Mrs. Masterson says. "I told you to go home an hour ago, Gertrude. It's way past your suppertime, and your mother will be worried. Go home!" A door on the Babcocks' terrace flies open, and out comes Mrs. Babcock without any clothes on, pursued by her naked husband. (Their children are away at boarding school, and their terrace is screened by a hedge.) Over the terrace they go and in at the kitchen door, as passionate and handsome a nymph and satyr as you will find on any wall in Venice. Cutting the last of the roses in her garden, Julia hears old Mr. Nixon shouting at the squirrels in his bird-feeding station. "Rapscallions! Varmits! Avaunt and quit my sight!" A miserable cat wanders into the garden, sunk in spiritual and physical discomfort. Tied to its head is a small straw hat—a doll's hat—and it is securely buttoned into a doll's dress, from the skirts of which protrudes its long, hairy tail. As it walks, it shakes its feet, as if it had fallen into water.

"Here, pussy, pussy, pussy!" Julia calls.

"Here, pussy, here, poor pussy!" But the cat gives her a skeptical look and stumbles away in its skirts. The last to come is Jupiter. He prances through the tomato vines, holding in his generous mouth the remains of an evening slipper. Then it is dark; it is a night where kings in golden suits ride elephants over the mountains.

BERNARD MALAMUD

[1914–1986]

The Magic Barrel

(First published in *Partisan Review*, November, 1954; first book publication in 1954.)

NOT LONG AGO there lived in uptown New York, in a small, almost meager room, though crowded with books, Leo Finkle, a rabbinical student in the Yeshivah University. Finkle, after six years of study, was to be ordained in June and had been advised by an acquaintance that he might find it easier to win himself a congregation if he were married. Since he had no present prospects of marriage, after two tormented days of turning it over in his mind, he called in Pinye Salzman, a marriage broker, whose two-line advertisement he had read in the *Forward*.

The matchmaker appeared one night out of the dark fourth-floor hallway of the graystone rooming house, grasping a black, strapped portfolio that had been worn thin with use. Salzman, who had been long in the business, was of slight but dignified build, wearing an old hat and an overcoat too short and tight for him. He smelled frankly of fish, which he loved to eat, and although he was missing a few teeth, his presence was not displeasing, because of an amiable manner curiously contrasted by mournful eyes. His voice, his lips, his wisp of beard, his bony fingers were animated, but give him a moment of repose and his mild blue eyes soon revealed a depth of sadness, a characteristic that put Leo a little at ease although the situation, for him, was inherently tense.

He at once informed Salzman why he had asked him to come, explaining that his home was in Cleveland, and that but for his parents, who had married comparatively late in life, he was alone in the world. He had for six years devoted himself entirely to his studies, as a result of which, quite understandably, he had found himself without time for a social life and the company of young women. Therefore he thought it the better part of trial and error—of embarrassing fumbling—to call in an experienced person to advise him in these matters. He remarked in passing that the function of the marriage broker was ancient and honorable, highly approved in the Jewish community, because it made practical the necessary without hindering joy. Moreover, his own parents had been brought together by a matchmaker. They had made, if not a financially profitable marriage—since neither had possessed any worldly goods to speak of—at least a successful one in the sense of their everlasting devotion to one another. Salzman listened in embarrassed surprise, sensing a sort of apology. Later, however, he experienced a glow of pride in his work, an emotion that had left him years ago, and he heartily approved of Finkle.

The two men went to their business. Leo had led Salzman to the only clear place in the room, a table near a window that overlooked the lamplit city. He seated himself at the matchmaker's side but facing him, attempting by an act of will to suppress the unpleasant tickle in his throat. Salzman eagerly unstrapped his portfolio and removed a loose rubber band from a thin packet of much handled cards. As he flipped through them, a gesture and sound that physically hurt Leo, the student pretended not to see and gazed steadfastly out the window. Although it was still February, winter was on its last legs, signs of which he had for the first time in years begun to notice. He now observed the round white moon, moving high in the sky through a cloud menagerie, and watched with half-open mouth as it penetrated a huge hen, and dropped out of her like an egg laying itself. Salzman, though pretending through eyeglasses he had just slipped on to be engaged in scanning the writing on the cards, stole occasional glances at the young man's distinguished face, noting with pleasure the long, severe scholar's nose, brown eyes heavy with learning, sensitive yet ascetic lips, and a certain almost hollow quality of the dark cheeks. He gazed around at shelves upon shelves of books and let out a soft but happy sigh.

When Leo's eyes fell upon the cards, he counted six spread out in Salzman's hand.

"So few?" he said in disappointment.

"You wouldn't believe me how much cards I got in my office," Salzman replied. "The drawers are already filled to the top, so I keep them now in a barrel, but is every girl good for a new rabbi?"

Leo blushed at this, regretting all he had revealed of himself in a curriculum vitae he had sent to Salzman. He had thought it best to acquaint him with his strict standards and specifications, but in having done so now felt he had told the marriage broker more than was absolutely necessary.

He hesitantly inquired, "Do you keep photographs of your clients on file?"

"First comes family, amount of dowry, also what kind promises," Salzman replied, unbuttoning his tight coat and settling himself in the chair. "After comes pictures, rabbi."

"Call me Mr. Finkle. I'm not a rabbi yet."

Salzman said he would, but instead called him doctor, which he changed to rabbi when Leo was not listening too attentively.

Salzman adjusted his horn-rimmed spectacles, gently cleared his throat and read in an eager voice the contents of the top card:

"Sophie P. Twenty-four years. Widow for one year. No children. Educated high school and two years college. Father promises eight thousand dollars. Has wonderful wholesale business. Also real estate. On the mother's side comes teachers, also one actor. Well known on Second Avenue."

Leo gazed up in surprise. "Did you say a widow?"

"A widow don't mean spoiled, rabbi. She lived with her husband maybe four months. He was a sick boy, she made a mistake to marry him."

"Marrying a widow has never entered my mind."

"This is because you have no experience. A widow, specially if she is young and healthy like this girl, is a wonderful person to marry. She will be thankful to you the rest of her life. Believe me, if I was looking now for a bride, I would marry a widow."

Leo reflected, then shook his head.

Salzman hunched his shoulders in an almost imperceptible gesture of disappointment. He placed the card down on the wooden table and began to read another:

"Lily H. High school teacher. Regular. Not a substitute. Has savings and new Dodge car. Lived in Paris one year. Father is successful dentist thirty-five years. Interested in professional man. Well Americanized family. Wonderful opportunity.

"I know her personally," said Salzman. "I wish you could see this girl. She is a doll. Also very intelligent. All day you could talk to her about books and theyater and what not. She also knows current events."

"I don't believe you mentioned her age?"

"Her age?" Salzman said, raising his brows in surprise. "Her age is thirty-two years."

Leo said after a while, "I'm afraid that seems a little too old."

Salzman let out a laugh. "So how old are you, rabbi?"

"Twenty-seven."

"So what is the difference, tell me, between twenty-seven and thirty-two? My own wife is seven years older than me. So what did I suffer?—Nothing. If Rothschild's a daughter wants to marry you, would you say on account her age, no?"

"Yes," Leo said dryly.

Salzman shook off the no in the yes. "Five years don't mean a thing. I give you my word that when you will live with her for one week you will forget her age. What does it mean five years—that she lived more and knows more than somebody who is younger? On this girl, God bless her, years are not wasted. Each one that it comes makes better the bargain."

"What subject does she teach in high school?"

"Languages. If you heard the way she reads French, you will think it is music. I am in the business twenty-five years, and I recommend her with my whole heart. Believe me, I know what I'm talking, rabbi."

"What's on the next card?" Leo said abruptly.

Salzman reluctantly turned up the third card:

"Ruth K. Nineteen years. Honor student. Father offers thirteen thousand dollars cash to the right bridegroom. He is a medical doctor. Stomach specialist with marvelous practice. Brother-in-law owns own garment business. Particular people."

Salzman looked up as if he had read his trump card.

"Did you say nineteen?" Leo asked with interest.

"On the dot."

"Is she attractive?" He blushed. "Pretty?"

Salzman kissed his fingertips. "A little doll. On this I give you my word. Let me call the father tonight and you will see what means pretty."

But Leo was troubled. "You're sure she's that young?"

"This I am positive. The father will show you the birth certificate."

"Are you positive there isn't something wrong with her?" Leo insisted.

"Who says there is wrong?"

"I don't understand why an American girl her age should go to a marriage broker."

A smile spread over Salzman's face

"So for the same reason you went, she comes."

Leo flushed. "I am pressed for time."

Salzman, realizing he had been tactless, quickly explained. "The father came, not her. He wants she should have the best, so he looks around himself. When we will locate the right boy he will introduce him and encourage. This makes a better marriage than if a young girl without experience takes for herself. I don't have to tell you this."

"But don't you think this young girl believes in love?" Leo spoke uneasily.

Salzman was about to guffaw but caught himself and said soberly, "Love comes with the right person, not before."

Leo parted dry lips but did not speak. Noticing that Salzman had snatched a quick glance at the next card, he cleverly asked, "How is her health?"

"Perfect," Salzman said, breathing with difficulty. "Of course, she is a little lame on her right foot from an auto accident that it happened to her when she was twelve years, but nobody notices on account she is so brilliant and also beautiful."

Leo got up heavily and went to the window. He felt curiously bitter and upbraided himself for having called in the marriage broker. Finally, he shook his head.

"Why not?" Salzman persisted, the pitch of his voice rising.

"Because I hate stomach specialists."

"So what do you care what is his business? After you marry her, do you need him? Who says he must come every Friday night to your house?"

Ashamed of the way the talk was going, Leo dismissed Salzman, who went home with melancholy eyes.

Though he had felt only relief at the marriage broker's departure, Leo was in low spirits the next day. He explained it as arising from Salzman's failure to produce a suitable bride for him. He did not care for his type of clientele. But when Leo found himself hesitating over whether to seek out another matchmaker, one more polished than Pinye, he wondered if it could be—his protestations to the contrary, and although he honored his father and mother—that he did not, in essence, care for the matchmaking institution. This thought he quickly put out of mind yet found himself still upset. All day he ran around in a fog—missed an important appointment, forgot to give out his laundry, walked out of a Broadway cafeteria without paying and had to run back with the ticket in his hand; had even not recognized his landlady in the street when she passed with a friend and courteously called out, "A good evening to you, Doctor Finkle." By nightfall, however, he had regained sufficient calm to sink his nose into a book and there found peace from his thoughts.

Almost at once there came a knock on the door. Before Leo could say enter, Salzman, commerical cupid, was standing in the room. His face was gray and meager, his expression hungry, and he looked as if he would expire on his feet. Yet the marriage broker managed, by some trick of the muscles, to display a broad smile.

"So good evening. I am invited?"

Leo nodded, disturbed to see him again, yet unwilling to ask him to leave.

Beaming still, Salzman laid his portfolio on the table. "Rabbi, I got for you tonight good news."

"I've asked you not to call me rabbi. I'm still a student."

"Your worries are finished. I have for you a first-class bride."

"Leave me in peace concerning this subject." Leo pretended lack of interest.

"The world will dance at your wedding."

"Please, Mr. Salzman, no more."

"But first must come back my strength," Salzman said weakly. He fumbled with the portfolio straps and took out of the leather case an oily paper bag, from which he extracted a hard seeded roll and a small smoked whitefish. With one motion of his hand he stripped the fish out of its skin and began ravenously to chew. "All day in a rush," he muttered.

Leo watched him eat.

"A sliced tomato you have maybe?" Salzman hesitantly inquired.

"No."

The marriage broker shut his eyes and ate. When he had finished he carefully cleaned up the crumbs and rolled up the remains of the fish in the paper bag. His spectacled eyes roamed the room until he discovered, amid some piles of books, a one-burner gas stove. Lifting his hat he humbly asked, "A glass tea you got, rabbi?"

Conscience-stricken, Leo rose and brewed the tea. He served it with a chunk of lemon and two cubes of lump sugar, delighting Salzman.

After he had drunk his tea, Salzman's strength and good spirits were restored.

"So tell me, rabbi," he said amiably, "you considered any more the three clients I mentioned yesterday?"

"There was no need to consider."

"Why not?"

"None of them suits me."

"What, then, suits you?"

Leo let it pass because he could give only a confused answer.

Without waiting for a reply, Salzman asked, "You remember this girl I talked to you—the high school teacher?"

"Age thirty-two?"

But, surprisingly, Salzman's face lit in a smile. "Age twenty-nine."

Leo shot him a look. "Reduced from thirty-two?"

"A mistake," Salzman avowed. "I talked today with the dentist. He took me to his safety deposit box and showed me the birth certificate. She was twenty-nine years last August. They made her a party in the mountains where she went for her vacation. When her father spoke to me the first time I forgot to write the age and I told you thirty-two, but now I remember this was a different client, a widow."

"The same one you told me about ? I thought she was twenty-four?"

"A different. Am I responsible that the world is filled with widows?"

"No, but I'm not interested in them, nor for that matter, in schoolteachers."

Salzman passionately pulled his clasped hands to his breast. Looking at the ceiling he exclaimed, "Jewish children, what can I say to somebody that he is not interested in high school teachers? So what then you are interested?"

Leo flushed but controlled himself.

"In who else you will be interested," Salzman went on, "if you not interested in this fine girl that she speaks four languages and has personally in the bank ten thousand dollars? Also her father guarantees further twelve thousand. Also she has a new car, wonderful clothes, talks on all subjects, and she will give you a first-class home and children. How near do we come in our life to paradise?"

"If she's so wonderful, why wasn't she married ten years ago?"

"Why?" said Salzman with a heavy laugh "—Why? Because she is *partikler.* This is why. She wants only the *best.*"

Leo was silent, amused at how he had trapped himself. But Salzman had aroused his interest in Lily H., and he began seriously to consider calling on her. When the marriage broker observed how intently Leo's mind was at work on the facts he had supplied, he felt positive they would soon come to an agreement.

Late Saturday afternoon, conscious of Salzman, Leo Finkle walked with Lily Hirschorn along Riverside Drive. He walked briskly and erectly, wearing with distinction the black fedora he had that morning taken with trepidation out of the dusty hatbox on his closet shelf, and the heavy black Saturday coat he had thoroughly whisked clean. Leo also owned a walking stick, a present from a distant relative, but had decided not to use it. Lily, petite and not unpretty, had on something signifying the approach of spring. She was *au courant*, animatedly, with all subjects, and he weighed her words and found her surprisingly sound—score another for Salzman, whom he uneasily sensed to be somewhere around, hiding perhaps high in a tree along the street, flashing the lady signals; or perhaps a cloven-hoofed Pan, piping nuptial ditties as he danced his invisible way before them, strewing wild buds on the walk and purple summer grapes in their path, symbolizing fruit of a union, of which there was yet none.

Lily startled Leo by remarking, "I was thinking of Mr. Salzman, a curious figure, wouldn't you say?"

Not certain what to answer, he nodded.

She bravely went on, blushing, "I for one am grateful for his introducing us. Aren't you?"

He courteously replied, "I am."

"I mean," she said with a little laugh—and it was all in good taste, or at least gave the effect of being not in bad—"do you mind that we came together so?"

He was not afraid of her honesty, recognizing that she meant to set the relationship aright, and understanding that it took a certain amount of experience in life, and courage, to want to do it quite that way. One had to have some sort of past to make that kind of beginning.

He said that he did not mind. Salzman's function was traditional and honorable—valuable for what it might achieve, which, he pointed out, was frequently nothing.

Lily agreed with a sigh. They walked on for a while and she said after a long silence, again with a nervous laugh, "Would you mind if I asked you something a little bit personal? Frankly, I find the subject fascinating." Although Leo shrugged, she went on half embarrassedly, "How was it that you came to your calling? I mean was it a sudden passionate inspiration?"

Leo, after a time, slowly replied, "I was always interested in the Law."

"You saw revealed in it the presence of the Highest?"

He nodded and changed the subject. "I understand you spent a little time in Paris, Miss Hirschorn?"

"Oh, did Mr. Salzman tell you, Rabbi Finkle?" Leo winced but she went on, "It was ages and ages ago and almost forgotten. I remember I had to return for my sister's wedding."

But Lily would not be put off. "When," she asked in a trembly voice, "did you become enamored of God?"

He stared at her. Then it came to him that she was talking not about Leo Finkle, but a total stranger, some mystical figure, perhaps even passionate prophet that Salzman had conjured up for her—no relation to the living or dead. Leo trembled with rage and weakness. The trickster had obviously sold her a bill of goods, just as he had him, who'd expected to become acquainted with a young lady of twenty-nine, only to behold, the moment he laid eyes upon her strained and anxious face, a woman past thirty-five and aging very rapidly. Only his self-control, he thought, had kept him this long in her presence.

"I am not," he said gravely, "a talented religious person," and in seeking words to go on, found himself possessed by fear and shame. "I think," he said in a strained manner, "that I came to God not because I loved him, but because I did not."

This confession he spoke harshly because its unexpectedness shook him.

Lily wilted. Leo saw a profusion of loaves of bread sailing like ducks high over his head, not unlike the loaves by which he had counted himself to sleep last night. Mercifully, then, it snowed, which he would not put past Salzman's machinations.

He was infuriated with the marriage broker and swore he would throw him out of the room the moment he reappeared. But Salzman did not come that night, and when Leo's anger had subsided, an unaccountable despair grew in its place. At first he thought this was caused by his disappointment in Lily, but before long it became evident that he had involved himself with Salzman without a true knowledge of his own intent. He gradually realized—with an emptiness that seized him with six hands—that he had called in the broker to find him a bride because he was incapable of doing it himself. This terrifying insight he had derived as a result of his meeting and conversation with Lily Hirschorn. Her probing questions had somehow irritated him into revealing—to himself more than her—the true nature of his relationship with God, and from that it had come upon him, with shocking force, that apart from his parents, he had never loved anyone. Or perhaps it went the other way, that he did not love God so well as he might, because he had not loved man. It seemed to Leo that his whole life stood starkly revealed and he saw himself, for the first time, as he truly was—unloved and loveless. This bitter but somehow not fully unexpected revelation brought him to a point of panic controlled only by extraordinary effort. He covered his face with his hands and wept.

The week that followed was the worst of his life. He did not eat, and lost weight. His beard darkened and grew ragged. He stopped attending lectures and seminars and almost never opened a book. He seriously considered leaving the Yeshivah, although he was deeply troubled at the thought of the loss of all his years of study—saw them like pages from a book strewn over the city—and at the devastating effect of this decision upon his parents. But he had lived without knowledge of himself, and never in the Five Books and all the Commentaries—mea culpa—had the truth been revealed to him. He did not know where to turn, and in all this desolating loneliness there was no *to whom*, although he often thought of Lily but not once could bring himself to go downstairs and make the call. He became touchy and irritable, especially with his landlady, who asked him all manner of questions; on the other hand, sensing his own disagreeableness, he waylaid her on the stairs and apologized abjectly, until, mortified, she ran from him. Out of this, however, he drew the consolation that he was yet a Jew and that a Jew suffered. But gradually, as the long and terrible week drew to a close, he regained his composure and some idea of purpose in life: to go on as planned. Although he was imperfect, the ideal was not. As for his quest of a bride, the thought of continuing afflicted him with anxiety and heartburn, yet perhaps with this new knowledge of himself he would be more successful than in the past. Perhaps love would now come to him and a bride to that love. And for this sanctified seeking who needed a Salzman?

The marriage broker, a skeleton with haunted eyes, returned that very night. He looked, withal, the picture of frustrated expectancy—as if he had steadfastly waited the week at Miss Lily Hirschorn's side for a telephone call that never came.

Casually coughing, Salzman came immediately to the point: "So how did you like her?"

Leo's anger rose and he could not refrain from chiding the matchmaker: "Why did you lie to me, Salzman?"

Salzman's pale face went dead white, as if the world had snowed on him.

"Did you not state that she was twenty-nine?" Leo insisted.

"I give you my word—"

"She was thirty-five. *At least* thirty-five."

"Of this I would not be too sure. Her father told me—"

"Never mind. The worst of it was that you lied to her."

"How did I lie to her, tell me?"

"You told her things about me that weren't true. You made me out to be more, consequently less than I am. She had in mind a totally different person, a sort of semi-mystical Wonder Rabbi."

"All I said, you was a religious man."

"I can imagine."

Salzman sighed. "This is my weakness that I have," he confessed. "My wife says to me I shouldn't be a salesman, but when I have two fine people that they would be wonderful to be married, I am so happy that I talk too much." He smiled wanly. "This is why Salzman is a poor man."

Leo's anger went. "Well, Salzman, I'm afraid that's all."

The marriage broker fastened hungry eyes on him.

"You don't want any more a bride?"

"I do," said Leo, "but I have decided to seek her in a different way. I am no longer interested in an arranged marriage. To be frank, I now admit the necessity of premarital love. That is, I want to be in love with the one I marry."

"Love?" said Salzman, astounded. After a moment he said, "For us, our love is our life, not for the ladies. In the ghetto they–"

"I know, I know," said Leo. "I've thought of it often. Love, I have said to myself, should be a by-product of living and worship rather than its own end. Yet for myself I find it necessary to establish the level of my need and to fulfill it."

Salzman shrugged but answered, "Listen, rabbi, if you want love, this I can find for you also. I have such beautiful clients that you will love them the minute your eyes will see them."

Leo smiled unhappily. "I'm afraid you don't understand."

But Salzman hastily unstrapped his portfolio and withdrew a manila packet from it.

"Pictures," he said, quickly laying the envelope on the table.

Leo called after him to take the pictures away, but as if on the wings of the wind, Salzman had disappeared.

March came. Leo had returned to his regular routine. Although he felt not quite himself yet–lacked energy–he was making plans for a more active social life. Of course it would cost something, but he was an expert in cutting corners; and when there were no corners left he could make circles rounder. All the while Salzman's pictures had lain on the table, gathering dust. Occasionally as Leo sat studying, or enjoying a cup of tea, his eyes fell on the manila envelope, but he never opened it.

The days went by and no social life to speak of developed with a member of the opposite sex–it was difficult, given the circumstances of his situation. One morning Leo toiled up the stairs to his room and stared out the window at the city. Although the day was bright his view of it was dark. For some time he watched the people in the street below hurrying along and then turned with a heavy heart to his little room. On the table was the packet. With a sudden relentless gesture he tore it open. For a half-hour he stood there, in a state of excitement, examining the photographs of the ladies Salzman had included. Finally, with a deep sigh he put them down. There were six, of varying degrees of attractiveness, but look at them long enough and they all became Lily Hirschorn: all past their prime, all starved behind bright smiles, not a true personality in the lot. Life, despite their anguished struggles and frantic yoohooings, had passed them by; they were photographs in a briefcase that stank of fish. After a while, however, as Leo attempted to return the pictures into the envelope, he found another in it, a small snapshot of the type taken by a machine for a quarter. He gazed at it a moment and let out a cry.

Her face deeply moved him. Why, he could at first not say. It gave him the impression of youth—all spring flowers, yet age—a sense of having been used to the bone, wasted; this all came from the eyes, which were hauntingly familiar, yet absolutely strange. He had a strong impression that he had met her before, but try as he might he could not place her, although he could almost recall her name, as if he had read it written in her own handwriting. No, this couldn't be; he would have remembered her. It was not, he affirmed, that she had an extraordinary beauty—no, although her face was attractive enough; it was that *something* about her moved him. Feature for feature, even some of the ladies of the photographs could do better; but she leaped forth to the heart—had lived, or wanted to—more than just wanted, perhaps regretted it—had somehow deeply suffered: it could be seen in the depths of those reluctant eyes, and from the way the light enclosed and shone from her, and within her, opening whole realms of possibility: this was her own. Her he desired. His head ached and eyes narrowed with the intensity of his gazing, then, as if a black fog had blown up in the mind, he experienced fear of her and was aware that he had received an impression, somehow, of filth. He shuddered, saying softly, it is thus with us all. Leo brewed some tea in a small pot and sat sipping it, without sugar, to calm himself. But before he had finished drinking, again with excitement he examined the face and found it good: good for him. Only such a one could truly understand Leo Finkle and help him to seek whatever he was seeking. How she had come to be among the discards in Salzman's barrel he could never guess, but he knew he must urgently go find her.

Leo rushed downstairs, grabbed up the Bronx telephone book, and searched for Salzman's home address. He was not listed, nor was his office. Neither was he in the Manhattan book. But Leo remembered having written down the address on a slip of paper after he had read Salzman's advertisement in the "personals" column of the *Forward*. He ran up to his room and tore through his papers, without luck. It was exasperating. Just when he needed the matchmaker he was nowhere to be found. Fortunately Leo remembered to look in his wallet. There on a card he found his name written and a Bronx address. No phone number was listed, which, Leo now recalled, was the reason he had originally communicated with Salzman by letter. He got on his coat, put a hat on over his skull cap and hurried to the subway station. All the way to the far end of the Bronx he sat on the edge of the seat. He was more than once tempted to take out the picture and see if the girl's face was as he remembered it, but he refrained, allowing the snapshot to remain in his inside coat pocket, content to have her so close. When the train pulled into the station he was waiting at the door and bolted out. He quickly located the street Salzman had advertised.

The building he sought was less than a block from the subway, but it was not an office building, nor even a loft, nor a store in which one could rent office space. It was an old and grimy tenement. Leo found Salzman's name in pencil on a soiled tag under the bell and climbed three dark flights to his apartment. When he knocked, the door was opened by a thin, asthmatic, gray-haired woman, in felt slippers.

"Yes?" she said, expecting nothing. She listened without listening. He could have sworn he had seen her somewhere before but knew it was illusion.

"Salzman—does he live here? Pinye Salzman," he said, "the matchmaker?"

She stared at him a long time. "Of course."

He felt embarrassed. "Is he in?"

"No." Her mouth was open, but she offered nothing more.

"This is urgent. Can you tell me where his office is?"

"In the air." She pointed upward.

"You mean he has no office?" Leo said.

"In his socks."

He peered into the apartment. It was sunless and dingy, one large room divided by a half-open curtain, beyond which he could see a sagging metal bed. The near side of the room was crowded with rickety chairs, old bureaus, a three-legged table, racks of cooking utensils, and all the apparatus of a kitchen. But there was no sign of Salzman or his magic barrel, probably also a figment of his imagination. An odor of frying fish made Leo weak to the knees.

"Where is he?" he insisted. "I've got to see your husband."

At length she answered, "So who knows where he is? Every time he thinks a new thought he runs to a different place. Go home, he will find you."

"Tell him Leo Finkle."

She gave no sign that she had heard.

He went downstairs, deeply depressed.

But Salzman, breathless, stood waiting at his door.

Leo was overjoyed and astounded. "How did you get here before me?"

"I rushed."

"Come inside."

They entered. Leo fixed tea and a sardine sandwich for Salzman.

As they were drinking he reached behind him for the packet of pictures and handed them to the marriage broker.

Salzman put down his glass and said expectantly, "You found maybe somebody you like?"

"Not among these."

The marriage broker turned sad eyes away.

"Here's the one I like." Leo held forth the snapshot.

Salzman slipped on his glasses and took the picture into his trembling hand. He turned ghastly and let out a miserable groan.

"What's the matter?" cried Leo.

"Excuse me. Was an accident this picture. She is not for you."

Salzman frantically shoved the manila packet into his portfolio. He thrust the snapshot into his pocket and fled down the stairs.

Leo, after momentary paralysis, gave chase and cornered the marriage broker in the vestibule. The landlady made hysterical outcries but neither of them listened.

"Give me back the picture, Salzman."

"No." The pain in his eyes was terrible.

"Tell me who she is then."

"This I can't tell you. Excuse me."

He made to depart, but Leo, forgetting himself, seized the matchmaker by his tight coat and shook him frenziedly.

"Please," sighed Salzman. "*Please*."

Leo ashamedly let him go. "Tell me who she is," he begged. "It's very important for me to know."

"She is not for you. She is a wild one—wild, without shame. This is not a bride for a rabbi."

"What do you mean wild?"

"Like an animal. Like a dog. For her to be poor was a sin. This is why she is dead now."

"In God's name, what do you mean ?"

"Her I can't introduce to you," Salzman cried.

"Why are you so excited?"

"Why he asks," Salzman said, bursting into tears. "This is my baby, my Stella, she should burn in hell."

Leo hurried up to bed and hid under the covers. Under the covers he thought his whole life through. Although he soon fell asleep he could not sleep her out of his mind. He woke, beating his breast. Though he prayed to be rid of her, his prayers went unanswered. Through days of torment he struggled endlessly not to love her; fearing success, he escaped it. He then concluded to convert her to goodness, himself to God.The idea alternately nauseated and exalted him.

He perhaps did not know that he had come to a final decision until he encountered Salzman in a Broadway cafeteria. He was sitting alone at a rear table, sucking the bony remains of a fish. The marriage broker appeared haggard, and transparent to the point of vanishing.

Salzman looked up at first without recognizing him. Leo had grown a pointed beard and his eyes were weighted with wisdom.

"Salzman," he said, "love has at last come to my heart."

"Who can love from a picture?" mocked the marriage broker.

"It is not impossible."

"If you can love her, then you can love anybody. Let me show you some new clients that they just sent me their photographs. One is a little doll."

"Just her I want," Leo murmured.

"Don't be a fool, doctor. Don't bother with her."

"Put me in touch with her, Salzman," Leo said humbly. "Perhaps I can do her a service."

Salzman had stopped chewing, and Leo understood with emotion that it was now arranged.

Leaving the cafeteria, he was, however, afflicted by a tormenting suspicion that Salzman had planned it all to happen this way.

Leo was informed by letter that she would meet him on a certain corner, and she was there one spring night, waiting under a street lamp. He appeared, carrying a small bouquet of violets and rosebuds. Stella stood by the lamppost, smoking. She wore white with red shoes, which fitted his expectations, although in a troubled moment he had imagined the dress red, and only the shoes white. She waited uneasily and shyly. From afar he saw that her eyes—clearly her father's—were filled with desperate innocence. He pictured, in hers, his own redemption. Violins and lit candles revolved in the sky. Leo ran forward with the flowers outthrust.

Around the corner, Salzman, leaning against a wall, chanted prayers for the dead.

SAUL BELLOW

[1915–2005]

A Silver Dish

(First published in the *New Yorker*, September, 1978; first book publication in 1979.)

WHAT DO YOU do about death—in this case, the death of an old father? If you're a modern person, sixty years of age, and a man who's been around, like Woody Selbst, what do you do? Take this matter of mourning, and take it against a contemporary background. How, against a contemporary background, do you mourn an octogenarian father, nearly blind, his heart enlarged, his lungs filling with fluid, who creeps, stumbles, gives off the odors, the moldiness or gassiness, of old men. I *mean*! As Woody put it, be realistic. Think what times these are. The papers daily give it to you—the Lufthansa pilot in Aden is described by the hostages on his knees, begging the Palestinian terrorists not to execute him, but they shoot him through the head. Later they themselves are killed. And still others shoot others, or shoot themselves. That's what you read in the press, see on the tube, mention at dinner. We know now what goes daily through the whole of the human community, like a global death-peristalsis.

Woody, a businessman in South Chicago, was not an ignorant person. He knew more such phrases than you would expect a tile contractor (offices, lobbies, lavatories) to know. The kind of knowledge he had was not the kind for which you get academic degrees. Although Woody had studied for two years in a seminary, preparing to be a minister. Two years of college during the Depression was more than most high-school graduates could afford. After that, in his own vital, picturesque, original way (Morris, his old man, was also, in his days of nature, vital and picturesque), Woody had read up on many subjects, subscribed to *Science* and other magazines that gave real information, and had taken night courses at De Paul and Northwestern in ecology, criminology, existentialism. Also he had traveled extensively in Japan, Mexico, and Africa, and there was an African experience that was especially relevant to mourning. It was this: on a launch near the Murchison Falls in Uganda, he had seen a buffalo calf seized by a crocodile from the bank of the White Nile. There were giraffes along the tropical river, and hippopotamuses, and baboons, and flamingos and other brilliant birds crossing the bright air in the heat of the morning, when the calf, stepping into the river to drink, was grabbed by the hoof and dragged down. The parent buffaloes couldn't figure it out. Under the water the calf still threshed, fought, churned the mud. Woody, the robust traveler, took this in as he sailed by, and to him it looked as if the parent cattle were asking each other dumbly what had happened. He chose to assume that there was pain in this, he read brute grief into it. On the White Nile, Woody had the impression that he had gone back to the pre-Adamite past, and he brought reflections on this impression home to South Chicago. He brought also a bundle of hashish from Kampala. In this he took a chance with the customs inspectors, banking perhaps on his broad build, frank face, high color. He didn't look like a wrongdoer, a bad guy; he looked like a good guy. But he liked taking chances. Risk was a wonderful stimulus. He threw down his trenchcoat on the customs counter. If the inspectors searched the pockets, he was prepared to say that the coat wasn't his. But he got away with it, and the Thanksgiving turkey was stuffed with hashish. This was much enjoyed. That was practically the last feast at which Pop, who also relished risk or defiance, was present. The hashish Woody had tried to raise in his backyard from the Africa seeds didn't take. But behind his warehouse, where the Lincoln Continental was parked, he kept a patch of marijuana. There was no harm at all in Woody, but he didn't like being entirely within the law. It was simply a question of self-respect.

After that Thanksgiving, Pop gradually sank as if he had a slow leak. This went on for some years. In and out of the hospital, he dwindled, his mind wandered, he couldn't even concentrate enough to complain, except in exceptional moments on the Sundays Woody regularly devoted to him. Morris, an amateur who once was taken seriously by Willie Hoppe, the great pro himself, couldn't execute the simplest billiard shots anymore. He could only conceive shots; he began to theorize about impossible three-cushion combinations. Halina, the Polish woman with whom Morris had lived for over forty years as man and wife, was too old herself now to run to the hospital. So Woody had to do it. There was Woody's mother, too—a Christian convert—needing care; she was over eighty and frequently hospitalized. Everybody had diabetes and pleurisy and arthritis and cataracts and cardiac pacemakers. And everybody had lived by the body, but the body was giving out.

There were Woody's two sisters as well, unmarried, in their fifties, very Christian, very straight, still living with Mama in an entirely Christian bungalow. Woody, who took full responsibility for them all, occasionally had to put one of the girls (they had become sick girls) in a mental institution. Nothing severe. The sisters were wonderful women, both of them gorgeous once, but neither of the poor things was playing with a full deck. And all the factions had to be kept separate—Mama, the Christian convert; the fundamentalist sisters; Pop, who read the Yiddish paper as long as he could still see print; Halina, a good Catholic. Woody, the seminary forty years behind him, described himself as an agnostic. Pop had no more religion than you could find in the Yiddish paper, but he made Woody promise to bury him among Jews, and that was where he lay now, in the Hawaiian shirt Woody had bought for him at the tilers' convention in Honolulu. Woody would allow no undertaker's assistant to dress him, but came to the parlor and buttoned the stiff into the shirt himself, and the old man went down looking like Ben-Gurion in a simple wooden coffin, sure to rot fast. That was how Woody wanted it all. At the graveside, he had taken off and folded his jacket, rolled up his sleeves on thick freckled biceps, waved back the little tractor standing by, and shoveled the dirt himself. His big face, broad at the bottom, narrowed upward like a Dutch house. And, his small good lower teeth taking hold of the upper lip in his exertion, he performed the final duty of a son. He was very fit, so it must have been emotion, not the shoveling, that made him redden so. After the funeral, he went home with Halina and her son, a decent Polack like his mother, and talented, too–Mitosh played the organ at hockey and basketball games in the Stadium, which took a smart man because it was a rabble-rousing kind of occupation–and they had some drinks and comforted the old girl. Halina was true blue, always one hundred percent for Morris.

Then for the rest of the week Woody was busy, had jobs to run, office responsibilities, family responsibilities. He lived alone; as did his wife; as did his mistress: everybody in a separate establishment. Since his wife, after fifteen years of separation, had not learned to take care of herself, Woody did her shopping on Fridays, filled her freezer. He had to take her this week to buy shoes. Also, Friday night he always spent with Helen–Helen was his wife de facto. Saturday he did his big weekly shopping. Saturday night he devoted to Mom and his sisters. So he was too busy to attend to his own feelings except, intermittently, to note to himself, "First Thursday in the grave." "First Friday, and fine weather." "First Saturday; he's got to be getting used to it." Under his breath he occasionally said, "Oh, Pop."

But it was Sunday that hit him, when the bells rang all over South Chicago–the Ukrainian, Roman Catholic, Greek, Russian, African Methodist churches, sounding off one after another. Woody had his offices in his warehouse, and there had built an apartment for himself, very spacious and convenient, in the top story. Because he left every Sunday morning at seven to spend the day with Pop, he had forgotten by how many churches Selbst Tile Company was surrounded. He was still in bed when he heard the bells, and all at once he knew how heartbroken he was. This sudden big heartache in a man of sixty, a practical, physical, healthy-minded, and experienced man, was deeply unpleasant. When he had an unpleasant condition, he believed in taking something for it. So he thought: What shall I take? There were plenty of remedies available. His cellar was stocked with cases of Scotch whisky, Polish vodka, Armagnac, Moselle, Burgundy. There were also freezers with steaks and with game and with Alaskan king crab. He bought with a broad hand—by the crate and by the dozen. But in the end, when he got out of bed, he took nothing but a cup of coffee. While the kettle was heating, he put on his Japanese judo-style suit and sat down to reflect.

Woody was moved when things were *honest*. Bearing beams were honest, undisguised concrete pillars inside high-rise apartments were honest. It was bad to cover up anything. He hated faking. Stone was honest. Metal was honest. These Sunday bells were very straight. They broke loose, they wagged and rocked, and the vibrations and the banging did something for him—cleansed his insides, purified his blood. A bell was a one-way throat, had only one thing to tell you and simply told it. He listened.

He had had some connections with bells and churches. He was after all something of a Christian. Born a Jew, he was a Jew facially, with a hint of Iroquois or Cherokee, but his mother had been converted more than fifty years ago by her brother-in-law, the Reverend Doctor Kovner. Kovner, a rabbinical student who had left the Hebrew Union College in Cincinnati to become a minister and establish a mission, had given Woody a partly Christian upbringing. Now, Pop was on the outs with these fundamentalists. He said that the Jews came to the mission to get coffee, bacon, canned pineapple, day-old bread, and dairy products. And if they had to listen to sermons, that was okay—this was the Depression and you couldn't be too particular—but he knew they sold the bacon.

The Gospels said it plainly: "Salvation is from the Jews."

Backing the Reverend Doctor were wealthy fundamentalists, mainly Swedes, eager to speed up the Second Coming by converting all Jews. The foremost of Kovner's backers was Mrs. Skoglund, who had inherited a large dairy business from her late husband. Woody was under her special protection.

Woody was fourteen years of age when Pop took off with Halina, who worked in his shop, leaving his difficult Christian wife and his converted son and his small daughters. He came to Woody in the backyard one spring day and said, "From now on you're the man of the house." Woody was practicing with a golf club, knocking off the heads of dandelions. Pop came into the yard in his good suit, which was too hot for the weather, and when he took off his fedora the skin of his head was marked with a deep ring and the sweat was sprinkled over his scalp—more drops than hairs. He said, "I'm going to move out." Pop was anxious, but he was set to go—determined. "It's no use. I can't live a life like this." Envisioning the life Pop simply *had* to live, his free life, Woody was able to picture him in the billiard parlor, under the El tracks in a crap game, or playing poker at Brown and Koppel's upstairs. "You're going to be the man of the house," said Pop. "It's okay. I put you all on welfare. I just got back from Wabansia Avenue, from the relief station." Hence the suit and the hat. "They're sending out a caseworker." Then he said, "You got to lend me money to buy gasoline—the caddie money you saved."

Understanding that Pop couldn't get away without his help, Woody turned over to him all he had earned at the Sunset Ridge Country Club in Winnetka. Pop felt that the valuable life lesson he was transmitting was worth far more than these dollars, and whenever he was conning his boy a sort of high-priest expression came down over his bent nose, his ruddy face. The children, who got their finest ideas at the movies, called him Richard Dix. Later, when the comic strip came out, they said he was Dick Tracy.

As Woody now saw it, under the tumbling bells, he had bankrolled his own desertion. Ha ha! He found this delightful; and especially Pop's attitude of "That'll teach you to trust your father." For this was a demonstration on behalf of real life and free instincts, against religion and hypocrisy. But mainly it was aimed against being a fool, the disgrace of foolishness. Pop had it in for the Reverend Doctor Kovner, not because he was an apostate (Pop couldn't have cared less), not because the mission was a racket (he admitted that the Reverend Doctor was personally honest), but because Doctor Kovner behaved foolishly, spoke like a fool, and acted like a fiddler. He tossed his hair like a Paganini (this was Woody's addition; Pop had never even heard of Paganini). Proof that he was not a spiritual leader was that he converted Jewish women by stealing their hearts. "He works up all those broads," said Pop. "He doesn't even know it himself, I swear he doesn't know how he gets them."

From the other side, Kovner often warned Woody, "Your father is a dangerous person. Of course, you love him; you should love him and forgive him, Voodrow, but you are old enough to understand he is leading a life of wice."

It was all petty stuff: Pop's sinning was on a boy level and therefore made a big impression on a boy. And on Mother. Are wives children, or what? Mother often said, "I hope you put that brute in your prayers. Look what he has done to us. But only pray for him, don't see him." But he saw him all the time. Woodrow was leading a double life, sacred and profane. He accepted Jesus Christ as his personal redeemer. Aunt Rebecca took advantage of this. She made him work. He had to work under Aunt Rebecca. He filled in for the janitor at the mission and settlement house. In winter, he had to feed the coal furnace, and on some nights he slept near the furnace room, on the pool table. He also picked the lock of the storeroom. He took canned pineapple and cut bacon from the flitch with his pocketknife. He crammed himself with uncooked bacon. He had a big frame to fill out.

Only now, sipping Melitta coffee, he asked himself: Had he been so hungry? No, he loved being reckless. He was fighting Aunt Rebecca Kovner when he took out his knife and got on a box to reach the bacon. She didn't know, she couldn't prove that Woody, such a frank, strong, positive boy, who looked you in the eye, so direct, was a thief also. But he was also a thief. Whenever she looked at him, he knew that she was seeing his father. In the curve of his nose, the movements of his eyes, the thickness of his body, in his healthy face, she saw that wicked savage Morris.

Morris, you see, had been a street boy in Liverpool—Woody's mother and her sister were British by birth. Morris's Polish family, on their way to America, abandoned him in Liverpool because he had an eye infection and they would all have been sent back from Ellis Island. They stopped awhile in England, but his eyes kept running and they ditched him. They slipped away, and he had to make out alone in Liverpool at the age of twelve. Mother came of better people. Pop, who slept in the cellar of her house, fell in love with her. At sixteen, scabbing during a seamen's strike, he shoveled his way across the Atlantic and jumped ship in Brooklyn. He became an American, and America never knew it. He voted without papers, he drove without a license, he paid no taxes, he cut every corner. Horses, cards, billiards, and women were his lifelong interests, in ascending order. Did he love anyone (he was so busy)? Yes, he loved Halina. He loved his son. To this day, Mother believed that he had loved her most and always wanted to come back. This gave her a chance to act the queen, with her plump wrists and faded Queen Victoria face. "The girls are instructed never to admit him," she said. The Empress of India speaking.

Bell-battered Woodrow's soul was whirling this Sunday morning, indoors and out, to the past, back to his upper corner of the warehouse, laid out with such originality—the bells coming and going, metal on naked metal, until the bell circle expanded over the whole of steel-making, oil-refining, power-producing mid-autumn South Chicago, and all its Croatians, Ukrainians, Greeks, Poles, and respectable blacks heading for their churches to hear Mass or to sing hymns.

Woody himself had been a good hymn singer. He still knew the hymns. He had testified, too. He was often sent by Aunt Rebecca to get up and tell a churchful of Scandihoovians that he, a Jewish lad, accepted Jesus Christ. For this she paid him fifty cents. She made the disbursement. She was the bookkeeper, fiscal chief, general manager of the mission. The Reverend Doctor didn't know a thing about the operation. What the Doctor supplied was the fervor. He was genuine, a wonderful preacher. And what about Woody himself? He also had fervor. He was drawn to the Reverend Doctor. The Reverend Doctor taught him to lift up his eyes, gave him his higher life. Apart from this higher life, the rest was Chicago—the ways of Chicago, which came so natural that nobody thought to question them. So, for instance, in 1933 (what ancient, ancient times!), at the Century of Progress World's Fair, when Woody was a coolie and pulled a rickshaw, wearing a peaked straw hat and trotting with powerful, thick legs, while the brawny red farmers—his boozing passengers—were laughing their heads off and pestered him for whores, he, although a freshman at the seminary, saw nothing wrong, when girls asked him to steer a little business their way, in making dates and accepting tips from both sides. He necked in Grant Park with a powerful girl who had to go home quickly to nurse her baby. Smelling of milk, she rode beside him on the streetcar to the West Side, squeezing his rickshaw puller's thigh and wetting her blouse. This was the Roosevelt Road car. Then, in the apartment where she lived with her mother, he couldn't remember that there were any husbands around. What he did remember was the strong milk odor. Without inconsistency, next morning he did New Testament Greek: The light shineth in darkness—*to fos en te skotia fainei*—and the darkness comprehended it not.

And all the while he trotted between the shafts on the fairgrounds he had one idea, nothing to do with these horny giants having a big time in the city: that the goal, the project, the purpose was (and he couldn't explain why he thought so; all evidence was against it)—God's idea was that this world should be a love world, that it should eventually recover and be entirely a world of love. He wouldn't have said this to a soul, for he could see himself how stupid it was—personal and stupid. Nevertheless, there it was at the center of his feelings. And at the same time, Aunt Rebecca was right when she said to him, strictly private, close to his ear even, "You're a little crook, like your father."

There was some evidence for this, or what stood for evidence to an impatient person like Rebecca. Woody matured quickly—he had to—but how could you expect a boy of seventeen, he wondered, to interpret the viewpoint, the feelings, of a middle-aged woman, and one whose breast had been removed? Morris told him that this happened only to neglected women, and was a sign. Morris said that if titties were not fondled and kissed, they got cancer in protest. It was a cry of the flesh. And this had seemed true to Woody. When his imagination tried the theory on the Reverend Doctor, it worked out—he couldn't see the Reverend Doctor behaving in that way to Aunt Rebecca's breasts! Morris's theory kept Woody looking from bosoms to husbands and from husbands to bosoms. He still did that. It's an exceptionally smart man who isn't marked forever by the sexual theories he hears from his father, and Woody wasn't all that smart. He knew this himself. Personally, he had gone far out of his way to do right by women in this regard. What nature demanded. He and Pop were common, thick men, but there's nobody too gross to have ideas of delicacy.

The Reverend Doctor preached, Rebecca preached, rich Mrs. Skoglund preached from Evanston, Mother preached. Pop also was on a soapbox. Everyone was doing it. Up and down Division Street, under every lamp, almost, speakers were giving out: anarchists, Socialists, Stalinists, single-taxers, Zionists, Tolstoyans, vegetarians, and fundamentalist Christian preachers—you name it. A beef, a hope, a way of life or salvation, a protest. How was it that the accumulated gripes of all the ages took off so when transplanted to America?

And that fine Swedish immigrant Aase (Osie, they pronounced it), who had been the Skoglunds' cook and married the eldest son, to become his rich, religious widow—she supported the Reverend Doctor. In her time she must have been built like a chorus girl. And women seem to have lost the secret of putting up their hair in the high basketry fence of braid she wore. Aase took Woody under her special protection and paid his tuition at the seminary. And Pop said . . . But on this Sunday, at peace as soon as the bells stopped banging, this velvet autumn day when the grass was finest and thickest, silky green: before the first frost, and the blood in your lungs is redder than summer air can make it and smarts with oxygen, as if the iron in your system was hungry for it, and the chill was sticking it to you in every breath . . . Pop, six feet under, would never feel this blissful sting again. The last of the bells still had the bright air streaming with vibrations.

On weekends, the institutional vacancy of decades came back to the warehouse and crept under the door of Woody's apartment. It felt as empty on Sundays as churches were during the week. Before each business day, before the trucks and the crews got started, Woody jogged five miles in his Adidas suit. Not on this day still reserved for Pop, however. Although it was tempting to go out and run off the grief. Being alone hit Woody hard this morning. He thought: Me and the world; the world and me. Meaning that there always was some activity to interpose, an errand or a visit, a picture to paint (he was a creative amateur), a massage, a meal—a shield between himself and that troublesome solitude which used the world as its reservoir. But Pop! Last Tuesday, Woody had gotten into the hospital bed with Pop because he kept pulling out the intravenous needles. Nurses stuck them back, and then Woody astonished them all by climbing into bed to hold the struggling old guy in his arms. "Easy, Morris, Morris, go easy." But Pop still groped feebly for the pipes.

When the tolling stopped, Woody didn't notice that a great lake of quiet had come over his kingdom, the Selbst Tile warehouse. What he heard and saw was an old red Chicago streetcar, one of those trams the color of a stockyard steer. Cars of this type went out before Pearl Harbor—clumsy, big-bellied, with tough rattan seats and brass grips for the standing passengers. Those cars used to make four stops to the mile, and ran with a wallowing motion. They stank of carbolic or ozone and throbbed when the air compressors were being charged. The conductor had his knotted signal cord to pull, and the motorman beat the foot gong with his mad heel.

Woody recognized himself on the Western Avenue line and riding through a blizzard with his father, both in sheepskins and with hands and faces raw, the snow blowing in from the rear platform when the doors opened and getting into the longitudinal cleats of the floor. There wasn't warmth enough inside to melt it. And Western Avenue was the longest car line in the world, the boosters said, as if it was a thing to brag about. Twenty-three miles long, made by a draftsman with a T square, lined with factories, storage buildings, machine shops, used-car lots, trolley barns, gas stations, funeral parlors, six-flats, utility buildings, and junkyards, on and on from the prairies on the south to Evanston on the north. Woodrow and his father were going north to Evanston, to Howard Street, and then some, to see Mrs. Skoglund. At the end of the line they would still have about five blocks to hike. The purpose of the trip? To raise money for Pop. Pop had talked him into this. When they found out, Mother and Aunt Rebecca would be furious, and Woody was afraid, but he couldn't help it.

Morris had come and said, "Son, I'm in trouble. It's bad."

"What's bad, Pop?"

"Halina took money from her husband for me and has to put it back before old Bujak misses it. He could kill her."

"What did she do it for?"

"Son, you know how the bookies collect? They send a goon. They'll break my head open."

"Pop! You know I can't take you to Mrs. Skoglund."

"Why not? You're my kid, aren't you? The old broad wants to adopt you, doesn't she? Shouldn't I get something out of it for my trouble? What am I—outside? And what about Halina? She puts her life on the line, but my own kid says no."

"Oh, Bujak wouldn't hurt her."

"Woody, he'd beat her to death."

Bujak? Uniform in color with his dark-gray work clothes, short in the legs, his whole strength in his tool-and-die-maker's forearms and black fingers; and beat-looking—there was Bujak for you. But, according to Pop, there was big, big violence in Bujak, a regular boiling Bessemer inside his narrow chest. Woody could never see the violence in him. Bujak wanted no trouble. If anything, maybe he was afraid that Morris and Halina would gang up on him and kill him, screaming. But Pop was no desperado murderer. And Halina was a calm, serious woman. Bujak kept his savings in the cellar (banks were going out of business). The worst they did was to take some of his money, intending to put it back. As Woody saw him, Bujak was trying to be sensible. He accepted his sorrow. He set minimum requirements for Halina: cook the meals, clean the house, show respect. But at stealing Bujak might have drawn the line, for money was different, money was vital substance. If they stole his savings he might have had to take action, out of respect for the substance, for himself—self-respect. But you couldn't be sure that Pop hadn't invented the bookie, the goon, the theft—the whole thing. He was capable of it, and you'd be a fool not to suspect him. Morris knew that Mother and Aunt Rebecca had told Mrs. Skoglund how wicked he was. They had painted him for her in poster colors—purple for vice, black for his soul, red for Hell flames: a gambler, smoker, drinker, deserter, screwer of women, and atheist. So Pop was determined to reach her. It was risky for everybody. The Reverend Doctor's operating costs were met by Skoglund Dairies. The widow paid Woody's seminary tuition; she bought dresses for the little sisters.

Woody, now sixty, fleshy and big, like a figure for the victory of American materialism, sunk in his lounge chair, the leather of its armrests softer to his fingertips than a woman's skin, was puzzled and, in his depths, disturbed by certain blots within him, blots of light in his brain, a blot combining pain and amusement in his breast (how did *that* get there?). Intense thought puckered the skin between his eyes with a strain bordering on headache. Why had he let Pop have his way? Why did he agree to meet him that day, in the dim rear of the poolroom?

"But what will you tell Mrs. Skoglund?"

"The old broad? Don't worry, there's plenty to tell her, and it's all true. Ain't I trying to save my little laundry-and-cleaning shop? Isn't the bailiff coming for the fixtures next week?" And Pop rehearsed his pitch on the Western Avenue car. He counted on Woody's health and his freshness. Such a straightforward-looking body was perfect for a con.

Did they still have such winter storms in Chicago as they used to have? Now they somehow seemed less fierce. Blizzards used to come straight down from Ontario, from the Arctic, and drop five feet of snow in an afternoon. Then the rusty green platform cars, with revolving brushes at both ends, came out of the barns to sweep the tracks. Ten or twelve streetcars followed in slow processions, or waited, block after block.

There was a long delay at the gates of Riverview Park, all the amusements covered for the winter, boarded up—the dragon's-back high-rides, the Bobs, the Chute, the Tilt-a-Whirl, all the fun machinery put together by mechanics and electricians, men like Bujak the tool-and-die-maker, good with engines. The blizzard was having it all its own way behind the gates, and you couldn't see far inside; only a few bulbs burned behind the palings. When Woody wiped the vapor from the glass, the wire mesh of the window guards was stuffed solid at eye level with snow. Looking higher, you saw mostly the streaked wind horizontally driving from the north. In the seat ahead, two black coal heavers, both in leather Lindbergh flying helmets, sat with shovels between their legs, returning from a job. They smelled of sweat, burlap sacking, and coal. Mostly dull with black dust, they also sparkled here and there.

There weren't many riders. People weren't leaving the house. This was a day to sit legs stuck out beside the stove, mummified by both the outdoor and the indoor forces. Only a fellow with an angle, like Pop, would go and buck such weather. A storm like this was out of the compass, and you kept the human scale by having a scheme to raise fifty bucks. Fifty soldiers! Real money in 1933.

"That woman is crazy for you," said Pop.

"She's just a good woman, sweet to all of us."

"Who knows what she's got in mind. You're a husky kid. Not such a kid, either."

"She's a religious woman. She really has religion."

"Well, your mother isn't your only parent. She and Rebecca and Kovner aren't going to fill you up with their ideas. I know your mother wants to wipe me out of your life. Unless I take a hand, you won't even understand what life is. Because they don't know—those silly Christers."

"Yes, Pop."

"The girls I can't help. They're too young. I'm sorry about them, but I can't do anything. With you it's different."

He wanted me like himself, an American.

They were stalled in the storm, while the cattle-colored car waited to have the trolley reset in the crazy wind, which boomed, tingled, blasted. At Howard Street they would have to walk straight into it, due north.

"You'll do the talking at first," said Pop.

Woody had the makings of a salesman, a pitchman. He was aware of this when he got to his feet in church to testify before fifty or sixty people. Even though Aunt Rebecca made it worth his while, he moved his own heart when he spoke up about his faith. But occasionally, without notice, his heart went away as he spoke religion and he couldn't find it anywhere. In its absence, sincere behavior got him through. He had to rely for delivery on his face, his voice—on behavior. Then his eyes came closer and closer together. And in this approach of eye to eye he felt the strain of hypocrisy. The twisting of his face threatened to betray him. It took everything he had to keep looking honest. So, since he couldn't bear the cynicism of it, he fell back on mischievousness. Mischief was where Pop came in. Pop passed straight through all those divided fields, gap after gap, and arrived at his side, bent-nosed and broad-faced. In regard to Pop, you thought of neither sincerity nor insincerity. Pop was like the man in the song: he wanted what he wanted when he wanted it. Pop was physical; Pop was digestive, circulatory, sexual. If Pop got serious, he talked to you about washing under the arms or in the crotch or of drying between your toes or of cooking supper, of baked beans and fried onions, of draw poker or of a certain horse in the fifth race at Arlington. Pop was elemental. That was why he gave such relief from religion and paradoxes, and things like that. Now, Mother *thought* she was spiritual, but Woody knew that she was kidding herself. Oh, yes, in the British accent she never gave up she was always talking to God or about Him—please God, God willing, praise God. But she was a big substantial bread-and-butter down-to-earth woman, with down-to-earth duties like feeding the girls, protecting, refining, keeping pure the girls. And those two protected doves grew up so overweight, heavy in the hips and thighs, that their poor heads looked long and slim. And mad. Sweet but cuckoo—Paula cheerfully cuckoo, Joanna depressed and having episodes.

"I'll do my best by you, but you have to promise, Pop, not to get me in Dutch with Mrs. Skoglund."

"You worried because I speak bad English? Embarrassed? I have a mockie accent?"

"It's not that. Kovner has a heavy accent, and she doesn't mind."

"Who the hell are those freaks to look down on me? You're practically a man and your dad has a right to expect help from you. He's in a fix. And you bring him to her house because she's bighearted, and you haven't got anybody else to go to."

"I got you, Pop."

The two coal trimmers stood up at Devon Avenue. One of them wore a woman's coat. Men wore women's clothing in those years, and women men's, when there was no choice. The fur collar was spiky with the wet, and sprinkled with soot. Heavy, they dragged their shovels and got off at the front. The slow car ground on, very slow. It was after four when they reached the end of the line, and somewhere between gray and black, with snow spouting and whirling under the street lamps. In Howard Street, autos were stalled at all angles and abandoned. The sidewalks were blocked. Woody led the way into Evanston, and Pop followed him up the middle of the street in the furrows made earlier by trucks. For four blocks they bucked the wind and then Woody broke through the drifts to the snowbound mansion, where they both had to push the wrought-iron gate because of the drift behind it. Twenty rooms or more in this dignified house and nobody in them but Mrs. Skoglund and her servant Hjordis, also religious.

As Woody and Pop waited, brushing the slush from their sheepskin collars and Pop wiping his big eyebrows with the ends of his scarf, sweating and freezing, the chains began to rattle and Hjordis uncovered the air holes of the glass storm door by turning a wooden bar. Woody called her "monk-faced." You no longer see women like that, who put no female touch on the face. She came plain, as God made her. She said, "Who is it and what do you want?"

"It's Woodrow Selbst. Hjordis? It's Woody."

"You're not expected."

"No, but we're here."

"What do you want?"

"We came to see Mrs. Skoglund."

"What for do you want to see her?"

"Just tell her we're here."

"I have to tell her what you came for, without calling up first."

"Why don't you say it's Woody with his father, and we wouldn't come in a snowstorm like this if it wasn't important."

The understandable caution of women who live alone. Respectable old-time women, too. There was no such respectability now in those Evanston houses, with their big verandas and deep yards and with a servant like Hjordis, who carried at her belt keys to the pantry and to every closet and every dresser drawer and every padlocked bin in the cellar. And in High Episcopal Christian Science Women's Temperance Evanston, no tradespeople rang at the front door. Only invited guests. And here, after a ten-mile grind through the blizzard, came two tramps from the West Side. To this mansion where a Swedish immigrant lady, herself once a cook and now a philanthropic widow, dreamed, snowbound, while frozen lilac twigs clapped at her storm windows, of a new Jerusalem and a Second Coming and a Resurrection and a Last Judgment. To hasten the Second Coming, and all the rest, you had to reach the hearts of these scheming bums arriving in a snowstorm.

Sure, they let us in.

Then in the heat that swam suddenly up to their mufflered chins Pop and Woody felt the blizzard for what it was; their cheeks were frozen slabs. They stood beat, itching, trickling in the front hall that *was* a hall, with a carved newel post staircase and a big stained-glass window at the top. Picturing Jesus with the Samaritan woman. There was a kind of Gentile closeness to the air. Perhaps when he was with Pop, Woody made more Jewish observations than he would otherwise. Although Pop's most Jewish characteristic was that Yiddish was the only language he could read a paper in. Pop was with Polish Halina, and Mother was with Jesus Christ, and Woody ate uncooked bacon from the flitch. Still, now and then he had a Jewish impression.

Mrs. Skoglund was the cleanest of women—her fingernails, her white neck, her ears—and Pop's sexual hints to Woody all went wrong because she was so intensely clean, and made Woody think of a waterfall, large as she was, and grandly built. Her bust was big. Woody's imagination had investigated this. He thought she kept things tied down tight, very tight. But she lifted both arms once to raise a window and there it was, her bust, beside him, the whole unbindable thing. Her hair was like the raffia you had to soak before you could weave with it in a basket class—pale, pale. Pop, as he took his sheepskin off, was in sweaters, no jacket. His darting looks made him seem crooked. Hardest of all for these Selbsts with their bent noses and big, apparently straightforward faces was to look honest. All the signs of dishonesty played over them. Woody had often puzzled about it.

Did it go back to the muscles, was it fundamentally a jaw problem—the projecting angles of the jaws? Or was it the angling that went on in the heart? The girls called Pop Dick Tracy, but Dick Tracy was a good guy. Whom could Pop convince? Here Woody caught a possibility as it flitted by. Precisely because of the way Pop looked, a sensitive person might feel remorse for condemning unfairly or judging unkindly. Just because of a face? Some must have bent over backward. Then he had them. Not Hjordis. She would have put Pop into the street then and there, storm or no storm. Hjordis was religious, but she was wised up, too. She hadn't come over in steerage and worked forty years in Chicago for nothing.

Mrs. Skoglund, Aase (Osie), led the visitors into the front room. This, the biggest room in the house, needed supplementary heating. Because of fifteen-foot ceilings and high windows, Hjordis had kept the parlor stove burning. It was one of those elegant parlor stoves that wore a nickel crown, or miter, and this miter, when you moved it aside, automatically raised the hinge of an iron stove lid. That stove lid underneath the crown was all soot and rust, the same as any other stove lid. Into this hole you tipped the scuttle and the anthracite chestnut rattled down. It made a cake or dome of fire visible through the small isinglass frames. It was a pretty room, three-quarters paneled in wood. The stove was plugged into the flue of the marble fireplace, and there were parquet floors and Axminster carpets and cranberry-colored tufted Victorian upholstery, and a kind of Chinese étagère, inside a cabinet, lined with mirrors and containing silver pitchers, trophies won by Skoglund cows, fancy sugar tongs and cut-glass pitchers and goblets. There were Bibles and pictures of Jesus and the Holy Land and that faint Gentile odor, as if things had been rinsed in a weak vinegar solution.

"Mrs. Skoglund, I brought my dad to you. I don't think you ever met him," said Woody.

"Yes, Missus, that's me, Selbst."

Pop stood short but masterful in the sweaters, and his belly sticking out, not soft but hard. He was a man of the hard-bellied type. Nobody intimidated Pop. He never presented himself as a beggar. There wasn't a cringe in him anywhere. He let her see at once by the way he said "Missus" that he was independent and that he knew his way around. He communicated that he was able to handle himself with women. Handsome Mrs. Skoglund, carrying a basket woven out of her own hair, was in her fifties—eight, maybe ten years his senior.

"I asked my son to bring me because I know you do the kid a lot of good. It's natural you should know both of his parents."

"Mrs. Skoglund, my dad is in a tight corner and I don't know anybody else to ask for help."

This was all the preliminary Pop wanted. He took over and told the widow his story about the laundry-and-cleaning business and payments overdue, and explained about the fixtures and the attachment notice, and the bailiff's office and what they were going to do to him; and he said, "I'm a small man trying to make a living."

"You don't support your children," said Mrs. Skoglund.

"That's right," said Hjordis.

"I haven't got it. If I had it, wouldn't I give it? There's bread lines and soup lines all over town. Is it just me? What I have I divvy with. I give the kids. A bad father? You think my son would bring me if I was a bad father into your house? He loves his dad, he trusts his dad, he knows his dad is a good dad. Every time I start a little business going I get wiped out. This one is a good little business, if I could hold on to that little business. Three people work for me, I meet a payroll, and three people will be on the street, too, if I close down. Missus, I can sign a note and pay you in two months. I'm a common man, but I'm a hard worker and a fellow you can trust."

Woody was startled when Pop used the word "trust." It was as if from all four corners a Sousa band blew a blast to warn the entire world: "Crook! This is a crook!" But Mrs. Skoglund, on account of her religious preoccupations, was remote. She heard nothing. Although everybody in this part of the world, unless he was crazy, led a practical life, and you'd have nothing to say to anyone, your neighbors would have nothing to say to you, if communications were not of a practical sort, Mrs. Skoglund, with all her money, was unworldly—two-thirds out of this world.

"Give me a chance to show what's in me," said Pop, "and you'll see what I do for my kids."

So Mrs. Skoglund hesitated, and then she said she'd have to go upstairs, she'd have to go to her room and pray on it and ask for guidance—would they sit down and wait. There were two rocking chairs by the stove. Hjordis gave Pop a grim look (a dangerous person) and Woody a blaming one (he brought a dangerous stranger and disrupter to injure two kind Christian ladies). Then she went out with Mrs. Skoglund.

As soon as they left, Pop jumped up from the rocker and said in anger, "What's this with the praying? She has to ask God to lend me fifty bucks?"

Woody said, "It's not you, Pop, it's the way these religious people do."

"No," said Pop. "She'll come back and say that God wouldn't let her."

Woody didn't like that; he thought Pop was being gross and he said, "No, she's sincere. Pop, try to understand: she's emotional, nervous, and sincere, and tries to do right by everybody."

And Pop said, "That servant will talk her out of it. She's a toughie. It's all over her face that we're a couple of chiselers."

"What's the use of us arguing," said Woody. He drew the rocker closer to the stove. His shoes were wet through and would never dry. The blue flames fluttered like a school of fishes in the coal fire. But Pop went over to the Chinese-style cabinet or étagère and tried the handle, and then opened the blade of his penknife and in a second had forced the lock of the curved glass door. He took out a silver dish.

"Pop, what is this?" said Woody.

Pop, cool and level, knew exactly what this was. He relocked the étagère, crossed the carpet, listened. He stuffed the dish under his belt and pushed it down into his trousers. He put the side of his short thick finger to his mouth.

So Woody kept his voice down, but he was all shook up. He went to Pop and took him by the edge of his hand. As he looked into Pop's face, he felt his eyes growing smaller and smaller, as if something were contracting all the skin on his head. They call it hyperventilation when everything feels tight and light and close and dizzy. Hardly breathing, he said, "Put it back, Pop."

Pop said, "It's solid silver; it's worth dough."

"Pop, you said you wouldn't get me in Dutch."

"It's only insurance in case she comes back from praying and tells me no. If she says yes, I'll put it back."

"How?"

"It'll get back. If I don't put it back, you will."

"You picked the lock. I couldn't. I don't know how."

"There's nothing to it."

"We're going to put it back now. Give it here."

"Woody, it's under my fly, inside my underpants. Don't make such a noise about nothing."

"Pop, I can't believe this."

"For cry-ninety-nine, shut your mouth. If I didn't trust you I wouldn't have let you watch me do it. You don't understand a thing. What's with you?"

"Before they come down, Pop, will you dig that dish out of your long johns."

Pop turned stiff on him. He became absolutely military. He said, "Look, I order you!"

Before he knew it, Woody had jumped his father and begun to wrestle with him. It was outrageous to clutch your own father, to put a heel behind him, to force him to the wall. Pop was taken by surprise and said loudly, "You want Halina killed? Kill her! Go on, you be responsible." He began to resist, angry, and they turned about several times, when Woody, with a trick he had learned in a Western movie and used once on the playground, tripped him and they fell to the ground. Woody, who already outweighed the old man by twenty pounds, was on top. They landed on the floor beside the stove, which stood on a tray of decorated tin to protect the carpet. In this position, pressing Pop's hard belly, Woody recognized that to have wrestled him to the floor counted for nothing. It was impossible to thrust his hand under Pop's belt to recover the dish. And now Pop had turned furious, as a father has every right to be when his son is violent with him, and he freed his hand and hit Woody in the face. He hit him three or four times in midface. Then Woody dug his head into Pop's shoulder and held tight only to keep from being struck and began to say in his ear, "Jesus, Pop, for Christ sake remember where you are. Those women will be back!" But Pop brought up his short knee and fought and butted him with his chin and rattled Woody's teeth. Woody thought the old man was about to bite him. And because he was a seminarian, he thought: Like an unclean spirit. And held tight. Gradually Pop stopped threshing and struggling. His eyes stuck out and his mouth was open, sullen. Like a stout fish. Woody released him and gave him a hand up. He was then overcome with many many bad feelings of a sort he knew the old man never suffered. Never, never. Pop never had these groveling emotions. There was his whole superiority. Pop had no such feelings. He was like a horseman from Central Asia, a bandit from China. It was Mother, from Liverpool, who had the refinement, the English manners. It was the preaching Reverend Doctor in his black suit. You have refinements, and all they do is oppress you? The hell with that.

The long door opened and Mrs. Skoglund stepped in, saying, "Did I imagine, or did something shake the house?"

"I was lifting the scuttle to put coal on the fire and it fell out of my hand. I'm sorry I was so clumsy," said Woody.

Pop was too huffy to speak. With his eyes big and sore and the thin hair down over his forehead, you could see by the tightness of his belly how angrily he was fetching his breath, though his mouth was shut.

"I prayed," said Mrs. Skoglund.

"I hope it came out well," said Woody.

"Well, I don't do anything without guidance, but the answer was yes, and I feel right about it now. So if you'll wait, I'll go to my office and write a check. I asked Hjordis to bring you a cup of coffee. Coming in such a storm."

And Pop, consistently a terrible little man, as soon as she shut the door, said, "A check? Hell with a check. Get me the greenbacks."

"They don't keep money in the house. You can cash it in her bank tomorrow. But if they miss that dish, Pop, they'll stop the check, and then where are you?"

As Pop was reaching below the belt, Hjordis brought in the tray. She was very sharp with him. She said, "Is this a place to adjust clothing, Mister? A men's washroom?"

"Well, which way is the toilet, then?" said Pop.

She had served the coffee in the seamiest mugs in the pantry, and she bumped down the tray and led Pop down the corridor, standing guard at the bathroom door so that he shouldn't wander about the house.

Mrs. Skoglund called Woody to her office and after she had given him the folded check said that they should pray together for Morris. So once more he was on his knees, under rows and rows of musty marbled-cardboard files, by the glass lamp by the edge of the desk, the shade with flounced edges, like the candy dish. Mrs. Skoglund, in her Scandinavian accent—an emotional contralto—raising her voice to Jesus-uh Christ-uh, as the wind lashed the trees, kicked the side of the house, and drove the snow seething on the windowpanes, to send light-uh, give guidance-uh, put a new heart-uh in Pop's bosom. Woody asked God only to make Pop put the dish back. He kept Mrs. Skoglund on her knees as long as possible. Then he thanked her, shining with candor (as much as he knew how), for her Christian generosity and he said, "I know that Hjordis has a cousin who works at the Evanston YMCA. Could she please phone him and try to get us a room tonight so that we don't have to fight the blizzard all the way back? We're almost as close to the Y as to the car line. Maybe the cars have even stopped running."

Suspicious Hjordis, coming when Mrs. Skoglund called to her, was burning now. First they barged in, made themselves at home, asked for money, had to have coffee, probably left gonorrhea on the toilet seat. Hjordis, Woody remembered, was a woman who wiped the doorknobs with rubbing alcohol after guests had left. Nevertheless, she telephoned the Y and got them a room with two cots for six bits.

Pop had plenty of time, therefore, to reopen the étagère, lined with reflecting glass or German silver (something exquisitely delicate and tricky), and as soon as the two Selbsts had said thank you and goodbye and were in midstreet again up to the knees in snow, Woody said, "Well, I covered for you. Is that thing back?"

"Of course it is," said Pop.

They fought their way to the small Y building, shut up in wire grille and resembling a police station—about the same dimensions. It was locked, but they made a racket on the grille, and a small black man let them in and shuffled them upstairs to a cement corridor with low doors. It was like the small-mammal house in Lincoln Park. He said there was nothing to eat, so they took off their wet pants, wrapped themselves tightly in the khaki army blankets, and passed out on their cots.

First thing in the morning, they went to the Evanston National Bank and got the fifty dollars. Not without difficulties. The teller went to call Mrs. Skoglund and was absent a long time from the wicket. "Where the hell has he gone?" said Pop.

But when the fellow came back, he said, "How do you want it?"

Pop said, "Singles." He told Woody, "Bujak stashes it in one-dollar bills."

But by now Woody no longer believed Halina had stolen the old man's money.

Then they went into the street, where the snow-removal crews were at work. The sun shone broad, broad, out of the morning blue, and all Chicago would be releasing itself from the temporary beauty of those vast drifts.

"You shouldn't have jumped me last night, Sonny."

"I know, Pop, but you promised you wouldn't get me in Dutch."

"Well, it's okay. We can forget it, seeing you stood by me."

Only, Pop had taken the silver dish. Of course he had, and in a few days Mrs. Skoglund and Hjordis knew it, and later in the week they were all waiting for Woody in Kovner's office at the settlement house. The group included the Reverend Doctor Crabbie, head of the seminary, and Woody, who had been flying along, level and smooth, was shot down in flames. He told them he was innocent. Even as he was falling, he warned that they were wronging him. He denied that he or Pop had touched Mrs. Skoglund's property. The missing object–he didn't even know what it was–had probably been misplaced, and they would be very sorry on the day it turned up. After the others were done with him, Dr. Crabbie said that until he was able to tell the truth he would be suspended from the seminary, where his work had been unsatisfactory anyway. Aunt Rebecca took him aside and said to him, "You are a little crook, like your father. The door is closed to you here."

To this Pop's comment was "So what, kid?"

"Pop, you shouldn't have done it."

"No? Well, I don't give a care, if you want to know. You can have the dish if you want to go back and square yourself with all those hypocrites."

"I didn't like doing Mrs. Skoglund in the eye, she was so kind to us."

"Kind?"

"Kind."

"Kind has a price tag."

Well, there was no winning such arguments with Pop. But they debated it in various moods and from various elevations and perspectives for forty years and more, as their intimacy changed, developed, matured.

"Why did you do it, Pop? For the money? What did you do with the fifty bucks?" Woody, decades later, asked him that.

"I settled with the bookie, and the rest I put in the business."

"You tried a few more horses."

"I maybe did. But it was a double, Woody. I didn't hurt myself, and at the same time did you a favor."

"It was for me?"

"It was too strange of a life. That life wasn't *you*, Woody. All those women. . . Kovner was no man, he was an in between. Suppose they made you a minister? Some Christian minister! First of all, you wouldn't have been able to stand it, and second, they would throw you out sooner or later."

"Maybe so."

"And you wouldn't have converted the Jews, which was the main thing they wanted."

"And what a time to bother the Jews," Woody said. "At least *I* didn't bug them."

Pop had carried him back to his side of the line, blood of his blood, the same thick body walls, the same coarse grain. Not cut out for a spiritual life. Simply not up to it.

Pop was no worse than Woody, and Woody was no better than Pop. Pop wanted no relation to theory, and yet he was always pointing Woody toward a position—a jolly, hearty, natural, likable, unprincipled position. If Woody had a weakness, it was to be unselfish. This worked to Pop's advantage, but he criticized Woody for it, nevertheless. "You take too much on yourself," Pop was always saying. And it's true that Woody gave Pop his heart because Pop was so selfish. It's usually the selfish people who are loved the most. They do what you deny yourself, and you love them for it. You give them your heart.

Remembering the pawn ticket for the silver dish, Woody startled himself with a laugh so sudden that it made him cough. Pop said to him after his expulsion from the seminary and banishment from the settlement house, "You want in again? Here's the ticket. I hocked that thing. It wasn't so valuable as I thought."

"What did they give?"

"Twelve-fifty was all I could get. But if you want it you'll have to raise the dough yourself, because I haven't got it anymore."

"You must have been sweating in the bank when the teller went to call Mrs. Skoglund about the check."

"I was a little nervous," said Pop. "But I didn't think they could miss the thing so soon."

That theft was part of Pop's war with Mother. With Mother, and Aunt Rebecca, and the Reverend Doctor. Pop took his stand on realism. Mother represented the forces of religion and hypochondria. In four decades, the fighting never stopped. In the course of time, Mother and the girls turned into welfare personalities and lost their individual outlines. Ah, the poor things, they became dependents and cranks. In the meantime, Woody, the sinful man, was their dutiful and loving son and brother. He maintained the bungalow—this took in roofing, pointing, wiring, insulation, air-conditioning—and he paid for heat and light and food, and dressed them all out of Sears, Roebuck and Wieboldt's, and bought them a TV, which they watched as devoutly as they prayed. Paula took courses to learn skills like macramé-making and needlepoint, and sometimes got a little job as recreational worker in a nursing home. But she wasn't steady enough to keep it. Wicked Pop spent most of his life removing stains from people's clothing. He and Halina in the last years ran a Cleanomat in West Rogers Park—a so-so business resembling a laundromat—which gave him leisure for billiards, the horses, rummy and pinochle. Every morning he went behind the partition to check out the filters of the cleaning equipment. He found amusing things that had been thrown into the vats with the clothing–sometimes, when he got lucky, a locket chain or a brooch. And when he had fortified the cleaning fluid, pouring all that blue and pink stuff in from plastic jugs, he read the *Forward* over a second cup of coffee, and went out, leaving Halina in charge. When they needed help with the rent, Woody gave it.

After the new Disney World was opened in Florida, Woody treated all his dependents to a holiday. He sent them down in separate batches, of course. Halina enjoyed this more than anybody else. She couldn't stop talking about the address given by an Abraham Lincoln automaton. "Wonderful, how he stood up and moved his hands, and his mouth. So real! And how beautiful he talked." Of them all, Halina was the soundest, the most human, the most honest. Now that Pop was gone, Woody and Halina's son, Mitosh, the organist at the Stadium, took care of her needs over and above Social Security, splitting expenses. In Pop's opinion, insurance was a racket. He left Halina nothing but some out-of-date equipment.

Woody treated himself, too. Once a year, and sometimes oftener, he left his business to run itself, arranged with the trust department at the bank to take care of his gang, and went off. He did that in style, imaginatively, expensively. In Japan, he wasted little time on Tokyo. He spent three weeks in Kyoto and stayed at the Tawaraya Inn, dating from the seventeenth century or so. There he slept on the floor, the Japanese way, and bathed in scalding water. He saw the dirtiest strip show on earth, as well as the holy places and the temple gardens. He visited also Istanbul, Jerusalem, Delphi, and went to Burma and Uganda and Kenya on safari, on democratic terms with drivers, Bedouins, bazaar merchants. Open, lavish, familiar, fleshier and fleshier but (he jogged, he lifted weights) still muscular–in his naked person beginning to resemble a Renaissance courtier in full costume–becoming ruddier every year, an outdoor type with freckles on his back and spots across the flaming forehead and the honest nose. In Addis Ababa he took an Ethiopian beauty to his room from the street and washed her, getting into the shower with her to soap her with his broad, kindly hands. In Kenya he taught certain American obscenities to a black woman so that she could shout them out during the act. On the Nile, below Murchison Falls, those fever trees rose huge from the mud, and hippos on the sandbars belched at the passing launch, hostile. One of them danced on his spit of sand, springing from the ground and coming down heavy, on all fours. There, Woody saw the buffalo calf disappear, snatched by the crocodile.

Mother, soon to follow Pop, was being lightheaded these days. In company, she spoke of Woody as her boy–"What do you think of my Sonny?"–as though he was ten years old. She was silly with him, her behavior was frivolous, almost flirtatious. She just didn't seem to know the facts. And behind her all the others, like kids at the playground, were waiting their turn to go down the slide: one on each step, and moving toward the top.

Over Woody's residence and place of business there had gathered a pool of silence of the same perimeter as the church bells while they were ringing, and he mourned under it, this melancholy morning of sun and autumn. Doing a life survey, taking a deliberate look at the gross side of his case—of the other side as well, what there was of it. But if this heartache continued, he'd go out and run it off. A three-mile jog—five, if necessary. And you'd think that this jogging was an entirely physical activity, wouldn't you? But there was something else in it. Because, when he was a seminarian, between the shafts of his World's Fair rickshaw, he used to receive, pulling along (capable and stable), his religious experiences while he trotted. Maybe it was all a single experience repeated. He felt truth coming to him from the sun. He received a communication that was also light and warmth. It made him very remote from his horny Wisconsin passengers, those farmers whose whoops and whore cries he could hardly hear when he was in one of his states. And again out of the flaming of the sun would come to him a secret certainty that the goal set for this earth was that it should be filled with good, saturated with it. After everything preposterous, after dog had eaten dog, after the crocodile death had pulled everyone into his mud. It wouldn't conclude as Mrs. Skoglund, bribing him to round up the Jews and hasten the Second Coming, imagined it, but in another way. This was his clumsy intuition. It went no further. Subsequently, he proceeded through life as life seemed to want him to do it.

There remained one thing more this morning, which was explicitly physical, occurring first as a sensation in his arms and against his breast and, from the pressure, passing into him and going into his breast.

It was like this: When he came into the hospital room and saw Pop with the sides of his bed raised, like a crib, and Pop, so very feeble, and writhing, and toothless, like a baby, and the dirt already cast into his face, into the wrinkles—Pop wanted to pluck out the intravenous needles and he was piping his weak death noise. The gauze patches taped over the needles were soiled with dark blood. Then Woody took off his shoes, lowered the side of the bed, and climbed in and held him in his arms to soothe and still him. As if he were Pop's father, he said to him, "Now, Pop. Pop." Then it was like the wrestle in Mrs. Skoglund's parlor, when Pop turned angry like an unclean spirit and Woody tried to appease him, and warn him, saying, "Those women will be back!" Beside the coal stove, when Pop hit Woody in the teeth with his head and then became sullen, like a stout fish. But this struggle in the hospital was weak—so weak! In his great pity, Woody held Pop, who was fluttering and shivering. From those people, Pop had told him, you'll never find out what life is, because they don't know what it is. Yes, Pop—well, what is it, Pop? Hard to comprehend that Pop, who was dug in for eighty-three years and had done all he could to stay, should now want nothing but to free himself. How could Woody allow the old man to pull the intravenous needles out? Willful Pop, he wanted what he wanted when he wanted it. But what he wanted at the very last Woody failed to follow, it was such a switch.

After a time, Pop's resistance ended. He subsided and subsided. He rested against his son, his small body curled there. Nurses came and looked. They disapproved, but Woody, who couldn't spare a hand to wave them out, motioned with his head toward the door. Pop, whom Woody thought he had stilled, only had found a better way to get around him. Loss of heat was the way he did it. His heat was leaving him. As can happen with small animals while you hold them in your hand, Woody presently felt him cooling. Then, as Woody did his best to restrain him, and thought he was succeeding, Pop divided himself. And when he was separated from his warmth, he slipped into death. And there was his elderly, large, muscular son, still holding and pressing him when there was nothing anymore to press. You could never pin down that self-willed man. When he was ready to make his move, he made it—always on his own terms. And always, always, something up his sleeve. That was how he was.

SHIRLEY JACKSON

[1919–1965]

The Lottery

(First published in the *New Yorker*, June, 1948; first book publication in 1949.)

THE MORNING OF June 27th was clear and sunny, with the fresh warmth of a full-summer day; the flowers were blossoming profusely and the grass was richly green. The people of the village began to gather in the square, between the post office and the bank, around ten o'clock; in some towns there were so many people that the lottery took two days and had to be started on June 26th, but in this village, where there were only about three hundred people, the whole lottery took less than two hours, so it could begin at ten o'clock in the morning and still be through in time to allow the villagers to get home for noon dinner.

The children assembled first, of course. School was recently over for the summer, and the feeling of liberty sat uneasily on most of them; they tended to gather quietly for a while before they broke into boisterous play, and their talk was still of the classroom and the teacher, of books and reprimands. Bobby Martin had already stuffed his pockets full of stones, and the other boys soon followed his example, selecting the smoothest and roundest stones; Bobby and Harry Jones and Dickie Delacroix—the villagers pronounced this name "Dellacroy"—eventually made a great pile of stones in one corner of the square and guarded it against the raids of the other boys. The girls stood aside, talking among themselves, looking over their shoulders at the boys, and the very small children rolled in the dust or clung to the hands of their older brothers or sisters.

Soon the men began to gather surveying their own children, speaking of planting and rain, tractors and taxes. They stood together, away from the pile of stones in the corner, and their jokes were quiet and they smiled rather than laughed. The women, wearing faded house dresses and sweaters, came shortly after their menfolk. They greeted one another and exchanged bits of gossip as they went to join their husbands. Soon the women, standing by their husbands, began to call to their children, and the children came reluctantly, having to be called four or five times. Bobby Martin ducked under his mother's grasping hand and ran, laughing, back to the pile of stones. His father spoke up sharply, and Bobby came quickly and took his place between his father and his oldest brother.

The lottery was conducted—as were the square dances, the teen-age club, the Halloween program—by Mr. Summers, who had time and energy to devote to civic activities. He was a round-faced, jovial man and he ran the coal business, and people were sorry for him, because he had no children and his wife was a scold. When he arrived in the square, carrying the black wooden box, there was a murmur of conversation among the villagers, and he waved and called, "Little late today, folks." The postmaster, Mr. Graves, followed him, carrying a three-legged stool, and the stool was put in the center of the square and Mr. Summers set the black box down on it. The villagers kept their distance, leaving a space between themselves and the stool, and when Mr. Summers said, "Some of you fellows want to give me a hand?" there was a hesitation before two men, Mr. Martin and his oldest son, Baxter, came forward to hold the box steady on the stool while Mr. Summers stirred up the papers inside it.

The original paraphernalia for the lottery had been lost long ago, and the black box now resting on the stool had been put into use even before Old Man Warner, the oldest man in town, was born. Mr. Summers spoke frequently to the villagers about making a new box, but no one liked to upset even as much tradition as was represented by the black box. There was a story that the present box had been made with some pieces of the box that had preceded it, the one that had been constructed when the first people settled down to make a village here. Every year, after the lottery, Mr. Summers began talking again about a new box, but every year the subject was allowed to fade off without anything's being done. The black box grew shabbier each year; by now it was no longer completely black but splintered badly along one side to show the original wood color, and in some places faded or stained.

Mr. Martin and his oldest son, Baxter, held the black box securely on the stool until Mr. Summers had stirred the papers thoroughly with his hand. Because so much of the ritual had been forgotten or discarded, Mr. Summers had been successful in having slips of paper substituted for the chips of wood that had been used for generations. Chips of wood, Mr. Summers had argued, had been all very well when the village was tiny, but now that the population was more than three hundred and likely to keep on growing, it was necessary to use something that would fit more easily into the black box. The night before the lottery, Mr. Summers and Mr. Graves made up the slips of paper and put them in the box, and it was then taken to the safe of Mr. Summers' coal company and locked up until Mr. Summers was ready to take it to the square next morning. The rest of the year, the box was put away, sometimes one place, sometimes another; it had spent one year in Mr. Graves's barn and another year underfoot in the post office, and sometimes it was set on a shelf in the Martin grocery and left there.

There was a great deal of fussing to be done before Mr. Summers declared the lottery open. There were the lists to make up—of heads of families, heads of households in each family, members of each household in each family. There was the proper swearing-in of Mr. Summers by the postmaster, as the official of the lottery; at one time, some people remembered, there had been a recital of some sort, performed by the official of the lottery, a perfunctory, tuneless chant that had been rattled off duly each year; some people believed that the official of the lottery used to stand just so when he said or sang it, others believed that he was supposed to walk among the people, but years and years ago this part of the ritual had been allowed to lapse. There had been, also, a ritual salute, which the official of the lottery had had to use in addressing each person who came up to draw from the box, but this also had changed with time, until now it was felt necessary only for the official to speak to each person approaching. Mr. Summers was very good at all this; in his clean white shirt and blue jeans, with one hand resting carelessly on the black box, he seemed very proper and important as he talked interminably to Mr. Graves and the Martins.

Just as Mr. Summers finally left off talking and turned to the assembled villagers, Mrs. Hutchinson came hurriedly along the path to the square, her sweater thrown over her shoulders, and slid into place in the back of the crowd. "Clean forgot what day it was," she said to Mrs. Delacroix, who stood next to her, and they both laughed softly. "Thought my old man was out back stacking wood," Mrs. Hutchinson went on, "and then I looked out the window and the kids was gone, and then I remembered it was the twenty-seventh and came a-running." She dried her hands on her apron, and Mrs. Delacroix said, "You're in time, though. They're still talking away up there."

Mrs. Hutchinson craned her neck to see through the crowd and found her husband and children standing near the front. She tapped Mrs. Delacroix on the arm as a farewell and began to make her way through the crowd. The people separated good-humoredly to let her through; two or three people said, in voices just loud enough to be heard across the crowd, "Here comes your Missus, Hutchinson," and "Bill, she made it after all." Mrs. Hutchinson reached her husband, and Mr. Summers, who had been waiting, said cheerfully, "Thought we were going to have to get on without you, Tessie." Mrs. Hutchinson said, grinning, "Wouldn't have me leave m'dishes in the sink, now, would you, Joe?," and soft laughter ran through the crowd as the people stirred back into position after Mrs. Hutchinson's arrival.

"Well, now," Mr. Summers said soberly, "guess we better get started, get this over with, so's we can go back to work. Anybody ain't here?"

"Dunbar," several people said. "Dunbar, Dunbar."

Mr. Summers consulted his list. "Clyde Dunbar," he said. "That's right. He's broke his leg, hasn't he? Who's drawing for him?"

"Me, I guess," a woman said, and Mr. Summers turned to look at her. "Wife draws for her husband," Mr. Summers said. "Don't you have a grown boy to do it for you, Janey?" Although Mr. Summers and everyone else in the village knew the answer perfectly well, it was the business of the official of the lottery to ask such questions formally. Mr. Summers waited with an expression of polite interest while Mrs. Dunbar answered.

"Horace's not but sixteen yet," Mrs. Dunbar said regretfully. "Guess I gotta fill in for the old man this year."

"Right," Mr. Summers said. He made a note on the list he was holding. Then he asked, "Watson boy drawing this year?"

A tall boy in the crowd raised his hand. "Here," he said. "I'm drawing for m'mother and me." He blinked his eyes nervously and ducked his head as several voices in the crowd said things like "Good fellow, Jack," and "Glad to see your mother's got a man to do it."

"Well," Mr. Summers said, "guess that's everyone. Old Man Warner make it?"

"Here," a voice said, and Mr. Summers nodded.

A sudden hush fell on the crowd as Mr. Summers cleared his throat and looked at the list. "All ready?" he called. "Now, I'll read the names—heads of families first—and the men come up and take a paper out of the box. Keep the paper folded in your hand without looking at it until everyone has had a turn. Everything clear?"

The people had done it so many times that they only half listened to the directions; most of them were quiet, wetting their lips, not looking around. Then Mr. Summers raised one hand high and said, "Adams." A man disengaged himself from the crowd and came forward. "Hi, Steve," Mr. Summers said, and Mr. Adams said, "Hi, Joe." They grinned at one another humorlessly and nervously. Then Mr. Adams reached into the black box and took out a folded paper. He held it firmly by one corner as he turned and went hastily back to his place in the crowd, where he stood a little apart from his family, not looking down at his hand.

"Allen," Mr. Summers said. "Anderson . . . Bentham."

"Seems like there's no time at all between lotteries any more," Mrs. Delacroix said to Mrs. Graves in the back row. "Seems like we got through with the last one only last week."

"Time sure goes fast," Mrs. Graves said.

"Clark . . . Delacroix."

"There goes my old man," Mrs. Delacroix said. She held her breath while her husband went forward.

"Dunbar," Mr. Summers said, and Mrs. Dunbar went steadily to the box while one of the women said, "Go on, Janey," and another said, "There she goes."

"We're next," Mrs. Graves said. She watched while Mr. Graves came around from the side of the box, greeted Mr. Summers gravely, and selected a slip of paper from the box. By now, all through the crowd there were men holding the small folded papers in their large hands, turning them over and over nervously. Mrs. Dunbar and her two sons stood together, Mrs. Dunbar holding the slip of paper.

"Harburt . . . Hutchinson."

"Get up there, Bill," Mrs. Hutchinson said, and the people near her laughed.

"Jones."

"They do say," Mr. Adams said to Old Man Warner, who stood next to him, "that over in the north village they're talking of giving up the lottery."

Old Man Warner snorted. "Pack of crazy fools," he said. "Listening to the young folks, nothing's good enough for *them*. Next thing you know, they'll be wanting to go back to living in caves, nobody work any more, live *that* way for a while. Used to be a saying about 'Lottery in June, corn be heavy soon.' First thing you know, we'd all be eating stewed chickweed and acorns. There's *always* been a lottery," he added petulantly. "Bad enough to see young Joe Summers up there joking with everybody."

"Some places have already quit lotteries," Mrs. Adams said.

"Nothing but trouble in *that*," Old Man Warner said stoutly. "Pack of young fools."

"Martin." And Bobby Martin watched his father go forward. "Overdyke . . . Percy."

"I wish they'd hurry," Mrs. Dunbar said to her older son. "I wish they'd hurry."

"They're almost through," her son said.

"You get ready to run tell Dad," Mrs. Dunbar said.

Mr. Summers called his own name and then stepped forward precisely and selected a slip from the box. Then he called, "Warner."

"Seventy-seventh year I been in the lottery," Old Man Warner said as he went through the crowd. "Seventy-seventh time."

"Watson." The tall boy came awkwardly through the crowd. Someone said, "Don't be nervous, Jack," and Mr. Summers said, "Take your time, son."

"Zanini."

After that, there was a long pause, a breathless pause, until Mr. Summers, holding his slip of paper in the air, said, "All right, fellows." For a minute, no one moved, and then all the slips of paper were opened. Suddenly, all the women began to speak at once, saying, "Who is it?" "Who's got it?" "Is it the Dunbars?" "Is it the Watsons?" Then the voices began to say, "It's Hutchinson. It's Bill." "Bill Hutchinson's got it."

"Go tell your father," Mrs. Dunbar said to her older son.

People began to look around to see the Hutchinsons. Bill Hutchinson was standing quiet, staring down at the paper in his hand. Suddenly, Tessie Hutchinson shouted to Mr. Summers, "You didn't give him time enough to take any paper he wanted. I saw you. It wasn't fair!"

"Be a good sport, Tessie," Mrs. Delacroix called, and Mrs. Graves said, "All of us took the same chance."

"Shut up, Tessie," Bill Hutchinson said.

"Well, everyone," Mr. Summers said, "that was done pretty fast, and now we've got to be hurrying a little more to get done in time." He consulted his next list. "Bill," he said, "you draw for the Hutchinson family. You got any other households in the Hutchinsons?"

"There's Don and Eva," Mrs. Hutchinson yelled. "Make *them* take their chance!"

"Daughters draw with their husbands' families, Tessie," Mr. Summers said gently. "You know that as well as anyone else."

"It wasn't *fair*," Tessie said.

"I guess not, Joe," Bill Hutchinson said regretfully. "My daughter draws with her husband's family, that's only fair. And I've got no other family except the kids."

"Then, as far as drawing for families is concerned, it's you," Mr. Summers said in explanation, "and as far as drawing for households is concerned, that's you, too. Right?"

"Right," Bill Hutchinson said.

"How many kids, Bill?" Mr. Summers asked formally.

"Three," Bill Hutchinson said. "There's Bill, Jr., and Nancy, and little Dave. And Tessie and me."

"All right, then," Mr. Summers said. "Harry, you got their tickets back?"

Mr. Graves nodded and held up the slips of paper. "Put them in the box, then," Mr. Summers directed. "Take Bill's and put it in."

"I think we ought to start over," Mrs. Hutchinson said, as quietly as she could. "I tell you it wasn't *fair*. You didn't give him time enough to choose. *Every*body saw that."

Mr. Graves had selected the five slips and put them in the box, and he dropped all the papers but those onto the ground, where the breeze caught them and lifted them off.

"Listen, everybody," Mrs. Hutchinson was saying to the people around her.

"Ready, Bill?" Mr. Summers asked, and Bill Hutchinson, with one quick glance around at his wife and children, nodded.

"Remember," Mr. Summers said, "take the slips and keep them folded until each person has taken one. Harry, you help little Dave." Mr. Graves took the hand of the little boy, who came willingly with him up to the box. "Take a paper out of the box, Davy," Mr. Summers said. Davy put his hand into the box and laughed. "Take just *one* paper," Mr. Summers said. "Harry, you hold it for him." Mr. Graves took the child's hand and removed the folded paper from the tight fist and held it while little Dave stood next to him and looked up at him wonderingly.

"Nancy next," Mr. Summers said. Nancy was twelve, and her school friends breathed heavily as she went forward, switching her skirt, and took a slip daintily from the box. "Bill, Jr.," Mr. Summers said, and Billy, his face red and his feet overlarge, nearly knocked the box over as he got a paper out. "Tessie," Mr. Summers said. She hesitated for a minute, looking around defiantly, and then set her lips and went up to the box. She snatched a paper out and held it behind her.

"Bill," Mr. Summers said, and Bill Hutchinson reached into the box and felt around, bringing his hand out at last with the slip of paper in it.

The crowd was quiet. A girl whispered, "I hope it's not Nancy," and the sound of the whisper reached the edges of the crowd.

"It's not the, way it used to be," Old Man Warner said clearly. "People ain't the way they used to be."

"All right," Mr. Summers said. "Open the papers. Harry, you open little Dave's."

Mr. Graves opened the slip of paper and there was a general sigh through the crowd as he held it up and everyone could see that it was blank. Nancy and Bill, Jr., opened theirs at the same time, and both beamed and laughed, turning around to the crowd and holding their slips of paper above their heads.

"Tessie," Mr. Summers said. There was a pause, and then Mr. Summers looked at Bill Hutchinson, and Bill unfolded his paper and showed it. It was blank.

"It's Tessie," Mr. Summers said, and his voice was hushed. "Show us her paper, Bill."

Bill Hutchinson went over to his wife and forced the slip of paper out of her hand. It had a black spot on it, the black spot Mr. Summers had made the night before with the heavy pencil in the coal-company office. Bill Hutchinson held it up, and there was a stir in the crowd.

"All right, folks," Mr. Summers said. "Let's finish quickly."

Although the villagers had forgotten the ritual and lost the original black box, they still remembered to use stones. The pile of stones the boys had made earlier was ready; there were stones on the ground with the blowing scraps of paper that had come out of the box. Mrs. Delacroix selected a stone so large she had to pick it up with both hands and turned to Mrs. Dunbar. "Come on," she said. "Hurry up."

Mrs. Dunbar had small stones in both hands, and she said, gasping for breath, "I can't run at all. You'll have to go ahead and I'll catch up with you."

The children had stones already, and someone gave little Davy Hutchinson a few pebbles.

Tessie Hutchinson was in the center of a cleared space by now, and she held her hands out desperately as the villagers moved in on her. "It isn't fair," she said. A stone hit her on the side of the head.

Old Man Warner was saying, "Come on, come on, everyone." Steve Adams was in the front of the crowd of villagers, with Mrs. Graves beside him.

"It isn't fair, it isn't right," Mrs. Hutchinson screamed, and then they were upon her.

RAY BRADBURY

[1920–]

There Will Come Soft Rains

(First published in *Collier's*,
May, 1950; first book publication in 1950.)

IN THE LIVING room the voice-clock sang, *Tick-tock, seven o'clock, time to get up, time to get up, seven o'clock*! as if it were afraid that nobody would. The morning house lay empty. The clock ticked on, repeating and repeating its sounds into the emptiness. *Seven-nine, breakfast time, seven-nine!*

In the kitchen the breakfast stove gave a hissing sigh and ejected from its warm interior eight pieces of perfectly browned toast, eight eggs sunnyside up, sixteen slices of bacon, two coffees, and two cool glasses of milk.

"Today is August 4, 2026," said a second voice from the kitchen ceiling, "in the city of Allendale, California." It repeated the date three times for memory's sake. "Today is Mr. Featherstone's birthday. Today is the anniversary of Tilita's marriage. Insurance is payable, as are the water, gas, and light bills."

Somewhere in the walls, relays clicked, memory tapes glided under electric eyes.

Eight-one, tick-tock, eight-one o'clock, off to school, off to work, run, run, eight-one! But no doors slammed, no carpets took the soft tread of rubber heels. It was raining outside. The weather box on the front door sang quietly: "Rain, rain, go away; rubbers, raincoats for today . . ." And the rain tapped on the empty house, echoing.

Outside, the garage chimed and lifted its door to reveal the waiting car. After a long wait the door swung down again.

At eight-thirty the eggs were shriveled and the toast was like stone. An aluminum wedge scraped them into the sink, where hot water whirled them down a metal throat which digested and flushed them away to the distant sea. The dirty dishes were dropped into a hot washer and emerged twinkling dry.

Nine-fifteen, sang the clock, *time to clean.*

Out of warrens in the wall, tiny robot mice darted. The rooms were acrawl with the small cleaning animals, all rubber and metal. They thudded against chairs, whirling their mustached runners, kneading the rug nap, sucking gently at hidden dust. Then, like mysterious invaders, they popped into their burrows. Their pink electric eyes faded. The house was clean.

Ten o'clock. The sun came out from behind the rain. The house stood alone in a city of rubble and ashes. This was the one house left standing. At night the ruined city gave off a radioactive glow which could be seen for miles.

Ten-fifteen. The garden sprinklers whirled up in golden founts, filling the soft morning air with scatterings of brightness. The water pelted windowpanes running down the charred west side where the house had been burned evenly free of its white paint. The entire west face of the house was black, save for five places. Here the silhouette in paint of a man mowing a lawn. Here, as in a photograph, a woman bent to pick flowers. Still farther over, their images burned on wood in one titanic instant, a small boy, hands flung into the air; higher up, the image of a thrown ball, and opposite him a girl, hands raised to catch a ball which never came down.

The five spots of paint—the man, the woman, the children, the ball—remained. The rest was a thin charcoaled layer.

The gentle sprinkler rain filled the garden with falling light.

Until this day, how well the house had kept its peace. How carefully it had inquired, "Who goes there? What's the password?" and, getting no answer from lonely foxes and whining cats, it had shut up its windows and drawn shades in an old-maidenly preoccupation with self-protection which bordered on a mechanical paranoia.

It quivered at each sound, the house did. If a sparrow brushed a window, the shade snapped up. The bird, startled, flew off! No, not even a bird must touch the house!

The house was an altar with ten thousand attendants, big, small, servicing, attending, in choirs. But the gods had gone away, and the ritual of the religion continued senselessly, uselessly.

Twelve noon.

A dog whined, shivering, on the front porch.

The front door recognized the dog voice and opened. The dog, once huge and fleshy, but now gone to bone and covered with sores, moved in and through the house, tracking mud. Behind it whirred angry mice, angry at having to pick up mud, angry at inconvenience.

For not a leaf fragment blew under the door but what the wall panels flipped open and the copper scrap rats flashed swiftly out. The offending dust, hair, or paper, seized in miniature steel jaws, was raced back to the burrows. There, down tubes which fed into the cellar, it was dropped into the sighing vent of an incinerator which sat like evil Baal in a dark corner.

The dog ran upstairs, hysterically yelping to each door, at last realizing, as the house realized, that only silence was here.

It sniffed the air and scratched the kitchen door. Behind the door, the stove was making pancakes which filled the house with a rich baked odor and the scent of maple syrup.

The dog frothed at the mouth, lying at the door, sniffing, its eyes turned to fire. It ran wildly in circles, biting at its tail, spun in a frenzy, and died. It lay in the parlor for an hour.

Two o'clock, sang a voice.

Delicately sensing decay at last, the regiments of mice hummed out as softly as blown gray leaves in an electrical wind.

Two-fifteen.

The dog was gone.

In the cellar, the incinerator glowed suddenly and a whirl of sparks leaped up the chimney.

Two thirty-five.

Bridge tables sprouted from patio walls. Playing cards fluttered onto pads in a shower of pips. Martinis manifested on an oaken bench with egg-salad sandwiches. Music played.

But the tables were silent and the cards untouched.

At four o'clock the tables folded like great butterflies back through the paneled walls.

Four-thirty.

The nursery walls glowed.

Animals took shape: yellow giraffes, blue lions, pink antelopes, lilac panthers cavorting in crystal substance. The walls were glass. They looked out upon color and fantasy. Hidden films clocked through well-oiled sprockets, and the walls lived. The nursery floor was woven to resemble a crisp, cereal meadow. Over this ran aluminum roaches and iron crickets, and in the hot still air butterflies of delicate red tissue wavered among the sharp aroma of animal spoors! There was the sound like a great matted yellow hive of bees within a dark bellows, the lazy bumble of a purring lion. And there was the patter of okapi feet and the murmur of a fresh jungle rain, like other hoofs, falling upon the summer-starched grass. Now the walls dissolved into distances of parched weed, mile on mile, and warm endless sky. The animals drew away into thorn brakes and water holes.

It was the children's hour.

Five o'clock. The bath filled with clear hot water.

Six, seven, eight o'clock. The dinner dishes manipulated like magic tricks, and in the study a *click*. In the metal stand opposite the hearth where a fire now blazed up warmly, a cigar popped out, half an inch of salt gray ash on it, smoking, waiting.

Nine o'clock. The beds warmed their hidden circuits, for nights were cool here.

Nine-five. A voice spoke from the study ceiling:

"Mrs. McClellan, which poem would you like this evening?"

The house was silent.

The voice said at last, "Since you express no preference, I shall select a poem at random." Quiet music rose to back the voice. "Sara Teasdale. As I recall, your favorite. . . .

"There will come soft rains and the smell of the ground,
And swallows circling with their shimmering sound;

And frogs in the pools singing at night,
And wild plum-trees in tremulous white;

Robins will wear their feathery fire
Whistling their whims on a low fence-wire;

And not one will know of the war, not one
Will care at last when it is done.

Not one would mind, either bird nor tree
If mankind perished utterly;

And Spring herself, when she woke at dawn,
Would scarcely know that we were gone."

The fire burned on the stone hearth and the cigar fell away into a mound of quiet ash on its tray. The empty chairs faced each other between the silent walls, and the music played.

At ten o'clock the house began to die.

The wind blew. A falling tree bough crashed through the kitchen window. Cleaning solvent, bottled, shattered over the stove. The room was ablaze in an instant!

"Fire!" screamed a voice. The house lights flashed, water pumps shot water from the ceilings. But the solvent spread on the linoleum, licking, eating under the kitchen door, while the voices took it up in chorus: "Fire, fire, fire!"

The house tried to save itself. Doors sprang tightly shut, but the windows were broken by the heat and the wind blew and sucked upon the fire.

The house gave ground as the fire in ten billion angry sparks moved with flaming ease from room to room and then up the stairs. While scurrying water rats squeaked from the walls, pistoled their water, and ran for more. And the wall sprays let down showers of mechanical rain.

But too late. Somewhere, sighing, a pump shrugged to a stop. The quenching rain ceased. The reserve water supply which had filled baths and washed dishes for many quiet days was gone.

The fire crackled up the stairs. It fed upon Picassos and Matisses in the upper halls, like delicacies, baking off the oily flesh, tenderly crisping the canvases into black shavings.

Now the fire lay in beds, stood in windows, changed the colors of drapes!

And then, reinforcements.

From attic trapdoors, blind robot faces peered down with faucet mouths gushing green chemical.

The fire backed off, as even an elephant must at the sight of a dead snake. Now there were twenty snakes whipping over the floor, killing the fire with a clear cold venom of green froth.

But the fire was clever. It had sent flame outside the house, up through the attic to the pumps there. An explosion! The attic brain which directed the pumps was shattered into bronze shrapnel on the beams.

The fire rushed back into every closet and felt of the clothes hung there.

The house shuddered, oak bone on bone, its bared skeleton cringing from the heat, its wire, its nerves revealed as if a surgeon had torn the skin off to let the red veins and capillaries quiver in the scalded air. Help, help! Fire! Run, run! Heat snapped mirrors like the first brittle winter ice. And the voices wailed Fire, fire, run, run, like a tragic nursery rhyme, a dozen voices, high, low, like children dying in a forest, alone, alone. And the voices fading as the wires popped their sheathings like hot chestnuts. One, two, three, four, five voices died.

In the nursery the jungle burned. Blue lions roared, purple giraffes bounded off. The panthers ran in circles, changing color, and ten million animals, running before the fire, vanished off toward a distant steaming river. . . .

Ten more voices died. In the last instant under the fire avalanche, other choruses, oblivious, could be heard announcing the time, playing music, cutting the lawn by remote-control mower, or setting an umbrella frantically out and in the slamming and opening front door, a thousand things happening, like a clock shop when each clock strikes the hour insanely before or after the other, a scene of maniac confusion, yet unity; singing, screaming, a few last cleaning mice darting bravely out to carry the horrid ashes away! And one voice, with sublime disregard for the situation, read poetry aloud in the fiery study, until all the film spools burned, until all the wires withered and the circuits cracked.

The fire burst the house and let it slam flat down, puffing out skirts of spark and smoke.

In the kitchen, an instant before the rain of fire and timber, the stove could be seen making breakfasts at a psychopathic rate, ten dozen eggs, six loaves of toast, twenty dozen bacon strips, which, eaten by fire, started the stove working again, hysterically hissing!

The crash. The attic smashing into kitchen and parlor. The parlor into cellar, cellar into sub-cellar. Deep freeze, armchair, film tapes, circuits, beds, and all like skeletons thrown in a cluttered mound deep under.

Smoke and silence. A great quantity of smoke.

Dawn showed faintly in the east. Among the ruins, one wall stood alone. Within the wall, a last voice said, over and over again and again, even as the sun rose to shine upon the heaped rubble and steam:

"Today is August 5, 2026, today is August 5, 2026, today is . . ."

KURT VONNEGUT, JR.

[1922–]

Welcome to the Monkey House

(First published in *Playboy*, 1967; first book publication in 1967.)

So Pete Crocker, the sheriff of Barnstable County, which was the whole of Cape Cod, came into the Federal Ethical Suicide Parlor in Hyannis one May afternoon—and she told the two six-foot Hostesses there that they weren't to be alarmed, but that a notorious nothinghead named Billy the Poet was believed headed for the Cape.

A nothinghead was a person who refused to take his ethical birth-control pills three times a day. The penalty for that was $10,000 and ten years in jail.

This was at a time when the population on Earth was 17 billion human beings. That was far too many mammals that big for a planet that small. The people were virtually packed together like drupelets.

Drupelets are the pulpy little knobs that compose the outside of a raspberry.

So the World Government was making a two-pronged attack on overpopulation. One pronging was the encouragement of ethical suicide, which consisted of going to the nearest Suicide Parlor and asking a Hostess to kill you painlessly while you lay on a Barcalounger. The other pronging was compulsory ethical birth control.

The sheriff told the Hostesses, who were pretty, tough-minded, highly intelligent girls, that roadblocks were being set up and house-to-house searches were being conducted to catch Billy the Poet. The main difficulty was that the police didn't know what he looked like. The few people who had seen him and known him for what he was were women—and they disagreed fantastically as to his height, his hair color, his voice, his weight, the color of his skin.

"I don't need to remind you girls," the sheriff went on, "that a nothinghead is very sensitive from the waist down. If Billy the Poet somehow slips in here and starts making trouble, one good kick in the right place will do wonders."

He was referring to the fact that ethical birth-control pills, the only legal form of birth control, made people numb from the waist down.

Most men said their bottom halves felt like cold iron or balsawood. Most women said their bottom halves felt like wet cotton or stale ginger ale. The pills were so effective that you could blindfold a man who had taken one, tell him to recite the Gettysburg Address, kick him in the balls while he was doing it, and he wouldn't miss a syllable.

The pills were ethical because they didn't interfere with a person's ability to reproduce, which would have been unnatural and immoral. All the pills did was take every bit of pleasure out of sex.

Thus did science and morals go hand in hand.

The two Hostesses there in Hyannis were Nancy McLuhan and Mary Kraft. Nancy was a strawberry blonde. Mary was a glossy brunette. Their uniforms were white lipstick, heavy eye makeup, purple body stockings with nothing underneath, and black-leather boots. They ran a small operation—with only six suicide booths. In a really good week, say the one before Christmas, they might put sixty people to sleep. It was done with a hypodermic syringe.

"My main message to you girls," said Sheriff Crocker, "is that everything's well under control. You can just go about your business here."

"Didn't you leave out part of your main message?" Nancy asked him.

"I don't get you."

"I didn't hear you say he was probably headed straight for us."

He shrugged in clumsy innocence. "We don't know that for sure."

"I thought that was all anybody *did* know about Billy the Poet: that he specializes in deflowering Hostesses in Ethical Suicide Parlors." Nancy was a virgin. All Hostesses were virgins. They also had to hold advanced degrees in psychology and nursing. They also had to be plump and rosy, and at least six feet tall.

America had changed in many ways, but it had yet to adopt the metric system.

Nancy McLuhan was burned up that the sheriff would try to protect her and Mary from the full truth about Bill the Poet—as though they might panic if they heard it. She told the sheriff so.

"How long do you think a girl would last in the E. S. S.," she said, meaning the Ethical Suicide Service, "if she scared that easy?"

The sheriff took a step backward, pulled in his chin. "Not very long, I guess."

"That's very true," said Nancy, closing the distance between them and offering him a sniff of the edge of her hand, which was poised for a karate chop. All Hostesses were experts at judo and karate. "If you'd like to find out how helpless we are, just come toward me, pretending you're Billy the Poet."

The sheriff shook his head, gave her a glassy smile. "I'd rather not."

"That's the smartest thing you've said today," said Nancy, turning her back on him while Mary laughed. "We're not scared—we're *angry*. Or we're not even *that*. He isn't *worth* that. We're bored. How boring that he should come a great distance, should cause all this fuss, in order to—" She let the sentence die there. "It's just too absurd."

"I'm not as mad at *him* as I am at the women who let him do it to them without a struggle"—said Mary—"who let him do it and then couldn't tell the police what he looked like. Suicide Hostesses at that!"

"Somebody hasn't been keeping up with her karate," said Nancy.

It wasn't just Billy the Poet who was attracted to Hostesses in Ethical Suicide Parlors. All nothingheads were. Bombed out of their skulls with the sex madness that came from taking nothing, they thought the white lips and big eyes and body stocking and boots of a Hostess spelled *sex, sex, sex.*

The truth was, of course, that sex was the last thing any Hostess ever had in mind.

"If Billy follows his usual M. O.," said the sheriff, "he'll study your habits and the neighborhood. And then he'll pick one or the other of you and he'll send her a dirty poem in the mail."

"Charming," said Nancy.

"He has also been known to use the telephone."

"How brave," said Nancy. Over the sheriff's shoulder, she could see the mailman coming.

A blue light went on over the door of a booth for which Nancy was responsible. The person in there wanted something. It was the only booth in use at the time.

The sheriff asked her if there was a possibility that the person in there was Billy the Poet, and Nancy said, "Well, if it is, I can break his neck with my thumb and forefinger."

"Foxy Grandpa," said Mary, who'd seen him, too. A Foxy Grandpa was any old man, cute and senile, who quibbled and joked and reminisced for hours before he let a Hostess put him to sleep.

Nancy groaned. "We've spent the past two hours trying to decide on a last meal."

And then the mailman came in with just one letter. It was addressed to Nancy in smeary pencil. She was splendid with anger and disgust as she opened it, knowing it would be a piece of filth from Billy.

She was right. Inside the envelope was a poem. It wasn't an original poem. It was a song from olden days that had taken on new meanings since the numbness of ethical birth control had become universal. It went like this, in smeary pencil again:-

> *We were walking through the park,*
> A-goosing statues in the dark.
> If Sherman's horse can take it,
> So can you.

When Nancy came into the suicide booth to see what he wanted, the Foxy Grandpa was lying on the mint-green Barcalounger, where hundreds had died so peacefully over the years. He was studying the menu from the Howard Johnson's next door and beating time to the Muzak coming from the loudspeaker on the lemon-yellow wall. The room was painted cinder block. There was one barred window with a Venetian blind.

There was a Howard Johnson's next door to every Ethical Suicide Parlor, and vice versa. The Howard Johnson's had an orange roof and the Suicide Parlor had a purple roof, but they were both the Government. Practically everything was the Government.

Practically everything was automated, too. Nancy and Mary and the sheriff were lucky to have jobs. Most people didn't. The average citizen moped around home and watched television, which was the Government. Every fifteen minutes his television would urge him to vote intelligently or consume intelligently, or worship in the church of his choice, or love his fellowmen, or obey the laws—or pay a call to the nearest Ethical Suicide Parlor and find out how friendly and understanding a Hostess could be.

The Foxy Grandpa was something of a rarity, since he was marked by old age, was bald, was shaky, had spots on his hands. Most people looked twenty-two, thanks to antiaging shots they took twice a year. That the old man looked old was proof that the shots had been discovered after his sweet bird of youth had flown.

"Have we decided on a last supper yet?" Nancy asked him. She heard peevishness in her own voice, heard herself betray her exasperation with Billy the Poet, her boredom with the old man. She was ashamed, for this was unprofessional of her. "The breaded veal cutlet is very good."

The old man cocked his head. With the greedy cunning of second childhood, he had caught her being unprofessional, unkind, and he was going to punish her for it. "You don't sound very friendly. I thought you were all supposed to be friendly. I thought this was supposed to be a pleasant place to come."

"I beg your pardon," she said. "If I seem unfriendly, it has nothing to do with you."

"I thought maybe I bored you."

"No, no," she said gamely, "not at all. You certainly know some very interesting history." Among other things, the Foxy Grandpa claimed to have known J. Edgar Nation, the Grand Rapids druggist who was the father of ethical birth control.

"Then *look* like you're interested," he told her. He could get away with that sort of impudence. The thing was, he could leave any time he wanted to, right up to the moment he asked for the needle—and he had to *ask* for the needle. That was the law.

Nancy's art, and the art of every Hostess, was to see that volunteers didn't leave, to coax and wheedle and flatter them patiently, every step of the way.

So Nancy had to sit down there in the booth, to pretend to marvel at the freshness of the yarn the old man told, a story everybody knew, about how J. Edgar Nation happened to experiment with ethical birth control.

"He didn't have the slightest idea his pills would be taken by human beings someday," said the Foxy Grandpa. "His dream was to introduce morality into the monkey house at the Grand Rapids Zoo. Did you realize that?" he inquired severely.

"No. No, I didn't. That's very interesting."

"He and his eleven kids went to church one Easter. And the day was so nice and the Easter service had been so beautiful and pure that they decided to take a walk through the zoo, and they were just walking on clouds."

"Um." The scene described was lifted from a play that was performed on television every Easter.

The Foxy Grandpa shoehorned himself into the scene, had himself chat with the Nations just before they got to the monkey house. "'Good morning, Mr. Nation,' I said to him. 'It certainly is a nice morning.' 'And a good morning to *you*, Mr. Howard,' he said to me. 'There is nothing like an Easter morning to make a man feel clean and reborn and at one with God's intentions.'"

"Um." Nancy could hear the telephone ringing faintly, naggingly, through the nearly soundproof door.

"So we went on to the monkey house together, and what do you think we saw?"

"I can't imagine." Somebody had answered the phone.

"We saw a monkey playing with his private parts!"

"No!"

"Yes! And J. Edgar Nation was so upset he went straight home and he started developing a pill that would make monkeys in the springtime fit things for a Christian family to see."

There was a knock on the door.

"Yes—?" said Nancy.

"Nancy," said Mary, "telephone for you."

When Nancy came out of the booth, she found the sheriff choking on little squeals of law-enforcement delight. The telephone was tapped by agents hidden in the Howard Johnson's. Billy the Poet was believed to be on the line. His call had been traced. Police were already on their way to grab him.

"Keep him on, keep him on," the sheriff whispered to Nancy, and he gave her the telephone as though it were solid gold.

"Yes–?" said Nancy.

"Nancy McLuhan?" said a man. His voice was disguised. He might have been speaking through a kazoo. "I'm calling for a mutual friend."

"Oh?"

"He asked me to deliver a message."

"I see."

"It's a poem."

"All right."

"Ready?"

"Ready." Nancy could hear sirens screaming in the background of the call.

The caller must have heard the sirens, too, but he recited the poem without any emotion. It went like this:

"Soak yourself, in Jergen's Lotion.
Here comes the one-man population
explosion."

They got him. Nancy heard it all—the thumping and clumping, the argle-bargle and cries.

The depression she felt as she hung up was glandular. Her brave body had prepared for a fight that was not to be.

The sheriff bounded out of the Suicide Parlor, in such a hurry to see the famous criminal he'd helped catch that a sheaf of papers fell from the pocket of his trench coat.

Mary picked them up, called after the sheriff. He halted for a moment, said the papers didn't matter any more, asked her if maybe she wouldn't like to come along. There was a flurry between the two girls, with Nancy persuading Mary to go, declaring that she had no curiosity about Billy. So Mary left, irrelevantly handing the sheaf to Nancy.

The sheaf proved to be photocopies of poems Billy had sent to Hostesses in other places. Nancy read the top one. It made much of a peculiar side effect of ethical birth-control pills: They not only made people numb—they also made people piss blue. The poem was called *What the Somethinghead Said to the Suicide Hostess*, and it went like this:

I did not sow, I did not spin,
And thanks to pills I did not sin.
I loved the crowds, the stink, the noise.
And when I peed, I peed turquoise.

I ate beneath a roof of orange;
Swung with progress like a door hinge.
'Neath purple roof I've come today
To piss my azure life away.

Virgin hostess, death's recruiter,
Life is cute, but you are cuter.
Mourn my pecker, purple daughter–
All it passed was sky-blue water.

"You never heard that story before–about how J. Edgar Nation came to invent ethical birth control?" the Foxy Grandpa wanted to know. His voice cracked.

"Never did," lied Nancy.

"I thought everybody knew that."

"It was news to me."

"When he got through with the monkey house, you couldn't tell it from the Michigan Supreme Court. Meanwhile, there was this crisis going on in the United Nations. The people who understood science said people had to quit reproducing so much, and the people who understood morals said society would collapse if people used sex for nothing but pleasure."

The Foxy Grandpa got off his Barcalounger, went over to the window, pried two slats of the blind apart. There wasn't much to see out there. The view was blocked by the backside of a mocked-up thermometer twenty feet high, which faced the street. It was calibrated in billions of people on Earth, from zero to twenty. The make-believe column of liquid was a strip of translucent red plastic. It showed how many people there were on Earth. Very close to the bottom was a black arrow that showed what the scientists thought the population ought to be.

The Foxy Grandpa was looking at the setting sun through that red plastic, and through the blind, too, so that his face was banded with shadows and red

"Tell me–" he said, "when I die, how much will that thermometer go down? A foot?"

"No."

"An inch?"

"Not quite."

"You know what the answer is, don't you?" he said, and he faced her. The senility had vanished from his voice and eyes. "One inch on that thing equals 83,333 people. You knew that, didn't you?"

"That–that might be true," said Nancy, "but that isn't the right way to look at it, in my opinion."

He didn't ask her what the right way was, in her opinion. He completed a thought of his own, instead. "I'll tell you something else that's true: I'm Billy the Poet, and you're a very good-looking woman."

With one hand, he drew a snub-nosed revolver from his belt. With the other, he peeled off his bald dome and wrinkled forehead, which proved to be rubber. Now he looked twenty-two.

"The police will want to know exactly what I look like when this is all over," he told Nancy with a malicious grin. "In case you're not good at describing people, and it's surprising how many women aren't:

I'm five foot two,
With eyes of blue,
With Brown hair to my shoulders–
A manly elf
So full of self
The ladies say he smolders."

Billy was ten inches shorter than Nancy was. She had about forty pounds on him. She told him he didn't have a chance, but Nancy was much mistaken. He had unbolted the bars on the window the night before and he made her go out the window and then down a manhole that was hidden from the street by the big thermometer.

He took her down into the sewers of Hyannis. He knew where he was going. He had a flashlight and a map. Nancy had to go before him along the narrow catwalk, her own shadow dancing mockingly in the lead. She tried to guess where they were, relative to the real world above. She guessed correctly when they passed under the Howard Johnson's, guessed from noises she heard. The machinery that processed and served the food there was silent. But, so people wouldn't feel too lonesome when eating there, the designers had provided sound effects for the kitchen. It was these Nancy heard–a tape recording of the clashing of silverware and the laughter of Negroes and Puerto Ricans.

After that she was lost. Billy had very little to say to her other than "Right," or, "Left," or "Don't try anything funny, Juno, or I'll blow your great big fucking head off."

Only once did they have anything resembling a conversation. Billy began it, and ended it, too. "What in hell is a girl with hips like yours doing selling death?" he asked her from behind.

She dared to stop. "I can answer that," she told him. She was confident that she could give him an answer that would shrivel him like napalm.

But he gave her a shove, offered to blow her fucking head off again.

"You don't even want to hear my answer," she taunted him. "You're afraid to hear it."

"I never listen to a woman till the pills wear off," sneered Billy. That was his plan, then–to keep her a prisoner for at least eight hours. That was how long it took for the pills to wear off.

"That's a silly rule."

"A woman's not a woman till the pills wear off."

"You certainly manage to make a woman feel like an object rather than a person."

"Thank the pills for that," said Billy.

There were 80 miles of sewers under Greater Hyannis, which had a population of 400,000 drupelets, 400,000 souls. Nancy lost track of the time down there. When Billy announced that they had at last reached their destination, it was possible for Nancy to imagine that a year had passed.

She tested this spooky impression by pinching her own thigh, by feeling what the chemical clock of her body said. Her thigh was still numb.

Billy ordered her to climb iron rungs that were set in wet masonry. There was a circle of sickly light above. It proved to be moonlight filtered through the plastic polygons of an enormous geodesic dome. Nancy didn't have to ask the traditional victim's question, "Where am I?" There was only one dome like that on Cape Cod. It was in Hyannis Port and it sheltered the ancient Kennedy Compound.

It was a museum of how life had been lived in more expansive times. The museum was closed. It was open only in the summertime.

The manhole from which Nancy and then Billy emerged was set in an expanse of green cement, which showed where the Kennedy lawn had been. On the green cement, in front of the ancient frame houses, were statues representing the fourteen Kennedys who had been Presidents of the United States or the World. They were playing touch football.

The President of the World at the time of Nancy's abduction, incidentally, was an ex-Suicide Hostess named "Ma" Kennedy. Her statue would never join this particular touch-football game. Her name was Kennedy, all right, but she wasn't the real thing. People complained of her lack of style, found her vulgar. On the wall of her office was a sign that said, YOU DON'T HAVE TO BE CRAZY TO WORK HERE, BUT IT SURE HELPS, and another one that said THIMK!, and another one that said, SOME DAY WE'RE GOING TO HAVE TO GET ORGANIZED AROUND HERE.

Her office was in the Taj Mahal.

Until she arrived in the Kennedy Museum, Nancy McLuhan was confident that she would sooner or later get a chance to break every bone in Billy's little body, maybe even shoot him with his own gun. She wouldn't have minded doing those things. She thought he was more disgusting than a blood-filled tick.

It wasn't compassion that changed her mind. It was the discovery that Billy had a gang. There were at least eight people around the manhole, men and women in equal numbers, with stockings pulled over their heads. It was the women who laid firm hands on Nancy, told her to keep calm. They were all at least as tall as Nancy and they held her in places where they could hurt her like hell if they had to.

Nancy closed her eyes, but this didn't protect her from the obvious conclusion: These perverted women were sisters from the Ethical Suicide Service. This upset her so much that she asked loudly and bitterly, "How can you violate your oaths like this?"

She was promptly hurt so badly that she doubled up and burst into tears.

When she straightened up again, there was plenty more she wanted to say, but she kept her mouth shut. She speculated silently as to what on Earth could make Suicide Hostesses turn against every concept of human decency. Nothingheadedness alone couldn't begin to explain it. They had to be drugged besides.

Nancy went over in her mind all the terrible drugs she'd learned about in school, persuaded herself that the women had taken the worst one of all. That drug was so powerful, Nancy's teachers had told her, that even a person numb from the waist down would copulate repeatedly and enthusiastically after just one glass. That had to be the answer: The women, and probably the men, too, had been drinking gin.

They hastened Nancy into the middle frame house, which was dark like all the rest, and Nancy heard the men giving Billy the news. It was in this news that Nancy perceived a glint of hope. Help might be on its way.

The gang member who had phoned Nancy obscenely had fooled the police into believing that they had captured Billy the Poet, which was bad for Nancy. The police didn't know yet that Nancy was missing, two men told Billy, and a telegram had been sent to Mary Kraft in Nancy's name declaring that Nancy had been called to New York City on urgent family business.

That was where Nancy saw the glint of hope: Mary wouldn't believe that telegram. Mary knew Nancy had no family in New York. Not one of the 63,000,000 people living there was a relative of Nancy's.

The gang had deactivated the burglar-alarm system of the museum. They had also cut through a lot of the chains and ropes that were meant to keep visitors from touching anything of value. There was no mystery as to who and what had done the cutting. One of the men was armed with brutal lopping shears.

They marched Nancy into a servant's bedroom upstairs. The man with the shears cut the ropes that fenced off the narrow bed. They put Nancy into the bed and two men held Nancy while a woman gave her a knockout shot.

Billy the Poet had disappeared.

As Nancy was going under, the woman who had given her the shot asked her how old she was.

Nancy was determined not to answer, but discovered that the drug had made her powerless not to answer. "Sixty-three," she murmured.

"How does it feel to be a virgin at sixty-three?"

Nancy heard her own answer through a velvet fog. She was amazed by the answer, wanted to protest that it couldn't possibly be hers. "Pointless," she'd said.

Moments later, she asked the woman thickly, "What was in that needle?"

"What was in the needle, honey bunch? Why, honey bunch, they call that 'truth serum.'"

The moon was down when Nancy woke up—but the night was still out there. The shades were drawn and there was candlelight. Nancy had never seen a lit candle before.

What awakened Nancy was a dream of mosquitoes and bees. Mosquitoes and bees were extinct. So were birds. But Nancy dreamed that millions of insects were swarming about her from the waist down. They didn't sting. They fanned her. Nancy was a nothinghead.

She went to sleep again. When she awoke next time, she was being led into a bathroom by three women, still with stockings over their heads. The bathroom was already filled with the steam from somebody else's bath. There were somebody else's wet footprints crisscrossing the floor and the air reeked of pine-needle perfume.

Her will and intelligence returned as she was bathed and perfumed and dressed in a white nightgown. When the women stepped back to admire her, she said to them quietly, "I may be a nothinghead now. But that doesn't mean I have to think like one or act like one."

Nobody argued with her.

Nancy was taken downstairs and out of the house. She fully expected to be sent down a manhole again. It would be the perfect setting for her violation by Billy, she was thinking—down in a sewer.

But they took her across the green cement, where the grass used to be, and then across the yellow cement, where the beach used to be, and then out onto the blue cement, where the harbor used to be. There were twenty-six yachts that had belonged to various Kennedys, sunk up to their water lines in blue cement. It was to the most ancient of these yachts, the Marlin, once the property of Joseph P. Kennedy, that they delivered Nancy.

It was dawn. Because of the high-rise apartments all around the Kennedy Museum, it would be an hour before any direct sunlight would reach the microcosm under the geodesic dome.

Nancy was escorted as far as the companionway to the forward cabin of the Marlin. The women pantomimed that she was expected to go down the five steps alone.

Nancy froze for the moment and so did the women. And there were two actual statues in the tableau on the bridge. Standing at the wheel was a statue of Frank Wirtanen, once skipper of the Marlin. And next to him was his son and first mate, Carly. They weren't paying any attention to poor Nancy. They were staring out through the windshield at the blue cement.

Nancy, barefoot and wearing a thin white nightgown, descended bravely into the forward cabin, which was a pool of candlelight and pine-needle perfume. The companionway hatch was closed and locked behind her.

Nancy's emotions and the antique furnishings of the cabin were so complex that Nancy could not at first separate Billy the Poet from his surroundings, from all the mahogany and leaded glass. And then she saw him at the far end of the cabin, with his back against the door to the forward cockpit. He was wearing purple silk pajamas with a Russian collar. They were piped in red, and writhing across Billy's silken breast was a golden dragon. It was belching fire.

Anticlimactically, Billy was wearing glasses. He was holding a book.

Nancy poised herself on the next-to-the-bottom step, took a firm grip on the handholds in the companionway. She bared her teeth, calculated that it would take ten men Billy's size to dislodge her.

Between them was a great table. Nancy had expected the cabin to be dominated by a bed, possibly in the shape of a swan, but the Marlin was a day boat. The cabin was anything but a seraglio. It was about as voluptuous as a lower-middle-class dining room in Akron, Ohio, around 1910

A candle was on the table. So were an ice bucket and two glasses and a quart of champagne. Champagne was as illegal as heroin.

Billy took off his glasses, gave her a shy, embarrassed smile, said, "Welcome."

"This is as far as I come."

He accepted that. "You're very beautiful there."

"And what am I supposed to say—that you're stunningly handsome? That I feel an overwhelming desire to throw myself into your manly arms?"

"If you wanted to make me happy, that would certainly be the way to do it." He said that humbly.

"And what about *my* happiness?"

The question seemed to puzzle him. "Nancy—that's what this is all about."

"What if my idea of happiness doesn't coincide with yours?"

"And what do you think my idea of happiness is?"

"I'm not going to throw myself into your arms, and I'm not going to drink that poison, and I'm not going to budge from here unless somebody makes me," said Nancy. "So I think your idea of happiness is going to turn out to be eight people holding me down on that table, while you bravely hold a cocked pistol to my head—and do what you want. That's the way it's going to have to be, so call your friends and get it over with!"

Which he did.

He didn't hurt her. He deflowered her with a clinical skill she found ghastly. When it was all over, he didn't seem cocky or proud. On the contrary, he was terribly depressed, and he said to Nancy, "Believe me, if there'd been any other way—"

Her reply to this was a face like stone—and silent tears of humiliation.

His helpers let down a folding bunk from the wall. It was scarcely wider than a bookshelf and hung on chains. Nancy allowed herself to be put to bed in it, and she was left alone with Billy the Poet again. Big as she was, like a double bass wedged on that narrow shelf, she felt like a pitiful little thing. A scratchy, war-surplus blanket had been tucked in around her. It was her own idea to pull up a corner of the blanket to hide her face.

Nancy sensed from sounds what Billy was doing, which wasn't much. He was sitting at the table, sighing occasionally, sniffing occasionally, turning the pages of a book. He lit a cigar and the stink of it seeped under the blanket. Billy inhaled the cigar, then coughed and coughed and coughed.

When the coughing died down, Nancy said loathingly through the blanket, "You're so strong, so masterful, so healthy. It must be wonderful to be so manly."

Billy only sighed at this.

"I'm not a very typical nothinghead," she said. "I hated it—hated everything about it."

Billy sniffed, turned a page.

"I suppose all the other women just loved it—couldn't get enough of it."

"Nope."

She uncovered her face. "What do you mean, 'Nope'?"

"They've all been like you."

This was enough to make Nancy sit up and stare at him. "The women who helped you tonight—"

"What about them?"

"You've done to them what you did to me?"

He didn't look up from his book. "That's right."

"Then why don't they kill you instead of helping you?"

"Because they understand." And then he added mildly, "They're *grateful.*"

Nancy got out of bed, came to the table, gripped the edge of the table, leaned close to him. And she said to him tautly, "I am not grateful."

"You will be."

"And what could possibly bring about that miracle?"

"Time," said Billy.

Billy closed his book, stood up. Nancy was confused by his magnetism. Somehow he was very much in charge again.

"What you've been through, Nancy," he said, "is a typical wedding night for a strait-laced girl of a hundred years ago, when everybody was a nothinghead. The groom did without helpers, because the bride wasn't customarily ready to kill him. Otherwise, the spirit of the occasion was much the same. These are the pajamas my great-great-grandfather wore on his wedding night in Niagara Falls.

"According to his diary, his bride cried all that night, and threw up twice. But, with the passage of time, she became a sexual enthusiast."

It was Nancy's turn to reply by not replying. She understood the tale. It frightened her to understand so easily that, from gruesome beginnings, sexual enthusiasm could grow and grow.

"You're a very typical nothinghead," said Billy. "If you dare to think about it now, you'll realize that you're angry because I'm such a bad lover, and a funny-looking shrimp besides. And what you can't help dreaming about from now on is a really suitable mate for a Juno like yourself.

"You'll find him, too—tall and strong and gentle. The nothinghead movement is growing by leaps and bounds."

"But—" said Nancy, and she stopped there. She looked out a porthole at the rising sun.

"But what?"

"The world is in the mess it is today because of the nothingheadedness of olden times. Don't you see?" She was pleading weakly. "The world can't afford sex anymore."

"Of course it can afford sex," said Billy. "All it can't afford anymore is reproduction."

"Then why the laws?"

"They're bad laws," said Billy. "If you go back through history, you'll find that the people who have been most eager to rule, to make the laws, to enforce the laws and to tell everybody exactly how God Almighty wants things here on Earth—those people have forgiven themselves and their friends for anything and everything. But they have been absolutely disgusted and terrified by the natural sexuality of common men and women.

"Why this is, I do not know. That is one of the many questions I wish somebody would ask the machines. I do know this: The triumph of that sort of disgust and terror is now complete. Almost every man and woman looks and feels like something the cat dragged in. The only sexual beauty that an ordinary human being can see today is in the woman who will kill him. Sex is death. There's a short and nasty equation for you: 'Sex is death. Q. E. D.'

"So you see, Nancy," said Billy, "I have spent this night, and many others like it, attempting to restore a certain amount of innocent pleasure to the world, which is poorer in pleasure than it needs to be."

Nancy sat down quietly and bowed her head.

"I'll tell you what my grandfather did on the dawn of his wedding night," said Billy.

"I don't think I want to hear it."

"It isn't violent. It's—it's meant to be tender."

"Maybe that's why I don't want to hear it."

"He read his bride a poem." Billy took the book from the table, opened it. "His diary tells which poem it was. While we aren't bride and groom, and while we may not meet again for many years, I'd like to read this poem to you, to have you know I've loved you."

"Please—no. I couldn't stand it."

"All right, I'll leave the book here, with the place marked, in case you want to read it later. It's the poem beginning:

How do I love thee? Let me count the ways.
I love thee to the depth and breadth and height
My soul can reach, when feeling out of sight
For the ends of Being and ideal Grace."

Billy put a small bottle on top of the book. "I am also leaving you these pills. If you take one a month, you will never have children. And still you'll be a nothinghead."

And he left. And they all left but Nancy.

When Nancy raised her eyes at last to the book and bottle, she saw that there was a label on the bottle. What the label said was this: WELCOME TO THE MONKEY HOUSE.

TRUMAN CAPOTE

[1924–1984]

A Christmas Memory

(First published in *Mademoiselle*,
December, 1956; first book publication in 1958.)

IMAGINE A MORNING in late November. A coming of winter morning more than twenty years ago. Consider the kitchen of a spreading old house in a country town. A great black stove is its main feature; but there is also a big round table and a fireplace with two rocking chairs placed in front of it. Just today the fireplace commenced its seasonal roar.

A woman with shorn white hair is standing at the kitchen window. She is wearing tennis shoes and a shapeless gray sweater over a summery calico dress. She is small and sprightly, like a bantam hen; but, due to a long youthful illness, her shoulders are pitifully hunched. Her face is remarkable—not unlike Lincoln's, craggy like that, and tinted by sun and wind; but it is delicate too, finely boned, and her eyes are sherry-colored and timid. "Oh my," she exclaims, her breath smoking the windowpane, "it's fruitcake weather!"

The person to whom she is speaking is myself. I am seven; she is sixty-something. We are cousins, very distant ones, and we have lived together—well, as long as I can remember. Other people inhabit the house, relatives; and though they have power over us, and frequently make us cry, we are not, on the whole, too much aware of them. We are each other's best friend. She calls me Buddy, in memory of a boy who was formerly her best friend. The other Buddy died in the 1880's, when she was still a child. She is still a child.

"I knew it before I got out of bed," she says, turning away from the window with a purposeful excitement in her eyes. "The courthouse bell sounded so cold and clear. And there were no birds singing; they've gone to warmer country, yes indeed. Oh, Buddy, stop stuffing biscuit and fetch our buggy. Help me find my hat. We've thirty cakes to bake."

It's always the same: a morning arrives in November, and my friend, as though officially inaugurating the Christmas time of year that exhilarates her imagination and fuels the blaze of her heart, announces: "It's fruitcake weather! Fetch our buggy. Help me find my hat."

The hat is found, a straw cartwheel corsaged with velvet roses out-of-doors has faded: it once belonged to a more fashionable relative. Together, we guide our buggy, a dilapidated baby carriage, out to the garden and into a grove of pecan trees. The buggy is mine; that is, it was bought for me when I was born. It is made of wicker, rather unraveled, and the wheels wobble like a drunkard's legs. But it is a faithful object; springtimes, we take it to the woods and fill it with flowers, herbs, wild fern for our porch pots; in the summer, we pile it with picnic paraphernalia and sugar-cane fishing poles and roll it down to the edge of a creek; it has its winter uses, too: as a truck for hauling firewood from the yard to the kitchen, as a warm bed for Queenie, our tough little orange and white rat terrier who has survived distemper and two rattlesnake bites. Queenie is trotting beside it now.

Three hours later we are back in the kitchen hulling a heaping buggyload of windfall pecans. Our backs hurt from gathering them: how hard they were to find (the main crop having been shaken off the trees and sold by the orchard's owners, who are not us) among the concealing leaves, the frosted, deceiving grass. Caarackle! A cheery crunch, scraps of miniature thunder sound as the shells collapse and the golden mound of sweet oily ivory meat mounts in the milk-glass bowl. Queenie begs to taste, and now and again my friend sneaks her a mite, though insisting we deprive ourselves. "We mustn't, Buddy. If we start, we won't stop. And there's scarcely enough as there is. For thirty cakes." The kitchen is growing dark. Dusk turns the window into a mirror: our reflections mingle with the rising moon as we work by the fireside in the firelight. At last, when the moon is quite high, we toss the final hull into the fire and, with joined sighs, watch it catch flame. The buggy is empty, the bowl is brimful.

We eat our supper (cold biscuits, bacon, blackberry jam) and discuss tomorrow. Tomorrow the kind of work I like best begins: buying. Cherries and citron, ginger and vanilla and canned Hawaiian pineapple, rinds and raisins and walnuts and whiskey and oh, so much flour, butter, so many eggs, spices, flavorings: why, we'll need a pony to pull the buggy home.

But before these purchases can be made, there is the question of money. Neither of us has any. Except for skinflint sums persons in the house occasionally provide (a dime is considered very big money); or what we earn ourselves from various activities: holding rummage sales, selling buckets of hand-picked blackberries, jars of homemade jam and apple jelly and peach preserves, rounding up flowers for funerals and weddings. Once we won seventy-ninth prize, five dollars, in a national football contest. Not that we know a fool thing about football. It's just that we enter any contest we hear about: at the moment our hopes are centered on the fifty-thousand-dollar Grand Prize being offered to name a new brand of coffee (we suggested "A.M."; and, after some hesitation, for my friend thought it perhaps sacrilegious, the slogan "A.M.! Amen!"). To tell the truth, our only *really* profitable enterprise was the Fun and Freak Museum we conducted in a back-yard woodshed two summers ago. The Fun was a stereopticon with slide views of Washington and New York lent us by a relative who had been to those places (she was furious when she discovered why we'd borrowed it); the Freak was a three-legged biddy chicken hatched by one of our own hens. Everybody hereabouts wanted to see that biddy: we charged grownups a nickel, kids two cents. And took in a good twenty dollars before the museum shut down due to the decease of the main attraction.

But one way and another we do each year accumulate Christmas savings, a Fruitcake Fund. These moneys we keep hidden in an ancient bead purse under a loose board under the floor under a chamber pot under my friend's bed. The purse is seldom removed from this safe location except to make a deposit, or, as happens every Saturday, a withdrawal; for on Saturdays I am allowed ten cents to go to the picture show. My friend has never been to a picture show, nor does she intend to: "I'd rather hear you tell the story, Buddy. That way I can imagine it more. Besides, a person my age shouldn't squander their eyes. When the Lord comes, let me see Him clear." In addition to never having seen a movie, she has never: eaten in a restaurant, traveled more than five miles from home, received or sent a telegram, read anything except funny papers and the Bible, worn cosmetics, cursed, wished someone harm, told a lie on purpose, let a hungry dog go hungry. Here are a few things she has done, does do: killed with a hoe the biggest rattlesnake ever seen in this county (sixteen rattles), dip snuff (secretly), tame hummingbirds (just try it) till they balance on her finger, tell ghost stories (we both believe in ghosts) so tingling they chill you in July, talk to herself, take walks in the rain, grow the prettiest japonicas in town, know the recipe for every sort of old-time Indian cure, including a magical wart-remover.

Now, with supper finished, we retire to the room in a faraway part of the house where my friend sleeps in a scrap-quilt-covered iron bed painted rose pink, her favorite color. Silently, wallowing in the pleasures of conspiracy, we take the bead purse from its secret place and spill its contents on the scrap quilt. Dollar bills, tightly rolled and green as May buds. Somber fifty-cent pieces, heavy enough to weight a dead man's eyes. Lovely dimes, the liveliest coin, the one that really jingles. Nickels and quarters, worn smooth as creek pebbles. But mostly a hateful heap of bitter-odored pennies. Last summer others in the house contracted to pay us a penny for every twenty-five flies we killed. Oh, the carnage of August: the flies that flew to heaven! Yet it was not work in which we took pride. And, as we sit counting pennies, it is as though we were back tabulating dead flies. Neither of us has a head for figures; we count slowly, lose track, start again. According to her calculations, we have $12.73. According to mine, exactly $13. "I do hope you're wrong, Buddy. We can't mess around with thirteen. The cakes will fall. Or put somebody in the cemetery. Why, I wouldn't dream of getting out of bed on the thirteenth." This is true: she always spends thirteenths in bed. So, to be on the safe side, we subtract a penny and toss it out the window.

Of the ingredients that go into our fruitcakes, whiskey is the most expensive, as well as the hardest to obtain: State laws forbid its sale. But everybody knows you can buy a bottle from Mr. Haha Jones. And the next day, having completed our more prosaic shopping, we set out for Mr. Haha's business address, a "sinful" (to quote public opinion) fish-fry and dancing café down by the river. We've been there before, and on the same errand; but in previous years our dealings have been with Haha's wife, an iodine-dark Indian woman with brassy peroxided hair and a dead-tired disposition. Actually, we've never laid eyes on her husband, though we've heard that he's an Indian too. A giant with razor scars across his cheeks. They call him Haha because he's so gloomy, a man who never laughs. As we approach his café (a large log cabin festooned inside and out with chains of garish-gay naked light bulbs and standing by the river's muddy edge under the shade of river trees where moss drifts through the branches like gray mist) our steps slow down. Even Queenie stops prancing and sticks close by. People have been murdered in Haha's café. Cut to pieces. Hit on the head. There's a case coming up in court next month. Naturally these goings-on happen at night when the colored lights cast crazy patterns and the victrola wails. In the daytime Haha's is shabby and deserted. I knock at the door, Queenie barks, my friend calls: "Mrs. Haha, ma'am? Anyone to home?"

Footsteps. The door opens. Our hearts overturn. It's Mr. Haha Jones himself! And he *is* a giant; he *does* have scars; he *doesn't* smile. No, he glowers at us through Satan-tilted eyes and demands to know: "What you want with Haha?"

For a moment we are too paralyzed to tell. Presently my friend half-finds her voice, a whispery voice at best: "If you please, Mr. Haha, we'd like a quart of your finest whiskey."

His eyes tilt more. Would you believe it? Haha is smiling! Laughing, too. "Which one of you is a drinkin' man?"

"It's for making fruitcakes, Mr. Haha. Cooking."

This sobers him. He frowns. "That's no way to waste good whiskey." Nevertheless, he retreats into the shadowed café and seconds later appears carrying a bottle of daisy-yellow unlabeled liquor. He demonstrates its sparkle in the sunlight and says: "Two dollars."

We pay him with nickels and dimes and pennies. Suddenly, as he jangles the coins in his hand like a fistful of dice, his face softens. "Tell you what," he proposes, pouring the money back into our bead purse, "just send me one of them fruitcakes instead."

"Well," my friend remarks on our way home, "there's a lovely man. We'll put an extra cup of raisins in *his* cake."

The black stove, stoked with coal and firewood, glows like a lighted pumpkin. Eggbeaters whirl, spoons spin round in bowls of butter and sugar, vanilla sweetens the air, ginger spices it; melting, nose-tingling odors saturate the kitchen, suffuse the house, drift out to the world on puffs of chimney smoke. In four days our work is done. Thirty-one cakes, dampened with whiskey, bask on window sills and shelves.

Who are they for?

Friends. Not necessarily neighbor friends: indeed, the larger share is intended for persons we've met maybe once, perhaps not at all. People who've struck our fancy. Like President Roosevelt. Like the Reverend and Mrs. J. C. Lucey, Baptist missionaries to Borneo who lectured here last winter. Or the little knife grinder who comes through town twice a year. Or Abner Packer, the driver of the six o'clock bus from Mobile, who exchanges waves with us every day as he passes in a dust-cloud whoosh. Or the young Wistons, a California couple whose car one afternoon broke down outside the house and who spent a pleasant hour chatting with us on the porch (young Mr. Wiston snapped our picture, the only one we've ever had taken). Is it because my friend is shy with everyone *except* strangers that these strangers, and merest acquaintances, seem to us our truest friends? I think yes. Also, the scrapbooks we keep of thank-you's on White House stationery, time-to-time communications from California and Borneo, the knife grinder's penny post cards, make us feel connected to eventful worlds beyond the kitchen with its view of a sky that stops.

Now a nude December fig branch grates against the window. The kitchen is empty, the cakes are gone; yesterday we carted the last of them to the post office, where the cost of stamps turned our purse inside out. We're broke. That rather depresses me, but my friend insists on celebrating—with two inches of whiskey left in Haha's bottle. Queenie has a spoonful in a bowl of coffee (she likes her coffee chicory-flavored and strong). The rest we divide between a pair of jelly glasses. We're both quite awed at the prospect of drinking straight whiskey; the taste of it brings screwed-up expressions and sour shudders. But by and by we begin to sing, the two of us singing different songs simultaneously. I don't know the words to mine, just: *Come on along, come on along, to the dark-town strutters' ball.* But I can dance: that's what I mean to be, a tapdancer in the movies. My dancing shadow rollicks on the walls; our voices rock the chinaware; we giggle: as if unseen hands were tickling us. Queenie rolls on her back, her paws plow the air, something like a grin stretches her black lips. Inside myself, I feel warm and sparky as those crumbling logs, carefree as the wind in the chimney. My friend waltzes round the stove, the hem of her poor calico skirt pinched between her fingers as though it were a party dress: *Show me the way to go home*, she sings, her tennis shoes squeaking on the floor. *Show me the way to go home.*

Enter: two relatives. Very angry. Potent with eyes that scold, tongues that scald. Listen to what they have to say, the words tumbling together into a wrathful tune: "A child of seven! whiskey on his breath! are you out of your mind? feeding a child of seven! must be loony! road to ruination! remember Cousin Kate? Uncle Charlie? Uncle Charlie's brother-in-law? shame! scandal! humiliation! kneel, pray, beg the Lord!"

Queenie sneaks under the stove. My friend gazes at her shoes, her chin quivers, she lifts her skirt and blows her nose and runs to her room. Long after the town has gone to sleep and the house is silent except for the chimings of clocks and the sputter of fading fires, she is weeping into a pillow already as wet as a widow's handkerchief.

"Don't cry," I say, sitting at the bottom of her bed and shivering despite my flannel nightgown that smells of last winter's cough syrup, "don't cry," I beg, teasing her toes, tickling her feet, "you're too old for that."

"It's because," she hiccups, "I *am* too old. Old and funny."

"Not funny. Fun. More fun than anybody. Listen. If you don't stop crying you'll be so tired tomorrow we can't go cut a tree."

She straightens up. Queenie jumps on the bed (where Queenie is not allowed) to lick her cheeks. "I know where we'll find real pretty trees, Buddy. And holly, too. With berries big as your eyes. It's way off in the woods. Farther than we've ever been. Papa used to bring us Christmas trees from there: carry them on his shoulder. That's fifty years ago. Well, now: I can't wait for morning."

Morning. Frozen rime lusters the grass; the sun, round as an orange and orange as hot-weather moons, balances on the horizon, burnishes the silvered winter woods. A wild turkey calls. A renegade hog grunts in the undergrowth. Soon, by the edge of knee-deep, rapid-running water, we have to abandon the buggy. Queenie wades the stream first, paddles across barking complaints at the swiftness of the current, the pneumonia-making coldness of it. We follow, holding our shoes and equipment (a hatchet, a burlap sack) above our heads. A mile more: of chastising thorns, burs and briers that catch at our clothes; of rusty pine needles brilliant with gaudy fungus and molted feathers. Here, there, a flash, a flutter, an ecstasy of shrillings remind us that not all the birds have flown south. Always, the path unwinds through lemony sun pools and pitch-black vine tunnels. Another creek to cross: a disturbed armada of speckled trout froths the water round us, and frogs the size of plates practice belly flops; beaver workmen are building a dam. On the farther shore, Queenie shakes herself and trembles. My friend shivers, too: not with cold but enthusiasm. One of her hat's ragged roses sheds a petal as she lifts her head and inhales the pine-heavy air. "We're almost there; can you smell it, Buddy?" she says, as though we were approaching an ocean.

And, indeed, it is a kind of ocean. Scented acres of holiday trees, prickly-leafed holly. Red berries shiny as Chinese bells: black crows swoop upon them screaming. Having stuffed our burlap sacks with enough greenery and crimson to garland a dozen windows, we set about choosing a tree. "It should be," muses my friend, "twice as tall as a boy. So a boy can't steal the star." The one we pick is twice as tall as me. A brave handsome brute that survives thirty hatchet strokes before it keels with a creaking rending cry. Lugging it like a kill, we commence the long trek out. Every few yards we abandon the struggle, sit down and pant. But we have the strength of triumphant huntsmen; that and the tree's virile, icy perfume revive us, goad us on. Many compliments accompany our sunset return along the red clay road to town; but my friend is sly and noncommittal when passers-by praise the treasure perched in our buggy: what a fine tree and where did it come from? "Yonderways," she murmurs vaguely. Once a car stops and the rich mill owner's lazy wife leans out and whines: "Giveya two-bits cash for that ol tree." Ordinarily my friend is afraid of saying no; but on this occasion she promptly shakes her head: "We wouldn't take a dollar." The mill owner's wife persists. "A dollar, my foot! Fifty cents. That's my last offer. Goodness, woman, you can get another one." In answer, my friend gently reflects: "I doubt it. There's never two of anything."

Home: Queenie slumps by the fire and sleeps till tomorrow, snoring loud as a human.

A trunk in the attic contains: a shoebox of ermine tails (off the opera cape of a curious lady who once rented a room in the house), coils of frazzled tinsel gone gold with age, one silver star, a brief rope of dilapidated, undoubtedly dangerous candy-like light bulbs. Excellent decorations, as far as they go, which isn't far enough: my friend wants our tree to blaze "like a Baptist window," droop with weighty snows of ornament. But we can't afford the made-in-Japan splendors at the five-and-dime. So we do what we've always done: sit for days at the kitchen table with scissors and crayons and stacks of colored paper. I make sketches and my friend cuts them out: lots of cats, fish too (because they're easy to draw), some apples, some watermelons, a few winged angels devised from saved-up sheets of Hershey-bar tin foil. We use safety pins to attach these creations to the tree; as a final touch, we sprinkle the branches with shredded cotton (picked in August for this purpose). My friend, surveying the effect, clasps her hands together. "Now honest, Buddy. Doesn't it look good enough to eat?" Queenie tries to eat an angel.

After weaving and ribboning holly wreaths for all the front windows, our next project is the fashioning of family gifts. Tie-dye scarves for the ladies, for the men a home-brewed lemon and licorice and aspirin syrup to be taken "at the first Symptoms of a Cold and after Hunting." But when it comes time for making each other's gift, my friend and I separate to work secretly.

I would like to buy her a pearl-handled knife, a radio, a whole pound of chocolate-covered cherries (we tasted some once, and she always swears: "I could live on them, Buddy, Lord yes I could–and that's not taking His name in vain"). Instead, I am building her a kite. She would like to give me a bicycle (she's said so on several million occasions: "If only I could, Buddy. It's bad enough in life to do without something *you* want; but confound it, what gets my goat is not being able to give somebody something you want *them* to have. Only one of these days I will, Buddy. Locate you a bike. Don't ask how. Steal it, maybe"). Instead, I'm fairly certain that she is building me a kite–the same as last year, and the year before: the year before that we exchanged slingshots. All of which is fine by me. For we are champion kite-fliers who study the wind like sailors; my friend, more accomplished than I, can get a kite aloft when there isn't enough breeze to carry clouds.

Christmas Eve afternoon we scrape together a nickel and go to the butcher's to buy Queenie's traditional gift, a good gnawable beef bone. The bone, wrapped in funny paper, is placed high in the tree near the silver star. Queenie knows it's there. She squats at the foot of the tree staring up in a trance of greed: when bedtime arrives she refuses to budge. Her excitement is equaled by my own. I kick the covers and turn my pillow as though it were a scorching summer's night. Somewhere a rooster crows: falsely, for the sun is still on the other side of the world.

"Buddy, are you awake?" It is my friend, calling from her room, which is next to mine; and an instant later she is sitting on my bed holding a candle. "Well, I can't sleep a hoot," she declares. "My mind's jumping like a jack rabbit. Buddy, do you think Mrs. Roosevelt will serve our cake at dinner?" We huddle in the bed, and she squeezes my hand I-love-you. "Seems like your hand used to be so much smaller. I guess I hate to see you grow up. When you're grown up, will we still be friends ?" I say always. "But I feel so bad, Buddy. I wanted so bad to give you a bike. I tried to sell my cameo Papa gave me. Buddy"–she hesitates, as though embarrassed–"I made you another kite." Then I confess that I made her one, too; and we laugh. The candle burns too short to hold. Out it goes, exposing the starlight, the stars spinning at the window like a visible caroling that slowly, slowly daybreak silences. Possibly we doze; but the beginnings of dawn splash us like cold water: we're up, wide-eyed and wandering while we wait for others to waken. Quite deliberately my friend drops a kettle on the kitchen floor. I tap-dance in front of closed doors. One by one the household emerges, looking as though they'd like to kill us both; but it's Christmas, so they can't. First, a gorgeous breakfast: just everything you can imagine–from flapjacks and fried squirrel to hominy grits and honey-in-the-comb. Which puts everyone in a good humor except my friend and me. Frankly, we're so impatient to get at the presents we can't eat a mouthful.

Well, I'm disappointed. Who wouldn't be? With socks, a Sunday school shirt, some handkerchiefs, a hand-me-down sweater and a year's subscription to a religious magazine for children. *The Little Shepherd.* It makes me boil. It really does.

My friend has a better haul. A sack of Satsumas, that's her best present. She is proudest, however, of a white wool shawl knitted by her married sister. But she *says* her favorite gift is the kite I built her. And it *is* very beautiful; though not as beautiful as the one she made me, which is blue and scattered with gold and green Good Conduct stars; moreover, my name is painted on it, "Buddy."

"Buddy, the wind is blowing."

The wind is blowing, and nothing will do till we've run to a pasture below the house where Queenie has scooted to bury her bone (and where, a winter hence, Queenie will be buried, too). There, plunging through the healthy waist-high grass, we unreel our kites, feel them twitching at the string like sky fish as they swim into the wind. Satisfied, sun-warmed, we sprawl in the grass and peel Satsumas and watch our kites cavort. Soon I forget the socks and hand-me-down sweater. I'm as happy as if we'd already won the fifty-thousand-dollar Grand Prize in that coffee-naming contest.

"My, how foolish I am!" my friend cries, suddenly alert, like a woman remembering too late she has biscuits in the oven. "You know what I've always thought?" she asks in a tone of discovery, and not smiling at me but a point beyond. "I've always thought a body would have to be sick and dying before they saw the Lord. And I imagined that when He came it would be like looking at the Baptist window: pretty as colored glass with the sun pouring through, such a shine you don't know it's getting dark. And it's been a comfort: to think of that shine taking away all the spooky feeling. But I'll wager it never happens. I'll wager at the very end a body realizes the Lord has already shown Himself. That things as they are"—her hand circles in a gesture that gathers clouds and kites and grass and Queenie pawing earth over her bone—"just what they've always seen, was seeing Him. As for me, I could leave the world with today in my eyes."

This is our last Christmas together.

Life separates us. Those who Know Best decide that I belong in a military school. And so follows a miserable succession of bugle-blowing prisons, grim reveille-ridden summer camps. I have a new home too. But it doesn't-count. Home is where my friend is, and there I never go.

And there she remains, puttering around the kitchen. Alone with Queenie. Then alone. ("Buddy dear," she writes in her wild hard-to-read script, "yesterday Jim Macy's horse kicked Queenie bad. Be thankful she didn't feel much. I wrapped her in a Fine Linen sheet and rode her in the buggy down to Simpson's pasture where she can be with all her Bones . . ."). For a few Novembers she continues to bake her fruitcakes single-handed;

not as many, but some: and, of course, she always sends me "the best of the batch." Also, in every letter she encloses a dime wadded in toilet paper: "See a picture show and write me the story." But gradually in her letters she tends to confuse me with her other friend, the Buddy who died in the 1880's; more and more thirteenths are not the only days she stays in bed: a morning arrives in November, a leafless birdless coming of winter morning, when she cannot rouse herself to exclaim: "Oh my, it's fruitcake weather!"

And when that happens, I know it. A message saying so merely confirms a piece of news some secret vein had already received, severing from me an irreplaceable part of myself, letting it loose like a kite on a broken string. That is why, walking across a school campus on this particular December morning, I keep searching the sky. As if I expected to see, rather like hearts, a lost pair of kites hurrying toward heaven.

JAMES BALDWIN

[1924–1987]

Tell Me How Long the Train's Been Gone

(First published in *McCalls*, February, 1967; first book publication in 1968.)

My BROTHER, CALEB, was seventeen when I was ten. We were very good friends. In fact, he was my best friend and, for a very long time, my only friend.

I do not mean to say that he was always nice to me. I got on his nerves a lot, and he resented having to take me around with him and be responsible for me when there were so many other things he wanted to be doing. Therefore, his hand was often up against the side of my head, and my tears caused him to be punished many times. But I knew, somehow, anyway, that when he was being punished for my tears, he was not being punished for anything he had done to me; he was being punished because that was the way we lived; and his punishment, oddly, helped unite us. More oddly still, even as his great hand caused my head to stammer and dropped a flame-colored curtain before my eyes, I understood that he was not striking *me*. His hand leaped out because he could not help it, and I received the blow because I was there. And it happened, sometimes, before I could even catch my breath to howl, that the hand that had struck me grabbed me and held me, and it was difficult indeed to know which of us was weeping. He was striking, striking out, striking out; the hand asked me to forgive him. I felt his bewilderment through the membrane of my own. I also felt that he was trying to teach me something. And I had, God knows, no other teachers.

For our father—how shall I describe our father?—was a ruined Barbados peasant, exiled in a Harlem which he loathed, where he never saw the sun or sky he remembered, where life took place neither indoors nor without, and where there was no joy. By which I mean no joy that he remembered. Had he been able to bring with him any of the joy he had felt on that far-off island, then the air of the sea and the impulse to dancing would sometimes have transfigured our dreadful rooms. Our lives might have been very different.

But no, he brought with him from Barbados only black rum and blacker pride and magic incantations, which neither healed nor saved.

He did not understand the people among whom he found himself; they had no coherence, no stature and no pride. He came from a race which had been flourishing at the very dawn of the world—a race greater and nobler than Rome or Judea, mightier than Egypt—he came from a race of kings, kings who had never been taken in battle, kings who had never been slaves. He spoke to us of tribes and empires, battles, victories and monarchs of whom we had never heard—they were not mentioned in our textbooks—and invested us with glories in which we felt more awkward than in the secondhand shoes we wore. In the stifling room of his pretensions and expectations, we stumbled wretchedly about, stubbing our toes, as it were, on rubies, scraping our shins on golden caskets, bringing down, with a childish cry, the splendid purple tapestry on which, in pounding gold and scarlet, our destinies and our inheritance were figured. It could scarcely have been otherwise, since a child's major attention has to be concentrated on how to fit into a world which, with every passing hour, reveals itself as merciless.

If our father was of royal blood and we were royal children, our father was certainly the only person in the world who knew it. The landlord did not know it; our father never mentioned royal blood to *him*. When we were late with our rent, which was often, the landlord threatened, in terms no commoner had ever used before a king, to put us in the streets. He complained that our shiftlessness, which he did not hesitate to consider an attribute of the race, had forced him, an old man with a weak heart, to climb all these stairs to plead with us to give him the money we owed him. And this was the last time; he wanted to make sure we understood that this was the last time.

Our father was younger than the landlord, leaner, stronger and bigger. With one blow, he could have brought the landlord to his knees. And we knew how much he hated the man. For days on end, in the wintertime, we huddled around the gas stove in the kitchen, because the landlord gave us no heat. When windows were broken, the landlord took his time about fixing them; the wind made the cardboard we stuffed in the windows rattle all night long; and when snow came, the weight of the snow forced the cardboard inward and onto the floor. Whenever the apartment received a fresh coat of paint, we bought the paint and did the painting ourselves; we killed the rats. A great chunk of the kitchen ceiling fell one winter, narrowly missing our mother.

We all hated the landlord with a perfectly exquisite hatred, and we would have been happy to see our proud father kill him. We would have been glad to help. But our father did nothing of the sort. He stood before the landlord, looking unutterably weary. He made excuses. He apologized. He swore that it would never happen again. (We knew that it *would* happen again.) He begged for time. The landlord would finally go down the stairs, letting us and all the neighbors know how good-hearted he was, and our father would walk into the kitchen and pour himself a glass of rum.

But we knew that our father would never have allowed any black man to speak to him as the landlord did, as policemen did, as storekeepers and welfare workers and pawnbrokers did. No, not for a moment. He would have thrown him out of the house. He would certainly have made a black man know that he was not the descendant of slaves! He had made them know it so often that he had almost no friends among them, and if we had followed his impossible lead, we would have had no friends, either. It was scarcely worthwhile being the descendant of kings if the kings were black and no one had ever heard of them.

And it was because of our father, perhaps, that Caleb and I clung to each other, in spite of the great difference in our ages; or, in another way, it may have been precisely the difference in our ages that made the clinging possible. I don't know. It is really not the kind of thing anyone can ever know. I think it may be easier to love the really helpless younger brother, because he cannot enter into competition with one on one s own ground, or on any ground at all, and can never question one's role or jeopardize one's authority. In my own case, certainly, it did not occur to me to compete with Caleb, and I could not have questioned his role or his authority, because I needed both. He was my touchstone, my model and my only guide.

Anyway, our father, dreaming bitterly of Barbados, despised and mocked by his neighbors and all but ignored by his sons, held down his unspeakable factory job, spread his black gospel in bars on the weekends, and drank his rum. I do not know if he loved our mother. I think he did.

They had had five children—only Caleb and I, the first and the last, were left. We were both dark, like our father; but two of the three dead girls had been fair, like our mother.

She came from New Orleans. Her hair was not like ours. It was black, but softer and finer. The color of her skin reminded me of the color of bananas. Her skin was as bright as that, and contained that kind of promise, and she had tiny freckles around her nose and a small black mole just above her upper lip. It was the mole, I don't know why, which made her beautiful. Without it, her face might have been merely sweet, merely pretty. But the mole was funny. It had the effect of making one realize that our mother liked funny things, liked to laugh. The mole made one look at her eyes—large, extraordinary dark eyes, eyes which seemed always to be amused by something, eyes which looked straight out, seeming to see everything, seeming to be afraid of nothing. She was a soft, round, plump woman. She liked nice clothes and dangling jewelry, which she mostly didn't have, and she liked to cook for large numbers of people, and she loved our father.

She knew him—knew him through and through. I am not being coy or colloquial but bluntly and sadly matter-of-fact when I say that I will now never know what she saw in him. What she saw was certainly not for many eyes; what she saw got him through his working week and his Sunday rest; what she saw saved him. She saw that he was a man. For her, perhaps, he was a great man. I think, though, that, for our mother, any man was great who aspired to become a man: this meant that our father was very rare and precious. I used to wonder how she took it, how she bore it—his rages, his tears, his cowardice.

On Saturday nights, he was almost always evil, drunk and maudlin. He came home from work in the early afternoon and gave our mother some money. It was never enough, of course, but he always kept enough to go out and get drunk. She never protested, at least not as far as I know. Then she would go out shopping. I would usually go with her, for Caleb would almost always be out somewhere, and our mother didn't like the idea of leaving me alone in the house. And this was probably, after all, the best possible arrangement. People who disliked our father were sure (for that very reason) to like our mother; and people who felt that Caleb was growing to be too much like his father could feel that I, after all, might turn out like my mother. Besides, it is not, as a general rule, easy to hate a small child. One runs the risk of looking ridiculous, especially if the child is with his mother.

And especially if that mother is Mrs. Proudhammer. Mrs. Proudhammer knew very well what people thought of Mr. Proudhammer. She knew, too, exactly how much she owed in each store she entered, how much she was going to be able to pay, and what she had to buy. She entered with a smile, ready.

"Evening. Let me have some of them red beans there."

"Evening. You know, you folks been running up quite a little bill here."

"I'm going to give you something on it right now. I need some cornmeal and flour and some rice."

"You know, I got my bills to meet, too, Mrs. Proudhammer."

"Didn't I just tell you I was going to pay? I want some cornflakes too and some milk." Such merchandise as she could reach, she had already placed on the counter.

"When do you think you're going to be able to pay this bill? All of it, I mean."

"You know I'm going to pay it just as soon as I can. How much does it all come to? Give me that end you got there of that chocolate cake." The chocolate cake was for Caleb and me. "Well, now you put this against the bill."

Imperiously, as though it were the most natural thing in the world, she put two or three dollars on the counter.

"You lucky I'm softhearted, Mrs. Proudhammer."

"Things sure don't cost this much downtown—you think I don't know it? Here." And she paid him for what she had bought. "Thank you. You been mighty kind."

And we left the store. I often felt that in order to help her, I should have filled my pockets with merchandise while she was talking. But I never did, not only because the store was often crowded or because I was afraid of being caught by the storekeeper, but because I was afraid of humiliating her. When I began to steal, not very much later, I stole in stores that were not in our neighborhood, where we were not known.

When we had to do "heavy" shopping, we went marketing under the bridge at Park Avenue—Caleb, our mother and I; and sometimes, but rarely, our father came with us. The most usual reason for heavy shopping was that some relatives of our mother's, or old friends of both our mother's and our father's, were coming to visit. We were certainly not going to let them go away hungry—not even if it meant, as it often did, spending more than we had. In spite of what I have been suggesting about our father's temperament, and no matter how difficult he may sometimes have been with us, he was much too proud to offend any guest of his; on the contrary, his impulse was to make them feel that his home was theirs; and besides, he was lonely, lonely for his past, lonely for those faces which had borne witness to that past. Therefore, he would sometimes pretend that our mother did not know how to shop, and our father would come with us, under the bridge, in order to teach her.

There he would be, then, uncharacteristically, in shirt-sleeves, which made him look rather boyish; and as our mother showed no desire to take shopping lessons from him, he turned his attention to Caleb and me. He would pick up a fish, opening the gills and holding it close to his nose. "You see that? That fish looks fresh, don't it? Well, that fish ain't as fresh as I am, and I *been* out of the water. They done doctored that fish. Come on." And we would walk away, a little embarrassed but, on the whole, rather pleased that our father was so smart.

Meantime, our mother was getting the marketing done. She was very happy on days like this, because our father was happy. He was happy, odd as his expression of it may sound, to be out with his wife and his two sons. If we had been on the island that had been witness to his birth, instead of the unspeakable island of Manhattan, he felt that it would not have been so hard for us all to trust and love each other. He sensed, and I think he was right, that on that other, never to be recovered island, his sons would have looked on him very differently, and he would have looked very differently on his sons. Life would have been hard there, too; we would have fought there, too, and more or less blindly suffered and more or less blindly died. But we would not have been (or so it was to seem to all of us forever) so wickedly menaced by the mere fact of our relationship, would not have been so frightened of entering into the central, most beautiful and valuable facts of our lives. We would have been laughing and cursing and tussling in the water, instead of stammering under the bridge; we would have known less about vanished African kingdoms and more about each other. Or, not at all impossibly, more about both.

If it was summer, we bought a watermelon, which either Caleb or our father carried home, fighting with each other for this privilege. They looked very like each other on those days—both big, both black, both laughing.

Caleb always looked absolutely helpless when he laughed. He laughed with all his body, perhaps touching his shoulder against yours, or putting his head on your chest for a moment, and then careening off you, halfway across the room or down the block. I will always hear his laughter. He was always happy on such days, too. If our father needed his son, Caleb certainly needed his father. Such days, however, were rare—one of the reasons, probably, that I remember them now.

Eventually, we all climbed the stairs into that hovel which, at such moments, was our castle. One very nearly felt the drawbridge rising behind us as our father locked the door.

The bathtub could not yet be filled with cold water and the melon placed in the tub, because this was Saturday, and, come evening, we all had to bathe. The melon was covered with a blanket and placed on the fire escape. Then we unloaded what we had bought, rather impressed by our opulence, though our father was always, by this time, appalled by the money we had spent. I was always sadly aware that there would be nothing left of all this once tomorrow had come and gone and that most of it, after all, was not for us, but for others.

Our mother was calculating the pennies she would need all week—carfare for our father and for Caleb, who went to a high school out of our neighborhood; money for the life insurance; money for milk for me at school; money for light and gas; money put away, if possible, toward the rent. She knew just about what our father had left in *his* pockets and was counting on him to give me the money I would shortly be demanding to go to the movies. Caleb had a part-time job after school and already had his movie money. Anyway, unless he was in a very good mood or needed me for something, he would not be anxious to go to the movies with me.

Our mother never insisted that Caleb tell her where he was going, nor did she question him as to how he spent the money he made. She was afraid of hearing him lie, and she did not want to risk forcing him to lie. She was operating on the assumption that he was sensible and had been raised to be honorable and that he, now more than ever, needed his privacy.

But she was very firm with him, nevertheless. "I do not want to see you rolling in here at three in the morning, Caleb. I want you here in time to eat, and you know you got to take your bath."

"Yes, indeed, ma'am. Why can't I take my bath in the morning?"

"Don't you start being funny. You know you ain't going to get up in time to take no bath in the morning."

"Don't nobody want you messing around in that bathroom all morning long, man," said our father. "You just git back in the house like your ma's telling you."

"Besides," I said, "you never wash out the tub."

Caleb looked at me in mock surprise and from a great height, allowing his chin and his lids simultaneously to drop and swiveling his head away from me.

"I see," he said, "that everyone in this family is ganging up on me. All right, Leo. I was planning to take you to the show with me, but now I've changed my mind."

"I'm sorry," I said quickly. "I take it back."

"You take *what* back?"

"What I said–about you not washing out the tub."

"Ain't no need to take it back," our father said stubbornly. "It's true. A man don't take back nothing that's true."

"So *you* say," Caleb said, with a hint of a sneer. But before anyone could possibly react to this, he picked me up, scowling into my face, which he held just above his own. "You take it back?"

"Leo ain't going to take it back," our father said.

Now I was in trouble. Caleb watched me, a small grin on his face. "You take it back?"

"Stop teasing that child, and put him down," our mother said. "The trouble ain't that Caleb don't wash out the tub–he just don't wash it out very clean."

"I never knew him to wash it out," our father said, "unless I was standing behind him."

"Well, ain't neither one of you much good around the house," our mother said.

Caleb laughed and set me down. "You didn't take it back," he said.

I said nothing.

"I guess I'm just going to have to go on without you."

Still, I said nothing.

"You going to have that child to crying in a minute," our mother said. "If you going to take him go on and take him. Don't do him like that."

Caleb laughed again. "I'm going to take him. The way he got them eyes all ready to water, I'd better take him somewhere." We walked toward the door. "But you got to make up *your* mind," he said to me, "to say what *you* think is right."

I grabbed Caleb's hand, the signal for the descent of the drawbridge. Our mother watched us cheerfully as we walked out; our father watched us balefully. Yet there was a certain humor in his face, too, and a kind of pride.

"Dig you later," Caleb said, and the door closed behind us.

The hall was dark, smelling of cooking, of stale wine, of rotting garbage. We dropped down the stairs, Caleb going two at a time, pausing at each landing, briefly, to glance back up at me. I dropped down behind him as fast as I could. When I reached the street level, Caleb was already on the stoop, joking with some of his friends, who were standing in the doorway—who seemed always to be in the doorway.

I didn't like Caleb's friends, because I was afraid of them. I knew the only reason they didn't try to make life hell for me, the way they made life hell for a lot of the other kids, was because they were afraid of Caleb. I went through the door, passing between my brother and his friends, down to the sidewalk, feeling, as they looked briefly at me and then continued joking with Caleb, what they felt—that here was Caleb's round-eyed, frail and useless sissy of a little brother. They pitied Caleb for having to take me out. On the other hand, they also wanted to go to the show, but didn't have the money. Therefore, in silence, I could crow over them even as they despised me. But this was always a terribly risky, touch-and-go business, for Caleb might, at any moment, change his mind and drive me away.

I always stood, those Saturday afternoons, in fear and trembling, holding on to the small shield of my bravado, while waiting for Caleb to come down the steps of the stoop, away from his friends, to me. I braced myself, always, for the moment when he would turn to me, saying, "Okay, kid. You run along. I'll see you later."

This meant that I would have to go the movies by myself and hang around in front of the box office, wailing for some grown-up to take me in. I could not go back upstairs, for this would be informing my mother and father that Caleb had gone off somewhere after promising to take me to the movies.

Neither could I simply hang around, playing with the kids on the block. For one thing, my demeanor, as I came out of the house, very clearly indicated that I had better things to do than play with *them*; for another, they were not terribly anxious to play with *me*; and, finally, my remaining on the block would have had exactly the same effect as my going upstairs. To remain on the block after Caleb's dismissal was to put myself at the mercy of the block and to put Caleb at the mercy of our parents.

So I prepared myself, those Saturdays, to respond with a cool "Okay. See you later," and then to turn indifferently away, and walk. This was surely the most terrible moment. The moment I turned away, I was committed, I was trapped, and I then had miles to walk, so it seemed to me, before I would be out of sight, before the block ended and I could turn onto the avenue. I wanted to run out of that block, but I never did. I never looked back. I forced myself to walk very slowly, looking neither right nor left, striving to seem at once distracted and offhand; concentrating on the cracks in the sidewalk and stumbling over them; trying to whistle, feeling every muscle in my body, feeling that all the block was watching me, and feeling, which was odd, that I deserved it.

And then I reached the avenue, and turned, still not looking back, and was released from those eyes at least; but now I faced other eyes, eyes coming toward me. These eyes were the eyes of children stronger than me, who would steal my movie money; these eyes were the eyes of white cops, whom I feared, whom I hated with a literally murderous hatred; these eyes were the eyes of old folks, who might wonder what I was doing on this avenue by myself.

And then I got to the show. Sometimes someone would take me in right away, and sometimes I would have to stand there and wait, watching the faces coming to the box office. And this was not easy, since I didn't, after all, want everyone in the neighborhood to know I was loitering outside the movie house waiting for someone to take me in. If it came to our father's attention, he would kill both Caleb and me.

Eventually, I would see a face which looked susceptible. I would rush up to him—it was usually a man, for men were less likely to be disapproving—and whisper, "Take me in," and give him my dime. Sometimes the man simply took the dime and disappeared inside; sometimes he gave my dime back to me and took me in anyway. Sometimes I ended up wandering around the streets—but I couldn't wander into a strange neighborhood, because I would be beaten up if I did—until I figured the show was out. It was dangerous to get home too early, and, of course, it was practically lethal to arrive too late. If all went well, I could cover for Caleb, saying that I had left him with some boys on the stoop. Then, if *he* came in too late, it could not be considered my fault.

But if wandering around this way was not without its dangers, neither was it without its discoveries and delights. I discovered subways. I discovered, that is, that I could ride on subways by myself and, furthermore, that I could usually ride for nothing. Sometimes, when I ducked under the turnstile, I was caught, and sometimes great black ladies seized on me as a pretext for long, very loud, ineffably moral lectures about wayward children breaking their parents' hearts. Sometimes, doing everything in my power not to attract their attention, I endeavored to look as though I were in the charge of a respectable-looking man or woman, entering the subway in their shadow and sitting very still beside them. It was best to try to sit *between* two such people, for each would automatically assume that I was with the other. There I would sit, then, in a precarious anonymity, watching the people, listening to the roar, watching the lights of stations flash by. It seemed to me that nothing was faster than a subway train, and I loved the speed, because the speed was dangerous.

For a time, during these expeditions, I simply sat and watched the people. Lots of people would be dressed up, for this was Saturday night. The women's hair would be all curled and straightened, and the lipstick on their full lips looked purple and make-believe against the dark skins of their faces. They wore very fancy capes or coats, in wonderful colors, and long dresses, and sometimes they had jewels in their hair, and sometimes they wore flowers on their dresses. They were almost as beautiful as movie stars. And so the men with them seemed to think.

The hair of the men was slick and wavy, brushed up into pompadours; or they wore very sharp hats, brim flicked down dangerously over one eye, with perhaps one flower in the lapel of their many-colored suits. They laughed and talked with their girls, but quietly, for there were white people in the car. The white people would scarcely ever be dressed up and did not speak to each other at all—only read their papers and stared at the advertisements. But they fascinated me more than the colored people did, because I knew nothing at all about them and could not imagine what they were like.

Underground, I received my first apprehension of New York neighborhoods and, underground, first felt what may be called a civic terror. I very soon realized that after the train had passed a certain point, going uptown or downtown, all the colored people disappeared. The first time I realized this, I panicked and got lost. I rushed off the train, terrified of what these white people might do to me, with no colored person around to protect me—even to scold me, even to beat me; at least, their touch was familiar, and I knew that they did not, after all, intend to kill me—and got on another train only because I saw a black man on it. But almost everyone else was white.

The train did not stop at any of the stops I remembered. I became more and more frightened, frightened of getting off the train and frightened of staying on it, frightened of saying anything to the man and frightened that he would get off the train before I could say anything to him. He was my salvation, and he stood there in the unapproachable and frightening form that salvation so often takes. At each stop, I watched him with despair.

To make matters worse, I suddenly realized that I had to pee. Once I realized it, this need became a torment; the horror of wetting my pants in front of all these people made the torment greater. Finally, I tugged at the man's sleeve. He looked down at me with a gruff, amused concern; then, reacting, no doubt to the desperation in my face, he bent closer.

I asked him if there was a bathroom on the train.

He laughed. "No," he said, "but there's a bathroom in the station." He looked at me again. "Where are you going?"

I told him that I was going home. "And where's home?"

I told him.

This time he did not laugh. "Do you know where you are?" he said.

I shook my head. At that moment, the train came into a station, and after several hours, it rolled to a stop. The doors opened, and the man led me to the bathroom. I ran in, and I hurried, because I was afraid he would disappear. But I was glad he had not come in with me.

When I came out, he stood waiting for me. "Now," he said, "you in Brooklyn. You ever hear of Brooklyn? What you doing out here by yourself?"

"I got lost," I said.

"I *know* you got lost. What I want to know is how *come* you got lost? Where's your mama? Where's your daddy?"

I almost said that I didn't have any, because I liked his face and his voice and was half hoping to hear him say that *he* didn't have any little boy and would just as soon take a chance on me. But I told him that my mama and daddy were at home.

"And do they know where *you* are?"

I said, "No." There was a pause.

"Well, I know they going to make your tail hot when they see you." He took my hand. "Come on."

And he led me along the platform and then down some steps and along a narrow passage and then up some steps onto the opposite platform. I was very impressed by this maneuver; in order to accomplish the same purpose, I had always left the subway station and gone up into the street. Now that the emergency was over, I was in no great hurry to leave my savior. I asked him if he had a little boy.

"Yes," he said, "and if *you* was my little boy, I'd paddle your behind so you couldn't sit down for a week."

I asked him how old was his little boy, what was his name and if his little boy was at home.

"He *better* be at home!" He looked at me and laughed. "His name is Jonathan. He ain't but five years old." His gaze refocused, sharpened. "How old are you?"

I told him that I was ten, going on eleven.

"You a pretty bad little fellow," he said then.

I tried to look repentant, but I would not have dreamed of denying it.

"Now, look here," he said, "this here's the uptown side. Can you read, or don't you never go to school?" I assured him that I could read.

"Now, to get where you going, you got to change trains." He told me where. "Here, I'll write it down for you." He found some paper in his pockets but no pencil. We heard the train coming. He looked about him in helpless annoyance, looked at his watch, looked at me. "It's all right. I'll tell the conductor."

But the conductor, standing between two cars, had rather a mean pink face.

My savior looked at him dubiously. "He *might* be all right. But we better not take no chances." He pushed me ahead of him into the train. "You know you right lucky that I got a little boy? If I didn't, I swear I'd just let you go on and *be* lost. You don't know the kind of trouble you going to get me in at home. My wife ain't *never* going to believe *this* story."

I told him to give me his name and address and I would write a letter to his wife and to his little boy, too.

This caused him to laugh harder than ever. "You only say that because you know I ain't got no pencil. You are one *hell* of a shrewd little boy."

I told him that then maybe we should get off the train and that I would go back home with him.

This made him grave. "What does your father do?"

This question made me uneasy. I stared at him for a long time before I answered. "He works in a–" I could not pronounce the word–"he has a job."

He nodded. "I see. Is he home now?"

I really did not know, and I said I did not know.

"And what does your mother do?"

"She stays home."

Again he nodded. "You got any brothers or sisters?"

I told him no.

"I see. What's your name?"

"Leo."

"Leo what?"

"Leo Proudhammer."

He saw something in my face. "What do you want to be when you grow up, Leo?"

"I want to be–" and I had never said this before–"I want to be a–a movie actor. I want to be a–actor."

"You pretty skinny for that," he said.

"That's all right," I told him. "Caleb's going to teach me to swim. That's how you get big."

"Who's Caleb?"

I opened my mouth, I started to speak. I checked myself as the train roared into a station. He glanced out the window, but did not move. "He swims," I said.

"Oh," he said after a very long pause, during which the doors slammed and the train began to move. "Is he a good swimmer?"

I said that Caleb was the best swimmer in the world.

"Okay," my savior said, "okay," and put his hand on my head again and smiled at me.

I asked him what his name was.

"Charles," he said, "Charles Williams. But you better call me *Uncle* Charles, you little devil, because you have certainly ruined my Saturday night." The train came into a station. "Here's where we change," he said.

We got out of the train and crossed the platform and waited.

"Now," he said, "this train stops exactly where you going. Tell me where you going."

I stared at him.

"I want you," he said, "to tell me exactly where you *going*. I can't be fooling with you all night."

I told him.

"You sure that's right?"

I told him I was sure.

"I got a very good memory," he said. "Give me your address. Just say it, I'll remember it."

So I said it, staring into his face as the train came roaring in.

"If you don't go straight home," he said, "I'm going to come see your daddy, and when we find you, you'll be mighty sorry." He pushed me into the train and put one shoulder against the door. "Go on, now," he said, loud enough for all the car to hear. "Your mama'll meet you at the station where I told you to get off." He repeated my subway stop, pushed the angry door with his shoulder, and then said gently, "Sit down, Leo." He remained in the door until I sat down. "So long, Leo," he said then, and stepped backward out. The doors closed. He grinned at me and waved, and the train began to move.

I waved back. Then he was gone, the station was gone, and I was on my way back home.

I never saw that man again, but I made up stories about him, I dreamed about him, I even wrote a letter to him and his wife and his little boy, but I never mailed it.

I never told Caleb anything about my solitary expeditions. I don't know why. I think that he might have liked to know about them. I suppose, finally, at bottom, I said nothing because my expeditions belonged to me.

Another time, it was raining, and it was still too early for me to go home. I felt very, very low that day. It was one of the times that my tongue and my body refused to obey me, and I had not been able to work up the courage to ask anyone to take me in to the show. The ticket taker was watching me, or so I thought, with a hostile suspicion. Actually, it's very unlikely he was thinking at all, and certainly not of me. But I walked away from the show, because I could no longer bear his eyes, or anybody's eyes.

I walked the long block east from the movie house. The street was empty, black and glittering. The water soaked through my coat at the shoulders, and water dripped down my neck from my cap. I began to be afraid. I could not stay out in the rain, because then my father and mother would know I had been wandering the streets. I would get a beating, and, though Caleb was too old to get a beating, he and my father would have a terrible fight, and Caleb would blame it all on me and would not speak to me for days.

I began to hate Caleb. I wondered where he was. I started in the direction of our house, only because I did not know what else to do. Perhaps Caleb would be waiting for me on the stoop.

The avenue, too, was very long and silent. Somehow, it seemed old, like a picture in a book. It stretched straight before me, endless, and the streetlights did not so much illuminate it as prove how dark it was. The rain was falling harder. Cars sloshed by, sending up sheets of water. From the bars, I heard music, faintly, and many voices. Straight ahead of me a woman walked, very fast, head down, carrying a shopping bag. I reached my corner and crossed the wide avenue. There was no one on my stoop.

Now I was not even certain what time it was; but I knew it wasn't time yet for the show to be over. I walked into my hallway and wrung out my cap. I was sorry that I had not made someone take me in to the show, because now I did not know what to do. I *could* go upstairs and say that we had not liked the movie and had left early and that Caleb was with some boys on the stoop. But this would sound strange, and Caleb, who would not know what story I had told, would, therefore, be greatly handicapped when he came home.

I could not stay in my hallway, because my father might not be at home and might come in. I could not go into the hallway of another building, because if any of the kids who lived in the building found me, they would have the right to beat me up. I could not go back out into the rain. I stood next to the big, cold radiator, and I began to cry. But crying wasn't going to do me any good, either, especially as there was no one to hear me.

So I stepped out on my stoop again and stood there for a long time, wondering what to do. Then I thought of a condemned house, around the corner from us. We played there sometimes, though it was very dangerous and we were not supposed to. What possessed me to go there now, I don't know, except that I could not think of another dry place in the whole world. I started running east, down our block. I turned two corners and came to the house, with its black window sockets. The house was completely dark. I had forgotten how afraid I was of the dark, but the rain was drenching me. I ran down the cellar steps and clambered into the house through one of the broken windows. I squatted there in a still, dry dread, not daring to look into the house but staring outward. I was holding my breath. I heard an endless scurrying in the darkness, a perpetual busyness, and I thought of rats, of their teeth and ferocity and fearful size, and I began to cry again.

I don't know how long I squatted there this way or what was in my mind. I listened to the rain and the rats. Then I was aware of another sound—I had been hearing it for a while without realizing it. This was a moaning sound, a sighing sound, a sound of strangling, which mingled with the sound of the rain and with a muttering, cursing human voice. The sounds came from the door that led to the backyard.

I wanted to stand, but I crouched lower; wanted to run, but could not move. Sometimes the sounds seemed to come closer, and I knew that this meant my death; sometimes they diminished or ceased altogether, and then I knew that my assailant was looking for me. I looked toward the backyard door, and I seemed to see, silhouetted against the driving rain, a figure, half bent, moaning, leaning against the wall, in indescribable torment; then there seemed to be two figures, sighing and grappling, moving so quickly that it was impossible to tell which was which, two creatures, each in a dreadful, absolute, silent single-mindedness attempting to strangle the other!

I watched, crouching low. A very powerful and curious excitement mingled itself with my terror and made the terror greater. I could not move. I did not dare move. The figures were quieter now. It seemed to me that one of them was a woman, and she seemed to be crying, pleading for her life. But her sobbing was answered only by a growling sound. The muttered, joyous curses began again; the murderous ferocity began again, more bitterly than ever. The sobbing began to rise in pitch, like a song.

Then everything was still, all movement ceased. Then I heard only the rain and the scurrying of the rats. It was over; one of them, or both of them, lay stretched out, dead or dying in this filthy place. It happened in Harlem every Saturday night. I could not catch my breath to scream. Then I heard a laugh, a low, happy, wicked laugh, and the figure turned in my direction and seemed to start toward me.

Then I screamed and stood up straight, bumping my head on the window frame and losing my cap, and scrambled up the cellar steps. I ran head down, like a bull, away from that house and out of that block. I ran up the steps of my stoop and bumped into Caleb.

"Where the hell have you been? Hey! What's the matter with you?"

I had jumped up on him, almost knocking him down, trembling and sobbing.

"You're *soaked.* Leo, what's the matter? Where's your cap?"

But I could not say anything. I held him around the neck with all my might, and I could not stop shaking.

"Come on, Leo," Caleb said, in a different tone, "tell me what's the matter." He pried my arms loose and held me away from him, so that he could look into my face. "Oh, little Leo. Little Leo. What's the matter, baby?" He looked at though he were about to cry himself, and this made me cry harder than ever. He took out his handkerchief and wiped my face and made me blow my nose. My sobs began to lessen, but I could not stop trembling. He thought that I was trembling from cold, and he rubbed his hands roughly up and down my back and rubbed my hands between his. "What's the matter?"

I did not know how to tell him.

"Somebody try to beat you up?"

I shook my head. "No."

"What movie did you see?"

"I didn't go. I couldn't find nobody to take me in."

"And you just been wandering around in the rain all night?"

"Yes."

He sat down on the hallway steps. "Oh, Leo." Then, "You mad at me?"

I said, "No. I was scared."

He nodded. "I reckon you were, man." He wiped my face again. "You ready to go upstairs? It's getting late."

"Okay."

"How'd you lose your cap?"

"I went in a hallway to wring it out–and–I put it on the radiator, and I heard some people coming–and–I ran away, and I forgot it."

"We'll say you forgot it in the movies."

"Okay."

We started up the stairs.

"Leo," he said, "I'm sorry about tonight. I'm really sorry. I won't let it happen again. You believe me?"

"Sure. I believe you." I smiled up at him.

He squatted down. "Give us a kiss."

I kissed him.

"Okay. Climb up. I'll give you a ride. Hold on, now."

He carried me piggyback up the stairs.

Thereafter, we evolved a system, which did not, in fact, work too badly. When things went wrong and he could not be found, I was to leave a message for him at a certain store on the avenue. This store had a bad reputation–more than candy and hot dogs and soda pop were sold there; Caleb himself had told me this and told me not to hang out there. But he said he would see to it that they treated me all right.

I went in the store one Saturday night, and one of the boys who was always there, a boy about Caleb's age, looked up and smiled and said, "You looking for your brother? Come on, I'll take you to him."

This was not the agreed-on formula. I was to be *taken* to Caleb only in cases of real emergency, which wasn't the case this time. I was there because the show was over a little earlier than usual, and since it was only about a quarter past eleven, I figured I had about half an hour to wait for Caleb.

When the boy made his invitation, I assumed it was because of some prearrangement with the owner of the store, a very dour, silent black man, who looked at me from behind his counter and said nothing.

I said, "Okay," and the boy, whose name was Arthur, said, "Come on, Sonny. I'm going to take you to a party." He took my hand and led me across the avenue and into a long, dark block.

We walked the length of the block in silence, crossed another avenue and went into a big house in the middle of the block. We were in a big vestibule, with four locked apartment doors staring away from each other. It was not really clean, but it was fairly clean. We climbed three flights of stairs. Arthur knocked on the door, a very funny knock, not loud. After a moment, I heard a scraping sound, then the sound of a chain rattling and a bolt being pulled back. The door opened.

A lady, very black and rather fat, wearing a blue dress, held the door for us. She said, "Come on in. Now, what you doing here with this child?"

"Had to do it. It's all right. It's Caleb's brother."

We started down a long, dark hall, with closed rooms on either side of it, toward the living room. One of the rooms was the kitchen. A smell of barbecue made me realize that I was hungry. The living room was really two living rooms. The far one looked out on the street. There were six or seven people in the room, women and men. They looked exactly like the men and women who frightened me when I saw them standing on the corners, laughing and joking in front of the bars. But they did not seem frightening here. A record player was going, not very loud. They had drinks in their hands, and there were half-empty plates of food around the room. Caleb was sitting on the sofa, with his arm around a girl in a yellow dress.

"Here's your little brother," said the fat black lady in blue.

Arthur said to Caleb, "It was just better for him not to have to wait there tonight."

Caleb smiled at me. I was tremendously relieved that he was not angry. I was delighted by this party, even though it made me shy. "Come on over here," Caleb said. I went to the sofa. "This is my kid brother. His name is Leo. Leo, this is Dolores. Say hello to Dolores."

Dolores smiled at me—I thought she was very pretty—and said, "I'm very happy to meet you, Leo. How've you been?"

"Just fine," I said.

"Don't you want to know how *she's* been?" Caleb grinned.

"No," said the fat black lady, and laughed. "I'm sure he don't want to know that. I bet he's hungry. You been stuffing yourself all night, Caleb. Let me give him a little bit of my barbecue and a glass of ginger ale." She already was beginning to propel me out of the room.

I looked at Caleb. Caleb said, "Just remember we ain't got all night. Leo, this is Miss Mildred. She cooked everything, and she's a might good friend of mine. What do you say to Miss Mildred, Leo?"

"Dig Caleb being the big brother," Arthur muttered, and laughed.

"Thank you, Miss Mildred," I said.

"Come on in the kitchen," she said, "and let me try to put some flesh on them bones." She walked me into the kitchen. "Now, you sit right over there," she said. "Won't take me but a minute to warm this up." She sat me at the kitchen table and gave me a napkin and poured the ginger ale. "What grade you in at school, Leo?" I told her. "You must be a right smart boy, then," she said, with a pleased smile. "Do you like school, Leo?"

I told her what I liked best was Spanish and history and English composition.

This caused her to look more pleased than ever. "What do you want to be when you grow up?"

Somehow, I could not tell her what I had told the man, my friend, on the train. I said I wasn't sure, that maybe I would be a schoolteacher.

"That's just what I wanted to be," she said proudly, "and I studied right hard for it, too, and I believe I would have made it, but then I had to go and get myself mixed up with some no-count nigger. I didn't have no sense. I didn't have no better sense but to marry him. Can you beat that?" And she laughed and set my plate in front of me. "Go on, now, eat. Foolish me. Now, your brother," she said suddenly, "he's a right fine boy. He wants to make something of himself. He's got ambition. That's what I like—*ambition.* Don't you let him be foolish. Like me. You like my barbecue?"

"Yes, ma'am," I said. "It's good."

"Let me give you some more ginger ale," she said, and poured it.

I was beginning to be full. But I didn't want to go, although I knew that, now, it was really beginning to be late. While Miss Mildred talked and moved about the kitchen, I listened to the voices coming from the other room, the voices and the music. They were playing a kind of purple, lazy dance music, a music that was already in my bones, along with the wilder music from which the purple music sprang. The voices were not like the music, though they corroborated it. I listened to a girl's voice, gravelly and low, indignant and full of laughter. The room was full of laughter. It exploded, at intervals, and rolled through the living room and hammered at the walls of the kitchen.

Every once in a while, I heard Caleb, booming like a trumpet, drowning out the music. I wondered how often Caleb came here and how he had met these people, who were so different, at least as it seemed to me, from any of the people who ever came to our house.

Then Caleb's hand was on my neck. Dolores stood in the doorway, smiling. "You stuffed yourself enough, little brother?" Caleb said. "Because we got to get out of here now."

We walked slowly down the hall, Miss Mildred, Dolores and Caleb and me. We reached the door, which had a metal pole built into it in such a way as to prevent its being opened from the outside, and a heavy piece of chain around the top of the three locks.

Miss Mildred began, patiently, to open the door. "Leo," she said, "don't you be no stranger. You make your brother bring you back to see me, you hear?" She got the pole out of the way and then undid the chain. To Caleb, she said, "Bring him by some afternoon. I ain't got nothing to do. I'll be glad to look after him." The last lock yielded, and Miss Mildred opened the door. We were facing the bright hall lights: no, the building was not very clean. "Good night, Leo," Miss Mildred said, and then she said good night to Dolores and Caleb. She closed the door.

I heard the scraping sound again, and we walked down the stairs.

"She's nice," I said.

Caleb said, yawning, "Yeah, she's a very nice lady." Then he said, "Now, I don't want you telling nobody at home about this, you hear?" I swore I wouldn't tell. "It's our secret," Caleb said.

It was colder in the streets than it had been before.

Caleb took Dolores' arm. "Let's get you to your subway," he said.

We started walking up the wide, dark avenue. We reached the brightly lit kiosk, which came up out of the sidewalk like some unbelievably malevolent awning or the suction apparatus of a monstrous vacuum cleaner.

"Bye-bye," Caleb said, and kissed Dolores on the nose. "I got to run. See you Monday after school."

"Bye-bye," Dolores said. She bent down and kissed me quickly on the cheek. "Bye-bye, Leo. Be good." She hurried down the steps.

Caleb and I began walking very fast, down the avenue, toward our block. The subway station was near the movie house, and the movie house was dark. We knew we were late; we did not think we were *that* late.

"It was a *very* long show, wasn't it?" Caleb said.

"Yes," I said.

"What did we see? Better tell me about *both* pictures. Just in case."

I told him as well as I could as we hurried down the avenue. Caleb had great powers of concentration and could figure out enough from what I said to know what to say if the necessity arose.

But our troubles, that night, came from a very different source than our parents. I had just reached the point in my breathless narration where the good girl is murdered by the Indians and the hero vows revenge. We were hurrying down the long block that led east to our house when we heard a car braking and were blinded by bright lights and were pushed up against a wall.

"Turn around," a voice said. "And keep your hands in the air."

It may seem funny, but I felt as though Caleb and I had conjured up a movie—that if I had not been describing a movie to him, we would not have suddenly found ourselves in the middle of one. Or was it the end? I had never been so frightened in my life.

We did as we were told. I felt the grainy brick beneath my fingers. A hand patted me all over my body, every touch humiliating. Beside me, I heard Caleb catch his breath.

"Turn around," the voice said.

The great lights of the police car had gone out; I could see the car at the curb, the doors open. I did not dare look at Caleb, for I felt that this would, somehow, be used against us. I stared at the two policemen, young, white, tight-lipped and self-important.

They turned a flashlight first on Caleb, then on me. "Where you boys going?"

"Home," Caleb said. I could hear his breathing. "We live in the next block." And he gave the address.

"Where've you been?"

Now I heard the effort Caleb was making not to surrender either to rage or panic. "We just took my girl to the subway station. We were at the movies." And then, forced out of him, weary, dry and bitter, "This here's my brother. I got to get him home. He ain't but ten years old."

"What movie did you see?"

And Caleb told them. I marveled at his memory. But I also knew that the show had let out about an hour or so before. I feared that the policemen might also know this. But they didn't.

"You got any identification?"

"My brother doesn't. I do."

"Let's see it."

Caleb took out his wallet and handed it over.

They looked at his wallet, looked at us, handed it back. "Get on home," one of them said. They got into their car and drove off.

"Thanks," Caleb said. "Thanks, all you scum-bag Christians." His accent was now as irredeemably of the islands as was the accent of our father. I had never heard this sound in his voice before. And then, suddenly, he looked down at me and laughed and hugged me. "Come on, let's get home. Little Leo. Were you scared?"

"Yes," I said. "Were you?"

"Damn right, I was scared. But—damn!—they must have seen that you weren't but ten years old."

"You didn't *act* scared," I said.

We were in our own block, approaching our stoop. "Well. We certainly have a good excuse for being late," he said. He grinned. Then he said, "Leo,

I'll tell you something. I'm glad this happened. It had to happen one day, and I'm glad it happened while I was with you—of course, I'm glad you were with *me*, too, because it it hadn't been for you, they'd have pulled me."

"What for?"

"Because I'm black," Caleb said. "That's what for."

I said nothing. I said nothing, because what he said was true, and I knew it. It seemed, now, that I had always known it, though I had never been able to say it. But I did not understand it. I was filled with an awful wonder; it hurt my chest and paralyzed my tongue. *Because you're black.* I tried to think, but I couldn't. I only saw the policemen, those murderous eyes again, those hands. Were they people?

"Caleb," I asked, "are white people people?"

"What are you talking about, Leo?"

"I mean, are white people—*people*? People like us?"

He looked down at me. His face was very strange and sad. It was a face I had never seen before. We were in the house now, and we climbed a few more stairs, very slowly. Then, "All I can tell you, Leo, is—well, *they* don't think they are."

I thought of the landlord. Then I thought of my schoolteacher, a lady named Mrs. Nelson. I liked her very much. I thought she was very pretty. She had long yellow hair, like someone I had seen in the movies, and a nice laugh, and we all liked her, all the kids I knew. The kids who were not in her class wished they were. I liked to write compositions for her, because she seemed really interested. But she was white. Would she hate me all my life because I was black? It didn't seem possible. She didn't hate me now; I was pretty sure of that. And yet, what Caleb had said was true.

"Caleb," I asked, "are all white people the same?"

"I never met a good one."

I asked, "Not even when you were little? In school?"

Caleb said, "Maybe. I don't remember." He smiled at me. "I never met a good one, Leo. But that's not saying that *you* won't. Don't look so frightened."

We were in front of our door. Caleb raised his hand to knock.

I held his hand. "Caleb," I whispered, "what about Mama?"

"What do you mean, what about Mama?"

"Well, Mama." I stared at him; he watched me very gravely. "Mama—Mama's almost white."

"But that don't make her white. You got to be *all* white to be white." He laughed. "Poor Leo. Don't feel bad. I know you don't understand it now. I'll try to explain it to you, little by little." He paused. "But our mama is a colored woman. You can tell she's a colored woman because she's married to a colored *man*, and she's got two colored *children*. Now, you know ain't no white lady going to do a thing like that." He watched me, smiling. "You understand that?" I nodded. "Well, you going to keep me here all night with your questions, or can we go on in now?"

He knocked, and our mother opened the door. "About time," she said drily. She had her hair piled in a knot on the top of her head. I liked her hair that way. "You must have sat through that movie four or five times. You're going to ruin your eyes, and that'll just be too bad for you, because you know we ain't got no money to be buying you no glasses. Leo, you go on inside and get ready to take your bath."

"Let him come over here a minute," our father said. He was sitting in the one easy chair, near the window. He was drunk, but not as drunk as I had seen him, and this was a good-mood drunk. In this mood, he talked about the islands, his mother and father and kinfolk and friends, the feast days, the singing, the dancing and the sea.

I approached him, and he pulled me to him, smiling, and held me between his thighs. "How's my big man?" he asked, smiling and rubbing his hand, gently, over my hair. "Did you have a good time tonight?"

Caleb sat on a straight chair near him, leaning forward. "Let Leo tell you why we so late. Tell them what happened, Leo."

"We were coming down the block," I began—and I watched my father's face. Suddenly, I did not want to tell him. Something in Caleb's tone had alerted him, and he watched me with a stern and frightened apprehension. My mother came and stood beside him, one hand on his shoulder. I looked at Caleb. "Maybe you could tell it better," I said.

"Go on, start. I'll fill in."

"We were coming down the block," I said, "coming from the movies." I looked at Caleb.

"It's not the way we usually come," Caleb said.

My father and I stared at each other. There was, suddenly, between us, an overwhelming sorrow. It had come from nowhere. "We got stopped by the cops," I said. Then I could not continue. I looked helplessly at Caleb, and Caleb told the story.

As Caleb spoke, I watched my father's face. I don't know how to describe what I saw. I felt his arm tighten, tighten; his lips became bitter, and his eyes grew dull. It was as though—after indescribable, nearly mortal effort, after grim years of fasting and prayer, after the loss of all he had, and after having been promised by the Almighty that he had paid the price and no more would be demanded of his soul, which was harbored now—it was as though in the midst of his joyful feasting and dancing, crowned and robed, a messenger arrived to tell him that a great error had been made, and that it was all to be done again. Before his eyes, then, the banquet and the banquet wines and the banquet guests departed, the robe and crown were lifted, and he was alone, frozen out of his dream, with all that before him which he had thought was behind him.

My father looked as stunned and still and as close to madness as that, and his encircling arm began to hurt me, but I did not complain. I put my hand on his face, and he turned to me; he smiled—he was very beautiful then!—and he put his great hand on top of mine. He turned to Caleb. "That's all that happened? You didn't say nothing?"

"What could I say? It might have been different if I'd been by myself. But I had Leo with me, and I was afraid of what they might do to Leo."

"No, you did right, man. I got no fault to find. You didn't take their badge number?"

Caleb snickered. "What for? You know a friendly judge? We got money for a lawyer? Somebody they going to *listen* to? They get us in that precinct house and make us confess to all kinds of things and sometimes even kill us, and don't nobody give a damn. Don't nobody care what happens to a black man. If they didn't need us for work, they'd have killed us all off a long time ago. They did it to the Indians."

"That's the truth," our mother said. "I wish I could say different, but it's the truth." She stroked our father's shoulder. "We just thank the Lord is wasn't no worse. We just got to say: Well, the boys got home safe tonight."

I asked, "Daddy, how come they do us like they do?"

My father looked at us for a long time. Finally, he said, "Leo, if I could tell you that, maybe I'd be able to make them stop. But don't let them make you afraid. You hear?"

I said, "Yes, sir." But I knew that I was already afraid.

"Let's not talk about it no more," our mother said. "If you two is hungry, I got some pork chops back there."

Caleb grinned at me. "Little Leo might be hungry. He stuffs himself like a pig. But I ain't hungry. Hey, old man—" he nudged my father's shoulder; nothing would be refused us tonight—"why don't we have a taste of your rum? All right?"

Our mother laughed. "I'll go get it," she said. She started out of the room.

"Reckon we can give Leo a little bit, too?" our father asked. He pulled me onto his lap.

"In a big glass of water," our mother said, laughing. She took one last look at us before she went into the kitchen. "My," she said, "I sure am surrounded by some pretty men! My, my, my!"

FLANNERY O'CONNOR

[1925–1964]

A Good Man Is Hard to Find

(1953)

THE GRANDMOTHER DIDN'T want to go to Florida. She wanted to visit some of her connections in east Tennessee and she was seizing at every chance to change Bailey's mind. Bailey was the son she lived with, her only boy. He was sitting on the edge of his chair at the table, bent over the orange sports section of the *Journal.* "Now look here, Bailey," she said, "see here, read this," and she stood with one hand on her thin hip and the other rattling the newspaper at his bald head. "Here this fellow that calls himself The Misfit is aloose from the Federal Pen and headed toward Florida and you read here what it says he did to these people. Just you read it. I wouldn't take my children in any direction with a criminal like that aloose in it. I couldn't answer to my conscience if I did."

Bailey didn't look up from his reading so she wheeled around then and faced the children's mother, a young woman in slacks, whose face was as broad and innocent as a cabbage and was tied around with a green headkerchief that had two points on the top like rabbit's ears. She was sitting on the sofa, feeding the baby his apricots out of a jar. "The children have been to Florida before," the old lady said. "You all ought to take them somewhere else for a change so they would see different parts of the world and be broad. They never have been to east Tennessee."

The children's mother didn't seem to hear her but the eight-year-old boy, John Wesley, a stocky child with glasses, said, "If you don't want to go to Florida, why dontcha stay at home?" He and the little girl, June Star, were reading the funny papers on the floor.

"She wouldn't stay at home to be queen for a day," June Star said without raising her yellow head.

"Yes and what would you do if this fellow, The Misfit, caught you?" the grandmother asked.

"I'd smack his face," John Wesley said.

"She wouldn't stay at home for a million bucks," June Star said. "Afraid she'd miss something. She has to go everywhere we go."

"All right, Miss," the grandmother said. "Just remember that the next time you want me to curl your hair."

June Star said her hair was naturally curly.

The next morning the grandmother was the first one in the car, ready to go. She had her big black valise that looked like the head of a hippopotamus in one corner, and underneath it she was hiding a basket with Pitty Sing, the cat, in it. She didn't intend for the cat to be left alone in the house for three days because he would miss her too much and she was afraid he might brush against one of the gas burners and accidentally asphyxiate himself. Her son, Bailey, didn't like to arrive at a motel with a cat.

She sat in the middle of the back seat with John Wesley and June Star on either side of her. Bailey and the children's mother and the baby sat in front and they left Atlanta at eight forty-five with the mileage on the car at 55,890. The grandmother wrote this down because she thought it would be interesting to say how many miles they had been when they got back. It took them twenty minutes to reach the outskirts of the city.

The old lady settled herself comfortably, removing her white cotton gloves and putting them up with her purse on the shelf in front of the back window. The children's mother still had on slacks and still had her head tied up in a green kerchief, but the grandmother had on a navy blue straw sailor hat with a bunch of white violets on the brim and a navy blue dress with a small white dot in the print. Her collars and cuffs were white organdy trimmed with lace and at her neckline she had pinned a purple spray of cloth violets containing a sachet. In case of an accident, anyone seeing her dead on the highway would know at once that she was a lady.

She said she thought it was going to be a good day for driving, neither too hot nor too cold, and she cautioned Bailey that the speed limit was fifty-five miles an hour and that the patrolmen hid themselves behind billboards and small clumps of trees and sped out after you before you had a chance to slow down. She pointed out interesting details of the scenery: Stone Mountain; the blue granite that in some places came up to both sides of the highway; the brilliant red clay banks slightly streaked with purple; and the various crops that made rows of green lace-work on the ground. The trees were full of silver-white sunlight and the meanest of them sparkled. The children were reading comic magazines and their mother had gone back to sleep.

"Let's go through Georgia fast so we won't have to look at it much," John Wesley said.

"If I were a little boy," said the grandmother, "I wouldn't talk about my native state that way. Tennessee has the mountains and Georgia has the hills."

"Tennessee is just a hillbilly dumping ground," John Wesley said, "and Georgia is a lousy state too."

"You said it," June Star said.

"In my time," said the grandmother, folding her thin veined fingers, "children were more respectful of their native states and their parents and everything else. People did right then. Oh look at the cute little pickaninny!" she said and pointed to a Negro child standing in the door of a shack. "Wouldn't that make a picture, now?" she asked and they all turned and looked at the little Negro out of the back window. He waved.

"He didn't have any britches on," June Star said.

"He probably didn't have any," the grandmother explained. "Little niggers in the country don't have things like we do. If I could paint, I'd paint that picture," she said.

The children exchanged comic books.

The grandmother offered to hold the baby and the children's mother passed him over the front seat to her. She set him on her knee and bounced him and told him about the things they were passing. She rolled her eyes and screwed up her mouth and stuck her leathery thin face into his smooth bland one. Occasionally he gave her a far-away smile. They passed a large cotton field with five or six graves fenced in the middle of it, like a small island. "Look at the graveyard!" the grandmother said, pointing it out. "That was the old family burying ground. That belonged to the plantation."

"Where's the plantation?" John Wesley asked.

"Gone With the Wind," said the grandmother. "Ha. Ha."

When the children finished all the comic books they had brought, they opened the lunch and ate it. The grandmother ate a peanut butter sandwich and an olive and would not let the children throw the box and the paper napkins out the window. When there was nothing else to do they played a game by choosing a cloud and making the other two guess what shape it suggested. John Wesley took one the shape of a cow and June Star guessed a cow and John Wesley said, no, an automobile, and June Star said he didn't play fair, and they began to slap each other over the grandmother.

The grandmother said she would tell them a story if they would keep quiet. When she told a story, she rolled her eyes and waved her head and was very dramatic. She said once when she was a maiden lady she had been courted by a Mr. Edgar Atkins Teagarden from Jasper, Georgia. She said he was a very good-looking man and a gentleman and that he brought her a watermelon every Saturday afternoon with his initials cut in it. E. A. T. Well, one Saturday, she said, Mr. Teagarden brought the watermelon and there was nobody at home and he left it on the front porch and returned in his buggy to Jasper, but she never got the watermelon, she said, because a nigger boy ate it when he saw the initials, E. A. T.! This story tickled John Wesley's funny bone and he giggled and giggled but June Star didn't think it was any good. She said she wouldn't marry a man that just brought her a watermelon on Saturday. The grandmother said she would have done well to marry Mr. Teagarden because he was a gentleman and had bought Coca-Cola stock when it first came out and that he had died only a few years ago, a very wealthy man.

They stopped at The Tower for barbecued sandwiches. The Tower was a part stucco and part wood filling station and dance hall set in a clearing outside of Timothy. A fat man named Red Sammy Butts ran it and there were signs stuck here and there on the building and for miles up and down the highway saying, TRY RED SAMMY'S FAMOUS BARBECUE. NONE LIKE FAMOUS RED SAMMY'S! RED SAM! THE FAT BOY WITH THE HAPPY LAUGH. A VETERAN! RED SAMMY'S YOUR MAN!

Red Sammy was lying on the bare ground outside The Tower with his head under a truck while a gray monkey about a foot high, chained to a small chinaberry tree, chattered nearby. The monkey sprang back into the tree and got on the highest limb as soon as he saw the children jump out of the car and run toward him.

Inside, The Tower was a long dark room with a counter at one end and tables at the other and dancing space in the middle. They all sat down at a board table next to the nickelodeon and Red Sam's wife, a tall burnt-brown woman with hair and eyes lighter than her skin, came and took their order. The children's mother put a dime in the machine and played "The Tennessee Waltz," and the grandmother said that tune always made her want to dance. She asked Bailey if he would like to dance but he only glared at her. He didn't have a naturally sunny disposition like she did and trips made him nervous. The grandmother's brown eyes were very bright. She swayed her head from side to side and pretended she was dancing in her chair. June Star said play something she could tap to so the children's mother put in another dime and played a fast number and June Star stepped out onto the dance floor and did her tap routine.

"Ain't she cute?" Red Sam's wife said, leaning over the counter. "Would you like to come be my little girl?"

"No I certainly wouldn't," June Star said "I wouldn't live in a broken-down place like this for a million bucks!" and she ran back to the table.

"Ain't she cute?" the woman repeated, stretching her mouth politely.

"Aren't you ashamed?" hissed the grandmother.

Red Sam came in and told his wife to quit lounging on the counter and hurry up with these people's order. His khaki trousers reached just to his hip bones and his stomach hung over them like a sack of meal swaying under his shirt. He came over and sat down at a table nearby and let out a combination sigh and yodel. "You can't win," he said. "You can't win," and he wiped his sweating red face off with a gray handkerchief. "These days you don't know who to trust," he said. "Ain't that the truth?"

"People are certainly not nice like they used to be," said the grandmother.

"Two fellers come in here last week," Red Sammy said, "driving a

Chrysler. It was a old beat-up car but it was a good one and these boys looked all right to me. Said they worked at the mill and you know I let them fellers charge the gas they bought? Now why did I do that?"

"Because you're a good man!" the grandmother said at once.

"Yes'm, I suppose so," Red Sam said as if he were struck with this answer.

His wife brought the orders, carrying the five plates all at once without a tray, two in each hand and one balanced on her arm. "It isn't a soul in this green world of God's that you can trust," she said. "And I don't count nobody out of that, not nobody," she repeated, looking at Red Sammy.

"Did you read about that criminal, The Misfit, that's escaped?" asked the grandmother.

"I wouldn't be a bit surprised if he didn't attact this place right here," said the woman. "If he hears about it being here, I wouldn't be none surprised to see him. If he heard it's two cent in the cash register, I wouldn't be a tall surprised if he . . ."

"That'll do," Red Sam said. "Go bring these people their Co'-Colas," and the woman went off to get the rest of the order.

"A good man is hard to find," Red Sammy said. "Everything is getting terrible. I remember the day you could go off and leave your screen door unlatched. Not no more."

He and the grandmother discussed better times. The old lady said that in her opinion Europe was entirely to blame for the way things were now. She said the way Europe acted you would think we were made of money and Red Sam said it was no use talking about it, she was exactly right. The children ran outside into the white sunlight and looked at the monkey in the lacy chinaberry tree. He was busy catching fleas on himself and biting each one carefully between his teeth as if it were a delicacy.

They drove off again into the hot afternoon. The grandmother took cat naps and woke up every few minutes with her own snoring. Outside of Toombsboro she woke up and recalled an old plantation that she had visited in this neighborhood once when she was a young lady. She said the house had six white columns across the front and that there was an avenue of oaks leading up to it and two little wooden trellis arbors on either side in front where you sat down with your suitor after a stroll in the garden. She recalled exactly which road to turn off to get to it. She knew that Bailey would not be willing to lose any time looking at an old house, but the more she talked about it, the more she wanted to see it once again and find out if the little twin arbors were still standing. "There was a secret panel in this house," she said craftily, not telling the truth but wishing that she were, "and the story went that all the family silver was hidden in it when Sherman came through but it was never found."

"Hey!" John Wesley said. "Let's go see it! We'll find it! We'll poke all the woodwork and find it! Who lives there? Where do you turn off at? Hey Pop, can't we turn off there?"

"We never have seen a house with a secret panel!" June Star shrieked. "Let's go to the house with the secret panel! Hey Pop, can't we go see the house with the secret panel!"

"It's not far from here, I know," the grandmother said. "It wouldn't take over twenty minutes."

Bailey was looking straight ahead. His jaw was as rigid as a horseshoe. "No," he said.

The children began to yell and scream that they wanted to see the house with the secret panel. John Wesley kicked the back of the front seat and June Star hung over her mother's shoulder and whined desperately into her ear that they never had any fun even on their vacation, that they could never do what THEY wanted to do. The baby began to scream and John Wesley kicked the back of the seat so hard that his father could feel the blows in his kidney.

"All right!" he shouted and drew the car to a stop at the side of the road. "Will you all shut up? Will you all just shut up for one second? If you don't shut up, we won't go anywhere."

"It would be very educational for them," the grandmother murmured.

"All right," Bailey said, "but get this: this is the only time we're going to stop for anything like this. This is the one and only time."

"The dirt road that you have to turn down is about a mile back," the grandmother directed. "I marked it when we passed."

"A dirt road," Bailey groaned.

After they had turned around and were headed toward the dirt road, the grandmother recalled other points about the house, the beautiful glass over the front doorway and the candle-lamp in the hall. John Wesley said that the secret panel was probably in the fireplace.

"You can't go inside this house," Bailey said. "You don't know who lives there."

"While you all talk to the people in front, I'll run around behind and get in a window," John Wesley suggested.

"We'll all stay in the car," his mother said.

They turned onto the dirt road and the car raced roughly along in a swirl of pink dust. The grandmother recalled the times when there were no paved roads and thirty miles was a day's journey. The dirt road was hilly and there were sudden washes in it and sharp curves on dangerous embankments. All at once they would be on a hill, looking down over the blue tops of trees for miles around, then the next minute, they would be in a red depression with the dust-coated trees looking down on them.

"This place had better turn up in a minute," Bailey said, "or I'm going to turn around."

The road looked as if no one had traveled on it in months.

"It's not much farther," the grandmother said and just as she said it, a horrible thought came to her. The thought was so embarrassing that she turned red in the face and her eyes dilated and her feet jumped up, upsetting her valise in the corner. The instant the valise moved, the newspaper top she had over the basket under it rose with a snarl and Pitty Sing, the cat, sprang onto Bailey's shoulder.

The children were thrown to the floor and their mother, clutching the baby, was thrown out the door onto the ground; the old lady was thrown into the front seat. The car turned over once and landed right-side-up in a gulch off the side of the road. Bailey remained in the driver's seat with the cat—gray-striped with a broad white face and an orange nose—clinging to his neck like a caterpillar.

As soon as the children saw they could move their arms and legs, they scrambled out of the car, shouting, "We've had an ACCIDENT!" The grandmother was curled up under the dashboard, hoping she was injured so that Bailey's wrath would not come down on her all at once. The horrible thought she had had before the accident was that the house she had remembered so vividly was not in Georgia but in Tennessee.

Bailey removed the cat from his neck with both hands and flung it out the window against the side of a pine tree. Then he got out of the car and started looking for the children's mother. She was sitting against the side of the red gutted ditch, holding the screaming baby, but she only had a cut down her face and a broken shoulder. "We've had an ACCIDENT!" the children screamed in a frenzy of delight.

"But nobody's killed," June Star said with disappointment as the grandmother limped out of the car, her hat still pinned to her head but the broken front brim standing up at a jaunty angle and the violet spray hanging off the side. They all sat down in the ditch, except the children, to recover from the shock. They were all shaking.

"Maybe a car will come along," said the children's mother hoarsely.

"I believe I have injured an organ," said the grandmother, pressing her side, but no one answered her. Bailey's teeth were clattering. He had on a yellow sport shirt with bright blue parrots designed in it and his face was as yellow as the shirt. The grandmother decided that she would not mention that the house was in Tennessee.

The road was about ten feet above and they could see only the tops of the trees on the other side of it. Behind the ditch they were sitting in there were more woods, tall and dark and deep. In a few minutes they saw a car some distance away on top of a hill, coming slowly as if the occupants were watching them. The grandmother stood up and waved both arms dramatically to attract their attention. The car continued to come on slowly, disappeared around a bend and appeared again, moving even slower, on top of the hill they had gone over. It was a big black battered hearse-like automobile. There were three men in it.

It came to a stop just over them and for some minutes, the driver looked down with a steady expressionless gaze to where they were sitting, and didn't speak. Then he turned his head and muttered something to the other two and they got out. One was a fat boy in black trousers and a red sweat shirt with a silver stallion embossed on the front of it. He moved around on the right side of them and stood staring, his mouth partly open in a kind of loose grin. The other had on khaki pants and a blue striped coat and a gray hat pulled down very low, hiding most of his face. He came around slowly on the left side. Neither spoke.

The driver got out of the car and stood by the side of it, looking down at them. He was an older man than the other two. His hair was just beginning to gray and he wore silver-rimmed spectacles that gave him a scholarly look. He had a long creased face and didn't have on any shirt or undershirt. He had on blue jeans that were too tight for him and was holding a black hat and a gun. The two boys also had guns.

"We've had an ACCIDENT!" the children screamed.

The grandmother had the peculiar feeling that the bespectacled man was someone she knew. His face was as familiar to her as if she had known him all her life but she could not recall who he was. He moved away from the car and began to come down the embankment, placing his feet carefully so that he wouldn't slip. He had on tan and white shoes and no socks, and his ankles were red and thin. "Good afternoon," he said. "I see you all had you a little spill."

"We turned over twice!" said the grandmother.

"Oncet," he corrected. "We seen it happen. Try their car and see will it run, Hiram," he said quietly to the boy with the gray hat.

"What you got that gun for?" John Wesley asked. "Whatcha gonna do with that gun?"

"Lady," the man said to the children's mother, "would you mind calling them children to sit down by you? Children make me nervous. I want all you all to sit down right together there where you're at."

"What are you telling US what to do for?" June Star asked.

Behind them the line of woods gaped like a dark open mouth. "Come here," said their mother.

"Look here now," Bailey began suddenly, "we're in a predicament! We're in . . ."

The grandmother shrieked. She scrambled to her feet and stood staring. "You're The Misfit!" she said. "I recognized you at once!"

"Yes'm," the man said, smiling slightly as if he were pleased in spite of himself to be known, "but it would have been better for all of you, lady, if you hadn't of reckernized me."

Bailey turned his head sharply and said something to his mother that shocked even the children. The old lady began to cry and The Misfit reddened.

"Lady," he said, "don't you get upset. Sometimes a man says things he don't mean. I don't reckon he meant to talk to you thataway."

"You wouldn't shoot a lady, would you?" the grandmother said and removed a clean handkerchief from her cuff and began to slap at her eyes with it.

The Misfit pointed the toe of his shoe into the ground and made a little hole and then covered it up again. "I would hate to have to," he said.

"Listen," the grandmother almost screamed, "I know you're a good man. You don't look a bit like you have common blood. I know you must come from nice people!"

"Yes mam," he said, "finest people in the world." When he smiled he showed a row of strong white teeth. "God never made a finer woman than my mother and my daddy's heart was pure gold," he said. The boy with the red sweat shirt had come around behind them and was standing with his gun at his hip. The Misfit squatted down on the ground. "Watch them children, Bobby Lee," he said. "You know they make me nervous." He looked at the six of them huddled together in front of him and he seemed to be embarrassed as if he couldn't think of anything to say. "Ain't a cloud in the sky," he remarked, looking up at it. "Don't see no sun but don't see no cloud neither."

"Yes, it's a beautiful day," said the grandmother. "Listen," she said, "you shouldn't call yourself The Misfit because I know you're a good man at heart. I can just look at you and tell."

"Hush!" Bailey yelled. "Hush! Everybody shut up and let me handle this!" He was squatting in the position of a runner about to sprint forward but he didn't move.

"I pre-chate that, lady," The Misfit said and drew a little circle in the ground with the butt of his gun.

"It'll take a half a hour to fix this here car," Hiram called, looking over the raised hood of it.

"Well, first you and Bobby Lee get him and that little boy to step over yonder with you," The Misfit said, pointing to Bailey and John Wesley. "The boys want to ast you something," he said to Bailey. "Would you mind stepping back in them woods there with them?"

"Listen," Bailey began, "we're in a terrible predicament! Nobody realizes what this is," and his voice cracked. His eyes were as blue and intense as the parrots in his shirt and he remained perfectly still.

The grandmother reached up to adjust her hat brim as if she were going to the woods with him but it came off in her hand. She stood staring at it and after a second she let it fall on the ground. Hiram pulled Bailey up by the arm as if he were assisting an old man. John Wesley caught hold of his father's hand and Bobby Lee followed. They went off toward the woods and just as they reached the dark edge, Bailey turned and supporting himself against a gray naked pine trunk, he shouted, "I'll be back in a minute, Mamma, wait on me!"

"Come back this instant!" his mother shrilled but they all disappeared into the woods.

"Bailey Boy!" the grandmother called in a tragic voice but she found she was looking at The Misfit squatting on the ground in front of her. "I just know you're a good man," she said desperately. "You're not a bit common!"

"Nome, I ain't a good man," The Misfit said after a second as if he had considered her statement carefully, "but I ain't the worst in the world neither. My daddy said I was a different breed of dog from my brothers and sisters. 'You know,' Daddy said, 'it's some that can live their whole life out without asking about it and it's others has to know why it is, and this boy is one of the latters. He's going to be into everything!'" He put on his black hat and looked up suddenly and then away deep into the woods as if he were embarrassed again. "I'm sorry I don't have on a shirt before you ladies," he said, hunching his shoulders slightly. "We buried our clothes that we had on when we escaped and we're just making do until we can get better. We borrowed these from some folks we met," he explained.

"That's perfectly all right," the grandmother said. "Maybe Bailey has an extra shirt in his suitcase."

"I'll look and see terrectly," The Misfit said.

"Where are they taking him?" the children's mother screamed.

"Daddy was a card himself," The Misfit said. "You couldn't put anything over on him. He never got in trouble with the Authorities though. Just had the knack of handling them."

"You could be honest too if you'd only try," said the grandmother. "Think how wonderful it would be to settle down and live a comfortable life and not have to think about somebody chasing you all the time."

The Misfit kept scratching in the ground with the butt of his gun as if he were thinking about it. "Yes'm, somebody is always after you," he murmured.

The grandmother noticed how thin his shoulder blades were just behind his hat because she was standing up looking down on him. "Do you ever pray?" she asked.

He shook his head. All she saw was the black hat wiggle between his shoulder blades. "Nome," he said.

There was a pistol shot from the woods, followed closely by another. Then silence. The old lady's head jerked around. She could hear the wind move through the tree tops like a long satisfied insuck of breath. "Bailey Boy!" she called.

"I was a gospel singer for a while," The Misfit said. "I been most everything. Been in the arm service, both land and sea, at home and abroad, been twict married, been an undertaker, been with the railroads, plowed Mother Earth, been in a tornado, seen a man burnt alive oncet," and he looked up at the children's mother and the little girl who were sitting close together, their faces white and their eyes glassy; "I even seen a woman flogged," he said.

"Pray, pray," the grandmother began, "pray, pray . . ."

"I never was a bad boy that I remember of," The Misfit said in an almost dreamy voice, "but somewheres along the line I done something wrong and got sent to the penitentiary. I was buried alive," and he looked up and held her attention to him by a steady stare.

"That's when you should have started to pray," she said. "What did you do to get sent to the penitentiary that first time?"

"Turn to the right, it was a wall," The Misfit said, looking up again at the cloudless sky. "Turn to the left, it was a wall. Look up it was a ceiling, look down it was a floor. I forget what I done, lady. I set there and set there, trying to remember what it was I done and I ain't recalled it to this day. Oncet in a while, I would think it was coming to me, but it never come."

"Maybe they put you in by mistake," the old lady said vaguely.

"Nome," he said. "It wasn't no mistake. They had the papers on me."

"You must have stolen something," she said.

The Misfit sneered slightly. "Nobody had nothing I wanted," he said. "It was a head-doctor at the penitentiary said what I had done was kill my daddy but I known that for a lie. My daddy died in nineteen ought nineteen of the epidemic flu and I never had a thing to do with it. He was buried in the Mount Hopewell Baptist churchyard and you can go there and see for yourself."

"If you would pray," the old lady said, "Jesus would help you."

"That's right," The Misfit said.

"Well then, why don't you pray?" she asked trembling with delight suddenly.

"I don't want no hep," he said. "I'm doing all right by myself."

Bobby Lee and Hiram came ambling back from the woods. Bobby Lee was dragging a yellow shirt with bright blue parrots in it.

"Thow me that shirt, Bobby Lee," The Misfit said. The shirt came flying at him and landed on his shoulder and he put it on. The grandmother couldn't name what the shirt reminded her of. "No, lady," The Misfit said while he was buttoning it up, "I found out the crime don't matter. You can do one thing or you can do another, kill a man or take a tire off his car, because sooner or later you're going to forget what it was you done and just be punished for it."

The children's mother had begun to make heaving noises as if she couldn't get her breath. "Lady," he asked, "would you and that little girl like to step off yonder with Bobby Lee and Hiram and join your husband?"

"Yes, thank you," the mother said faintly. Her left arm dangled helplessly and she was holding the baby, who had gone to sleep, in the other. "Hep that lady up, Hiram," The Misfit said as she struggled to climb out of the ditch, "and Bobby Lee, you hold onto that little girl's hand."

"I don't want to hold hands with him," June Star said. "He reminds me of a pig."

The fat boy blushed and laughed and caught her by the arm and pulled her off into the woods after Hiram and her mother.

Alone with The Misfit, the grandmother found that she had lost her voice. There was not a cloud in the sky nor any sun. There was nothing around her but woods. She wanted to tell him that he must pray. She opened and closed her mouth several times before anything came out. Finally she found herself saying, "Jesus. Jesus," meaning, Jesus will help you, but the way she was saying it, it sounded as if she might be cursing.

"Yes'm," The Misfit said as if he agreed. "Jesus thown everything off balance. It was the same case with Him as with me except He hadn't committed any crime and they could prove I had committed one because they had the papers on me. Of course," he said, "they never shown me my papers. That's why I sign myself now. I said long ago, you get you a signature and sign everything you do and keep a copy of it. Then you'll know what you done and you can hold up the crime to the punishment and see do they match and in the end you'll have something to prove you ain't been treated right. I call myself The Misfit," he said, "because I can't make what all I done wrong fit what all I gone through in punishment."

There was a piercing scream from the woods, followed closely by a pistol report. "Does it seem right to you, lady, that one is punished a heap and another ain't punished at all?"

"Jesus!" the old lady cried. "You've got good blood! I know you wouldn't shoot a lady! I know you come from nice people! Pray! Jesus, you ought not to shoot a lady. I'll give you all the money I've got!"

"Lady," The Misfit said, looking beyond her far into the woods, "there never was a body that give the undertaker a tip."

There were two more pistol reports and the grandmother raised her head like a parched old turkey hen crying for water and called, "Bailey Boy, Bailey Boy!" as if her heart would break.

"Jesus was the only One that ever raised the dead," The Misfit continued, "and He shouldn't have done it. He thown everything off balance. If He did what He said, then it's nothing for you to do but thow away everything and follow Him, and if He didn't, then it's nothing for you to do but enjoy the few minutes you got left the best way you can—by killing somebody or burning down his house or doing some other meanness to him. No pleasure but meanness," he said and his voice had become almost a snarl.

"Maybe He didn't raise the dead," the old lady mumbled, not knowing what she was saying and feeling so dizzy that she sank down in the ditch with her legs twisted under her.

"I wasn't there so I can't say He didn't," The Misfit said. "I wisht I had of been there," he said, hitting the ground with his fist. "It ain't right I wasn't there because if I had of been there I would of known. Listen lady," he said in a high voice, "if I had of been there I would of known and I wouldn't be like I am now." His voice seemed about to crack and the grandmother's head cleared for an instant. She saw the man's face twisted close to her own as if he were going to cry and she murmured, "Why you're one of my babies. You're one of my own children!" She reached out and touched him on the shoulder. The Misfit sprang back as if a snake had bitten him and shot her three times through the chest. Then he put his gun down on the ground and took off his glasses and began to clean them.

Hiram and Bobby Lee returned from the woods and stood over the ditch, looking down at the grandmother who half sat and half lay in a puddle of blood with her legs crossed under her like a child's and her face smiling up at the cloudless sky.

Without his glasses, The Misfit's eyes were red-rimmed and pale and defenseless-looking. "Take her off and thow her where you thown the others," he said, picking up the cat that was rubbing itself against his leg.

"She was a talker, wasn't she?" Bobby Lee said, sliding down the ditch with a yodel.

"She would of been a good woman," The Misfit said, "if it had been somebody there to shoot her every minute of her life."

"Some fun!" Bobby Lee said.

"Shut up, Bobby Lee," The Misfit said. "It's no real pleasure in life."

JOHN UPDIKE

[1932–]

Pigeon Feathers

(First published in the *New Yorker*, August, 1961; first book publication in 1962.)

WHEN THEY MOVED to Firetown, things were upset, displaced, rearranged. A red cane-back sofa that had been the chief piece in the living room at Olinger was here banished, too big for the narrow country parlor, to the barn, and shrouded under a tarpaulin. Never again would David lie on its length all afternoon eating raisins and reading mystery novels and science fiction and P. G. Wodehouse. The blue wing chair that had stood for years in the ghostly, immaculate guest bedroom in town, gazing through windows curtained with dotted swiss at the telephone wires and horse-chestnut trees and opposite houses, was here established importantly in front of the smutty little fireplace that supplied, in those first cold April days, their only heat. As a child, David had always been afraid of the guest bedroom—it was there that he, lying sick with the measles, had seen a black rod the size of a yardstick jog along at a slight slant beside the edge of the bed, and vanish when he screamed—and it was disquieting to have one of the elements of its haunted atmosphere basking by the fire, in the center of the family, growing sooty with use. The books that at home had gathered dust in the case beside the piano were here hastily stacked, all out of order, in the shelves that the carpenters had built low along one wall. David, at fourteen, had been more moved than a mover; like the furniture, he had to find a new place, and on the Saturday of the second week tried to work off some of his disorientation by arranging the books.

It was a collection obscurely depressing to him, mostly books his mother had acquired when she was young: college anthologies of Greek plays and Romantic poetry; Will Durant's *Story of Philosophy*; a soft-leather set of Shakespeare with string bookmarks sewed to the bindings; *Green Mansions*, boxed and illustrated with woodcuts; *I, the Tiger*, by Manuel Komroff; novels by names like Galsworthy and Ellen Glasgow and Irvin S. Cobb and Sinclair Lewis and "Elizabeth." The odor of faded taste made him feel the ominous gap between himself and his parents, the insulting gulf of time that existed before he was born. Suddenly he was tempted to dip into this time. From the heaps of books around him on the broad old floorboards, he picked up Volume II of a four-volume set of *An Outline of History*, by H. G. Wells. The book's red binding had faded to orange-pink in the spine. When he lifted the cover, there was a sweetish, atticlike smell, and his mother's maiden name written in unfamiliar handwriting on the flyleaf—an upright, bold, yet careful signature, bearing a faint relation to the quick scrunched backslant that flowed with marvelous consistency across her shopping lists and budget accounts and notes on Christmas cards to college friends from this same, vaguely menacing long ago.

He leafed through, pausing at drawings, done in an old-fashioned stippled style, of bas-reliefs, masks, Romans without pupils in their eyes, articles of ancient costume, fragments of pottery found in unearthed homes. The print was determinedly legible, and smug, like a lesson book. As he bent over the pages, yellow at the edges, they were like rectangles of dusty glass through which he looked down into unreal and irrelevant worlds. He could see things sluggishly move, and an unpleasant fullness came into his throat. His mother and grandmother fussed in the kitchen; the puppy, which they had just acquired, "for protection in the country," was cowering, with a sporadic panicked scrabble of claws, under the dining table that in their old home had been reserved for special days but that here was used for every meal.

Then, before he could halt his eyes, David slipped into Wells's account of Jesus. He had been an obscure political agitator, a kind of hobo, in a minor colony of the Roman Empire. By an accident impossible to reconstruct, he (the small *h* horrified David) survived his own crucifixion and presumably died a few weeks later. A religion was founded on the freakish incident. The credulous imagination of the times retrospectively assigned miracles and supernatural pretensions to Jesus; a myth grew, and then a church, whose theology at most points was in direct contradiction of the simple, rather communistic teachings of the Galilean.

It was as if a stone that for weeks and even years had been gathering weight in the web of David's nerves snapped them, plunged through the page, and a hundred layers of paper underneath. These fantastic falsehoods (plainly untrue; churches stood everywhere, the entire nation was founded "under God") did not at first frighten him; it was the fact that they had been permitted to exist in an actual human brain. This was the initial impact—that at a definite spot in time and space a brain black with the denial of Christ's divinity had been suffered to exist; that the universe had not spit out this ball of tar but allowed it to continue in its blasphemy, to grow old, win honors, wear a hat, write books that, if true, collapsed everything into a jumble of horror. The world outside the deep-silled windows—a rutted lawn, a whitewashed barn, a walnut tree frothy with fresh green—seemed a haven from which he was forever sealed off. Hot washrags seemed pressed against his cheeks.

He read the account again. He tried to supply out of his ignorance objections that would defeat the complacent march of these black words, and found none. Survivals and misunderstandings more farfetched were reported daily in the papers. But none of them caused churches to be built in every town. He tried to work backward through the churches, from their brave high fronts through their shabby, ill-attended interiors back into the events at Jerusalem, and felt himself surrounded by shifting gray shadows, centuries of history, where he knew nothing. The thread dissolved in his hands. Had Christ ever come to him, David Kern, and said, "Here. Feel the wound in My side"? No; but prayers had been answered. What prayers? He had prayed that Rudy Mohn, whom he had purposely tripped so he cracked his head on their radiator, not die, and he had not died. But for all the blood, it was just a cut; Rudy came back the same day, wearing a bandage and repeating the same teasing words. He could never have died. Again, David had prayed for two separate photographs of movie stars he had sent away for to arrive tomorrow, and though they did not, they did arrive, some days later, together, popping through the clacking letter slot like a rebuke from God's mouth: *I answer your prayers in My way, in My time.* After that, he had made his prayers less definite, less susceptible of being twisted into a scolding. But what a tiny, ridiculous coincidence this was, after all, to throw into battle against H. G. Wells's engines of knowledge! Indeed, it proved the enemy's point: Hope bases vast premises on foolish accidents, and reads a word where in fact only a scribble exists.

His father came home. They had supper. It got dark. He had to go to the bathroom, and took a flashlight down through the wet grass to the outhouse. For once, his fear of spiders there felt trivial. He set the flashlight, burning, beside him, and an insect alighted on its lens, a tiny insect, a mosquito or flea, so fragile and fine that the weak light projected its X-ray onto the wall boards: the faint rim of its wings, the blurred strokes, magnified, of its long hinged legs, the dark cone at the heart of its anatomy. The tremor must be its heart beating. Without warning, David was visited by an exact vision of death: a long hole in the ground, no wider than your body, down which you are drawn while the white faces above recede. You try to reach them but your arms are pinned. Shovels pour dirt into your face. There you will be forever, in an upright position, blind and silent, and in time no one will remember you, and you will never be called. As strata of rock shift, your fingers elongate, and your teeth are distended sidewise in a great underground grimace indistinguishable from a strip of chalk. And the earth tumbles on, and the sun expires, and unaltering darkness reigns where once there were stars.

Sweat broke out on his back. His mind seemed to rebound off of a solidness. Such extinction was not another threat, a graver sort of danger, a kind of pain; it was qualitatively different. It was not even a conception that could be voluntarily pictured; it entered you from outside. His protesting nerves swarmed on its surface like lichen on a meteor. The skin of his chest was soaked with the effort of rejection. At the same time that the fear was dense and internal, it was dense and all around him; a tide of clay had swept up to the stars; space was crushed into a mass. When he stood up, automatically hunching his shoulders to keep his head away from the spider webs, it was with a numb sense of being cramped between two huge volumes of rigidity. That he had even this small freedom to move surprised him. In the narrow shelter of that rank shack, adjusting his pants, he felt—his first spark of comfort—too small to be crushed.

But in the open, as the beam of the flashlight skidded with frightened quickness across the remote surfaces of the barn wall and the grape arbor and the giant pine that stood by the path to the woods, the terror descended. He raced up through the clinging grass pursued not by one of the wild animals the woods might hold, or one of the goblins his superstitious grandmother had communicated to his childhood, but by specters out of science fiction, where gigantic cinder moons fill half the turquoise sky. As David ran, a gray planet rolled inches behind his neck. If he looked back, he would be buried. And in the momentum of his terror, hideous possibilities—the dilation of the sun, the triumph of the insects —wheeled out of the vacuum of make-believe and added their weight to his impending oblivion.

He wrenched the door open; the lamps within the house flared. The wicks burning here and there seemed to mirror one another. His mother was washing the dishes in a little pan of heated pump water; Granmom fluttered near her elbow apprehensively. In the living room—the downstairs of the little square house was two long rooms—his father sat in front of the black fireplace restlessly folding and unfolding a newspaper.

David took from the shelf, where he had placed it this afternoon, the great unabridged Webster's Dictionary that his grandfather had owned. He turned the big thin pages, floppy as cloth, to the entry he wanted, and read:

soul . . . **1.** An entity conceived as the essence, substance, animating principle, or actuating cause of life, or of the individual life, esp. of life manifested in physical activities; the vehicle of individual existence, separate in nature from the body and usually held to be separable in existence.

The definition went on, into Greek and Egyptian conceptions, but David stopped short on the treacherous edge of antiquity. He needed to read no farther. The careful overlapping words shingled a temporary shelter for him. "Usually held to be separable in existence"—what could be fairer, more judicious, surer?

Upstairs, he seemed to be lifted above his fears. The sheets on his bed were clean. Granmom had ironed them with a pair of flatirons saved from the Olinger attic; she plucked them hot off the stove alternately, with a wooden handle called a goose. It was a wonder, to see how she managed. In the next room, his parents made comforting scratching noises as they carried a little lamp back and forth. Their door was open a crack, so he saw the light shift and swing. Surely there would be, in the last five minutes, in the last second, a crack of light, showing the door from the dark room to another, full of light. Thinking of it this vividly frightened him. His own dying, in a specific bed in a specific room, specific walls mottled with wallpaper, the dry whistle of his breathing, the murmuring doctors, the nervous relatives going in and out, but for him no way out but down into the funnel. Never touch a doorknob again. A whisper, and his parents' light was blown out. David prayed to be reassured. Though the experiment frightened him, he lifted his hands high into the darkness above his face and begged Christ to touch them. Not hard or long; the faintest, quickest grip would be final for a lifetime. His hands waited in the air, itself a substance, which seemed to move through his fingers; or was it the pressure of his pulse? He returned his hands to beneath the covers uncertain if they had been touched or not. For would not Christ's touch *be* infinitely gentle?

Through all the eddies of its aftermath, David clung to this thought about his revelation of extinction: that there, in the outhouse, he had struck a solidness *qualitatively different*, a rock of horror firm enough to support any height of construction. All he needed was a little help; a word, a gesture, a nod of certainty and he would be sealed in, safe. The assurance from the dictionary had melted in the night. Today was Sunday, a hot fair day. Across a mile of clear air the church bells called, *Celebrate, celebrate*. Only Daddy went. He put on a coat over his rolled-up shirtsleeves and got into the little old black Plymouth parked by the barn and went off, with the same pained, hurried grimness of all his actions. His churning wheels, as he shifted too hastily into second, raised plumes of red dust on the dirt road. Mother walked to the far field, to see what bushes needed cutting. David, though he usually preferred to stay in the house, went with her. The puppy followed at a distance, whining as it picked its way through the stubble but floundering off timidly if one of them went back to pick it up and carry it. When they reached the crest of the far field, his mother asked, "David, what's troubling you?"

"Nothing. Why?"

She looked at him sharply. The greening woods cross-hatched the space beyond her half-gray hair. Then she turned her profile, and gestured toward the house, which they had left a half mile behind them. "See how it sits in the land? They don't know how to build with the land any more. Pop always said the foundations were set with the compass. We must try to get a compass and see. It's supposed to face due south; but south feels a little more *that* way to me." From the side, as she said these things, she seemed handsome and young. The smooth sweep of her hair over her ear seemed white with a purity and calm that made her feel foreign to him. He had never regarded his parents as consolers of his troubles; from the beginning they had seemed to have more troubles than he. Their confusion had flattered him into an illusion of strength; so now on this high clear ridge he jealously guarded the menace all around them, blowing like a breeze on his fingertips, the possibility of all this wide scenery sinking into darkness. The strange fact that though she came to look at the brush she carried no clippers, for she had a fixed prejudice against working on Sundays, was the only consolation he allowed her to offer.

As they walked back, the puppy whimpering after them, the rising dust behind a distant line of trees announced that Daddy was speeding home from church. When they reached the house he was there. He had brought back the Sunday paper and the vehement remark "Dobson's too intelligent for these farmers. They just sit there with their mouths open and don't hear a thing he's saying."

David hid in the funny papers and sports section until one-thirty. At two, the catechetical class met at the Firetown church. He had transferred from the catechetical class of the Lutheran church in Olinger, a humiliating comedown. In Olinger they met on Wednesday nights, spiffy and spruce, in the atmosphere of a dance. Afterward, blessed by the brickfaced minister from whose lips the word "Christ" fell like a burning stone, the more daring of them went with their Bibles to a luncheonette and smoked. Here in Firetown, the girls were dull white cows and the boys narrow-faced brown goats in old men's suits, herded on Sunday afternoons into a threadbare church basement that smelled of stale hay. Because his father had taken the car on one of his countless errands to Olinger, David walked, grateful for the open air and the silence. The catechetical class embarrassed him, but today he placed hope in it, as the source of the nod, the gesture, that was all he needed.

Reverend Dobson was a delicate young man with great dark eyes and small white shapely hands that flickered like protesting doves when he preached; he seemed a bit misplaced in the Lutheran ministry. This was his first call. It was a split parish; he served another rural church twelve miles away. His iridescent green Ford, new six months ago, was spattered to the windows with red mud and rattled from bouncing on the rude back roads, where he frequently got lost, to the malicious satisfaction of many. But David's mother liked him, and, more pertinent to his success, the Haiers, the sleek family of feed merchants and innkeepers and tractor salesmen who dominated the Firetown church liked him. David liked him, and felt liked in turn; sometimes in class, after some special stupidity, Dobson directed toward him out of those wide black eyes a mild look of disbelief, a look that, though flattering, was also delicately disquieting.

Catechetical instruction consisted of reading aloud from a work booklet answers to problems prepared during the week, problems like "I am the ——, the–, and the——, saith the Lord." Then there was a question period in which no one ever asked any questions. Today's theme was the last third of the Apostles' Creed. When the time came for questions, David blushed and asked, "About the Resurrection of the Body—are we conscious between the time when we die and the Day of Judgment?"

Dobson blinked, and his fine little mouth pursed, suggesting that David was making difficult things more difficult. The faces of the other students went blank, as if an indiscretion had been committed.

"No, I suppose not," Reverend Dobson said.

"Well, where is our soul, then, in this gap?"

The sense grew, in the class, of a naughtiness occurring. Dobson's shy eyes watered, as if he were straining to keep up the formality of attention, and one of the girls, the fattest, simpered toward her twin, who was a little less fat. Their chairs were arranged in a rough circle. The current running around the circle panicked David. Did everybody know something he didn't know?

"I suppose you could say our souls are asleep," Dobson said.

"And then they wake up, and there is the earth like it always is, and all the people who have ever lived? Where will Heaven be?"

Anita Haier giggled. Dobson gazed at David intently, but with an awkward, puzzled flicker of forgiveness, as if there existed a secret between them that David was violating. But David knew of no secret. All he wanted was to hear Dobson repeat the words he said every Sunday morning. This he would not do. As if these words were unworthy of the conversational voice.

"David, you might think of Heaven this way: as the way the goodness Abraham Lincoln did lives after him."

"But is Lincoln conscious of it living on?" He blushed no longer with embarrassment but in anger; he had walked here in good faith and was being made a fool.

"Is he conscious now? I would have to say no; but I don't think it matters." Dobson's voice had a coward's firmness; he was hostile now.

"You don't?"

"Not in the eyes of God, no." The unction, the stunning impudence, of this reply sprang tears of outrage in David's eyes. He bowed them to his book, where short words like Duty, Love, Obey, Honor were stacked in the form of a cross.

"Were there any other questions, David?" Dobson asked with renewed gentleness. The others were rustling, collecting their books.

"No." He made his voice firm, though he could not bring up his eyes.

"Did I answer your question fully enough?"

"Yes."

In the minister's silence the shame that should have been his crept over David; the burden and fever of being a fraud were placed upon *him*, who was innocent, and it seemed, he knew, a confession of this guilt that on the way out he was unable to face Dobson's stirred gaze, though he felt it probing the side of his head.

Anita Haier's father gave him a ride down the highway as far as the dirt road. David said he wanted to walk the rest, and figured that his offer was accepted because Mr. Haier did not want to dirty his bright blue Buick with dust. This was all right; everything was all right, as long as it was clear. His indignation at being betrayed, at seeing Christianity betrayed, had hardened him. The straight dirt road reflected his hardness. Pink stones thrust up through its packed surface. The April sun beat down from the center of the afternoon half of the sky; already it had some of summer's heat. Already the fringes of weeds at the edges of the road were bedraggled with dust. From the reviving grass and scruff of the fields he walked between, insects were sending up a monotonous, automatic chant. In the distance a tiny figure in his father's coat was walking along the edge of the woods. His mother. He wondered what joy she found in such walks; to him the brown stretches of slowly rising and falling land expressed only a huge exhaustion.

Flushed with fresh air and happiness, she returned from her walk earlier than he had expected, and surprised him at his grandfather's Bible. It was a stumpy black book, the boards worn thin where the old man's fingers had held them; the spine hung by one weak hinge of fabric. David had been looking for the passage where Jesus says to the one thief on the cross "Today shalt thou be with me in paradise." He had never tried reading the Bible for himself before. What was so embarrassing about being caught at it was that he detested the apparatus of piety. Fusty churches, creaking hymns, ugly Sunday-school teachers and their stupid leaflets—he hated everything about them but the promise they held out, a promise that in the most perverse way, as if the homeliest crone in the kingdom were given the prince's hand, made every good and real thing, ball games and jokes and big-breasted girls, possible. He couldn't explain this to his mother. Her solicitude was upon him.

"David, what are you doing at Granpop's Bible?"

"Trying to read it. This is supposed to he a Christian country, isn't it?"

She sat down on the green sofa that used to be in the sun parlor at Olinger, under the fancy mirror. A little smile still lingered on her face from the walk. "David, I wish you'd talk to me."

"What about?"

"About whatever it is that's troubling you. Your father and I have both noticed it."

"I asked Reverend Dobson about Heaven and he said it was like Abraham Lincoln's goodness living after him."

He waited for the shock to strike her. "Yes?" she said, expecting more.

"That's all."

"And why didn't you like it?"

"Well; don't you see? It amounts to saying there isn't any Heaven at all."

"I don't see that it amounts to that. What do you want Heaven to be?"

"Well, I don't know. I want it to be *some*thing. I thought *he'd* tell me what it was. I thought that was his job." He was becoming angry, sensing her surprise at him. She had assumed that Heaven had faded from his head years ago. She had imagined that he had already entered, in the secrecy of silence, the conspiracy that he now knew to be all around him.

"David," she asked gently, "don't you ever want to rest?"

"No. Not forever."

"David, you're so young. When you get older, you'll feel differently."

"Grandpa didn't. Look how tattered this book is."

"I never understood your grandfather."

"Well, I don't understand ministers who say it's like Lincoln's memory going on and on. Suppose you're not Lincoln?"

"I think Reverend Dobson made a mistake. You must try to forgive him."

"It's not a *question* of his making a mistake! It's a question of dying and never moving or seeing or hearing anything ever again."

"But"—in exasperation—"darling, it's so *greedy* of you to want more. When God has given us this wonderful April day, and given us this farm, and you have your whole life ahead of you—"

"You think, then, that there is God?"

"Of course I do"—with deep relief that smoothed her features into a reposeful oval. He was standing, and above her, too near for his comfort. He was afraid she would reach out and touch him.

"He made everthing? You feel that?"

"Yes."

"Then who made Him?"

"Why, Man. Man." The happiness of this answer lit up her face radiantly, until she saw his gesture of disgust.

"Well that amounts to saying there is none."

Her hand reached for his wrist but he backed away. "David, it's a mystery. A miracle. It's a miracle more beautiful than any Reverend Dobson could have told you about. You don't say houses don't exist because Man made them."

"No. God has to be different."

"But, David, you have the *evidence*. Look out the window at the sun; at the fields."

"Mother, good grief. Don't you see"—he gasped away the roughness in his throat—"if when we die there's nothing, all your sun and fields and what not are all, ah *horror*? It's just an ocean of horror."

"But David, it's not. It's so clearly not that." And she made an urgent opening gesture with her hands that expressed, with its suggestion of a willingness to receive his helplessness, all her grace, her gentleness, her love of beauty gathered into a passive intensity that made him intensely hate her. He would not be wooed away from the truth. *I am the Way, the Truth—*

"No," he told her. "Just let me alone."

He found his tennis ball behind the piano and went outside to throw it against the side of the house. There was a patch high up where the brown stucco that had been laid over the sandstone masonry was crumbling away; he kept trying with the tennis ball to chip more pieces off. Superimposed upon his deep ache was a smaller but more immediate worry that he had hurt his mother. He heard his father's car rattling on the straightaway, and went into the house, to make peace before he arrived. To his relief, she was not giving off the stifling damp heat of her anger but instead was cool, decisive, maternal. She handed him an old green book, her college text of Plato.

"I want you to read the Parable of the Cave," she said.

"All right," he said, though he knew it would do no good. Some story by a dead Greek just vague enough to please her. "Don't worry about it, Mother."

"I am worried. Honestly, David, I'm sure there will be something for us. As you get older, these things seem to matter a great deal less."

"That may be. It's a dismal thought, though."

His father bumped at the door. The locks and jambs stuck here. But before Granmom could totter to the catch and let him in, he had knocked it open. Although Mother usually kept her talks with David a confidence, a treasure between them, she called instantly, "George, David is worried about death!"

He came to the doorway of the living room, his shirt pocket bristling with pencils, holding in one hand a pint box of melting ice cream and in the other the knife with which he was about to divide it into four sections, their Sunday treat. "Is the kid worried about death? Don't give it a thought, David. I'll be lucky if I live till tomorrow, and I'm not worried. If they'd taken a buckshot gun and shot me in the cradle I'd be better off. The *world'd* be better off. Hell, I think death is a wonderful thing. I look forward to it. Get the garbage out of the way. If I had the man here who invented death, I'd pin a medal on him."

"Hush, George. You'll frighten the child worse than he is."

This was not true; he never frightened David. There was no harm in his father, no harm at all. Indeed, in the man's steep self-disgust the boy felt a kind of ally. A distant ally. He saw his position with a certain strategic coldness. Nowhere in the world of other people would he find the hint, the nod, he needed to begin to build his fortress against death. They none of them believed. He was alone. In a deep hole.

In the months that followed, his position changed little. School was some comfort. All those sexy, perfumed people, wisecracking, chewing gum, all of them doomed to die, and none of them noticing. In their company David felt that they would carry him along into the bright, cheap paradise reserved for them. In any crowd, the fear ebbed a little; he had reasoned that somewhere in the world there must exist a few people who believed what was necessary, and the larger the crowd, the greater the chance that he was near such a soul, within calling distance, if only he was not too ignorant, too ill-equipped, to spot him. The sight of clergymen cheered him; whatever they themselves thought, their collars were still a sign that somewhere, at some time, someone had recognized that we cannot, *cannot,* submit to death. The sermon topics posted outside churches, the flip hurried pieties of disc jockeys, the cartoons in magazines showing angels or devils—on such scraps he kept alive the possibility of hope.

For the rest, he tried to drown his hopelessness in clatter and jostle. The pinball machine at the luncheonette was a merciful distraction; as he bent over its buzzing, flashing board of flippers and cushions, the weight and constriction in his chest lightened and loosened. He was grateful for all the time his father wasted in Olinger. Every delay postponed the moment when they must ride together down the dirt road into the heart of the dark farmland, where the only light was the kerosene lamp waiting on the dining room table, a light that made their food shadowy, scrabbled, sinister.

He lost his appetite for reading. He was afraid of being ambushed again. In mystery novels people died like dolls being discarded; in science fiction enormities of space and time conspired to crush the humans; and even in P. G. Wodehouse he felt a hollowness, a turning away from reality that was implicitly bitter and became explicit in the comic figures of futile clergymen. All gaiety seemed minced out on the skin of a void. All quiet hours seemed invitations to dread.

School stopped. His father took the car in the opposite direction, to a construction job where he had been hired for the summer as a timekeeper, and David was stranded in the middle of acres of heat and greenery and blowing pollen and the strange, mechanical humming that lay invisibly in the weeds and alfalfa and dry orchard grass.

For his fifteenth birthday his parents gave him, with jokes about his being a hillbilly now, a Remington .22. It was somewhat like a pinball machine to take it out to the old kiln in the woods, where they dumped their trash, and set up tin cans on the kiln's sandstone shoulder and shoot them off one by one. He'd take the puppy, who had grown long legs and a rich coat of reddish fur—he was part chow. Copper hated the gun but loved David enough to accompany him. When the flat acrid crack rang out, he would race in terrified circles that would tighten and tighten until they brought him, shivering, against David's legs. Depending upon his mood, David would shoot again or drop to his knees and comfort the dog. Giving this comfort to a degree returned comfort to him. The dog's ears, laid flat against his skull in fear, were folded so intricately, so—he groped for the concept—*surely*. Where the dull-studded collar made his fur stand up, each hair showed a root of soft white under the length, black-tipped, of the metal color that had given the dog its name. In his agitation Copper panted through nostrils that were elegant slits, like two healed cuts, or like the keyholes of a dainty lock of black, grained wood. His whole whorling, knotted, jointed body was a wealth of such embellishments. And in the smell of the dog's hair David seemed to descend through many finely differentiated layers of earth: mulch, soil, sand, clay, and the glittering mineral base.

But when he returned to the house, and saw the books arranged on the low shelves, fear returned. The four adamant volumes of Wells like four thin bricks, the green Plato that had puzzled him with its queer softness and tangled purity, the dead Galsworthy and "Elizabeth," Grandpa's mammoth dictionary, Grandpa's Bible, the Bible that he himself had received on becoming a member of the Firetown Lutheran Church—at the sight of these, the memory of his fear reawakened and came around him. He had grown stiff and stupid in its embrace. His parents tried to think of ways to entertain him.

"David, I have a job for you to do," his mother said one evening at the table.

"What?"

"If you're going to take that tone perhaps we'd better not talk."

"What tone? I didn't take any tone."

"Your grandmother thinks there are too many pigeons in the barn."

"Why?" David turned to look at his grandmother, but she sat there staring at the orange flame of the burning lamp with her usual expression of bewilderment.

Mother shouted, "Mom, he wants to know why?"

Granmom made a jerky, irritable motion with her bad hand, as if generating the force for utterance, and said, "They foul the furniture."

"That's right," Mother said. "She's afraid for that old Olinger furniture that we'll never use. David, she's been after me for a month about those poor pigeons. She wants you to shoot them."

"I don't want to kill anything especially," David said.

Daddy said, "The kid's like you are, Elsie. He's too good for this world. Kill or be killed, that's my motto."

His mother said loudly, "Mother, he doesn't want to do it."

"Not?" The old lady's eyes distended as if in horror, and her claw descended slowly to her lap.

"Oh, I'll do it, I'll do it tomorrow," David snapped, and a pleasant crisp taste entered his mouth with the decision.

"And I had thought, when Boyer's men made the hay, it would be better if the barn doesn't look like a rookery," his mother added needlessly.

A barn, in day, is a small night. The splinters of light between the dry shingles pierce the high roof like stars, and the rafters and crossbeams and built-in ladders seem, until your eyes adjust, as mysterious as the branches of a haunted forest. David entered silently, the gun in one hand. Copper whined desperately at the door, too frightened to come in with the gun yet unwilling to leave the boy. David stealthily turned, said, "Go away," shut the door on the dog, and slipped the bolt across. It was a door within a door; the double door for wagons and tractors was as high and wide as the face of a house.

The smell of old straw scratched his sinuses. The red sofa, half hidden under its white-splotched tarpaulin, seemed assimilated into this smell, sunk in it, buried. The mouths of empty bins gaped like caves. Rusty oddments of farming—coils of baling wire, some spare tines for a harrow, a handleless shovel—hung on nails driven here and there in the thick wood. He stood stock-still a minute; it took a while to separate the cooing of the pigeons from the rustling in his ears. When he had focused on the cooing, it flooded the vast interior with its throaty, bubbling outpour: there seemed no other sound. They were up behind the beams. What light there was leaked through the shingles and the dirty glass windows at the far end and the small round holes, about as big as basketballs, high on the opposite stone side walls, under the ridge of the roof.

A pigeon appeared in one of these holes, on the side toward the house. It flew in, with a battering of wings, from the outside, and waited there, silhouetted against its pinched bit of sky, preening and cooing in a throbbing, thrilled, tentative way. David tiptoed four steps to the side, rested his gun against the lowest rung of a ladder pegged between two upright beams, and lowered the gunsight into the bird's tiny, jauntily cocked head. The slap of the report seemed to come off the stone wall behind him, and the pigeon did not fall. Neither did it fly. Instead it stuck in the round hole, pirouetting rapidly and nodding its head as if in frantic agreement. David shot the bolt back and forth and had aimed again before the spent cartridge stopped jingling on the boards by his feet. He eased the tip of the sight a little lower, into the bird's breast, and took care to squeeze the trigger with perfect evenness. The slow contraction of his hand, abruptly sprang the bullet; for a half second there was doubt, and then the pigeon fell like a handful of rags, skimming down the barn wall into the layer of straw that coated the floor of the mow on this side.

Now others shook loose from the rafters, and whirled in the dim air with a great blurred hurtle of feathers and noise. They would go for the hole; he fixed his sights on the little moon of blue, and when a pigeon came to it, shot him as he was walking the ten inches or so of stone that would carry him into the open air. This pigeon lay down in that tunnel of stone, unable to fall either one way or the other, although he was alive enough to lift one wing and cloud the light. It would sink back, and he would suddenly lift it again, the feathers flaring. His body blocked that exit. David raced to the other side of the barn's main aisle, where a similar ladder was symmetrically placed, and rested his gun on the same rung. Three birds came together to this hole; he got one, and two got through. The rest resettled in the rafters.

There was a shallow triangular space behind the crossbeams supporting the roof. It was here they roosted and hid. But either the space was too small, or they were curious, for now that his eyes were at home in the dusty gloom David could see little dabs of gray popping in and out. The cooing was shriller now; its apprehensive tremolo made the whole volume of air seem liquid. He noticed one little smudge of a head that was especially persistent in peeking out; he marked the place, and fixed his gun on it, and when the head appeared again, had his finger tightened in advance on the trigger. A parcel of fluff slipped off the beam and fell the barn's height onto a canvas covering some Olinger furniture, and where its head had peeked out there was a fresh prick of light in the shingles.

Standing in the center of the floor, fully master now, disdaining to steady the barrel with anything but his arm, he killed two more that way. He felt like a beautiful avenger. Out of the shadowy ragged infinity of the vast barn roof these impudent things dared to thrust their heads, presumed to dirty its starred silence with their filthy timorous life, and he cut them off, tucked them back neatly into the silence. He had the sensations of a creator; these little smudges and flickers that he was clever to see and even cleverer to hit in the dim recesses of the rafters—out of each of them he was making a full bird. A tiny peek, probe, dab of life, when he hit it, blossomed into a dead enemy, falling with good, final weight.

The imperfection of the second pigeon he had shot, who was still lifting his wing now and then up in the round hole, nagged him. He put a new clip into the stock. Hugging the gun against his body, he climbed the ladder. The barrel sight scratched his ear; he had a sharp, bright vision, like a color slide, of shooting himself and being found tumbled on the barn floor among his prey. He locked his arm around the top rung—a fragile, gnawed rod braced between uprights—and shot into the bird's body from a flat angle. The wing folded, but the impact did not, as he had hoped, push the bird out of the hole. He fired again, and again, and still the little body, lighter than air when alive, was too heavy to budge from its high grave. From up here he could see green trees and a brown corner of the house through the hole. Clammy with the cobwebs that gathered between the rungs, he pumped a full clip of eight bullets into the stubborn shadow, with no success. He climbed down, and was struck by the silence in the barn. The remaining pigeons must have escaped out the other hole. That was all right; he was tired of it.

He stepped with his rifle into the light. His mother was coming to meet him, and it amused him to see her shy away from the carelessly held gun. "You took a chip out of the house," she said. "What were those last shots about?"

"One of them died up in that little round window and I was trying to shoot it down."

"Copper's hiding behind the piano and won't come out. I had to leave him."

"Well, don't blame me. *I* didn't want to shoot the poor devils."

"Don't smirk. You look like your father. How many did you get?"

"Six."

She went into the barn, and he followed. She listened to the silence. Her hair was scraggly, perhaps from tussling with the dog. "I don't suppose the others will be back," she said wearily. "Indeed, I don't know why I let Mother talk me into it. Their cooing was such a comforting noise." She began to gather up the dead birds. Though he didn't want to touch them, David went into the mow and picked up by its tepid, horny, coral-colored feet the first bird he had killed. Its wings unfolded disconcertingly, as if the creature had been held together by threads that now were slit. It did not weigh much. He retrieved the one on the other side of the barn; his mother got the three in the middle, and led the way across the road to the little southern slope of land that went down toward the foundations of the vanished tobacco shed. The ground was too steep to plant or mow; wild strawberries grew in the tangled grass. She put her burden down and said, "We'll have to bury them. The dog will go wild."

He put his two down on her three; the slick feathers let the bodies slide liquidly on one another. He asked, "Shall I get you the shovel?"

"Get it for yourself; *you* bury them. They're your kill," she said. "And be sure to make the hole deep enough so he won't dig them up."

While he went to the tool shed for the shovel, she went into the house. Unlike her, she did not look up, either at the orchard to the right of her or at the meadow on her left, but instead held her head rigidly, tilted a little, as if listening to the ground.

He dug the hole, in a spot where there were no strawberry plants, before he studied the pigeons. He had never seen a bird this close before. The feathers were more wonderful than dog's hair; for each filament was shaped within the shape of the feather, and the feathers in turn were trimmed to fit a pattern that flowed without error across the bird's body. He lost himself in the geometrical tides as the feathers now broadened and stiffened to make an edge for flight, now softened and constricted to cup warmth around the mute flesh. And across the surface of the infinitely adjusted yet somehow effortless mechanics of the feathers played idle designs of color, no two alike, designs executed, it seemed, in a controlled rapture, with a joy that hung level in the air above and behind him. Yet these birds bred in the millions and were exterminated as pests. Into the fragrant, open earth he dropped one broadly banded in shades of slate blue, and on top of it another, mottled all over with rhythmic patches of lilac and gray. The next was almost wholly white, yet with a salmon glaze at the throat. As he fitted the last two, still pliant, on the top, and stood up, crusty coverings were lifted from him, and with a feminine, slipping sensation along his nerves that seemed to give the air hands, he was robed in this certainty: that the God who had lavished such craft upon these worthless birds would not destroy His whole Creation by refusing to let David live forever.

JOYCE CAROL OATES

[1938–]

Where Are You Going, Where Have You Been?

TO BOB DYLAN

(First published in *Epoch*, Fall, 1965; first book publication in 1965.)

HER NAME WAS Connie. She was fifteen and she had a quick nervous giggling habit of craning her neck to glance into mirrors, or checking other people's faces to make sure her own was all right. Her mother, who noticed everything and knew everything and who hadn't much reason any longer to look at her own face, always scolded Connie about it. "Stop gawking at yourself, who are you? You think you're so pretty?" she would say. Connie would raise her eyebrows at these familiar complaints and look right through her mother, into a shadowy vision of herself as she was right at that moment: she knew she was pretty and that was everything. Her mother had been pretty once too, if you could believe those old snapshots in the album, but now her looks were gone and that was why she was always after Connie.

"Why don't you keep your room clean like your sister? How've you got your hair fixed—what the hell stinks? Hair spray? You don't see your sister using that junk."

Her sister June was twenty-four and still lived at home. She was a secretary in the high school Connie attended, and if that wasn't bad enough—with her in the same building—she was so plain and chunky and steady that Connie had to hear her praised all the time by her mother and her mother's sisters. June did this, June did that, she saved money and helped clean the house and cooked and Connie couldn't do a thing, her mind was all filled with trashy daydreams. Their father was away at work most of the time and when he came home he wanted supper and he read the newspaper at supper and after supper he went to bed. He didn't bother talking much to them, but around his bent head Connie's mother kept picking at her until Connie wished her mother were dead and she herself were dead and it were all over. "She makes me want to throw up sometimes," she complained to her friends.

She had a high, breathless, amused voice which made everything she said sound a little forced, whether it was sincere or not.

There was one good thing: June went places with girlfriends of hers, girls who were just as plain and steady as she, and so when Connie wanted to do that her mother had no objections. The father of Connie's best girlfriend drove the girls the three miles to town and left them off at a shopping plaza, so that they could talk through the stores or go to a movie, and when he came to pick them up again at eleven he never bothered to ask what they had done.

They must have been familiar sights, walking around that shopping plaza in their shorts and flat ballerina slippers that always scuffed the sidewalk, with charm bracelets jingling on their thin wrists; they would lean together to whisper and laugh secretly if someone passed by who amused or interested them. Connie had long dark blond hair that drew anyone's eye to it, and she wore part of it pulled up on her head and puffed out and the rest of it she let fall down her back. She wore a pullover jersey blouse that looked one way when she was at home and another way when she was away from home. Everything about her had two sides to it, one for home and one for anywhere that was not home: her walk that could be childlike and bobbing, or languid enough to make anyone think she was hearing music in her head, her mouth which was pale and smirking most of the time, but bright and pink on these evenings out, her laugh which was cynical and drawling at home—"Ha, ha, very funny"—but high-pitched and nervous anywhere else, like the jingling of the charms on her bracelet.

Sometimes they did go shopping or to a movie, but sometimes they went across the highway, ducking fast across the busy road, to a drive-in restaurant where older kids hung out. The restaurant was shaped like a big bottle, though squatter than a real bottle, and on its cap was a revolving figure of a grinning boy who held a hamburger aloft. One night in midsummer they ran across, breathless with daring, and right away someone leaned out a car window and invited them over, but it was just a boy from high school they didn't like. It made them feel good to be able to ignore him. They went up through the maze of parked and cruising cars to the bright-lit, fly-infested restaurant, their faces pleased and expectant as if they were entering a sacred building that loomed out of the night to give them what haven and what blessing they yearned for. They sat at the counter and crossed their legs at the ankles, their thin shoulders rigid with excitement, and listened to the music that made everything so good: the music was always in the background like music at a church service, it was something to depend upon.

A boy named Eddie came in to talk with them. He sat backward on his stool, turning himself jerkily around in semicircles and then stopping and turning again, and after awhile he asked Connie if she would like something to eat. She said she did and so she tapped her friend's arm on her way out—

her friend pulled her face up into a brave droll look—and Connie said she would meet her at eleven, across the way. "I just hate to leave her like that," Connie said earnestly, but the boy said that she wouldn't be alone for long. So they went out to his car and on the way Connie couldn't help but let her eyes wander over the windshields and faces all around her, her face gleaming with a joy that had nothing to do with Eddie or even this place; it might have been the music. She drew her shoulders up and sucked in her breath with the pure pleasure of being alive, and just at that moment she happened to glance at a face just a few feet from hers. It was a boy with shaggy black hair, in a convertible jalopy painted gold. He stared at her and then his lips widened into a grin. Connie slit her eyes at him and turned away, but she couldn't help glancing back and there he was still watching her. He wagged a finger and laughed and said, "Gonna get you, baby," and Connie turned away again without Eddie noticing anything.

She spent three hours with him, at the restaurant where they ate hamburgers and drank Cokes in wax cups that were always sweating, and then down an alley a mile or so away, and when he left her off at five to eleven only the movie house was still open at the plaza. Her girlfriend was there, talking with a boy. When Connie came up the two girls smiled at each other and Connie said, "How was the movie?" and the girl said, "*You* should know." They rode off with the girl's father, sleepy and pleased, and Connie couldn't help but look at the darkened shopping plaza with its big empty parking lot and its signs that were faded and ghostly now, and over at the drive-in restaurant where cars were still circling tirelessly. She couldn't hear the music at this distance.

Next morning June asked her how the movie was and Connie said, "So-so."

She and that girl and occasionally another girl went out several times a week that way, and the rest of the time Connie spent around the house—it was summer vacation—getting in her mother's way and thinking, dreaming, about the boys she met. But all the boys fell back and dissolved into a single face that was not even a face, but an idea, a feeling, mixed up with the urgent insistent pounding of the music and the humid night air of July. Connie's mother kept dragging her back to the daylight by finding things for her to do or saying, suddenly, "What's this about the Pettinger girl?"

And Connie would say nervously, "Oh, her. That dope." She always drew thick clear lines between herself and such girls, and her mother was simple and kindly enough to believe her. Her mother was so simple, Connie thought, that it was maybe cruel to fool her so much. Her mother went scuffling around the house in old bedroom slippers and complained over the telephone to one sister about the other, then the other called up and the two of them complained about the third one. If June's name was mentioned her mother's tone was approving and if Connie's name was mentioned it was disapproving. This did not really mean she disliked Connie and actually Connie thought that her mother preferred her to June because she was prettier, but the two of them kept up a pretense of exasperation, a sense that they were tugging and struggling over something of little value to either of them. Sometimes, over coffee, they were almost friends, but something would come up—some vexation that was like a fly buzzing suddenly around their heads—and their faces went hard with contempt.

One Sunday Connie got up at eleven—none of them bothered with church—and washed her hair so that it could dry all day long, in the sun. Her parents and sisters were going to a barbecue at an aunt's house and Connie said no, she wasn't interested, rolling her eyes to let mother know just what she thought of it. "Stay home alone then," her mother said sharply. Connie sat out back in a lawn chair and watched them drive away, her father quiet and bald, hunched around so that he could back the car out, her mother with a look that was still angry and not at all softened through the windshield, and in the back seat poor old June all dressed up as if she didn't know what a barbecue was, with all the running yelling kids and the flies. Connie sat with her eyes closed in the sun, dreaming and dazed with the warmth about her as if this were a kind of love, the caresses of love, and her mind slipped over onto thoughts of the boy she had been with the night before and how nice he had been, how sweet it always was, not the way someone like June would suppose but sweet, gentle, the way it was in movies and promised in songs; and when she opened her eyes she hardly knew where she was, the back yard ran off into weeds and a fence-line of trees and behind it the sky was perfectly blue and still. The asbestos "ranch house" that was now three years old startled her—it looked small. She shook her head as if to get awake.

It was too hot. She went inside the house and turned on the radio to drown out the quiet. She sat on the edge of her bed, barefoot, and listened for an hour and a half to a program called XYZ Sunday Jamboree, record after record of hard, fast, shrieking songs she sang along with, interspersed by exclamations from "Bobby King": "An' look here you girls at Napoleon's—Son and Charley want you to pay real close attention to this song coming up!"

And Connie paid close attention herself, bathed in a glow of slow-pulsed joy that seemed to rise mysteriously out of the music itself and lay languidly about the airless little room, breathed in and breathed out with each gentle rise and fall of her chest.

After a while she heard a car coming up the drive. She sat up at once, startled, because it couldn't be her father so soon. The gravel kept crunching all the way in from the road—the driveway was long—and Connie ran to the window. It was a car she didn't know. It was an open jalopy, painted a bright gold that caught the sunlight opaquely. Her heart began to pound and her fingers snatched at her hair, checking it, and she whispered "Christ. Christ," wondering how bad she looked. The car came to a stop at the side door and the horn sounded four short taps as if this were a signal Connie knew.

She went into the kitchen and approached the door slowly, then hung out the screen door, her bare toes curling down off the step. There were two boys in the car and now she recognized the driver: he had shaggy, shabby black hair that looked crazy as a wig and he was grinning at her.

"I ain't late, am I?" he said.

"Who the hell do you think you are?" Connie said.

"Toldja I'd be out, didn't I?"

"I don't even know who you are."

She spoke sullenly, careful to show no interest or pleasure, and he spoke in a fast bright monotone. Connie looked past him to the other boy, taking her time. He had fair brown hair, with a lock that fell onto his forehead. His sideburns gave him a fierce, embarrassed look, but so far he hadn't even bothered to glance at her. Both boys wore sunglasses. The driver's glasses were metallic and mirrored everything in miniature.

"You wanta come for a ride?" he said.

Connie smirked and let her hair fall loose over one shoulder.

"Don'tcha like my car? New paint job," he said. "Hey."

"What?"

"You're cute."

She pretended to fidget, chasing flies away from the door.

"Don'tcha believe me, or what?" he said.

"Look, I don't even know who you are," Connie said in disgust.

"Hey, Ellie's got a radio, see. Mine's broke down." He lifted his friend's arm and showed her the little transistor the boy was holding, and now Connie began to hear the music. It was the same program that was playing inside the house.

"Bobby King?" she said.

"I listen to him all the time. I think he's great."

"He's kind of great," Connie said reluctantly.

"Listen, that guy's *great*. He knows where the action is."

Connie blushed a little, because the glasses made it impossible for her to see just what this boy was looking at. She couldn't decide if she liked him or if he was just a jerk, and so she dawdled in the doorway and wouldn't come down or go back inside. She said, "What's all that stuff painted on your car?"

"Can'tcha read it?" He opened the door very carefully, as if he was afraid it might fall off. He slid out just as carefully, planting his feet firmly on the ground, the tiny metallic world in his glasses slowing down like gelatine hardening and in the midst of it Connie's bright green blouse. "This here is my name, to begin with," he said. ARNOLD FRIEND was written in tarlike black letters on the side, with a drawing of a round grinning face that reminded Connie of a pumpkin, except it wore sunglasses. "I wanta introduce myself, I'm Arnold Friend and that's my real name and I'm gonna be your friend, honey, and inside the car's Ellie Oscar, he's kinda shy." Ellie brought his transistor radio up to his shoulder and balanced it there. "Now these numbers are a secret code, honey," Arnold Friend explained. He read off the numbers 33, 19, 17 and raised his eyebrows at her to see what she thought of that, but she didn't think much of it. The left rear fender had been smashed and around it was written, on the gleaming gold background: DONE BY CRAZY WOMAN DRIVER. Connie had to laugh at that. Arnold Friend was pleased at her laughter and looked up at her. "Around the other side's a lot more—you wanta come and see them?"

"No."

"Why not?"

"Why should I?"

"Don'tcha wanta see what's on the car? Don'tcha wanta go for a ride?"

"I don't know."

"Why not?"

"I got things to do."

"Like what?"

"Things."

He laughed as if she had said something funny. He slapped his thighs. He was standing in a strange way, leaning back against the cars as if he were balancing himself. He wasn't tall, only an inch or so taller than she would be if she came down to him. Connie liked the way he was dressed, which was the way all of them dressed: tight faded jeans stuffed into black, scuffed boots, a belt that pulled his waist in and showed how lean he was, and a white pullover shirt that was a little soiled and showed the hard small muscles of his arms and shoulders. He looked as if he probably did hard work, lifting and carrying things. Even his neck looked muscular. And his face was a familiar face, somehow: the jaw and chin and cheeks slightly darkened, because he hadn't shaved for a day or two, and the nose long and hawklike, sniffing as if she were a treat he was going to gobble up and it was all a joke.

"Connie, you ain't telling the truth. This is your day set aside for a ride with me and you know it," he said, still laughing. The way he straightened and recovered from his fit of laughing showed that it had been all fake.

"How do you know what my name is?" she said suspiciously.

"It's Connie."

"Maybe and maybe not."

"I know my Connie," he said, wagging his finger. Now she remembered him even better, back at the restaurant, and her cheeks warmed at the thought of how she sucked in her breath just at the moment she passed him—how she must have looked to him. And he had remembered her. "Ellie and I come out here especially for you," he said. "Ellie can sit in back. How about it?"

"Where?"

"Where what?"

"Where're we going?"

He looked at her. He took off the sunglasses and she saw how pale the skin around his eyes was, like holes that were not in shadow but instead in light. His eyes were like chips of broken glass that catch the light in an amiable way. He smiled. It was as if the idea of going for a ride somewhere, to some place, was a new idea to him.

"Just for a ride, Connie sweetheart."

"I never said my name was Connie," she said.

"But I know what it is. I know your name and all about you, lots of things," Arnold Friend said. He had not moved yet but stood still leaning back against the side of his jalopy. "I took a special interest in you, such a pretty girl, and found out all about you like I know your parents and sister are gone somewheres and I know where and how long they're going to be gone, and I know who you were with last night, and your best girlfriend's name is Betty. Right?"

He spoke in a simple lilting voice, exactly as if he were reciting the words to a song. His smile assured her that everything was fine. In the car Ellie turned up the volume on his radio and did not bother to look around at them.

"Ellie can sit in the back seat," Arnold Friend said. He indicated his friend with a casual jerk of his chin, as if Ellie did not count and she should not bother with him.

"How'd you find out all that stuff?" Connie said.

"Listen: Betty Schultz and Tony Fitch and Jimmy Pettinger and Nancy Pettinger," he said, in a chant. "Raymond Stanley and Bob Hutter—"

"Do you know all those kids?"

"I know everybody."

"Look, you're kidding. You're not from around here."

"Sure."

"But—how come we never saw you before?"

"Sure you saw me before," he said. He looked down at his boots, as if he were a little offended. "You just don't remember."

"I guess I'd remember you," Connie said.

"Yeah?" He looked up at this, beaming. He was pleased. He began to mark time with the music from Ellie's radio, tapping his fists lightly together. Connie looked away from his smile to the car, which was painted so bright it almost hurt her eyes to look at it. She looked at that name, ARNOLD FRIEND. And up at the front fender was an expression that was familiar—

MAN THE FLYING SAUCERS. It was an expression kids had used the year before, but didn't use this year. She looked at it for a while as if the words meant something to her that she did not yet know.

"What're you thinking about? Huh?" Arnold Friend demanded. "Not worried about your hair blowing around in the car, are you?"

"No."

"Think I maybe can't drive good?"

"How do I know?"

"You're a hard girl to handle. How come?" he said. "Don't you know I'm your friend? Didn't you see me put my sign in the air when you walked by?"

"What sign?"

"My sign." And he drew an X in the air, leaning out toward her. They were maybe ten feet apart. After his hand fell back to his side the X was still in the air, almost visible. Connie let the screen door close and stood perfectly still inside it, listening to the music from her radio and the boy's blend together. She stared at Arnold Friend. He stood there so stiffly relaxed, pretending to be relaxed, with one hand idly on the door handle as if he were keeping himself up that way and had no intention of ever moving again. She recognized most things about him, the tight jeans that showed his thighs and buttocks and the greasy leather boots and the tight shirt, and even that slippery friendly smile of his, that sleepy dreamy smile that all the boys used to get across ideas they didn't want to put into words. She recognized all this and also the singsong way he talked, slightly mocking, kidding, but serious and a little melancholy, and she recognized the way he tapped one fist against the other in homage to the perpetual music behind him. But all these things did not come together.

She said suddenly, "Hey, how old are you?"

His smile faded. She could see then that he wasn't a kid, he was much older—thirty, maybe more. At this knowledge her heart began to pound faster.

"That's a crazy thing to ask. Can'tcha see I'm your own age?"

"Like hell you are."

"Or maybe a coupla years older, I'm eighteen."

"Eighteen?" she said doubtfully.

He grinned to reassure her and lines appeared at the corners of his mouth. His teeth were big and white. He grinned so broadly his eyes became slits and she saw how thick the lashes were, thick and black as if painted with a black tarlike material. Then he seemed to become embarrassed, abruptly, and looked over his shoulder at Ellie. "*Him*, he's crazy," he said. "Ain't he a riot, he's a nut, a real character." Ellie was still listening to the music. His sunglasses told nothing about what he was thinking. He wore a bright orange shirt unbuttoned halfway to show his chest, which was a pale, bluish chest and not muscular like Arnold Friend's. His shirt collar was turned up all around and the very tips of the collar pointed out past his chin as if they were protecting him. He was pressing the transistor radio up against his ear and sat there in a kind of daze, right in the sun.

"He's kinda strange," Connie said.

"Hey, she says you're kinda strange! Kinda strange!" Arnold Friend cried. He pounded on the car to get Ellie's attention. Ellie turned for the first time and Connie saw with shock that he wasn't a kid either—he had a fair, hairless face, cheeks reddened slightly as if the veins grew too close to the surface of his skin, the face of a forty-year-old baby. Connie felt a wave of dizziness rise in her at this sight and she stared at him as if waiting for something to change the shock of the moment, make it all right again. Ellie's lips kept shaping words, mumbling along with the words blasting in his ear.

"Maybe you two better go away," Connie said faintly.

"What? How come?" Arnold Friend cried. "We come out here to take you for a ride. It's Sunday." He had the voice of the man on the radio now. It was the same voice, Connie thought. "Don'tcha know it's Sunday all day and honey, no matter who you were with last night today you're with Arnold Friend and don't you forget it!—Maybe you better step out here," he said, and this last was in a different voice. It was a little flatter, as if the heat was finally getting to him.

"No. I got things to do."

"Hey."

"You two better leave."

"We ain't leaving until you come with us."

"Like hell I am—"

"Connie, don't fool around with me. I mean, I mean, don't fool *around*," he said, shaking his head. He laughed incredulously. He placed his sunglasses on top of his head, carefully, as if he were indeed wearing a wig, and brought the stems down behind his ears. Connie stared at him, another wave of dizziness and fear rising in her so that for a moment he wasn't even in focus but was just a blur, standing there against his gold car, and she had the idea that he had driven up the driveway all right but had come from nowhere before that and belonged nowhere and that everything about him and even about the music that was so familiar to her was only half real.

"If my father comes and sees you—"

"He ain't coming. He's at a barbecue."

"How do you know that?"

"Aunt Tillie's. Right now they're—uh—they're drinking. Sitting around," he said vaguely, squinting as if he were staring all the way to town and over to Aunt Tillie's back yard. Then the vision seemed to get clear and he nodded energetically. "Yeah. Sitting around. There's your sister in a blue dress, huh? And high heels, the poor sad bitch—nothing like you, sweetheart! And your mother's helping some fat woman with the corn, they're cleaning the corn—husking the corn—"

"What fat woman?" Connie cried.

"How do I know what fat woman, I don't know every goddam fat woman in the world!" Arnold laughed.

"Oh, that's Mrs. Hornby . . . Who invited her?" Connie said. She felt a little light-headed. Her breath was coming quickly.

"She's too fat. I don't like them fat. I like them the way you are, honey," he said, smiling sleepily at her. They stared at each other for a while, through the screen door. He said softly, "Now what you're going to do is this: you're going to come out that door. You're going to sit up front with me and Ellie's going to sit in the back, the hell with Ellie, right? This isn't Ellie's date. You're my date. I'm your lover, honey."

"What? You're crazy—"

"Yes, I'm your lover. You don't know what that is but you will," he said. "I know that too. I know all about you. But look: it's real nice and you couldn't ask for nobody better than me, or more polite. I always keep my word. I'll tell you how it is, I'm always nice at first, the first time. I'll hold you so tight you won't think you have to try to get away or pretend anything because you'll know you can't. And I'll come inside you where it's all secret and you'll give in to me and you'll love me—"

"Shut up! You're crazy!" Connie said. She backed away from the door. She put her hands against her ears as if she'd heard something terrible, something not meant for her. "People don't talk like that, you're crazy," she muttered. Her heart was almost too big now for her chest and its pumping made sweat break out all over her. She looked out to see Arnold Friend pause and then take a step toward the porch lurching. He almost fell. But, like a clever drunken man, he managed to catch his balance. He wobbled in his high boots and grabbed hold of one of the porch posts.

"Honey?" he said. "You still listening?"

"Get the hell out of here!"

"Be nice, honey. Listen."

"I'm going to call the police—"

He wobbled again and out of the side of his mouth came a fast spat curse, an aside not meant for her to hear. But even this "Christ!" sounded forced. Then he began to smile again. She watched this smile come, awkward as if he were smiling from inside a mask. His whole face was a mask, she thought wildly, tanned down onto his throat but then running out as if he had plastered makeup on his face but had forgotten about his throat.

"Honey—? Listen, here's how it is. I always tell the truth and I promise you this: I ain't coming in that house after you."

"You better not! I'm going to call the police if you—if you don't—"

"Honey," he said, talking right through her voice, "honey, I'm not coming in there but you are coming out here. You know why?"

She was panting. The kitchen looked like a place she had never seen before, some room she had run inside but which wasn't good enough, wasn't going to help her. The kitchen window had never had a curtain, after three years, and there were dishes in the sink for her to do—probably—and if you ran your hand across the table you'd probably feel something sticky there.

"You listening, honey? Hey?"

"—going to call the police—"

"Soon as you touch the phone I don't need to keep my promise and can come inside. You won't want that."

She rushed forward and tried to lock the door. Her fingers were shaking. "But why lock it," Arnold Friend said gently, talking right into her face. "It's just a screen door. It's just nothing." One of his boots was at a strange angle, as if his foot wasn't in it. It pointed out to the left, bent at the ankle. "I mean, anybody can break through a screen door and glass and wood and iron or anything else if he needs to, anybody at all and specially Arnold Friend. If the place got lit up with a fire honey you'd come runnin' out into my arms, right into my arms an' safe at home—like you knew I was your lover and'd stopped fooling around. I don't mind a nice shy girl but I don't like no fooling around." Part of those words were spoken with a slight rhythmic lilt, and Connie somehow recognized them—the echo of a song from last year, about a girl rushing into her boyfriend's arms and coming home again—

Connie stood barefoot on the linoleum floor, staring at him. "What do you want?" she whispered.

"I want you," he said.

"What?"

"Seen you that night and thought, that's the one, yes sir. I never needed to look any more."

"But my father's coming back. He's coming to get me. I had to wash my hair first—" She spoke in a dry, rapid voice, hardly raising it for him to hear.

"No, your Daddy is not coming and yes, you had to wash your hair and you washed it for me. It's nice and shining and all for me, I thank you, sweetheart," he said, with a mock bow, but again he almost lost his balance. He had to bend and adjust his boots. Evidently his feet did not go all the way down; the boots must have been stuffed with something so that he would seem taller. Connie stared out at him and behind him Ellie in the car, who seemed to be looking off toward Connie's right, into nothing. This Ellie said, pulling the words out of the air one after another as if he were just discovering them, "You want me to pull out the phone?"

"Shut your mouth and keep it shut," Arnold Friend said, his face red from bending over or maybe from embarrassment because Connie had seen his boots. "This ain't none of your business."

"What—what are you doing? What do you want?" Connie said. "If I call the police they'll get you, they'll arrest you—"

"Promise was not to come in unless you touch that phone, and I'll keep that promise," he said. He resumed his erect position and tried to force his shoulders back. He sounded like a hero in a movie, declaring something important. He spoke too loudly and it was as if he were speaking to someone behind Connie. "I ain't made plans for coming in that house where I don't belong but just for you to come out to me, the way you should. Don't you know who I am?"

"You're crazy," she whispered. She backed away from the door but did not want to go into another part of the house, as if this would give him permission to come through the door. "What do you . . . You're crazy, you . . ."

"Huh? What're you saying, honey?"

Her eyes darted everywhere in the kitchen. She could not remember what it was, this room.

"This is how it is, honey: you come out and we'll drive away, have a nice ride. But if you don't come out we're gonna wait till your people come home and then they're all going to get it."

"You want that telephone pulled out?" Ellie said. He held the radio away from his ear and grimaced, as if without the radio the air was too much for him.

"I toldja shut up, Ellie," Arnold Friend said, "you're deaf, get a hearing aid, right? Fix yourself up. This little girl's no trouble and's gonna be nice to me, so Ellie keep to yourself, this ain't your date—right? Don't hem in on me. Don't hog. Don't crush. Don't bird dog. Don't trail me," he said in a rapid meaningless voice, as if he were running through all the expressions he'd learned but was no longer sure which one of them was in style, then rushing on to new ones, making them up with his eyes closed, "Don't crawl under my fence, don't squeeze in my chipmunk hole, don't sniff my glue, suck my popsicle, keep your own greasy fingers on yourself!" He shaded his eyes and peered in at Connie, who was backed against the kitchen table. "Don't mind him honey he's just a creep. He's a dope. Right? I'm the boy for you and like I said you come out here nice like a lady and give me your hand, and nobody else gets hurt, I mean, your nice old bald-headed daddy and your mummy and your sister in her high heels. Because listen: why bring them in this?"

"Leave me alone," Connie whispered.

"Hey, you know that old woman down the road, the one with the chickens and stuff—you know her?"

"She's dead!"

"Dead? What? You know her?" Arnold Friend said.

"She's dead—"

"Don't you like her?"

"She's dead—she's—she isn't here any more—"

"But don't you like her, I mean, you got something against her? Some grudge or something?" Then his voice dipped as if he were conscious of a rudeness. He touched the sunglasses perched on top of his head as if to make sure they were still there. "Now you be a good girl."

"What are you going to do?"

"Just two things, or maybe three," Arnold Friend said. "But I promise it won't last long and you'll like me the way you get to like people you're close to. You will. It's all over for you here, so come on out. You don't want your people in any trouble, do you?"

She turned and bumped against a chair or something, hurting her leg, but she ran into the back room and picked up the telephone. Something roared in her ear, a tiny roaring, and she was so sick with fear that she could do nothing but listen to it—the telephone was clammy and very heavy and her fingers groped down to the dial but were too weak to touch it. She began to scream into the phone, into the roaring. She cried out, she cried for her mother, she felt her breath start jerking back and forth in her lungs as if it were something Arnold Friend were stabbing her with again and again with no tenderness. A noisy sorrowful wailing rose all about her and she was locked inside it the way she was locked inside this house.

After a while she could hear again. She was sitting on the floor with her wet back against the wall.

Arnold Friend was saying from the door, "That's a good girl. Put the phone back."

She kicked the phone away from her.

"No, honey. Pick it up. Put it back right."

She picked it up and put it back. The dial tone stopped.

"That's a good girl. Now you come outside."

She was hollow with what had been fear, but what was now just an emptiness. All that screaming had blasted it out of her. She sat, one leg cramped under her, and deep inside her brain was something like a pinpoint of light that kept going and would not let her relax.

She thought, I'm not going to see my mother again. She thought, I'm not going to sleep in my bed again. Her bright green blouse was all wet.

Arnold Friend said, in a gentle-loud voice that was like a stage voice, "The place where you came from ain't there any more, and where you had in mind to go is canceled out. This place you are now—inside your daddy's house—is nothing but a cardboard box I can knock down any time. You know that and always did know it. You hear me?"

She thought, I have got to think. I have to know what to do.

"We'll go out to a nice field, out in the country here where it smells so nice and it's sunny," Arnold Friend said. "I'll have my arms tight around you so you won't need to try to get away and I'll show you what love is like, what it does. The hell with this house! It looks solid all right," he said. He ran a fingernail down the screen and the noise did not make Connie shiver, as it would have the day before. "Now put your hand on your heart, honey. Feel that? That feels solid too but we know better, be nice to me, be sweet like you can because what else is there for a girl like you but to be sweet and pretty and give in?—and get away before her people come back?"

She felt her pounding heart. Her hand seemed to enclose it. She thought for the first time in her life that it was nothing that was hers, that belonged to her, but just a pounding, living thing inside this body that wasn't really hers either.

"You don't want them to get hurt," Arnold Friend went on. "Now get up, honey. Get up all by yourself."

She stood.

"Now turn this way. That's right. Come over here to me—Ellie, put that away, didn't I tell you? You dope. You miserable creepy dope," Arnold Friend said. His words were not angry but only part of an incantation. The incantation was kindly. "Now come out through the kitchen to me honey and let's see a smile, try it, you're a brave sweet little girl and now they're eating corn and hot dogs cooked to bursting over an outdoor fire, and they don't know one thing about you and never did and honey you're better than them because not a one of them would have done this for you."

Connie felt the linoleum under her feet; it was cool. She brushed her hair back out of her eyes. Arnold Friend let go of the post tentatively and opened his arms for her, his elbows pointing in toward each other and his wrists limp, to show that this was an embarrassed embrace and a little mocking, he didn't want to make her self-conscious.

She put out her hand against the screen. She watched herself push the door slowly open as if she were safe back somewhere in the other doorway, watching this body and this head of long hair moving out into the sunlight where Arnold Friend waited.

"My sweet little blue-eyed girl," he said, in a half-sung sigh that had nothing to do with her brown eyes but was taken up just the same by the vast sunlit reaches of the land behind him and on all sides of him, so much land that Connie had never seen before and did not recognize except to know that she was going to it.